EVERYMAN,
I WILL GO WITH THEE,
AND BE THY GUIDE,
IN THY MOST NEED
TO GO BY THY SIDE

RAYMOND CHANDLER

Collected Stories

with an Introduction by
John Bayley

EVERYMAN'S LIBRARY

Alfred A. Knopf New York Toronto

257

THIS IS A BORZOI BOOK

PUBLISHED BY ALFRED A. KNOPF

First included in Everyman's Library, 2002
Collected Stories copyright 2002 by Philip Marlowe BV
'Blackmailers Don't Shoot' copyright 1933 by Raymond Chandler.
Copyright Philip Marlowe BV. Reprinted by permission of the
Estate of Raymond Chandler.
'English Summer' copyright 1976 by Helga Greene for the Estate of
Raymond Chandler
All other stories copyright 1934, 1935, 1936, 1937, 1938, 1939, 1941,
1944, 1950, 1951, 1959, 1961 by Raymond Chandler
Copyright 1939 by the Curtis Publishing Company
Introduction Copyright © 2002 by John Bayley
Bibliography and Chronology Copyright © 2002 by Everyman
Publishers plc
Typography by Peter B. Willberg

www.randomhouse.com/everymans

ISBN 0-375-41500-9

Book Design by Barbara de Wilde and Carol Devine Carson

Printed and bound in Germany
by GGP Media, Pössneck

RAYMOND CHANDLER

C O N T E N T S

vii

INTRODUCTION

When my wife Iris Murdoch – a novelist and herself a
Chandler fan – was at school, the headmistress, a rather
formidable woman, used periodically to descend on the girls
in their recreation time, and if one of them happened to
be reading anything, assume an interested and approving
expression and ask what it was. One of Iris's schoolmates was
found in this way with her nose in a book, and obviously
deeply absorbed. 'And what are you reading, Clare?' enquired
the great lady benevolently, expecting the answer to be something high-minded on world politics (the school was both
Quakerish and left-wing in tone) or perhaps some modern
thinker of that time like H. G. Wells or Aldous Huxley.
'Detection, Mystery and Howwor, Miss Baker,' reported the
maiden brightly and quite unabashed, her demure inability to
manage the Rs somehow lending her girlish tastes an extra
dimension of depravity. Her schoolfellows, Iris among them,
were too polite to start giggling, at least at that moment; and
the great lady herself had for once no comeback (or so Iris
reported to me, many years later) but swept off with the sound
usually represented by the monosyllable 'Tchah!'

One would like to think that the 'Detection, Mystery and
Howwor' omnibus in which the enterprising girl was immersed
might have included an early tale or two by the great master
of the form – if the blanket title of the young lady's book
could be said to describe a form – but given the time (the
1930s) and the place that seems unlikely. Chandler's apprentice
tales from the *Black Mask* magazine did not find their way to
England or into an English collection of his own until some
time after the war, when the true stature of his mature
masterpieces had already been appreciated by a discerning
audience of English critics and writers – fellow professionals,
as it were – among whom were such varied performers in
their own line as W. H. Auden and T. S. Eliot, J. B. Priestley,
Graham Greene and Elizabeth Bowen. In the wake of his
rising fame, publication of the early stories naturally followed.

ix

Among these English devotees was a young journalist and man about town called Ian Fleming, who would himself shortly win fame of a much more spectacular and popular kind with the creation of his hero James Bond. As narrator and character Bond is not in the same class as Philip Marlowe, but he, or rather his creator, does possess an unbounded admiration for Marlowe and for Chandler's personality and achievements. Towards the end of *Goldfinger*, in the moment of deceptive calm before the final crisis, James Bond finds time at the airport to buy Ben Hogan's *The Modern Fundamentals of Golf*. Although content himself to be an amateur, this is a sport in which he is seriously interested, but he is just as interested in the latest Raymond Chandler, which he also buys. *Goldfinger* was written in 1959, the year of Chandler's death, but neither Bond nor his creator would have worried about a little mistiming like that.

Fleming's books were beginning by then to be increasingly successful, although he was still a long way from the best seller he was ultimately to become. But the example of Chandler, and the admiration Fleming felt for his work, continued to act as an inspiration, although Fleming may well have wished that his hero Bond, with whom his public not unjustifiably identified him, had been more up to the intellectual level of Chandler and his Marlowe. Yet he had undoubtedly begun to see himself as carrying the great man's torch, and writing in the same tradition. The example of Chandler had indeed taught his English disciple how to create a world unmistakably his own, not by means of plot device or story line, but by the build-up of atmosphere, and the attentive accumulation of local colour. Both writers relegate the story to a decidedly subordinate position: what tells is not our curiosity about the plot, or the ingenuities of the whodunit, but the creation of a unique and autonomous domain, with the denizens appropriate to it.

Much more than Bond, of course, Marlowe is an inhabitant of a particular world, Chandler's own in so far as it is his own brilliant imaginative creation, but a world none the less observed as meticulously from life as are the properties of a Vermeer picture. Within the nature and quality of Chandler's writing the paradox comes to seem quite normal. The Southern Californian landscape, the settings urban and semi-urban, as if the whole huge colourful country were a single town; the gardens sprawling and richly outlandish, or sinister and compact; the house interiors, as naturally and as closely observed as Vermeer's own, with their furniture and carpets and fittings ... These are the scenes in which Chandler and his hero are at home, and his sense of place is immaculate, a pleasure unique and all of its own, whether we are in the opulent mansions of Bel-Air, the grand ranch-type dwellings in the hills miles away from Hollywood, or the sleazy back-streets of 'Bay City', as Santa Monica is usually referred to in the stories.

In her book *Good Bones* (1992), Margaret Atwood presents a picture as full of admiration as it is of amusement at the almost sensuous charms of Chandler's still-life interiors, implying that he would have been the ideal editor and contributor to a sort of Californian version of *House & Garden*. She imagines too the pleasures of having 'An Affair with Raymond Chandler', along the lines of those English gentlemen who dreamed of an afternoon with Elinor Glyn on her famous tiger skin. She would fall in love with his interest in upholstery, with the bouquet of sunlight on ageing cloth, with his sofas 'stuffed to roundness, satin-covered, pale-blue, like the eyes of his cold blonde unbodied murderous women'. Together they would drive out to some motel, and come to grips only after they had lovingly appraised the furniture, and inhaled the odour of dusty drapes and worn carpets, ancient cigarette and cigar smoke, Martinis mixed and spilled long ago.

This is a world which is inescapably cosy even when it is at its most sinister. In one sense it is almost an elaborate transfiguration of that more simply and robustly cosy world in which Sherlock Holmes and Dr Watson go about their familiar business, returning to 221b Baker Street for relaxation over a well-roasted partridge and a bottle of Burgundy. Both Holmes and Marlowe are domestic pipe-smokers, but although Marlowe is both an austere and a dedicated drinking man he despises all drugs and their addicts: Holmes's cocaine would not have been for him. His pipe, his chess problem and his tumbler of Scotch are none the less the equivalents of Holmes's solitary violin and his pistol practice. Chandler is an adept both at following the conventions of the form in which he writes, and abandoning them in his own fashion, and with the subtle individuality of his own style.

That style was initiated and formed in England. Chandler was educated at Dulwich College on the outskirts of London, a school whose pupils were well-taught along old-fashioned lines, and particularly well-grounded in the classics. It had been founded in 1619 by Edward Alleyn, the celebrated actor-manager whose company, 'the Admiral's Men', included the poet and playwright Christopher Marlowe, forerunner of Shakespeare and author of *Tamburlaine* and *Dr Faustus*. It seems likely that Chandler had the name of the playwright in his mind when he finally christened his own narrator-hero Philip Marlowe, after bestowing on him in earlier stories tough pseudo-Irish names, suited to shamuses and private eyes, such as 'John Dalmas'. Chandler's mother was in fact Irish, although paradoxically Quaker rather than Catholic Irish, but his upbringing and his earliest writing were very much English, and almost of the *fin de siècle* period.

By coincidence, two other writers, P. G. Wodehouse and C. S. Forester, both of whom were to become masters of their own particular literary genre, were near-contemporaries of Chandler at Dulwich,* and at a later date Chandler corresponded with Wodehouse and admired him as a fellow crafts-man, in however different a style. Chandler was gratified, too, that his first recognition as a serious and original artist came from English authors and critics. But although his sympathies and so much of his culture lay in England, Chandler, both as man and as writer, was very much an American at heart. In a sense, and perhaps ironically, he was the opposite of those English butlers he does so well in his stories and novels, like the sublime Norris who seems to brood over the action of *The Big Sleep*.

The fine quality of Chandler's writing is shown by the

*Wodehouse left the year Chandler entered the school (1900). Forester went to Dulwich in 1915.

subtlety and precision that went into a minor character like Norris (Sir John Norris, or Norreys, was, incidentally, a famous and chivalrous Elizabethan commander) who makes an obvious contrast with the stock comic butler figures of Wodehouse, and other genre writers of his time. (Chandleresque humour appears early, too, in the 'rogue' butler of one story, whose British accent has a habit of slipping. 'Dartmouth?, or Dannemora?' enquires detective Dalmas sardonically.)

The culture mix in Chandler himself is certainly an exotic one. Dashiell Hammett, the forerunner in Chandler's chosen manner, was the most obvious literary influence, as he was also a source of personal inspiration, introducing Chandler to *Black Mask* and its 'Fellowship' (the word seems curiously apt in the context of the crime and mystery tradition.) Afterwards came Ross Macdonald, a talented and avowed disciple of Chandler, making extensive use of his locations and his atmosphere, but with his own line, in a sense a more traditional and conventional one when it came to plots and solutions, and to the old detective tale technique of keeping the reader guessing. Chandler goes, as it were, through the motions of this technique, but it is clear that his interest is not really in it, nor does he require his reader's to be. What he expects instead is for his reader to be fully and sensitively alert to all the rich pleasures of being in Chandler country, and meeting Chandler people.

And these, as I have said, are in a sense an imaginative exploration, even exaggeration, of the characters and properties inherent in the old-fashioned mystery thriller, but never so fully exploited. Their tradition of place and event was always ritualized, but Chandler gives this ritualization the polish and the density of his own manner and his own highly original kind of awareness. He dispenses with the traditional confidant, assistant or faithful friend, whose function was often to provide light relief and to be a bit of a buffoon, as even the much esteemed Dr Watson can be to Holmes at times; and as Ricardo is to Inspector Hanaud in A. E. W. Mason's novels, or his bluff colleague Petrie is to Sir Dennis Nayland Smith of Scotland Yard in Sax Rohmer's Fu Manchu stories.

Unlike his many predecessors Philip Marlowe is a lone wolf,

a single operator walking on his own 'down mean streets', as Chandler was to put it, in his wry, cynical, understated endeavour not only to find out the truth but to make justice prevail in a corrupt world, a world which neither knows nor cares for the meaning of the word. Cosiness none the less breaks in, just as it does in the earlier, less stylishly ethical world of Holmes and Watson, and the solitary knight of the mean streets, who has no friend but his pipe, the chessboard and the whiskey bottle, who has every man's hand against him, the police as well as the criminal and the villain, will in the evening return home, in the old style, but to his solitary lodging, to recruit himself for further trouble next day. ('Trouble', as the title of one of the earlier stories claims, 'Is My Business.')

This rhythmical alternation of comfort and cosiness with danger and thrills is the most effective feature of the tradition. James Bond will return to his Chelsea flat where his veteran Scottish housekeeper will serve him boiled eggs done just as he likes them, a curiously innocent form of celebration for the victor of a hundred clashes with the evil power of SMERSH. True, for him there will have been the brief but satisfying encounter, no more than ritually erotic, with the heroine of the tale. For Marlowe there is not even that, although he too, after a heavy night, is a believer in the restorative powers of lightly boiled eggs. Nevertheless, neither sex nor riches will reward his efforts; only the meagre wages of the upright man – twenty-five dollars a day and expenses* – and perhaps the unspoken knowledge that he has struck some sort of blow for freedom, truth and justice, and let light and air, however briefly, into the murky underworld in which it is his lot to operate.

Towards the end of Marlowe's career, as we know it, this unspoken monastic regime, whose routine in a subtle way is very satisfying to the reader, shows ominous signs of collapsing. The trouble, which is not the sort which Marlowe has always made his business, began in 1954, the year which saw the

---

*By the time of *The Little Sister* (1949) Marlowe's rates have gone up to forty dollars a day.

publication of *The Long Goodbye*, a novel whose length, unusual for Chandler, does not belie its title. Ominously too, the victim here is himself a writer, a writer who has made a fortune with a succession of bodice-ripping romances. He longs to write much better, but finds himself condemned to imitating his earlier successes, and reading 'my old stuff for inspiration', an oblique but ironic comment on the dilemma of many a successful author, as Chandler must himself have been becoming aware. His last completed novel, *Playback*, reveals the problem more than ever, even though Chandler himself remains an artist to his fingertips, and every sentence he wrote at this time still shows it.

Chandler may have thought that the notion of Marlowe succumbing eventually to a woman's charms would be a good way for both writer and reader to bid him a graceful goodbye. However that may be, Marlowe does at last subside into full-blown matrimony in *Poodle Springs*, the final and very much unfinished novel. His personality as we know it would hardly have been capable of sustaining such a transformation, any more than one of Henry James's unmarried heroes or heroines could have gone to the altar and yet survived as a character. Somebody once said that Sherlock Holmes might have miraculously survived the Reichenbach Falls, but he was never again quite the same man. With Chandler's Marlowe, a man at least as much of a legend to his readers today as Holmes had once been, the case is different, and rather more complex; indeed it poses a general problem to which I shall return.

The point meanwhile is that the reader's loyalty to the world created by Chandler, a world to which the reader has by now become so happily accustomed, is tested almost to breaking-point in *Poodle Springs*. Chandler's unique interior landscape, and our belief in it, are both under threat, even though the story line and its conventions remain as strong as ever and readers who most enjoy the machinery of his plotting still find it perfectly adequate for ordinary enjoyment. Even in *The Long Goodbye* there is no longer any of Chandler's lightness of touch – Marlowe's grim virtue and integrity begin by the end of the novel to get the reader down a bit, as does a general tendency, even more marked in *Playback*, to hold forth at length about society and its ills – and yet the narrative is still gripping. Chandler remained master, too, of what might be termed the Scheherazade effect. That wily princess told the Sultan only a little of her story at a time. In the same way Chandler's masterpieces should ideally be sampled slowly, in small appreciative mouthfuls. They depend upon Scheherazade's sense of timing, instead of baffling readers and compelling them, sometimes out of sheer exasperation, to press on to some unlikely solution presented in the last pages. A Chandler novel is a far cry from the kind of mystery the reader only wants to be finished and done with. If there should be a mild surprise in store it comes with quizzical courtesy, as if to show the author is aware of the conventions of his genre, and prepared to respect them in the letter if not in the spirit. What happened to Rusty Regan in *The Big Sleep*, and who projected whom through the high window which gives that novel its title, we shall find out in due course, but in the meantime we need not feel any great curiosity about the matter. The text offers too much else to be appreciated at our leisure.

Pleasure comes from the elaboration of what was originally a much shorter and brisker type of narrative, often one of the *Black Mask* tales, in which Chandler twice used the death by cyanosis which also figures in *The Big Sleep*. Chandler relied heavily on these tales for the outlines of his later novel plots, and the fusion of short-story terseness with the rich leisurely pace of the novel proved an effective formula. A later fiction like *The Long Goodbye* develops in a more leisurely manner, independent of the earlier story technique, and the results of this are not entirely beneficial.

Like Shakespeare, Chandler was happy to take his plots where he found them. His tongue-in-cheek recipe for bracing up any tale whose pace seemed to be slackening was for a man to burst in pointing a gun. But he could be a shrewd and serious critic of the genre in which he wrote, most notably in an essay called 'The Simple Art of Murder'. 'Fiction in any form', he begins, 'has always intended to be realistic.' Only afterwards does the critic point out that it is in fact hidebound by conventions of all kinds. But the writer himself should not, must not, be too conscious of these. (That Chandler himself was both creator and an admirable critic was one of his peculiar strengths.) 'All art forms can be practised badly, and it is exceedingly hard to practise any of them well, but really good specimens of the detective writer's art are much rarer than good serious novels.' The good novel, says Chandler, is not at all the same sort of thing as the bad: it is about different things, whereas the good and the bad detective story are necessarily about just the same things.

There is a difference none the less. The good writer in the genre simply cannot be bothered with the labours of his colleague, the ingenious constructionist who has both to invent and to break down apparently unbreakable alibis. The good writer's labours and difficulties are of a more complex and intractable kind. Chandler wrote slowly, embroidering and enriching the fabric of his narrative as he went along.

At a decisive point in 'The Simple Art of Murder' Chandler puts on, as it were, the black cap. However ingenious it may be, no detective story is really an intellectual success as a problem, and usually it does not come off artistically as a fiction. The real weakness of the form is that its very nature makes it impossible for the writer to give his characters their heads. That is indeed the crux of the matter and the clue to the art of Chandler's own novels. His characters invariably give what Henry James calls 'the blessed illusion' of being free and independent people, perfectly capable of leading a free and normal life outside the dimension of a detective story. In *War and Peace*, or in Jane Austen's great novels, or in Chekhov's plays, it seems that no artificial literary genre has determined – pre-determined – the way the characters shall live and behave. So it is in Chandler at his best.

This freedom of the character, or the illusion of freedom if we prefer to call it so, is related to another source of strength in Chandler's writing. He has not only created a world of his own but a world which, even if we ourselves are wholly ignorant of it, we know to be in some vital sense true to the facts as they are. Chandler's world is not, like the world of James Bond, a purely fantasy world. It is more like Kafka's. As Kafka's world can freely be compared with our own experiences, so in its more modest, less absolute way, can

Chandler's. However pleasurably exotic and unfamiliar it may be, we feel we could live in it: indeed that we actually *are* living in it as we read; and this illusion of a complete reality must be all but unique in the annals of detective fiction.

We may even imagine that we could lead a perfectly ordinary humdrum life inside a Chandler novel, quite outside the usual excitements and preoccupations of a detective story. We should not ourselves be shooting or being shot at, slugged on the head, or threatened by corrupt policemen, but just driving about in the Oldsmobile, visiting quick lunch counters, and surveying with the eye of a connoisseur the streets and house interiors of Santa Monica. The permit supplied by Chandler would even entitle us to visit such opulent palaces as the Sternwood residence, to admire the family portraits and to wonder at the magnificence of the entrance hall, wide enough to accommodate 'a troop of Indian elephants' and decorated by a giant stained-glass panel 'showing a knight in dark armor rescuing a lady who was tied to a tree and didn't have any clothes on but some very long and convenient hair.'

At once, in the opening paragraphs of *The Big Sleep*, the reader finds himself given the freedom of Chandler country, richly sinister and weirdly funny, humorous and foreboding at the same time. Marlowe is indeed a kind of knight, a knight who travels down mean streets, as well as to the houses of the rich with their English butlers and their festering secrets. But the lady he finds himself having to rescue lives in a world a very long way indeed from medieval romance. The knight of the stained-glass window, we might notice, goes to work in dark – rather than in the traditional knightly shining – armour and Marlowe is an operator who operates without show and with none of the traditional glamour of the detective. No detail of that sort is ever random or irrelevant in Chandler's world. The marvellous detail is as meticulously pointed as it is unobtrusive.

Carmen Sternwood, the spoilt little rich girl and drug-taker, who displays herself naked for the camera of the creepiest of photographers, is the best – or the worst – that the real world of Hollywood runs to in the way of a damsel in distress. She is a far cry from the sentimental fantasy world of 1930s cinema.

Because he declined to make love to her and politely turned down her degraded charms, she has disposed of one doomed representative of the contemporary knightly world, her sister's husband, the ex-bootlegger and IRA man. He lies dishonoured in the old oil sump which has helped to enrich the Sternwood family – a family whose patriarch still clings to an old-fashioned and outdated code of honour.

Marlowe, the ironic knight-errant for twenty-five dollars a day, can save himself from her fatal embrace by quick thinking – another ironic touch out of the medieval romance. But as a further twist of irony he has himself had to be rescued by another lady, who appears in the role of damsel in distress, yet who turns out to be in love with her gangster husband and captor. Like some maimed king in an ancient legend, old General Sternwood presides over this domain, powerless to control his family, or to exercise authority in the modern world; while Norris the family butler, an honourable hireling like Marlowe himself, can only keep faith, and stay silent.

Chandler never wrote anything better than *The Big Sleep*. In the best of the novels which followed (he wrote three in fairly quick succession during the war years), he was able successfully to 'cannibalize', to use his own expression, many of the events and dramatic sequences he had used in earlier *Black Mask* stories. Writing in greater detail and with the sophisticated and elaborate sense of place and people which he had now developed so successfully, he produced other masterpieces like *Farewell, My Lovely* in 1940 and *The Lady in the Lake* three years later. Both have bravura openings, each of a quite different sort, rivalling that of *The Big Sleep* and transporting the reader at once into a new and vivid kind of Chandler landscape. The mountain setting of *The Lady in the Lake* is especially memorable. The California mountains, with their lakes and fish, birds and animals, come instantly alive, and, together with the ambiguous figure of the caretaker at the mountain property, form a perfect and brilliantly realized background to the discovery of the body. Indeed, as so often happens in the best of Chandler, the detail of background and setting is more gripping than the mystery itself and its solution. In this novel these are, none the less, effective enough, reminding us that the author, during this period, was a highly talented and inventive screenwriter, who worked with success on the script of such screen masterpieces as *Double Indemnity*, and had a hand in bringing to the cinema Dashiell Hammett's *The Maltese Falcon*, and his own novels as well.

Like all writers in the genre, Chandler made use of his favourite formulae. The villain invariably turns out to be a woman, young or old, who in terms of the story is all the more aesthetically effective for being female. By the time of *The Long Goodbye* in 1954 the formula had become rather too stereotyped, but it nevertheless remains an aesthetic plot device rather than a symptom of deeper misogyny on the part of the author. Chandler's sense of people is too acute and thus too sympathetic to lay him open to any crude charge of disliking women and making use of them in a monotonously wicked role for that reason. His humanity towards all his creations is never in doubt, but the female monster is a convenience he came increasingly to depend upon.

In becoming modern classics his best books contradict his own stated opinion, in 'The Simple Art of Murder', that both the good and the bad detective story are alike in that they are necessarily about the same things, and treated in a way which does not allow a wide degree of variation. Every fictional murder requires its own style of mystery, and, as *The Lady in the Lake* shows, Chandler cannot but select one among a number of traditional solutions and possibilities. And yet, in the background of *The Big Sleep* and the novels which succeed it there is always the same impression of moral alertness, of reflection, query and discernment – the impression that lies behind all the masterpieces of fiction in any period.

All Chandler's novels possess not only an extraordinarily vivid sense of place, but what in addition might be termed the *atmosphere* of characterization. There is a special and sensitive awareness of the sort of people usually found almost as stock types in detective fiction – policemen, big-time crooks and their bodyguards, secretaries, butlers, business people and hopeful rogues, predatory men and women, or those who have lost out and given up the struggle. Together they make up a world in which individuality, and often a measure of eccentricity, play a natural and unforced part. People in the novels are naturally peculiar, or bad, or even good; but there is no need here, as there would have been in an older and simpler tradition descended from Dickens and G. K. Chesterton, to keep drawing our attention to the fact.

In achieving this overall atmosphere of characterization Chandler has enlarged the scope and enterprise of a not usually very elevated form of fiction on its own terms, and yet without any recourse to the characteristic ingenuities and exaggerated new ploys of the normal detective novel; in fact, he turns out to be not a new kind of thriller-writer but a sober, authoritative and unobtrusively sensitive straight novelist with a world, a style and a personality which are all his own.

His rare and indispensable gift of humour is dissolved, as it were, in this personal and original mode of discourse. His minor personae, always both unusual and alive, are similarly dissolved, together with the rich wealth of background detail, in an atmosphere that is pungently sardonic and yet sympathetic at the same time. His wisecracks and *bon mots* can be deliciously precise, almost surrealistic ('she was a blonde to make a bishop kick a hole in a stained-glass window') though, as a minor villainness tartly points out, Marlowe's addiction to the routine wisecrack can be a little mechanical at times, and even a trifle wearing. But that is all part of a persona which seems both effortlessly natural and carefully crafted at the same time.

What works upon the reader with such effect, and makes him aware that he is experiencing a unique kind of literary pleasure, is the seamless garment of Chandler's style, always and at the same moment serious, humorous, and discreetly erudite. Unlike his older schoolfellow, P. G. Wodehouse, he never seems to draw attention to his own wit, or the part that apt quotation and a meticulous literary sense play in the fine flow of his narrative and his stylistic manner. That overt sentimentality becomes all too visible in the last pair of completed novels – *The Long Goodbye* and *Playback* – is a charge that can hardly be denied, although the old magic is still very much there: Chandler remained Chandler to the end, just as Marlowe remained Marlowe. But in the earlier novels any touch of sentiment is kept fastidiously under control, only emerging briefly in such admirable moments as our brief encounter in *The Big Sleep* with the miniature but valorous Harry Jones, and his big blonde Agnes, the bad picker and eternal loser. Harry Jones is a hero whose death touches us, without requiring a moment's more emotion that the action gives him.

Chandler had always been too good a writer and too independent of fashion to bring what were becoming routine sex scenes into the Marlowe novels. Whatever arrangements Marlowe might have had in that line were not disclosed by himself as narrator, and were no business of the novelist either. Between the assignments that were the subject of a novel, Marlowe might have had any number of disastrous or successful love affairs, but his readers would know nothing about them. But eventually – and the change was even more unfortunate than the drift to a burgeoning sentimentality – the standard thriller's obligation to make its hero a master of the bedroom scene, as well as of mystery solution and crime detection, began to catch up with Chandler. His style, his wit, his masterly impressions of places and people, none of them can help him in this context; and when in *Playback* he seems to make up his mind to attempt the new mode he sounds like any other thriller-writer jumping through the obligatory hoops. (Marlowe's brisk and wholly uncharacteristic bedding of the lawyer's secretary in *Playback* appears actually to copy the standard formalities of a seduction to be found at the time in the novels of every standard thriller-writer, including Ian Fleming.)

Together with sex there goes a more general demoralization of style. Although *Playback* is as sharp-eyed and sharp-talking as ever, and almost as much pleasure to read, there is about it an unmistakable atmosphere of valediction and farewell. Chandler's alcohol problem was becoming more acute, and he had lost the wife to whom he had for a great many years been devoted. The slackening of tempo evident in *The Long Goodbye* of 1954 is in fact arrested three years later in *Playback*, but that novel none the less retains the air of a swansong, and the newly imported sex and sententiousness are far from helpful.

Despite its many good qualities, *The Long Goodbye* had become over-expansive, even verbose at times, with more than a hint of what can seem involuntary self-parody, although the story's grasp of locale, and the individuals that go with it, like the dubious doctors Marlowe has to investigate, is as sure and satisfying as ever. The theme of betrayal, brilliantly handled in an early story called 'Red Wind', is exaggerated and too long drawn-out in the novel. However elaborate his descriptions and his witticisms, a laconic tone is the lifeblood of Chandler's best fiction. He can wonderfully combine an almost *fin de siècle* luxuriance of description with the terseness and ironic understatement learnt from Hemingway. In Hemingway the display of restraint is self-promoting, but as Chandler grew into his own literary personality the quietly ironic style came naturally, embodied in the completely realized figure of Marlowe himself.

The sense equally of aesthetic satisfaction and of a deeper sort of understanding which the reading of these novels leaves with us is the gift of an artistically unique and also a humanely delicate vision: this totality is a far cry from the author who seeks merely to enliven a worn-out genre by means of a new technique. On the contrary, by making an enlightened and intelligent use of his genre, Chandler wrote novels which not only transcend it but will certainly be read as long as the best novels of any kind, or of any age.

John Bayley

JOHN BAYLEY is former Thomas Warton Professor of English Literature at the University of Oxford. His many books include *The Characters of Love, The Short Story: Henry James to Elizabeth Bowen, Shakespeare and Tragedy* and *Tolstoy and the Novel*. He has written several novels, and is the author of the best-selling *Iris*, a memoir of Iris Murdoch.

SELECT BIBLIOGRAPHY

NOVELS
The Big Sleep. New York: Alfred A. Knopf, 1939; London: Hamish Hamilton, 1939.
Farewell, My Lovely. New York: Alfred A. Knopf, 1940; London: Hamish Hamilton, 1940.
The High Window. New York: Alfred A. Knopf, 1942; London: Hamish Hamilton, 1943.
The Lady in the Lake. New York: Alfred A. Knopf, 1943; London: Hamish Hamilton, 1944.
The Little Sister. London: Hamish Hamilton, 1949; Boston: Houghton Mifflin, 1949.
The Long Goodbye. London: Hamish Hamilton, 1953; Boston: Houghton Mifflin, 1954.
Playback. London: Hamish Hamilton, 1958; Boston: Houghton Mifflin, 1958.

STORIES
'Blackmailers Don't Shoot'. *Black Mask*, December 1933.
'Smart-Aleck Kill'. *Black Mask*, July 1934.
'Finger Man'. *Black Mask*, October 1934.
'Killer in the Rain'. *Black Mask*, January 1935.
'Nevada Gas'. *Black Mask*, June 1935.
'Spanish Blood'. *Black Mask*, November 1935.
'Guns at Cyrano's'. *Black Mask*, January 1936.
'The Man Who Liked Dogs'. *Black Mask*, March 1936.
'Noon Street Nemesis' (republished as 'Pickup on Noon Street'. *Detective Fiction Weekly*, May 30, 1936.
'Goldfish'. *Black Mask*, June 1936.
'The Curtain'. *Black Mask*, September 1936.
'Try the Girl'. *Black Mask*, January 1937.
'Mandarin's Jade'. *Dime Detective Magazine*, November 1937.
'Red Wind'. *Dime Detective Magazine*, January 1938.
'The King in Yellow'. *Dime Detective Magazine*, March 1938.
'Bay City Blues'. *Dime Detective Magazine*, June 1938.
'The Lady in the Lake'. *Dime Detective Magazine*, January 1939.
'Pearls Are a Nuisance'. *Dime Detective Magazine*, April 1939.
'Trouble Is My Business'. *Dime Detective Magazine*, August 1939.
'I'll Be Waiting'. *Saturday Evening Post*, October 14, 1939.

'The Bronze Door'. Unknown Magazine, November 1939.
'No Crime in the Mountains'. *Detective Story*, September 1941.
'Professor Bingo's Snuff'. *Park East*, June–August 1951; *Go*, June–July 1951.
'Marlowe Takes on the Syndicate'. *London Daily Mail*, April 6–10 1959, also published as 'Wrong Pidgeon'. *Manhunt*, February 1961. Reprinted as 'The Pencil'.
'English Summer'. First published posthumously in *The Notebooks of Raymond Chandler and English Summer: A Gothic Romance by Raymond Chandler*, ed. Frank MacShane, The Ecco Press, New York, 1976.

BIOGRAPHY
There are several biographies, including *The Life of Raymond Chandler* by Frank MacShane (Cape, 1976), *Raymond Chandler* by William Marling (Twayne, 1986) and Tom Hiney's *Raymond Chandler: An Authorized Biography* (Chatto & Windus, 1997; Grove Atlantic, 2001). *The Raymond Chandler Papers* (ed. Tom Hiney and Frank MacShane, Hamish Hamilton, 2000) includes letters, essays and stories. Miriam Gross's *The World of Raymond Chandler* (Weidenfeld & Nicolson, 1977) offers a pictorial biography and a lavishly illustrated study of the milieu of the Marlowe novels. Jerry Speir's *Raymond Chandler* (Ungar, 1981) contains a useful bibliography.

CHRONOLOGY

DATE	AUTHOR'S LIFE	LITERARY CONTEXT
1888	Raymond Thornton Chandler born 23 July in Chicago.	
1892		1892 James M. Cain born.
1894		1894 Dashiell Hammett born.
1895	Parents divorce. Moves to London with his mother.	1895 Twain: *Pudd'nhead Wilson*. Conan Doyle: *The Memoirs of Sherlock Holmes*. Hardy: *Jude the Obscure*.
1896		1896 Chekhov: *The Seagull*. Fitzgerald born.
1899		1899 Chopin: *The Awakening*. James: *The Awkward Age*. Hornung: *Raffles: The Amateur Cracksman*. Hemingway born. Nabokov born.
1900	Attends Dulwich College, as a day student (to 1904).	1900 Dreiser: *Sister Carrie*. Conrad: *Lord Jim*. Freud: *The Interpretation of Dreams*.
1901		1901 Mann: *Buddenbrooks*. Kipling: *Kim*.
1902		1902 Conan Doyle: *The Hound of the Baskervilles*. Steinbeck born.
1904		1904 James: *The Golden Bowl*. Chekhov dies.
1905–6	Attends language schools in France and Germany in preparation for British Civil Service examinations.	1905 Conan Doyle: *The Return of Sherlock Holmes*. 1906 Wharton: *The House of Mirth*. Beckett born.
1907	Returns to London. Works as a civil servant for the Admiralty.	1907 Conrad: *The Secret Agent*. Auden born.
1909–12	Resigns from Admiralty and works as a literary journalist, contributing poems, reviews, sketches and translations to *The Westminster Gazette* and *The Academy*.	1909 Stein: *Three Lives*. 1910 Forster: *Howards End*. Wells: *The History of Mr Polly*.

HISTORICAL EVENTS

1888 The US becomes the leading manufacturing nation in the world.

1892 California earthquake disaster.
1894 Nicholas II becomes Tsar of Russia.
1895 Beginning of Freudian psychoanalysis.

1896 William McKinley elected US president. Klondike Gold Rush.

1899 Outbreak of Boer War. Alfred Hitchcock born.

1900 US population 76 million. US rail network just less than 200,000 miles. First International Socialist Congress in Paris. Planck's quantum theory.

1901 President McKinley assassinated. Succeeded by Theodore Roosevelt, in a progressive era in American politics. Marconi transmits message across the Atlantic. Death of Queen Victoria. Accession of Edward VII.

1904 War breaks out between Japan and Russia.

1905 Einstein's theory of relativity. General strikes, mutiny and incipient revolution in Russia.
1906 San Francisco earthquake.

1907 Cubist exhibition in Paris.

1909 First Ford Model T car.
1910 Death of Edward VII; accession of George V.

DATE	AUTHOR'S LIFE	LITERARY CONTEXT
1912	Returns to America, spends time in St Louis and Omaha, then settles in California. Does odd jobs, including working for a sporting goods firm and on a ranch.	1912 Dreiser: *The Financier.* Mann: *Death in Venice.*
1913–17	Enrols in night-school bookkeeping course and works as an accountant for the Los Angeles Creamery. His mother comes from England to live with him.	1913 Frost: *A Boy's Will.* Cather: *O Pioneers!* Lawrence: *Sons and Lovers.* 1914 Burroughs: *Tarzan of the Apes.* Joyce: *Dubliners.* 1915 Ford: *The Good Soldier.* Lawrence: *The Rainbow.* Kafka: *Metamorphosis.*
1917	Enlists in Canadian army, is assigned to 7th Batallion of Canadian Expeditionary Force, serves in trenches and is made sergeant.	1917 Conan Doyle: *His Last Bow.* Eliot: 'The Love Song of J. Alfred Prufrock'.
1918	In June is transferred to Royal Air Force.	1918 Cather: *My Ántonia.*
1919–22	Discharged and takes a job in a bank in San Francisco before returning to Los Angeles and working for *The Daily Express.* Has an affair with Cissy Pascal, who is seventeen years his senior and now gets a second divorce.	1919 *Black Mask*, pulp magazine, set up. Anderson: *Winesburg, Ohio.* Wodehouse: *My Man Jeeves.* 1920 Fitzgerald: *This Side of Paradise.* Lewis: *Main Street.* Wharton: *The Age of Innocence.* Pound: *Hugh Selwyn Mauberley.* Christie: *The Mysterious Affair at Styles* (first novel). 1921 Dos Passos: *Three Soldiers.* Lawrence: *Women in Love.* Pirandello: *Six Characters in Search of an Author.*
1922	Takes job with Dabney Oil Syndicate as bookkeeper and soon rises to Vice-President.	1922 Carroll John Daly creates the first hard-boiled detective in 'The False Burton Combs'. Eliot: *The Waste Land.* Joyce: *Ulysses.* Mansfield: *The Garden Party.* Hemingway: *In Our Time.*

CHRONOLOGY

1912 Woodrow Wilson elected US president. Sinking of *Titanic*. Charlie Chaplin's first film.

1913 Completion of new Grand Central Terminal, New York. Post-Impressionist exhibition in New York.

1914 Outbreak of World War I. President Wilson proclaims US neutrality. Panama Canal opens.

1917 US declares war on Germany. Russian October Revolution.

1918 World War I ends. Civil war in Russia (to 1921).

1919 Versailles Peace Conference, with Wilson's Fourteen Points. Eighteenth Amendment, prohibiting the manufacture and sale of intoxicating liquors, is ratified. The 'Red Scare' in the US and a yearlong strike by steelworkers. Nineteenth Amendment (Female Suffrage) passed.
1920 League of Nations formed. Warren G. Harding elected US president. The Slump and the 'jazz age' begin.

1921 Washington Conference on disarmament (to 1922).

1922 Establishment of USSR. Mussolini forms a Fascist government in Italy. Stalin becomes General Secretary of Communist Party. Quota laws restrict immigration to the US. Revival of Ku Klux Klan. Radio broadcasting starts. Talking pictures developed.

DATE	AUTHOR'S LIFE	LITERARY CONTEXT
1923		
1924	Mother dies. Marries Cissy.	1924 Forster: *A Passage to India*. Ford: *Parade's End* (to 1928).
1925		1925 Dreiser: *An American Tragedy*. Fitzgerald: *The Great Gatsby*. Loos: *Gentlemen Prefer Blondes*. Stein: *The Making of Americans*. Dos Passos: *Manhattan Transfer*. Woolf: *Mrs Dalloway*. Kafka: *The Trial*.
1926		1926 Fitzgerald: *All the Sad Young Men*. Faulkner: *Soldier's Pay*. Hemingway: *The Sun Also Rises*. Christie: *The Murder of Roger Ackroyd*.
1927		1927 Cather: *Death Comes for the Archbishop*. Wilder: *The Bridge of San Luis Rey*. Woolf: *To the Lighthouse*. Conan Doyle: *The Case Book of Sherlock Holmes*. Proust: *Remembrance of Things Past*.
1928		1928 O'Neill: *Strange Interlude*. Lawrence: *Lady Chatterley's Lover*. Waugh: *Decline and Fall*.
1929		
1930		1930 Faulkner: *As I Lay Dying*. Hammett: *The Maltese Falcon*. Crane: *The Bridge*. Freud *Civilization and its Discontents*. Lawrence dies.
1931		1931 Hammett: *The Glass Key*.
1932	Sacked for drinking and absenteeism, goes to Seattle without Cissy but returns when he becomes ill.	1932 Caldwell: *Tobacco Road*. Erle Stanley Gardner: *The Case of the Velvet Claws* (first Perry Mason novel). Huxley: *Brave New World*. Crane dies.

CHRONOLOGY

1923 Calvin Coolidge elected president after Harding's death.
1924 Death of Lenin. First Labour government in UK.

1925 Al Capone is a powerful force in Chicago.
The 'Monkey Trial' in Dayton, Tennessee, finds for *Genesis*, signalling the withdrawal of Southern culture into otherworldliness.

1926 Television invented by John Logie Baird. First liquid fuel rocket. General strike in the UK.

1927 Lindbergh's solo Atlantic flight. Trotsky expelled from Communist Party in USSR.

1928 First full-length film; first television broadcast; 13 million radios and 26 million cars in use in US. Herbert Hoover elected US president. Amelia Earhart is the first woman to fly the Atlantic solo. Gershwin: *An American in Paris.*
1929 Wall Street Crash on 24 October. Beginning of world depression. US establishes Federal Loans. Museum of Modern Art in New York founded. Land speed record set at 231 mph.
1930 US Unemployment at 13 million. US tariff raised. France begins Maginot Line. Gandhi embarks on civil disobedience campaign in India. Empire State Building opened.

1931 Al Capone found guilty of tax evasion and imprisoned. Britain abandons Gold Standard. Invention of electric razor.
1932 Lindbergh's son kidnapped. Franklin D. Roosevelt elected US president and inaugurates New Deal. Stock prices in US fall to 20% of 1929 value.

DATE	AUTHOR'S LIFE	LITERARY CONTEXT
1933	Studies Erle Stanley Gardner and other representatives of pulp fiction, and spends five months writing his first story, 'Blackmailers Don't Shoot', which is published by pulp detective magazine, *Black Mask*.	1933 Nathaniel West: *Miss Lonelyhearts*. Book burnings in Germany.
1934–39	Lives in and around Los Angeles, writing a total of twenty pulp stories for *Black Mask* and other magazines.	1934 Cain: *The Postman Always Rings Twice* (banned in Boston). Hammett: *The Thin Man*. Fitzgerald: *Tender is the Night*. Miller: *Tropic of Cancer*. Waugh: *A Handful of Dust*. Christie: *Murder on the Orient Express*. 1935 Wolfe: *Of Time and the River*. Lewis: *It Can't Happen Here*. 1936 Cain: *Double Indemnity*. Mitchell: *Gone with the Wind*. Dos Passos: *The Big Money*. Faulkner: *Absalom, Absalom!* Eliot: *Collected Poems*. Wodehouse: *Laughing Gas*. Lorca killed by Fascist militia in Spain. 1937 Hemingway: *To Have and Have Not*. Steinbeck: *Of Mice and Men*. Stevens: *The Man with the Blue Guitar*. Dos Passos: *U.S.A.* Erle Stanley Gardner: *The D.A. Calls it Murder* (first D.A. Douglas Selby novel). Christie: *Death on the Nile* C. S. Forester: *The Happy Return* (first Hornblower novel). 1938 Cummings: *Collected Poems*. Waugh: *Scoop*. Sartre: *Nausea*. Beckett: *Murphy*.
1939	Publishes his first full-length detective story, *The Big Sleep*.	1939 Joyce: *Finnegans Wake*. Steinbeck: *The Grapes of Wrath*.

CHRONOLOGY

1933 The Twenty-First Amendment, repealing Prohibition, ratified. Hitler appointed Chancellor in Germany. USSR recognized by US.

1934 Depth of Great Depression in US; half of the banks have failed. Al Capone sent to Alcatraz.

1935: Nuremberg Laws depriving Jews of rights and citizenship in Germany. Mussolini invades Abyssinia. Transcontinental air service begins in US. Gershwin: *Porgy and Bess*.
1936 Roosevelt re-elected by landslide. Spanish Civil War (to 1939). Abdication of King Edward VIII who wishes to marry the American divorcee Wallis Simpson. Hitler and Mussolini form Rome–Berlin axis. Stalin's Great Purge of Communist Party in Russia (to 1938).

1937 Japanese invasion of China. First jet engine and nylon stockings. In the US around 75 million visit the movies every week. Strikes against Republic Steel in Chicago: four strikers killed and forty-four injured.

1938 Germany annexes Austria; Munich crisis. Hitchcock: *The Lady Vanishes*.

1939 Nazi-Soviet Pact. Hitler invades Poland: World War II begins. First commercial transatlantic flights. Vivien Leigh and Clark Gable star in *Gone with the Wind*.

DATE	AUTHOR'S LIFE	LITERARY CONTEXT
1940–43	Continues with pulp writing and also publishes three full-length works: *Farewell, My Lovely* (1940), *The High Window* (1942) and *The Lady in the Lake* (1943).	1940 Hemingway: *For Whom the Bell Tolls*. Greene: *The Power and the Glory*. Fitzgerald dies. 1941 Fitzgerald: *The Last Tycoon* (posthumous). Cain: *Mildred Pierce*. Nabokov: *The Real Life of Sebastian Knight*. Brecht: *Mother Courage*. Woolf and Joyce die. 1942 Paul: *A Narrow Street*. Camus: *The Stranger*.
1943	Adapts James Cain's crime novel *Double Indemnity* with Billy Wilder for Paramount Studios.	
1944–46	Works for various film studios but is open about his dislike for the industry. Wins Edgar Allen Poe Award in 1946 (and again in 1956).	1944 Williams: *The Glass Menagerie*. Eliot: *Four Quartets*. 1945 Thurber: *The Thurber Carnival*. Orwell: *Animal Farm*. Waugh: *Brideshead Revisited*. Borges: *Fictions*. Dreiser dies.
1946	Moves to La Jolla and begins to detach himself from movie industry.	1946 Cain: *Past All Dishonor*. Goodis: *Dark Passage*.
1947		1947 Williams: *A Streetcar Named Desire*. Cain: *Butterfly*.
1948		1948 Mailer: *The Naked and the Dead*. Cain: *The Moth*. Eliot wins Nobel Prize.
1949	Publishes first post-Hollywood novel, *The Little Sister*. Works on *The Long Goodbye* (to 1952) as Cissy's health deteriorates.	1949 Miller: *Death of a Salesman*. Orwell: *Nineteen Eighty-Four*. Greene: *The Third Man*. Faulkner wins Nobel Prize.
1950	'The Simple Act of Murder' published. Works with Hitchcock on a film version of Patricia Highsmith's *Strangers on a Train*.	1950 Eliot: *The Cocktail Party*.

CHRONOLOGY

1940 France surrenders to Germany. The Battle of Britain. Trotsky assassinated in Mexico. Churchill prime minister in UK. Penicillin developed. Extraction of plutonium from uranium.

1941 Japanese attack Pearl Harbor. US enters war on 11 December. Hitler invades Russia. US introduces 'lease-lend' system of aid to Britain. Orson Welles: *Citizen Kane*. Irving Berlin: 'White Christmas'. Beginnings of 'bebop'.

1942 Rommel defeated at El Alamein. Build-up of American air force in Free China. World's first nuclear reactor constructed at Chicago University.
1943 Russians defeat Germans at Stalingrad. Allied armies victorious in North Africa. Allied invasion of Italy.

1944 Allied landings in Normandy; German retreat; liberation of Paris. Roosevelt elected for fourth term.

1945 Unconditional surrender of Germany and suicide of Hitler. Bombing of Hiroshima and Nagasaki. End of World War II. United Nations founded. Death of Roosevelt. Truman president of US. Attlee prime minister in UK.

1946 Churchill makes 'Iron Curtain' speech. Cold War begins. Film of *The Big Sleep* released with Humphrey Bogart and Lauren Bacall.

1947 India proclaimed independent. Marshall Plan (US aid for European post-war recovery).

1948 Jewish state of Israel comes into existence. Soviet blockade of West Berlin. Gandhi assassinated. Apartheid introduced in South Africa. Month-long strike of coal miners in US. Hitchcock: *Rope*.

1949 Chinese Revolution. North Atlantic Treaty signed in Washington. Orson Welles stars in *The Third Man*.

1950 Senator Joseph McCarthy accuses State Department of being riddled with Communists and begins period of Communist witch-hunts in US (to 1954). Korean War begins (to 1953).

DATE	AUTHOR'S LIFE	LITERARY CONTEXT
1951		1951 Jones: *From Here to Eternity*. Salinger: *The Catcher in the Rye*. Frost: *Complete Poems*.
1952		1952 Beckett: *Waiting for Godot*. Ellison: *The Invisible Man*. O'Connor: *Wise Blood*. Steinbeck: *East of Eden*
1953	*The Long Goodbye* published, cementing Chandler's literary standing among critics on both sides of the Atlantic.	1953 Bellow: *The Adventures of Augie March*. Faulkner: *Requiem for a Nun*. Williams: *Camino Real*. Fleming: *Casino Royale*.
1954	Cissy dies and Chandler attempts suicide shortly afterwards. Briefly admitted to a psychiatric hospital.	1954 Amis: *Lucky Jim*. Fleming: *Live and Let Die*. Hemingway wins Nobel Prize.
1955–57	Lives between La Jolla and Europe, mostly in hotels. Drinks heavily.	1955 Nabokov: *Lolita*. Williams: *Cat on a Hot Tin Roof*. Miller: *A View from the Bridge*. 1956 Highsmith: *The Talented Mr Ripley*. Goodis: *Shoot the Piano Player*. Osborne: *Look Back in Anger*. Fleming: *Diamonds are Forever*. 1957 Kerouac: *On the Road*. Nabokov: *Pnin*.
1958	Publishes *Playback*.	1958 Pasternak: *Doctor Zhivago*. Capote: *Breakfast at Tiffany's*.
1959	Dies in La Jolla on 26 March, aged seventy.	1959 Burroughs: *Naked Lunch*. Bellow: *Henderson the Rain King*. Grass: *The Tin Drum*.

CHRONOLOGY

1951 President Truman dismisses General MacArthur as commander of the UN forces in Korea. Rogers and Hammerstein: *South Pacific*. Churchill elected prime minister in UK.

1952 Eisenhower elected US president. Gary Cooper stars in *High Noon*. China accuses US of waging germ warfare in Korea. Batista overthrows Cuban government. Accession of Elizabeth II. First contraceptive pill.

1953 Experiments in colour television. Stalin dies. European Court of Human Rights set up in Strasbourg.

1954 Communist Party outlawed in US. Vietnamese Communists defeat French at Dien Bien Phu. Vietnam War begins. Marlon Brando stars in *On the Waterfront*. Hitchcock: *Dial M for Murder* and *Rear Window*.

1956 Soviets invade Hungary. Suez Crisis. Eisenhower re-elected as US president. Transatlantic telephone service linking Britain and US.

1957 Civil Rights Commission established in US to safeguard voting rights. Race riots in the south.
1958 Alaska becomes 49th State. Beginning of space exploration. Bernstein: *West Side Story*. Hitchcock: *Vertigo*.
1959 Batista flees Cuba; Castro seizes power.

BLACKMAILERS DON'T SHOOT

1

THE MAN IN the powder-blue suit – which wasn't powder-blue under the lights of the Club Bolivar – was tall, with wide-set gray eyes, a thin nose, a jaw of stone. He had a rather sensitive mouth. His hair was crisp and black, ever so faintly touched with gray, as by an almost diffident hand. His clothes fitted him as though they had a soul of their own, not just a doubtful past. His name happened to be Mallory.

He held a cigarette between the strong, precise fingers of one hand. He put the other hand flat on the white table-cloth, and said:

"The letters will cost you ten grand, Miss Farr. That's not too much."

He looked at the girl opposite him very briefly; then he looked across empty tables towards the heart-shaped space of floor where the dancers prowled under shifting colored lights.

They crowded the customers around the dance-floor so closely that the perspiring waiters had to balance themselves like tightrope walkers to get between the tables. But near where Mallory sat were only four people.

A slim, dark woman was drinking a highball across the table from a man whose fat red neck glistened with damp bristles. The woman stared into her glass morosely, and fiddled with a big silver flask in her lap. Farther along two bored, frowning men smoked long thin cigars, without speaking to each other.

Mallory said thoughtfully: "Ten grand does it nicely, Miss Farr."

Rhonda Farr was very beautiful. She was wearing, for this occasion, all black, except a collar of white fur, light as thistledown, on her evening wrap. Except also a white wig which, meant to disguise her, made her look very girlish. Her eyes were cornflower blue, and she had the sort of skin an old rake dreams of.

She said nastily, without raising her head: "That's ridiculous."

"Why is it ridiculous?" Mallory asked, looking mildly surprised and rather annoyed.

Rhonda Farr lifted her face and gave him a look as hard as marble. Then she picked a cigarette out of a silver case that lay open on the table, and fitted it into a long slim holder, also black. She went on:

"The love letters of a screen star? Not so much anymore. The public has stopped being a sweet old lady in long lace panties."

A light danced contemptuously in her purplish-blue eyes. Mallory gave her a hard look.

"But you came here to talk about them quick enough," he said, "with a man you never heard of."

She waved the cigarette holder, and said: "I must have been nuts."

Mallory smiled with his eyes, without moving his lips. "No, Miss Farr. You had a damn good reason. Want me to tell you what it is?"

Rhonda Farr looked at him angrily. Then she looked away, almost appeared to forget him. She held up her hand, the one with the cigarette holder, looked at it, posing. It was a beautiful hand, without a ring. Beautiful hands are as rare as jacaranda-trees in bloom, in a city where pretty faces are as common as runs in dollar stockings.

She turned her head and glanced at the stiff-eyed woman, beyond her towards the mob around the dance-floor. The orchestra went on being saccharine and monotonous.

4

"I loathe these dives," she said thinly. "They look as if they only existed after dark, like ghouls. The people are dissipated without grace, sinful without irony." She lowered her hand to the white cloth. "Oh yes, the letters, what makes them so dangerous, blackmailer?"

Mallory laughed. He had a ringing laugh with a hard quality in it, a grating sound. "You're good," he said. "The letters are not so much perhaps. Just sexy tripe. The memoirs of a schoolgirl who's been seduced and can't stop talking about it."

"That's lousy," Rhonda Farr said in a voice like iced velvet.

"It's the man they're written to that makes them important," Mallory said coldly. "A racketeer, a gambler, a fast-money boy. And all that goes with it. A guy you couldn't be seen talking to — and stay in the cream."

"I don't talk to him, blackmailer. I haven't talked to him in years. Landrey was a pretty nice boy when I knew him. Most of us have something behind us we'd rather not go into. In my case it *is* behind."

"Oh yes? Make mine strawberry," Mallory said with a sudden sneer. "You just got through asking him to help you get your letters back."

Her head jerked. Her face seemed to come apart, to become merely a set of features without control. Her eyes looked like the prelude to a scream but only for a second.

Almost instantly she got her self-control back. Her eyes were drained of color, almost as gray as his own. She put the black cigarette holder down with exaggerated care, laced her fingers together. The knuckles looked white.

"You know Landrey that well?" she said bitterly.

"Maybe I just get around, find things out. . . . Do we deal, or do we just go on snarling at each other?"

"Where did you get the letters?" Her voice was still rough and bitter.

Mallory shrugged. "We don't tell things like that in our business."

5

"I had a reason for asking. Some other people have been trying to sell me these same damned letters. That's why I'm here. It made me curious. But I guess you're just one of them trying to scare me into action by stepping the price."

Mallory said: "No; I'm on my own."

She nodded. Her voice was scarcely more than a whisper. "That makes it nice. Perhaps some bright mind thought of having a private edition of my letters made. Photostats . . . Well, I'm not paying. It wouldn't get me anywhere. I don't deal, blackmailer. So far as I'm concerned you can go out some dark night and jump off the dock with your lousy letters!"

Mallory wrinkled his nose, squinted down it with an air of deep concentration. "Nicely put, Miss Farr. But it doesn't get us anywhere."

She said deliberately: "It wasn't meant to. I could put it better. And if I'd thought to bring my little pearl-handled gun I could say it with slugs and get away with it! But I'm not looking for that kind of publicity."

Mallory held up two lean fingers and examined them critically. He looked amused, almost pleased. Rhonda Farr put her slim hand up to her white wig, held it there a moment, and dropped it.

A man sitting at a table some way off got up at once and came towards them.

He came quickly, walking with a light, lithe step and swinging a soft black hat against his thigh. He was sleek in dinner clothes.

While he was coming Rhonda Farr said: "You didn't expect me to walk in here alone, did you? Me, I don't go to night-clubs alone."

Mallory grinned. "You shouldn't ought to have to, baby," he said dryly.

The man came up to the table. He was small, neatly put together, dark. He had a little black mustache, shiny like satin, and the clear pallor that Latins prize above rubies.

With a smooth gesture, a hint of drama, he leaned across the table and took one of Mallory's cigarettes out of the silver case. He lit it with a flourish.

Rhonda Farr put her hand to her lips and yawned. She said, "This is Erno, my bodyguard. He takes care of me. Nice, isn't it?"

She stood up slowly. Erno helped her with her wrap. Then he spread his lips in a mirthless smile, looked at Mallory, said:

"Hello, baby."

He had dark, almost opaque eyes with hot lights in them.

Rhonda Farr gathered her wrap about her, nodded slightly, sketched a brief sarcastic smile with her delicate lips, and turned off along the aisle between the tables. She went with her head up and proud, her face a little tense and wary, like a queen in jeopardy. Not fearless, but disdaining to show fear. It was nicely done.

The two bored men gave her an interested eye. The dark woman brooded glumly over the task of mixing herself a highball that would have floored a horse. The man with the fat sweaty neck seemed to have gone to sleep.

Rhonda Farr went up the five crimson-carpeted steps to the lobby, past a bowing head waiter. She went through looped-back gold curtains, and disappeared.

Mallory watched her out of sight, then he looked at Erno. He said: "Well, punk, what's on your mind?"

He said it insultingly, with a cold smile. Erno stiffened. His gloved left hand jerked the cigarette that was in it so that some ash fell off.

"Kiddin' yourself, baby?" he inquired swiftly.

"About what, punk?"

Red spots came into Erno's pale cheeks. His eyes narrowed to black slits. He moved his ungloved right hand a little, curled the fingers so that the small pink nails glittered. He said thinly:

"About some letters, baby. Forget it! It's out, baby, out!"

Mallory looked at him with elaborate, cynical interest, ran his fingers through his crisp black hair. He said slowly:

7

"Perhaps I don't know what you mean, little one."

Erno laughed. A metallic sound, a strained deadly sound. Mallory knew that kind of laugh; the prelude to gun-music in some places. He watched Erno's quick little right hand. He spoke raspingly.

"On your way, red hot. I might take a notion to slap that fuzz off your lip."

Erno's face twisted. The red patches showed startlingly in his cheeks. He lifted the hand that held his cigarette, lifted it slowly, and snapped the burning cigarette straight at Mallory's face. Mallory moved his head a little, and the white tube arched over his shoulder.

There was no expression on his lean, cold face. Distantly, dimly, as though another voice spoke, he said:

"Careful, punk. People get hurt for things like that."

Erno laughed the same metallic, strained laugh. "Blackmailers don't shoot, baby," he snarled. "Do they?"

"Beat it, you dirty little wop!"

The words, the cold sneering tone, stung Erno to fury. His right hand shot up like a striking snake. A gun whisked into it from a shoulder-holster. Then he stood motionless, glaring. Mallory bent forward a little, his hands on the edge of the table, his fingers curled below the edge. The corners of his mouth sketched a dim smile.

There was a dull screech, not loud, from the dark woman. The color drained from Erno's cheeks, leaving them pallid, sunk in. In a voice that whistled with fury he said:

"Okay, baby. We'll go outside. March, you – !"

One of the bored men three tables away made a sudden movement of no significance. Slight as it was it caught Erno's eye. His glance flickered. Then the table rose into his stomach, knocked him sprawling.

It was a light table, and Mallory was not a lightweight. There was a complicated thudding sound. A few dishes clattered, some silver. Erno was spread on the floor with the table across his thighs. His gun settled a foot from his clawing hand. His face was convulsed.

For a poised instant of time it was as though the scene were imprisoned in glass, and would never change. Then the dark woman screeched again, louder. Everything became a swirl of movement. People on all sides came to their feet. Two waiters put their arms straight up in the air and began to spout violent Neapolitan. A moist, overdriven bus-boy charged up, more afraid of the head waiter than of sudden death. A plump, reddish man with corn-colored hair hurried down steps, waving a bunch of menus.

Erno jerked his legs clear, weaved to his knees, snatched up his gun. He swiveled, spitting curses. Mallory, alone, indifferent in the center of the babel, leaned down and cracked a hard fist against Erno's flimsy jaw.

Consciousness evaporated from Erno's eyes. He collapsed like a half-filled sack of sand.

Mallory observed him carefully for a couple of seconds. Then he picked his cigarette case up off the floor. There were still two cigarettes in it. He put one of them between his lips, put the case away. He took some bills out of his trouser pocket, folded one lengthwise and poked it at a waiter.

He walked away without haste, towards the five crimson-carpeted steps and the entrance.

The man with the fat neck opened a cautious and fishy eye. The drunken woman staggered to her feet with a cackle of inspiration, picked up a bowl of ice cubes in her thin jeweled hands, and dumped it on Erno's stomach, with fair accuracy.

2

MALLORY CAME OUT from under the canopy with his soft hat under his arm. The doorman looked at him inquiringly. He shook his head and walked a little way down the curving sidewalk that bordered the semi-circular private driveway. He stood at the edge of the curbing, in the darkness, thinking hard. After a little while an Isotta-Fraschini went by him slowly.

It was an open phaeton, huge even for the calculated swank of Hollywood. It glittered like a Ziegfeld chorus as it passed the entrance lights, then it was dull gray and silver. A liveried chauffeur sat behind the wheel as stiff as a poker, with a peaked cap cocked rakishly over one eye. Rhonda Farr sat in the back seat, under the half-deck, with the rigid stillness of a wax figure.

The car slid soundlessly down the driveway, passed between a couple of squat stone pillars and was lost among the lights of the boulevard. Mallory put on his hat absently.

Something stirred in the darkness behind him, between tall Italian cypresses. He swung around, looked at faint light on a gun barrel.

The man who held the gun was very big and broad. He had a shapeless felt hat on the back of his head, and an indistinct overcoat hung away from his stomach. Dim light from a high-up, narrow window outlined bushy eyebrows, a hooked nose. There was another man behind him.

He said: "This is a gun, buddy. It goes boom-boom, and guys fall down. Want to try it?"

Mallory looked at him emptily, and said: "Grow up, flattie! What's the act?"

The big man laughed. His laughter had a dull sound, like the sea breaking on rocks in a fog. He said with heavy sarcasm:

"Bright boy has us spotted, Jim. One of us must look like a cop." He eyed Mallory, and added: "Saw you pull a rod on a little guy inside. Was that nice?"

Mallory tossed his cigarette away, watched it arc through the darkness. He said carefully:

"Would twenty bucks make you see it some other way?"

"Not tonight, mister. Most any other night, but not tonight."

"A C note?"

"Not even that, mister."

"That," Mallory said gravely, "must be damn tough."

The big man laughed again, came a little closer. The man behind him lurched out of the shadows and planted a soft fattish hand on Mallory's shoulder. Mallory slid sideways without moving his feet. The hand fell off. He said:

"Keep your paws off me, gumshoe!"

The other man made a snarling sound. Something swished through the air. Something hit Mallory very hard behind his left ear. He went to his knees. He kneeled swaying for a moment, shaking his head violently. His eyes cleared. He could see the lozenge design in the sidewalk. He got to his feet again rather slowly.

He looked at the man who had blackjacked him and cursed him in a thick dull voice, with a concentration of ferocity that set the man back on his heels with his slack mouth working like melting rubber.

The big man said: "Damn your soul, Jim! What in hell'd you do that for?"

The man called Jim put his soft fat hand to his mouth and gnawed at it. He shuffled the blackjack into the side pocket of his coat.

"Forget it!" he said. "Let's take the —— and get on with it. I need a drink."

He plunged down the walk. Mallory turned slowly, followed him with his eyes, rubbing the side of his head. The big man moved his gun in a businesslike way and said:

"Walk, buddy. We're takin' a little ride in the moonlight."

Mallory walked. The big man fell in beside him. The man called Jim fell in on the other side. He hit himself hard in the pit of the stomach, said:

"I need a drink, Mac. I've got the jumps."

The big man said peacefully: "Who don't, you poor egg?"

They came to a touring car that was double-parked near the squat pillars at the edge of the boulevard. The man who had hit Mallory got in behind the wheel. The big man prodded Mallory into the back seat and got in beside him. He held his gun across his big thigh, tilted his hat a little further back, and got out a crumpled pack of cigarettes. He lit one carefully, with his left hand.

The car went out into the sea of lights, rolled east a short way, then turned south down the long slope. The lights of the city were an endless glittering sheet. Neon signs glowed and flashed. The languid ray of a searchlight prodded about among high faint clouds.

"It's like this," the big man said, blowing smoke from his wide nostrils. "We got you spotted. You were tryin' to peddle some phony letters to this Farr twist."

Mallory laughed shortly, mirthlessly. He said: "You flatties give me an ache."

The big man appeared to think it over, staring in front of him. Passing electroliers threw quick waves of light across his broad face. After a while he said:

"You're the guy all right. We got to know these things in our business."

Mallory's eyes narrowed in the darkness. His lips smiled. He said: "What business, copper?"

The big man opened his mouth wide, shut it with a click. He said:

"Maybe you better talk, bright boy. Now would be a hell of a good time. Jim and me ain't tough to get on with, but we got friends who ain't so dainty."

Mallory said: "What would I talk about, Lieutenant?"

The big man shook with silent laughter, made no answer. The car went past the oil well that stands in the middle of La Cienega Boulevard, then turned off on to a quiet street fringed with palm trees. It stopped half-way down the block, in front of an empty lot. Jim cut the motor and the lights.

Then he got a flat bottle out of the door-pocket and held it to his mouth, sighed deeply, passed the bottle over his shoulder.

The big man took a drink, waved the bottle, said:

"We got to wait here for a friend. Let's talk. My name's Macdonald — detective bureau. You was tryin' to shake the Farr girl down. Then her protection stepped in front of her. You bopped him. That was nice routine and we liked it. But we didn't like the other part."

Jim reached back for the whiskey bottle, took another drink, sniffed at the neck, said: "We was stashed out for you. But we don't figure your play out in the open like that. It don't listen."

Mallory leaned an arm on the side of the car, and looked out and up at the calm, blue, star-spattered sky. He said:

"You know too much, copper. And you didn't get your dope from Miss Farr. No screen star would go to the police on a matter of blackmail."

Macdonald jerked his big head around. His eyes gleamed faintly in the dark interior of the car.

"We didn't say how we got our dope, bright boy. So you *was* tryin' to shake her down, huh?"

Mallory said gravely: "Miss Farr is an old friend of mine. Somebody is trying to blackmail her, but not me. I just have a hunch."

Macdonald said swiftly: "What the wop pull a gun on you for?"

"He didn't like me," Mallory said in a bored voice. "I was mean to him."

Macdonald said: "Horse-feathers!" He rumbled angrily. The man in the front seat said: "Smack him in the kisser, Mac. Make the —— like it!"

Mallory stretched his arms downward, twisting his shoulders like a man cramped from sitting. He felt the bulge of his Luger under his left arm. He said slowly:

"You said I was trying to peddle some phony letters. What makes you think the letters would be phony?"

Macdonald said softly: "Maybe we know where the right ones are."

Mallory drawled: "That's what I thought, copper," and laughed.

Macdonald moved suddenly, jerked his balled fist up, hit him in the face, but not very hard. Mallory laughed again, then he touched the bruised place behind his ear with careful fingers.

"That went home, didn't it?" he said.

Macdonald swore dully. "Maybe you're just a bit too damn smart, bright boy. I guess we'll find out after a while."

He fell silent. The man in the front seat took off his hat and scratched at a mat of gray hair. Staccato horn blasts came from the boulevard a half block away. Headlights streamed past the end of the street. After a time a pair of them swung around in a wide curve, speared white beams along below the palm trees. A dark bulk drifted down the half block, slid to the curb in front of the touring car. The lights went off.

A man got out and walked back. Macdonald said: "Hi, Slippy. How'd it go?"

The man was a tall thin figure with a shadowy face under a pulled-down cap. He lisped a little when he spoke. He said:

"Nothin' to it. Nobody got mad."

"Okay," Macdonald grunted. "Ditch the hot one and drive this heap."

Jim got into the back of the touring car and sat on Mallory's left, digging a hard elbow into him. The lanky man slid under the wheel, started the motor, and drove back to La Cienega, then south to Wilshire, then west again. He drove fast and roughly.

They went casually through a red light, passed a big movie palace with most of its lights out and its glass cashier's cage empty; then through Beverly Hills, over interurban tracks. The exhaust got louder on a hill with high banks paralleling the road Macdonald spoke suddenly:

"Hell, Jim, I forgot to frisk this baby. Hold the gun a minute."

He leaned in front of Mallory, close to him, blowing whiskey breath in his face. A big hand went over his pockets, down inside his coat around the hips, up under his left arm. It stopped there a moment, against the Luger in the shoulder-holster. It went on to the other side, went away altogether.

"Okay, Jim. No gun on bright boy."

A sharp light of wonder winked into being deep in Mallory's brain. His eyebrows drew together. His mouth felt dry.

"Mind if I light up a cigarette?" he asked, after a pause.

Macdonald said with mock politeness: "Now why would we mind a little thing like that, sweetheart?"

3

THE APARTMENT HOUSE stood on a hill above Westward Village, and was new and rather cheap-looking. Macdonald and Mallory and Jim got out in front of it, and the touring car went on around the corner, disappeared.

The three men went through a quiet lobby past a switch-board where no one sat at the moment, up to the seventh floor in the automatic elevator. They went along a corridor, stopped before a door. Macdonald took a loose key out of his pocket, unlocked the door. They went in.

It was a very new room, very bright, very foul with cigarette smoke. The furniture was upholstered in loud colors, the carpet was a mess of fat green and yellow lozenges. There was a mantel with bottles on it.

Two men sat at an octagonal table with tall glasses at their elbows. One had red hair, very dark eyebrows, and a dead white face with deep-set dark eyes. The other one had a

ludicrous big bulbous nose, no eyebrows at all, hair the color
of the inside of a sardine can. This one put some cards down
slowly and came across the room with a wide smile. He had
a loose, good-natured mouth, an amiable expression.

"Have any trouble, Mac?" he said.

Macdonald rubbed his chin, shook his head sourly. He
looked at the man with the nose as if he hated him. The man
with the nose went on smiling. He said:

"Frisk him?"

Macdonald twisted his mouth to a thick sneer and stalked
across the room to the mantel and the bottles. He said in a
nasty tone:

"Bright boy don't pack a gun. He works with his head.
He's smart."

He re-crossed the room suddenly and smacked the back of
his rough hand across Mallory's mouth. Mallory smiled thinly,
did not stir. He stood in front of a big bile-colored davenport spotted with angry-looking red squares. His hands hung
down at his sides, and cigarette smoke drifted up from
between his fingers to join the haze that already blanketed the
rough, arched ceiling.

"Keep your pants on, Mac," the man with the nose said.
"You've done your act. You and Jim check out now. Oil the
wheels and check out."

Macdonald snarled: "Who you givin' orders to, big shot?
I'm stickin' around till this chiseler gets what's coming to
him, Costello."

The man called Costello shrugged his shoulders briefly.
The red-haired man at the table turned a little in his chair and
looked at Mallory with the impersonal air of a collector
studying an impaled beetle. Then he took a cigarette out of a
neat black case and lit it carefully with a gold lighter.

Macdonald went back to the mantel, poured some whiskey
out of a square bottle into a glass, and drank it raw. He leaned,
scowling, with his back to the mantel.

Costello stood in front of Mallory, cracking the joints of long, bony fingers.

He said: "Where do you come from?"

Mallory looked at him dreamily and put his cigarette in his mouth. "McNeil's Island," he said with vague amusement.

"How long since?"

"Ten days."

"What were you in for?"

"Forgery." Mallory gave the information in a soft, pleased voice.

"Been here before?"

Mallory said: "I was born here. Didn't you know?"

Costello's voice was gentle, almost soothing. "No-o, I didn't know that," he said. "What did you come for – ten days ago?"

Macdonald heaved across the room again, swinging his thick arms. He slapped Mallory across the mouth a second time, leaning past Costello's shoulder to do it. A red mark showed on Mallory's face. He shook his head back and forth. Dull fire was in his eyes.

"Jeeze, Costello, this crumb ain't from McNeil. He's ribbin' you." His voice blared. "Bright boy's just a cheap chiseler from Brooklyn or K.C. – one of those hot towns where the cops are all cripples."

Costello put a hand up and pushed gently at Macdonald's shoulder. He said: "You're not needed in this, Mac," in a flat, toneless voice.

Macdonald balled his fist angrily. Then he laughed, lunged forward and ground his heel on Mallory's foot. Mallory said: " —— damn!" and sat down hard on the davenport.

The air in the room was drained of oxygen. Windows were in one wall only, and heavy net curtains hung straight and still across them. Mallory got out a handkerchief and wiped his forehead, patted his lips.

Costello said: "You and Jim check out, Mac," in the same flat voice.

Macdonald lowered his head, stared at him steadily through a fringe of eyebrow. His face was shiny with sweat. He had not taken his shabby, crumpled overcoat off. Costello didn't even turn his head. After a moment Macdonald barged back to the mantel, elbowed the gray-haired cop out of the way and grabbed at the square bottle of Scotch.

"Call the boss, Costello," he blared over his shoulder. "You ain't got the brains for this deal. For —— sake do something besides talk!" He turned a little towards Jim, thumped him on the back, said sneeringly: "Did you want just one more drink, copper?"

"What did you come here for?" Costello asked Mallory again.

"Looking for a connection." Mallory stared up at him lazily. The fire had died out of his eyes.

"Funny way you went about it, boy."

Mallory shrugged. "I thought if I made a play I might get in touch with the right people."

"Maybe you made the wrong kind of play," Costello said quietly. He closed his eyes and rubbed his nose with a thumbnail. "These things are hard to figure sometimes."

Macdonald's harsh voice boomed across the close room. "Bright boy don't make mistakes, mister. Not with his brains."

Costello opened his eyes and glanced back over his shoulder at the red-haired man. The red-haired man swiveled loosely in his chair. His right hand lay along his leg, slack, half closed. Costello turned the other way, looked straight at Macdonald.

"Move out!" he snapped coldly. "Move out now. You're drunk, and I'm not arguing with you."

Macdonald ground his shoulders against the mantel and put his hands in the side pockets of his suit coat. His hat hung formless and crumpled on the back of his big, square head.

Jim, the gray-haired cop, moved a little away from him, stared at him strainedly, his mouth working.

"Call the boss, Costello!" Macdonald shouted. "You ain't givin' me orders. I don't like you well enough to take 'em."

Costello hesitated, then moved across to the telephone. His eyes stared at a spot high up on the wall. He lifted the instrument off the prongs and dialed with his back to Macdonald. Then he leaned against the wall, smiling thinly at Mallory over the cup. Waiting.

"Hello . . . yes . . . Costello. Everything's oke except Mac's loaded. He's pretty hostile . . . won't move out. Don't know yet . . . some out-of-town boy. Okay."

Macdonald made a motion, said: "Hold it . . ."

Costello smiled and put the phone aside without haste. Macdonald's eyes gleamed at him with a greenish fire. He spit on the carpet, in the corner between a chair and the wall. He said:

"That's lousy. Lousy. You can't dial Montrose from here." Costello moved his hands vaguely. The red-haired man got to his feet. He moved away from the table and stood laxly, tilting his head back so that the smoke from his cigarette rose clear of his eyes.

Macdonald rocked angrily on his heels. His jawbone was a hard white line against his flushed face. His eyes had a deep, hard glitter.

"I guess we'll play it this way," he stated. He took his hands out of his pockets in a casual manner, and his blued service revolver moved in a tight, businesslike arc.

Costello looked at the red-haired man and said: "Take him, Andy."

The red-haired man stiffened, spit his cigarette straight out from between his pale lips, flashed a hand up like lightning.

Mallory said: "Not fast enough. Look at this one."

He had moved so quickly and so little that he had not seemed to move at all. He leaned forward a little on the davenport. The long black Luger lined itself evenly on the red-haired man's belly.

The red-haired man's hand came down slowly from his lapel, empty. The room was very quiet. Costello looked once at Macdonald with infinite disgust, then he put his hands out in front of him, palms up, and looked down at them with a blank smile.

Macdonald spoke slowly, bitterly. "The kidnapping is one too many for me, Costello. I don't want any part of it. I'm takin' a powder from this toy mob. I took a chance that bright boy might side me."

Mallory stood up and moved sideways towards the red-haired man. When he had gone about half the distance the gray-haired cop, Jim, let out a strangled sort of yell and jumped for Macdonald, clawing at his pocket. Macdonald looked at him with quick surprise. He put his big left hand out and grabbed both lapels of Jim's overcoat tight together, high up. Jim flailed at him with both fists, hit him in the face twice. Macdonald drew his lips back over his teeth. Calling to Mallory, "Watch those birds," he very calmly laid his gun down on the mantel, reached down into the pocket of Jim's coat and took out the woven leather blackjack. He said:

"You're a louse, Jim. You always were a louse."

He said it rather thoughtfully, without rancor. Then he swung the blackjack and hit the gray-haired man on the side of the head. The gray-haired man sagged slowly to his knees. He clawed freely at the skirts of Macdonald's coat. Macdonald stooped over and hit him again with the blackjack, in the same place, very hard.

Jim crumpled down sideways and lay on the floor with his hat off and his mouth open. Macdonald swung the blackjack slowly from side to side. A drop of sweat ran down the side of his nose.

Costello said: "Rough boy, ain't you, Mac?" He said it dully, absently, as though he had very little interest in what went on.

Mallory went on towards the red-haired man. When he was behind him he said:

"Put the hands way up, wiper."

When the red-haired man had done this, Mallory put his free hand over his shoulder, down inside his coat. He jerked a gun loose from a shoulder-holster and dropped it on the floor behind him. He felt the other side, patted pockets. He stepped back and circled to Costello. Costello had no gun.

Mallory went to the other side of Macdonald, stood where everyone in the room was in front of him. He said:

"Who's kidnapped?"

Macdonald picked up his gun and glass of whiskey. "The Farr girl," he said. "They got her on her way home, I guess. It was planned when they knew from the wop bodyguard about the date at the Bolivar. I don't know where they took her."

Mallory planted his feet wide apart and wrinkled his nose. He held his Luger easily, with a slack wrist. He said:

"What does your little act mean?"

Macdonald said grimly: "Tell me about yours. I gave you a break."

Mallory nodded, said: "Sure – for your own reasons. I was hired to look for some letters that belong to Rhonda Farr." He looked at Costello. Costello showed no emotion.

Macdonald said: "Okay by me. I thought it was some kind of a plant. That's why I took the chance. Me, I want an out from this connection, that's all." He waved his hand around to take in the room and everything in it.

Mallory picked up a glass, looked into it to see if it was clean, then poured a little Scotch into it and drank it in sips, rolling his tongue around in his mouth.

"Let's talk about kidnapping," he said. "Who was Costello phoning to?"

"Atkinson. Big Hollywood lawyer. Front for the boys. He's the Farr girl's lawyer, too. Nice guy, Atkinson. A louse."

"He in on the kidnapping?"

Macdonald laughed and said: "Sure."

Mallory shrugged, said: "It seems like a dumb trick – for him."

He went past Macdonald, along the wall to where Costello stood. He stuck the muzzle of the Luger against Costello's chin, pushed his head back against the rough plaster.

"Costello's a nice old boy," he said thoughtfully. "He wouldn't kidnap a girl. Would you, Costello? A little quiet extortion maybe, but nothing rough. That right, Costello?"

Costello's eyes went blank. He swallowed. He said between his teeth: "Can it. You're not funny."

Mallory said: "It gets funnier as it goes on. But perhaps you don't know it all."

He lifted the Luger and drew the muzzle down the side of Costello's big nose, hard. It left a white mark that turned to a red weal. Costello looked a little worried.

Macdonald finished pushing a nearly full bottle of Scotch into his overcoat pocket, and said:

"Let me work on the —— !"

Mallory shook his head gravely from side to side, looking at Costello.

"Too noisy. You know how these places are built. Atkinson is the boy to see. Always see the head man – if you can get to him."

Jim opened his eyes, flapped his hands on the floor, tried to get up. Macdonald lifted a large foot and planted it carelessly in the gray-haired man's face. Jim lay down again. His face was a muddy gray color.

Mallory glanced at the red-haired man and went over to the telephone stand. He lifted the instrument down and dialed a number awkwardly, with his left hand.

He said: "I'm calling the man who hired me . . . He has a big fast car . . . We'll put these boys in soak for a while."

4

LANDREY'S BIG BLACK Cadillac rolled soundlessly up the long grade to Montrose. Lights shone low on the left, in the lap of the valley. The air was cool and clear, and the stars were very bright. Landrey looked back from the front seat, draped an arm over the back of the seat, a long black arm that ended in a white glove.

He said, for the third or fourth time: "So it's her own mouthpiece shaking her down. Well, well, well."

He smiled smoothly, deliberately. All his movements were smooth and deliberate. Landrey was a tall, pale man with white teeth and jet-black eyes that sparkled under the dome light.

Mallory and Macdonald sat in the back seat. Mallory said nothing; he stared out of the car window. Macdonald took a pull at his square bottle of Scotch, lost the cork on the floor of the car, and swore as he bent over to grope for it. When he found it he leaned back and looked morosely at Landrey's clear, pale face above the white silk scarf.

He said: "You still got that place on Highland Drive?"

Landrey said: "Yes, copper, I have. And it's not doin' so well."

Macdonald growled. He said: "That's a damn shame, Mr. Landrey."

Then he put his head back against the upholstery and closed his eyes.

The Cadillac turned off the highway. The driver seemed to know just where he was going. He circled around into a landscaped subdivision of rambling elaborate homes. Tree frogs sounded in the darkness, and there was a smell of orange blossoms.

Macdonald opened his eyes and leaned forward. "The house on the corner," he told the driver.

The house stood well back from a wide curve. It had a lot of tiled roof, an entrance like a Norman arch, and wrought-iron lanterns lit on either side of the door. By the sidewalk there was a pergola covered with climbing roses. The driver cut his lights and drifted expertly up to the pergola.

Mallory yawned and opened the car door. Cars were parked along the street around the corner. The cigarette tips of a couple of lounging chauffeurs spotted the soft bluish dark.

"Party," he said. "That makes it nice."

He got out, stood a moment looking across the lawn. Then he walked over soft grass to a pathway of dull bricks spaced so that the grass grew between them. He stood between the wrought-iron lanterns and rang the bell.

A maid in cap and apron opened the door. Mallory said:

"Sorry to disturb Mr. Atkinson, but it's important. Macdonald is the name."

The maid hesitated, then went back into the house, leaving the front door open a crack. Mallory pushed it open carelessly, looked into a roomy hallway with Indian rugs on the floor and walls. He went in.

A few yards down the hallway a doorway gave on a dim room lined with books, smelling of good cigars. Hats and coats were spread around on the chairs. From the back of the house a radio droned dance music.

Mallory took his Luger out and leaned against the jamb of the door, inside.

A man in evening dress came along the hall. He was a plump man with thick white hair above a shrewd, pink, irritable face. Beautifully tailored shoulders failed to divert attention from rather too much stomach. His heavy eyebrows were drawn together in a frown. He walked fast and looked mad.

Mallory stepped out of the doorway and put his gun in Atkinson's stomach.

"You're looking for me," he said.

Atkinson stopped, heaved a little, made a choked sound in his throat. His eyes were wide and startled. Mallory moved the Luger up, put the cold muzzle into the flesh at Atkinson's throat, just above the V of his wing collar. The lawyer partly lifted one arm, as though to make a sweep of the gun. Then he stood quite still, holding the arm up in the air.

Mallory said: "Don't talk. Just think. You're sold out. Macdonald has ratted on you. Costello and two other boys are taped up at Westwood. We want Rhonda Farr."

Atkinson's eyes were dull blue, opaque, without interior light. The mention of Rhonda Farr's name did not seem to make much impression on him. He squirmed against the gun and said:

"Why do you come to me?"

"We think you know where she is," Mallory said tonelessly. "But we won't talk about it here. Let's go outside."

Atkinson jerked, sputtered. "No . . . no, I have guests."

Mallory said coldly: "The guest we want isn't here." He pressed on the gun.

A sudden wave of emotion went over Atkinson's face. He took a short step back and snatched at the gun. Mallory's lips tightened. He twisted his wrist in a tight circle, and the gun sight flicked across Atkinson's mouth. Blood came out on his lips. His mouth began to puff. He got very pale.

Mallory said: "Keep your head, fat boy, and you may live through the night."

Atkinson turned and walked straight out of the open door, swiftly, blindly.

Mallory took his arm and jerked him to the left, on to the grass. "Make it slow," he said softly.

They rounded the pergola. Atkinson put his hands out in front of him and floundered at the car. A long arm came out of the open door and grabbed him. He went in, fell against the seat. Macdonald clapped a hand over his face and forced him back against the upholstery. Mallory got in and slammed the car door.

Tires squealed as the car circled rapidly and shot away. The driver drove a block before he switched the lights on again. Then he turned his head a little, said: "Where to, boss?"

Mallory said: "Anywhere. Back to town. Take it easy."

The Cadillac turned on to the highway again and began to drop down the long grade. Lights showed in the valley once more, little white lights that moved ever so slowly along the floor of the valley. Headlights.

Atkinson heaved up in the seat, got a handkerchief out and dabbed at his mouth. He peered at Macdonald and said in a composed voice:

"What's the frame, Mac? Shakedown?"

Macdonald laughed gruffly. Then he hiccoughed. He was a little drunk. He said thickly:

"Hell, no. The boys hung a snatch on the Farr girl tonight. Her friends here don't like it. But you wouldn't know anything about it, would you, big shot?" He laughed again, jeeringly.

Atkinson said slowly: "It's funny . . . but I wouldn't." He lifted his white head higher, went on: "Who are these men?"

Macdonald didn't answer him. Mallory lit a cigarette, guarding the match flame with cupped hands. He said slowly:

"That's not important, is it? Either you know where Rhonda Farr was taken, or you can give us a lead. Think it out. There's lots of time."

Landrey turned his head and looked back. His face was a pale blur in the dark.

"It's not much to ask, Mr. Atkinson," he said gravely. His voice was cool, suave, pleasant. He tapped on the seat-back with his gloved fingers.

Atkinson stared towards him for a while, then put his head back against the upholstery. "Suppose I don't know anything about it," he said wearily.

Macdonald lifted his hand and hit him in the face. The lawyer's head jerked against the cushions. Mallory said in a cold, unpleasant voice:

"A little less of your crap, copper."

Macdonald swore at him, turned his head away. The car went on.

They were down in the valley now. A three-colored airport beacon swung through the sky not far away. There began to be wooded slopes and little beginnings of valley between dark hills. A train roared down from the Newhall tunnel, gathered speed and went by with a long shattering crash.

Landrey said something to his driver. The Cadillac turned off on to a dirt road. The driver switched the lights off and picked his way by moonlight. The dirt road ended in a spot of dead brown grass with low bushes around it. There were old cans and torn discolored newspapers faintly visible on the ground.

Macdonald got his bottle out, hefted it, and gurgled a drink. Atkinson said thickly:

"I'm a bit faint. Give me one."

Macdonald turned, held the bottle out, then growled: "Aw, go to hell!" and put it away in his coat. Mallory took a flash out of the door pocket, clicked it on, and put the beam on Atkinson's face. He said:

"Talk."

Atkinson put his hands on his knees and stared straight at the beacon of the flashlight. His eyes were glassy and there was blood on his chin. He spoke:

"This is a frame by Costello. I don't know what it's all about. But if it's Costello, a man named Slippy Morgan will be in on it. He has a shack on the mesa by Baldwin Hills. They might have taken Rhonda Farr there."

He closed his eyes, and a tear showed in the glare of the flash. Mallory said slowly:

"Macdonald should know that."

Atkinson kept his eyes shut, said: "I guess so." His voice was dull and without any feeling.

Macdonald balled his first, lurched sideways and hit him in the face again. The lawyer groaned, sagged to one side. Mallory's hand jerked; jerked the flash. His voice shook with fury. He said:

"Do that again and I'll put a slug in your guts, copper. So help me I will."

Macdonald rolled away, with a foolish laugh. Mallory snapped off the light. He said, more quietly:

"I think you're telling the truth, Atkinson. We'll case this shack of Slippy Morgan's."

The driver swung and backed the car, picked his way back to the highway again.

5

A WHITE PICKET fence showed up for a moment before the headlights went off. Behind it on a rise the gaunt shapes of a couple of derricks groped towards the sky. The darkened car went forward slowly, stopped across the street from a small frame house. There were no houses on that side of the street, nothing between the car and the oil-field. The house showed no light.

Mallory got to the ground and went across. A gravel driveway led along to a shed without a door. There was a touring car parked under the shed. There was thin worn grass along the driveway and a dull patch of something that had once been a lawn at the back. There was a wire clothes line and a small stoop with a rusted screen door. The moon showed all this.

Beyond the stoop there was a single window with the blind drawn; two thin cracks of light showed along the edges of the blind. Mallory went back to the car, walking on the dry grass and the dirt road surface without sound.

He said: "Let's go, Atkinson."

Atkinson got out heavily, stumbled across the street like a man half asleep. Mallory grabbed his arm. The two men went up the wooden steps, crossed the porch quietly. Atkinson fumbled and found the bell. He pressed it. There was a dull buzz inside the house. Mallory flattened himself against the wall, on the side where he would not be blocked by the opening screen door.

Then the house door came open without sound, and a figure loomed behind the screen. There was no light behind the figure. The lawyer said mumblingly:

"It's Atkinson."

The screen hook was undone. The screen door came outward.

"What's the big idea?" said a lisping voice that Mallory had heard before.

Mallory moved, holding his Luger waist-high. The man in the doorway whirled at him. Mallory stepped in on him swiftly, making a clucking sound with tongue and teeth, shaking his head reprovingly.

"You wouldn't have a gun, would you, Slippy," he said, nudging the Luger forward. "Turn slow and easy, Slippy. When you feel something against your spine, go on in, Slippy. We'll be right with you."

The lanky man put his hands up and turned. He walked back into the darkness, Mallory's gun in his back. A small living-room smelled of dust and casual cooking. A door had light under it. The lanky man put one hand down slowly and opened the door.

An unshaded light bulb hung from the middle of the ceiling. A thin woman in a dirty white smock stood under it, limp arms at her sides. Dull colorless eyes brooded under a mop of rusty hair. Her fingers fluttered and twitched in involuntary contractions of the muscles. She made a thin plaintive sound, like a starved cat.

The lanky man went and stood against the wall on the opposite side of the room, pressing the palms of his hands against wallpaper. There was a fixed, meaningless smile on his face.

Landrey's voice said from behind: "I'll take care of Atkinson's pals."

He came into the room with a big automatic in his gloved hand. "Nice little home," he added pleasantly.

There was a metal bed in a corner of the room. Rhonda Farr was lying on it, wrapped to the chin in a brown army blanket. Her white wig was partly off her head and damp golden curls showed. Her face was bluish-white, a mask in which the rouge and lip-paint glared. She was snoring.

Mallory put his hand under the blanket, felt for her pulse. Then he lifted an eyelid and looked closely at the upturned pupil.

He said: "Doped."

The woman in the smock wetted her lips. "A shot of M," she said in a slack voice. "No harm done, mister."

Atkinson sat down on a hard chair that had a dirty towel on the back of it. His dress shirt was dazzling under the unshaded light. The lower part of his face was smeared with dry blood. The lanky man looked at him contemptuously, and patted the stained wallpaper with the flat of his hands. Then Macdonald came into the room.

His face was flushed and sweaty. He staggered a little and put a hand up along the door-frame. "Hi ho, boys," he said vacantly. "I ought to rate a promotion for this."

The lanky man stopped smiling. He ducked sideways very fast, and a gun jumped into his hand. Roar filled the room, a great crashing roar. And again a roar.

The lanky man's duck became a slide and the slide degenerated into a fall. He spread himself out on the bare carpet in a leisurely sort of way. He lay quite still, one half-open eye apparently looking at Macdonald. The thin woman opened her mouth wide, but no sound came out of it.

Macdonald put his other hand up to the door-frame, leaned forward and began to cough. Bright red blood came out on his chin. His hands came down the door-frame slowly. Then his shoulder twitched forward, he rolled like a swimmer in a breaking wave, and crashed. He crashed on his face, his hat still on his head, the mouse-colored hair at the nape of his neck showing below it in an untidy curl.

Mallory said: "Two down," and looked at Landrey with a disgusted expression. Landry looked down at his big automatic and put it away out of sight, in the side pocket of his thin dark overcoat.

Mallory stooped over Macdonald, put a finger to his temple. There was no heartbeat. He tried the jugular vein with the same result. Macdonald was dead, and he still smelled violently of whiskey.

There was a faint trace of smoke under the light bulb, an acrid fume of powder. The thin woman bent forward at the waist and scrambled towards the door. Mallory jerked a hard hand against her chest and threw her back.

"You're fine where you are."

Atkinson took his hands off his knees and rubbed them together as if all the feeling had gone out of them. Landrey went over to the bed, put his gloved hand down and touched Rhonda Farr's hair.

"Hello, baby," he said lightly. "Long time no see." He went out of the room, saying: "I'll get the car over on this side of the street."

Mallory looked at Atkinson. He said casually: "Who has the letters, Atkinson? The letters belonging to Rhonda Farr?"

Atkinson lifted his blank face slowly, squinted as though the light hurt his eyes. He spoke in a vague, far-off sort of voice.

"I – I don't know. Costello, maybe. I never saw them."

Mallory let out a short harsh laugh which made no change in the hard cold lines of his face. "Wouldn't it be funny as hell if that's true!"

He stooped over the bed in the corner and wrapped the brown blanket closely around Rhonda Farr. When he lifted her she stopped snoring, but she did not wake.

6

A WINDOW OR two in the front of the apartment house showed light. Mallory held his wrist up and looked at the curved watch on the inside of it. The faintly glowing hands were at half-past three. He spoke back into the car:

"Give me ten minutes or so. Then come on up. I'll fix the doors."

The street entrance to the apartment house was locked. Mallory unlocked it with a loose key, put it on the latch. There was a little light in the lobby, from one bulb in a floor lamp and from a hooded light above the switchboard. A wizened, white-haired little man was asleep in a chair by the switchboard, with his mouth open and his breath coming in long, wailing snores, like the sounds of an animal in pain.

Mallory walked up one flight of carpeted steps. On the second floor he pushed the button for the automatic elevator. When it came rumbling down from above he got in and pushed the button marked "7." He yawned. His eyes were dull with fatigue.

The elevator lurched to a stop, and Mallory went down the bright, silent corridor. He stopped at a gray olive-wood door and put his ear to the panel. Then he fitted the loose key slowly into the lock, turned it slowly, moved the door back an inch or two. He listened again, went in.

There was light from a lamp with a red shade that stood beside an easy chair. A man was sprawled in the chair and the light splashed on his face. He was bound at the wrists and ankles with strips of wide adhesive tape. There was a strip of adhesive across his mouth.

Mallory fixed the door latch and shut the door. He went across the room with quick silent steps. The man in the chair was Costello. His face was a purplish color above the white adhesive that plastered his lips together. His chest moved in jerks and his breath made a snorting noise in his big nose.

Mallory yanked the tape off Costello's mouth, put the heel of one hand on the man's chin, forced his mouth wide open. The cadence of the breathing changed a bit. Costello's chest stopped jerking, and the purplish color of his face faded to pallor. He stirred, made a groaning sound.

Mallory took an unopened pint bottle of rye off the mantel and tore the metal strip from the cap with his teeth. He pushed Costello's head far back, poured some whiskey into his open mouth, slapped his face hard. Costello choked, swallowed convulsively. Some of the whiskey ran out of his nostrils. He opened his eyes, focused them slowly. He mumbled something confused.

Mallory went through velour curtains that hung across a doorway at the inner end of the room, into a short hall. The first door led into a bedroom with twin beds. A light burned, and a man was lying bound on each of the beds.

Jim, the gray-haired cop, was asleep or still unconscious. The side of his head was stiff with congealed blood. The skin of his face was a dirty gray.

The eyes of the red-haired man were wide open, diamond bright, angry. His mouth worked under the tape, trying to chew it. He had rolled over on his side and almost off the bed. Mallory pushed him back towards the middle, and said:

"It's all in the game."

He went back to the living-room and switched on more light. Costello had struggled up in the easy chair. Mallory took out a pocket knife and reached behind him, sawed the tape that bound his wrists. Costello jerked his hands apart, grunted, and rubbed the backs of his wrists together where the tape had pulled hairs out. Then he bent over and tore tape off his ankles. He said:

"That didn't do me any good. I'm a mouth breather." His voice was loose, flat and without cadence.

He got to his feet and poured two inches of rye into a glass, drank it at a gulp, sat down again and leaned his head against the high back of the chair. Life came into his face; glitter came into his washed-out eyes.

He said: "What's new?"

Mallory spooned at a bowl of water that had been ice, frowned and drank some whiskey straight. He rubbed the left side of his head gently with his finger-tips and winced. Then he sat down and lit a cigarette.

He said: "Several things. Rhonda Farr is home. Macdonald and Slippy Morgan got gunned. But that's not important. I'm after some letters you were trying to peddle to Rhonda Farr. Dig 'em up."

Costello lifted his head and grunted. He said: "I don't have the letters."

Mallory said: "Get the letters, Costello. Now." He sprinkled cigarette ash carefully in the middle of a green and yellow diamond in the carpet design.

Costello made an impatient movement. "I don't have them," he insisted. "I never saw them."

Mallory's eyes were slate-gray, very cold, and his voice was brittle. He said: "What you heels don't know about your racket is just pitiful. . . . I'm tired, Costello. I don't feel like an argument. You'd look lousy with that big beezer smashed over on one side of your face with a gun barrel."

Costello put his bony hand up and rubbed the reddened skin around his mouth where the tape had chafed it. He glanced down the room. There was a slight movement of the velour curtains across the end door, as though a breeze had stirred them. But there was no breeze. Mallory was staring down at the carpet.

34

Costello stood up from the chair, slowly. He said: "I've got a wall safe. I'll open it up."

He went across the room to the wall in which the outside door was, lifted down a picture and worked the dial of a small inset circular safe. He swung the little round door open and thrust his arm into the safe.

Mallory said: "Stay just like that, Costello."

He stepped lazily across the room, and passed his left hand down Costello's arm, into the safe. It came out again holding a small pearl-handled automatic. He made a sibilant sound with his lips and put the little gun into his pocket.

"Just can't learn, can you, Costello?" he said in a tired voice.

Costello shrugged, went back across the room. Mallory plunged his hands into the safe and tumbled the contents out onto the floor. He dropped on one knee. There were some long white envelopes, a bunch of clippings fastened with a paper-clip, a narrow, thick check-book, a small photograph album, an address book, some loose papers, some yellow bank statements with check inside. Mallory spread one of the long envelopes carelessly, without much interest.

The curtains over the end door moved again. Costello stood rigid in front of the mantel. A gun came through the curtains in a small hand that was very steady. A slim body followed the hand, a white face with blazing eyes – Erno.

Mallory came to his feet, his hands breast-high, empty.

"Higher, baby," Erno croaked. "Much higher, baby!"

Mallory raised his hands a little more. His forehead was wrinkled in a hard frown. Erno came forward into the room. His face glistened. A lock of oily black hair drooped over one eyebrow. His teeth showed in a stiff grin.

He said: "I think we'll give it to you right here, two-timer."

His voice had a questioning inflection, as if he waited Costello's confirmation.

Costello didn't say anything.

35

Mallory moved his head a little. His mouth felt very dry. He watched Erno's eyes, saw them tense. He said rather quickly:

"You've been crossed, mug, but not by me."

Erno's grin widened to a snarl, and his head went back. His trigger finger whitened at the first joint. Then there was a noise outside the door, and it came open.

Landrey came in. He shut the door with a jerk of his shoulder, and leaned against it, dramatically. Both his hands were in the side pockets of his thin dark overcoat. His eyes under the soft black hat were bright and devilish. He looked pleased. He moved his chin in the white silk evening scarf that was tucked carelessly about his neck. His handsome pale face was like something carved out of old ivory.

Erno moved his gun slightly and waited. Landrey said cheerfully:

"Bet you a grand you hit the floor first!"

Erno's lips twitched under his shiny little mustache. Two guns went off at the same time. Landrey swayed like a tree hit by a gust of wind; the heavy roar of his .45 sounded again, muffled a little by cloth and the nearness to his body.

Mallory went down behind the davenport, rolled and came up with the Luger straight out in front of him. But Erno's face had already gone blank.

He went down slowly; his light body seemed to be drawn down by the weight of the gun in his right hand. He bent at the knees as he fell, and slid forward on the floor. His back arched once, and then went loose.

Landrey took his left hand out of his coat pocket and spread the fingers away from him as though pushing at something. Slowly and with difficulty he got the big automatic out of the other pocket and raised it inch by inch, turning on the balls of his feet. He swiveled his body towards Costello's rigid figure and squeezed the trigger again. Plaster jumped from the wall at Costello's shoulder.

Landrey smiled vaguely, said: "Damn!" in a soft voice.

Then his eyes went up in his head and the gun plunged down from his nerveless fingers, bounded on the carpet. Landrey went down joint by joint, smoothly and gracefully, kneeled, swaying a moment before he melted over sideways, spread himself on the floor almost without sound. Mallory looked at Costello, and said in a strained, angry voice: "Boy, are you lucky!"

★

The buzzer droned insistently. Three little lights glowed red on the panel of the switchboard. The wizened, white-haired little man shut his mouth with a snap and struggled sleepily upright.

Mallory jerked past him with his head turned the other way, shot across the lobby, out of the front door of the apartment house, down the three marble-faced steps, across the sidewalk and the street. The driver of Landrey's car had already stepped on the starter. Mallory swung in beside him, breathing hard, and slammed the car door.

"Get goin' fast!" he rasped. "Stay off the boulevard. Cops here in five minutes!"

The driver looked at him and said: "Where's Landrey? . . . I heard shootin'."

Mallory held the Luger up, said swiftly and coldly: "Move, baby!"

The gears went in, the Cadillac jumped forward, the driver took a corner recklessly, the tail of his eye on the gun.

Mallory said: "Landrey stopped lead. He's cold." He held the Luger up, put the muzzle under the driver's nose. "But not from my gun. Smell that, friend. It hasn't been fired!"

The driver said: "Jeeze!" in a shattered voice, swung the big car wildly, missing the curb by inches.

It was getting to be daylight.

7

RHONDA FARR SAID: "Publicity, darling. Just publicity. Any kind is better than none at all. I'm not so sure my contract is going to be renewed and I'll probably need it."

She was sitting in a deep chair, in a large, long room. She looked at Mallory with lazy, indifferent, purplish-blue eyes and moved her hand to a tall, misted glass. She took a drink.

The room was enormous. Mandarin rugs in soft colors swathed the floor. There was a lot of teakwood and red lacquer. Gold frames glinted high up on the walls, and the ceiling was remote and vague, like the dusk of a hot day. A huge carved radio gave forth muted and unreal strains.

Mallory wrinkled his nose and looked amused in a grim sort of way. He said:

"You're a nasty little rat. I don't like you."

Rhonda Farr said: "Oh, yes, you do, darling. You're crazy about me."

She smiled and fitted a cigarette into a jade-green holder that matched her jade-green lounging pajamas. Then she reached out her beautifully shaped hand and pushed the button of a bell that was set into the top of a low nacre and teakwood table at her side. A silent, white-coated Japanese butler drifted into the room and mixed more highballs.

"You're a pretty wise lad, aren't you, darling?" Rhonda Farr said, when he had gone out again. "And you have some letters in your pocket you think are body and soul to me. Nothing like it, mister, nothing like it." She took a sip of the fresh highball. "The letters you have are phony. They were written about a month ago. Landrey never had them. He gave *his* letters back a long time ago. . . . What you have are just props." She put a hand to her beautifully waved hair. The experience of the previous night seemed to have left no trace on her.

Mallory looked at her carefully. He said: "How do you prove that?"

"The notepaper – if I have to prove it. There's a little man down at Fourth and Spring who makes a study of that kind of thing."

Mallory said: "The writing?"

Rhonda Farr smiled dimly. "Writing's easy to fake, if you have plenty of time. Or so I'm told. That's my story anyhow."

Mallory nodded, sipped at his own highball. He put his hand into his inside breast pocket and took out a flat manila envelope, legal size. He laid it on his knee.

"Four men got gunned out last night on account of these phony letters," he said carelessly.

Rhonda Farr looked at him mildly. "Two crooks, a double-crossing policeman, make three of them. I should lose my sleep over that trash! Of course, I'm sorry about Landrey."

Mallory said politely: "It's nice of you to be sorry about Landrey."

She said peacefully: "Landrey, as I told you once, was a pretty nice boy a few years ago, when he was trying to get into pictures. But he chose another business, and in that business he was bound to stop a bullet some time."

Mallory rubbed his chin. "It's funny he didn't remember he'd given you back your letters. Very funny."

"He wouldn't care, darling. He was that kind of actor, and he'd like the show. It gave him a chance for a swell pose. He'd like that terribly."

Mallory let his face get hard and disgusted. He said: "The job looked on the level to me. I didn't know much about Landrey, but he knew a good friend of mine in Chicago. He figured a way to the boys who were working on you, and I played his hunch. Things happened that made it easier – but a lot noisier."

Rhonda Farr tapped little bright nails against her little bright teeth. She said: "What are you back where you live, darling? One of those hoods they call private dicks?"

Mallory laughed harshly, made a vague movement and ran his fingers through his crisp dark hair. "Let it go, baby," he said softly. "Let it go."

Rhonda Farr looked at him with a surprised glance, then laughed rather shrilly. "It gets mad, doesn't it?" she cooed. She went on, in a dry voice: "Atkinson has been bleeding me for years, one way and another. I fixed the letters up and put them where he could get hold of them. They disappeared. A few days afterwards a man with one of those tough voices called up and began to apply the pressure. I let it ride. I figured I'd hang a pinch on Atkinson somehow, and our two reputations put together would be good for a write-up that wouldn't hurt me too much. But the thing seemed to be spreading out, and I got scared. I thought of asking Landrey to help me out. I was sure he would like it."

Mallory said roughly: "Simple, straightforward kid, ain't you? Like hell!"

"You don't know much about this Hollywood racket, do you darling?" Rhonda Farr said. She put her head on one side and hummed softly. The strains of a dance band floated idly through the quiet air. "That's a gorgeous melody. . . . It's swiped from a Weber sonata. . . . Publicity has to hurt a bit out here. Otherwise nobody believes it."

Mallory stood up, lifting the manila envelope off his knee. He dropped it in her lap.

"Five grand these are costing you," he said.

Rhonda Farr leaned back and crossed her jade-green legs. One little green slipper fell off her bare foot to the rug, and the manila envelope fell down beside it. She didn't stir towards either one.

She said: "Why?"

"I'm a business man, baby. I get paid for my work. Landrey didn't pay me. Five grand was the price. The price to him, and now the price to you."

She looked at him almost casually, out of placid, cornflower-blue eyes, and said: "No deal . . . blackmailer. Just like I told you at the Bolivar. You have all my thanks, but I'm spending my money myself."

Mallory said curtly: "This might be a damn good way to spend some of it."

He leaned over and picked up her highball, drank a little of it. When he put the glass down he tapped the nails of two fingers against the side for a moment. A small tight smile wrinkled the corners of his mouth. He lit a cigarette and tossed the match into a bowl of hyacinths.

He said slowly: "Landrey's driver talked, of course. Landrey's friends want to see me. They want to know how come Landrey got rubbed out in Westwood. The cops will get around to me after a while. Someone is sure to tip them off. I was right beside four killings last night, and naturally I'm not going to run out on them. I'll probably have to spill the whole story. The cops will give you plenty of publicity, baby. Landrey's friends – I don't know what they'll do. Something that will hurt a lot, I should say."

Rhonda Farr jerked to her feet, fumbling with her toe for the green slipper. Her eyes had gone wide and startled.

"You'd . . . sell me out?" she breathed.

Mallory laughed. His eyes were bright and hard. He stared along the floor at a splash of light from one of the standing lamps. He said in a bored voice:

"Why the hell should I protect you? I don't owe you anything. And you're too damn tight with your dough to hire me. I haven't a record, but you know how the law boys love my sort. And Landrey's friends will just see a dirty plant that got a good lad killed. —— sake, why should I front for a chiseler like you?"

He snorted angrily. Red spots showed in his tanned cheeks.

Rhonda Farr stood quite still and shook her head slowly from side to side. She said: "No deal, blackmailer . . . no deal." Her voice was small and tired, but her chin stuck out hard and brave.

Mallory reached out and picked up his hat. "You're a hell of a guy," he said, grinning, "Christ! but you Hollywood frails must be hard to get on with!"

He leaned forward suddenly, put his left hand behind her head and kissed her on the mouth hard. Then he flipped the tips of his fingers across her cheek.

"You're a nice kid – in some ways," he said. "And a fair liar. Just fair. You didn't fake any letters, baby. Atkinson wouldn't fall for a trick like that."

Rhonda Farr stooped over, snatched the manila envelope off the rug, and tumbled out what was in it – a number of closely written grey pages, deckle-edged, with thin gold monograms. She stared down at them with quivering nostrils.

She said slowly: "I'll send you the money."

Mallory put his hand against her chin, and pushed her head back.

He said rather gently:

"I was kidding you, baby. I have that bad habit. But there are two funny things about these letters. They haven't any envelopes, and there's nothing to show who they were written to – nothing at all. The second thing is, Landrey had them in his pocket when he was killed."

He nodded and turned away. Rhonda Farr said sharply: "Wait!" Her voice was suddenly terrified.

Mallory said: "It gets you when it's over. Take a drink."

He went a little way down the room, turned his head. He said: "I have to go. Got a date with a big black spot. . . . Send me some flowers. Wild, blue flowers, like your eyes."

He went out under an arch. A door opened and shut heavily. Rhonda Farr sat without moving for a long time.

8

CIGARETTE SMOKE LACED the air. A group of people in evening clothes stood sipping cocktails at one side of a curtained opening that led to the gambling rooms. Beyond the curtains light blazed down on one end of a roulette table.

Mallory put his elbows on the bar, and the bartender left two young girls in party gowns and slid a white towel along the polished wood towards him. He said:

"What'll it be, chief?"

Mallory said: "A small beer."

The bartender gave it to him, smiled, went back to the two girls. Mallory sipped the beer, made a face, and looked into the long mirror that ran all the way behind the bar and slanted forward a little, so that it showed the floor all the way over to the far wall. A door opened in the wall and a man in dinner clothes came through. He had a wrinkled brown face and hair the color of steel wool. He met Mallory's glance in the mirror and came across the room nodding.

He said: "I'm Mardonne. Nice of you to come." He had a soft, husky voice, the voice of a fat man, but he was not fat.

Mallory said: "It's not a social call."

Mardonne said: "Let's go up to my office."

Mallory drank a little more of the beer, made another face, and pushed the glass away from him across the bar top. They went through the door, up a carpeted staircase that met another staircase half-way up. An open door shone light on the landing. They went in where the light was.

The room had been a bedroom, and no particular trouble had been taken to make it over into an office. It had gray walls, two or three prints in narrow frames. There was a big filing cabinet, a good safe, chairs. A parchment-shaded lamp stood on a walnut desk. A very blond young man sat on a corner of the desk swinging one leg over the other. He was wearing a soft hat with a gay band.

Mardonne said: "All right, Henry. I'll be busy."

The blond young man got off the desk, yawned, put his hand to his mouth with an affected flirt of the wrist. There was a large diamond on one of his fingers. He looked at

Mallory, smiled, and went slowly out of the room, closing the door.

Mardonne sat down in a blue leather swivel-chair. He lit a thin cigar and pushed a humidor across the grained top of the desk. Mallory took a chair at the end of the desk, between the door and a pair of open windows. There was another door, but the safe stood in front of it. He lit a cigarette, said:

"Landrey owed me some money. Five grand. Anybody here interested in paying it?"

Mardonne put his brown hands on the arms of his chair and rocked back and forth. "We haven't come to that," he said.

Mallory said: "Right. What have we come to?"

Mardonne narrowed his dull eyes. His voice was flat and without tone. "To how Landrey got killed."

Mallory put his cigarette in his mouth and clasped his hands together behind his head. He puffed smoke and talked through it at the wall above Mardonne's head.

"He crossed everybody up and then he crossed himself. He played too many parts and got his lines mixed. He was gun-drunk. When he got a rod in his hand he had to shoot somebody. Somebody shot back."

Mardonne went on rocking, said: "Maybe you could make it a little more definite."

"Sure . . . I could tell you a story . . . about a girl who wrote some letters once. She thought she was in love. They were reckless letters, the sort a girl would write who had more guts than was good for her. Time passed, and somehow the letters got on the blackmail market. Some workers started to shake the girl down. Not a high stake, nothing that would have bothered her, but it seems she liked to do things the hard way. Landrey thought he would help her out. He had a plan and the plan needed a man who could wear a tux, keep a spoon out of a coffee-cup, and wasn't known in this town. He got me. I run a small agency in Chicago."

Mardonne swiveled towards the open windows and stared out at the tops of some trees. "Private dick, huh?" he grunted impassively. "From Chicago."

Mallory nodded, looked at him briefly, looked back at the same spot on the wall. "And supposed to be on the level, Mardonne. You wouldn't think it from some of the company I've been keeping lately."

Mardonne made a quick impatient gesture, said nothing.

Mallory went on: "Well, I gave the job a tumble, which was my first and worst mistake. I was making a little headway when the shakedown turned into a kidnapping. Not so good. I got in touch with Landrey and he decided to show with me. We found the girl without a lot of trouble. We took her home. We still had to get the letters. While I was trying to pry them loose from the guy I thought had them one of the bad boys got in the back way and wanted to play with his gun. Landrey made a swell entrance, struck a pose and shot it out with the hood, toe to toe. He stopped some lead. It was pretty, if you like that sort of thing, but it left me in a spot. So perhaps I'm prejudiced. I had to lam out and collect my ideas."

Mardonne's dull brown eyes showed a passing flicker of emotion. "The girl's story might be interesting, too," he said coolly.

Mallory blew a pale cloud of smoke. "She was doped and doesn't know anything. She wouldn't talk, if she did. And I don't know her name."

"I do," Mardonne said. "Landrey's driver also talked to me. So I won't have to bother you about that."

Mallory talked on, placidly. "That's the tale from the outside, without notes. The notes make it funnier — and a hell of a lot dirtier. The girl didn't ask Landrey for help, but he knew about the shakedown. He'd once had the letters, because they were written to him. His scheme to get on their trail was for me to make a wrong pass at the girl myself, make her think *I* had the letters, talk her into a meeting at a night-club where we could be watched by the people who were working on her. She'd come, because she had that kind of guts. She'd be watched, because there would be an inside – maid, chauffeur or something. The boys would want to know about me. They'd pick me up, and if I didn't get conked out of hand, I might learn who was who in the racket. Sweet set-up, don't you think so?"

Mardonne said coldly: "A bit loose in places. . . . Go on talking."

"When the decoy worked I knew it was fixed. I stayed with it, because for the time being I had to. After a while there was another sour play, unrehearsed this time. A big flattie who was taking graft money from the gang got cold feet and threw the boys for a loss. He didn't mind a little extortion, but a snatch was going off the deep end on a dark night. The break made things easier for me, and it didn't hurt Landrey any, because the flattie wasn't in on the clever stuff. The hood who got Landrey wasn't either, I guess. That one was just sore, thought he was being chiseled out of his cut."

Mardonne flipped his brown hands up and down on the chair arms, like a purchasing agent getting restless under a sales talk. "Were you supposed to figure things out this way?" he asked with a sneer.

"I used my head, Mardonne. Not soon enough, but I used it. Maybe I wasn't hired to think, but that wasn't explained to me, either. If I got wise, it was Landrey's hard luck. He'd have to figure an out to that one. If I didn't, I was the nearest thing to an honest stranger he could afford to have around."

Mardonne said smoothly: "Landrey had plenty of dough. He had some brains. Not a lot, but some. He wouldn't go for a cheap shake like that."

Mallory laughed harshly: "It wasn't so cheap to him, Mardonne. He wanted the girl. She'd got away from him, out of his class. He couldn't pull himself up, but he could pull her down. The letters were not enough to bring her into line. Add

a kidnapping and a fake rescue by an old flame turned racketeer, and you have a story no rag could be made to soft-
pedal. If it was spilled, it would blast her right out of her job.
You guess the price for not spilling it, Mardonne."

Mardonne said: "Uh-huh," and kept on looking out of the
window.

Mallory said: "But all that's on the cuff, now. I was hired to
get some letters, and I got them – out of Landrey's pocket
when he was bumped. I'd like to get paid for my time."

Mardonne turned in his chair and put his hands flat on the
top of the desk. "Pass them over," he said. "I'll see what they're
worth to me."

Mallory's eyes got sharp and bitter. "The trouble with you
heels is that you can't figure anybody to be on the up and up.
. . . The letters are withdrawn from circulation. They passed
around too much and they wore out."

"It's a sweet thought," Mardonne sneered. "For somebody
else. Landrey was my partner, and I thought a lot of him. . . .
So you give the letters away, and I pay you dough for letting
Landrey get gunned. I ought to write that one in my diary.
My hunch is you've been paid plenty already – by Miss
Rhonda Farr."

Mallory said, sarcastically: "I figured it would look like that
to you. Maybe *you'd* like the story better this way . . . The girl
got tired of having Landrey trail her around. She faked some
letters and put them where her smart lawyer could lift them,
pass them along to a man who was running a strong-arm
squad the lawyer used in his business sometimes. The girl
wrote to Landrey for help and he got me. The girl got to me
with a better bid. She hired me to put Landrey on the spot.
I played along with him until I got him under the gun of a
wiper that was pretending to make a pass at me. The wiper let
him have it, and I shot the wiper with Landrey's gun, to make
it look good. Then I had a drink and went home to get some
sleep."

Mardonne leaned over and pressed a buzzer on the side of his desk. He said: "I like that one a lot better. I'm wondering if I could make it stick."

"You could try," Mallory said lazily. "I don't guess it would be the first lead quarter you've tried to pass."

9

THE ROOM DOOR came open and the blond boy strolled in. His lips were spread in a pleased grin and his tongue came out between them. He had an automatic in his hand.

Mardonne said: "I'm not busy anymore, Henry."

The blond boy shut the door. Mallory stood up and backed slowly towards the wall. He said grimly:

"Now for the funny stuff, eh?"

Mardonne put brown fingers up and pinched the fat part of his chin. He said curtly:

"There won't be any shooting here. Nice people come to this house. Maybe you didn't spot Landrey, but I don't want you around. You're in my way."

Mallory kept on backing until he had his shoulders against the wall. The blond boy frowned, took a step towards him. Mallory said:

"Stay right where you are, Henry. I need room to think. You might get a slug into me, but you wouldn't stop my gun from talking a little. The noise wouldn't bother me at all."

Mardonne bent over his desk, looking sideways. The blond boy slowed up. His tongue still peeped out between his lips. Mardonne said:

"I've got some C notes in the desk here. I'm giving Henry ten of them. He'll go to your hotel with you. He'll even help you pack. When you get on the train East he'll pass you the dough. If you come back after that, it will be a new deal – from a cold deck". He put his hand down slowly and opened the desk drawer.

Mallory kept his eyes on the blond boy. "Henry might make a change in the continuity," he said pleasantly. "Henry looks kind of unstable to me."

Mardonne stood up, brought his hand from the drawer. He dropped a packet of notes on top of the desk. He said:

"I don't think so. Henry usually does what he is told."

Mallory grinned tightly. "Perhaps *that's* what I'm afraid of," he said. His grin got tighter still, and crookeder. His teeth glittered between his pale lips. "You said you thought a lot of Landrey, Mardonne. That's hooey. You don't care a thin dime about Landrey, now he's dead. You probably stepped right into his half of the joint, and nobody around to ask questions. It's like that in the rackets. You want me out because you think you can still peddle your dirt – in the right place – for more than this small-time joint would net in a year. But you can't peddle it, Mardonne. The market's closed. Nobody's going to pay you a plugged nickel either to spill it or not to spill it."

Mardonne cleared his throat softly. He was standing in the same position, leaning forward a little over the desk, both hands on top of it, and the packet of notes between his hands. He licked his lips, said:

"All right, master mind. Why not?"

Mallory made a quick but expressive gesture with his right thumb.

"I'm the sucker in this deal. *You're* the smart guy. I told you a straight story the first time and my hunch says Landrey wasn't in that sweet frame alone. *You* were in it up to your fat neck! . . . But you aced yourself backwards when you let Landrey pack those letters around with him. The girl can talk now. Not a whole lot, but enough to get backing from an outfit that isn't going to scrap a million-dollar reputation because some cheap gambler wants to get smart. . . . If your money says different, you're going to get a jolt that'll have you picking your eye-teeth out of your socks. You're going to see the sweetest cover-up even Hollywood ever fixed."

49

He paused, flashed a quick glance at the blond boy. "Something else, Mardonne. When you figure on gun play get yourself a loogan that knows what it's all about. The gay caballero here forgot to thumb back his safety."

Mardonne stood frozen. The blond boy's eyes flinched down to his gun for a split second of time. Mallory jumped fast along the wall, and his Luger snapped into his hand. The blond boy's face tensed, his gun crashed. Then the Luger cracked, and a slug went into the wall beside the blond boy's gay felt hat. Henry faded down gracefully, squeezed lead again. The shot knocked Mallory back against the wall. His left arm went dead.

His lips writhed angrily. He steadied himself; the Luger talked twice, very rapidly.

The blond boy's gun arm jerked up and the gun sailed against the wall high up. His eyes widened, his mouth came open in a yell of pain. Then he whirled, wrenched the door open and pitched straight out on the landing with a crash.

Light from the room streamed after him. Somebody shouted somewhere. A door banged. Mallory looked at Mardonne, saying evenly:

"Got me in the arm! ——— I could have killed the bastard four times!"

Mardonne's hand came up from the desk with a blued revolver in it. A bullet splashed into the floor at Mallory's feet. Mardonne lurched drunkenly, threw the gun away like something red hot. His hands groped high in the air. He looked scared stiff.

Mallory said: "Get in front of me, big shot! I'm moving out of here."

Mardonne came out from behind the desk. He moved jerkily, like a marionette. His eyes were as dead as stale oysters. Saliva drooled down his chin.

Something loomed in the doorway. Mallory heaved sideways, firing blindly at the door. But the sound of the Luger was overborne by the terrific flat booming of a shotgun.

Searing flame stabbed down Mallory's right side. Mardonne got the rest of the load.

He plunged to the floor on his face, dead before he landed.

A sawed-off shotgun dumped itself in through the open door. A thick-bellied man in shirtsleeves eased himself down in the door-frame, clutching and rolling as he fell. A strangled sob came out of his mouth, and blood spread on the pleated front of a dress shirt.

Sudden noise flared out down below. Shouting, running feet, a shrilling off-key laugh, a high sound that might have been a shriek. Cars started outside, tires screeched on the driveway. The customers were getting away. A pane of glass went out somewhere. There was a loose clatter of running feet on a sidewalk.

Across the lighted patch of landing nothing moved. The blond boy groaned softly, out there on the floor, behind the dead man in the doorway.

Mallory plowed across the room, sank into the chair at the end of the desk. He wiped sweat from his eyes with the heel of his gun hand. He leaned his ribs against the desk, panting, watching the door.

His left arm was throbbing now, and his right leg felt like the plagues of Egypt. Blood ran down his sleeve inside, down on his hand, off the tips of two fingers.

After a while he looked away from the door, at the packet of notes lying on the desk under the lamp. Reaching across he pushed them into the open drawer with the muzzle of the Luger. Grinning with pain he leaned far enough over to pull the drawer shut. Then he opened and closed his eyes quickly, several times, squeezing them tight together, then snapping them open wide. That cleared his head a little. He drew the telephone towards him.

There was silence below stairs now. Mallory put the Luger down, lifted the phone off the prongs and put it down beside the Luger.

He said out loud: "Too bad, baby. . . . Maybe I played it wrong after all. . . . Maybe the louse hadn't the guts to hurt you at that . . . well . . . there's got to be talking done now."

As he began to dial, the wail of a siren got louder.

10

THE UNIFORMED OFFICER behind the typewriter desk talked into a dictaphone, then looked at Mallory and jerked his thumb towards a glass-paneled door that said: "Captain of Detectives. Private."

Mallory got up stiffly from a hard chair and went across the room, leaned against the wall to open the glass-paneled door, went on in.

The room he went into was paved with dirty brown linoleum, furnished with the peculiar sordid hideousness only municipalities can achieve. Cathcart, the captain of detectives, sat in the middle of it alone, between a littered roll-top desk that was not less than twenty years old and a flat oak table large enough to play ping-pong on.

Cathcart was a big shabby Irishman with a sweaty face and a loose-lipped grin. His white mustache was stained in the middle by nicotine. His hands had a lot of warts on them.

Mallory went towards him slowly, leaning on a heavy cane with a rubber tip. His right leg felt large and hot. His left arm was in a sling made from a black silk scarf. He was freshly shaved. His face was pale and his eyes were as dark as slate.

He sat down across the table from the captain of detectives, put his cane on the table, tapped a cigarette and lit it. Then he said casually:

"What's the verdict, chief?"

Cathcart grinned. "How you feel, kid? You look kinda pulled down."

"Not bad. A bit stiff."

Cathcart nodded, cleared his throat, fumbled unnecessarily with some papers that were in front of him. He said:

"You're clear. It's a lulu, but you're clear. Chicago gives you a clean sheet – damn clean. Your Luger got Mike Corliss, a two-time loser. I'm keepin' the Luger for a souvenir. Okay?"

Mallory nodded. "Okay. I'm getting me a .25 with copper slugs. A sharpshooter's gun. No shock effect, but it goes better with evening clothes."

Cathcart looked at him closely for a minute, then went on: "Mike's prints are on the shotgun. The shotgun got Mardonne. Nobody's cryin' about that much. The blond kid ain't hurt bad. That automatic we found on the floor had his prints and that will take care of him for a while."

Mallory rubbed his chin wearily. "How about the others?"

The captain raised tangled eyebrows, and his eyes looked absent. He said: "I don't know of nothin' to connect you there. Do you?"

"Not a thing," Mallory said apologetically. "I was just wondering."

The captain said firmly: "Don't wonder. And don't get to guessin', if anybody should ask you. . . . Take that Baldwin Hills thing. The way we figure it Macdonald got killed in the line of duty, takin' with him a dope-peddler named Slippy Morgan. We have a tag out for Slippy's wife, but I don't guess we'll make her. Mac wasn't on the narcotic detail, but it was his night off and he was a great guy to gum-shoe around on his night off. Mac loved his work."

Mallory smiled faintly, said politely: "Is that so?"

"Yeah," the captain said. "In the other one it seems this Landrey, a known gambler – he was Mardonne's partner too – that's kind of a funny coincidence – went down to Westwood to collect dough from a guy called Costello that ran a book on the Eastern tracks. Jim Ralston, one of our boys, went with him. Hadn't ought to, but he knew Landrey pretty well. There was a little trouble about the money. Jim got beaned with a blackjack and Landrey and some little hood fogged each other. There was another guy there we don't trace. We got Costello, but he won't talk, and we don't like to beat up an old guy. He's got a rap comin' on account of the blackjack. He'll plead, I guess."

Mallory slumped down in his chair until the back of his neck rested on top of it. He blew smoke straight up towards the stained ceiling. He said:

"How about night before last? Or was that the time the roulette wheel backfired and the trick cigar blew a hole in the garage floor?"

The captain of detectives rubbed both his moist cheeks briskly, then hauled out a very large handkerchief and snorted into it.

"Oh that," he said negligently, "that wasn't nothin'. The blond kid – Henry Anson or something like that – says it was all his fault. He was Mardonne's bodyguard, but that didn't mean he could go shootin' anyone he might want to. That takes care of him, but we let him down easy for tellin' a straight story."

The captain stopped short and stared at Mallory hard-eyed. Mallory was grinning. "Of course if you don't *like* his story . . ." the captain went on coldly.

Mallory said: "I haven't heard it yet. I'm sure I'll like it fine."

"Okay," Cathcart rumbled, mollified. "Well, this Anson says Mardonne buzzed him in where you and the boss were talkin'. You was makin' a kick about something, maybe a crooked wheel downstairs. There was some money on the desk and Anson got the idea it was a shake. You looked pretty fast to him, and not knowing you was a dick he gets kinda nervous. His gun went off. You didn't shoot right away, but the poor sap lets off another round and plugs you. Then, by —— you drilled him in the shoulder, as who wouldn't, only if it had been me, I'd of pumped his guts. Then the shotgun boy comes bargin' in, lets go without asking any questions, fogs

Mardonne and stops one from you. We kinda thought at first the guy might of got Mardonne on purpose, but the kid says no, he tripped in the door comin' in. . . . Hell, we don't like for you to do all that shooting, you being a stranger and all that, but a man ought to have a right to protect himself against illegal weapons."

Mallory said gently: "There's the D.A. and the coroner. How about them? I'd kind of like to go back as clean as I came away."

Cathcart frowned down at the dirty linoleum and bit his thumb as if he liked hurting himself.

"The coroner don't give a damn about that trash. If the D.A. wants to get funny, I can tell him about a few cases his office didn't clean up so good."

Mallory lifted his cane off the table, pushed his chair back, put weight on the cane and stood up. "You have a swell police department here," he said. "I shouldn't think you'd have any crime at all."

He moved across towards the outer door. The captain said to his back:

"Goin' on to Chicago?"

Mallory shrugged carefully with his right shoulder, the good one. "I might stick around," he said. "One of the studios made me a proposition. Private extortion detail. Blackmail and so on."

The captain grinned heartily. "Swell," he said. "Eclipse Films is a swell outfit. They always been swell to me. . . . Nice easy work, blackmail. Oughtn't to run into any rough stuff."

Mallory nodded solemnly. "Just light work, Chief. Almost effeminate, if you know what I mean."

He went on out, down the hall to the elevator, down to the street. He got into a taxi. It was hot in the taxi. He felt faint and dizzy going back to his hotel.

SMART-ALECK KILL

1

THE DOORMAN OF the Kilmarnock was six foot two. He wore a pale blue uniform, and white gloves made his hands look enormous. He opened the door of the Yellow taxi as gently as an old maid stroking a cat.

Johnny Dalmas got out and turned to the red-haired driver. He said: "Better wait for me around the corner, Joey."

The driver nodded, tucked a toothpick a little farther back in the corner of his mouth, and swung his cab expertly away from the white-marked loading zone. Dalmas crossed the sunny sidewalk and went into the enormous cool lobby of the Kilmarnock. The carpets were thick, soundless. Bellboys stood with folded arms and the two clerks behind the marble desk looked austere.

Dalmas went across to the elevator lobby. He got into a paneled car and said: "End of the line, please."

The penthouse floor had a small quiet lobby with three doors opening off it, one to each wall. Dalmas crossed to one of them and rang the bell.

Derek Walden opened the door. He was about forty-five, possibly a little more, and had a lot of powdery gray hair and a handsome, dissipated face that was beginning to go pouchy. He had on a monogrammed lounging robe and a glass full of whiskey in his hand. He was a little drunk.

He said thickly, morosely: "Oh, it's you. C'mon in, Dalmas."

He went back into the apartment, leaving the door open. Dalmas shut it and followed him into a long, high-ceilinged room with a balcony at one end and a line of french windows along the left side. There was a terrace outside.

Derek Walden sat down in a brown and gold chair against the wall and stretched his legs across a foot stool. He swirled the whiskey around in his glass, looking down at it.

"What's on your mind?" he asked.

Dalmas stared at him a little grimly. After a moment he said: "I dropped in to tell you I'm giving you back your job."

Walden drank the whiskey out of his glass and put it down on the corner of a table. He fumbled around for a cigarette, stuck it in his mouth and forgot to light it.

"Tha' so?" His voice was blurred but indifferent.

Dalmas turned away from him and walked over to one of the windows. It was open and an awning flapped outside. The traffic noise from the boulevard was faint.

He spoke over his shoulder:

"The investigation isn't getting anywhere — because you don't want it to get anywhere. *You* know why you're being blackmailed. *I* don't. Eclipse Films is interested because they have a lot of sugar tied up in a film you have made."

"To hell with Eclipse Films," Walden said, almost quietly.

Dalmas shook his head and turned around. "Not from my angle. They stand to lose if you get in a jam the publicity hounds can't handle. You took me on because you were asked to. It was a waste of time. You haven't cooperated worth a cent."

Walden said in an unpleasant tone: "I'm handling this my own way and I'm not gettin' into any jam. I'll make my own deal — when I can buy something that'll stay bought . . . And all you have to do is make the Eclipse people think the situation's bein' taken care of. That clear?"

Dalmas came partway back across the room. He stood with one hand on top of a table, beside an ashtray littered with cigarette stubs that had very dark lip rouge on them. He looked down at these absently.

"That wasn't explained to me, Walden," he said coldly.

"I thought you were smart enough to figure it out," Walden sneered. He leaned sidewise and slopped some more whiskey into his glass. "Have a drink?"

Dalmas said: "No, thanks."

Walden found the cigarette in his mouth and threw it on the floor. He drank. "What the hell!" he snorted. "You're a private detective and you're being paid to make a few motions that don't mean anything. It's a clean job — as your racket goes."

Dalmas said: "That's another crack I could do without hearing."

Walden made an abrupt, angry motion. His eyes glittered. The corners of his mouth drew down and his face got sulky. He avoided Dalmas' stare.

Dalmas said: "I'm not against you, but I never was for you. You're not the kind of guy I could go for, ever. If you had played with me, I'd have done what I could. I still will — but not for your sake. I don't want your money — and you can pull your shadows off my tail any time you like."

Walden put his feet on the floor. He laid his glass down very carefully on the table at his elbow. The whole expression of his face changed.

"Shadows? . . . I don't get you." He swallowed. "I'm not having you shadowed."

Dalmas stared at him. After a moment he nodded. "Okay, then. I'll backtrack on the next one and see if I can make him tell who he's working for . . . I'll find out."

Walden said very quietly: "I wouldn't do that, if I were you. You're — you're monkeying with people that might get nasty . . . I know what I'm talking about."

"That's something I'm not going to let worry me," Dalmas said evenly. "If it's the people that want *your* money, they were nasty a long time ago."

He held his hat out in front of him and looked at it. Walden's face glistened with sweat. His eyes looked sick. He opened his mouth to say something.

The door buzzer sounded.

Walden scowled quickly, swore. He stared down the room but did not move.

"Too damn many people come here without bein' announced," he growled. "My Jap boy is off for the day."

The buzzer sounded again, and Walden started to get up. Dalmas said: "I'll see what it is. I'm on my way anyhow."

He nodded to Walden, went down the room and opened the door.

Two men came in with guns in their hands. One of the guns dug sharply into Dalmas' ribs, and the man who was holding it said urgently: "Back up, and make it snappy. This is one of those stick-ups you read about."

He was dark and good-looking and cheerful. His face was as clear as a cameo, almost without hardness. He smiled.

The one behind him was short and sandy-haired. He scowled. The dark one said: "This is Walden's dick, Noddy. Take him over and go through him for a gun."

The sandy-haired man, Noddy, put a short-barreled revolver against Dalmas' stomach and his partner kicked the door shut, then strolled carelessly down the room toward Walden.

Noddy took a .38 Colt from under Dalmas' arm, walked around him and tapped his pockets. He put his own gun away and transferred Dalmas' Colt to his business hand.

"Okay, Ricchio. This one's clean," he said in a grumbling voice. Dalmas let his arms fall, turned and went back into the room. He looked thoughtfully at Walden. Walden was leaning forward with his mouth open and an expression of intense concentration on his face. Dalmas looked at the dark stick-up and said softly: "Ricchio?"

The dark boy glanced at him. "Over there by the table, sweetheart. I'll do all the talkin'."

Walden made a hoarse sound in his throat. Ricchio stood in front of him, looking down at him pleasantly, his gun dangling from one finger by the trigger guard.

"You're too slow on the pay-off, Walden. Too damn slow! So we came to tell you about it. Tailed your dick here too. Wasn't that cute?"

Dalmas said gravely, quietly: "This punk used to be your bodyguard, Walden – if his name is Ricchio."

Walden nodded silently and licked his lips. Ricchio snarled at Dalmas: "Don't crack wise, dick. I'm tellin' you again." He stared with hot eyes, then looked back at Walden, looked at a watch on his wrist.

"It's eight minutes past three, Walden. I figure a guy with your drag can still get dough out of the bank. We're giving you an hour to raise ten grand. Just an hour. And we're takin' your shamus along to arrange about delivery."

Walden nodded again, still silent. He put his hands down on his knees and clutched them until his knuckles whitened.

Ricchio went on: "We'll play clean. Our racket wouldn't be worth a squashed bug if we didn't. You'll play clean too. If you don't your shamus will wake up on a pile of dirt. Only he won't wake up. Get it?"

Dalmas said contemptuously: "And if he pays up – I suppose you turn me loose to put the finger on you."

Smoothly, without looking at him, Ricchio said: "There's an answer to that one, too . . . Ten grand today, Walden. The other ten the first of the week. Unless we have trouble . . . If we do, we'll get paid for our trouble."

Walden made an aimless, defeated gesture with both hands outspread. "I guess I can arrange it," he said hurriedly.

"Swell. We'll be on our way then."

Ricchio nodded shortly and put his gun away. He took a brown kid glove out of his pocket, put it on his right hand, moved across then took Dalmas' Colt away from the sandy-haired man. He looked it over, slipped it into his side pocket and held it there with the gloved hand.

"Let's drift," he said with a jerk of his head.

They went out. Derek Walden stared after them bleakly.

The elevator car was empty except for the operator. They got off at the mezzanine and went across a silent writing room past a stained-glass window with lights behind it to give the effect of sunshine. Ricchio walked half a step behind on Dalmas' left. The sandy-haired man was on his right, crowding him.

They went down carpeted steps to an arcade of luxury shops, along that, out of the hotel through the side entrance. A small brown sedan was parked across the street. The sandy-haired man slid behind the wheel, stuck his gun under his leg and stepped on the starter. Ricchio and Dalmas got in the back. Ricchio drawled: "East on the boulevard, Noddy. I've got to figure."

Noddy grunted. "That's a kick," he growled over his shoulder. "Ridin' a guy down Wilshire in daylight."

"Drive the heap, bozo."

The sandy-haired man grunted again and drove the small sedan away from the curb, slowed a moment later for the boulevard stop. An empty Yellow pulled away from the west curb, swung around in the middle of the block and fell in behind. Noddy made his stop, turned right and went on. The taxi did the same. Ricchio glanced back at it without interest. There was a lot of traffic on Wilshire.

Dalmas leaned back against the upholstery and said thoughtfully: "Why wouldn't Walden use his telephone while we were coming down?"

Ricchio smiled at him. He took his hat off and dropped it in his lap, then took his right hand out of his pocket and held it under the hat with the gun in it.

"He wouldn't want us to get mad at him, dick."

"So he lets a couple of punks take me for the ride."

Ricchio said coldly: "It's not that kind of a ride. We need you in our business . . . And we ain't punks, see?"

Dalmas rubbed his jaw with a couple of fingers. He smiled quickly and snapped: "Straight ahead at Robertson?"

"Yeah. I'm still figuring," Ricchio said.

"What a brain!" the sandy-haired man sneered.

Ricchio grinned tightly and showed even white teeth. The light changed to red half a block ahead. Noddy slid the sedan forward and was first in the line at the intersection. The empty Yellow drifted up on his left. Not quite level. The driver of it had red hair. His cap was balanced on one side of his head and he whistled cheerfully past a toothpick.

Dalmas drew his feet back against the seat and put his weight on them. He pressed his back hard against the upholstery. The tall traffic light went green and the sedan started forward, then hung a moment for a car that crowded into a fast left turn. The Yellow slipped forward on the left and the red-haired driver leaned over his wheel, yanked it suddenly to the right. There was a grinding, tearing noise. The riveted fender of the taxi plowed over the low-swung fender of the brown sedan, locked over its left front wheel. The two cars jolted to a stop.

Horn blasts behind the two cars sounded angrily, impatiently.

Dalmas' right fist crashed against Ricchio's jaw. His left hand closed over the gun in Ricchio's lap. He jerked it loose as Ricchio sagged in the corner. Ricchio's head wobbled. His eyes opened and shut flickeringly. Dalmas slid away from him along the seat and slipped the Colt under his arm.

Noddy was sitting quite still in the front seat. His right hand moved slowly towards the gun under his thigh. Dalmas opened the door of the sedan and got out, shut the door, took two steps and opened the door of the taxi. He stood beside the taxi and watched the sandy-haired man.

Horns of the stalled cars blared furiously. The driver of the Yellow was out in front tugging at the two cars with a great show of energy and with no result at all. His toothpick waggled up and down in his mouth. A motorcycle officer in amber glasses threaded the traffic, looked the situation over wearily, jerked his head at the driver.

"Get in and back up," he advised. "Argue it out somewhere else – we use this intersection."

The driver grinned and scuttled around the front end of his Yellow. He climbed into it, threw it in gear and worried it backwards with a lot of tooting and arm-waving. It came clear. The sandy-haired man peered woodenly from the sedan. Dalmas got into the taxi and pulled the door shut.

The motorcycle officer drew a whistle out and blew two sharp blasts on it, spread his arms from east to west. The brown sedan went through the intersection like a cat chased by a police dog.

The Yellow went after it. Half a block on, Dalmas leaned forward and tapped on the glass.

"Let 'em go, Joey. You can't catch them and I don't want them . . . That was a swell routine back there."

The redhead leaned his chin towards the opening in the panel. "Cinch, chief," he said, grinning. "Try me on a hard one some time."

2

THE TELEPHONE RANG at twenty minutes to five. Dalmas was lying on his back on the bed. He was in his room at the Merrivale. He reached for the phone without looking at it, said: "Hello."

The girl's voice was pleasant and a little strained. "This is Mianne Crayle. Remember?"

Dalmas took a cigarette from between his lips. "Yes, Miss Crayle."

"Listen. You must please go over and see Derek Walden. He's worried stiff about something and he's drinking himself blind. Something's got to be done."

Dalmas stared past the phone at the ceiling. The hand holding his cigarette beat a tattoo on the side of the bed. He said slowly: "He doesn't answer his phone, Miss Crayle. I've tried to call him a time or two."

There was a short silence at the other end of the line. Then the voice said: "I left my key under the door. You'd better just go on in."

Dalmas' eyes narrowed. The fingers of his right hand became still. He said slowly: "I'll get over there right away, Miss Crayle. Where can I reach you?"

"I'm not sure . . . At John Sutro's, perhaps. We were supposed to go there."

Dalmas said: "That's fine." He waited for the click, then hung up and put the phone away on the night table. He sat up on the side of the bed and stared at a patch of sunlight on the wall for a minute or two. Then he shrugged, stood up. He finished a drink that stood beside the telephone, put on his hat, went down in the elevator and got into the second taxi in the line outside the hotel.

"Kilmarnock again, Joey. Step on it."

It took fifteen minutes to get to Kilmarnock.

The tea dance had let out and the streets around the big hotel were a mess of cars bucking their way out from the three entrances. Dalmas got out of the taxi half a block away and walked past groups of flushed débutantes and their escorts to the arcade entrance. He went in, walked up the stairs to the mezzanine, crossed the writing room and got into an elevator full of people. They all got out before the penthouse floor.

Dalmas rang Walden's bell twice. Then he bent over and looked under the door. There was a fine thread of light broken by an obstruction. He looked back at the elevator indicators, then stooped and teased something out from under the door with the blade of a penknife. It was a flat key. He went in with it . . . stopped . . . stared . . .

There was death in the big room. Dalmas went towards it slowly, walking softly, listening. There was a hard light in his gray eyes and the bone of his jaw made a sharp line that was pale against the tan of his cheek.

Derek Walden was slumped almost casually in the brown and gold chair. His mouth was slightly open. There was a blackened hole in his right temple, and a lacy pattern of blood spread down the side of his face and across the hollow of his neck as far as the soft collar of his shirt. His right hand trailed in the thick nap of the rug. The fingers held a small, black automatic.

The daylight was beginning to fade in the room. Dalmas stood perfectly still and stared at Derek Walden for a long time. There was no sound anywhere. The breeze had gone down and the awnings outside the french windows were still.

Dalmas took a pair of thin suede gloves from his left hip pocket and drew them on. He kneeled on the rug beside Walden and gently eased the gun from the clasp of his stiffening fingers. It was a .32, with a walnut grip, a black finish. He turned it over and looked at the stock. His mouth tightened. The number had been filed off and the patch of file marks glistened faintly against the dull black of the finish. He put the gun down on the rug and stood up, walked slowly towards the telephone that was on the end of a library table, beside a flat bowl of cut flowers.

He put his hand towards the phone but didn't touch it. He let the hand fall to his side. He stood there a moment, then turned and went quickly back and picked up the gun again. He slipped the magazine out and ejected the shell that was in the breech, picked that up and pressed it into the magazine. He forked two fingers of his left hand over the barrel, held the cocking piece back, twisted the breech block and broke the gun apart. He took the butt piece over to the window.

The number that was duplicated on the inside of the stock had not been filed off.

He reassembled the gun quickly, put the empty shell into the chamber, pushed the magazine home, cocked the gun and fitted it back into Derek Walden's dead hand. He pulled the suede gloves off his hands and wrote the number down in a small notebook.

He left the apartment, went down in the elevator, left the hotel. It was half-past five and some of the cars on the boulevard had switched on their lights.

3

THE BLOND MAN who opened the door at Sutro's did it very thoroughly. The door crashed back against the wall and the blond man sat down on the floor – still holding on to the knob. He said indignantly: "Earthquake, by gad!"

Dalmas looked down at him without amusement.

"Is Miss Mianne Crayle here – or wouldn't you know?" he asked.

The blond man got off the floor and hurled the door away from him. It went shut with another crash. He said in a loud voice: "Everybody's here but the Pope's tomcat – and he's expected."

Dalmas nodded. "You ought to have a swell party."

He went past the blond man down the hall and turned under an arch into a big old-fashioned room with built-in china closets and a lot of shabby furniture. There were seven or eight people in the room and they were all flushed with liquor.

A girl in shorts and a green polo shirt was shooting craps on the floor with a man in dinner clothes. A fat man with nose-glasses was talking sternly into a toy telephone. He was saying: "Long Distance – Sioux City – and put some snap into it, sister!"

The radio blared "Sweet Madness."

Two couples were dancing around carelessly bumping into each other and the furniture. A man who looked like Al Smith was dancing all alone, with a drink in his hand and an absent expression on his face. A tall, white-faced blonde weaved towards Dalmas, slopping liquor out of her glass. She shrieked: "Darling! Fancy meeting you here!"

Dalmas went around her, went towards a saffron-colored woman who had just come into the room with a bottle of gin in each hand. She put the bottles on the piano and leaned against it, looking bored. Dalmas went up to her and asked for Miss Crayle.

The saffron-colored woman reached a cigarette out of an open box on the piano. "Outside – in the yard," she said tonelessly.

Dalmas said: "Thank you, Mrs. Sutro."

She stared at him blankly. He went under another arch, into a darkened room with wicker furniture in it. A door led to a glassed-in porch and a door out of that led down steps to a path that wound off through dim trees. Dalmas followed the path to the edge of a bluff that looked out over the lighted part of Hollywood. There was a stone seat at the edge of the bluff. A girl sat on it with her back to the house. A cigarette tip glowed in the darkness. She turned her head slowly and stood up.

She was small and dark and delicately made. Her mouth showed dark with rouge, but there was not enough light to see her face clearly. Her eyes were shadowed.

Dalmas said: "I have a cab outside, Miss Crayle. Or did you bring a car?"

"No car. Let's go. It's rotten here, and I don't drink gin."

They went back along the path and passed around the side of the house. A trellis-topped gate let them out on the sidewalk, and they went along by the fence to where the taxi was waiting. The driver was leaning against it with one heel hooked on the edge of the running board. He opened the cab door. They got in.

Dalmas said: "Stop at a drugstore for some butts, Joey."

"Okay."

Joey slid behind his wheel and started up. The cab went down a steep, winding hill. There was a little moisture on the surface of the asphalt pavement and the store fronts echoed back the swishing sound of the tires.

After a while Dalmas said: "What time did you leave Walden?"

The girl spoke without turning her head towards him. "About three o'clock."

"Put it a little later, Miss Crayle. He was alive at three o'clock – and there was somebody else with him."

The girl made a small, miserable sound like a strangled sob. Then, she said very softly: "I know . . . he's dead." She lifted her gloved hands and pressed them against her temples.

Dalmas said: "Sure. Let's not get any more tricky than we have to . . . Maybe we'll have to – enough."

She said very slowly, in a low voice: "I was there after he was dead."

Dalmas nodded. He did not look at her. The cab went on and after a while it stopped in front of a corner drugstore. The driver turned in his seat and looked back. Dalmas stared at him, but spoke to the girl.

"You ought to have told me more over the phone. I might have got in a hell of a jam. I may be in a hell of a jam now."

The girl swayed forward and started to fall. Dalmas put his arm out quickly and caught her, pushed her back against the cushions. Her head wobbled on her shoulders and her mouth was a dark gash in her stone-white face. Dalmas held her shoulder and felt her pulse with his free hand. He said sharply, grimly: "Let's go on to Carli's, Joey. Never mind the butts . . . This party has to have a drink – in a hurry."

Joey slammed the cab in gear and stepped on the accelerator.

4

CARLI'S WAS A small club at the end of a passage between a sporting-goods store and a circulating library. There was a grilled door and a man behind it who had given up trying to look as if it mattered who came in.

Dalmas and the girl sat in a small booth with hard seats and looped-back green curtains. There were high partitions between the booths. There was a long bar down the other side of the room and a big juke box at the end of it. Now and then, when there wasn't enough noise, the bartender put a nickel in the juke box.

The waiter put two small glasses of brandy on the table and Mianne Crayle downed hers at a gulp. A little light came into her shadowed eyes. She peeled a black and white gauntlet off her right hand and sat playing with the empty fingers of it, staring down at the table. After a little while the waiter came back with a couple of brandy highballs.

When he had gone away again Mianne Crayle began to speak in a low, clear voice, without raising her head: "I wasn't the first of his women by several dozen. I wouldn't have been the last – by that many more. But he had his decent side. And believe it or not he didn't pay my room rent."

Dalmas nodded, didn't say anything. The girl went on without looking at him: "He was a heel in a lot of ways. When he was sober he had the dark blue sulks. When he was lit up he was vile. When he was nicely edged he was a pretty good sort of guy besides being the best smut director in Hollywood. He could get more smooth sexy tripe past the Hays office than any other three men."

Dalmas said without expression: "He was on his way out. Smut is on its way out, and that was all he knew."

The girl looked at him briefly, lowered her eyes again and drank a little of her highball. She took a tiny handkerchief out of the pocket of her sports jacket and patted her lips.

The people on the other side of the partition were making a great deal of noise.

Mianne Crayle said: "We had lunch on the balcony. Derek was drunk and on the way to get drunker. He had something on his mind. Something that worried him a lot."

Dalmas smiled faintly. "Maybe it was the twenty grand

somebody was trying to pry loose from him — or didn't you know about that?"

"It might have been that. Derek was a bit tight about money."

"His liquor cost him a lot," Dalmas said dryly. "And that motor cruiser he liked to play about in — down below the border."

The girl lifted her head with a quick jerk. There were sharp lights of pain in her dark eyes. She said very slowly: "He bought all his liquor at Ensenada. Brought it in himself. He had to be careful — with the quantity he put away."

Dalmas nodded. A cold smile played about the corners of his mouth. He finished his drink and put a cigarette in his mouth, felt in his pocket for a match. The holder on the table was empty.

"Finish your story, Miss Crayle," he said.

"We went up to the apartment. He got two fresh bottles out and said he was going to get good and drunk . . . Then we quarreled . . . I couldn't stand any more of it. I went away. When I got home I began to worry about him. I called up but he wouldn't answer the phone. I went back finally . . . and let myself in with the key I had . . . and he was dead in the chair."

After a moment Dalmas said: "Why didn't you tell me some of that over the phone?"

She pressed the heels of her hands together, said very softly: "I was terribly afraid . . . And there was something . . . wrong."

Dalmas put his head back against the partition, stared at her with his eyes half closed.

"It's an old gag," she said. "I'm almost ashamed to spring it. But Derek Walden was left-handed . . . I'd know about that, wouldn't I?"

Dalmas said very softly: "A lot of people must have known that — but one of them might have got careless."

Dalmas stared at Mianne Crayle's empty glove. She was twisting it between her fingers.

"Walden was left-handed," he said slowly. "That means he didn't suicide. The gun was in his other hand. There was no sign of a struggle and the hole in his temple was powder-burned, looked as if the shot came from about the right angle. That means whoever shot him was someone who could get in there and get close to him. Or else he was paralyzed drunk, and in that case whoever did it had to have a key."

Mianne Crayle pushed the glove away from her. She clenched her hands. "Don't make it any plainer," she said sharply. "I know the police will think I did it. Well – I didn't. I loved the poor damn fool. What do you think of that?"

Dalmas said without emotion: "You *could* have done it, Miss Crayle. They'll think of that, won't they? And you might be smart enough to act the way you have afterwards. They'll think of that, too."

"That wouldn't be smart," she said bitterly. "Just smart-aleck."

"Smart-aleck kill!" Dalmas laughed grimly. "Not bad." He ran his fingers through his crisp hair. "No, I don't think we can pin it on you – and maybe the cops won't know he was left-handed . . . until somebody else gets a chance to find things out."

He leaned over the table a little, put his hands on the edge as if to get up. His eyes narrowed thoughtfully on her face.

"There's one man downtown that might give me a break. He's all cop, but he's an old guy and don't give a damn about his publicity. Maybe if you went down with me, let him size you up and hear the story, he'd stall the case a few hours and hold out on the papers."

He looked at her questioningly. She drew her glove on and said quietly: "Let's go."

5

WHEN THE ELEVATOR doors at the Merrivale closed, the big man put his newspaper down from in front of his face and yawned. He got up slowly from the settee in the corner and loafed across the small but sedate lobby. He squeezed himself into a booth at the end of a row of house phones. He dropped a coin in the slot and dialed with a thick forefinger, forming the number with his lips.

After a pause he leaned close to the mouthpiece and said: "This is Denny. I'm at the Merrivale. Our man just came in. I lost him outside and came here to wait for him to get back."

He had a heavy voice with a burr in it. He listened to the voice at the other end, nodded and hung up without saying anything more. He went out of the booth, crossed to the elevators. On the way he dropped a cigar butt into a glazed jar full of white sand.

In the elevator he said: "Ten," and took his hat off. He had straight black hair that was damp with perspiration, a wide, flat face and small eyes. His clothes were unpressed, but not shabby. He was a studio dick and he worked for Eclipse Films.

He got out at the tenth floor and went along a dim corridor, turned a corner and knocked at a door. There was a sound of steps inside. The door opened. Dalmas opened it.

The big man went in, dropped his hat casually on the bed, sat down in an easy chair by the window without being asked.

He said: "Hi, boy. I hear you need some help."

Dalmas looked at him for a moment without answering. Then he said slowly, frowningly: "Maybe – for a tail. I asked for Collins. I thought you'd be too easy to spot."

He turned away and went into the bathroom, came out with two glasses. He mixed the drinks on the bureau, handed one. The big man drank, smacked his lips and put his glass down on the sill of the open window. He took a short, chubby cigar out of his vest pocket.

"Collins wasn't around," he said. "And I was just countin' my thumbs. So the big cheese give me the job. Is it footwork?"

"I don't know. Probably not," Dalmas said indifferently.

"If it's a tail in a car, I'm okay. I brought my little coupe."

Dalmas took his glass and sat down on the side of the bed. He stared at the big man with a faint smile. The big man bit the end off his cigar and spit it out.

Then he bent over and picked up the piece, looked at it, tossed it out of the window.

"It's a swell night. A bit warm for so late in the year," he said.

Dalmas said slowly: "How well do you know Derek Walden, Denny?"

Denny looked out of the window. There was a sort of haze in the sky and the reflection of a red neon sign behind a nearby building looked like a fire.

He said: "I don't what you call know him. I've seen him around. I know he's one of the big money guys on the lot."

"Then you won't fall over if I tell you he's dead," Dalmas said evenly.

Denny turned around slowly. The cigar, still unlighted, moved up and down in his wide mouth. He looked mildly interested.

Dalmas went on: "It's a funny one. A blackmail gang has been working on him, Denny. Looks like it got his goat. He's dead – with a hole in his head and a gun in his hand. It happened this afternoon."

Denny opened his small eyes a little wider. Dalmas sipped his drink and rested the glass on his thigh.

"His girl friend found him. She had a key to the apartment in the Kilmarnock. The Jap boy was away and that's all the help he kept. The gal didn't tell anyone. She beat it and called me up. I went over . . . I didn't tell anybody either."

76

The big man said very slowly: "For Pete's sake! The cops'll stick it into you and break it off, brother. You can't get away with that stuff."

Dalmas stared at him, then turned his head away and stared at a picture on the wall. He said coldly: "I'm doing it – and you're helping me. We've got a job, and a damn powerful organization behind us. There's a lot of sugar at stake."

"How do you figure?" Denny asked grimly. He didn't look pleased.

"The girl friend doesn't think Walden suicided, Denny. I don't either, and I've got a sort of lead. But it has to be worked fast, because it's as good a lead for the law as us. I didn't expect to be able to check it right away, but I got a break."

Denny said: "Uh-huh. Don't make it too clever. I'm a slow thinker."

He struck a match and lit his cigar. His hand shook just a little.

Dalmas said: "It's not clever. It's kind of dumb. The gun that killed Walden is a filed gun. But I broke it and the inside number wasn't filed. And Headquarters has the number, in the special permits."

"And you just went in and asked for it and they gave it to you," Denny said grimly. "And when they pick Walden up and trace the gun themselves, they'll just think it was swell of you to beat them to it." He made a harsh noise in his throat.

Dalmas said: "Take it easy, boy. The guy that did the checking rates. I don't have to worry about that."

"Like hell you don't! And what would a guy like Walden be doin' with a filed gun? That's a felony rap."

Dalmas finished his drink and carried his empty glass over to the bureau. He held the whiskey bottle out. Denny shook his head. He looked very disgusted.

"If he had the gun, he might not have known about that, Denny. And it could be that it wasn't his gun at all. If it was a killer's gun, then the killer was an amateur. A professional wouldn't have that kind of artillery."

The big man said slowly: "Okay, what you get on the rod?"

Dalmas sat down on the bed again. He dug a package of cigarettes out of his pocket, lit one, and leaned forward to toss the match through the open window. He said: "The permit was issued about a year ago to a newshawk on the Press-Chronicle, name of Dart Burwand. This Burwand was bumped off last April on the ramp of the Arcade Depot. He was all set to leave town, but he didn't make it. They never cracked the case, but the hunch is that this Burwand was tied to some racket – like the Lingle killing in Chi – and that he tried to shake one of the big boys. The big boy backfired on the idea. Exit Burwand."

The big man was breathing deeply. He had let his cigar go out. Dalmas watched him gravely while he talked.

"I got that from Westfalls, on the Press-Chronicle," Dalmas said. "He's a friend of mine. There's more of it. This gun was given back to Burwand's wife – probably. She still lives here – out on North Kenmore. She might tell me what she did with the gun . . . and she might be tied to some racket herself, Denny. In that case she wouldn't tell me, but after I talk to her she might make some contacts we ought to know about. Get the idea?"

Denny struck another match and held it on the end of his cigar. His voice said thickly: "What do I do – tail the broad after you put the idea to her, about the gun?"

"Right."

The big man stood up, pretended to yawn. "Can do," he grunted. "But why all the hush-hush about Walden? Why not let the cops work it out? We're just goin' to get ourselves a lot of bad marks at Headquarters."

Dalmas said slowly: "It's got to be risked. We don't know what the blackmail crowd had on Walden, and the studio stands to lose too much money if it comes out in the investigation and gets a front-page spread all over the country."

Denny said: "You talk like Walden was spelled Valentino. Hell, the guy's only a director. All they got to do is take his name off a couple of unreleased pictures."

"They figure different," Dalmas said. "But maybe that's because they haven't talked to you."

Denny said roughly: "Okay. But me, I'd let the girl friend take the damn rap! All the law ever wants is a fall guy."

He went around the bed to get his hat, crammed it on his head.

"Swell," he said sourly. "We gotta find out all about it before the cops even know Walden is dead." He gestured with one hand and laughed mirthlessly. "Like they do in the movies."

Dalmas put the whiskey bottle away in the bureau drawer and put his hat on. He opened the door and stood aside for Denny to go out. He switched off the lights.

It was ten minutes to nine.

6

THE TALL BLONDE looked at Dalmas out of greenish eyes with very small pupils. He went in past her quickly, without seeming to move quickly. He pushed the door shut with his elbow.

He said: "I'm a dick – private – Mrs. Burwand. Trying to dig up a little dope you might know about."

The blonde said: "The name is Dalton, Helen Dalton. Forget the Burwand stuff."

Dalmas smiled and said: "I'm sorry. I should have known."

The blonde shrugged her shoulders and drifted away from the door. She sat down on the edge of a chair that had a cigarette burn on the arm. The room was a furnished-apartment living-room with a lot of department store bric-à-brac spread around. Two floor lamps burned. There were flounced pillows on the floor, a French doll sprawled against the base of one lamp, and a row of gaudy novels went across the mantel, above the gas fire.

Dalmas said politely, swinging his hat: "It's about a gun Dart Burwand used to own. It's showed up on a case I'm working. I'm trying to trace it – from the time you had it."

Helen Dalton scratched the upper part of her arm. She had half-inch-long fingernails. She said curtly: "I don't have an idea what you're talking about."

Dalmas stared at her and leaned against the wall. His voice got on edge.

"Maybe you remember that you used to be married to Dart Burwand and that he got bumped off last April . . . Or is that too far back?"

The blonde bit one of her knuckles and said: "Smart guy, huh?"

"Not unless I have to be. But don't fall asleep from that last shot in the arm."

Helen Dalton sat up very straight, suddenly. All the vagueness went out of her expression. She spoke between tight lips.

"What's the howl about the gun?"

"It killed a guy, that's all," Dalmas said carelessly.

She stared at him. After a moment she said: "I was broke. I hocked it. I never got it out. I had a husband that made sixty bucks a week but didn't spend any of it on me. I never had a dime."

Dalmas nodded. "Remember the pawnshop where you left it?" he asked. "Or maybe you still have the ticket."

"No. It was on Main. The street's lined with them. And I don't have the ticket."

Dalmas said: "I was afraid of that."

He walked slowly across the room, looked at the titles of some of the books on the mantel. He went on and stood in front of a small, folding desk. There was a photo in a silver frame on the desk. Dalmas stared at it for some time. He turned slowly.

"It's too bad about the gun, Helen. A pretty important name was rubbed out with it this afternoon. The number was filed off the outside. If you hocked it, I'd figure some hood bought it from the hock-shop guy, except that a hood wouldn't file a gun that way. He'd know there was another number inside. So it wasn't a hood — and the man it was found with wouldn't be likely to get a gun in a hock shop."

The blonde stood up slowly. Red spots burned in her cheeks. Her arms were rigid at her sides and her breath whispered. She said slowly, strainedly: "You can't maul me around, dick. I don't want any part of any police business — and I've got some good friends to take care of me. Better scram."

Dalmas looked back towards the frame on the desk. He said: "Johnny Sutro oughtn't to leave his mug around in a broad's apartment that way. Somebody might think he was cheating."

The blonde walked stiff-legged across the room and slammed the photo into the drawer of the desk. She slammed the drawer shut, and leaned her hips against the desk.

"You're all wet, shamus. That's not anybody called Sutro. Get on out, will you, for gawd's sake?"

Dalmas laughed unpleasantly. "I saw you at Sutro's house this afternoon. You were so drunk you don't remember."

The blonde made a movement as though she were going to jump at him. Then she stopped, rigid. A key turned in the room door. It opened and a man came in. He stood just inside the door and pushed it shut very slowly. His right hand was in the pocket of a light tweed overcoat. He was dark-skinned, high-shouldered, angular, with a sharp nose and chin.

Dalmas looked at him quietly and said: "Good evening, Councilman Sutro."

The man looked past Dalmas at the girl. He took no notice of Dalmas. The girl said shakily: "This guy says he's a dick. He's giving me a third about some gun he says I had. Throw him out, will you?"

Sutro said: "A dick, eh?"

He walked past Dalmas without looking at him. The blonde backed away from him and fell into a chair. Her face got a pasty look and her eyes were scared. Sutro looked down at her for a moment, then turned around and took a small automatic out of his pocket. He held it loosely, pointed down at the floor.

He said: "I haven't a lot of time."

Dalmas said: "I was just going." He moved near the door. Sutro said sharply: "Let's have the story first."

Dalmas said: "Sure."

He moved lithely, without haste, and threw the door wide open. The gun jerked up in Sutro's hand. Dalmas said: "Don't be a sap. You're not starting anything here and you know it."

The two men stared at each other. After a moment or two Sutro put the gun back into his pocket and licked his thin lips. Dalmas said: "Miss Dalton had a gun once that killed a man — recently. But she hasn't had it for a long time. That's all I wanted to know."

Sutro nodded slowly. There was a peculiar expression in his eyes.

"Miss Dalton is a friend of my wife's. I wouldn't want her to be bothered," he said coldly.

"That's right. You wouldn't," Dalmas said. "But a legitimate dick has a right to ask legitimate questions. I didn't break in here."

Sutro eyed him slowly: "Okay, but take it easy on my friends. I draw water in this town and I could hang a sign on you."

Dalmas nodded. He went quietly out of the door and shut it. He listened a moment. There was no sound inside that he could hear. He shrugged and went on down the hall, down three steps and across a small lobby that had no switchboard. Outside the apartment house he looked along the street. It was an apartment-house district and there were cars parked up and down the street. He went towards the lights of the taxi that was waiting for him.

Joey, the red-haired driver, was standing on the edge of the curb in front of his hack. He was smoking a cigarette, staring across the street, apparently at a big, dark coupe that was parked with its left side to the curb. As Dalmas came up to him he threw his cigarette away and came to meet him.

He spoke quickly: "Listen, boss. I got a look at the guy in that Cad – "

Pale flame broke in bitter streaks from above the door of the coupe. A gun racketed between the buildings that faced each other across the street. Joey fell against Dalmas. The coupe jerked into sudden motion. Dalmas went down side-wise, on to one knee, with the driver clinging to him. He tried to reach his gun, couldn't make it. The coupe went around the corner with a squeal of rubber, and Joey fell down Dalmas' side and rolled over on his back on the sidewalk. He beat his hands up and down on the cement and a hoarse, anguished sound came from deep inside him.

Tires screeched again and Dalmas flung up to his feet, swept his hand to his left armpit. He relaxed as a small car skidded to a stop and Denny fell out of it, charged across the intervening space towards him.

Dalmas bent over the driver. Light from the lanterns beside the entrance to the apartment house showed blood on the front of Joey's whipcord jacket, blood that was seeping out through the material. Joey's eyes opened and shut like the eyes of a dying bird.

Denny said: "No use to follow that bus. Too fast."

"Get on a phone and call an ambulance," Dalmas said quickly. "The kid's got a bellyful . . . Then take a plant on the blonde."

The big man hurried back to his car, jumped into it and tore off around the corner. A window went open somewhere and a man yelled down. Some cars stopped.

Dalmas bent down over Joey and muttered: "Take it easy, oldtimer . . . Easy, boy . . . easy."

7

THE HOMICIDE LIEUTENANT'S name was Weinkassel. He had thin, blond hair, icy blue eyes and a lot of pockmarks. He sat in a swivel chair with his feet on the edge of a pulled-out drawer and a telephone scooped close to his elbow. The room smelled of dust and cigar butts.

A man named Lonergan, a bulky dick with gray hair and a gray mustache, stood near an open window, looking out of it morosely.

Weinkassel chewed on a match, stared at Dalmas, who was across the desk from him. He said: "Better talk a bit. The hack driver can't. You've had luck in this town and you wouldn't want to run it into the ground."

Lonergan said: "He's hard. He won't talk." He didn't turn around when he said it.

"A little less of your crap would go farther, Lonnie," Weinkassel said in a dead voice.

Dalmas smiled faintly and rubbed the palm of his hand against the side of the desk. It made a squeaking sound.

"What would I talk about?" he asked. "It was dark and I didn't get a flash of the man behind the gun. The car was a Cadillac coupe, without lights. I've told you this already, Lieutenant."

"It don't listen," Weinkassel grumbled. "There's something screwy about it. You gotta have some kind of a hunch who it could be. It's a cinch the gun was for you."

Dalmas said: "Why? The hack driver was hit and I wasn't. Those lads get around a lot. One of them might be in wrong with some tough boys."

"Like you," Lonergan said. He went on staring out of the window.

84

Weinkassel frowned at Lonergan's back and said patiently: "The car was outside while you was still inside. The hack driver was outside. If the guy with the gun had wanted him, he didn't have to wait for you to come out."

Dalmas spread his hands and shrugged. "You boys think I know who it was?"

"Not exactly. We think you could give us some names to check on, though. Who'd you go to see in them apartments?"

Dalmas didn't say anything for a moment. Lonergan turned away from the window, sat on the end of the desk and swung his legs. There was a cynical grin on his flat face.

"Come through, baby," he said cheerfully.

Dalmas tilted his chair back and put his hands into his pockets. He stared at Weinkassel speculatively, ignored the gray-haired dick as though he didn't exist.

He said slowly: "I was there on business for a client. You can't make me talk about that."

Weinkassel shrugged and stared at him coldly. Then he took the chewed match out of his mouth, looked at the flattened end of it, tossed it away.

"I might have a hunch your business had something to do with the shootin'," he said grimly. "That way the hush-hush would be out. Wouldn't it?"

"Maybe," Dalmas said. "If that's the way it's going to work out. But I ought to have a chance to talk to my client."

Weinkassel said: "Okay. You can have till the morning. Then you put your papers on the desk, see."

Dalmas nodded and stood up. "Fair enough, Lieutenant."

"Hush-hush is all a shamus knows," Lonergan said roughly.

Dalmas nodded to Weinkassel and went out of the office. He walked down a bleak corridor and up steps to the lobby floor. Outside the City Hall he went down a long flight of concrete steps and across Spring Street to where a blue Packard roadster, not very new, was parked. He got into it and drove around the corner, then though the Second Street tunnel, dropped over a block and drove out west. He watched in the mirror as he drove.

At Alvarado he went into a drugstore and called his hotel. The clerk gave him a number to call. He called it and heard Denny's heavy voice at the other end of the line. Denny said urgently: "Where you been? I've got that broad out here at my place. She's drunk. Come on out and we'll get her to tell us what you want to know."

Dalmas stared out through the glass of the phone booth without seeing anything. After a pause he said slowly: "The blonde? How come?"

"It's a story, boy. Come on out and I'll give it to you. Fourteen-fifty-four South Livesay. Know where that is?"

"I've got a map. I'll find it," Dalmas said in the same tone.

Denny told him just how to find it, at some length. At the end of the explanation he said: "Make it fast. She's asleep now, but she might wake up and start yellin' murder."

Dalmas said: "Where you live it probably wouldn't matter much . . . I'll be right out, Denny."

He hung up and went out to his car. He got a pint bottle of bourbon out of the car pocket and took a long drink. Then he started up and drove towards Fox Hills. Twice on the way he stopped and sat still in the car, thinking. But each time he went on again.

8

THE ROAD TURNED off Pico into a scattered subdivision that spread itself out over rolling hills between two golf courses. It followed the edge of one of the golf courses, separated from it by a high wire fence. There were bungalows here and there dotted about the slopes. After a while the road dipped into a hollow and there was a single bungalow in the hollow, right across the street from the golf course.

Dalmas drove past it and parked under a giant eucalyptus that etched deep shadow on the moonlit surface of the road. He got out and walked back, turned up a cement path to the bungalow. It was wide and low and had cottage windows across the front. Bushes grew halfway up the screens. There was faint light inside and the sound of a radio, turned low, came through the open windows.

A shadow moved across the screens and the front door came open. Dalmas went into a living-room built across the front of the house. One small bulb burned in a lamp and the luminous dial of the radio glowed. A little moonlight came into the room.

Denny had his coat off and his sleeves rolled up on his big arms.

He said: "The broad's still asleep. I'll wake her up when I've told you how I got her here."

Dalmas said: "Sure you weren't tailed?"

"Not a chance." Denny spread a big hand.

Dalmas sat down in a wicker chair in the corner, between the radio and the end of the line of windows. He put his hat on the floor, pulled out the bottle of bourbon and regarded it with a dissatisfied air.

"Buy us a real drink, Denny. I'm tired as hell. Didn't get any dinner."

Denny said: "I've got some Three-Star Martel. Be right up."

He went out of the room and light went on in the back part of the house. Dalmas put the bottle on the floor beside his hat and rubbed two fingers across his forehead. His head ached. After a little while the light went out in the back and Denny came back with two tall glasses.

The brandy tasted clean and hard. Denny sat down in another wicker chair. He looked very big and dark in the half-lit room. He began to talk slowly, in his gruff voice.

"It sounds goofy, but it worked. After the cops stopped milling around I parked in the alley and went in the back way.

87

I knew which apartment the broad had but I hadn't seen her. I thought I'd make some kind of a stall and see how she was makin' out. I knocked on her door, but she wouldn't answer. I could hear her movin' around inside, and in a minute I could hear a telephone bein' dialed. I went back along the hall and tried the service door. It opened and I went in. It fastened with one of them screw bolts that get out of line and don't fasten when you think they do."

Dalmas nodded, said: "I get the idea, Denny."

The big man drank out of his glass and rubbed the edge of it up and down on his lower lip. He went on.

"She was phoning a guy named Gayn Donner. Know him?"

"I've heard of him," Dalmas said. "So she has that kind of connections."

"She was callin' him by name and she sounded mad," Denny said. "That's how I knew. Donner has that place on Mariposa Canyon Drive – the Mariposa Club. You hear his band over the air – Hank Munn and his boys."

Dalmas said: "I've heard it, Denny."

"Okay. When she hung up I went in on her. She looked snowed, weaved around funny, didn't seem to know much what was going on. I looked around and there was a photo of John Sutro, the Councilman, in a desk there. I used that for a stall. I said that Sutro wanted her to duck out for a while and that I was one of his boys and she was to come along. She fell for it. Screwy. She wanted some liquor. I said I had some in the car. She got her little hat and coat."

Dalmas said softly: "It was that easy, huh?"

"Yeah," Denny said. He finished his drink and put the glass somewhere. "I bottle-fed her in the car to keep her quiet and we came out here. She went to sleep and that's that. What do you figure? Tough downtown?"

"Tough enough," Dalmas said. "I didn't fool the boys much."

"Anything on the Walden kill?"

Dalmas shook his head slowly.

"I guess the Jap didn't get home yet, Denny."

"Want to talk to the broad?"

The radio was playing a waltz. Dalmas listened to it for a moment before he answered. Then he said in a tired voice: "I guess that's what I came out here for."

Denny got up and went out of the room. There was the sound of a door opening and muffled voices.

Dalmas took his gun out from under his arm and put it down in the chair beside his leg.

The blonde staggered a little too much as she came in. She stared around, giggled, made vague motions with her long hands. She blinked at Dalmas, stood swaying a moment, then slid down into the chair Denny had been sitting in. The big man kept near her and leaned against a library table that stood by the inside wall.

She said drunkenly: "My old pal the dick. Hey, hey, stranger! How about buyin' a lady a drink?"

Dalmas stared at her without expression. He said slowly: "Got any new ideas about that gun? You know, the one we were talking about when Johnny Sutro crashed in . . . The filed gun . . . The gun that killed Derek Walden."

Denny stiffened, then made a sudden motion towards his hip. Dalmas brought his Colt up and came to his feet with it. Denny looked at it and became still, relaxed. The girl had not moved at all, but the drunkenness dropped away from her like a dead leaf. Her face was suddenly tense and bitter.

Dalmas said evenly: "Keep the hands in sight, Denny, and everything'll be jake . . . Now suppose you two cheap crossers tell me what I'm here for."

The big man said thickly: "For gawd's sake! What's eatin' you? You scared me when you said 'Walden' to the girl."

Dalmas grinned. "That's all right, Denny. Maybe she never heard of him. Let's get this ironed out in a hurry. I have an idea I'm here for trouble."

"You're crazy as hell!" the big man snarled.

Dalmas moved the gun slightly. He put his back against the end wall of the room, leaned over and turned the radio off with his left hand. Then he spoke bitterly: "You sold out, Denny. That's easy. You're too big for a tail and I've spotted you following me around half a dozen times lately. When you horned in on the deal tonight I was pretty sure . . . And when you told me that funny story about how you got baby out here I was *damn* sure . . . Hell's sake, do you think a guy that's stayed alive as long as I have would believe that one? Come on, Denny, be a sport and tell me who you're working for . . . I might let you take a powder . . . Who you working for? Donner? Sutro? Or somebody I don't know? And why the plant out here in the woods?"

The girl shot to her feet suddenly and sprang at him. He threw her off with his free hand and she sprawled on the floor. She yelled: "Get him, you big punk? Get him!"

Denny didn't move. "Shut up, snow-bird!" Dalmas snapped. "Nobody's getting anybody. This is just a talk between friends. Get up on your feet and stop throwing curves!"

The blonde stood up slowly.

Denny's face had a stony, immovable look in the dimness. His voice came with a dull rasp. He said: "I sold out. It was lousy. Okay, that's that. I got fed up with watchin' a bunch of extra girls trying to pinch each other's lipstick . . . You can take a plug at me, if you feel like it."

He still didn't move. Dalmas nodded slowly and said again: "Who is it, Denny? Who you working for?"

Denny said: "I don't know. I call a number, get orders, and report that way. I get dough in the mail. I tried to break the twist here, but no luck . . . I don't think you're on the spot and I don't know a damn thing about that shootin' in the street."

Dalmas stared at him. He said slowly: "You wouldn't be stalling – to keep me here – would you, Denny?"

The big man raised his head slowly. The room suddenly seemed to get very still. A car had stopped outside. The faint throbbing of its motor died.

A red spotlight hit the top of the screens.

It was blinding. Dalmas slid down on one knee, shifted his position sidewise very quickly, silently. Denny's harsh voice in the silence said: "Cops, for gawd's sake!"

The red light dissolved the wire mesh of the screens into a rosy glow, threw a great splash of vivid color on the oiled finish of the inside wall. The girl made a choked sound and her face was a red mask for an instant before she sank down out of the fan of light. Dalmas looked into the light, his head low behind the sill of the end window. The leaves of the bushes were black spearpoints in the red glare.

Steps sounded on the walk.

A harsh voice rasped: "Everybody out! Mitts in the air!"

There was a sound of movement inside the house. Dalmas swung his gun – uselessly. A switch clicked and a porch light went on. For a moment, before they dodged back, two men in blue police uniforms showed up in the cone of the porch light. One of them held a sub-machine gun and the other had a long Luger with a special magazine fitted to it.

There was a grating sound. Denny was at the door, opening the peep panel. A gun came up in his hand and crashed.

Something heavy clattered on the cement and a man swayed forward into the light, swayed back again. His hands were against his middle. A stiff-vizored cap fell down and rolled on the walk.

Dalmas hit the floor low down against the baseboard as the machine gun cut loose. He ground his face into the wood of the floor. The girl screamed behind him.

The chopper raked the room swiftly from end to end and the air filled with plaster and splinters. A wall mirror crashed down. A sharp stench of powder fought with the sour smell of the plaster dust. This seemed to go on for a very long time.

Something fell across Dalmas' legs. He kept his eyes shut and his face pressed against the floor.

The stuttering and crashing stopped. The rain of plaster inside the walls kept on. A voice yelled: "How d'you like it, pals?"

Another voice far back snapped angrily: "Come on — let's go!"

Steps sounded again, and a dragging sound. More steps. The motor of the car roared into life. A door slammed heavily. Tires screeched on the gravel of the road and the song of the motor swelled and died swiftly.

Dalmas got up on his feet. His ears boomed and his nostrils were dry. He got his gun off the floor, unclipped a thin flash from an inside pocket, snapped it on. It probed weakly through the dusty air. The blonde lay on her back with her eyes wide open and her mouth twisted into a sort of grin. She was sobbing. Dalmas bent over her. There didn't seem to be a mark on her.

He went on down the room. He found his hat untouched beside the chair that had half the top shot off. The bottle of bourbon lay beside the hat. He picked them both up. The man with the chopper had raked the room waist-high, back and forth, without lowering it far enough. Dalmas went on farther, came to the door.

Denny was on his knees in front of the door. He was swaying backwards and forwards and holding one of his hands in the other. Blood dribbled between his thick fingers.

Dalmas got the door open and went out. There was a smear of blood and a litter of shells on the walk. There was nobody in sight. He stood there with the blood beating in his face, like little hammers. The skin around his nose prickled.

He drank some whiskey out of the bottle and turned and went back into the house. Denny was up on his feet now. He had a handkerchief out and was tying it around his bloody hand. He looked dazed, drunk. He swayed on his feet. Dalmas put the beam of the flash on his face.

He said: "Hurt much?"

"No. Clipped on the hand," the big man said thickly. His fingers were clumsy on the handkerchief.

"The blonde's scared blind," Dalmas said. "It's your party, boy. Nice pals you have. They meant to get all three of us. You rattled them when you took a pot out of the peephole. I guess I owe you something for that, Denny . . . The gunner wasn't so good."

Denny said: "Where you goin'?"

"Where d'you think?"

Denny looked at him. "Sutro's your man," he said slowly. "I'm through – washed up. They can all go to hell."

Dalmas went through the door again, down the path to the street. He got into his car and drove away without lights. When he had turned corners and gone some distance he switched the lights on and got out and dusted himself off.

9

BLACK AND SILVER curtains opened in an inverted V against a haze of cigarette and cigar smoke. The brasses of the dance band shot brief flashes of color through the haze. There was a smell of food and liquor and perfume and face powder. The dance floor was an empty splash of amber light and looked slightly larger than a screen star's bath mat.

Then the band started up and the lights went down, and a headwaiter came up the carpeted steps tapping a gold pencil against the satin stripe of his trousers. He had narrow, lifeless eyes and blond-white hair sleeked back off a bony forehead.

Dalmas said: "I'd like to see Mister Donner."

The headwaiter tapped his teeth with his gold pencil. "I'm afraid he's busy. What name?"

"Dalmas. Tell him I'm a special friend of Johnny Sutro's."

The headwaiter said: "I'll try."

He went across to a panel that had a row of buttons on it and a small one-piece phone. He took it off the hook and put it to his ear, staring at Dalmas across the cup with the impersonal stare of a stuffed animal.

Dalmas said: "I'll be in the lobby."

He went back through the curtains and prowled over to the Men's Room. Inside he got out the bottle of bourbon and drank what was left of it, tilting his head back and standing splay-legged in the middle of the tiled floor. A wizened Negro in a white jacket fluttered at him, said anxiously: "No drinkin' in here, boss."

Dalmas threw the empty bottle into a receptacle for towels. He took a clean towel off the glass shelf, wiped his lips with it, put a dime down on the edge of the basin and went out.

There was a space between an inner and outer door. He leaned against the outer door and took a small automatic about four inches long out of his vest pocket. He held it with three fingers against the inside of his hat and went on out, swinging the hat gently beside his body.

After a while a tall Filipino with silky black hair came into the lobby and looked around. Dalmas went towards him. The headwaiter looked out through the curtains and nodded at the Filipino.

The Filipino spoke to Dalmas: "This way, boss."

They went down a long, quiet corridor. The sound of the dance band died away behind them. Some deserted green-topped tables showed through an open door. The corridor turned into another that was at right angles, and at the end of this one some light came out through a doorway.

The Filipino paused in midstride and made a graceful, complicated movement, at the end of which he had a big, black automatic in his hand. He prodded it politely into Dalmas' ribs.

"Got to frisk you, boss. House rules."

Dalmas stood still and held his arms out from his sides. The Filipino took Dalmas' Colt away from him and dropped it into his pocket. He patted the rest of Dalmas' pockets, stepped back and holstered his own cannon.

Dalmas lowered his arms and let his hat fall on the floor and the little automatic that had been inside the hat peered neatly at the Filipino's belly. The Filipino looked down at it with a shocked grin.

Dalmas said: "That was fun, spig. Let me do it."

He put his Colt back where it belonged, took the big automatic from under the Filipino's arm, slipped the magazine out of it and ejected the shell that was in the chamber. He gave the empty gun back to the Filipino.

"You can still use it for a sap. If you stay in front of me, your boss don't have to know that's all it's good for."

The Filipino licked his lips. Dalmas felt him for another gun, and they went on along the corridor, went in at the door that was partly open. The Filipino went first.

It was a big room with walls paneled in diagonal strips of wood. A yellow Chinese rug on the floor, plenty of good furniture, countersunk doors that told of soundproofing, and no windows. There were several gilt gratings high up and a built-in ventilator fan made a faint, soothing murmur. Four men were in the room. Nobody said anything.

Dalmas sat down on a leather divan and stared at Ricchio, the smooth boy who had walked him out of Walden's apartment. Ricchio was tied to a high-backed chair. His arms were pulled around behind it and fastened together at the wrists. His eyes were mad and his face was a welter of blood and bruises. He had been pistol whipped. The sandy-haired man, Noddy, who had been with him at the Kilmarnock sat on a sort of stool in the corner, smoking.

John Sutro was rocking slowly in a red leather rocker, staring down at the floor. He did not look up when Dalmas came into the room.

The fourth man sat behind a desk that looked as if it had cost a lot of money. He had soft brown hair parted in the middle and brushed back and down; thin lips and reddish-brown eyes that had hot lights in them. He watched Mallory while he sat down and looked around. Then he spoke, glancing at Ricchio.

"The punk got a little out of hand. We've been telling him about it. I guess you're not sorry."

Dalmas laughed shortly, without mirth. "All right as far as it goes, Donner. How about the other one? I don't see any marks on him."

"Noddy's all right. He worked under orders," Donner said evenly. He picked up a long-handled file and began to file one of his nails. "You and I have things to talk about. That's why you got in here. You look all right to me – if you don't try to cover too much ground with your private-dick racket."

Dalmas' eyes widened a little. He said: "I'm listening, Donner."

Sutro lifted his eyes and stared at the back of Donner's head. Donner went on talking in a smooth indifferent voice.

"I know all about the play at Derek Walden's place and I know about the shooting on Kenmore. If I'd thought Ricchio would go that crazy, I'd have stopped him before. As it is, I figure it's up to me to straighten things out . . . And when we get through here Mister Ricchio will go downtown and speak his piece.

"Here's how it happened. Ricchio used to work for Walden when the Hollywood crowd went in for body-guards. Walden bought his liquor in Ensenada – still does, for all I know – and brought it in himself. Nobody bothered him. Ricchio saw a chance to bring in some white goods under good cover. Walden caught him at it. He didn't want a scandal, so he just showed Ricchio the gate. Ricchio took advantage of that by trying to shake Walden down, on the theory that he wasn't clean enough to stand the working-over the

Feds would give him. Walden didn't shake fast enough to suit Ricchio, so he went hog wild and decided on a strong-arm play. You and your driver messed it up and Ricchio went gunning for you."

Donner put down his file and smiled. Dalmas shrugged and glanced at the Filipino, who was standing by the wall, at the end of the divan.

Dalmas said: "I don't have your organization, Donner, but I get around. I think that's a smooth story and it would have got by – with a little co-operation downtown. But it won't fit the facts as they are now."

Donner raised his eyebrows. Sutro began to swing the tip of his polished shoe up and down in front of his knee.

Dalmas said: "How does Mister Sutro fit into all this?"

Sutro stared at him and stopped rocking. He made a swift, impatient movement. Donner smiled. "He's a friend of Walden's. Walden talked to him a little and Sutro knows Ricchio worked for me. But being a councilman he didn't want to tell Walden everything he knew."

Dalmas said grimly: "I'll tell you what's wrong with your story, Donner. There's not enough fear in it. Walden was too scared to help me even when I was working for him . . . And this afternoon somebody was so scared of him that he got shot."

Donner leaned forward and his eyes got small and tight. His hands balled into fists on the desk before him.

"Walden is – dead?" he almost whispered.

Dalmas nodded. "Shot in the right temple . . . with a thirty-two. It looks like suicide. It isn't."

Sutro put his hand up quickly and covered his face. The sandy-haired man got rigid on his stool in the corner.

Dalmas said: "Want to hear a good honest guess, Donner? . . . We'll call it a guess . . . Walden was in the dope-smuggling racket himself – and not all by his lonesome. But after Repeal he wanted to quit. The coast guards wouldn't have to spend so

97

much time watching liquor ships, and dope-smuggling up the coast wasn't going to be gravy any more. And Walden got sweet on a gal that had good eyes and could add up to ten. So he wanted to walk out on the dope racket."

Donner moistened his lips and said: "What dope racket?"

Dalmas eyed him. "You wouldn't know about anything like that, would you, Donner? Hell, no, that's something for the bad boys to play with. And the bad boys didn't like the idea of Walden quitting that way. He was drinking too much – and he might start to broadcast to his girl friend. They wanted him to quit the way he did – on the receiving end of a gun."

Donner turned his head slowly and stared at the bound man on the high-backed chair. He said very softly: "Ricchio."

Then he got up and walked around his desk. Sutro took his hand down from his face and watched with his lips shaking.

Donner stood in front of Ricchio. He put his hand out against Ricchio's head and jarred it back against the chair. Ricchio moaned. Donner smiled down at him.

"I must be slowing up. *You* killed Walden, you bastard! You went back and croaked him. You forgot to tell us about that part, baby."

Ricchio opened his mouth and spit a stream of blood against Donner's hand and wrist. Donner's face twitched and he stepped back and away, holding the hand straight out in front of him. He took out a handkerchief and wiped it off carefully, dropped the handkerchief on the floor.

"Lend me your gun, Noddy," he said quietly, going towards the sandy-haired man.

Sutro jerked and his mouth fell open. His eyes looked sick. The tall Filipino flicked his empty automatic into his hand as if he had forgotten it was empty. Noddy took a blunt revolver from under his right arm, held it out to Donner.

Donner took it from him and went back to Ricchio. He raised the gun.

Dalmas said: "Ricchio didn't kill Walden."

The Filipino took a quick step forward and slashed at him with his big automatic. The gun hit Dalmas on the point of the shoulder, and a wave of pain billowed down his arm. He rolled away and snapped his Colt into his hand. The Filipino swung at him again, missed.

Dalmas slid to his feet, side-stepped and laid the barrel of the Colt along the side of the Filipino's head, with all his strength. The Filipino grunted, sat down on the floor, and the whites showed all around his eyes. He fell over slowly, clawing at the divan.

There was no expression on Donner's face and he held his blunt revolver perfectly still. His long upper lip was beaded with sweat.

Dalmas said: "Ricchio didn't kill Walden. Walden was killed with a filed gun and the gun was planted in his hand. Ricchio wouldn't go within a block of a filed gun."

Sutro's face was ghastly. The sandy-haired man had got down off his stool and stood with his right hand swinging at his side.

"Tell me more," Donner said evenly.

"The filed gun traces to a broad named Helen Dalton or Burwand," Dalmas said. "It was her gun. She told me that she hocked it long ago. I didn't believe her. She's a good friend of Sutro's and Sutro was so bothered by my going to see her that he pulled a gat on me himself. Why do you suppose Sutro was bothered, Donner, and how do you suppose he knew I was likely to go see the broad?"

Donner said: "Go ahead and tell me." He looked at Sutro very quietly.

Dalmas took a step closer to Donner and held his Colt down at his side, not threateningly.

"I'll tell you how and why. I've been tailed ever since I started to work for Walden – tailed by a clumsy ox of a studio dick I could spot a mile off. He was bought, Donner. The guy that killed Walden bought him. He figured the studio dick had a chance to get next to me, and I let him do just that — to give him rope and spot his game. His boss was Sutro. Sutro killed Walden — with his own hand. It was that kind of a job. An amateur job — a smart-aleck kill. The thing that made it smart was the thing that gave it away — the suicide plant, with a filed gun that the killer thought couldn't be traced because he didn't know most guns have numbers inside."

Donner swung the blunt revolver until it pointed midway between the sandy-haired man and Sutro. He didn't say anything. His eyes were thoughtful and interested.

Dalmas shifted his weight a little, on to the balls of his feet. The Filipino on the floor put a hand along the divan and his nails scratched on the leather.

"There's more of it, Donner, but what the hell! Sutro was Walden's pal, and he could get close to him, close enough to stick a gun to his head and let go. A shot wouldn't be heard on the penthouse floor of the Kilmarnock, one little shot from a thirty-two. So Sutro put the gun in Walden's hand and went on his way. But he forgot that Walden was left-handed and he didn't know the gun could be traced. When it was — and his bought man wised him up — and I tapped the girl — he hired himself a chopper squad and angled all three of us out to a house in Palms to button our mouths for good . . . Only the chopper squad, like everything else in this play, didn't do its stuff so good."

Donner nodded slowly. He looked at a spot in the middle of Sutro's stomach and lined his gun on it.

"Tell us about it, Johnny," he said softly. "Tell us how you got clever in your old age — "

The sandy-haired man moved suddenly. He dodged down behind the desk and as he went down his right hand swept for his other gun. It roared from behind the desk. The bullet came through the kneehole and pinged into the wall with a sound of striking metal behind the paneling.

Dalmas jerked his Colt and fired twice into the desk. A few splinters flew. The sandy-haired man yelled behind the desk and came up fast with his gun flaming in his hand. Donner staggered. His gun spoke twice, very quickly. The sandy-haired man yelled again, and blood jumped straight out from one of his cheeks. He went down behind the desk and stayed quiet.

Donner backed until he touched the wall. Sutro stood up and put his hands in front of his stomach and tried to scream.

Donner said: "Okay, Johnny. Your turn."

Then Donner coughed suddenly and slid down the wall with a dry rustle of cloth. He bent forward and dropped his gun and put his hands on the floor and went on coughing. His face got gray.

Sutro stood rigid, his hands in front of his stomach, and bent back at the wrists, the fingers curved clawlike. There was no light behind his eyes. They were dead eyes. After a moment his knees buckled and he fell down on the floor on his back.

Donner went on coughing quietly.

Dalmas crossed swiftly to the door of the room, listened at it, opened it and looked out. He shut it again quickly.

"Soundproof – and how!" he muttered.

He went back to the desk and lifted the telephone off its prongs. He put his Colt down and dialed, waited, said into the phone: "Captain Cathcart . . . Got to talk to him . . . Sure, it's important . . . very important."

He waited, drumming on the desk, staring hard-eyed around the room. He jerked a little as a sleepy voice came over the wire.

"Dalmas, Chief. I'm at the Casa Mariposa, in Gayn Donner's private office. There's been a little trouble, but nobody hurt bad . . . I've got Derek Walden's killer for you . . . Johnny Sutro did it . . . Yeah, the councilman . . . Make it fast, Chief . . . I wouldn't want to get in a fight with the help, you know. . . . "

He hung up and picked his Colt off the top of the desk, held it on the flat of his hand and stared across at Sutro.

"Get off the floor, Johnny," he said wearily. "Get up and tell a poor dumb dick how to cover this one up – smart guy!"

10

THE LIGHT ABOVE the big oak table at Headquarters was too bright. Dalmas ran a finger along the wood, looked at it, wiped it off on his sleeve. He cupped his chin in his lean hands and stared at the wall above the roll-top desk that was beyond the table. He was alone in the room.

The loudspeaker on the wall droned: "Calling Car 71W in 72's district . . . at Third and Berendo . . . at the drugstore . . . meet a man . . . "

The door opened and Captain Cathcart came in, shut the door carefully behind him. He was a big, battered man with a wide, moist face, a strained mustache, gnarled hands.

He sat down between the oak table and the roll-top desk and fingered a cold pipe that lay in the ashtray.

Dalmas raised his head from between his hands. Cathcart said: "Sutro's dead."

Dalmas stared, said nothing.

"His wife did it. He wanted to stop by his house a minute. The boys watched him good but they didn't watch her. She slipped him the dose before they could move."

Cathcart opened and shut his mouth twice. He had strong, dirty teeth.

"She never said a damn word. Brought a little gun around from behind her and fed him three slugs. One, two, three. Win, place, show. Just like that. Then she turned the gun around in her hand as nice as you could think of and handed it to the boys . . . What in hell she do that for?"

Dalmas said: "Get a confession?"

Cathcart stared at him and put the cold pipe in his mouth. He sucked on it noisily. "From him? Yeah — not on paper, though . . . What you suppose she done that for?"

"She knew about the blonde," Dalmas said. "She thought it was her last chance. Maybe she knew about his rackets."

The captain nodded slowly. "Sure," he said. "That's it. She figured it was her last chance. And why shouldn't she bop the bastard? If the D.A.'s smart, he'll let her take a manslaughter plea. That'd be about fifteen months at Tchachapi. A rest cure."

Dalmas moved in his chair. He frowned.

Cathcart went on: "It's a break for all of us. No dirt your way, no dirt on the administration. If she hadn't done it, it would have been a kick in the pants all around. She ought to get a pension."

"She ought to get a contract from Eclipse Films," Dalmas said. "When I got to Sutro I figured I was licked on the publicity angle. I might have gunned Sutro myself — if he hadn't been so yellow — and if he hadn't been a councilman."

"Nix on that, baby. Leave that stuff to the law," Cathcart growled. "Here's how it looks. I don't figure we can get Walden on the book as a suicide. The filed gun is against it and we got to wait for the autopsy and the gun-shark's report. And a paraffin test of the hand ought to show he didn't fire the gun at all. On the other hand, the case is closed on Sutro and what has to come out ought not to hurt too bad. Am I right?"

Dalmas took out a cigarette and rolled it between his fingers. He lit it slowly and waved the match until it went out.

"Walden was no lily," he said. "It's the dope angle that would raise hell — but that's cold. I guess we're jake, except for a few loose ends."

"Hell with the loose ends." Cathcart grinned. "Nobody's getting away with any fix that I can see. That sidekick of yours, Denny, will fade in a hurry and if I ever get my paws on the Dalton frail, I'll send her to Mendocino for the cure.

We might get something on Donner — after the hospital gets through with him. We've got to put the rap on those hoods, for the stick-up and the taxi driver, whichever of 'em did that, but they won't talk. They still got a future to think about, and the taxi driver ain't so bad hurt. That leaves the chopper squad." Cathcart yawned. "Those boys must be from Frisco. We don't run to choppers around here much."

Dalmas sagged in his chair. "You wouldn't have a drink, would you, Chief ?" he said dully.

Cathcart stared at him. "There's just one thing," he said grimly. "I want you to stay told about that. It was okay for you to break that gun — if you didn't spoil the prints. And I guess it was okay for you not to tell me, seein' the jam you were in. But I'll be damned if it's okay for you to beat our time by chiselin' on our own records."

Dalmas smiled thoughtfully at him. "You're right all the way, Chief," he said humbly. "It was the job — and that's all a guy can say."

Cathcart rubbed his cheeks vigorously. His frown went away and he grinned. Then he bent over and pulled out a drawer and brought up a quart bottle of rye. He put it on the desk and pressed a buzzer. A very large uniformed torso came part way into the room.

"Hey, Tiny!" Cathcart boomed. "Loan me that corkscrew you swiped out of my desk." The torso disappeared and came back.

"What'll we drink to?" the captain asked a couple of minutes later.

Dalmas said: "Let's just drink."

FINGER MAN

1

I GOT AWAY from the Grand Jury a little after four, and then sneaked up the back stairs to Fenweather's office. Fenweather, the D.A., was a man with severe, chiseled features and the gray temples women love. He played with a pen on his desk and said: "I think they believed you. They might even indict Manny Tinnen for the Shannon kill this afternoon. If they do, then is the time you begin to watch your step."

I rolled a cigarette around in my fingers and finally put it in my mouth. "Don't put any men on me, Mr. Fenweather. I know the alleys in this town pretty well, and your men couldn't stay close enough to do me any good."

He looked towards one of the windows. "How well do you know Frank Dorr?" he asked, with his eyes away from me.

"I know he's a big politico, a fixer you have to see if you want to open a gambling hell or a bawdy house – or if you want to sell honest merchandise to the city."

"Right." Fenweather spoke sharply, and brought his head around towards me. Then he lowered his voice. "Having the goods on Tinnen was a surprise to a lot of people. If Frank Dorr had an interest in getting rid of Shannon who was the head of the Board where Dorr's supposed to get his contracts, it's close enough to make him take chances. And I'm told he and Manny Tinnen had dealings. I'd sort of keep an eye on him, if I were you."

I grinned. "I'm just one guy," I said. "Frank Dorr covers a lot of territory. But I'll do what I can."

Fenweather stood up and held his hand across the desk. He said: "I'll be out of town for a couple of days, I'm leaving tonight, if this indictment comes through. Be careful – and if anything should happen to go wrong, see Bernie Ohls, my chief investigator."

I said: "Sure."

We shook hands and I went out past a tired-looking girl who gave me a tired smile and wound one of her lax curls up on the back of her neck as she looked at me. I got back to my office soon after four-thirty. I stopped outside the door of the little reception room for a moment, looking at it. Then I opened it and went in, and of course there wasn't anybody there.

There was nothing there but an old red davenport, two odd chairs, a bit of carpet, and a library table with a few old magazines on it. The reception room was left open for visitors to come in and sit down and wait – if I had any visitors and they felt like waiting.

I went across and unlocked the door into my private office, lettered "*Philip Marlowe . . . Investigations.*"

Lou Harger was sitting on a wooden chair on the side of the desk away from the window. He had bright yellow gloves clamped on the crook of a cane, a green snap-brim hat set too far back on his head. Very smooth black hair showed under the hat and grew too low on the nape of his neck.

"Hello. I've been waiting," he said, and smiled languidly.

"'Lo, Lou. How did you get in here?"

"The door must have been unlocked. Or maybe I had a key that fitted. Do you mind?"

I went around the desk and sat down in the swivel chair. I put my hat down on the desk, picked up a bulldog pipe out of an ashtray and began to fill it up.

"It's all right as long as it's you," I said. "I just thought I had a better lock."

He smiled with his full red lips. He was a very good-looking boy. He said: "Are you still doing business, or will you spend the next month in a hotel room drinking liquor with a couple of Headquarters boys?"

"I'm still doing business – if there's any business for me to do."

I lit a pipe, leaned back and stared at his clear olive skin, straight, dark eyebrows.

He put his cane on top of the desk and clasped his yellow gloves on the glass. He moved his lips in and out.

"I have a little something for you. Not a hell of a lot. But there's carfare in it."

I waited.

"I'm making a little play at Las Olindas tonight," he said. "At Canales' place."

"The white smoke?"

"Uh-huh. I think I'm going to be lucky – and I'd like to have a guy with a rod."

I took a fresh pack of cigarettes out of a top drawer and slid them across the desk. Lou picked them up and began to break the pack open.

I said: "What kind of a play?"

He got a cigarette halfway out and stared down at it. There was a little something in his manner I didn't like.

"I've been closed up for a month now. I wasn't makin' the kind of money it takes to stay open in this town. The Headquarters boys have been putting the pressure on since repeal. They have bad dreams when they see themselves trying to live on their pay."

I said: "It doesn't cost any more to operate here than anywhere else. And here you pay it all to one organization. That's something."

Lou Harger jabbed the cigarette in his mouth. "Yeah – Frank Dorr," he snarled. "That fat, bloodsuckin' sonofabitch!"

I didn't say anything. I was way past the age when it's fun to swear at people you can't hurt. I watched Lou light his cigarette with my desk lighter. He went on, through a puff of smoke: "It's a laugh, in a way. Canales bought a new wheel –

from some grafters in the sheriff's office. I know Pina, Canales' head croupier, pretty well. The wheel is one they took away from me. It's got bugs – and I know the bugs."

"And Canales don't . . . That sounds just like Canales," I said.

Lou didn't look at me. "He gets a nice crowd down there," he said. "He has a small dance floor and a five-piece Mexican band to help the customers relax. They dance a bit and then go back for another trimming, instead of going away disgusted."

I said: "What do *you* do?"

"I guess you might call it a system," he said softly, and looked at me under his long lashes.

I looked away from him, looked around the room. It had a rust-red carpet, five green filing cases in a row under an advertising calendar, an old costumer in the corner, a few walnut chairs, net curtains over the windows. The fringe of the curtains was dirty from blowing about in the draft. There was a bar of late sunlight across my desk and it showed up the dust.

"I get it like this," I said. "You think you have that roulette wheel tamed and you expect to win enough money so that Canales will be mad at you. You'd like to have some protection along – me. I think it's screwy."

"It's not screwy at all," Lou said. "Any roulette wheel has a tendency to work in a certain rhythm. If you know the wheel very well indeed – "

I smiled and shrugged. "Okay, I wouldn't know about that. I don't know enough roulette. It sounds to me like you're being a sucker for your own racket, but I could be wrong. And that's not the point anyway."

"What is?" Lou asked thinly.

"I'm not much stuck on bodyguarding – but maybe that's not the point either. I take it I'm supposed to think this play is on the level. Suppose I don't, and walk out on you, and you get in a box? Or suppose I think everything is aces, but Canales don't agree with me and gets nasty."

"That's why I need a guy with a rod," Lou said, without moving a muscle except to speak.

I said evenly: "If I'm tough enough for the job – and I didn't know I was – that still isn't what worries me."

"Forget it," Lou said. "It breaks me up enough to know you're worried."

I smiled a little more and watched his yellow gloves moving around on top of the desk, moving too much. I said slowly: "You're the last guy in the world to be getting expense money that way just now. I'm the last guy to be standing behind you while you do it. That's all."

Lou said: "Yeah." He knocked some ash off his cigarette down on the glass top, bent his head to blow it off. He went on, as if it was a new subject: "Miss Glenn is going with me. She's a tall redhead, a swell looker. She used to model. She's nice people in any kind of a spot and she'll keep Canales from breathing on my neck. So we'll make out. I just thought I'd tell you."

I was silent for a minute, then I said: "You know damn well I just got through telling the Grand Jury it was Manny Tinnen I saw lean out of that car and cut the ropes on Art Shannon's wrists after they pushed him on the roadway, filled with lead."

Lou smiled faintly at me. "That'll make it easier for the grafters on the big time; the fellows who take the contracts and don't appear in the business. They say Shannon was square and kept the Board in line. It was a nasty bump-off."

I shook my head. I didn't want to talk about that. I said: "Canales has a noseful of junk a lot of the time. And maybe he doesn't go for redheads."

Lou stood up slowly and lifted his cane off the desk. He stared at the tip of one yellow finger. He had an almost sleepy expression. Then he moved towards the door, swinging his cane.

"Well, I'll be seein' you some time," he drawled.

I let him get his hand on the knob before I said: "Don't go away sore, Lou. I'll drop down to Las Olindas, if you have to have me. But I don't want any money for it, and for Pete's sake don't pay any more attention to me than you have to."

He licked his lips softly and didn't quite look at me. "Thanks, keed. I'll be careful as hell."

He went out then and his yellow glove disappeared around the edge of the door.

I sat still for about five minutes and then my pipe got too hot. I put it down, looked at my strap watch, and got up to switch on a small radio in the corner beyond the end of the desk. When the A.C. hum died down the last tinkle of a chime came out of the horn, then a voice was saying: "KLI now brings you its regular early evening broadcast of local news releases. An event of importance this afternoon was the indictment returned late today against Maynard J. Tinnen by the Grand Jury. Tinnen is a well-known City Hall lobbyist and man about town. The indictment, a shock to his many friends, was based almost entirely on the testimony – "

My telephone rang sharply and a girl's cool voice said in my ear: "One moment, please. Mr. Fenweather is calling you."

He came on at once. "Indictment returned. Take care of the boy."

I said I was just getting it over the radio. We talked a short moment and then he hung up, after saying he had to leave at once to catch a plane.

I leaned back in my chair again and listened to the radio without exactly hearing it. I was thinking what a damn fool Lou Harger was and that there wasn't anything I could do to change that.

2

IT WAS A good crowd for a Tuesday but nobody was dancing. Around ten o'clock the little five-piece band got tired of messing around with a rhumba that nobody was paying any attention to. The marimba player dropped his sticks and reached under his chair for a glass. The rest of the boys lit cigarettes and just sat there looking bored.

I leaned sidewise against the bar, which was on the same side of the room as the orchestra stand. I was turning a small glass of tequila around on the top of the bar. All the business was at the center one of the three roulette tables.

The bartender leaned beside me, on his side of the bar.

"The flame-top gal must be pickin' them," he said.

I nodded without looking at him. "She's playing with fistfuls now," I said. "Not even counting it."

The red-haired girl was tall. I could see the burnished copper of her hair between the heads of the people behind her. I could see Lou Harger's sleek head beside hers. Everybody seemed to be playing standing up.

"You don't play?" the bartender asked me.

"Not on Tuesdays. I had some trouble on a Tuesday once."

"Yeah? Do you like that stuff straight, or could I smooth it out for you?"

"Smooth it out with what?" I said. "You got a wood rasp handy?"

He grinned. I drank a little more of the tequila and made a face.

"Did anybody invent this stuff on purpose?"

"I wouldn't know, mister."

"What's the limit over there?"

"I wouldn't know that either. How the boss feels, I guess."

The roulette tables were in a row near the far wall. A low railing of gilt metal joined their ends and the players were outside the railing.

Some kind of a confused wrangle started at the center table. Half a dozen people at the two end tables grabbed their chips up and moved across.

Then a clear, very polite voice, with a slightly foreign accent, spoke out: "If you will just be patient, madame . . . Mr. Canales will be here in a minute."

I went across, squeezed near the railing. Two croupiers stood near me with their heads together and their eyes looking sidewise. One moved a rake slowly back and forth beside the idle wheel. They were staring at the red-haired girl.

She wore a high-cut black evening gown. She had fine white shoulders, was something less than beautiful and more than pretty. She was leaning on the edge of the table, in front of the wheel. Her long eyelashes were twitching. There was a big pile of money and chips in front of her.

She spoke monotonously, as if she had said the same thing several times already.

"Get busy and spin that wheel! You take it away fast enough, but you don't like to dish it out."

The croupier in charge smiled a cold, even smile. He was tall, dark, disinterested: "The table can't cover your bet," he said with calm precision. "Mr. Canales, perhaps – " He shrugged neat shoulders.

The girl said: "It's your money, highpockets. Don't you want it back?"

Lou Harger licked his lips beside her, put a hand on her arm, stared at the pile of money with hot eyes. He said gently: "Wait for Canales . . ."

"To hell with Canales! I'm hot – and I want to stay that way."

A door opened at the end of the tables and a very slight, very pale man came into the room. He had straight, lusterless black hair, a high bony forehead, flat, impenetrable eyes. He had a thin mustache that was trimmed in two sharp lines almost at right angles to each other. They came down below the corners of his mouth a full inch. The effect was Oriental. His skin had a thick, glistening pallor.

He slid behind the croupiers, stopped at a corner of the center table, glanced at the red-haired girl and touched the ends of his mustache with two fingers, the nails of which had a purplish tint.

He smiled suddenly, and the instant after it was as though he had never smiled in his life. He spoke in a dull, ironic voice.

"Good evening, Miss Glenn. You must let me send somebody with you when you go home. I'd hate to see any of that money get in the wrong pockets."

The red-haired girl looked at him, not very pleasantly.

"I'm not leaving – unless you're throwing me out."

Canales said: "No? What would you like to do?"

"Bet the wad – dark meat!"

The crowd noise became a deathly silence. There wasn't a whisper of any kind of sound. Harger's face slowly got ivory-white.

Canales' face was without expression. He lifted a hand, delicately, gravely, slipped a large wallet from his dinner jacket and tossed it in front of the tall croupier.

"Ten grand," he said in a voice that was a dull rustle of sound. "That's my limit – always."

The tall croupier picked the wallet up, spread it, drew out two flat packets of crisp bills, riffled them, refolded the wallet and passed it along the edge of the table to Canales.

Canales did not move to take it. Nobody moved, except the croupier.

The girl said: "Put it on the red."

The croupier leaned across the table and very carefully stacked her money and chips. He placed her bet for her on the red diamond. He placed his hand along the curve of the wheel.

"If no one objects," Canales said, without looking at anyone, "this is just the two of us."

Heads moved. Nobody spoke. The croupier spun the wheel and sent the ball skimming in the groove with a light flirt of his left wrist. Then he drew his hands back and placed them in full view on the edge of the table, on top of it.

The red-haired girl's eyes shone and her lips slowly parted.

The ball drifted along the groove, dipped past one of the bright metal diamonds, slid down the flank of the wheel and chattered along the tines beside the numbers. Movement went out of it suddenly, with a dry click. It fell next the double-zero, in red twenty-seven. The wheel was motionless.

The croupier took up his rake and slowly pushed the two packets of bills across, added them to the stake, pushed the whole thing off the field of play.

Canales put his wallet back in his breast pocket, turned and walked slowly back to the door, went through it.

I took my cramped fingers off the top of the railing, and a lot of people broke for the bar.

3

WHEN LOU CAME up I was sitting at a little tile-top table in a corner, fooling with some more of the tequila. The little orchestra was playing a thin, brittle tango and one couple was maneuvering self-consciously on the dance floor.

Lou had a cream-colored overcoat on, with the collar turned up around a lot of white silk scarf. He had a fine-drawn glistening expression. He had white pigskin gloves this time and he put one of them down on the table and leaned at me.

"Over twenty-two thousand," he said softly. "Boy, what a take!"

I said: "Very nice money, Lou. What kind of car are you driving?"

"See anything wrong with it?"

"The play?" I shrugged, fiddled with my glass. "I'm not wised up on roulette, Lou . . . I saw plenty wrong with your broad's manners."

"She's not a broad," Lou said. His voice got a little worried.

"Okay. She made Canales look like a million. What kind of car?"

"Buick sedan. Nile green, with two spotlights and those little fender lights on rods." His voice was still worried.

I said: "Take it kind of slow through town. Give me a chance to get in the parade."

He moved his glove and went away. The red-haired girl was not in sight anywhere. I looked down at the watch on my wrist. When I looked up again Canales was standing across the table. His eyes looked at me lifelessly above his trick mustache.

"You don't like my place," he said.

"On the contrary."

"You don't come here to play." He was telling me, not asking me.

"Is it compulsory?" I asked dryly.

A very faint smile drifted across his face. He leaned a little down and said: "I think you are a dick. A smart dick."

"Just a shamus," I said. "And not so smart. Don't let my long upper lip fool you. It runs in the family."

Canales wrapped his fingers around the top of a chair, squeezed on it. "Don't come here again — for anything." He spoke very softly, almost dreamily. "I don't like pigeons."

I took the cigarette out of my mouth and looked it over before I looked at him. I said: "I heard you insulted a while back. You took it nicely . . . So we won't count this one."

He had a queer expression for a moment. Then he turned and slid away with a little sway of the shoulders. He put his feet down flat and turned them out a good deal as he walked. His walk, like his face, was a little negroid.

I got up and went out through the big white double doors into a dim lobby, got my hat and coat and put them on. I went out through another pair of double doors onto a wide veranda with scrollwork along the edge of its roof. There was sea fog in the air and the windblown Monterey cypresses in front of the house dripped with it. The grounds sloped gently into the dark for a long distance. Fog hid the ocean.

I had parked the car out on the street, on the other side of the house. I drew my hat down and walked soundlessly on the damp moss that covered the driveway, rounded a corner of the porch, and stopped rigidly.

A man just in front of me was holding a gun – but he didn't see me. He was holding the gun down at his side, pressed against the material of his overcoat, and his big hand made it look quite small. The dim light that reflected from the barrel seemed to come out of the fog, to be part of the fog. He was a big man, and he stood very still, poised on the balls of his feet.

I lifted my right hand very slowly and opened the top two buttons of my coat, reached inside and drew out a long .38 with a six-inch barrel. I eased it into my overcoat pocket.

The man in front of me moved, reached his left hand up to his face. He drew on a cigarette cupped inside his hand and the glow put brief light on a heavy chin, wide, dark nostrils, and a square, aggressive nose, the nose of a fighting man.

Then he dropped the cigarette and stepped on it and a quick, light step made faint noise behind me. I was far too late turning.

Something swished and I went out like a light.

4

WHEN I CAME to I was cold and wet and had a headache a yard wide. There was a soft bruise behind my right ear that wasn't bleeding. I had been put down with a sap.

I got up off my back and saw that I was a few yards from the driveway, between two trees that were wet with fog. There was some mud on the backs of my shoes. I had been dragged off the path, but not very far.

I went through my pockets. My gun was gone, of course, but that was all – that and the idea that this excursion was all fun.

I nosed around through the fog, didn't find anything or see anyone, gave up bothering about that, and went along the blank side of the house to a curving line of palm trees and an old type arc light that hissed and flickered over the entrance to a sort of lane where I had stuck the 1925 Marmon touring car I still used for transportation. I got into it after wiping the seat off with a towel, teased the motor alive, and choked it along to a big empty street with disused car tracks in the middle.

I went from there to De Cazens Boulevard, which was the main drag of Las Olindas and was called after the man who built Canales' place long ago. After a while there was town, buildings, dead-looking stores, a service station with a night-bell, and at last a drugstore which was still open.

A dolled-up sedan was parked in front of the drugstore and I parked behind that, got out, and saw that a hatless man was sitting at the counter, talking to a clerk in a blue smock. They seemed to have the world to themselves. I started to go in, then I stopped and took another look at the dolled-up sedan.

It was a Buick and of a color that could have been Nile-green in daylight. It had two spotlights and two little egg-shaped amber lights stuck up on thin nickel rods clamped to the front fenders. The window by the driver's seat was down. I went back to the Marmon and got a flash, reached in and twisted the license holder of the Buick around, put the light on it quickly, then off again.

It was registered to Louis N. Harger.

I got rid of the flash and went into the drugstore. There was a liquor display at one side, and the clerk in the blue smock sold me a pint of Canadian Club, which I took over to the counter and opened. There were ten seats at the counter, but I sat down on the one next to the hatless man. He began to look me over, in the mirror, very carefully.

I got a cup of black coffee two-thirds full and added plenty of the rye. I drank it down and waited for a minute, to let it warm me up. Then I looked the hatless man over.

He was about twenty-eight, a little thin on top, had a healthy red face, fairly honest eyes, dirty hands and looked as if he wasn't making much money. He wore a gray whipcord jacket with metal buttons on it, pants that didn't match.

I said carelessly, in a low voice: "Your bus outside?"

He sat very still. His mouth got small and tight and he had trouble pulling his eyes away from mine, in the mirror.

"My brother's," he said, after a moment.

I said: "Care for a drink? . . . Your brother is an old friend of mine."

He nodded slowly, gulped, moved his hand slowly, but finally got the bottle and curdled his coffee with it. He drank the whole thing down. Then I watched him dig up a crumpled pack of cigarettes, spear his mouth with one, strike a match on the counter, after missing twice on his thumbnail, and inhale with a lot of very poor nonchalance that he knew wasn't going over.

I leaned close to him and said evenly: "This doesn't *have* to be trouble."

He said: "Yeah . . . Wh-what's the beef ?"

The clerk sidled towards us. I asked for more coffee. When I got it I stared at the clerk until he went and stood in front of the display window with his back to me. I laced my second cup of coffee and drank some of it. I looked at the clerk's back and said: "The guy the car belongs to doesn't have a brother."

He held himself tightly, but turned towards me. "You think it's a hot car?"

"No."

"You don't think it's a hot car?"

I said: "No. I just want the story."

"You a dick?"

"Uh-huh – but it isn't a shakedown, if that's what worries you."

He drew hard on his cigarette and moved his spoon around in his empty cup.

"I can lose my job over this," he said slowly. "But I needed a hundred bucks. I'm a hack driver."

"I guessed that," I said.

He looked surprised, turned his head and stared at me. "Have another drink and let's get on with it," I said. "Car thieves don't park them on the main drag and then sit around in drugstores."

The clerk came back from the window and hovered near us, busying himself with rubbing a rag on the coffee urn. A heavy silence fell. The clerk put the rag down, went along to the back of the store, behind the partition, and began to whistle aggressively.

The man beside me took some more of the whiskey and drank it, nodding his head wisely at me. "Listen – I brought a fare out and was supposed to wait for him. A guy and a jane come up alongside me in the Buick and the guy offers me a hundred bucks to let him wear my cap and drive my hack into town. I'm to hang around here an hour, then take his heap to the Hotel Carillon on Towne Boulevard. My cab will be there for me. He gives me the hundred bucks."

"What was his story?" I asked.

"He said they'd been to a gambling joint and had some luck for a change. They're afraid of holdups on the way in. They figure there's always spotters watchin' the play."

I took one of his cigarettes and straightened it out in my fingers. "It's a story I can't hurt much," I said. "Could I see your cards?"

He gave them to me. His name was Tom Sneyd and he was a driver for the Green Top Cab Company. I corked my pint, slipped it into my side pocket, and danced a half-dollar on the counter.

The clerk came along and made change. He was almost shaking with curiosity.

"Come on, Tom," I said in front of him. "Let's go get that cab. I don't think you should wait around here any longer."

We went out, and I let the Buick lead me away from the straggling lights of Las Olindas, through a series of small beach towns with little houses built on sandlots close to the ocean, and bigger ones built on the slopes of the hills behind. A window was lit here and there. The tires sang on the moist concrete and the little amber lights on the Buick's fenders peeped back at me from the curves.

At West Cimarron we turned inland, chugged on through Canal City, and met the San Angelo Cut. It took us almost an hour to get to 5640 Towne Boulevard, which is the number of the Hotel Carillon. It is a big, rambling slate-roofed building with a basement garage and a forecourt fountain on which they play a pale green light in the evening.

Green Top Cab No. 469 was parked across the street, on the dark side. I couldn't see where anybody had been shooting into it. Tom Sneyd found his cap in the driver's compartment, climbed eagerly under the wheel.

"Does that fix me up? Can I go now?" His voice was strident with relief.

I told him it was all right with me, and gave him my card. It was twelve minutes past one as he took the corner. I climbed into the Buick and tooled it down the ramp to the garage and left it with a colored boy who was dusting cars in slow motion. I went around to the lobby.

The clerk was an ascetic-looking young man who was reading a volume of *California Appellate Decisions* under the switchboard light. He said Lou was not in and had not been in since eleven, when he came on duty. After a short argument about the lateness of the hour and the importance of my visit, he rang Lou's apartment, but there wasn't any answer.

I went out and sat in my Marmon for a few minutes, smoked a cigarette, imbibed a little from my pint of Canadian Club. Then I went back into the Carillon and shut myself in a pay booth. I dialed the *Telegram*, asked for the City Desk, got a man named Von Ballin.

He yelped at me when I told him who I was. "You still walking around? That ought to be a story. I thought Manny

Tinnen's friends would have had you laid away in old lavender by this time."

I said: "Can that and listen to this. Do you know a man
named Lou Harger? He's a gambler. Had a place that was
raided and closed up a month ago."

Von Ballin said he didn't know Lou personally, but he
knew who he was.

"Who around your rag would know him real well?"

He thought a moment. "There's a lad named Jerry Cross
here," he said, "that's supposed to be an expert on night life.
What did you want to know?"

"Where would he go to celebrate," I said. Then I told him
some of the story, not too much. I left out the part where
I got sapped and the part about the taxi. "He hasn't shown at
his hotel," I ended. "I ought to get a line on him."

"Well, if you're a friend of his – "

"Of his – not of his crowd," I said sharply.

Von Ballin stopped to yell at somebody to take a call, then
said to me softly, close to the phone: "Come through, boy.
Come through."

"All right. But I'm talking to you, not to your sheet. I got
sapped and lost my gun outside Canales' joint. Lou and his girl
switched his car for a taxi they picked up. Then they dropped
out of sight. I don't like it too well. Lou wasn't drunk enough
to chase around town with that much dough in his pockets.
And if he was, the girl wouldn't let him. She had the practical eye."

"I'll see what I can do," Von Ballin said. "But it don't sound
promising. I'll give you a buzz."

I told him I lived at the Merritt Plaza, in case he had forgotten, went out and got into the Marmon again. I drove
home and put hot towels on my head for fifteen minutes, then
sat around in my pajamas and drank hot whiskey and lemon
and called the Carillon every once in a while. At two-thirty
Von Ballin called me and said no luck. Lou hadn't been

pinched, he wasn't in any of the Receiving Hospitals, and he hadn't shown at any of the clubs Jerry Cross could think of.

At three I called the Carillon for the last time. Then I put my light out and went to sleep.

In the morning it was the same way. I tried to trace the red-haired girl a little. There were twenty-eight people named Glenn in the phone book, and three women among them. One didn't answer, the other two assured me they didn't have red hair. One offered to show me.

I shaved, showered, had breakfast, walked three blocks down the hill to the Condor Building.

Miss Glenn was sitting in my little reception room.

5

I UNLOCKED THE other door and she went in and sat in the chair where Lou had sat the afternoon before. I opened some windows, locked the outer door of the reception room, and struck a match for the unlighted cigarette she held in her ungloved and ringless left hand.

She was dressed in a blouse and plaid skirt with a loose coat over them, and a close-fitting hat that was far enough out of style to suggest a run of bad luck. But it hid almost all of her hair. Her skin was without make-up and she looked about thirty and had the set face of exhaustion.

She held her cigarette with a hand that was almost too steady, a hand on guard. I sat down and waited for her to talk.

She stared at the wall over my head and didn't say anything. After a little while I packed my pipe and smoked for a minute. Then I got up and went across to the door that opened into the hallway and picked up a couple of letters that had been pushed through the slot.

I sat down at the desk again, looked them over, read one of them twice, as if I had been alone. While I was doing this I didn't look at her directly or speak to her, but I kept an eye on her all the same. She looked like a lady who was getting nerved for something.

Finally she moved. She opened up a big black patent-leather bag and took out a fat manila envelope, pulled a rubber band off it and sat holding the envelope between the palms of her hands, with her head tilted way back and the cigarette dribbling gray smoke from the corners of her mouth.

She said slowly: "Lou said if I ever got caught in the rain, you were the boy to see. It's raining hard where I am."

I stared at the manila envelope. "Lou is a pretty good friend of mine," I said. "I'd do anything in reason for him. Some things not in reason – like last night. That doesn't mean Lou and I always play the same games."

She dropped her cigarette into the glass bowl of the ashtray and left it to smoke. A dark flame burned suddenly in her eyes, then went out.

"Lou is dead." Her voice was quite toneless.

I reached over with a pencil and stabbed at the hot end of the cigarette until it stopped smoking.

She went on: "A couple of Canales' boys got him in my apartment – with one shot from a small gun that looked like my gun. Mine was gone when I looked for it afterwards. I spent the night there with him dead . . . I had to."

She broke quite suddenly. Her eyes turned up in her head and her head came down and hit the desk. She lay still, with the manila envelope in front of her lax hands.

I jerked a drawer open and brought up a bottle and a glass, poured a stiff one and stepped around with it, heaved her up in her chair. I pushed the edge of the glass hard against her mouth – hard enough to hurt. She struggled and swallowed. Some of it ran down her chin, but life came back into her eyes.

I left the whiskey in front of her and sat down again. The flap of the envelope had come open enough for me to see currency inside, bales of currency.

She began to talk to me in a dreamy sort of voice.

"We got all big bills from the cashier, but it makes quite a package at that. There's twenty-two thousand even in the envelope. I kept out a few odd hundreds.

"Lou was worried. He figured it would be pretty easy for Canales to catch up with us. You might be right behind and not be able to do very much about it."

I said: "Canales lost the money in full view of everybody there. It was good advertising – even if it hurt."

She went on exactly as though I had not spoken. "Going through the town we spotted a cab driver sitting in his parked cab and Lou had a brain wave. He offered the boy a C note to let him drive the cab into San Angelo and bring the Buick to the hotel after a while. The boy took us up and we went over on another street and made the switch. We were sorry about ditching you, but Lou said you wouldn't mind. And we might get a chance to flag you.

"Lou didn't go into his hotel. We took another cab over to my place. I live at the Hobart Arms, eight hundred block on South Minter. It's a place where you don't have to answer questions at the desk. We went up to my apartment and put the lights on and two guys with masks came around the half-wall between the living-room and the dinette. One was small and thin and the other one was a big slob with a chin that stuck out under his mask like a shelf. Lou made a wrong motion and the big one shot him just the once. The gun just made a flat crack, not very loud, and Lou fell down on the floor and never moved."

I said: "It might be the ones that made a sucker out of me. I haven't told you about that yet."

She didn't seem to hear that either. Her face was white and composed, but as expressionless as plaster. "Maybe I'd better have another finger of the hooch," she said.

I poured us a couple of drinks, and we drank them. She went on: "They went through us, but we didn't have the money. We had stopped at an all-night drugstore and had it weighed and mailed it at a branch post office. They went through the apartment, but of course we had just come in and hadn't had time to hide anything. The big one slammed me down with his fist, and when I woke up again they were gone and I was alone with Lou dead on the floor."

She pointed to a mark on the angle of her jaw. There was something there, but it didn't show much. I moved around in my chair a little and said: "They passed you on the way in. Smart boys would have looked a taxi over on that road. How did they know where to go?"

"I thought that out during the night," Miss Glenn said. "Canales knows where I live. He followed me home once and tried to get me to ask him up."

"Yeah," I said, "but why did they go to your place and how did they get in?"

"That's not hard. There's a ledge just below the windows and a man could edge along it to the fire escape. They probably had other boys covering Lou's hotel. We thought of that chance, but we didn't think about my place being known to them."

"Tell me the rest of it," I said.

"The money was mailed to me," Miss Glenn explained. "Lou was a swell boy, but a girl has to protect herself. That's why I had to stay there last night with Lou dead on the floor. Until the mail came. Then I came over here."

I got up and looked out of the window. A fat girl was pounding a typewriter across the court. I could hear the clack of it. I sat down again, stared at my thumb.

"Did they plant the gun?" I asked.

"Not unless it's under him. I didn't look there."

"They let you off too easy. Maybe it wasn't Canales at all. Did Lou open his heart to you much?"

She shook her head quietly. Her eyes were slate-blue now, and thoughtful, without the blank stare.

"All right," I said. "Just what did you think of having me do about it all?"

She narrowed her eyes a little, then put a hand out and pushed the bulging envelope slowly across the desk.

"I'm no baby and I'm in a jam. But I'm not going to the cleaners just the same. Half of this money is mine, and I want it with a clean getaway. One-half net. If I'd called the law last night, there'd have been a way to chisel me out of it . . . I think Lou would like you to have his half, if you want to play with me."

I said: "It's big money to flash at a private dick, Miss Glenn," and smiled wearily. "You're a little worse off for not calling cops last night. But there's an answer to anything they might say. I think I'd better go over there and see what's broken, if anything."

She leaned forward quickly and said: "Will you take care of the money? . . . Dare you?"

"Sure. I'll pop downstairs and put it in a safe-deposit box. You can hold one of the keys – and we'll talk split later on. I think it would be a swell idea if Canales knew he had to see me, and still sweller if you hid out in a little hotel where I have a friend – at least until I nose around a bit."

She nodded. I put my hat on and put the envelope inside my belt. I went out, telling her there was a gun in the top left-hand drawer, if she felt nervous.

When I got back she didn't seem to have moved. But she said she had phoned Canales' place and left a message for him she thought he would understand.

We went by rather devious ways to the Lorraine, at Brant and Avenue C. Nobody shot at us going over, and as far as I could see we were not trailed.

I shook hands with Jim Dolan, the day clerk at the Lorraine, with a twenty folded in my hand. He put his hand in his pocket and said he would be glad to see that "Miss Thompson" was not bothered.

I left. There was nothing in the noon paper about Lou Harger of the Hobart Arms.

6

THE HOBART ARMS was just another apartment house, in a block lined with them. It was six stories high and had a buff front. A lot of cars were parked at both curbs all along the block. I drove through slowly and looked things over. The neighborhood didn't have the look of having been excited about anything in the immediate past. It was peaceful and sunny, and the parked cars had a settled look, as if they were right at home.

I circled into an alley with a high board fence on each side and a lot of flimsy garages cutting it. I parked beside one that had a For Rent sign and went between two garbage cans into the concrete yard of the Hobart Arms, along the side to the street. A man was putting golf clubs into the back of a coupe. In the lobby a Filipino was dragging a vacuum cleaner over the rug and a dark Jewess was writing at the switchboard.

I used the automatic elevator and prowled along an upper corridor to the last door on the left. I knocked, waited, knocked again, went in with Miss Glenn's key.

Nobody was dead on the floor.

I looked at myself in the mirror that was the back of a pull-down bed, went across and looked out of a window. There was a ledge below that had once been a coping. It ran along to the fire escape. A blind man could have walked in. I didn't notice anything like footmarks in the dust on it.

There was nothing in the dinette or kitchen except what belonged there. The bedroom had a cheerful carpet and painted gray walls. There was a lot of junk in the corner, around a wastebasket, and a broken comb on the dresser held a few strands of red hair. The closets were empty except for some gin bottles.

I went back to the living-room, looked behind the wall bed, stood around for a minute, left the apartment.

The Filipino in the lobby had made about three yards with the vacuum cleaner. I leaned on the counter beside the switchboard.

"Miss Glenn?"

The dark Jewess said: "Five-two-four," and made a check mark on the laundry list.

"She's not in. Has she been in lately?"

She glanced up at me. "I haven't noticed. What is it – a bill?"

I said I was just a friend, thanked her and went away. That established the fact that there had been no excitement in Miss Glenn's apartment. I went back to the alley and the Marmon.

I hadn't believed it quite the way Miss Glenn told it anyhow.

I crossed Cordova, drove a block and stopped beside a forgotten drugstore that slept behind two giant pepper trees and a dusty, cluttered window. It had a single pay booth in the corner. An old man shuffled towards me wistfully, then went away when he saw what I wanted, lowered a pair of steel spectacles on to the end of his nose and sat down again with his newspaper.

I dropped my nickel, dialed, and a girl's voice said: "Telegrayam!" with a tinny drawl. I asked for Von Ballin.

When I got him and he knew who it was, I could hear him clearing his throat. Then his voice came close to the phone and said very distinctly: "I've got something for you, but it's bad. I'm sorry as all hell. Your friend Harger is in the morgue. We got a flash about ten minutes ago."

I leaned against the wall of the booth and felt my eyes getting haggard. I said: "What else did you get?"

"Couple of radio cops picked him up in somebody's front yard or something, in West Cimarron. He was shot through the heart. It happened last night, but for some reason they only just put out the identification."

I said: "West Cimarron, huh? . . . Well, that takes care of that. I'll be in to see you."

I thanked him and hung up, stood for a moment looking out through the glass at a middle-aged gray-haired man who had come into the store and was pawing over the magazine rack.

Then I dropped another nickel and dialed the Lorraine, asked for the clerk.

I said: "Get your girl to put me on to the redhead, will you, Jim?"

I got a cigarette out and lit it, puffed smoke at the glass of the door. The smoke flattened out against the glass and swirled about in the close air. Then the line clicked and the operator's voice said: "Sorry, your party does not answer."

"Give me Jim again," I said. Then, when he answered, "Can you take time to run up and find out why she doesn't answer the phone? Maybe she's just being cagey."

Jim said: "You bet. I'll shoot right up with a key."

Sweat was coming out all over me. I put the receiver down on a little shelf and jerked the booth door open. The gray-haired man looked up quickly from the magazines, then scowled and looked at his watch. Smoke poured out of the booth. After a moment I kicked the door shut and picked up the receiver again.

Jim's voice seemed to come to me from a long way off. "She's not here. Maybe she went for a walk."

I said: "Yeah – or maybe it was a ride."

I pronged the receiver and pushed on out of the booth. The gray-haired stranger slammed a magazine down so hard that it fell to the floor. He stooped to pick it up as I went past him. Then he straightened up just behind me and said quietly, but very firmly: "Keep the hands down, and quiet. Walk on out to your heap. This is business."

Out of the corner of my eye I could see the old man peeking short-sightedly at us. But there wasn't anything for him to see, even if he could see that far. Something prodded my back. It might have been a finger, but I didn't think it was.

We went out of the store very peacefully.

A long gray car had stopped close behind the Marmon. Its rear door was open and a man with a square face and a crooked mouth was standing with one foot out on the running board. His right hand was behind him, inside the car.

My man's voice said: "Get in your car and drive west. Take this first corner and go about twenty-five, not more."

The narrow street was sunny and quiet and the pepper trees whispered. Traffic threshed by on Cordova a short block away. I shrugged, opened the door of my car and got under the wheel. The gray-haired man got in very quickly beside me, watching my hands. He swung his right hand around, with a snub-nosed gun in it.

"Careful getting your keys out, buddy."

I was careful. As I stepped on the starter a car door slammed behind, there were rapid steps, and someone got into the back seat of the Marmon. I let in the clutch and drove around the corner. In the mirror I could see the gray car making the turn behind. Then it dropped back a little.

I drove west on a street that paralleled Cordova and when we had gone a block and a half a hand came down over my shoulder from behind and took my gun away from me. The gray-haired man rested his short revolver on his leg and felt me over carefully with his free hand. He leaned back satisfied.

"Okay. Drop over to the main drag and snap it up," he said. "But that don't mean trying to sideswipe a prowl car, if you lamp one . . . Or if you think it does, try it and see."

I made the two turns, speeded up to thirty-five and held it there. We went through some nice residential districts, and then the landscape began to thin out. When it was quite thin the gray car behind dropped back, turned towards town and disappeared.

"What's the snatch for?" I asked.

The gray-haired man laughed and rubbed his broad red chin. "Just business. The big boy wants to talk to you."

"Canales?"

"Canales – hell! I said the *big boy*."

I watched traffic, what there was of it that far out, and didn't speak for a few minutes. Then I said: "Why didn't you pull it in the apartment, or in the alley?"

"Wanted to make sure you wasn't covered."

"Who's this big boy?"

"Skip that – till we get you there. Anything else?"

"Yes. Can I smoke?"

He held the wheel while I lit up. The man in the back seat hadn't said a word at any time. After a while the gray-haired man made me pull up and move over, and he drove.

"I used to own one of these, six years ago, when I was poor," he said jovially.

I couldn't think of a really good answer to that, so I just let smoke seep down into my lungs and wondered why, if Lou had been killed in West Cimarron, the killers didn't get the money. And if he really had been killed at Miss Glenn's apartment, why somebody had taken the trouble to carry him back to West Cimarron.

7

IN TWENTY MINUTES we were in the foothills. We went over a hogback, drifted down a long white concrete ribbon, crossed a bridge, went halfway up the next slope and turned off on a gravel road that disappeared around a shoulder of scrub oak and manzanita. Plumes of pampas grass flared on the side of the hill, like jets of water. The wheels crunched on the gravel and skidded on the curves.

We came to a mountain cabin with a wide porch and cemented boulder foundations. The windmill of a generator turned slowly on the crest of a spur a hundred feet behind the cabin. A mountain blue jay flashed across the road, zoomed, banked sharply, and fell out of sight like a stone.

The gray-haired man tooled the car up to the porch, beside a tan-colored Lincoln coupe, switched off the ignition and set the Marmon's long parking brake. He took the keys out, folded them carefully in their leather case, put the case away in his pocket.

The man in the back seat got out and held the door beside me open. He had a gun in his hand. I got out. The gray-haired man got out. We all went into the house.

There was a big room with walls of knotted pine, beautifully polished. We went across it walking on Indian rugs and the gray-haired man knocked carefully on a door.

A voice shouted: "What is it?"

The gray-haired man put his face against the door and said: "Beasley – and the guy you wanted to talk to."

The voice inside said to come on in. Beasley opened the door, pushed me through it and shut it behind me.

It was another big room with knotted pine walls and Indian rugs on the floor. A driftwood fire hissed and puffed on a stone hearth.

The man who sat behind a flat desk was Frank Dorr, the politico.

He was the kind of man who liked to have a desk in front of him, and shove his fat stomach against it, and fiddle with things on it, and look very wise. He had a fat, muddy face, a thin fringe of white hair that stuck up a little, small sharp eyes, small and very delicate hands.

What I could see of him was dressed in a slovenly gray suit, and there was a large black Persian cat on the desk in front of him. He was scratching the cat's head with one of his little neat hands and the cat was leaning against his hand. Its busy tail flowed over the edge of the desk and fell straight down.

He said: "Sit down," without looking away from the cat.

I sat down in a leather chair with a very low seat. Dorr said: "How do you like it up here? Kind of nice, ain't it? This is Toby, my girl friend. Only girl friend I got. Ain't you, Toby?"

I said: "I like it up here – but I don't like the way I got here."

Dorr raised his head a few inches and looked at me with his mouth slightly open. He had beautiful teeth, but they hadn't grown in his mouth. He said: "I'm a busy man, brother. It was simpler than arguing. Have a drink?"

"Sure I'll have a drink," I said.

He squeezed the cat's head gently between his two palms, then pushed it away from him and put both hands down on the arms of his chair. He shoved hard and his face got a little red and he finally got up on his feet. He waddled across to a built-in cabinet and took out a squat decanter of whiskey and two gold-veined glasses.

"No ice today," he said, waddling back to the desk. "Have to drink it straight."

He poured two drinks, gestured, and I went over and got mine. He sat down again. I sat down with my drink. Dorr lit a long brown cigar, pushed the box two inches in my direction, leaned back and stared at me with complete relaxation.

"You're the guy that fingered Manny Tinnen," he said. "It won't do."

I sipped my whiskey. It was good enough to sip.

"Life gets complicated at times," Dorr went on, in the same even, relaxed voice. "Politics – even when it's a lot of fun – is tough on the nerves. You know me. I'm tough and I get what I want. There ain't a hell of a lot I want any more, but what I want – I want bad. And ain't so damn particular how I get it."

"You have that reputation," I said politely.

Dorr's eyes twinkled. He looked around for the cat, dragged it towards him by the tail, pushed it down on its side and began to rub its stomach. The cat seemed to like it.

Dorr looked at me and said very softly: "You bumped Lou Harger."

"What makes you think so?" I asked, without any particular emphasis.

"You bumped Lou Harger. Maybe he needed the bump – but you gave it to him. He was shot once through the heart, with a thirty-eight. You wear a thirty-eight and you're known to be a fancy shot with it. You were with Harger at Las Olindas last night and saw him win a lot of money. You were supposed to be acting as bodyguard for him, but you got a better idea. You caught up with him and that girl in West Cimarron, slipped Harger the dose and got the money."

I finished my whiskey, got up and poured myself some more of it.

"You made a deal with the girl," Dorr said, "but the deal didn't stick. She got a cute idea. But that don't matter, because the police got your gun along with Harger. And you got the dough."

I said: "Is there a tag out for me?"

"Not till I give the word . . . And the gun hasn't been turned in . . . I got a lot of friends, you know."

I said slowly: "I got sapped outside Canales' place. It served me right. My gun was taken from me. I never caught up with Harger, never saw him again. The girl came to me this morning with the money in an envelope and a story that Harger had been killed in her apartment. That's how I have the money – for safekeeping. I wasn't sure about the girl's story, but her bringing the money carried a lot of weight. And Harger was a friend of mine. I started out to investigate."

"You should have let the cops do that," Dorr said with a grin.

"There was a chance the girl was being framed. Besides there was a possibility I might make a few dollars – legitimately. It has been done, even in San Angelo."

Dorr stuck a finger towards the cat's face and the cat bit it, with an absent expression. Then it pulled away from him, sat down on a corner of the desk and began to lick one toe.

"Twenty-two grand, and the jane passed it over to you to keep," Dorr said. "Ain't that just like a jane?

"You got the dough," Dorr said. "Harger was killed with your gun. The girl's gone – but I could bring her back. I think she'd make a good witness, if we needed one."

"Was the play at Las Olindas crooked?" I asked.

Dorr finished his drink and curled his lips around his cigar again. "Sure," he said carelessly. "The croupier – a guy named Pina – was in on it. The wheel was wired for the double-zero. The old crap. Copper button on the floor, copper button on Pina's shoe sole, wires up his leg, batteries in his hip pockets. The old crap."

I said: "Canales didn't act as if he knew about it."

Dorr chuckled. "He knew the wheel was wired. He didn't know his head croupier was playin' on the other team."

"I'd hate to be Pina," I said.

Dorr made a negligent motion with his cigar. "He's taken care of . . . The play was careful and quiet. They didn't make any fancy long shots, just even money bets, and they didn't win all the time. They couldn't. No wired wheel is that good."

I shrugged, moved around in my chair. "You know a hell of a lot about it," I said. "Was all this just to get me set for a squeeze?"

He grinned softly: "Hell, no! Some of it just happened – the way the best plans do." He waved his cigar again, and a pale gray tendril of smoke curled past his cunning little eyes. There was a muffled sound of talk in the outside room. "I got connections I got to please – even if I don't like all their capers," he added simply.

"Like Manny Tinnen?" I said. "He was around City Hall a lot, knew too much. Okay, Mister Dorr. Just what do you figure on having me do for you? Commit suicide?"

He laughed. His fat shoulders shook cheerfully. He put one of his small hands out with the palm towards me. "I wouldn't think of that," he said dryly, "and the other way's better business. The way public opinion is about the Shannon kill, I ain't sure that louse of a D.A. wouldn't convict Tinnen without you – if he could sell the folks the idea you'd been knocked off to button your mouth."

I got up out of my chair, went over and leaned on the desk, leaned across it towards Dorr.

He said: "No funny business!" a little sharply and breathlessly. His hand went to a drawer and got it half open. His movements with his hands were very quick in contrast with the movements of his body.

I smiled down at the hand and he took it away from the drawer. I saw a gun just inside the drawer.

I said: "I've already talked to the Grand Jury."

Dorr leaned back and smiled at me. "Guys make mistakes," he said. "Even smart private dicks . . . You could have a change of heart – and put it in writing."

I said very softly: "No. I'd be under a perjury rap – which I couldn't beat. I'd rather be under a murder rap – which I can beat. Especially as Fenweather will *want* me to beat it. He won't want to spoil me as a witness. The Tinnen case is too important to him."

Dorr said evenly: "Then you'll have to try and beat it, brother. And after you get through beating it there'll still be enough mud on your neck so no jury'll convict Manny on your say-so alone."

I put my hand out slowly and scratched the cat's ear. "What about the twenty-two grand?"

"It *could* be all yours, if you want to play. After all, it ain't my money . . . If Manny gets clear, I might add a little something that *is* my money."

I tickled the cat under its chin. It began to purr. I picked it up and held it gently in my arms.

"Who did kill Lou Harger, Dorr?" I asked, not looking at him.

He shook his head. I looked at him, smiling. "Swell cat you have," I said.

Dorr licked his lips. "I think the little bastard likes you," he grinned. He looked pleased at the idea.

I nodded — and threw the cat in his face.

He yelped, but his hands came up to catch the cat. The cat twisted neatly in the air and landed with both front paws working. One of them split Dorr's cheek like a banana peel. He yelled very loudly.

I had the gun out of the drawer and the muzzle of it into the back of Dorr's neck when Beasley and the square-faced man dodged in.

For an instant there was a sort of tableau. Then the cat tore itself loose from Dorr's arms, shot to the floor and went under the desk. Beasley raised his snub-nosed gun, but he didn't look as if he was certain what he meant to do with it.

I shoved the muzzle of mine hard into Dorr's neck and said: "Frankie gets it first, boys . . . And that's not a gag."

Dorr grunted in front of me. "Take it easy," he growled to his hoods. He took a handkerchief from his breast pocket and began to dab at his split and bleeding cheek with it. The man with the crooked mouth began to sidle along the wall.

I said: "Don't get the idea I'm enjoying this, but I'm not fooling either. You heels stay put."

The man with the crooked mouth stopped sidling and gave me a nasty leer. He kept his hands low.

Dorr half turned his head and tried to talk over his shoulder to me. I couldn't see enough of his face to get any expression, but he didn't seem scared. He said: "This won't get you anything. I could have you knocked off easy enough, if that was what I wanted. Now where are you? You can't shoot anybody without getting in a worse jam than if you did what I asked you to. It looks like a stalemate to me."

I thought that over for a moment while Beasley looked at me quite pleasantly, as though it was all just routine to him.

There was nothing pleasant about the other man. I listened hard, but the rest of the house seemed to be quite silent.

Dorr edged forward from the gun and said: "Well?"

I said: "I'm going out. I have a gun and it looks like a gun that I could hit somebody with, if I have to. I don't want to very much, and if you'll have Beasley throw my keys over and the other one turn back the gun he took from me, I'll forget about the snatch."

Dorr moved his arms in the lazy beginning of a shrug. "Then what?"

"Figure out your deal a little closer," I said. "If you get enough protection behind me, I might throw in with you . . . And if you're as tough as you think you are, a few hours won't cut any ice one way or the other."

"It's an idea," Dorr said and chuckled. Then to Beasley: "Keep your rod to yourself and give him his keys. Also his gun – the one you got today."

Beasley sighed and very carefully inserted a hand into his pants. He tossed my leather keycase across the room near the end of the desk. The man with the twisted mouth put his hand up, edged it inside his side pocket and I eased down behind Dorr's back, while he did it. He came out with my gun, let it fall to the floor and kicked it away from him.

I came out from behind Dorr's back, got my keys and the gun up from the floor, moved sidewise towards the door of the room. Dorr watched with an empty stare that meant nothing. Beasley followed me around with his body and stepped away from the door as I neared it. The other man had trouble holding himself quiet.

I got to the door and reversed a key that was in it. Dorr said dreamily: "You're just like one of those rubber balls on the end of an elastic. The farther you get away, the suddener you'll bounce back."

I said: "The elastic might be a little rotten," and went through the door, turned the key in it and braced myself for shots that didn't come. As a bluff, mine was thinner than the gold on a week-end wedding ring. It worked because Dorr let it, and that was all.

I got out of the house, got the Marmon started and wrangled it around and sent it skidding past the shoulder of the hill and so on down to the highway. There was no sound of anything coming after me.

When I reached the concrete highway bridge it was a little past two o'clock, and I drove with one hand for a while and wiped the sweat off the back of my neck.

8

THE MORGUE WAS at the end of a long and bright and silent corridor that branched off from behind the main lobby of the County Building. The corridor ended in two doors and a blank wall faced with marble. One door had "Inquest Room" lettered on a glass panel behind which there was no light. The other opened into a small, cheerful office.

A man with gander-blue eyes and rust-colored hair parted in the exact center of his head was pawing over some printed forms at a table. He looked up, looked me over, and then suddenly smiled.

I said: "Hello, Landon . . . Remember the Shelby case?"

The bright blue eyes twinkled. He got up and came around the table with his hand out. "Sure. What can we do – " He broke off suddenly and snapped his fingers. "Hell! You're the guy that put the bee on that hot rod."

I tossed a butt through the open door into the corridor. "That's not why I'm here," I said. "Anyhow not this time. There's a fellow named Louis Harger . . . picked up shot last night or this morning, in West Cimarron, as I get it. Could I take a look-see?"

"They can't stop you," Landon said.

He led the way through a door on the far side of his office into a place that was all white paint and white enamel and glass and bright light. Against one wall was a double tier of large bins with glass windows in them. Through the peepholes showed bundles in white sheeting, and, further back, frosted pipes.

A body covered with a sheet lay on a table that was high at the head and sloped down to the foot. Landon pulled the sheet down casually from a man's dead, placid, yellowish face. Long black hair lay loosely on a small pillow, with the dankness of water still in it. The eyes were half open and stared incuriously at the ceiling.

I stepped close, looked at the face, Landon pulled the sheet on down and rapped his knuckles on a chest that rang hollowly, like a board. There was a bullet hole over the heart.

"Nice clean shot," he said.

I turned away quickly, got a cigarette out and rolled it around in my fingers. I stared at the floor.

"Who identified him?"

"Stuff in his pockets," Landon said. "We're checking his prints, of course. You know him?"

I said: "Yes."

Landon scratched the base of his chin softly with his thumbnail. We walked back into the office and Landon went behind his table and sat down.

He thumbed over some papers, separated one from the pile and studied it for a moment.

He said: "A sheriff's radio car found him at twelve thirty-five A.M., on the side of the old road out of West Cimarron, a quarter of a mile from where the cutoff starts. That isn't traveled much, but the prowl car takes a slant down it now and then looking for petting parties."

I said: "Can you say how long he had been dead?"

"Not very long. He was still warm, and the nights are cool along there."

I put my unlighted cigarette in my mouth and moved it up and down with my lips. "And I bet you took a long thirty-eight out of him," I said.

"How did you know that?" Landon asked quickly.

"I just guess. It's that sort of hole."

He stared at me with bright, interested eyes. I thanked him, said I'd be seeing him, went through the door and lit my cigarette in the corridor. I walked back to the elevators and got into one, rode to the seventh floor, then went along another corridor exactly like the one below except that it didn't lead to the morgue. It led to some small, bare offices that were used by the District Attorney's investigators. Halfway along I opened a door and went into one of them.

Bernie Ohls was sitting humped loosely at a desk placed against the wall. He was the chief investigator Fenweather had told me to see, if I got into any kind of a jam. He was a medium-sized bland man with white eyebrows and an out-thrust, very deeply cleft chin. There was another desk against the other wall, a couple of hard chairs, a brass spittoon on a rubber mat and very little else.

Ohls nodded casually at me, got out of his chair and fixed the door latch. Then he got a flat tin of little cigars out of his desk, lit one of them, pushed the tin along the desk and stared at me along his nose. I sat down in one of the straight chairs and tilted it back.

Ohls said: "Well?"

"It's Lou Harger," I said. "I thought maybe it wasn't."

"The hell you did. I could have told you it was Harger."

Somebody tried the handle of the door, then knocked. Ohls paid no attention. Whoever it was went away.

I said slowly: "He was killed between eleven-thirty and twelve thirty-five. There was just time for the job to be done where he was found. There wasn't time for it to be done the way the girl said. There wasn't time for me to do it."

Ohls said: "Yeah. Maybe you could prove that. And then maybe you could prove a friend of yours didn't do it with your gun."

I said: "A friend of mine wouldn't be likely to do it with my gun – if he was a friend of mine."

Ohls grunted, smiled sourly at me sidewise. He said: "Most anyone would think that. That's why he might have done it."

I let the legs of my chair settle to the floor. I stared at him.

"Would I come and tell you about the money and the gun – everything that ties me to it?"

Ohls said expressionlessly: "You would – if you knew damn well somebody else had already told it for you."

I said: "Dorr wouldn't lose much time."

I pinched my cigarette out and flipped it towards the brass cuspidor. Then I stood up.

"Okay. There's no tag out for me yet – so I'll go over and tell my story."

Ohls said: "Sit down a minute."

I sat down. He took his little cigar out of his mouth and flung it away from him with a savage gesture. It rolled along the brown linoleum and smoked in the corner. He put his arms down on the desk and drummed with the fingers of both hands. His lower lip came forward and pressed his upper lip back against his teeth.

"Dorr probably knows you're here now," he said. "The only reason you ain't in the tank upstairs is they're not sure but it would be better to knock you off and take a chance. If Fenweather loses the election, I'll be all washed up – if I mess around with you."

I said: "If he convicts Manny Tinnen, he won't lose the election."

Ohls took another of the little cigars out of the box and lit it. He picked his hat off the desk, fingered it a moment, put it on.

"Why'd the redhead give you that song and dance about the bump in her apartment, the stiff on the floor – all that hot comedy?"

"They wanted me to go over there. They figured I'd go to see if a gun was planted – maybe just to check up on her. That got me away from the busy part of town. They could tell better if the D.A. had any boys watching my blind side."

"That's just a guess," Ohls said sourly.

I said: "Sure."

Ohls swung his thick legs around, planted his feet hard and leaned his hands on his knees. The little cigar twitched in the corner of his mouth.

"I'd like to get to know some of these guys that let loose of twenty-two grand just to color up a fairy tale," he said nastily.

I stood up again and went past him towards the door.

Ohls said: "What's the hurry?"

I turned around and shrugged, looked at him blankly. "You don't act very interested," I said.

He climbed to his feet, said wearily: "The hack driver's most likely a dirty little crook. But it might just be Dorr's lads don't know he rates in this. Let's go get him while his memory's fresh."

9

THE GREEN TOP Garage was on Deviveras, three blocks east of Main. I pulled the Marmon up in front of a fireplug and got out. Ohls slumped in the seat and growled: "I'll stay here. Maybe I can spot a tail."

I went into a huge echoing garage, in the inner gloom of which a few brand-new paint jobs were splashes of sudden color. There was a small, dirty, glass-walled office in the corner and a short man sat there with a derby hat on the back of his head and a red tie under his stubbled chin. He was whittling tobacco into the palm of his hand.

I said: "You the dispatcher?"

"Yeah."

"I'm looking for one of your drivers," I said. "Name of Tom Sneyd."

He put down the knife and the plug and began to grind the cut tobacco between his two palms. "What's the beef?" he asked cautiously.

"No beef. I'm a friend of his."

"More friends, huh? . . . He works nights, mister . . . So he's gone I guess. Seventeen twenty-three Renfrew. That's over by Gray Lake."

I said: "Thanks. Phone?"

"No phone."

I pulled a folded city map from an inside pocket and unfolded part of it on the table in front of his nose. He looked annoyed.

"There's a big one on the wall," he growled, and began to pack a short pipe with his tobacco.

"I'm used to this one," I said. I bent over the spread map, looking for Renfrew Street. Then I stopped and looked suddenly at the face of the man in the derby. "You remembered that address damn quick," I said.

He put his pipe in his mouth, bit hard on it, and pushed two quick fingers into the pocket of his open vest.

"Couple other mugs was askin' for it a while back."

I folded the map very quickly and shoved it back into my pocket as I went through the door. I jumped across the sidewalk, slid under the wheel and plunged at the starter.

"We're headed," I told Bernie Ohls. "Two guys got the kid's address there a while back. It might be – "

Ohls grabbed the side of the car and swore as we took the corner on squealing tires. I bent forward over the wheel and drove hard. There was a red light at Central. I swerved into a corner service station, went through the pumps, popped out on Central and jostled through some traffic to make a right turn east again.

A colored traffic cop blew a whistle at me and then stared hard as if trying to read the license number. I kept on going.

Warehouses, a produce market, a big gas tank, more warehouses, railroad tracks, and two bridges dropped behind us. I beat three traffic signals by a hair and went right through a fourth. Six blocks on I got the siren from a motorcycle cop. Ohls passed me a bronze star and I flashed it out of the car, twisting it so the sun caught it. The siren stopped. The motorcycle kept right behind us for another dozen blocks, then sheered off.

Gray Lake is an artificial reservoir in a cut between two groups of hills, on the east fringe of San Angelo. Narrow but expensively paved streets wind around in the hills, describing elaborate curves along their flanks for the benefit of a few cheap and scattered bungalows.

We plunged up into the hills, reading street signs on the run. The gray silk of the lake dropped away from us and the exhaust of the old Marmon roared between crumbling banks that shed dirt down on the unused sidewalks. Mongrel dogs quartered in the wild grass among the gopher holes.

Renfrew was almost at the top. Where it began there was a small neat bungalow in front of which a child in a diaper and nothing else fumbled around in a wire pen on a patch of lawn. Then there was a stretch without houses. Then there were two houses, then the road dropped, slipped in and out of sharp turns, went between banks high enough to put the whole street in shadow.

Then a gun roared around a bend ahead of us.

Ohls sat up sharply, said: "Oh-oh! That's no rabbit gun," slipped his service pistol out and unlatched the door on his side.

We came out of the turn and saw two more houses on the down side of the hill, with a couple of steep lots between them.

A long gray car was slewed across the street in the space between the two houses. Its left front tire was flat and both its front doors were wide open, like the spread ears of an elephant.

A small, dark-faced man was kneeling on both knees in the street beside the open right-hand door. His right arm hung loose from his shoulder and there was blood on the hand that belonged to it. With his other hand he was trying to pick up an automatic from the concrete in front of him.

I skidded the Marmon to a fast stop and Ohls tumbled out.

"Drop that, you!" he yelled.

The man with the limp arm snarled, relaxed, fell back against the running board, and a shot came from behind the car and snapped in the air not very far from my ear. I was out on the road by that time. The gray car was angled enough towards the houses so that I couldn't see any part of its left side except the open door. The shot seemed to come from about there. Ohls put two slugs into the door. I dropped, looked under the car and saw a pair of feet. I shot at them and missed.

About that time there was a thin but very sharp crack from the corner of the nearest house. Glass broke in the gray car. The gun behind it roared and plaster jumped out of the corner of the house wall, above the bushes. Then I saw the upper part of a man's body in the bushes. He was lying downhill on his stomach and he had a light rifle to his shoulder.

He was Tom Sneyd, the taxi driver.

Ohls grunted and charged the gray car. He fired twice more into the door, then dodged down behind the hood. More explosions occurred behind the car. I kicked the wounded man's gun out of his way, slid past him and sneaked a look over the gas tank. But the man behind had had too many angles to figure.

He was a big man in a brown suit and he made a clatter running hard for the lip of the hill between the two bunga-lows. Ohls' gun roared. The man whirled and snapped a shot without stopping. Ohls was in the open now. I saw his hat jerk off his head. I saw him stand squarely on well-spread feet, steady his pistol as if he was on the police range.

But the big man was already sagging. My bullet had drilled through his neck. Ohls fired at him very carefully and he fell and the sixth and last slug from his gun caught the man in the chest and twisted him around. The side of his head slapped the curb with a sickening crunch.

We walked towards him from opposite ends of the car. Ohls leaned down, heaved the man over on his back. His face in death had a loose, amiable expression, in spite of the blood all over his neck. Ohls began to go through his pockets.

I looked back to see what the other one was doing. He wasn't doing anything but sitting on the running board holding his right arm against his side and grimacing with pain.

Tom Sneyd scrambled up the bank and came towards us.

Ohls said: "It's a guy named Poke Andrews. I've seen him around the poolrooms." He stood up and brushed off his knee. He had some odds and ends in his left hand. "Yeah, Poke Andrews. Gun work by the day, hour or week. I guess there was a livin' in it – for a while."

"It's not the guy that sapped me," I said. "But it's the guy I was looking at when I got sapped. And if the redhead was giving out any truth at all this morning, it's likely the guy that shot Lou Harger."

Ohls nodded, went over and got his hat. There was a hole in the brim. "I wouldn't be surprised at all," he said, putting his hat on calmly.

Tom Sneyd stood in front of us with his little rifle held rigidly across his chest. He was hatless and coatless, and had sneakers on his feet. His eyes were bright and mad, and he was beginning to shake.

"I knew I'd get them babies!" he crowed. "I knew I'd fix them lousy bastards!" Then he stopped talking and his face began to change color. It got green. He leaned down slowly, dropped his rifle, put both his hands on his bent knees.

Ohls said: "You better go lay down somewhere, buddy. If I'm any judge of color, you're goin' to shoot your cookies."

10

TOM SNEYD WAS lying on his back on a day bed in the front room of his little bungalow. There was a wet towel across his forehead. A little girl with honey-colored hair was sitting beside him, holding his hand. A young woman with hair a couple of shades darker than the little girl's sat in the corner and looked at Tom Sneyd with tired ecstasy.

It was very hot when we came in. All the windows were shut and all the blinds down. Ohls opened a couple of front windows and sat down beside them, looked out towards the gray car. The dark Mexican was anchored to its steering wheel by his good wrist.

"It was what they said about my little girl," Tom Sneyd said from under the towel. "That's what sent me screwy. They said they'd come back and get her, if I didn't play with them."

Ohls said: "Okay, Tom. Let's have it from the start." He put one of his little cigars in his mouth, looked at Tom Sneyd doubtfully, and didn't light it.

I sat in a very hard Windsor chair and looked down at the cheap, new carpet.

"I was readin' a mag, waiting for time to eat and go to work," Tom Sneyd said carefully. "The little girl opened the door. They come in with guns on us, got us all in here and shut the windows. They pulled down all the blinds but one and the Mex sat by that and kept looking out. He never said a word. The big guy sat on the bed here and made me tell him all about last night — twice. Then he said I was to forget I'd met anybody or come into town with anybody. The rest was okay."

Ohls nodded and said: "What time did you first see this man here?"

"I didn't notice," Tom Sneyd said. "Say eleven-thirty, quarter of twelve. I checked in to the office at one-fifteen, right after I got my hack at the Carillon. It took us a good hour to make town from the beach. We was in the drugstore talkin' say fifteen minutes, maybe longer."

"That figures back to around midnight when you met him," Ohls said.

Tom Sneyd shook his head and the towel fell down over his face. He pushed it back up again.

"Well, no," Tom Sneyd said. "The guy in the drugstore told me he closed up at twelve. He wasn't closing up when we left."

Ohls turned his head and looked at me without expression. He looked back at Tom Sneyd. "Tell us the rest about the two gunnies," he said.

"The big guy said most likely I wouldn't have to talk to anybody about it. If I did and talked right, they'd be back with some dough. If I talked wrong, they'd be back for my little girl."

"Go on," Ohls said. "They're full of crap."

"They went away. When I saw them go on up the street I got screwy. Renfrew is just a pocket — one of them graft jobs. It goes on around the hill half a mile, then stops. There's no way to get off it. So they had to come back this way . . . I got my twenty-two, which is all the gun I have, and hid in the bushes. I got the tire with the second shot. I guess they thought it was a blowout. I missed with the next and that put 'em wise. They got guns loose. I got the Mex then, and the big guy ducked behind the car . . . That's all there was to it. Then you come along."

Ohls flexed his thick, hard fingers and smiled grimly at the girl in the corner. "Who lives in the next house, Tom?"

"A man named Grandy, a motorman on the interurban. He lives all alone. He's at work now."

"I didn't guess he was home." Ohls grinned. He got up and went over and patted the little girl on the head. "You'll have to come down and make a statement, Tom."

"Sure." Tom Sneyd's voice was tired, listless. "I guess I lose my job, too, for rentin' out the hack last night."

"I ain't so sure about that," Ohls said softly. "Not if your boss likes guys with a few guts to run his hacks."

He patted the little girl on the head again, went towards the door and opened it. I nodded at Tom Sneyd and followed Ohls out of the house. Ohls said quietly: "He don't know about the kill yet. No need to spring it in front of the kid."

We went over to the gray car. We had got some sacks out of the basement and spread them over the late Andrews, weighted them down with stones. Ohls glanced that way and said absently: "I got to get to where there's a phone pretty quick."

He leaned on the door of the car and looked in at the Mexican. The Mexican sat with his head back and his eyes half-closed and a drawn expression on his brown face. His left wrist was shackled to the spider of the wheel.

"What's your name?" Ohls snapped at him.

"Luis Cadena." The Mexican said it in a soft voice without opening his eyes any wider.

"Which one of you heels scratched the guy at West Cimarron last night?"

"No understand, señor," the Mexican said purringly.

"Don't go dumb on me, spig," Ohls said dispassionately. "It gets me sore." He leaned on the window and rolled his little cigar around in his mouth.

The Mexican looked faintly amused and at the same time very tired. The blood on his right hand had dried black.

Ohls said: "Andrews scratched the guy in a taxi at West Cimarron. There was a girl along. We got the girl. You have a lousy chance to prove you weren't in on it."

Light flickered and died behind the Mexican's half-open eyes. He smiled with a glint of small white teeth.

Ohls said: "What did he do with the gun?"

"No understand, señor."

Ohls said: "He's tough. When they get tough it scares me."

He walked away from the car and scuffed some loose dirt from the sidewalk beside the sacks that draped the dead man. His toe gradually uncovered the contractor's stencil in the cement. He read it out loud: "Dorr Paving and Construction Company, San Angelo. It's a wonder the fat louse wouldn't stay in his own racket."

I stood beside Ohls and looked down the hill between the two houses. Sudden flashes of light darted from the windshields of cars going along the boulevard that fringed Gray Lake, far below.

Ohls said: "Well?"

I said: "The killers knew about the taxi – maybe – and the girl friend reached town with the swag. So it wasn't Canales' job. Canales isn't the boy to let anybody play around with twenty-two grand of his money. The redhead was in on the kill, and it was done for a reason."

Ohls grinned. "Sure. It was done so you could be framed for it."

I said: "It's a shame how little account some folks take of human life – or twenty-two grand. Harger was knocked off so I could be framed and the dough was passed to me to make the frame tighter."

"Maybe they thought you'd highball," Ohls grunted. "That would sew you up right."

I rolled a cigarette around in my fingers. "That would have been a little too dumb, even for me. What do we do now? Wait till the moon comes up so we can sing – or go down the hill and tell some more little white lies?"

Ohls spat on one of Poke Andrews' sacks. He said gruffly: "This is county land here. I could take all this mess over to the sub-station at Solano and keep it hush-hush for a while. The hack driver would be tickled to death to keep it under the hat. And I've gone far enough so I'd like to get the Mex in the goldfish room with me personal."

"I'd like it that way too," I said. "I guess you can't hold it down there for long, but you might hold it down long enough for me to see a fat boy about a cat."

11

IT WAS LATE afternoon when I got back to the hotel. The clerk handed me a slip which read: "Please phone F. D. as soon as possible."

I went upstairs and drank some liquor that was in the bottom of a bottle. Then I phoned down for another pint, scraped my chin, changed clothes and looked up Frank Dorr's number in the book. He lived in a beautiful old house on Greenview Park Crescent.

I made myself a tall smooth one with a tinkle and sat down in an easy chair with the phone at my elbow. I got a maid first. Then I got a man who spoke Mister Dorr's name as though he thought it might blow up in his mouth. After him I got a voice with a lot of silk in it. Then I got a long silence and at the end of the silence I got Frank Dorr himself. He sounded glad to hear from me.

He said: "I've been thinking about our talk this morning, and I have a better idea. Drop out and see me . . . And you might bring that money along. You just have time to get it out of the bank."

I said: "Yeah. The safe-deposit closes at six. But it's not your money."

I heard him chuckle. "Don't be foolish. It's all marked, and I wouldn't want to have to accuse you of stealing it."

I thought that over, and didn't believe it – about the currency being marked. I took a drink out of my glass and said: "I *might* be willing to turn it over to the party I got it from – in your presence."

He said: "Well – I told you that party left town. But I'll see what I can do. No tricks, please."

I said of course no tricks, and hung up. I finished my drink, called Von Ballin of the *Telegram*. He said the sheriff's people didn't seem to have any ideas about Lou Harger – or give a damn. He was a little sore that I still wouldn't let him use my story. I could tell from the way he talked that he hadn't got the doings over near Gray Lake.

I called Ohls, couldn't reach him.

I mixed myself another drink, swallowed half of it and began to feel it too much. I put my hat on, changed my mind about the other half of my drink, went down to my car. The early evening traffic was thick with householders riding home to dinner. I wasn't sure whether two cars tailed me or just one. At any rate nobody tried to catch up and throw a pineapple in my lap.

The house was a square two-storied place of old red brick, with beautiful grounds and a red brick wall with a white stone coping around them. A shiny black limousine was parked under the porte-cochère at the side. I followed a red-flagged walk up over two terraces, and a pale wisp of a man in a cutaway coat let me into a wide, silent hall with dark old furniture and a glimpse of garden at the end. He led me along that and along another hall at right angles and ushered me softly into a paneled study that was dimly lit against the gathering dusk. He went away, leaving me alone.

The end of the room was mostly open french windows, through which a brass-colored sky showed behind a line of quiet trees. In front of the trees a sprinkler swung slowly on a patch of velvety lawn that was already dark. There were large dim oils on the walls, a huge black desk with books across one end, a lot of deep lounging chairs, a heavy soft rug that went from wall to wall. There was a faint smell of good cigars and beyond that somewhere a smell of garden flowers and moist earth. The door opened and a youngish man in nose-glasses came in, gave me a slight formal nod, looked around vaguely, and said that Mr. Dorr would be there in a moment. He went out again, and I lit a cigarette.

In a little while the door opened again and Beasley came in, walked past me with a grin and sat down just inside the windows. Then Dorr came in and behind him Miss Glenn.

Dorr had his black cat in his arms and two lovely red scratches, shiny with collodion, down his right cheek. Miss Glenn had on the same clothes I had seen on her in the morning. She looked dark and drawn and spiritless, and she went past me as though she had never seen me before.

Dorr squeezed himself into the high-backed chair behind the desk and put the cat down in front of him. The cat strolled over to one corner of the desk and began to lick its chest with a long, sweeping, businesslike motion.

Dorr said: "Well, well. Here we are," and chuckled pleasantly.

The man in the cutaway came in with a tray of cocktails, passed them around, put the tray with the shaker down on a low table beside Miss Glenn. He went out again, closing the door as if he was afraid he might crack it.

We all drank and looked very solemn.

I said: "We're all here but two. I guess we have a quorum."

Dorr said: "What's that?" sharply and put his head to one side.

I said: "Lou Harger's in the morgue and Canales is dodging cops. Otherwise we're all here. All the interested parties."

Miss Glenn made an abrupt movement, then relaxed suddenly and picked at the arm of her chair.

Dorr took two swallows of his cocktail, put the glass aside and folded his small neat hands on the desk. His face looked a little sinister.

"The money," he said coldly. "I'll take charge of it now."

I said: "Not now or any other time. I didn't bring it."

Dorr stared at me and his face got a little red. I looked at Beasley. Beasley had a cigarette in his mouth and his hands in his pockets and the back of his head against the back of his chair. He looked half asleep.

Dorr said softly, meditatively: "Holding out, huh?"

"Yes," I said grimly. "While I have it I'm fairly safe. You overplayed your hand when you let me get my paws on it. I'd be a fool not to hold what advantage it gives me."

Dorr said: "Safe?" with a gently sinister intonation.

I laughed. "Not safe from a frame," I said. "But the last one didn't click so well . . . Not safe from being gun-walked again. But that's going to be harder next time too . . . But fairly safe from being shot in the back and having you sue my estate for the dough."

Dorr stroked the cat and looked at me under his eyebrows.

"Let's get a couple of more important things straightened out," I said. "Who takes the rap for Lou Harger?"

"What makes you so sure *you* don't?" Dorr asked nastily.

"My alibi's been polished up. I didn't know how good it was until I knew how close Lou's death could be timed. I'm clear now . . . regardless of who turns in what gun with what fairy tale . . . And the lads that were sent to scotch my alibi ran into some trouble."

Dorr said: "That so?" without any apparent emotion.

"A thug named Andrews and a Mexican calling himself Luis Cadena. I daresay you've heard of them."

"I don't know such people," Dorr said sharply.

"Then it won't upset you to hear Andrews got very dead, and the law has Cadena."

"Certainly not," Dorr said. "They were from Canales. Canales had Harger killed."

I said: "So that's your new idea. I think it's lousy."

I leaned over and slipped my empty glass under my chair. Miss Glenn turned her head towards me and spoke very gravely, as if it was very important to the future of the race for me to believe what she said: "Of course — *of course* Canales had Lou killed . . . At least, the men he sent after us killed Lou."

157

I nodded politely. "What for? A packet of money they didn't get? They wouldn't have killed him. They'd have brought him in, brought both of you in. You arranged for that kill, and the taxi stunt was to sidetrack me, not to fool Canales' boys."

She put her hand out quickly. Her eyes were shimmering. I went ahead.

"I wasn't very bright, but I didn't figure on anything so flossy. Who the hell would? Canales had no motive to gun Lou, unless it got back the money he had been gypped out of. Supposing he could know that quick he *had* been gypped."

Dorr was licking his lips and quivering his chins and looking from one of us to the other with his small tight eyes. Miss Glenn said drearily: "Lou knew all about the play. He planned it with the croupier, Pina. Pina wanted some getaway money, wanted to move on to Havana. Of course Canales would have got wise, but not too soon, if I hadn't got noisy and tough. *I* got Lou killed – but not the way you mean."

I dropped an inch of ash off a cigarette I had forgotten all about. "All right," I said grimly. "Canales takes the rap . . . And I suppose you two chiselers think that's all I care about . . . Where was Lou going to be when Canales was *supposed* to find out he'd been gypped?"

"He was going to be gone," Miss Glenn said tonelessly. "A damn long way off. And I was going to be gone with him."

I said: "Nerts! You seem to forget *I* know *why* Lou was killed."

Beasley sat up in his chair and moved his right hand rather delicately towards his left shoulder. "This wise guy bother you, chief?"

Dorr said: "Not yet. Let him rant."

I moved so that I faced a little more towards Beasley. The sky had gone dark outside and the sprinkler had been turned off. A damp feeling came slowly into the room. Dorr opened a cedarwood box and put a long brown cigar in his mouth, bit the end off with a dry snap of his false teeth. There was the harsh noise of a match striking, then the slow, rather labored puffing of his breath in the cigar.

He said slowly, through a cloud of smoke: "Let's forget all this and make a deal about that money . . . Manny Tinnen hung himself in his cell this afternoon."

Miss Glenn stood up suddenly, pushing her arms straight down at her sides. Then she sank slowly down into the chair again, sat motionless. I said: "Did he have any help?" Then I made a sudden, sharp movement – and stopped.

Beasley jerked a swift glance at me, but I wasn't looking at Beasley. There was a shadow outside one of the windows – a lighter shadow than the dark lawn and darker trees. There was a hollow, bitter, coughing plop; a thin spray of whitish smoke in the window.

Beasley jerked, rose halfway to his feet, then fell on his face with one arm doubled under him.

Canales stepped through the windows, past Beasley's body, came three steps further, and stood silent, with a long, black, small-calibered gun in his hand, the larger tube of a silencer flaring from the end of it.

"Be very still," he said. "I am a fair shot – even with this elephant gun."

His face was so white that it was almost luminous. His dark eyes were all smoke-gray iris, without pupils.

"Sound carries well at night, out of open windows," he said tonelessly.

Dorr put both his hands down on the desk and began to pat it. The black cat put its body very low, drifted down over the end of the desk and went under a chair. Miss Glenn turned her head towards Canales very slowly, as if some kind of mechanism moved it.

Canales said: "Perhaps you have a buzzer on that desk. If the door of the room opens, I shoot. It will give me a lot of pleasure to see blood come out of your fat neck."

I moved the fingers of my right hand two inches on the arm of my chair. The silenced gun swayed towards me and I stopped moving my fingers. Canales smiled very briefly under his angular mustache.

"You are a smart dick," he said. "I thought I had you right. But there are things about you I like."

I didn't say anything. Canales looked back at Dorr. He said very precisely: "I have been bled by your organization for a long time. But this is something else again. Last night I was cheated out of some money. But this is trivial too. I am wanted for the murder of this Harger. A man named Cadena has been made to confess that I hired him . . . That is just a little too much fix."

Dorr swayed gently over his desk, put his elbows down hard on it, held his face in his small hands and began to shake. His cigar was smoking on the floor.

Canales said: "I would like to get my money back, and I would like to get clear of this rap – but most of all I would like you to say something – so I can shoot you with your mouth open and see blood come out of it."

Beasley's body stirred on the carpet. His hands groped a little. Dorr's eyes were agony trying not to look at him. Canales was rapt and blind in his act by this time. I moved my fingers a little more on the arm of my chair. But I had a long way to go.

Canales said: "Pina has talked to me. I saw to that. You killed Harger. Because he was a secret witness against Manny Tinnen. The D.A. kept the secret, and the dick here kept it. But Harger could not keep it himself. He told his broad – and the broad told you . . . So the killing was arranged, in a way to throw suspicion with a motive on me. First on this dick, and if that wouldn't hold, on me."

There was silence. I wanted to say something, but I couldn't get anything out. I didn't think anybody but Canales would ever again say anything.

Canales said: "You fixed Pina to let Harger and his girl win my money. It was not hard – because I don't play my wheels crooked."

Dorr had stopped shaking. His face lifted, stone-white, and turned towards Canales, slowly, like the face of a man about to have an epileptic fit. Beasley was up on one elbow. His eyes were almost shut but a gun was laboring upwards in his hand.

Canales leaned forward and began to smile. His trigger finger whitened at the exact moment Beasley's gun began to pulse and roar.

Canales arched his back until his body was a rigid curve. He fell stiffly forward, hit the edge of the desk and slid along it to the floor, without lifting his hands.

Beasley dropped his gun and fell down on his face again. His body got soft and his fingers moved fitfully, then were still.

I got motion into my legs, stood up and went to kick Canales' gun under the desk – senselessly. Doing this I saw that Canales had fired at least once, because Frank Dorr had no right eye.

He sat still and quiet with his chin on his chest and a nice touch of melancholy on the good side of his face.

The door of the room came open and the secretary with the nose-glasses slid in pop-eyed. He staggered back against the door, closing it again. I could hear his rapid breathing across the room.

He gasped: "Is – is anything wrong?"

I thought that very funny, even then. Then I realized that he might be short-sighted and from where he stood Frank Dorr looked natural enough. The rest of it could have been just routine to Dorr's help.

I said: "Yes – but we'll take care of it. Stay out of here."

He said: "Yes, sir," and went out again. That surprised me so much that my mouth fell open. I went down the room and bent over the gray-haired Beasley. He was unconscious, but had a fair pulse. He was bleeding from the side, slowly.

Miss Glenn was standing up and looked almost as dopy as Canales had looked. She was talking to me quickly, in a brittle, very distinct voice: "I didn't know Lou was to be killed, but I couldn't have done anything about it anyway. They burned me with a branding iron — just for a sample of what I'd get. Look!"

I looked. She tore her dress down in front and there was a hideous burn on her chest almost between her two breasts.

I said: "Okay, sister. That's nasty medicine. But we've got to have some law here now and an ambulance for Beasley."

I pushed past her towards the telephone, shook her hand off my arm when she grabbed at me. She went on talking to my back in a thin, desperate voice.

"I thought they'd just hold Lou out of the way until after the trial. But they dragged him out of the cab and shot him without a word. Then the little one drove the taxi into town and the big one brought me up into the hills to a shack. Dorr was there. He told me how you had to be framed. He promised me the money, if I went through with it, and torture till I died, if I let them down."

It occurred to me that I was turning my back too much to people. I swung around, got the telephone in my hands, still on the hook, and put my gun down on the desk.

"Listen! Give me a break," she said wildly. "Dorr framed it all with Pina, the croupier. Pina was one of the gang that got Shannon where they could fix him. I didn't — "

I said: "Sure — that's all right. Take it easy."

The room, the whole house seemed very still, as if a lot of people were hunched outside the door, listening.

"It wasn't a bad idea," I said, as if I had all the time in the world. "Lou was just a white chip to Frank Dorr. The play he figured put us both out as witnesses. But it was too elaborate, took in too many people. That sort always blows up in your face."

"Lou was getting out of the state," she said, clutching at her dress "He was scared. He thought the roulette trick was some kind of a pay-off to him."

I said: "Yeah," lifted the phone and asked for police head-quarters.

The room door came open again then and the secretary barged in with a gun. A uniformed chauffeur was behind him with another gun.

I said very loudly into the phone: "This is Frank Dorr's house. There's been a killing . . ."

The secretary and the chauffeur dodged out again. I heard running in the hall. I clicked the phone, called the *Telegram* office and got Von Ballin. When I got through giving him the flash Miss Glenn was gone out of the window into the dark garden.

I didn't go after her. I didn't mind very much if she got away.

I tried to get Ohls, but they said he was still down at Solano. And by that time the night was full of sirens.

★

I had a little trouble but not too much. Fenweather pulled too much weight. Not all of the story came out, but enough so that the City Hall boys in the two-hundred-dollar suits had their left elbows in front of their faces for some time.

Pina was picked up in Salt Lake City. He broke and impli-cated four others of Manny Tinnen's gang. Two of them were killed resisting arrest, the other two got life without parole.

Miss Glenn made a clean getaway and was never heard of again. I think that's about all, except that I had to turn the twenty-two grand over to the Public Administrator. He allowed me two hundred dollars fee and nine dollars and twenty cents mileage. Sometimes I wonder what he did with the rest of it.

KILLER IN THE RAIN

1

WE WERE SITTING in a room at the Berglund. I was on the side of the bed, and Dravec was in the easy chair. It was my room.

Rain beat very hard against the windows. They were shut tight and it was hot in the room and I had a little fan going on the table. The breeze from it hit Dravec's face high up, lifted his heavy black hair, moved the longer bristles in the fat path of eyebrow that went across his face in a solid line. He looked like a bouncer who had come into money.

He showed me some of his gold teeth and said: "What you got on me?"

He said it importantly, as if anyone who knew anything would know quite a lot about him.

"Nothing," I said. "You're clean, as far as I know."

He lifted a large hairy hand and stared at it solidly for a minute.

"You don't get me. A feller named M'Gee sent me here. Violets M'Gee."

"Fine. How is Violets these days?" Violets M'Gee was a homicide dick in the sheriff's office.

He looked at his large hand and frowned. "No – you still don't get it. I got a job for you."

"I don't go out much any more," I said. "I'm getting kind of frail."

He looked around the room carefully, bluffing a bit, like a man not naturally observant.

"Maybe it's money," he said.

"Maybe it is," I said.

He had a belted suede raincoat on. He tore it open carelessly and got out a wallet that was not quite as big as a bale of hay. Currency stuck out of it at careless angles. When he slapped it down on his knee it made a fat sound that was pleasant to the ear. He shook money out of it, selected a few bills from the bunch, stuffed the rest back, dropped the wallet on the floor and let it lie, arranged five century notes like a tight poker hand and put them under the base of the fan on the table.

That was a lot of work. It made him grunt.

"I got lots of sugar," he said.

"So I see. What do I do for that, if I get it?"

"You know me now, huh?"

"A little better."

I got an envelope out of an inside pocket and read to him aloud from some scribbling on the back.

"Dravec, Anton or Tony. Former Pittsburgh steelworker, truck guard, all-round muscle stiff. Made a wrong pass and got shut up. Left town, came West. Worked on an avocado ranch at El Seguro. Came up with a ranch of his own. Sat right on the dome when the El Seguro oil boom burst. Got rich. Lost a lot of it buying into other people's dusters. Still has enough. Serbian by birth, six feet, two hundred and forty, one daughter, never known to have had a wife. No police record of any consequence. None at all since Pittsburgh."

I lit a pipe.

"Jeeze," he said. "Where you promote all that?"

"Connections. What's the angle?"

He picked the wallet off the floor and moused around inside it with a couple of square fingers for a while, with his tongue sticking out between his thick lips. He finally got out a slim brown card and some crumpled slips of paper. He pushed them at me.

The card was in golf type, very delicately done. It said: "Mr. Harold Hardwicke Steiner," and very small in the corner, "Rare Books and De Luxe Editions." No address or phone number.

The white slips, three in number, were simple IOU's for a thousand dollars each, signed: "Carmen Dravec" in a sprawling, moronic handwriting.

I gave it all back to him and said: "Blackmail?"

He shook his head slowly and something gentle came into his face that hadn't been there before.

"It's my little girl – Carmen. This Steiner, he bothers her. She goes to his joint all the time, makes whoopee. He makes love to her, I guess. I don't like it."

I nodded. "How about the notes?"

"I don't care nothin' about the dough. She plays games with him. The hell with that. She's what you call man-crazy. You go tell this Steiner to lay off Carmen. I break his neck with my hands. See?"

All this in a rush, with deep breathing. His eyes got small and round, and furious. His teeth almost chattered.

I said: "Why have me tell him? Why not tell him yourself?"

"Maybe I get mad and kill the —— !" he yelled.

I picked a match out of my pocket and prodded the loose ash in the bowl of my pipe. I looked at him carefully for a moment, getting hold of an idea.

"Nerts, you're scared to," I told him.

Both fists came up. He held them shoulder high and shook them, great knots of bone and muscle. He lowered them slowly, heaved a deep honest sigh, and said: "Yeah. I'm scared to. I dunno how to handle her. All the time some new guy and all the time a punk. A while back I gave a guy called Joe Marty five grand to lay off her. She's still mad at me."

I stared at the window, watched the rain hit it, flatten out, and slide down in a thick wave, liked melted gelatin. It was too early in the fall for that kind of rain.

"Giving them sugar doesn't get you anywhere," I said. "You could be doing that all your life. So you figure you'd like to have me get rough with this one, Steiner."

"Tell him I break his neck!"

"I wouldn't bother," I said. "I know Steiner. I'd break his neck for you myself, if it would do any good."

He leaned forward and grabbed my hand. His eyes got childish. A gray tear floated in each of them.

"Listen, M'Gee says you're a good guy. I tell you something I ain't told nobody – ever. Carmen – she's not my kid at all. I just picked her up in Smoky, a little baby in the street. She didn't have nobody. I guess maybe I steal her, huh?"

"Sounds like it," I said, and had to fight to get my hand loose. I rubbed feeling back into it with the other one. The man had a grip that would crack a telephone pole.

"I go straight then," he said grimly, and yet tenderly. "I come out here and make good. She grows up. I love her."

I said: "Uh-huh. That's natural."

"You don't get me. I wanta marry her."

I stared at him.

"She gets older, get some sense. Maybe she marry me, huh?"

His voice implored me, as if I had the settling of that.

"Ever ask her?"

"I'm scared to," he said humbly.

"She soft on Steiner, do you think?"

He nodded. "But that don't mean nothin'."

I could believe that. I got off the bed, threw a window up and let the rain hit my face for a minute.

"Let's get this straight," I said, lowering the window again and going back to the bed. "I can take Steiner off your back. That's easy. I just don't see what it buys you."

He grabbed for my hand again, but I was a little too quick for him this time.

"You came in here a little tough, flashing your wad," I said. "You're going out soft. Not from anything I've said. You knew it already. I'm not Dorothy Dix, and I'm only partly a prune. But I'll take Steiner off you, if you really want that."

He stood up clumsily, swung his hat and stared down at my feet.

"You take him off my back, like you said. He ain't her sort, anyway."

"It might hurt your back a little."

"That's okay. That's what it's for," he said.

He buttoned himself up, dumped his hat on his big shaggy head, and rolled on out. He shut the door carefully, as if he was going out of a sickroom.

I thought he was as crazy as a pair of waltzing mice, but I liked him.

I put his goldbacks in a safe place, mixed myself a long drink, and sat down in the chair that was still warm from him.

While I played with the drink I wondered if he had any idea what Steiner's racket was.

Steiner had a collection of rare and half-rare smut books which he loaned out as high as ten dollars a day – to the right people.

2

IT RAINED ALL the next day. Late in the afternoon I sat parked in a blue Chrysler roadster, diagonally across the Boulevard from a narrow store front, over which a green neon sign in script letters said: "H. H. Steiner."

The rain splashed knee-high off the sidewalks, filled the gutters, and big cops in slickers that shone like gun barrels had a lot of fun carrying little girls in silk stockings and cute little rubber boots across the bad places, with a lot of squeezing.

The rain drummed on the hood of the Chrysler, beat and tore at the taut material of the top, leaked in at the buttoned places, and made a pool on the floorboards for me to keep my feet in.

I had a big flask of Scotch with me. I used it often enough to keep interested.

Steiner did business, even in that weather; perhaps especially in that weather. Very nice cars stopped in front of his store, and very nice people dodged in, then dodged out again with wrapped parcels under their arms. Of course they could have been buying rare books and de luxe editions.

At five-thirty a pimply-faced kid in a leather windbreaker came out of the store and sloped up the side street at a fast trot. He came back with a neat cream-and-gray coupe. Steiner came out and got into the coupe. He wore a dark green leather raincoat, a cigarette in an amber holder, no hat. I couldn't see his glass eye at that distance but I knew he had one. The kid in the windbreaker held an umbrella over him across the sidewalk, then shut it up and handed it into the coupe.

Steiner drove west on the Boulevard. I drove west on the Boulevard. Past the business district, at Pepper Canyon, he turned north, and I tailed him easily from a block back. I was pretty sure he was going home, which was natural.

He left Pepper Drive and took a curving ribbon of wet cement called La Verne Terrace, climbed up it almost to the top. It was a narrow road with a high bank on one side and a few well-spaced cabinlike houses built down the steep slope on the other side. Their roofs were not much above road level. The fronts of them were masked by shrubs. Sodden trees dripped all over the landscape.

Steiner's hideaway had a square box hedge in front of it, more than window-high. The entrance was a sort of maze, and the house door was not visible from the road. Steiner put his gray-and-cream coupe in a small garage, locked up, went through the maze with his umbrella up, and light went on in the house.

While he was doing this I had passed him and gone to the top of the hill. I turned around there and went back and parked in front of the next house above his. It seemed to be closed up or empty, but had no signs on it. I went into a conference with my flask of Scotch, and then just sat.

At six-fifteen lights bobbed up the hill. It was quite dark by then. A car stopped in front of Steiner's hedge. A slim, tall girl in a slicker got out of it. Enough light filtered out through the hedge for me to see that she was dark-haired and possibly pretty.

Voices drifted on the rain and a door shut. I got out of the Chrysler and strolled down the hill, put a pencil flash into the car. It was a dark maroon or brown Packard convertible. Its license read to Carmen Dravec, 3596 Lucerne Avenue. I went back to my heap.

A solid, slow-moving hour crawled by. No more cars came up or down the hill. It seemed to be a very quiet neighborhood.

Then a single flash of hard white light leaked out of Steiner's house, like a flash of summer lightning. As the darkness fell again a thin tinkling scream trickled down the darkness and echoed faintly among the wet trees. I was out of the Chrysler and on my way before the last echo of it died.

There was no fear in the scream. It held the note of a half-pleasurable shock, an accent of drunkenness, and a touch of pure idiocy.

The Steiner mansion was perfectly silent when I hit the gap in the hedge, dodged around the elbow that masked the front door, and put my hand up to bang on the door.

At that exact moment, as if somebody had been waiting for it, three shots racketed close together behind the door. After that there was a long, harsh sigh, a soft thump, rapid steps, going away into the back of the house.

I wasted time hitting the door with my shoulder, without enough start. It threw me back like a kick from an army mule.

The door fronted on a narrow runway, like a small bridge, that led from the banked road. There was no side porch, no way to get at the windows in a hurry. There was no way around to the back except through the house or up a long flight of wooden steps that went up to the back door from the alleylike street below. On these steps I now heard a clatter of feet.

That gave me the impulse and I hit the door again, from the feet up. It gave at the lock and I pitched down two steps into a big, dim, cluttered room. I didn't see much of what was in the room then. I wandered through to the back of the house.

I was pretty sure there was death in it.

A car throbbed in the street below as I reached the back porch. The car went away fast, without lights. That was that. I went back to the living-room.

3

THAT ROOM REACHED all the way across the front of the house and had a low, beamed ceiling, walls painted brown. Strips of tapestry hung all around the walls. Books filled low shelves. There was a thick, pinkish rug on which some light fell from two standing lamps with pale green shades. In the middle of the rug there was a big, low desk and a black chair with a yellow satin cushion at it. There were books all over the desk.

On a sort of dais near one end wall there was a teakwood chair with arms and a high back. A dark-haired girl was sitting in the chair, on a fringed red shawl.

She sat very straight, with her hands on the arms of the chair, her knees close together, her body stiffly erect, her chin level. Her eyes were wide open and mad and had no pupils.

She looked unconscious of what was going on, but she didn't have the pose of unconsciousness. She had a pose as if she was doing something very important and making a lot of it.

Out of her mouth came a tinny chuckling noise, which didn't change her expression or move her lips. She didn't seem to see me at all.

She was wearing a pair of long jade earrings, and apart from those she was stark naked.

I looked away from her to the other end of the room.

Steiner was on his back on the floor, just beyond the edge of the pink rug, and in front of a thing that looked like a small totem pole. It had a round open mouth in which the lens of a camera showed. The lens seemed to be aimed at the girl in the teakwood chair.

There was a flashbulb apparatus on the floor beside Steiner's outflung hand in a loose silk sleeve. The cord of the flashbulb went behind the totem pole thing.

Steiner was wearing Chinese slippers with thick white felt soles. His legs were in black satin pajamas and the upper part of him in an embroidered Chinese coat. The front of it was mostly blood. His glass eye shone brightly and was the most lifelike thing about him. At a glance none of the three shots had missed.

The flashbulb was the sheet lightning I had seen leak out of the house and the half-giggling scream was the doped and naked girl's reaction to that. The three shots had been somebody else's idea of how the proceedings ought to be punctuated. Presumably the idea of the lad who had gone very fast down the back steps.

I could see something in his point of view. At that stage I thought it was a good idea to shut the front door and fasten it with the short chain that was on it. The lock had been spoiled by my violent entrance.

A couple of thin purple glasses stood on a red lacquer tray on one end of the desk. Also a potbellied flagon of something brown. The glasses smelled of ether and laudanum, a mixture I had never tried, but it seemed to fit the scene pretty well.

I found the girl's clothes on a divan in the corner, picked up a brown sleeved dress to begin with, and went over to her. She smelled of ether also, at a distance of several feet.

The tinny chuckling was still going on and a little froth was oozing down her chin. I slapped her face, not very hard.

I didn't want to bring her out of whatever kind of trance she was in, into a screaming fit.

"Come on," I said brightly. "Let's be nice. Let's get dressed."

She said: "G-g-go – ta – hell," without any emotion that I could notice.

I slapped her a little more. She didn't mind the slaps, so I went to work getting the dress on her.

She didn't mind the dress either. She let me hold her arms up but she spread her fingers wide, as if that was very cute. It made me do a lot of finagling with the sleeves. I finally got the dress on. I got her stockings on, and her shoes, and then got her up on her feet.

"Let's take a little walk," I said. "Let's take a nice little walk."

We walked. Part of the time her earrings banged against my chest and part of the time we looked like a couple of adagio dancers doing the splits. We walked over to Steiner's body and back. She didn't pay any attention to Steiner and his bright glass eye.

She found it amusing that she couldn't walk and tried to tell me about it, but only bubbled. I put her arm on the divan while I wadded her underclothes up and shoved them into a deep pocket of my raincoat, put her handbag in my other deep pocket. I went through Steiner's desk and found a little blue notebook written in code that looked interesting. I put that in my pocket, too.

Then I tried to get at the back of the camera in the totem pole, to get the plate, but couldn't find the catch right away. I was getting nervous, and I figured I could build up a better excuse if I ran into the law when I came back later to look for it than for any reason I could give if caught there now.

I went back to the girl and got her slicker on her, nosed around to see if anything else of hers was there, wiped away a lot of fingerprints I probably hadn't made, and at least some of those Miss Dravec must have made. I opened the door and put out both the lamps.

I got my left arm around her again and we struggled out into the rain and piled into her Packard. I didn't like leaving my own bus there very well, but that had to be. Her keys were in her car. We drifted off down the hill.

Nothing happened on the way to Lucerne Avenue except that Carmen stopped bubbling and giggling and went to snoring. I couldn't keep her head off my shoulder. It was all I could do to keep it out of my lap. I had to drive rather slowly and it was a long way anyhow, clear over to the west edge of the city.

The Dravec home was a large old-fashioned brick house in large grounds with a wall around them. A gray composition driveway went through iron gates and up a slope past flower beds and lawns to a big front door with narrow leaded panels on each side of it. There was dim light behind the panels as if nobody much was home.

I pushed Carmen's head into the corner and shed her belongings in the seat, and got out.

A maid opened the door. She said Mr. Dravec wasn't in and she didn't know where he was. Downtown somewhere. She had a long, yellowish, gentle face, a long nose, no chin and large wet eyes. She looked like a nice old horse that had been turned out to pasture after long service, and as if she would do the right thing by Carmen.

I pointed into the Packard and growled: "Better get her to bed. She's lucky we don't throw her in the can — drivin' around with a tool like that on her."

She smiled sadly and I went away.

I had to walk five blocks in the rain before a narrow apartment house let me into its lobby to use a phone. Then I had to wait another twenty-five minutes for a taxi. While I waited I began to worry about what I hadn't completed.

I had yet to get the used plate out of Steiner's camera.

4

I PAID THE taxi off on Pepper Drive, in front of a house where there was company, and walked back up the curving hill of La Verne Terrace to Steiner's house behind its shrubbery.

Nothing looked any different. I went in through the gap in the hedge, pushed the door open gently, and smelled cigarette smoke.

It hadn't been there before. There had been a complicated set of smells, including the sharp memory of smokeless powder. But cigarette smoke hadn't stood out from the mixture.

I closed the door and slipped down on one knee and listened, holding my breath. I didn't hear anything but the sound of the rain on the roof. I tried throwing the beam of my pencil flash along the floor. Nobody shot at me.

I straightened up, found the dangling tassel of one of the lamps and made light in the room.

The first thing I noticed was that a couple of strips of tapestry were gone from the wall. I hadn't counted them, but the spaces where they had hung caught my eye.

Then I saw Steiner's body was gone from in front of the totem pole thing with the camera eye in its mouth. On the floor below, beyond the margin of the pink rug, somebody had spread down a rug over the place where Steiner's body had been. I didn't have to lift the rug to know why it had been put there.

I lit a cigarette and stood there in the middle of the dimly lighted room and thought about it. After a while I went to the camera in the totem pole. I found the catch this time. There wasn't any plate-holder in the camera.

My hand went towards the mulberry-colored phone on Steiner's low desk, but didn't take hold of it.

I crossed into the little hallway beyond the living-room and poked into a fussy-looking bedroom that looked like a woman's room more than a man's. The bed had a long cover with a flounced edge. I lifted that and shot my flash under the bed.

Steiner wasn't under the bed. He wasn't anywhere in the house. Somebody had taken him away. He couldn't very well have gone by himself.

It wasn't the law, or somebody would have been there still. It was only an hour and a half since Carmen and I left the place. And there was none of the mess police photographers and fingerprint men would have made.

I went back to the living-room, pushed the flashbulb apparatus around the back of the totem pole with my foot, switched off the lamp, left the house, got into my rain-soaked car and choked it to life.

It was all right with me if somebody wanted to keep the Steiner kill hush-hush for a while. It gave me a chance to find out whether I could tell it leaving Carmen Dravec and the nude photo angle out.

It was after ten when I got back to the Berglund and put my heap away and went upstairs to the apartment. I stood under a shower, then put pajamas on and mixed up a batch of hot grog. I looked at the phone a couple of times, thought about calling to see if Dravec was home yet, thought it might be a good idea to let him alone until the next day.

I filled a pipe and sat down with my hot grog and Steiner's little blue notebook. It was in code, but the arrangement of the entries and the indented leaves made it a list of names and addresses. There were over four hundred and fifty of them. If this was Steiner's sucker list, he had a gold mine – quite apart from the blackmail angles.

Any name on the list might be a prospect as the killer. I didn't envy the cops their job when it was handed to them.

I drank too much whiskey trying to crack the code. About midnight I went to bed, and dreamed about a man in a Chinese coat with blood all over the front who chased a naked girl with long jade earrings while I tried to photograph the scene with a camera that didn't have any plate in it.

5

VIOLETS M'GEE CALLED me up in the morning, before I was dressed, but after I had seen the paper and not found anything about Steiner in it. His voice had the cheerful sound of a man who had slept well and didn't owe too much money.

"Well, how's the boy?" he began.

I said I was all right except that I was having a little trouble with my Third Reader. He laughed a little absently, and then his voice got too casual.

"This guy Dravec that I sent over to see you – done anything for him yet?"

"Too much rain," I answered, if that was an answer.

"Uh-huh. He seems to be a guy that things happen to. A car belongin' to him is washin' about in the surf off Lido fish pier."

I didn't say anything. I held the telephone very tightly.

"Yeah," M'Gee went on cheerfully. "A nice new Cad all messed up with sand and sea water. . . . Oh, I forgot. There's a guy inside it."

I let my breath out slowly, very slowly. "Dravec?" I whispered.

"Naw. A young kid. I ain't told Dravec yet. It's under the fedora. Wanta run down and look at it with me?"

I said I would like to do that.

"Snap it up. I'll be in my hutch," M'Gee told me and hung up.

Shaved, dressed and lightly breakfasted I was at the County Building in half an hour or so. I found M'Gee staring at a yellow wall and sitting at a little yellow desk on which there was nothing but M'Gee's hat and one of the M'Gee feet. He took both of them off the desk and we went down to the official parking lot and got into a small black sedan.

The rain had stopped during the night and the morning was all blue and gold. There was enough snap in the air to make life simple and sweet, if you didn't have too much on your mind. I had.

It was thirty miles to Lido, the first ten of them through city traffic. M'Gee made it in three-quarters of an hour. At the end of that time we skidded to a stop in front of a stucco arch beyond which a long black pier extended. I took my feet out of the floorboards and we got out.

There were a few cars and people in front of the arch. A motorcycle officer was keeping the people off the pier. M'Gee showed him a bronze star and we went out along the pier, into a loud smell that even two days' rain had failed to wash away.

"There she is – on the tug," M'Gee said.

A low black tug crouched off the end of the pier. Something large and green and nickeled was on its deck in front of the wheelhouse. Men stood around it.

We went down slimy steps to the deck of the tug.

M'Gee said hello to a deputy in green khaki and another man in plain clothes. The tug crew of three moved over to the wheelhouse, and set their backs against it, watching us.

We looked at the car. The front bumper was bent, and one headlight and the radiator shell. The paint and the nickel were scratched up by sand and the upholstery was sodden and black. Otherwise the car wasn't much the worse for wear. It was a big job in two tones of green, with a wine-colored stripe and trimming.

M'Gee and I looked into the front part of it. A slim, dark-haired kid who had been good-looking was draped around the steering post, with his head at a peculiar angle to the rest of his body. His face was bluish white. His eyes were a faint dull gleam under the lowered lids. His open mouth had sand in it. There were traces of blood on the side of his head which the sea water hadn't quite washed away.

M'Gee backed away slowly, made a noise in his throat and began to chew on a couple of the violet-scented breath purifiers that gave him his nickname.

"What's the story?" he asked quietly.

The uniformed deputy pointed up to the end of the pier. Dirty white railings made of two-by-fours had been broken through in a wide space and the broken wood showed up yellow and bright.

"Went through there. Must have hit pretty hard, too. The rain stopped early down here, about nine, and the broken wood is dry inside. That puts it after the rain stopped. That's all we know except she fell in plenty of water not to be banged up worse: at least half-tide, I'd say. That would be right after the rain stopped. She showed under the water when the boys came down to fish this morning. We got the tug to lift her out. Then we find the dead guy."

The other deputy scuffed at the deck with the toe of his shoe. M'Gee looked sideways at me with foxy little eyes. I looked blank and didn't say anything.

"Pretty drunk that lad," M'Gee said gently. "Showin' off all alone in the rain. I guess he must have been fond of driving. Yeah – pretty drunk."

"Drunk, hell," the plainclothes deputy said. "The hand throttle's set halfway down and the guy's been sapped on the side of the head. Ask me and I'll call it murder."

M'Gee looked at him politely, then at the uniformed man. "What you think?"

"It could be suicide, I guess. His neck's broke and he could have hurt his head in the fall. And his hand could have knocked the throttle down. I kind of like murder myself, though."

M'Gee nodded, said: "Frisked him? Know who he is?"

The two deputies looked at me, then at the tug crew.

"Okay. Save that part," M'Gee said. "I *know* who he is."

A small man with glasses and a tired face and a black bag came slowly along the pier and down the slimy steps. He picked out a fairly clean place on the deck and put his bag down. He took his hat off and rubbed the back of his neck and smiled wearily.

"'Lo, Doc. There's your patient," M'Gee told him. "Took a dive off the pier last night. That's all we know now."

The medical examiner looked in at the dead man morosely. He fingered the head, moved it around a little, felt the man's ribs. He lifted one lax hand and stared at the fingernails. He let it fall, stepped back and picked his bag up again.

"About twelve hours," he said. "Broken neck, of course. I doubt if there's any water in him. Better get him out of there before he starts to get stiff on us. I'll tell you the rest when I get him on a table."

He nodded around, went back up the steps and along the pier. An ambulance was backing into position beside the stucco arch at the pier head.

The two deputies grunted and tugged to get the dead man out of the car and lay him down on the deck, on the side of the car away from the beach.

"Let's go," M'Gee told me. "That ends this part of the show."

We said goodbye and M'Gee told the deputies to keep their chins buttoned until they heard from him. We went back along the pier and got into the small black sedan and drove back towards the city along a white highway washed clean by the rain, past low rolling hills of yellow-white sand terraced with moss. A few gulls wheeled and swooped over something in the surf. Far out to sea a couple of white yachts on the horizon looked as if they were suspended in the sky.

We laid a few miles behind us without saying anything to each other. Then M'Gee cocked his chin at me and said: "Got ideas?"

"Loosen up," I said. "I never saw the guy before. Who is he?"

"Hell, I thought you were going to tell me about it."

"Loosen up, Violets," I said.

He growled, shrugged, and we nearly went off the road into the loose sand.

"Dravec's chauffeur. A kid named Carl Owen. How do I know? We had him in the cooler a year ago on a Mann Act rap. He run Dravec's hotcha daughter off to Yuma. Dravec went after them and brought them back and had the guy heaved in the goldfish bowl. Then the girl gets to him, and next morning the old man steams downtown and begs the guy off. Says the kid meant to marry her, only she wouldn't. Then, by heck, the kid goes back to work for him and been there ever since. What you think of that?"

"It sounds just like Dravec," I said.

"Yeah – but the kid could have had a relapse."

M'Gee had silvery hair and a knobby chin and a little pouting mouth made to kiss babies with. I looked at his face sideways, and suddenly I got his idea. I laughed.

"You think maybe Dravec killed him?" I asked.

"Why not? The kid makes another pass at the girl and Dravec cracks down at him too hard. He's a big guy and could break a neck easy. Then he's scared. He runs the car down to Lido in the rain and lets it slide off the end of the pier. Thinks it won't show. Maybe don't think at all. Just rattled."

"It's a kick in the pants," I said. "Then all he had to do was walk home thirty miles in the rain."

"Go on. Kid me."

"Dravec killed him, sure," I said. "But they were playing leapfrog. Dravec fell on him."

"Okay, pal. Some day you'll want to play with *my* catnip mouse."

"Listen, Violets," I said seriously. "If the kid was murdered – and you're not sure it's murder at all – it's not Dravec's kind of crime. He might kill a man in a temper – but he'd let him lay. He wouldn't go to all that fuss."

We shuttled back and forth across the road while M'Gee thought about that.

"What a pal," he complained. "I have me a swell theory and look what you done to it. I wish the hell I hadn't brought you. Hell with you. I'm goin' after Dravec just the same."

"Sure," I agreed. "You'd have to do that. But Dravec never killed that boy. He's too soft inside to cover up on it."

It was noon when we got back to town. I hadn't had any dinner but whisky the night before and very little breakfast that morning. I got off on the Boulevard and let M'Gee go on alone to see Dravec.

I was interested in what had happened to Carl Owen; but I wasn't interested in the thought that Dravec might have murdered him.

I ate lunch at a counter and looked casually at an early afternoon paper. I didn't expect to see anything about Steiner in it, and I didn't.

After lunch I walked along the Boulevard six blocks to have a look at Steiner's store.

6

IT WAS A half-store frontage, the other half being occupied by a credit jeweler. The jeweler was standing in his entrance, a big, white-haired, black-eyed Jew with about nine carats of diamond on his hand. A faint, knowing smile curved his lips as I went past him into Steiner's.

A thick blue rug paved Steiner's from wall to wall. There were blue leather easy chairs with smoke stands beside them. A few sets of tooled leather books were put out on narrow tables. The rest of the stock was behind glass. A paneled partition with a single door in it cut off a back part of the store, and in the corner by this a woman sat behind a small desk with a hooded lamp on it.

She got up and came towards me, swinging lean thighs in a tight dress of some black material that didn't reflect any light. She was an ash-blonde, with greenish eyes under heavily mascaraed lashes. There were large jet buttons in the lobes of her ears; her hair waved back smoothly from behind them. Her fingernails were silvered.

She gave me what she thought was a smile of welcome, but what I thought was a grimace of strain.

"Was it something?"

I pulled my hat low over my eyes and fidgeted. I said: "Steiner?"

"He won't be in today. May I show you – "

"I'm selling," I said. "Something he's wanted for a long time."

The silvered fingernails touched the hair over one ear. "Oh, a salesman. . . . Well, you might come in tomorrow."

"He sick? I could go up to the house," I suggested hopefully. "He'd want to see what I have."

That jarred her. She had to fight for her breath for a minute. But her voice was smooth enough when it came.

"That – that wouldn't be any use. He's out of town today."

I nodded, looked properly disappointed, touched my hat and started to turn away when the pimply-faced kid of the night before stuck his head through the door in the paneling. He went back as soon as he saw me, but not before I saw some loosely packed cases of books behind him on the floor of the back room.

The cases were small and open and packed any old way. A man in very new overalls was fussing with them. Some of Steiner's stock was being moved out.

I left the store and walked down to the corner, then back to the alley. Behind Steiner's stood a small black truck with wire sides. It didn't have any lettering on it. Boxes showed through the wire sides and, as I watched, the man in overalls came out with another one and heaved it up.

I went back to the Boulevard. Half a block on, a fresh-faced kid was reading a magazine in a parked Green Top. I showed him money and said: "Tail job?"

He looked me over, swung his door open, and stuck his magazine behind the rear-vision mirror.

"My meat, boss," he said brightly.

We went around to the end of the alley and waited beside a fireplug.

There were about a dozen boxes on the truck when the man in the very new overalls got up in front and gunned his motor. He went down the alley fast and turned left on the street at the end. My driver did the same. The truck went north to Garfield, then east. It went very fast and there was a lot of traffic on Garfield. My driver tailed from too far back.

I was telling him about that when the truck turned north off Garfield again. The street at which it turned was called Brittany. When we got to Brittany there wasn't any truck.

The fresh-faced kid who was driving me made comforting sounds through the glass panel of the cab and we went up Brittany at four miles an hour looking for the truck behind bushes. I refused to be comforted.

Brittany bore a little to the east two blocks up and met the next street, Randall Place, in a tongue of land on which there was a white apartment house with its front on Randall Place and its basement garage entrance on Brittany, a story lower. We were going past that and my driver was telling me the truck couldn't be very far away when I saw it in the garage.

We went around to the front of the apartment house and I got out and went into the lobby.

There was no switchboard. A desk was pushed back against the wall, as if it wasn't used any more. Above it names were on a panel of gilt mailboxes.

The name that went with Apartment 405 was Joseph Marty. Joe Marty was the name of the man who played with Carmen Dravec until her papa gave him five thousand dollars to go away and play with some other girl. It could be the same Joe Marty.

I went down steps and pushed through a door with a wired glass panel into the dimness of the garage. The man in the very new overalls was stacking boxes in the automatic elevator.

I stood near him and lit a cigarette and watched him. He didn't like it very well, but he didn't say anything. After a while I said: "Watch the weight, buddy. She's only tested for half a ton. Where's it goin'?"

"Marty, four-o-five," he said, and then looked as if he was sorry he had said it.

"Fine," I told him. "It looks like a nice lot of reading."

I went back up the steps and out of the building, got into my Green Top again.

We drove back downtown to the building where I have an office. I gave the driver too much money and he gave me a dirty card which I dropped into the brass spittoon beside the elevators.

Dravec was holding up the wall outside the door of my office.

7

AFTER THE RAIN, it was warm and bright but he still had the belted suede raincoat on. It was open down the front, as were his coat, and vest underneath. His tie was under one ear. His face looked like a mask of gray putty with a black stubble on the lower part of it.

He looked awful.

I unlocked the door and patted his shoulder and pushed him in and got him into a chair. He breathed hard but didn't say anything. I got a bottle of rye out of the desk and poured a couple of ponies. He drank both of them without a word. Then he slumped in the chair and blinked his eyes and groaned and took a square white envelope out of an inner pocket. He put it down on the desk top and held his big hairy hand over it.

"Tough about Carl," I said. "I was with M'Gee this morning."

He looked at me emptily. After a little while he said:

"Yeah. Carl was a good kid. I ain't told you about him much."

I waited, looking at the envelope under his hand. He looked down at it himself.

"I gotta let you see it," he mumbled. He pushed it slowly across the desk and lifted his hand off it as if with the movement he was giving up most everything that made life worth living. Two tears welled up in his eyes and slid down his unshaven cheeks.

I lifted the square envelope and looked at it. It was addressed to him at his house, in neat pen-and-ink printing, and bore a Special Delivery stamp. I opened it and looked at the shiny photograph that was inside.

Carmen Dravec sat in Steiner's teakwood chair, wearing her jade earrings. Her eyes looked crazier, if anything, than as I had seen them. I looked at the back of the photo, saw that it was blank, and put the thing face down on my desk.

"Tell me about it," I said carefully.

Dravec wiped the tears off his face with his sleeve, put his hands flat on the desk and stared down at the dirty nails. His fingers trembled on the desk.

"A guy called me," he said in a dead voice. "Ten grand for the plate and the prints. The deal's got to be closed tonight, or they give the stuff to some scandal sheet."

"That's a lot of hooey," I said. "A scandal sheet couldn't use it, except to back up a story. What's the story?"

He lifted his eyes slowly, as if they were very heavy. "That ain't all. The guy say there's a jam to it. I better come through fast, or I'd find my girl in the cooler."

"What's the story?" I asked again, filling my pipe. "What does Carmen say?"

He shook his big shaggy head. "I ain't asked her. I ain't got the heart. Poor little girl. No clothes on her. . . . No, I ain't got the heart. . . . You ain't done nothin' on Steiner yet, I guess."

"I didn't have to," I told him. "Somebody beat me to it."

He stared at me open-mouthed, uncomprehending. It was obvious he knew nothing about the night before.

"Did Carmen go out at all last night?" I asked carelessly.

He was still staring with his mouth open, groping in his mind.

"No. She's sick. She's sick in bed when I get home. She don't go out at all. . . . What you mean – about Steiner?"

I reached for the bottle of rye and poured us each a drink. Then I lit my pipe.

"Steiner's dead," I said. "Somebody got tired of his tricks and shot him full of holes. Last night, in the rain."

"Jeeze," he said wonderingly. "You was there?"

I shook my head. "Not me. Carmen was there. That's the jam your man spoke of. She didn't do the shooting, of course."

Dravec's face got red and angry. He balled his fists. His breath made a harsh sound and a pulse beat visibly in the side of his neck.

"That ain't true! She's sick. She don't go out at all. She's sick in bed when I get home!"

"You told me that," I said. "*That's* not true. I brought Carmen home myself. The maid knows, only she's trying to be decent about it. Carmen was at Steiner's house and I was watching outside. A gun went off and someone ran away. I didn't see him. Carmen was too drunk to see him. That's why she's sick."

His eyes tried to focus on my face, but they were vague and empty, as if the light behind them had died. He took hold of the arms of the chair. His big knuckles strained and got white.

"She don't tell me," he whispered. "She don't tell me. Me, that would do anything for her." There was no emotion in his voice; just the dead exhaustion of despair.

He pushed his chair back a little. "I go get the dough," he said. "The ten grand. Maybe the guy don't talk."

Then he broke. His big rough head came down on the desk and sobs shook his whole body. I stood up and went around the desk and patted his shoulder, kept on patting it, not saying anything. After a while he lifted his face smeared with tears and grabbed for my hand.

"Jeeze, you're a good guy," he sobbed.

"You don't know the half of it."

I pulled my hand away from him and got a drink into his paw, helped him lift it and down it. Then I took the empty glass out of his hand and put it back on the desk. I sat down again.

"You've got to brace up," I told him grimly. "The law doesn't know about Steiner yet. I brought Carmen home and kept my mouth shut. I wanted to give you and Carmen a break. That puts me in a jam. You've got to do your part."

He nodded slowly, heavily. "Yeah, I do what you say – anything you say."

"Get the money," I said. "Have it ready for the call. I've got ideas and you may not have to use it. But it's no time to get foxy. . . . Get the money and sit tight and keep your mouth shut. Leave the rest to me. Can you do that?"

"Yeah," he said. "Jeeze, you're a good guy."

"Don't talk to Carmen," I said. "The less she remembers out of her drunk, the better. This picture – " I touched the back of the photo on the desk – "shows somebody was working with Steiner. We've got to get him and get him quick – even if it costs ten grand to do it."

He stood up slowly. "That's nothin'. That's just dough. I go get it now. Then I go home. You do it like you want to. Me, I do just like you say."

He grabbed for my hand again, shook it, and went slowly out of the office. I heard his heavy steps drag down the hall.

I drank a couple of drinks fast and mopped my face.

8

I DROVE MY Chrysler slowly up La Verne Terrace towards Steiner's house.

In the daylight, I could see the steep drop of the hill and the flight of wooden steps down which the killer had made his escape. The street below was almost as narrow as an alley. Two small houses fronted on it, not very near Steiner's place. With the noise the rain had been making it was doubtful if anyone in them had paid much attention to the shots.

Steiner's looked peaceful under the afternoon sun. The unpainted shingles of the roof were still damp from the rain. The trees on the other side of the street had new leaves on them. There were no cars on the street.

Something moved behind the square growth of box hedge that screened Steiner's front door.

Carmen Dravec, in a green and white checkered coat and no hat, came out through the opening, stopped suddenly, looked at me wild-eyed, as if she hadn't heard the car. She went back quickly behind the hedge. I drove on and parked in front of the empty house.

I got out and walked back. In the sunlight it felt like an exposed and dangerous thing to do.

I went in through the hedge and the girl stood there very straight and silent against the half-open house door. One hand went slowly to her mouth, and her teeth bit at a funny-looking thumb that was like an extra finger. There were deep purple-black smudges under her frightened eyes.

I pushed her back into the house without saying anything, shut the door. We stood looking at each other inside. She dropped her hand slowly and tried to smile. Then all expression went out of her white face and it looked as intelligent as the bottom of a shoe box.

I got gentleness into my voice and said: "Take it easy. I'm pals. Sit down in that chair by the desk. I'm a friend of your father's. Don't get panicky."

She went and sat down in the yellow cushion in the black chair at Steiner's desk.

The place looked decadent and off-color by daylight. It still stank of the ether.

Carmen licked the corners of her mouth with the tip of a whitish tongue. Her dark eyes were stupid and stunned rather than scared now. I rolled a cigarette around in my fingers and pushed some books out of the way to sit on the edge of the desk. I lit my cigarette, puffed it slowly for a moment, then asked: "What are you doing here?"

She picked at the material of her coat, didn't answer. I tried again.

"How much do you remember about last night?"

She answered that. "Remember what? I was sick last night – at home." Her voice was a cautious, throaty sound that only just reached my ears.

"Before that," I said. "Before I brought you home. Here."

A slow flush crept up her throat and her eyes widened. "You – you were the one?" she breathed, and began to chew on her funny thumb again.

"Yeah, I was the one. How much of it all stays with you?"

She said: "Are you the police?"

"No. I told you I was a friend of your father's."

"You're not the police?"

"No."

It finally registered. She let out a long sigh. "What – what do you want?"

"Who killed him?"

193

Her shoulders jerked in the checkered coat, but nothing changed much in her face. Her eyes slowly got furtive.

"Who – who else knows?"

"About Steiner? I don't know. Not the police, or someone would be here. Maybe Marty."

It was just a stab in the dark, but it got a sudden, sharp cry out of her.

"Marty!"

We were both silent for a minute. I puffed on my cigarette and she chewed on her thumb.

"Don't get clever," I said. "Did Marty kill him?"

Her chin came down an inch. "Yes."

"Why did he do it?"

"I – I don't know," very dully.

"Seen much of him lately?"

Her hands clenched. "Just once or twice."

"Know where he lives?"

"Yes!" She spat it at me.

"What's the matter? I thought you liked Marty."

"I hate him!" she almost yelled.

"Then you'd like him for the spot," I said.

She was blank to that. I had to explain it. "I mean, are you willing to tell the police it was Marty?"

Sudden panic flamed in her eyes.

"If I kill the nude photo angle," I said soothingly.

She giggled.

That gave me a nasty feeling. If she had screeched, or turned white, or even keeled over, that would have been fairly natural. But she just giggled.

I began to hate the sight of her. Just looking at her made me feel dopey.

Her giggles went on, ran around the room like rats. They gradually got hysterical. I got off the desk, took a step towards her, and slapped her face.

"Just like last night," I said.

The giggling stopped at once and the thumb-chewing started again. She still didn't mind my slaps apparently. I sat on the end of the desk once more.

"You came here to look for the camera plate – for the birthday suit photo," I told her.

Her chin went up and down again.

"Too late. I looked for it last night. It was gone then. Probably Marty has it. You're not kidding me about Marty?"

She shook her head vigorously. She got out of the chair slowly. Her eyes were narrow and sloe-black and as shallow as an oyster shell.

"I'm going now," she said, as if we had been having a cup of tea.

She went over to the door and was reaching out to open it when a car came up the hill and stopped outside the house. Somebody got out of the car.

She turned and stared at me, horrified.

The door opened casually and a man looked in at us.

9

HE WAS A hatchet-faced man in a brown suit and a black felt hat. The cuff of his left sleeve was folded under and pinned to the side of his coat with a big black safety pin.

He took his hat off, closed the door by pushing it with his shoulder, looked at Carmen with a nice smile. He had close-cropped black hair and a bony skull. He fitted his clothes well. He didn't look tough.

"I'm Guy Slade," he said. "Excuse the casual entrance. The bell didn't work. Is Steiner around?"

He hadn't tried the bell. Carmen looked at him blankly, then at me, then back at Slade. She licked her lips but didn't say anything.

I said: "Steiner isn't here, Mr. Slade. We don't know just where he is."

He nodded and touched his long chin with the brim of his hat.

"You friends of his?"

"We just dropped by for a book," I said, and gave him back his smile. "The door was half open. We knocked, then stepped inside. Just like you."

"I see," Slade said thoughtfully. "Very simple."

I didn't say anything. Carmen didn't say anything. She was staring fixedly at his empty sleeve.

"A book, eh?" Slade went on. The way he said it told me things. He knew about Steiner's racket, maybe.

I moved over towards the door. "Only *you* didn't knock," I said.

He smiled with faint embarrassment. "That's right. I ought to have knocked. Sorry."

"We'll trot along now," I said carelessly. I took hold of Carmen's arm.

"Any message – if Steiner comes back?" Slade asked softly.

"We won't bother you."

"That's too bad," he said, with too much meaning.

I let go of Carmen's arm and took a slow step away from her. Slade still had his hat in his hand. He didn't move. His deep-set eyes twinkled pleasantly.

I opened the door again.

Slade said: "The girl can go. But I'd like to talk to you a little."

I stared at him, trying to look very blank.

"Kidder, eh?" Slade said nicely.

Carmen made a sudden sound at my side and ran out through the door. In a moment I heard her steps going down the hill. I hadn't seen her car, but I guessed it was around somewhere.

I began to say: "What the hell – "

"Save it," Slade interrupted coldly. "There's something wrong here. I'll just find out what it is."

He began to walk around the room carelessly – too carelessly. He was frowning, not paying much attention to me. That made me thoughtful. I took a quick glance out of the window, but I couldn't see anything but the top of his car above the hedge.

Slade found the potbellied flagon and the two thin purple glasses on the desk. He sniffed at one of them. A disgusted smile wrinkled his thin lips.

"The lousy pimp," he said tonelessly.

He looked at the books on the desk, touched one or two of them, went on around the back of the desk and was in front of the totem pole thing. He stared at that. Then his eyes went down to the floor, to the thin rug that was over the place where Steiner's body had been. Slade moved the rug with his foot and suddenly tensed, staring down.

It was a good act – or else Slade had a nose I could have used in my business. I wasn't sure which – yet, but I was giving it a lot of thought.

He went slowly down to the floor on one knee. The desk partly hid him from me.

I slipped a gun out from under my arm and put both hands behind my body and leaned against the wall.

There was a sharp, swift exclamation, then Slade shot to his feet. His arm flashed up. A long, black Luger slid into it expertly. I didn't move. Slade held the Luger in long, pale fingers, not pointing it at me, not pointing it at anything in particular.

"Blood," he said quietly, grimly, his deep-set eyes black and hard now. "Blood on the floor there, under a rug. A lot of blood."

I grinned at him. "I noticed it," I said. "It's old blood. Dried blood."

He slid sideways into the black chair behind Steiner's desk and raked the telephone towards him by putting the Luger around it. He frowned at the telephone, then frowned at me.

"I think we'll have some law," he said.

"Suits me."

Slade's eyes were narrow and as hard as jet. He didn't like my agreeing with him. The veneer had flaked off him, leaving a well-dressed hard boy with a Luger. Looking as if he could use it.

"Just who the hell are you?" he growled.

"A shamus. The name doesn't matter. The girl is my client. Steiner's been riding her with some blackmail dirt. We came to talk to him. He wasn't here."

"Just walk in, huh?"

"Correct. So what? Think we gunned Steiner, Mr. Slade?"

He smiled slightly, thinly, but said nothing.

"Or do you think Steiner gunned somebody and ran away?" I suggested.

"Steiner didn't gun anybody," Slade said. "Steiner didn't have the guts of a sick cat."

I said: "You don't see anybody here, do you? Maybe Steiner had chicken for dinner, and liked to kill his chickens in the parlor."

"I don't get it. I don't get your game."

I grinned again. "Go ahead and call your friends downtown. Only you won't like the reaction you'll get."

He thought that over without moving a muscle. His lips went back against his teeth.

"Why not?" he asked finally, in a careful voice.

I said: "I know you, Mr. Slade. You run the Aladdin Club down on the Palisades. Flash gambling. Soft lights and evening clothes and a buffet supper on the side. You know Steiner well enough to walk into his house without knocking. Steiner's racket needed a little protection now and then. You could be that."

Slade's finger tightened on the Luger, then relaxed. He put the Luger down on the desk, kept his fingers on it. His mouth became a hard white grimace.

"Somebody got to Steiner," he said softly, his voice and the expression on his face seeming to belong to two different people. "He didn't show at the store today. He didn't answer his phone. I came up to see about it."

"Glad to hear you didn't gun Steiner yourself," I said.

The Luger swept up again and made a target of my chest. I said:

"Put it down, Slade. You don't know enough to pop off yet. Not being bullet-proof is an idea I've had to get used to. Put it down. I'll tell you something — if you don't know it. Somebody moved Steiner's books out of his store today — the books he did his real business with."

Slade put his gun down on the desk for the second time. He leaned back and wrestled an amiable expression onto his face.

"I'm listening," he said.

"I think somebody got to Steiner too," I told him. "I think that blood is his blood. The books being moved out from Steiner's store gives us a reason for moving his body away from here. Somebody is taking over the racket and doesn't want Steiner found till he's all set. Whoever it was ought to have cleaned up the blood. He didn't."

Slade listened silently. The peaks of his eyebrows made sharp angles against the white skin of his indoor forehead.

I went on: "Killing Steiner to grab his racket was a dumb trick, and I'm not sure it happened that way. But I *am* sure that whoever took the books knows about it, and that the blonde down in the store is scared stiff about something."

"Any more?" Slade asked evenly.

"Not right now. There's a piece of scandal dope I want to trace. If I get it, I might tell you where. That will be your muscler in."

"Now would be better," Slade said. Then he drew his lips back against his teeth and whistled sharply, twice.

I jumped. A car door opened outside. There were steps.

I brought the gun around from behind my body. Slade's face convulsed and his hand snatched for the Luger that lay in front of him, fumbled at the butt.

I said: "Don't touch it!"

He came to his feet rigid, leaning over, his hand on the gun, but the gun not in his hand. I dodged past him into the hallway and turned as two men came into the room.

One had short red hair, a white, lined face, unsteady eyes. The other was an obvious pug; a good-looking boy except for a flattened nose and one ear as thick as a club steak.

Neither of the newcomers had a gun in sight. They stopped, stared.

I stood behind Slade in the doorway. Slade leaned over the desk in front of me, didn't stir.

The pug's mouth opened in a wide snarl, showing sharp, white teeth. The redhead looked shaky and scared.

Slade had plenty of guts. In a smooth, low, but very clear voice he said:

"This heel gunned Steiner, boys. Take him!"

The redhead took hold of his lower lip with his teeth and snatched for something under his left arm. He didn't get it. I was all set and braced. I shot him through the right shoulder, hating to do it. The gun made a lot of noise in the closed room. It seemed to me that it would be heard all over the city. The redhead went down on the floor and writhed and threshed about as if I had shot him in the belly.

The pug didn't move. He probably knew there wasn't enough speed in his arm. Slade grabbed his Luger up and started to whirl. I took a step and slammed him behind the ear. He sprawled forward over the desk and the Luger shot against a row of books.

Slade didn't hear me say: "I hate to hit a one-armed man from behind, Slade. And I'm not crazy about the show-off. You made me do it."

The pug grinned at me and said: "Okay, pal. What next?"

"I'd like to get out of here, if I can do it without any more shooting. Or I can stick around for some law. It's all one to me."

He thought it over calmly. The redhead was making moaning noises on the floor. Slade was very still.

The pug put his hands up slowly and clasped them behind his neck. He said coolly: "I don't know what it's all about, but I don't give a good —— damn where you go or what you do when you get there. And this ain't my idea of a spot for a lead party. Drift!"

"Wise boy. You've more sense than your boss."

I edged around the desk, edged over towards the open door. The pug turned slowly, facing me, keeping his hands behind his neck. There was a wry but almost good-natured grin on his face.

I skinned through the door and made a fast break through the gap in the hedge and up the hill, half expecting lead to fly after me. None came.

I jumped into the Chrysler and chased it up over the brow of the hill and away from that neighborhood.

10

IT WAS AFTER five when I stopped opposite the apartment house on Randall Place. A few windows were lit up already and radios bleated discordantly on different programs. I rode the automatic elevator to the fourth floor. Apartment 405 was at the end of a long hall that was carpeted in green and paneled in ivory. A cool breeze blew through the hall from open doors to the fire escape.

There was a small ivory push button beside the door marked 405. I pushed it.

After a long time a man opened the door a foot or so. He was a long-legged, thin man with dark brown eyes in a very brown face. Wiry hair grew far back on his head, giving him a great deal of domed brown forehead. His brown eyes probed at me impersonally.

I said: "Steiner?"

Nothing in the man's face changed. He brought a cigarette from behind the door and put it slowly between tight brown lips. A puff of smoke came towards me, and behind it words in a cool, unhurried voice, without inflection. "You said what?"

"Steiner. Harold Hardwicke Steiner. The guy that has the books."

The man nodded. He considered my remark without haste. He glanced at the tip of his cigarette, said: "I think I know him. But he doesn't visit here. Who sent you?"

I smiled. He didn't like that. I said: "You're Marty?"

The brown face got harder. "So what? Got a grift – or just amusin' yourself?"

I moved my left foot casually, enough so that he couldn't slam the door.

"You got the books," I said. "I got the sucker list. How's to talk it over?"

Marty didn't shift his eyes from my face. His right hand went behind the panel of the door again, and his shoulder had a look as if he was making motions with a hand. There was a faint sound in the room behind him – very faint. A curtain ring clicked lightly on a rod.

Then he opened the door wide. "Why not? If you think you've got something," he said coolly.

I went past him into the room. It was a cheerful room, with good furniture and not too much of it. French windows in the end wall looked across a stone porch at the foothills, already getting purple in the dusk. Near the windows a door was shut. Another door in the same wall at the near end of the room had curtains drawn across it, on a brass rod below the lintel.

I sat down on a davenport against the wall in which there were no doors. Marty shut the door and walked sideways to a tall oak writing desk studded with square nails. A cedarwood cigar box with gilt hinges rested on the lowered leaf of the desk. Marty picked it up without taking his eyes off me, carried it to a low table beside an easy chair. He sat down in the easy chair.

I put my hat beside me and opened the top button of my coat and smiled at Marty.

"Well – I'm listening," he said.

He snubbed his cigarette out, lifted the lid of the cigar box and took out a couple of fat cigars.

"Cigar?" he suggested casually, and tossed one at me.

I reached for it and that made me a sap. Marty dropped the other cigar back into the box and came up very swiftly with a gun.

I looked at the gun politely. It was a black police Colt, a .38. I had no argument against it at the moment.

"Stand up a minute," Marty said. "Come forward just about two yards. You might grab a little air while you're doing that." His voice was elaborately casual.

I was mad inside, but I grinned at him. I said: "You're the second guy I've met today that thinks a gun in the hand means the world by the tail. Put it away, and let's talk."

Marty's eyebrows came together and he pushed his chin forward a little. His brown eyes were vaguely troubled.

We stared at each other. I didn't look at the pointed black slipper that showed under the curtains across the doorway to my left.

Marty was wearing a dark blue suit, a blue shirt and a black tie. His brown face looked somber above the dark colors. He said softly, in a lingering voice: "Don't get me wrong. I'm not a tough guy – just careful. I don't know hell's first thing about you. You might be a life-taker for all I know."

"You're not careful enough," I said. "The play with the books was lousy."

He drew a long breath and let it out silently. Then he leaned back and crossed his long legs and rested the Colt on his knee.

"Don't kid yourself I won't use this, if I have to. What's your story?"

"Tell your friend with the pointed shoes to come on in," I said. "She gets tired holding her breath."

Without turning his head Marty called out: "Come on in, Agnes."

The curtains over the door swung aside and the green-eyed blonde from Steiner's store joined us in the room. I wasn't very much surprised to see her there. She looked at me bitterly.

"I knew damn well you were trouble," she told me angrily. "I told Joe to watch his step."

"Save it," Marty snapped. "Joe's watchin' his step plenty. Put some light on so I can see to pop this guy, if it works out that way."

The blonde lit a large floor lamp with a square red shade. She sat down under it, in a big velours chair and held a fixed painful smile on her face. She was scared to the point of exhaustion.

I remembered the cigar I was holding and put it in my mouth. Marty's Colt was very steady on me while I got matches out and lit it.

I puffed smoke and said through the smoke: "The sucker list I spoke of is in code. So I can't read the names yet, but there's about five hundred of them. You got twelve boxes of books, say three hundred. There'll be that many more out on loan. Say five hundred altogether, just to be conservative. If it's a good active list and you could run it around all the books, that would be a quarter of a million rentals. Put the average rental low – say a dollar. That's too low, but say a dollar. That's a lot of money these days. Enough to spot a guy for."

The blonde yelped sharply: "You're crazy, if you – "

"Shut up!" Marty swore at her.

The blonde subsided and put her head back against the back of her chair. Her face was tortured with strain.

"It's no racket for bums," I went on telling them. "You've got to get confidence and keep it. Personally I think the blackmail angles are a mistake. I'm for shedding all that."

Marty's dark brown stare held coldly on my face. "You're a funny guy," he drawled smoothly. "Who's got this lovely racket?"

"You have," I said. "Almost."

Marty didn't say anything.

"You shot Steiner to get it," I said. "Last night in the rain. It was good shooting weather. The trouble is, he wasn't alone when it happened. Either you didn't see that, or you got scared. You ran out. But you had nerve enough to come back and hide the body somewhere – so you could tidy up on the books before the case broke."

The blonde made one strangled sound and then turned her face and stared at the wall. Her silvered fingernails dug into her palms. Her teeth bit her lip tightly.

Marty didn't bat an eye. He didn't move and the Colt didn't move in his hand. His brown face was as hard as a piece of carved wood.

"Boy, you take chances," he said softly, at last. "It's lucky as all hell for you I didn't kill Steiner."

I grinned at him, without much cheer. "You might step off for it just the same," I said.

Marty's voice was a dry rustle of sound. "Think you've got me framed for it?"

"Positive."

"How come?"

"There's somebody who'll tell it that way."

Marty swore then. "That – damned little ——— ! She would – just that – damn her!"

I didn't say anything. I let him chew on it. His face cleared slowly, and he put the Colt down on the table, kept his hand near it.

"You don't sound like chisel as I know chisel," he said slowly, his eyes a tight shine between dark narrowed lids. "And I don't see any coppers here. What's your angle?"

I drew on my cigar and watched his gun hand. "The plate that was in Steiner's camera. All the prints that have been made. Right here and right now. You've got it – because that's the only way you could have known who was there last night."

Marty turned his head slightly to look at Agnes. Her face was still to the wall and her fingernails were still spearing her palms. Marty looked back at me.

"You're cold as a night watchman's feet on that one, guy," he told me.

I shook my head. "No. You're a sap to stall, Marty. You can be pegged for the kill easy. It's a natural. If the girl has to tell her story, the pictures won't matter. But she don't want to tell it."

"You a shamus?" he asked.

"Yeah."

"How'd you get to me?"

"I was working on Steiner. He's been working on Dravec. Dravec leaks money. You had some of it. I tailed the books here from Steiner's store. The rest was easy when I had the girl's story."

"She say I gunned Steiner?"

I nodded. "But she could be mistaken."

Marty sighed. "She hates my guts," he said. "I gave her the gate. I got paid to do it, but I'd have done it anyway. She's too screwy for me."

I said: "Get the pictures, Marty."

He stood up slowly, looked down at the Colt, put it in his side pocket. His hand moved slowly up to his breast pocket.

Somebody rang the door buzzer and kept on ringing it.

11

MARTY DIDN'T LIKE that. His lower lip went in under his teeth and his eyebrows drew down at the corners. His whole face got mean.

The buzzer kept on buzzing.

The blonde stood up quickly. Nerve tension made her face old and ugly.

Watching me, Marty jerked a small drawer open in the tall desk and got a small, white-handled automatic out of it. He held it out to the blonde. She went to him and took it gingerly, not liking it.

"Sit down next to the shamus," he rasped. "Hold the gun on him. If he gets funny, feed him a few."

The blonde sat down on the davenport about three feet from me, on the side away from the door. She lined the gun on my leg. I didn't like the jerky look in her green eyes.

The door buzzer stopped and somebody started a quick, light, impatient rapping on the panel. Marty went across and opened the door. He slid his right hand into his coat pocket and opened the door with his left hand, threw it open quickly.

Carmen Dravec pushed him back into the room with the muzzle of a small revolver against his brown face.

Marty backed away from her smoothly, lightly. His mouth was open and an expression of panic was on his face. He knew Carmen pretty well.

Carmen shut the door, then bored ahead with her little gun. She didn't look at anyone but Marty, didn't seem to see anything but Marty. Her face had a dopey look.

The blonde shivered the full length of her body and swung the white-handled automatic up and towards Carmen. I shot my hand out and grabbed her hand, closed my fingers down over it quickly, thumbed the safety to the on position, and held it there. There was a short tussle, which neither Marty nor Carmen paid any attention to. Then I had the gun.

The blonde breathed deeply and stared at Carmen Dravec. Carmen looked at Marty with doped eyes and said: "I want my pictures."

Marty swallowed and tried to smile at her. He said: "Sure, kid, sure," in a small, flat voice that wasn't like the voice he had used in talking to me.

Carmen looked almost as crazy as she had looked in Steiner's chair. But she had control of her voice and muscles this time. She said: "You shot Hal Steiner."

"Wait a minute, Carmen!" I yelped.

Carmen didn't turn her head. The blonde came to life with a rush, ducked her head at me as if she was going to butt me, and sank her teeth in my right hand, the one that had her gun in it.

I yelped some more. Nobody minded that either.

Marty said: "Listen, kid, I didn't – "

The blonde took her teeth out of my hand and spat my own blood at me. Then she threw herself at my leg and tried to bite that. I cracked her lightly on the head with the barrel of the gun and tried to stand up. She rolled down my legs and wrapped her arms around my ankles. I fell back on the davenport again. The blonde was strong with the madness of fear.

Marty grabbed for Carmen's gun with his left hand, missed. The little revolver made a dull, heavy sound that was not loud. A bullet missed Marty and broke glass in one of the folded-back french windows.

Marty stood perfectly still again. He looked as if all his muscles had gone back on him.

"Duck and knock her off her feet, you damn' fool!" I yelled at him.

Then I hit the blonde on the side of the head again, much harder, and she rolled off my feet. I got loose and slid away from her.

Marty and Carmen were still facing each other like a couple of images.

Something very large and heavy hit the outside of the door and the panel split diagonally from top to bottom.

That brought Marty to life. He jerked the Colt out of his pocket and jumped back. I snapped a shot at his right shoulder and missed, not wanting to hurt him much. The heavy thing hit the door again with a crash that seemed to shake the whole building.

I dropped the little automatic and got my own gun loose as Dravec came in with the smashed door.

He was wild-eyed, raging drunk, berserk. His big arms were flailing. His eyes were glaring and bloodshot and there was froth on his lips.

He hit me very hard on the side of the head without even looking at me. I fell against the wall, between the end of the davenport and the broken door.

I was shaking my head and trying to get level again when Marty began to shoot.

Something lifted Dravec's coat away from his body behind, as if a slug had gone clean through him. He stumbled, straightened immediately, charged like a bull.

I lined my gun and shot Marty through the body. It shook him, but the Colt in his hand continued to leap and roar. Then Dravec was between us and Carmen was knocked out of the way like a dead leaf and there was nothing more that anybody could do about it.

Marty's bullets couldn't stop Dravec. Nothing could. If he had been dead, he would still have got Marty.

He got him by the throat as Marty threw his empty gun in the big man's face. It bounced off like a rubber ball. Marty yelled shrilly, and Dravec took him by the throat and lifted him clean off his feet.

For an instant Marty's brown hands fought for a hold on the big man's wrists. Something cracked sharply, and Marty's hands fell away limply. There was another, duller crack. Just before Dravec let go of Marty's neck I saw that Marty's face was a purple-black color. I remembered, almost casually, that men whose necks are broken sometimes swallow their tongues before they die.

Then Marty fell down in the corner and Dravec started to back away from him. He backed like a man losing his balance, not able to keep his feet under his center of gravity. He took four clumsy backward steps like that. Then his big body tipped over backwards and he fell on his back on the floor with his arms flung out wide.

Blood came out of his mouth. His eyes strained upwards as if to see through a fog.

Carmen Dravec went down beside him and began to wail like a frightened animal.

There was noise outside in the hall, but nobody showed at the open door. Too much casual lead had been flipped around.

I went quickly over to Marty and leaned over him and got my hand into his breast pocket. I got out a thick, square envelope that had something stiff and hard in it. I straightened up with it and turned.

Far off the wail of a siren sounded faintly on the evening air, seemed to be getting louder. A white-faced man peeped cautiously in through the doorway. I knelt down beside Dravec.

He tried to say something, but I couldn't hear the words. Then the strained look went out of his eyes and they were aloof and indifferent like the eyes of a man looking at something a long way off, across a wide plain.

Carmen said stonily: "He was drunk. He made me tell him where I was going. I didn't know he followed me."

"You wouldn't," I said emptily.

I stood up again and broke the envelope open. There were a few prints in it and a glass negative. I dropped the plate on the floor and ground it to pieces with my heel.

I began to tear up the prints and let the pieces flutter down out of my hands.

"They'll print plenty of photos of you now, girlie," I said. "But they won't print this one."

"I didn't know he was following me," she said again, and began to chew on her thumb.

The siren was loud outside the building now. It died to a penetrating drone and then stopped altogether, just about the time I finished tearing up the prints.

I stood still in the middle of the room and wondered why I had taken the trouble. It didn't matter any more now.

12

LEANING HIS ELBOW on the end of the big walnut table in Inspector Isham's office, and holding a burning cigarette idly between his fingers, Guy Slade said, without looking at me:

"Thanks for putting me on the pan, shamus. I like to see the boys at Headquarters once in a while." He crinkled the corners of his eyes in an unpleasant smile.

I was sitting at the long side of the table across from Isham. Isham was lanky and gray and wore nose glasses. He didn't look, act or talk copper. Violets M'Gee and a merry-eyed Irish dick named Grinnell were in a couple of round-backed chairs against a glass-topped partition wall that cut part of the office off into a reception room.

I said to Slade: "I figured you found that blood a little too soon. I guess I was wrong. My apologies, Mr. Slade."

"Yeah. That makes it just like it never happened." He stood up, picked a malacca cane and one glove off the table. "That all for me, Inspector?"

"That's all tonight, Slade." Isham's voice was dry, cool, sardonic.

Slade caught the crook of his cane over his wrist to open the door. He smiled around before he strolled out. The last thing his eyes rested on was probably the back of my neck, but I wasn't looking at him.

Isham said: "I don't have to tell you how a police department looks at that kind of a cover-up on a murder."

I sighed. "Gunfire," I said. "A dead man on the floor. A naked, doped girl in a chair not knowing what had happened. A killer I couldn't have caught and you couldn't have caught – then. Behind all this a poor old roughneck that was breaking his heart trying to do the right thing in a miserable spot. Go ahead – stick it into me. I'm not sorry."

Isham waved all that aside. "Who did kill Steiner?"

"The blonde girl will tell you."

"I want you to tell me."

I shrugged. "If you want me to guess – Dravec's driver, Carl Owen."

Isham didn't look too surprised. Violets M'Gee grunted loudly.

"What makes you think so?" Isham asked.

"I thought for a while it could be Marty, partly because the girl said so. But that doesn't mean anything. She didn't know, and jumped at the chance to stick a knife into Marty. And she's a type that doesn't let loose of an idea very easily. But Marty didn't act like a killer. And a man as cool as Marty wouldn't have run out that way. I hadn't even banged on the door when the killer started to scram.

"Of course I thought of Slade, too. But Slade's not quite the type either. He packs two gunmen around with him, and they'd have made some kind of a fight of it. And Slade seemed genuinely surprised when he found the blood on the floor this afternoon. Slade was in with Steiner and keeping tabs on him, but he didn't kill him, didn't have any reason to kill him, and wouldn't have killed him that way, in front of a witness, if he had a reason.

"But Carl Owen would. He was in love with the girl once, probably never got over it. He had chances to spy on her, find out where she went and what she did. He lay for Steiner, got in the back way, saw the nude photo stunt and blew his top. He let Steiner have it. Then the panic got him and he just ran."

"Ran all the way to Lido pier, and then off the end of that," Isham said dryly. "Aren't you forgetting that the Owen boy had a sap wound on the side of his head?"

I said: "No. And I'm not forgetting that somehow or other Marty knew what was on that camera plate – or nearly enough to make him go in and get it and then hide a body in Steiner's garage to give him room."

Isham said: "Get Agnes Laurel in here, Grinnell."

Grinnell heaved up out of his chair and strolled the length of the office, disappeared through a door.

Violets M'Gee said: "Baby, are you a pal!"

I didn't look at him. Isham pulled the loose skin in front of his Adam's apple and looked down at the fingernails of his other hand.

Grinnell came back with the blonde. Her hair was untidy above the collar of her coat. She had taken the jet buttons out of her ears. She looked tired but she didn't look scared any more. She let herself down slowly into the chair at the end of the table where Slade had sat, folded her hands with the silvered nails in front of her.

Isham said quietly: "All right, Miss Laurel. We'd like to hear from you now."

The girl looked down at her folded hands and talked without hesitation, in a quiet, even voice.

"I've known Joe Marty about three months. He made friends with me because I was working for Steiner, I guess. I thought it was because he liked me. I told him all I knew about Steiner. He already knew a little. He had been spending money he had got from Carmen Dravec's father, but it was gone and he was down to nickels and dimes, ready for something else. He decided Steiner needed a partner and he was watching him to see if he had any tough friends in the background.

"Last night he was in his car down on the street back of Steiner's house. He heard the shots, saw the kid tear down the steps, jump into a big sedan and take it on the lam. Joe chased him. Halfway to the beach, he caught him and ran him off the road. The kid came up with a gun, but his nerve was bad and Joe sapped him down. While he was out Joe went through him and found out who he was. When he came around Joe played copper and the kid broke and gave him the story. While Joe was wondering what to do about it the kid came to life and knocked him off the car and scrammed again. He drove like a crazy guy and Joe let him go. He went back to Steiner's house. I guess you know the rest. When Joe had the plate developed and saw what he had he went for a quick touch so we could get out of town before the law found Steiner. We were going to take some of Steiner's books and set up shop in another city."

Agnes Laurel stopped talking. Isham tapped with his fingers, said: "Marty told you everything, didn't he?"

"Uh-huh."

"Sure he didn't murder this Carl Owen?"

"I wasn't there. Joe didn't act like he'd killed anybody."

Isham nodded. "That's all for now, Miss Laurel. We'll want all that in writing. We'll have to hold you, of course."

The girl stood up. Grinnell took her out. She went out without looking at anyone.

Isham said: "Marty couldn't have known Carl Owen was dead. But he was sure he'd try to hide out. By the time we got to him Marty would have collected from Dravec and moved on. I think the girl's story sounds reasonable."

Nobody said anything. After a moment Isham said to me: "You made one bad mistake. You shouldn't have mentioned Marty to the girl until you were sure he was your man. That got two people killed quite unnecessarily."

I said: "Uh-huh. Maybe I better go back and do it over again."

"Don't get tough."

"I'm not tough. I was working for Dravec and trying to save him from a little heartbreak. I didn't know the girl was as screwy as all that, or that Dravec would have a brainstorm. I wanted the pictures. I didn't care a lot about trash like Steiner or Joe Marty and his girl friend, and still don't."

"Okay. Okay," Isham said impatiently. "I don't need you any more tonight. You'll probably be panned plenty at the inquest."

He stood up and I stood up. He held out his hand.

"But that will do you a hell of a lot more good than harm," he added dryly.

I shook hands with him and went out. M'Gee came out after me. We rode down in the elevator together without speaking to each other. When we got outside the building M'Gee went around to the right side of my Chrysler and got into it.

"Got any liquor at your dump?"

"Plenty," I said.

"Let's go get some of it."

I started the car and drove west along First Street, through a long echoing tunnel. When we were out of that, M'Gee said: "Next time I send you a client I won't expect you to snitch on him, boy."

We went on through the quiet evening to the Berglund. I felt tired and old and not much use to anybody.

NEVADA GAS

1

HUGO CANDLESS STOOD in the middle of the squash court bending his big body at the waist, holding the little black ball delicately between left thumb and forefinger. He dropped it near the service line and flicked at it with the long-handled racket.

The black ball hit the front wall a little less than halfway up, floated back in a high, lazy curve, skimmed just below the white ceiling and the lights behind wire protectors. It slid languidly down the back wall, never touching it enough to bounce out.

George Dial made a careless swing at it, whanged the end of his racket against the cement back wall. The ball fell dead.

He said: "That's the story, chief. 12–14. You're just too good for me."

George Dial was tall, dark, handsome, Hollywoodish. He was brown and lean, and had a hard, outdoor look. Everything about him was hard except his full, soft lips and his large, cow-like eyes.

"Yeah. I always was too good for you," Hugo Candless chortled.

He leaned far back from his thick waist and laughed with his mouth wide open. Sweat glistened on his chest and belly. He was naked except for blue shorts, white wool socks and heavy sneakers with crêpe soles. He had gray hair and a broad moon face with a small nose and mouth, sharp twinkly eyes.

"Want another lickin'?" he asked.

"Not unless I have to."

Hugo Candless scowled. "Okay," he said shortly. He stuck his racket under his arm and got an oilskin pouch out of his shorts, took a cigarette and a match from it. He lit the cigarette with a flourish and threw the match into the middle of the court, where somebody else would have to pick it up.

He threw the door of the squash court open and paraded down the corridor to the locker room with his chest out. Dial walked behind him silently; catlike, soft-footed, with a lithe grace. They went to the showers.

Candless sang in the showers, covered his big body with thick suds, showered dead-cold after the hot, and liked it. He rubbed himself dry with immense leisure, took another towel and stalked out of the shower room yelling for the attendant to bring ice and ginger ale.

A Negro in a stiff white coat came hurrying with a tray. Candless signed the check with a flourish, unlocked his big double locker and planked a bottle of Johnny Walker on the round green table that stood in the locker aisle.

The attendant mixed drinks carefully, two of them, said: "Yes, suh, Mista Candless," and went away palming a quarter.

George Dial, already fully dressed in smart gray flannels, came around the corner and lifted one of the drinks.

"Through for the day, chief?" He looked at the ceiling light through his drink, with tight eyes.

"Guess so," Candless said largely. "Guess I'll go home and give the little woman a treat." He gave Dial a swift, sidewise glance from his little eyes.

"Mind if I don't ride home with you?" Dial asked carelessly.

"With me it's okay. It's tough on Naomi," Candless said unpleasantly.

Dial made a soft sound with his lips, shrugged, said: "You like to burn people up, don't you chief?"

Candless didn't answer, didn't look at him. Dial stood silent with his drink and watched the big man put on monogrammed satin underclothes, purple socks with gray clocks, a monogrammed silk shirt, a suit of tiny black and white checks that made him look as big as a barn.

By the time he got to his purple tie he was yelling for the Negro to come and mix another drink.

Dial refused the second drink, nodded, went away softly along the matting between the tall green lockers.

Candless finished dressing, drank his second highball, locked his liquor away and put a fat brown cigar in his mouth. He had the Negro light the cigar for him. He went off with a strut and several loud greetings here and there.

It seemed very quiet in the locker room after he went out. There were a few snickers.

★

It was raining outside the Delmar Club. The liveried doorman helped Hugo Candless on with his belted white slicker and went out for his car. When he had it in front of the canopy he held an umbrella over Hugo across the strip of wooden matting to the curb. The car was a royal blue Lincoln limousine, with buff striping. The license number was 5A6.

The chauffeur, in a black slicker turned up high around his ears, didn't look around. The doorman opened the door and Hugo Candless got in and sank heavily on the back seat.

" 'Night, Sam. Tell him to go on home."

The doorman touched his cap, shut the door, and relayed the orders to the driver, who nodded without turning his head. The car moved off in the rain.

The rain came down slantingly and at the intersection sudden gusts blew it rattling against the glass of the limousine. The street corners were clotted with people trying to get across Sunset without being splashed. Hugo Candless grinned out at them, pityingly.

The car went out Sunset, through Sherman, then swung towards the hills. It began to go very fast. It was on a boulevard where traffic was thin now.

It was very hot in the car. The windows were all shut and the glass partition behind the driver's seat was shut all the way across. The smoke of Hugo's cigar was heavy and choking in the tonneau of the limousine.

Candless scowled and reached out to lower a window. The window lever didn't work. He tried the other side. That didn't work either. He began to get mad. He grabbed for the little telephone dingus to bawl his driver out. There wasn't any little telephone dingus.

The car turned sharply and began to go up a long straight hill with eucalyptus trees on one side and no houses. Candless felt something cold touch his spine, all the way up and down his spine. He bent forward and banged on the glass with his fist. The driver didn't turn his head. The car went very fast up the long dark hill road.

Hugo Candless grabbed viciously for the door handle. The doors didn't have any handles – either side. A sick, incredulous grin broke over Hugo's broad moon face.

The driver bent over to the right and reached for something with his gloved hand. There was a sudden sharp hissing noise. Hugo Candless began to smell the odor of almonds.

Very faint at first – very faint, and rather pleasant. The hissing noise went on. The smell of almonds got bitter and harsh and very deadly. Hugo Candless dropped his cigar and banged with all his strength on the glass of the nearest window. The glass didn't break.

The car was up in the hills now, beyond even the infrequent street lights of the residential sections.

Candless dropped back on the seat and lifted his foot to kick hard at the glass partition in front of him. The kick was never finished. His eyes no longer saw. His face twisted into a snarl and his head went back against the cushions, crushed down against his thick shoulders. His soft white felt hat was shapeless on his big square skull.

The driver looked back quickly, showing a lean, hawklike face for a brief instant. Then he bent to his right again and the hissing noise stopped.

He pulled over to the side of the deserted road, stopped the car, switched off all the lights. The rain made a dull noise pounding on the roof.

The driver got out in the rain and opened the rear door of the car, then backed away from it quickly, holding his nose.

He stood a little way off for a while and looked up and down the road.

In the back of the limousine Hugo Candless didn't move.

2

FRANCINE LEY SAT in a low red chair beside a small table on which there was an alabaster bowl. Smoke from the cigarette she had just discarded into the bowl floated up and made patterns in the still, warm air. Her hands were clasped behind her head and her smoke-blue eyes were lazy, inviting. She had dark auburn hair set in loose waves. There were bluish shadows in the troughs of the waves.

George Dial leaned over and kissed her on the lips, hard. His own lips were hot when he kissed her, and he shivered. The girl didn't move. She smiled up at him lazily when he straightened again.

In a thick, clogged voice Dial said: "Listen, Francy. When do you ditch this gambler and let me set you up?"

Francine Ley shrugged, without taking her hands from behind her head. "He's a square gambler, George," she drawled. "That's something nowadays and you don't have enough money."

"I can get it."

"How?" Her voice was low and husky. It moved George Dial like a cello.

"From Candless. I've got plenty on that bird."

"As for instance?" Francine Ley suggested lazily.

Dial grinned softly down at her. He widened his eyes in a deliberately innocent expression. Francine Ley thought the whites of his eyes were tinged ever so faintly with some color that was not white.

Dial flourished an unlighted cigarette. "Plenty – like he sold out a tough boy from Reno last year. The tough boy's half-brother was under a murder rap here and Candless took twenty-five grand to get him off. He made a deal with the D.A. on another case and let the tough boy's brother go up."

"And what did the tough boy do about all that?" Francine Ley asked gently.

"Nothing – yet. He thinks it was on the up and up, I guess. You can't always win."

"But he might do plenty, if he knew," Francine Ley said, nodding. "Who was the tough boy, Georgie?"

Dial lowered his voice and leaned down over her again. "I'm a sap to tell you that. A man named Zapparty. I've never met him."

"And never want to – if you've got sense, Georgie. No, thanks. I'm not walking myself into any jam like that with you."

Dial smiled lightly, showing even teeth in a dark, smooth face. "Leave it to me, Francy. Just forget the whole thing except how I'm nuts about you."

"Buy us a drink," the girl said.

The room was a living-room in a hotel apartment. It was all red and white, with embassy decorations, too stiff. The white walls had red designs painted on them, the white venetian blinds were framed in white box drapes, there was a half-round red rug with a white border in front of the gas fire. There was a kidney-shaped white desk against one wall, between the windows.

Dial went over to the desk and poured Scotch into two glasses, added ice and charged water, carried the glasses back across the room to where a thin wisp of smoke still plumed upward from the alabaster bowl.

"Ditch the gambler," Dial said, handing her a glass. "He's the one will get you in a jam."

She sipped the drink, nodded. Dial took the glass out of her hand, sipped from the same place on the rim, leaned over holding both glasses and kissed her on the lips again.

There were red curtains over a door to a short hallway. They were parted a few inches and a man's face appeared in the opening, cool gray eyes stared in thoughtfully at the kiss. The curtains fell together again without sound.

After a moment a door shut loudly and steps came along the hallway. Johnny De Ruse came through the curtains into the room. By that time Dial was lighting his cigarette.

Johnny De Ruse was tall, lean, quiet, dressed in dark clothes dashingly cut. His cool gray eyes had fine laughter wrinkles at the corners. His thin mouth was delicate but not soft, and his long chin had a cleft in it.

Dial stared at him, made a vague motion with his hand. De Ruse walked over to the desk without speaking, poured some whiskey into a glass and drank it straight.

He stood a moment with his back to the room, tapping on the edge of the desk. Then he turned around, smiled faintly, said: " 'Lo, people," in a gentle, rather drawling voice and went out of the room through an inner door.

He was in a big overdecorated bedroom with twin beds. He went to a closet and got a tan calfskin suitcase out of it, opened it on the nearest bed. He began to rob the drawers of a highboy and put things in the suitcase, arranging them carefully, without haste. He whistled quietly through his teeth while he was doing it.

When the suitcase was packed he snapped it shut and lit a cigarette. He stood for a moment in the middle of the room without moving. His gray eyes looked at the wall without seeing it.

After a little while he went back into the closet and came out with a small gun in a soft leather harness with two short straps. He pulled up the left leg of his trousers and strapped the holster on his leg. Then he picked up the suitcase and went back to the living-room.

Francine Ley's eyes narrowed swiftly when she saw the suitcase.

"Going some place?" she asked in her low, husky voice.

"Uh-huh. Where's Dial?"

"He had to leave."

"That's too bad," De Ruse said softly. He put the suitcase down on the floor and stood beside it, moving his cool gray eyes over the girl's face, up and down her slim body, from her ankles to her auburn head. "That's too bad," he said. "I like to see him around. I'm kind of dull for you."

"Maybe you are, Johnny."

He bent to the suitcase, but straightened without touching it and said casually: "Remember Mops Parisi? I saw him in town today."

Her eyes widened and then almost shut. Her teeth clicked lightly. The line of her jawbone stood out very distinctly for a moment.

De Ruse kept moving his glance up and down her face and body.

"Going to do anything about it?" she asked.

"I thought of taking a trip," De Ruse said. "I'm not so scrappy as I was once."

"A powder," Francine Ley said softly. "Where do we go?"

"Not a powder – a trip," De Ruse said tonelessly. "And not we – *me*. I'm going alone."

She sat still, watching his face, not moving a muscle.

De Ruse reached inside his coat and got out a long wallet that opened like a book. He tossed a tight sheaf of bills into the girl's lap, put the wallet away. She didn't touch the bills.

"That'll hold you for longer than you'll need to find a new playmate," he said, without expression. "I wouldn't say I won't send you more, if you need it."

She stood up slowly and the sheaf of bills slid down her skirt to the floor. She held her arms straight down at the sides, the hands clenched so that the tendons on the backs of them were sharp. Her eyes were as dull as slate.

"That means we're through, Johnny?"

He lifted his suitcase. She stepped in front of him swiftly, with two long steps. She put a hand against his coat. He stood quite still, smiling gently with his eyes, but not with his lips. The perfume of Shalimar twitched at his nostrils.

"You know what you are, Johnny?" Her husky voice was almost a lisp.

He waited.

"A pigeon, Johnny. A pigeon."

He nodded slightly. "Check. I called copper on Mops Parisi. I don't like the snatch racket, baby. I'd call copper on it any day. I might even get myself hurt blocking it. That's old stuff. Through?"

"You called copper on Mops Parisi and you don't think he knows it, but maybe he does. So you're running away from him . . . That's a laugh, Johnny. I'm kidding you. That's not why you're leaving me."

"Maybe I'm just tired of you, baby."

She put her head back and laughed sharply, almost with a wild note. De Ruse didn't budge.

"You're not a tough boy, Johnny. You're soft. George Dial is harder than you are. Gawd, how soft you are, Johnny!"

She stepped back, staring at his face. Some flicker of almost unbearable emotion came and went in her eyes.

"You're such a handsome pup, Johnny. Gawd, but you're handsome. It's too bad you're soft."

De Ruse said gently, without moving: "Not soft, baby — just a bit sentimental. I like to clock the ponies and play seven-card stud and mess around with little red cubes with white spots on them. I like games of chance, including women. But when I lose I don't get sore and I don't chisel. I just move on to the next table. Be seein' you."

He stooped, hefted the suitcase, and walked around her. He went across the room and through the red curtains without looking back.

Francine Ley stared with stiff eyes at the floor.

3

STANDING UNDER THE scalloped glass canopy of the side entrance to the Chatterton, De Ruse looked up and down Irolo, towards the flashing lights of Wilshire and towards the dark quiet end of the side street.

The rain fell softly, slantingly. A light drop blew in under the canopy and hit the red end of his cigarette with a sputter. He hefted the suitcase and went along Irolo towards his sedan. It was parked almost at the next corner, a shiny black Packard with a little discreet chromium here and there.

He stopped and opened the door and a gun came up swiftly from inside the car. The gun prodded against his chest. A voice said sharply: "Hold it! The mitts high, sweets!"

De Ruse saw the man dimly inside the car. A lean hawk-like face on which some reflected light fell without making it distinct. He felt a gun hard against his chest, hurting his breast-bone. Quick steps came up behind him and another gun prodded his back.

"Satisfied?" another voice inquired.

De Ruse dropped the suitcase, lifted his hands and put them against the top of the car.

"Okay," he said wearily. "What is it – a heist?"

A snarling laugh came from the man in the car. A hand smacked De Ruse's hips from behind.

"Back up – slow!"

De Ruse backed up, holding his hands very high in the air.

"Not so high, punk," the man behind said dangerously. "Just shoulder high."

De Ruse lowered them. The man in the car got out, straightened. He put his gun against De Ruse's chest again, put out a long arm and unbuttoned De Ruse's overcoat. De Ruse leaned backwards. The hand belonging to the long arm explored his pockets, his armpits. A .38 in a spring holster ceased to make weight under his arm.

"Got one, Chuck. Anything your side?"

"Nothin' on the hip."

The man in front stepped away and picked up the suitcase.

"March sweets. We'll ride in our heap."

They went farther along Irolo. A big Lincoln limousine loomed up, a blue car with a lighter stripe. The hawk-faced man opened the rear door.

"In."

De Ruse got in listlessly, spitting his cigarette end into the wet darkness, as he stooped under the roof of the car. A faint smell assailed his nose, a smell that might have been overripe peaches or almonds. He got into the car.

"In beside him, Chuck."

"Listen. Let's all ride up front. I can handle – "

"Nix. In beside him, Chuck," the hawk-faced one snapped.

Chuck growled, got into the back seat beside De Ruse. The other man slammed the door hard. His lean face showed through the closed window in a sardonic grin. Then he went around to the driver's seat and started the car, tooled it away from the curb.

DeRuse wrinkled his nose, sniffing at the queer smell.

They spun at the corner, went east on Eighth to Normandie, north on Normandie across Wilshire, across other streets, up over a steep hill and down the other side to Melrose. The big Lincoln slid through the light rain without a whisper. Chuck sat in the corner, held his gun on his knee, scowled. Street lights showed a square, arrogant red face, a face that was not at ease.

The back of the driver's head was motionless beyond the glass partition. They passed Sunset and Hollywood, turned east on Franklin, swung north to Los Feliz and down Los Feliz towards the river bed.

Cars coming up the hill threw sudden brief glares of white light into the interior of the Lincoln. De Ruse tensed, waited. At the next pair of lights that shot squarely into the car he bent over swiftly and jerked up the left leg of his trousers. He was back against the cushions before the blinding light was gone.

Chuck hadn't moved, hadn't noticed movement.

Down at the bottom of the hill, at the intersection of Riverside Drive, a whole phalanx of cars surged towards them as a light changed. De Ruse waited, timed the impact of the headlights. His body stooped briefly, his hand swooped down, snatched the small gun from the leg holster.

He leaned back once more, the gun against the bulk of his left thigh, concealed behind it from where Chuck sat.

The Lincoln shot over on to Riverside and passed the entrance to Griffith Park.

"Where we going, punk?" De Ruse asked casually.

"Save it," Chuck snarled. "You'll find out."

"Not a stick-up, huh?"

"Save it," Chuck snarled again.

"Mops Parisi's boys?" De Ruse asked thinly, slowly.

The red-faced gunman jerked, lifted the gun off his knee. "I said – save it!"

De Ruse said: "Sorry, punk."

He turned the gun over his thigh, lined it swiftly, squeezed the trigger left-handed. The gun made a small flat sound – almost an unimportant sound.

Chuck yelled and his hand jerked wildly. The gun kicked out of it and fell on the floor of the car. His left hand raced for his right shoulder.

De Ruse shifted the little Mauser to his right hand and put it deep into Chuck's side.

"Steady, boy, steady. Keep your hands out of trouble. Now – kick that cannon over this way – fast!"

Chuck kicked the big automatic along the floor of the car. De Ruse reached down for it swiftly, got it. The lean-faced driver jerked a look back and the car swerved, then straightened again.

De Ruse hefted the big gun. The Mauser was too light for a sap. He slammed Chuck hard on the side of the head. Chuck groaned, sagged forward, clawing.

"The gas!" he bleated. "The gas! He'll turn on the gas!"

De Ruse hit him again, harder. Chuck was a tumbled heap on the floor of the car.

The Lincoln swung off Riverside, over a short bridge and a bridle path, down a narrow dirt road that split a golf course. It went into darkness and among trees. It went fast, rocketed from side to side, as if the driver wanted it to do just that.

De Ruse steadied himself, felt for the door handle. There wasn't any door handle. His lips curled and he smashed at a window with the gun. The heavy glass was like a wall of stone.

The hawk-faced man leaned over and there was a hissing sound. Then there was a sudden sharp increase of intensity of the smell of almonds.

De Ruse tore a handkerchief out of his pocket and pressed it to his nose. The driver had straightened again now and was driving hunched over, trying to keep his head down.

De Ruse held the muzzle of the big gun close to the glass partition behind the driver's head, who ducked sidewise. He squeezed lead four times quickly, shutting his eyes and turning his head away, like a nervous woman.

No glass flew. When he looked again there was a jagged round hole in the glass and the windshield in a line with it was starred but not broken.

He slammed the gun at the edges of the hole and managed to knock a piece of glass loose. He was getting the gas now, through the handkerchief. His head felt like a balloon. His vision waved and wandered.

The hawk-faced driver, crouched, wrenched the door open at his side, swung the wheel of the car the opposite way and jumped clear.

The car tore over a low embankment, looped a little and smacked sidewise against a tree. The body twisted enough for one of the rear doors to spring open.

De Ruse went through the door in a headlong dive. Soft earth smacked him, knocked some of the wind out of him. Then his lungs breathed clean air. He rolled up on his stomach and elbows, kept his head down, his gun hand up.

The hawk-faced man was on his knees a dozen yards away. De Ruse watched him drag a gun out of his pocket and lift it.

Chuck's gun pulsed and roared in De Ruse's hand until it was empty.

The hawk-faced man folded down slowly and his body merged with the dark shadows and the wet ground. Cars went by distantly on Riverside Drive. Rain dripped off the trees. The Griffith Park beacon turned in the thick sky. The rest was darkness and silence.

De Ruse took a deep breath and got up on his feet. He dropped the empty gun, took a small flash out of his overcoat pocket and pulled his overcoat up against his nose and mouth, pressing the thick cloth hard against his face. He went to the car, switched off the lights and threw the beam of the flash into the driver's compartment. He leaned in quickly and turned a petcock on a copper cylinder like a fire extinguisher. The hissing noise of the gas stopped.

He went over to the hawk-faced man. He was dead. There was some loose money, currency and silver in his pockets, cigarettes, a folder of matches from the Club Egypt, no wallet, a couple of extra clips of cartridges, De Ruse's .38. De Ruse put the last back where it belonged and straightened from the sprawled body.

He looked across the darkness of the Los Angeles river bed towards the lights of Glendale. In the middle distance a green neon sign far from any other light winked on and off: Club Egypt.

De Ruse smiled quietly to himself, and went back to the Lincoln. He dragged Chuck's body out onto the wet ground. Chuck's red face was blue now, under the beam of the small flash. His open eyes held an empty stare. His chest didn't move. De Ruse put the flash down and went through some more pockets.

He found the usual things a man carries, including a wallet showing a driver's license issued to Charles Le Grand, Hotel Metropole, Los Angeles. He found more Club Egypt matches and a tabbed hotel key marked 809, Hotel Metropole.

He put the key in his pocket, slammed the sprung door of the Lincoln, got in under the wheel. The motor caught. He backed the car away from the tree with a wrench of broken fender metal, swung it around slowly over the soft earth and got it back again on the road.

When he reached Riverside again he turned the lights on and drove back to Hollywood. He put the car under some pepper trees in front of a big brick apartment house on Kenmore half a block north of Hollywood Boulevard, locked the ignition and lifted out his suitcase.

Light from the entrance of the apartment house rested on the front license plate as he walked away. He wondered why gunmen would use a car with plate numbers reading 5A6, almost a privilege number.

In a drugstore he phoned for a taxi. The taxi took him back to the Chatterton.

4

THE APARTMENT WAS empty. The smell of Shalimar and cigarette smoke lingered on the warm air, as if someone had been there not long before. De Ruse pushed into the bedroom, looked at clothes in two closets, articles on a dresser, then went back to the red and white living room and mixed himself a stiff highball.

He put the night latch on the outside door and carried his drink into the bedroom, stripped off his muddy clothes and put on another suit of somber material but dandified cut. He sipped his drink while he knotted a black four-in-hand in the opening of a soft white linen shirt.

He swabbed the barrel of the little Mauser, reassembled it, and added a shell to the small clip, slipped the gun back into the leg holster. Then he washed his hands and took his drink to the telephone.

The first number he called was the *Chronicle*. He asked for the City Room, Werner.

A drawly voice dripped over the wire: "Werner talkin'. Go ahead. Kid me."

De Ruse said: "This is John De Ruse, Claude. Look up California License 5A6 on your list for me."

"Must be a bloody politician," the drawly voice said, and went away.

De Ruse sat motionless, looking at a fluted white pillar in the corner. It had a red and white bowl of red and white artificial roses on top of it. He wrinkled his nose at it disgustedly.

Werner's voice came back on the wire: "1930 Lincoln limousine registered to Hugo Candless, Casa de Oro Apartments, 2942 Clearwater Street, West Hollywood."

De Ruse said in a tone that meant nothing: "That's the mouthpiece, isn't it?"

"Yeah. The big lip. Mister Take the Witness." Werner's voice came down lower. "Speaking to you, Johnny, and not for publication – a big crooked tub of guts that's not even smart; just been around long enough to know who's for sale . . . Story in it?"

"Hell, no," De Ruse said softly. "He just sideswiped me and didn't stop."

He hung up and finished his drink, stood up to mix another. Then he swept a telephone directory onto the white desk and looked up the number of the Casa de Oro. He dialed it. A switchboard operator told him Mr. Hugo Candless was out of town.

"Give me his apartment," De Ruse said.

A woman's cool voice answered the phone. "Yes. This is Mrs. Hugo Candless speaking. What is it, please?"

De Ruse said: "I'm a client of Mr. Candless, very anxious to get hold of him. Can you help me?"

"I'm very sorry," the cool, almost lazy voice told him. "My husband was called out of town quite suddenly. I don't even know where he went, though I expect to hear from him later this evening. He left his club – "

"What club was that?" De Ruse asked casually.

"The Delmar Club. I say he left there without coming home. If there is any message – "

De Ruse said: "Thank you, Mrs. Candless. Perhaps I may call you again later."

He hung up, smiled slowly and grimly, sipped his fresh drink and looked up the number of the Hotel Metropole. He called it and asked for "Mister Charles Le Grand in Room 809."

"Six-o-nine," the operator said casually. "I'll connect you." A moment later: "There is no answer."

De Ruse thanked her, took the tabbed key out of his pocket, looked at the number on it. The number was 809.

5

SAM, THE DOORMAN at the Delmar Club, leaned against the buff stone of the entrance and watched the traffic swish by on

Sunset Boulevard. The headlights hurt his eyes. He was tired and he wanted to go home. He wanted a smoke and a big slug of gin. He wished the rain would stop. It was dead inside the club when it rained.

He straightened away from the wall and walked the length of the sidewalk canopy a couple of times, slapping together his big black hands in big white gloves. He tried to whistle the "Skaters Waltz," couldn't get within a block of the tune, whistled "Low Down Lady" instead. That didn't have any tune.

De Ruse came around the corner from Hudson Street and stood beside him near the wall.

"Hugo Candless inside?" he asked, not looking at Sam.

Sam clicked his teeth disapprovingly. "He ain't."

"Been in?"

"Ask at the desk'side, please, mistah."

De Ruse took gloved hands out of his pocket and began to roll a five-dollar bill around his left forefinger.

"What do they know that you don't know?"

Sam grinned slowly, watched the bill being wound tightly around the gloved finger.

"That's a fac', boss. Yeah — he was in. Comes most every day."

"What time he leave?"

"He leave 'bout six-thirty, Ah reckon."

"Drive his blue Lincoln limousine?"

"Shuah. Only he don't drive it hisself. What for you ask?"

"It was raining then," De Ruse said calmly. "Raining pretty hard. Maybe it wasn't the Lincoln."

" 'Twas, too, the Lincoln," Sam protested. "Ain't I tucked him in? He never rides nothin' else."

"License 5A6?" De Ruse bored on relentlessly.

"That's it," Sam chortled. "Just like a councilman's number that number is."

"Know the driver?"

"Shuah — " Sam began, and then stopped cold. He raked a black jaw with a white finger the size of a banana. "Well, Ah'll be a big black slob if he ain't got hisself a new driver again. I ain't *know* that man, sure'nough."

De Ruse poked the rolled bill into Sam's big white paw. Sam grabbed it but his large eyes suddenly got suspicious.

"Say, for what you ask all of them questions, mistah man?"

De Ruse said: "I paid my way, didn't I?"

He went back around the corner to Hudson and got into his black Packard sedan. He drove it out on to Sunset, then west on Sunset almost to Beverly Hills, then turned towards the foothills and began to peer at the signs on street corners. Clearwater Street ran along the flank of a hill and had a view of the entire city. The Casa de Oro, at the corner of Parkinson, was a tricky block of high-class bungalow apartments surrounded by an adobe wall with red tiles on top. It had a lobby in a separate building, a big private garage on Parkinson, opposite one length of the wall.

De Ruse parked across the street from the garage and sat looking through the wide window into a glassed-in office where an attendant in spotless white coveralls sat with his feet on the desk, reading a magazine and spit over his shoulder at an invisible cuspidor.

De Ruse got out of the Packard, crossed the street farther up, came back and slipped into the garage without the attendant seeing him.

The cars were in four rows. Two rows backed against the white walls, two against each other in the middle. There were plenty of vacant stalls, but plenty of cars had gone to bed also. They were mostly big, expensive closed models, with two or three flashy open jobs.

There was only one limousine. It had License No. 5A6.

It was a well-kept car, bright and shiny; royal blue with a buff trimming. De Ruse took a glove off and rested his hand on the radiator shell. Quite cold. He felt the tires, looked at his fingers. A little fine dry dust adhered to the skin. There was no mud in the treads, just bone-dry dust.

He went back along the row of dark car bodies and leaned in the open door of the little office. After a moment the attendant looked up, almost with a start.

"Seen the Candless chauffeur around?" De Ruse asked him.

The man shook his head and spit deftly into a copper spittoon.

"Not since I came on – three o'clock."

"Didn't he go down to the club for the old man?"

"Nope, I guess not. The big hack ain't been out. He always takes that."

"Where does he hang his hat?"

"Who? Mattick? They got servants' quarters in back of the jungle. But I think I heard him say he parks at some hotel. Let's see – " A brow got furrowed.

"The Metropole?" De Ruse suggested.

The garage man thought it over while De Ruse stared at the point of his chin.

"Yeah. I think that's it. I ain't just positive though. Mattick don't open up much."

De Ruse thanked him and crossed the street and got into the Packard again. He drove downtown.

It was twenty-five minutes past nine when he got to the corner of Seventh and Spring, where the Metropole was.

It was an old hotel that had once been exclusive and was now steering a shaky course between a receivership and a bad name at Headquarters. It had too much oily dark wood paneling, too many chipped gilt mirrors. Too much smoke hung below its low beamed lobby ceiling and too many grifters bummed around in its worn leather rockers.

The blonde who looked after the big horseshoe cigar counter wasn't young any more and her eyes were cynical from standing off cheap dates. De Ruse leaned on the glass and pushed his hat back on his crisp black hair.

"Camels, honey," he said in his low-pitched gambler's voice.

The girl smacked the pack in front of him, rang up fifteen cents and slipped the dime change under his elbow, with a faint smile. Her eyes said they liked him. She leaned opposite him and put her head near enough so that he could smell the perfume in her hair.

"Tell me something," De Ruse said.

"What?" she asked softly.

"Find out who lives in eight-o-nine, without telling any answers to the clerk."

The blonde looked disappointed. "Why don't you ask him yourself, mister?"

"I'm too shy," De Ruse said.

"Yes you are!"

She went to her telephone and talked into it with languid grace, came back to De Ruse.

"Name of Mattick. Mean anything?"

"Guess not," De Ruse said. "Thanks a lot. How do you like it in this nice hotel?"

"Who said it was a nice hotel?"

De Ruse smiled, touched his hat, strolled away. Her eyes looked after him sadly. She leaned her sharp elbows on the counter and cupped her chin in her hands to stare after him.

De Ruse crossed the lobby and went up three steps and got into an open-cage elevator that started with a lurch.

"Eight," he said, and leaned against the cage with his hands in his pockets.

Eight was as high as the Metropole went. De Ruse followed a long corridor that smelled of varnish. A turn at the end brought him face to face with 809. He knocked on the dark wood panel. Nobody answered. He bent over, looked through an empty keyhole, knocked again.

Then he took the tabbed key out of his pocket and unlocked the door and went in.

Windows were shut in two walls. The air reeked of whiskey. Lights were on in the ceiling. There was a wide brass bed, a dark bureau, a couple of brown leather rockers, a stiff-looking desk with a flat brown quart of Four Roses on it, nearly empty, without a cap. De Ruse sniffed it and set his hips against the edge of the desk, let his eyes prowl the room.

His glance traversed from the dark bureau across the bed and the wall with the door in it to another door behind which light showed. He crossed to that and opened it.

The man lay on his face, on the yellowish brown wood-stone floor of the bathroom. Blood on the floor looked sticky and black. Two soggy patches on the back of the man's head were the points from which rivulets of dark red had run down the side of his neck to the floor. The blood had stopped flowing a long time ago.

De Ruse slipped a glove off and stooped to hold two fingers against the place where an artery would beat. He shook his head and put his hand back into his glove.

He left the bathroom, shut the door and went to open one of the windows. He leaned out, breathing clean rain-wet air, looking down along slants of thin rain into the dark slit of an alley.

After a little while he shut the window again, switched off the light in the bathroom, took a "Do Not Disturb" sign out of the top bureau drawer, doused the ceiling lights, and went out.

He hung the sign on the knob and went back along the corridor to the elevators and left the Hotel Metropole.

6

FRANCINE LEY HUMMED low down in her throat as she went along the silent corridor of the Chatterton. She hummed unsteadily without knowing what she was humming, and her left hand with its cherry-red fingernails held a green velvet cape from slipping down off her shoulders. There was a wrapped bottle under her other arm.

She unlocked the door, pushed it open and stopped, with a quick frown. She stood still, remembering, trying to remember. She was still a little tight.

She had left the lights on, that was it. They were off now. Could be the maid service, of course. She went on in, fumbled through the red curtains into the living-room.

The glow from the heater prowled across the red and white rug and touched shiny black things with a ruddy gleam. The shiny black things were shoes. They didn't move.

Francine Ley said: "Oh – oh," in a sick voice. The hand holding the cape almost tore into her neck with its long, beautifully molded nails.

Something clicked and light glowed in a lamp beside an easy chair. De Ruse sat in the chair, looking at her woodenly. He had his coat and hat on. His eyes shrouded, far away, filled with a remote brooding.

He said: "Been out, Francy?"

She sat down slowly on the edge of a half-round settee, put the bottle down beside her.

"I got tight," she said. "Thought I'd better eat. Then I thought I'd get tight again." She patted the bottle.

De Ruse said: "I think your friend Dial's boss has been snatched." He said it casually, as if it was of no importance to him.

Francine Ley opened her mouth slowly and as she opened it all the prettiness went out of her face. Her face became a blank haggard mask on which rouge burned violently. Her mouth looked as if it wanted to scream.

After a while it closed again and her face got pretty again and her voice, from far off, said: "Would it do any good to say I don't know what you're talking about?"

De Ruse didn't change his wooden expression. He said: "When I went down to the street from here a couple of hoods jumped me. One of them was stashed in the car. Of course they could have spotted me somewhere else – followed me here."

"They did," Francine Ley said breathlessly. "They did, Johnny."

His long chin moved an inch. "They piled me into a big Lincoln, a limousine. It was quite a car. It had heavy glass that didn't break easily and no door handles and it was all shut up tight. In the front seat it had a tank of Nevada gas, cyanide, which the guy driving could turn into the back part without getting it himself. They took me out Griffith Parkway, towards the Club Egypt. That's that joint on county land, near the airport." He paused, rubbed the end of one eyebrow, went on: "They overlooked the Mauser I sometimes wear on my leg. The driver crashed the car and I got loose."

He spread his hands and looked down at them. A faint metallic smile showed at the corners of his lips.

Francine Ley said: "I didn't have anything to do with it, Johnny." Her voice was as dead as the summer before last.

De Ruse said: "The guy that rode in the car before I did probably didn't have a gun. He was Hugo Candless. The car was a ringer for his car – same model, same paint job, same plates – but it wasn't his car. Somebody took a lot of trouble. Candless left the Delmar Club in the wrong car about six-thirty. His wife says he's out of town. I talked to her an hour ago. His car hasn't been out of the garage since noon . . . Maybe his wife knows he's snatched by now, maybe not."

Francine Ley's nails clawed at her skirt. Her lips shook.

De Ruse went on calmly, tonelessly: "Somebody gunned the Candless chauffeur in a downtown hotel tonight or this afternoon. The cops haven't found it yet. Somebody took a lot of trouble, Francy. You wouldn't want to be in on that kind of a set-up, would you, precious?"

Francine Ley bent her head forward and stared at the floor. She said thickly: "I need a drink. What I had is dying in me. I feel awful."

De Ruse stood up and went to the white desk. He drained a bottle into a glass and brought it across to her. He stood in front of her, holding the glass out of her reach.

"I only get tough once in a while, baby, but when I get tough I'm not so easy to stop, if I say it myself. If you know anything about all this, now would be a good time to spill it."

He handed her the glass. She gulped the whiskey and a little more light came into her smoke-blue eyes. She said slowly: "I don't know anything about it, Johnny. Not in the way you mean. But George Dial made me a love-nest proposition tonight and he told me he could get money out of Candless by threatening to spill a dirty trick Candless played on some tough boy from Reno."

"Damn clever, these greasers," De Ruse said. "Reno's my town, baby. I know all the tough boys in Reno. Who was it?"

"Somebody named Zapparty."

De Ruse said very softly: "Zapparty is the name of the man who runs the Club Egypt."

Francine Ley stood up suddenly and grabbed his arm. "Stay out of it, Johnny! For Christ sake, can't you stay out of it for just this once?"

De Ruse shook his head, smiled delicately, lingeringly at her. Then he lifted her hand off his arm and stepped back.

"I had a ride in their gas car, baby, and I didn't like it. I smelled their Nevada gas. I left my lead in somebody's gun punk. That makes me call copper or get jammed up with the law. If someody's snatched and I call copper, there'll be another kidnap victim bumped off, more likely than not. Zapparty's a tough boy from Reno and that could tie in with what Dial told you, and if Mops Parisi is playing with

Zapparty, that could make a reason to pull me into it. Parisi loathes my guts."

"You don't have to be a one-man riot squad, Johnny," Francine Ley said desperately.

He kept on smiling, with tight lips and solemn eyes. "There'll be two of us, baby. Get yourself a long coat. It's still raining a little."

She goggled at him. Her outstretched hand, the one that had been on his arm, spread its fingers stiffly, bent back from the palm, straining back. Her voice was hollow with fear.

"Me, Johnny? . . . Oh, please, not . . ."

De Ruse said gently: "Get that coat, honey. Make yourself look nice. It might be the last time we'll go out together."

She staggered past him. He touched her arm softly, held it a moment, said almost in a whisper:

"*You* didn't put the finger on me, did you, Francy?"

She looked back stonily at the pain in his eyes, made a hoarse sound under her breath and jerked her arm loose, went quickly into the bedroom.

After a moment the pain went out of De Ruse's eyes and the metallic smile came back to the corners of his lips.

7

DE RUSE HALF closed his eyes and watched the croupier's fingers as they slid back across the table and rested on the edge. They were round, plump, tapering fingers, graceful fingers. De Ruse raised his head and looked at the croupier's face. He was a bald-headed man of no particular age, with quiet blue eyes. He had no hair on his head at all, not a single hair.

De Ruse looked down at the croupier's hands again. The right hand turned a little on the edge of the table. The buttons on the sleeve of the croupier's brown velvet coat – cut like a dinner coat – rested on the edge of the table. De Ruse smiled his thin metallic smile.

He had three blue chips on the red. On that play the ball stopped at Black 2. The croupier paid off two of the four other men who were playing.

De Ruse pushed five blue chips forward and settled them on the red diamond. Then he turned his head to the left and watched a huskily built blond young man put three red chips on the zero.

De Ruse licked his lips and turned his head farther, looked towards the side of the rather small room. Francine Ley was sitting on a couch backed to the wall, with her head leaning against it.

"I think I've got it, baby," De Ruse said to her. "I think I've got it."

Francine Ley blinked and lifted her head away from the wall. She reached for a drink on a low round table in front of her.

She sipped the drink, looked at the floor, didn't answer.

De Ruse looked back at the blond man. The three other men had made bets. The croupier looked impatient and at the same time watchful.

De Ruse said: "How come you always hit zero when I hit red, and double zero when I hit black?"

The blond young man smiled, shrugged, said nothing.

De Ruse put his hand down on the layout and said very softly: "I asked you a question, mister."

"Maybe I'm Jesse Livermore," the blond young man grunted. "I like to sell short."

"What is this – slow motion?" one of the other men snapped.

"Make your plays, please, gentlemen," the croupier said.

De Ruse looked at him, said: "Let it go."

The croupier spun the wheel left-handed, flicked the ball with the same hand the opposite way. His right hand rested on the edge of the table.

The ball stopped at black 28, next to zero. The blond man laughed. "Close," he said, "close."

De Ruse checked his chips, stacked them carefully. "I'm down six grand," he said. "It's a little raw, but I guess there's money in it. Who runs this clip joint?"

The croupier smiled slowly and stared straight into De Ruse's eyes. He asked quietly: "Did you say clip joint?"

De Ruse nodded. He didn't bother to answer.

"I thought you said clip joint," the croupier said, and moved one foot, put weight on it.

Three of the men who had been playing picked their chips up quickly and went over to a small bar in the corner of the room. They ordered drinks and leaned their backs against the wall by the bar, watching De Ruse and the croupier. The blond man stayed put and smiled sarcastically at De Ruse.

"Tsk, tsk," he said thoughtfully. "Your manners."

Francine Ley finished her drink and leaned her head back against the wall again. Her eyes came down and watched De Ruse furtively, under the long lashes.

A paneled door opened after a moment and a very big man with a black mustache and very rough black eyebrows came in. The croupier moved his eyes to him, then to De Ruse, pointing with his glance.

"Yes, I thought you said clip joint," he repeated tonelessly.

The big man drifted to De Ruse's elbow, touched him with his own elbow.

"Out," he said impassively.

The blond man grinned and put his hands in the pockets of his dark gray suit. The big man didn't look at him.

De Ruse glanced across the layout at the croupier and said: "I'll take back my six grand and call it a day."

"Out," the big man said wearily, jabbing his elbow into De Ruse's side.

The bald-headed croupier smiled politely.

"You," the big man said to De Ruse, "ain't goin' to get tough, are you?"

De Ruse looked at him with sarcastic surprise.

"Well, well, the bouncer," he said softly. "Take him, Nicky."

The blond man took his right hand out of his pocket and swung it. The sap looked black and shiny under the bright lights. It hit the big man on the back of the head with a soft thud. The big man clawed at De Ruse, who stepped away from him quickly and took a gun out from under his arm. The big man clawed at the edge of the roulette table and fell heavily on the floor.

Francine Ley stood up and made a strangled sound in her throat.

The blond man skipped sidewise, whirled and looked at the bartender. The bartender put his hands on top of the bar. The three men who had been playing roulette looked very interested, but they didn't move.

De Ruse said: "The middle button on his right sleeve, Nicky. I think it's copper."

"Yeah." The blond man drifted around the end of the table putting the sap back in his pocket. He went close to the croupier and took hold of the middle of three buttons on his right cuff, jerked it hard. At the second jerk it came away and a thin wire followed it out of the sleeve.

"Correct," the blond man said casually, letting the croupier's arm drop.

"I'll take my six grand now," De Ruse said. "Then we'll go talk to your boss."

The croupier nodded slowly and reached for the rack of chips beside the roulette table.

The big man on the floor didn't move. The blond man put his right hand behind his hip and took a .45 automatic out from inside his waistband at the back.

He swung it in his hand, smiling pleasantly around the room.

8

THEY WENT ALONG a balcony that looked down over the dining room and the dance floor. The lisp of hot jazz came up to them from the lithe, swaying bodies of a high-yaller band. With the lisp of jazz came the smell of food and cigarette smoke and perspiration. The balcony was high and the scene down below had a patterned look, like an overhead camera shot.

The bald-headed croupier opened a door in the corner of the balcony and went through without looking back. The blond man De Ruse had called Nicky went after him. Then De Ruse and Francine Ley.

There was a short hall with a frosted light in the ceiling. The door at the end of that looked like painted metal. The croupier put a plump finger on the small push button at the side, rang it in a certain way. There was a buzzing noise like the sound of an electric door release. The croupier pushed on the edge and opened it.

Inside was a cheerful room, half den and half office. There was a grate fire and a green leather davenport at right angles to it, facing the door. A man sitting on the davenport put a newspaper down and looked up and his face suddenly got livid. He was a small man with a tight round head, a tight round dark face. He had little lightless black eyes like buttons of jet.

There was a big flat desk in the middle of the room and a very tall man stood at the end of it with a cocktail shaker in his hands. His head turned slowly and he looked over his shoulder at the four people who came into the room while his hands continued to agitate the cocktail shaker in gentle rhythm. He had a cavernous face with sunken eyes, loose grayish skin, and close-cropped reddish hair without shine or parting. A thin crisscross scar like a German *Mensur* scar showed on his left cheek.

The tall man put the cocktail shaker down and turned his body around and stared at the croupier. The man on the davenport didn't move. There was a crouched tensity in his not moving.

The croupier said: "I think it's a stick-up. But I couldn't help myself. They sapped Big George."

The blond man smiled gaily and took his .45 out of his pocket. He pointed it at the floor.

"He thinks it's a stick-up," he said. "Wouldn't that positively slay you?"

De Ruse shut the heavy door. Francine Ley moved away from him, towards the side of the room away from the fire. He didn't look at her. The man on the davenport looked at her, looked at everybody.

De Ruse said quietly: "The tall one is Zapparty. The little one is Mops Parisi."

The blond man stepped to one side, leaving the croupier alone in the middle of the room. The .45 covered the man on the davenport.

"Sure, I'm Zapparty," the tall man said. He looked at De Ruse curiously for a moment.

Then he turned his back and picked the cocktail shaker up again, took out the plug and filled a shallow glass. He drained the glass, wiped his lips with a sheer lawn handkerchief and tucked the handkerchief back into his breast pocket very carefully, so that three points showed.

De Ruse smiled his thin metallic smile and touched one end of his left eyebrow with his forefinger. His right hand was in his jacket pocket.

"Nicky and I put on a little act," he said. "That was so the boys outside would have something to talk about if the going got too noisy when we came in to see you."

249

"It sounds interesting," Zapparty agreed. "What did you want to see me about?"

"About that gas car you take people for rides in," De Ruse said.

The man on the davenport made a very sudden movement and his hand jumped off his leg as if something had stung it. The blond man said: "No . . . or yes, if you'd rather, Mister Parisi. It's all a matter of taste."

Parisi became motionless again. His hand dropped back to his short thick thigh.

Zapparty widened his deep eyes a little. "Gas car?" His tone was of mild puzzlement.

De Ruse went forward into the middle of the room near the croupier. He stood balanced on the balls of his feet. His gray eyes had a sleepy glitter but his face was drawn and tired, not young.

He said: "Maybe somebody just tossed it in your lap, Zapparty, but I don't think so. I'm talking about the blue Lincoln, License 5A6, with the tank of Nevada gas in front. You know, Zapparty, the stuff they use on killers in our state."

Zapparty swallowed and his large Adam's apple moved in and out. He puffed his lips, then drew them back against his teeth, then puffed them again.

The man on the davenport laughed out loud, seemed to be enjoying himself.

A voice that came from no one in the room said sharply: "Just drop that gat, blondie. The rest of you grab air."

De Ruse looked up towards an opened panel in the wall beyond the desk. A gun showed in the opening, and a hand, but no body or face. Light from the room lit up the hand and the gun.

The gun seemed to point directly at Francine Ley. De Ruse said: "Okay," quickly, and lifted his hands, empty.

The blond man said: "That'll be Big George — all rested and ready to go." He opened his hand and let the .45 thud to the floor in front of him.

Parisi stood up very swiftly from the davenport and took a gun from under his arm. Zapparty took a revolver out of the desk drawer, leveled it. He spoke towards the panel: "Get out, and stay out."

The panel clicked shut. Zapparty jerked his head at the bald-headed croupier, who had not seemed to move a muscle since he came into the room.

"Back on the job, Louis. Keep the chin up."

The croupier nodded and turned and went out of the room, closing the door carefully behind him.

Francine Ley laughed foolishly. Her hand went up and pulled the collar of her wrap close around her throat, as if it was cold in the room. But there were no windows and it was very warm, from the fire.

Parisi made a whistling sound with his lips and teeth and went quickly to De Ruse and stuck the gun he was holding in De Ruse's face, pushing his head back. He felt in De Ruse's pockets with his left hand, took the Colt, felt under his arms, circled around him, touched his hips, came to the front again.

He stepped back a little and hit De Ruse on the cheek with the flat of one gun. De Ruse stood perfectly still except that his head jerked a little when the hard metal hit his face.

Parisi hit him again the same place. Blood began to run down De Ruse's cheek from the cheekbone, lazily. His head sagged a little and his knees gave way. He went down slowly, leaned with his left hand on the floor, shaking his head. His body was crouched, his legs doubled under him. His right hand dangled loosely beside his left foot.

Zapparty said: "All right, Mops. Don't get blood-hungry. We want words out of these people."

Francine Ley laughed again, rather foolishly. She swayed along the wall, holding one hand up against it.

Parisi breathed hard and backed away from De Ruse with a happy smile on his round swart face.

"I been waitin' a long time for this," he said.

When he was about six feet from De Ruse something small and darkly glistening seemed to slide out of the left leg of De Ruse's trousers into his hand. There was a sharp, snapping explosion, a tiny orange-green flame down on the floor.

Parisi's head jerked back. A round hole appeared under his chin. It got large and red almost instantly. His hands opened laxly and the two guns fell out of them. His body began to sway. He fell heavily.

Zapparty said: "Holy Christ!" and jerked up his revolver.

Francine Ley screamed flatly and hurled herself at him – clawing, kicking, shrilling.

The revolver went off twice with a heavy crash. Two slugs plunked into a wall. Plaster rattled.

Francine Ley slid down to the floor, on her hands and knees. A long slim leg sprawled out from under her dress.

The blond man, down on one knee with his .45 in his hand again, rasped: "She got the bastard's gun!"

Zapparty stood with his hands empty, a terrible expression on his face. There was a long red scratch on the back of his right hand. His revolver lay on the floor beside Francine Ley. His horrified eyes looked down at it unbelievingly.

Parisi coughed once on the floor and after that was still.

De Ruse got up on his feet. The little Mauser looked like a toy in his hand. His voice seemed to come from far away saying: "Watch that panel, Nicky. . . ."

There was no sound outside the room, no sound anywhere. Zapparty stood at the end of the desk, frozen, ghastly.

De Ruse bent down and touched Francine Ley's shoulder. "All right, baby?"

She drew her legs under her and got up, stood looking down at Parisi. Her body shook with a nervous chill.

"I'm sorry, baby," De Ruse said softly beside her. "I guess I had a wrong idea about you."

He took a handkerchief out of his pocket and moistened it with his lips, then rubbed his left cheek lightly and looked at blood on the handkerchief.

Nicky said: "I guess Big George went to sleep again. I was a sap not to blast at him."

De Ruse nodded a little, and said:

"Yeah. The whole play was lousy. Where's your hat and coat, Mister Zapparty? We'd like to have you go riding with us."

9

IN THE SHADOWS under the pepper trees De Ruse said: "There it is, Nicky. Over there. Nobody's bothered it. Better take a look around."

The blond man got out from under the wheel of the Packard and went off under the trees. He stood a little while on the same side of the street as the Packard, then he slipped across to where the big Lincoln was parked in front of the brick apartment house on North Kenmore.

De Ruse leaned forward across the back of the front seat and pinched Francine Ley's cheek. "You're going home now, baby – with this bus. I'll see you later."

"Johnny" – she clutched at his arm – "what are you going to do? For Pete's sake, can't you stop having fun for tonight?"

"Not yet, baby. Mister Zapparty wants to tell us things. I figure a little ride in that gas car will pep him up. Anyway I need it for evidence."

He looked sidewise at Zapparty in the corner of the back seat. Zapparty made a harsh sound in his throat and stared in front of him with a shadowed face.

Nicky came back across the road, stood with one foot on the running board.

"No keys," he said. "Go 'em?"

De Ruse said: "Sure." He took keys out of his pocket and handed them to Nicky. Nicky went around to Zapparty's side of the car and opened the door.

"Out, mister."

Zapparty got out stiffly, stood in the soft, slanting rain, his mouth working. De Ruse got out after him.

"Take it away, baby."

Francine Ley slid along the seat under the steering wheel of the Packard and pushed the starter. The motor caught with a soft whirr.

"So long, baby," De Ruse said gently. "Get my slippers warmed for me. And do me a big favor, honey. Don't phone anyone."

The Packard went off along the dark street, under the big pepper trees. De Ruse watched it turn a corner. He prodded Zapparty with his elbow.

"Let's go. You're going to ride in the back of your gas car. We can't feed you much gas on account of the hole in the glass, but you'll like the smell of it. We'll go off in the country somewhere. We've got all night to play with you."

"I guess you know this is a snatch," Zapparty said harshly.

"Don't I love to think it," De Ruse purred.

They went across the street, three men walking together without haste. Nicky opened the good rear door of the Lincoln. Zapparty got into it. Nicky banged the door shut, got under the wheel and fitted the ignition key in the lock. De Ruse got in beside him and sat with his legs straddling the tank of gas.

The whole car still smelled of the gas.

Nicky started the car, turned it in the middle of the block and drove north to Franklin, back over Los Feliz towards Glendale. After a little while Zapparty leaned forward and banged on the glass. De Ruse put his ear to the hole in the glass behind Nicky's head.

Zapparty's harsh voice said: "Stone house – Castle Road – in the La Crescenta flood area."

"Jeeze, but he's a softy," Nicky grunted, his eyes on the road ahead.

De Ruse nodded, said thoughtfully: "There's more to it than that. With Parisi dead he'd clam up unless he figured he had an out."

Nicky said: "Me, I'd rather take a beating and keep my chin buttoned. Light me a pill, Johnny."

De Ruse lit two cigarettes and passed one to the blond man. He glanced back at Zapparty's long body in the corner of the car. Passing light touched up his taut face, made the shadows on it look very deep.

The big car slid noiselessly through Glendale and up the grade towards Montrose. From Montrose over to the Sunland highway and across that into the almost deserted flood area of La Crescenta.

They found Castle Road and followed it towards the mountains. In a few minutes they came to the stone house.

It stood back from the road, across a wide space which might once have been lawn but which was now packed sand, small stones and a few large boulders. The road made a square turn just before they came to it. Beyond it the road ended in a clean edge of concrete chewed off by the flood of New Year's Day, 1934.

Beyond this edge was the main wash of the flood. Bushes grew in it and there were many huge stones. On the very edge a tree grew with half its roots in the air eight feet above the bed of the wash.

Nicky stopped the car and turned off the lights and took a big nickeled flash out of the car pocket. He handed it to De Ruse.

De Ruse got out of the car and stood for a moment with his hand on the open door, holding the flash. He took a gun out of his overcoat pocket and held it down at his side.

"Looks like a stall," he said. "I don't think there's anything stirring here."

He glanced in at Zapparty, smiled sharply and walked off across the ridges of sand, towards the house. The front door stood half open, wedged that way by sand. De Ruse went towards the corner of the house, keeping out of line with the door as well as he could. He went along the side wall, looking at boarded-up windows behind which there was no trace of light.

At the back of the house was what had been a chicken house. A piece of rusted junk in a squashed garage was all that remained of the family sedan. The back door was nailed up like the windows. De Ruse stood silent in the rain, wondering why the front door was open. Then he remembered that there had been another flood a few months before, not such a bad one. There might have been enough water to break open the door on the side towards the mountains.

Two stucco houses, both abandoned, loomed on the adjoining lots. Farther away from the wash, on a bit of higher ground, there was a lighted window. It was the only light anywhere in the range of De Ruse's vision.

He went back to the front of the house and slipped through the open door, stood inside it and listened. After quite a long time he snapped the flash on.

The house didn't smell like a house. It smelled like out of doors. There was nothing in the front room but sand, a few pieces of smashed furniture, some marks on the walls, above the dark line of the flood water, where pictures had hung.

De Ruse went through a short hall into a kitchen that had a hole in the floor where the sink had been and a rusty gas stove stuck in the hole. From the kitchen he went into a bedroom. He had not heard any whisper of sound in the house so far.

The bedroom was square and dark. A carpet stiff with old mud was plastered to the floor. There was a metal bed with a rusted spring, and a waterstained mattress over part of the spring.

Feet stuck out from under the bed.

They were large feet in walnut brown brogues, with purple socks above them. The socks had gray clocks down the sides. Above the socks were trousers of black and white check.

De Ruse stood very still and played the flash down on the feet. He made a soft sucking sound with his lips. He stood like that for a couple of minutes, without moving at all. Then he stood the flash on the floor, on its end, so that the light it shot against the ceiling was reflected down to make dim light all over the room.

He took hold of the mattress and pulled it off the bed. He reached down and touched one of the hands of the man who was under the bed. The hand was ice cold. He took hold of the ankles and pulled, but the man was large and heavy.

It was easier to move the bed from over him.

10

ZAPPARTY LEANED HIS head back against the upholstery and shut his eyes and turned his head away a little. His eyes were shut very tight and he tried to turn his head far enough so that the light from the big flash wouldn't shine through his eyelids.

Nicky held the flash close to his face and snapped it on, off again, on, off again, monotonously, in a kind of rhythm.

De Ruse stood with one foot on the running board by the open door and looked off through the rain. On the edge of the murky horizon an airplane beacon flashed weakly.

Nicky said carelessly: "You never know what'll get a guy. I saw one break once because a cop held his fingernail against the dimple in his chin."

De Ruse laughed under his breath. "This one is tough," he said. "You'll have to think of something better than a flashlight."

Nicky snapped the flash on, off, on, off. "I could," he said, "But I don't want to get my hands dirty."

After a little while Zapparty raised his hands in front of him and let them fall slowly and began to talk. He talked in a low monotonous voice, keeping his eyes shut against the flash.

"Parisi worked the snatch. I didn't know anything about it until it was done. Parisi muscled in on me about a month ago, with a couple of tough boys to back him up. He had found out somehow that Candless beat me out of twenty-five grand to defend my half-brother on a murder rap, then sold the kid out. I didn't tell Parisi that. I didn't know he knew until tonight.

"He came into the club about seven or a little after and said: 'We've got a friend of yours, Hugo Candless. It's a hundred-grand job, a quick turnover. All you have to do is help spread the pay-off across the tables here, get it mixed up with a bunch of other money. You have to do that because we give you a cut – and because the caper is right up your alley, if anything goes sour.' That's about all. Parisi sat around then and chewed his fingers and waited for his boys. He got pretty jumpy when they didn't show. He went out once to make a phone call from a beer parlor."

De Ruse drew on a cigarette he held cupped inside a hand.

He said: "Who fingered the job, and how did you know Candless was up here?"

Zapparty said: "Mops told me. But I didn't know he was dead."

Nicky laughed and snapped the flash several times quickly.

De Ruse said: "Hold it steady for a minute." Nicky held the beam steady on Zapparty's white face. Zapparty moved his lips in and out. He opened his eyes once. They were blind eyes, like the eyes of a dead fish.

Nicky said: "It's damn cold up here. What do we do with his nibs?"

De Ruse said: "We'll take him into the house and tie him to Candless. They can keep each other warm. We'll come up again in the morning and see if he's got any fresh ideas."

Zapparty shuddered. The gleam of something like a tear showed in the corner of his nearest eye. After a moment of silence he said: "Okay. I planned the whole thing. The gas car was my idea. I didn't want the money. I wanted Candless, and I wanted him dead. My kid brother was hanged in Quentin a week ago Friday."

There was a little silence. Nicky said something under his breath. De Ruse didn't move or make a sound.

Zapparty went on: "Mattick, the Candless driver, was in on it. He hated Candless. He was supposed to drive the ringer car to make everything look good and then take a powder. But he lapped up too much corn getting set for the job and Parisi got leery of him, had him knocked off. Another boy drove the car. It was raining and that helped."

De Ruse said: "Better – but still not all of it, Zapparty."

Zapparty shrugged quickly, slightly opened his eyes against the flash, almost grinned.

"What the hell do you want? Jam on both sides?"

De Ruse said: "I want a finger put on the bird that had me grabbed . . . Let it go. I'll do it myself."

He took his foot off the running board and snapped his butt away into the darkness. He slammed the car door shut, got in the front. Nicky put the flash away and slid around under the wheel, started the engine.

De Ruse said: "Somewhere where I can phone for a cab, Nicky. Then you take this riding for another hour and then call Francy. I'll have a word for you there."

The blond man shook his head slowly from side to side. "You're a good pal, Johnny, and I like you. But this has gone far enough this way. I'm taking it down to Headquarters. Don't forget I've got a private-dick license under my old shirts at home."

De Ruse said: "Give me an hour, Nicky. Just an hour."

The car slid down the hill and crossed the Sunland Highway, started down another hill towards Montrose. After a while Nicky said: "Check."

11

IT WAS TWELVE minutes past one by the stamping clock on
the end of the desk in the lobby of the Casa de Oro. The
lobby was antique Spanish, with black and red Indian rugs,
nail-studded chairs with leather cushions and leather tassels
on the corners of the cushions; the gray-green olivewood
doors were fitted with clumsy wrought-iron strap hinges.

A thin, dapper clerk with a waxed blond mustache and a
blond pompadour leaned on the desk and looked at the clock
and yawned, tapping his teeth with the backs of his bright
fingernails.

The door opened from the street and De Ruse came
in. He took off his hat and shook it, put it on again and
yanked the brim down. His eyes looked slowly around the
deserted lobby and he went to the desk, slapped a gloved
palm on it.

"What's the number of the Hugo Candless bungalow?" he
asked.

The clerk looked annoyed. He glanced at the clock, at De
Ruse's face, back at the clock. He smiled superciliously, spoke
with a slight accent.

"Twelve C. Do you wish to be announced – at this hour?"
De Ruse said: "No."

He turned away from the desk and went towards a large
door with a diamond of glass in it. It looked like the door of
a very high-class privy.

As he put his hand out to the door a bell rang sharply
behind him.

De Ruse looked back over his shoulder, turned and went
back to the desk. The clerk took his hand away from the bell,
rather quickly.

His voice was cold, sarcastic, insolent, saying: "It's not that
kind of apartment house, if you please."

Two patches above De Ruse's cheekbones got a dusky red. He leaned across the counter and took hold of the braided lapel of the clerk's jacket, pulled the man's chest against the edge of the desk.

"What was that crack, nance?"

The clerk paled but managed to bang his bell again with a flailing hand.

A pudgy man in a baggy suit and a seal-brown toupee came around the corner of the desk, put out a plump finger and said: "Hey."

De Ruse let the clerk go. He looked expressionlessly at cigar ash on the front of the pudgy man's coat.

The pudgy man said: "I'm the house man. You gotta see me if you want to get tough."

De Ruse said: "You speak my language. Come over in the corner."

They went over in the corner and sat down beside a palm. The pudgy man yawned amiably and lifted the edge of his toupee and scratched under it.

"I'm Kuvalick," he said. "Times I could bop that Swiss myself. What's the beef?"

De Ruse said: "Are you a guy that can stay clammed?"

"No. I like to talk. It's all the fun I get around this dude ranch." Kuvalick got half of a cigar out of a pocket and burned his nose lighting it.

De Ruse said: "This is one time you stay clammed."

He reached inside his coat, got his wallet out, took out two tens. He rolled them around his forefinger, then slipped them off in a tube and tucked the tube into the outside pocket of the pudgy man's coat.

Kuvalick blinked, but didn't say anything.

De Ruse said: "There's a man in the Candless apartment named George Dial. His car's outside, and that's where he would be. I want to see him and I don't want to send a name in. You can take me in and stay with me."

The pudgy man said cautiously: "It's kind of late. Maybe he's in bed."

"If he is, he's in the wrong bed," De Ruse said. "He ought to get up."

The pudgy man stood up. "I don't like what I'm thinkin', but I like your tens," he said. "I'll go in and see if they're up. You stay put."

De Ruse nodded. Kuvalick went along the wall and slipped through a door in the corner. The clumsy square butt of a hip holster showed under the back of his coat as he walked. The clerk looked after him, then looked contemptuously towards De Ruse and got out a nail file.

Ten minutes went by, fifteen. Kuvalick didn't come back. De Ruse stood up suddenly, scowled and marched towards the door in the corner. The clerk at the desk stiffened, and his eyes went to the telephone on the desk, but he didn't touch it.

De Ruse went through the door and found himself under a roofed gallery. Rain dripped softly off the slanting tiles of the roof. He went along a patio the middle of which was an oblong pool framed in a mosaic of gaily colored tiles. At the end of that, other patios branched off. There was a window light at the far end of the one to the left. He went towards it, at a venture, and when he came close to it made out the number 12C on the door.

He went up two flat steps and punched a bell that rang in the distance. Nothing happened. In a little while he rang again, then tried the door. It was locked. Somewhere inside he thought he heard a faint muffled thumping sound.

He stood in the rain a moment, then went around the corner of the bungalow, down a narrow, very wet passage to the back. He tried the service door; locked also. De Ruse swore, took his gun out from under his arm, held his hat against the glass panel of the service door and smashed the pane with the butt of the gun. Glass fell tinkling lightly inside.

He put the gun away, straightened his hat on his head and reached in through the broken pane to unlock the door.

The kitchen was large and bright with black and yellow tiling, looked as if it was used mostly for mixing drinks. Two bottles of Haig and Haig, a bottle of Hennessy, three or four kinds of fancy cordial bottles stood on the tiled drainboard. A short hall with a closed door led to the living-room. There was a grand piano in the corner with a lamp lit beside it. Another lamp on a low table with drinks and glasses. A wood fire was dying on the hearth.

The thumping noise got louder.

De Ruse went across the living-room and through a door framed in a valance into another hallway, thence into a beautifully paneled bedroom. The thumping noise came from a closet. De Ruse opened the door of the closet and saw a man.

He was sitting on the floor with his back in a forest of dresses on hangers. A towel was tied around his face. Another held his ankles together. His wrists were tied behind him. He was a very bald man, as bald as the croupier at the Club Egypt.

De Ruse stared down at him harshly, then suddenly grinned, bent and cut him loose.

The man spit a washcloth out of his mouth, swore hoarsely and dived into the clothes at the back of the closet. He came up with something furry clutched in his hand, straightened it out, and put it on his hairless head.

That made him Kuvalick, the house dick.

He got up still swearing and backed away from De Ruse, with a stiff alert grin on his fat face. His right hand shot to his hip holster.

De Ruse spread his hands, said: "Tell it," and sat down in a small chintz-covered slipper chair.

Kuvalick stared at him quietly for a moment, then took his hand away from his gun.

"There's lights," he said, "So I push the buzzer. A tall dark guy opens. I seen him around here a lot. That's Dial. I say to him there's a guy outside in the lobby wants to see him hush-hush, won't give a name."

"That made you a sap," De Ruse commented dryly.

"Not yet, but soon," Kuvalick grinned, and spit a shred of cloth out of his mouth. "I describe you. *That* makes me a sap. He smiled kind of funny and asks me to come in a minute. I go in past him and he shuts the door and sticks a gun in my kidney. He says: 'Did you say he wore all dark clothes?' I say: 'Yes. And what's that gat for?' He says: 'Does he have gray eyes and sort of crinkly black hair and is he hard around the teeth?' I say: 'Yes, you bastard and what's the gat for?'

"He says: 'For this,' and lets me have it on the back of the head. I go down, groggy, but not out. Then the Candless broad comes out from a doorway and they tie me up and shove me in the closet and that's that. I hear them fussin' around for a little while and then I hear silence. That's all until you ring the bell."

De Ruse smiled lazily, pleasantly. His whole body was lax in the chair. His manner had become indolent and unhurried.

"They faded," he said softly. "They got tipped off. I don't think that was very bright."

Kuvalick said: "I'm an old Wells Fargo dick and I can stand a shock. What they been up to?"

"What kind of woman is Mrs. Candless?"

"Dark, a looker. Sex hungry, as the fellow says. Kind of worn and tight. They get a new chauffeur every three months. There's a couple guys in the Casa she likes too. I guess there's this gigolo that bopped me."

De Ruse looked at his watch, nodded, leaned forward to get up. "I guess it's about time for some law. Got any friends downtown you'd like to give a snatch story to?"

A voice said: "Not quite yet."

George Dial came quickly into the room from the hallway and stood quietly inside it with a long, thin, silenced automatic in his hand. His eyes were bright and mad, but his lemon-colored finger was very steady on the trigger of the small gun.

"We didn't fade," he said "We weren't quite ready. But it might not have been a bad idea – for you two."

Kuvalick's pudgy hand swept for his hip holster.

The small automatic with the black tube on it made two flat dull sounds.

A puff of dust jumped from the front of Kuvalick's coat. His hands jerked sharply away from the sides and his small eyes snapped very wide open, like seeds bursting from a pod. He fell heavily on his side against the wall, lay quite still on his left side, with his eyes half open and his back against the wall. His toupee was tipped over rakishly.

De Ruse looked at him swiftly, looked back at Dial. No emotion showed in his face, not even excitement.

He said: "You're a crazy fool, Dial. That kills your last chance. You could have bluffed it out. But that's not your only mistake."

Dial said calmly: "No. I see that now. I shouldn't have sent the boys after you. I did that just for the hell of it. That comes of not being a professional."

De Ruse nodded slightly, looked at Dial almost with friendliness. "Just for the fun of it – who tipped you off the game had gone smash?"

"Francy – and she took her damn time about it," Dial said savagely. "I'm leaving, so I won't be able to thank her for a while."

"Not ever," De Ruse said. "You won't get out of the state. You won't ever touch a nickel of the big boy's money. Not you or your sidekicks or your woman. The cops are getting the story – right now."

Dial said: "We'll get clear. We have enough to tour on, Johnny. So long."

Dial's face tightened and his hand jerked up, with the gun in it. De Ruse half closed his eyes, braced himself for the shock.

The little gun didn't go off. There was a rustle behind Dial and a tall dark woman in a gray fur coat slid into the room. A small hat was balanced on dark hair knotted on the nape of her neck. She was pretty, in a thin, haggard sort of way. The lip rouge on her mouth was as black as soot; there was no color in her cheeks.

She had a cool lazy voice that didn't match with her taut expression. "Who is Francy?" she asked coldly.

De Ruse opened his eyes wide and his body got stiff in the chair and his right hand began to slide up towards his chest.

"Francy is my girl friend," he said. "Mister Dial has been trying to get her away from me. But that's all right. He's a handsome lad and ought to be able to pick his spots."

The tall woman's face suddenly became dark and wild and furious. She grabbed fiercely at Dial's arm, the one that held the gun.

De Ruse snatched for his shoulder holster, got his .38 loose. But it wasn't his gun that went off. It wasn't the silenced automatic in Dial's hand. It was a huge frontier Colt with an eight-inch barrel and a boom like an exploding bomb. It went off from the floor, from beside Kuvalick's right hip, where Kuvalick's plump hand held it.

It went off just once. Dial was thrown back against the wall as if by a giant hand. His head crashed against the wall and instantly his darkly handsome face was a mask of blood.

He fell laxly down the wall and the little automatic with the black tube on it fell in front of him. The dark woman dived for it, down on her hands and knees in front of Dial's sprawled body.

She got it, began to bring it up. Her face was convulsed, her lips were drawn back over thin wolfish teeth that shimmered.

Kuvalick's voice said: "I'm a tough guy. I used to be a Wells Fargo dick."

His great cannon slammed again. A shrill scream was torn from the woman's lips. Her body was flung against Dial's. Her

eyes opened and shut, opened and shut. Her face got white
and vacant.

"Shoulder shot. She's okay," Kuvalick said, and got up on
his feet. He jerked open his coat and patted his chest.

"Bullet-proof vest," he said proudly. "But I thought I'd
better lie quiet for a while or he'd popped me in the face."

12

FRANCINE LEY YAWNED and stretched out a long green
pajama-clad leg and looked at a slim green slipper on her bare
foot. She yawned again, got up and walked nervously across
the room to the kidney-shaped desk. She poured a drink,
drank it quickly, with a sharp nervous shudder. Her face was
drawn and tired, her eyes hollow; there were dark smudges
under her eyes.

She looked at the tiny watch on her wrist. It was almost
four o'clock in the morning. Still with her wrist up she
whirled at a sound, put her back to the desk and began to
breathe very quickly, pantingly.

De Ruse came in through the red curtains. He stopped and
looked at her without expression, then slowly took off his hat
and overcoat and dropped them on a chair. He took off his
suit coat and his tan shoulder harness and walked over to the
drinks.

He sniffed at a glass, filled it a third full of whiskey, put it
down in a gulp.

"So you had to tip the louse off," he said somberly, looking down into the empty glass he held.

Francine Ley said: "Yes. I had to phone him. What happened?"

"You had to phone the louse," De Ruse said in exactly the
same tone. "You knew damn well he was mixed up in it. You'd
rather he got loose, even if he cooled me off doing it."

"You're all right, Johnny?" She asked softly, tiredly.

De Ruse didn't speak, didn't look at her. He put the glass down slowly and poured some more whiskey into it, added charged water, looked around for some ice. Not finding any he began to sip the drink with his eyes on the white top of the desk.

Francine Ley said: "There isn't a guy in the world that doesn't rate a start on you, Johnny. It wouldn't do him any good, but he'd have to have it, if I knew him."

De Ruse said slowly: "That's swell. Only I'm not quite that good. I'd be a stiff right now except for a comic hotel dick that wears a Buntline Special and a bullet-proof vest to work."

After a little while Francine Ley said: "Do you want me to blow?"

De Ruse looked at her quickly, looked away again. He put his glass down and walked away from the desk. Over his shoulder he said: "Not so long as you keep on telling me the truth."

He sat down in a deep chair and leaned his elbows on the arms of it, cupped his face in his hands. Francine Ley watched him for a moment, then went over and sat on an arm of the chair. She pulled his head back gently until it was against the back of the chair. She began to stroke his forehead.

De Ruse closed his eyes. His body became loose and relaxed. His voice began to sound sleepy.

"You saved my life over at the Club Egypt maybe. I guess that gave you the right to let handsome have a shot at me."

Francine Ley stroked his head, without speaking.

"Handsome is dead," De Ruse went on. "The peeper shot his face off."

Francine Ley's hand stopped. In a moment it began again, stroking his head.

"The Candless frau was in on it. Seems she's a hot number. She wanted Hugo's dough, and she wanted all the men in the world except Hugo. Thank heaven she didn't get bumped. She talked plenty. So did Zapparty."

"Yes, honey," Francine Ley said quietly.

De Ruse yawned. "Candless is dead. He was dead before we started. They never wanted him anything else but dead. Parisi didn't care one way or the other, as long as he got paid."

Francine Ley said. "Yes, honey."

"Tell you the rest in the morning," De Ruse said thickly. "I guess Nicky and I are all square with the law . . . Let's go to Reno, get married . . . I'm sick of this tomcat life . . . Get me 'nother drink, baby."

Francine Ley didn't move except to draw her fingers softly and soothingly across his forehead and back over his temples. De Ruse moved lower in the chair. His head rolled to one side.

"Yes, honey."

"Don't call me honey," De Ruse said thickly. "Just call me pigeon."

When he was quite asleep she got off the arm of the chair and went and sat down near him. She sat very still and watched him, her face cupped in her long delicate hands with the cherry-colored nails.

SPANISH BLOOD

1

BIG JOHN MASTERS was large, fat, oily. He had sleek blue jowls and very thick fingers on which the knuckles were dimples. His brown hair was combed straight back from his forehead and he wore a wine-colored suit with patch pockets, a wine-colored tie, a tan silk shirt. There was a lot of red and gold band around the thick brown cigar between his lips.

He wrinkled his nose, peeped at his hole card again, tried not to grin. He said: "Hit me again, Dave – and don't hit me with the City Hall."

A four and a deuce showed. Dave Aage looked at them solemnly across the table, looked down at his own hand. He was very tall and thin, with a long bony face and hair the color of wet sand. He held the deck flat on the palm of his hand, turned the top card slowly, and flicked it across the table. It was the queen of spades.

Big John Masters opened his mouth wide, waved his cigar about, chuckled.

"Pay me, Dave. For once a lady was right." He turned his hole card with a flourish. A five.

Dave Aage smiled politely, didn't move. A muted telephone bell rang close to him, behind long silk drapes that bordered the very high lancet windows. He took a cigarette out of his mouth and laid it carefully on the edge of a tray on a tabouret beside the card table, reached behind the curtain for the phone.

He spoke into the cup with a cool, almost whispering voice, then listened for a long time. Nothing changed in his greenish eyes, no flicker of emotion showed on his narrow face. Masters squirmed, bit hard on his cigar.

After a long time Aage said, "Okay, you'll hear from us." He pronged the instrument and put it back behind the curtain.

He picked his cigarette up, pulled the lobe of his ear. Masters swore. "What's eating you, for Pete's sake? Gimme ten bucks."

Aage smiled dryly and leaned back. He reached for a drink, sipped it, put it down, spoke around his cigarette. All his movements were slow, thoughtful, almost absent-minded. He said: "Are we a couple of smart guys, John?"

"Yeah. We own the town. But it don't help my blackjack game any."

"It's just two months to election, isn't it, John?"

Masters scowled at him, fished in his pocket for a fresh cigar, jammed it into his mouth.

"So what?"

"Suppose something happened to our toughest opposition. Right now. Would that be a good idea, or not?"

"Huh?" Masters raised eyebrows so thick that his whole face seemed to have to work to push them up. He thought for a moment, sourly. "It would be lousy — if they didn't catch the guy pronto. Hell, the voters would figure we hired it done."

"You're talking about murder, John," Aage said patiently. "I didn't say anything about murder."

Masters lowered his eyebrows and pulled at a coarse black hair that grew out of his nose.

"Well, spit it out!"

Aage smiled, blew a smoke ring, watched it float off and come apart in frail wisps.

"I just had a phone call," he said very softly. "Donegan Marr is dead."

Masters moved slowly. His whole body moved slowly towards the card table, leaned far over it. When his body couldn't go any farther his chin came out until his jaw muscles stood out like thick wires.

"Huh?" he said thickly. "Huh?"

Aage nodded, calm as ice. "But you were right about murder, John. It *was* murder. Just half an hour ago, or so. In his office. They don't know who did it – yet."

Masters shrugged heavily and leaned back. He looked around him with a stupid expression. Very suddenly he began to laugh. His laughter bellowed and roared around the little turretlike room where the two men sat, overflowed into an enormous living-room beyond, echoed back and forth through a maze of heavy dark furniture, enough standing lamps to light a boulevard, a double row of oil paintings in massive gold frames.

Aage sat silent. He rubbed his cigarette out slowly in the tray until there was nothing of the fire left but a thick dark smudge. He dusted his bony fingers together and waited.

Masters stopped laughing as abruptly as he had begun. The room was very still. Masters looked tired. He mopped his big face.

"We got to do something, Dave," he said quietly. "I almost forgot. We got to break this fast. It's dynamite."

Aage reached behind the curtain again and brought the phone out, pushed it across the table over the scattered cards.

"Well – we know how, don't we?" he said calmly.

A cunning light shone in Big John Masters' muddy brown eyes. He licked his lips, reached a big hand for the phone.

"Yeah," he said purringly, "we do, Dave. We do at that, by —— !"

He dialed with a thick finger that would hardly go into the holes.

2

DONEGAN MARR'S FACE looked cool, neat, poised, even then. He was dressed in soft gray flannels and his hair was the same soft gray color as his suit, brushed back from a ruddy, youngish face. The skin was pale on the frontal bones where the hair would fall when he stood up. The rest of the skin was tanned.

He was lying back in a padded blue office chair. A cigar had gone out in a tray with a bronze greyhound on its rim. His left hand dangled beside the chair and his right hand held a gun loosely on the desk top. The polished nails glittered in sunlight from the big closed window behind him.

Blood had soaked the left side of his vest, made the gray flannel almost black. He was quite dead, had been dead for some time.

A tall man, very brown and slender and silent, leaned against a brown mahogany filing cabinet and looked fixedly at the dead man. His hands were in the pockets of a neat blue serge suit. There was a straw hat on the back of his head. But there was nothing casual about his eyes or his tight, straight mouth.

A big sandy-haired man was groping around on the blue rug. He said thickly, stooped over: "No shells, Sam."

The dark man didn't move, didn't answer. The other stood up, yawned, looked at the man in the chair.

"Hell! This one will stink. Two months to election. Boy, is this a smack in the puss for somebody."

The dark man said slowly: "We went to school together. We used to be buddies. We carried the torch for the same girl. He won, but we stayed good friends, all three of us. He was always a great kid . . . Maybe a shade too smart."

The sandy-haired man walked around the room without touching anything. He bent over and sniffed at the gun on the desk, shook his head, said: "Not used – this one." He wrinkled his nose, sniffed at the air. "Air-conditioned. The three top floors. Soundproofed too. High-grade stuff. They tell me this whole building is electric-welded. Not a rivet in it. Ever hear that, Sam?"

The dark man shook his head slowly.

"Wonder where the help was," the sandy-haired man went on. "A big shot like him would have more than one girl."

The dark man shook his head again. "That's all, I guess. She was out to lunch. He was a lone wolf, Pete. Sharp as a weasel. In a few more years he'd have taken the town over."

The sandy-haired man was behind the desk now, almost leaning over the dead man's shoulder. He was looking down at a leather-backed appointment pad with buff leaves. He said slowly: "Somebody named Imlay was due here at twelve-fifteen. Only date on the pad."

He glanced at a cheap watch on his wrist. "One-thirty. Long gone. Who's Imlay? . . . Say, wait a minute! There's an assistant D.A. named Imlay. He's running for judge on the Masters–Aage ticket. D'you figure – "

There was a sharp knock on the door. The office was so long that the two men had to think a moment before they placed which of the three doors it was. Then the sandy-haired man went towards the most distant of them, saying over his shoulder: "M.E.'s man maybe. Leak this to your favorite newshawk and you're out a job. Am I right?"

The dark man didn't answer. He moved slowly to the desk, leaned forward a little, spoke softly to the dead man.

"Goodbye, Donny. Just let it all go. I'll take care of it. I'll take care of Belle."

The door at the end of the office opened and a brisk man with a bag came in, trotted down the blue carpet and put his bag on the desk. The sandy-haired man shut the door against a bulge of faces. He strolled back to the desk.

The brisk man cocked his head on one side, examining the corpse. "Two of them," he muttered. "Look like about .32's – hard slugs. Close to the heart but not touching. He must have died pretty soon. Maybe a minute or two."

The dark man made a disgusted sound and walked to the window, stood with his back to the room, looking out at the tops of high buildings and a warm blue sky. The sandy-haired man watched the examiner lift a dead eyelid. He said: "Wish the powder guy would get here. I wanta use the phone. This Imlay – "

The dark man turned his head slightly, with a dull smile. "Use it. This isn't going to be any mystery."

"Oh I don't know," the M.E.'s man said, flexing a wrist, then holding the back of his hand against the skin of the dead man's face. "Might not be so damn political as you think, Delaguerra. He's a good-looking stiff."

The sandy-haired man took hold of the phone gingerly, with a handkerchief, laid the receiver down, dialed, picked the receiver up with the handkerchief and put it to his ear.

After a moment he snapped his chin down, said: "Pete Marcus. Wake the Inspector." He yawned, waited again, then spoke in a different tone: "Marcus and Delaguerra, Inspector, from Donegan Marr's office. No print or camera men here yet . . . Huh? . . . Holding off till the Commissioner gets here? . . . Okay . . . Yeah, he's here."

The dark man turned. The man at the phone gestured at him. "Take it, Spanish."

Sam Delaguerra took the phone, ignoring the careful handkerchief, listened. His face got hard. He said quietly: "Sure I knew him – but I didn't sleep with him . . . Nobody's here but his secretary, a girl. She phoned the alarm in. There's a name on a pad – Imlay, a twelve-fifteen appointment. No, we haven't touched anything yet . . . No . . . Okay, right away."

He hung up so slowly that the click of the instrument was barely audible. His hand stayed on it, then fell suddenly and heavily to his side. His voice was thick.

"I'm called off it, Pete. You're to hold it down until Commissioner Drew gets here. Nobody gets in. White, black or Cherokee Indian."

"What you called in for?" the sandy-haired man yelped angrily.

"Don't know. It's an order," Delaguerra said tonelessly.

The M.E.'s man stopped writing on a form pad to look curiously at Delaguerra, with a sharp, sidelong look.

Delaguerra crossed the office and went through the communicating door. There was a smaller office outside, partly partitioned off for a waiting room, with a group of leather chairs and a table with magazines. Inside a counter was a typewriter desk, a safe, some filing cabinets. A small dark girl sat at the desk with her head down on a wadded handkerchief. Her hat was crooked on her head. Her shoulders jerked and her thick sobs were like panting.

Delaguerra patted her shoulder. She looked up at him with a tear-bloated face, a twisted mouth. He smiled down at her questioning face, said gently: "Did you call Mrs. Marr yet?"

She nodded, speechless, shaken with rough sobs. He patted her shoulder again, stood a moment beside her, then went on out, with his mouth tight and a hard, dark glitter in his black eyes.

3

THE BIG ENGLISH house stood a long way back from the narrow, winding ribbon of concrete that was called De Neve Lane. The lawn had rather long grass with a curving path of stepping stones half hidden in it. There was a gable over the front door and ivy on the wall. Trees grew all around the house, close to it, made it a little dark and remote.

All the houses in De Neve Lane had that same calculated air of neglect. But the tall green hedge that hid the driveway and the garages was trimmed as carefully as a French poodle, and there was nothing dark or mysterious about the mass of yellow and flame-colored gladioli that flared at the opposite end of the lawn.

Delaguerra got out of a tan-colored Cadillac touring car that had no top. It was an old model, heavy and dirty. A taut canvas formed a deck over the back part of the car. He wore a white linen cap and dark glasses and had changed his blue serge for a gray cloth outing suit with a jerkin-style zipper jacket.

He didn't look very much like a cop. He hadn't looked very much like a cop in Donegan Marr's office. He walked slowly up the path of stepping stones, touched a brass knocker on the front door of the house, then didn't knock with it. He pushed a bell at the side, almost hidden by the ivy.

There was a long wait. It was very warm, very silent. Bees droned over the warm bright grass. There was the distant whirring of a lawnmower.

The door opened slowly and a black face looked out at him, a long, sad black face with tear streaks on its lavender face powder. The black face almost smiled, said haltingly: "Hello there, Mistah Sam. It's sure good to see you."

Delaguerra took his cap off, swung the dark glasses at his side. He said: "Hello, Minnie. I'm sorry. I've got to see Mrs. Marr."

"Sure. Come right in, Mistah Sam."

The maid stood aside and he went into a shadowy hall with a tile floor. "No reporters yet?"

The girl shook her head slowly. Her warm brown eyes were stunned, doped with shock.

"Ain't been nobody yet . . . She ain't been in long. She ain't said a word. She just stand there in that there sun room that ain't got no sun."

Delaguerra nodded, said: "Don't talk to anybody, Minnie. They're trying to keep this quiet for a while, out of the papers."

"Ah sure won't, Mistah Sam. Not nohow."

Delaguerra smiled at her, walked noiselessly on crêpe soles along the tiled hall to the back of the house, turned into another hall just like it at right angles. He knocked at a door. There was no answer. He turned the knob and went into a long narrow room that was dim in spite of many windows. Trees grew close to the windows, pressing their leaves against the glass. Some of the windows were masked by long cretonne drapes.

The tall girl in the middle of the room didn't look at him. She stood motionless, rigid. She stared at the windows. Her hands were tightly clenched at her sides.

She had red-brown hair that seemed to gather all the light there was and make a soft halo around her coldly beautiful face. She wore a sportily cut blue velvet ensemble with patch pockets. A white handkerchief with a blue border stuck out of the breast pocket, arranged carefully in points, like a foppish man's handkerchief.

Delaguerra waited, letting his eyes get used to the dimness. After a while the girl spoke through the silence, in a low, husky voice.

"Well . . . they got him, Sam. They got him at last. Was he so much hated?"

Delaguerra said softly: "He was in a tough racket, Belle. I guess he played it as clean as he could, but he couldn't help but make enemies."

She turned her head slowly and looked at him. Lights shifted in her hair. Gold glinted in it. Her eyes were vividly, startlingly blue. Her voice faltered a little, saying: "Who killed him, Sam? Have they any ideas?"

Delaguerra nodded slowly, sat down in a wicker chair, swung his cap and glasses between his knees.

"Yeah. We think we know who did it. A man named Imlay, an assistant in the D.A.'s office."

"My God!" the girl breathed. "What's this rotten city coming to?"

Delaguerra went on tonelessly: "It was like this — if you're sure you want to know . . . yet."

"I do, Sam. His eyes stare at me from the wall, wherever I look. Asking me to do something. He was pretty swell to me, Sam. We had our troubles, of course, but . . . they didn't mean anything."

Delaguerra said: "This Imlay is running for judge with the backing of the Masters–Aage group. He's in the gay forties and it seems he's been playing house with a night-club number called Stella La Motte. Somehow, someway, photos were taken of them together, very drunk and undressed. Donny got the photos, Belle. They were found in his desk. According to his desk pad he had a date with Imlay at twelve-fifteen. We figure they had a row and Imlay beat him to the punch."

"You found those photos, Sam?" the girl asked, very quietly.

He shook his head, smiled crookedly. "No. If I had, I guess I might have ditched them. Commissioner Drew found them – after I was pulled off the investigation."

Her head jerked at him. Her vivid blue eyes got wide. "Pulled off the investigation? You – Donny's friend?"

"Yeah. Don't take it too big. I'm a cop, Belle. After all I take orders."

She didn't speak, didn't look at him any more. After a little while he said: "I'd like to have the keys to your cabin at Puma Lake. I'm detailed to go up there and look around, see if there's any evidence. Donny had conferences there."

Something changed in the girl's face. It got almost contemptuous. Her voice was empty. "I'll get them. But you won't find anything there. If you're helping them to find dirt on Donny – so they can clear this Imlay person. . . ."

He smiled a little, shook his head slowly. His eyes were very deep, very sad.

"That's crazy talk, kid. I'd turn my badge in before I did that."

"I see." She walked past him to the door, went out of the room. He sat quite still while she was gone, looked at the wall with an empty stare. There was a hurt look on his face. He swore very softly, under his breath.

The girl came back, walked up to him and held her hand out. Something tinkled into his palm.

"The keys, copper."

Delaguerra stood up, dropped the keys into a pocket. His face got wooden. Belle Marr went over to a table and her nails scratched harshly on a cloisonné box, getting a cigarette out of it. With her back turned she said: "I don't think you'll have any luck, as I said. It's too bad you've only got blackmailing on him so far."

Delaguerra breathed out slowly, stood a moment, then turned away. "Okay," he said softly. His voice was quite off-hand now, as if it was a nice day, as if nobody had been killed.

At the door he turned again. "I'll see you when I get back, Belle. Maybe you'll feel better."

She didn't answer, didn't move. She held the unlighted cigarette rigidly in front of her mouth, close to it. After a moment Delaguerra went on: "You ought to know how I feel about it. Donny and I were like brothers once. I – I heard you were not getting on so well with him . . . I'm glad as all hell that was wrong. But don't let yourself get too hard, Belle. There's nothing to be hard about – with me."

He waited a few seconds, staring at her back. When she still didn't move or speak he went on out.

4

A NARROW ROCKY road dropped down from the highway and ran along the flank of the hill above the lake. The tops of cabins showed here and there among the pines. An open shed was cut into the side of the hill. Delaguerra put his dusty Cadillac under it and climbed down a narrow path towards the water.

The lake was deep blue but very low. Two or three canoes drifted about on it and the chugging of an outboard motor sounded in the distance, around a bend. He went along between thick walls of undergrowth, walking on pine needles, turned around a stump and crossed a small rustic bridge to the Marr cabin.

It was built of half-round logs and had a wide porch on the lake side. It looked very lonely and empty. The spring that ran under the bridge curved around beside the house and one end of the porch dropped down sheer to the big flat stones through which the water trickled. The stones would be covered when the water was high, in the spring.

Delaguerra went up wooden steps and took the keys out of his pocket, unlocked the heavy front door, then stood on the porch a little while and lit a cigarette before he went in. It was very still, very pleasant, very cool and clear after the heat of the city. A mountain bluejay sat on a stump and pecked at its wings. Somebody far out on the lake fooled with a ukulele. He went into the cabin.

He looked at some dusty antlers, a big rough table splattered with magazines, an old-fashioned battery-type radio, a box-shaped phonograph with a disheveled pile of records beside it. There were tall glasses that hadn't been washed and a half-bottle of Scotch beside them, on a table near the big stone fireplace. A car went along the road up above and stopped somewhere not far off. Delaguerra frowned around, said: "Stall," under his breath, with a defeated feeling. There wasn't any sense in it. A man like Donegan Marr wouldn't leave anything that mattered in a mountain cabin.

He looked into a couple of bedrooms, one just a shake-down with a couple of cots, one better furnished, with a make-up bed, and a pair of women's gaudy pajamas tossed across it. They didn't look quite like Belle Marr's.

At the back there was a small kitchen with a gasoline stove and a wood stove. He opened the back door with another key and stepped out on a small porch flush with the ground, near a big pile of cordwood and a double-bitted axe on a chopping block.

The he saw the flies.

A wooden walk went down the side of the house to a woodshed under it. A beam of sunlight had slipped through the trees and lay across the walk. In the sunlight there a clotted mass of flies festered on something brownish, sticky. The flies didn't want to move. Delaguerra bent down, then put his hand down and touched the sticky place, sniffed at his finger. His face got shocked and stiff.

There was another smaller patch of the brownish stuff farther on, in the shade, outside the door of the shed. He took the keys out of his pocket very quickly and found the one that unlocked the big padlock of the woodshed. He yanked the door open.

There was a big loose pile of cordwood inside. Not split wood – cordwood. Not stacked, just thrown in anyhow. Delaguerra began to toss the big rough pieces to one side.

After he had thrown a lot of it aside he was able to reach down and take hold of two cold stiff ankles in lisle socks and drag the dead man out into the light.

He was a slender man, neither tall nor short, in a well-cut basket weave suit. His small neat shoes were polished, a little dust over the polish. He didn't have any face, much. It was broken to pulp by a terrific smash. The top of his head was split open and brains and blood were mixed in the thin grayish-brown hair.

Delaguerra straightened quickly and went back into the house to where the half-bottle of Scotch stood on the table in the living-room. He uncorked it, drank from the neck, waited a moment, drank again.

He said: "Phew!" out loud, and shivered as the whiskey whipped at his nerves.

He went back to the woodshed, leaned down again as an automobile motor started up somewhere. He stiffened. The motor swelled in sound, then the sound faded and there was silence again. Delaguerra shrugged, went through the dead man's pockets. They were empty. One of them, with cleaner's marks on it probably, had been cut away. The tailor's label had been cut from the inside pocket of the coat, leaving ragged stitches.

The man was stiff. He might have been dead twenty-four hours, not more. The blood on his face had coagulated thickly but had not dried completely.

Delaguerra squatted beside him for a little while, looking at the bright glitter of Puma Lake, the distant flash of a paddle from a canoe. Then he went back into the woodshed and pawed around for a heavy block of wood with a great deal of blood on it, didn't find one. He went back into the house and out on the front porch, went to the end of the porch, stared down the drop, then at the big flat stones in the spring.

"Yeah," he said softly.

There were flies clotted on two of the stones, a lot of flies. He hadn't noticed them before. The drop was about thirty feet, enough to smash a man's head open if he landed just right.

He sat down in one of the big rockers and smoked for several minutes without moving. His face was still with thought, his black eyes withdrawn and remote. There was a tight, hard smile, ever so faintly sardonic, at the corners of his mouth.

At the end of that he went silently back through the house and dragged the dead man into the woodshed again, covered him up loosely with the wood. He locked the woodshed, locked the house up, went back along the narrow, steep path to the road and to his car.

It was past six o'clock, but the sun was still bright as he drove off.

5

AN OLD STORE counter served as bar in the roadside beer-stube. Three low stools stood against it. Delaguerra sat on the end one near the door, looked at the foamy inside of an empty beer glass. The bartender was a dark kid in overalls, with shy eyes and lank hair. He stuttered. He said: "Sh-should I d-draw you another g-glass, mister?"

Delaguerra shook his head, stood up off the stool. "Racket beer, sonny," he said sadly. "Tasteless as a roadhouse blonde."

"P-portola B-brew, mister. Supposed to be the b-best."

"Uh-huh. The worst. You use it, or you don't have a license. So long, sonny."

He went across to the screen door, looked out at the sunny highway on which the shadows were getting quite long. Beyond the concrete there was a graveled space edged by a white fence of four-by-fours. There were two cars parked there: Delaguerra's old Cadillac and a dusty hard-bitten Ford. A tall, thin man in khaki whipcord stood beside the Cadillac, looking at it.

Delaguerra got a bulldog pipe out, filled it half full from a zipper pouch, lit it with slow care and flicked the match into the corner. Then he stiffened a little, looking out through the screen.

The tall, thin man was unsnapping the canvas that covered the back part of Delaguerra's car. He rolled part of it back, stood peering down in the space underneath.

Delaguerra opened the screen door softly and walked in long, loose strides across the concrete of the highway. His crêpe soles made sound on the gravel beyond, but the thin man didn't turn. Delaguerra came up beside him.

"Thought I noticed you behind me," he said dully. "What's the grift?"

The man turned without any haste. He had a long, sour face, eyes the color of seaweed. His coat was open, pushed back by a hand on a left hip. That showed a gun worn butt to the front in a belt holster, cavalry style.

He looked Delaguerra up and down with a faint crooked smile.

"This your crate?"

"What do you think?"

The thin man pulled his coat back farther and showed a bronze badge on his pocket.

"I think I'm a Toluca County game warden, mister. I think this ain't deer-hunting time and it ain't ever deer-hunting time for does."

Delaguerra lowered his eyes very slowly, looked into the back of his car, bending over to see past the canvas. The body of a young deer lay there on some junk, beside a rifle. The soft eyes of the dead animal, unglazed by death, seemed to look at him with a gentle reproach. There was dried blood on the doe's slender neck.

Delaguerra straightened, said gently: "That's damn cute."

"Got a hunting license?"

"I don't hunt," Delaguerra said.

"Wouldn't help much. I see you got a rifle."

"I'm a cop."

"Oh – cop, huh? Would you have a badge?"

"I would."

Delaguerra reached into his breast pocket, got the badge out, rubbed it on his sleeve, held it in the palm of his hand. The thin game warden stared down at it, licking his lips.

"Detective lieutenant, huh? City police." His face got distant and lazy. "Okay, Lieutenant. We'll ride about ten miles down-grade in your heap. I'll thumb a ride back to mine."

Delaguerra put the badge away, knocked his pipe out carefully, stamped the embers into the gravel. He replaced the canvas loosely.

"Pinched?" he asked gravely.

"Pinched, Lieutenant."

"Let's go."

He got in under the wheel of the Cadillac. The thin warden went around the other side, got in beside him. Delaguerra started the car, backed around and started off down the smooth concrete of the highway. The valley was a deep haze in the distance. Beyond the haze other peaks were enormous on the skyline. Delaguerra coasted the big car easily, without haste. The two men stared straight before them without speaking.

After a long time Delaguerra said: "I didn't know they had deer at Puma Lake. That's as far as I've been."

"There's a reservation by there, Lieutenant," the warden said calmly. He stared through the dusty windshield. "Part of the Toluca County Forest – or wouldn't you know that?"

Delaguerra said: "I guess I wouldn't know it. I never shot a deer in my life. Police work hasn't made me that tough."

The warden grinned, said nothing. The highway went through a saddle, then the drop was on the right side of the highway. Little canyons began to open out into the hills on the left. Some of them had rough roads in them, half overgrown, with wheel tracks.

Delaguerra swung the big car hard and suddenly to the left, shot it into a cleared space of reddish earth and dry grass, slammed the brake on. The car skidded, swayed, ground to a lurching stop.

The warden was flung violently to the right, then forward against the windshield. He cursed, jerked up straight and threw his right hand across his body at the holstered gun.

Delaguerra took hold of a thin, hard wrist and twisted it sharply towards the man's body. The warden's face whitened behind the tan. His left hand fumbled at the holster, then relaxed. He spoke in a tight, hurt voice.

"Makin' it worse, copper. I got a phone tip at Salt Springs. Described your car, said where it was. Said there was a doe carcass in it. I – "

Delaguerra loosed the wrist, snapped the belt holster open and jerked the Colt out of it. He tossed the gun from the car.

"Get out, County! Thumb that ride you spoke of. What's the matter – can't you live on your salary any more? You planted it yourself, back at Puma Lake, you goddamn chiseler!"

The warden got out slowly, stood on the ground with his face blank, his jaw loose and slack.

"Tough guy," he muttered. "You'll be sorry for this, copper. I'll swear a complaint."

Delaguerra slid across the seat, got out of the right-hand door. He stood close to the warden, said very slowly: "Maybe I'm wrong, mister. Maybe you did get a call. Maybe you did."

He swung the doe's body out of the car, laid it down on the ground, watching the warden. The thin man didn't move, didn't try to get near his gun lying on the grass a dozen feet away. His seaweed eyes were dull, very cold.

Delaguerra got back into the Cadillac, snapped the brake off, started the engine. He backed to the highway. The warden still didn't make a move.

The Cadillac leaped forward, shot down the grade, out of sight. When it was quite gone the warden picked his gun up and holstered it, dragged the doe behind some bushes, and started to walk back along the highway towards the crest of the grade.

6

THE GIRL AT the desk in the Kenworthy said: "This man called you three times, Lieutenant, but he wouldn't give a number. A lady called twice. Wouldn't leave name or number."

Delaguerra took three slips of paper from her, read the name "Joey Chill" on them and the various times. He picked up a couple of letters, touched his cap to the desk girl and got into the automatic elevator. He got off at four, walked down a narrow, quiet corridor, unlocked a door. Without switching on any lights he went across to a big french window, opened it wide, stood there looking at the thick dark sky, the flash of neon lights, the stabbing beams of headlamps on Ortega Boulevard, two blocks over.

He lit a cigarette and smoked half of it without moving. His face in the dark was very long, very troubled. Finally he left the window and went into a small bedroom, switched on a table lamp and undressed to the skin. He got under the shower, toweled himself, put on clean linen and went into the kitchenette to mix a drink. He sipped that and smoked another cigarette while he finished dressing. The telephone in the living-room rang as he was strapping on his holster.

It was Belle Marr. Her voice was blurred and throaty, as if she had been crying for hours.

"I'm so glad to get you, Sam. I — I didn't mean the way I talked. I was shocked and confused, absolutely wild inside. You knew that, didn't you, Sam?"

"Sure, kid," Delaguerra said. "Think nothing of it. Anyway you were right. I just got back from Puma Lake and I think I was just sent up there to get rid of me."

"You're all I have now, Sam. You won't let them hurt you, will you?"

"Who?"

"You know. I'm no fool, Sam. I know this was all a plot, a vile political plot to get rid of him."

Delaguerra held the phone very tight. His mouth felt stiff and hard. For a moment he couldn't speak. Then he said: "It might be just what it looks like, Belle. A quarrel over those pictures. After all Donny had a right to tell a guy like that to get off the ticket. That wasn't blackmail . . . And he had a gun in his hand, you know."

"Come out and see me when you can, Sam." Her voice lingered with a spent emotion, a note of wistfulness.

He drummed on the desk, hesitated again, said: "Sure. . . When was anybody at Puma Lake last, at the cabin?"

"I don't know. I haven't been there in a year. He went . . . alone. Perhaps he met people there. I don't know."

He said something vaguely, after a moment said goodbye and hung up. He stared at the wall over the writing desk. There was a fresh light in his eyes, a hard glint. His whole face was tight, not doubtful any more.

He went back to the bedroom for his coat and straw hat. On the way out he picked up the three telephone slips with the name "Joey Chill" on them, tore them into small pieces and burned the pieces in an ashtray.

7

PETE MARCUS, THE big, sandy-haired dick, sat sidewise at a small littered desk in a bare office in which there were two such desks, faced to opposite walls. The other desk was neat and tidy, had a green blotter with an onyx pen set, a small brass calendar and an abalone shell for an ashtray.

A round straw cushion that looked something like a target was propped on end in a straight chair by the window. Pete Marcus had a handful of bank pens in his left hand and he was flipping them at the cushion, like a Mexican knife thrower. He was doing it absently, without much skill.

The door opened and Delaguerra came in. He shut the door and leaned against it, looking woodenly at Marcus. The sandy-haired man creaked his chair around and tilted it back against the desk, scratched his chin with a broad thumbnail.

"Hi, Spanish. Nice trip? The Chief's yappin' for you."

Delaguerra grunted, stuck a cigarette between his smooth brown lips.

"Were you in Marr's office when those photos were found, Pete?"

"Yeah, but I didn't find them. The Commish did. Why?"

"Did you see him find them?"

Marcus stared a moment, then said quietly, guardedly: "He found them all right, Sam. He didn't plant them — if that's what you mean."

Delaguerra nodded, shrugged. "Anything on the slugs?"

"Yeah. Not thirty-twos — twenty-fives. A damn vest-pocket rod. Copper-nickel slugs. An automatic, though, and we didn't find any shells."

"Imlay remembered those," Delaguerra said evenly, "but he left without the photos he killed for."

Marcus lowered his feet to the floor and leaned forward, looking up past his tawny eyebrows.

"That could be. They give him a motive, but with the gun in Marr's hand they kind of knock a premeditation angle."

"Good headwork, Pete." Delaguerra walked over to the small window, stood looking out of it. After a moment Marcus said dully: "You don't see me doin' any work, do you, Spanish?"

Delaguerra turned slowly, went over and stood close to Marcus, looking down at him.

"Don't be sore, kid. You're my partner, and I'm tagged as Marr's line into Headquarters. You're getting some of that. You're sitting still and I was hiked up to Puma Lake for no good reason except to have a deer carcass planted in the back of my car and have a game warden nick me with it."

Marcus stood up very slowly, knotting his fists at his sides. His heavy gray eyes opened very wide. His big nose was white at the nostrils.

"Nobody here'd go *that* far, Sam."

Delaguerra shook his head. "I don't think so either. But they could take a hint to send me up there. And somebody outside the department could do the rest."

Pete Marcus sat down again. He picked up one of the pointed bank pens and flipped it viciously at the round straw cushion. The point stuck, quivered, broke, and the pen rattled to the floor.

"Listen," he said thickly, not looking up, "this is a job to me. That's all it is. A living. I don't have any ideals about this police work like you have. Say the word and I'll heave the goddamn badge in the old boy's puss."

Delaguerra bent down, punched him in the ribs. "Skip it, copper. I've got ideas. Go on home and get drunk."

He opened the door and went out quickly, walked along a marble-faced corridor to a place where it widened into an alcove with three doors. The middle one said: CHIEF OF DETECTIVES. ENTER. Delaguerra went into a small reception room with a plain railing across it. A police stenographer behind the railing looked up, then jerked his head at an inner door. Delaguerra opened a gate in the railing and knocked at the inner door, then went in.

Two men were in the big office. Chief of Detectives Tod McKim sat behind a heavy desk, looked at Delaguerra hard-eyed as he came in. He was a big, loose man who had gone saggy. He had a long, petulantly melancholy face. One of his eyes was not quite straight in his head.

The man who sat in a round-backed chair at the end of the desk was dandyishly dressed, wore spats. A pearl-gray hat and gray gloves and an ebony cane lay beside him on another chair. He had a shock of soft white hair and a handsome dissipated face kept pink by constant massaging. He smiled at Delaguerra, looked vaguely amused and ironical, smoked a cigarette in a long amber holder.

Delaguerra sat down opposite McKim. Then he looked at the white-haired man briefly and said: "Good evening, Commissioner."

Commissioner Drew nodded offhandedly, didn't speak.

McKim leaned forward and clasped blunt, nail-chewed fingers on the shiny desk top. He said quietly: "Took your time reporting back. Find anything?"

Delaguerra stared at him, a level expressionless stare.

"I wasn't meant to – except maybe a doe carcass in the back of my car."

Nothing changed in McKim's face. Not a muscle of it moved. Drew dragged a pink and polished fingernail across the front of his throat and made a tearing sound with his tongue and teeth.

"That's no crack to be makin' at your boss, lad."

Delaguerra kept on looking at McKim, waited. McKim spoke slowly, sadly: "You've got a good record, Delaguerra. Your grandfather was one of the best sheriffs this county ever had. You've blown a lot of dirt on it today. You're charged with violating game laws, interfering with a Toluca County officer in the performance of his duty, and resisting arrest. Got anything to say to all that?"

Delaguerra said tonelessly: "Is there a tag out for me?"

McKim shook his head very slowly. "It's a department charge. There's no formal complaint. Lack of evidence, I guess." He smiled dryly, without humor.

Delaguerra said quietly: "In that case I guess you'll want my badge."

McKim nodded, silent. Drew said: "You're a little quick on the trigger. Just a shade fast on the snap-up."

Delaguerra took his badge out, rubbed it on his sleeve, looked at it, pushed it across the smooth wood of the desk.

"Okay, Chief," he said very softly. "My blood is Spanish, pure Spanish. Not nigger-Mex and not Yaqui-Mex. My grandfather would have handled a situation like this with fewer words and more powder smoke, but that doesn't mean I think it's funny. I've been deliberately framed into this spot because I was a close friend of Donegan Marr once. You know and I know that never counted for anything on the job. The Commissioner and his political backers may not feel so sure."

Drew stood up suddenly. "By God, you'll not talk like that to me," he yelped.

Delaguerra smiled slowly. He said nothing, didn't look towards Drew at all. Drew sat down again, scowling, breathing hard.

After a moment McKim scooped the badge into the middle drawer of his desk and got to his feet.

"You're suspended for a board, Delaguerra. Keep in touch with me." He went out of the room quickly, by the inner door, without looking back.

Delaguerra pushed his chair back and straightened his hat on his head. Drew cleared his throat, assumed a conciliatory smile and said: "Maybe I was a little hasty myself. The Irish in me. Have no hard feelings. The lesson you're learning is something we've all had to learn. Might I give you a word of advice?"

Delaguerra stood up, smiled at him, a small dry smile that moved the corners of his mouth and left the rest of his face wooden.

"I know what it is, Commissioner. Lay off the Marr case."

Drew laughed, good-humored again. "Not exactly. There isn't any Marr case. Imlay has admitted the shooting through his attorney, claiming self-defense. He's to surrender in the morning. No, my advice was something else. Go back to Toluca County and tell the warden you're sorry. I think that's all that's needed. You might try it and see."

Delaguerra moved quietly to the corridor and opened it. Then he looked back with a sudden flashing grin that showed all his white teeth.

"I know a crook when I see one, Commissioner. He's been paid for his trouble already."

He went out. Drew watched the door close shut with a faint whoosh, a dry click. His face was stiff with rage. His pink skin had turned a doughy gray. His hand shook furiously, holding the amber holder, and ash fell on the knee of his immaculate knife-edged trousers.

"By God," he said rigidly, in the silence, "you may be a damn-smooth Spaniard. You may be smooth as plate glass – but you're a hell of a lot easier to poke a hole through!"

He rose, awkward with anger, brushed the ashes from his trousers carefully and reached a hand out for hat and cane. The manicured fingers of the hand were trembling.

8

NEWTON STREET, BETWEEN Third and Fourth, was a block of cheap clothing stores, pawnshops, arcades of slot machines, mean hotels in front of which furtive-eyed men slid words delicately along their cigarettes, without moving their lips.

Midway of the block a jutting wooden sign on a canopy said, STOLL'S BILLIARD PARLORS. Steps went down from the side-walk edge. Delaguerra went down the steps.

It was almost dark in the front of the poolroom. The tables were sheeted, the cues racked in rigid lines. But there was light far at the back, hard white light against which clus-tered heads and shoulders were silhouetted. There was noise, wrangling, shouting of odds. Delaguerra went towards the light.

Suddenly, as if at a signal, the noise stopped and out of the silence came the sharp click of balls, the dull thud of cue ball against cushion after cushion, the final click of a three-bank carom. Then the noise flared up again.

Delaguerra stopped beside a sheeted table and got a ten-dollar bill from his wallet, got a small gummed label from a pocket in the wallet. He wrote on it: "Where is Joe?" pasted it to the bill, folded the bill in four. He went on to the fringe of the crowd and inched his way through until he was close to the table.

A tall, pale man with an impassive face and neatly parted brown hair was chalking a cue, studying the set-up on the table. He leaned over, bridged with strong white fingers. The betting ring noise dropped like a stone. The tall man made a smooth, effortless three-cushion shot.

A chubby-faced man on a high stool intoned: "Forty for Chill. Eight's the break."

The tall man chalked his cue again, looked around idly. His eyes passed over Delaguerra without sign. Delaguerra stepped closer to him, said: "Back yourself, Max? Five-spot against the next shot."

The tall man nodded. "Take it."

Delaguerra put the folded bill on the edge of the table. A youth in a striped shirt reached for it. Max Chill blocked him off without seeming to, tucked the bill in a pocket of his vest, said tonelessly: "Five bet," and bent to make another shot.

It was a clean crisscross at the top of the table, a hairline shot. There was a lot of applause. The tall man handed his cue to his helper in the striped shirt, said: "Time out. I got to go a place."

He went back through the shadows, through a door marked MEN. Delaguerra lit a cigarette, looked around at the usual Newton Street riffraff. Max Chill's opponent, another tall, pale, impassive man, stood beside the marker and talked to him without looking at him. Near them, alone and supercilious, a very good-looking Filipino in a smart tan suit was puffing at a chocolate-colored cigarette.

Max Chill came back to the table, reached for his cue, chalked it. He reached a hand into his vest, said lazily: "Owe you five, buddy," passed a folded bill to Delaguerra.

He made three caroms in a row, almost without stopping. The marker said: "Forty-four for Chill. Twelve's the break."

Two men detached themselves from the edge of the crowd, started towards the entrance. Delaguerra fell in behind them, followed them among the sheeted tables to the foot of the steps. He stopped there, unfolded the bill in his hand, read the address scribbled on the label under his question. He crumpled the bill in his hand, started it towards his pocket.

Something hard poked into his back. A twangy voice like a plucked banjo string said: "Help a guy out, huh?"

Delaguerra's nostrils quivered, got sharp. He looked up the steps at the legs of the two men ahead, at the reflected glare of street lights.

"Okay," the twangy voice said grimly.

Delaguerra dropped sidewise, twisting in the air. He shot a snakelike arm back. His hand grabbed an ankle as he fell. A swept gun missed his head, cracked the point of his shoulder and sent a dart of pain down his left arm. There was hard, hot breathing. Something without force slammed his straw hat. There was a thin tearing snarl close to him. He rolled, twisted the ankle, tucked a knee under him and lunged up. He was on his feet, catlike, lithe. He threw the ankle away from him, hard.

The Filipino in the tan suit hit the floor with his back. A gun wobbled up. Delaguerra kicked it out of a small brown hand and it skidded under a table. The Filipino lay still on his back, his head straining up, his snap-brim hat still glued to his oily hair.

At the back of the poolroom the three-cushion match went on peacefully. If anyone noticed the scuffling sound, at least no one moved to investigate. Delaguerra jerked a thonged blackjack from his hip pocket, bent over. The Filipino's tight brown face cringed.

"Got lots to learn. On the feet, baby."

Delaguerra's voice was chilled but casual. The dark man scrambled up, lifted his arms, then his left hand snaked for his right shoulder. The blackjack knocked it down, with a careless flip of Delaguerra's wrist. The brown man screamed thinly, like a hungry kitten.

Delaguerra shrugged. His mouth moved in a sardonic grin.

"Stick-up, huh? Okay, yellowpuss, some other time. I'm busy now. Dust!"

The Filipino slid back among the tables, crouched down. Delaguerra shifted the blackjack to his left hand, shot his right to a gun butt. He stood for a moment like that, watching the Filipino's eyes. Then he turned and went quickly up the steps, out of sight.

The brown man darted forward along the wall, crept under the table for his gun.

9

JOEY CHILL, WHO jerked the door open, held a short, worn gun without a foresight. He was a small man, hardbitten, with a tight, worried face. He needed a shave and a clean shirt. A harsh animal smell came out of the room behind him.

He lowered the gun, grinned sourly, stepped back into the room.

"Okay, copper. Took your sweet time gettin' here."

Delaguerra went in and shut the door. He pushed his straw hat far back on his wiry hair, and looked at Joey Chill without any expression. He said: "Am I supposed to remember the address of every punk in town? I had to get it from Max."

The small man growled something and went and lay down on the bed, shoved his gun under the pillow. He clasped his hands behind his head and blinked at the ceiling.

"Got a C note on you, copper?"

Delaguerra jerked a straight chair in front of the bed and straddled it. He got his bulldog pipe out, filled it slowly, looking with distaste at the shut window, the chipped enamel of the bed frame, the dirty, tumbled bedclothes, the wash bowl in the corner with two smeared towels hung over it, the bare dresser with half a bottle of gin planked on top of the Gideon Bible.

"Holed up?" he inquired, without much interest.

"I'm hot, copper. I mean I'm hot. I got something see. It's worth a C note."

Delaguerra put his pouch away slowly, indifferently, held a lighted match to his pipe, puffed with exasperating leisure. The small man on the bed fidgeted, watching him with side-long looks. Delaguerra said slowly: "You're a good stoolie, Joey. I'll always say that for you. But a hundred bucks is important money to a copper."

"Worth it, guy. If you like the Marr killing well enough to want to break it right."

Delaguerra's eyes got steady and very cold. His teeth clamped on the pipe stem. He spoke very quietly, very grimly.

"I'll listen, Joey. I'll pay if it's worth it. It better be right, though."

The small man rolled over on his elbow. "Know who the girl was with Imlay in those pajama–pajama snaps?"

"Know her name," Delaguerra said evenly. "I haven't seen the pictures."

"Stella La Motte's a hoofer name. Real name Stella Chill. My kid sister."

Delaguerra folded his arms on the back of the chair. "That's nice," he said. "Go on."

"She framed him, copper. Framed him for a few bindles of heroin from a slant-eyed Flip."

"Flip?" Delaguerra spoke the word swiftly, harshly. His face was tense now.

"Yeah, a little brown brother. A looker, a neat dresser, a snow peddler. A goddamn dodo. Name, Toribo. They call him the Caliente Kid. He had a place across the hall from Stella. He got to feedin' her the stuff. Then he works her into the frame. She puts heavy drops in Imlay's liquor and he passes out. She lets the Flip in to shoot pictures with a Minny camera. Cute, huh? . . . And then, just like a broad, she gets sorry and spills the whole thing to Max and me."

Delaguerra nodded, silent, almost rigid.

The little man grinned sharply, showed his small teeth. "What do I do? I take a plant on the Flip. I live in his shadow, copper. And after a while I tail him bang into Dave Aage's skyline apartment in the Vendome . . . I guess that rates a yard."

Delaguerra nodded slowly, shook a little ash into the palm of his hand and blew it off. "Who else knows this?"

"Max. He'll back me up, if you handle him right. Only he don't want any part of it. He don't play those games. He gave Stella dough to leave town and signed off. Because those boys are tough."

"Max couldn't know where you followed the Filipino to, Joey."

The small man sat up sharply, swung his feet to the floor. His face got sullen.

"I'm not kidding you, copper. I never have."

Delaguerra said quietly, "I believe you, Joey. I'd like more proof, though. What do you make of it?"

The little man snorted. "Hell, it sticks up so hard it hurts. Either the Flip's working for Masters and Aage before or he makes a deal with them after he gets the snaps. Then Marr gets the pictures and it's a cinch he don't get them unless they say so and he don't know they had them. Imlay was running for judge, on their ticket. Okay, he's their punk, but he's still a punk. It happens he's a guy who drinks and has a nasty temper. That's known."

Delaguerra's eyes glistened a little. The rest of his face was like carved wood. The pipe in his mouth was as motionless as though set in cement.

Joey Chill went on, with his sharp little grin: "So they deal the big one. They get the pictures to Marr without Marr's knowing where they came from. Then Imlay gets tipped off who has them, what they are, that Marr is set to put the squeeze on him. What would a guy like Imlay do? He'd go hunting, copper – and Big John Masters and his sidekick would eat the ducks."

"Or the venison," Delaguerra said absently.

"Huh? Well, does it rate?"

Delaguerra reached for his wallet, shook the money out of it, counted some bills on his knee. He rolled them into a tight wad and flipped them on to the bed.

"I'd like a line to Stella pretty well, Joey. How about it?"

The small man stuffed the money in his shirt pocket, shook his head. "No can do. You might try Max again. I think she's left town, and me, I'm doin' that too, now I've got the scratch. Because those boys are tough like I said – and maybe I didn't tail so good . . . Because some mug's been tailin' me." He stood up, yawned, added: "Snort of gin?"

Delaguerra shook his head, watched the little man go over to the dresser and lift the gin bottle, pour a big dose into a thick glass. He drained the glass, started to put it down.

Glass tinkled at the window. There was a sound like the loose slap of a glove. A small piece of the window glass dropped to the bare stained wood beyond the carpet, almost at Joey Chill's feet.

The little man stood quite motionless for two or three seconds. Then the glass fell from his hand, bounced and rolled against the wall. Then his legs gave. He went down on his side, slowly, rolled slowly over on his back.

Blood began to move sluggishly down his cheek from a hole over his left eye. It moved faster. The hole got large and red. Joey Chill's eyes looked blankly at the ceiling, as if those things no longer concerned him at all.

Delaguerra slipped quietly down out of the chair to his hands and knees. He crawled along the side of the bed, over to the wall by the window, reached out from there and groped inside Joey Chill's shirt. He held fingers against his heart for a little while, took them away, shook his head. He squatted down low, took his hat off, and pushed his head up very carefully until he could see over a lower corner of the window.

He looked at the high blank wall of a storage warehouse, across an alley. There were scattered windows in it, high up, none of them lighted. Delaguerra pulled his head down again, said quietly, under his breath: "Silenced rifle, maybe. And very sweet shooting."

His hand went forward again, diffidently, took the little roll of bills from Joey Chill's shirt. He went back along the wall to the door, still crouched, reached up and got the key from the door, opened it, straightened and stepped through quickly, locked the door from the outside.

He went along a dirty corridor and down four flights of steps to a narrow lobby. The lobby was empty. There was a desk and a bell on it, no one behind it. Delaguerra stood behind the plate-glass street door and looked across the street at a frame rooming house where a couple of old men rocked on the porch, smoking. They looked very peaceful. He watched them for a couple of minutes.

He went out, searched both sides of the block quickly with sharp glances, walked along beside parked cars to the next

corner. Two blocks over he picked up a cab and rode back to
Stoll's Billiard Parlors on Newton Street.

Lights were lit all over the poolroom now. Balls clicked
and spun, players weaved in and out of a thick haze of
cigarette smoke. Delaguerra looked around, then went to
where a chubby-faced man sat on a high stool beside a cash
register.

"You Stoll?"

The chubby-faced man nodded.

"Where did Max Chill get to?"

"Long gone, brother. They only played a hundred up.
Home, I guess."

"Where's home?"

The chubby-faced man gave him a swift, flickering glance
that passed like a finger of light.

"I wouldn't know."

Delaguerra lifted a hand to the pocket where he carried
his badge. He dropped it again – tried not to drop it too
quickly. The chubby-faced man grinned.

"Flattie, eh? Okay, he lives at the Mansfield, three blocks
west on Grand."

10

CEFARINO TORIBO, THE good-looking Filipino in the well-
cut tan suit, gathered two dimes and three pennies off the
counter in the telegraph office, smiled at the bored blonde
who was waiting on him.

"That goes out right away, Sugar?"

She glanced at the message icily. "Hotel Mansfield? Be
there in twenty minutes – and save the sugar."

"Okay, Sugar."

Toribo dawdled elegantly out of the office. The blonde
spiked the message with a jab, said over her shoulder: "Guy
must be nuts. Sending a wire to a hotel three blocks away."

Cefarino Toribo strolled along Spring Street, trailing smoke over his neat shoulder from a chocolate-colored cigarette. At Fourth he turned west, went three blocks more, turned into the side entrance of the Mansfield, by the barber-shop. He went up some marble steps to a mezzanine, along the back of a writing room and up carpeted steps to the third floor. He passed the elevators and swaggered down a long corridor to the end, looking at the numbers on doors.

He came back halfway to the elevators, sat down in an open space where there was a pair of windows on the court, a glass-topped table and chairs. He lit a fresh cigarette from his stub, leaned back and listened to the elevators.

He leaned forward sharply whenever one stopped at that floor, listening for steps. The steps came in something over ten minutes. He stood up and went to the corner of the wall where the widened-out space began. He took a long thin gun out from under his right arm, transferred it to his right hand, held it down against the wall beside his leg.

A squat, pockmarked Filipino in bellhop's uniform came along the corridor, carrying a small tray. Toribo made a hissing noise, lifted the gun. The squat Filipino whirled. His mouth opened and his eyes bulged at the gun.

Toribo said, "What room, punk?"

The squat Filipino smiled very nervously, placatingly. He came close, showed Toribo a yellow envelope on his tray. The figures 338 were penciled on the window of the envelope.

"Put it down," Toribo said calmly.

The squat Filipino put the telegram on the table. He kept his eyes on the gun.

"Beat it," Toribo said. "You put it under the door, see?"

The squat Filipino ducked his round black head, smiled nervously again, and went away very quickly towards the elevators.

Toribo put the gun in his jacket pocket, took out a folded white paper. He opened it very carefully, shook glistening white powder from it on to the hollow place formed between his left thumb and forefinger when he spread his hand. He sniffed the powder sharply up his nose, took out a flame-colored silk handkerchief and wiped his nose.

He stood still for a little while. His eyes got the dullness of slate and the skin on his brown face seemed to tighten over his high cheekbones. He breathed audibly between his teeth.

He picked the yellow envelope up and went along the corridor to the end, stopped in front of the last door, knocked.

A voice called out. He put his lips close to the door, spoke in a high-pitched, very deferential voice.

"Mail for you, sar."

Bedsprings creaked. Steps came across the floor inside. A key turned and the door opened. Toribo had his thin gun out again by this time. As the door opened he stepped swiftly into the opening, sidewise, with a graceful sway of his hips. He put the muzzle of the thin gun against Max Chill's abdomen.

"Back up!" he snarled, and his voice now had the metallic twang of a plucked banjo string.

Max Chill backed away from the gun. He backed across the room to the bed, sat down on the bed when his legs struck the side of it. Springs creaked and a newspaper rustled. Max Chill's pale face under the neatly parted brown hair had no expression at all.

Toribo shut the door softly, snapped the lock. When the door latch snapped, Max Chill's face suddenly became a sick face. His lips began to shake, kept on shaking.

Toribo said mockingly, in his twangy voice: "You talk to the cops, huh? *Adios*."

The thin gun jumped in his hand, kept on jumping. A little pale smoke lisped from the muzzle. The noise the gun made was no louder than a hammer striking a nail or knuckles rapping sharply on wood. It made that noise seven times.

Max Chill lay down on the bed very slowly. His feet stayed on the floor. His eyes went blank, and his lips parted and a pinkish froth seethed on them. Blood showed in several places on the front of his loose shirt. He lay quite still on his back and looked at the ceiling with his feet touching the floor and the pink froth bubbling on his blue lips.

Toribo moved the gun to his left hand and put it away under his arm. He sidled over to the bed and stood beside it, looking down at Max Chill. After a while the pink froth stopped bubbling and Max Chill's face became the quiet, empty face of a dead man.

Toribo went back to the door, opened it, started to back out, his eyes still on the bed. There was a stir of movement behind him.

He started to whirl, snatching a hand up. Something looped at his head. The floor tilted queerly before his eyes, rushed up at his face. He didn't know when it struck his face.

Delaguerra kicked the Filipino's legs into the room, out of the way of the door. He shut the door, locked it, walked stiffly over to the bed, swinging a thonged sap at his side. He stood beside the bed for quite a long time. At last he said under his breath: "They clean up. Yeah – they clean up."

He went back to the Filipino, rolled him over and went through his pockets. There was a well-lined wallet without any identification, a gold lighter set with garnets, a gold cigarette case, keys, a gold pencil and knife, the flame-colored handkerchief, loose money, two guns and spare clips for them, and five bindles of heroin powder in the ticket pocket of the tan jacket.

He left it thrown around on the floor, stood up. The Filipino breathed heavily, with his eyes shut, a muscle twitching in one cheek. Delaguerra took a coil of thin wire out of his pocket and wired the brown man's wrists behind him. He dragged him over to the bed, sat him up against the leg, looped a strand of the wire around his neck and around the bedpost. He tied the flame-colored handkerchief to the looped wire.

He went into the bathroom and got a glass of water and threw it into the Filipino's face as hard as he could throw it.

Toribo jerked, gagged sharply as the wire caught his neck. His eyes jumped open. He opened his mouth to yell.

Delaguerra jerked the wire taut against the brown throat. The yell was cut off as though by a switch. There was a strained anguished gurgle. Toribo's mouth drooled.

Delaguerra let the wire go slack again and put his head down close to the Filipino's head. He spoke to him gently, with a dry, very deadly gentleness.

"You want to talk to me, spig. Maybe not right away, maybe not even soon. But after a while you want to talk to me."

The Filipino's eyes rolled yellowly. He spat. Then his lips came together, tight.

Delaguerra smiled a faint, grim smile. "Tough boy," he said softly. He jerked the handkerchief back, held it tight and hard, biting into the brown throat above the Adam's apple.

The Filipino's legs began to jump on the floor. His body moved in sudden lunges. The brown of his face became a thick congested purple. His eyes bulged, shot with blood.

Delaguerra let the wire go loose again.

The Filipino gasped air into his lungs. His head sagged, then jerked back against the bedpost. He shook with a chill.

"Sí . . . I talk," he breathed.

11

WHEN THE BELL rang Ironhead Toomey very carefully put a black ten down on a red jack. Then he licked his lips and put all the cards down and looked around towards the front door of the bungalow, through the dining-room arch. He stood up slowly, a big brute of a man with loose gray hair and a big nose.

In the living-room beyond the arch a thin blonde girl was lying on a davenport, reading a magazine under a lamp with a torn red shade. She was pretty, but too pale, and her thin, high-arched eyebrows gave her face a startled look. She put the magazine down and swung her feet to the floor and looked at Ironhead Toomey with sharp, sudden fear in her eyes.

Toomey jerked his thumb silently. The girl stood up and went very quickly through the arch and through a swing door into the kitchen. She shut the swing door slowly, so that it made no noise.

The bell rang again, longer. Toomey shoved his white-socked feet into carpet slippers, hung a pair of glasses on his big nose, took a revolver off a chair beside him. He picked a crumpled newspaper off the floor and arranged it loosely in front of the gun, which he held in his left hand. He strolled unhurriedly to the front door.

He was yawning as he opened it, peering with sleepy eyes through the glasses at the tall man who stood on the porch.

"Okay," he said wearily. "Talk it up."

Delaguerra said: "I'm a police officer. I want to see Stella La Motte."

Ironhead Toomey put an arm like a Yule log across the door frame and leaned solidly against it. His expression remained bored.

"Wrong dump, copper. No broads here."

Delaguerra said: "I'll come in and look."

Toomey said cheerfully: "You will – like hell."

Delaguerra jerked a gun out of his pocket very smoothly and swiftly, smashed it at Toomey's left wrist. The newspaper and the big revolver fell down on the floor of the porch. Toomey's face got a less bored expression.

"Old gag," Delaguerra snapped. "Let's go in."

Toomey shook his left wrist, took his other arm off the door frame and swung hard at Delaguerra's jaw. Delaguerra moved his head about four inches. He frowned, made a dis-approving noise with his tongue and lips.

Toomey dived at him. Delaguerra sidestepped and chopped the gun at a big gray head. Toomey landed on his stomach, half in the house and half out on the porch. He grunted, planted his hands firmly and started to get up again, as if nothing had hit him.

Delaguerra kicked Toomey's gun out of the way. A swing door inside the house made a light sound. Toomey was up on one knee and one hand as Delaguerra looked towards the noise. He took a swing at Delaguerra's stomach, hit him. Delaguerra grunted and hit Toomey on the head again, hard. Toomey shook his head, growled: "Sappin' me is a waste of time, bo."

He dived sidewise, got hold of Delaguerra's leg, jerked the leg off the floor. Delaguerra sat down on the boards of the porch, jammed in the doorway. His head hit the side of the doorway, dazed him.

The thin blonde rushed through the arch with a small automatic in her hand. She pointed it at Delaguerra, said furiously: "Reach, damn you!"

Delaguerra shook his head, started to say something, then caught his breath as Toomey twisted his foot. Toomey set his teeth hard and twisted the foot as if he was all alone in the world with it and it was his foot and he could do what he liked with it.

Delaguerra's head jerked back again and his face got white. His mouth twisted into a harsh grimace of pain. He heaved up, grabbed Toomey's hair with his left hand, dragged the big head up and over until his chin came up, straining. Delaguerra smashed the barrel of his Colt on the skin.

Toomey became limp, an inert mass, fell across his legs and pinned him to the floor. Delaguerra couldn't move. He was propped on the floor on his right hand, trying to keep from being pushed flat by Toomey's weight. He couldn't get his right hand with the gun in it off the floor. The blonde was closer to him now, wild-eyed, white-faced with rage.

Delaguerra said in a spent voice: "Don't be a fool, Stella. Joey – "

The blonde's face was unnatural. Her eyes were unnatural, with small pupils, a queer flat glitter in them.

"Cops!" she almost screamed. "Cops! God, how I hate cops!"

The gun in her hand crashed. The echoes of it filled the room, went out of the open front door, died against the high-board fence across the street.

A sharp blow like the blow of a club hit the left side of Delaguerra's head. Pain filled his head. Light flared – blinding white light that filled the world. Then it was dark. He fell soundlessly, into bottomless darkness.

12

LIGHT CAME BACK as a red fog in front of his eyes. Hard, bitter pain racked the side of his head, his whole face, ground in his teeth. His tongue was hot and thick when he tried to move it. He tried to move his hands. They were far away from him, not his hands at all.

Then he opened his eyes and the red fog went away and he was looking at a face. It was a big face, very close to him, a huge face. It was fat and had sleek blue jowls and there was a cigar with a bright band in a grinning, thick-lipped mouth. The face chuckled. Delaguerra closed his eyes again and the pain washed over him, submerged him. He passed out.

Seconds, or years, passed. He was looking at the face again. He heard a thick voice.

"Well, he's with us again. A pretty tough lad at that."

The face came closer, the end of the cigar glowed cherry-red. Then he was coughing rackingly, gagging on smoke. The side of his head seemed to burst open. He felt fresh blood slide down his cheekbone, tickling the skin, then slide over stiff dried blood that had already caked on his face.

"That fixes him up swell," the thick voice said.

Another voice with a touch of brogue to it said something gentle and obscene. The big face whirled towards the sound, snarling.

Delaguerra came wide awake then. He saw the room clearly, saw the four people in it. The big face was the face of Big John Masters.

The thin blonde girl was hunched on one end of the davenport, staring at the floor with a doped expression, her arms stiff at her sides, her hands out of sight in the cushions.

Dave Aage had his long lank body propped against a wall beside a curtained window. His wedge-shaped face looked bored. Commissioner Drew was on the other end of the davenport, under the frayed lamp. The light made silver in his hair. His blue eyes were very bright, very intent.

There was a shiny gun in Big John Masters' hand. Delaguerra blinked at it, started to get up. A hard hand jerked at his chest, jarred him back. A wave of nausea went over him. The thick voice said harshly: "Hold it, pussyfoot. You've had your fun. This is our party."

Delaguerra licked his lips, said: "Give me a drink of water."

Dave Aage stood away from the wall and went through the dining-room arch. He came back with a glass, held it to Delaguerra's mouth. Delaguerra drank.

Masters said: "We like your guts, copper. But you don't use them right. It seems you're a guy that can't take a hint. That's too bad. That makes you through. Get me?"

The blonde turned her head and looked at Delaguerra with heavy eyes, looked away again. Aage went back to his wall. Drew began to stroke the side of his face with quick nervous fingers, as if Delaguerra's bloody head made his own face hurt.

Delaguerra said slowly: "Killing me will just hang you a little higher, Masters. A sucker on the big time is still a sucker. You've had two men killed already for no reason at all. You don't even know what you're trying to cover."

The big man swore harshly, jerked the shiny gun up, then lowered it slowly, with a heavy leer. Aage said indolently: "Take it easy, John. Let him speak his piece."

Delaguerra said in the same slow, careless voice: "The lady over there is the sister of the two men you've had killed. She told them her story, about framing Imlay, who got the pictures, how they got to Donegan Marr. Your little Filipino hood has done some singing. I get the general idea all right. You couldn't be sure Imlay would kill Marr. Maybe Marr would get Imlay. It would work out all right either way. Only, if Imlay did kill Marr, the case had to be broken fast. That's where you slipped. You started to cover up before you really knew what happened."

Masters said harshly: "Crummy, copper, crummy. You're wasting my time."

The blonde turned her head towards Delaguerra, towards Masters' back. There was hard green hate in her eyes now. Delaguerra shrugged very slightly, went on: "It was routine stuff for you to put killers on the Chill brothers. It was routine stuff to get me off the investigation, get me framed, and suspended because you figured I was on Marr's payroll. But it wasn't routine when you couldn't find Imlay – and that crowded you."

Masters' hard black eyes got wide and empty. His thick neck swelled. Aage came away from the wall a few feet and stood rigidly. After a moment Masters snapped his teeth, spoke very quietly: "That's a honey, copper. Tell us about that one."

Delaguerra touched his smeared face with the tips of two fingers, looked at the fingers. His eyes were depthless, ancient.

"Imlay is dead, Masters. He was dead before Marr was killed."

The room was very still. Nobody moved in it. The four people Delaguerra looked at were frozen with shock. After a long time Masters drew in a harsh breath and blew it out and almost whispered: "Tell it, copper. Tell it fast, or by God I'll – "

Delaguerra's voice cut in on him coldly, without any emotion at all: "Imlay went to see Marr all right. Why wouldn't he? He didn't know he was double-crossed. Only he went to see him last night, not today. He rode up to the cabin at Puma Lake with him, to talk things over in a friendly way. That was the gag, anyhow. Then, up there, they had their fight and Imlay got killed, got dumped off the end of the porch, got his head smashed open on some rocks. He's dead as last Christmas, in the woodshed of Marr's cabin . . . Okay, Marr hid him and came back to town. Then today he got a phone call, mentioning the name Imlay, making a date for twelve-fifteen. What would Marr do? Stall, of course, send his office girl off to lunch, put a gun where he could reach it in a hurry. He was all set for trouble then. Only the visitor fooled him and he didn't use the gun."

Masters said gruffly: "Hell, man, you're just cracking wise. You couldn't know all those things."

He looked back at Drew. Drew was gray-faced, taut. Aage came a little farther away from the wall and stood close to Drew. The blonde girl didn't move a muscle.

Delaguerra said wearily: "Sure, I'm guessing, but I'm guessing to fit the facts. It had to be like that. Marr was no slouch with a gun and he was on edge, all set. Why didn't he get a shot in? Because it was a woman that called on him."

He lifted an arm, pointed at the blonde. "There's your killer. She loved Imlay even though she framed him. She's a junkie and junkies are like that. She got sad and sorry and she went after Marr herself. Ask her!"

The blonde stood up in a smooth lunge. Her right hand jerked up from the cushions with a small automatic in it, the one she had shot Delaguerra with. Her green eyes were pale and empty and staring. Masters whirled around, flailed at her arm with the shiny revolver.

She shot him twice, point-blank, without a flicker of hesitation. Blood spurted from the side of his thick neck, down the front of his coat. He staggered, dropped the shiny revolver, almost at Delaguerra's feet. He fell outwards towards the wall behind Delaguerra's chair, one arm groping out for the wall. His hand hit the wall and trailed down it as he fell. He crashed heavily, didn't move again.

Delaguerra had the shiny revolver almost in his hand.

Drew was on his feet yelling. The girl turned slowly towards Aage, seemed to ignore Delaguerra. Aage jerked a Luger from under his arm and knocked Drew out of the way with his arm. The small automatic and the Luger roared at the same time. The small gun missed. The girl was flung down on the davenport, her left hand clutching at her breast. She rolled her eyes, tried to lift the gun again. Then she fell sidewise on the cushions and her left hand went lax, dropped away from her breast. The front of her dress was a sudden welter of blood. Her eyes opened and shut, opened and stayed open.

Aage swung the Luger towards Delaguerra. His eyebrows were twisted up into a sharp grin of intense strain. His smoothly combed, sand-colored hair flowed down his bony scalp as tightly as though it were painted on it.

Delaguerra shot him four times, so rapidly that the explosions were like the rattle of a machine gun.

In the instant of time before he fell Aage's face became the thin, empty face of an old man, his eyes the vacant eyes of an idiot. Then his long body jackknifed to the floor, the Luger still in his hand. One leg doubled under him as if there was no bone in it.

Powder smell was sharp in the air. The air was stunned by the sound of guns. Delaguerra got to his feet slowly, motioned to Drew with the shiny revolver.

"Your party, Commissioner. Is this anything like what you wanted?"

Drew nodded slowly, white-faced, quivering. He swallowed, moved slowly across the floor, past Aage's sprawled body. He looked down at the girl on the davenport, shook his head. He went over to Masters, went down on one knee, touched him. He stood up again.

"All dead, I think," he muttered.

Delaguerra said: "That's swell. What happened to the big boy? The bruiser?"

"They sent him away. I – I don't think they meant to kill you, Delaguerra."

Delaguerra nodded a little. His face began to soften, the rigid lines began to go out of it. The side that was not a bloodstained mask began to look human again. He sopped at his face with a handkerchief. It came away bright red with blood. He threw it away and lightly fingered his matted hair into place. Some of it was caught in the dried blood.

"The hell they didn't," he said.

The house was very still. There was no noise outside. Drew listened, sniffed, went to the front door and looked out. The street outside was dark, silent. He came back close to Delaguerra. Very slowly a smile worked itself on to his face.

"It's a hell of a note," he said, "when a commissioner of police has to be his own undercover man – and a square cop had to be framed off the force to help him."

Delaguerra looked at him without expression. "You want to play it that way?"

Drew spoke calmly now. The pink was back in his face. "For the good of the department, man, and the city – and ourselves, it's the only way to play it."

Delaguerra looked him straight in the eyes.

"I like it that way too," he said in a dead voice. "If it gets played – *exactly* that way."

13

MARCUS BRAKED THE car to a stop and grinned admiringly at the big tree-shaded house.

"Pretty nice," he said. "I could go for a long rest there myself."

Delaguerra got out of the car slowly, as if he was stiff and very tired. He was hatless, carried his straw under his arm. Part of the left side of his head was shaved and the shaved part covered by a thick pad of gauze and tape, over the stitches. A wick of wiry black hair stuck up over one edge of the bandage, with a ludicrous effect.

He said: "Yeah – but I'm not staying here, sap. Wait for me."

He went along the path of stones that wound through the grass. Trees speared long shadows across the lawn, through the morning sunlight. The house was very still, with drawn blinds, a dark wreath on the brass knocker. Delaguerra didn't go up to the door. He turned off along another path under the windows and went along the side of the house past the gladioli beds.

There were more trees at the back, more lawn, more flowers, more sun and shadow. There was a pond with water lilies in it and a big stone bullfrog. Beyond was a half-circle of lawn chairs around an iron table with a tile top. In one of the chairs Belle Marr sat.

She wore a black-and-white dress, loose and casual, and there was a wide-brimmed garden hat on her chestnut hair. She sat very still, looking into the distance across the lawn. Her face was white. The make-up glared on it.

She turned her head slowly, smiled a dull smile, motioned to a chair beside her. Delaguerra didn't sit down. He took his straw from under his arm, snapped a finger at the brim, said: "The case is closed. There'll be inquests, investigations, threats, a lot of people shouting their mouths off to horn in on the publicity, that sort of thing. The papers will play it big for a while. But underneath, on the record, it's closed. You can begin to try to forget it."

The girl looked at him suddenly, widened her vivid blue eyes, looked away again, over the grass.

"Is your head very bad, Sam?" she asked softly.

Delaguerra said: "No. It's fine . . . What I mean is the La Motte girl shot Masters — and she shot Donny. Aage shot her. I shot Aage. All dead, ring around the rosy. Just how Imlay got killed we'll not know ever, I guess. I can't see that it matters now."

Without looking up at him Belle Marr said quietly: "But how did you know it was Imlay up at the cabin? The paper said — " She broke off, shuddered suddenly.

He stared woodenly at the hat he was holding. "I didn't. I thought a woman shot Donny. It looked like a good hunch that was Imlay up at the lake. It fitted his description."

"How did you know it was a woman . . . that killed Donny?" Her voice had a lingering, half-whispered stillness.

"I just knew."

He walked away a few steps, stood looking at the trees. He turned slowly, came back, stood beside her chair again. His face was very weary.

"We had great times together — the three of us. You and Donny and I. Life seems to do nasty things to people. It's all gone now — all the good part."

Her voice was still a whisper saying: "Maybe not all gone, Sam. We must see a lot of each other, from now on."

A vague smile moved the corners of his lips, went away again. "It's my first frame-up," he said quietly. "I hope it will be my last."

Belle Marr's head jerked a little. Her hands took hold of the arms of the chair, looked white against the varnished wood. Her whole body seemed to get rigid.

After a moment Delaguerra reached in his pocket and something gold glittered in his hand. He looked down at it dully.

"Got the badge back," he said. "It's not quite as clean as it was. Clean as most, I suppose. I'll try to keep it that way." He put it back in his pocket.

Very slowly the girl stood up in front of him. She lifted her chin, stared at him with a long level stare. Her face was a mask of white plaster behind the rouge.

She said: "My God, Sam — I begin to understand."

Delaguerra didn't look at her face. He looked past her shoulder at some vague spot in the distance. He spoke vaguely, distantly.

"Sure . . . I thought it was a woman because it was a small gun such as a woman would use. But not only on that account. After I went up to the cabin I knew Donny was primed for trouble and it wouldn't be that easy for a man to get the drop on him. But it was a perfect set-up for Imlay to have done it. Masters and Aage assumed he'd done it and had a lawyer phone in admitting he did it and promising to surrender him in the morning. So it was natural for anyone who didn't know Imlay was dead to fall in line. Besides, no cop would expect a woman to pick up her shells.

"After I got Joey Chill's story I thought it might be the La Motte girl. But I didn't think so when I said it in front of her. That was dirty. It got her killed, in a way. Though I wouldn't give much for her chances anyway, with that bunch."

Belle Marr was still staring at him. The breeze blew a wisp of her hair and that was the only thing about her that moved.

He brought his eyes back from the distance, looked at her gravely for a brief moment, looked away again. He took a small bunch of keys out of his pocket, tossed them down on the table.

"Three things were tough to figure until I got completely wise. The writing on the pad, the gun in Donny's hand, the missing shells. Then I tumbled to it. He didn't die right away. He had guts and he used them to the last flicker — to protect somebody. The writing on the pad was a bit shaky. He wrote it afterwards, when he was alone, dying. He had been thinking of Imlay and writing the name helped mess the trial. Then he got the gun out of his desk to die with it in his hand. That left the shells. I got that too, after a while.

"The shots were fired close, across the desk, and there were books on one end of the desk. The shells fell there, stayed on the desk where he could get them. He couldn't have got them off the floor. There's a key to the office on your ring. I went there last night, late. I found the shells in a humidor with his cigars. Nobody looked for them there. You only find what you expect to find, after all."

He stopped talking and rubbed the side of his face. After a moment he added: "Donny did the best he could – and then he died. It was a swell job – and I'm letting him get away with it."

Belle Marr opened her mouth slowly. A kind of babble came out of it first, then words, clear words.

"It wasn't just women, Sam. It was the kind of women he had." She shivered. "I'll go downtown now and give myself up."

Delaguerra said: "No. I told you I was letting him get away with it. Downtown they like it the way it is. It's swell politics. It gets the city out from under the Masters–Aage mob. It puts Drew on top for a little while, but he's too weak to last. So that doesn't matter . . . You're not going to do anything about any of it. You're going to do what Donny used his last strength to show he wanted. You're staying out. Goodbye."

He looked at her white shattered face once more, very quickly. Then he swung around, walked away over the lawn, past the pool with the lily pads and the stone bullfrog along the side of the house and out to the car.

Pete Marcus swung the door open. Delaguerra got in and sat down and put his head far back against the seat, slumped down in the car and closed his eyes. He said flatly: "Take it easy, Pete. My head hurts like hell."

Marcus started the car and turned into the street, drove slowly back along De Neve Lane towards town. The tree-shaded house disappeared behind them. The tall trees finally hid it.

When they were a long way from it Delaguerra opened his eyes again.

GUNS AT CYRANO'S

1

TED CARMADY LIKED the rain; liked the feel of it; the sound of it, the smell of it. He got out of his LaSalle coupe and stood for a while by the side entrance to the Carondelet, the high collar of his blue suede ulster tickling his ears, his hands in his pockets and a limp cigarette sputtering between his lips. Then he went in past the barbershop and the drugstore and the perfume shop with its rows of delicately lighted bottles, ranged like the ensemble in the finale of a Broadway musical.

He rounded a gold-veined pillar and got into an elevator with a cushioned floor.

" 'Lo Albert. A swell rain. Nine."

The slim tired-looking kid in pale blue and silver held a white-gloved hand against the closing doors, said: "Jeeze, you think I don't know your floor, Mister Carmady?"

He shot the car up to nine without looking at his signal light, whooshed the doors open, then leaned suddenly against the cage and closed his eyes.

Carmady stopped on his way out, flicked a sharp glance from bright brown eyes. "What's the matter, Albert? Sick?"

The boy worked a pale smile on his face. "I'm workin' double shift. Corky's sick. He's got boils. I guess maybe I didn't eat enough."

The tall, brown-eyed man fished a crumpled five-spot out of his pocket, snapped it under the boy's nose. The boy's eyes bulged. He heaved upright.

"Jeeze, Mister Carmady. I didn't mean – "

"Skip it, Albert. What's a fin between pals? Eat some extra meals on me."

He got out of the car and started along the corridor. Softly, under his breath, he said: "Sucker . . ."

The running man almost knocked him off his feet. He rounded the turn fast, lurched past Carmady's shoulder, ran for the elevator.

"Down!" He slammed through the closing doors.

Carmady saw a white set face under a pulled-down hat that was wet with rain; two empty black eyes set very close. Eyes in which there was a peculiar stare he had seen before. A load of dope.

The car dropped like lead. Carmady looked at the place where it had been for a long moment, then he went on down the corridor and around the turn.

He saw the girl lying half in and half out of the open door of 914.

She lay on her side, in a sheen of steel-gray lounging pajamas, her cheek pressed into the nap of the hall carpet, her head a mass of thick corn-blond hair, waved with glassy precision. Not a hair looked out of place. She was young, very pretty, and she didn't look dead.

Carmady slid down beside her, touched her cheek. It was warm. He lifted the hair softly away from her head and saw the bruise.

"Sapped." His lips pressed back against his teeth.

He picked her up in his arms, carried her through a short hallway to the living-room of a suite, put her down on a big velour davenport in front of some gas logs.

She lay motionless, her eyes shut, her face bluish behind the make-up. He shut the outer door and looked through the apartment, then went back to the hallway and picked up something that gleamed white against the baseboard. It was a bone-handled .22 automatic, sevenshot. He sniffed it, dropped it into his pocket and went back to the girl.

He took a big hammered-silver flask out of his inside breast pocket and unscrewed the top, opened her mouth with his fingers and poured whiskey against her small white teeth. She gagged and her head jerked out of his hand. Her eyes opened. They were deep blue, with a tint of purple. Light came into them and the light was brittle.

He lit a cigarette and stood looking down at her. She moved a little more. After a while she whispered: "I like your whiskey. Could I have a little more?"

He got a glass from the bathroom, poured whiskey into it. She sat up very slowly, touched her head, groaned. Then she took the glass out of his hand and put the liquor down with a practised flip of the wrist.

"I still like it," she said. "Who are you?"

She had a deep soft voice. He liked the sound of it. He said: "Ted Carmady. I live down the hall in 937."

"I got a dizzy spell, I guess."

"Uh-huh. You got sapped, angel." His bright eyes looked at her probingly. There was a smile tucked to the corners of his lips.

Her eyes got wider. A glaze came over them, the glaze of a protective enamel.

He said: "I saw the guy. He was snowed to the hairline. And here's your gun."

He took it out of his pocket, held it on the flat of his hand.

"I suppose that makes me think up a bedtime story," the girl said slowly.

"Not for me. If you're in a jam, I might help you. It all depends."

"Depends on what?" Her voice was colder, sharper.

"On what the racket is," he said softly. He broke the magazine from the small gun, glanced at the top cartridge. "Copper-nickel, eh? You know your ammunition, angel."

"Do you have to call me angel?"

"I don't know your name."

He grinned at her, then walked over to a desk in front of the windows, put the gun down on it. There was a leather photo frame on the desk, with two photos side by side. He looked at them casually at first, then his gaze tightened. A handsome dark woman and a thin blondish cold-eyed man whose high stiff collar, large knotted tie and narrow lapels dated the photo back many years. He stared at the man.

The girl was talking behind him. "I'm Jean Adrian. I do a number at Cyrano's, in the floor show."

Carmady still stared at the photo. "I know Benny Cyrano pretty well," he said absently. "These your parents?"

He turned and looked at her. She lifted her head slowly. Something that might have been fear showed in her deep blue eyes.

"Yes. They've been dead for years," she said dully. "Next question?"

He went quickly back to the davenport and stood in front of her. "Okay," he said thinly. "I'm nosey. So what? This is my town. My dad used to run it. Old Marcus Carmady, the People's Friend; this is my hotel. I own a piece of it. That snowed-up hoodlum looked like a life-taker to me. Why wouldn't I want to help out?"

The blonde girl stared at him lazily. "I still like your whiskey," she said. "Could I – "

"Take it from the neck, angel. You get it down faster," he grunted.

She stood up suddenly and her face got a little white. "You talk to me as if I was a crook," she snapped. "Here it is, if you have to know. A boy friend of mine has been getting threats. He's a fighter, and they want him to drop a fight. Now they're trying to get at him through me. Does that satisfy you a little?"

Carmady picked his hat off a chair, took the cigarette end out of his mouth and rubbed it out in a tray. He nodded quietly, said in a changed voice: "I beg your pardon." He started towards the door.

The giggle came when he was halfway there. The girl said behind him softly: "You have a nasty temper. And you've forgotten your flask."

He went back and picked the flask up. Then he bent suddenly, put a hand under the girl's chin and kissed her on the lips.

"To hell with you, angel. I like you," he said softly.

He went back to the hallway and out. The girl touched her lips with one finger, rubbed it slowly back and forth. There was a shy smile on her face.

2

TONY ACOSTA, THE bell captain, was slim and dark and slight as a girl, with small delicate hands and velvety eyes and a hard little mouth. He stood in the doorway and said: "Seventh row was the best I could get, Mister Carmady. This Deacon Werra ain't bad and Duke Targo's the next light heavy champ."

Carmady said: "Come in and have a drink, Tony." He went over to the window, stood looking out at the rain. "If they buy it for him," he added over his shoulder.

"Well – just a short one, Mister Carmady."

The dark boy mixed a highball carefully at a tray on an imitation Sheraton desk. He held the bottle against the light and gauged his drink carefully, tinkled ice gently with a long spoon, sipped, smiled, showing small white teeth.

"Targo's a lu, Mister Carmady. He's fast, clever, got a sock in both mitts, plenty guts, don't ever take a step back."

"He has to hold up the bums they feed him," Carmady drawled.

"Well, they ain't fed him no lion meat yet," Tony said.

The rain beat against the glass. The thick drops flattened out and washed down the pane in tiny waves.

Carmady said: "He's a bum. A bum with color and looks, but still a bum."

Tony sighed deeply. "I wisht I was goin'. It's my night off, too."

Carmady turned slowly and went over to the desk, mixed a drink. Two dusky spots showed in his cheeks and his voice was tired, drawling.

"So that's it. What's stopping you?"

"I got a headache."

"You're broke again," Carmady almost snarled.

The dark boy looked sidewise under his long lashes, said nothing.

Carmady clenched his left hand, unclenched it slowly. His eyes were sullen.

"Just ask Carmady," he sighed. "Good old Carmady. He leaks dough. He's soft. Just ask Carmady. Okay, Tony, take the ducat back and get a pair together."

He reached into his pocket, held a bill out. The dark boy looked hurt.

"Jeeze, Mister Carmady, I wouldn't have you think – "

"Skip it! What's a fight ticket between pals? Get a couple and take your girl. To hell with this Targo."

Tony Acosta took the bill. He watched the older man carefully for a moment. Then his voice was very soft, saying: "I'd rather go with you, Mister Carmady. Targo knocks them over, and not only in the ring. He's got a peachy blonde right on this floor, Miss Adrian, in 914."

Carmady stiffened. He put his glass down slowly, turned it on the top of the desk. His voice got a little hoarse.

"He's still a bum, Tony. Okay, I'll meet you for dinner, in front of your hotel at seven."

"Jeeze, that's swell, Mister Carmady."

Tony Acosta went out softly, closed the outer door without a sound.

Carmady stood by the desk, his fingertips stroking the top of it, his eyes on the floor. He stood like that for a long time.

"Carmady, the All-American sucker," he said grimly, out loud. "A guy that plays with the help and carries the torch for stray broads. Yeah."

He finished his drink, looked at his wrist watch, put on his hat and the blue suede raincoat, went out. Down the corridor in front of 914 he stopped, lifted his hand to knock, then dropped it without touching the door.

He went slowly on to the elevators and rode down to the street and his car.

★

The *Tribune* office was at Fourth and Spring. Carmady parked around the corner, went in at the employees' entrance and rode to the fourth floor in a rickety elevator operated by an old man with a dead cigar in his mouth and a rolled magazine which he held six inches from his nose while he ran the elevator.

On the fourth floor big double doors were lettered City Room. Another old man sat outside them at a small desk with a call box.

Carmady tapped on the desk, said: "Adams. Carmady calling."

The old man made noises into the box, released a key, pointed with his chin.

Carmady went through the doors, past a horseshoe copy desk, then past a row of small desks at which typewriters were being banged. At the far end a lanky red-haired man was doing nothing with his feet on a pulled-out drawer, the back of his neck on the back of a dangerously tilted swivel chair and a big pipe in his mouth pointed straight at the ceiling.

When Carmady stood beside him he moved his eyes down without moving any other part of his body and said around the pipe: "Greetings, Carmady. How's the idle rich?"

Carmady said: "How's a glance at your clips on a guy named Courtway? State Senator John Myerson Courtway, to be precise."

Adams put his feet on the floor. He raised himself erect by pulling on the edge of his desk. He brought his pipe down level, took it out of his mouth and spit into a wastebasket. He said: "That old icicle? When was he ever news? Sure." He stood up wearily, added: "Come along, Uncle," and started along the end of the room.

They went along another row of desks, past a fat girl in smudged make-up who was typing and laughing at what she was writing.

They went through a door into a big room that was mostly six-foot tiers of filing cases with an occasional alcove in which there was a small table and a chair.

Adams prowled the filing cases, jerked one out and set a folder on a table.

"Park yourself. What's the graft?"

Carmady leaned on the table on an elbow, scuffed through a thick wad of cuttings. They were monotonous, political in nature, not front page. Senator Courtway said this and that on this and that matter of public interest, addressed this and that meeting, went or returned from this and that place. It all seemed very dull.

He looked at a few halftone cuts of a thin, white-haired man with a blank, composed face, deep-set dark eyes in which there was no light or warmth. After a while he said: "Got a print I could sneeze? A real one, I mean."

Adams sighed, stretched himself, disappeared down the line of file walls. He came back with a shiny black-and-white photograph, tossed it down on the table.

"You can keep it," he said. "We got dozens. The guy lives forever. Shall I have it autographed for you?"

Carmady looked at the photo with narrow eyes, for a long time. "It's right," he said slowly. "Was Courtway ever married?"

"Not since I left off my diapers," Adams growled. "Probably not ever. Say, what'n hell's the mystery?"

Carmady smiled slowly at him. He reached his flask out, set it on the table beside the folder. Adams' face brightened swiftly and his long arm reached.

"Then he never had a kid," Carmady said.

Adams leered over the flask. "Well – not for publication, I guess. If I'm any judge of a mug, not at all." He drank deeply, wiped his lips, drank again.

"And that," Carmady said, "is very funny indeed. Have three more drinks – and forget you ever saw me."

3

THE FAT MAN put his face close to Carmady's face. He said with a wheeze: "You think it's fixed, neighbor?"

"Yeah. For Werra."

"How much says so?"

"Count your poke."

"I got five yards that want to grow."

"Take it," Carmady said tonelessly, and kept on looking at the back of a corn-blond head in a ringside seat. A white wrap with white fur was below the glassily waved hair. He couldn't see the face. He didn't have to.

The fat man blinked his eyes and got a thick wallet carefully out of a pocket inside his vest. He held it on the edge of his knee, counted out ten fifty-dollar bills, rolled them up, edged the wallet back against his ribs.

"You're on, sucker," he wheezed. "Let's see your dough."

Carmady brought his eyes back, reached out a flat pack of new hundreds, riffled them. He slipped five from under the printed band, held them out.

"Boy, this is from home," the fat man said. He put his face close to Carmady's face again. "I'm Skeets O'Neal. No little powders, huh?"

Carmady smiled very slowly and pushed his money into the fat man's hand. "You hold it, Skeets. I'm Carmady. Old

Marcus Carmady's son. I can shoot faster than you can run – and fix it afterwards."

The fat man took a long hard breath and leaned back in his seat. Tony Acosta stared soft-eyed at the money in the fat man's pudgy tight hand. He licked his lips and turned a small embarrassed smile on Carmady.

"Gee, that's lost dough, Mister Carmady," he whispered. "Unless – unless you got something inside."

"Enough to be worth a five-yard plunge," Carmady growled.

The buzzer sounded for the sixth.

The first five had been anybody's fight. The big blond boy, Duke Targo, wasn't trying. The dark one, Deacon Werra, a powerful, loose-limbed Polack with bad teeth and only two cauliflower ears, had the physique but didn't know anything but rough clinching and a giant swing that started in the basement and never connected. He had been good enough to hold Targo off so far. The fans razzed Targo a good deal.

When the stool swung back out of the ring Targo hitched at his black and silver trunks, smiled with a small tight smile at the girl in the white wrap. He was very good-looking, without a mark on him. There was blood on his left shoulder from Werra's nose.

The bell rang and Werra charged across the ring, slid off Targo's shoulder, got a left hook in. Targo got more of the hook than was in it. He piled back into the ropes, bounced out, clinched.

Carmady smiled quietly in the darkness.

The referee broke them easily. Targo broke clean, Werra tried for an uppercut and missed. They sparred for a minute. There was waltz music from the gallery. Then Werra started a swing from his shoetops. Targo seemed to wait for it, to wait for it to hit him. There was a queer strained smile on his face. The girl in the white wrap stood up suddenly.

Werra's swing grazed Targo's jaw. It barely staggered him. Targo lashed a long right that caught Werra over the eye. A left hook smashed Werra's jaw, then a right cross almost to the same spot.

The dark boy went down on his hands and knees, slipped slowly all the way to the floor, lay with both his gloves under him. There were catcalls as he was counted out.

The fat man struggled to his feet, grinning hugely. He said: "How you like it, pal? Still think it was a set piece?"

"It came unstuck," Carmady said in a voice as toneless as a police radio.

The fat man said: "So long, pal. Come around lots." He kicked Carmady's ankle climbing over him.

Carmady sat motionless, watched the auditorium empty. The fighters and their handlers had gone down the stairs under the ring. The girl in the white wrap had disappeared in the crowd. The lights went out and the barnlike structure looked cheap, sordid.

Tony Acosta fidgeted, watching a man in striped overalls picking up papers between the seats.

Carmady stood up suddenly, said: "I'm going to talk to that bum, Tony. Wait outside in the car for me."

He went swiftly up the slope to the lobby, through the remnants of the gallery crowd to a gray door marked "No Admittance." He went through that and down a ramp to another door marked the same way. A special cop in faded and unbuttoned khaki stood in front of it, with a bottle of beer in one hand and a hamburger in the other.

Carmady flashed a police card and the cop lurched out of the way without looking at the card. He hiccoughed peacefully as Carmady went through the door, then along a narrow passage with numbered doors lining it. There was noise behind the doors. The fourth door on the left had a scribbled card with the name "Duke Targo" fastened to the panel by a thumbtack.

Carmady opened it into the heavy sound of a shower going, out of sight.

In a narrow and utterly bare room a man in a white sweater was sitting on the end of a rubbing table that had clothes scattered on it. Carmady recognized him as Targo's chief second.

He said: "Where's the Duke?"

The sweatered man jerked a thumb towards the shower noise. Then a man came around the door and lurched very close to Carmady. He was tall and had curly brown hair with hard gray color in it. He had a big drink in his hand. His face had the flat glitter of extreme drunkenness. His hair was damp, his eyes bloodshot. His lips curled and uncurled in rapid smiles without meaning. He said thickly: "Scramola, umpchay."

Carmady shut the door calmly and leaned against it and started to get his cigarette case from his vest pocket, inside his open blue raincoat. He didn't look at the curly-haired man at all.

The curly-haired man lunged his free right hand up suddenly, snapped it under his coat, out again. A blue steel gun shone dully against his light suit. The glass in his left hand slopped liquor.

"None of that!" he snarled.

Carmady brought the cigarette case out very slowly, showed it in his hand, opened it and put a cigarette between his lips. The blue gun was very close to him, not very steady. The hand holding the glass shook in a sort of jerky rhythm.

Carmady said loosely: "You *ought* to be looking for trouble."

The sweatered man got off the rubbing table. Then he stood very still and looked at the gun. The curly-haired man said: "We like trouble. Frisk him, Mike."

The sweatered man said: "I don't want any part of it, Shenvair. For Pete's sake, take it easy. You're lit like a ferry boat."

Carmady said: "It's okay to frisk me. I'm not rodded."

"Nix," the sweatered man said. "This guy is the Duke's bodyguard. Deal me out."

The curly-haired man said: "Sure, I'm drunk," and giggled.

"You're a friend of the Duke?" the sweatered man asked.

"I've got some information for him," Carmady said.

"About what?"

Carmady didn't say anything. "Okay," the sweatered man said. He shrugged bitterly.

"Know what, Mike?" the curly-haired man said suddenly and violently. "I think this sonofabitch wants my job. Hell, yes." He punched Carmady with the muzzle of the gun. "You ain't a shamus, are you, mister?"

"Maybe," Carmady said: "And keep your iron next to your own belly."

The curly-haired man turned his head a little and grinned back over his shoulder.

"What d'you know about that, Mike? He's a shamus. Sure he wants my job. Sure he does."

"Put the heater up, you fool," the sweatered man said disgustedly.

The curly-haired man turned a little more. "I'm his protection, ain't I?" he complained.

Carmady knocked the gun aside almost casually, with the hand that held his cigarette case. The curly-haired man snapped his head around again. Carmady slid close to him, sank a stiff punch in his stomach, holding the gun away with his forearm. The curly-haired man gagged, sprayed liquor down the front of Carmady's raincoat. His glass shattered on the floor. The blue gun left his hand and went over in a corner. The sweatered man went after it.

The noise of the shower had stopped unnoticed and the blond fighter came out toweling himself vigorously. He stared open-mouthed at the tableau.

Carmady said: "I don't need this any more."

He heaved the curly-haired man away from him and laced his jaw with a hard right as he went back. The curly-haired man staggered across the room, hit the wall, slid down it and sat on the floor.

The sweatered man snatched the gun up and stood rigid, watching Carmady.

Carmady got out a handkerchief and wiped the front of his coat, while Targo shut his large well-shaped mouth slowly and began to move the towel back and forth across his chest. After a moment he said: "Just who the hell may you be?"

Carmady said: "I used to be a private dick. Carmady's the name. I think you need help."

Targo's face got a little redder than the shower had left it. "Why?"

"I heard you were supposed to throw it, and I think you tried to. But Werra was too lousy. You couldn't help yourself. That means you're in a jam."

Targo said very slowly: "People get their teeth kicked in for saying things like that."

The room was very still for a moment. The drunk sat up on the floor and blinked, tried to get his feet under him, and gave it up.

Carmady added quietly: "Benny Cyrano is a friend of mine. He's your backer, isn't he?"

The sweatered man laughed harshly. Then he broke the gun and slid the shells out of it, dropped the gun on the floor. He went to the door, went out, slammed the door shut.

Targo looked at the shut door, looked back at Carmady. He said very slowly: "What did you hear?"

"Your friend Jean Adrian lives in my hotel, on my floor. She got sapped by a hood this afternoon. I happened by and saw the hood running away, picked her up. She told me a little of what it was all about."

Targo had put on his underwear and socks and shoes. He reached into a locker for a black satin shirt, put that on. He said: "She didn't tell me."

"She wouldn't – before the fight."

Targo nodded slightly. Then he said: "If you know Benny, you may be all right. I've been getting threats. Maybe it's a lot of birdseed and maybe it's some Spring Street punter's idea of how to make himself a little easy dough. I fought my fight the way I wanted to. Now you can take the air, mister."

He put on high-waisted black trousers and knotted a white tie on his black shirt. He got a white serge coat trimmed with black braid out of the locker, put that on. A black and white handkerchief flared from the pocket in three points.

Carmady stared at the clothes, moved a little towards the door and looked down at the drunk.

"Okay," he said. "I see you've got a bodyguard. It was just an idea I had. Excuse it, please."

He went out, closed the door gently, and went back up the ramp to the lobby, out to the street. He walked through the rain around the corner of the building to a big graveled parking lot.

The lights of a car blinked at him and his coupe slid along the wet gravel and pulled up. Tony Acosta was at the wheel.

Carmady got in at the right side and said: "Let's go out to Cyrano's and have a drink, Tony."

"Jeeze, that's swell. Miss Adrian's in the floor show there. You know, the blonde I told you about."

Carmady said: "I saw Targo. I kind of liked him – but I didn't like his clothes."

4

GUS NEISHACKER WAS a two-hundred-pound fashion plate with very red cheeks and thin, exquisitely penciled eyebrows – eyebrows from a Chinese vase. There was a red carnation in the lapel of his wide-shouldered dinner jacket and he kept sniffing at it while he watched the headwaiter seat a party of guests. When Carmady and Tony Acosta came through the foyer arch he flashed a sudden smile and went to them with his hand out.

"How's a boy, Ted? Party?"

Carmady said: "Just the two of us. Meet Mister Acosta. Gus Neishacker, Cyrano's floor manager."

Gus Neishacker shook hands with Tony without looking at him. He said: "Let's see, the last time you dropped in – "

"She left town," Carmady said. "We'll sit near the ring but not too near. We don't dance together."

Gus Neishacker jerked a menu from under the head-waiter's arm and led the way down five crimson steps, along the tables that skirted the oval dance floor.

They sat down. Carmady ordered rye highballs and Denver sandwiches. Neishacker gave the order to a waiter, pulled a chair out and sat down at the table. He took a pencil out and made triangles on the inside of a match cover.

"See the fights?" he asked carelessly.

"Was that what they were?"

Gus Neishacker smiled indulgently. "Benny talked to the Duke. He says you're wise." He looked suddenly at Tony Acosta.

"Tony's all right," Carmady said.

"Yeah. Well do us a favor, will you? See it stops right here. Benny likes this boy. He wouldn't let him get hurt. He'd put protection all around him – real protection – if he thought that threat stuff was anything but some pool-hall bum's idea of a very funny joke. Benny never backs but one boxfighter at a time, and he picks them damn careful."

Carmady lit a cigarette, blew smoke from a corner of his mouth, said quietly: "It's none of my business, but I'm telling you it's screwy. I have a nose for that sort of thing."

Gus Neishacker stared at him a minute, then shrugged. He said: "I hope you're wrong," stood up quickly and walked away among the tables. He bent to smile here and there, and speak to a customer.

Tony Acosta's velvet eyes shone. He said: "Jeeze, Mister Carmady, you think it's rough stuff?"

Carmady nodded, didn't say anything. The waiter put their drinks and sandwiches on the table, went away. The band on the stage at the end of the oval floor blared out a long chord and a slick, grinning m.c. slid out on the stage and put his lips to a small open mike.

The floor show began. A line of half-naked girls ran out under a rain of colored lights. They coiled and uncoiled in a long sinuous line, their bare legs flashing, their navels little dimples of darkness in soft white, very nude flesh.

A hard-boiled redhead sang a hard-boiled song in a voice that could have been used to split firewood. The girls came back in black tights and silk hats, did the same dance with a slightly different exposure.

The music softened and a tall high-yaller torch singer drooped under an amber light and sang of something very far away and unhappy, in a voice like old ivory.

Carmady sipped his drink, poked at his sandwich in the dim light. Tony Acosta's hard young face was a small tense blur beside him.

The torch singer went away and there was a little pause and then suddenly all the lights in the place went out except the lights over the music racks of the band and little pale amber lights at the entrances to the radiating aisles of booths beyond the tables.

There were squeals in the thick darkness. A single white spot winked on, high up under the roof, settled on a runway beside the stage. Faces were chalk-white in the reflected glare. There was the red glow of a cigarette tip here and there. Four tall black men moved in the light, carrying a white mummy case on their shoulders. They came slowly, in rhythm, down the runway. They wore white Egyptian headdresses and loincloths of white leather and white sandals laced to the knee. The black smoothness of their limbs was like black marble in the moonlight.

They reached the middle of the dance floor and slowly upended the mummy case until the cover tipped forward and fell and was caught. Then slowly, very slowly, a swathed white figure tipped forward and fell – slowly, like the last leaf from a dead tree. It tipped in the air, seemed to hover, then plunged towards the floor under a shattering roll of drums.

The light went off, went on. The swathed figure was upright on the floor, spinning, and one of the blacks was spinning the opposite way, winding the white shroud around his body. Then the shroud fell away and a girl was all tinsel and smooth white limbs under the hard light and her body shot through the air glittering and was caught and passed around swiftly among the four black men, like a baseball handled by a fast infield.

Then the music changed to a waltz and she danced among the black men slowly and gracefully, as though among four ebony pillars, very close to them but never touching them.

The act ended. The applause rose and fell in thick waves. The light went out and it was dark again, and then all the lights went up and the girl and the four black men were gone.

"Keeno," Tony Acosta breathed. "Oh, keeno. That was Miss Adrian, wasn't it?"

Carmady said slowly: "A little daring." He lit another cigarette, looked around. "There's another black and white number, Tony. The Duke himself, in person."

Duke Targo stood applauding violently at the entrance to one of the radiating booth aisles. There was a loose grin on his face. He looked as if he might have had a few drinks.

An arm came down over Carmady's shoulder. A hand planted itself in the ashtray at his elbow. He smelled Scotch in heavy gusts. He turned his head slowly, looked up at the liquor-shiny face of Shenvair, Duke Targo's drunken bodyguard.

"Smokes and a white gal," Shenvair said thickly. "Lousy. Crummy. Godawful crummy."

Carmady smiled slowly, moved his chair a little. Tony Acosta stared at Shenvair round-eyed, his little mouth a thin line.

"Blackface, Mister Shenvair. Not real smokes. I liked it."

"And who the hell cares what you like?" Shenvair wanted to know.

Carmady smiled delicately, laid his cigarette down on the edge of a plate. He turned his chair a little more.

"Still think I want your job, Shenvair?"

"Yeah. I owe you a smack in the puss too." He took his hand out of the ashtray, wiped it off on the tablecloth. He doubled it into a fist. "Like it now?"

A waiter caught him by the arm, spun him around.

"You lost your table, sir? This way."

Shenvair patted the waiter on the shoulder, tried to put an arm around his neck. "Swell, let's go nibble a drink. I don't like these people."

They went away, disappeared among the tables.

Carmady said: "To hell with this place, Tony," and stared moodily towards the band stage. Then his eyes became intent.

A girl with corn-blond hair, in a white wrap with a white fur collar, appeared at the edge of the shell, went behind it, reappeared nearer. She came along the edge of the booths to the place where Targo had been standing. She slipped in between the booths there, disappeared.

Carmady said: "To hell with this place. Let's go Tony," in a low angry voice. Then very softly, in a tensed tone: "No – wait a minute. I see another guy I don't like."

The man was on the far side of the dance floor, which was empty at the moment. He was following its curve around, past the tables that fringed it. He looked a little different without his hat. But he had the same flat white expressionless face, the same close-set eyes. He was youngish, not more than thirty, but already having trouble with his bald spot. The slight bulge of a gun under his left arm was barely noticeable. He was the man who had run away from Jean Adrian's apartment in the Carondelet.

He reached the aisle into which Targo had gone, into which a moment before Jean Adrian had gone. He went into it.

Carmady said sharply: "Wait here, Tony." He kicked his chair back and stood up.

Somebody rabbit-punched him from behind. He swiveled, close to Shenvair's grinning sweaty face.

"Back again, pal," the curly-haired man chortled, and hit him on the jaw.

It was a short jab, well placed for a drunk. It caught Carmady off balance, staggered him. Tony Acosta came to his feet snarling, catlike. Carmady was still rocking when Shenvair let go with the other fist. That was too slow, too wide. Carmady slid inside it, uppercut the curly-haired man's nose savagely, got a handful of blood before he could get his hand away. He put most of it back on Shenvair's face.

Shenvair wobbled, staggered back a step and sat down on the floor, hard. He clapped a hand to his nose.

"Keep an eye on this bird, Tony," Carmady said swiftly.

Shenvair took hold of the nearest tablecloth and yanked it. It came off the table. Silver and glasses and china followed it to the floor. A man swore and a woman squealed. A waiter ran towards them with a livid, furious face.

Carmady almost didn't hear the two shots.

They were small and flat, close together, a small-caliber gun. The rushing waiter stopped dead, and a deeply etched white line appeared around his mouth as instantly as though the lash of a whip had cut it there.

A dark woman with a sharp nose opened her mouth to yell and no sound came from her. There was the instant when nobody makes a sound, when it almost seems as if there will never again be any sound – after the sound of a gun. Then Carmady was running.

He bumped into people who stood up and craned their necks. He reached the entrance to the aisle into which the white-faced man had gone. The booths had high walls and swing doors not so high. Heads stuck out over the doors, but no one was in the aisle yet. Carmady charged up a shallow carpeted slope, at the far end of which booth doors stood wide open.

Legs in dark cloth showed past the doors, slack on the floor, the knees sagged. The toes of black shoes were pointed into the booth.

Carmady shook an arm off, reached the place.

The man lay across the end of a table, his stomach and one side of his face on the white cloth, his left hand dropped between the table and the padded seat. His right hand on top of the table didn't quite hold a big black gun, a .45 with a cut barrel. The bald spot on his head glistened under the light, and the oily metal of the gun glistened beside it.

Blood leaked from under his chest, vivid scarlet on the white cloth, seeping into it as into blotting paper.

Duke Targo was standing up, deep in the booth. His left arm in the white serge coat was braced on the end of the table. Jean Adrian was sitting down at his side. Targo looked at Carmady blankly, as if he had never seen him before. He pushed his big right hand forward.

A small white-handled automatic lay on his palm.

"I shot him," Targo said. "He pulled a gun on us and I shot him."

Jean Adrian was scrubbing her hands together on a scrap of handkerchief. Her face was strained, cold, not scared. Her eyes were dark.

"I shot him," Targo said. He threw the small gun down on the cloth. It bounced, almost hit the fallen man's head. "Let's – let's get out of here."

Carmady put a hand against the side of the sprawled man's neck, held it there a second or two, took it away.

"He's dead," he said. "When a citizen drops a redhot – that's news."

Jean Adrian was staring at him stiff-eyed. He flashed a smile at her, put a hand against Targo's chest, pushed him back.

"Sit down, Targo. You're not going any place."

Targo said: "Well – okay. I shot him, see."

"That's all right," Carmady said. "Just relax."

People were close behind him now, crowding him. He leaned back against the press of bodies and kept on smiling at the girl's white face.

5

BENNY CYRANO WAS shaped like two eggs, a little one that was his head on top of a big one that was his body. His small dapper legs and feet in patent-leather shoes were pushed into the kneehole of a dark sheenless desk. He held a corner of a handkerchief tightly between his teeth and pulled against it with his left hand and held his right hand out pudgily in front of him, pushing against the air. He was saying in a voice muffled by the handkerchief: "Now wait a minute, boys. Now wait a minute."

There was a striped built-in sofa in one corner of the office, and Duke Targo sat in the middle of it, between two Headquarters dicks. He had a dark bruise over one cheek-bone, his thick blond hair was tousled and his black satin shirt looked as if somebody had tried to swing him by it.

One of the dicks, the gray-haired one, had a split lip. The young one with hair as blond as Targo's had a black eye. They both looked mad, but the blond one looked madder.

Carmady straddled a chair against the wall and looked sleepily at Jean Adrian, near him in a leather rocker. She was twisting a handkerchief in her hands, rubbing her palms with it. She had been doing this for a long time, as if she had forgotten she was doing it. Her small firm mouth was angry.

Gus Neishacker leaned against the closed door smoking.

"Now wait a minute, boys," Cyrano said. "If you didn't get tough with him, he wouldn't fight back. He's a good boy – the best I ever had. Give him a break."

Blood dribbled from one corner of Targo's mouth, in a fine thread down to his jutting chin. It gathered there and glistened. His face was empty, expressionless.

Carmady said coldly: "You wouldn't want the boys to stop playing blackjack pinochle, would you, Benny?"

The blond dick snarled: "You still got that private-dick license, Carmady?"

"It's lying around somewhere, I guess," Carmady said.

"Maybe we could take it away from you," the blond dick snarled.

"Maybe you could do a fan dance, copper. You might be all kinds of a smart guy for all I'd know."

The blond dick started to get up. The older one said: "Leave him be. Give him six feet. If he steps over that, we'll take the screws out of him."

Carmady and Gus Neishacker grinned at each other. Cyrano made helpless gestures in the air. The girl looked at Carmady under her lashes. Targo opened his mouth and spat blood straight before him on the blue carpet.

Something pushed against the door and Neishacker stepped to one side, opened it a crack, then opened it wide. McChesney came in.

McChesney was a lieutenant of detectives, tall, sandy-haired, fortyish, with pale eyes and a narrow suspicious face. He shut the door and turned the key in it, went slowly over and stood in front of Targo.

"Plenty dead," he said. "One under the heart, one in it. Nice snap shooting. In any league."

"When you've got to deliver you've got to deliver," Targo said dully.

"Make him?" the gray-haired dick asked his partner, moving away along the sofa.

McChesney nodded. "Torchy Plant. A gun for hire. I haven't seen him round for all of two years. Tough as an ingrowing toenail with his right load. A bindle punk."

"He'd have to be that to throw his party in here," the gray-haired dick said.

McChesney's long face was serious, not hard. "Got a permit for the gun, Targo?"

Targo said: "Yes. Benny got me one two weeks ago. I been getting a lot of threats."

"Listen, Lieutenant," Cyrano chirped, "some gamblers try to scare him into a dive, see? He wins nine straight fights by knockouts so they get a swell price. I told him he should take one at that maybe."

"I almost did," Targo said sullenly.

"So they sent the redhot to him," Cyrano said.

McChesney said: "I wouldn't say no. How'd you beat his draw, Targo? Where was your gun?"

"On my hip."

"Show me."

Targo put his hand back into his right hip pocket and jerked a handkerchief out quickly, stuck his finger through it like a gun barrel.

"That handkerchief in the pocket?" McChesney asked. "With the gun?"

Targo's big reddish face clouded a little. He nodded.

McChesney leaned forward casually and twitched the handkerchief from his hand. He sniffed at it, unwrapped it, sniffed at it again, folded it and put it away in his own pocket. His face said nothing.

"What did he say, Targo?"

"He said: 'I got a message for you, punk, and this is it.' Then he went for the gat and it stuck a little in the clip. I got mine out first."

McChesney smiled faintly and leaned far back, teetering on his heels. His faint smile seemed to slide off the end of his long nose. He looked Targo up and down.

"Yeah," he said softly. "I'd call it damn nice shooting with a twenty-two. But you're fast for a big guy . . . Who got these threats?"

"I did," Targo said. "Over the phone."

"Know the voice?"

"It might have been this same guy. I'm not just positive."

McChesney walked stiff-legged to the other end of the office, stood a moment looking at a hand-tinted sporting print. He came back slowly, drifted over to the door.

"A guy like that don't mean a lot," he said quietly, "but we got to do our job. The two of you will have to come downtown and make statements. Let's go."

He went out. The two dicks stood up, with Duke Targo between them. The gray-haired one snapped: "You goin' to act nice, bo?"

Targo sneered: "If I get to wash my face."

They went out. The blond dick waited for Jean Adrian to pass in front of him. He swung the door, snarled back at Carmady: "As for you — nuts!"

Carmady said softly: "I like them. It's the squirrel in me, copper."

Gus Neishacker laughed, then shut the door and went to the desk.

"I'm shaking like Benny's third chin," he said. "Let's all have a shot of cognac."

He poured three glasses a third full, took one over to the striped sofa and spread his long legs out on it, leaned his head back and sipped the brandy.

Carmady stood up and downed his drink. He got a cigarette out and rolled it around in his fingers, staring at Cyrano's smooth white face with an up-from-under look.

"How much would you say changed hands on that fight tonight?" he asked softly. "Bets."

Cyrano blinked, massaged his lips with a fat hand. "A few grand. It was just a regular weekly show. It don't listen, does it?"

Carmady put the cigarette in his mouth and leaned over the desk to strike a match. He said: "If it does, murder's getting awfully cheap in this town."

Cyrano didn't say anything. Gus Neishacker sipped the last of his brandy and carefully put the empty glass down on a round cork table beside the sofa. He stared at the ceiling, silently.

After a moment Carmady nodded at the two men, crossed the room and went out, closed the door behind him. He went along a corridor off which dressing rooms opened, dark now. A curtained archway let him out at the back of the stage.

In the foyer the headwaiter was standing at the glass doors, looking out at the rain and the back of a uniformed policeman. Carmady went into the empty cloakroom, found his hat and coat, put them on, came out to stand beside the headwaiter.

He said: "I guess you didn't notice what happened to the kid I was with?"

The headwaiter shook his head and reached forward to unlock the door.

"There was four hundred people here – and three hundred scrammed before the law checked in. I'm sorry."

Carmady nodded and went out into the rain. The uniformed man glanced at him casually. He went along the street to where the car had been left. It wasn't there. He looked up and down the street, stood for a few moments in the rain, then walked towards Melrose.

After a little while he found a taxi.

6

THE RAMP OF the Carondelet garage curved down into semi-darkness and chilled air. The dark bulks of stalled cars looked ominous against the whitewashed walls, and the single drop-light in the small office had the relentless glitter of the death house.

A big Negro in stained overalls came out rubbing his eyes, then his face split in an enormous grin.

"Hello, there, Mistuh Carmady. You kinda restless tonight?"

Carmady said: "I get a little wild when it rains. I bet my heap isn't here."

"No, it ain't, Mistuh Carmady. I been all around wipin' off and yours ain't here aytall."

Carmady said woodenly: "I lent it to a pal. He probably wrecked it . . ."

He flicked a half-dollar through the air and went back up the ramp to the side street. He turned towards the back of the hotel, came to an alleylike street one side of which was the rear wall of the Carondelet. The other side had two frame houses and a four-story brick building. Hotel Blaine was lettered on a round milky globe over the door.

Carmady went up three cement steps and tried the door. It was locked. He looked through the glass panel into a small dim empty lobby. He got out two passkeys; the second one moved the lock a little. He pulled the door hard towards him, tried the first one again. That snicked the bolt far enough for the loosely fitted door to open.

He went in and looked at an empty counter with a sign "Manager" beside a plunger bell. There was an oblong of empty numbered pigeonholes on the wall. Carmady went around behind the counter and fished a leather register out of a space under the top. He read names back three pages, found the boyish scrawl: "Tony Acosta," and a room number in another writing.

He put the register away and went past the automatic elevator and upstairs to the fourth floor.

The hallway was very silent. There was weak light from a ceiling fixture. The last door but one on the left-hand side had a crack of light showing around its transom. That was the door – 411. He put his hand out to knock, then withdrew it without touching the door.

The doorknob was heavily smeared with something that looked like blood.

Carmady's eyes looked down and saw what was almost a pool of blood on the stained wood before the door, beyond the edge of the runner.

His hand suddenly felt clammy inside his glove. He took the glove off, held the hand stiff, clawlike for a moment, then shook it slowly. His eyes had a sharp strained light in them.

He got a handkerchief out, grasped the doorknob inside it, turned it slowly. The door was unlocked. He went in.

He looked across the room and said very softly: "Tony . . . oh, Tony."

Then he shut the door behind him and turned a key in it, still with the handkerchief.

There was light from the bowl that hung on three brass chains from the middle of the ceiling. It shone on a made-up bed, some painted, light-colored furniture, a dull green carpet, a square writing desk of eucalyptus wood.

Tony Acosta sat at the desk. His head was slumped forward on his left arm. Under the chair on which he sat, between the legs of the chair and his feet, there was a glistening brownish pool.

Carmady walked across the room so rigidly that his ankles ached after the second step. He reached the desk, touched Tony Acosta's shoulder.

"Tony," he said thickly, in a low, meaningless voice. "My God, Tony!"

Tony didn't move. Carmady went around to his side. A blood-soaked bath towel glared against the boy's stomach, across his pressed-together thighs. His right hand was crouched against the front edge of the desk, as if he was trying to push himself up. Almost under his face there was a scrawled envelope.

Carmady pulled the envelope towards him slowly, lifted it like a thing of weight, read the wandering scrawl of words.

"Tailed him . . . woptown . . . 28 Court Street . . . over garage . . . shot me . . . think I got . . . him . . . your car . . . "

The line trailed over the edge of the paper, became a blot there. The pen was on the floor. There was a bloody thumbprint on the envelope.

Carmady folded it meticulously to protect the print, put the envelope in his wallet. He lifted Tony's head, turned it a little towards him. The neck was still warm; it was beginning to stiffen. Tony's soft dark eyes were open and they held the quiet brightness of a cat's eyes. They had that effect the eyes of the new-dead have of almost, but not quite, looking at you.

Carmady lowered the head gently on the outstretched left arm. He stood laxly, his head on one side, his eyes almost sleepy. Then his head jerked back and his eyes hardened.

He stripped off his raincoat and the suitcoat underneath, rolled his sleeves up, wet a face towel in the basin in the corner of the room and went to the door. He wiped the knobs off, bent down and wiped up the smeared blood from the floor outside.

He rinsed the towel and hung it up to dry, wiped his hands carefully, put his coat on again. He used his handkerchief to open the transom, to reverse the key and lock the door from the outside. He threw the key in over the top of the transom, heard it tinkle inside.

He went downstairs and out of the Hotel Blaine. It still rained. He walked to the corner, looked along a tree-shaded block. His car was a dozen yards from the intersection, parked carefully, the lights off, the keys in the ignition. He drew them out, felt the seat under the wheel. It was wet, sticky. Carmady wiped his hand off, ran the windows up and locked the car. He left it where it was.

Going back to the Carondelet he didn't meet anybody. The hard slanting rain still pounded down into the empty streets.

7

THERE WAS A thin thread of light under the door of 914. Carmady knocked lightly, looking up and down the hall, moved his gloved fingers softly on the panel while he waited. He waited a long time. Then a voice spoke wearily behind the wood of the door.

"Yes? What is it?"

"Carmady, angel. I have to see you. It's strictly business."

The door clicked, opened. He looked at a tired white face, dark eyes that were slatelike, not violet-blue. There were smudges under them as though mascara had been rubbed into the skin. The girl's strong little hand twitched on the edge of the door.

"You," she said wearily. "It would be you. Yes . . . Well, I've simply got to have a shower. I smell of policemen."

"Fifteen minutes?" Carmady asked casually, but his eyes were very sharp on her face.

She shrugged slowly, then nodded. The closing door seemed to jump at him. He went along to his own rooms, threw off his hat and coat, poured whiskey into a glass and went into the bathroom to get ice water from the small tap over the basin.

He drank slowly, looking out of the windows at the dark breadth of the boulevard. A car slid by now and then, two beams of white light attached to nothing, emanating from nowhere.

He finished the drink, stripped to the skin, went under a shower. He dressed in fresh clothes, refilled his big flask and put it in his inner pocket, took a snub-nosed automatic out of a suitcase and held it in his hand for a minute staring at it. Then he put it back in the suitcase, lit a cigarette and smoked it through.

He got a dry hat and a tweed coat and went back to 914.

The door was almost insidiously ajar. He slipped in with a light knock, shut the door, went on into the living-room and looked at Jean Adrian.

She was sitting on the davenport with a freshly scrubbed look, in loose plum-colored pajamas and a Chinese coat. A tendril of damp hair drooped over one temple. Her small even features had the cameo-like clearness that tiredness gives to the very young.

Carmady said: "Drink?"

She gestured emptily. "I suppose so."

He got glasses, mixed whiskey and ice water, went to the davenport with them.

"Are they keeping Targo on ice?"

She moved her chin an eighth of an inch, staring into her glass.

"He cut loose again, knocked two cops halfway through the wall. They love that boy."

Carmady said: "He has a lot to learn about cops. In the morning the cameras will be all set for him. I can think of some nice headlines, such as: 'Well-known Fighter Too Fast for Gunman.' 'Duke Targo Puts Crimp in Underworld Hot Rod.'"

The girl sipped her drink. "I'm tired," she said. "And my foot itches. Let's talk about what makes this your business."

"Sure." He flipped his cigarette case open, held it under her chin. Her hand fumbled at it and while it still fumbled he said: "When you light that tell me why you shot him."

Jean Adrian put the cigarette between her lips, bent her head to the match, inhaled and threw her head back. Color awakened slowly in her eyes and a small smile curved the line of her pressed lips. She didn't answer.

Carmady watched her for a minute, turning his glass in his hands. Then he stared at the floor, said: "It was your gun – the gun I picked up here in the afternoon. Targo said he drew it from his hip pocket, the slowest draw in the world. Yet he's supposed to have shot twice, accurately enough to kill a man, while the man wasn't even getting his gun loose from a shoulder holster. That's hooey. But you, with the gun in a bag in your lap, and knowing the hood, might just have managed it. He would have been watching Targo."

The girl said emptily: "You're a private dick, I hear. You're the son of a boss politician. They talked about you downtown. They act a little afraid of you, of people you might know. Who sicked you on me?"

Carmady said: "They're not afraid of me, angel. They just talked like that to see how you'd react, if I was involved, so on. They don't know what it's all about."

"They were told plainly enough what it was all about."

Carmady shook his head. "A cop never believes what he gets without a struggle. He's too used to cooked-up stories. I think McChesney's wise you did the shooting. He knows by now if that handkerchief of Targo's had been in a pocket with a gun."

Her limp fingers discarded her cigarette half-smoked. A curtain eddied at the window and loose flakes of ash crawled around in the ashtray. She said slowly: "All right. I shot him. Do you think I'd hesitate after this afternoon?"

Carmady rubbed the lobe of his ear. "I'm playing this too light," he said softly. "You don't know what's in my heart. Something has happened, something nasty. Do you think the hood meant to kill Targo?"

"I thought so – or I wouldn't have shot a man."

"I think maybe it was just a scare, angel. Like the other one. After all a night club is a poor place for a getaway."

She said sharply: "They don't do many low tackles on forty-fives. He'd have got away all right. Of course he meant to kill somebody. And of course I didn't mean Duke to front for me. He just grabbed the gun out of my hand and slammed into his act. What did it matter? I knew it would all come out in the end."

She poked absently at the still burning cigarette in the tray, kept her eyes down. After a moment she said, almost in a whisper: "Is that all you wanted to know?"

Carmady let his eyes crawl sidewise, without moving his head, until he could just see the firm curve of her cheek, the strong line of her throat. He said thickly: "Shenvair was in on it. The fellow I was with at Cyrano's followed Shenvair to a hideout. Shenvair shot him. He's dead. He's dead, angel – just a young kid that worked here in the hotel. Tony, the bell captain. The cops don't know that yet."

The muffled clang of elevator doors was heavy through the silence. A horn tooted dismally out in the rain on the boulevard. The girl sagged forward suddenly, then sidewise, fell across Carmady's knees. Her body was half turned and she lay almost on her back across his thighs, her eyelids flickering. The small blue veins in them stood out rigid in the soft skin.

He put his arms around her slowly, loosely, then they tightened, lifted her. He brought her face close to his own face. He kissed her on the side of the mouth.

Her eyes opened, stared blankly, unfocused. He kissed her again, tightly, then pushed her upright on the davenport.

He said quietly: "That wasn't just an act, was it?"

She leaped to her feet, spun around. Her voice was low, tense and angry.

"There's something horrible about you! Something – satanic. You come here and tell me another man has been killed – and then you kiss me. It isn't real."

Carmady said dully: "There's something horrible about any man that goes suddenly gaga over another man's woman."

"I'm not his woman!" she snapped. "I don't even like him – and I don't like you."

Carmady shrugged. They stared at each other with bleak hostile eyes. The girl clicked her teeth shut, then said almost violently: "Get out! I can't talk to you any more. I can't stand you around. Will you get out?"

Carmady said: "Why not?" He stood up, went over and got his hat and coat.

The girl sobbed once sharply, then she went in light quick strides across the room to the windows, became motionless with her back to him.

Carmady looked at her back, went over near her and stood looking at the soft hair low down on her neck. He said: "Why the hell don't you let me help? I know there's something wrong. I wouldn't hurt you."

The girl spoke to the curtain in front of her face, savagely: "Get out! I don't want your help. Go away and stay away. I won't be seeing you – ever."

Carmady said slowly: "I think you've got to have help. Whether you like it or not. That man in the photo frame on the desk there – I think I know who he is. And I don't think he's dead."

The girl turned. Her face now was as white as paper. Her eyes strained at his eyes. She breathed thickly, harshly. After what seemed a long time she said: "I'm caught. Caught. There's nothing you can do about it."

Carmady lifted a hand and drew his fingers slowly down her cheek, down the angle of her tight jaw. His eyes held a hard brown glitter, his lips a smile. It was cunning, almost a dishonest smile.

He said: "I'm wrong, angel. I don't know him at all. Good night."

He went back across the room, through the little hallway, opened the door. When the door opened the girl clutched at the curtain and rubbed her face against it slowly.

Carmady didn't shut the door. He stood quite still halfway through it, looking at two men who stood there with guns.

They stood close to the door, as if they had been about to knock. One was thick, dark, saturnine. The other one was an albino with sharp red eyes, a narrow head that showed shining snow-white hair under a rain-spattered dark hat. He had the thin sharp teeth and the drawn-back grin of a rat.

Carmady started to close the door behind him. The albino said: "Hold it, rube. The door, I mean. We're goin' in."

The other man slid forward and pressed his left hand up and down Carmady's body carefully. He stepped away, said: "No gat, but a swell flask under his arm."

The albino gestured with his gun. "Back up, rube. We want the broad, too."

Carmady said tonelessly: "It doesn't take a gun, Critz. I know you and I know your boss. If he wants to see me, I'll be glad to talk to him."

He turned and went back into the room with the two gunmen behind him.

Jean Adrian hadn't moved. She stood by the window still, the curtain against her cheek, her eyes closed, as if she hadn't heard the voices at the door at all.

Then she heard them come in and her eyes snapped open. She turned slowly, stared past Carmady at the two gunmen. The albino walked to the middle of the room, looked around it without speaking, went on into the bedroom and bathroom. Doors opened and shut. He came back on quiet catlike feet, pulled his overcoat open and pushed his hat back on his head.

"Get dressed, sister. We have to go for a ride in the rain. Okay?"

The girl stared at Carmady now. He shrugged, smiled a little, spread his hands.

"That's how it is, angel. Might as well fall in line."

The lines of her face got thin and contemptuous. She said slowly: "You — You ——— ." Her voice trailed off into a sibilant, meaningless mutter. She went across the room stiffly and out of it into the bedroom.

The albino slipped a cigarette between his sharp lips, chuckled with a wet, gurgling sound, as if his mouth was full of saliva.

"She don't seem to like you, rube."

Carmady frowned. He walked slowly to the writing desk, leaned his hips against it, stared at the floor.

"She thinks I sold her out," he said dully.

"Maybe you did, rube," the albino drawled.

Carmady said: "Better watch her. She's neat with a gun."

His hands, reaching casually behind him on the desk, tapped the top of it lightly, then without apparent change of movement folded the leather photo frame down on its side and edged it under the blotter.

8

THERE WAS A padded arm rest in the middle of the rear seat of the car, and Carmady leaned an elbow on it, cupped his chin in his hand, stared through the half-misted windows at the rain. It was thick white spray in the headlights, and the noise of it on the top of the car was like drum fire very far off.

Jean Adrian sat on the other side of the arm rest, in the corner. She wore a black hat and a gray coat with tufts of silky hair on it, longer than caracul and not so curly. She didn't look at Carmady or speak to him.

The albino sat on the right of the thick dark man, who drove. They went through silent streets, past blurred houses, blurred trees, the blurred shine of street lights. There were neon signs behind the thick curtains of mist. There was no sky.

Then they climbed and a feeble arc light strung over an intersection threw light on a signpost, and Carmady read the name "Court Street."

He said softly: "This is woptown, Critz. The big guy can't be so dough-heavy as he used to be."

Lights flickered from the albino's eyes as he glanced back. "You should know, rube."

The car slowed in front of a big frame house with a trellised porch, walls finished in round shingles, blind, lightless windows. Across the street, a stencil sign on a brick building built sheer to the sidewalk said: "Paolo Perrugini Funeral Parlors."

The car swung out to make a wide turn into a gravel driveway. Lights splashed into an open garage. They went in, slid to a stop beside a big shiny undertaker's ambulance.

The albino snapped: "All out!"

Carmady said: "I see our next trip is all arranged for."

"Funny guy," the albino snarled. "A wise monkey."

"Uh-uh. I just have nice scaffold manners," Carmady drawled.

The dark man cut the motor and snapped on a big flash, then cut the lights, got out of the car. He shot the beam of the flash up a narrow flight of wooden steps in the corner. The albino said: "Up you go, rube. Push the girl ahead of you. I'm behind with my rod."

Jean Adrian got out of the car past Carmady, without looking at him. She went up the steps stiffly, and the three men made a procession behind her.

There was a door at the top. The girl opened it and hard white light came out at them. They went into a bare attic with exposed studding, a square window in front and rear, shut tight, the glass painted black. A bright bulb hung on a drop cord over a kitchen table and a big man sat at the table with a saucer of cigarette butts at his elbow. Two of them still smoked.

A thin loose-lipped man sat on a bed with a Luger beside his left hand. There was a worn carpet on the floor, a few sticks of furniture, a half-opened clapboard door in the corner through which a toilet seat showed, and one end of a big old-fashioned bathtub standing up from the floor on iron legs.

The man at the kitchen table was large but not handsome. He had carroty hair and eyebrows a shade darker, a square aggressive face, a strong jaw. His thick lips held his cigarette brutally. His clothes looked as if they had cost a great deal of money and had been slept in.

He glanced carelessly at Jean Adrian, said around the cigarette: "Park the body, sister. Hi, Carmady. Gimme that rod, Lefty, and you boys drop down below again."

The girl went quietly across the attic and sat down in a straight wooden chair. The man on the bed stood up, put the Luger at the big man's elbow on the kitchen table. The three gunmen went down the stairs, leaving the door open.

The big man touched the Luger, stared at Carmady, said sarcastically: "I'm Doll Conant. Maybe you remember me."

Carmady stood loosely by the kitchen table, with his legs spread wide, his hands in his overcoat pockets, his head tilted back. His half-closed eyes were sleepy, very cold.

He said: "Yeah. I helped my dad hang the only rap on you that ever stuck."

"It didn't stick, mug. Not with the Court of Appeals."

"Maybe this one will," Carmady said carelessly. "Kidnapping is apt to be a sticky rap in this state."

Conant grinned without opening his lips. His expression was grimly good-humored. He said: "Let's not barber. We got business to do and you know better than that last crack. Sit down — or rather take a look at Exhibit One first. In the bathtub, behind you. Yeah, take a look at that. Then we can get down to tacks."

Carmady turned, went across to the clapboard door, pushed through it. There was a bulb sticking out of the wall, with a key switch. He snapped it on, bent over the tub.

For a moment his body was quite rigid and his breath was held rigidly. Then he let it out very slowly, and reached his left hand back and pushed the door almost shut. He bent farther over the big iron tub.

It was long enough for a man to stretch out in, and a man was stretched out in it, on his back. He was fully dressed even to a hat, although his head didn't look as if he had put it on himself. He had thick, gray-brown curly hair. There was blood on his face and there was a gouged, red-rimmed hole at the inner corner of his left eye.

He was Shenvair and he was long since dead.

Carmady sucked in his breath and straightened slowly, then suddenly bent forward still further until he could see into the space between the tub and the wall. Something blue and metallic glistened down there in the dust. A blue steel gun. A gun like Shenvair's gun.

Carmady glanced back quickly. The not quite shut door showed him a part of the attic, the top of the stairs, one of Doll Conant's feet square and placid on the carpet, under the kitchen table. He reached his arm out slowly down behind the tub, gathered the gun up. The four exposed chambers had steel-jacketed bullets in them.

Carmady opened his coat, slipped the gun down inside the waistband of his trousers, tightened his belt, and buttoned his coat again. He went out of the bathroom, shut the clapboard door carefully.

Doll Conant gestured at a chair across the table from him: "Sit down."

Carmady glanced at Jean Adrian. She was staring at him with a kind of rigid curiosity, her eyes dark and colorless in a stone-white face under the black hat.

He gestured at her, smiled faintly. "It's Mister Shenvair, angel. He met with an accident. He's – dead."

The girl stared at him without any expression at all. Then she shuddered once, violently. She stared at him again, made no sound of any kind.

Carmady sat down in the chair across the table from Conant.

Conant eyed him, added a smoking stub to the collection in the white saucer, lit a fresh cigarette, streaking the match the whole length of the kitchen table.

He puffed, said casually: "Yeah, he's dead. You shot him."

Carmady shook his head very slightly, smiled. "No."

"Skip the baby eyes, feller. You shot him. Perrugini, the wop undertaker across the street, owns this place, rents it out now and then to a right boy for a quick dust. Incidentally, he's a friend of mine, does me a lot of good among the other wops. He rented it to Shenvair. Didn't know him, but Shenvair got a right ticket into him. Perrugini heard shooting over here tonight, took a look out of his window, saw a guy make it to a car. He saw the license number of the car. Your car."

Carmady shook his head again. "But I didn't shoot him, Conant."

"Try and prove it . . . The wop ran over and found Shenvair halfway up the stairs, dead. He dragged him up and stuck him in the bathtub. Some crazy idea about the blood, I suppose. Then he went through him, found a police card, a private-dick license, and that scared him. He got me on the phone and when I got the name, I came steaming."

Conant stopped talking, eyed Carmady steadily. Carmady said very softly: "You hear about the shooting at Cyrano's tonight?"

Conant nodded.

Carmady went on: "I was there, with a kid friend of mine from the hotel. Just before the shooting this Shenvair threw a punch at me. The kid followed Shenvair here and they shot each other. Shenvair was drunk and scared and I'll bet he shot first. I didn't even know the kid had a gun. Shenvair shot him through the stomach. He got home, died there. He left me a note. I have the note."

After a moment Conant said: "You killed Shenvair, or hired that boy to do it. Here's why. He tried to copper his bet on your blackmail racket. He sold out to Courtway."

Carmady looked startled. He snapped his head around to look at Jean Adrian. She was leaning forward staring at him with color in her cheeks, a shine in her eyes. She said very softly: "I'm sorry – angel. I had you wrong."

Carmady smiled a little, turned back to Conant. He said: "She thought I was the one that sold out. Who's Courtway? Your bird dog, the state senator?"

Conant's face turned a little white. He laid his cigarette down very carefully in the saucer, leaned across the table and hit Carmady in the mouth with his fist. Carmady went over backwards in the rickety chair. His head struck the floor.

Jean Adrian stood up quietly and her teeth made a sharp clicking sound. Then she didn't move.

Carmady rolled over on his side and got up and set the chair upright. He got a handkerchief out, patted his mouth, looked at the handkerchief.

Steps clattered on the stairs and the albino poked his narrow head into the room, poked a gun still farther in.

"Need any help, boss?"

Without looking at him, Conant said: "Get out – and shut that door – and stay out!"

The door was shut. The albino's steps died down the stairs. Carmady put his left hand on the back of the chair and moved it slowly back and forth. His right hand still held the handkerchief. His lips were getting puffed and darkish. His eyes looked at the Luger by Conant's elbow.

Conant picked up his cigarette and put it in his mouth. He said: "Maybe you think I'm going to neck this blackmail racket. I'm not, brother. I'm going to kill it – so it'll stay killed. You're going to spill your guts. I have three boys downstairs who need exercise. Get busy and talk."

Carmady said: "Yeah – but your three boys are downstairs." He slipped the handkerchief inside his coat. His hand came out with the blued gun in it. He said: "Take that Luger by the barrel and push it across the table so I can reach it."

Conant didn't move. His eyes narrowed to slits. His hard mouth jerked the cigarette in it once. He didn't touch the Luger. After a moment he said: "Guess you know what will happen to you now."

Carmady shook his head slightly. He said: "Maybe I'm not particular about that. If it does happen, you won't know anything about it."

Conant stared at him, didn't move. He stared at him for quite a long time, stared at the blue gun. "Where did you get it? Didn't the heels frisk you?"

Carmady said: "They did. This is Shenvair's gun. Your wop friend must have kicked it behind the bathtub. Careless."

Conant reached two thick fingers forward and turned the Luger around and pushed it to the far edge of the table. He nodded and said tonelessly: "I lose this hand. I ought to have thought of that. That makes me do the talking."

Jean Adrian came quickly across the room and stood at the end of the table. Carmady reached forward across the chair and took the Luger in his left hand and slipped it down into his overcoat pocket, kept his hand on it. He rested the hand holding the blue gun on the top of the chair.

Jean Adrian said: "Who is this man?"

"Doll Conant, a local bigtimer. Senator John Myerson Courtway is his pipe line into the state senate. And Senator Courtway, angel, is the man in your photo frame on your desk. The man you said was your father, that you said was dead."

The girl said very quietly: "He is my father. I knew he wasn't dead. I'm blackmailing him – for a hundred grand. Shenvair and

Targo and I. He never married my mother, so I'm illegitimate. But I'm still his child. I have rights and he won't recognize them. He treated my mother abominably, left her without a nickel. He had detectives watch me for years. Shenvair was one of them. He recognized my photos when I came here and met Targo. He remembered. He went up to San Francisco and got a copy of my birth certificate. I have it here."

She fumbled at her bag, felt around in it, opened a small zipper pocket in the lining. Her hand came out with a folded paper. She tossed it on the table.

Conant stared at her, reached a hand for the paper, spread it out and studied it. He said slowly: "This doesn't prove anything."

Carmady took his left hand out of his pocket and reached for the paper. Conant pushed it towards him.

It was a certified copy of a birth certificate, dated originally in 1912. It recorded the birth of a girl child, Adriana Gianni Myerson, to John and Antonina Gianni Myerson. Carmady dropped the paper again.

He said: "Adriana Gianni – Jean Adrian. Was that the tip-off, Conant?"

Conant shook his head. "Shenvair got cold feet. He tipped Courtway. He was scared. That's why he had this hideout lined up. I thought that was why he got killed. Targo couldn't have done it, because Targo's still in the can. Maybe I had you wrong, Carmady."

Carmady stared at him woodenly, didn't say anything. Jean Adrian said: "It's my fault. I'm the one that's to blame. It was pretty rotten. I see that now. I want to see him and tell him I'm sorry and that he'll never hear from me again. I want to make him promise he won't do anything to Duke Targo. May I?"

Carmady said: "You can do anything you want to, angel. I have two guns that say so. But why did you wait so long? And why didn't you go at him through the courts? You're in show business. The publicity would have made you – even if he beat you out."

The girl bit her lip, said in a low voice: "My mother never really knew who he was, never knew his last name even. He was John Myerson to her. I didn't know until I came here and happened to see a picture in the local paper. He had changed, but I knew the face. And of course the first part of his name – "

Conant said sneeringly: "You didn't go at him openly because you knew damn well you weren't his kid. That your mother just wished you on to him like any cheap broad who sees herself out of a swell meal ticket. Courtway says he can prove it, and that he's going to prove it and put you where you belong. And believe me, sister, he's just the stiff-necked kind of sap who would kill himself in public life raking up a twenty-year-old scandal to do that little thing."

The big man spit his cigarette stub out viciously, added: "It cost me money to put him where he is and I aim to keep him there. That's why I'm in it. No dice, sister. I'm putting the pressure on. You're going to take a lot of air and keep on taking it. As for your two-gun friend – maybe he didn't know, but he knows now and that ties him up in the same package."

Conant banged on the table top, leaned back, looking calmly at the blue gun in Carmady's hand.

Carmady stared into the big man's eyes, said very softly: "That hood at Cyrano's tonight – he wasn't your idea of putting on the pressure by any chance, Conant, was he?"

Conant grinned harshly, shook his head. The door at the top of the stairs opened a little, silently. Carmady didn't see it. He was staring at Conant. Jean Adrian saw it.

Her eyes widened and she stepped back with a startled exclamation, that jerked Carmady's eyes to her.

The albino stepped softly through the door with a gun leveled.

His red eyes glistened, his mouth was drawn wide in a

snarling grin. He said: "The door's kind of thin, boss. I listened. Okay? . . . Shed the heater, rube, or I blow you both in half."

Carmady turned slightly and opened his right hand and let the blue gun bounce on the thin carpet. He shrugged, spread his hands out wide, didn't look at Jean Adrian.

The albino stepped clear of the door, came slowly forward and put his gun against Carmady's back.

Conant stood up, came around the table, took the Luger out of Carmady's coat pocket and hefted it. Without a word or change of expression he slammed it against the side of Carmady's jaw.

Carmady sagged drunkenly, then went down on the floor on his side.

Jean Adrian screamed, clawed at Conant. He threw her off, changed the gun to his left hand and slapped the side of her face with a hard palm.

"Pipe down, sister. You've had all your fun."

The albino went to the head of the stairs and called down it. The two other gunmen came up into the room, stood grinning.

Carmady didn't move on the floor. After a little while Conant lit another cigarette and rattled a knuckle on the table top beside the birth certificate. He said gruffly: "She wants to see the old man. Okay, she can see him. We'll all go see him. There's still something in this that stinks." He raised his eyes, looked at the stocky man. "You and Lefty go downtown and spring Targo, get him out to the Senator's place as soon as you can. Step on it."

The two hoods went back down the stairs.

Conant looked down at Carmady, kicked him in the ribs lightly, kept on kicking them until Carmady opened his eyes and stirred.

9

THE CAR WAITED at the top of a hill, before a pair of tall wrought-iron gates, inside which there was a lodge. A door of the lodge stood open and yellow light framed a big man in an overcoat and pulled-down hat. He came forward slowly into the rain, his hands down in his pockets.

The rain slithered about his feet and the albino leaned against the uprights of the gate, clicking his teeth. The big man said: "What yuh want? I can see yuh."

"Shake it up, rube. Mister Conant wants to call on your boss."

The man inside spit into the wet darkness. "So what? Know what time it is?"

Conant opened the car door suddenly and went over to the gates. The rain made noise between the car and the voices.

Carmady turned his head slowly and patted Jean Adrian's hand. She pushed his hand away from her quickly.

Her voice said softly: "You fool – oh, you fool!"

Carmady sighed. "I'm having a swell time, angel. A swell time."

The man inside the gates took out keys on a long chain, unlocked the gates and pushed them back until they clicked on the chocks. Conant and the albino came back to the car.

Conant stood in the rain with a heel hooked on the running board. Carmady took his big flask out of his pocket, felt it over to see if it was dented, then unscrewed the top. He held it out towards the girl, said: "Have a little bottle courage."

She didn't answer him, didn't move. He drank from the flask, put it away, looked past Conant's broad back at acres of dripping trees, a cluster of lighted windows that seemed to hang in the sky.

A car came up the hill stabbing the wet dark with its headlights, pulled behind the sedan and stopped. Conant went over to it, put his head into it and said something. The car backed, turned into the driveway, and its lights splashed on retaining walls, disappeared, reappeared at the top of the drive as a hard white oval against a stone porte-cochère.

Conant got into the sedan and the albino swung it into the driveway after the other car. At the top, in a cement parking circle ringed with cypresses, they all got out.

At the top of steps a big door was open and a man in a bathrobe stood in it. Targo, between two men who leaned hard against him, was halfway up the steps. He was bareheaded and without an overcoat. His big body in the white coat looked enormous between the two gunmen.

The rest of the party went up the steps and into the house and followed the bathrobed butler down a hall lined with portraits of somebody's ancestors, through a still oval foyer to another hall and into a paneled study with soft lights and heavy drapes and deep leather chairs.

A man stood behind a big dark desk that was set in an alcove made by low, outjutting bookcases. He was enormously tall and thin. His white hair was so thick and fine that no single hair was visible in it. He had a small straight bitter mouth, black eyes without depth in a white lined face. He stooped a little and a blue corduroy bathrobe faced with satin was wrapped around his almost freakish thinness.

The butler shut the door and Conant opened it again and jerked his chin at the two men who had come in with Targo. They went out. The albino stepped behind Targo and pushed him down into a chair. Targo looked dazed, stupid. There was a smear of dirt on one side of his face and his eyes had a drugged look.

The girl went over to him quickly, said: "Oh, Duke – are you all right, Duke?"

Targo blinked at her, half-grinned. "So you had to rat, huh? Skip it. I'm fine." His voice had an unnatural sound.

Jean Adrian went away from him and sat down and hunched herself together as if she was cold.

The tall man stared coldly at everyone in the room in turn, then said lifelessly: "Are these the blackmailers – and was it necessary to bring them here in the middle of the night?"

Conant shook himself out of his coat, threw it on the floor behind a lamp. He lit a fresh cigarette and stood spread-legged in the middle of the room, a big, rough, rugged man very sure of himself. He said: "The girl wanted to see you and tell you she was sorry and wants to play ball. The guy in the ice-cream coat is Targo, the fighter. He got himself in a shooting scrape at a night spot and acted so wild downtown they fed him sleep tablets to quiet him. The other guy is Carmady, old Marcus Carmady's boy. I don't figure him yet."

Carmady said dryly: "I'm a private detective, Senator. I'm here in the interests of my client, Miss Adrian." He laughed.

The girl looked at him suddenly, then looked at the floor.

Conant said gruffly: "Shenvair, the one you know about, got himself bumped off. Not by us. That's still to straighten out."

The tall man nodded coldly. He sat down at his desk and picked up a white quill pen, tickled one ear with it.

"And what is your idea of the way to handle this matter, Conant?" he asked thinly.

Conant shrugged. "I'm a rough boy, but I'd handle this one legal. Talk to the D.A., toss them in a coop on suspicion of extortion. Cook up a story for the papers, then give it time to cool. Then dump these birds across the state line and tell them not to come back – or else."

Senator Courtway moved the quill around to his other ear. "They could attack me again, from a distance," he said icily. "I'm in favor of a showdown, put them where they belong."

"You can't try them, Courtway. It would kill you politically."

"I'm tired of public life, Conant. I'll be glad to retire." The tall thin man curved his mouth into a faint smile.

"The hell you are," Conant growled. He jerked his head around, snapped: "Come here, sister."

Jean Adrian stood up, came slowly across the room, stood in front of the desk.

"Make her?" Conant snarled.

Courtway stared at the girl's set face for a long time, without a trace of expression. He put his quill down on the desk, opened a drawer and took out a photograph. He looked from the photo to the girl, back to the photo, said tonelessly: "This was taken a number of years ago, but there's a very strong resemblance. I don't think I'd hesitate to say it's the same face."

He put the photo down on the desk and with the same unhurried motion took an automatic out of the drawer and put it down on the desk beside the photo.

Conant stared at the gun. His mouth twisted. He said thickly: "You won't need that, Senator. Listen, your show-down idea is all wrong. I'll get detailed confessions from these people and we'll hold them. If they ever act up again, it'll be time enough then to crack down with the big one."

Carmady smiled a little and walked across the carpet until he was near the end of the desk. He said: "I'd like to see that photograph" and leaned over suddenly and took it.

Courtway's thin hand dropped to the gun, then relaxed. He leaned back in his chair and stared at Carmady.

Carmady stared at the photograph, lowered it, said softly to Jean Adrian: "Go sit down."

She turned and went back to her chair, dropped into it wearily.

Carmady said: "I like your showdown idea, Senator. It's clean and straightforward and a wholesome change in policy from Mr. Conant. But it won't work." He snicked a fingernail at the photo. "This has a superficial resemblance, no more. I don't think it's the same girl at all myself. Her ears are differently shaped and lower on her head. Her eyes are closer together than Miss Adrian's eyes, the line of her jaw is longer.

Those things don't change. So what have you got? An extortion letter. Maybe, but you can't tie it to anyone or you'd have done it already. The girl's name. Just coincidence. What else?"

Conant's face was granite hard, his mouth bitter. His voice shook a little saying: "And how about that certificate the gal took out of her purse, wise guy?"

Carmady smiled faintly, rubbed the side of his jaw with his fingertips. "I thought you got that from Shenvair?" he said slyly. "And Shenvair is dead."

Conant's face was a mask of fury. He balled his fist, took a jerky step forward. "Why you – damn louse – "

Jean Adrian was leaning forward staring round-eyed at Carmady. Targo was staring at him, with a loose grin, pale hard eyes. Courtway was staring at him. There was no expression of any kind on Courtway's face. He sat cold, relaxed, distant.

Conant laughed suddenly, snapped his fingers. "Okay, toot your horn," he grunted.

Carmady said slowly: "I'll tell you another reason why there'll be no showdown. That shooting at Cyrano's. Those threats to make Targo drop an unimportant fight. That hood that went to Miss Adrian's hotel room and sapped her, left her lying on her doorway. Can't you tie all that in, Conant? I can."

Courtway leaned forward suddenly and placed his hand on his gun, folded it around the butt. His black eyes were holes in a white frozen face.

Conant didn't move, didn't speak.

Carmady went on: "Why did Targo get those threats, and after he didn't drop the fight, why did a gun go to see him at Cyrano's, a night club, a very bad place for that kind of play? Because at Cyrano's he was with the girl, and Cyrano was his backer, and if anything happened at Cyrano's the law would get the threat story before they had time to think of anything else. That's why. The threats were a build-up for a killing. When the shooting came off Targo was to be with the girl, so the hood could get the girl and it would look as if Targo was the one he was after.

"He would have tried for Targo, too, of course, but above all he would have got the girl. Because she was the dynamite behind this shakedown, without her it meant nothing, and with her it could always be made over into a legitimate paternity suit. If it didn't work the other way. You know about her and about Targo, because Shenvair got cold feet and sold out. And Shenvair knew about the hood — because when the hood showed, and I saw him — and Shenvair knew I knew him, because he had heard me tell Targo about him — then Shenvair tried to pick a drunken fight with me and keep me from trying to interfere."

Carmady stopped, rubbed the side of his head again, very slowly, very gently. He watched Conant with an up-from-under look.

Conant said slowly, very harshly: "I don't play those games, buddy. Believe it or not — I don't."

Carmady said: "Listen. The hood could have killed the girl at the hotel with his sap. He didn't because Targo wasn't there and the fight hadn't been fought, and the build-up would have been all wasted. He went there to have a close look at her, without make-up. And she was scared about something, and had a gun with her. So he sapped her down and ran away. That visit was just a finger."

Conant said again: "I don't play those games, buddy." Then he took the Luger out of his pocket and held it down at his side.

Carmady shrugged, turned his head to stare at Senator Courtway.

"No, but he does," he said softly. "He had the motive, and the play wouldn't look like him. He cooked it up with Shenvair — and if it went wrong, as it did, Shenvair would have breezed and if the law got wise, big tough Doll Conant is the boy whose nose would be in the mud."

Courtway smiled a little and said in an utterly dead voice: "The young man is very ingenious, but surely – "

Targo stood up. His face was a stiff mask. His lips moved slowly and he said: "It sounds pretty good to me. I think I'll twist your goddamn neck, Mister Courtway."

The albino snarled, "Sit down, punk," and lifted his gun. Targo turned slightly and slammed the albino on the jaw. He went over backwards, smashed his head against the wall. The gun sailed along the floor from his limp hand.

Targo started across the room.

Conant looked at him sidewise and didn't move. Targo went past him, almost touching him. Conant didn't move a muscle. His big face was blank, his eyes narrowed to a faint glitter between the heavy lids.

Nobody moved but Targo. Then Courtway lifted his gun and his finger whitened on the trigger and the gun roared.

Carmady moved across the room very swiftly and stood in front of Jean Adrian, between her and the rest of the room.

Targo looked down at his hands. His face twisted into a silly smile. He sat down on the floor and pressed both his hands against his chest.

Courtway lifted his gun again and then Conant moved. The Luger jerked up, flamed twice. Blood flowed down Courtway's hand. His gun fell behind his desk. His long body seemed to swoop down after the gun. It jackknifed until only his shoulders showed humped above the line of the desk.

Conant said: "Stand up and take it, you goddamn double-crossing swine!"

There was a shot behind the desk. Courtway's shoulders went down out of sight.

After a moment Conant went around behind the desk, stooped, straightened.

"He ate one," he said very calmly. "Through the mouth . . . And I lose me a nice clean senator."

Targo took his hands from his chest and fell over sidewise on the floor and lay still.

The door of the room slammed open. The butler stood in it, tousle-headed, his mouth gaping. He tried to say something, saw the gun in Conant's hand, saw Targo slumped on the floor. He didn't say anything.

The albino was getting to his feet, rubbing his chin, feeling his teeth, shaking his head. He went slowly along the wall and gathered up his gun.

Conant snarled at him: "Swell gut you turned out to be. Get on the phone. Get Malloy, the night captain – and snap it up!"

Carmady turned, put his hand down and lifted Jean Adrian's cold chin.

"It's getting light, angel. And I think the rain has stopped," he said slowly. He pulled his inevitable flask out. "Let's take a drink – to Mister Targo."

The girl shook her head, covered her face with her hands. After a long time there were sirens.

10

THE SLIM, TIRED-LOOKING kid in the pale and silver of the Carondelet held his white glove in front of the closing doors and said: "Corky's boils is better, but he didn't come to work, Mister Carmady. Tony the bell captain ain't showed this morning neither. Pretty soft for some guys."

Carmady stood close to Jean Adrian in the corner of the car. They were alone in it. He said: "That's what you think."

The boy turned red. Carmady moved over and patted his shoulder, said: "Don't mind me, son. I've been up all night with a sick friend. Here, buy yourself a second breakfast."

"Jeeze, Mister Carmady, I didn't mean – "

The doors opened at nine and they went down the corridor to 914. Carmady took the key and opened the door, put the key on the inside, held the door, said: "Get some sleep and wake up with your fist in your eye. Take my flask and get a mild toot on. Do you good."

The girl went in through the door, said over her shoulder: "I don't want liquor. Come in a minute. There's something I want to tell you."

He shut the door and followed her in. A bright bar of sunlight lay across the carpet all the way to the davenport. He lit a cigarette and stared at it.

Jean Adrian sat down and jerked her hat off and rumpled her hair. She was silent a moment, then she said slowly, carefully: "It was swell of you to go to all that trouble for me. I don't know why you should do it."

Carmady said: "I can think of a couple of reasons, but they didn't keep Targo from getting killed, and that was my fault in a way. Then in another way it wasn't. I didn't ask him to twist Senator Courtway's neck."

The girl said: "You think you're hard-boiled but you're just a big slob that argues himself into a jam for the first tramp he finds in trouble. Forget it. Forget Targo and forget me. Neither of us was worth any part of your time. I wanted to tell you that because I'll be going away as soon as they let me, and I won't be seeing you any more. This is goodbye."

Carmady nodded, stared at the sun on the carpet. The girl went on: "It's a little hard to tell. I'm not looking for sympathy when I say I'm a tramp. I've smothered in too many hall bedrooms, stripped in too many filthy dressing rooms, missed too many meals, told too many lies to be anything else. That's why I wouldn't want to have anything to do with you, ever."

Carmady said: "I like the way you tell it. Go on."

She looked at him quickly, looked away again. "I'm not the Gianni girl. You guessed that. But I knew her. We did a cheap sister act together when they still did sister acts. Ada and Jean Adrian. We made up our names from hers. That flopped, and we went in a road show and that flopped too. In New Orleans. The going was a little too rough for her. She swallowed bichloride. I kept her photos because I knew her story. And looking at that thin cold guy and thinking what he could have done for her I got to hate him. She was his kid all right. Don't ever think she wasn't. I even wrote letters to him, asking for help for her, just a little help, signing her name. But they didn't get any answer. I got to hate him so much I wanted to do something to him, after she took the bichloride. So I came out here when I got a stake."

She stopped talking and laced her fingers together tightly, then pulled them apart violently, as if she wanted to hurt herself. She went on: "I met Targo through Cyrano and Shenvair through him. Shenvair knew the photos. He'd worked once for an agency in Frisco that was hired to watch Ada. You know all the rest of it."

Carmady said: "It sounds pretty good. I wondered why the touch wasn't made sooner. Do you want me to think you didn't want his money?"

"No. I'd have taken his money all right. But that wasn't what I wanted most. I said I was a tramp."

Carmady smiled very faintly and said: "You don't know a lot about tramps, angel. You made an illegitimate pass and you got caught. That's that, but the money wouldn't have done you any good. It would have been dirty money. I know."

She looked up at him, stared at him. He touched the side of his face and winced and said: "I know because that's the kind of money mine is. My dad made it out of crooked sewerage and paving contracts, out of gambling concessions, appointment pay-offs, even vice, I daresay. He made it every rotten way there is to make money in city politics. And when it was made and there was nothing left to do but sit and look at it, he died and left it to me. It hasn't brought me any fun either. I always hope it's going to, but it never does. Because I'm his pup, his blood, reared in the same gutter. I'm worse than a tramp, angel. I'm a guy that lives on crooked dough and doesn't even do his own stealing."

He stopped, flicked ash on the carpet, straightened his hat on his head.

"Think that over, and don't run too far, because I have all the time in the world and it wouldn't do you any good. It would be so much more fun to run away together."

He went a little way towards the door, stood looking down at the sunlight on the carpet, looked back at her quickly and then went on out.

When the door shut she stood up and went into the bedroom and lay down on the bed just as she was, with her coat on. She stared at the ceiling. After a long time she smiled. In the middle of the smile she fell asleep.

THE MAN WHO LIKED DOGS

1

THERE WAS A brand-new aluminum-gray DeSoto sedan in front of the door. I walked around that and went up three white steps, through a glass door and up three more carpeted steps. I rang a bell on the wall.

Instantly a dozen dog voices began to shake the roof. While they bayed and howled and yapped I looked at a small alcove office with a roll-top desk and a waiting room with mission leather chairs and three diplomas on the wall, at a mission table scattered with copies of the *Dog Fancier's Gazette*.

Somebody quieted the dogs out back, then an inner door opened and a small pretty-faced man in a tan smock came in on rubber soles, with a solicitous smile under a pencil-line mustache. He looked around and under me, didn't see a dog. His smile got more casual.

He said: "I'd like to break them of that, but I can't. Every time they hear a buzzer they start up. They get bored and they know the buzzer means visitors."

I said: "Yeah," and gave him my card. He read it, turned it over and looked at the back, turned it back and read the front again.

"A private detective," he said softly, licking his moist lips. "Well – I'm Dr. Sharp. What can I do for you?"

"I'm looking for a stolen dog."

His eyes flicked at me. His soft little mouth tightened. Very slowly his whole face flushed. I said: "I'm not suggesting *you* stole the dog, Doc. Almost anybody could plant an animal in a place like this and you wouldn't think about that chance they didn't own it, would you?"

"One doesn't just like the idea," he said stiffly. "What kind of dog?"

"Police dog."

He scuffed a toe on the thin carpet, looked at a corner of the ceiling. The flush went off his face, leaving it with a sort of shiny whiteness. After a long moment he said: "I have only one police dog here, and I know the people he belongs to. So I'm afraid – "

"Then you won't mind my looking at him," I cut in, and started towards the inner door.

Dr. Sharp didn't move. He scuffed some more. "I'm not sure that's convenient," he said softly. "Perhaps later in the day."

"Now would be better for me," I said, and reached for the knob.

He scuttled across the waiting room to his little roll-top desk. His small hand went around the telephone there.

"I'll – I'll just call the police if you want to get tough," he said hurriedly.

"That's jake," I said. "Ask for Chief Fulwider. Tell him Carmady's here. I just came from his office."

Dr. Sharp took his hand away from the phone. I grinned at him and rolled a cigarette around in my fingers.

"Come on, Doc," I said. "Shake the hair out of your eyes and let's go. Be nice and maybe I'll tell you the story."

He chewed both his lips in turn, stared at the brown blotter on his desk, fiddled with a corner of it, stood up and crossed the room in his white bucks, opened the door in front of me and we went along a narrow gray hallway. An operating table showed through an open door. We went through a door farther along, into a bare room with a concrete floor, a gas heater in the corner with a bowl of water beside it, and all along one wall two tiers of stalls with heavy wire mesh doors.

Dogs and cats stared at us silently, expectantly, behind the mesh. A tiny chihuahua snuffled under a big red Persian with a wide sheep-skin collar around its neck. There was a sour-faced Scottie and a mutt with all the skin off one leg and a silky-gray Angora and a Sealyham and two more mutts and a razor-sharp fox terrier with a barrel snout and just the right droop to the last two inches of it.

Their noses were wet and their eyes were bright and they wanted to know whose visitor I was.

I looked them over. "These are toys, Doc," I growled. "I'm talking police dog. Gray and black, no brown. A male. Nine years old. Swell points all around except that his tail is too short. Do I bore you?"

He stared at me, made an unhappy gesture. "Yes, but — " he mumbled. "Well, this way."

We went back out of the room. The animals looked disappointed, especially the chihuahua, which tried to climb through the wire mesh and almost made it. We went back out of a rear door into a cement yard with two garages fronting on it. One of them was empty. The other, with its door open a foot, was a box of gloom at the back of which a big dog clanked a chain and put his jaw down flat on the old comforter that was his bed.

"Be careful," Sharp said. "He's pretty savage at times. I had him inside, but he scared the others."

I went into the garage. The dog growled. I went towards him and he hit the end of his chain with a bang. I said: "Hello there, Voss. Shake hands."

He put his head back down on the comforter. His ears came forward halfway. He was very still. His eyes were wolfish, black-rimmed. Then the curved, too-short tail began to thump the floor slowly. I said: "Shake hands, boy," and put mine out. In the doorway behind me the little vet was telling me to be careful. The dog came up slowly on his big rough paws, swung his ears back to normal and lifted his left paw. I shook it.

The little vet complained: "This is a great surprise to me, Mr. — Mr. — "

"Carmady," I said. "Yeah, it would be."

I patted the dog's head and went back out of the garage.

383

We went into the house, into the waiting room. I pushed magazines out of the way and sat on a corner of the mission table, looked the pretty little man over.

"Okay," I said. "Give. What's the name of his folks and where do they live?"

He thought it over sullenly. "Their name is Voss. They've moved East and they are to send for the dog when they're settled."

"Cute at that," I said. "The dog's named Voss after a German war flier. The folks are named after the dog."

"You think I'm lying," the little man said hotly.

"Uh-uh. You scare too easy for a crook. I think somebody wanted to ditch the dog. Here's my story. A girl named Isobel Snare disappeared from her home in San Angelo, two weeks ago. She lives with her great-aunt, a nice old lady in gray silk who isn't anybody's fool. The girl had been stepping out with some pretty shady company in the night spots and gambling joints. So the old lady smelled a scandal and didn't go to the law. She didn't get anywhere until a girl friend of the Snare girl happened to see the dog in your joint. She told the aunt. The aunt hired me – because when the niece drove off in her roadster and didn't come back she had the dog with her."

I mashed out my cigarette on my heel and lit another. Dr. Sharp's little face was as white as dough. Perspiration twinkled in his cute little mustache.

I added gently: "It's not a police job yet. I was kidding you about Chief Fulwider. How's for you and me to keep it under the hat?"

"What – what do you want me to do?" the little man stammered.

"Think you'll hear anything more about the dog?"

"Yes," he said quickly. "The man seemed very fond of him. A genuine dog lover. The dog was gentle with him."

"Then you'll hear from him," I said. "When you do I want to know. What's the guy look like?"

"He was tall and thin with very sharp black eyes. His wife is tall and thin like him. Well-dressed, quiet people."

"The Snare girl is a little runt," I said. "What made it so hush-hush?"

He stared at his foot and didn't say anything.

"Okay," I said. "Business is business. Play ball with me and you won't get any adverse publicity. Is it a deal?" I held my hand out.

"I'll play with you," he said softly, and put a moist fishy little paw in mine. I shook it carefully, so as not to bend it.

I told him where I was staying and went back out to the sunny street and walked a block down to where I had left my Chrysler. I got into it and poked it forward from around the corner, far enough so that I could see the DeSoto and the front of Sharp's place.

I sat like that for half an hour. Then Dr. Sharp came out of his place in street clothes and got into the DeSoto. He drove it off around the corner and swung into the alley that ran behind his yard.

I got the Chrysler going and shot up the block the other way, took a plant at the other end of the alley.

A third of the way down the block I heard growling, barking, snarling. This went on for some time. Then the DeSoto backed out of the concrete yard and came towards me. I ran away from it to the next corner.

The DeSoto went south to Arguello Boulevard, then east on that. A big police dog with a muzzle on his head was chained in the back of the sedan. I could just see his head straining at the chain.

I trailed the DeSoto.

2

CAROLINA STREET WAS away off at the edge of the little beach city. The end of it ran into a disused interurban right of way, beyond which stretched a waste of Japanese truck farms. There were just two houses in the last block, so I hid behind the first, which was on the corner, with a weedy grass plot and a high dusty red and yellow lantana fighting with a honeysuckle vine against the front wall.

Beyond that two or three burned over lots with a few weed stalks sticking up out of the charred grass and then a ramshackle mud-colored bungalow with a wire fence. The DeSoto stopped in front of that.

Its door slammed open and Dr. Sharp dragged the muzzled dog out of the back and fought him through a gate and up the walk. A big barrel-shaped palm tree kept me from seeing him at the front door of the house. I backed my Chrysler and turned it in the shelter of the corner house, went three blocks over and turned along a street parallel to Carolina. This street also ended at the right of way. The rails were rusted in a forest of weeds, came down the other side on to a dirt road, and started back towards Carolina.

The dirt road dropped until I couldn't see over the embankment. When I had gone what felt like three blocks I pulled up and got out, went up the side of the bank and sneaked a look over it.

The house with the wire gate was half a block from me. The DeSoto was still in front of it. Boomingly on the afternoon air came the deep-toned woof-woofing of the police dog. I put my stomach down in the weeds and sighted on the bungalow and waited.

Nothing happened for about fifteen minutes except that the dog kept right on barking. Then the barking suddenly got harder and harsher. Then somebody shouted. Then a man screamed.

I picked myself up out of the weeds and sprinted across the right of way, down the other side to the street end. As I got near the house I heard the low, furious growling of the dog worrying something, and behind it the staccato rattle of a woman's voice in anger, more than in fear.

Behind the wire gate was a patch of lawn mostly dandelions and devil grass. There was a shred of cardboard hanging from the barrel-shaped palm, the remains of a sign. The roots of the tree had wrecked the walk, cracked it wide open and lifted the rough edges into steps.

I went through the gate and thumped up wooden steps to a sagging porch. I banged on the door.

The growling was still going on inside, but the scolding voice had stopped. Nobody came to the door.

I tried the knob, opened the door and went in. There was a heavy smell of chloroform.

In the middle of the floor, on a twisted rug, Dr. Sharp lay spread-eagled on his back, with blood pumping out of the side of his neck. The blood had made a thick glossy pool around his head. The dog leaned away from it, crouched on his forelegs, his ears flat to his head, fragments of a torn muzzle hanging about his neck. His throat bristled and the hair on his spine stood up and there was a low pulsing growl deep in his throat.

Behind the dog a closet door was smashed back against the wall and on the floor of the closet a big wad of cotton-wool sent sickening waves of chloroform out on the air.

A dark handsome woman in a print house dress held a big automatic pointed at the dog and didn't fire it.

She threw a quick glance at me over her shoulder, started to turn. The dog watched her, with narrow, black-rimmed eyes. I took my Luger out and held it down at my side.

Something creaked and a tall black-eyed man in faded blue overalls and a blue work shirt came through the swing door at the back with a sawed-off double-barrel shotgun in his hands. He pointed it at me.

"Hey, you! Drop that gat!" he said angrily.

I moved my jaw with the idea of saying something. The man's finger tightened on the front trigger. My gun went off – without my having much to do with it. The slug hit the stock of the shotgun, knocked it clean out of the man's hands. It pounded on the floor and the dog jumped sideways about seven feet and crouched again.

With an utterly incredulous look on his face the man put his hands up in the air.

I couldn't lose. I said: "Down yours too, lady."

She worked her tongue along her lips and lowered the automatic to her side and walked away from the body on the floor.

The man said: "Hell, don't shoot him. I can handle him."

I blinked, then I got the idea. He had been afraid I was going to shoot the dog. He hadn't been worrying about himself.

I lowered the Luger a little. "What happened?"

"That —— tried to chloroform – *him*, a fighting dog!"

I said: "Yeah. If you've got a phone, you'd better call an ambulance. Sharp won't last long with that tear in his neck."

The woman said tonelessly: "I thought *you* were law."

I didn't say anything. She went along the wall to a window seat full of crumpled newspapers, reached down for a phone at one end of it.

I looked down at the little vet. The blood had stopped coming out of his neck. His face was the whitest face I had ever seen.

"Never mind the ambulance," I told the woman. "Just call Police Headquarters."

The man in the overalls put his hands down and dropped on one knee, began to pat the floor and talk soothingly to the dog.

"Steady, old-timer. Steady. We're all friends now – all friends. Steady, Voss."

The dog growled and swung his hind end a little. The man kept on talking to him. The dog stopped growling and the hackles on his back went down. The man in overalls kept on crooning to him.

The woman on the window seat put the phone aside and said: "On the way. Think you can handle it, Jerry?"

"Sure," the man said, without taking his eyes off the dog.

The dog let his belly touch the floor now and opened his mouth and let his tongue hang out. The tongue dripped saliva, pink saliva with blood mixed in it. The hair at the side of the dog's mouth was stained with blood.

3

THE MAN CALLED Jerry said: "Hey, Voss. Hey, Voss old kid. You're fine now. You're fine."

The dog panted, didn't move. The man straightened up and went close to him, pulled one of the dog's ears. The dog turned his head sideways and let his ear be pulled. The man stroked his head, unbuckled the chewed muzzle and got it off.

He stood up with the end of the broken chain and the dog came up on his feet obediently, went out through the swing door into the back part of the house, at the man's side.

I moved a little, out of line with the swing door. Jerry might have more shotguns. There was something about Jerry's face that worried me. As if I had seen him before, but not very lately, or in a newspaper photo.

I looked at the woman. She was a handsome brunette in her early thirties. Her print house dress didn't seem to belong with her finely arched eyebrows and her long soft hands.

"How did it happen?" I asked casually, as if it didn't matter very much.

Her voice snapped at me, as if she was aching to turn it loose. "We've been in the house about a week. Rented it furnished. I was in the kitchen, Jerry in the yard. The car stopped out front and the little guy marched in just as if he lived here. The door didn't happen to be locked, I guess. I opened the swing door a crack and saw him pushing the dog into the closet. Then I smelled the chloroform. Then things began to happen all at once and I went for a gun and called Jerry out of the window. I got back in here about the time you crashed in. Who are you?"

"It was all over then?" I said. "He had Sharp chewed up on the floor?"

"Yes – if Sharp is his name."

"You and Jerry didn't know him?"

"Never saw him before. Or the dog. But Jerry loves dogs."

"Better change a little of that," I said. "Jerry knew the dog's name. Voss."

Her eyes got tight and her mouth got stubborn. "I think you must be mistaken," she said in a sultry voice. "I asked you who you were, mister."

"Who's Jerry?" I asked. "I've seen him somewhere. Maybe on a reader. Where'd he get the sawed-off? You going to let the cops see that?"

She bit her lip, then stood up suddenly, went towards the fallen shotgun. I let her pick it up, saw she kept her hand away from the triggers. She went back to the window seat and pushed it under the pile of newspapers.

She faced me. "Okay, what's the pay-off?" she asked grimly.

I said slowly: "The dog is stolen. His owner, a girl, happens to be missing. I'm hired to find her. The people Sharp said he got the dog from sounded like you and Jerry. Their name was Voss. They moved East. Ever heard of a lady called Isobel Snare?"

The woman said "No," tonelessly, and stared at the end of my chin.

The man in overalls came back through the swing door wiping his face on the sleeve of his blue work shirt. He didn't have any fresh guns with him. He looked me over without much concern.

I said: "I could do you a lot of good with the law, if you had any ideas about this Snare girl."

The woman stared at me, curled her lips. The man smiled, rather softly, as if he held all the cards. Tires squealed, taking a distant corner in a hurry.

"Aw, loosen up," I said quickly. "Sharp was scared. He brought the dog back to where he got him. He must have thought the house was empty. The chloroform idea wasn't so good, but the little guy was all rattled."

They didn't make a sound, either of them. They just stared at me.

"Okay," I said, and stepped over to the corner of the room. "I think you're a couple of lamsters. If whoever's coming isn't law, I'll start shooting. Don't ever think I won't."

The woman said very calmly: "Suit yourself, kibitzer."

Then a car rushed along the block and ground to a harsh stop before the house. I sneaked a quick glance out, saw the red spotlight on the windshield, the P.D. on the side. Two big bruisers in plain clothes tumbled out and slammed through the gate, up the steps.

A fist pounded the door. "It's open," I shouted.

The door swung wide and the two dicks charged in, with drawn guns.

They stopped dead, stared at what lay on the floor. Their guns jerked at Jerry and me. The one who covered me was a big red-faced man in a baggy gray suit.

"Reach — and reach empty!" he yelled in a large tough voice.

I reached, but held on to my Luger. "Easy," I said. "A dog killed him, not a gun. I'm a private dick from San Angelo. I'm on a case here."

"Yeah?" He closed in on me heavily, bored his gun into my stomach. "Maybe so, bud. We'll know all that later on."

He reached up and jerked my gun loose from my hand, sniffed at it, leaning his gun into me.

"Fired, huh? Sweet! Turn around."

"Listen — "

391

"Turn around, bud."

I turned slowly. Even as I turned he was dropping his gun into a side pocket and reaching for his hip.

That should have warned me, but it didn't. I may have heard the swish of the blackjack. Certainly I must have felt it. There was a sudden pool of darkness at my feet. I dived into it and dropped . . . and dropped . . . and dropped . . .

4

WHEN I CAME to the room was full of smoke. The smoke hung in the air, in thin lines straight up and down, like a bead curtain. Two windows seemed to be open in an end wall, but the smoke didn't move. I had never seen the room before.

I lay a little while thinking, then I opened my mouth and yelled: "Fire!" at the top of my lungs.

Then I fell back on the bed and started laughing. I didn't like the sound I made laughing. It had a goofy ring, even to me.

Steps ran along somewhere and a key turned in the door and the door opened. A man in a short white coat looked in at me, hard-eyed. I turned my head a little and said: "Don't count that one, Jack. It slipped out."

He scowled sharply. He had a hard small face, beady eyes. I didn't know him.

"Maybe you want some more strait jacket," he sneered.

"I'm fine, Jack," I said. "Just fine. I'm going to have me a short nap now."

"Better be just that," he snarled.

The door shut, the key turned, the steps went away.

I lay still and looked at the smoke. I knew now that there wasn't any smoke there really. It must have been night because a porcelain bowl hanging from the ceiling on three chains had light behind it. It had little colored lumps around the edge, orange and blue alternating. While I watched them they opened like tiny portholes and heads stuck out of them, tiny heads like the heads on dolls, but alive heads. There was a man in a yachting cap and a large fluffy blonde and a thin man with a crooked bow tie who kept saying: "Would you like your steak rare or medium, sir?"

I took hold of the corner of the rough sheet and wiped the sweat off my face. I sat up, put my feet down on the floor. They were bare. I was wearing canton flannel pajamas. There was no feeling in my feet when I put them down. After a while they began to tingle and then got full of pins and needles.

Then I could feel the floor. I took hold of the side of the bed and stood up and walked.

A voice that was probably my own was saying to me: "You have the D.T.s . . . you have the D.T.s . . . you have the D.T.s . . ."

I saw a bottle of whiskey on a small white table between the two windows. I started towards it. It was a Johnnie Walker bottle, half full. I got it up, took a long drink from the neck. I put the bottle down again.

The whisky had a funny taste. While I was realizing that it had a funny taste I saw a washbowl in the corner. I just made it to the washbowl before I vomited.

I got back to the bed and lay there. The vomiting had made me very weak, but the room seemed a little more real, a little less fantastic. I could see bars on the two windows, a heavy wooden chair, no other furniture but the white table with the doped whiskey on it. There was a closet door, shut, probably locked.

The bed was a hospital bed and there were two leather straps attached to the sides, about where a man's wrists would be. I knew I was in some kind of prison ward.

My left arm suddenly began to feel sore. I rolled up the loose sleeve, looked at half a dozen pinpricks on the upper arm, and a black and blue circle around each one.

I had been shot so full of dope to keep me quiet that I was having the French fits coming out of it. That accounted for

393

the smoke and the little heads on the ceiling light. The doped whiskey was probably part of somebody else's cure.

I got up again and walked, kept on walking. After a while I drank a little water from the tap, kept it down, drank more. Half an hour or more of that and I was ready to talk to somebody.

The closet door was locked and the chair was too heavy for me. I stripped the bed, slid the mattress to one side. There was a mesh spring underneath, fastened at the top and bottom by heavy coil springs about nine inches long. It took me half an hour and much misery to work one of these loose.

I rested a little and drank a little more cold water and went over to the hinge side of the door.

I yelled "Fire!" at the top of my voice, several times.

I waited, but not long. Steps ran along the hallway outside. The key jabbed into the door, the lock clicked. The hard-eyed little man in the short white coat dodged in furiously, his eyes on the bed.

I laid the coil spring on the angle of his jaw, then on the back of his head as he went down. I got him by the throat. He struggled a good deal. I used a knee on his face. It hurt my knee.

He didn't say how his face felt. I got a blackjack out of his right hip pocket and reversed the key in the door and locked it from the inside. There were other keys on the ring. One of them unlocked my closet. I looked in at my clothes.

I put them on slowly, with fumbling fingers. I yawned a great deal. The man on the floor didn't move.

I locked him in and left him.

5

FROM A WIDE silent hallway, with a parquetry floor and a narrow carpet down its middle, flat white oak banisters swept down in long curves to the entrance hall. There were closed doors, big, heavy, old-fashioned. No sounds behind them. I went down the carpet runner, walking on the balls of my feet.

There were stained-glass inner doors to a vestibule from which the front door opened. A telephone rang as I got that far. A man's voice answered it, from behind a half-open door through which light came out into the dim hall.

I went back, sneaked a glance around the edge of the open door, saw a man at a desk, talking into the phone. I waited until he hung up. Then I went in.

He had a pale, bony, high-crowned head, across which a thin wave of brown hair curled and was plastered to his skull. He had a long, pale, joyless face. His eyes jumped at me. His hand jumped towards a button on his desk.

I grinned, growled at him: "Don't. I'm a desperate man, warden." I showed him the blackjack.

His smile was as stiff as a frozen fish. His long pale hands made gestures like sick butterflies over the top of his desk. One of them began to drift towards a side drawer of the desk.

He worked his tongue loose – "You've been a very sick man, sir. A very sick man. I wouldn't advise – "

I flicked the blackjack at his wandering hand. It drew into itself like a slug on a hot stone. I said: "Not sick, warden, just doped within an inch of my reason. Out is what I want, and some clean whiskey. Give."

He made vague motions with his fingers. "I'm Dr. Sundstrand," he said. "This is a private hospital – not a jail."

"Whiskey," I croaked. "I get all the rest. Private funny house. A lovely racket. Whiskey."

"In the medicine cabinet," he said with a drifting, spent breath.

"Put your hands behind your head."

"I'm afraid you'll regret this." He put his hands behind his head.

I got to the far side of the desk, opened the drawer his hand had wanted to reach, took an automatic out of it. I put the blackjack away, went back round the desk to the medicine cabinet on the wall. There was a pint bottle of bond bourbon in it, three glasses. I took two of them.

I poured two drinks. "You first, warden."

"I – I don't drink. I'm a total abstainer," he muttered, his hands still behind his head.

I took the blackjack out again. He put a hand down quickly, gulped from one of the glasses. I watched him. It didn't seem to hurt him. I smelled my dose, then put it down my throat. It worked, and I had another, then slipped the bottle into my coat pocket.

"Okay," I said. "Who put me in here? Shake it up. I'm in a hurry."

"The – the police, of course."

"What police?"

He hunched his shoulders down in the chair. He looked sick. "A man named Galbraith signed as complaining witness. Strictly legal, I assure you. He is an officer."

I said: "Since when can a cop sign as complaining witness on a psycho case?"

He didn't say anything.

"Who gave me the dope in the first place?"

"I wouldn't know that. I presume it has been going on a long time."

I felt my chin. "All of two days," I said. "They ought to have gunned me. Less kickback in the long run. So long, warden."

"If you go out of here," he said thinly, "you will be arrested at once."

"Not just for going out," I said softly.

As I went out he still had his hands behind his head.

There was a chain and a bolt on the front door, beside the lock. But nobody tried to stop me from opening it. I crossed a big old-fashioned porch, went down a wide path fringed with flowers. A mockingbird sang in a dark tree. There was a white picket fence on the street. It was a corner house, on Twenty-ninth and Descanso.

I walked four blocks east to a bus line and waited for a bus. There was no alarm, no cruising car looking for me. The bus came and I rode downtown, went to a Turkish Bath establishment, had a steam bath, a needle shower, a rub-down, a shave, and the rest of the whiskey.

I could eat then. I ate and went to a strange hotel, registered under a fake name. It was half past eleven. The local paper, which I read over more whiskey and water, informed me that one Dr. Richard Sharp, who had been found dead in a vacant furnished house on Carolina Street, was still causing the police much headache. They had no clue to the murderer as yet.

The date on the paper informed me that over forty-eight hours had been abstracted from my life without my knowledge or consent.

I went to bed and to sleep, had nightmares and woke up out of them covered with cold sweat. That was the last of the withdrawal symptoms. In the morning I was a well man.

6

CHIEF OF POLICE FULWIDER was a hammered down, fattish heavyweight, with restless eyes and that shade of red hair that is almost pink. It was cut very short and his pink scalp glistened among the pink hairs. He wore a fawn-colored flannel suit with patch pockets and lapped seams, cut as every tailor can't cut flannel.

He shook hands with me and turned his chair sideways and crossed his legs. That showed me French lisle socks at three or four dollars a pair, and hand-made English walnut brogues at fifteen to eighteen, depression prices.

I figured that probably his wife had money.

"Ah, Carmady," he said, chasing my card over the glass top of his desk, "with two *a*'s, eh? Down here on a job?"

"A little trouble," I said. "You can straighten it out, if you will."

He stuck his chest out, waved a pink hand and lowered his voice a couple of notches.

"Trouble," he said, "is something our little town don't have a lot of. Our little city is small, but very, very clean. I look out of my west window and I see the Pacific Ocean. Nothing cleaner than that. On the north Arguello Boulevard and the foothills. On the east the finest little business section you would want to see and beyond it a paradise of well-kept homes and gardens. On the south – if I had a south window, which I don't have – I would see the finest little yacht harbor in the world, for a small yacht harbor."

"I brought my trouble with me," I said. "That is, some of it. The rest went on ahead. A girl named Isobel Snare ran off from home in the big city and her dog was seen here. I found the dog, but the people who had the dog went to a lot of trouble to sew me up."

"Is that so?" the chief asked absently. His eyebrows crawled around on his forehead. I wasn't sure whether I was kidding him or he was kidding me.

"Just turn the key in the door, will you?" he said. "You're a younger man than I am."

I got up and turned the key and sat down again and got a cigarette out. By that time the chief had a right-looking bottle and two pony glasses on the desk, and a handful of cardamom seeds.

We had a drink and he cracked three or four of the cardamom seeds and we chewed them and looked at one another.

"Just tell me about it," he said then. "I can take it now."

"Did you ever hear of a guy called Farmer Saint?"

"*Did* I?" He banged his desk and the cardamom seeds jumped. "Why there's a thousand berries on that bimbo. A bank stickup, ain't he?"

I nodded, trying to look behind his eyes without seeming to. "He and his sister work together. Diana is her name. They dress up like country folks and smack down small-town banks, state banks. That's why he's called Farmer Saint. There's a grand on the sister too."

"I would certainly like to put the sleeves on that pair," the chief said firmly.

"Then why the hell didn't you?" I asked him.

He didn't quite hit the ceiling, but he opened his mouth so wide I was afraid his lower jaw was going to fall in his lap. His eyes stuck out like peeled eggs. A thin trickle of saliva showed in the fat crease at the corner. He shut his mouth with all the deliberation of a steam shovel.

It was a great act, if it was an act.

"Say that again," he whispered.

I opened a folded newspaper I had with me and pointed to a column.

"Look at this Sharp killing. Your local paper didn't do so good on it. It says some unknown rang the department and the boys ran out and found a dead man in an empty house. That's a lot of noodles. I was there. Farmer Saint and his sister were there. Your cops were there when we were there."

"Treachery!" he shouted suddenly. "Traitors in the department." His face was now as gray as arsenic flypaper. He poured two more drinks, with a shaking hand.

It was my turn to crack the cardamom seeds.

He put his drink down in one piece and lunged for a mahogany call box on his desk. I caught the name Galbraith. I went over and unlocked the door.

We didn't wait very long, but long enough for the chief to have two more drinks. His face got a better color.

Then the door opened and the big red-faced dick who had sapped me loafed through it, with a bulldog pipe clamped in his teeth and his hands in his pockets. He shouldered the door shut, leaned against it casually.

I said: "Hello, Sarge."

He looked at me as if he would like to kick me in the face and not have to hurry about it.

"Badge!" the fat chief yelled. "Badge! Put it on the desk. You're fired!"

Galbraith went over to the desk slowly and put an elbow down on it, put his face about a foot from the chief's nose.

"What was that crack?" he asked thickly.

"You had Farmer Saint under your hand and let him go," the chief yelled. "You and that saphead Duncan. You let him stick a shotgun in your belly and get away. You're through. Fired. You ain't got no more job than a canned oyster. Gimme your badge!"

"Who the hell is Farmer Saint?" Galbraith asked, unimpressed, and blew pipe smoke in the chief's face.

"He don't know," the chief whined at me. "He don't know. That's the kind of material I got to work with."

"What do you mean, work?" Galbraith inquired loosely.

The fat chief jumped as though a bee had stung the end of his nose. Then he doubled a meaty fist and hit Galbraith's jaw with what looked like a lot of power. Galbraith's head moved about half an inch.

"Don't do that," he said. "You'll bust a gut and then where would the department be?" He shot a look at me, looked back at Fulwider. "Should I tell him?"

Fulwider looked at me, to see how the show was going over. I had my mouth open and a blank expression on my face, like a farm boy at a Latin lesson.

"Yeah, tell him," he growled, shaking his knuckles back and forth.

Galbraith stuck a thick leg over a corner of the desk and knocked his pipe out, reached for the whiskey and poured himself a drink in the chief's glass. He wiped his lips, grinned. When he grinned he opened his mouth wide, and he had a mouth a dentist could have got both hands in, up to the elbows.

He said calmly: "When me and Dunc crash the joint you was cold on the floor and the lanky guy was over you with a sap. The broad was on a window seat, with a lot of newspapers around her. Okay. The lanky guy starts to tell us some yarn when a dog begins to howl out back and we look that way and the broad slips a sawed-off 12-gauge out of the newspapers and shows it to us. Well, what could we do except be nice? She couldn't have missed and we could. So the guy gets more guns out of his pants and they tie knots around us and stick us in a closet that has enough chloroform in it to make us quiet, without the ropes. After a while we hear 'em leave, in two cars. When we get loose the stiff has the place to himself. So we fudge it a bit for the papers. We don't get no new line yet. How's it tie to yours?"

"Not bad," I told him. "As I remember the woman phoned for some law herself. But I could be mistaken. The rest of it ties in with me being sapped on the floor and not knowing anything about it."

Galbraith gave me a nasty look. The chief looked at his thumb.

"When I came to," I said, "I was in a private dope and hooch cure out on Twenty-ninth. Run by a man named Sundstrand. I was shot so full of hop myself I could have been Rockefeller's pet dime trying to spin myself."

"That Sundstrand," Galbraith said heavily. "That guy's been a flea in our pants for a long time. Should we go out and push him in the face, Chief?"

"It's a cinch Farmer Saint put Carmady in there," Fulwider said solemnly. "So there must be some tie-up. I'd say yes, and take Carmady with you. Want to go?" he asked me.

"Do I?" I said heartily.

Galbraith looked at the whiskey bottle. He said carefully: "There's a grand each on this Saint and his sister. If we gather them in, how do we cut it?"

"You cut me out," I said. "I'm on a straight salary and expenses."

Galbraith grinned again. He teetered on his heels, grinning with thick amiability.

"Okydoke. We got your car in the garage downstairs. Some Jap phoned in about it. We'll use that to go in – just you and me."

"Maybe you ought to have more help, Gal," the chief said doubtfully.

"Uh-uh. Just me and him's plenty. He's a tough baby or he wouldn't be walkin' around."

"Well, all right," the chief said brightly. "And we'll just have a little drink on it."

But he was still rattled. He forgot the cardamom seeds.

7

IT WAS A cheerful spot by daylight. Tea-rose begonias made a solid mass under the front windows and pansies were a round carpet about the base of an acacia. A scarlet climbing rose covered a trellis to one side of the house, and a bronze-green hummingbird was prodding delicately in a mass of sweet peas that grew up the garage wall.

It looked like the home of a well-fixed elderly couple who had come to the ocean to get as much sun as possible in their old age.

Galbraith spit on my running board and shook his pipe out and tickled the gate open, stamped up the path and flattened his thumb against a neat copper bell.

We waited. A grille opened in the door and a long sallow face looked out at us under a starched nurse's cap.

"Open up. It's the law," the big cop growled.

A chain rattled and a bolt slid back. The door opened. The nurse was a six-footer with long arms and big hands, an ideal torturer's assistant. Something happened to her face and I saw she was smiling.

"Why, it's Mr. Galbraith," she chirped, in a voice that was high-pitched and throaty at the same time. "How are you, Mr. Galbraith? Did you want to see Doctor?"

"Yeah, and sudden," Galbraith growled, pushing past her.

We went along the hall. The door of the office was shut. Galbraith kicked it open, with me at his heels and the big nurse chirping at mine.

Dr. Sundstrand, the total abstainer, was having a morning bracer out of a fresh quart bottle. His thin hair was stuck in wicks with perspiration and his bony mask of a face seemed to have a lot of lines in it that hadn't been there the night before.

He took his hand off the bottle hurriedly and gave us his frozen-fish smile. He said fussily: "What's this? What's this? I thought I gave orders – "

"Aw, pull your belly in," Galbraith said, and yanked a chair near the desk. "Dangle, sister."

The nurse chirped something more and went back through the door. The door was shut. Dr. Sundstrand worked his eyes up and down my face and looked unhappy.

Galbraith put both his elbows on the desk and took hold of his bulging jowls with his fists. He stared fixedly, venomously, at the squirming doctor.

After what seemed a very long time he said, almost softly: "Where's Farmer Saint?"

The doctor's eyes popped wide. His Adam's apple bobbled above the neck of his smock. His greenish eyes began to look bilious.

"Don't stall!" Galbraith roared. "We know all about your private hospital racket, the crook hideout you're runnin', the dope and women on the side. You made one slip too many when you hung a snatch on this shamus from the big town. Your big city protection ain't going to do you no good on this one. Come on, where is Saint? And where's that girl?"

I remembered, quite casually, that I had not said anything about Isobel Snare in front of Galbraith – if that was the girl he meant.

Dr. Sundstrand's hand flopped about on his desk. Sheer astonishment seemed to be adding a final touch of paralysis to his uneasiness.

"Where are they?" Galbraith yelled again.

The big door opened and the big nurse fussed in again. "Now, Mr. Galbraith, the patients. Please remember the patients, Mr. Galbraith."

"Go climb up your thumb," Galbraith told her, over his shoulder.

She hovered by the door. Sundstrand found his voice at last. It was a mere wisp of a voice. It said wearily: "As if you didn't know."

Then his darting hand swept into his smock, and out again, with a gun glistening in it. Galbraith threw himself sideways, clean out of the chair. The doctor shot at him twice, missed twice. My hand touched a gun, but didn't draw it. Galbraith laughed on the floor and his big right hand snatched at his armpit, came up with a Luger. It looked like my Luger. It went off, just once.

Nothing changed in the doctor's long face. I didn't see where the bullet hit him. His head came down and hit the desk and his gun made a thud on the floor. He lay with his face on the desk, motionless.

Galbraith pointed his gun at me, and got up off the floor. I looked at the gun again. I was sure it was my gun.

"That's a swell way to get information," I said aimlessly.

"Hands down, shamus. You don't want to play."

I put my hands down. "Cute," I said. "I suppose this whole scene was framed just to put the chill on Doc."

"He shot first, didn't he?"

"Yeah," I said thinly. "He shot first."

The nurse was sidling along the wall towards me. No sound had come from her since Sundstrand pulled his act. She was almost at my side. Suddenly, much too late, I saw the flash of knuckles on her good right hand, and hair on the back of the hand.

I dodged, but not enough. A crunching blow seemed to split my head wide open. I brought up against the wall, my knees full of water and my brain working hard to keep my right hand from snatching at a gun.

I straightened. Galbraith leered at me.

"Not so very smart," I said. "You're still holding my Luger. That sort of spoils the plant, doesn't it?"

"I see you get the idea, shamus."

The chirpy-voiced nurse said, in a blank pause: "Jeeze, the guy's got a jaw like a elephant's foot. Damn if I didn't split a knuck on him."

Galbraith's little eyes had death in them. "How about upstairs?" he asked the nurse.

"All out last night. Should I try one more swing?"

"What for? He didn't go for his gat, and he's too tough for you, baby. Lead is his meat."

I said: "You ought to shave baby twice a day on this job."

The nurse grinned, pushed the starched cap and the stringy blond wig askew on a bullet head. She – or more properly he – reached a gun from under the white nurse's uniform.

Galbraith said: "It was self-defense, see? You tangled with Doc, but he shot first. Be nice and me and Dunc will try to remember it that way."

I rubbed my jaw with my left hand. "Listen, Sarge. I can take a joke as well as the next fellow. You sapped me in that house on Carolina Street and didn't tell about it. Neither did I. I figured you had reasons and you'd let me in on them at the right time. Maybe I can guess what the reasons are. I think you know where Saint is, or can find out. Saint knows where the Snare girl is, because he had her dog. Let's put a little more into this deal, something for both of us."

"We've got ours, sappo. I promised Doc I'd bring you back and let him play with you. I put Dunc in here in the nurse's rig to handle you for him. But *he* was the one we really wanted to handle."

"All right," I said. "What do I get out of it?"

"Maybe a little more living."

I said: "Yeah. Don't think I'm kidding you – but look at that little window in the wall behind you."

Galbraith didn't move, didn't take his eyes off me. A thick sneer curved his lips.

Duncan, the female impersonator, looked – and yelled.

A small, square, tinted glass window high up in the corner of the back wall had swung open quite silently. I was looking straight at it, past Galbraith's ear, straight at the black snout of a tommy gun, on the sill, at the two hard black eyes behind the gun.

A voice I had last heard soothing a dog said: "How's to drop the rod, sister? And you at the desk – grab a cloud."

8

THE BIG COP'S mouth sucked for air. Then his whole face tightened and he jerked around and the Luger gave one hard, sharp cough.

I dropped to the floor as the tommy gun cut loose in a short burst. Galbraith crumpled beside the desk, fell on his back with his legs twisted. Blood came out of his nose and mouth.

The cop in nurse's uniform turned as white as the starched cap. His gun bounced. His hands tried to claw at the ceiling.

There was a queer, stunned silence. Powder smoke reeked. Farmer Saint spoke downward from his perch at the window, to somebody outside the house.

A door opened and shut distinctly and running steps came along the hall. The door of our room was pushed wide. Diana Saint came in with a brace of automatics in her hands. A tall, handsome woman, neat and dark, with a rakish black hat, and two gloved hands holding guns.

I got up off the floor, keeping my hands in sight. She tossed her voice calmly at the window, without looking towards it.

"Okay, Jerry. I can hold them."

Saint's head and shoulders and his sub-machine gun went away from the frame of the window, leaving blue sky and the thin, distant branches of a tall tree.

There was a thud, as if feet dropped off a ladder to a wooden porch. In the room we were five statues, two fallen.

Somebody had to move. The situation called for two more killings. From Saint's angle I couldn't see it any other way. There had to be a cleanup.

The gag hadn't worked when it wasn't a gag. I tried it again when it was. I looked past the woman's shoulder, kicked a hard grin on to my face, said hoarsely:

"Hello, Mike. Just in time."

It didn't fool her, of course, but it made her mad. She stiffened her body and snapped a shot at me from the right-hand gun. It was a big gun for a woman and it jumped. The other gun jumped with it. I didn't see where the shot went. I went in under the guns.

My shoulder hit her thigh and she tipped back and hit her head against the jamb of the door. I wasn't too nice about knocking the guns out of her hands. I kicked the door shut, reached up and yanked the key around, then scrambled back from a high-heeled shoe that was doing its best to smash my nose for me.

Duncan said: "Keeno," and dived for his gun on the floor.

"Watch that little window, if you want to live," I snarled at him.

Then I was behind the desk, dragging the phone away from Dr. Sundstrand's dead body, dragging it as far from the line of the door as the cord would let me. I lay down on the floor with it and started to dial, on my stomach.

Diana's eyes came alive on the phone. She screeched: "They've got me, Jerry! They've got me!"

The machine gun began to tear the door apart as I bawled into the ear of a bored desk sergeant.

Pieces of plaster and wood flew like fists at an Irish wedding. Slugs jerked the body of Dr. Sundstrand as though a chill was shaking him back to life. I threw the phone away from me and grabbed Diana's guns and started in on the door for our side. Through a wide crack I could see cloth. I shot at that.

I couldn't see what Duncan was doing. Then I knew. A shot that couldn't have come through the door smacked Diana Saint square on the end of her chin. She went down again, stayed down.

Another shot that didn't come through the door lifted my hat. I rolled and yelled at Duncan. His gun moved in a stiff arc, following me. His mouth was an animal snarl. I yelled again.

Four round patches of red appeared in a diagonal line across the nurse uniform, chest high. They spread even in the short time it took Duncan to fall.

There was a siren somewhere. It was my siren, coming my way, getting louder.

The tommy gun stopped and a foot kicked at the door. It shivered, but held at the lock. I put four more slugs into it, well away from the lock.

The siren got louder. Saint had to go. I heard his step running away down the hall. A door slammed. A car started out back in an alley. The sound of its going got less as the approaching siren screeched into a crescendo.

I crawled over to the woman and looked at blood on her face and hair and soft soggy places on the front of her coat.

I touched her face. She opened her eyes slowly, as if the lids were very heavy.

"Jerry – " she whispered.

"Dead," I lied grimly. "Where's Isobel Snare, Diana?"

The eyes closed. Tears glistened, the tears of the dying.

"Where's Isobel, Diana?" I pleaded. "Be regular and tell me. I'm no cop. I'm her friend. Tell me, Diana."

I put tenderness and wistfulness into it, everything I had.

The eyes half opened. The whisper came again: "Jerry – " then it trailed off and the eyes shut. Then the lips moved once more, breathed a word that sounded like "Monty."

That was all. She died.

I stood up slowly and listened to the sirens.

9

IT WAS GETTING late and lights were going on here and there in a tall office building across the street. I had been in Fulwider's office all the afternoon. I had told my story twenty times. It was all true – what I told.

Cops had been in and out, ballistics and print men, record men, reporters, half a dozen city officials, even an A.P. correspondent. The correspondent didn't like his handout and said so.

The fat chief was sweaty and suspicious. His coat was off and his armpits were black and his short red hair curled as if it had been singed. Not knowing how much or little I knew he didn't dare lead me. All he could do was yell at me and whine at me by turns, and try to get me drunk in between.

I was getting drunk and liking it.

"Didn't nobody say anything at all!" he wailed at me for the hundredth time.

I took another drink, flopped my hand around, looked silly. "Not a word, Chief," I said owlishly. "I'm the boy that would tell you. They died too sudden."

He took hold of his jaw and cranked it. "Damn funny," he sneered. "Four dead ones on the floor and you not even nicked."

"I was the only one," I said, "that lay down on the floor while still healthy."

He took hold of his right ear and worried that. "You been here three days," he howled. "In them three days we got more crime than in three years before you come. It ain't human. I must be having a nightmare."

"You can't blame me, Chief," I grumbled. "I came down here to look for a girl. I'm still looking for her. I didn't tell Saint and his sister to hide out in your town. When I spotted him I tipped you off, though your own cops didn't. I didn't shoot Doc Sundstrand before anything could be got out of him. I still haven't any idea why the phony nurse was planted there."

"Nor me," Fulwider yelled. "But it's my job that's shot full of holes. For all the chance I got to get out of this I might as well go fishin' right now."

I took another drink, hiccoughed cheerfully. "Don't say that, Chief," I pleaded. "You cleaned the town up once and you can do it again. This one was just a hot grounder that took a bad bounce."

He took a turn around the office and tried to punch a hole in the end wall, then slammed himself back in his chair. He eyed me savagely, grabbed for the whiskey bottle, then didn't touch it – as though it might do him more good in my stomach.

"I'll make a deal with you," he growled. "You run on back to San Angelo and I'll forget it was your gun croaked Sundstrand."

"That's not a nice thing to say to a man that's trying to earn his living, Chief. You know how it happened to be my gun."

His face looked gray again, for a moment. He measured me for a coffin. Then the mood passed and he smacked his desk, said heartily:

"You're right, Carmady. I couldn't do that, could I? You still got to find that girl, ain't you? Okay, you run on back to the hotel and get some rest. I'll work on it tonight and see you in the A.M."

I took another short drink, which was all there was left in the bottle. I felt fine. I shook hands with him twice and staggered out of his office. Flash bulbs exploded all over the corridor.

I went down the City Hall steps and around the side of the building to the police garage. My blue Chrysler was home again. I dropped the drunk act and went on down the side streets to the ocean front, walked along the wide cement walk towards the two amusement piers and the Grand Hotel.

It was getting dusk now. Lights on the piers came out. Masthead lights were lit on the small yachts riding at anchor behind the yacht harbor breakwater. In a white barbecue stand a man tickled wienies with a long fork and droned: "Get hungry, folks. Nice hot doggies here. Get hungry, folks."

I lit a cigarette and stood there looking out to sea. Very suddenly, far out, lights shone from a big ship. I watched them, but they didn't move. I went over to the hot dog man.

"Anchored?" I asked him, pointing.

He looked around the end of his booth, wrinkled his nose with contempt.

"Hell, that's the gambling boat. The Cruise to Nowhere, they call the act, because it don't go no place. If Tango ain't crooked enough, try that. Yes, sir, that's the good ship *Montecito*. How about a nice warm puppy?"

I put a quarter on his counter. "Have one yourself," I said softly. "Where do the taxis leave from?"

I had no gun. I went on back to the hotel to get my spare.

The dying Diana Saint had said "Monty."

Perhaps she just hadn't lived long enough to say "Montecito."

At the hotel I lay down and fell asleep as though I had been anaesthetized. It was eight o'clock when I woke up, and I was hungry.

I was tailed from the hotel, but not very far. Of course the clean little city didn't have enough crime for the dicks to be very good shadows.

10

IT WAS A long ride for forty cents. The water taxi, an old speedboat without trimmings, slid through the anchored yachts and rounded the breakwater. The swell hit us. All the company I had besides the tough-looking citizen at the wheel was two spooning couples who began to peck at each other's faces as soon as the darkness folded down.

I stared back at the lights of the city and tried not to bear down too hard on my dinner. Scattered diamond points at first, the lights drew together and became a jeweled wristlet laid out in the show window of the night. Then they were a soft orange yellow blur above the top of the swell. The taxi smacked in the invisible waves and bounced like a surf boat. There was cold fog in the air.

The portholes of the *Montecito* got large and the taxi swept out in a wide turn, tipped to an angle of forty-five degrees and careened neatly to the side of a brightly lit stage. The taxi engine idled down and backfired in the fog.

A sloe-eyed boy in a tight blue mess jacket and a gangster mouth handed the girls out, swept their escorts with a keen glance, sent them on up. The look he gave me told me something about him. The way he bumped into my gun holster told me more.

"Nix," he said softly. "Nix."

He jerked his chin at the taxi man. The taxi man dropped a short noose over a bitt, turned his wheel a little and climbed on the stage. He got behind me.

"Nix," the one in the mess jacket purred. "No gats on this boat, mister. Sorry."

"Part of my clothes," I told him. "I'm a private dick. I'll check it."

"Sorry, bo. No checkroom for gats. On your way."

The taxi man hooked a wrist through my right arm. I shrugged.

"Back in the boat," the taxi man growled behind me. "I owe you forty cents, mister. Come on."

I got back into the boat.

"Okay," I sputtered at Mess Jacket. "If you don't want my money, you don't want it. This is a hell of a way to treat a visitor. This is — "

His sleek, silent smile was the last thing I saw as the taxi cast off and hit the swell on the way back. I hated to leave that smile.

The way back seemed longer. I didn't speak to the taxi man and he didn't speak to me. As I got out on to the float at the pier he sneered at my back: "Some other night when we ain't so busy, shamus."

Half a dozen customers waiting to go out stared at me. I went past them, past the door of the waiting room on the float, towards the steps at the landward end.

A big redheaded roughneck in dirty sneakers and tarry pants and a torn blue jersey straightened from the railing and bumped into me casually.

I stopped, got set. He said softly: " 's matter, dick? No soap on the hell ship?"

"Do I have to tell you?"

"I'm a guy that can listen."

"Who are you?"

"Just call me Red."

"Out of the way, Red. I'm busy."

He smiled sadly, touched my left side. "The gat's kind of bulgy under the light suit," he said. "Want to get on board? It can be done, if you got a reason."

"How much is the reason?" I asked him.

"Fifty bucks. Ten more if you bleed in my boat."

I started away. "Twenty-five out," he said quickly. "Maybe you come back with friends, huh?"

I went four steps away from him before I half turned, said: "Sold," and went on.

At the foot of the bright amusement pier there was a flaring Tango Parlor, jammed full even at that still early hour. I went into it, leaned against a wall and watched a couple of numbers go up on the electric indicator, watched a house player with an inside straight give the high sign under the counter with his knee.

A large blueness took form beside me and I smelled tar. A soft, deep, sad voice said: "Need help out there?"

"I'm looking for a girl, but I'll look alone. What's your racket?" I didn't look at him.

"A dollar here, a dollar there. I like to eat. I was on the cops but they bounced me."

I liked his telling me that. "You must have been leveling," I said, and watched the house player slip his card across with his thumb over the wrong number, watched the counter man get his own thumb in the same spot and hold the card up.

I could feel Red's grin. "I see you been around our little city. Here's how it works. I got a boat with an underwater bypass. I know a loading port I can open. I take a load out for a guy once in a while. There ain't many guys below decks. That suit you?"

I got my wallet out and slipped a twenty and a five from it, passed them over in a wad. They went into a tarry pocket.

Red said: "Thanks," softly, and walked away. I gave him a small start and went after him. He was easy to follow by his size, even in a crowd.

We went past the yacht harbor and the second amusement pier and beyond that the lights got fewer and the crowd thinned to nothing. A short black pier stuck out into the water with boats moored all along it. My man turned out on that.

He stopped almost at the end, at the head of a wooden ladder.

"I'll bring her down to here," he said. "Got to make noise warmin' up."

"Listen," I said urgently. "I have to phone a man. I forgot."

"Can do. Come on."

He led the way farther along the pier, knelt, rattled keys on a chain, and opened a padlock. He lifted a small trap and took a phone out, listened to it.

"Still working," he said with a grin in his voice. "Must belong to some crooks. Don't forget to snap the lock back on."

He slipped away silently into the darkness. For ten minutes I listened to water slapping the piles of the pier, the occasional whirr of a seagull in the gloom. Then far off a motor roared and kept on roaring for minutes. Then the noise stopped abruptly. More minutes passed. Something thudded at the foot of the ladder and a low voice called up to me: "All set."

I hurried back to the phone, dialed a number, asked for Chief Fulwider. He had gone home. I dialed another number, got a woman, asked her for the chief, said I was headquarters.

I waited again. Then I heard the fat chief's voice. It sounded full of baked potato.

"Yeah? Can't a guy even eat? Who is it?"

"Carmady, Chief. Saint is on the *Montecito*. Too bad that's over your line."

He began to yell like a wild man. I hung up in his face, put the phone back in its zinc-lined cubbyhole and snapped the padlock. I went down the ladder to Red.

His big black speedboat slid out over the oily water. There was no sound from its exhaust but a steady bubbling along the side of the shell.

The city lights again became a yellow blur low on the black water and the ports of the good ship *Montecito* again got large and bright and round out to sea.

11

THERE WERE NO floodlights on the seaward side of the ship. Red cut his motor to half of nothing and curved in under the overhang of the stern, sidled up to the greasy plates as coyly as a clubman in a hotel lobby.

Double iron doors loomed high over us, forward a little from the slimy links of a chain cable. The speedboat scuffed the *Montecito*'s ancient plates and the sea water slapped loosely at the bottom of the speedboat under our feet. The shadow of the big ex-cop rose over me. A coiled rope flicked against the dark, caught on something, and fell back into the boat. Red pulled it tight, made a turn around something on the engine cowling.

He said softly: "She rides as high as a steeplechaser. We gotta climb them plates."

I took the wheel and held the nose of the speedboat against the slippery hull, and Red reached for an iron ladder flat to the side of the ship, hauled himself up into the darkness, grunting, his big body braced at right angles, his sneakers slipping on the wet metal rungs.

After a while something creaked up above and feeble yellow light trickled out into the foggy air. The outline of a heavy door showed, and Red's crouched head against the light.

I went up the ladder after him. It was hard work. It landed me panting in a sour, littered hold full of cases and barrels. Rats skittered out of sight in the dark corners. The big man put his lips to my ear: "From here we got an easy way to the boiler-room catwalk. They'll have steam up in one auxiliary, for hot water and the generators. That means one guy. I'll handle him. The crew doubles in brass upstairs. From the boiler room I'll show you a ventilator with no grating in it. Goes to the boat deck. Then it's all yours."

"You must have relatives on board," I said.

"Never no mind. A guy gets to know things when he's on the beach. Maybe I'm close to a bunch that's set to knock the tub over. Will you come back fast?"

"I ought to make a good splash from the boat deck," I said. "Here."

I fished more bills out of my wallet, pushed them at him.

He shook his red head. "Uh-uh. That's for the trip back."

"I'm buying it now," I said. "Even if I don't use it. Take the dough before I bust out crying."

"Well – thanks, pal. You're a right guy."

We went among the cases and barrels. The yellow light came from a passage beyond, and we went along the passage to a narrow iron door. That led to the catwalk. We sneaked along it, down an oily steel ladder, heard the slow hiss of oil burners and went among mountains of iron towards the sound.

Around a corner we looked at a short, dirty Italian in a purple silk shirt who sat in a wired-together office chair, under a naked bulb, and read the paper with the aid of steel-rimmed spectacles and a black forefinger.

Red said gently: "Hi, Shorty. How's all the little bambinos?"

The Italian opened his mouth and reached swiftly. Red hit him. We put him down on the floor and tore his purple shirt into shreds for ties and a gag.

"You ain't supposed to hit a guy with glasses on," Red said. "But the idea is you make a hell of a racket goin' up a ventilator – to a guy down here. Upstairs they won't hear nothing."

I said that was the way I would like it, and we left the Italian bound up on the floor and found the ventilator that had no grating in it. I shook hands with Red, said I hoped to see him again, and started up the ladder inside the ventilator.

It was cold and black and the foggy air rushed down it and the way up seemed a long way. After three minutes that felt like an hour I reached the top and poked my head out cautiously. Canvas-sheeted boats loomed near by on the boatdeck davits. There was a soft whispering in the dark between a pair of them. The heavy throb of music pulsed up from below. Overhead a masthead light, and through the thin, high layers of the mist a few bitter stars stared down.

I listened, but didn't hear any police-boat sirens. I got out of the ventilator, lowered myself to the deck.

The whispering came from a necking couple huddled under a boat. They didn't pay any attention to me. I went along the deck past the closed doors of three or four cabins. There was a little light behind the shutters of two of them. I listened, didn't hear anything but the merrymaking of the customers down below on the main deck.

I dropped into a dark shadow, took a lungful of air and let it out in a howl – the snarling howl of a gray timber wolf, lonely and hungry and far from home, and mean enough for seven kinds of trouble.

The deep-toned woof-woofing of a police dog answered me. A girl squealed along the dark deck and a man's voice said: "I thought all the shellac drinkers was dead."

I straightened and unshipped my gun and ran towards the barking. The noise came from a cabin on the other side of the deck.

I put an ear to the door, listened to a man's voice soothing the dog. The dog stopped barking and growled once or twice, then was silent. A key turned in the door I was touching.

I dropped away from it, down on one knee. The door opened a foot and a sleek head came forward past its edge. Light from a hooded deck lamp made a shine on the black hair.

I stood up and slammed the head with my gun barrel. The man fell softly out of the doorway into my arms. I dragged him back into the cabin, pushed him down on a made-up berth.

I shut the door again, locked it. A small, wide-eyed girl crouched on the other berth. I said: "Hello, Miss Snare. I've had a lot of trouble finding you. Want to go home?"

Farmer Saint rolled over and sat up, holding his head. Then he was very still, staring at me with his sharp black eyes. His mouth had a strained smile, almost good-humored.

I ranged the cabin with a glance, didn't see where the dog was, but saw an inner door behind which he could be. I looked at the girl again.

She was not much to look at, like most of the people that make most of the trouble. She was crouched on the berth with her knees drawn up and hair falling over one eye. She wore a knitted dress and golf socks and sport shoes with wide tongues that fell down over the instep. Her knees were bare and bony under the hem of the dress. She looked like a schoolgirl.

I went over Saint for a gun, didn't find one. He grinned at me.

The girl lifted her hand and threw her hair back. She looked at me as if I was a couple of blocks away. Then her breath caught and she began to cry.

"We're married," Saint said softly. "She thinks you're set to blow holes in me. That was a smart trick with the wolf howl."

I didn't say anything. I listened. No noises outside.

"How'd you know where to come?" Saint asked.

"Diana told me — before she died," I said brutally.

His eyes looked hurt. "I don't believe it, shamus."

"You ran out and left her in the ditch. What would you expect?"

"I figured the cops wouldn't bump a woman and I could make some kind of a deal on the outside. Who got her?"

"One of Fulwider's cops. You got him."

His head jerked back and a wild look came over his face, then went away. He smiled sideways at the weeping girl.

"Hello, sugar. I'll get you clear." He looked back at me. "Suppose I come in without a scrap. Is there a way for her to get loose?"

"What do you mean, scrap?" I sneered.

"I got plenty friends on this boat, shamus. You ain't even started yet."

"You got her into it," I said. "You can't get her out. That's part of the pay-off."

12

HE NODDED SLOWLY, looked down at the floor between his feet. The girl stopped crying long enough to mop at her cheeks, then started in again.

"Fulwider know I'm here?" Saint asked me slowly.

"Yeah."

"You give him the office?"

"Yeah."

He shrugged. "That's okay from your end. Sure. Only I'll never get to talk, if Fulwider pinches me. If I could get to talk to a D.A. I could maybe convince him *she's* not hep to my stuff."

"You could have thought of that, too," I said heavily. "You didn't have to go back to Sundstrand's and cut loose with your stutter gun."

He threw his head back and laughed. "No? Suppose you paid a guy ten grand for protection and he crossed you up by grabbing your wife and sticking her in a crooked dope hospital and telling you to run along far away and be good, or the tide would wash her up on the beach? What would you do — smile, or trot over with some heavy iron to talk to the guy?"

"She wasn't there then," I said. "You were just kill-screwy. And if you hadn't hung on to that dog until he killed a man, the protection wouldn't have been scared into selling you out."

"I like dogs," Saint said quietly. "I'm a nice guy when I'm not workin', but I can get shoved around just so much."

420

I listened. Still no noises on deck outside.

"Listen," I said quickly. "If you want to play ball with me, I've got a boat at the back door and I'll try to get the girl home before they want her. What happens to you is past me. I wouldn't lift a finger for you, even if you do like dogs."

The girl said suddenly, in a shrill, little-girl voice: "I don't want to go home! I won't go home!"

"A year from now you'll thank me," I snapped at her.

"He's right, sugar," Saint said. "Better beat it with him."

"I won't," the girl shrilled angrily. "I just won't. That's all."

Out of the silence on the deck something hard slammed the outside of the door. A grim voice shouted: "Open up! It's the law!"

I backed swiftly to the door, keeping my eyes on Saint. I spoke back over my shoulder: "Fulwider there?"

"Yeah," the chief's fat voice growled. "Carmady?"

"Listen, Chief. Saint's in here and he's ready to surrender. There's a girl here with him, the one I told you about. So come in easy, will you?"

"Right," the chief said. "Open the door."

I twisted the key, jumped across the cabin and put my back against the inner partition, beside the door behind which the dog was moving around now, growling a little.

The outer door whipped open. Two men I hadn't seen before charged in with drawn guns. The fat chief was behind them. Briefly, before he shut the door, I caught a glimpse of ship's uniforms.

The two dicks jumped on Saint, slammed him around, put cuffs on him. Then they stepped back beside the chief. Saint grinned at them, with blood trickling down his lower lip.

Fulwider looked at me reprovingly and moved a cigar around in his mouth. Nobody seemed to take an interest in the girl.

"You're a hell of a guy, Carmady. You didn't give me no idea where to come," he growled.

"I didn't know," I said. "I thought it was outside your jurisdiction, too."

"Hell with that. We tipped the Feds. They'll be out."

One of the dicks laughed. "But not too soon," he said roughly. "Put the heater away, shamus."

"Try and make me," I told him.

He started forward, but the chief waved him back. The other dick watched Saint, looked at nothing else.

"How'd you find him then?" Fulwider wanted to know.

"Not by taking his money to hide him out," I said.

Nothing changed in Fulwider's face. His voice became almost lazy. "Oh, oh, you've been peekin'," he said very gently.

I said disgustedly: "Just what kind of a sap did you and your gang take me for? Your clean little town stinks. It's the well-known whited sepulcher. A crook sanctuary where the hot rods can lie low – if they pay off nice and don't pull any local capers – and where they can jump off for Mexico in a fast boat, if the finger waves towards them."

The chief said very carefully: "Any more?"

"Yeah," I shouted. "I've saved it for you too damn long. *You* had me doped until I was half goofy and stuck me in a private jail. When that didn't hold me *you* worked a plant up with Galbraith and Duncan to have my gun kill Sundstrand, your helper, and then have me killed resisting some arrest. Saint spoiled that party for you and saved my life. Not intending to, perhaps, but he did it. *You* knew all along where the little Snare girl was. She was Saint's wife and you were holding her yourself to make him stay in line. Hell, why do you suppose I tipped you he was out here? That was something you *didn't* know!"

The dick who had tried to make me put up my gun said: "Now, Chief. We better make it fast. Those Feds – "

Fulwider's jaw shook. His face was gray and his ears were far back in his head. The cigar twitched in his fat mouth.

"Wait a minute," he said thickly, to the man beside. Then to me: "Well – why did you tip me?"

"To get you where you're no more law than Billy the Kid," I said, "and see if you have the guts to go through with murder on the high seas."

Saint laughed. He shot a low, snarling whistle between his teeth. A tearing animal growl answered him. The door beside me crashed open as though a mule had kicked it. The big police dog came through the opening in a looping spring that carried him clear across the cabin. The gray body twisted in mid-air. A gun banged harmlessly.

"Eat 'em up, Voss!" Saint yelled. "Eat 'em alive, boy!"

The cabin filled with gunfire. The snarling of the dog blended with a thick, choked scream. Fulwider and one of the dicks were down on the floor and the dog was at Fulwider's throat.

The girl screamed and plunged her face into a pillow. Saint slid softly down from the bunk and lay on the floor with blood running slowly down his neck in a thick wave.

The dick who hadn't gone down jumped to one side, almost fell headlong on the girl's berth, then caught his balance and pumped bullets into the dog's long gray body – wildly without pretense of aim.

The dick on the floor pushed at the dog. The dog almost bit his hand off. The man yelled. Feet pounded on the deck. Yelling outside. Something was running down my face that tickled. My head felt funny, but I didn't know what had hit me.

The gun in my hand felt large and hot. I shot the dog, hating to do it. The dog rolled off Fulwider and I saw where a stray bullet had drilled the chief's forehead between the eyes, with the delicate exactness of pure chance.

The standing dick's gun hammer clicked on a discharged shell. He cursed, started to reload frantically.

I touched the blood on my face and looked at it. It seemed very black. The light in the cabin seemed to be failing.

The bright corner of an axe blade suddenly split the cabin door, which was wedged shut by the chief's body, and that of the groaning man beside him. I stared at the bright metal, watched it go away and reappear in another place.

Then all the lights went out very slowly, as in a theater just as the curtain goes up. Just as it got quite dark my head hurt me, but I didn't know then that a bullet had fractured my skull.

I woke up two days later in the hospital. I was there three weeks. Saint didn't live long enough to hang, but he lived long enough to tell his story. He must have told it well, because they let Mrs. Jerry (Farmer) Saint go home to her aunt.

By that time the County Grand Jury had indicted half the police force of the little beach city. There were a lot of new faces around the City Hall, I heard. One of them was a big red-headed detective-sergeant named Norgard who said he owed me twenty-five dollars but had had to use it to buy a new suit when he got his job back. He said he would pay me out of his first check. I said I would try to wait.

PICKUP ON NOON STREET

1

THE MAN AND the girl walked slowly, close together, past a dim stencil sign that said. Surprise Hotel. The man wore a purple suit, a Panama hat over his shiny, slicked-down hair. He walked splay-footed, soundlessly.

The girl wore a green hat and a short skirt and sheer stockings, four-and-a-half-inch French heels. She smelled of Midnight Narcissus.

At the corner the man leaned close, said something in the girl's ear. She jerked away from him, giggled.

"You gotta buy liquor if you take *me* home, Smiler."

"Next time, baby. I'm fresh outa dough."

The girl's voice got hard. "Then I tells you goodbye in the next block, handsome."

"Like hell, baby," the man answered.

The arc at the intersection threw light on them. They walked across the street far apart. At the other side the man caught the girl's arm. She twisted away from him.

"Listen, you cheap grifter!" she shrilled. "Keep your paws down, see! Tinhorns are dust to me. Dangle!"

"How much liquor you gotta have, baby?"

"Plenty."

"Me bein' on the nut, where do I collect it?"

"You got hands, ain't you?" the girl sneered. Her voice dropped the shrillness. She leaned close to him again. "Maybe you got a gun, big boy. Got a gun?"

"Yeah. And no shells for it."

"The goldbricks over on Central don't know that."

"Don't be that way," the man in the purple suit snarled. Then he snapped his fingers and stiffened. "Wait a minute. I got me a idea."

He stopped and looked back along the street toward the dim stencil hotel sign. The girl slapped a glove across his chin caressingly. The glove smelled to him of the perfume, Midnight Narcissus.

The man snapped his fingers again, grinned widely in the dim light. "If that drunk is still holed up in Doc's place – I collect. Wait for me, huh?"

"Maybe, at home. If you ain't gone too long."

"Where's home, baby?"

The girl stared at him. A half-smile moved along her full lips, died at the corners of them. The breeze picked a sheet of newspaper out of the gutter and tossed it against the man's leg. He kicked at it savagely.

"Calliope Apartments. Four-B, Two-Forty-Six East Forty-Eight. How soon you be there?"

The man stepped very close to her, reached back and tapped his hip. His voice was low, chilling.

"You wait for me, baby."

She caught her breath, nodded. "Okay, handsome. I'll wait."

The man went back along the cracked sidewalk, across the intersection, along to where the stencil sign hung out over the street. He went through a glass door into a narrow lobby with a row of brown wooden chairs pushed against the plaster wall. There was just space to walk past them to the desk. A bald-headed colored man lounged behind the desk, fingering a large green pin in his tie.

The Negro in the purple suit leaned across the counter and his teeth flashed in a quick, hard smile. He was very young, with a thin, sharp jaw, a narrow bony forehead, the flat brilliant eyes of the gangster. He said softly: "That pug with the husky voice still here? The guy that banked the crap game last night."

The bald-headed clerk looked at the flies on the ceiling fixture. "Didn't see him go out, Smiler."

"Ain't what I asked you, Doc."

"Yeah. He still here."

"Still drunk?"

"Guess so. Hasn't been out."

"Three-forty-nine, ain't it?"

"You been there, ain't you? What you wanta know for?"

"He cleaned me down to my lucky piece. I gotta make a touch."

The bald-headed man looked nervous. The Smiler stared softly at the green stone in the man's tie pin.

"Get rolling, Smiler. Nobody gets bent around here. We ain't no Central Avenue flop."

The Smiler said very softly: "He's my pal, Doc. He'll lend me twenty. You touch half."

He put his hand out palm up. The clerk stared at the hand for a long moment. Then he nodded sourly, went behind a ground-glass screen, came back slowly, looking toward the street door.

His hand went out and hovered over the palm. The palm closed over a passkey, dropped inside the cheap purple suit.

The sudden flashing grin on the Smiler's face had an icy edge to it.

"Careful, Doc – while I'm up above."

The clerk said: "Step on it. Some of the customers get home early." He glanced at the green electric clock on the wall. It was seven-fifteen. "And the walls ain't any too thick," he added.

The thin youth gave him another flashing grin, nodded, went delicately back along the lobby to the shadowy staircase. There was no elevator in the Surprise Hotel.

At one minute past seven Pete Anglich, narcotic squad under-cover man, rolled over on the hard bed and looked at the cheap strap watch on his left wrist. There were heavy shadows under his eyes, a thick dark stubble on his broad chin. He swung his bare feet to the floor and stood up in cheap cotton pajamas, flexed his muscles, stretched, bent over stiff-kneed and touched the floor in front of his toes with a grunt.

He walked across to a chipped bureau, drank from a quart bottle of cheap rye whiskey, grimaced, pushed the cork into the neck of the bottle, and rammed it down hard with the heel of his hand.

"Boy, have I got a hangover," he grumbled huskily.

He stared at his face in the bureau mirror, at the stubble on his chin, the thick white scar on his throat close to the wind-pipe. His voice was husky because the bullet that had made the scar had done something to his vocal cords. It was a smooth huskiness, like the voice of a blues singer.

He stripped his pajamas off and stood naked in the middle of the room, his toes fumbling the rough edge of a big rip in the carpet. His body was very broad, and that made him look a little shorter than he was. His shoulders sloped, his nose was a little thick, the skin over his cheekbones looked like leather. He had short, curly, black hair, utterly steady eyes, the small set mouth of a quick thinker.

He went into a dim, dirty bathroom, stepped into the tub and turned the shower on. The water was warmish, but not hot. He stood under it and soaped himself, rubbed his whole body over, kneaded his muscles, rinsed off.

He jerked a dirty towel off the rack and started to rub a glow into his skin.

A faint noise behind the loosely closed bathroom door stopped him. He held his breath, listened, heard the noise again, a creak of boarding, a click, a rustle of cloth. Pete Anglich reached for the door and pulled it open slowly.

The Negro in the purple suit and Panama hat stood beside the bureau, with Pete Anglich's coat in his hand. On the bureau in front of him were two guns. One of them was Pete Anglich's old worn Colt. The room door was shut and a key with a tag lay on the carpet near it, as though it had fallen out of the door, or been pushed out from the other side.

The Smiler let the coat fall to the floor and held a wallet in his left hand. His right hand lifted the Colt. He grinned.

"Okay, white boy. Just go on dryin' yourself off after your shower," he said.

Pete Anglich toweled himself. He rubbed himself dry, stood naked with the wet towel in his left hand.

The Smiler had the billfold empty on the bureau, was counting the money with his left hand. His right still clutched the Colt.

"Eighty-seven bucks. Nice money. Some of it's mine from the crap game, but I'm lifting it all, pal. Take it easy. I'm friends with the management here."

"Gimme a break, Smiler," Pete Anglich said hoarsely. "That's every dollar I got in the world. Leave a few bucks, huh?" He made his voice thick, coarse, heavy as though with liquor.

The Smiler gleamed his teeth, shook his narrow head. "Can't do it, pal. Got me a date and I need the kale."

Pete Anglich took a loose step forward and stopped, grinning sheepishly. The muzzle of his own gun had jerked at him.

The Smiler sidled over to the bottle of rye and lifted it.

"I can use this, too. My baby's got a throat for liquor. Sure has. What's in your pants is yours, pal. Fair enough?"

Pete Anglich jumped sideways, about four feet. The Smiler's face convulsed. The gun jerked around and the bottle of rye slid out of his left hand, slammed down on his foot. He yelped, kicked out savagely, and his toe caught in the torn place in the carpet.

Pete Anglich flipped the wet end of the bathtowel straight at the Smiler's eyes.

The Smiler reeled and yelled with pain. Then Pete Anglich held the Smiler's gun wrist in his hard left hand. He twisted up, around. His hand started to slide down over the Smiler's hand, over the gun. The gun turned inward and touched the Smiler's side.

A hard knee kicked viciously at Pete Anglich's abdomen. He gagged, and his finger tightened convulsively on the Smiler's trigger finger.

The shot was dull, muffled against the purple cloth of the suit. The Smiler's eyes rolled whitely and his narrow jaw fell slack.

Pete Anglich let him down on the floor and stood panting, bent over, his face greenish. He groped for the fallen bottle of rye, got the cork out, got some of the fiery liquid down his throat.

The greenish look went away from his face. His breathing slowed. He wiped sweat off his forehead with the back of his hand.

He felt the Smiler's pulse. The Smiler didn't have any pulse. He was dead. Pete Anglich loosened the gun from his hand, went over to the door and glanced out into the hallway. Empty. There was a passkey in the outside of the lock. He removed it, locked the door from the inside.

He put his underclothes and socks and shoes on, his worn blue serge suit, knotted a black tie around the crumpled shirt collar, went back to the dead man and took a roll of bills from his pocket. He packed a few odds and ends of clothes and toilet articles in a cheap fiber suitcase, stood it by the door.

He pushed a torn scrap of sheet through his revolver barrel with a pencil, replaced the used cartridge, crushed the empty shell with his heel on the bathroom floor and then flushed it down the toilet.

He locked the door from the outside and walked down the stairs to the lobby.

The bald-headed clerk's eyes jumped at him, then dropped. The skin of his face turned gray. Pete Anglich leaned on the counter and opened his hand to let two keys tinkle on the scarred wood. The clerk stared at the keys, shuddered.

Pete Anglich said in his slow, husky voice: "Hear any funny noises?"

The clerk shook his head, gulped.

"Creep joint, eh?" Pete Anglich said.

The clerk moved his head painfully, twisted his neck in his collar. His bald head winked darkly under the ceiling light.

"Too bad," Pete Anglich said. "What name did I register under last night?"

"You ain't registered," the clerk whispered.

"Maybe I wasn't here even," Pete Anglich said softly.

"Never saw you before, mister."

"You're not seeing me now. You never will see me – to know me – will you, Doc?"

The clerk moved his neck and tried to smile.

Pete Anglich drew his wallet out and shook three dollar bills from it.

"I'm a guy that likes to pay his way," he said slowly. "This pays for Room 349 – till way in the morning, kind of late. The lad you gave the passkey to looks like a heavy sleeper." He paused, steadied his cool eyes on the clerk's face, added thoughtfully: "Unless, of course, he's got friends who would like to move him out."

Bubbles showed on the clerk's lips. He stuttered: "He ain't – ain't – "

"Yeah," Pete Anglich said. "What would you expect?"

He went across to the street door, carrying his suitcase, stepped out under the stencil sign, stood a moment looking toward the hard white glare of Central Avenue.

Then he walked the other way. The street was very dark, very quiet. There were four blocks of frame houses before he came to Noon Street. It was all a Negro quarter.

He met only one person on the way, a brown girl in a green hat, very sheer stockings, and four-and-a-half-inch heels, who smoked a cigarette under a dusty palm tree and stared back toward the Surprise Hotel.

2

THE LUNCH WAGON was an old buffet car without wheels, set end to the street in a space between a machine shop and a rooming house. The name Bella Donna was lettered in faded gold on the sides. Pete Anglich went up the two iron steps at the end, into a smell of fry grease.

The Negro cook's fat white back was to him. At the far end of the low counter a white girl in a cheap brown felt hat and a shabby polo coat with a high turned-up collar was sipping coffee, her cheek propped in her left hand. There was nobody else in the car.

Pete Anglich put his suitcase down and sat on a stool near the door, saying: "Hi, Mopsy!"

The fat cook turned a shiny black face over his white shoulder. The face split in a grin. A thick bluish tongue came out and wiggled between the cook's thick lips.

"How's a boy? W'at you eat?"

"Scramble two light, coffee, toast, no spuds."

"Dat ain't no food for a he-guy," Mopsy complained.

"I been drunk," Pete Anglich said.

The girl at the end of the counter looked at him sharply, looked at the cheap alarm clock on the shelf, at the watch on her gloved wrist. She drooped, stared into her coffee cup again.

The fat cook broke eggs into a pan, added milk, stirred them around. "You want a shot, boy?"

Pete Anglich shook his head.

"I'm driving the wagon, Mopsy."

The cook grinned. He reached a brown bottle from under the counter, and poured a big drink into a water glass, set the glass down beside Pete Anglich.

Pete Anglich reached suddenly for the glass, jerked it to his lips, drank the liquor down.

434

"Guess I'll drive the wagon some other time." He put the glass down empty.

The girl stood up, came along the stools, put a dime on the counter. The fat cook punched his cash register, put down a nickel change. Pete Anglich stared casually at the girl. A shabby, innocent-eyed girl, brown hair curling on her neck, eyebrows plucked clean as a bone and startled arches painted above the place where they had been.

"Not lost, are you, lady?" he asked in his softly husky voice.

The girl had tumbled her bag open to put the nickel away. She started violently, stepped back and dropped the bag. It spilled its contents on the floor. She stared down at it, wide-eyed.

Pete Anglich went down on one knee and pushed things into the bag. A cheap nickel compact, cigarettes, a purple match-folder lettered in gold: The Juggernaut Club. Two colored handkerchiefs, a crumpled dollar bill and some silver and pennies.

He stood up with the closed bag in his hand, held it out to the girl.

"Sorry," he said softly. "I guess I startled you."

Her breath made a rushing sound. She caught the bag out of his hand, ran out of the car, and was gone.

The fat cook looked after her. "That doll don't belong in Tough Town," he said slowly.

He dished up the eggs and toast, poured coffee in a thick cup, put them down in front of Pete Anglich.

Pete Anglich touched the food, said absently: "Alone, and matches from the Juggernaut. Trimmer Waltz's spot. You know what happens to girls like that when he gets hold of them."

The cook licked his lips, reached under the counter for the whiskey bottle. He poured himself a drink, added about the same amount of water to the bottle, put it back under the counter.

"I ain't never been a tough guy, and don' want to start," he said slowly. "But I'se all tired of white boys like dat guy. Some day he gonna get cut."

Pete Anglich kicked his suitcase.

"Yeah. Keep the keister for me, Mopsy."

He went out.

Two or three cars flicked by in the crisp fall night, but the sidewalks were dark and empty. A colored night watchman moved slowly along the street, trying the doors of a small row of dingy stores. There were frame houses across the street, and a couple of them were noisy.

Pete Anglich went on past the intersection. Three blocks from the lunch wagon he saw the girl again.

She was pressed against a wall, motionless. A little beyond her, dim yellow light came from the stairway of a walk-up apartment house. Beyond that a small parking lot with billboards across most of its front. Faint light from somewhere touched her hat, her shabby polo coat with the turned-up collar, one side of her face. He knew it was the same girl.

He stepped into a doorway, watched her. Light flashed on her upraised arm, on something bright, a wrist watch. Somewhere not far off a clock struck eight, low, pealing notes.

Lights stabbed into the street from the corner behind. A big car swung slowly into view and as it swung its headlights dimmed. It crept along the block, a dark shininess of glass and polished paint.

Pete Anglich grinned sharply in his doorway. A custom-built Duesenberg, six blocks from Central Avenue! He stiffened at the sharp sound of running steps, clicking high heels.

The girl was running toward him along the sidewalk. The car was not near enough for its dimmed lights to pick her up. Pete Anglich stepped out of the doorway, grabbed her arm, dragged her back into the doorway. A gun snaked from under his coat.

The girl panted at his side.

The Duesenberg passed the doorway slowly. No shots came from it. The uniformed driver didn't slow down.

"I can't do it. I'm scared," the girl gasped in Pete Anglich's ear. Then she broke away from him and ran farther along the sidewalk, away from the car.

Pete Anglich looked after the Duesenberg. It was opposite the row of billboards that screened the parking lot. It was barely crawling now. Something sailed from its left front window, fell with a dry slap on the sidewalk. The car picked up speed soundlessly, purred off into the darkness. A block away its headlights flashed up full again.

Nothing moved. The thing that had been thrown out of the car lay on the inner edge of the sidewalk, almost under one of the billboards.

Then the girl was coming back again, a step at a time, haltingly. Pete Anglich watched her come, without moving. When she was level with him he said softly: "What's the racket? Could a fellow help?"

She spun around with a choked sound, as though she had forgotten all about him. Her head moved in the darkness at his side. There was a swift shine as her eyes moved. There was a pale flicker across her chin. Her voice was low, hurried, scared.

"You're the man from the lunch wagon. I saw you."

"Open up. What is it — a pay-off?"

Her head moved again in the darkness at his side, up and down.

"What's in the package?" Pete Anglich growled. "Money?"

Her words came in a rush. "Would you get it for me? Oh, would you please? I'd be so grateful: I'd – "

He laughed. His laugh had a low growling sound. "Get it for *you*, baby? I use money in my business, too. Come on, what's the racket? Spill."

She jerked away from him, but he didn't let go of her arm. He slid the gun out of sight under his coat, held her with both

437

hands. Her voice sobbed as she whispered: "He'll kill me, if I don't get it."

Very sharply, coldly, Pete Anglich said, "Who will? Trimmer Waltz?"

She started violently, almost tore out of his grasp. Not quite. Steps shuffled on the sidewalk. Two dark forms showed in front of the billboards, didn't pause to pick anything up. The steps came near, cigarette tips glowed.

A voice said softly: "'Lo there, sweets. Yo' want to change yo'r boy frien', honey?"

The girl shrank behind Pete Anglich. One of the Negroes laughed gently, waved the red end of his cigarette.

"Hell, it's a white gal," the other one said quickly. "Le's dust."

They went on, chuckling. At the corner they turned, were gone.

"There you are," Pete Anglich growled. "Shows you where you are." His voice was hard, angry. "Oh, hell, stay here and I'll get your damn pay-off for you."

He left the girl and went lightly along close to the front of the apartment house. At the edge of the billboards he stopped, probed the darkness with his eyes, saw the package. It was wrapped in dark material, not large but large enough to see. He bent down and looked under the billboards. He didn't see anything behind them.

He went on four steps, leaned down and picked up the package, felt cloth and two thick rubber bands. He stood quite still, listening.

Distant traffic hummed on a main street. A light burned across the street in a rooming house, behind a glass-paneled door. A window was open and dark above it.

A woman's voice screamed shrilly behind him.

He stiffened, whirled, and the light hit him between the eyes. It came from the dark window across the street, a blinding white shaft that impaled him against the billboard.

His face leered in it, his eyes blinked. He didn't move any more.

Shoes dropped on cement and a smaller spot stabbed at him sideways from the end of the billboards. Behind the spot a casual voice spoke: "Don't shift an eyelash, bud. You're all wrapped up in law."

Men with revolvers out closed in on him from both ends of the line of billboards. Heels clicked far off on concrete. Then it was silent for a moment. Then a car with a red spotlight swung around the corner and bore down on the group of men with Pete Anglich in their midst.

The man with the casual voice said: "I'm Angus, detective-lieutenant. I'll take the packet, if you don't mind. And if you'll just keep your hands together a minute – "

The handcuffs clicked dryly on Pete Anglich's wrists.

He listened hard for the sound of the heels far off, running away. But there was too much noise around him now.

Doors opened and dark people began to boil out of the houses.

3

JOHN VIDAURY WAS six feet two inches in height and had the most perfect profile in Hollywood. He was dark, winsome, romantic, with an interesting touch of gray at his temples. His shoulders were wide, his hips narrow. He had the waist of an English guards officer, and his dinner clothes fit him so beautifully that it hurt.

So he looked at Pete Anglich as if he was about to apologize for not knowing him. Pete Anglich looked at his handcuffs, at his worn shoes on the thick rug, at the tall chiming clock against the wall. There was a flush on his face and his eyes were bright.

In a smooth, clear, modulated voice Vidaury said, "No, I've never seen him before." He smiled at Pete Anglich.

Angus, the plainclothes lieutenant, leaned against one end of a carved library table and snapped a finger against the brim of his hat. Two other detectives stood near a side wall. A fourth sat at a small desk with a stenographer's notebook in front of him.

Angus said, "Oh, we just thought you might know him. We can't get much of anything out of him."

Vidaury raised his eyebrows, smiled very faintly. "Really I'm surprised at that." He went around collecting glasses, and took them over to a tray, started to mix more drinks.

"It happens," Angus said.

"I thought you had ways," Vidaury said delicately, pouring Scotch into the glasses.

Angus looked at a fingernail. "When I say he won't tell us anything, Mr. Vidaury, I mean anything that counts. He says his name is Pete Anglich, that he used to be a fighter, but hasn't fought for several years. Up to about a year ago he was a private detective, but has no work now. He won some money in a crap game and got drunk, and was just wandering about. That's how he happened to be on Noon Street. He saw the package tossed out of your car and picked it up. We can vag him, but that's about all."

"It could happen that way," Vidaury said softly. He carried the glasses two at a time to the four detectives, lifted his own, and nodded slightly before he drank. He drank gracefully, with a superb elegance of movement. "No, I don't know him," he said again. "Frankly, he doesn't look like an acid-thrower to me." He waved a hand. "So I'm afraid bringing him here – "

Pete Anglich lifted his head suddenly, stared at Vidaury. His voice sneered.

"It's a great compliment, Vidaury. They don't often use up the time of four coppers taking prisoners around to call on people."

Vidaury smiled amiably. "That's Hollywood," he smiled. "After all, one had a reputation."

"Had," Pete Anglich said. "Your last picture was a pain where you don't tell the ladies."

Angus stiffened Vidaury's face went white. He put his glass down slowly, let his hand fall to his side. He walked springily across the rug and stood in front of Pete Anglich.

"That's your opinion," he said harshly, "but I warn you – "

Pete Anglich scowled at him. "Listen, big shot. You put a grand on the line because some punk promised to throw acid at you if you didn't. I picked up the grand, but I didn't get any of your nice, new money. So you got it back. You get ten grand worth of publicity and it won't cost you a nickel. I call that pretty swell."

Angus said sharply, "That's enough from you, mug."

"Yeah?" Pete Anglich sneered. "I thought you wanted me to talk. Well, I'm talking, and I hate pikers, see?"

Vidaury breathed hard. Very suddenly he balled his fist and swung at Pete Anglich's jaw. Pete Anglich's head rolled under the blow, and his eyes blinked shut, then wide open. He shook himself and said coolly: "Elbow up and thumb down, Vidaury. You break a hand hitting a guy that way."

Vidaury stepped back and shook his head, looked at his thumb. His face lost its whiteness. His smile stole back.

"I'm sorry," he said contritely. "I am very sorry. I'm not used to being insulted. As I don't know this man, perhaps you'd better take him away, Lieutenant. Handcuffed, too. Not very sporting, was it?"

"Tell that to your polo ponies," Pete Anglich said. "I don't bruise so easy."

Angus walked over to him, tapped his shoulder. "Up on the dogs, bo. Let's drift. You're not used to nice people, are you?"

"No. I like bums," Pete Anglich said.

He stood up slowly, scuffed at the pile of the carpet.

The two dicks against the wall fell in beside him, and they walked away down the huge room, under an arch. Angus and the other man came behind. They waited in the small private lobby for the elevator to come up.

"What was the idea?" Angus snapped. "Getting gashouse with him?"

Pete Anglich laughed. "Jumpy," he said. "Just jumpy."

The elevator came up and they rode down to the huge, silent lobby of the Chester Towers. Two house detectives lounged at the end of the marble desk, two clerks stood alert behind it.

Pete Anglich lifted his manacled hands in the fighter's salute. "What, no newshawks yet?" he jeered. "Vidaury won't like hush-hush on this."

"Keep goin', smartie," one of the dicks snapped, jerking his arm.

They went down a corridor and out of a side entrance to a narrow street that dropped almost sheer to treetops. Beyond the treetops the lights of the city were a vast golden carpet, stitched with brilliant splashes of red and green and blue and purple.

Two starters whirred. Pete Anglich was pushed into the back seat of the first car. Angus and another man got in on either side of him. The cars drifted down the hill, turned east on Fountain, slid quietly through the evening for mile after mile. Fountain met Sunset, and the cars dropped downtown toward the tall, white tower of the City Hall. At the plaza the first car swung over to Los Angeles Street and went south. The other car went on.

After a while Pete Anglich dropped the corners of his mouth and looked sidways at Angus.

"Where you taking me? This isn't the way to headquarters."

Angus' dark, austere face turned toward him slowly. After a moment the big detective leaned back and yawned at the night. He didn't answer.

The car slid along Los Angeles to Fifth, east to San Pedro, south again for block after block, quiet blocks and loud blocks, block where silent men sat on shaky front porches and blocks where noisy young toughs of both colors snarled and wisecracked at one another in front of cheap restaurants and drugstores and beer parlors full of slot machines.

At Santa Barbara the police car turned east again, drifted slowly along the curb to Noon Street. It stopped at the corner above the lunch wagon. Pete Anglich's face tightened again, but he didn't say anything.

"Okay," Angus drawled. "Take the nippers off."

The dick on Pete Anglich's other side dug a key out of his vest, unlocked the handcuffs, jangled them pleasantly before he put them away on his hip. Angus swung the door open and stepped out of the car.

"Out," he said over his shoulder.

Pete Anglich got out. Angus walked a little way from the street light, stopped, beckoned. His hand moved under his coat, came out with a gun. He said softly: "Had to play it this way. Otherwise we'd tip the town. Pearson's the only one that knows you. Any ideas?"

Pete Anglich took his gun, shook his head slowly, slid the gun under his own coat, keeping his body between it and the car at the curb behind.

"The stake-out was spotted, I guess," he said slowly. "There was a girl hanging around there, but maybe that just happened, too."

Angus stared at him silently for a moment, then nodded and went back to the car. The door slammed shut, and the car drifted off down the street and picked up speed.

Pete Anglich walked along Santa Barbara to Central, south on Central. After a while a bright sign glared at him in violet letters – Juggernaut Club. He went up broad carpeted stairs toward noise and dance music.

4

THE GIRL HAD to go sideways to get between the close-set tables around the small dance floor. Her hips touched the

443

back of a man's shoulder and he reached out and grabbed her hand, grinning. She smiled mechanically, pulled her hand away and came on.

She looked better in the bronze metal-cloth dress with bare arms and the brown hair curling low on her neck; better than in the shabby polo coat and cheap felt hat, better even than in skyscraper heels, bare legs and thighs, the irreducible minimum above the waistline, and a dull gold opera hat tipped rakishly over one ear.

Her face looked haggard, small, pretty, shallow. Her eyes had a wide stare. The dance band made a sharp racket over the clatter of dishes, the thick hum of talk, the shuffling feet on the dance floor. The girl came slowly up to Pete Anglich's table, pulled the other chair out and sat down.

She propped her chin on the backs of her hands, put her elbows on the tablecloth, stared at him.

"Hello there," she said in a voice that shook a little.

Pete Anglich pushed a pack of cigarettes across the table, watched her shake one loose and get it between her lips. He struck a match. She had to take it out of his hand to light her cigarette.

"Drink?"

"I'll say."

He signaled the fuzzy-haired, almond-eyed waiter, ordered a couple of sidecars. The waiter went away. Pete Anglich leaned back on his chair and looked at one of his blunt fingertips.

The girl said very softly: "I got your note, mister."

"Like it?" His voice was stiffly casual. He didn't look at her.

She laughed off key. "We've got to please the customers."

Pete Anglich looked past her shoulder at the corner of the band shell. A man stood there smoking, beside a small microphone. He was heavily built, old for an m.c., with slick gray hair and a big nose and the thickened complexion of a steady drinker. He was smiling at everything and everybody. Pete

Anglich looked at him a little while, watching the direction of his glances. He said stiffly, in the same casual voice, "But you'd be here anyway."

The girl stiffened, then slumped. "You don't have to insult me, mister."

He looked at her slowly, with an empty up-from-under look. "You're down and out, knee-deep in nothing, baby. I've been that way often enough to know the symptoms. Besides, you got me in plenty jam tonight. I owe you a couple insults."

The fuzzy-haired waiter came back and slid a tray on the cloth, wiped the bottoms of two glasses with a dirty towel, set them out. He went away again.

The girl put her hand around a glass, lifted it quickly and took a long drink. She shivered a little as she put the glass down. Her face was white.

"Wisecrack or something," she said rapidly. "Don't just sit there. I'm watched."

Pete Anglich touched his fresh drink, smiled very deliberately toward the corner of the band shell.

"Yeah, I can imagine. Tell me about that pickup on Noon Street."

She reached out quickly and touched his arm. Her sharp nails dug into it. "Not here," she breathed. "I don't know how you found me and I don't care. You looked like the kind of Joe that would help a girl out. I was scared stiff. But don't talk about it here. I'll do anything you want, go anywhere you want. Only not here."

Pete Anglich took his arm from under her hand, leaned back again. His eyes were cold, but his mouth was kind.

"I get it. Trimmer's wishes. Was he tailing the job?"

She nodded quickly. "I hadn't gone three blocks before he picked me up. He thought it was a swell gag, what I did, but he won't think so when he sees you here. That makes you wise."

Pete Anglich sipped his drink. "He is coming this way," he said, coolly.

445

The gray-haired m.c. was moving among the tables, bowing and talking, but edging toward the one where Pete Anglich sat with the girl. The girl was staring into a big gilt mirror behind Pete Anglich's head. Her face was suddenly distorted, shattered with terror. Her lips were shaking uncontrollably.

Trimmer Waltz idled casually up to the table, leaned a hand down on it. He poked his big-veined nose at Pete Anglich. There was a soft, flat grin on his face.

"Hi, Pete. Haven't seen you around since they buried McKinley. How's tricks?"

"Not bad, not good," Pete Anglich said huskily. "I been on a drunk."

Trimmer Waltz broadened his smile, turned it on the girl. She looked at him quickly, looked away, picking at the tablecloth.

Waltz's voice was soft, cooing. "Know the little lady before – or just pick her out of the line-up?"

Pete Anglich shrugged, looked bored. "Just wanted somebody to share a drink with, Trimmer. Sent her a note. Okay?"

"Sure. Perfect." Waltz picked one of the glasses up, sniffed at it. He shook his head sadly. "Wish we could serve better stuff. At four bits a throw it can't be done. How about tipping a few out of a right bottle, back in my den?"

"Both of us?" Pete Anglich asked gently.

"Both of you is right. In about five minutes. I got to circulate a little first."

He pinched the girl's cheek, went on, with a loose swing of his tailored shoulders.

The girl said slowly, thickly, hopelessly, "So Pete's your name. You must want to die young, Pete. Mine's Token Ware. Silly name, isn't it?"

"I like it," Pete Anglich said softly.

The girl stared at a point below the white scar on Pete Anglich's throat. Her eyes slowly filled with tears.

Trimmer Waltz drifted among the tables, speaking to a customer here and there. He edged over to the far wall, came along it to the band shell, stood there ranging the house with his eyes until he was looking directly at Pete Anglich. He jerked his head, stepped back through a pair of thick curtains.

Pete Anglich pushed his chair back and stood up. "Let's go," he said.

Token Ware crushed a cigarette out in a glass tray with jerky fingers, finished the drink in her glass, stood up. They went back between the tables, along the edge of the dance floor, over to the side of the band shell.

The curtains opened on to a dim hallway with doors on both sides. A shabby red carpet masked the floor. The walls were chipped, the doors cracked.

"The one at the end on the left," Token Ware whispered.

They came to it. Pete Anglich knocked. Trimmer Waltz's voice called out to come in. Pete Anglich stood a moment looking at the door, then turned his head and looked at the girl with his eyes hard and narrow. He pushed the door open, gestured at her. They went in.

The room was not very light. A small oblong reading lamp on the desk shed glow on polished wood, but less on the shabby red carpet, and the long heavy red drapes across the outer wall. The air was close, with a thick, sweetish smell of liquor.

Trimmer Waltz sat behind the desk with his hands touching a tray that contained a cut-glass decanter, some gold-veined glasses, an ice bucket and a siphon of charged water.

He smiled, rubbed one side of his big nose.

"Park yourselves, folks. Liqueur Scotch at six-ninety a fifth. That's what it costs me – wholesale."

Pete Anglich shut the door, looked slowly around the room, at the floor-length window drapes, at the unlighted ceiling light. He unbuttoned the top button of his coat with a slow, easy movement.

"Hot in here," he said softly. "Any windows behind those drapes?"

The girl sat in a round chair on the opposite side of the desk from Waltz. He smiled at her very gently.

"Good idea," Waltz said. "Open one up, will you?"

Pete Anglich went past the end of the desk, toward the curtains. As he got beyond Waltz, his hand went up under his coat and touched the butt of his gun. He moved softly toward the red drapes. The tips of wide, square-toed black shoes just barely showed under the curtains, in the shadow between the curtains and the wall.

Pete Anglich reached the curtains, put his left hand out and jerked them open.

The shoes on the floor against the wall were empty. Waltz laughed dryly behind Pete Anglich. Then a thick, cold voice said: "Put 'em high, boy."

The girl made a strangled sound, not quite a scream. Pete Anglich dropped his hands and turned slowly and looked. The Negro was enormous in stature, gorillalike, and wore a baggy checked suit that made him even more enormous. He had come soundlessly on shoeless feet out of a closet door, and his right hand almost covered a huge black gun.

Trimmer Waltz held a gun too, a Savage. The two men stared quietly at Pete Anglich. Pete Anglich put his hands up in the air, his eyes blank, his small mouth set hard.

The Negro in the checked suit came toward him in long, loose strides, pressed the gun against his chest, then reached under his coat. His hand came out with Pete Anglich's gun. He dropped it behind him on the floor. He shifted his own gun casually and hit Pete Anglich on the side of the jaw with the flat of it.

Pete Anglich staggered and the salt taste of blood came under his tongue. He blinked, said thickly: "I'll remember you a long time, big boy."

The Negro grinned. "Not so long, pal. Not so long."

He hit Pete Anglich again with the gun, then suddenly he jammed it into a side pocket and his two big hands shot out, clamped themselves on Pete Anglich's throat.

"When they's tough I likes to squeeze 'em," he said almost softly.

Thumbs that felt as big and hard as doorknobs pressed into the arteries on Pete Anglich's neck. The face before him and above him grew enormous, an enormous shadowy face with a wide grin in the middle of it. It waved in lessening light, an unreal, a fantastic face.

Pete Anglich hit the face, with puny blows, the blows of a toy balloon. His fists didn't feel anything as they hit the face. The big man twisted him around and put a knee into his back, and bent him down over the knee.

There was no sound for a while except the thunder of blood threshing in Pete Anglich's head. Then, far away, he seemed to hear a girl scream thinly. From still farther away the voice of Trimmer Waltz muttered: "Easy now, Rufe. Easy."

A vast blackness shot with hot red filled Pete Anglich's world. The darkness grew silent. Nothing moved in it now, not even blood.

The Negro lowered Pete Anglich's limp body to the floor, stepped back and rubbed his hands together.

"Yeah, I likes to squeeze 'em," he said.

5

THE NEGRO IN the checked suit sat on the side of the daybed and picked languidly at a five-stringed banjo. His large face was solemn and peaceful, a little sad. He plucked the banjo strings slowly, with his bare fingers, his head on one side, a crumpled cigarette-end sticking barely past his lips at one corner of his mouth.

Low down in his throat he was making a kind of droning sound. He was singing.

A cheap electric clock on the mantel said 11:35. It was a small living-room with bright, overstuffed furniture, a red floor lamp with a cluster of French dolls at its base, a gay carpet with large diamond shapes in it, two curtained windows with a mirror between them.

A door at the back was ajar. A door near it opening into the hall was shut.

Pete Anglich lay on his back on the floor, with his mouth open and his arms outflung. His breath was a thick snore. His eyes were shut, and his face in the reddish glow of the lamp looked flushed and feverish.

The Negro put the banjo down out of his immense hands, stood up and yawned and stretched. He walked across the room and looked at a calendar over the mantel.

"This ain't August," he said disgustedly.

He tore a leaf from the calendar, rolled it into a ball and threw it at Pete Anglich's face. It hit the unconscious man's cheek. He didn't stir. The Negro spit the cigarette-end into his palm, held his palm out flat, and flicked a fingernail at it, sent it sailing in the same direction as the paper ball.

He loafed a few steps and leaned down, fingering a bruise on Pete Anglich's temple. He pressed the bruise, grinning softly. Pete Anglich didn't move.

The Negro straightened and kicked the unconscious man in the ribs thoughtfully, over and over again, not very hard. Pete Anglich moved a little, gurgled, and rolled his head to one side. The Negro looked pleased, left him, went back to the daybed. He carried his banjo over to the hall door and leaned it against the wall. There was a gun lying on a newspaper on a small table. He went through a partly open inner door and came back with a pint bottle of gin, half full. He rubbed the bottle over carefully with a handkerchief, set it on the mantel.

"About time now, pal," he mused out loud. "When you wake up, maybe you don't feel so good. Maybe need a shot . . . Hey, I gotta better hunch."

He reached for the bottle again, went down on one big knee, poured gin over Pete Anglich's mouth and chin, slopped it loosely on the front of his shirt. He stood the bottle on the floor, after wiping it off again, and flicked the glass stopper under the daybed.

"Grab it, white boy," he said softly. "Prints don't never hurt."

He got the newspaper with the gun on it, slid the gun off on the carpet, and moved it with his foot until it lay just out of reach of Pete Anglich's outflung hand.

He studied the layout carefully from the door, nodded, picked his banjo up. He opened the door, peeped out, then looked back.

"So long, pal," he said softly. "Time for me to breeze. You ain't got a lot of future comin', but what you got you get sudden."

He shut the door, went along the hallway to stairs and down the stairs. Radios made faint sound behind shut doors. The entrance lobby of the apartment house was empty. The Negro in the checked suit slipped into a pay booth in the dark corner of the lobby, dropped his nickel and dialed.

A heavy voice said: "Police department."

The Negro put his lips close to the transmitter and got a whine into his voice.

"This the cops? Say, there's been a shootin' scrape in the Calliope Apartments, Two-Forty-Six East Forty-Eight, Apartment Four-B. Got it? . . . Well, do somethin' about it, flatfoot!"

He hung up quickly, giggling, ran down the front steps of the apartment house and jumped into a small, dirty sedan. He kicked it to life and drove toward Central Avenue. He was a block from Central Avenue when the red eye of a prowl car swung around from Central on to East Forty-Eight Street.

The Negro in the sedan chuckled and went on his way. He was singing down in his throat when the prowl car whirred past him.

*

The instant the door latch clicked Pete Anglich opened his eyes halfway. He turned his head slowly, and a grin of pain came on his face and stayed on it, but he kept on turning his head until he could see the emptiness of one end of the room and the middle. He tipped his head far back on the floor, saw the rest of the room.

He rolled toward the gun and took hold of it. It was his own gun. He sat up and snapped the gate open mechanically. His face stiffened out of the grin. One shell in the gun had been fired. The barrel smelled of powder fumes.

He came to his feet and crept toward the slightly open inner door, keeping his head low. When he reached the door he bent still lower, and slowly pushed the door wide open. Nothing happened. He looked into a bedroom with twin beds, made up and covered with rose damask with a gold design in it.

Somebody lay on one of the beds. A woman. She didn't move. The hard, tight grin came back on Pete Anglich's face. He rose straight up and walked softly on the balls of his feet over to the side of the bed. A door beyond was open on a bathroom, but no sound came from it. Pete Anglich looked down at the colored girl on the bed.

He caught his breath and let it out slowly. The girl was dead. Her eyes were half open, uninterested, her hands lazy at her sides. Her legs were twisted a little and bare skin showed above one sheer stocking, below the short skirt. A green hat lay on the floor. She had four-and-a-half-inch French heels. There was a scent of Midnight Narcissus in the room. He remembered the girl outside the Surprise Hotel.

She was quite dead, dead long enough for the blood to have clotted over the powder-scorched hole below her left breast.

Pete Anglich went back to the living-room, grabbed up the gin bottle, and emptied it without stopping or choking. He stood a moment, breathing hard, thinking. The gun hung slack in his left hand. His small, tight mouth hardly showed at all.

He worked his fingers on the glass of the gin bottle, tossed it empty on top of the daybed, slid his gun into the underarm holster, went to the door and stepped quietly into the hall.

The hall was long and dim and yawning with chill air. A single bracket light loomed yellowly at the top of the stairs. A screen door led to a balcony over the front porch of the building. There was a gray splash of cold moonlight on one corner of the screen.

Pete Anglich went softly down the stairs to the front hall, put his hand out to the knob of the glass door.

A red spot hit the front of the door. It sifted a hard red glare through the glass and the sleazy curtain that masked it.

Pete Anglich slid down the door, below the panel, hunched along the wall to the side. His eyes ranged the place swiftly, held on the dark telephone booth.

"Man trap," he said softly, and dodged over to the booth, into it. He crouched and almost shut the door.

Steps slammed on the porch and the front door squeaked open. The steps hammered into the hallway, stopped.

A heavy voice said: "All quiet, huh? Maybe a phony."

Another voice said: "Four-B. Let's give it the dust, anyway."

The steps went along the lower hall, came back. They sounded on the stairs going up. They drummed in the upper hall.

Pete Anglich pushed the door of the booth back, slid over to the front door, crouched and squinted against the red glare.

The prowl car at the curb was a dark bulk. Its headlights burned along the cracked sidewalk. He couldn't see into it. He sighed, opened the door and walked quickly, but not too quickly, down the wooden steps from the porch.

The prowl car was empty, with both front doors hanging open. Shadowy forms were converging cautiously from across the street. Pete Anglich marched straight to the prowl car and got into it. He shut the doors quietly, stepped on the starter, threw the car in gear.

He drove off past the gathering crowd of neighbors. At the first corner he turned and switched off the red spot. Then he drove fast, wound in and out of blocks, away from Central, after a while turned back toward it.

When he was near its lights and chatter and traffic he pulled over to the side of the dusty tree-lined street, left the prowl car standing.

He walked towards Central.

6

TRIMMER WALTZ CRADLED the phone with his left hand. He put his right index finger along the edge of his upper lip, pushed the lip out of the way, and rubbed his finger slowly along his teeth and gums. His shallow, colorless eyes looked across the desk at the big Negro in the checked suit.

"Lovely," he said in a dead voice. "Lovely. He got away before the law jumped him. A very swell job, Rufe."

The Negro took a cigar stub out of his mouth and crushed it between a huge flat thumb and a huge flat forefinger.

"Hell, he was out cold," he snarled. "The prowlies passed me before I got to Central. Hell, he *can't* get away."

"That was him talking," Waltz said lifelessly. He opened the top drawer of his desk and laid his heavy Savage in front of him.

The Negro looked at the Savage. His eyes got dull and lightless, like obsidian. His lips puckered and gouged at each other.

"That gal's been cuttin' corners on me with three, four other guys," he grumbled. "I owed her the slug. Oky-doke. That's jake. Now, I go out and collect me the smart monkey."

He started to get up. Waltz barely touched the butt of his gun with two fingers. He shook his head, and the Negro sat down again. Waltz spoke.

"He got away, Rufe. And you called the buttons to find a dead woman. Unless they get him with the gun on him – one

454

chance in a thousand — there's no way to tie it to him. That makes you the fall guy. You live there."

The Negro grinned and kept his dull eyes on the Savage.

He said: "That makes me get cold feet. And my feet are big enough to get plenty cold. Guess I take me a powder, huh?"

Waltz sighed. He said thoughtfully: "Yeah, I guess you leave town for a while. From Glendale. The 'Frisco late train will be about right."

The Negro looked sulky. "Nix on 'Frisco, boss. I put my thumbs on a frail there. She croaked. Nix on 'Frisco, boss."

"You've got ideas, Rufe," Waltz said calmly. He rubbed the side of his veined nose with one finger, then slicked his gray hair back with his palm. "I see them in your big brown eyes. Forget it. I'll take care of you. Get the car in the alley. We'll figure the angles on the way to Glendale."

The Negro blinked and wiped cigar ash off his chin with his huge hand.

"And better leave your big shiny gun here," Waltz added. "It needs a rest."

Rufe reached back and slowly drew his gun from a hip pocket. He pushed it across the polished wood of the desk with one finger. There was a faint, sleepy smile at the back of his eyes.

"Okay, boss," he said, almost dreamily.

He went across to the door, opened it, and went out. Waltz stood up and stepped over to the closet, put on a dark felt hat and a light-weight overcoat, a pair of dark gloves. He dropped the Savage into his left-hand pocket, Rufe's gun into the right. He went out of the room down the hall toward the sound of the dance band.

At the end he parted the curtains just enough to peer through. The orchestra was playing a waltz. There was a good crowd, a quiet crowd for Central Avenue. Waltz sighed, watched the dancers for a moment, let the curtains fall together again.

He went back along the hall past his office to a door at the end that gave on stairs. Another door at the bottom of the stairs opened on a dark alley behind the building.

Waltz closed the door gently, stood in the darkness against the wall. The sound of an idling motor came to him, the light clatter of loose tappets. The alley was blind at one end, at the other turned at right angles toward the front of the building. Some of the light from Central Avenue splashed on a brick wall at the end of the cross alley, beyond the waiting car, a small sedan that looked battered and dirty even in the darkness.

Waltz reached his right hand into his overcoat pocket, took out Rufe's gun and held it down in the cloth of his overcoat. He walked to the sedan soundlessly, went around to the right-hand door, opened it to get in.

Two huge hands came out of the car and took hold of his throat. Hard hands, hands with enormous strength in them. Waltz made a faint gurgling sound before his head was bent back and his almost blind eyes were groping at the sky.

Then his right hand moved, moved like a hand that had nothing to do with his stiff, straining body, his tortured neck, his bulging blind eyes. It moved forward cautiously, delicately, until the muzzle of the gun it held pressed against something soft. It explored the something soft carefully, without haste, seemed to be making sure just what it was.

Trimmer Waltz didn't see, he hardly felt. He didn't breathe. But his hand obeyed his brain like a detached force beyond the reach of Rufe's terrible hands. Waltz's finger squeezed the trigger.

The hands fell slack on his throat, dropped away. He staggered back, almost fell across the alley, hit the far wall with his shoulder. He straightened slowly, gasping deep down in his tortured lungs. He began to shake.

He hardly noticed the big gorilla's body fall out of the car and slam the concrete at his feet. It lay at his feet, limp, enormous, but no longer menacing. No longer important.

Waltz dropped the gun on the sprawled body. He rubbed his throat gently for a little while. His breathing was deep, racking, noisy. He searched the inside of his mouth with his tongue, tasted blood. His eyes looked up wearily at the indigo slit of the night sky above the alley.

After a while he said huskily, "I thought of that, Rufe. . . You see, I thought of that."

He laughed, shuddered, adjusted his coat collar, went around the sprawled body to the car and reached in to switch the motor off. He started back along the alley to the rear door of the Juggernaut Club.

A man stepped out of the shadows at the back of the car. Waltz's left hand flashed to his overcoat pocket. Shiny metal blinked at him. He let his hand fall loosely at his side.

Pete Anglich said, "Thought that call would bring you out, Trimmer. Thought you might come this way. Nice going."

After a moment Waltz said thickly: "He choked me. It was self-defense."

"Sure. There's two of us with sore necks. Mine's a pip."

"What do you want, Pete?"

"You tried to frame me for bumping off a girl."

Waltz laughed suddenly, almost crazily. He said quietly: "When I'm crowded I get nasty, Pete. You should know that. Better lay off little Token Ware."

Pete Anglich moved his gun so that the light flickered on the barrel. He came up to Waltz, pushed the gun against his stomach.

"Rufe's dead," he said softly. "Very convenient. Where's the girl?"

"What's it to you?"

"Don't be a bunny. I'm wise. You tried to pick some jack off John Vidaury. I stepped in front of Token. I want to know the rest of it."

Waltz stood very still with the gun pressing his stomach. His fingers twisted in the gloves.

"Okay," he said dully. "How much to button your lip – and keep it buttoned?"

"Couple of centuries. Rufe lifted my poke."

"What does it buy me?" Waltz asked slowly.

"Not a damn thing. I want the girl, too."

Waltz said very gently: "Five C's. But not the girl. Five C's is heavy dough for a Central Avenue punk. Be smart and take it, and forget the rest."

The gun went away from his stomach. Pete Anglich circled him deftly, patted pockets, took the Savage, made a gesture with his left hand, holding it.

"Sold," he said grudgingly. "What's a girl between pals? Feed it to me."

"Have to go up to the office," Waltz said.

Pete Anglich laughed shortly. "Better play ball, Trimmer. Lead on."

They went back along the upstairs hall. The dance band beyond the distant curtains was wailing a Duke Ellington lament, a forlorn monotone of stifled brasses, bitter violins, softly clicking gourds. Waltz opened his office door, snapped the light on, went across to his desk and sat down. He tilted his hat back, smiled, opened a drawer with a key.

Pete Anglich watched him, reached back to turn the key in the door, went along the wall to the closet and looked into it, went behind Waltz to the curtains that masked the windows. He still had his gun out.

He came back to the end of the desk. Waltz was pushing a loose sheaf of bills away from him.

Pete Anglich ignored the money, leaned down over the end of the desk.

"Keep that and give me the girl, Trimmer."

Waltz shook his head, kept on smiling.

"The Vidaury squeeze was a grand, Trimmer – or started with a grand. Noon Street is almost in your alley. Do you have to scare women into doing your dirty work? I think you wanted something on the girl, so you could make her say uncle."

Waltz narrowed his eyes a little, pointed to the sheaf of bills.

Pete Anglich said slowly: "A shabby, lonesome, scared kid. Probably lives in a cheap furnished room. No friends, or she wouldn't be working in your joint. Nobody would wonder about her, except me. You wouldn't have put her in a house, would you, Trimmer?"

"Take your money and beat it," Waltz said thinly. "You know what happens to rats in this district."

"Sure, they run night clubs," Pete Anglich said gently.

He put his gun down, started to reach for the money. His fist doubled, swept upward casually. His elbow went up with the punch, the fist turned, landed almost delicately on the angle of Waltz's jaw.

Waltz became a loose bag of clothes. His mouth fell open. His hat fell off the back of his head. Pete Anglich stared at him, grumbled: "Lot of good that does me."

The room was very still. The dance band sounded faintly, like a turned-down radio. Pete Anglich moved behind Waltz and reached down under his coat into his breast pocket. He took a wallet out, shook out money, a driver's license, a police pistol permit, several insurance cards.

He put the stuff back, stared morosely at the desk, rubbed a thumbnail on his jaw. There was a shiny buff memo pad in front of him. Impressions of writing showed on the top blank sheet. He held it sideways against the light, then picked up a pencil and began to make light loose strokes across the paper. Writing came out dimly. When the sheet was shaded all over Pete Anglich read: 4623 Noon Street. Ask for Reno.

He tore the sheet off, folded it into a pocket, picked his gun up and crossed to the door. He reversed the key, locked the room from the outside, went back to the stairs and down them to the alley.

The body of the Negro lay as it had fallen, between the small sedan and the dark wall. The alley was empty. Pete Anglich stooped, searched the dead man's pockets, came up with a roll of money. He counted the money in the dim light of a match, separated eighty-seven dollars from what there was, and started to put the few remaining bills back. A piece of torn paper fluttered to the pavement. One side only was torn, jaggedly.

Pete Anglich crouched beside the car, struck another match, looked at a half-sheet from a buff memo pad on which was written, beginning with the tear: —— t. Ask for Reno.

He clicked his teeth and let the match fall. "Better," he said softly.

He got into the car, started it and drove out of the alley.

7

THE NUMBER WAS on a front-door transom, faintly lit from behind, the only light the house showed. It was a big frame house, in the block above where the stakeout had been. The windows in front were closely curtained. Noise came from behind them, voices and laughter, the high-pitched whine of a colored girl's singing. Cars were parked along the curb, on both sides of the street.

A tall thin Negro in dark clothes and gold nose-glasses opened the door. There was another door behind him, shut. He stood in a dark box between the two doors.

Pete Anglich said: "Reno?"

The tall Negro nodded, said nothing.

"I've come for the girl Rufe left, the white girl."

The tall Negro stood a moment quite motionless, looking over Pete Anglich's head. When he spoke, his voice was a lazy rustle of sound that seemed to come from somewhere else.

"Come in and shut the do'."

Pete Anglich stepped into the house, shut the outer door behind him. The tall Negro opened the inner door. It was thick, heavy. When he opened it sound and light jumped at them. A purplish light. He went through the inner door, into a hallway.

The purplish light came through a broad arch from a long living-room. It had heavy velour drapes, davenports and deep chairs, a glass bar in the corner, and a white-coated Negro behind the bar. Four couples lounged about the room drinking; slim, slick-haired Negro sheiks and girls with bare arms, sheer silk legs, plucked eyebrows. The soft, purplish light made the scene unreal.

Reno stared vaguely past Pete Anglich's shoulder, dropped his heavy-lidded eyes, said wearily: "You says which?"

The Negroes beyond the arch were quiet, staring. The barman stooped and put his hands down under the bar.

Pete Anglich put his hand into his pocket slowly, brought out a crumpled piece of paper.

"This any help?"

Reno took the paper, studied it. He reached languidly into his vest and brought out another piece of the same color. He fitted the pieces together. His head went back and he looked at the ceiling.

"Who send you?"

"Trimmer."

"I don' like it," the tall Negro said. "He done write my name. I don' like that. That ain't sma't. Apa't from that I guess I check you."

He turned and started up a long, straight flight of stairs. Pete Anglich followed him. One of the Negro youths in the living-room snickered loudly.

Reno stopped suddenly, turned and went back down the steps, through the arch. He went up to the snickerer.

"This is business," he said exhaustedly. "Ain't no white folks comin' heah. Git me?"

The boy who had laughed said, "Okay, Reno," and lifted a tall, misted glass.

Reno came up the stairs again, talking to himself. Along the upper hall were many closed doors. There was faint pink light from flame-colored wall lamps. At the end Reno took a key out and unlocked the door.

He stood aside. "Git her out," he said tersely. "I don' handle no white cargo heah."

Pete Anglich stepped past him into a bedroom. An orange floor lamp glowed in the far corner near a flounced, gaudy bed. The windows were shut, the air heavy, sickish.

Token Ware lay on her side on the bed, with her face to the wall, sobbing quietly.

Pete Anglich stepped to the side of the bed, touched her. She whirled, cringed. Her head jerked around at him, her eyes dilated, her mouth half open as if to yell.

"Hello, there," he said quietly, very gently. "I've been looking all over for you."

The girl stared back at him. Slowly all the fear went out of her face.

8

THE *NEWS* PHOTOGRAPHER held the flashbulb holder high up in his left hand, leaned down over his camera.

"Now, the smile, Mr. Vidaury," he said. "The sad one – that one that makes 'em pant."

Vidaury turned in the chair and set his profile. He smiled at the girl in the red hat, then turned his face to the camera with the smile still on.

The bulb flared and the shutter clicked.

"Not bad, Mr. Vidaury. I've seen you do better."

"I've been under a great strain," Vidaury said gently.

"I'll say. Acid in the face is no fun," the photographer said.

The girl in the red hat tittered, then coughed, behind a gauntleted glove with red stitching on the back.

The photographer packed his stuff together. He was an oldish man in shiny blue serge, with sad eyes. He shook his gray head and straightened his hat.

"No, acid in the puss is no fun," he said. "Well, I hope our boys can see you in the morning, Mr. Vidaury."

"Delighted," Vidaury said wearily. "Just tell them to ring me from the lobby before they come up. And have a drink on your way out."

"I'm crazy," the photographer said. "I don't drink."

He hoisted his camera bag over his shoulder and trudged down the room. A small Jap in a white coat appeared from nowhere and let him out, then went away.

"Acid in the puss," the girl in the red hat said. "Ha, ha, ha! That's positively excruciating, if a nice girl may say so. Can I have a drink?"

"Nobody's stopping you," Vidaury growled.

"Nobody ever did, sweets."

She walked sinuously over to a table with a square Chinese tray on it. She mixed a stiff one. Vidaury said half absently: "That should be all till morning. The *Bulletin*, the *Press-Tribune*, the three wire services, the *News*. Not bad."

"I'd call it a perfect score," the girl in the red hat said.

Vidaury scowled at her. "But nobody caught," he said softly, "except an innocent passer-by. *You* wouldn't know anything about this squeeze, would you, Irma?"

Her smile was lazy, but cold. "Me take you for a measly grand? Be your forty years plus, Johnny. I'm a home-run hitter, always."

Vidaury stood up and crossed the room to a carved wood cabinet, unlocked a small drawer and took a large ball of crystal out of it. He went back to his chair, sat down, and leaned forward, holding the ball in his palms and staring into it, almost vacantly.

The girl in the red hat watched him over the rim of her glass. Her eyes widened, got a little glassy.

463

"Hell! He's gone psychic on the folks," she breathed. She put her glass down with a sharp slap on the tray, drifted over to his side and leaned down. Her voice was cooing, edged. "Ever hear of senile decay, Johnny? It happens to exceptionally wicked men in their forties. They get ga-ga over flowers and toys, cut out paper dolls and play with glass balls . . . Can it, for God's sake, Johnny! You're not a punk yet."

Vidaury stared fixedly into the crystal ball. He breathed slowly, deeply.

The girl in the red hat leaned still closer to him. "Let's go riding, Johnny," she cooed. "I like the night air. It makes me remember my tonsils."

"I don't want to go riding," Vidaury said vaguely. "I – I feel something. Something imminent."

The girl bent suddenly and knocked the ball out of his hands. It thudded heavily on the floor, rolled: sluggishly in the deep nap of the rug.

Vidaury shot to his feet, his face convulsed.

"I want to go riding, handsome," the girl said coolly. "It's a nice night, and you've got a nice car. So I want to go riding."

Vidaury stared at her with hate in his eyes. Slowly he smiled. The hate went away. He reached out and touched her lips with two fingers.

"Of course we'll go riding, baby," he said softly.

He got the ball, locked it up in the cabinet, went through an inner door. The girl in the red hat opened a bag and touched her lips with rouge, pursed them, made a face at herself in the mirror of her compact, found a rough wool coat in beige braided with red, and shrugged into it carefully, tossed a scarflike collar end over her shoulder.

Vidaury came back with a hat and coat on, a fringed muffler hanging down his coat.

They went down the room.

"Let's sneak out the back way," he said at the door. "In case any more newshawks are hanging around."

"Why, Johnny!" The girl in the red hat raised mocking eyebrows. "People saw me come in, saw me here. Surely you wouldn't want them to think your girl friend stayed the night?"

"Hell!" Vidaury said violently and wrenched the door open.

The telephone bell jangled back in the room. Vidaury swore again, took his hand from the door and stood waiting while the little Jap in the white jacket came in and answered the phone.

The boy put the phone down, smiled deprecatingly and gestured with his hands.

"You take, prease? I not understand."

Vidaury walked back and lifted the instrument. He said, "Yes? This is John Vidaury." He listened.

Slowly his fingers tightened on the phone. His whole face tightened, got white. He said slowly, thickly: "Hold the line a minute."

He put the phone down on its side, put his hand down on the table and leaned on it. The girl in the red hat came up behind him.

"Bad news, handsome? You look like a washed egg."

Vidaury turned his head slowly and stared at her. "Get the hell out of here," he said tonelessly.

She laughed. He straightened, took a single long step and slapped her across the mouth, hard.

"I said, get the hell out of here," he repeated in an utterly dead voice.

She stopped laughing and touched her lips with fingers in the gauntleted glove. Her eyes were round, but not shocked.

"Why, Johnny. You sweep me right off my feet," she said wonderingly. "You're simply terrific. Of course I'll go."

She turned quickly, with a light toss of her head, went back along the room to the door, waved her hand, and went out.

Vidaury was not looking at her when she waved. He

465

lifted the phone as soon as the door clicked shut after her, said into it grimly: "Get over here, Waltz – and get over here quick!"

He dropped the phone on its cradle, stood a moment blank-eyed. He went back through the inner door, reappeared in a moment without his hat and overcoat. He held a thick, short automatic in his hand. He slipped it nose-down into the inside breast pocket of his dinner jacket, lifted the phone again slowly, said into it coldly and firmly: "If a Mr. Anglich calls to see me, send him up. Anglich." He spelled the name out, put the phone down carefully, and sat down in the easy chair beside it.

He folded his arms and waited.

9

THE WHITE-JACKETED JAPANESE boy opened the door, bobbed his head, smiled, hissed politely: "Ah, you come inside, prease. Quite so, prease."

Pete Anglich patted Token Ware's shoulder, pushed her through the door into the long, vivid room. She looked shabby and forlorn against the background of handsome furnishings. Her eyes were reddened from crying, her mouth was smeared.

The door shut behind them and the little Japanese stole away.

They went down the stretch of thick, noiseless carpet, past quiet brooding lamps, bookcases sunk into the wall, shelves of alabaster and ivory, and porcelain and jade knickknacks, a huge mirror framed in blue glass, and surrounded by a frieze of lovingly autographed photos, low tables with lounging chairs, high tables with flowers, more books, more chairs, more rugs – and Vidaury sitting remotely with a glass in his hand, staring at them coldly.

He moved his hand carelessly, looked the girl up and down.

"Ah, yes, the man the police had here. Of course. Something I can do for you? I heard they made a mistake."

Pete Anglich turned a chair a little, pushed Token Ware into it. She sat down slowly, stiffly, licked her lips and stared at Vidaury with a frozen fascination.

A touch of polite distaste curled Vidaury's lips. His eyes were watchful.

Pete Anglich sat down. He drew a stick of gum out of his pocket, unwrapped it, slid it between his teeth. He looked worn, battered, tired. There were dark bruises on the side of his face and on his neck. He still needed a shave.

He said slowly, "This is Miss Ware. The girl that was supposed to get your dough."

Vidaury stiffened. A hand holding a cigarette began to tap restlessly on the arm of his chair. He stared at the girl, but didn't say anything. She half smiled at him, then flushed.

Pete Anglich said: "I hang around Noon Street. I know the sharpshooters, know what kind of folks belong there and what kind don't. I saw this little girl in a lunchwagon on Noon Street this evening. She looked uneasy and she was watching the clock. She didn't belong. When she left I followed her."

Vidaury nodded slightly. A gray tip of ash fell off the end of his cigarette. He looked down at it vaguely, nodded again.

"She went up Noon Street," Pete Anglich said. "A bad street for a white girl. I found her hiding in a doorway. Then a big Duesenberg slid around the corner and doused lights, and your money was thrown out on the sidewalk. She was scared. She asked me to get it. I got it."

Vidaury said smoothly, not looking at the girl: "She doesn't look like a crook. Have you told the police about her? I suppose not, or you wouldn't be here."

Pete Anglich shook his head, ground the gum around in his jaws. "Tell the law? A couple of times nix. This is velvet for us. We want our cut."

Vidaury started violently, then he was very still. His hand stopped beating the chair arm. His face got cold and white and grim. Then he reached up inside his dinner jacket and quietly took the short automatic out, held it on his knees. He leaned forward a little and smiled.

"Blackmailers," he said gravely, "are always rather interesting. How much would your cut be – and what have you got to sell?"

Pete Anglich looked thoughtfully at the gun. His jaws moved easily, crunching the gum. His eyes were unworried.

"Silence," he said gravely. "Just silence."

Vidaury made a sharp sudden gesture with the gun. "Talk," he said. "And talk fast. I don't like silence."

Pete Anglich nodded, said: "The acid-throwing threats were just a dream. You didn't get any. The extortion attempt was a phony. A publicity stunt. That's all." He leaned back in his chair.

Vidaury looked down the room past Pete Anglich's shoulder. He started to smile, then his face got wooden.

Trimmer Waltz had slid into the room through an open side door. He had his big Savage in his hand. He came slowly along the carpet without sound. Pete Anglich and the girl didn't see him.

Pete Anglich said, "Phony all the way through. Just a build-up. Guessing? Sure I am, but look a minute, see how soft it was played first – and how tough it was played afterward, after I showed in it. The girl works for Trimmer Waltz at the Juggernaut. She's down and out, and she scares easily. So Waltz sends her on a caper like that. Why? Because she's supposed to be nabbed. The stake-out's all arranged. If she squawks about Waltz, he laughs it off, points to the fact that the plant was almost in his alley, that it was a small stake at best, and his joint's doing all right. He points to the fact that a dumb girl goes to get it, and would he, a smart guy, pull anything like that? Certainly not.

"The cops will half believe him, and you'll make a big gesture and refuse to prosecute the girl. If she doesn't spill, you'll refuse to prosecute anyway, and you'll get your publicity just the same, either way. You need it bad, because you're slipping, and you'll get it, and all it will cost you is what you pay Waltz – or that's what you think. Is that crazy? Is that too far for a Hollywood heel to stretch? Then tell me why no Feds were on the case. Because those lads would keep on digging until they found the mouse, and then you'd be up for obstructing justice. That's why. The local law don't give a damn. They're so used to movie build-ups they just yawn and turn over and go to sleep again."

Waltz was halfway down the room now. Vidaury didn't look at him. He looked at the girl, smiled at her faintly.

"Now, see how tough it was played after I got into it," Pete Anglich said. "I went to the Juggernaut and talked to the girl. Waltz got us into his office and a big ape that works for him damn near strangled me. When I came to I was in an apartment and a dead girl was there, and she was shot, and a bullet was gone from my gun. The gun was on the floor beside me, and I stank of gin, and a prowl car was booming around the corner. And Miss Ware here was locked up in a whore house on Noon Street.

"Why all that hard stuff? Because Waltz had a perfectly swell blackmail racket lined up for you, and he'd have bled you whiter than an angel's wing. As long as you had a dollar, half of it would have been his. And you'd have paid it and liked it, Vidaury. You'd have had publicity, and you'd have had protection, but how you'd have paid for it!"

Waltz was close now, almost too close. Vidaury stood up suddenly. The short gun jerked at Pete Anglich's chest. Vidaury's voice was thin, an old man's voice. He said dreamily: "Take him, Waltz. I'm too jittery for this sort of thing."

Pete Anglich didn't even turn. His face became the face of a wooden Indian.

Waltz put his gun into Pete Anglich's back. He stood there half smiling, with the gun against Pete Anglich's back, looking across his shoulder at Vidaury.

"Dumb, Pete," he said dryly. "You had enough evening already. You ought to have stayed away from here – but I figured you couldn't pass it up."

Vidaury moved a little to one side, spread his legs, flattened his feet to the floor. There was a queer, greenish tint to his handsome face, a sick glitter in his deep eyes.

Token Ware stared at Waltz. Her eyes glittered with panic, the lids straining away from the eyeballs, showing the whites all around the iris.

Waltz said, "I can't do anything here, Vidaury. I'd rather not walk him out alone, either. Get your hat and coat."

Vidaury nodded very slightly. His head just barely moved. His eyes were still sick.

"What about the girl?" he asked whisperingly.

Waltz grinned, shook his head, pressed the gun hard into Pete Anglich's back.

Vidaury moved a little more to the side, spread his feet again. The thick gun was very steady in his hand, but not pointed at anything in particular.

He closed his eyes, held them shut a brief instant, then opened them wide. He said slowly, carefully: "It looked all right as it was planned. Things just as far-fetched, just as unscrupulous, have been done before in Hollywood, often. I just didn't expect it to lead to hurting people, to killing. I'm – I'm just not enough of a heel to go on with it, Waltz. Not any further. You'd better put your gun up and leave."

Waltz shook his head; smiled a peculiar strained smile. He stepped back from Pete Anglich and held the Savage a little to one side.

"The cards are dealt," he said coldly. "You'll play 'em. Get going."

Vidaury sighed, sagged a little. Suddenly he was a lonely, forlorn man, no longer young.

"No," he said softly. "I'm through. The last flicker of a not-so-good reputation. It's my show, after all. Always the ham, but still my show. Put the gun up, Waltz. Take the air."

Waltz's face got cold and hard and expressionless. His eyes became the expressionless eyes of the killer. He moved the Savage a little more.

"Get – your – hat, Vidaury," he said very clearly.

"Sorry," Vidaury said, and fired.

Waltz's gun flamed at the same instant, the two explosions blended. Vidaury staggered to his left and half turned, then straightened his body again.

He looked steadily at Waltz. "Beginner's luck," he said, and waited.

Pete Anglich had his Colt out now, but he didn't need it. Waltz fell slowly on his side. His cheek and the side of his big-veined nose pressed the nap of the rug. He moved his left arm a little, tried to throw it over his back. He gurgled, then was still.

Pete Anglich kicked the Savage away from Waltz's sprawled body.

Vidaury asked draggingly: "Is he dead?"

Pete Anglich grunted, didn't answer. He looked at the girl. She was standing up with her back against the telephone table, the back of her hand to her mouth in the conventional attitude of startled horror. So conventional it looked silly.

Pete Anglich looked at Vidaury. He said sourly: "Beginner's luck – yeah. But suppose you'd missed him? He was bluffing. Just wanted you in a little deeper, so you wouldn't squawk. As a matter of fact, I'm his alibi on a kill."

Vidaury said: "Sorry . . . I'm sorry." He sat down suddenly, leaned his head back and closed his eyes.

"God, but he's handsome!" Token Ware said reverently. "And brave."

Vidaury put his hand to his left shoulder, pressed it hard against his body. Blood oozed slowly between his fingers. Token Ware let out a stifled screech.

Pete Anglich looked down the room. The little Jap in the white coat had crept into the end of it, stood silently, a small huddled figure against the wall. Pete Anglich looked at Vidaury again. Very slowly, as though unwillingly, he said: "Miss Ware has folks in 'Frisco. You can send her home, with a little present. That's natural – and open. She turned Waltz up to me. That's how I came into it. I told him you were wise and he came here to shut you up. Tough-guy stuff. The coppers will laugh at it, but they'll laugh in their cuffs. After all, they're getting publicity too. The phony angle is out. Check?"

Vidaury opened his eyes, said faintly, "You're – you're very decent about it. I won't forget." His head lolled.

"He's fainted," the girl cried.

"So he has," Pete Anglich said. "Give him a nice big kiss and he'll snap out of it . . . And you'll have something to remember all your life."

He ground his teeth, went to the phone, and lifted it.

GOLDFISH

1

I WASN'T DOING any work that day, just catching up on my foot-dangling. A warm gusty breeze was blowing in at the office window and the soot from the Mansion House Hotel oil burners across the alley was rolling across the glass top of my desk in tiny particles, like pollen drifting over a vacant lot.

I was just thinking about going to lunch when Kathy Horne came in.

She was a tall, seedy, sad-eyed blonde who had once been a policewoman and had lost her job when she married a cheap little check bouncer named Johnny Horne, to reform him. She hadn't reformed him, but she was waiting for him to come out so she could try again. In the meantime she ran the cigar counter at the Mansion House, and watched the grifters go by in a haze of nickel cigar smoke. And once in a while lent one of them ten dollars to get out of town. She was just that soft. She sat down and opened her big shiny bag and got out a package of cigarettes and lit one with my desk lighter. She blew a plume of smoke, wrinkled her nose at it.

"Did you ever hear of the Leander pearls?" she asked. "Gosh, that blue serge shines. You must have money in the bank, the clothes you wear."

"No," I said, "to both your ideas. I never heard of the Leander pearls and don't have any money in the bank."

"Then you'd like to make yourself a cut of twenty-five grand maybe."

I lit one of her cigarettes. She got up and shut the window, saying: "I get enough of that hotel smell on the job."

She sat down again, went on: "It's nineteen years ago. They had the guy in Leavenworth fifteen and it's four since they let him out. A big lumberman from up north named Sol Leander bought them for his wife – the pearls, I mean – just two of them. They cost two hundred grand."

"It must have taken a hand truck to move them," I said.

"I see you don't know a lot about pearls," Kathy Horne said. "It's not just size. Anyhow they're worth more today and the twenty-five-grand reward the Reliance people put out is still good."

"I get it," I said. "Somebody copped them off."

"Now you're getting yourself some oxygen." She dropped her cigarette into a tray and let it smoke, as ladies will. I put it out for her. "That's what the guy was in Leavenworth for, only they never proved he got the pearls. It was a mail-car job. He got himself hidden in the car somehow and up in Wyoming he shot the clerk, cleaned out the registered mail and dropped off. He got to B.C. before he was nailed. But they didn't get any of the stuff – not then. All they got was him. He got life."

"If it's going to be a long story, let's have a drink."

"I never drink until sundown. That way you don't get to be a heel."

"Tough on the Eskimos," I said. "In the summertime anyway."

She watched me get my little flat bottle out. Then she went on: "His name was Sype – Wally Sype. He did it alone. And he wouldn't squawk about the stuff, not a peep. Then after fifteen long years they offered him a pardon, if he would loosen up with the loot. He gave up everything but the pearls."

"Where did he have it?" I asked. "In his hat?"

"Listen, this ain't just a bunch of gag lines, I've had a lead to those marbles."

I shut my mouth with my hand and looked solemn.

"He said he never had the pearls and they must have halfway believed him because they gave him the pardon. Yet the pearls were in the load, registered mail, and they were never seen again."

My throat began to feel a little thick. I didn't say anything.

Kathy Horne went on: "One time in Leavenworth, just one time in all those years, Wally Sype wrapped himself around a can of white shellac and got as tight as a fat lady's girdle. His cell mate was a little man they called Peeler Mardo. He was doing twenty-seven months for splitting twenty-dollar bills. Sype told him he had the pearls buried somewhere in Idaho."

I leaned forward a little.

"Beginning to get to you, eh?" she said. "Well, get this. Peeler Mardo is rooming at my house and he's a coke hound and he talks in his sleep."

I leaned back again. "Good grief," I said. "And I was practically spending the reward money."

She stared at me coldly. Then her face softened. "All right," she said a little hopelessly. "I know it sounds screwy. All those years gone by and all the smart heads that must have worked on the case, postal men and private agencies and all. And then a cokehead to turn it up. But he's a nice little runt and somehow I believe him. He knows where Sype is."

I said: "Did he talk all this in his sleep?"

"Of course not. But you know me. An old policewoman's got ears. Maybe I was nosey, but I guessed he was an ex-con and I worried about him using the stuff so much. He's the only roomer I've got now and I'd kind of go in by his door and listen to him talking to himself. That way I got enough to brace him. He told me the rest. He wants help to collect."

I leaned forward again. "Where's Sype?"

Kathy Horne smiled, and shook her head. "That's the one thing he wouldn't tell, that and the name Sype is using now. But it's somewhere up north, in or near Olympia, Washington. Peeler saw him up there and found out about him and he says Sype didn't see him."

"What's Peeler doing down here?" I asked.

"Here's where they put the Leavenworth rap on him. You know an old con always goes back to look at the piece of sidewalk he slipped on. But he doesn't have any friends here now."

I lit another cigarette and had another little drink.

"Sype has been out four years, you say. Peeler did twenty-seven months. What's he been doing with all the time since?"

Kathy Horne widened her china-blue eyes pityingly. "Maybe you think there's only one jailhouse he could get into."

"Okay," I said. "Will he talk to me? I guess he wants help to deal with the insurance people, in case there are any pearls and Sype will put them right in Peeler's hand and so on. Is that it?"

Kathy Horne sighed. "Yes, he'll talk to you. He's aching to. He's scared about something. Will you go out now, before he gets junked up for the evening?"

"Sure — if that's what you want."

She took a flat key out of her bag and wrote an address on my pad. She stood up slowly.

"It's a double house. My side's separate. There's a door in between, with the key on my side. That's just in case he won't come to the door."

"Okay," I said. I blew smoke at the ceiling and stared at her.

She went towards the door, stopped, came back. She looked down at the floor.

"I don't rate much in it," she said. "Maybe not anything. But if I could have a grand or two waiting for Johnny when he came out, maybe — "

"Maybe you could hold him straight," I said. "It's a dream, Kathy. It's all a dream. But if it isn't, you cut an even third."

She caught her breath and glared at me to keep from crying. She went towards the door, stopped and came back again.

"That isn't all," she said. "It's the old guy – Sype. He did fifteen years. He paid. Paid hard. Doesn't it make you feel kind of mean?"

I shook my head. "He stole them, didn't he? He killed a man. What does he do for a living?"

"His wife has money," Kathy Horne said. "He just plays around with goldfish."

"Goldfish?" I said. "To hell with him."

She went on out.

2

THE LAST TIME I had been in the Gray Lake district I had helped a D.A.'s man named Bernie Ohls shoot a gunman named Poke Andrews. But that was higher up the hill, farther away from the lake. This house was on the second level, in a loop the street made rounding a spur of the hill. It stood on a terrace, with a cracked retaining wall in front and several vacant lots behind.

Being originally a double house it had two front doors and two sets of front steps. One of the doors had a sign tacked over the grating that masked the peep window: Ring 1432.

I parked my car and went up right-angle steps, passed between two lines of pinks, went up more steps to the side with the sign. That should be the roomer's side. I rang the bell. Nobody answered it, so I went across to the other door. Nobody answered that one either.

While I was waiting a gray Dodge coupe whished around the curve and a small neat girl in blue looked up at me for a second. I didn't see who else was in the car. I didn't pay much attention. I didn't know it was important.

I took out Kathy Horne's key and let myself into a closed living-room that smelled of cedar oil. There was just enough furniture to get by, net curtains, a quiet shaft of sunlight under the drapes in front. There was a tiny breakfast room, a kitchen, a bedroom in the back that was obviously Kathy's, a bath-room, another bedroom in front that seemed to be used as a sewing room. It was this room that had the door cut through to the other side of the house.

I unlocked it and stepped, as it were, through a mirror. Everything was backwards, except the furniture. The living-room on that side had twin beds, didn't have the look of being lived in.

I went towards the back of the house, past the second bath-room, knocked at the shut door that corresponded to Kathy's bedroom.

No answer. I tried the knob and went in. The little man on the bed was probably Peeler Mardo. I noticed his feet first, because although he had on trousers and a shirt, his feet were bare and hung over the end of the bed. They were tied there by a rope around the ankles.

They had been burned raw on the soles. There was a smell of scorched flesh in spite of the open window. Also a smell of scorched wood. An electric iron on a desk was still connected. I went over and shut it off.

I went back to Kathy Horne's kitchen and found a pint of Brooklyn Scotch in the cooler. I used some of it and breathed deeply for a little while and looked out over the vacant lots. There was a narrow cement walk behind the house and green wooden steps down to the street.

I went back to Peeler Mardo's room. The coat of a brown suit with a red pin stripe hung over a chair with the pockets turned out and what had been in them on the floor.

He was wearing the trousers of the suit, and their pockets were turned out also. Some keys and change and a handker-chief lay on the bed beside him, and a metal box like a woman's compact, from which some glistening white powder had spilled. Cocaine.

He was a little man, not more than five feet four, with thin brown hair and large ears. His eyes had no particular color.

They were just eyes, and very wide open and quite dead. His arms were pulled out from him and tied at the wrists by a rope that went under the bed.

I looked him over for bullet or knife wounds, didn't find any. There wasn't a mark on him except his feet. Shock or heart failure or a combination of the two must have done the trick. He was still warm. The gag in his mouth was both warm and wet.

I wiped off everything I had touched, looked out of Kathy's front window for a while before I left the house.

It was three-thirty when I walked into the lobby of the Mansion House, over to the cigar counter in the corner. I leaned on the glass and asked for Camels.

Kathy Horne flicked the pack at me, dropped the change into my outside breast pocket, and gave me her customer's smile.

"Well? You didn't take long," she said, and looked sidewise along her eyes at a drunk who was trying to light a cigar with the old-fashioned flint and steel lighter.

"It's heavy," I told her. "Get set."

She turned away quickly and flipped a pack of paper matches along the glass to the drunk. He fumbled for them, dropped both matches and cigar, scooped them angrily off the floor and went off looking back over his shoulder, as if he expected a kick.

Kathy looked past my head, her eyes cool and empty.

"I'm set," she whispered.

"You cut a full half," I said. "Peeler's out. He's been bumped off – in his bed."

Her eyes twitched. Two fingers curled on the glass near my elbow. A white line showed around her mouth. That was all.

"Listen," I said. "Don't say anything until I'm through. He died of shock. Somebody burned his feet with a cheap electric iron. Not yours, I looked. I'd say he died rather quickly and couldn't have said much. The gag was still in his mouth. When I went out there, frankly, I thought it was all hooey.

Now I'm not so sure. If he opened up, we're through, and so is Sype, unless I can find him first. Those workers didn't have any inhibitions at all. If he didn't give up, there's still time."

Her head turned, her set eyes looked towards the revolving door at the lobby entrance. White patches glared in her cheeks.

"What do I do?" she breathed.

I poked at a box of wrapped cigars, dropped her key into it. Her long fingers got it out smoothly, hid it.

"When you get home you find him. You don't know a thing. Leave the pearls out, leave me out. When they check his prints they'll know he had a record and they'll just figure it was something caught up with him."

I broke my cigarettes open and lit one, watched her for a moment. She didn't move an inch.

"Can you face it down?" I asked. "If you can't, now's the time to speak."

"Of course." Her eyebrows arched. "Do I look like a torturer?"

"You married a crook," I said grimly.

She flushed, which was what I wanted. "He isn't! He's just a damn fool! Nobody thinks any the worse of me, not even the boys down at Headquarters."

"All right. I like it that way. It's not our murder, after all. And if we talk now, you can say goodbye to any share in any reward – even if one is ever paid."

"Darn tootin'," Kathy Horne said pertly. "Oh, the poor little runt," she almost sobbed.

I patted her arm, grinned as heartily as I could and left the Mansion House.

3

THE RELIANCE INDEMNITY Company had offices in the Graas Building, three small rooms that looked like nothing at all. They were a big enough outfit to be as shabby as they liked.

The resident manager was named Lutin, a middle-aged bald-headed man with quiet eyes, dainty fingers that caressed a dappled cigar. He sat behind a large, well-dusted desk and stared peacefully at my chin.

"Marlowe, eh? I've heard of you." He touched my card with a shiny little finger. "What's on your mind?"

I rolled a cigarette around in my fingers and lowered my voice. "Remember the Leander pearls?"

His smile was slow, a little bored. "I'm not likely to forget them. They cost this company one hundred and fifty thousand dollars. I was a cocky young adjuster then."

I said: "I've got an idea. It may be all haywire. It very likely is. But I'd like to try it out. Is your twenty-five-grand reward still good?"

He chuckled. "Twenty grand, Marlowe. We spent the difference ourselves. You're wasting time."

"It's my time. Twenty it is then. How much co-operation can I get?"

"What kind of co-operation?"

"Can I have a letter identifying me to your other branches? In case I have to go out of the state. In case I need kind words from some local law."

"Which way out of the state?"

I smiled at him. He tapped his cigar on the edge of a tray and smiled back. Neither of our smiles was honest.

"No letter," he said. "New York wouldn't stand for it. We have our own tie-up. But all the co-operation you can use, under the hat. And the twenty grand, if you click. Of course you won't."

I lit my cigarette and leaned back, puffed smoke at the ceiling.

"No? Why not? You never got those marbles. They existed, didn't they?"

"Darn right they existed. And if they still do, they belong to us. But two hundred grand doesn't get buried for twenty years — and then get dug up."

"All right. It's still my own time."

He knocked a little ash off his cigar and looked down his eyes at me. "I like your front," he said, "even if you are crazy. But we're a large organization. Suppose I have you covered from now on. What then?"

"I lose. I'll know I'm covered. I'm too long in the game to miss that. I'll quit, give up what I know to the law, and go home."

"Why would you do that?"

I leaned forward over the desk again. "Because," I said slowly, "the guy that had the lead got bumped off today."

"Oh – oh." Lutin rubbed his nose.

"I didn't bump him off," I added.

We didn't talk any more for a little while. Then Lutin said: "You don't want any letter. You wouldn't even carry it. And after your telling me that you know damn well I won't dare give it you."

I stood up, grinned, started for the door. He got up himself, very fast, ran around the desk and put his small neat hand on my arm.

"Listen, I know you're crazy, but if you do get anything, bring it in through our boys. We need the advertising."

"What the hell do you think I live on?" I growled.

"Twenty-five grand."

"I thought it was twenty."

"Twenty-five. And you're still crazy. Sype never had those pearls. If he had, he'd have made some kind of terms with us many years ago."

"Okay," I said. "You've had plenty of time to make up your mind."

We shook hands, grinned at each other like a couple of wise boys who know they're not kidding anybody, but won't give up trying.

It was a quarter to five when I got back to the office. I had a couple of short drinks and stuffed a pipe and sat down to interview my brains. The phone rang.

A woman's voice said: "Marlowe?" It was a small, tight, cold voice. I didn't know it.

"Yeah."

"Better see Rush Madder. Know him?"

"No," I lied. "Why should I see him?"

There was a sudden tinkling, icy-cold laugh on the wire. "On account of a guy had sore feet," the voice said.

The phone clicked. I put my end of it aside, struck a match and stared at the wall until the flame burned my fingers.

Rush Madder was a shyster in the Quorn Building. An ambulance chaser, a small-time fixer, an alibi builder-upper, anything that smelled a little and paid a little more. I hadn't heard of him in connection with any big operations like burning people's feet.

4

IT WAS GETTING toward quitting time on lower Spring Street. Taxis were dawdling close to the curb, stenographers were getting an early start home, streetcars were clogging up, and traffic cops were preventing people from making perfectly legal right turns.

The Quorn Building was a narrow front, the color of dried mustard, with a large case of false teeth in the entrance. The directory held the names of painless dentists, people who teach you how to become a letter carrier, just names, and numbers without any names. Rush Madder, Attorney-at-Law, was in Room 619.

I got out of a jolting open-cage elevator, looked at a dirty spittoon on a dirty rubber mat, walked down a corridor that smelled of butts, and tried the knob below the frosted glass panel of 619. The door was locked. I knocked.

A shadow came against the glass and the door was pulled back with a squeak. I was looking at a thick-set man with a soft round chin, heavy black eyebrows, an oily complexion and a Charlie Chan mustache that made his face look fatter than it was.

He put out a couple of nicotined fingers. "Well, well, the old dog catcher himself. The eye that never forgets. Marlowe is the name, I believe?"

I stepped inside and waited for the door to squeak shut. A bare carpetless room paved in brown linoleum, a flat desk and a roll-top at right angles to it, a big green safe that looked as fireproof as a delicatessen bag, two filing cases, three chairs, a built-in closet and washbowl in the corner by the door.

"Well, well, sit down," Madder said. "Glad to see you." He fussed around behind his desk and adjusted a burst-out seat cushion, sat on it. "Nice of you to drop around. Business?"

I sat down and put a cigarette between my teeth and looked at him. I didn't say a word. I watched him start to sweat. It started up in his hair. Then he grabbed a pencil and made marks on his blotter. Then he looked at me with a quick darting glance, down at his blotter again. He talked – to the blotter.

"Any ideas?" he asked softly.

"About what?"

He didn't look at me. "About how we could do a little business together. Say, in stones."

"Who was the wren?" I asked.

"Huh? What wren?" He still didn't look at me.

"The one that phoned me."

"Did somebody phone you?"

I reached for his telephone, which was the old-fashioned gallows type. I lifted off the receiver and started to dial the number of Police Headquarters, very slowly. I knew he would know that number about as well as he knew his hat.

He reached over and pushed the hook down. "Now, listen," he complained. "You're too fast. What you calling copper for?"

I said slowly: "They want to talk to you. On account of you know a broad that knows a man had sore feet."

"Does it have to be that way?" His collar was too tight now. He yanked at it.

"Not from my side. But if you think I'm going to sit here and let you play with my reflexes, it does."

Madder opened a flat tin of cigarettes and pushed one past his lips with a sound like somebody gutting a fish. His hand shook.

"All right," he said thickly. "All right. Don't get sore."

"Just stop trying to count clouds with me," I growled. "Talk sense. If you've got a job for me, it's probably too dirty for me to touch. But I'll at least listen."

He nodded. He was comfortable now. He knew I was bluffing. He puffed a pale swirl of smoke and watched it float up.

"That's all right," he said evenly. "I play dumb myself once in a while. The thing is we're wise. Carol saw you go to the house and leave it again. No law came."

"Carol?"

"Carol Donovan. Friend of mine. She called you up."

I nodded. "Go ahead."

He didn't say anything. He just sat there and looked at me owlishly.

I grinned and leaned across the desk a little and said: "Here's what's bothering you. You don't know why I went to the house or why, having gone, I didn't yell police. That's easy. I thought it was a secret."

"We're just kidding each other," Madder said sourly.

"All right," I said. "Let's talk about pearls. Does that make it any easier?"

His eyes shone. He wanted to let himself get excited, but he didn't. He kept his voice down, said coolly: "Carol picked him up one night, the little guy. A crazy little number, full of snow, but way back in his noodle an idea. He'd talk about pearls, about an old guy up in the northwest or Canada that swiped them a long time ago and still had them. Only he wouldn't say who the old guy was or where he was. Foxy about that. Holding out. I wouldn't know why."

"He wanted to get his feet burned," I said.

Madder's lips shook and another fine sweat showed in his hair.

"I didn't do that," he said thickly.

"You or Carol, what's the odds? The little guy died. They can make murder out of it. You didn't find out what you wanted to know. That's why I'm here. You think I have information you didn't get. Forget it. If I knew enough, I wouldn't be here, and if you knew enough, you wouldn't want me here. Check?"

He grinned, very slowly, as if it hurt him. He struggled up in his chair and dragged a deeper drawer out from the side of his desk, put a nicely molded brown bottle up on the desk, and two striped glasses. He whispered: "Two-way split. You and me. I'm cutting Carol out. She's too damn rough, Marlowe. I've seen hard women, but she's the bluing on armor plate. And you'd never think it to look at her, would you?"

"Have I seen her?"

"I guess so. She says you did."

"Oh, the girl in the Dodge."

He nodded, and poured two good-sized drinks, put the bottle down and stood up. "Water? I like it in mine."

"No," I said, "but why cut me in? I don't know any more than you mentioned. Or very little. Certainly not as much as you must know to go that far."

He leered across the glasses. "I know where I can get fifty grand for the Leander pearls, twice what you could get. I can give you yours and still have mine. You've got the front I need to work in the open. How about the water?"

"No water," I said.

He went across to the built-in wash place and ran the water and came back with his glass half full. He sat down again, grinned, lifted it.

We drank.

5

SO FAR I had only made four mistakes. The first was mixing in at all, even for Kathy Horne's sake. The second was staying mixed after I found Peeler Mardo dead. The third was letting Rush Madder see I knew what he was talking about. The fourth, the whiskey, was the worst.

It tasted funny even on the way down. Then there was that sudden moment of sharp lucidity when I knew, exactly as though I had seen it, that he had switched his drink for a harmless one cached in the closet.

I sat still for a moment, with the empty glass at my fingers' ends, gathering my strength. Madder's face began to get large and moony and vague. A fat smile jerked in and out under his Charlie Chan mustache as he watched me.

I reached back into my hip pocket and pulled out a loosely wadded handkerchief. The small sap inside it didn't seem to show. At least Madder didn't move, after his first grab under the coat.

I stood up and swayed forward drunkenly and smacked him square on the top of the head.

He gagged. He started to get up. I tapped him on the jaw. He became limp and his hand sweeping down from under his coat knocked his glass over on the desk top. I straightened it, stood silent, listening, struggling with a rising wave of nauseous stupor.

I went over to a communicating door and tried the knob. It was locked. I was staggering by now. I dragged an office chair to the entrance door and propped the back of it under the knob. I leaned against the door panting, gritting my teeth, cursing myself. I got handcuffs out and started back towards Madder.

A very pretty black-haired, gray-eyed girl stepped out of the clothes closet and poked a .32 at me.

She wore a blue suit cut with a lot of snap. An inverted saucer of a hat came down in a hard line across her forehead. Shiny black hair showed at the sides. Her eyes were slate-gray, cold, and yet lighthearted. Her face was fresh and young and delicate, and as hard as a chisel.

"All right, Marlowe. Lie down and sleep it off. You're through."

I stumbled towards her waving my sap. She shook her head. When her face moved it got large before my eyes. Its outlines changed and wobbled. The gun in her hand looked like anything from a tunnel to a toothpick.

"Don't be a goof, Marlowe," she said. "A few hours' sleep for you, a few hours' start for us. Don't make me shoot. I would."

"Damn you," I mumbled. "I believe you would."

"Right as rain, toots. I'm a lady that wants her own way. That's fine. Sit down."

The floor rose up and bumped me. I sat on it as on a raft in a rough sea. I braced myself on flat hands. I could hardly feel the floor. My hands were numb. My whole body was numb.

I tried to stare her down. "Ha-a! L-lady K-killer!" I giggled.

She threw a chilly laugh at me which I only just barely heard. Drums were beating in my head now, war drums from a far-off jungle. Waves of light were moving, and dark shadows and a rustle as of a wind in treetops. I didn't want to lie down. I lay down.

The girl's voice came from very far off, an elfin voice.

"Two-way split, eh? He doesn't like my method, eh? Bless his big soft heart. We'll see about him."

Vaguely as I floated off I seemed to feel a dull jar that might have been a shot. I hoped she had shot Madder, but she hadn't. She had merely helped me on my way out – with my own sap.

★

When I came around again it was night. Something clacked overhead with a heavy sound. Through the open window beyond the desk yellow light splashed on the high side walls of a building. The thing clacked again and the light went off. An advertising sign on the roof.

I got up off the floor like a man climbing out of thick mud. I waded over to the washbowl, sloshed water on my face, felt the top of my head and winced, waded back to the door and found the light switch.

Strewn papers lay around the desk, broken pencils, envelopes, an empty brown whiskey bottle, cigarette ends and ashes. The débris of hastily emptied drawers. I didn't bother going through any of it. I left the office, rode down to the street in the shuddering elevator, slid into a bar and had a brandy, then got my car and drove on home.

I changed clothes, packed a bag, had some whiskey and answered the telephone. It was about nine-thirty.

Kathy Horne's voice said: "So you're not gone yet. I hoped you wouldn't be."

"Alone?" I asked, still thick in the voice.

"Yes, but I haven't been. The house has been full of coppers for hours. They were very nice, considering. Old grudge of some kind, they figured."

"And the line is likely bugged now," I growled. "Where was I supposed to be going?"

"Well – you know. Your girl told me."

"Little dark girl? Very cool? Name of Carol Donovan?"

"She had your card. Why, wasn't it – "

"I don't have any girl," I said grimly. "And I bet that just very casually, without thinking at all, a name slipped past your lips – the name of a town up north. Did it?"

"Ye-es," Kathy Horne admitted weakly.

I caught the night plane north.

It was a nice trip except that I had a sore head and a raging thirst for ice water.

6

THE SNOQUALMIE HOTEL in Olympia was on Capitol Way, fronting on the usual square city block of park. I left by the coffee-shop door and walked down a hill to where the last, loneliest reach of Puget Sound died and decomposed against a line of disused wharves. Corded firewood filled the foreground and old men pottered about in the middle of the stacks, or sat on boxes with pipes in their mouths and signs behind their heads reading: "Firewood and Split Kindling. Free Delivery."

Behind them a low cliff rose and the vast pines of the north loomed against a gray-blue sky.

Two of the old men sat on boxes about twenty feet apart, ignoring each other. I drifted near one of them. He wore corduroy pants and what had been a red and black Mackinaw. His felt hat showed the sweat of twenty summers. One of his hands clutched a short black pipe, and with the grimed fingers of the other he slowly, carefully, ecstatically jerked at a long curling hair that grew out of his nose.

I set a box on end, sat down, filled my own pipe, lit it, puffed a cloud of smoke. I waved a hand at the water and said: "You'd never think that ever met the Pacific Ocean."

He looked at me.

I said: "Dead end – quiet, restful, like your town. I like a town like this." He went on looking at me.

"I'll bet," I said, "that a man that's been around a town like this knows everybody in it and in the country near it."

He said: "How much you bet?"

I took a silver dollar out of my pocket. They still had a few up there. The old man looked it over, nodded, suddenly yanked the long hair out of his nose and held it up against the light.

"You'd lose," he said.

I put the dollar down on my knee. "Know anybody around here that keeps a lot of goldfish?" I asked.

He stared at the dollar. The other old man near by was wearing overalls and shoes without any laces. He stared at the dollar. They both spit at the same instant. The first old man said: "Leetle deef." He got up slowly and went over to a shack built of old boards of uneven lengths. He went into it, banged the door.

The second old man threw his axe down pettishly, spit in the direction of the closed door and went off among the stacks of cordwood.

The door of the shack opened, the man in the Mackinaw poked his head out of it.

"Sewer crabs is all," he said, and slammed the door again.

I put my dollar in my pocket and went back up the hill. I figured it would take too long to learn their language.

Capitol Way ran north and south. A dull green streetcar shuttled past on the way to a place called Tumwater. In the distance I could see the government buildings. Northward the street passed two hotels and some stores and branched right and left. Right went to Tacoma and Seattle. Left went over a bridge and out to the Olympic Peninsula.

Beyond this right and left turn the street suddenly became old and shabby, with broken asphalt paving, a Chinese restaurant, a boarded-up movie house, a pawnbroker's establishment. A sign jutting over the dirty sidewalk said "Smoke Shop," and in small letters underneath, as if it hoped nobody was looking, "Pool."

I went in past a rack of gaudy magazines and a cigar showcase that had flies inside it. There was a long wooden counter on the left, a few slot machines, a single pool table. Three kids fiddled with the slot machines and a tall thin man with a long nose and no chin played pool all by himself, with a dead cigar in his face.

I sat on a stool and a hard-eyed bald-headed man behind the counter got up from a chair, wiped his hands on a thick gray apron, showed me a gold tooth.

"A little rye," I said. "Know anybody that keeps goldfish?"

"Yeah," he said. "No."

He poured something behind the counter and shoved a thick glass across.

"Two bits."

I sniffed the stuff, wrinkled my nose. "Was it the rye the 'yeah' was for?"

The bald-headed man held up a large bottle with a label that said something about: "Cream of Dixie Straight Rye Whiskey Guaranteed at Least Four Months Old."

"Okay," I said. "I see it just moved in."

I poured some water in it and drank it. It tasted like a cholera culture. I put a quarter on the counter. The barman showed me a gold tooth on the other side of his face and took hold of the counter with two hard hands and pushed his chin at me.

"What was that crack?" he asked, almost gently.

"I just moved in," I said. "I'm looking for some goldfish for the front window. Goldfish."

The barman said very slowly: "Do I look like a guy would know a guy would have goldfish?" His face was a little white.

The long-nosed man who had been playing himself a round of pool racked his cue and strolled over to the counter beside me and threw a nickel on it.

"Draw me a Coke before you wet yourself," he told the barman.

The barman pried himself loose from the counter with a good deal of effort. I looked down to see if his fingers had made any dents in the wood. He drew a Coke, stirred it with a swizzle-stick, dumped it on the bar top, took a deep breath and let it out through his nose, grunted and went away towards a door marked "Toilet."

The long-nosed man lifted his Coke and looked into the smeared mirror behind the bar. The left side of his mouth twitched briefly. A dim voice came from it, saying: "How's Peeler?"

I pressed my thumb and forefinger together, put them to my nose, sniffed, shook my head sadly.

"Hitting it high, huh?"

"Yeah," I said. "I didn't catch the name."

"Call me Sunset. I'm always movin' west. Think he'll stay clammed?"

"He'll stay clammed," I said.

"What's your handle?"

"Dodge Willis, El Paso," I said.

"Got a room somewhere?"

"Hotel."

He put his glass down empty. "Let's dangle."

7

WE WENT UP to my room and sat down and looked at each other over a couple of glasses of Scotch and ice water. Sunset studied me with his close-set expressionless eyes, a little at a time, but very thoroughly in the end, adding it all up.

I sipped my drink and waited. At last he said in his lipless "stir" voice: "How come Peeler didn't come hisself?"

"For the same reason he didn't stay when he was here."

"Meaning which?"

"Figure it out for yourself," I said.

He nodded, just as though I had said something with a meaning. Then: "What's the top price?"

"Twenty-five grand."

"Nuts." Sunset was emphatic, even rude.

I leaned back and lit a cigarette, puffed smoke at the open window and watched the breeze pick it up and tear it to pieces.

"Listen," Sunset complained. "I don't know you from last Sunday's sports section. You may be all to the silk. I just don't know."

"Why'd you brace me?" I asked.

"You had the word, didn't you?"

This was where I took the dive. I grinned at him. "Yeah. Goldfish was the password. The Smoke Shop was the place."

His lack of expression told me I was right. It was one of those breaks you dream of, but don't handle right even in dreams.

"Well, what's the next angle?" Sunset inquired, sucking a piece of ice out of his glass and chewing on it.

I laughed. "Okay, Sunset, I'm satisfied you're cagey. We could go on like this for weeks. Let's put our cards on the table. Where is the old guy?"

Sunset tightened his lips, moistened them, tightened them again. He set his glass down very slowly and his right hand hung lax on his thigh. I knew I had made a mistake, that Peeler knew where the old guy was, exactly. Therefore I should know.

Nothing in Sunset's voice showed I had made a mistake. He said crossly: "You mean why don't I put my cards on the table and you just sit back and look 'em over. Nix."

"Then how do you like this?" I growled. "Peeler's dead."

One eyebrow twitched, and one corner of his mouth. His eyes got a little blanker than before, if possible. His voice rasped lightly, like a finger on dry leather.

"How come?"

"Competition you two didn't know about." I leaned back, smiled.

The gun made a soft metallic blue in the sunshine. I hardly saw where it came from. Then the muzzle was round and dark and empty looking at me.

"You're kidding the wrong guy," Sunset said lifelessly. "I ain't no soft spot for chiselers to lie on."

I folded my arms, taking care that my right hand was outside, in view.

"I would be – if I was kidding. I'm not. Peeler played with a girl and she milked him – up to a point. He didn't tell her where to find the old fellow. So she and her top man went to see Peeler where he lived. They used a hot iron on his feet. He died of the shock."

Sunset looked unimpressed. "I got a lot of room in my ears yet," he said.

"So have I," I snarled, suddenly pretending anger. "Just what the hell have you said that means anything – except that you know Peeler?"

He spun his gun on his trigger finger, watched it spin. "Old man Sype's at Westport," he said casually. "That mean anything to you?"

"Yeah. Has he got the marbles?"

"How the hell would I know?" He steadied the gun again, dropped it to his thigh. It wasn't pointing at me now. "Where's this competish you mentioned?"

"I hope I ditched them," I said. "I'm not too sure. Can I put my hands down and take a drink?"

"Yeah, go ahead. How did you cut in?"

"Peeler roomed with the wife of a friend of mine who's in stir. A straight girl, one you can trust. He let her in and she passed it to me – afterwards."

"After the bump? How many cuts your side? My half is set."

I took my drink, shoved the empty glass away. "The hell it is."

The gun lifted an inch, dropped again. "How many altogether?" he snapped.

"Three, now Peeler's out. If we can hold off the competition."

497

"The feet-toasters? No trouble about that. What they look like?"

"Man named Rush Madder, a shyster down south, fifty, fat, thin down-curving mustache, dark hair thin on top, five-nine, a hundred and eighty, not much guts. The girl, Carol Donovan, black hair, long bob, gray eyes, pretty, small features, twenty-five to -eight, five-two, hundred-twenty, last seen wearing blue, hard as they come. The real iron in the combination."

Sunset nodded indifferently and put his gun away. "We'll soften her, if she pokes her snoot in," he said. "I've got a heap at the house. Let's take the air Westport way and look it over. You might be able to ease in on the goldfish angle. They say he's nuts about them. I'll stay under cover. He's too stir-wise for me. I smell of the bucket."

"Swell," I said heartily. "I'm an old goldfish fancier myself."

Sunset reached for the bottle, poured two fingers of Scotch and put it down. He stood up, twitched his collar straight, then shot his chinless jaw forward as far as it would go.

"But don't make no error, bo. It's goin' to take pressure. It's goin' to mean a run out in the deep woods and some thumb-twisting. Snatch stuff, likely."

"That's okay," I said. "The insurance people are behind us."

Sunset jerked down the points of his vest and rubbed the back of his thin neck. I put my hat on, locked the Scotch in the bag by the chair I'd been sitting in, went over and shut the window.

We started towards the door. Knuckles rattled on it just as I reached for the knob. I gestured Sunset back along the wall. I stared at the door for a moment and then I opened it up.

The two guns came forward almost on the same level, one small – a .32, one a big Smith & Wesson. They couldn't come into the room abreast, so the girl came in first.

"Okay, hot shot," she said dryly. "Ceiling zero. See if you can reach it."

8

I BACKED SLOWLY into the room. The two visitors bored in on me, either side. I tripped over my bag and fell backwards, hit the floor and rolled on my side groaning.

Sunset said casually: "H'ist 'em folks. Pretty now!"

Two heads jerked away from looking down at me and then I had my gun loose, down at my side. I kept on groaning.

There was a silence. I didn't hear any guns fall. The door of the room was still wide open and Sunset was flattened against the wall more or less behind it.

The girl said between her teeth: "Cover the shamus, Rush – and shut the door. Skinny can't shoot here. Nobody can." Then, in a whisper I barely caught, she added: "Slam it!"

Rush Madder waddled backwards across the room keeping the Smith & Wesson pointed my way. His back was to Sunset and the thought of that made his eyes roll. I could have shot him easily enough, but it wasn't the play. Sunset stood with his feet spread and his tongue showing. Something that could have been a smile wrinkled his flat eyes.

He stared at the girl and she stared at him. Their guns stared at each other.

Rush Madder reached the door, grabbed the edge of it and gave it a hard swing. I knew exactly what was going to happen. As the door slammed the .32 was going to go off. It wouldn't be heard if it went off at the right instant. The explosion would be lost in the slamming of the door.

I reached out and took hold of Carol Donovan's ankle and jerked it hard.

The door slammed. Her gun went off and chipped the ceiling.

She whirled on me kicking. Sunset said in his tight but somewhat penetrating drawl: "If this is it, this is it. Let's go!" The hammer clicked back on his Colt.

Something in his voice steadied Carol Donovan. She relaxed, let her automatic fall to her side and stepped away from me with a vicious look back.

Madder turned the key in the door and leaned against the wood, breathing noisily. His hat had tipped over one ear and the ends of two strips of adhesive showed under the brim.

Nobody moved while I had these thoughts. There was no sound of feet outside in the hall, no alarm. I got up on my knees, slid my gun out of sight, rose on my feet and went over to the window. Nobody down on the sidewalk was staring up at the upper floors of the Snoqualmie Hotel.

I sat on the broad old-fashioned sill and looked faintly embarrassed, as though the minister had said a bad word.

The girl snapped at me: "Is this lug your partner?"

I didn't answer. Her face flushed slowly and her eyes burned. Madder put a hand out and fussed: "Now listen, Carol, now listen here. This sort of act ain't the way – "

"Shut up!"

"Yeah," Madder said in a clogged voice. "Sure."

Sunset looked the girl over lazily for the third or fourth time. His gun hand rested easily against his hipbone and his whole attitude was of complete relaxation. Having seen him pull his gun once I hoped the girl wasn't fooled.

He said slowly: "We've heard about you two. What's your offer? I wouldn't listen even, only I can't stand a shooting rap."

The girl said: "There's enough in it for four." Madder nodded his big head vigorously, almost managed a smile.

Sunset glanced at me. I nodded. "Four it is," he sighed.

"But that's the top. We'll go to my place and gargle. I don't like it here."

"We must look simple," the girl said nastily.

"Kill-simple," Sunset drawled. "I've met lots of them. That's why we're going to talk it over. It's not a shooting play."

Carol Donovan slipped a suede bag from under her left

arm and tucked her .32 into it. She smiled. She was pretty when she smiled.

"My ante is in," she said quietly. "I'll play. Where is the place?"

"Out Water Street. We'll go in a hack."

"Lead on, sport."

We went out of the room and down in the elevator, four friendly people walking out through a lobby full of antlers and stuffed birds and pressed wildflowers in glass frames. The taxi went out Capitol Way, past the square, past a big red apartment house that was too big for the town except when the Legislature was sitting. Along car tracks past the distant Capitol buildings and the high closed gates of the governor's mansion.

Oak trees bordered the sidewalks. A few largish residences showed behind garden walls. The taxi shot past them and veered on to a road that led towards the tip of the Sound. In a short while a house showed in a narrow clearing between tall trees. Water glistened far back behind the tree trunks. The house had a roofed porch, a small lawn rotten with weeds and overgrown bushes. There was a shed at the end of a dirt driveway and an antique touring car squatted under the shed.

We got out and I paid the taxi. All four of us carefully watched it out of sight. Then Sunset said: "My place is upstairs. There's a schoolteacher lives down below. She ain't home. Let's go up and gargle."

We crossed the lawn to the porch and Sunset threw a door open, pointed up narrow steps.

"Ladies first. Lead on, beautiful. Nobody locks a door in this town."

The girl gave him a cool glance and passed him to go up the stairs. I went next, then Madder, Sunset last.

The single room that made up most of the second floor was dark from the trees, had a dormer window, a wide daybed pushed back under the slope of the roof, a table, some wicker chairs, a small radio and a round black stove in the middle of the floor.

Sunset drifted into a kitchenette and came back with a square bottle and some glasses. He poured drinks, lifted one and left the others on the table.

We helped ourselves and sat down.

Sunset put his drink down in a lump, leaned over to put his glass on the floor and came up with his Colt out.

I heard Madder's gulp in the sudden cold silence. The girl's mouth twitched as if she were going to laugh. Then she leaned forward, holding her glass on top of her bag with her left hand.

Sunset slowly drew his lips into a thin straight line. He said slowly and carefully: "Feet-burners, huh?"

Madder choked, started to spread his fat hands. The Colt flicked at him. He put his hands on his knees and clutched his kneecaps.

"And suckers at that," Sunset went on tiredly. "Burn a guy's feet to make him sing and then walk right into the parlor of one of his pals. You couldn't tie that with Christmas ribbon."

Madder said jerkily: "All r-right. W-what's the p-pay-off?" The girl smiled slightly but she didn't say anything.

Sunset grinned. "Rope," he said softly. "A lot of rope tied in hard knots, with water on it. Then me and my pal trundle off to catch fire-flies – pearls to you – and when we come back – " He stopped, drew his left hand across the front of his throat. "Like the idea?" He glanced at me.

"Yeah, but don't make a song about it," I said. "Where's the rope?"

"Bureau," Sunset answered, and pointed with one ear at the corner.

I started in that direction, by way of the walls. Madder made a sudden thin whimpering noise and his eyes turned up in his head and he fell straight forward off the chair on his face, in a dead faint.

That jarred Sunset. He hadn't expected anything so foolish. His right hand jerked around until the Colt was pointing down at Madder's back.

The girl slipped her hand under her bag. The bag lifted an inch. The gun that was caught there in a trick clip – the gun that Sunset thought was inside the bag – spat and flamed briefly.

Sunset coughed. His Colt boomed and a piece of wood detached itself from the back of the chair Madder had been sitting in. Sunset dropped the Colt and put his chin down on his chest and tried to look at the ceiling. His long legs slid out in front of him and his heels made a rasping sound on the floor. He sat like that limp, his chin on his chest, his eyes looking upward. Dead as a pickled walnut.

I kicked Miss Donovan's chair out from under her and she banged down on her side in a swirl of silken legs. Her hat went crooked on her head. She yelped. I stood on her hand and then shifted suddenly and kicked her gun clear across the attic.

"Get up."

She got up slowly, backed away from me biting her lip, savage-eyed, suddenly a nasty-faced little brat at bay. She kept on backing until the wall stopped her. Her eyes glittered in a ghastly face.

I glanced down at Madder, went over to a closed door. A bathroom was behind it. I reversed a key and gestured at the girl.

"In."

She walked stiff-legged across the floor and passed in front of me, almost touching me.

"Listen a minute, shamus – "

I pushed her through the door and slammed it and turned the key. It was all right with me if she wanted to jump out of the window. I had seen the windows from below.

I went across to Sunset, felt him, felt the small hard lump of keys on a ring in his pocket, and got them out without quite knocking him off his chair. I didn't look for anything else.

There were car keys on the ring.

I looked at Madder again, noticed that his fingers were as white as snow. I went down the narrow dark stairs to the porch, around to the side of the house and got into the old touring car under the shed. One of the keys on the ring fitted its ignition lock.

The car took a beating before it started up and let me back it down the dirt driveway to the curb. Nothing moved in the house that I saw or heard. The tall pines behind and beside the house stirred their upper branches listlessly and a cold heartless sunlight sneaked through them intermittently as they moved.

I drove back to Capitol Way and downtown again as fast as I dared, past the square and the Snoqualmie Hotel and over the bridge towards the Pacific Ocean and Westport.

9

AN HOUR'S FAST driving through thinned-out timberland, interrupted by three stops for water and punctuated by the cough of a head gasket leak, brought me within sound of surf. The broad white road, striped with yellow down the center, swept around the flank of a hill, a distant cluster of buildings loomed up in front of the shine of the ocean, and the road forked. The left fork was signposted: "Westport – 9 Miles," and didn't go towards the buildings. It crossed a rusty cantilever bridge and plunged into a region of wind-distorted apple orchards.

Twenty minutes more and I chugged into Westport, a sandy spit of land with scattered frame houses dotted over rising ground behind it. The end of the spit a long narrow pier, and the end of the pier a cluster of sailing boats with half-lowered sails flapping against their single masts. And beyond them a buoyed channel and a long irregular line where the water creamed on a hidden sandbar.

Beyond the sandbar the Pacific rolled over to Japan. This was the last outpost of the coast, the farthest west a man could go and still be on the mainland of the United States. A swell place for an ex-convict to hide out with a couple of somebody else's pearls the size of new potatoes — if he didn't have any enemies.

I pulled up in front of a cottage that had a sign in the front yard: "*Luncheons, Teas, Dinners.*" A small rabbit-faced man with freckles was waving a garden rake at two black chickens. The chickens appeared to be sassing him back. He turned when the engine of Sunset's car coughed itself still.

I got out, went through a wicket gate, pointed to the sign. "Luncheon ready?"

He threw the rake at the chickens, wiped his hands on his trousers and leered. "The wife put that up," he confided to me in a thin, impish voice. "Ham and eggs is what it means."

"Ham and eggs get along with me," I said.

We went into the house. There were three tables covered with patterned oilcloth, some chromos on the walls, a full-rigged ship in a bottle on the mantel. I sat down. The host went away through a swing door and somebody yelled at him and a sizzling noise was heard from the kitchen. He came back and leaned over my shoulder, put some cutlery and a paper napkin on the oilcloth.

"Too early for apple brandy, ain't it?" he whispered.

I told him how wrong he was. He went away again and came back with glasses and a quart of clear amber fluid. He sat down with me and poured. A rich baritone voice in the kitchen was singing "Chloe," over the sizzling.

We clinked glasses and drank and waited for the heat to crawl up our spines.

"Stranger, ain't you?" the little man asked.

I said I was.

"From Seattle maybe? That's a nice piece of goods you got on."

"Seattle," I agreed.

"We don't git many strangers," he said, looking at my left ear. "Ain't on the way to nowheres. Now before repeal – " he stopped, shifted his sharp woodpecker gaze to my other ear.

"Ah, before repeal," I said with a large gesture, and drank knowingly.

He leaned over and breathed on my chin. "Hell, you could load up in any fish stall on the pier. The stuff come in under catches of crabs and oysters. Hell, Westport was lousy with it. They give the kids cases of Scotch to play with. There wasn't a car in this town that slept in a garage, mister. The garages was full to the roof of Canadian hooch. Hell, they had a coastguard cutter off the pier watchin' the boats unload one day every week. Friday. Always the same day." He winked.

I puffed a cigarette and the sizzling noise and the baritone rendering of "Chloe" went on in the kitchen.

"But hell, you wouldn't be in the liquor business," he said.

"Hell, no. I'm a goldfish buyer," I said.

"Okay," he said sulkily.

I poured us another round of the apple brandy. "This bottle is on me," I said. "And I'm taking a couple more with me."

He brightened up. "What did you say the name was?"

"Marlowe. You think I'm kidding you about the goldfish. I'm not."

"Hell, there ain't a livin' in them little fellers, is there?"

I held my sleeve out. "You said it was a nice piece of goods. Sure there's a living out of the fancy brands. New brands, new types all the time. My information is there's an old guy down here somewhere that has a real collection. Maybe would sell it. Some he'd bred himself."

A large woman with a mustache kicked the swing door open a foot and yelled: "Pick up the ham and eggs!"

My host scuttled across and came back with my food. I ate. He watched me minutely. After a time he suddenly smacked his skinny leg under the table.

"Old Wallace," he chuckled. "Sure, you come to see old Wallace. Hell, we don't know him right well. He don't act neighborly."

He turned around in his chair and pointed out through the sleazy curtains at a distant hill. On top of the hill was a yellow and white house that shone in the sun.

"Hell, that's where he lives. He's got a mess of them. Goldfish, huh? Hell, you could bend me with an eye dropper."

That ended my interest in the little man. I gobbled my food, paid off for it and for three quarts of apple brandy at a dollar a quart, shook hands and went back out to the touring car.

There didn't seem to be any hurry. Rush Madder would come out of his faint, and he would turn the girl loose. But they didn't know anything about Westport. Sunset hadn't mentioned the name in their presence. They didn't know it when they reached Olympia or they would have gone there at once. And if they had listened outside my room at the hotel, they would have known I wasn't alone. They hadn't acted as if they knew that when they charged in.

I had lots of time. I drove down to the pier and looked it over. It looked tough. There were fish stalls, drinking dives, a tiny honkytonk for the fishermen, a pool room, an arcade of slot machines and smutty peep shows. Bait fish squirmed and darted in big wooden tanks down in the water along the piles. There were loungers and they looked like trouble for anyone that tried to interfere with them. I didn't see any law enforcement around.

I drove back up the hill to the yellow and white house. It stood very much alone, four blocks from the next nearest dwelling. There were flowers in front, a trimmed green lawn, a rock garden. A woman in a brown and white print dress was popping at aphids with a spray gun.

I let my heap stall itself, got out and took my hat off.

"Mister Wallace live here?"

She had a handsome face, quiet, firm-looking. She nodded.

"Would you like to see him?" She had a quiet firm voice, a good accent.

It didn't sound like the voice of a train robber's wife.

I gave her my name, said I'd been hearing about his fish down in the town. I was interested in fancy goldfish.

She put the spray gun down and went into the house. Bees buzzed around my head, large fuzzy bees that wouldn't mind the cold wind off the sea. Far off like background music the surf pounded on the sandbars. The northern sunshine seemed bleak to me, had no heat in the core of it.

The woman came out of the house and held the door open.

"He's at the top of the stairs," she said, "if you'd like to go up."

I went past a couple of rustic rockers and into the house of the man who had stolen the Leander pearls.

10

FISH TANKS WERE all around the big room, two tiers of them on braced shelves, big oblong tanks with metal frames, some with lights over them and some with lights down in them. Water grasses were festooned in careless patterns behind the algae-coated glass and the water held a ghostly greenish light and through the greenish light moved fish of all the colors of rainbow.

There were long slim fish like golden darts and Japanese Veiltails with fantastic trailing tails, and X-ray fish as transparent as colored glass, tiny guppies half an inch long, calico popeyes spotted like a bride's apron, and big lumbering Chinese Moors with telescope eyes, froglike faces and unnecessary fins, waddling through the green water like fat men going to lunch.

Most of the light came from a big sloping skylight. Under the skylight at a bare wooden table a tall gaunt man stood with a squirming red fish in his left hand, and in his right hand a safety-razor blade backed with adhesive tape.

He looked at me from under wide gray eyebrows. His eyes were sunken, colorless, opaque. I went over beside him and looked down at the fish he was holding.

"Fungus?" I asked.

He nodded slowly. "White fungus." He put the fish down on the table and carefully spread its dorsal fin. The fin was ragged and split and the ragged edges had a mossy white color.

"White fungus," he said, "ain't so bad. I'll trim this feller up and he'll be right as rain. What can I do for you, mister?"

I rolled a cigarette around in my fingers and smiled at him.

"Like people," I said. "The fish, I mean. They get things wrong with them."

He held the fish against the wood and trimmed off the ragged part of the fin. He spread the tail and trimmed that. The fish had stopped squirming.

"Some you can cure," he said, "and some you can't. You can't cure swimming-bladder disease, for instance." He glanced up at me. "This don't hurt him, 'case you think it does," he said. "You can shock a fish to death but you can't hurt it like a person."

He put the razor blade down and dipped a cotton swab in some purplish liquid, painted the cut places. Then he dipped a finger in a jar of white vaseline and smeared that over. He dropped the fish in a small tank off to one side of the room. The fish swam around peacefully, quite content.

The gaunt man wiped his hands, sat down at the edge of a bench and stared at me with lifeless eyes. He had been good-looking once, a long time ago.

"You interested in fish?" he asked. His voice had the quiet careful murmur of the cell block and the exercise yard.

I shook my head. "Not particularly. That was just an excuse. I came a long way to see you, Mister Sype."

He moistened his lips and went on staring at me. When his voice came again it was tired and soft.

"Wallace is the name, mister."

I puffed a smoke ring and poked my finger through it. "For my job it's got to be Sype."

He leaned forward and dropped his hands between his spread bony knees, clasped them together. Big gnarled hands that had done a lot of hard work in their time. His head tipped up at me and his dead eyes were cold under the shaggy brows. But his voice stayed soft.

"Haven't seen a dick in a year. To talk to. What's your lay?"

"Guess," I said.

His voice got still softer. "Listen, dick. I've got a nice home here, quiet. Nobody bothers me any more. Nobody's got a right to. I got a pardon straight from the White House. I've got the fish to play with and a man gets fond of anything he takes care of. I don't owe the world a nickel. I paid up. My wife's got enough dough for us to live on. All I want is to be let alone, dick." He stopped talking, shook his head once. "You can't burn me up – not any more."

I didn't say anything. I smiled a little and watched him.

"Nobody can touch me," he said. "I got a pardon straight from the President's study. I just want to be let alone."

I shook my head and kept on smiling at him. "That's the one thing you can never have – until you give in."

"Listen," he said softly. "You may be new on this case. It's kind of fresh to you. You want to make a rep for yourself. But me, I've had almost twenty years of it, and so have a lot of other people, some of 'em pretty smart people too. They know I don't have nothing that don't belong to me. Never did have. Somebody else got it."

"The mail clerk," I said. "Sure."

"Listen," he said, still softly. "I did my time. I know all the angles. I know they ain't going to stop wondering – long as anybody's alive that remembers. I know they're going to send some punk out once in a while to kind of stir it up. That's okay. No hard feelings. Now what do I do to get you to go home again?"

I shook my head and stared past his shoulder at the fish drifting in their big silent tanks. I felt tired. The quiet of the house made ghosts in my brain, ghosts of a lot of years ago. A train pounding through the darkness, a stick-up hidden in a mail car, a gun flash, a dead clerk on the floor, a silent drop off at some water tank, a man who had kept a secret for nineteen years – almost kept it.

"You made one mistake," I said slowly. "Remember a fellow named Peeler Mardo?"

He lifted his head. I could see him searching in his memory. The name didn't seem to mean anything to him.

"A fellow you knew in Leavenworth," I said. "A little runt that was in there for splitting twenty-dollar bills and putting phony backs on them."

"Yeah," he said. "I remember."

"You told him you had the pearls," I said.

I could see he didn't believe me. "I must have been kidding him," he said slowly, emptily.

"Maybe. But here's the point. He didn't think so. He was up in this country a while ago with a pal, a guy who called himself Sunset. They saw you somewhere and Peeler recognized you. He got to thinking how he could make himself some jack. But he was a coke hound and he talked in his sleep. A girl got wise and then another girl and a shyster. Peeler got his feet burned and he's dead."

Sype stared at me unblinkingly. The lines at the corners of his mouth deepened.

I waved my cigarette and went on: "We don't know how much he told, but the shyster and a girl are in Olympia. Sunset's in Olympia, only he's dead. They killed him. I wouldn't know if they know where you are or not. But they will sometime, or others like them. You can wear the cops down, if they can't find the pearls and you don't try to sell them. You can wear the insurance company down and even the postal men."

Sype didn't move a muscle. His big knotty hands clenched between his knees didn't move. His dead eyes just stared.

"But you can't wear the chiselers down," I said. "They'll never lay off. There'll always be a couple or three with time enough and money enough and meanness enough to bear down. They'll find out what they want to know some way. They'll snatch your wife or take you out in the woods and give you the works. And you'll have to come through . . . Now I've got a decent, square proposition."

"Which bunch are you?" Sype asked suddenly. "I thought you smelled of dick, but I ain't so sure now."

"Insurance," I said. "Here's the deal. Twenty-five grand reward in all. Five grand to the girl that passed me the info. She got it on the square and she's entitled to that cut. Ten grand to me. I've done all the work and looked into all the guns. Ten grand to you, through me. You couldn't get a nickel direct. Is there anything in it? How does it look?"

"It looks fine," he said gently. "Except for one thing, I don't have no pearls, dick."

I scowled at him. That was my wad. I didn't have any more. I straightened away from the wall and dropped a cigarette end on the wood floor, crushed it out. I turned to go.

He stood up and put a hand out. "Wait a minute," he said gravely, "and I'll prove it to you."

He went across the floor in front of me and out of the room. I stared at the fish and chewed my lip. I heard the sound of a car engine somewhere, not very close. I heard a drawer open and shut, apparently in a nearby room.

Sype came back into the fish room. He had a shiny Colt

.45 in his gaunt fist. It looked as long as a man's forearm.

He pointed it at me and said: "I got pearls in this, six of them. Lead pearls. I can comb a fly's whiskers at sixty yards. You ain't no dick. Now get up and blow – and tell your red-hot friends I'm ready to shoot their teeth out any day of the week and twice on Sunday."

I didn't move. There was a madness in the man's dead eyes. I didn't dare move.

"That's grandstand stuff," I said slowly. "I can prove I'm a dick. You're an ex-con and it's a felony just having that rod. Put it down and talk sense."

The car I had heard seemed to be stopping outside the house. Brakes whined on drums. Feet clattered, up a walk, up steps. Sudden sharp voices, a caught exclamation.

Sype backed across the room until he was between the table and a big twenty- or thirty-gallon tank. He grinned at me, the wide clear grin of a fighter at bay.

"I see your friends kind of caught up with you," he drawled. "Take your gat out and drop it on the floor while you still got time – and breath."

I didn't move. I looked at the wiry hair above his eyes. I looked into his eyes. I knew if I moved – even to do what he told me – he would shoot.

Steps came up the stairs. They were clogged, shuffling steps, with a hint of struggle in them.

Three people came into the room.

11

MRS. SYPE CAME in first, stiff-legged, her eyes glazed, her arms bent rigidly at the elbows and the hands clawing straight forward at nothing, feeling for something that wasn't there. There was a gun in her back, Carol Donovan's small .32, held efficiently in Carol Donovan's small ruthless hand.

Madder came last. He was drunk, brave from the bottle, flushed and savage. He threw the Smith & Wesson down on me and leered.

Carol Donovan pushed Mrs. Sype aside. The older woman stumbled into the corner and sank down on her knees, blank-eyed.

Sype stared at the Donovan girl. He was rattled because she was a girl and young and pretty. He hadn't been used to the type. Seeing her took the fire out of him. If men had come in he would have shot them to pieces.

The small dark white-faced girl faced him coldly, said in her tight chilled voice: "All right, Dad. Shed the heater. Make it smooth now."

Sype leaned down slowly, not taking his eyes off her. He put his enormous frontier Colt on the floor.

"Kick it away from you, Dad."

Sype kicked it. The gun skidded across the bare boards, over towards the center of the room.

"That's the way, old-timer. You hold on him, Rush, while I unrod the dick."

The two guns swiveled and the hard gray eyes were looking at me now. Madder went a little way towards Sype and pointed his Smith & Wesson at Sype's chest.

The girl smiled, not a nice smile. "Bright boy, eh? You sure stick your neck out all the time, don't you? Made a beef, shamus. Didn't frisk your skinny pal. He had a little map in one shoe."

"I didn't need one," I said smoothly, and grinned at her.

I tried to make the grin appealing, because Mrs. Sype was moving her knees on the floor, and every move took her nearer to Sype's Colt.

"But you're all washed up now, you and your big smile. Hoist the mitts while I get your iron. Up, mister."

She was a girl, about five feet two inches tall, and weighed around a hundred and twenty. Just a girl. I was six feet and a half-inch, weighed one-ninety-five. I put my hands up and hit her on the jaw.

That was crazy, but I had all I could stand of the Donovan–Madder act, the Donovan–Madder guns, the Donovan–Madder tough talk. I hit her on the jaw.

She went back a yard and her popgun went off. A slug burned my ribs. She started to fall. Slowly, like a slow motion picture, she fell. There was something silly about it.

Mrs. Sype got the Colt and shot her in the back.

Madder whirled and the instant he turned Sype rushed him. Madder jumped back and yelled and covered Sype again. Sype stopped cold and the wide crazy grin came back on his gaunt face.

The slug from the Colt knocked the girl forward as though a door had whipped in a high wind. A flurry of blue cloth, something thumped my chest – her head. I saw her face for a moment as she bounced back, a strange face that I had never seen before.

Then she was a huddled thing on the floor at my feet, small, deadly, extinct, with redness coming out from under her, and the tall quiet woman behind her with the smoking Colt held in both hands.

Madder shot Sype twice. Sype plunged forward still grinning and hit the end of the table. The purplish liquid he had used on the sick fish sprayed up over him. Madder shot him again as he was falling.

I jerked my Luger out and shot Madder in the most painful place I could think of that wasn't likely to be fatal – the back of the knee. He went down exactly as if he had tripped over a hidden wire. I had cuffs on him before he even started to groan.

I kicked guns here and there and went over to Mrs. Sype and took the big Colt out of her hands.

It was very still in the room for a little while. Eddies of smoke drifted towards the skylight, filmy gray, pale in the afternoon sun. I heard the surf booming in the distance. Then I heard a whistling sound close at hand.

It was Sype trying to say something. His wife crawled across to him, still on her knees, huddled beside him. There was blood on his lips and bubbles. He blinked hard, trying to clear his head. He smiled up at her. His whistling voice said very faintly: "The Moors, Hattie – the Moors."

Then his neck went loose and the smile melted off his face. His head rolled to one side on the bare floor.

Mrs. Sype touched him, then got very slowly to her feet and looked at me, calm, dry-eyed.

She said in a low clear voice: "Will you help me carry him to the bed? I don't like him here with these people."

I said: "Sure. What was that he said?"

"I don't know. Some nonsense about his fish, I think."

I lifted Sype's shoulders and she took his feet and we carried him into the bedroom and put him on the bed. She folded his hands on his chest and shut his eyes. She went over and pulled the blinds down.

"That's all, thank you," she said, not looking at me. "The telephone is downstairs."

She sat down in a chair beside the bed and put her head down on the coverlet near Sype's arm.

I went out of the room and shut the door.

12

MADDER'S LEG WAS bleeding slowly, not dangerously. He stared at me with fear-crazed eyes while I tied a tight handkerchief above his knee. I figured he had a cut tendon and maybe a chipped kneecap. He might walk a little lame when they came to hang him.

I went downstairs and stood on the porch looking at the two cars in front, then down the hill towards the pier. Nobody could have told where the shots came from, unless he happened to be passing. Quite likely nobody had even noticed them. There was probably shooting in the woods around there a good deal.

I went back into the house and looked at the crank telephone on the living-room wall, but didn't touch it yet. Something was bothering me. I lit a cigarette and stared out of the window and a ghost voice said in my ears: "The Moors, Hattie. The Moors."

I went back up to the fish room. Madder was groaning now, thick panting groans. What did I care about a torturer like Madder?

The girl was quite dead. None of the tanks was hit. The fish swam peacefully in their green water, slow and peaceful and easy. They didn't care about Madder either.

The tank with the black Chinese Moors in it was over in the corner, about ten-gallon size. There were just four of them, big fellows, about four inches body length, coal black all over. Two of them were sucking oxygen on top of the water and two were waddling sluggishly on the bottom. They had thick deep bodies with a lot of spreading tail and high dorsal fins and their bulging telescope eyes that made them look like frogs when they were head towards you.

I watched them fumbling around in the green stuff that was growing in the tank. A couple of red pond snails were window-cleaning. The two on the bottom looked thicker and more sluggish than the two on the top. I wondered why.

There was a long-handled strainer made of woven string lying between two of the tanks. I got it and fished down in the tank, trapped one of the big Moors and lifted it out. I turned it over in the net, looked at its faintly silver belly. I saw something that looked like a suture. I felt the place. There was a hard lump under it.

I pulled the other one off the bottom. Same suture, same hard round lump. I got one of the two that had been sucking air on top. No suture, no hard round lump. It was harder to catch too.

I put it back in the tank. My business was with the other two. I like goldfish as well as the next man, but business is business and crime is crime. I took my coat off and rolled my sleeves up and picked the razor blade backed with adhesive tape off the table.

It was a very messy job. It took about five minutes. Then they lay in the palm of my hand, three-quarters of an inch in diameter, heavy, perfectly round, milky white and shimmering with that inner light no other jewel has. The Leander pearls.

I washed them off, wrapped them in my handkerchief, rolled down my sleeves and put my coat back on. I looked at Madder, at his little pain-and fear-tortured eyes, the sweat on his face. I didn't care anything about Madder. He was a killer, a torturer.

I went out of the fish room. The bedroom door was still shut. I went down below and cranked the wall telephone.

"This is the Wallace place at Westport," I said. "There's been an accident. We need a doctor and we'll have to have the police. What can you do?"

The girl said: "I'll try and get you a doctor, Mr. Wallace. It may take a little time though. There's a town marshal at Westport. Will he do?"

"I suppose so," I said and thanked her and hung up. There were points about a country telephone after all.

I lit another cigarette and sat down in one of the rustic rockers on the porch. In a little while there were steps and Mrs. Sype came out of the house. She stood a moment looking off down the hills, then she sat down in the other rocker beside me. Her dry eyes looked at me steadily.

"You're a detective, I suppose," she said slowly, diffidently.

"Yes, I represent the company that insured the Leander pearls."

She looked off into the distance. "I thought he would have peace here," she said. "That nobody would bother him any more. That this place would be a sort of sanctuary."

"He ought not to have tried to keep the pearls."

She turned her head, quickly this time. She looked blank now, then she looked scared.

I reached down in my pocket and got out the wadded handkerchief, opened it up on the palm of my hand. They lay there together on the white linen, two hundred grand worth of murder.

"He could have had his sanctuary," I said. "Nobody wanted to take it away from him. But he wasn't satisfied with that."

She looked slowly, lingeringly at the pearls. Then her lips twitched. Her voice got hoarse.

"Poor Wally," she said. "So you did find them. You're pretty clever, you know. He killed dozens of fish before he learned how to do that trick." She looked up into my face. A little wonder showed at the back of her eyes.

She said: "I always hated the idea. Do you remember the old Bible theory of the scapegoat?"

I shook my head, no.

"The animal on which the sins of a man were laid and then it was driven off into the wilderness. The fish were his scapegoat."

She smiled at me. I didn't smile back.

She said, still smiling faintly: "You see, he once had the pearls, the real ones, and suffering seemed to him to make them his. But he couldn't have had any profit from them, even if he had found them again. It seems some landmark changed, while he was in prison, and he never could find the spot in Idaho where they were buried."

An icy finger was moving slowly up and down my spine. I opened my mouth and something I supposed might be my voice said: "Huh?"

She reached a finger out and touched one of the pearls. I was still holding them out, as if my hand was a shelf nailed to the wall.

"So he got these," she said. "In Seattle. They're hollow, filled with white wax. I forget what they call the process.

They look very fine. Of course I never saw any really valuable pearls."

"What did he get them for?" I croaked.

"Don't you see? They were his sin. He had to hide them in the wilderness, this wilderness. He hid them in the fish. And do you know – " she leaned towards me again and her eyes shone. She said very slowly, very earnestly: "Sometimes I think that in the very end, just the last year or so, he actually believed they were the real pearls he was hiding. Does all this mean anything to you?"

I looked down at my pearls. My hand and the handkerchief closed over them slowly.

I said: "I'm a plain man, Mrs. Sype. I guess the scapegoat idea is a bit over my head. I'd say he was just trying to kid himself a bit – like any healthy loser."

She smiled again. She was handsome when she smiled. Then she shrugged quite lightly.

"Of course, you would see it that way. But me – " She spread her hands. "Oh, well, it doesn't matter much now. May I have them for a keepsake?"

"Have them?"

"The – the phony pearls. Surely you don't – "

I stood up. An old Ford roadster without a top was chugging up the hill. A man in it had a big star on his vest. The chatter of the motor was like the chatter of some old angry bald-headed ape in the zoo.

Mrs. Sype was standing beside me, with her hand half out, a thin, beseeching look on her face.

I grinned at her with sudden ferocity.

"Yeah, you were pretty good in there for a while," I said. "I damn near fell for it. And was I cold down the back, lady! But you helped. 'Phony' was a shade out of character for you. Your work with the Colt was fast and kind of ruthless. Most of all Sype's last words queered it. 'The Moors, Hattie – the Moors.' He wouldn't have bothered with that if the stones had been ringers. And he wasn't sappy enough to kid himself all the way."

For a moment her face didn't change at all. Then it did. Something horrible showed in her eyes. She put her lips out and spit at me. Then she slammed into the house.

I tucked twenty-five thousand dollars into my vest pocket. Twelve thousand five hundred for me and twelve thousand five hundred for Kathy Horne. I could see her eyes when I brought her the check, and when she put it in the bank, to wait for Johnny to get paroled from Quentin.

The Ford had pulled up behind the other cars. The man driving spit over the side, yanked his emergency brake on, got out without using the door. He was a big fellow in shirt sleeves.

I went down the steps to meet him.

THE CURTAIN

1

THE FIRST TIME I ever saw Larry Batzel he was drunk outside Sardi's in a secondhand Rolls-Royce. There was a tall blonde with him who had eyes you wouldn't forget. I helped her argue him out from under the wheel so that she could drive.

The second time I saw him he didn't have any Rolls-Royce or any blonde or any job in pictures. All he had was the jitters and a suit that needed pressing. He remembered me. He was that kind of drunk.

I bought him enough drinks to do him some good and gave him half my cigarettes. I used to see him from time to time "between pictures." I got to lending him money. I don't know just why. He was a big, handsome brute with eyes like a cow and something innocent and honest in them. Something I don't get much of in my business.

The funny part was he had been a liquor runner for a pretty hard mob before Repeal. He never got anywhere in pictures, and after a while I didn't see him around any more.

Then one day out of the clear blue I got a check for all he owed me and a note that he was working on the tables – gambling not dining – at the Dardanella Club, and to come out and look him up. So I knew he was back in the rackets.

I didn't go to see him, but I found out somehow or other that Joe Mesarvey owned the place, and that Joe Mesarvey was married to the blonde with the eyes, the one Larry Batzel had been with in the Rolls that time. I still didn't go out there.

Then very early one morning there was a dim figure standing by my bed, between me and the windows. The blinds had been pulled down. That must have been what wakened me. The figure was large and had a gun.

I rolled over and rubbed my eyes.

"Okay," I said sourly. "There's twelve bucks in my pants and my wrist watch cost twenty-seven fifty. You couldn't get anything on that."

The figure went over to the window and pulled a blind aside an inch and looked down at the street. When he turned again I saw that it was Larry Batzel.

His face was drawn and tired and he needed a shave. He had dinner clothes on still and a dark double-breasted overcoat with a dwarf rose drooping in the lapel.

He sat down and held the gun on his knee for a moment before he put it away, with a puzzled frown, as if he didn't know how it got into his hand.

"You're going to drive me to Berdoo," he said. "I've got to get out of town. They've put the pencil on me."

"Okay," I said. "Tell me about it."

I sat up and felt the carpet with my toes and lit a cigarette. It was a little after five-thirty.

"I jimmied your lock with a piece of celluloid," he said. "You ought to use your night latch once in a while. I wasn't sure which was your flop and I didn't want to rouse the house."

"Try the mailboxes next time," I said. "But go ahead. You're not drunk, are you?"

"I'd like to be, but I've got to get away first. I'm just rattled. I'm not so tough as I used to be. You read about the O'Mara disappearance of course."

"Yeah."

"Listen, anyway. If I keep talking I won't blow up. I don't think I'm spotted here."

"One drink won't hurt either of us," I said. "The Scotch is on the table there."

He poured a couple of drinks quickly and handed me one. I put on a bathrobe and slippers. The glass rattled against his teeth when he drank.

He put his empty glass down and held his hands tight together.

"I used to know Dud O'Mara pretty well. We used to run stuff together down from Hueneme Point. We even carried the torch for the same girl. She's married to Joe Mesarvey now. Dud married five million dollars. He married General Dade Winslow's rickety-rackety divorcée daughter."

"I know all that," I said.

"Yeah. Just listen. She picked him out of a speak, just like I'd pick up a cafeteria tray. But he didn't like the life. I guess he used to see Mona. He got wise Joe Mesarvey and Lash Yeager had a hot car racket on the side. They knocked him off."

"The hell they did," I said. "Have another drink."

"No. Just listen. There's just two points. The night O'Mara pulled down the curtain – no, the night the papers got it – Mona Mesarvey disappeared too. Only she didn't. They hid her out in a shack a couple of miles beyond Realito in the orange belt. Next door to a garage run by a heel named Art Huck, a hot car drop. I found out. I trailed Joe there."

"What made it your business?" I asked.

"I'm still soft on her. I'm telling you this because you were pretty swell to me once. You can make something of it after I blow. They hid her out there so it would look as if Dud had blown with her. Naturally the cops were not too dumb to see Joe after the disappearance. But they didn't find Mona. They have a system on disappearances and they play the system."

He got up and went over to the window again, looked through the side of the blind.

"There's a blue sedan down there I think I've seen before," he said. "But maybe not. There's a lot like it."

He sat down again. I didn't speak.

"This place beyond Realito is on the first side road north from the Foothill Boulevard. You can't miss it. It stands all alone, the garage and the house next door. There's an old cyanide plant up above there. I'm telling you this – "

"That's point one," I said. "What was the second point?"

"The punk that used to drive for Lash Yeager lit out a couple of weeks back and went East. I lent him fifty bucks. He was broke. He told me Yeager was out to the Winslow estate the night Dud O'Mara disappeared."

I stared at him. "It's interesting, Larry. But not enough to break eggs over. After all we do have a police department."

"Yeah. Add this. I got drunk last night and told Yeager what I knew. Then I quit the job at the Dardanella. So somebody shot at me outside where I live when I got home. I've been on the dodge ever since. Now, will you drive me to Berdoo?"

I stood up. It was May but I felt cold. Larry Batzel looked cold, even with his overcoat on.

"Absolutely," I said. "But take it easy. Later will be much safer than now. Have another drink. You don't *know* they knocked O'Mara off."

"If he found out about the hot car racket, with Mona married to Joe Mesarvey, they'd have to knock him off. He was that kind of guy."

I stood up and went towards the bathroom. Larry went over to the window again.

"It's still there," he said over his shoulder. "You might get shot at riding with me."

"I'd hate that," I said.

"You're a good sort of heel, Carmady. It's going to rain. I'd hate like hell to be buried in the rain, wouldn't you?"

"You talk too damn much," I said, and went into the bathroom.

It was the last time I ever spoke to him.

2

I HEARD HIM moving around while I was shaving, but not after I got under the shower, of course. When I came out he was gone. I padded over and looked into the kitchenette. He wasn't in there. I grabbed a bathrobe and peeked out into the hall. It was empty except for a milkman starting down the back stairs with his wiry tray of bottles, and the fresh folded papers leaning against the shut doors.

"Hey," I called out to the milkman, "did a guy just come out of here and go by you?"

He looked back at me from the corner of the wall and opened his mouth to answer. He was a nice-looking boy with fine large white teeth. I remember his teeth well, because I was looking at them when I heard the shots.

They were not very near or very far. Out back of the apartment house, by the garages, or in the alley, I thought. There were two quick, hard shots and then the riveting machine. A burst of five or six, all a good chopper should ever need. Then the roar of the car going away.

The milkman shut his mouth as if a winch controlled it. His eyes were huge and empty looking at me. Then he very carefully set his bottles down on the top step and leaned against the wall.

"That sounded like shots," he said.

All this took a couple of seconds and felt like half an hour. I went back into my place and threw clothes on, grabbed odds and ends off the bureau, barged out into the hall. It was still empty, even of the milkman. A siren was dying somewhere near. A bald head with a hangover under it poked out of a door and made a snuffling noise.

I went down the back stairs.

There were two or three people out in the lower hall. I went out back. The garages were in two rows facing each other across a cement space, then two more at the end, leaving a space to go out to the alley. A couple of kids were coming over a fence three houses away.

Larry Batzel lay on his face, with his hat a yard away from his head, and one hand flung out to within a foot of a big black automatic. His ankles were crossed, as if he had spun as he fell. Blood was thick on the side of his face, on his blond hair, especially on his neck. It was also thick on the cement yard.

Two radio cops and the milk driver and a man in a brown sweater and bibless overalls were bending over him. The man in overalls was our janitor.

I went up to them, about the same time the two kids from over the fence hit the yard. The milk driver looked at me with a queer, strained expression. One of the cops straightened up and said: "Either of you guys know him? He's still got half his face."

He wasn't talking to me. The milk driver shook his head and kept on looking at me from the corner of his eyes. The janitor said: "He ain't a tenant here. He might of been a visitor. Kind of early for visitors, though, ain't it?"

"He's got party clothes on. You know your flophouse better'n I do," the cop said heavily. He got out a notebook.

The other cop straightened up too and shook his head and went towards the house, with the janitor trotting beside him.

The cop with the notebook jerked a thumb at me and said harshly: "You was here first after these two guys. Anything from you?"

I looked at the milkman. Larry Batzel wouldn't care, and a man has a living to earn. It wasn't a story for a prowl car anyway.

"I just heard the shots and came running," I said.

The cop took that for an answer. The milk driver looked up at the lowering gray sky and said nothing.

After a while I got back into my apartment and finished my dressing. When I picked my hat up off the window table by the Scotch bottle there was a small rosebud lying on a piece of scrawled paper.

The note said: "You're a good guy, but I think I'll go it alone. Give the rose to Mona, if you ever should get a chance. Larry."

I put those things in my wallet, and braced myself with a drink.

3

ABOUT THREE O'CLOCK that afternoon I stood in the main hallway of the Winslow place and waited for the butler to come back. I had spent most of the day not going near my office or apartment, and not meeting any homicide men. It was only a question of time until I had to come through, but I wanted to see General Dade Winslow first. He was hard to see.

Oil paintings hung all around me, mostly portraits. There were a couple of statues and several suits of time-darkened armor on pedestals of dark wood. High over the huge marble fireplace hung two bullet-torn – or moth-eaten – cavalry pennants crossed in a glass case, and below them the painted likeness of a thin, spry-looking man with a black beard and mustachios and full regimentals of about the time of the Mexican War. This might be General Dade Winslow's father. The general himself, though pretty ancient, couldn't be quite that old.

Then the butler came back and said General Winslow was in the orchid house and would I follow him, please.

We went out of the french doors at the back and across the lawns to a big glass pavilion well beyond the garages. The butler opened the door into a sort of vestibule and shut it when I was inside, and it was already hot. Then he opened the inner door and it was really hot.

The air steamed. The walls and ceiling of the greenhouse dripped. In the half light enormous tropical plants spread their blooms and branches all over the place, and the smell of them was almost as overpowering as the smell of boiling alcohol.

The butler, who was old and thin and very straight and white-haired, held branches of the plants back for me to pass, and we came to an opening in the middle of the place. A large reddish Turkish rug was spread down on the hexagonal flagstones. In the middle of the rug, in a wheel chair, a very old man sat with a traveling rug around his body and watched us come.

Nothing lived in his face but the eyes. Black eyes, deep-set, shining, untouchable. The rest of his face was the leaden mask of death, sunken temples, a sharp nose, outward-turning ear lobes, a mouth that was a thin white slit. He was wrapped partly in a reddish and very shabby bathrobe and partly in the rug. His hands had purple fingernails and were clasped loosely, motionless on the rug. He had a few scattered wisps of white hair on his skull.

The butler said: "This is Mr. Carmady, General."

The old man stared at me. After a while a sharp, shrewish voice said: "Place a chair for Mr. Carmady."

The butler dragged a wicker chair out and I sat down. I put my hat on the floor. The butler picked it up.

"Brandy," the general said. "How do you like your brandy, sir?"

"Any way at all," I said.

He snorted. The butler went away. The general stared at me with his unblinking eyes. He snorted again.

"I always take champagne with mine," he said. "A third of a glass of brandy under the champagne, and the champagne as cold as Valley Forge. Colder, if you can get it colder."

A noise that might have been a chuckle came out of him.

"Not that I was at Valley Forge," he said. "Not quite that bad. You may smoke, sir."

I thanked him and said I was tired of smoking for a while. I got a handkerchief out and mopped my face.

"Take your coat off, sir. Dud always did. Orchids require heat, Mr. Carmady – like sick old men."

I took my coat off, a raincoat I had brought along. It looked like rain. Larry Batzel had said it was going to rain.

"Dud is my son-in-law. Dudley O'Mara. I believe you had something to tell me about him."

"Just hearsay," I said. "I wouldn't want to go into it, unless I had your O.K., General Winslow."

The basilisk eyes stared at me. "You are a private detective. You want to be paid, I suppose."

"I'm in that line of business," I said. "But that doesn't mean I have to be paid for every breath I draw. It's just something I heard. You might like to pass it on yourself to the Missing Persons Bureau."

"I see," he said quietly. "A scandal of some sort."

The butler came back before I could answer. He wheeled a tea wagon in through the jungle, set it at my elbow and mixed me a brandy and soda. He went away.

I sipped the drink. "It seems there was a girl," I said. "He knew her before he knew your daughter. She's married to a racketeer now. It seems – "

"I've heard all that," he said. "I don't give a damn. What I want to know is where he is and if he's all right. If he's happy."

I stared at him popeyed. After a moment I said weakly: "Maybe I could find the girl, or the boys downtown could, with what I could tell them."

He plucked at the edge of his rug and moved his head about an inch. I think he was nodding. Then he said very slowly: "Probably I'm talking too much for my health, but I want to make something clear. I'm a cripple. I have two ruined legs and half my lower belly. I don't eat much or sleep much. I'm a bore to myself and a damn nuisance to everybody else. So I miss Dud. He used to spend a lot of time with me. Why, God only knows."

"Well – " I began.

"Shut up. You're a young man to me, so I can be rude to you. Dud left without saying goodbye to me. That wasn't like him. He drove his car away one evening and nobody has heard from him since. If he got tired of my fool daughter and her brat, if he wanted some other woman, that's all right. He got a brainstorm and left without saying goodbye to me, and now he's sorry. That's why I don't hear from him. Find him and tell him I understand. That's all – unless he needs money. If he does, he can have all he wants."

His leaden cheeks almost had a pink tinge now. His black eyes were brighter, if possible. He leaned back very slowly and closed his eyes.

I drank a lot of my drink in one long swallow. I said: "Suppose he's in a jam. Say, on account of the girl's husband. This Joe Mesarvey."

He opened his eyes and winked. "Not an O'Mara," he said. "It's the other fellow would be in a jam."

"Okay. Shall I just pass on to the Bureau where I heard this girl was?"

"Certainly not. They've done nothing. Let them go on doing it. Find him yourself. I'll pay you a thousand dollars – even if you only have to walk across the street. Tell him everything is all right here. The old man's doing fine and sends his love. That's all."

I couldn't tell him. Suddenly I couldn't tell him anything Larry Batzel had told me, or what had happened to Larry, or anything about it. I finished my drink and stood up and put my coat back on. I said: "That's too much money for the job, General Winslow. We can talk about that later. Have I your authority to represent you in my own way?"

He pressed a bell on his wheel chair. "Just tell him," he said. "I want to know he's all right and I want him to know I'm all right. That's all – unless he needs money. Now you'll have to excuse me. I'm tired."

He closed his eyes. I went back through the jungle and the butler met me at the door with my hat.

I breathed in some cool air and said: "The general wants me to see Mrs. O'Mara."

4

THIS ROOM HAD a white carpet from wall to wall. Ivory drapes of immense height lay tumbled casually on the white carpet inside the many windows. The windows stared towards the dark foothills, and the air beyond the glass was dark too. It hadn't started to rain yet, but there was a feeling of pressure in the atmosphere.

Mrs. O'Mara was stretched out on a white chaise longue with both her slippers off and her feet in the net stockings they don't wear any more. She was tall and dark, with a sulky mouth. Handsome, but this side of beautiful.

She said: "What in the world can *I* do for you? It's all known. Too damn known. Except that I don't know you, do I?"

"Well, hardly," I said. "I'm just a private copper in a small way of business."

She reached for a glass I hadn't noticed but would have looked for in a moment, on account of her way of talking and the fact she had her slippers off. She drank languidly, flashing a ring.

"I met him in a speakeasy," she said with a sharp laugh. "A very handsome bootlegger, with thick curly hair and an Irish grin. So I married him. Out of boredom. As for him, the bootlegging business was even then uncertain – if there were no other attractions."

She waited for me to say there were, but not as if she cared a lot whether I came through. I just said: "You didn't see him leave on the day he disappeared?"

"No. I seldom saw him leave, or come back. It was like that." She drank some more of her drink.

"Huh," I grunted. "But, of course, you didn't quarrel." They never do.

"There are so many ways of quarreling, Mr. Carmady."

"Yeah. I like your saying that. Of course you knew about the girl."

"I'm glad I'm being properly frank to an old family detective. Yes, I knew about the girl." She curled a tendril of inky hair behind her ear.

"Did you know about her before he disappeared?" I asked politely.

"Certainly."

"How?"

"You're pretty direct, aren't you? Connections, as they say. I'm an old speak fancier. Or didn't you know that?"

"Did you know the bunch at the Dardanella?"

"I've been there." She didn't look startled, or even surprised. "In fact I practically lived there for a week. That's where I met Dudley O'Mara."

"Yeah. Your father married pretty late in life, didn't he?"

I watched color fade in her cheeks. I wanted her mad, but there was nothing doing. She smiled and the color came back and she rang a push bell on a cord down in the swansdown cushions of the chaise longue.

"Very late," she said, "if it's any of your business."

"It's not," I said.

A coy-looking maid came in and mixed a couple of drinks at a side table. She gave one to Mrs. O'Mara, put one down beside me. She went away again, showing a nice pair of legs under a short skirt.

Mrs. O'Mara watched the door shut and then said: "The whole thing has got Father into a mood. I wish Dud would wire or write or something."

I said slowly: "He's an old, old man, crippled, half buried already. One thin thread of interest held him to life. The thread snapped and nobody gives a damn. He tries to act as if he didn't give a damn himself. I don't call that a mood. I call that a pretty swell display of intestinal fortitude."

"Gallant," she said, and her eyes were daggers. "But you haven't touched your drink."

"I have to go," I said. "Thanks all the same."

She held a slim, tinted hand out and I went over and touched it. The thunder burst suddenly behind the hills and she jumped. A gust of air shook the windows.

I went down a tiled staircase to the hallway and the butler appeared out of a shadow and opened the door for me.

I looked down a succession of terraces decorated with flower beds and imported trees. At the bottom a high metal railing with gilded spearheads and a six-foot hedge inside. A sunken driveway crawled down to the main gates and a lodge inside them.

Beyond the estate the hill sloped down to the city and the old oil wells of La Brea, now partly a park, partly a deserted stretch of fenced-in wild land. Some of the wooden derricks still stood. These had made the wealth of the Winslow family and then the family had run away from them up the hill, far enough to get away from the smell of the sumps, not too far for them to look out of the front windows and see what made them rich.

I walked down brick steps between the terraced lawns. On one of them a dark-haired, pale-faced kid of ten or eleven was throwing darts at a target hung on a tree. I went along near him.

"You young O'Mara?" I asked.

He leaned against a stone bench with four darts in his hand and looked at me with cold, slaty eyes, old eyes.

"I'm Dade Winslow Trevillyan," he said grimly.

"Oh, then Dudley O'Mara's not your dad."

"Of course not." His voice was full of scorn. "Who are you?"

"I'm a detective. I'm going to find your – I mean, Mr. O'Mara."

That didn't bring us any closer. Detectives were nothing to him. The thunder was tumbling about in the hills like a bunch of elephants playing tag. I had another idea.

"Bet you can't put four out of five into the gold at thirty feet."

He livened up sharply. "With these?"

"Uh-huh."

"How much you bet?" he snapped.

"Oh, a dollar."

He ran to the target and cleaned darts off it, came back and took a stance by the bench.

"That's not thirty feet," I said.

He gave me a sour look and went a few feet behind the bench. I grinned, then I stopped grinning.

His small hand darted so swiftly I could hardly follow it. Five darts hung in the gold center of the target in less than that made seconds. He stared at me triumphantly.

"Gosh, you're pretty good, Master Trevillyan," I grunted, and got my dollar out.

His small hand snapped at it like a trout taking the fly. He had it out of sight like a flash.

"That's nothing," he chuckled. "You ought to see me on our target range back of the garages. Want to go over there and bet some more?"

I looked back up the hill and saw part of a low white building backed up to a bank.

"Well, not today," I said. "Next time I visit here maybe. So Dud O'Mara is not your dad. If I find him anyway, will it be all right with you?"

He shrugged his thin, sharp shoulders in a maroon sweater. "Sure. But what can you do the police can't do?"

"It's a thought," I said, and left him.

I went on down the brick walk to the bottom of the lawns and along inside the hedge towards the gatehouse. I could see glimpses of the street through the hedge. When I was halfway to the lodge I saw the blue sedan outside. It was a small neat car, low-slung, very clean, lighter than a police car, but about the same size. Over beyond it I could see my roadster waiting under the pepper tree.

I stood looking at the sedan through the hedge. I could see the drift of somebody's cigarette smoke against the windshield inside the car. I turned my back to the lodge and looked up the hill. The Trevillyan kid had gone somewhere out of sight, to salt his dollar down maybe, though a dollar shouldn't have meant much to him.

I bent over and unsheathed the 7.65 Luger I was wearing that day and stuck it nose-down inside my left sock, inside my shoe. I could walk that way, if I didn't walk too fast. I went on to the gates.

They kept them locked and nobody got in without identification from the house. The lodge keeper, a big husky with a gun under his arm, came out and let me through a small postern at the side of the gates. I stood talking to him through the bars for a minute, watching the sedan.

It looked all right. There seemed to be two men in it. It was about a hundred feet along in the shadow of the high wall on the other side. It was a very narrow street, without sidewalks. I didn't have far to go to my roadster.

I walked a little stiffly across the dark pavement and got in, grabbed quickly down into a small compartment in the front part of the seat where I kept a spare gun. It was a police Colt. I slid it inside my under-arm holster and started the car.

I eased the brake off and pulled away. Suddenly the rain let go in big splashing drops and the sky was as black as Carrie Nation's bonnet. Not so black but that I saw the sedan wheel away from the curb behind me.

I started the windshield wiper and built up to forty miles an hour in a hurry. I had gone about eight blocks when they gave me the siren. That fooled me. It was a quiet street, deadly quiet. I slowed down and pulled over to the curb. The sedan slid up beside me and I was looking at the black snout of a sub-machine gun over the sill of the rear door.

Behind it a narrow face with reddened eyes, a fixed mouth. A voice above the sound of the rain and the windshield wiper and the noise of the two motors said: "Get in here with us. Be nice, if you know what I mean."

They were not cops. It didn't matter now. I shut off the ignition, dropped my car keys on the floor and got out on the running board. The man behind the wheel of the sedan didn't look at me. The one behind kicked a door open and slid away along the seat, holding the tommy gun nicely.

I got into the sedan.

"Okay, Louie. The frisk."

The driver came out from under his wheel and got behind me. He got the Colt from under my arm, tapped my hips and pockets, my belt line.

"Clean," he said, and got back into the front of the car.

The man with the tommy reached forward with his left hand and took my Colt from the driver, then lowered the tommy to the floor of the car and draped a brown rug over it. He leaned back in the corner again, smooth and relaxed, holding the Colt on his knee.

"Okay, Louie. Now let's ride."

5

WE RODE — IDLY, GENTLY, the rain drumming on the roof and streaming down the windows on one side. We wound along curving hill streets, among estates that covered acres, whose houses were distant clusters of wet gables beyond blurred trees.

A tang of cigarette smoke floated under my nose and the red-eyed man said: "What did he tell you?"

"Little enough," I said. "That Mona blew town the night the papers got it. Old Winslow knew it already."

"He wouldn't have to dig very deep for that," Red-eyes said. "The buttons didn't. What else?"

"He said he'd been shot at. He wanted me to ride him out of town. At the last moment he ran off alone. I don't know why."

"Loosen up, peeper," Red-eyes said dryly. "It's your only way out."

"That's all there is," I said, and looked out of the window at the driving rain.

"You on the case for the old guy?"

"No. He's tight."

Red-eyes laughed. The gun in my shoe felt heavy and unsteady, and very far away. I said: "That might be all there is to know about O'Mara."

The man in the front seat turned his head a little and growled: "Where the hell did you say that street was?"

"Top of Beverly Glen, stupid. Mulholland Drive."

"Oh, that. Jeeze, that ain't paved worth a damn."

"We'll pave it with the peeper," Red-eyes said.

The estates thinned out and scrub oak took possession of the hillsides.

"You ain't a bad guy," Red-eyes said. "You're just tight, like the old man. Don't you get the idea? We want to know *everything* he said, so we'll know whether we got to blot you or no."

"Go to hell," I said. "You wouldn't believe me anyway."

"Try us. This is just a job to us. We just do it and pass on."

"It must be nice work," I said. "While it lasts."

"You'll crack wise once too often, guy."

"I did – long ago, while you were still in Reform School. I'm still getting myself disliked."

Red-eyes laughed again. There seemed to be very little bluster about him.

"Far as we know you're clean with the law. Didn't make no cracks this morning. That right?"

"If I say yes, you can blot me right now. Okay."

"How about a grand pin money and forget the whole thing?"

"You wouldn't believe that either."

"Yeah, we would. Here's the idea. We do the job and pass on. We're an organization. But you live here, you got goodwill and a business. You'd play ball."

"Sure," I said. "I'd play ball."

"We don't," Red-eyes said softly, "never knock off a legit. Bad for the trade."

He leaned back in the corner, the gun on his right knee, and reached into an inner pocket. He spread a large tan wallet on his knee and fished two bills out of it, slid them folded along the seat. The wallet went back into his pocket.

"Yours," he said gravely. "You won't last twenty-four hours if you slip your cable."

I picked the bills up. Two five hundreds. I tucked them in my vest. "Right," I said. "I wouldn't be a legit any more then, would I?"

"Think that over, dick."

We grinned at each other, a couple of nice lads getting along in a harsh, unfriendly world. Then Red-eyes turned his head sharply.

"Okay, Louie. Forget the Mulholland stuff. Pull up."

The car was halfway up a long bleak twist of hill. The rain drove in gray curtains down the slope. There was no ceiling, no horizon. I could see a quarter of a mile and I could see nothing outside our car that lived.

The driver edged over to the side of the bank and shut his motor off. He lit a cigarette and draped an arm on the back seat.

He smiled at me. He had a nice smile – like an alligator.

"We'll have a drink on it," Red-eyes said. "I wish I could make me a grand that easy. Just tyin' my nose to my chin."

"You ain't got no chin," Louie said, and went on smiling.

Red-eyes put the Colt down on the seat and drew a flat half-pint out of his side pocket. It looked like good stuff, green stamp, bottled in bond. He unscrewed the top with his teeth, sniffed at the liquor and smacked his lips.

"No Crow McGee in this," he said. "This is the company spread. Tilt her."

He reached along the seat and gave me the bottle. I could have had his wrist, but there was Louie, and I was too far from my ankle.

I breathed shallowly from the top of my lungs and held the bottle near my lips, sniffed carefully. Behind the charred smell of the bourbon there was something else, very faint, a fruity odor that would have meant nothing to me in another place. Suddenly and for no reason at all I remembered something Larry Batzel had said, something like: "East of Realito, towards the mountains, near the old cyanide plant." Cyanide. That was the word.

There was a swift tightness in my temples as I put the bottle to my mouth. I could feel my skin crawling, and the air was suddenly cold on it. I held the bottle high up around the liquor level and took a long gurgling drag at it. Very hearty and relaxing. About half a teaspoonful went into my mouth and none of that stayed there.

I coughed sharply and lurched forward gagging. Red-eyes laughed.

"Don't say you're sick from just one drink, pal."

I dropped the bottle and sagged far down in the seat, gagging violently. My legs slid way to the left, the left one underneath. I sprawled down on top of them, my arms limp. I had the gun.

I shot him under my left arm, almost without looking. He never touched the Colt except to knock it off the seat. The one shot was enough. I heard him lurch. I snapped a shot upward towards where Louie would be.

Louie wasn't there. He was down behind the front seat. He was silent. The whole car, the whole landscape was silent. Even the rain seemed for a moment to be utterly silent rain.

I still didn't have time to look at Red-eyes, but he wasn't doing anything. I dropped the Luger and yanked the tommy gun out from under the rug, got my left hand on the front grip, got it set against my shoulder low down. Louie hadn't made a sound.

"Listen, Louie," I said softly, "I've got the stutter gun. How's about it?"

A shot came through the seat, a shot that Louie knew wasn't going to do any good. It starred a frame of unbreakable glass. There was more silence. Louie said thickly: "I got a pineapple here. Want it?"

"Pull the pin and hold it," I said. "It will take care of both of us."

"Hell!" Louie said violently. "Is he croaked? I ain't got no pineapple."

I looked at Red-eyes then. He looked very comfortable in the corner of the seat, leaning back. He seemed to have three eyes, one of them redder even than the other two. For under-arm shooting that was something to be almost bashful about. It was too good.

"Yeah, Louie, he's croaked," I said. "How do we get to-gether?"

I could hear his hard breathing now, and the rain had stopped being silent. "Get out of the heap," he growled. "I'll blow."

"You get out, Louie. I'll blow."

"Jeeze, I can't walk home from here, pal."

"You won't have to, Louie. I'll send a car for you."

"Jeeze, I ain't done nothing. All I done was drive."

"Then reckless driving will be the charge, Louie. You can fix that – you and your organization. Get out before I uncork this popgun."

A door latch clicked and feet thumped on the running board, then on the roadway. I straightened up suddenly with the chopper. Louie was in the road in the rain, his hands empty and the alligator smile still on his face.

I got out past the dead man's neatly shod feet, got my Colt and the Luger off the floor, laid the heavy twelve-pound tommy gun back on the car floor. I got handcuffs off my hip, motioned to Louie. He turned around sulkily and put his hands behind him.

"You got nothing on me," he complained. "I got protection."

I clicked the cuffs on him and went over him for guns, much more carefully than he had gone over me. He had one besides the one he had left in the car.

I dragged Red-eyes out of the car and let him arrange himself on the wet roadway. He began to bleed again, but he was quite dead. Louie eyed him bitterly.

"He was a smart guy," he said. "Different. He liked tricks. Hello, smart guy."

I got my handcuff key out and unlocked one cuff, dragged it down and locked it to the dead man's lifted wrist.

Louie's eyes got round and horrified and at last his smile went away.

"Jeeze," he whined. "Holy —— ! Jeeze. You ain't going to leave me like this, pal?"

"Goodbye, Louie," I said. "That was a friend of mine you cut down this morning."

"Holy —— !" Louie whined.

I got into the sedan and started it, drove on to a place where I could turn, drove back down the hill past him. He stood stiffly as a scorched tree, his face as white as snow; with the dead man at his feet, one linked hand reaching up to Louie's hand. There was the horror of a thousand nightmares in his eyes.

I left him there in the rain.

It was getting dark early. I left the sedan a couple of blocks from my own car and locked it up, put the keys in the oil strainer. I walked back to my roadster and drove downtown.

I called the homicide detail from a phone booth, asked for a man named Grinnell, told him quickly what had happened and where to find Louie and the sedan. I told him I thought they were the thugs that machine-gunned Larry Batzel. I didn't tell him anything about Dud O'Mara.

"Nice work," Grinnell said in a queer voice. "But you better come in fast. There's a tag out for you, account of what some milk driver phoned in an hour ago."

"I'm all in," I said. "I've got to eat. Keep me off the air and I'll come in after a while."

"You better come in, boy. I'm sorry, but you better."

"Well, okay," I said.

I hung up and left the neighborhood without hanging around. I had to break it now. I had to, or get broken myself.

I had a meal down near the Plaza and started for Realito.

6

AT ABOUT EIGHT o'clock two yellow vapor lamps glowed high up in the rain and a dim stencil sign strung across the highway read: "Welcome to Realito."

Frame houses on the main street, a sudden knot of stores, the lights of the corner drugstore behind fogged glass, a flying-cluster of cars in front of a tiny movie palace, and a dark bank on another corner, with a knot of men standing in front of it in the rain. That was Realito. I went on. Empty fields closed in again.

This was past the orange country; nothing but the empty fields and the crouched foothills, and the rain.

It was a smart mile, more like three, before I spotted a side road and a faint light on it, as if from behind drawn blinds in a house. Just at that moment my left front tire let go with an angry hiss. That was cute. Then the right rear let go the same way.

I stopped almost exactly at the intersection. Very cute indeed. I got out, turned my raincoat up a little higher, unshipped a flash, and looked at a flock of heavy galvanized tacks with heads as big as dimes. The flat shiny butt of one of them blinked at me from my tire.

Two flats and one spare. I tucked my chin down and started towards the faint light up the side road.

It was the place all right. The light came from the tilted skylight on the garage roof. Big double doors in front were shut tight, but light showed at the cracks, strong white light. I tossed the beam of the flash up and read: "Art Huck – Auto Repairs and Refinishing."

Beyond the garage a house sat back from the muddy road behind a thin clump of trees. That had light too. I saw a small buttoned-up coupe in front of the wooden porch.

The first thing was the tires, if it could be worked, and they didn't know me. It was a wet night for walking.

I snapped the flash out and rapped on the doors with it. The light inside went out. I stood there licking rain off my upper lip, the flash in my left hand, my right inside my coat. I had the Luger back under my arm again.

A voice spoke through the door, and didn't sound pleased. "What you want? Who are you?"

"Open up," I said. "I've got two flat tires on the highway and only one spare. I need help."

"We're closed up, mister. Realito's a mile west of here."

I started to kick the door. There was swearing inside, then another, much softer voice.

"A wise guy, huh? Open up, Art."

A bolt squealed and half of the door sagged inward. I snapped the flash again and it hit a gaunt face. Then an arm swept and knocked it out of my hand. A gun had just peeked at me from the flailing hand.

I dropped low, felt around for the flash and was still. I just didn't pull a gun.

"Kill the spot, mister. Guys get hurt that way."

The flash was burning down in the mud. I snapped it off, stood up with it. Light went on inside the garage, outlined a tall man in coveralls. He backed inward and his gun held on me.

"Come on in and shut the door."

I did that. "Tacks all over the end of your street," I said. "I thought you wanted the business."

"Ain't you got any sense? A bank job was pulled at Realito this afternoon."

"I'm a stranger here," I said, remembering the knot of men in front of the bank in the rain.

"Okay, okay. Well there was and the punks are hid out somewhere in the hills, they say. You stepped on their tacks, huh?"

"So it seems." I looked at the other man in the garage.

He was short, heavy-set, with a cool brown face and cool brown eyes. He wore a belted raincoat of brown leather. His brown hat had the usual rakish tilt and was dry. His hands were in his pockets and he looked bored.

There was a hot sweetish smell of pyroxylin paint on the air. A big sedan over in the corner had a paint gun lying on its fender. It was a Buick, almost new. It didn't need the paint it was getting.

The man in coveralls tucked his gun out of sight through a flap in the side of his clothes. He looked at the brown man. The brown man looked at me and said gently: "Where you from, stranger?"

"Seattle," I said.

"Going west – to the big city?" He had a soft voice, soft and dry, like the rustle of well-worn leather.

"Yes. How far is it?"

"About forty miles. Seems farther in this weather. Come the long way, didn't you? By Tahoe and Lone Pine?"

"Not Tahoe," I said. "Reno and Carson City."

"Still the long way." A fleeting smile touched the brown lips.

"Take a jack and get his flats, Art."

"Now, listen, Lash – " the man in the coveralls growled, and stopped as though his throat had been cut from ear to ear.

I could have sworn that he shivered. There was dead silence. The brown man didn't move a muscle. Something looked out of his eyes, and then his eyes lowered, almost shyly. His voice was the same soft, dry rustle of sound.

"Take two jacks, Art. He's got two flats."

The gaunt man swallowed. Then he went over to a corner and put a coat on, and a cap. He grabbed up a socket wrench and a handjack and wheeled a dolly jack over to the doors.

"Back on the highway, is it?" he asked me almost tenderly.

"Yeah. You can use the spare for one spot, if you're busy," I said.

"He's not busy," the brown man said and looked at his fingernails.

Art went out with his tools. The door shut again. I looked at the Buick. I didn't look at Lash Yeager. I knew it was Lash Yeager. There wouldn't be two men called Lash that came to that garage. I didn't look at him because I would be looking across the sprawled body of Larry Batzel, and it would show in my face. For a moment, anyway.

He glanced towards the Buick himself. "Just a panel job to start with," he drawled. "But the guy that owns it has dough and his driver needed a few bucks. You know the racket."

"Sure," I said.

The minutes passed on tiptoe. Long, sluggish minutes. Then feet crunched outside and the door was pushed open. The light hit pencils of rain and made silver wires of them. Art trundled two muddy flats in sulkily, kicked the door shut, let one of the flats fall on its side. The rain and fresh air had given him his nerve back. He looked at me savagely.

"Seattle," he snarled. "Seattle, my eye!"

The brown man lit a cigarette as if he hadn't heard. Art peeled his coat off and yanked my tire up on a rim spreader, tore it loose viciously, had the tube out and cold-patched in nothing flat. He strode scowling over to the wall near me and grabbed an air hose, let enough air into the tube to give it body, and hefted it in both hands to dip it in a washtub of water.

I was a sap, but their teamwork was very good. Neither had looked at the other since Art came back with my tires.

Art tossed the air-stiffened tube up casually, caught it with both hands wide, looked it over sourly beside the washtub of water, took one short easy step and slammed it down over my head and shoulders.

He jumped behind me in a flash, leaned his weight down on the rubber, dragged it tight against my chest and arms. I could move my hands, but I couldn't get near my gun.

The brown man brought his right hand out of his pocket and tossed a wrapped cylinder of nickels up and down on his palm as he stepped lithely across the floor.

I heaved back hard, then suddenly threw all my weight forward. Just as suddenly Art let go of the tube, and kneed me from behind.

I sprawled, but I never knew when I reached the floor. The fist with the weighted tube of nickels met me in mid-flight. Perfectly timed, perfectly weighted, and with my own weight to help it out.

I went out like a puff of dust in a draft.

7

IT SEEMED THERE was a woman and she was sitting beside a lamp. Light shone on my face, so I shut my eyes again and tried to look at her through my eyelashes. She was so platinumed that her head shone like a silver fruit bowl.

She wore a green traveling dress with a mannish cut to it and a broad white collar falling over the lapels. A sharp-angled glossy bag stood at her feet. She was smoking, and a drink was tall and pale at her elbow.

I opened my eye wider and said: "Hello there."

Her eyes were the eyes I remembered, outside Sardi's in a secondhand Rolls-Royce. Very blue eyes, very soft and lovely. Not the eyes of a hustler around the fast money boys.

"How do you feel?" Her voice was soft and lovely too.

"Great," I said. "Except somebody built a filling station on my jaw."

"What did you expect, Mr. Carmady? Orchids?"

"So you know my name."

"You slept well. They had plenty of time to go through your pockets. They did everything but embalm you."

"Right," I said.

I could move a little, not very much. My wrists were behind my back, handcuffed. There was a little poetic justice in that. From the cuffs a cord ran to my ankles, and tied them, and then dropped down out of sight over the end of the daven-port and was tied somewhere else. I was almost as helpless as if I had been screwed up in a coffin.

"What time is it?"

She looked sideways down at her wrist, beyond the spiral of her cigarette smoke.

"Ten-seventeen. Got a date?"

"Is this the house next the garage? Where are the boys – digging a grave?"

"You wouldn't care, Carmady. They'll be back."

"Unless you have the key to these bracelets you might spare me a little of that drink."

She rose all in one piece and came over to me, with the tall amber glass in her hand. She bent over me. Her breath was delicate. I gulped from the glass craning my neck up.

"I hope they don't hurt you," she said distantly, stepping back. "I hate killing."

"And you Joe Mesarvey's wife. Shame on you. Gimme some more of the hooch."

She gave me some more. Blood began to move in my stiffened body.

"I kind of like you," she said. "Even if your face does look like a collision mat."

"Make the most of it," I said. "It won't last long even this good."

She looked around swiftly and seemed to listen. One of the two doors was ajar. She looked towards that. Her face seemed pale. But the sounds were only the rain.

She sat down by the lamp again.

"Why did you come here and stick your neck out?" she asked slowly, looking at the floor.

The carpet was made of red and tan squares. There were bright green pine trees on the wallpaper and the curtains were blue. The furniture, what I could see of it, looked as if it came from one of those places that advertise on bus benches.

"I had a rose for you," I said. "From Larry Batzel."

She lifted something off the table and twirled it slowly, the dwarf rose he had left for her.

"I got it," she said quietly. "There was a note, but they didn't show me that. Was it for me?"

"No, for me. He left it on my table before he went out and got shot."

Her face fell apart like something you see in a nightmare. Her mouth and eyes were black hollows. She didn't make a sound. And after a moment her face settled back into the same calmly beautiful lines.

"They didn't tell me that either," she said softly.

"He got shot," I said carefully, "because he found out what Joe and Lash Yeager did to Dud O'Mara. Bumped him off."

That one didn't faze her at all. "Joe didn't do anything to Dud O'Mara," she said quietly. "I haven't seen Dud in two years. That was just newspaper hooey, about me seeing him."

"It wasn't in the papers," I said.

"Well, it was hooey wherever it was. Joe is in Chicago. He went yesterday by plane to sell out. If the deal goes through, Lash and I are to follow him. Joe is no killer."

I stared at her.

Her eyes got haunted again. "Is Larry — is he — ?"

"He's dead," I said. "It was a professional job, with a tommy gun. I didn't mean they did it personally."

She took hold of her lip and held it for a moment tight between her teeth. I could hear her slow, hard breathing. She jammed her cigarette in an ashtray and stood up.

"Joe didn't do it!" she stormed. "I know damn well he didn't. He — " She stopped cold, glared at me, touched her hair, then suddenly yanked it off. It was a wig. Underneath her own hair was short like a boy's, and streaked yellow and whitish brown, with darker tints at the roots. It couldn't make her ugly.

I managed a sort of laugh. "You just came out here to molt, didn't you, Silver-Wig? And I thought they were hiding you out — so it would look as if you had skipped with Dud O'Mara."

She kept on staring at me. As if she hadn't heard a word I said. Then she strode over to a wall mirror and put the wig back on, straightened it, turned and faced me.

"Joe didn't kill anybody," she said again, in a low, tight voice. "He's a heel — but not that kind of heel. He doesn't know anything more about where Dud O'Mara went than I do. And I don't know anything."

"He just got tired of the rich lady and scrammed," I said dully.

She stood near me now, her white fingers down at her sides, shining in the lamplight. Her head above me was almost in shadow. The rain drummed and my jaw felt large and hot and the nerve along the jawbone ached, ached.

"Lash has the only car that was here," she said softly. "Can you walk to Realito, if I cut the ropes?"

"Sure. Then what?"

"I've never been mixed up in a murder. I won't now. I won't ever."

She went out of the room very quickly, and came back with a long kitchen knife and sawed the cord that tied my ankles, pulled it off, cut the place where it was tied to the handcuffs. She stopped once to listen, but it was just the rain again.

I rolled up to a sitting position and stood up. My feet were numb, but that would pass. I could walk. I could run, if I had to.

"Lash has the key of the cuffs," she said dully.

"Let's go," I said. "Got a gun?"

"No. I'm not going. You beat it. He may be back any minute. They were just moving stuff out of the garage."

I went over close to her. "You're going to stay here after turning me loose? Wait for that killer? You're nuts. Come on, Silver-Wig, you're going with me."

"No."

"Suppose," I said, "he did kill O'Mara? Then he also killed Larry. It's got to be that way."

"Joe never killed anybody," she almost snarled at me.

"Well, suppose Yeager did."

"You're lying, Carmady. Just to scare me. Get out. I'm not afraid of Lash Yeager. I'm his boss's wife."

"Joe Mesarvey is a handful of mush," I snarled back. "The only time a girl like you goes for a wrong gee is when he's a handful of mush. Let's drift."

"Get out!" she said hoarsely.

"Okay." I turned away from her and went through the door.

She almost ran past me into the hallway and opened the front door, looked out into the black wetness. She motioned me forward.

"Goodbye," she whispered. "I hope you find Dud. I hope you find who killed Larry. But it wasn't Joe."

I stepped close to her, almost pushed her against the wall with my body.

"You're still crazy, Silver-Wig. Goodbye."

She raised her hands quickly and put them on my face. Cold hands, icy cold. She kissed me swiftly on the mouth with cold lips.

"Beat it, strong guy. I'll be seeing you some more. Maybe in heaven."

I went through the door and down the dark slithery wooden steps of the porch, across gravel to the round grass plot and the clump of thin trees. I came past them to the road-way, went back along it towards Foothill Boulevard. The rain touched my face with fingers of ice that were no colder than her fingers.

The curtained roadster stood just where I had left it, leaned over, the left front axle on the tarred shoulder of the highway. My spare and one stripped rim were thrown in the ditch.

They had probably searched it, but I still hoped. I crawled in backwards and banged my head on the steering post and rolled over to get the manacled hands into my little secret gun pocket. They touched the barrel. It was still there.

I got it out, got myself out of the car, got hold of the gun by the right end and looked it over.

I held it tight against my back to protect it a little from the rain and started back towards the house.

8

I WAS HALFWAY there when he came back. His lights turning quickly off the highway almost caught me. I flopped into the ditch and put my nose in the mud and prayed.

The car hummed past. I heard the wet rasp of its tires shouldering the gravel in front of the house. The motor died and lights went off. The door slammed. I didn't hear the house door shut, but I caught a feeble fringe of light through the trees as it opened.

I got up on my feet and went on. I came up beside the car, a small coupe, rather old. The gun was down at my side, pulled around my hip as far as the cuffs would let it come.

The coupe was empty. Water gurgled in the radiator. I listened and heard nothing from the house. No loud voices, no quarrel. Only the heavy bong-bong-bong of the raindrops hitting the elbows at the bottom of rain gutters.

Yeager was in the house. She had let me go and Yeager was in there with her. Probably she wouldn't tell him anything. She would just stand and look at him. She was his boss's wife. That would scare Yeager to death.

He wouldn't stay long, but he wouldn't leave her behind, alive or dead. He would be on his way and take her with him. What happened to her later on was something else.

All I had to do was wait for him to come out. I didn't do it.

I shifted the gun into my left hand and leaned down to scoop up some gravel. I threw it against the front window. It was a weak effort. Very little even reached the glass.

I ran back behind the coupe and got its door open and saw the keys in the ignition lock. I crouched down on the running board, holding on to the door post.

The house had already gone dark, but that was all. There wasn't any sound from it. No soap. Yeager was too cagey.

I reached it with my foot and found the starter, then strained back with one hand and turned the ignition key. The warm motor caught at once, throbbed gently against the pounding rain.

I got back to the ground and slid along to the rear of the car, crouched down.

The sound of the motor got him. He couldn't be left there without a car.

A darkened window slid up an inch, only some shifting of light on the glass showing it moved. Flame spouted from it, the racket of three quick shots. Glass broke in the coupe.

I screamed and let the scream die into a gurgling groan. I was getting good at that sort of thing. I let the groan die in a choked gasp. I was through, finished. He had got me. Nice shooting, Yeager.

Inside the house a man laughed. Then silence again, except for the rain and the quietly throbbing motor of the coupe.

Then the house door inched open. A figure showed in it. She came out on the porch, stiffly, the white showing at her collar, the wig showing a little but not so much. She came down the steps like a wooden woman. I saw Yeager crouched behind her.

She started across the gravel. Her voice said slowly, without any tone at all:

"I can't see a thing, Lash. The windows are all misted."

She jerked a little, as if a gun had prodded her, and came on. Yeager didn't speak. I could see him now past her shoulder, his hat, part of his face. But no kind of a shot for a man with cuffs on his wrists.

She stopped again, and her voice was suddenly horrified.

"He's behind the wheel!" she yelled. "Slumped over!"

He fell for it. He knocked her to one side and started to blast again. More glass jumped around. A bullet hit a tree on my side of the car. A cricket whined somewhere. The motor kept right on humming.

He was low, crouched against the black, his face a grayness without form that seemed to come back very slowly after the glare of the shots. His own fire had blinded him too – for a second. That was enough.

I shot him four times, straining the pulsing Colt against my ribs.

He tried to turn and the gun slipped away from his hand. He half snatched for it in the air, before both his hands suddenly went against his stomach and stayed there. He sat down on the wet gravel and his harsh panting dominated every other sound of the wet night.

I watched him lie down on his side, very slowly, without taking his hands away from his stomach. The panting stopped.

It seemed like an age before Silver-Wig called out to me. Then she was beside me, grabbing my arm.

"Shut the motor off!" I yelled at her. "And get the key of these damn irons out of his pocket."

"You d–darn fool," she babbled. "W-what did you come back for?"

9

CAPTAIN AL ROOF of the Missing Persons Bureau swung in his chair and looked at the sunny window. This was another day, and the rain had stopped long since.

He said gruffly: "You're making a lot of mistakes, brother. Dud O'Mara just pulled down the curtain. None of those people knocked him off. The Batzel killing had nothing to do with it. They've got Mesarvey in Chicago and he looks clean. The Heeb you anchored to the dead guy don't even know who they were pulling the job for. Our boys asked him enough to be sure of that."

"I'll bet they did," I said. "I've been in the same bucket all night and I couldn't tell much either."

He looked at me slowly, with large, bleak, tired eyes. "Killing Yeager was all right, I guess. And the chopper. In the circumstances. Besides I'm not homicide. I couldn't link any of that to O'Mara – unless you could."

I could, but I hadn't. Not yet. "No," I said. "I guess not." I stuffed and lit my pipe. After a sleepless night it tasted better.

"That all that's worrying you?"

"I wondered why you didn't find the girl, at Realito. It couldn't have been very hard – for you."

"We just didn't. We should have. I admit it. We didn't. Anything else?"

I blew smoke across his desk. "I'm looking for O'Mara because the general told me to. It wasn't any use my telling him you would do everything that could be done. He could afford a man with all his time on it. I suppose you resent that."

He wasn't amused. "Not at all, if he wants to waste money. The people that resent you are behind a door marked Homicide Bureau."

He planted his feet with a slap and elbowed his desk.

"O'Mara had fifteen grand in his clothes. That's a lot of jack but O'Mara would be the boy to have it. So he could take it out and have his old pals see him with it. Only they wouldn't think it was fifteen grand of real dough. His wife says it was. Now with any other guy but an ex-legger in the gravy that might indicate an intention to disappear. But not O'Mara. He packed it all the time."

He bit a cigar and put a match to it. He waved a large finger. "See?"

I said I saw.

"Okay. O'Mara had fifteen grand, and a guy that pulls down the curtain can keep it down only so long as his wad lasts. Fifteen grand is a good wad. I might disappear myself, if I had that much. But after it's gone we get him. He cashes a check, lays down a marker, hits a hotel or store for credit, gives a reference, writes a letter or gets one. He's in a new town and he's got a new name, but he's got the same old appetite. He has to get back into the fiscal system one way or another. A guy can't have friends everywhere, and if he had, they wouldn't all stay clammed forever. Would they?"

"No, they wouldn't," I said.

"He went far," Roof said. "But the fifteen grand was all the preparation he made. No baggage, no boat or rail or plane reservation, no taxi or private rental hack to a point out of town. That's all checked. His own car was found a dozen blocks from where he lived. But that means nothing. He knew people who would ferry him several hundred miles and keep quiet about it, even in the face of a reward. Here, but not everywhere. Not new friends."

"But you'll get him," I said.

"When he gets hungry."

"That could take a year or two. General Winslow may not live a year. That is a matter of sentiment, not whether you have an open file when you retire."

"You attend to the sentiment, brother." His eyes moved and bushy reddish eyebrows moved with them. He didn't like me. Nobody did, in the police department, that day.

"I'd like to," I said and stood up. "Maybe I'd go pretty far to attend to that sentiment."

"Sure," Roof said, suddenly thoughtful. "Well, Winslow is a big man. Anything I can do let me know."

"You could find out who had Larry Batzel gunned," I said. "Even if there isn't any connection."

"We'll do that. Glad to." He guffawed and flicked ash all over his desk. "You just knock off the guys who can talk and we'll do the rest. We like to work that way."

"It was self-defense," I growled. "I couldn't help myself."

"Sure. Take the air, brother. I'm busy."

But his large bleak eyes twinkled at me as I went out.

10

THE MORNING WAS all blue and gold and the birds in the ornamental trees of the Winslow estate were crazy with song after the rain.

The gatekeeper let me in through the postern and I walked up the driveway and along the top terrace to the huge carved Italian front door. Before I rang the bell I looked down the hill and saw the Trevillyan kid sitting on his stone bench with his head cupped in his hands, staring at nothing.

I went down the brick path to him. "No darts today, son?"

He looked up at me with his lean, slaty, sunken eyes.

"No. Did you find him?"

"Your dad? No, sonny, not yet."

He jerked his head. His nostrils flared angrily. "He's not my dad I told you. And don't talk to me as if I was four years old. My dad he's — he's in Florida or somewhere."

"Well, I haven't found him yet, whoever's dad he is," I said.

"Who smacked your jaw?" he asked, staring at me.

"Oh, a fellow with a roll of nickels in his hand."

"Nickels?"

"Yeah. That's as good as brass knuckles. Try it sometime, but not on me." I grinned.

"You won't find him," he said bitterly, staring at my jaw. "Him, I mean. My mother's husband."

"I bet I do."

"How much you bet?"

"More money than even you've got in your pants."

He kicked viciously at the edge of a red brick in the walk. His voice was still sulky, but more smooth. His eyes speculated.

"Want to bet on something else? C'mon over to the range. I bet you a dollar I can knock down eight out of ten pipes in ten shots."

I looked back towards the house. Nobody seemed impatient to receive me.

"Well," I said, "we'll have to make it snappy. Let's go."

We went along the side of the house under the windows. The orchid greenhouse showed over the tops of some bushy trees far back. A man in neat whipcord was polishing the chromium on a big car in front of the garages. We went past there to the low white building against the bank.

The boy took a key out and unlocked the door and we went into close air that still held traces of cordite fumes. The boy clicked a spring lock on the door.

"Me first," he snapped.

The place looked something like a small beach shooting gallery. There was a counter with a .22 repeating rifle on it and a long, slim target pistol. Both well oiled but dusty. About thirty feet beyond the counter was a waist-high, solid-looking partition across the building, and behind that a simple layout of clay pipes and ducks and two round white targets marked off with black rings and stained by lead bullets.

The clay pipes ran in an even line across the middle, and there was a big skylight, and a row of hooded overhead lights.

The boy pulled a cord on the wall and a thick canvas blind slid across the skylight. He turned on the hooded lights and then the place really looked like a beach shooting gallery.

He picked up the .22 rifle and loaded it quickly from a cardboard box of shells, .22 shorts.

"A dollar I get eight out of ten pipes?"

"Blast away," I said, and put my money on the counter.

He took aim almost casually, fired too fast, showing off. He missed three pipes. It was pretty fancy shooting at that. He threw the rifle down on the counter.

"Gee, go set up some more. Let's not count that one. I wasn't set."

"You don't aim to lose any money, do you, son? Go set 'em up yourself. It's your range."

His narrow face got angry and his voice got shrill. "You do it! I've got to relax, see. I've got to relax."

I shrugged at him, lifted a flap in the counter and went along the whitewashed side wall, squeezed past the end of the low partition. The boy clicked his reloaded rifle shut behind me.

"Put that down," I growled back at him. "Never touch a gun when there's anyone in front of you."

He put it down, looking hurt.

I bent down and grabbed a handful of clay pipes out of the sawdust in a big wooden box on the floor. I shook the yellow grains of wood off them and started to straighten up.

I stopped with my hat above the barrier, just the top of my hat. I never knew why I stopped. Blind instinct.

The .22 cracked and the lead bullet bonged into the target in front of my head. My hat stirred lazily on my head, as though a blackbird had swooped at it during the nesting season.

A nice kid. He was full of tricks, like Red-eyes. I dropped the pipes and took hold of my hat by the brim, lifted it straight up off my head a few inches. The gun cracked again. Another metallic bong on the target.

I let myself fall heavily to the wooden flooring, among the pipes.

A door opened and shut. That was all. Nothing else. The hard glare from the hooded lights beat down on me. The sun peeked in at the edges of the skylight blind. There were two bright new splashes on the nearest target, and there were four small round holes in my hat, two and two, on each side.

I crawled to the end of the barrier and peeked around it. The boy was gone. I could see the small muzzles of the two guns on the counter.

I stood up and went back along the wall, switched the lights off, turned the knob of the spring lock and went out. The Winslow chauffeur whistled at his polish job around in front of the garages.

I crushed my hat in my hand and went back along the side of the house, looking for the kid. I didn't see him. I rang the front door bell.

I asked for Mrs. O'Mara. I didn't let the butler take my hat.

11

SHE WAS IN an oyster-white something, with white fur at the cuffs and collar and around the bottom. A breakfast table on wheels was pushed to one side of her chair and she was flicking ashes among the silver.

The coy-looking maid with the nice legs came and took the table out and shut the tall white door. I sat down.

Mrs. O'Mara leaned her head back against a cushion and looked tired. The line of her throat was distant, cold. She stared at me with a cool, hard look, in which there was plenty of dislike.

"You seemed rather human yesterday," she said. "But I see you are just a brute like the rest of them. Just a brutal cop."

"I came to ask you about Lash Yeager," I said.

She didn't even pretend to be amused. "And why should you think of asking me?"

"Well – if you lived a week at the Dardanella Club – " I waved my crunched-together hat.

She looked at her cigarette fixedly. "Well, I did meet him, I believe. I remember the rather unusual name."

"They all have names like that, those animals," I said. "It seems that Larry Batzel – I guess you read in your paper about him too – was a friend of Dud O'Mara's once. I didn't tell you about him yesterday. Maybe that was a mistake."

A pulse began to throb in her throat. She said softly: "I have a suspicion you are about to become very insolent, that I may even have to have you thrown out."

"Not before I've said my piece," I said. "It seems that Mr. Yeager's driver – they have drivers as well as unusual names, those animals – told Larry Batzel that Mr. Yeager was out this way the night O'Mara disappeared."

The old army blood had to be good for something in her. She didn't move a muscle. She just froze solid.

I got up and took the cigarette from between her frozen fingers and killed it in a white jade ashtray. I laid my hat carefully on her white satin knee. I sat down again.

Her eyes moved after a while. They moved down and looked at the hat. Her face flushed very slowly, in two vivid patches over the cheekbones. She fought around with her tongue and lips.

"I know," I said. "It's not much of a hat. I'm not making you a present of it. But just look at the bullet holes in it once."

Her hand became alive and snatched at the hat. Her eyes became flames.

She spread the crown out, looked at the holes, and shuddered.

"Yeager?" she asked, very faintly. It was a wisp of a voice, an old voice.

I said very slowly: "Yeager wouldn't use a .22 target rifle, Mrs. O'Mara."

The flame died in her eyes. They were pools of darkness, much emptier than darkness.

"You're his mother," I said. "What do you want to do about it?"

"Merciful God! Dade! He . . . shot at you!"

"Twice," I said.

"But why? . . . Oh, why?"

"You think I'm a wise guy, Mrs. O'Mara. Just another hard-eyed boy from the other side of the tracks. It would be easy in this spot, if I was. But I'm not that at all, really. Do I have to tell why he shot at me!"

She didn't speak. She nodded slowly. Her face was a mask now.

"I'd say he probably can't help it," I said. "He didn't want me to find his stepfather, for one thing. Then he's a little lad that likes money. That seems small, but it's part of the picture. He almost lost a dollar to me on his shooting. It seems small, but he lives in a small world. Most of all, of course, he's a crazy little sadist with an itchy trigger finger."

"How dare you!" she flared. It didn't mean anything. She forgot it herself instantly.

"How dare I? I do dare. Let's not bother figuring why he shot at *me*. I'm not the first, am I? You wouldn't have known what I was talking about, you wouldn't have assumed he did it on purpose."

She didn't move or speak. I took a deep breath.

"So let's talk about why he shot Dud O'Mara," I said.

If I thought she would yell even this time, I fooled myself. The old man in the orchid house had put more into her than her tallness and her dark hair and her reckless eyes.

She pulled her lips back and tried to lick them, and it made her look like a scared little girl, for a second. The lines of her cheeks sharpened and her hand went up like an artificial hand moved by wires and took hold of the white fur at her throat and pulled it tight and squeezed it until her knuckles looked like bleached bone. Then she just stared at me.

Then my hat slid off her knee on to the floor, without her moving. The sound it made falling was one of the loudest sounds I had ever heard.

"Money," she said in a dry croak. "Of course you want money."

"How much money do I want?"

"Fifteen thousand dollars."

I nodded, stiff-necked as a floorwalker trying to see with his back.

"That would be about right. That would be the established retainer. That would be about what he had in his pockets and what Yeager got for getting rid of him."

"You're too – damned smart," she said horribly. "I could kill you myself and like it."

I tried to grin. "That's right. Smart and without a feeling in the world. It happened something like this. The boy got O'Mara where he got me, by the same simple ruse. I don't think it was a plan. He hated his stepfather, but he wouldn't exactly plan to kill him."

"He hated him," she said.

"So they're in the little shooting gallery and O'Mara is dead on the floor, behind the barrier, out of sight. The shots, of course, meant nothing there. And very little blood, with a head shot, small caliber. So the boy goes out and locks the door and hides. But after a while he has to tell somebody. He has to. He tells you. You're his mother. You're the one to tell."

"Yes," she breathed. "He did just that." Her eyes had stopped hating me.

"You think about calling it an accident, which is okay, except for one thing. The boy's not a normal boy, and you know it. The general knows it, the servants know. There must be other people that know it. And the law, dumb as you think they are, are pretty smart with subnormal types. They get to handle so many of them. And I think he would have talked. I think, after a while, he would even have bragged."

"Go on," she said.

"You wouldn't risk that," I said. "Not for your son and not for the sick old man in the orchid house. You'd do any awful criminal callous thing rather than risk that. You did it. You knew Yeager and you hired him to get rid of the body. That's all — except that hiding the girl, Mona Mesarvey, helped to make it look like a deliberate disappearance."

"He took him away after dark, in Dud's own car," she said hollowly.

I reached down and picked my hat off the floor. "How about the servants?"

"Norris knows. The butler. He'd die on the rack before he told."

"Yeah. Now you know why Larry Batzel was knocked off and why I was taken for a ride, don't you?"

"Blackmail," she said. "It hadn't come yet, but I was waiting for it. I would have paid anything, and he would know that."

"Bit by bit, year by year, there was a quarter of a million in it for him, easy. I don't think Joe Mesarvey was in it at all. I know the girl wasn't."

She didn't say anything. She just kept her eyes on my face.

"Why in hell," I groaned, "didn't you take the guns away from him?"

"He's worse than you think. That would have started something worse. I'm – I'm almost afraid of him myself."

"Take him away." I said. "From here. From the old man. He's young enough to be cured, by the right handling. Take him to Europe. Far away. Take him now. It would kill the general out of hand to know his blood was in that."

She got up draggingly and dragged herself across to the windows. She stood motionless, almost blending into the heavy white drapes. Her hands hung at her sides, very motionless also. After a while she turned and walked past me. When she was behind me she caught her breath and sobbed just once.

"It was very vile. It was the vilest thing I ever heard of. Yet I would do it again. Father would not have done it. He would have spoken right out. It would, as you say, have killed him."

"Take him away," I pounded on. "He's hiding out there now. He thinks he got me. He's hiding somewhere like an animal. Get him. He can't help it."

"I offered you money," she said, still behind me. "That's nasty. I wasn't in love with Dudley O'Mara. That's nasty too. I can't thank you. I don't know what to say."

"Forget it," I said. "I'm just an old workhorse. Put *your* work on the boy."

"I promise. Goodbye, Mr. Carmady."

We didn't shake hands. I went back down the stairs and the butler was at the front door as usual. Nothing in his face but politeness.

"You will not want to see the general today, sir?"

"Not today, Norris."

I didn't see the boy outside. I went through the postern and got into my rented Ford and drove on down the hill, past where the old oil wells were.

Around some of them, not visible from the street, there were still sumps in which waste water lay and festered with a scum of oil on top.

They would be ten or twelve feet deep, maybe more. There would be dark things in them. Perhaps in one of them –

I was glad I had killed Yeager.

On the way back downtown I stopped at a bar and had a couple of drinks. They didn't do me any good.

All they did was make me think of Silver-Wig, and I never saw her again.

TRY THE GIRL

THE BIG GUY wasn't any of my business. He never was, then or later, least of all then.

I was over on Central, which is the Harlem of Los Angeles, on one of the "mixed" blocks, where there were still both white and colored establishments. I was looking for a little Greek barber named Tom Aleidis whose wife wanted him to come home and was willing to spend a little money to find him. It was a peaceful job. Tom Aleidis was not a crook.

I saw the big guy standing in front of Shamey's, an all-colored drink and dice second-floor, not too savory. He was looking up at the broken stencils in the electric sign, with a sort of rapt expression, like a hunky immigrant looking at the Statue of Liberty, like a man who had waited a long time and come a long way.

He wasn't just big. He was a giant. He looked seven feet high, and he wore the loudest clothes I ever saw on a really big man.

Pleated maroon pants, a rough grayish coat with white billiard balls for buttons, brown suede shoes with explosions in white kid on them, a brown shirt, a yellow tie, a large red carnation, and a front-door handkerchief the color of the Irish flag. It was neatly arranged in three points, under the red carnation. On Central Avenue, not the quietest dressed street in the world, with that size and that make-up he looked about as unobtrusive as a tarantula on a slice of angel food.

He went over and swung back the doors into Shamey's. The doors didn't stop swinging before they exploded outward again. What sailed out and landed in the gutter and made a high, keening noise, like a wounded rat, was a slick-haired colored youth in a pinchback suit. A "brown," the color of coffee with rather thin cream in it. His face, I mean.

It still wasn't any of my business. I watched the colored boy creep away along the walls. Nothing more happened. So I made my mistake.

I moved along the sidewalk until I could push the swing door myself. Just enough to look in. Just too much.

A hand I could have sat in took hold of my shoulder and hurt and lifted me through the doors and up three steps.

A deep, soft voice said in my ear easily, "Smokes in here, pal. Can you tie that?"

I tried for a little elbow room to get to my sap. I wasn't wearing a gun. The little Greek barber business hadn't seemed to be that sort of job.

He took hold of my shoulder again.

"It's that kind of place," I said quickly.

"Don't say that, pal. Beulah used to work here. Little Beulah."

"Go on up and see for yourself."

He lifted me up three more steps.

"I'm feeling good," he said. "I wouldn't want anybody to bother me. Let's you and me go on up and maybe nibble a drink."

"They won't serve you," I said.

"I ain't seen Beulah in eight years, pal," he said softly, tearing my shoulder to pieces without noticing what he was doing. "She ain't even wrote in six. But she'll have a reason. She used to work here. Let's you and me go on up."

"All right," I said. "I'll go up with you. Just let me walk. Don't carry me. I'm fine. Carmady's the name. I'm all grown up. I go to the bathroom alone and everything. Just don't carry me."

"Little Beulah used to work here," he said softly. He wasn't listening to me.

We went on up. He let me walk.

A crap table was in the far corner beyond the bar, and scattered tables and a few customers were here and there. The whiny voices chanting around the crap table stopped instantly. Eyes looked at us in that dead, alien silence of another race.

A large Negro was leaning against the bar in shirt-sleeves with pink garters on his arms. An ex-pug who had been hit by everything but a concrete bridge. He pried himself loose from the bar edge and came towards us in a loose fighter's crouch.

He put a large brown hand against the big man's gaudy chest. It looked like a stud there.

"No white folks, brother. Jes' fo' the colored people. I'se sorry."

"Where's Beulah?" the big man asked in his deep, soft voice that went with his big white face and his depthless black eyes.

The Negro didn't quite laugh. "No Beulah, brother. No hooch, no gals, jes' the scram, brother. Jes' the scram."

"Kind of take your goddam mitt off me," the big man said.

The bouncer made a mistake, too. He hit him. I saw his shoulder drop, his body swing behind the punch. It was a good clean punch. The big man didn't even try to block it.

He shook his head and took hold of the bouncer by the throat. He was quick for his size. The bouncer tried to knee him. The big man turned him and bent him, took hold of the back of his belt. That broke. So the big man just put his huge hand flat against the bouncer's spine and threw him, clear across the narrow room. The bouncer hit the wall on the far side with a crash that must have been heard in Denver. Then he slid softly down the wall and lay there, motionless.

"Yeah," the big man said. "Let's you and me nibble one."

We went over to the bar. The barman swabbed the bar hurriedly. The customers, by ones and twos and threes, drifted out, silent across the bare floor, silent down the dim uncarpeted stairs. Their departing feet scarcely rustled.

"Whiskey sour," the big man said.

We had whiskey sours.

"You know where Beulah is?" the big man asked the barman impassively, licking his whiskey sour down the side of the thick glass.

"Beulah, you says?" the barman whined. "I ain't seen her roun' heah lately. Not right lately, no suh."

"How long you been here?"

"'Bout a yeah, Ah reckon. 'Bout a yeah. Yes suh. 'Bout – "

"How long's this coop been a dinge box?"

"Says which?"

The big man made a fist down at his side, about the size of a bucket.

"Five years anyway," I put in. "This fellow wouldn't know anything about a white girl named Beulah."

The big man looked at me as if I had just hatched out. His whiskey sour didn't seem to improve his temper.

"Who the hell asked you to stick your face in?"

I smiled. I made it a big, friendly smile. "I'm the fellow came in here with you. Remember?"

He grinned back, a flat, white grin. "Whiskey sour," he told the barman. "Get them fleas outa your pants. Service."

The barman scuttled around, hating us with the whites of his eyes.

The place was empty now, except for the two of us and the barman, and the bouncer over against the far wall.

The bouncer groaned and stirred. He rolled over and began to crawl softly along the baseboard, like a fly with one wing. The big man paid no attention to him.

"There ain't nothing left of the joint," he complained. "They was a stage and a band and cute little rooms where you could have fun. Beulah did some warbling. A redhead. Awful cute. We was to of been married when they hung the frame on me."

We had two more whiskey sours before us now. "What frame?" I asked.

"Where you figure I been them eight years I told you about?"

"In somebody's Stony Lonesome," I said.

"Right." He prodded his chest with a thumb like a base-ball bat. "Steve Skalla. The Great Bend job in Kansas. Just me. Forty grand. They caught up with me right here. I was what that — hey!"

The bouncer had made a door at the back and fallen through it. A lock clicked.

"Where's that door lead to?" the big man demanded.

"Tha — tha's Mistah Montgom'ry's office, suh. He's the boss. He's got his office back — "

"He might know," the big man said. He wiped his mouth on the Irish flag handkerchief and arranged it carefully back in his pocket. "He better not crack wise neither. Two more whiskey sours."

He crossed the room to the door behind the crap table. The lock gave him a little argument for a moment, then a piece of the panel dropped off and he went through, shut the door after him.

It was very silent in Shamey's now. I looked at the barman.

"This guy's tough," I said quickly. "And he's liable to go mean. You can see the idea. He's looking for an old sweetie who used to work here when it was a place for whites. Got any artillery back there?"

"I thought you was with him," the barman said suspiciously.

"Couldn't help myself. He dragged me up. I didn't feel like being thrown over any houses."

"Shuah. Ah got me a shotgun," the barman said, still suspicious.

He began to stoop behind the bar, then stayed in that position rolling his eyes.

There was a dull flat sound at the back of the place, behind the shut door. It might have been a slammed door. It might have been a gun. Just the one sound. No other followed it.

The barman and I waited too long, wondering what the sound was. Not liking to think what it could be.

The door at the back opened and the big man came through quickly, with a Colt army .45 automatic looking like a toy in his hand.

He looked the room over with one swift glance. His grin was taut. He looked like the man who could take forty grand singlehanded from the Great Bend Bank.

He came over to us in swift, almost soundless steps, for all his size.

"Rise up, nigger!"

The barman came up slowly, gray; his hands empty, high.

The big man felt me over, stepped away from us.

"Mr. Montgomery didn't know where Beulah was either," he said softly. "He tried to tell me – with this." He waggled the gun. "So long, punks. Don't forget your rubbers."

He was gone, down the stairs, very quickly, very quietly.

I jumped around the bar and took the sawed-off shotgun that lay there, on the shelf. Not to use on Steve Skalla. That was not my job. So the barman wouldn't use it on me. I went back across the room and through that door.

The bouncer lay on the floor of a hall with a knife in his hand. He was unconscious. I took the knife out of his hand and stepped over him through a door marked Office.

Mr. Montgomery was in there, behind a small scarred desk, close to a partly boarded-up window. Just folded, like a handkerchief or a hinge.

A drawer was open at his right hand. The gun would have come from there. There was a smear of oil on the paper that lined it.

Not a smart idea, but he would never have a smarter one – not now.

Nothing happened while I waited for the police.

When they came both the barman and the bouncer were gone. I had locked myself in with Mr. Montgomery and the shotgun. Just in case.

Hiney got it. A lean-jawed, complaining, overslow detective lieutenant, with long yellow hands that he held on his knees while he talked to me in his cubicle at Headquarters. His shirt was darned under the points of his old-fashioned stiff collar. He looked poor and sour and honest.

This was an hour or so later. They knew all about Steve Skalla then, from their own records. They even had a ten-year-old photo that made him look as eyebrowless as a French roll. All they didn't know was where he was.

"Six foot six and a half," Hiney said. "Two hundred sixty-four pounds. A guy that size can't get far, not in them fancy duds. He couldn't buy anything else in a hurry. Whyn't you take him?"

I handed the photo back and laughed.

Hiney pointed one of his long yellow fingers at me bitterly. "Carmady, a tough shamus, huh? Six feet of man, and a jaw you could break rocks on. Whyn't you take him?"

"I'm getting a little gray at the temples," I said. "And I didn't have a gun. He had. I wasn't on a gun-toting job over there. Skalla just picked me up. I'm kind of cute sometimes."

Hiney glared at me.

"All right," I said. "Why argue? I've seen the guy. He could wear an elephant in his vest pocket. And I didn't know he'd killed anybody. You'll get him all right."

"Yeah," Hiney said. "Easy. But I just don't like to waste my time on these shine killings. No pix. No space. Not even three lines in the want-ad section. Heck, they was five smokes – five, mind you – carved Harlem sunsets all over each other over on East Eighty-four one time. All dead. Cold meat. And the —— newshawks wouldn't even go out there."

"Pick him up nice," I said. "Or he'll knock off a brace of prowlies for you. Then you'll get space."

"And I wouldn't have the case then neither," Hiney jeered. "Well, the hell with him. I got him on the air. Ain't nothing else to do but just sit."

"Try the girl," I said. "Beulah. Skalla will. That's what he's after. That's what started it all. Try her."

"You try her," Hiney said. "I ain't been in a joy house in twenty years."

"I suppose I'd be right at home in one. How much will you pay?"

"Jeeze, guy, coppers don't hire private dicks. What with?" He rolled a cigarette out of a can of tobacco. It burned down one side like a forest fire. A man yelled angrily into a telephone in the next cubbyhole. Hiney made another cigarette with more care and licked it and lighted it. He clasped his bony hands on his bony knees again.

"Think of your publicity," I said. "I bet you twenty-five I find Beulah before you put Skalla under glass."

He thought it over. He seemed almost to count his bank balance on his cigarette puffs.

"Ten is top," he said. "And she's all mine – private."

I stared at him.

"I don't work for that kind of money," I said. "But if I can do it in one day – and you let me alone – I'll do it for nothing. Just to show you why you've been a lieutenant for twenty years."

He didn't like that crack much better than I liked his about the joy house. But we shook hands on it.

I got my old Chrysler roadster out of the official parking lot and drove back towards the Central Avenue district.

Shamey's was closed up, of course. An obvious plain-clothes man sat in a car in front of it, reading a paper with one eye. I didn't know why. Nobody there knew anything about Skalla.

I parked around the corner and went into the diagonal lobby of a Negro hotel called the Hotel Sans Souci. Two rows of hard, empty chairs stared at each other across a strip of fiber carpet. Behind a desk a bald-headed man had his eyes shut and his hands clasped on the desk top. He dozed. He wore an ascot tie that had been tied about 1880, and the green stone in his stickpin was not quite as large as a trash barrel. His large, loose chin folded down on it gently, and his brown hands were soft, peaceful, and clean.

A metal embossed sign at his elbow said: *This Hotel Is Under the Protection of the International Consolidated Agencies, Inc.*

When he opened one eye I pointed to the sign and said: "H.P.D. man checking up. Any trouble here?"

H.P.D. means Hotel Protective Department, which is the part of a large agency that looks after check bouncers and people who move out by the back stairs, leaving second-hand suitcases full of bricks.

"Trouble, brother," he said, in a high, sonorous voice, "is something we is fresh out of." He lowered the voice four or five notches and added, "We don't take no checks."

I leaned on the counter across from his folded hands and started to spin a quarter on the bare, scarred wood.

"Heard what happened over at Shamey's this morning?"

"Brother, I forgit." Both his eyes were open now and he was watching the blur of light made by the spinning quarter.

"The boss got bumped off," I said. "Montgomery. Got his neck broken."

"May the Lawd receive his soul, brother." The voice went down again. "Cop?"

"Private – on a confidential lay. And I know a man who can keep one that way when I see one."

He looked me over, closed his eyes again. I kept spinning the quarter. He couldn't resist looking at it.

"Who done it?" he asked softly. "Who fixed Sam?"

"A tough guy out of the jailhouse got sore because it wasn't a white joint. It used to be. Remember?"

He didn't say anything. The coin fell over with a light whirr and lay still.

"Call your play," I said. "I'll read you a chapter of the Bible or buy you a drink. Either one."

"Brother," he said sonorously, "I kinda like to read my Bible in the seclusion of my family." Then he added swiftly, in his business voice, "Come around to this side of the desk."

I went around there and pulled a pint of bonded bourbon off my hip and handed it to him in the shelter of the desk. He poured two small glasses, quickly, sniffed his with a smooth, expert manner, and tucked it away.

"What you want to know?" he asked. "Ain't a crack in the sidewalk I don't know. Mebbe I ain't tellin' though. This liquor's been in the right company."

"Who ran Shamey's before it was a colored place?"

He stared at me, surprised. "The name of that pore sinner was Shamey, brother."

I groaned. "What have I been using for brains?"

"He's daid, brother, gathered to the Lawd. Died in nineteen and twenty-nine. A wood alcohol case, brother. And him in the business." He raised his voice to the sonorous level. "The same year the rich folks lost their goods and chattels, brother." The voice went down again. "I didn't lose me a nickel."

"I'll bet you didn't. Pour some more. He leave any folks – anybody that's still around?"

He poured another small drink, corked the bottle firmly. "Two is all – before lunch," he said. "I thank you, brother. Yo' method of approach is soothin' to a man's dignity." He cleared his throat. "Had a wife," he said. "Try the phone book."

He wouldn't take the bottle. I put it back on my hip. He shook hands with me, folded his on the desk once more and closed his eyes.

The incident, for him, was over.

There was only one Shamey in the phone book. Violet Lu Shamey, 1644 West Fifty-fourth Place. I spent a nickel in a booth.

After a long time a dopey voice said, "Uh-huh. Wh-what is it?"

"Are you the Mrs. Shamey whose husband once ran a place on Central Avenue – a place of entertainment?"

"Wha – what? My goodness sakes alive! My husband's been gone these seven years. Who did you say you was?"

"Detective Carmady. I'll be right out. It's important."

"Wh-who did you say – "

It was a thick, heavy, clogged voice.

It was a dirty brown house with a dirty brown lawn in front of it. There was a large bare patch around a tough-looking palm tree. On the porch stood one lonely rocker.

The afternoon breeze made the unpruned shoots of last year's poinsettias tap-tap against the front wall. A line of stiff, yellowish, half-washed clothes jittered on a rusty wire in the side yard.

I drove on a little way and parked my roadster across the street, and walked back.

The bell didn't work, so I knocked. A woman opened the door blowing her nose. A long yellow face with weedy hair growing down the sides of it. Her body was shapeless in a flannel bathrobe long past all color and design. It was just something around her. Her toes were large and obvious in a pair of broken man's slippers.

I said, "Mrs. Shamey?"

"You the – ?"

"Yeah. I just called you."

She gestured me in wearily. "I ain't had time to get cleaned up yet," she whined.

We sat down in a couple of dingy mission rockers and looked at each other across a living-room in which everything was junk except a small new radio droning away behind its dimly lighted panel.

"All the company I got," she said. Then she tittered. "Bert ain't done nothing, has he? I don't get cops calling on me much."

"Bert?"

"Bert Shamey, mister. My husband."

She tittered again and flopped her feet up and down. In her titter was a loose alcoholic overtone. It seemed I was not to get away from it that day.

"A joke, mister," she said. "He's dead. I hope to Christ there's enough cheap blondes where he is. He never got enough of them here."

"I was thinking more about a redhead," I said.

"I guess he'd use one of those too." Her eyes, it seemed to me, were not so loose now. "I don't call to mind. Any special one?"

"Yeah. A girl named Beulah. I don't know her last name. She worked at the Club on Central. I'm trying to trace her for her folks. It's a colored place now and, of course, the people there never heard of her."

"I never went there," the woman yelled, with unexpected violence. "I wouldn't know."

"An entertainer," I said. "A singer. No chance you'd know her, eh?"

She blew her nose again, on one of the dirtiest handkerchiefs I ever saw. "I got a cold."

"You know what's good for it," I said.

She gave me a swift, raking glance. "I'm fresh out of that."

"I'm not."

"Gawd," she said. "You're no cop. No cop ever bought a drink."

I brought out my pint of bourbon and balanced it on my knee. It was almost full still. The clerk at the Hotel Sans Souci was no reservoir. The woman's seaweed-colored eyes jumped at the bottle. Her tongue coiled around her lips.

"Man, that's liquor," she sighed. "I don't care who you are. Hold it careful, mister."

584

She heaved up and waddled out of the room and came back with two thick, smeared glasses.

"No fixin's," she said. "Just what you brought." She held the glasses out.

I poured her a slug that would have made me float over a wall. A smaller one for me. She put hers down like an aspirin tablet and looked at the bottle. I poured her another. She took that over to her chair. Her eyes had turned two shades browner.

"This stuff dies painless with me," she said. "It never knows what hit it. What was we talkin' about?"

"A red-haired girl named Beulah. Used to work at the joint. Remember better now?"

"Yeah." She used her second drink. I went over and stood the bottle on the table beside her. She used some out of that.

"Hold on to your chair and don't step on no snakes," she said. "I got me a idea."

She got up out of the chair, sneezed, almost lost her bathrobe, slapped it back against her stomach and stared at me coldly.

"No peekin'," she said, and wagged a finger at me and went out of the room again, hitting the side of the door casement on her way.

From the back of the house presently there were various types of crashes. A chair seemed to be kicked over. A bureau drawer was pulled out too far and smashed to the floor. There was fumbling and thudding and loud language. After a while, then, there was the slow click of a lock and what seemed to be the screech of a trunk top going up. More fumbling and banging things around. A tray landed on the floor, I thought. Then a chortle of satisfaction.

She came back into the room holding a package tied with faded pink tape. She threw it in my lap.

"Look 'em over, Lou. Photos. Newspaper stills. Not that them tramps ever got in no newspapers except by way of the police blotter. They're people from the joint. By God, they're all the —— left me. Them and his old clothes."

She sat down and reached for the whiskey again.

I untied the tape and looked through a bunch of shiny photos of people in professional poses. Not all of them were women. The men had foxy faces and racetrack clothes or make-up. Hoofers and comics from the filling-station circuits. Not many of them ever got west of Main Street. The women had good legs and displayed them more than Will Hays would have liked. But their faces were as threadbare as a book-keeper's coat. All but one.

She wore a Pierrot costume, at least from the waist up. Under the high conical white hat her fluffed-out hair might have been red. Her eyes had laughter in them. I won't say her face was unspoiled. I'm not that good at faces. But it wasn't like the others. It hadn't been kicked around. Somebody had been nice to that face. Perhaps just a tough mug like Steve Skalla. But he had been nice. In the laughing eyes there was still hope.

I threw the others aside and carried this one over to the sprawled, glassy-eyed woman in the chair. I poked it under her nose.

"This one," I said. "Who is she? What happened to her?"

She stared at it fuzzily, then chuckled.

"Tha's Steve Skalla's girl, Lou. Heck, I forgot her name."

"Beulah," I said. "Beulah's her name."

She watched me under her tawny, mangled eyebrows. She wasn't so drunk.

"Yeah?" she said. "Yeah?"

"Who's Steve Skalla?" I rapped.

"Bouncer down at the joint, Lou." She giggled again. "He's in the pen."

"Oh no, he isn't," I said. "He's in town. He's out. I know him. He just got in."

Her face went to pieces like a clay pigeon. Instantly I knew who had turned Skalla up to the local law. I laughed.

I couldn't miss. Because she knew. If she hadn't known, she wouldn't have bothered to be cagey about Beulah. She couldn't have forgotten Beulah. Nobody could.

Her eyes went far back into her head. We stared into each other's faces. Then her hand snatched at the photo.

I stepped back and tucked it away in an inside pocket.

"Have another drink," I said. I handed her the bottle.

She took it, lingered over it, gurgled it slowly down her throat, staring at the faded carpet.

"Yeah," she said whisperingly "I turned him in but he never knew. Money in the bank he was. Money in the bank."

"Give me the girl," I said. "And Skalla knows nothing from me."

"She's here," the woman said. "She's in radio. I heard her once on KLBL. She's changed her name, though. I dunno."

I had another hunch. "You do know," I said. "You're bleeding her still. Shamey left you nothing. What do you live on? You're bleeding her because she pulled herself up in the world, from people like you and Skalla. That's it, isn't it?"

"Money in the bank," she croaked. "Hundred a month. Reg'lar as rent. Yeah."

The bottle was on the floor again. Suddenly, without being touched, it fell over on its side. Whiskey gurgled out. She didn't move to get it.

"Where is she?" I pounded on. "What's her name?"

"I dunno, Lou. Part of the deal. Get the money in a cashier's check. I dunno. Honest."

"The hell you don't!" I snarled. "Skalla — "

She came to her feet in a surge and screamed at me, "Get out, you! Get out before I call a cop! Get out, you —— —— !"

"Okay, okay." I put a hand out soothingly. "Take it easy. I won't tell Skalla. Just take it easy."

She sat down again slowly and retrieved the almost empty bottle. After all I didn't have to have a scene now. I could find out other ways.

She didn't even look towards me as I went out. I went out into the crisp fall sunlight and got into my car. I was a nice boy, trying to get along. Yes, I was a swell guy. I liked knowing myself. I was the kind of guy who chiseled a sodden old wreck out of her life secrets to win a ten-dollar bet.

I drove down to the neighborhood drugstore and shut myself in its phone booth to call Hiney.

"Listen," I told him, "the widow of the man that ran Shamey's when Skalla worked there is still alive. Skalla might call to see her, if he thinks he dares."

I gave him the address. He said sourly, "We almost got him. A prowl car was talkin' to a Seventh Street conductor at the end of the line. He mentioned a guy that size and with them clothes. He got off at Third and Alexandria, the conductor says. What he'll do is break into some big house where the folks is away. So we got him bottled."

I told him that was fine.

KLBL was on the western fringe of that part of the city that melts into Beverly Hills. It was housed in a flat stucco building, quite unpretentious, and there was a service station in the form of a Dutch windmill on the corner of the lot. The call letters of the station revolved in neon letters on the sails of the windmill.

I went into a ground-floor reception room, one side of which was glass and showed an empty broadcasting studio with a stage and ranged chairs for an audience. A few people sat around the reception room trying to look magnetic, and the blonde receptionist was spearing chocolates out of a large box with nails that were almost royal purple in color.

I waited half an hour and then got to see a Mr. Dave Marineau, studio manager. The station manager and the day-program manager were both too busy to see me. Marineau had a small sound-proofed office behind the organ. It was papered with signed photographs.

Marineau was a handsome tall man, somewhat in the

Levantine style, with red lips a little too full, a tiny silky mustache, large limpid brown eyes, shiny black hair that might or might not have been marceled, and long, pale, nicotined fingers.

He read my card while I tried to find my Pierrot girl on his wall and didn't.

"A private detective, eh? What can we do for you?"

I took my Pierrot out and placed it down on his beautiful brown blotter. It was fun watching him stare at it. All sorts of minute things happened to his face, none of which he wanted known. The sum total of them was that he knew the face and that it meant something to him. He looked up at me with a bargaining expression.

"Not very recent," he said. "But nice. I don't know whether we could use it or not. Legs, aren't they?"

"It's at least eight years old," I said. "What would you use it for?"

"Publicity, of course. We get one in the radio column about every second month. We're a small station still."

"Why?"

"You mean you don't know who it is?"

"I know who she was," I said.

"Vivian Baring, of course. Star of our Jumbo Candy Bar program. Don't you know it? A triweekly serial, half an hour."

"Never heard of it," I said. "A radio serial is my idea of the square root of nothing."

He leaned back and lit a cigarette, although one was burning on the edge of his glass-lined tray.

"All right," he said sarcastically. "Stop being fulsome and get to business. What is it you want?"

"I'd like her address."

"I can't give you that, of course. And you won't find it in any phone book or directory. I'm sorry." He started to gather papers together and then saw the second cigarette and that made him feel like a sap. So he leaned back again.

"I'm in a spot," I said. "I have to find the girl. Quickly. And I don't want to look like a blackmailer."

He licked his very full and very red lips. Somehow I got the idea he was pleased at something.

He said softly, "You mean you know something that might hurt Miss Baring – and incidentally the program?"

"You can always replace a star in radio, can't you?"

He licked his lips some more. Then his mouth tried to get tough. "I seem to smell something nasty," he said.

"It's your mustache burning," I said.

It wasn't the best gag in the world, but it broke the ice. He laughed. Then he did wingovers with his hands. He leaned forward and got as confidential as a tipster.

"We're going at this wrong," he said. "Obviously. You're probably on the level – you look it – so let me make my play." He grabbed a leatherbound pad and scribbled on it, tore the leaf off and passed it across.

I read: *1737 North Flores Avenue.*

"That's her address," he said. "I won't give the phone number without her O.K. Now treat me like a gentleman. That is, if it concerns the station."

I tucked his paper into my pocket and thought it over. He had suckered me neatly, put me on my few remaining shreds of decency. I made my mistake.

"How's the program going?"

"We're promised network audition. It's simple, everyday stuff called 'A Street in Our Town,' but it's done beautifully. It'll wow the country some day. And soon." He wiped his hand across his fine white brow. "Incidentally, Miss Baring writes the scripts herself."

"Ah," I said. "Well, here's your dirt. She had a boy friend in the big house. That is he used to be. She got to know him in a Central Avenue joint where she worked once. He's out and he's looking for her and he's killed a man. Now wait a minute – "

He hadn't turned as white as a sheet, because he didn't have the right skin. But he looked bad.

"Now wait a minute," I said. "It's nothing against the girl and you know it. She's okay. You can see that in her face. It might take a little counterpublicity, if it all came out. But that's nothing. Look how they gild some of those tramps in Hollywood."

"It costs money," he said. "We're a poor studio. And the network audition would be off." There was something faintly dishonest about his manner that puzzled me.

"Nuts," I said, leaning forward and pounding the desk. "The real thing is to protect her. This tough guy – Steve Skalla is his name – is in love with her. He kills people with his bare hands. He won't hurt her, but if she has a boy friend or a husband – "

"She's not married," Marineau put in quickly, watching the rise and fall of my pounding hand.

"He might wring his neck for him. That would put it a little too close to her. Skalla doesn't know where she is. He's on the dodge, so it's harder for him to find out. The cops are your best bet, if you have enough drag to keep them from feeding it to the papers."

"Nix," he said. "Nix on the cops. You want the job, don't you?"

"When do you need her here again?"

"Tomorrow night. She's not on tonight."

"I'll hide her for you until then," I said. "If you want me to. That's as far as I'd go alone."

He grabbed my card again, read it, dropped it into a drawer.

"Get out there and dig her out," he snapped. "If she's not home, stick till she is. I'll get a conference upstairs and then we'll see. Hurry it!"

I stood up. "Want a retainer?" he snapped.

"That can wait."

He nodded, made some more wingovers with his hands and reached for his phone.

That number on Flores would be up near Sunset Towers, across town from where I was. Traffic was pretty thick, but I hadn't gone more than twelve blocks before I was aware that a blue coupe which had left the studio parking lot behind me was still behind me.

I jockeyed around in a believable manner, enough to feel sure it was following me. There was one man in it. Not Skalla. The head was a foot too low over the steering wheel.

I jockeyed more and faster and lost it. I didn't know who it was, and at the moment, I hadn't time to bother figuring it out.

I reached the Flores Avenue place and tucked my roadster into the curb.

Bronze gates opened into a nice bungalow court, and two rows of bungalows with steep roofs of molded shingles gave an effect a little like the thatched cottages in old English sporting prints. A very little.

The grass was almost too well kept. There was a wide walk and an oblong pool framed in colored tiles and stone benches along its sides. A nice place. The late sun made interesting shadows over its lawns, and except for the motor horns, the distant hum of traffic up on Sunset Boulevard wasn't unlike the drone of bees.

My number was the last bungalow on the left. Nobody answered the bell, which was set in the middle of the door so that you would wonder how the juice got to where it had to go. That was cute too. I rang time after time, then I started back to the stone benches by the pool to sit down and wait.

A woman passed me walking fast, not in a hurry, but like a woman who always walks fast. She was a thin, sharp brunette in burnt-orange tweeds and a black hat that looked like a pageboy's hat. It looked like the devil with the burnt-orange tweeds. She had a nose that would be in things and tight lips and she swung a key container.

She went up to my door, unlocked it, went in. She didn't look like Beulah.

I went back and pushed the bell again. The door opened at once. The dark, sharp-faced woman gave me an up-and-down look and said: "Well?"

"Miss Baring? Miss Vivian Baring?"

"Who?" It was like a stab.

"Miss Vivian Baring – of KLBL," I said. "I was told – "

She flushed tightly and her lips almost bit her teeth. "If this is a gag, I don't care for it," she said. She started the door towards my nose.

I said hurriedly, "Mr. Marineau sent me."

That stopped the door closing. It opened again, very wide. The woman's mouth was as thin as a cigarette paper. Thinner.

"I," she said very distinctly, "happen to be Mr. Marineau's wife. This happens to be Mr. Marineau's residence. I wasn't aware that this – this – "

"Miss Vivian Baring," I said. But it wasn't uncertainty about the name that had stopped her. It was plain, cold fury.

" – that this Miss Baring," she went on, exactly as though I had not said a word, "had moved in here. Mr. Marineau must be feeling very amusing today."

"Listen, lady. This isn't – "

The slamming door almost made a wave in the pool down the walk. I looked at it for a moment, and then I looked at the other bungalows. If we had an audience, it was keeping out of sight. I rang the bell again.

The door jumped open this time. The brunette was livid. "Get off my porch!" she yelled. "Get off before I have you thrown off!"

"Wait a minute," I growled. "This may be a gag for him, but it's no gag to the police."

That got her. Her whole expression got soft and interested. "Police?" she cooed.

"Yeah. It's serious. It involves a murder. I've got to find this Miss Baring. Not that she, you understand – "

The brunette dragged me into the house and shut the door and leaned against it, panting.

"Tell me," she said breathlessly. "Tell me. Has that red-headed something got herself mixed up in a murder?" Suddenly her mouth snapped wide open and her eyes jumped at me.

I slapped a hand over her mouth. "Take it easy!" I pleaded. "It's not your Dave. Not Dave, lady."

"Oh." She got rid of my hand and let out a sigh and looked silly. "No, of course. Just for a moment . . . Well, *who* is it?"

"Nobody you know. I can't broadcast things like that, any-way. I want Miss Baring's address. Have you got it?"

I didn't know any reason why she would have. Or rather, I might be able to think of one, if I shook my brains hard enough.

"Yes," she said. "Yes, I have. Indeed, I have. Mister Smarty doesn't know that. Mister Smarty doesn't know as much as he thinks he knows, does Mister Smarty? He – "

"The address is all I can use right now," I growled. "And I'm in a bit of a hurry, Mrs. Marineau. Later on – " I gave her a meaning look. "I'm sure I'll want to talk to you."

"It's on Heather Street," she said. "I don't know the num-ber. But I've been there. I've been *past* there. It's only a short street, with four or five houses, and only one of them on the downward side of the hill." She stopped, added, "I don't think the house has a number. Heather Street is at the top of Beachwood Drive."

"Has she a phone?"

"Of course, but a restricted number. She would have. They all do, those —— . If I knew it – "

"Yeah," I said. "You'd call her up and chew her ear off. Well, thank you very much, Mrs. Marineau. This is confiden-tial, of course. I mean confidential."

"Oh, by all means!"

She wanted to talk longer but I pushed past her out of the house and went back down the flagged walk. I could feel her eyes on me all the way, so I didn't do any laughing.

The lad with the restless hands and the full red lips had had what he thought was a very cute idea. He had given me the first address that came into his head, his own. Probably he had expected his wife to be out. I didn't know. It looked awfully silly, however I thought about it — unless he was pressed for time.

Wondering why he should be pressed for time, I got careless. I didn't see the blue coupe double-parked almost at the gates until I also saw the man step from behind it.

He had a gun in his hand.

He was a big man, but not anything like Skalla's size. He made a sound with his lips and held his left palm out and something glittered in it. It might have been a piece of tin or a police badge.

Cars were parked along both sides of Flores. Half a dozen people should have been in sight. There wasn't one — except the big man with the gun and myself.

He came closer, making soothing noises with his mouth.

"Pinched," he said. "Get in my hack and drive it, like a nice lad." He had a soft, husky voice, like an overworked rooster trying to croon.

"You all alone?"

"Yeah, but I got the gun," he sighed. "Act nice and you're as safe as the bearded woman at a Legion convention. Safer."

He was circling slowly, carefully. I saw the metal thing now.

"That's a special badge," I said. "You've got no more right to pinch me than I have to pinch you."

"In the hack, bo. Be nice or your guts lie on this here street. I got orders." He started to pat me gently. "Hell, you ain't even rodded."

"Skip it!" I growled. "Do you think you could take me if I was?"

I walked over to his blue coupe and slid under its wheel. The motor was running. He got in beside me and put his gun in my side and we went on down the hill.

"Take her west on Santa Monica," he husked. "Then up, say, Canyon Drive to Sunset. Where the bridle path is."

I took her west on Santa Monica, past the bottom of Holloway, then a row of junk yards and some stores. The street widened and became a boulevard past Doheney. I let the car out a little to feel it. He stopped me doing that. I swung north to Sunset and then west again. Lights were being lit in big houses up the slopes. The dusk was full of radio music.

I eased down and took a look at him before it got too dark. Even under the pulled-down hat on Flores I had seen the eyebrows, but I wanted to be sure. So I looked again. They were the eyebrows, all right.

They were almost as even, almost as smoothly black, and fully as wide as a half-inch strip of black plush pasted across his broad face above the eyes and nose. There was no break in the middle. His nose was large and coarse-grained and had hung out over too many beers.

"Bub McCord," I said. "Ex-copper. So you're in the snatch racket now. It's Folsom for you this time, baby."

"Aw, can it." He looked hurt and leaned back in the corner. Bub McCord, caught in a graft tangle, had done a three in Quentin. Next time he would go to the recidivist prison, which is Folsom in our state.

He leaned his gun on his left thigh and cuddled the door with his fat back. I let the car drift and he didn't seem to mind. It was betweentimes, after the homeward rush of the office man, before the evening crowd came out.

"This ain't no snatch," he complained. "We just don't want no trouble. You can't expect to go up against an organization like KLBL with a two-bit shakedown, and get no kickback. It ain't reasonable." He spit out of the window without turning his head. "Keep her rollin', bo."

"What shakedown?"

"You wouldn't know, would you? Just a wandering peeper with his head stuck in a knothole, huh? That's you. Innocent, as the guy says."

"So you work for Marineau. That's all I wanted to know. Of course I knew it already, after I back-alleyed you, and you showed up again."

"Neat work, bo – but keep her rollin'. Yeah, I had to phone in. Just caught him."

"Where do we go from here?"

"I take care of you till nine-thirty. After that we go to a place."

"What place?"

"It ain't nine-thirty. Hey, don't go to sleep in that there corner."

"Drive it yourself, if you don't like my work."

He pushed the gun at me hard. It hurt. I kicked the coupe out from under him and set him back in his corner, but he kept his gun in a good grip. Somebody called out archly on somebody's front lawn.

Then I saw a red light winking ahead, and a sedan just passing it, and through the rear window of the sedan two flat caps side by side.

"You'll get awfully tired of holding that gun," I told McCord. "You don't dare use it anyway. You're copper-soft. There's nothing so soft as a copper who's had his badge torn off. Just a big heel. Copper-soft."

We weren't near to the sedan, but I wanted his attention. I got it. He slammed me over the head and grabbed the wheel and yanked the brake on. We ground to a stop. I shook my head woozily. By the time I came out of it he was away from me again, in his corner.

"Next time," he said thinly, for all his huskiness, "I put you to sleep in the rumble. Just try it, bo. Just try it. Now roll – and keep the wisecracks down in your belly."

I drove ahead, between the hedge that bordered the bridle path and the wide parkway beyond the curbing. The cops in the sedan tooled on gently, drowsing, listening with half an ear to their radio, talking of this and that. I could almost hear them in my mind, the sort of thing they would be saying.

"Besides," McCord growled. "I don't need no gun to handle you. I never see the guy I couldn't handle without no gun."

"I saw one this morning," I said. I started to tell him about Steve Skalla.

Another red stoplight showed. The sedan ahead seemed loath to leave it. McCord lit a cigarette with his left hand, bending his head a little.

I kept telling him about Skalla and the bouncer at Shamey's.

Then I tramped on the throttle.

The little car shot ahead without a quiver. McCord started to swing his gun at me. I yanked the wheel hard to the right and yelled: "Hold tight! It's a crash!"

We hit the prowl car almost on the left rear fender. It waltzed around on one wheel, apparently, and loud language came out of it. It slewed, rubber screamed, metal made a grinding sound, the left taillight splintered and probably the gas tank bulged.

The little coupe sat back on its heels and quivered like a scared rabbit.

McCord could have cut me in half. His gun muzzle was inches from my ribs. But he wasn't a hard guy, really. He was just a broken cop who had done time and got himself a cheap job after it and was on an assignment he didn't understand.

He tore the right-hand door open, and jumped out of the car.

One of the cops was out by this time, on my side. I ducked down under the wheel. A flash beam burned across the top of my hat.

It didn't work. Steps came near and the flash jumped into my face.

"Come on out of that," a voice snarled. "What the hell you think this is − a racetrack?"

I got out sheepishly. McCord was crouched somewhere behind the coupe, out of sight.

"Lemme smell of your breath."

I let him smell my breath.

"Whiskey," he said. "I thought so. Walk, baby. Walk." He prodded me with the flashlight.

I walked.

The other cop was trying to jerk his sedan loose from the coupe. He was swearing, but he was busy with his own troubles.

"You don't walk like no drunk," the cop said. "What's the matter? No brakes?" The other cop had got the bumpers free and was climbing back under his wheel.

I took my hat off and bent my head. "Just an argument," I said. "I got hit. It made me woozy for a minute."

McCord made a mistake. He started running when he heard that. He vaulted across the parkway, jumped the wall and crouched. His footsteps thudded on turf.

That was my cue. "Holdup!" I snapped at the cop who was questioning me. "I was afraid to tell you!"

"Jeeze, the howling − !" he yelled, and tore a gun out of his holster. "Why'n't you say so?" He jumped for the wall. "Circle the heap! We want that guy!" he yelled at the man in the sedan.

He was over the wall. Grunts. More feet pounding on the turf. A car stopped half a block away and a man started to get out of it but kept his foot on the running board. I could barely see him behind his dimmed headlights.

The cop in the prowl car charged at the hedge that bordered the bridle path, backed furiously, swung around and was off with screaming siren.

I jumped into McCord's coupe, and jerked the starter.

Distantly there was a shot, then two shots, then a yell. The siren died at a corner and picked up again.

I gave the coupe all it had and left the neighborhood. Far off, to the north, a lonely sound against the hills, a siren kept on wailing.

I ditched the coupe half a block from Wilshire and took a taxi in front of the Beverly-Wilshire. I knew I could be traced. That wasn't important. The important thing was how soon.

From a cocktail bar in Hollywood I called Hiney. He was still on the job and still sour.

"Anything new on Skalla?"

"Listen," he said nastily, "was you over to talk to that Shamey woman? Where are you?"

"Certainly I was," I said. "I'm in Chicago."

"You better come on home. Why was you there?"

"I thought she might know Beulah, of course. She did. Want to raise that bet a little?"

"Can the comedy. She's dead."

"Skalla — " I started to say.

"That's the funny side," he grunted. "He was there. Some nosy old —— next door seen him. Only there ain't a mark on her. She died natural. I kind of got tied up here, so I didn't get over to see her."

"I know how busy you are," I said in what seemed to me a dead voice.

"Yeah. Well, hell, the doc don't even know what she died of. Not yet."

"Fear," I said. "She's the one that turned Skalla up eight years ago. Whiskey may have helped a little."

"Is that so?" Hiney said. "Well, well. We got him now anyways. We make him at Girard, headed north in a rent hack. We got the county and state law in on it. If he drops over to the Ridge, we nab him at Castaic. She was the one turned him up, huh? I guess you better come in, Carmady."

"Not me," I said. "Beverly Hills wants me for a hit-and-run. I'm a criminal myself now."

I had a quick snack and some coffee before I took a taxi to Las Flores and Santa Monica and walked up to where I had left my roadster parked.

Nothing was happening around there except that some kid in the back of a car was strumming a ukulele.

I pointed my roadster towards Heather Street.

Heather Street was a gash in the side of a steep flat slope, at the top of Beachwood Drive. It curved around the shoulder enough so that even by daylight you couldn't have seen much more than half a block of it at one time while you were on it.

The house I wanted was built downward, one of those clinging-vine effects, with a front door below the street level, a patio on the roof, a bedroom or two possibly in the basement, and a garage as easy to drive into as an olive bottle.

The garage was empty, but a big shiny sedan had its two right wheels off the road, on the shoulder of the bank. There were lights in the house.

I drove around the curb, parked, walked back along the smooth, hardly used cement and poked a fountain pen flash into the sedan. It was registered to one David Marineau, 1737 North Flores Avenue, Hollywood, California. That made me go back to my heap and get a gun out of a locked pocket.

I repassed the sedan, stepped down three rough stone steps and looked at the bell beside a narrow door topped by a lancet arch.

I didn't push it, I just looked at it. The door wasn't quite shut. A fairly wide crack of dim light edged around its panel. I pushed it an inch. Then I pushed it far enough to look in.

Then I listened. The silence of that house was what made me go in. It was one of those utterly dead silences that come after an explosion. Or perhaps I hadn't eaten enough dinner. Anyway I went in.

The long living-room went clear to the back, which wasn't very far as it was a small house. At the back there were french doors and the metal railing of a balcony showed through the glass. The balcony would be very high above the slope of the hill, built as the house was.

There were nice lamps, nice chairs with deep sides, nice tables, a thick apricot-colored rug, two small cozy davenports, one facing and one right-angled to a fireplace with an ivory mantel and a miniature Winged Victory on that. A fire was laid behind the copper screen, but not lit.

The room had a hushed, warm smell. It looked like a room where people got made comfortable. There was a bottle of Vat 69 on a low table with glasses and a copper bucket, and tongs.

I fixed the door about as I had found it and just stood. Silence. Time passed. It passed in the dry whirr of an electric clock on a console radio, in the far-off hoot of an auto horn down on Beachwood half a mile below, in the distant hornet drone of a night-flying plane, in the metallic wheeze of a cricket under the house.

Then I wasn't alone any longer.

Mrs. Marineau slid into the room at the far end, by a door beside the french doors. She didn't make any more noise than a butterfly. She still wore the pillbox black hat and the burnt-orange tweeds, and they still looked like hell together. She had a small glove in her hand wrapped around the butt of a gun. I don't know why. I never did find that out.

She didn't see me at once and when she did it didn't mean anything much. She just lifted the gun a little and slid along the carpet towards me, her lip clutched back so far that I couldn't even see the teeth that clutched it.

But I had a gun out now myself. We looked at each other across our guns. Maybe she knew me. I hadn't any idea from her expression.

I said, "You got them, huh?"

She nodded a little. "Just him," she said.

"Put the gun down. You're all through with it."

She lowered it a little. She hadn't seemed to notice the Colt I was pushing through the air in her general direction. I lowered that too.

She said, "She wasn't here."

Her voice had a dry, impersonal sound, flat, without timbre.

"Miss Baring wasn't here?" I asked.

"No."

"Remember me?"

She took a better look at me but her face didn't light up with any pleasure.

"I'm the guy that was looking for Miss Baring," I said. "You told me where to come. Remember? Only Dave sent a loogan to put the arm on me and ride me around while he came up here himself and promoted something. I couldn't guess what."

The brunette said, "You're no cop. Dave said you were a fake."

I made a broad, hearty gesture and moved a little closer to her, unobtrusively. "Not a city cop," I admitted. "But a cop. And that was a long time ago. Things have happened since then. Haven't they?"

"Yes," she said. "Especially to Dave. Hee, hee."

It wasn't a laugh. It wasn't meant to be a laugh. It was just a little steam escaping through a safety valve.

"Hee, hee," I said. We looked at each other like a couple of nuts being Napoleon and Josephine.

The idea was to get close enough to grab her gun. I was still too far.

"Anybody here besides you?" I asked.

"Just Dave."

"I had an idea Dave was here." It wasn't clever, but it was good for another foot.

"Oh, Dave's here," she agreed. "Yes. You'd like to see him?"

"Well – if it isn't too much trouble."

"Hee, hee," she said. "No trouble at all. Like this."

She jerked the gun up and snapped the trigger at me. She did it without moving a muscle of her face.

The gun not going off puzzled her, in a sort of vague, week-before-last manner. Nothing immediate or important. I wasn't there any more. She lifted the gun up, still being very careful about the black kid glove wrapped about its butt, and peered into the muzzle. That didn't get her anywhere. She shook the gun. Then she was aware of me again. I hadn't moved. I didn't have to, now.

"I guess it's not loaded," she said.

"Maybe just all used up," I said. "Too bad. These little ones only hold seven. My shells won't fit, either. Let's see if I can do anything?"

She put the gun in my hand. Then she dusted her hands together. Her eyes didn't seem to have any pupils, or to be all pupils. I wasn't sure which.

The gun wasn't loaded. The magazine was quite empty. I sniffed the muzzle. The gun hadn't been fired since it was last cleaned.

That got me. Up to that point it had looked fairly simple, if I could get by without any more murder. But this threw it. I hadn't any idea what either of us was talking about now.

I dropped her pistol into my side pocket and put mine back on my hip and chewed my lip for a couple of minutes, to see what might turn up. Nothing did.

The sharp-faced Mrs. Marineau merely stood still and stared at a spot between my eyes, fuzzily, like a rather blotto tourist seeing a swell sunset on Mount Whitney.

"Well," I said at last, "let's kind of look through the house and see what's what."

"You mean Dave?"

"Yeah, we could take that in."

"He's in the bedroom." She tittered. "He's at home in bed-rooms."

I touched her arm and turned her around. She turned obediently, like a small child.

"But this one will be the last one he'll be at home in," she said. "Hee, hee."

"Oh, yeah. Sure," I said.

My voice sounded to me like the voice of a midget.

Dave Marineau was dead all right – if there had been any doubt about it.

A white bowl lamp with raised figures shone beside a large bed in a green and silver bedroom. It was the only light in the room. It filtered a hushed kind of light down at his face. He hadn't been dead long enough to get the corpse look.

He lay sprawled casually on the bed, a little sideways, as though he had been standing in front of it when he was shot. One arm was flung out as loose as a strand of kelp and the other was under him. His open eyes were flat and shiny and almost seemed to hold a self-satisfied expression. His mouth was open a little and the lamplight glistened on the edges of his upper teeth.

I didn't see the wound at all at first. It was high up, on the right side of his head, in the temple, but back rather far, almost far enough to drive the petrosal bone through the brain. It was powder-burned, rimmed with dusky red, and a fine trickle spidered down from it and got browner as it got thinner against his cheek.

"Hell, that's a contact wound," I snapped at the woman. "A suicide wound."

She stood at the foot of the bed and stared at the wall above his head. If she was interested in anything besides the wall, she didn't show it.

I lifted his still limp right hand and sniffed at the place where the base of the thumb joins the palm. I smelled cordite, then I didn't smell cordite, then I didn't know whether

I smelled cordite or not. It didn't matter, of course. A paraffin test would prove it one way or the other.

I put the hand down again, carefully, as though it were a fragile thing of great value. Then I plowed around on the bed, went down on the floor, got halfway under the bed, swore, got up again and rolled the dead man to one side enough to look under him. There was a bright, brassy shell-case but no gun.

It looked like murder again. I liked that better. He wasn't the suicide type.

"See any gun?" I asked her.

"No." Her face was as blank as a pie pan.

"Where's the Baring girl? What are you supposed to be doing here?"

She bit the end of her left little finger. "I'd better confess," she said. "I came here to kill them both."

"Go on," I said.

"Nobody was here. Of course, after I phoned him and he told me you were not a real cop and there was no murder and you were a blackmailer and just trying to scare me out of the address – " She stopped and sobbed once, hardly more than a sniff, and moved her line of sight to a corner of the ceiling.

Her words had a tumbled arrangement, but she spoke them like a drugstore Indian.

"I came here to kill both of them," she said. "I don't deny that."

"With an empty gun?"

"It wasn't empty two days ago. I looked. Dave must have emptied it. He must have been afraid."

"That listens," I said. "Go on."

"So I came here. That was the last insult – his sending you to me to get her *address*. That was more than I would – "

"The story," I said. "I know how you felt. I've read it in the love mags myself."

606

"Yes. Well, he said there was something about Miss Baring he had to see her about on account of the studio and it was nothing personal, never had been, never would be – "

"My Gawd," I said, "I know that too. I know what he'd feed you. We've got a dead man lying around here. We've got to do something, even if he was just your husband."

"You ——— ," she said.

"Yeah," I said. "That's better than the dopey talk. Go on."

"The door wasn't shut. I came in. That's all. Now, I'm going. And you're not going to stop me. You know where I live, you ——— ." She called me the same name again.

"We'll talk to some law first," I said. I went over and shut the door and turned the key on the inside of it and took it out. Then I went over to the french doors. The woman gave me looks, but I couldn't hear what her lips were calling me now.

French doors on the far side of the bed opened on the same balcony as the living-room. The telephone was in a niche in the wall there, by the bed, where you could yawn and reach out for it in the morning and order a tray of diamond necklaces sent up to try on.

I sat down on the side of the bed and reached for the phone, and a muffled voice came to me through the glass and said: "Hold it, pal! Just hold it!"

Even muffled by the glass it was a deep, soft voice. I had heard it before. It was Skalla's voice.

I was in line with the lamp. The lamp was right behind me. I dived off the bed on to the floor, clawing at my hip.

A shot roared and glass sprinkled the back of my neck. I couldn't figure it. Skalla wasn't on the balcony. I had looked.

I rolled over and started to snake away along the floor away from the french doors, my only chance with the lamp where it was.

Mrs. Marineau did just the right thing – for the other side. She jerked a slipper off and started slamming me with the heel of it. I grabbed for her ankles and we wrestled around and she cut the top of my head to pieces.

I threw her over. It didn't last long. When I started to get up Skalla was in the room, laughing at me. The .45 still had a home in his fist. The french door and the locked screen outside looked as though a rogue elephant had passed that way.

"Okay," I said. "I give up."

"Who's the twist? She sure likes you, pal."

I got up on my feet. The woman was over in a corner somewhere. I didn't even look at her.

"Turn around, pal, while I give you the fan."

I hadn't worked my gun loose yet. He got that. I didn't say anything about the door key, but he took it. So he must have been watching from somewhere. He left me my car keys. He looked at the little empty gun and dropped it back in my pocket.

"Where'd you come from?" I asked.

"Easy. Clumb up the balcony and held on, looking through the grill at you. Cinch to an old circus man. How you been, pal?"

Blood from the top of my head was leaking down my face. I got a handkerchief out and mopped at it. I didn't answer him.

"Jeeze, you sure was funny on the bed grabbin' for the phone with the stiff at your back."

"I was a scream," I growled. "Take it easy. He's her husband."

He looked at her. "She's his woman?"

I nodded and wished I hadn't.

"That's tough. If I'd a known — but I couldn't help meself. The guy asked for it."

"You — " I started to say, staring at him. I heard a queer, strained whine behind me, from the woman.

"Who else, pal? Who else? Let's all go back in that livin'-room. Seems to me they was a bottle of nice-looking hooch there. And you need some stuff on that head."

"You're crazy to stick around here," I growled. "There's a general pickup out for you. The only way out of this canyon is back down Beachwood or over the hills – on foot."

Skalla looked at me and said very quietly, "Nobody's phoned no law from here, pal."

Skalla watched me while I washed and put some tape on my head in the bathroom. Then we went back to the living-room. Mrs. Marineau, curled up on one of the davenports, looked blankly at the unlit fire. She didn't say anything.

She hadn't run away because Skalla had her in sight all the time. She acted resigned, indifferent, as if she didn't care what happened now.

I poured three drinks from the Vat 69 bottle, handed one to the brunette. She held her hand out for the glass, half smiled at me, crumpled off the davenport to the floor with the smile still on her face.

I put the glass down, lifted her and put her back on the davenport with her head low. Skalla stared at her. She was out cold, as white as paper.

Skalla took his drink, sat down on the other davenport and put the .45 beside him. He drank his drink looking at the woman, with a queer expression on his big pale face.

"Tough," he said. "Tough. But the louse was cheatin' on her anyways. The hell with him." He reached for another drink, swallowed it, sat down near her on the other davenport right-angled to the one she lay on.

"So you're a dick," he said.

"How'd you guess?"

"Lu Shamey told me about a guy goin' there. He sounded like you. I been around and looked in your heap outside. I walk silent."

"Well – what now?" I asked.

He looked more enormous than ever in the room in his sports clothes. The clothes of a smart-aleck kid. I wondered how long it had taken him to get them together. They couldn't have been ready-made. He was much too big for that.

His feet were spread wide on the apricot rug, he looked down sadly at the white kid explosions on the suede. They were the worst-looking shoes I ever saw.

"What you doin' here?" he asked gruffly.

"Looking for Beulah. I thought she might need a little help. I had a bet with a city cop I'd find her before he found you. But I haven't found her yet."

"You ain't seen her, huh?"

I shook my head, slowly, very carefully.

He said softly, "Me neither, pal. I been around for hours. She ain't been home. Only the guy in the bedroom come here. How about the dinge manager up at Shamey's?"

"That's what the tag's for."

"Yeah. A guy like that. They would. Well, I gotta blow. I'd like to take the stiff, account of Beulah. Can't leave him around to scare her. But I guess it ain't any use now. The dinge kill queers that."

He looked at the woman at his elbow on the other little davenport. Her face was still greenish white, her eyes shut. There was a movement of her breast.

"Without her," he said, "I guess I'd clean up right and button you good." He touched the .45 at his side. "No hard feelings, of course. Just for Beulah. But the way it is – heck, I can't knock the frail off."

"Too bad," I snarled, feeling my head.

He grinned. "I guess I'll take your heap. For a short ways. Throw them keys over."

I threw them over. He picked them up and laid them beside the big Colt. He leaned forward a little. Then he reached back into one of his patch pockets and brought out a small pearl-handled gun, about .25 caliber. He held it on the flat of his hand.

"This done it," he said. "I left a rent hack I had on the street below and come up the bank and around the house. I hear the bell ring. This guy is at the front door. I don't come up far enough for him to see me. Nobody answers. Well, what do you think? The guy's got a key. A key to Beulah's house!"

His huge face became one vast scowl. The woman on the davenport was breathing a little more deeply, and I thought I saw one of her eyelids twitch.

"What the hell," I said. "He could get that a dozen ways. He's a boss at KLBL where she works. He could get at her bag, take an impression. Hell, she didn't have to give it to him."

"That's right, pal." He beamed. "O' course, she didn't have to give it to the —— . Okay, he went in, and I made it fast after him. But he had the door shut. I opened it my way. After that it didn't shut so good, you might of noticed. He was in the middle of this here room, over there by a desk. He's been here before all right though" – the scowl came back again, although not quite so black – "because he slipped a hand into the desk drawer and come up with this." He danced the pearlhandled thing on his enormous palm.

Mrs. Marineau's face now had distinct lines of tensity.

"So I start for him. He lets one go. A miss. He's scared and runs into the bedroom. Me after. He lets go again. Another miss. You'll find them slugs in the wall somewheres."

"I'll make a point of it," I said.

"Yeah, then I got him. Well, hell, the guy's only a punk in a white muffler. If she's washed up with me, okay. I want it from her, see? Not from no greasy-faced piece of cheese like him. So I'm sore. But the guy's got guts at that."

He rubbed his chin. I doubted the last bit.

"I say: 'My woman lives here, pal. How come?' He says: 'Come back tomorrow. This here is my night.' "

Skalla spread his free left hand in a large gesture. "After that nature's got to take its course, ain't it? I pull his arms and legs off. Only while I'm doing it the damn little gat pops off and he's as limp as – as – " He glanced at the woman and didn't finish what he was going to say. "Yeah, he was dead."

One of the woman's eyelids flickered again. I said, "Then?"

"I scrammed. A guy does. But I come back. I got to thinkin' it's tough on Beulah, with that stiff on her bed. So I'll just go back and ferry him out to the desert and then crawl in a hole for a while. Then this frail comes along and spoils that part."

The woman must have been shamming for quite a long time. She must have been moving her legs and feet and turning her body a fraction of an inch at a time, to get in the right position, to get leverage against the back of the davenport.

The pearl-handled gun still lay on Skalla's flat hand when she moved. She shot off the davenport in a flat dive, gathering herself in the air like an acrobat. She brushed his knees and picked the gun off his hand as neatly as a chipmunk peels a nut.

He stood up and swore as she rolled against his legs. The big Colt was at his side, but he didn't touch it or reach for it. He stooped to take hold of the woman with his big hands empty.

She laughed just before she shot him.

She shot him four times, in the lower belly, then the hammer clicked. She threw the gun at his face and rolled away from him.

He stepped over her without touching her. His big pale face was quite empty for a moment, then it settled into stiff lines of torture, lines that seemed to have been there always.

He walked erectly along the rug towards the front door. I jumped for the big Colt and got it. To keep it from the woman. At the fourth step he took, blood showed on the yellowish nap of the rug. After that it showed at every step he took.

He reached the door and put his big hand flat against the wood and leaned there for a moment. Then he shook his head and turned back. His hand left a bloody smear on the door from where he had been holding his belly.

He sat down in the first chair he came to and leaned forward and held himself tightly with his hands. The blood came between his fingers slowly, like water from an overflowing basin.

"Them little slugs," he said, "hurt just like the big ones, down below anyways."

The dark woman walked towards him like a marionette. He watched her come unblinkingly, under his half-lowered, heavy lids.

When she got close enough she leaned over and spit in his face.

He didn't move. His eyes didn't change. I jumped for her and threw her into a chair. I wasn't nice about it.

"Leave her alone," he grunted at me. "Maybe she loved the guy."

Nobody tried to stop me from telephoning this time.

Hours later I sat on a red stool at Lucca's, at Fifth and Western, and sipped a martini and wondered how it felt to be mixing them all day and never drink one.

I took another martini over and ordered a meal. I guess I ate it. It was late, past one. Skalla was in the prison ward of the General Hospital. Miss Baring hadn't showed up yet, but they knew she would, as soon as she heard Skalla was under glass, and no longer dangerous.

KLBL, who didn't know anything about it at first, had got a nice hush working. They were to have twenty-four clear hours to decide how to release the story.

Lucca's was almost as full as at noon. After a while an Italian brunette with a grand nose and eyes you wouldn't fool with came over and said: "I have a table for you now."

My imagination put Skalla across the table from me. His flat black eyes had something in them that was more than mere pain, something he wanted me to do. Part of the time he was trying to tell me what it was, and part of the time he was holding his belly in one piece and saying again: "Leave her alone. Maybe she loved the guy."

I left there and drove north to Franklin and over Franklin to Beachwood and up to Heather Street. It wasn't staked. They were that sure of her.

I drifted along the street below and looked up the scrubby slope spattered with moonlight and showing her house from behind as if it were three stories high. I could see the metal brackets that supported the porch. They looked high enough off the ground so that a man would need a balloon to reach them. But there was where he had gone up. Always the hard way with him.

He could have run away and had a fight for his money or even bought himself a place to live up in. There were plenty of people in the business, and they wouldn't fool with Skalla. But he had come back instead to climb her balcony, like Romeo, and get his stomach full of slugs. From the wrong woman, as usual.

I drove around a white curve that looked like moonlight itself and parked and walked up the hill the rest of the way. I carried a flash, but I didn't need it to see there was nobody on the doorstep waiting for the milk. I didn't go in the front way. There might just happen to be some snooper with night glasses up on the hill.

I sneaked up the bank from behind, between the house and the empty garage. I found a window I could reach and made not much noise breaking it with a gun inside my hat. Nothing happened except that the crickets and tree frogs stopped for a moment.

I picked a way to the bedroom and prowled my flash around discreetly, after lowering the shades and pulling the drapes across them. The light dropped on a tumbled bed, on daubs of print powder, on cigarette butts on the window sills and heel marks in the nap of the carpet. There was a green and silver toilet set on the dressing table and three suitcases in the closet. There was a built-in bureau back in there with a lock that meant business. I had a chilled-steel screwdriver with me as well as the flash. I jimmied it.

The jewelry wasn't worth a thousand dollars. Perhaps not half. But it meant a lot to a girl in show business. I put it back where I got it.

The living-room had shut windows and a queer, unpleasant, sadistic smell. The law enforcement had taken care of the Vat 69, to make it easier for the fingerprint men. I had to use my own. I got a chair that hadn't been bled on into a corner, wet my throat and waited in the darkness.

A shade flapped in the basement or somewhere. That made me wet my throat again. Somebody came out of a house half a dozen blocks away and whooped. A door banged. Silence. The tree frogs started again, then the crickets. Then the electric clock on the radio got louder than all the other sounds together.

Then I went to sleep.

When I woke up the moon had gone from the front windows and a car had stopped somewhere. Light, delicate, careful steps separated themselves from the night. They were outside the front door. A key fumbled in the lock.

In the opening door the dim sky showed a head without a hat. The slope of the hill was too dark to outline any more. The door clicked shut.

Steps rustled on the rug. I already had the lamp cord in my fingers. I yanked it and there was light.

The girl didn't make a sound, not a whisper of sound. She just pointed the gun at me.

I said, "Hello, Beulah."

She was worth waiting for.

Not too tall, not too short; that girl. She had the long legs that can walk and dance. Her hair even by the light of the one lamp was like a brush fire at night. Her face had laughter wrinkles at the corner of the eyes. Her mouth could laugh.

The features were shadowed and had that drawn look that makes some faces more beautiful because it makes them more delicate. I couldn't see her eyes. They might have been blue enough to make you jump, but I couldn't see.

The gun looked about a .32, but had the extreme right-angled grip of a Mauser.

After a while she said very softly, "Police, I suppose."

She had a nice voice, too. I still think of it, at times.

I said, "Let's sit down and talk. We're all alone here. Ever drink out of the bottle?"

She didn't answer. She looked down at the gun she was holding, half smiled, shook her head.

"You wouldn't make two mistakes," I said. "Not a girl as smart as you are."

She tucked the gun into the side pocket of a long ulster-like coat with a military collar.

"Who are you?"

"Just a shamus. Private detective to you. Carmady is the name. Need a lift?"

I held my bottle out. It hadn't grown to my hand yet. I still had to hold it.

"I don't drink. Who hired you?"

"KLBL. To protect you from Steve Skalla."

"So they know," she said. "So they know about him."

I digested that and said nothing.

"Who's been here?" she went on sharply. She was still standing in the middle of the room, with her hands in her coat pockets now, and no hat.

"Everybody but the plumber," I said. "He's a little late, as usual."

"You're one of *those* men." Her nose seemed to curl a little. "Drugstore comics."

"No," I said. "Not really. It's just a way I get talking to the people I have to talk to. Skalla came back again and ran into trouble and got shot up and arrested. He's in the hospital. Pretty bad."

She didn't move. "How bad?"

"He might live if he'd have surgery. Doubtful, even with that. Hopeless without. He has three in the intestines and one in the liver."

She moved at last and started to sit down. "Not in that chair," I said quickly. "Over here."

She came over and sat near me, on one of the davenports. Lights twisted in her eyes. I could see them now. Little twisting lights like Catherine wheels spinning brightly.

She said, "Why did he come back?"

"He thought he ought to tidy up. Remove the body and so on. A nice guy, Skalla."

"Do you think so?"

"Lady, if nobody else in the world thinks so, I do."

"I'll take that drink," she said.

I handed her the bottle. I grabbed it away in a hurry. "Gosh," I said. "You have to break in on this stuff."

She looked towards the side door that led to the bedroom back of me.

"Gone to the morgue," I said. "You can go in there."

She stood up at once and went out of the room. She came back almost at once.

"What have they got on Steve?" she asked. "If he recovers."

"He killed a nigger over on Central this morning. It was more or less self-defense on both sides. I don't know. Except for Marineau he might get a break."

"Marineau?" she said.

"Yeah. You knew he killed Marineau."

"Don't be silly," she said. "I killed Dave Marineau."

"Okay," I said. "But that's not the way Steve wants it."

She stared at me. "You mean Steve came back here deliberately to take the blame?"

"If he had to, I guess. I think he really meant to cart Marineau off to the desert and lose him. Only a woman showed up here – Mrs. Marineau."

"Yes," the girl said tonelessly. "She thinks I was his mistress. That greasy spoon."

"Were you?" I asked.

"Don't try that again," she said. "Even if I did work on Central Avenue once." She went out of the room again.

Sounds of a suitcase being yanked about came into the living-room. I went in after her. She was packing pieces of cobweb and packing them as if she liked nice things nicely packed.

"You don't wear that stuff down in the tank," I told her, leaning in the door.

She ignored me some more. "I was going to make a break for Mexico," she said. "Then South America. I didn't mean to shoot him. He roughed me up and tried to blackmail me into something and I went and got the gun. Then we struggled again and it went off. Then I ran away."

"Just what Skalla said he did," I said. "Hell, couldn't you just have shot the —— on purpose?"

"Not for your benefit," she said. "Or any cop. Not when I did eight months in Dalhart, Texas, once for rolling a drunk. Not with that Marineau woman yelling her head off that I seduced him and then got sick of him."

"A lot she'll say," I grunted. "After I tell how she spit in Skalla's face when he had four slugs in him."

She shivered. Her face whitened. She went on taking the things out of the suitcase and putting them in again.

"Did you roll the drunk really?"

She looked up at me, then down. "Yes," she whispered.

I went over nearer to her. "Got any bruises or torn clothes to show?" I asked.

"No."

"Too bad," I said, and took hold of her.

Her eyes flamed at first and then turned to black stone. I tore her coat off, tore her up plenty, put hard fingers into her arms and neck and used my knuckles on her mouth. I let her go, panting. She reeled away from me, but didn't quite fall.

"We'll have to wait for the bruises to set and darken," I said. "Then we'll go downtown."

She began to laugh. Then she went over to the mirror and looked at herself. She began to cry.

"Get out of here while I change my clothes!" she yelled. "I'll give it a tumble. But if it makes any difference to Steve I'm going to tell it right."

"Aw, shut up and change your clothes," I said.

I went out and banged the door.

I hadn't even kissed her. I could have done that, at least. She wouldn't have minded any more than the rest of the knocking about I gave her.

We rode the rest of the night, first in separate cars to hide hers in my garage, then in mine. We rode up the coast and had coffee and sandwiches at Malibu, then on up and over. We had breakfast at the bottom of the Ridge Route, just north of San Fernando.

Her face looked like a catcher's mitt after a tough season. She had a lower lip the size of a banana and you could have cooked steaks on the bruises on her arms and neck, they were so hot.

With the first strong daylight we went to the City Hall.

They didn't even think of holding her or checking her up. They practically wrote the statement themselves. She signed it blank-eyed, thinking of something else. Then a man from KLBL and his wire came down to get her.

So I didn't get to ride her to a hotel. She didn't get to see Skalla either, not then. He was under morphine.

He died at two-thirty the same afternoon. She was holding one of his huge, limp fingers, but he didn't know her from the Queen of Siam.

MANDARIN'S JADE

1 300 CARATS OF FEI TSUI

I WAS SMOKING my pipe and making faces at the back of my name on the glass part of the office door when Violets M'Gee called me up. There hadn't been any business in a week.

"How's the sleuth racket, huh?" Violets asked. He's a homicide dick in the sheriff's office. "Take a little flutter down at the beach? Body guarding or something, it is."

"Anything that goes with a dollar," I said. "Except murder. I get three-fifty for that."

"I bet you do nice neat work too. Here's the lay, John."

He gave me the name, address and telephone number of a man named Lindley Paul who lived at Castellamare, was a socialite and went everywhere except to work, lived alone with a Jap servant, and drove a very large car. The sheriff's office had nothing against him except that he had too much fun.

Castellamare was in the city limits, but didn't look it, being a couple of dozen houses of various sizes hanging by their eyebrows to the side of a mountain, and looking as if a good sneeze would drop them down among the box lunches on the beach. There was a sidewalk café up on the highway, and beside that a cement arch which was really a pedestrian bridge. From the inner end of this a flight of white concrete steps went straight as a ruler up the side of the mountain.

Quinonal Avenue, Mr. Lindley Paul had told me over the phone, was the third street up, if I cared to walk. It was, he said, the easiest way to find his place the first time, the streets being designed in a pattern of interesting but rather intricate curves. People had been known to wander about in them for several hours without making any more yardage than an angleworm in a bait can.

So I parked my old blue Chrysler down below and walked up. It was a fine evening and there was still some sparkle on the water when I started. It had all gone when I reached the top. I sat down on the top step and rubbed my leg muscles and waited for my pulse to come down into the low hundreds. After that I shook my shirt loose from my back and went along to the house, which was the only one in the foreground.

It was a nice enough house, but it didn't look like really important money. There was a salt-tarnished iron staircase going up to the front door and the garage was underneath the house. A long black battleship of a car was backed into it, an immense streamlined boat with enough hood for three cars and a coyote tail tied to the radiator cap. It looked as if it had cost more than the house.

The man who opened the door at the top of the iron stairs wore a white flannel suit with a violet satin scarf arranged loosely inside the collar. He had a soft brown neck, like the neck of a very strong woman. He had pale blue-green eyes, about the color of an aquamarine, features on the heavy side but very handsome, three precise ledges of thick blond hair rising from a smooth brown forehead, an inch more of height than I had – which made him six feet one – and the general look of a guy who would wear a white flannel suit with a violet satin scarf inside the collar.

He cleared his throat, looked over my left shoulder, and said: "Yes?"

"I'm the man you sent for. The one Violets M'Gee recommended."

"Violets? Gracious, what a peculiar nickname. Let me see, your name is –"

He hesitated and I let him work at it until he cleared his throat again and moved his blue-green eyes to a spot several miles beyond my other shoulder.

"Dalmas," I said. "The same as it was this afternoon."

"Oh, come in, Mr. Dalmas. You'll excuse me, I'm sure. My houseboy is away this evening. So I —" He smiled deprecatingly at the closing door, as though opening and closing it himself sort of dirtied him.

The door put us on a balcony that ran around three sides of a big living-room, only three steps above it in level. We went down the steps and Lindley Paul pointed with his eyebrows at a pink chair, and I sat down on it and hoped I wouldn't leave a mark.

It was the kind of room where people sit on floor cushions with their feet in their laps and sip absinthe through lumps of sugar and talk from the backs of their throats, and some of them just squeak. There were bookshelves all around the balcony and bits of angular sculpture in glazed clay on pedestals. There were cozy little divans and bits of embroidered silk tossed here and there against the bases of lamps and so on. There was a big rosewood grand piano and on it a very tall vase with just one yellow rose in it, and under its leg there was a peach-colored Chinese rug a gopher could have spent a week in without showing his nose above the nap.

Lindley Paul leaned in the curve of the piano and lit a cigarette without offering me one. He put his head back to blow smoke at the tall ceiling and that made his throat look more than ever like the throat of a woman.

"It's a very slight matter," he said negligently. "Really hardly worth bothering you about. But I thought I might as well have an escort. You must promise not to flash any guns or anything like that. I suppose you do carry a gun."

"Oh, yes," I said. "Yes." I looked at the dimple in his chin. You could have lost a marble in it.

"Well, I won't want you to use it, you know, or anything like that. I'm just meeting a couple of men and buying something from them. I shall be carrying a little money in cash."

"How much money and what for?" I asked, putting one of my own matches to one of my own cigarettes.

"Well, really —" It was a nice smile, but I could have put the heel of my hand in it without feeling bad. I just didn't like the man.

"It's rather a confidential mission I'm undertaking for a friend. I'd hardly care to go into the details," he said.

"You just want me to go along to hold your hat," I suggested.

His hand jerked and some ash fell on his white suit cuff. That annoyed him. He frowned down at it, then he said softly, in the manner of a sultan suggesting a silk noose for a harem lady whose tricks have gone stale: "You are not being impertinent, I hope."

"Hope is what keeps us alive," I said.

He stared at me for a while. "I've a damned good mind to give you a sock on the nose," he said.

"That's more like it," I said. "You couldn't do it without hardening up a bit, but I like the spirit. Now let's talk business."

He was still a bit sore. "I ordered a bodyguard," he said coldly. "If I employed a private secretary I shouldn't tell him all my personal business."

"He'd know it if he worked for you steady. He'd know it upside down and backwards. But I'm just day labor. You've got to tell me. What is it — blackmail?"

After a long time he said: "No. It's a necklace of Fei Tsui jade worth at least seventy-five thousand dollars. Did you ever hear of Fei Tsui jade?"

"No."

"We'll have a little brandy and I'll tell you about it. Yes, we'll have a little brandy."

He leaned away from the piano and went off like a dancer, without moving his body above the waist. I put my cigarette out and sniffed at the air and thought I smelled sandalwood, and then Lindley Paul came back with a nice-looking bottle and a couple of sniffing glasses. He poured a table-spoonful in each and handed me a glass.

I put mine down in one piece and waited for him to get through rolling his spoonful under his nose and talk. He got around to it after a while.

He said in a pleasant enough tone: "Fei Tsui jade is the only really valuable kind. The others are valuable for the workmanship put on them, chiefly. Fei Tsui is valuable in itself. There are no known unworked deposits, very little of it in existence, all the known deposits having been exhausted hundreds of years ago. A friend of mine had a necklace of this jade. Fifty-one carved mandarin beads, perfectly matched, about six carats each. It was taken in a holdup some time ago. It was the only thing taken, and we were warned – I happened to be with this lady, which is one reason why I'm taking the risk of making the pay-off – not to tell the police or any insurance company, but wait for a phone call. The call came in a couple of days, the price was set at ten thousand dollars, and the time is tonight at eleven. I haven't heard the place yet. But it's to be somewhere fairly near here, somewhere along the Palisades."

I looked into my empty sniffing glass and shook it. He put a little more brandy in it for me. I sent that after the first dose and lit another cigarette, one of his this time, a nice Virginia Straight Cut with his monogram on the paper.

"Jewel ransom racket," I said. "Well organized, or they wouldn't know where and when to pull the job. People don't wear valuable jewels out very much, and half of the time, when they do, they're phonies. Is jade hard to imitate?"

"As to material, no," Lindley Paul said. "As to workmanship – that would take a lifetime."

"So the stuff can't be cut," I said. "Which means it can't be fenced except for a small fraction of the value. So the ransom money is the gang's only pay-off. I'd say they'll play ball. You left your bodyguard problem pretty late, Mr. Paul. How do you know they'll stand for a bodyguard?"

"I don't," he said rather wearily. "But I'm no hero. I like company in the dark. If the thing misses – it misses. I thought of going it alone and then I thought, why not have a man hidden in the back of my car, just in case?"

"In case they take your money and give you a dummy package? How could I prevent that? If I start shooting and come out on top and it *is* a dummy package, you'll never see your jade again. The contact men won't know who's behind the gang. And if I don't open up, they'll be gone before you can see what they've left you. They may not even give you anything. They may tell you your stuff will come to you through the mail after the money has been checked for markings. Is it marked?"

"My God, no!"

"It ought to be," I growled. "It can be marked these days so that only a microscope and black light could show the markings up. But that takes equipment, which means cops. Okay. I'll take a flutter at it. My part will cost you fifty bucks. Better give it to me now, in case we don't come back. I like to feel money."

His broad, handsome face seemed to turn a little white and glistening. He said swiftly: "Let's have some more brandy."

He poured a real drink this time.

We sat around and waited for the phone to ring. I got my fifty bucks to play with.

The phone rang four times and it sounded from his voice as if women were talking to him. The call we wanted didn't come through until ten-forty.

2 I LOSE MY CLIENT

I DROVE. Or rather I held the wheel of the big black car and let it drive itself. I was wearing a sporty light-colored overcoat and hat belonging to Lindley Paul. I had ten grand in hundred-dollar bills in one of the pockets. Paul was in the back seat. He had a silver-mounted Luger that was a pip to look at, and I hoped he knew how to use it. There wasn't anything about the job I liked.

The meeting place was a hollow at the head of Purissima Canyon, about fifteen minutes from the house. Paul said he knew the spot fairly well and wouldn't have any trouble directing me.

We switchbacked and figure-eighted around on the side of the mountain until I got dizzy and then all of a sudden we were out on the state highway, and the lights of the streaming cars were a solid white beam as far as you could see in either direction. The long-haul trucks were on their way.

We turned inland past a service station at Sunset Boulevard. There was loneliness then, and for a while the smell of kelp, not very strong, and the smell of wild sage dripping down the dark slopes much stronger. A dim, distant yellow window would peek down at us from the crest of some realtor's dream. A car would growl by and its white glare would hide the hills for a moment. There was a half-moon and wisps of cold fog chasing it down the sky.

"Off here is the Bel-Air Beach Club," Paul said. "The next canyon is Las Pulgas and the next after that is Purissima. We turn off at the top of the next rise." His voice was hushed, taut. It didn't have any of the Park Avenue brass of our earlier acquaintance.

"Keep your head down," I growled back at him. "We may be watched all the way. This car sticks out like spats at an Iowa picnic."

The car purred on in front of me until, "Turn right here," he whispered sharply at the top of the next hill.

I swung the black car into a wide, weed-grown boulevard that had never jelled into a traffic artery. The black stumps of unfinished electroliers jutted up from the crusted sidewalk.

Brush leaned over the concrete from the waste land behind. I could hear crickets chirp and tree frogs drone behind them. The car was that silent.

There was a house to a block now, all dark. The folks out there went to bed with the chickens it seemed. At the end of this road the concrete stopped abruptly and we slid down a dirt slope to a dirt terrace, then down another slope, and a barricade of what looked like four-by-fours painted white loomed across the dirt road.

I heard a rustling behind me and Paul leaned over the seat, with a sigh in his whispered voice. "This is the spot. You've got to get out and move that barricade and drive on down into the hollow. That's probably so that we can't make a quick exit, as we'd have to back out with this car. They want their time to get away."

"Shut up and keep down unless you hear me yell," I said.

I cut the almost noiseless motor and sat there listening. The crickets and tree frogs got a little louder. I heard nothing else. Nobody was moving nearby, or the crickets would have been still. I touched the cold butt of the gun under my arm, opened the car door and slid out on to the hard clay, stood there. There was brush all around. I could smell the sage. There was enough of it to hide an army. I went towards the barricade.

Perhaps this was just a tryout, to see if Paul did what he was told to do.

I put my hands out – it took both of them – and started to lift a section of the white barrier to one side. It wasn't a try-out. The largest flashlight in the world hit me square in the face from a bush not fifteen feet away.

A thin, high, niggerish voice piped out of the darkness behind the flash: "Two of us with shotguns. Put them mitts up high an' empty. We ain't takin' no chances."

I didn't say anything. For a moment I just stood holding the barricade inches off the ground. Nothing from Paul or the car. Then the weight of the four-by-fours pulled my muscles and my brain said let go and I put the section down again. I put my hands slowly into the air. The flash pinned me like a fly squashed on the wall. I had no particular thought except a vague wonder if there hadn't been a better way for us to work it.

"Tha's fine," the thin, high, whining voice said. "Jes' hold like that until I git aroun' to you."

The voice awakened vague echoes in my brain. It didn't mean anything though. My memory had too many such echoes. I wondered what Paul was doing. A thin, sharp figure detached itself from the fan of light, immediately ceased to be sharp or of any shape at all, and became a vague rustling off to the side. Then the rustling was behind me. I kept my hands in the air and blinked at the glare of the flash.

A light finger touched my back, then the hard end of a gun. The half-remembered voice said: "This may hurt jes' a little."

A giggle and a swishing sound. A white, hot glare jumped through the top of my head. I piled down on the barricade and clawed at it and yelled. My right hand tried to jerk down under my left arm.

I didn't hear the swishing sound the second time. I only saw the white glare get larger and larger, until there was nothing else anywhere but hard, aching white light. Then there was darkness in which something red wriggled like a germ under the microscope. Then there was nothing red and nothing wriggling, just darkness, and emptiness, and a falling sensation.

I woke up looking fuzzily at a star and listening to two goblins talking in a black hat.

"Lou Lid."

"What's that?"

"Lou Lid."

"Who's Lou Lid?"

"A tough dinge gunman you saw third-degreed once down at the Hall."

"Oh . . . Lou Lid."

I rolled over and clawed at the ground and crawled up on one knee. I groaned. There wasn't anybody there. I was talking to myself, coming out of it. I balanced myself, holding my hands flat on the ground, listening, not hearing anything. When I moved my hands, dried burrs stuck to the skin and the sticky ooze from the purple sage from which wild bees get most of their honey.

Honey was sweet. Much, much too sweet, and too hard on the stomach. I leaned down and vomited.

Time passed and I gathered my insides together again. I still didn't hear anything but the buzzing in my own ears. I got up very cautiously, like an old man getting out of a tub bath. My feet didn't have much feeling in them and my legs were rubbery. I wobbled and wiped the cold sweat of nausea off my forehead and felt the back of my head. It was soft and pulpy, like a bruised peach. When I touched it I could feel the pain clear down to my ankles. I could feel every pain I ever felt since the first time I got kicked in the rear in grade school.

Then my eyes cleared enough for me to see the outlines of the shallow bowl of wild land, with brush growing on the banks all around like a low wall, and a dirt road, indistinct under the sinking moon, crawling up one side. Then I saw the car.

It was quite close to me, not more than twenty feet away. I just hadn't looked in that direction. It was Lindley Paul's car, lightless. I stumbled over to it and instinctively grabbed under my arm for a gun. Of course there wasn't any gun there now. The whiny guy whose voice reminded me of someone would have seen to that. But I still had a fountain-pen flash. I unshipped it, opened the rear door of the car and poked the light in.

It didn't show anything – no blood, no torn upholstery, no starred or splintered glass, no bodies. The car didn't seem to have been the scene of a battle. It was just empty. The keys hung on the ornate panel. It had been driven down there and left. I pointed my little flash at the ground and began to prowl, looking for him. He'd be around there all right, if the car was.

Then in the cold silence a motor throbbed above the rim of the bowl. The light in my hand went out. Other lights – headlights – tilted up over the frayed bushes. I dropped and crawled swiftly behind the hood of Lindley Paul's car.

The lights tilted down, got brighter. They were coming down the slope of the dirt road into the bowl. I could hear the dull, idling sound of a small motor now.

Halfway down the car stopped. A spotlight at the side of the windshield clicked on and swung to one side. It lowered, held steady on some point I couldn't see. The spot clicked off again and the car came slowly on down the slope.

At the bottom it turned a little so that its headlights raked the black sedan. I took my upper lip between my teeth and didn't feel myself biting it until I tasted the blood.

The car swung a little more. Its lights went out abruptly. Its motor died and once more the night became large and empty and black and silent. Nothing – no movement, except the crickets and tree frogs far off that had been droning all the time, only I hadn't been hearing them. Then a door latch snapped and there was a light, quick step on the ground and a beam of light cut across the top of my head like a sword.

Then a laugh. A girl's laugh – strained, taut as a mandolin wire. And the white beam jumped under the big black car and hit my feet.

The girl's voice said sharply: "All right, you. Come out of there with your hands up – and very damned empty! I've got you covered!"

I didn't move.

The voice stabbed at me again. "Listen, I've got three slugs for your feet, mister, and seven more for your tummy, and spare clips, and I change them plenty fast. Coming?"

"Put that toy up!" I snarled. "Or I'll blow it out of your hand." My voice sounded like somebody else's voice. It was hoarse and thick.

"Oh, a hard-boiled gentleman." There was a little quaver in the voice now. Then it hardened again. "Coming? I'll count three. Look at all the odds I'm giving you – twelve big fat cylinders to hide behind – or is it sixteen? Your feet will hurt you though. And anklebones take years to get well when they've been hurt, and sometimes –"

I straightened up and looked into her flashlight. "I talk too much when I'm scared, too," I said.

"Don't – don't move another inch! Who are you?"

"A bum private dick – detective to you. Who cares?"

I started around the car towards her. She didn't shoot. When I was six feet from her I stopped.

"You stay right there!" she snapped angrily – after I had stopped.

"Sure. What were you looking at back there, with your windshield spotlight?"

"A man."

"Hurt bad?"

"I'm afraid he's dead," she said simply. "And you look half dead yourself."

"I've been sapped," I said. "It always makes me dark under the eyes."

"A nice sense of humor," she said. "Like a morgue attendant."

"Let's look him over," I said gruffly. "You can stay behind me with your popgun, if it makes you feel any safer."

"I never felt safer in my life," she said angrily, and backed away from me.

I circled the little car she had come in. An ordinary little car, nice and clean and shiny under what was left of the moon. I heard her steps behind me but I didn't pay any attention to her. About halfway up the slope a few feet off to the side I saw his foot.

I put my own little flash on him and then the girl added hers. I saw him all. He was smeared to the ground, on his back, at the base of a bush. He was in that bag-of-clothes position that always means the same thing.

The girl didn't speak. She kept away from me and breathed hard and held her light as steadily as any tough old homicide veteran.

One of his hands was flung out in a frozen gesture. The fingers were curled. The other hand was under him and his overcoat was twisted as though he had been thrown out and rolled. His thick blond hair was matted with blood, black as shoe polish under the moon, and there was more of it on his face and there was a gray ooze mixed in with the blood. I didn't see his hat.

Then was when I ought to have got shot. Up to that instant I hadn't even thought of the packet of money in my pocket. The thought came to me so quickly now, jarred me so hard, that I jammed a hand down into my pocket. It must have looked exactly like a hand going for a gun.

The pocket was quite empty. I took the hand out and looked back at her.

"Mister," she half sighed, "if I hadn't made my mind up about your face –"

"I had ten grand," I said. "It was his money. I was carrying it for him. It was a pay-off. I just remembered the money. And you've got the sweetest set of nerves I ever met on a woman. I didn't kill him."

"I didn't think you killed him," she said. "Somebody hated him to smash his head open like that."

"I hadn't known him long enough to hate him," I said. "Hold the flash down again."

I knelt and went through his pockets, trying not to move him much. He had loose silver and bills, keys in a tooled leather case, the usual billfold with the usual window for a driver's license and the usual insurance cards behind the license. No money in the folder. I wondered why they had missed his trouser pockets. Panicked by the light, perhaps. Otherwise they'd have stripped him down to his coat lining. I held more stuff up in her light: two fine handkerchiefs as white and crisp as dry snow; half a dozen paper match folders from swank night traps; a silver cigarette case as heavy as a buggy weight and full of his imported straightcuts; another cigarette case, with a tortoise-shell frame and embroidered silk sides, each side a writhing dragon. I tickled the catch open and there were three long cigarettes under the elastic, Russians, with hollow mouthpieces. I pinched one. It felt old, dry.

"Maybe for ladies," I said. "He smoked others."

"Or maybe jujus," the girl said behind me, breathing on my neck. "I knew a lad who smoked them once. Could I look?"

I passed the case up to her and she poked her flash into it until I growled at her to put it on the ground again. There wasn't anything else to examine. She snapped the case shut and handed it back and I put it in his breast pocket.

"That's all. Whoever tapped him down was afraid to wait and clean up. Thanks."

I stood up casually and turned and speared the little gun out of her hand.

"Darn it, you didn't have to get rough!" she snapped.

"Give," I said. "Who are you, and how come you ride around this place at midnight?"

She pretended I had hurt her hand, put the flash on it and looked at it carefully.

"I've been nice to you, haven't I?" she complained. "I'm burning up with curiosity and scared and I haven't asked you a single question, have I?"

"You've been swell," I said. "But I'm in a spot where I can't fool around. Who are you? And douse the flash now. We don't need light any more."

She put it out and the darkness lightened for us gradually until we could see the outlines of the bushes and the dead man's sprawled body and the glare in the southeastern sky that would be Santa Monica.

"My name is Carol Pride," she said. "I live in Santa Monica. I try to do feature stories for a newspaper syndicate. Sometimes I can't get sleepy at night and I go out riding – just anywhere. I know all this country like a book. I saw your little light flickering around down in the hollow and it seemed to me it was pretty cold for young love – if they use lights."

"I wouldn't know," I said. "I never did. So you have spare clips for this gun. Would you have a permit for it?"

I hefted the little weapon. It felt like a Colt .25 in the dark. It had a nice balance for a small gun. Plenty of good men have been put to sleep with .25's.

"Certainly I have a permit. That was just bluff about the spare clips though."

"Not afraid of things, are you, Miss Pride? Or would it be Mrs.?"

"No, it wouldn't. . . . This neighborhood isn't dangerous. People don't even lock their doors around here. I guess some bad men just happened to get wise how lonely it is."

I turned the little gun around and held it out. "Here. It's not my night to be clever. Now if you'll be good enough to ride me down to Castellamare, I'll take my car there and go find some law."

"Shouldn't somebody stay with him?"

I looked at the radiolite dial of my wrist watch. "It's a quarter to one," I said. "We'll leave him with the crickets and the stars. Let's go."

She tucked the gun in her bag and we went back down the slope and got into her car. She jockeyed it around without lights and drove it back up the slope. The big black car looked like a monument standing there behind us.

At the top of the rise I got out and dragged the section of white barricade back into position across the road. He was safe for the night now, and likely enough for many nights.

The girl didn't speak until we had come near the first house. Then she put the lights on and said quietly: "There's blood on your face, Mr. Whatever-Your-Name-Is, and I never saw a man who needed a drink worse. Why not go back to my house and phone West Los Angeles from there? There's nothing but a fire station in this neighborhood."

"John Dalmas is the name," I said. "I like the blood on my face. You wouldn't want to be mixed up in a mess like this. I won't even mention you."

She said: "I'm an orphan and live all alone. It wouldn't matter in the slightest."

"Just keep going down to the beach," I said. "I'll play it solo after that."

But we had to stop once before we got to Castellamare. The movement of the car made me go off into the weeds and be sick again.

When we came to the place where my car was parked and the steps started up the hill I said good night to her and sat in the Chrysler until I couldn't see her tail-lights any more.

The sidewalk café was still open. I could have gone in there and had a drink and phoned. But it seemed smarter to do what I did half an hour later – walk into the West Los Angeles Police Station cold sober and green, with the blood still on my face.

Cops are just people. And their whiskey is just as good as what they push across bars at you.

3 LOU LID

I DIDN'T TELL it well. It tasted worse all the time. Reavis, the man who came out from the downtown homicide bureau, listened to me with his eyes on the floor, and two plainclothes men lounged behind him like a bodyguard. A prowl-car unit had gone out long before to guard the body.

Reavis was a thin, narrow-faced, quiet man about fifty, with smooth gray skin and immaculate clothes. His trousers had a knife-edge crease and he pulled them up carefully after he sat down. His shirt and tie looked as if he had put them on new ten minutes ago and his hat looked as if he had bought it on the way over.

We were in the day captain's room at the West Los Angeles Police Station, just off Santa Monica Boulevard, near Sawtelle. There were just the four of us in it. Some drunk in a cell, waiting to go down to the city drunk tank for sunrise court, kept giving the Australian bush call all the time we were talking.

"So I was his bodyguard for the evening," I said at the end. "And a sweet job I made of it."

"I wouldn't give any thought to that," Reavis said carelessly. "It could happen to anybody. Seems to me they took you for this Lindley Paul, slugged you to save argument and to get plenty of time, perhaps didn't have the stuff with them at all and didn't mean to give it up so cheap. When they found you were not Paul they got sore and took it out on him."

"He had a gun," I said. "A swell Luger, but two shotguns staring at you don't make you warlike."

"About this darktown brother," Reavis said. He reached for a phone on the desk.

"Just a voice in the dark. I couldn't be sure."

"Yeah, but we'll find what he was doing about that time. Lou Lid. A name that would linger."

He lifted the phone off its cradle and told the PBX man: "Desk at headquarters, Joe. . . . This is Reavis out in West L.A. on that stick-up murder. I want a Negro or half-Negro gunman name of Lou Lid. About twenty-two to twenty-four, a lightish brown, neat-appearing, small, say one hundred thirty, cast in one eye, I forget which. There's something on him, but not much, and he's been in and out plenty times. The boys at Seventy-seventh will know him. I want to check his movements for this evening. Give the colored squad an hour, then put him on the air."

He cradled the phone and winked at me. "We got the best shine dicks west of Chicago. If he's in town, they'll pick him off without even looking. Will we move out there now?"

We went downstairs and got into a squad car and went back through Santa Monica to the Palisades.

Hours later, in the cold gray dawn, I got home. I was guzzling aspirin and whiskey and bathing the back of my head with very hot water when my phone jangled. It was Reavis.

"Well, we got Lou Lid," he said. "Pasadena got him and a Mex named Fuente. Picked them up on Arroyo Seco Boulevard – not exactly with shovels, but kind of careful."

"Go on," I said, holding the phone tight enough to crack it, "give me the punch line."

"You guessed it already. They found them under the Colorado Street Bridge. Gagged, trussed fore and aft with old wire. And smashed like ripe oranges. Like it?"

I breathed hard. "It's just what I needed to make me sleep like a baby," I said.

The hard concrete pavement of Arroyo Seco Boulevard is some seventy-five feet directly below Colorado Street Bridge – sometimes also known as Suicide Bridge.

"Well," Reavis said after a pause, "it looks like you bit into something rotten. What do you say now?"

"Just for a quick guess I'd say an attempted hijack of the pay-off money by a couple of smart-alecks that got a lead to it somehow, picked their own spot and got smeared with the cash."

"That would need inside help," Reavis said. "You mean guys that knew the beads were taken, but didn't have them. I like better that they tried to leave town with the whole take instead of passing it to the boss. Or even that the boss thought he had too many mouths to feed."

He said good night and wished me pleasant dreams. I drank enough whiskey to kill the pain in my head. Which was more than was good for me.

I got down to the office late enough to be elegant, but not feeling that way. Two stitches in the back of my scalp had begun to draw and the tape over the shaved place felt as hot as a bartender's bunion.

My office was two rooms hard by the coffee-shop smell of the Mansion House Hotel. The little one was a reception room I always left unlocked for a client to go in and wait, in case I had a client and he wanted to wait.

Carol Pride was in there, sniffing at the faded red davenport, the two odd chairs, the small square of carpet and the boy's-size library table with the pre-Repeal magazines on it.

She wore brownish speckled tweeds with wide lapels and a mannish shirt and tie, nice shoes, a black hat that might have cost twenty dollars for all I knew, and looked as if you could have made it with one hand out of an old desk blotter.

"Well, you do get up," she said. "That's nice to know. I was beginning to think perhaps you did all your work in bed."

"Tut, tut," I said. "Come into my boudoir."

I unlocked the communicating door, which looked better than just kicking the lock lightly – which had the same effect – and we went into the rest of the suite, which was a rust-red carpet with plenty of ink on it, five green filing cases, three of them full of California climate, an advertising calendar showing the Dionne quintuplets rolling around on a sky-blue floor, a few near walnut chairs, and the usual desk with the usual heel marks on it and the usual squeaky swivel chair behind it. I sat down in that and put my hat on the telephone.

I hadn't really seen her before, even by the lights down at Castellamare. She looked about twenty-six and as if she hadn't slept very well. She had a tired, pretty little face under fluffed-out brown hair, a rather narrow forehead with more height than is considered elegant, a small inquisitive nose, an upper lip a shade too long and a mouth more than a shade too wide. Her eyes could be very blue if they tried. She looked quiet, but not mousy-quiet. She looked smart, but not Hollywood-smart.

"I read it in the evening paper that comes out in the morning," she said. "What there was of it."

"And that means the law won't break it as a big story. They'd have held it for the morning sheets."

"Well, anyhow, I've been doing a little work on it for you," she said.

I stared hard at her, poked a flat box of cigarettes across the desk, and filled my pipe. "You're making a mistake," I said. "I'm not on this case. I ate my dirt last night and banged myself to sleep with a bottle. This is a police job."

"I don't think it is," she said. "Not all of it. And anyway you have to earn your fee. Or didn't you get a fee?"

"Fifty bucks," I said. "I'll return it when I know who to return it to. Even my mother wouldn't think I earned it."

"I like you," she said. "You look like a guy who was almost a heel and then something stopped him – just at the last minute. Do you know who that jade necklace belonged to?"

I sat up with a jerk that hurt. "What jade necklace?" I almost yelled. I hadn't told her anything about a jade necklace. There hadn't been anything in the paper about a jade necklace.

"You don't have to be clever. I've been talking to the man on the case – Lieutenant Reavis. I told him about last night. I get along with policemen. He thought I knew more than I did. So he told me things."

"Well – who does it belong to?" I asked, after a heavy silence.

"A Mrs. Philip Courtney Prendergast, a lady who lives in Beverly Hills – part of the year at least. Her husband has a million or so and a bad liver. Mrs. Prendergast is a black-eyed blonde who goes places while Mr. Prendergast stays home and takes calomel."

"Blondes don't like blonds," I said. "Lindley Paul was as blond as a Swiss yodeler."

"Don't be silly. That comes of reading movie magazines. This blonde liked that blond. I *know*. The society editor of the *Chronicle* told me. He weighs two hundred pounds and has a mustache and they call him Giddy Gertie."

"He tell you about the necklace?"

"No. The manager of Blocks Jewelry Company told me about that. I told him I was doing an article on rare jade – for the *Police Gazette*. Now you've got me doing the wisecracks."

I lit my pipe for the third time and squeaked my chair back and nearly fell over backwards.

"Reavis knows all this?" I asked, trying to stare at her without seeming to.

"He didn't tell me he did. He can find out easily enough. I've no doubt he will. He's nobody's fool."

"Except yours," I said. "Did he tell you about Lou Lid and Fuente the Mex?"

"No. Who are they?"

I told her about them. "Why, that's terrible," she said, and smiled.

"Your old man wasn't a cop by any chance, was he?" I asked suspiciously.

"Police Chief of Pomona for almost fifteen years."

I didn't say anything. I remembered that Police Chief John Pride of Pomona had been shot dead by two kid bandits about four years before.

After a while I said: "I should have thought of that. All right, what next?"

"I'll lay you five to one Mrs. Prendergast didn't get her necklace back and that her bilious husband has enough drag to keep that part of the story and their name out of the papers, and that she needs a nice detective to help her get straightened out – without any scandal."

"What scandal?"

"Oh, I don't know. She's the type that would have a basket of it in her dressing room."

"I suppose you had breakfast with her," I said. "What time did you get up?"

"No, I can't see her till two o'clock. I got up at six."

"My God," I said, and got a bottle out of the deep drawer of my desk. "My head hurts me something terrible."

"Just one," Carol Pride said sharply. "And only because you were beaten up. But I daresay that happens quite often."

I put the drink inside me, corked the bottle but not too tightly, and drew a deep breath.

The girl groped in her brown bag and said: "There's something else. But maybe you ought to handle this part of it yourself."

"It's nice to know I'm still working here," I said.

She rolled three long Russian cigarettes across the desk. She didn't smile.

"Look inside the mouthpieces," she said, "and draw your own conclusions. I swiped them out of that Chinese case last night. They all have that something to make you wonder."

"And you a cop's daughter," I said.

She stood up, wiped a little pipe ash off the edge of my desk with her bag and went towards the door.

"I'm a woman too. Now I've got to go see another society editor and find out more about Mrs. Philip Courtney Prendergast and her love life. Fun, isn't it?"

The office door and my mouth shut at about the same moment.

I picked up one of the Russian cigarettes. I pinched it between my fingers and peeped into the hollow mouthpiece. There seemed to be something rolled up in there, like a piece of paper or card, something that wouldn't have improved the drawing of the cigarette. I finally managed to dig it out with the nail-file blade of my pocketknife.

It was a card all right, a thin ivory calling card, man's size. Three words were engraved on it, nothing else.

Soukesian the Psychic

I looked into the other mouthpieces, found identical cards in each of them. It didn't mean a thing to me. I had never heard of Soukesian the Psychic. After a while I looked him up in the phone book. There was a man named Soukesian on West Seventh. It sounded Armenian so I looked him up again under *Oriental Rugs* in the classified section. He was there all right, but that didn't prove anything. You don't have to be a psychic to sell oriental rugs. You only have to be a psychic to buy them. And something told me this Soukesian on the card didn't have anything to do with oriental rugs.

I had a rough idea what his racket would be and what kind of people would be his customers. And the bigger he was the less he would advertise. If you gave him enough time and paid him enough, he would cure anything from a tired husband to a grasshopper plague. He would be an expert in frustrated women, in tricky, tangled, love affairs, in wandering boys who hadn't written home, in whether to sell the property now or hold it another year, in whether this part will hurt my type with my public or improve it. Even men would go to him – guys who bellowed like bulls around their own offices and were all cold mush inside just the same. But most of all, women – women with money, women with jewels, women who could be twisted like silk thread around a lean Asiatic finger.

I refilled my pipe and shook my thoughts around without moving my head too much, and fished for a reason why a man would carry a spare cigarette case, with three cigarettes in it not meant for smoking, and in each of those three cigarettes the name of another man concealed. Who would find that name?

I pushed the bottle to one side and grinned. Anyone would find those cards who went through Lindley Paul's pockets with a fine tooth comb – carefully and taking time. Who would do that? A cop. And when? If Mr. Lindley Paul died or was badly hurt in mysterious circumstances.

I took my hat off the telephone and called a man named Willy Peters who was in the insurance business, so he said, and did a sideline selling unlisted telephone numbers bribed from maids and chauffeurs. His fee was five bucks. I figured Lindley Paul could afford it out of his fifty.

Willy Peters had what I wanted. It was a Brentwood Heights number.

I called Reavis down at headquarters. He said everything was fine except his sleeping time and for me just to keep my mouth shut and not worry, but I ought really to have told him about the girl. I said that was right but maybe he had a daughter himself and wouldn't be so keen to have a lot of camera hounds jumping out at her. He said he had and the case didn't make me look very good but it could happen to anyone and so long.

I called Violets M'Gee to ask him to lunch some day when he had just had his teeth cleaned and his mouth was sore. But he was up in Ventura returning a prisoner. Then I called the Brentwood Heights number of Soukesian the Psychic.

After a while a slightly foreign woman's voice said: " 'Allo."

"May I speak to Mr. Soukesian?"

"I am ver-ry sor-ry. Soukesian he weel never speak upon the telephone. I am hees secretar-ry. Weel I take the message?"

"Yeah. Got a pencil?"

"But of course I 'ave the pencil. The message, eef you please?"

I gave her my name and address and occupation and telephone number first. I made sure she had them spelled right. Then I said: "It's about the murder of a man named Lindley

Paul. It happened last night down on the Palisades near Santa Monica. I'd like to consult Mr. Soukesian."

"He weel be ver-ry pleased." Her voice was as calm as an oyster. "But of course I cannot give you the appointment today. Soukesian he ees always ver-ry busy. Per'aps tomorrow –"

"Next week will be fine," I said heartily. "There's never any hurry about a murder investigation. Just tell him I'll give him two hours before I go to the police with what I know."

There was a silence. Maybe a breath caught sharply and maybe it was just wire noise. Then the slow foreign voice said: "I weel tell him. I do not understand –"

"Give it the rush, angel. I'll be waiting in my office."

I hung up, fingered the back of my head, put the three cards away in my wallet and felt as if I could eat some hot food. I went out to get it.

4 SECOND HARVEST

THE INDIAN SMELLED. He smelled clear across my little reception room when I heard the outer door open and got up to see who it was. He stood just inside the door looking as if he had been cast in bronze. He was a big man from the waist up and had a big chest.

Apart from that he looked like a bum. He wore a brown suit, too small for him. His hat was at least two sizes too small, and had been perspired in freely by someone it fitted better than it fitted him. He wore it about where a house wears a weathercock. His collar had the snug fit of a horse collar and was about the same shade of dirty brown. A tie dangled from it, outside his buttoned coat, and had apparently been tied with a pair of pliers in a knot the size of a pea. Around his bare throat above the collar he wore what looked like a piece of black ribbon.

He had a big, flat face, a big, high-bridged, fleshy nose that looked as hard as the prow of a cruiser. He had lidless eyes, drooping jowls, the shoulders of a blacksmith. If he had been cleaned up a little and dressed in a white nightgown, he would have looked like a very wicked Roman senator.

His smell was the earthy smell of the primitive man; dirty, but not the dirt of cities. "Huh," he said. "Come quick. Come now."

I jerked my thumb at the inner office and went back into it. He followed me ponderously and made as much noise walking as a fly makes. I sat down behind my desk, pointed at the chair opposite, but he didn't sit down. His small black eyes were hostile.

"Come where?" I wanted to know.

"Huh. Me Second Harvest. Me Hollywood Indian."

"Take a chair, Mr. Harvest."

He snorted and his nostrils got very wide. They had been wide enough for mouseholes in the first place.

"Name Second Harvest. No Mr. Harvest. Nuts."

"What do you want?"

"He say come quick. Big white father say come now. He say —"

"Don't give me any more of that pig Latin," I said. "I'm no schoolmarm at the snake dances."

"Nuts," he said.

He removed his hat with slow disgust and turned it upside down. He rolled a finger around under the sweatband. That turned the sweatband up into view. He removed a paper clip from the edge of the leather and moved near enough to throw a dirty fold of tissue paper on the desk. He pointed at it angrily. His lank, greasy black hair had a shelf all around it, high up, from the too-tight hat.

I unfolded the bit of tissue paper and found a card which read: *Soukesian the Psychic*. It was in thin script, nicely engraved. I had three just like it in my wallet.

I played with my empty pipe, stared at the Indian, tried to ride him with my stare. "Okay. What does he want?"

"He want you come now. Quick."

"Nuts," I said. The Indian liked that. That was the fraternity grip. He almost grinned. "It will cost him a hundred bucks as a retainer," I added.

"Huh?"

"Hundred dollars. Iron men. Bucks to the number one hundred. Me no money, me no come. Savvy?" I began to count by opening and closing both fists.

The Indian tossed another fold of tissue paper on the desk. I unfolded it. It contained a brand-new hundred-dollar bill.

"Psychic is right," I said. "A guy that smart I'm scared of, but I'll go nevertheless."

The Indian put his hat back on his head without bothering to fold the sweatband under. It looked only very slightly more comical that way.

I took a gun from under my arm, not the one I had had the night before unfortunately — I hate to lose a gun — dropped the magazine into the heel of my hand, rammed it home again, fiddled with the safety and put the gun back in its holster.

This meant no more to the Indian than if I had scratched my neck.

"I gottum car," he said. "Big car. Nuts."

"Too bad," I said. "I don't like big cars any more. However, let's go."

I locked up and we went out. In the elevator the Indian smelled very strong indeed. Even the elevator operator noticed it.

The car was a tan Lincoln touring, not new but in good shape, with glass gypsy curtains in the back. It dipped down past a shining green polo field, zoomed up the far side, and the dark, foreign-looking driver swung it into a narrow paved ribbon of white concrete that climbed almost as steeply as Lindley Paul's steps, but not as straight. This was well out of town, beyond Westwood, in Brentwood Heights.

We climbed past two orange groves, rich man's pets, as that is not orange country, past houses molded flat to the side of the foothills, like bas-reliefs.

Then there were no more houses, just the burnt foothills and the cement ribbon and a sheer drop on the left into the coolness of a nameless canyon, and on the right heat bouncing off the seared clay bank at whose edge a few unbeatable wild flowers clawed and hung on like naughty children who won't go to bed.

And in front of me two backs, a slim, whipcord back with a brown neck, black hair, a vizored cap on the black hair, and a wide, untidy back in an old brown suit with the Indian's thick neck and heavy head above that, and on his head the ancient greasy hat with the sweatband still showing.

Then the ribbon of road twisted into a hairpin, the big tires skidded on loose stones, and the tan Lincoln tore through an open gate and up a steep drive lined with pink geraniums growing wild. At the top of the drive there was an eyrie, an eagle's nest, a hilltop house of white plaster and glass and chromium, as modernistic as a fluoroscope and as remote as a lighthouse.

The car reached the top of the driveway, turned, stopped before a blank white wall in which there was a black door. The Indian got out, glared at me. I got out, nudging the gun against my side with the inside of my left arm.

The black door in the white wall opened slowly, untouched from outside, and showed a narrow passage ending far back. A bulb glowed in the ceiling.

The Indian said: "Huh. Go in, big shot."

"After you, Mr. Harvest."

He went in scowling and I followed him and the black door closed noiselessly of itself behind us. A bit of mumbo-jumbo for the customers. At the end of the narrow passage there was an elevator. I had to get into it with the Indian. We went up slowly, with a gentle purring sound, the faint hum of a small motor. The elevator stopped, its door opened without a whisper and there was daylight.

I got out of the elevator. It dropped down again behind me with the Indian still in it. I was in a turret room that was almost all windows, some of them close-draped against the afternoon glare. The rugs on the floor had the soft colors of old Persians, and there was a desk made of carved panels that probably came out of a church. And behind the desk there was a woman smiling at me, a dry, tight, withered smile that would turn to powder if you touched it.

She had sleek, black, coiled hair, a dark Asiatic face. There were pearls in her ears and rings on her fingers, large, rather cheap rings, including a moonstone and a square-cut emerald that looked as phony as a ten-cent-store slave bracelet. Her hands were little and dark and not young and not fit for rings.

"Ah, Meester Dalmas, so ver-ry good of you to come. Soukesian he weel be so pleased."

"Thanks," I said. I took the new hundred-dollar bill out of my wallet and laid it on her desk, in front of her dark, glittering hands. She didn't touch it or look at it. "My party," I said. "But thanks for the thought."

She got up slowly, without moving the smile, swished around the desk in a tight dress that fitted her like a mermaid's skin, and showed that she had a good figure, if you liked them four sizes bigger below the waist than above it.

"I weel conduct you," she said.

She moved before me to a narrow paneled wall, all there was of the room besides the windows and the tiny elevator shaft. She opened a narrow door beyond which there was a silky glow that didn't seem to be daylight. Her smile was older than Egypt now. I nudged my gun holster again and went in.

The door shut silently behind me. The room was octagonal, draped in black velvet, windowless, with a remote black ceiling. In the middle of the black rug there stood a white octagonal table, and on either side of that a stool that was a

651

smaller edition of the table. Over against the black drapes there was one more such stool. There was a large milky ball on a black stand on the white table. The light came from this. There was nothing else in the room.

I stood there for perhaps fifteen seconds, with that obscure feeling of being watched. Then the velvet drapes parted and a man came into the room and walked straight over to the other side of the table and sat down. Only then did he look at me.

He said: "Be seated opposite me, please. Do not smoke and do not move around or fidget, if you can avoid it. How may I serve you?"

5 SOUKESIAN THE PSYCHIC

HE WAS A tall man, straight as steel, with the blackest eyes I had ever seen and the palest and finest blond hair I had ever seen. He might have been thirty or sixty. He didn't look any more like an Armenian than I did. His hair was brushed straight back from as good a profile as John Barrymore had at twenty-eight. A matinee idol, and I expected something furtive and dark and greasy that rubbed its hands.

He wore a black double-breasted business suit cut like nobody's business, a white shirt, a black tie. He was as neat as a gift book.

I gulped and said: "I don't want a reading. I know all about this stuff."

"Yes?" he said delicately. "And what do you know about it?"

"Let it pass," I said. "I can figure the secretary because she's a sweet buildup for the shock people get when they see you. The Indian stumps me a bit, but it's none of my business anyhow. I'm not a bunko squad cop. What I came about is a murder."

"The Indian happens to be a natural medium," Soukesian said mildly. "They are much rarer than diamonds and, like diamonds, they are sometimes found in dirty places. That might not interest you either. As to the murder you may inform me. I never read the papers."

"Come, come," I said. "Not even to see who's pulling the big checks at the front office? Oke, here it is."

And I laid it in front of him, the whole damn story, and about his cards and where they had been found.

He didn't move a muscle. I don't mean that he didn't scream or wave his arms or stamp on the floor or bite his nails. I mean he simply didn't move at all, not even an eyelid, not even an eye. He just sat there and looked at me, like a stone lion outside the Public Library.

When I was all done he put his finger right down on the spot. "You kept those cards from the police? Why?"

"You tell me. I just did."

"Obviously the hundred dollars I sent you was not nearly enough."

"That's an idea too," I said. "But I hadn't really got around to playing with it."

He moved enough to fold his arms. His black eyes were as shallow as a cafeteria tray or as deep as a hole to China – whichever you like. They didn't say anything, either way.

He said: "You wouldn't believe me if I said I only knew this man in the most casual manner – professionally?"

"I'd take it under advisement," I said.

"I take it you haven't much faith in me. Perhaps Mr. Paul had. Was anything on those cards besides my name?"

"Yeah," I said. "And you wouldn't like it." This was kindergarten stuff, the kind the cops pull on radio crime dramatizations. He let it go without even looking at it.

"I'm in a sensitive profession," he said. "Even in this paradise of fakers. Let me see one of those cards."

"I was kidding you," I said. "There's nothing on them but your name." I got my wallet out and withdrew one card and laid it in front of him. I put the wallet away. He turned the card over with a fingernail.

"You know what I figure?" I said heartily. "I figure Lindley Paul thought you would be able to find out who did him in, even if the police couldn't. Which means he was afraid of somebody."

Soukesian unfolded his arms and folded them the other way. With him that was probably equivalent to climbing up the light fixture and biting off a bulb.

"You don't think anything of the sort," he said. "How much – quickly – for the three cards and a signed statement that you searched the body before you notified the police?"

"Not bad," I said, "for a guy whose brother is a rug peddler."

He smiled, very gently. There was something almost nice about his smile. "There are honest rug dealers," he said. "But Arizmian Soukesian is not my brother. Ours is a common name in Armenia."

I nodded.

"You think I'm just another faker, of course," he added.

"Go ahead and prove you're not."

"Perhaps it is not money you want after all," he said carefully.

"Perhaps it isn't."

I didn't see him move his foot, but he must have touched a floor button. The black velvet drapes parted and the Indian came into the room. He didn't look dirty or funny any more.

He was dressed in loose white trousers and a white tunic embroidered in black. There was a black sash around his waist and a black fillet around his forehead. His black eyes were sleepy. He shuffled over to the stool beside the drapes and sat down and folded his arms and leaned his head on his chest. He looked bulkier than ever, as if these clothes were over his other clothes.

Soukesian held his hands above the milky globe that was between us on the white table. The light on the remote black ceiling was broken and began to weave into odd shapes and patterns, very faint because the ceiling was black. The Indian kept his head low and his chin on his chest but his eyes turned up slowly and stared at the weaving hands.

The hands moved in a swift, graceful, intricate pattern that meant anything or nothing, that was like Junior Leaguers doing Greek dances, or coils of Christmas ribbon tossed on the floor – whatever you liked.

The Indian's solid jaw rested on his solid chest and slowly, like a toad's eyes, his eyes shut.

"I could have hypnotized him without all that," Soukesian said softly. "It's merely part of the show."

"Yeah." I watched his lean, firm throat.

"Now, something Lindley Paul touched," he said. "This card will do."

He stood up noiselessly and went across to the Indian and pushed the card inside the fillet against the Indian's forehead, left it there. He sat down again.

He began to mutter softly in a guttural language I didn't know. I watched his throat.

The Indian began to speak. He spoke very slowly and heavily, between motionless lips, as though the words were heavy stones he had to drag up hill in a blazing hot sun.

"Lindley Paul bad man. Make love to squaw of chief. Chief very angry. Chief have necklace stolen. Lindley Paul have to get um back. Bad man kill. *Grrrr.*"

The Indian's head jerked as Soukesian clapped his hands. The little lidless black eyes snapped open again. Soukesian looked at me with no expression at all on his handsome face.

"Neat," I said. "And not a darn bit gaudy." I jerked a thumb at the Indian. "He's a bit heavy to sit on your knee, isn't he? I haven't seen a good ventriloquist act since the chorus girls quit wearing tights."

Soukesian smiled very faintly.

"I watched your throat muscles," I said. "No matter. I guess I get the idea. Paul had been cutting corners with somebody's wife. The somebody was jealous enough to have him put away. It has points, as a theory. Because this jade necklace she was wearing wouldn't be worn often and somebody had to know she was wearing it that particular night when the stick-up was pulled off. A husband would know that."

"It is quite possible," Soukesian said. "And since you were not killed perhaps it was not the intent to kill Lindley Paul. Merely to beat him up."

"Yeah," I said. "And here's another idea. I ought to have had it before. If Lindley Paul really did fear somebody and wanted to leave a message, then there might still be something written on those cards – in invisible ink."

That got to him. His smile hung on but it had a little more wrinkle at the corners than at first. The time was short for me to judge that.

The light inside the milky globe suddenly went out. Instantly the room was pitch dark. You couldn't see your own hand. I kicked my stool back and jerked my gun free and started to back away.

A rush of air brought a strong earthy smell with it. It was uncanny. Without the slightest error of timing or space, even in that complete blackness, the Indian hit me from behind and pinned my arms. He started to lift me. I could have jerked a hand up and fanned the room in front of me with blind shots. I didn't try. There wasn't any point in it.

The Indian lifted me with his two hands holding my arms against my sides as though a steam crane was lifting me. He set me down again, hard, and he had my wrists. He had them behind me, twisting them. A knee like the corner of a foundation stone went into my back. I tried to yell. Breath panted in my throat and couldn't get out.

The Indian threw me sideways, wrapped my legs with his legs as we fell, and had me in a barrel. I hit the floor hard, with part of his weight on me.

I still had the gun. The Indian didn't know I had it. At least he didn't act as if he knew. It was jammed down between us. I started to turn it.

The light flicked on again.

Soukesian was standing beyond the white table, leaning on it. He looked older. There was something on his face I didn't like. He looked like a man who had something to do he didn't relish, but was going to do it all the same.

"So," he said softly. "Invisible writing."

Then the curtains swished apart and the thin dark woman rushed into the room with a reeking white cloth in her hands and slapped it around my face, leaning down to glare at me with hot black eyes.

The Indian grunted a little behind me, straining at my arms.

I had to breathe the chloroform. There was too much weight dragging my throat tight. The thick, sweetish reek of it ate into me.

I went away from there.

Just before I went somebody fired a gun twice. The sound didn't seem to have anything to do with me.

I was lying out in the open again, just like the night before. This time it was daylight and the sun was burning a hole in my right leg. I could see the hot blue sky, the lines of a ridge, scrub oak, yuccas in bloom spouting from the side of a hill, more hot blue sky.

I sat up. Then my left leg began to tingle with tiny needle points. I rubbed it. I rubbed the pit of my stomach. The chloroform stank in my nose. I was as hollow and rank as an old oil drum.

I got up on my feet, but didn't stay there. The vomiting was worse than last night. More shakes to it, more chills, and my stomach hurt worse. I got back up on my feet.

The breeze off the ocean lifted up the slope and put a little frail life into me. I staggered around dopily and looked at some tire marks on red clay, then at a big galvanized-iron cross, once white but with the paint flaked off badly. It was studded with empty sockets for light bulbs, and its base was of cracked concrete with an open door, inside which a verdigris-coated copper switch showed.

Beyond this concrete base I saw the feet.

They stuck out casually from under a bush. They were in hard-toed shoes, the kind college boys used to wear about the year before the war. I hadn't seen shoes like that for years, except once.

I went over there and parted the bushes and looked down at the Indian.

His broad, blunt hands lay at his sides, large and empty and limp. There were bits of clay and dead leaf and wild oyster-plant seeds in his greasy black hair. A tracery of sunlight skimmed along his brown cheek. On his stomach the flies had found a sodden patch of blood. His eyes were like other eyes I had seen – too many of them – half open, clear, but the play behind them was over.

He had his comic street clothes on again and his greasy hat lay near him, with the sweatband still wrong side out. He wasn't funny any more, or tough, or nasty. He was just a poor simple dead guy who had never known what it was all about.

I had killed him, of course. Those were my shots I had heard, from my gun.

I didn't find the gun. I went through my clothes. The other two Soukesian cards were missing. Nothing else. I followed the tire tracks to a deeply rutted road and followed that down the hill. Cars glittered by far below as the sunlight caught their windshields or the curve of a headlight. There was a service station and a few houses down there too. Farther off still the blue of water, piers, the long curve of the shore line towards Point Firmin. It was a little hazy. I couldn't see Catalina Island.

The people I was dealing with seemed to like operating in that part of the country.

It took me half an hour to reach the service station. I phoned for a taxi and it had to come from Santa Monica. I drove all the way home to my place in the Berglund, three blocks above the office, changed clothes, put my last gun in the holster and sat down to the phone.

Soukesian wasn't home. Nobody answered that number. Carol Pride didn't answer her number. I didn't expect her to. She was probably having tea with Mrs. Philip Courtney Prendergast. But police headquarters answered their number, and Reavis was still on the job. He didn't sound pleased to hear from me.

"Anything new on the Lindley Paul killing?" I asked him.

"I thought I told you to forget it. I meant to." His voice was nasty.

"You told me all right, but it keeps worrying at me. I like a clean job. I think her husband had it done."

He was silent for a moment. Then, "Whose husband, smart boy?"

"The husband of the frail that lost the jade beads, naturally."

"And of course you've had to poke your face into who she is."

"It sort of drifted to me," I said. "I just had to reach out."

He was silent again. This time so long that I could hear the loudspeaker on his wall put out a police bulletin on a stolen car.

Then he said very smoothly and distinctly: "I'd like to sell you an idea, shamus. Maybe I can. There's a lot of peace of mind in it. The Police Board gave you a license once and the sheriff gave you a special badge. Any acting captain with a peeve can get both of them taken away from you overnight. Maybe even just a lieutenant — like me. Now what did you have when you got that license and that badge? Don't answer,

I'm telling you. You had the social standing of a cockroach. You were a snooper for hire. All in the world you had to do then was to spend your last hundred bucks on a down payment on some rent and office furniture and sit on your tail until somebody brought a lion in – so you could put your head in the lion's mouth to see if he would bite. If he bit your ear off, you got sued for mayhem. Are you beginning to get it?"

"It's a good line," I said. "I used it years ago. So you don't want to break the case?"

"If I could trust you, I'd tell you we want to break up a very smart jewel gang. But I can't trust you. Where are you – in a poolroom?"

"I'm in bed," I said. "I've got a telephone jag."

"Well, you just fill yourself a nice hot-water bottle and put it on your face and go to sleep like a good little boy, will you please?"

"Naw, I'd rather go out and shoot an Indian, just for practice."

"Well, just one Indian, Junior."

"Don't forget that bite," I yelled, and hung the phone in his face.

6 LADY IN LIQUOR

I HAD A drink on the way down to the boulevard, black coffee laced with brandy, in a place where they knew me. It made my stomach feel like new, but I still had the same shopworn head. And I could still smell chloroform in my whiskers.

I went up to the office and into the little reception room. There were two of them this time, Carol Pride and a blonde. A blonde with black eyes. A blonde to make a bishop kick a hole in a stained-glass window.

Carol Pride stood up and scowled at me and said: "This is Mrs. Philip Courtney Prendergast. She has been waiting quite some time. And she's not used to being kept waiting. She wants to employ you."

The blonde smiled at me and put a gloved hand out. I touched the hand. She was perhaps thirty five and she had that wide-eyed, dreamy expression, as far as black eyes can have it. Whatever you need, whatever you are — she had it. I didn't pay much attention to her clothes. They were black and white. They were what the guy had put on her and he would know or she wouldn't have gone to him.

I unlocked the door of my private thinking-parlor and ushered them in.

There was a half-empty quart of hooch standing on the corner of my desk.

"Excuse me for keeping you waiting, Mrs. Prendergast," I said. "I had to go out on a little business."

"I don't see why you had to go out," Carol Pride said icily. "There seems to be all you can use right in front of you."

I placed chairs for them and sat down and reached for the bottle and the phone rang at my left elbow.

A strange voice took its time saying: "Dalmas? Okay. We have the gat. I guess you'll want it back, won't you?"

"Both of them. I'm a poor man."

"We only got one," the voice said smoothly. "The one the johns would like to have. I'll be calling you later. Think things over."

"Thanks." I hung up and put the bottle down on the floor and smiled at Mrs. Prendergast.

"I'll do the talking," Carol Pride said. "Mrs. Prendergast has a slight cold. She has to save her voice."

She gave the blonde one of those sidelong looks that women think men don't understand, the kind that feel like a dentist's drill.

"Well —" Mrs. Prendergast said, and moved a little so that she could see along the end of the desk, where I had put the whiskey bottle down on the carpet.

"Mrs. Prendergast has taken me into her confidence," Carol Pride said. "I don't know why, unless it is that I have shown her where a lot of unpleasant notoriety can be avoided."

I frowned at her. "There isn't going to be any of that. I talked to Reavis a while ago. He has a hush on it that would make a dynamite explosion sound like a pawnbroker looking at a dollar watch."

"Very funny," Carol Pride said, "for people who dabble in that sort of wit. But it just happens Mrs. Prendergast would like to get her jade necklace back – without Mr. Prendergast knowing it was stolen. It seems he doesn't know yet."

"That's different," I said. (The hell he didn't know!)

Mrs. Prendergast gave me a smile I could feel in my hip pocket. "I just love straight rye," she cooed. "Could we – just a little one?"

I got out a couple of pony glasses and put the bottle up on the desk again. Carol Pride leaned back and lit a cigarette contemptuously and looked at the ceiling. She wasn't so hard to look at herself. You could look at her longer without getting dizzy. But Mrs. Prendergast had it all over her for a quick smash.

I poured a couple of drinks for the ladies. Carol Pride didn't touch hers at all.

"In case you don't know," she said distantly, "Beverly Hills, where Mrs. Prendergast lives, is peculiar in some ways. They have two-way radio cars and only a small territory to cover and they cover it like a blanket, because there's plenty of money for police protection in Beverly Hills. In the better homes they even have direct communication with headquarters, over wires that can't be cut."

Mrs. Prendergast put her drink to sleep with one punch and looked at the bottle. I milked it again.

"That's nothing," she glowed. "We even have photo-cell connections on our safes and fur closets. We can fix the house so that even the servants can't go near certain places without police knocking at the door in about thirty seconds. Marvelous, isn't it?"

"Yes, marvelous," Carol Pride said. "But that's only in Beverly Hills. Once outside – and you can't spend your entire life in Beverly Hills – that is, unless you're an ant – your jewels are not so safe. So Mrs. Prendergast had a duplicate of her jade necklace – in soapstone."

I sat up straighter. Lindley Paul had let something drop about it taking a lifetime to duplicate the workmanship on Fei Tsui beads – even if material were available.

Mrs. Prendergast fiddled with her second drink, but not for long. Her smile got warmer and warmer.

"So when she went to a party outside Beverly Hills, Mrs. Prendergast was supposed to wear the imitation. That is, when she wanted to wear jade at all. Mr. Prendergast was very particular about that."

"And he has a lousy temper," Mrs. Prendergast said.

I put some more rye under her hand. Carol Pride watched me do it and almost snarled at me: "But on the night of the holdup she made a mistake and was wearing the real one."

I leered at her.

"I know what you're thinking," she snapped. "Who knew she had made that mistake? It happened that Mr. Paul knew it, soon after they left the house. He was her escort."

"He – er – touched the necklace a little," Mrs. Prendergast sighed. "He could tell real jade by the feel of it. I've heard some people can. He knew a lot about jewels."

I leaned back again in my squeaky chair. "Hell," I said disgustedly, "I ought to have suspected that guy long ago. The gang had to have a society finger. How else could they tell when the good things were out of the icebox? He must have pulled a cross on them and they used this chance to put him away."

"Rather wasteful of such a talent, don't you think?" Carol Pride said sweetly. She pushed her little glass along the desk top with one finger. "I don't really care for this, Mrs. Prendergast – if you'd like another –"

"Moths in your ermine," Mrs. Prendergast said, and threw it down the hatch.

"Where and how was the stick-up?" I rapped.

"Well, that seems a little funny too," Carol Pride said, beating Mrs. Prendergast by half a word. "After the party, which was in Brentwood Heights, Mr. Paul wanted to drop in at the Trocadero. They were in his car. At that time they were widening Sunset Boulevard all through the County Strip, if you remember. After they had killed a little time at the Troc –"

"And a few snifters." Mrs. Prendergast giggled, reaching for the bottle. She refilled one of her glasses. That is, some of the whiskey went into the glass.

"– Mr. Paul drove her home by way of Santa Monica Boulevard."

"That was the natural way to go," I said. "Almost the only way to go unless you wanted a lot of dust."

"Yes, but it also took them past a certain down-at-the-heels hotel called the Tremaine and a beer parlor across the street from it. Mrs. Prendergast noticed a car pull away from in front of the beer parlor and follow them. She's pretty sure it was that same car that crowded them to the curb a little later – and the holdup men knew just what they wanted. Mrs. Prendergast remembers all this very well."

"Well, naturally," Mrs. Prendergast said. "You don't mean I was drunk, I hope. This baby carries her hooch. You don't lose a string of beads like that every night."

She put her fifth drink down her throat.

"I wouldn't know a darn thing about wha – what those men looked like," she told me a little thickly. "Lin – tha's Mr. Paul – I called him Lin, y'know, felt kinda bad about it. That's why he stuck his neck out."

"It was your money – the ten thousand for the pay-off?" I asked her.

664

"It wasn't the butler's, honey. And I want those beads back before Court gets wise. How about lookin' over that beer parlor?"

She grabbled around in her black and white bag and pushed some bills across the desk in a lump. I straightened them out and counted them. They added to four hundred and sixty-seven dollars. Nice money. I let them lie.

"Mr. Prendergast," Carol Pride plowed on sweetly, "whom Mrs. Prendergast calls 'Court,' thinks the imitation necklace was taken. He can't tell one from the other, it seems. He doesn't know anything about last night except that Lindley Paul was killed by some bandits."

"The hell he doesn't." I said it out loud this time, and sourly. I pushed the money back across the desk. "I believe you think you're being blackmailed, Mrs. Prendergast. You're wrong. I think the reason this story hasn't broken in the press the way it happened is because pressure has been brought on the police. They'd be willing anyhow, because what they want is the jewel gang. The punks that killed Paul are dead already."

Mrs. Prendergast stared at me with a hard, bright, alcoholic stare. "I hadn't the slightest idea of bein' blackmailed," she said. She was having trouble with her s's now. "I want my beads and I want them quick. It's not a question of money. Not 'tall. Gimme a drink."

"It's in front of you," I said. She could drink herself under the desk for all I cared.

Carol Pride said: "Don't you think you ought to go out to that beer parlor and see what you can pick up?"

"A piece of chewed pretzel," I said. "Nuts to that idea."

The blonde was waving the bottle over her two glasses. She got herself a drink poured finally, drank it, and pushed the handful of currency around on the desk with a free and easy gesture, like a kid playing with sand.

I took it away from her, put it together again and went around the desk to put it back into her bag.

"If I do anything, I'll let you know," I told her. "I don't need a retainer from *you*, Mrs. Prendergast."

She liked that. She almost took another drink, thought better of it with what she still had to think with, got to her feet and started for the door.

I got to her in time to keep her from opening it with her nose. I held her arm and opened the door for her and there was a uniformed chauffeur leaning against the wall outside.

"Oke," he said listlessly, snapped a cigarette into the distance and took hold of her. "Let's go, baby. I ought to paddle your behind. Damned if I oughtn't."

She giggled and held on to him and they went down the corridor and turned a corner out of sight. I went back into the office and sat down behind my desk and looked at Carol Pride. She was mopping the desk with a dustcloth she had found somewhere.

"You and your office bottle," she said bitterly. Her eyes hated me.

"To hell with her," I said angrily. "I wouldn't trust her with my old socks. I hope she gets raped on the way home. To hell with her beer-parlor angle too."

"Her morals are neither here nor there, Mr. John Dalmas. She has pots of money and she's not tight with it. I've seen her husband and he's nothing but a beanstalk with a checkbook that never runs dry. If any fixing has been done, she has done it herself. She told me she's suspected for some time that Paul was a Raffles. She didn't care as long as he let her alone."

"This Prendergast is a prune, huh? He would be, of course."

"Tall, thin, yellow. Looks as if his first drink of milk soured on his stomach and he could still taste it."

"Paul didn't steal her necklace."

"No?"

"No. And she didn't have any duplicate of it."

Her eyes got narrower and darker. "I suppose Soukesian the Psychic told you all this."

"Who's he?"

She leaned forward a moment and then leaned back and pulled her bag tight against her side.

"I see," she said slowly. "You don't like my work. Excuse me for butting in. I thought I was helping you a little."

"I told you it was none of my business. Go on home and write yourself a feature article. I don't need any help."

"I thought we were friends," she said. "I thought you liked me." She stared at me for a minute with bleak, tired eyes.

"I've got a living to make. I don't make it bucking the police department."

She stood up and looked at me a moment longer without speaking. Then she went to the door and went out. I heard her steps die along the mosaic floor of the corridor.

I sat there for ten or fifteen minutes almost without moving. I tried to guess why Soukesian hadn't killed me. None of it made any sense. I went down to the parking lot and got into my car.

7 I CROSS THE BAR

THE HOTEL TREMAINE was far out of Santa Monica, near the junk yards. An interurban right-of-way split the street in half, and just as I got to the block that would have the number I had looked up, a two-car train came racketing by at forty-five miles an hour, making almost as much noise as a transport plane taking off. I speeded up beside it and passed the block, pulled into the cement space in front of a market that had gone out of business. I got out and looked back from the corner of the wall.

I could see the Hotel Tremaine's sign over a narrow door between two store fronts, both empty – an old two-story walk-up. Its woodwork would smell of kerosene, its shades would be cracked, its curtains would be a sleazy cotton lace and its bedsprings would stick into your back. I knew all about places like the Hotel Tremaine, I had slept in them, staked out in them, fought with bitter, scrawny landladies in them, got shot at in them, and might yet get carried out of one of them to the morgue wagon. They are flops where you find the cheap ones, the sniffers and pin-jabbers, the gowed-up runts who shoot you before you can say hello.

The beer parlor was on my side of the street. I went back to the Chrysler and got inside it while I moved my gun to my waistband, then I went along the sidewalk.

There was a red neon sign – BEER – over it. A wide pulled-down shade masked the front window, contrary to the law. The place was just a made-over store, half-frontage. I opened the door and went in.

The barman was playing the pin game on the house's money and a man sat on a stool with a brown hat on the back of his head reading a letter. Prices were scrawled in white on the mirror back of the bar.

The bar was just a plain, heavy wooden counter, and at each end of it hung an old frontier .44 in a flimsy cheap holster no gunfighter would ever have worn. There were printed cards on the walls, about not asking for credit and what to take for a hangover and a liquor breath, and there were some nice legs in photographs.

The place didn't look as if it even paid expenses.

The barkeep left the pin game and went behind the bar. He was fiftyish, sour. The bottoms of his trousers were frayed and he moved as if he had corns. The man on the stool kept right on chuckling over his letter, which was written in green ink on pink paper.

The barkeep put both his blotched hands on the bar and looked at me with the expression of a dead-pan comedian, and I said: "Beer."

He drew it slowly, raking the glass with an old dinner knife.

I sipped my beer and held my glass with my left hand. After a while I said: "Seen Lou Lid lately?" This seemed to be in order. There had been nothing in any paper I had seen about Lou Lid and Fuente the Mex.

The barkeep looked at me blankly. The skin over his eyes was grained like lizard skin. Finally he spoke in a husky whisper. "Don't know him."

There was a thick white scar on his throat. A knife had gone in there once which accounted for the husky whisper.

The man who was reading the letter guffawed suddenly and slapped his thigh. "I gotta tell this to Moose," he roared. "This is right from the bottom of the bucket."

He got down off his stool and ambled over to a door in the rear wall and went through it. He was a husky dark man who looked like anybody. The door shut behind him.

The barkeep said in his husky whisper: "Lou Lid, huh? Funny moniker. Lots a guys come in here. I dunno their names. Copper?"

"Private," I said. "Don't let it bother you. I'm just drinking beer. This Lou Lid was a shine. Light brown. Young."

"Well, maybe I seen him sometime. I don't recall."

"Who's Moose?"

"Him? That's the boss. Moose Magoon."

He dipped a thick towel down in a bucket and folded it and wrung it out and pushed it along the bar holding it by the ends. That made a club about two inches thick and eighteen inches long. You can knock a man into the next county with a club like that if you know how.

The man with the pink letter came back through the rear door, still chuckling, shoved the letter into his side pocket and strolled to the pin game. That put him behind me. I began to get a little worried.

I finished my beer quickly and stood down off the stool. The barkeep hadn't rung up my dime yet. He held his twisted towel and moved it back and forth slowly.

"Nice beer," I said. "Thanks all the same."

"Come again," he whispered, and knocked my glass over.

That took my eyes for a second. When I looked up again the door at the back was open and a big man stood in it with a big gun in his hand.

He didn't say anything. He just stood there. The gun looked at me. It looked like a tunnel. The man was very broad, very swarthy. He had a build like a wrestler. He looked plenty tough. He didn't look as if his real name was Magoon.

Nobody said anything. The barkeep and the man with the big gun just stared at me fixedly. Then I heard a train coming on the interurban tracks. Coming fast and coming noisy. That would be the time. The shade was down all across the front window and nobody could see into the place. The train would make a lot of noise as it went by. A couple of shots would be lost in it.

The noise of the approaching train got louder. I had to move before it got quite loud enough.

I went head first over the bar in a rolling dive.

Something banged faintly against the roar of the train and something rattled overhead, seemingly on the wall. I never knew what it was. The train went on by in a booming crescendo.

I hit the barkeep's legs and the dirty floor about the same moment. He sat down on my neck.

That put my nose in a puddle of stale beer and one of my ears into some very hard concrete floor. My head began to howl with pain. I was low down along a sort of duckboard behind the bar and half turned on my left side. I jerked the gun loose from my waistband. For a wonder it hadn't slipped and jammed itself down my trouser leg.

The barkeep made a kind of annoyed sound and something hot stung me and I didn't hear any more shots just at the moment. I didn't shoot the barkeep. I rammed the gun muzzle into a part of him where some people are sensitive. He was one of them.

He went up off me like a foul fly. If he didn't yell it was not for want of trying. I rolled a little more and put the gun in the seat of his pants. "Hold it!" I snarled at him. "I don't want to get vulgar with you."

Two more shots roared. The train was off in the distance, but somebody didn't care. These cut through wood. The bar was old and solid but not solid enough to stop .45 slugs. The barkeep sighed above me. Something hot and wet fell on my face. "You've shot me, boys," he whispered, and started to fall down on top of me.

I wriggled away just in time, got to the end of the bar nearest the front of the beer parlor and looked around it. A face with a brown hat over it was about nine inches from my own face, on the same level.

We looked at each other for a fraction of a second that seemed long enough for a tree to grow to maturity in, but was actually so short a time that the barkeep was still foundering in the air behind me.

This was my last gun. Nobody was going to get it. I got it up before the man I was facing had even reacted to the situation. He didn't do anything. He just slid off to one side and as he slid a thick gulp of red came out of his mouth.

I heard this shot. It was so loud it was like the end of the world, so loud that I almost didn't hear the door slam towards the back. I crawled farther around the end of the bar, knocked somebody's gun along the floor peevishly, stuck my hat around the corner of the wood. Nobody shot at it. I stuck one eye and part of my face out.

The door at the back was shut and the space in front of it was empty. I got up on my knees and listened. Another door slammed, and a car motor roared.

I went crazy. I tore across the room, threw the door open and plunged through it. It was a phony. They had slammed the door and started the car just for a come-on. I saw that the flailing arm held a bottle.

For the third time in twenty-four hours I took the count.

I came out of this one yelling, with the harsh bite of ammonia in my nose. I swung at a face. But I didn't have anything to swing with. My arms were a couple of four-ton anchors. I threshed around and groaned.

The face in front of me materialized into the bored yet attentive pan of a man with a white coat, a fast-wagon medico.

"Like it?" he grinned. "Some people used to drink it — with a wine-tonic chaser."

He pulled at me and something nipped at my shoulder and a needle stung me.

"Light shot," he said. "That head of yours is pretty bad. You won't go out."

His face went away. I prowled my eyes. Beyond there was a vagueness. Then I saw a girl's face, hushed, sharp, attentive. Carol Pride.

"Yeah," I said. "You followed me. You would."

She smiled and moved. Then her fingers were stroking my cheek and I couldn't see her.

"The prowl-car boys just made it," she said. "The crooks had you all wrapped up in a carpet — for shipment in a truck out back."

I couldn't see very well. A big red-faced man in blue slid in front of me. He had a gun in his hand with the gate open. Somebody groaned somewhere in the background.

She said: "They had two others wrapped up. But they were dead. Ugh!"

"Go on home," I grumbled woozily. "Go write yourself a feature story."

"You used that one before, sap." She went on stroking my cheek. "I thought you made them up as you went along. Drowsy?"

"That's all taken care of," a voice said sharply. "Get this shot guy down to where you can work on him. I want him to live."

Reavis came towards me as out of a mist. His face formed itself slowly, gray, attentive, rather stern. It lowered, as if he sat down in front of me, close to me.

"So you had to play it smart," he said in a sharp, edgy voice. "All right, talk. The hell with how your head feels. You asked for it and you got it."

"Gimme a drink."

Vague motion, a flicker of bright light, the lip of a flask touched my mouth. Hot strength ran down my throat. Some of it ran cold on my chin and I moved my head away from the flask.

"Thanks. Get Magoon – the biggest one?"

"He's full of lead, but still turning over. On his way down-town now."

"Get the Indian?"

"Huh?" he gulped.

"In some bushes under Peace Cross down on the Palisades. I shot him. I didn't mean to."

"Holy ——."

Reavis went away again and the fingers moved slowly and rhythmically on my cheek.

Reavis came back and sat down again. "Who's the Indian?" he snapped.

"Soukesian's strong-arm man. Soukesian the Psychic. He –"

"We know about him," Reavis interrupted bitterly. "You've been out a whole hour, shamus. The lady told us about those cards. She says it's her fault but I don't believe it. Screwy any-how. But a couple of the boys have gone out there."

"I was there," I said. "At his house. He knows something. I don't know what. He was afraid of me – yet he didn't knock me off. Funny."

"Amateur," Reavis said dryly. "He left that for Moose

Magoon. Moose Magoon was tough – up till lately. A record from here to Pittsburgh. . . . Here. But take it easy. This is *ante mortem* confession liquor. Too damn good for you."

The flask touched my lips again.

"Listen," I said thickly. "This was the stick-up squad. Soukesian was the brains. Lindley Paul was the finger. He must have crossed them on something –"

Reavis said, "Nuts," and just then a phone rang distantly and a voice said: "You, Lieutenant."

Reavis went away. When he came back again he didn't sit down.

"Maybe you're right," he said softly. "Maybe you are, at that. In a house on top of a hill in Brentwood Heights there's a golden-haired guy dead in a chair with a woman crying over him. Dutch act. There's a jade necklace on a table beside him."

"Too much death," I said, and fainted.

I woke up in an ambulance. At first I thought I was alone in it. Then I felt her hand and knew I wasn't. I was stone blind now. I couldn't even see light. It was just bandages.

"The doctor's up front with the driver," she said. "You can hold my hand. Would you like me to kiss you?"

"If it doesn't obligate me to anything."

She laughed softly. "I guess you'll live," she said. She kissed me. "Your hair smells of Scotch. Do you take baths in it? The doctor said you weren't to talk."

"They beaned me with a full bottle. Did I tell Reavis about the Indian?"

"Yes."

"Did I tell him Mrs. Prendergast thought Paul was mixed up –"

"You didn't even mention Mrs. Prendergast," she said quickly.

I didn't say anything to that. After a while she said: "This Soukesian, did he look like a lady's man?"

"The doctor said I wasn't to talk," I said.

674

8 POISON BLONDE

IT WAS A couple of weeks later that I drove down to Santa Monica. Ten days of the time I had spent in the hospital, at my own expense, getting over a bad concussion. Moose Magoon was in the prison ward at the County Hospital about the same time, while they picked seven or eight police slugs out of him. At the end of that time they buried him.

The case was pretty well buried by this time, too. The papers had had their play with it and other things had come along and after all it was just a jewel racket that went sour from too much double-crossing. So the police said, and they ought to know. They didn't find any more jewels, but they didn't expect to. They figured the gang pulled just one job at a time, with coolie labor mostly, and sent them on their way with their cut. That way only three people really knew what it was all about: Moose Magoon, who turned out to be an Armenian; Soukesian, who used his connections to find out who had the right kind of jewels; and Lindley Paul, who fingered the jobs and tipped the gang off when to strike. Or so the police said, and they ought to know.

It was a nice warm afternoon. Carol Pride lived on Twenty-fifth Street, in a neat little red brick house trimmed with white with a hedge in front of it.

Her living-room had a tan figured rug, white-and-rose chairs, a black marble fireplace with tall brass andirons, very high bookcases built back into the walls, rough cream-colored drapes against shades of the same color.

There was nothing womanish in it except a full-length mirror with a clear sweep of floor in front.

I sat down in a nice soft chair and rested what was left of my head and sipped Scotch and soda while I looked at her fluffed-out brown hair above a high-collar dress that made her face look small, almost childish.

"I bet you didn't get all this writing," I said.

"And my dad didn't get it grafting on the cops either," she snapped. "We had a few lots at Playa Del Rey, if you have to know."

"A little oil," I said. "Nice. I didn't have to know. Don't start snapping at me."

"Have you still got your license?"

"Oh, yes," I said. "Well, this is nice Scotch. You wouldn't like to go riding in an old car, would you?"

"Who am I to sneer at an old car?" she asked. "The laundry must have put too much starch in your neck."

I grinned at the thin line between her eyebrows.

"I kissed you in that ambulance," she said. "If you remember, don't take it too big. I was just sorry for the way you got your head bashed in."

"I'm a career man," I said. "I wouldn't build on anything like that. Let's go riding. I have to see a blonde in Beverly Hills. I owe her a report."

She stood up and glared at me. "Oh, the Prendergast woman," she said nastily. "The one with the hollow wooden legs."

"They may be hollow," I said.

She flushed and tore out of the room and came back in what seemed about three seconds with a funny little octagonal hat that had a red button on it, and a plaid overcoat with a suede collar and cuffs. "Let's go," she said breathlessly.

The Philip Courtney Prendergasts lived on one of those wide, curving streets where the houses seem to be too close together for their size and the amount of money they represent. A Jap gardener was manicuring a few acres of soft green lawn with the usual contemptuous expression Jap gardeners have. The house had an English slate roof and a porte-cochère, some nice imported trees, a trellis with bougainvillea. It was a nice place and not loud. But Beverly Hills is

Beverly Hills, so the butler had a wing collar and an accent like Alan Mowbray.

He ushered us through zones of silence into a room that was empty at the moment. It had large chesterfields and lounging chairs done in pale yellow leather and arranged around a fireplace, in front of which, on the glossy but not slippery floor, lay a rug as thin as silk and as old as Aesop's aunt. A jet of flowers in the corner, another jet on a low table, walls of dully painted parchment, silence, comfort, space, coziness, a dash of the very modern and a dash of the very old. A very swell room.

Carol Pride sniffed at it.

The butler swung half of a leather-covered door and Mrs. Prendergast came in. Pale blue, with a hat and bag to match, all ready to go out. Pale blue gloves slapping lightly at a pale blue thigh. A smile, hints of depths in the black eyes, a high color, and even before she spoke a nice edge.

She flung both her hands out at us. Carol Pride managed to miss her share. I squeezed mine.

"Gorgeous of you to come," she cried. "How nice to see you both again. I can still taste that whiskey you had in your office. Terrible, wasn't it?"

We all sat down.

I said: "I didn't really need to take up your time by coming in person, Mrs. Prendergast. Everything turned out all right and you got your beads back."

"Yes. That strange man. How curious of him to be what he was. I knew him too. Did you know that?"

"Soukesian? I thought perhaps you knew him," I said.

"Oh, yes. Quite well. I must owe you a lot of money. And your poor head. How is it?"

Carol Pride was sitting close to me.

She said tinnily, between her teeth, almost to herself, but not quite: "Sawdust and creosote. Even at that the termites are getting her."

I smiled at Mrs. Prendergast and she returned my smile with an angel on its back.

"You don't owe me a nickel," I said. "There was just one thing –"

"Impossible. I must. But let's have a little Scotch, shall we?" She held her bag on her knees, pressed something under the chair, said: "A little Scotch and soda, Vernon." She beamed. "Cute, eh? You can't even see the mike. This house is just full of little things like that. Mr. Prendergast loves them. This one talks in the butler's pantry."

Carol Pride said: "I bet the one that talks by the chauffeur's bed is cute too."

Mrs. Prendergast didn't hear her. The butler came in with a tray and mixed drinks, handed them around and went out.

Over the rim of her glass Mrs. Prendergast said: "You were nice not to tell the police I suspected Lin Paul of being – well, you know. Or that I had anything to do with your going to that awful beer parlor. By the way, how did you explain that?"

"Easy. I told them Paul told me himself. He was with you, remember?"

"But he didn't, of course?" I thought her eyes were a little sly now.

"He told me practically nothing. That was the whole truth. And of course he didn't tell me he'd been blackmailing you."

I seemed to be aware that Carol Pride had stopped breathing. Mrs. Prendergast went on looking at me over the rim of her glass. Her face had, for a brief moment, a sort of half-silly, nymph-surprised-while-bathing expression. Then she put her glass down slowly and opened her bag in her lap and got a handkerchief out and bit it. There was silence.

"That," she said in a low voice, "is rather fantastic, isn't it?"

I grinned at her coldly. "The police are a lot like the newspapers, Mrs. Prendergast. For one reason and another they can't use everything they get. But that doesn't make them dumb. Reavis isn't dumb. He doesn't really think, any more than I do, that this Soukesian person was really running a tough jewel-heist gang. He couldn't have handled people like Moose Magoon for five minutes. They'd have walked all over his face just for exercise. Yet Soukesian did have the necklace. That needs explaining. I think he bought it – from Moose Magoon. For the ten-grand pay-off supplied by you – and for some other little consideration likely paid in advance to get Moose to pull the job."

Mrs. Prendergast lowered her lids until her eyes were almost shut, then she lifted them again and smiled. It was a rather ghastly smile. Carol Pride didn't move beside me.

"Somebody *wanted* Lindley Paul killed," I said. "That's obvious. You might kill a man accidentally with a blackjack, by not knowing how hard to hit with it. But you won't put his brains all over his face. And if you beat him up just to teach him to be good, you wouldn't beat him about the head at all. Because that way he wouldn't know how badly you were hurting him. And you'd want him to know that – if you were just teaching him a lesson."

"Wha – what," the blonde woman asked huskily, "has all this to do with me?"

Her face was a mask. Her eyes held a warm bitterness like poisoned honey. One of her hands was roving around inside her bag. It became quiet, inside the bag.

"Moose Magoon would pull a job like that," I bored on, "if he was paid for it. He'd pull any kind of a job. And Moose was an Armenian, so Soukesian might have known how to reach him. And Soukesian was just the type to go skirt-simple over a roto queen and be willing to do anything she wanted him to do, even have a man killed, especially if that man was a rival, especially if he was the kind of man who rolled around on floor cushions and maybe even took candid camera photos of his lady friends when they got a little too close to the Garden of Eden. That wouldn't be too hard to understand, would it, Mrs. Prendergast?"

"Take a drink," Carol Pride said icily. "You're drooling. You don't have to tell this baby she's a tramp. She knows it. But how the hell could anybody blackmail her? You've got to have a reputation to be blackmailed."

"Shut up!" I snapped. "The less you've got the more you'll pay to keep it." I watched the blonde woman's hand move suddenly inside her bag. "Don't bother to pull the gun," I told her. "I know they won't hang you. I just wanted you to know you're not kidding anybody and that that trap in the beer parlor was rigged to finish me off when Soukesian lost his nerve and that you were the one that sent me in there to get what they had for me. The rest of it's dead wood now."

But she pulled the gun out just the same and held it on her pale blue knee and smiled at me.

Carol Pride threw a glass at her. She dodged and the gun went off. A slug went softly and politely into the parchment-covered wall, high up, making no more sound than a finger going into a glove.

The door opened and an enormously tall, thin man strolled into the room.

"Shoot me," he said. "I'm only your husband."

The blonde looked at him. For just a short moment I thought she might be going to take him up on it.

Then she just smiled a little more and put the gun back into her bag and reached for her glass. "Listening in again?" she said dully. "Someday you'll hear something you won't like."

The tall, thin man took a leather checkbook out of his pocket and cocked an eyebrow at me and said: "How much will keep you quiet – permanently?"

I gawked at him. "You heard what I said in here?"

"I think so. The pickup's pretty good this weather. I believe you were accusing my wife of having something to do with somebody's death, was it not?"

I kept on gawking at him.

"Well – how much do you want?" he snapped. "I won't argue with you. I'm used to blackmailers."

"Make it a million," I said. "And she just took a shot at us. That will be four bits extra."

The blonde laughed crazily and the laugh turned into a screech and then into a yell. The next thing she was rolling on the floor screaming and kicking her legs around.

The tall man went over to her quickly and bent down and hit her in the face with his open hand. You could have heard that smack a mile. When he straightened up again his face was a dusky red and the blonde was lying there sobbing.

"I'll show you to the door," he said. "You can call at my office tomorrow."

"What for?" I asked, and took my hat. "You'll still be a sap, even at your office."

I took Carol Pride's arm and steered her out of the room. We left the house silently. The Jap gardener had just pulled a bit of weed root out of the lawn and was holding it up and sneering at it.

We drove away from there, towards the foothills. A red spotlight near the old Beverly Hills Hotel stopped me after a while. I just sat there holding the wheel. The girl beside me didn't move either. She didn't say anything. She just looked straight ahead.

"I didn't get the big warm feeling," I said. "I didn't get to smack anybody down. I didn't make it stick."

"She probably didn't plan it in cold blood," she whispered. "She just got mad and resentful and somebody sold her an idea. A woman like that takes men and gets tired of them and throws them away and they go crazy trying to get her back. It might have been just between the two lovers – Paul and Soukesian. But Mr. Magoon played rough."

"She sent me to that beer parlor," I said. "That's enough for me. And Paul had ideas about Soukesian. I knew she'd miss. With the gun, I mean."

I grabbed her. She was shivering.

A car came up behind us and the driver stood on his horn. I listened to it for a little while, then I let go of Carol Pride and got out of the roadster and walked back. He was a big man, behind the wheel of a sedan.

"That's a boulevard stop," he said sharply. "Lover's Lane is farther up in the hills. Get out of there before I push you out."

"Blow your horn just once more," I begged him. "Just once. Then tell me which side you want the shiner on."

He took a police captain's badge out of his vest pocket. Then he grinned. Then we both grinned. It wasn't my day.

I got back into the roadster and turned it around and started back towards Santa Monica. "Let's go home and drink some more Scotch," I said. "Your Scotch."

RED WIND

1

THERE WAS A desert wind blowing that night. It was one of those hot dry Santa Anas that come down through the mountain passes and curl your hair and make your nerves jump and your skin itch. On nights like that every booze party ends in a fight. Meek little wives feel the edge of the carving knife and study their husbands' necks. Anything can happen. You can even get a full glass of beer at a cocktail lounge.

I was getting one in a flossy new place across the street from the apartment house where I lived. It had been open about a week and it wasn't doing any business. The kid behind the bar was in his early twenties and looked as if he had never had a drink in his life.

There was only one other customer, a souse on a bar stool with his back to the door. He had a pile of dimes stacked neatly in front of him, about two dollars' worth. He was drinking straight rye in small glasses and he was all by himself in a world of his own.

I sat farther along the bar and got my glass of beer and said: "You sure cut the clouds off them, buddy. I will say that for you."

"We just opened up," the kid said. "We got to build up trade. Been in before, haven't you, mister?"

"Uh-huh."

"Live around here?"

"In the Berglund Apartments across the street," I said. "And the name is Philip Marlowe."

"Thanks, mister. Mine's Lew Petrolle." He leaned close to me across the polished dark bar. "Know that guy?"

"No."

"He ought to go home, kind of. I ought to call a taxi and send him home. He's doing his next week's drinking too soon."

"A night like this," I said. "Let him alone."

"It's not good for him," the kid said, scowling at me.

"Rye!" the drunk croaked, without looking up. He snapped his fingers so as not to disturb his piles of dimes by banging on the bar.

The kid looked at me and shrugged. "Should I?"

"Whose stomach is it? Not mine."

The kid poured him another straight rye and I think he doctored it with water down behind the bar because when he came up with it he looked as guilty as if he'd kicked his grandmother. The drunk paid no attention. He lifted coins off his pile with the exact care of a crack surgeon operating on a brain tumor.

The kid came back and put more beer in my glass. Outside the wind howled. Every once in a while it blew the stained-glass door open a few inches. It was a heavy door.

The kid said: "I don't like drunks in the first place and in the second place I don't like them getting drunk in here, and in the third place I don't like them in the first place."

"Warner Brothers could use that," I said.

"They did."

Just then we had another customer. A car squeaked to a stop outside and the swinging door came open. A fellow came in who looked a little in a hurry. He held the door and ranged the place quickly with flat, shiny, dark eyes. He was well set up, dark, good-looking in a narrow-faced, tight-lipped way. His clothes were dark and a white handkerchief peeped coyly from his pocket and he looked cool as well as under a tension of some sort. I guessed it was the hot wind. I felt a bit the same myself only not cool.

He looked at the drunk's back. The drunk was playing checkers with his empty glasses. The new customer looked at me, then he looked along the line of half-booths at the other side of the place. They were all empty. He came on in – down past where the drunk sat swaying and muttering to himself – and spoke to the bar kid.

"Seen a lady in here, buddy? Tall, pretty, brown hair, in a print bolero jacket over a blue crêpe silk dress. Wearing a wide-brimmed straw hat with a velvet band." He had a tight voice I didn't like.

"No, sir. Nobody like that's been in," the bar kid said.

"Thanks. Straight Scotch. Make it fast, will you?"

The kid gave it to him and the fellow paid and put the drink down in a gulp and started to go out. He took three or four steps and stopped, facing the drunk. The drunk was grinning. He swept a gun from somewhere so fast that it was just a blur coming out. He held it steady and he didn't look any drunker than I was. The tall dark guy stood quite still and then his head jerked back a little and then he was still again.

A car tore by outside. The drunk's gun was a .22 target automatic, with a large front sight. It made a couple of hard snaps and a little smoke curled – very little.

"So long, Waldo," the drunk said.

Then he put the gun on the barman and me.

The dark guy took a week to fall down. He stumbled, caught himself, waved one arm, stumbled again. His hat fell off, and then he hit the floor with his face. After he hit it he might have been poured concrete for all the fuss he made.

The drunk slid down off the stool and scooped his dimes into a pocket and slid towards the door. He turned sideways, holding the gun across his body. I didn't have a gun. I hadn't thought I needed one to buy a glass of beer. The kid behind the bar didn't move or make the slightest sound.

The drunk felt the door lightly with his shoulder, keeping his eyes on us, then pushed through it backwards. When it was wide a hard gust of air slammed in and lifted the hair of the man on the floor. The drunk said: "Poor Waldo. I bet I made his nose bleed."

The door swung shut. I started to rush it – from long practice in doing the wrong thing. In this case it didn't matter. The car outside let out a roar and when I got onto the sidewalk it was flicking a red smear of taillight around the nearby corner. I got its license number the way I got my first million.

There were people and cars up and down the blocks as usual. Nobody acted as if a gun had gone off. The wind was making enough noise to make the hard quick rap of .22 ammunition sound like a slammed door, even if anyone heard it. I went back into the cocktail bar.

The kid hadn't moved, even yet. He just stood with his hands flat on the bar, leaning over a little and looking down at the dark guy's back. The dark guy hadn't moved either. I bent down and felt his neck artery. He wouldn't move – ever.

The kid's face had as much expression as a cut of round steak and was about the same color. His eyes were more angry than shocked.

I lit a cigarette and blew smoke at the ceiling and said shortly: "Get on the phone."

"Maybe he's not dead," the kid said.

"When they use a twenty-two that means they don't make mistakes. Where's the phone?"

"I don't have one. I got enough expenses without that. Boy, can I kick eight hundred bucks in the face!"

"You own this place?"

"I did till this happened."

He pulled his white coat off and his apron and came around the inner end of the bar. "I'm locking this door," he said, taking keys out.

He went out, swung the door to and jiggled the lock from the outside until the bolt clicked into place. I bent down and rolled Waldo over. At first I couldn't even see where the shots went in. Then I could. A couple of tiny holes in his coat, over his heart. There was a little blood on his shirt.

The drunk was everything you could ask – as a killer.

The prowl-car boys came in about eight minutes. The kid, Lew Petrolle, was back behind the bar by then. He had his white coat on again and he was counting his money in the register and putting it in his pocket and making notes in a little book.

I sat at the edge of one of the half-booths and smoked cigarettes and watched Waldo's face get deader and deader. I wondered who the girl in the print coat was, why Waldo had left the engine of his car running outside, why he was in a hurry, whether the drunk had been waiting for him or just happened to be there.

The prowl-car boys came in perspiring. They were the usual large size and one of them had a flower stuck under his cap and his cap on a bit crooked. When he saw the dead man he got rid of the flower and leaned down to feel Waldo's pulse.

"Seems to be dead," he said, and rolled him around a little more. "Oh yeah, I see where they went in. Nice clean work. You two see him get it?"

I said yes. The kid behind the bar said nothing. I told them about it, that the killer seemed to have left in Waldo's car.

The cop yanked Waldo's wallet out, went through it rapidly and whistled. "Plenty jack and no driver's license." He put the wallet away. "Okay, we didn't touch him, see? Just a chance we could find did he have a car and put it on the air."

"The hell you didn't touch him," Lew Patrolle said.

The cop gave him one of those looks. "Okay, pal," he said softly. "We touched him."

The kid picked up a clean highball glass and began to polish it. He polished it all the rest of the time we were there.

In another minute a homicide fast-wagon sirened up and screeched to a stop outside the door and four men came in, two dicks, a photographer and a laboratory man. I didn't know either of the dicks. You can be in the detecting business a long time and not know all the men on a big city force.

One of them was a short, smooth, dark, quiet, smiling man, with curly black hair and soft intelligent eyes. The other was big, raw-boned, long-jawed, with a veined nose and glassy eyes. He looked like a heavy drinker. He looked tough, but he looked as if he thought he was a little tougher than he was. He shooed me into the last booth against the wall and his partner got the kid up front and the bluecoats went out. The fingerprint man and photographer set about their work.

A medical examiner came, stayed just long enough to get sore because there was no phone for him to call the morgue wagon.

The short dick emptied Waldo's pockets and then emptied his wallet and dumped everything into a large handkerchief on a booth table. I saw a lot of currency, keys, cigarettes, another handkerchief, very little else.

The big dick pushed me back into the end of the half-booth. "Give," he said. "I'm Copernik, Detective Lieutenant."

I put my wallet in front of him. He looked at it, went through it, tossed it back, made a note in a book.

"Philip Marlowe, huh? A shamus. You here on business?"

"Drinking business," I said. "I live just across the street in the Berglund."

"Know this kid up front?"

"I've been in here once since he opened up."

"See anything funny about him now?"

"No."

"Takes it too light for a young fellow, don't he? Never mind answering. Just tell the story."

I told it – three times. Once for him to get the outline, once for him to get the details and once for him to see if I had it too pat. At the end he said: "This dame interests me.

690

And the killer called the guy Waldo, yet didn't seem to be anyways sure he would be in. I mean, if Waldo wasn't sure the dame would be here, nobody could be sure Waldo would be here."

"That's pretty deep," I said.

He studied me. I wasn't smiling. "Sounds like a grudge job, don't it? Don't sound planned. No getaway except by accident. A guy don't leave his car unlocked much in this town. And the killer works in front of two good witnesses. I don't like that."

"I don't like being a witness," I said. "The pay's too low."

He grinned. His teeth had a freckled look. "Was the killer drunk really?"

"With that shooting? No."

"Me too. Well, it's a simple job. The guy will have a record and he's left plenty prints. Even if we don't have his mug here we'll make him in hours. He had something on Waldo, but he wasn't meeting Waldo tonight. Waldo just dropped in to ask about a dame he had a date with and had missed connections on. It's a hot night and this wind would kill a girl's face. She'd be apt to drop in somewhere to wait. So the killer feeds Waldo two in the right place and scrams and don't worry about you boys at all. It's that simple."

"Yeah," I said.

"It's so simple it stinks," Copernik said.

He took his felt hat off and tousled up his ratty blond hair and leaned his head on his hands. He had a long mean horse face. He got a handkerchief out and mopped it, and the back of his neck and the back of his hands. He got a comb out and combed his hair – he looked worse with it combed – and put his hat back on.

"I was just thinking," I said.

"Yeah? What?"

"This Waldo knew just how the girl was dressed. So he must already have been with her tonight."

"So, what? Maybe he had to go to the can. And when he came back she's gone. Maybe she changed her mind about him."

"That's right," I said.

But that wasn't what I was thinking at all. I was thinking that Waldo had described the girl's clothes in a way the ordinary man wouldn't know how to describe them. Printed bolero jacket over blue crêpe silk dress. I didn't even know what a bolero jacket was. And I might have said blue dress or even blue silk dress, but never blue crêpe silk dress.

After a while two men came with a basket. Lew Petrolle was still polishing his glass and talking to the short dark dick.

We all went down to Headquarters.

Lew Petrolle was all right when they checked on him. His father had a grape ranch near Antioch in Contra Costa County. He had given Lew a thousand dollars to go into business and Lew had opened the cocktail bar, neon sign and all, on eight hundred flat.

They let him go and told him to keep the bar closed until they were sure they didn't want to do any more printing. He shook hands all around and grinned and said he guessed the killing would be good for business after all, because nobody believed a newspaper account of anything and people would come to him for the story and buy drinks while he was telling it.

"There's a guy won't ever do any worrying," Copernik said, when he was gone. "Over anybody else."

"Poor Waldo," I said. "The prints any good?"

"Kind of smudged," Copernik said sourly. "But we'll get a classification and teletype it to Washington some time tonight. If it don't click, you'll be in for a day on the steel picture racks downstairs."

I shook hands with him and his partner, whose name was Ybarra, and left. They didn't know who Waldo was yet either. Nothing in his pockets told.

692

2

I GOT BACK to my street about 9 P.M. I looked up and down the block before I went into the Berglund. The cocktail bar was farther down on the other side, dark, with a nose or two against the glass, but no real crowd. People had seen the law and the morgue wagon, but they didn't know what had happened. Except the boys playing pinball games in the drugstore on the corner. They know everything, except how to hold a job.

The wind was still blowing, oven-hot, swirling dust and torn paper up against the walls.

I went into the lobby of the apartment house and rode the automatic elevator up to the fourth floor. I unwound the doors and stepped out and there was a tall girl standing there waiting for the car.

She had brown wavy hair under a wide-brimmed straw hat with a velvet band and loose bow. She had wide blue eyes and eyelashes that didn't quite reach her chin. She wore a blue dress that might have been crêpe silk, simple in lines but not missing any curves. Over it she wore what might have been a print bolero jacket.

I said: "Is that a bolero jacket?"

She gave me a distant glance and made a motion as if to brush a cobweb out of the way.

"Yes. Would you mind – I'm rather in a hurry. I'd like – "

I didn't move. I blocked her off from the elevator. We stared at each other and she flushed very slowly.

"Better not go out on the street in those clothes," I said.

"Why, how dare you – "

The elevator clanked and started down again. I didn't know what she was going to say. Her voice lacked the edgy twang of a beer-parlor frill. It had a soft light sound, like spring rain.

"It's not a make," I said. "You're in trouble. If they come to this floor in the elevator, you have just that much time to get off the hall. First take off the hat and jacket – and snap it up!"

She didn't move. Her face seemed to whiten a little behind the not-too-heavy make-up.

"Cops," I said, "are looking for you. In those clothes. Give me the chance and I'll tell you why."

She turned her head swiftly and looked back along the corridor. With her looks I didn't blame her for trying one more bluff.

"You're impertinent, whoever you are. I'm Mrs. Leroy in Apartment Thirty-one. I can assure – "

"That you're on the wrong floor," I said. "This is the fourth." The elevator had stopped down below. The sound of doors being wrenched open came up the shaft.

"Off !" I rapped. "Now!"

She switched her hat off and slipped out of the bolero jacket, fast. I grabbed them and wadded them into a mess under my arm. I took her elbow and turned her and we were going down the hall.

"I live in Forty-two. The front one across from yours, just a floor up. Take your choice. Once again – I'm not on the make."

She smoothed her hair with that quick gesture, like a bird preening itself. Ten thousand years of practice behind it.

"Mine," she said, and tucked her bag under her arm and strode down the hall fast. The elevator stopped at the floor below. She stopped when it stopped. She turned and faced me.

"The stairs are back by the elevator shaft," I said gently.

"I don't have an apartment," she said.

"I didn't think you had."

"Are they searching for me?"

"Yes, but they won't start gouging the block stone by stone before tomorrow. And then only if they don't make Waldo."

She stared at me. "Waldo?"

"Oh, you don't know Waldo," I said.

She shook her head slowly. The elevator started down in the shaft again. Panic flicked in her blue eyes like a ripple on water.

"No," she said breathlessly, "but take me out of this hall."

We were almost at my door. I jammed the key in and shook the lock around and heaved the door inward. I reached in far enough to switch lights on. She went in past me like a wave. Sandalwood floated on the air, very faint.

I shut the door, threw my hat into a chair and watched her stroll over to a card table on which I had a chess problem set out that I couldn't solve. Once inside, with the door locked, her panic had left her.

"So you're a chess player," she said, in that guarded tone, as if she had come to look at my etchings. I wished she had.

We both stood still then and listened to the distant clang of elevator doors and then steps – going the other way.

I grinned, but with strain, not pleasure, went out into the kitchenette and started to fumble with a couple of glasses and then realized I still had her hat and bolero jacket under my arm. I went into the dressing room behind the wall bed and stuffed them into a drawer, went back out to the kitchenette, dug out some extra-fine Scotch and made a couple of highballs.

When I went in with the drinks she had a gun in her hand. It was a small automatic with a pearl grip. It jumped up at me and her eyes were full of horror.

I stopped, with a glass in each hand, and said: "Maybe this hot wind has got you crazy too. I'm a private detective. I'll prove it if you let me."

She nodded slightly and her face was white. I went over slowly and put a glass down beside her, and went back and set mine down and got a card out that had no bent corners. She was sitting down, smoothing one blue knee with her left hand, and holding the gun on the other. I put the card down beside her drink and sat with mine.

"Never let a guy get that close to you," I said. "Not if you mean business. And your safety catch is on."

She flashed her eyes down, shivered, and put the gun back in her bag. She drank half the drink without stopping, put the glass down hard and picked the card up.

"I don't give many people that liquor," I said. "I can't afford to."

Her lips curled. "I supposed you would want money."

"Huh?"

She didn't say anything. Her hand was close to her bag again.

"Don't forget the safety catch," I said. Her hand stopped. I went on: "This fellow I called Waldo is quite tall, say five-eleven, slim, dark, brown eyes with a lot of glitter. Nose and mouth too thin. Dark suit, white handkerchief showing, and in a hurry to find you. Am I getting anywhere?"

She took her glass again. "So that's Waldo," she said. "Well, what about him?" Her voice seemed to have a slight liquor edge now.

"Well, a funny thing. There's a cocktail bar across the street . . . Say, where have you been all evening?"

"Sitting in my car," she said coldly, "most of the time."

"Didn't you see a fuss across the street up the block?"

Her eyes tried to say no and missed. Her lips said: "I knew there was some kind of disturbance. I saw policemen and red searchlights. I supposed someone had been hurt."

"Someone was. And this Waldo was looking for you before that. In the cocktail bar. He described you and your clothes."

Her eyes were set like rivets now and had the same amount of expression. Her mouth began to tremble and kept on trembling.

"I was in there," I said, "talking to the kid that runs it. There was nobody in there but a drunk on a stool and the kid and myself. The drunk wasn't paying any attention to anything. Then Waldo came in and asked about you and we said no, we hadn't seen you and he started to leave."

I sipped my drink. I like an effect as well as the next fellow. Her eyes ate me.

"Just started to leave. Then this drunk that wasn't paying any attention to anyone called him Waldo and took a gun out. He shot him twice" – I snapped my fingers twice – "like that. Dead."

She fooled me. She laughed in my face. "So my husband hired you to spy on me," she said. "I might have known the whole thing was an act. You and your Waldo."

I gawked at her.

"I never thought of him as jealous," she snapped. "Not of a man who had been our chauffeur anyhow. A little about Stan, of course – that's natural. But Joseph Coates – "

I made motions in the air. "Lady, one of us has this book open at the wrong page," I grunted. "I don't know anybody named Stan or Joseph Coates. So help me, I didn't even know you had a chauffeur. People around here don't run to them. As for husbands – yeah, we do have a husband once in a while. Not often enough."

She shook her head slowly and her hand stayed near her bag and her blue eyes had glitters in them.

"Not good enough, Mr. Marlowe. No, not nearly good enough. I know you private detectives. You're all rotten. You tricked me into your apartment, if it is your apartment. More likely it's the apartment of some horrible man who will swear anything for a few dollars. Now you're trying to scare me. So you can blackmail me – as well as get money from my husband. All right," she said breathlessly, "how much do I have to pay?"

I put my empty glass aside and leaned back. "Pardon me if I light a cigarette," I said. "My nerves are frayed."

I lit it while she watched me without enough fear for any real guilt to be under it. "So Joseph Coates is his name," I said.

"The guy that killed him in the cocktail bar called him Waldo."

She smiled a bit disgustedly, but almost tolerantly. "Don't stall. How much?"

"Why were you trying to meet this Joseph Coates?"

"I was going to buy something he stole from me, of course. Something that's valuable in the ordinary way too. Almost fifteen thousand dollars. The man I loved gave it to me. He's dead. There! He's dead! He died in a burning plane. Now, go back and tell my husband that, you slimy little rat!"

"I'm not little and I'm not a rat," I said.

"You're still slimy. And don't bother about telling my husband. I'll tell him myself. He probably knows anyway."

I grinned. "That's smart. Just what was I supposed to find out?"

She grabbed her glass and finished what was left of her drink. "So he thinks I'm meeting Joseph. Well, perhaps I was. But not to make love. Not with a chauffeur. Not with a bum I picked off the front step and gave a job to. I don't have to dig down that far, if I want to play around."

"Lady," I said, "you don't indeed."

"Now, I'm going," she said. "You just try and stop me." She snatched the pearl-handled gun out of her bag. I didn't move.

"Why, you nasty little string of nothing," she stormed. "How do I know you're a private detective at all? You might be a crook. This card you gave me doesn't mean anything. Anybody can have cards printed."

"Sure," I said. "And I suppose I'm smart enough to live here two years because you were going to move in today so I could blackmail you for not meeting a man named Joseph Coates who was bumped off across the street under the name of Waldo. Have you got the money to buy this something that cost fifteen grand?"

"Oh! You think you'll hold me up, I suppose!"

"Oh!" I mimicked her, "I'm a stick-up artist now, am I? Lady, will you please either put that gun away or take the safety catch off? It hurts my professional feelings to see a nice gun made a monkey of that way."

"You're a full portion of what I don't like," she said. "Get out of my way."

I didn't move. She didn't move. We were both sitting down – and not even close to each other.

"Let me in on one secret before you go," I pleaded. "What in hell did you take the apartment down on the floor below for? Just to meet a guy down on the street?"

"Stop being silly," she snapped. "I didn't. I lied. It's his apartment."

"Joseph Coates'?"

She nodded sharply.

"Does my description of Waldo sound like Joseph Coates?"

She nodded sharply again.

"All right. That's one fact learned at last. Don't you realize Waldo described your clothes before he was shot – when he was looking for you – that the description was passed on to the police – that the police don't know who Waldo is – and are looking for somebody in those clothes to help tell them? Don't you get that much?"

The gun suddenly started to shake in her hand. She looked down at it, sort of vacantly, and slowly put it back in her bag.

"I'm a fool," she whispered, "to be even talking to you." She stared at me for a long time, then pulled in a deep breath. "He told me where he was staying. He didn't seem afraid. I guess blackmailers are like that. He was to meet me on the street, but I was late. It was full of police when I got here. So I went back and sat in my car for a while. Then I came up to Joseph's apartment and knocked. Then I went back to my car and waited again. I came up here three times in all. The last time I walked up a flight to take the elevator.

I had already been seen twice on the third floor. I met you. That's all."

"You said something about a husband," I grunted. "Where is he?"

"He's at a meeting."

"Oh, a meeting," I said, nastily.

"My husband's a very important man. He has lots of meetings. He's a hydroelectric engineer. He's been all over the world. I'd have you know – "

"Skip it," I said. "I'll take him to lunch some day and have him tell me himself. Whatever Joseph had on you is dead stock now. Like Joseph."

"He's really dead?" she whispered. "Really?"

"He's dead," I said. "Dead, dead, dead. Lady, he's dead."

She believed it at last. I hadn't thought she ever would somehow. In the silence, the elevator stopped at my floor.

I heard steps coming down the hall. We all have hunches. I put my finger to my lips. She didn't move now. Her face had a frozen look. Her big blue eyes were as black as the shadows below them. The hot wind boomed against the shut windows. Windows have to be shut when a Santa Ana blows, heat or no heat.

The steps that came down the hall were the casual ordinary steps of one man. But they stopped outside my door, and somebody knocked.

I pointed to the dressing room behind the wall bed. She stood up without a sound, her bag clenched against her side. I pointed again, to her glass. She lifted it swiftly, slid across the carpet, through the door, drew the door quietly shut after her.

I didn't know just what I was going to all this trouble for.

The knocking sounded again. The backs of my hands were wet. I creaked my chair and stood up and made a loud yawning sound. Then I went over and opened the door – without a gun. That was a mistake.

3

I DIDN'T KNOW him at first. Perhaps for the opposite reason Waldo hadn't seemed to know him. He'd had a hat on all the time over at the cocktail bar and he didn't have one on now. His hair ended completely and exactly where his hat would start. Above that line was hard white sweatless skin almost as glaring as scar tissue. He wasn't just twenty years older. He was a different man.

But I knew the gun he was holding, the .22 target automatic with the big front sight. And I knew his eyes. Bright, brittle, shallow eyes like the eyes of a lizard.

He was alone. He put the gun against my face very lightly and said between his teeth: "Yeah, me. Let's go on in."

I backed in just far enough and stopped. Just the way he would want me to, so he could shut the door without moving much. I knew from his eyes that he would want me to do just that.

I wasn't scared. I was paralyzed.

When he had the door shut he backed me some more, slowly, until there was something against the back of my legs. His eyes looked into mine.

"That's a card table," he said. "Some goon here plays chess. You?"

I swallowed. "I don't exactly play it. I just fool around."

"That means two," he said with a kind of hoarse softness, as if some cop had hit him across the windpipe with a black-jack once, in a third-degree session.

"It's a problem," I said. "Not a game. Look at the pieces."

"I wouldn't know."

"Well, I'm alone," I said, and my voice shook just enough.

"It don't make any difference," he said. "I'm washed up anyway. Some nose puts the bulls on me tomorrow, next week, what the hell? I just didn't like your map, pal. And that

701

smug-faced pansy in the bar coat that played left tackle for Fordham or something. To hell with guys like you guys."

I didn't speak or move. The big front sight raked my cheek lightly, almost caressingly. The man smiled.

"It's kind of good business too," he said. "Just in case. An old con like me don't make good prints, all I got against me is two witnesses. The hell with it."

"What did Waldo do to you?" I tried to make it sound as if I wanted to know, instead of just not wanting to shake too hard.

"Stooled on a bank job in Michigan and got me four years. Got himself a nolle prosse. Four years in Michigan ain't no summer cruise. They make you be good in them lifer states."

"How'd you know he'd come in there?" I croaked.

"I didn't. Oh yeah, I was lookin' for him. I was wanting to see him all right. I got a flash of him on the street night before last but I lost him. Up to then I wasn't lookin' for him. Then I was. A cute guy, Waldo. How is he?"

"Dead," I said.

"I'm still good," he chuckled. "Drunk or sober. Well, that don't make no doughnuts for me now. They make me downtown yet?"

I didn't answer him quick enough. He jabbed the gun into my throat and I choked and almost grabbed for it by instinct.

"Naw," he cautioned me softly. "Naw. You ain't that dumb."

I put my hands back, down at my sides, open, the palms towards him. He would want them that way. He hadn't touched me, except with the gun. He didn't seem to care whether I might have one too. He wouldn't – if he just meant the one thing.

He didn't seem to care very much about anything, coming back on that block. Perhaps the hot wind did something to him. It was booming against my shut windows like the surf under a pier.

"They got prints," I said. "I don't know how good."

"They'll be good enough – but not for teletype work. Take 'em airmail time to Washington and back to check 'em right. Tell me why I came here, pal."

"You heard the kid and me talking in the bar. I told him my name, where I lived."

"That's how, pal. I said why." He smiled at me. It was a lousy smile to be the last one you might see.

"Skip it," I said. "The hangman won't ask you to guess why he's there."

"Say, you're tough at that. After you, I visit that kid. I tailed him home from Headquarters, but I figure you're the guy to put the bee on first. I tail him home from the city hall, in the rent car Waldo had. From Headquarters, pal. Them funny dicks. You can sit in their laps and they don't know you. Start runnin' for a streetcar and they open up with machine guns and bump two pedestrians, a hacker asleep in his cab, and an old scrubwoman on the second floor workin' a mop. And they miss the guy they're after. Them funny lousy dicks."

He twisted the gun muzzle in my neck. His eyes looked madder than before.

"I got time," he said. "Waldo's rent car don't get a report right away. And they don't make Waldo very soon. I know Waldo. Smart he was. A smooth boy, Waldo."

"I'm going to vomit," I said, "if you don't take that gun out of my throat."

He smiled and moved the gun down to my heart. "This about right? Say when."

I must have spoken louder than I meant to. The door of the dressing room by the wall bed showed a crack of darkness. Then an inch. Then four inches. I saw eyes, but didn't look at them. I stared hard into the bald-headed man's eyes. Very hard. I didn't want him to take his eyes off mine.

"Scared?" he asked softly.

I leaned against his gun and began to shake. I thought he would enjoy seeing me shake. The girl came out through the door. She had her gun in her hand again. I was sorry as hell for her. She'd try to make the door – or scream. Either way it would be curtains – for both of us.

"Well, don't take all night about it," I bleated. My voice sounded far away, like a voice on a radio on the other side of a street.

"I like this, pal," he smiled. "I'm like that."

The girl floated in the air, somewhere behind him. Nothing was ever more soundless than the way she moved. It wouldn't do any good though. He wouldn't fool around with her at all. I had known him all my life but I had been looking into his eyes for only five minutes.

"Suppose I yell," I said.

"Yeah, suppose you yell. Go ahead and yell," he said with his killer's smile.

She didn't go near the door. She was right behind him.

"Well – here's where I yell," I said.

As if that was the cue, she jabbed the little gun hard into his short ribs, without a single sound.

He had to react. It was like a knee reflex. His mouth snapped open and both his arms jumped out from his sides and he arched his back just a little. The gun was pointing at my right eye.

I sank and kneed him with all my strength, in the groin.

His chin came down and I hit it. I hit it as if I was driving the last spike on the first transcontinental railroad. I can still feel it when I flex my knuckles.

His gun raked the side of my face but it didn't go off. He was already limp. He writhed down gasping, his left side against the floor. I kicked his right shoulder – hard. The gun jumped away from him, skidded on the carpet, under a chair. I heard the chessmen tinkling on the floor behind me somewhere.

The girl stood over him, looking down. Then her wide dark horrified eyes came up and fastened on mine.

"That buys me," I said. "Anything I have is yours — now and forever."

She didn't hear me. Her eyes were strained open so hard that the whites showed under the vivid blue iris. She backed quickly to the door with her little gun up, felt behind her for the knob and twisted it. She pulled the door open and slipped out.

The door shut.

She was bareheaded and without her bolero jacket.

She had only the gun, and the safety catch on that was still set so that she couldn't fire it.

It was silent in the room then, in spite of the wind. Then I heard him gasping on the floor. His face had a greenish pallor. I moved behind him and pawed him for more guns, and didn't find any. I got a pair of store cuffs out of my desk and pulled his arms in front of him and snapped them on his wrists. They would hold if he didn't shake them too hard.

His eyes measured me for a coffin, in spite of their suffering. He lay in the middle of the floor, still on his left side, a twisted, wizened, bald-headed little guy with drawn-back lips and teeth spotted with cheap silver fillings. His mouth looked like a black pit and his breath came in little waves, choked, stopped, came on again, limping.

I went into the dressing room and opened the drawer of the chest. Her hat and jacket lay there on my shirts. I put them underneath, at the back, and smoothed the shirts over them. Then I went out to the kitchenette and poured a stiff jolt of whiskey and put it down and stood a moment listening to the hot wind howl against the window glass. A garage door banged, and a power-line wire with too much play between the insulators thumped the side of the building with a sound like somebody beating a carpet.

The drink worked on me. I went back into the living-room and opened a window. The guy on the floor hadn't smelled her sandalwood, but somebody else might.

I shut the window again, wiped the palms of my hands and used the phone to dial Headquarters.

Copernik was still there. His smart-aleck voice said: "Yeah? Marlowe? Don't tell me. I bet you got an idea."

"Make that killer yet?"

"We're not saying, Marlowe. Sorry as all hell and so on. You know how it is."

"Okay, I don't care who he is. Just come and get him off the floor of my apartment."

"Holy Christ!" Then his voice hushed and went down low. "Wait a minute, now. Wait a minute." A long way off I seemed to hear a door shut. Then his voice again. "Shoot," he said softly.

"Handcuffed," I said. "All yours. I had to knee him, but he'll be all right. He came here to eliminate a witness."

Another pause. The voice was full of honey. "Now listen, boy, who else is in this with you?"

"Who else? Nobody. Just me."

"Keep it that way, boy. All quiet. Okay?"

"Think I want all the bums in the neighborhood in here sightseeing?"

"Take it easy, boy. Easy. Just sit tight and sit still. I'm practically there. No touch nothing. Get me?"

"Yeah." I gave him the address and apartment number again to save him time.

I could see his big bony face glisten. I got the .22 target gun from under the chair and sat holding it until feet hit the hallway outside my door and knuckles did a quiet tattoo on the door panel.

Copernik was alone. He filled the doorway quickly, pushed me back into the room with a tight grin and shut the door. He stood with his back to it, his hand under the left side of his coat. A big hard bony man with flat cruel eyes.

He lowered them slowly and looked at the man on the floor. The man's neck was twitching a little. His eyes moved in short stabs – sick eyes.

"Sure it's the guy?" Copernik's voice was hoarse.

"Positive. Where's Ybarra?"

"Oh, he was busy." He didn't look at me when he said that. "Those your cuffs?"

"Yeah."

"Key."

I tossed it to him. He went down swiftly on one knee beside the killer and took my cuffs off his wrists, tossed them to one side. He got his own off his hip, twisted the bald man's hands behind him and snapped the cuffs on.

"All right, you bastard," the killer said tonelessly.

Copernik grinned and balled his fist and hit the handcuffed man in the mouth a terrific blow. His head snapped back almost enough to break his neck. Blood dribbled from the lower corner of his mouth.

"Get a towel," Copernik ordered.

I got a hand towel and gave it to him. He stuffed it between the handcuffed man's teeth, viciously, stood up and rubbed his bony fingers through his ratty blond hair.

"All right. Tell it."

I told it — leaving the girl out completely. It sounded a little funny. Copernik watched me, said nothing. He rubbed the side of his veined nose. Then he got his comb out and worked on his hair just as he had done earlier in the evening, in the cocktail bar.

I went over and gave him the gun. He looked at it casually, dropped it into his side pocket. His eyes had something in them and his face moved in a hard bright grin.

I bent down and began picking up my chessmen and dropping them into the box. I put the box on the mantel, straightened out a leg of the card table, played around for a while. All the time Copernik watched me. I wanted him to think something out.

At last he came out with it. "This guy uses a twenty-two," he said. "He uses it because he's good enough to get by with

707

that much gun. That means he's good. He knocks at your door, pokes that gat in your belly, walks you back into the room, says he's here to close your mouth for keeps — and yet you take him. You not having any gun. You take him alone. You're kind of good yourself, pal."

"Listen," I said, and looked at the floor. I picked up another chessman and twisted it between my fingers. "I was doing a chess problem," I said. "Trying to forget things."

"You got something on your mind, pal," Copernik said softly. "You wouldn't try to fool an old copper, would you, boy?"

"It's a swell pinch and I'm giving it to you," I said. "What the hell more do you want?"

The man on the floor made a vague sound behind the towel. His bald head glistened with sweat.

"What's the matter, pal? You been up to something?" Copernik almost whispered.

I looked at him quickly, looked away again. "All right," I said. "You know damn well I couldn't take him alone. He had the gun on me and he shoots where he looks."

Copernik closed one eye and squinted at me amiably with the other. "Go on, pal. I kind of thought of that too."

I shuffled around a little more, to make it look good. I said, slowly: "There was a kid here who pulled a job over in Boyle Heights, a heist job. It didn't take. A two-bit service station stick-up. I know his family. He's not really bad. He was here trying to beg train money off me. When the knock came he sneaked in — there."

I pointed at the wall bed and the door beside. Copernik's head swiveled slowly, swiveled back. His eyes winked again. "And this kid had a gun," he said.

I nodded. "And he got behind him. That takes guts, Copernik. You've got to give the kid a break. You've got to let him stay out of it."

"Tag out for this kid?" Copernik asked softly.

"Not yet, he says. He's scared there will be."

Copernik smiled. "I'm a homicide man," he said. "I wouldn't know – or care."

I pointed down at the gagged and handcuffed man on the floor. "You took him, didn't you?" I said gently.

Copernik kept on smiling. A big whitish tongue came out and massaged his thick lower lip. "How'd I do it?" he whispered.

"Get the slugs out of Waldo?"

"Sure. Long twenty-two's. One smashed a rib, one good."

"You're a careful guy. You don't miss any angles. You know anything about me? You dropped in on me to see what guns I had."

Copernik got up and went down on one knee again beside the killer. "Can you hear me, guy?" he asked with his face close to the face of the man on the floor.

The man made some vague sound. Copernik stood up and yawned. "Who the hell cares what he says? Go on, pal."

"You wouldn't expect to find I had anything, but you wanted to look around my place. And while you were mousing around in there" – I pointed to the dressing room – "and me not saying anything, being a little sore, maybe, a knock came on the door. So he came in. So after a while you sneaked out and took him."

"Ah," Copernik grinned widely, with as many teeth as a horse. "You're on, pal. I socked him and I kneed him and I took him. You didn't have no gun and the guy swiveled on me pretty sharp and I left-hooked him down the backstairs. Okay,?"

"Okay," I said.

"You'll tell it like that downtown?"

"Yeah," I said.

"I'll protect you, pal. Treat me right and I'll always play ball. Forget about that kid. Let me know if he needs a break."

He came over and held out his hand. I shook it. It was as clammy as a dead fish. Clammy hands and the people who own them make me sick.

"There's just one thing," I said. "This partner of yours – Ybarra. Won't he be a bit sore you didn't bring him along on this?"

Copernik tousled his hair and wiped his hatband with a large yellowish silk handkerchief.

"That guinea?" he sneered. "To hell with him!" He came close to me and breathed in my face. "No mistakes, pal – about that story of ours."

His breath was bad. It would be.

4

THERE WERE JUST five of us in the chief-of-detectives' office when Copernik laid it before them. A stenographer, the chief, Copernik, myself, Ybarra. Ybarra sat on a chair tilted against the side wall. His hat was down over his eyes but their softness loomed underneath, and the small still smile hung at the corners of the clean-cut Latin lips. He didn't look directly at Copernik. Copernik didn't look at him at all.

Outside in the corridor there had been photos of Copernik shaking hands with me, Copernik with his hat on straight and his gun in his hand and a stern, purposeful look on his face.

They said they knew who Waldo was, but they wouldn't tell me. I didn't believe they knew, because the chief-of-detectives had a morgue photo of Waldo on his desk. A beautiful job, his hair combed, his tie straight, the light hitting his eyes just right to make them glisten. Nobody would have known it was a photo of a dead man with two bullet holes in his heart. He looked like a dance-hall sheik making up his mind whether to take the blonde or the redhead.

It was about midnight when I got home. The apartment door was locked and while I was fumbling for my keys a low voice spoke to me out of the darkness.

All it said was: "Please!" but I knew it. I turned and looked at a dark Cadillac coupe parked just off the loading zone. It had no lights. Light from the street touched the brightness of a woman's eyes.

I went over there. "You're a darn fool," I said.

She said: "Get in."

I climbed in and she started the car and drove it a block and a half along Franklin and turned down Kingsley Drive. The hot wind still burned and blustered. A radio lilted from an open, sheltered side window of an apartment house. There were a lot of parked cars but she found a vacant space behind a small brand-new Packard cabriolet that had the dealer's sticker on the windshield glass. After she'd jockeyed us up to the curb she leaned back in the corner with her gloved hands on the wheel.

She was all in black now, or dark brown, with a small foolish hat. I smelled the sandalwood in her perfume.

"I wasn't very nice to you, was I?" she said.

"All you did was save my life."

"What happened?"

"I called the law and fed a few lies to a cop I don't like and gave him all the credit for the pinch and that was that. That guy you took away from me was the man who killed Waldo."

"You mean – you didn't tell them about me?"

"Lady," I said again, "all you did was save my life. What else do you want done? I'm ready, willing, and I'll try to be able."

She didn't say anything, or move.

"Nobody learned who you are from me," I said. "Incidentally, I don't know myself."

"I'm Mrs. Frank C. Barsaly, Two-twelve Fremont Place, Olympia Two-four-five-nine-six. Is that what you wanted?"

"Thanks," I mumbled, and rolled a dry unlit cigarette around in my fingers. "Why did you come back?" Then I snapped the fingers of my left hand. "The hat and jacket," I said. "I'll go up and get them."

"It's more than that," she said. "I want my pearls." I might have jumped a little. It seemed as if there had been enough without pearls.

A car tore by down the street going twice as fast as it should. A thin bitter cloud of dust lifted in the street lights and whirled and vanished. The girl ran the window up quickly against it.

"All right," I said. "Tell me about the pearls. We have had a murder and a mystery woman and a mad killer and a heroic rescue and a police detective framed into making a false report. Now we will have pearls. All right – feed it to me."

"I was to buy them for five thousand dollars. From the man you call Waldo and I call Joseph Coates. He should have had them."

"No pearls," I said. "I saw what came out of his pockets. A lot of money, but no pearls."

"Could they be hidden in his apartment?"

"Yes," I said. "So far as I know he could have had them hidden anywhere in California except in his pockets. How's Mr. Barsaly this hot night?"

"He's still downtown at his meeting. Otherwise I couldn't have come."

"Well, you could have brought him," I said. "He could have sat in the rumble seat."

"Oh, I don't know," she said. "Frank weighs two hundred pounds and he's pretty solid. I don't think he would like to sit in the rumble seat, Mr. Marlowe."

"What the hell are we talking about anyway?"

She didn't answer. Her gloved hands tapped lightly, provokingly on the rim of the slender wheel. I threw the unlit cigarette out the window, turned a little and took hold of her.

When I let go of her, she pulled as far away from me as she could against the side of the car and rubbed the back of her glove against her mouth. I sat quite still.

We didn't speak for some time. Then she said very slowly: "I meant you to do that. But I wasn't always that way. It's only been since Stan Phillips was killed in his plane. If it hadn't been for that, I'd be Mrs. Phillips now. Stan gave me the pearls. They cost fifteen thousand dollars, he said once. White pearls, forty-one of them, the largest about a third of an inch across. I don't know how many grains. I never had them appraised or showed them to a jeweler, so I don't know those things. But I loved them on Stan's account. I loved Stan. The way you do just the one time. Can you understand?"

"What's your first name?" I asked.

"Lola."

"Go on talking, Lola." I got another dry cigarette out of my pocket and fumbled it between my fingers just to give them something to do.

"They had a simple silver clasp in the shape of a two-bladed propeller. There was one small diamond where the boss would be. I told Frank they were store pearls I had bought myself. He didn't know the difference. It's not so easy to tell, I dare say. You see – Frank is pretty jealous."

In the darkness she came closer to me and her side touched my side. But I didn't move this time. The wind howled and the trees shook. I kept on rolling the cigarette around in my fingers.

"I suppose you've read that story," she said. "About the wife and the real pearls and her telling her husband they were false?"

"I've read it," I said, "Maugham."

"I hired Joseph. My husband was in Argentina at the time. I was pretty lonely."

"*You* should be lonely," I said.

713

"Joseph and I went driving a good deal. Sometimes we had a drink or two together. But that's all. I don't go around – "

"You told him about the pearls," I said. "And when your two hundred pounds of beef came back from Argentina and kicked him out – he took the pearls, because he knew they were real. And then offered them back to you for five grand."

"Yes," she said simply. "Of course I didn't want to go to the police. And of course in the circumstance Joseph wasn't afraid of my knowing where he lived."

"Poor Waldo," I said. "I feel kind of sorry for him. It was a hell of a time to run into an old friend that had a down on you."

I struck a match on my shoe sole and lit the cigarette. The tobacco was so dry from the hot wind that it burned like grass. The girl sat quietly beside me, her hands on the wheel again.

"Hell with women – these fliers," I said. "And you're still in love with him, or think you are. Where did you keep the pearls?"

"In a Russian malachite jewelry box on my dressing table. With some other costume jewelry. I had to, if I ever wanted to wear them."

"And they were worth fifteen grand. And you think Joseph might have hidden them in his apartment. Thirty-one, wasn't it?"

"Yes," she said. "I guess it's a lot to ask."

I opened the door and got out of the car. "I've been paid," I said. "I'll go look. The doors in my apartment are not very obstinate. The cops will find out where Waldo lived when they publish his photo, but not tonight, I guess."

"It's awfully sweet of you," she said. "Shall I wait here?"

I stood with a foot on the running board, leaning in, looking at her. I didn't answer her question. I just stood there looking in at the shine of her eyes. Then I shut the car door and walked up the street towards Franklin.

Even with the wind shriveling my face I could still smell the sandalwood in her hair. And feel her lips.

I unlocked the Berglund door, walked through the silent lobby to the elevator, and rode up to Three. Then I soft-footed along the silent corridor and peered down at the sill of Apartment 31. No light. I rapped – the old light, confidential tattoo of the bootlegger with the big smile and the extra-deep hip pockets. No answer. I took the piece of thick hard celluloid that pretended to be a window over the driver's license in my wallet, and eased it between the lock and the jamb, leaning hard on the knob, pushing it toward the hinges. The edge of the celluloid caught the slope of the spring lock and snapped it back with a small brittle sound, like an icicle breaking. The door yielded and I went into near darkness. Street light filtered in and touched a high spot here and there.

I shut the door and snapped the light on and just stood. There was a queer smell in the air. I made it in a moment – the smell of dark-cured tobacco. I prowled over to a smoking stand by the window and looked down at four brown butts – Mexican or South American cigarettes.

Upstairs, on my floor, feet hit the carpet and somebody went into a bathroom. I heard the toilet flush. I went into the bathroom of Apartment 31. A little rubbish, nothing, no place to hide anything. The kitchenette was a longer job, but I only half searched. I knew there were no pearls in that apartment. I knew Waldo had been on his way out and that he was in a hurry and that something was riding him when he turned and took two bullets from an old friend.

I went back to the living-room and swung the wall bed and looked past its mirror side into the dressing room for signs of still current occupancy. Swinging the bed farther I was no longer looking for pearls. I was looking at a man.

He was small, middle-aged, iron-gray at the temples, with a very dark skin, dressed in a fawn-colored suit with a wine-colored tie. His neat little brown hands hung limply by his sides. His small feet, in pointed polished shoes, pointed almost at the floor.

He was hanging by a belt around his neck from the metal top of the bed. His tongue stuck out farther than I thought it possible for a tongue to stick out.

He swung a little and I didn't like that, so I pulled the bed shut and he nestled quietly between the two clamped pillows. I didn't touch him yet. I didn't have to touch him to know that he would be cold as ice.

I went around him into the dressing room and used my handkerchief on drawer knobs. The place was stripped clean except for the light litter of a man living alone.

I came out of there and began on the man. No wallet. Waldo would have taken that and ditched it. A flat box of cigarettes, half full, stamped in gold: "Louis Tapia y Cia, Calle de Paysandú, 19, Montevideo." Matches from the Spezia Club. An under-arm holster of dark-grained leather and in it a 9-millimeter Mauser.

The Mauser made him a professional, so I didn't feel so badly. But not a very good professional, or bare hands would not have finished him, with the Mauser – a gun you can blast through a wall with – undrawn in his shoulder holster.

I made a little sense of it, not much. Four of the brown cigarettes had been smoked, so there had been either waiting or discussion. Somewhere along the line Waldo had got the little man by the throat and held him in just the right way to make him pass out in a matter of seconds. The Mauser had been less useful to him than a toothpick. Then Waldo had hung him up by the strap, probably dead already. That would account for haste, cleaning out the apartment, for Waldo's anxiety about the girl. It would account for the car left unlocked outside the cocktail bar.

That is, it would account for these things if Waldo killed him, if this was really Waldo's apartment – if I wasn't just being kidded.

I examined some more pockets. In the left trouser one I found a gold penknife, some silver. In the left hip pocket a handkerchief, folded, scented. On the right hip another, unfolded but clean. In the right leg pocket four or five tissue handkerchiefs. A clean little guy. He didn't like to blow his nose on his handkerchief. Under these there was a small new keytainer holding four new keys – car keys. Stamped in gold on the keytainer was: Compliments of R. K. Vogelsang, Inc. "The Packard House."

I put everything as I had found it, swung the bed back, used my handkerchief on knobs and other projections, and flat surfaces, killed the light and poked my nose out the door. The hall was empty. I went down to the street and around the corner to Kingsley Drive. The Cadillac hadn't moved.

I opened the car door and leaned on it. She didn't seem to have moved, either. It was hard to see any expression on her face. Hard to see anything but her eyes and chin, but not hard to smell the sandalwood.

"That perfume," I said, "would drive a deacon nuts . . . no pearls."

"Well, thanks for trying," she said in a low, soft vibrant voice. "I guess I can stand it. Shall I . . . Do we . . . Or . . .?"

"You go on home now," I said. "And whatever happens you never saw me before. Whatever happens. Just as you may never see me again."

"I'd hate that."

"Good luck, Lola." I shut the car door and stepped back.

The lights blazed on, the motor turned over. Against the wind at the corner the big coupe made a slow contemptuous turn and was gone. I stood there by the vacant space at the curb where it had been.

It was quite dark there now. Windows had become blanks in the apartment where the radio sounded. I stood looking at the back of a Packard cabriolet which seemed to be brand-new. I had seen it before – before I went upstairs, in the same place, in front of Lola's car. Parked, dark, silent, with a blue sticker pasted to the right-hand corner of the shiny windshield.

And in my mind I was looking at something else, a set of brand-new car keys in a keytainer stamped: "The Packard House," upstairs, in a dead man's pocket.

I went up to the front of the cabriolet and put a small pocket flash on the blue slip. It was the same dealer all right. Written in ink below his name and slogan was a name and address – Eugénie Kolchenko, 5315 Arvieda Street, West Los Angeles.

It was crazy. I went back up to Apartment 31, jimmied the door as I had done before, stepped in behind the wall bed and took the keytainer from the trousers pocket of the neat brown dangling corpse. I was back down on the street beside the cabriolet in five minutes. The keys fitted.

5

IT WAS A small house, near a canyon rim out beyond Sawtelle, with a circle of writhing eucalyptus trees in front of it. Beyond that, on the other side of the street, one of those parties was going on where they come out and smash bottles on the sidewalk with a whoop like Yale making a touchdown against Princeton.

There was a wire fence at my number and some rose trees, and a flagged walk and a garage that was wide open and had no car in it. There was no car in front of the house either. I rang the bell. There was a long wait, then the door opened rather suddenly.

I wasn't the man she had been expecting. I could see it in her glittering kohl-rimmed eyes. Then I couldn't see anything in them. She just stood and looked at me, a long, lean, hungry brunette, with rouged cheekbones, thick black hair parted in the middle, a mouth made for three-decker sandwiches, coral-and-gold pajamas, sandals – and gilded toenails. Under her ear lobes a couple of miniature temple bells gonged lightly in the breeze. She made a slow disdainful motion with a cigarette in a holder as long as a baseball bat.

"We-el, what ees it, little man? You want sometheeng? You are lost from the bee-ootiful party across the street, hein?"

"Ha-ha," I said. "Quite a party, isn't it? No, I just brought your car home. Lost it, didn't you?"

Across the street somebody had delirium tremens in the front yard and a mixed quartet tore what was left of the night into small strips and did what they could to make the strips miserable. While this was going on the exotic brunette didn't move more than one eyelash.

She wasn't beautiful, she wasn't even pretty, but she looked as if things would happen where she was.

"You have said what?" she got out, at last, in a voice as silky as a burnt crust of toast.

"Your car." I pointed over my shoulder and kept my eyes on her. She was the type that uses a knife.

The long cigarette holder dropped very slowly to her side and the cigarette fell out of it. I stamped it out, and that put me in the hall. She backed away from me and I shut the door.

The hall was like the long hall of a railroad flat. Lamps glowed pinkly in iron brackets. There was a bead curtain at the end, a tiger skin on the floor. The place went with her.

"You're Miss Kolchenko?" I asked, not getting any more action.

"Ye-es. I am Mees Kolchenko. What the 'ell you want?"

She was looking at me now as if I had come to wash the windows, but at an inconvenient time.

I got a card out with my left hand, held it out to her. She read it in my hand, moving her head just enough. "A detect-ive?" she breathed.

"Yeah."

She said something in a spitting language. Then in English: "Come in! Thees damn wind dry up my skeen like so much teesue paper."

"We're in," I said. "I just shut the door. Snap out of it, Nazimova. Who was he? The little guy?"

Beyond the bead curtain a man coughed. She jumped as if she had been stuck with an oyster fork. Then she tried to smile. It wasn't very successful.

"A reward," she said softly. "You weel wait 'ere? Ten dollars it is fair to pay, no?"

"No," I said.

I reached a finger towards her slowly and added: "He's dead."

She jumped about three feet and let out a yell.

A chair creaked harshly. Feet pounded beyond the bead curtain, a large hand plunged into view and snatched it aside, and a big hard-looking blond man was with us. He had a purple robe over his pajamas, his right hand held something in his robe pocket. He stood quite still as soon as he was through the curtain, his feet planted solidly, his jaw out, his colorless eyes like gray ice. He looked like a man who would be hard to take out on an off-tackle play.

"What's the matter, honey?" He had a solid, burring voice, with just the right sappy tone to belong to a guy who would go for a woman with gilded toenails.

"I came about Miss Kolchenko's car," I said.

"Well, you could take your hat off," he said. "Just for a light workout."

I took it off and apologized.

"Okay," he said, and kept his right hand shoved down hard in the purple pocket. "So you came about Miss Kolchenko's car. Take it from there."

I pushed past the woman and went closer to him. She shrank back against the wall and flattened her palms against it. Camille in a high-school play. The long holder lay empty at her toes.

When I was six feet from the big man he said easily: "I can hear you from there. Just take it easy. I've got a gun in this pocket and I've had to learn to use one. Now about the car?"

"The man who borrowed it couldn't bring it," I said, and pushed the card I was still holding towards his face. He barely glanced at it. He looked back at me.

"So what?" he said.

"Are you always this tough?" I asked. "Or only when you have your pajamas on?"

"So why couldn't he bring it himself?" he asked. "And skip the mushy talk."

The dark woman made a stuffed sound at my elbow.

"It's all right, honeybunch," the man said. "I'll handle this. Go on."

She slid past both of us and flicked through the bead curtain.

I waited a little while. The big man didn't move a muscle. He didn't look any more bothered than a toad in the sun.

"He couldn't bring it because somebody bumped him off," I said. "Let's see you handle that."

"Yeah?" he said. "Did you bring him with you to prove it?"

"No," I said. "But if you put your tie and crush hat on, I'll take you down and show you."

"Who the hell did you say you were, now?"

"I didn't say. I thought maybe you could read." I held the card at him some more.

"Oh, that's right," he said. "Philip Marlowe, Private Investigator. Well, well. So I should go with you to look at who, why?"

"Maybe he stole the car," I said.

The big man nodded. "That's a thought. Maybe he did. Who?"

"The little brown guy who had the keys to it in his pocket, and had it parked around the corner from the Berglund Apartments."

He thought that over, without any apparent embarrassment. "You've got something there," he said. "Not much. But a little. I guess this must be the night of the Police Smoker. So you're doing all their work for them."

"Huh?"

"The card says private detective to me," he said. "Have you got some cops outside that were too shy to come in?"

"No, I'm alone."

He grinned. The grin showed white ridges in his tanned skin. "So you find somebody dead and take some keys and find a car and come riding out here – all alone. No cops. Am I right?"

"Correct."

He sighed. "Let's go inside," he said. He yanked the bead curtain aside and made an opening for me to go through. "It might be you have an idea I ought to hear."

I went past him and he turned, keeping his heavy pocket towards me. I hadn't noticed until I got quite close that there were beads of sweat on his face. It might have been the hot wind but I didn't think so.

We were in the living-room of the house.

We sat down and looked at each other across a dark floor, on which a few Navajo rugs and a few dark Turkish rugs made a decorating combination with some well-used over-stuffed furniture. There was a fireplace, a small baby grand, a Chinese screen, a tall Chinese lantern on a teakwood pedestal, and gold net curtains against lattice windows. The windows to the south were open. A fruit tree with a whitewashed trunk whipped about outside the screen, adding its bit to the noise from across the street.

The big man eased back into a brocaded chair and put his slippered feet on a footstool. He kept his right hand where it had been since I met him – on his gun.

The brunette hung around in the shadows and a bottle gurgled and her temple bells gonged in her ears.

"It's all right, honeybunch," the man said. "It's all under control. Somebody bumped somebody off and this lad thinks we're interested. Just sit down and relax."

The girl tilted her head and poured half a tumbler of whiskey down her throat. She sighed, said "Goddam," in a casual voice, and curled up on a davenport. It took all of the davenport. She had plenty of legs. Her gilded toenails winked at me from the shadowy corner where she kept herself quiet from then on.

I got a cigarette out without being shot at, lit it and went into my story. It wasn't all true, but some of it was. I told them about the Berglund Apartments and that I had lived there and that Waldo was living there in Apartment 31 on the floor below mine and that I had been keeping an eye on him for business reasons.

"Waldo what?" the blond man put in. "And what business reasons?"

"Mister," I said, "have you no secrets?" He reddened slightly.

I told him about the cocktail lounge across the street from the Berglund and what had happened there. I didn't tell him about the printed bolero jacket or the girl who had worn it. I left her out of the story altogether.

"It was an undercover job – from my angle," I said. "If you know what I mean." He reddened again, bit his teeth. I went on: "I got back from the city hall without telling anybody I knew Waldo. In due time, when I decided they couldn't find out where he lived that night, I took the liberty of examining his apartment."

"Looking for what?" the big man said thickly.

"For some letters. I might mention in passing there was nothing there at all – except a dead man. Strangled and hanging by a belt to the top of the wall bed – well out of sight.

A small man, about forty-five, Mexican or South American, well-dressed in a fawn-colored – "

"That's enough," the big man said. "I'll bite, Marlowe. Was it a blackmail job you were on?"

"Yeah. The funny part was this little brown man had plenty of gun under his arm."

"He wouldn't have five hundred bucks in twenties in his pocket, of course? Or are you saying?"

"He wouldn't. But Waldo had over seven hundred in currency when he was killed in the cocktail bar."

"Looks like I underrated this Waldo," the big man said calmly. "He took my guy and his pay-off money, gun and all. Waldo have a gun?"

"Not on him."

"Get us a drink, honeybunch," the big man said. "Yes, I certainly did sell this Waldo person shorter than a bargain-counter shirt."

The brunette unwound her legs and made two drinks with soda and ice. She took herself another gill without trimmings, wound herself back on the davenport. Her big glittering black eyes watched me solemnly.

"Well, here's how," the big man said, lifting his glass in salute. "I haven't murdered anybody, but I've got a divorce suit on my hands from now on. You haven't murdered anybody, the way you tell it, but you laid an egg down at police Headquarters. What the hell! Life's a lot of trouble, anyway you look at it. I've still got honeybunch here. She's a white Russian I met in Shanghai. She's safe as a vault and she looks as if she could cut your throat for a nickel. That's what I like about her. You get the glamor without the risk."

"You talk damn foolish," the girl spat at him.

"You look okay to me," the big man went on, ignoring her. "That is, for a keyhole peeper. Is there an out?"

"Yeah. But it will cost a little money."

"I expected that. How much?"

"Say another five hundred."

"Goddam, thees hot wind make me dry like the ashes of love," the Russian girl said bitterly.

"Five hundred might do," the blond man said. "What do I get for it?"

"If I swing it – you get left out of the story. If I don't – you don't pay."

He thought it over. His face looked lined and tired now. The small beads of sweat twinkled in his short blond hair.

"This murder will make you talk," he grumbled. "The second one, I mean. And I don't have what I was going to buy. And if it's a hush, I'd rather buy it direct."

"Who was the little brown man?" I asked.

"Name's Leon Valesanos, a Uruguayan. Another of my importations. I'm in a business that takes me a lot of places. He was working in the Spezzia Club in Chiseltown – you know, the strip of Sunset next to Beverly Hills. Working on roulette, I think. I gave him the five hundred to go down to this – this Waldo – and buy back some bills for stuff Miss Kolchenko had charged to my account and delivered here. That wasn't bright, was it? I had them in my briefcase and this Waldo got a chance to steal them. What's your hunch about what happened?"

I sipped my drink and looked at him down my nose. "Your Uruguayan pal probably talked curt and Waldo didn't listen good. Then the little guy thought maybe that Mauser might help his argument – and Waldo was too quick for him. I wouldn't say Waldo was a killer – not by intention. A blackmailer seldom is. Maybe he lost his temper and maybe he just held on to the little guy's neck too long. Then he had to take it on the lam. But he had another date, with more money coming up. And he worked the neighborhood looking for the party. And accidentally he ran into a pal who was hostile enough and drunk enough to blow him down."

"There's a hell of a lot of coincidence in all this business," the big man said.

"It's the hot wind," I grinned. "Everybody's screwy tonight."

"For the five hundred you guarantee nothing? If I don't get my cover-up, you don't get your dough. Is that it?"

"That's it," I said, smiling at him.

"Screwy is right," he said, and drained his highball. "I'm taking you up on it."

"There are just two things," I said softly, leaning forward in my chair. "Waldo had a getaway car parked outside the cocktail bar where he was killed, unlocked with the motor running. The killer took it. There's always the chance of a kickback from that direction. You see, all Waldo's stuff must have been in that car."

"Including my bills, and your letters."

"Yeah. But the police are reasonable about things like that – unless you're good for a lot of publicity. If you're not, I think I can eat some stale dog downtown and get by. If you are – that's the second thing. What did you say your name was?"

The answer was a long time coming. When it came I didn't get as much kick out of it as I thought I would. All at once it was too logical.

"Frank C. Barsaly," he said.

After a while the Russian girl called me a taxi. When I left, the party across the street was doing all that a party could do. I noticed the walls of the house were still standing. That seemed a pity.

6

WHEN I UNLOCKED the glass entrance door of the Berglund I smelled policeman. I looked at my wrist watch. It was nearly 3 A.M. In the dark corner of the lobby a man dozed in a chair with a newspaper over his face. Large feet stretched out before him. A corner of the paper lifted an inch, dropped again. The man made no other movement.

I went on along the hall to the elevator and rode up to my floor. I soft-footed along the hallway, unlocked my door, pushed it wide and reached in for the light switch.

A chain switch tinkled and light glared from a standing lamp by the easy chair, beyond the card table on which my chessmen were still scattered.

Copernik sat there with a stiff unpleasant grin on his face. The short dark man, Ybarra, sat across the room from him, on my left, silent, half smiling as usual.

Copernik showed more of his big yellow horse teeth and said: "Hi. Long time no see. Been out with the girls?"

I shut the door and took my hat off and wiped the back of my neck slowly, over and over again. Copernik went on grinning. Ybarra looked at nothing with his soft dark eyes.

"Take a seat, pal," Copernik drawled. "Make yourself at home. We got pow-wow to make. Boy, do I hate this night sleuthing. Did you know you were low on hooch?"

"I could have guessed it," I said. I leaned against the wall.

Copernik kept on grinning. "I always did hate private dicks," he said, "but I never had a chance to twist one like I got tonight."

He reached down lazily beside his chair and picked up a printed bolero jacket, tossed it on the card table. He reached down again and put a wide-brimmed hat beside it.

"I bet you look cuter than all hell with these on," he said.

I took hold of a straight chair, twisted it around and straddled it, leaned my folded arms on the chair and looked at Copernik.

He got up very slowly — with an elaborate slowness, walked across the room and stood in front of me smoothing his coat down. Then he lifted his open right hand and hit me across the face with it — hard. It stung but I didn't move.

Ybarra looked at the wall, looked at the floor, looked at nothing.

"Shame on you, pal," Copernik said lazily. "The way you was taking care of this nice exclusive merchandise. Wadded down behind your old shirts. You punk peepers always did make me sick."

He stood there over me for a moment. I didn't move or speak. I looked into his glazed drinker's eyes. He doubled a fist at his side, then shrugged and turned and went back to the chair.

"Okay," he said. "The rest will keep. Where did you get these things?"

"They belong to a lady."

"Do tell. They belong to a lady. Ain't you the lighthearted bastard! I'll tell you what lady they belong to. They belong to the lady a guy named Waldo asked about in a bar across the street – about two minutes before he got shot kind of dead. Or would that have slipped your mind?"

I didn't say anything.

"You was curious about her yourself," Copernik sneered on. "But you were smart, pal. You fooled me."

"That wouldn't make me smart," I said.

His face twisted suddenly and he started to get up. Ybarra laughed, suddenly and softly, almost under his breath. Copernik's eyes swung on him, hung there. Then he faced me again, bland-eyed.

"The guinea likes you," he said. "He thinks you're good."

The smile left Ybarra's face, but no expression took its place. No expression at all.

Copernik said: "You knew who the dame was all the time. You knew who Waldo was and where he lived. Right across the hall a floor below you. You knew this Waldo person had bumped a guy off and started to lam, only this broad came into his plans somewhere and he was anxious to meet up with her before he went away. Only he never got the chance.

A heist guy from back East named Al Tessilore took care of
that by taking care of Waldo. So you met the gal and hid her
clothes and sent her on her way and kept your trap glued.
That's the way guys like you make your beans. Am I right?"

"Yeah," I said. "Except that I only knew these things very
recently. Who was Waldo?"

Copernik bared his teeth at me. Red spots burned high on
his sallow cheeks. Ybarra, looking down at the floor, said very
softly: "Waldo Ratigan. We got him from Washington by
Teletype. He was a two-bit porch climber with a few small
terms on him. He drove a car in a bank stick-up job in
Detroit. He turned the gang in later and got a nolle prosse.
One of the gang was this Al Tessilore. He hasn't talked a
word, but we think the meeting across the street was purely
accidental."

Ybarra spoke in the soft quiet modulated voice of a man
for whom sounds have a meaning. I said: "Thanks, Ybarra. Can
I smoke – or would Copernik kick it out of my mouth?"

Ybarra smiled suddenly. "You may smoke, sure," he said.

"The guinea likes you all right," Copernik jeered. "You
never know what a guinea will like, do you?"

I lit a cigarette. Ybarra looked at Copernik and said very
softly: "The word guinea – you overwork it. I don't like it so
well applied to me."

"The hell with what you like, guinea."

Ybarra smiled a little more. "You are making a mistake," he
said. He took a pocket nail file out and began to use it,
looking down.

Copernik blared: "I smelled something rotten on you from
the start, Marlowe. So when we make these two mugs, Ybarra
and me think we'll drift over and dabble a few more words
with you. I bring one of Waldo's morgue photos – nice
work, the light just right in his eyes, his tie all straight and a
white handkerchief showing just right in his pocket. Nice
work. So on the way up, just as a matter of routine, we rout

out the manager here and let him lamp it. And he knows the guy. He's here as A. B. Hummel, Apartment Thirty-one. So we go in there and find a stiff. Then we go round and round with that. Nobody knows him yet, but he's got some swell finger bruises under that strap and I hear they fit Waldo's fingers very nicely."

"That's something," I said. "I thought maybe I murdered him."

Copernik stared at me a long time. His face had stopped grinning and was just a hard brutal face now. "Yeah. We got something else even," he said. "We got Waldo's getaway car – and what Waldo had in it to take with him."

I blew cigarette smoke jerkily. The wind pounded the shut windows. The air in the room was foul.

"Oh, we're bright boys," Copernik sneered. "We never figured you with that much guts. Take a look at this."

He plunged his bony hand into his coat pocket and drew something up slowly over the edge of the card table, drew it along the green top and left it there stretched out, gleaming. A string of white pearls with a clasp like a two-bladed propeller. They shimmered softly in the thick smoky air.

Lola Barsaly's pearls. The pearls the flier had given her. The guy who was dead, the guy she still loved.

I stared at them, but I didn't move. After a long moment Copernik said almost gravely: "Nice, ain't they? Would you feel like telling us a story about now, Mis-ter Marlowe?"

I stood up and pushed the chair from under me, walked slowly across the room and stood looking down at the pearls. The largest was perhaps a third of an inch across. They were pure white, iridescent, with a mellow softness. I lifted them slowly off the card table from beside her clothes. They felt heavy, smooth, fine.

"Nice," I said. "A lot of the trouble was about these. Yeah, I'll talk now. They must be worth a lot of money."

Ybarra laughed behind me. It was a very gentle laugh. "About a hundred dollars," he said. "They're good phonies – but they're phony."

I lifted the pearls again. Copernik's glassy eyes gloated at me. "How do you tell?" I asked.

"I know pearls," Ybarra said. "These are good stuff, the kind women very often have made on purpose, as a kind of insurance. But they are slick like glass. Real pearls are gritty between the edges of the teeth. Try."

I put two or three of them between my teeth and moved my teeth back and forth, then sideways. Not quite biting them. The beads were hard and slick.

"Yes. They are very good," Ybarra said. "Several even have little waves and flat spots, as real pearls might have."

"Would they cost fifteen grand – if they were real?" I asked.

"Sí, Probably. That's hard to say. It depends on a lot of things."

"This Waldo wasn't so bad," I said.

Copernik stood up quickly, but I didn't see him swing. I was still looking down at the pearls. His fist caught me on the side of the face, against the molars. I tasted blood at once. I staggered back and made it look like a worse blow than it was.

"Sit down and talk, you bastard!" Copernik almost whispered.

I sat down and used a handkerchief to pat my cheek. I licked at the cut inside my mouth. Then I got up again and went over and picked up the cigarette he had knocked out of my mouth. I crushed it out in a tray and sat down again.

Ybarra filed at his nails and held one up against the lamp. There were beads of sweat on Copernik's eyebrows, at the inner ends.

"You found the beads in Waldo's car," I said, looking at Ybarra. "Find any papers?"

He shook his head without looking up.

"I'd believe you," I said. "Here it is. I never saw Waldo until he stepped into the cocktail bar tonight and asked about the girl. I knew nothing I didn't tell. When I got home and stepped out of the elevator this girl, in the printed bolero jacket and the wide hat and the blue silk crêpe dress – all as he had described them – was waiting for the elevator, here on my floor. And she looked like a nice girl."

Copernik laughed jeeringly. It didn't make any difference to me. I had him cold. All he had to do was know that. He was going to know it now, very soon.

"I knew what she was up against as a police witness," I said. "And I suspected there was something else to it. But I didn't suspect for a minute that there was anything wrong with her. She was just a nice girl in a jam – and she didn't even know she was in a jam. I got her in here. She pulled a gun on me. But she didn't mean to use it."

Copernik sat up very suddenly and he began to lick his lips. His face had a stony look now. A look like wet gray stone. He didn't make a sound.

"Waldo had been her chauffeur," I went on. "His name was then Joseph Coates. Her name is Mrs. Frank C. Barsaly. Her husband is a big hydroelectric engineer. Some guy gave her the pearls once and she told her husband they were just store pearls. Waldo got wise somehow there was a romance behind them and when Barsaly came home from South America and fired him, because he was too good-looking, he lifted the pearls."

Ybarra lifted his head suddenly and his teeth flashed. "You mean he didn't know they were phony?"

"I thought he fenced the real ones and had imitations fixed up," I said.

Ybarra nodded. "It's possible."

"He lifted something else," I said. "Some stuff from Barsaly's briefcase that showed he was keeping a woman – out in Brentwood. He was blackmailing wife and husband both, without either knowing about the other. Get it so far?"

"I get it," Copernik said harshly, between his tight lips. His face was still wet gray stone. "Get the hell on with it."

"Waldo wasn't afraid of them," I said. "He didn't conceal where he lived. That was foolish, but it saved a lot of finagling, if he was willing to risk it. The girl came down here tonight with five grand to buy back her pearls. She didn't find Waldo. She came here to look for him and walked up a floor before she went back down. A woman's idea of being cagey. So I met her. So I brought her in here. So she was in that dressing room when Al Tessilore visited me to rub out a witness." I pointed to the dressing-room door. "So she came out with her little gun and stuck it in his back and saved my life," I said.

Copernik didn't move. There was something horrible in his face now. Ybarra slipped his nail file into a small leather case and slowly tucked it into his pocket.

"Is that all?" he said gently.

I nodded. "Except that she told me where Waldo's apartment was and I went in there and looked for the pearls. I found the dead man. In his pocket I found new car keys in a case from a Packard agency. And down on the street I found the Packard and took it to where it came from. Barsaly's kept woman. Barsaly had sent a friend from the Spezzia Club down to buy something and he had tried to buy it with his gun instead of the money Barsaly gave him. And Waldo beat him to the punch."

"Is that all?" Ybarra said softly.

"That's all," I said licking the torn place on the inside of my cheek.

Ybarra said slowly: "What do you want?"

Copernik's face convulsed and he slapped his long hard thigh. "This guy's good," he jeered. "He falls for a stray broad and breaks every law in the book and you ask him what does he want? I'll give him what he wants, guinea!"

Ybarra turned his head slowly and looked at him. "I don't think you will," he said. "I think you'll give him a clean bill of health and anything else he wants. He's giving you a lesson in police work."

Copernik didn't move or make a sound for a long minute. None of us moved. Then Copernik leaned forward and his coat fell open. The butt of his service gun looked out of his underarm holster.

"So what do you want?" he asked me.

"What's on the card table there. The jacket and hat and the phony pearls. And some names kept away from the papers. Is that too much?"

"Yeah—it's too much," Copernik said almost gently. He swayed sideways and his gun jumped neatly into his hand. He rested his forearm on his thigh and pointed the gun at my stomach.

"I like better that you get a slug in the guts resisting arrest," he said. "I like that better, because of a report I made out on Al Tessilore's arrest and how I made the pinch. Because of some photos of me that are in the morning sheets going out about now. I like it better that you don't live long enough to laugh about that baby."

My mouth felt suddenly hot and dry. Far off I heard the wind booming. It seemed like the sound of guns.

Ybarra moved his feet on the floor and said coldly: "You've got a couple of cases all solved, policeman. All you do for it is leave some junk here and keep some names from the papers. Which means from the D.A. If he gets them anyway, too bad for you."

Copernik said: "I like the other way." The blue gun in his hand was like a rock. "And God help you, if you don't back me up on it."

Ybarra said: "If the woman is brought out into the open, you'll be a liar on a police report and a chiseler on your own partner. In a week they won't even speak your name at Headquarters. The taste of it would make them sick."

The hammer clicked back on Copernik's gun and I watched his big finger slide in farther around the trigger.

Ybarra stood up. The gun jumped at him. He said: "We'll see how yellow a guinea is. I'm telling you to put that gun up, Sam."

He started to move. He moved four even steps. Copernik was a man without a breath of movement, a stone man.

Ybarra took one more step and quite suddenly the gun began to shake.

Ybarra spoke evenly: "Put it up, Sam. If you keep your head everything lies the way it is. If you don't – you're gone."

He took one more step. Copernik's mouth opened wide and made a gasping sound and then he sagged in the chair as if he had been hit on the head. His eyelids dropped.

Ybarra jerked the gun out of his hand with a movement so quick it was no movement at all. He stepped back quickly, held the gun low at his side.

"It's the hot wind, Sam. Let's forget it," he said in the same even, almost dainty voice.

Copernik's shoulders sagged lower and he put his face in his hands. "Okay," he said between his fingers.

Ybarra went softly across the room and opened the door. He looked at me with lazy, half-closed eyes. "I'd do a lot for a woman who saved my life, too," he said. "I'm eating this dish, but as a cop you can't expect me to like it."

I said: "The little man in the bed is called Leon Valesanos. He was a croupier at the Spezzia Club."

"Thanks," Ybarra said. "Let's go, Sam."

Copernik got up heavily and walked across the room and out of the open door and out of my sight. Ybarra stepped through the door after him and started to close it.

I said: "Wait a minute."

He turned his head slowly, his left hand on the door, the blue gun hanging down close to his right side.

"I'm not in this for money," I said. "The Barsalys live at Two-twelve Fremont Place. You can take the pearls to her.

If Barsaly's name stays out of the paper, I get five C's. It goes to the Police Fund. I'm not so damn smart as you think. It just happened that way – and you had a heel for a partner."

Ybarra looked across the room at the pearls on the card table. His eyes glistened. "You take them," he said. "The five hundred's okay, I think the fund has it coming."

He shut the door quietly and in a moment I heard the elevator doors clang.

7

I OPENED A window and stuck my head out into the wind and watched the squad car tool off down the block. The wind blew in hard and I let it blow. A picture fell off the wall and two chessmen rolled off the card table. The material of Lola Barsaly's bolero jacket lifted and shook.

I went out to the kitchenette and drank some Scotch and went back into the living-room and called her – late as it was.

She answered the phone herself, very quickly, with no sleep in her voice.

"Marlowe," I said. "Okay your end?"

"Yes . . . yes," she said. "I'm alone."

"I found something," I said. "Or rather the police did. But your dark boy gypped you. I have a string of pearls. They're not real. He sold the real ones, I guess, and made you up a string of ringers, with your clasp."

She was silent for a long time. Then, a little faintly: "The police found them?"

"In Waldo's car. But they're not telling. We have a deal. Look at the papers in the morning and you'll be able to figure out why."

"There doesn't seem to be anything more to say," she said. "Can I have the clasp?"

736

"Yes. Can you meet me tomorrow at four in the Club Esquire bar?"

"You're really rather sweet," she said in a dragged out voice. "I can. Frank is still at his meeting."

"Those meetings – they take it out of a guy," I said. We said goodbye.

I called a West Los Angeles number. He was still there, with the Russian girl.

"You can send me a check for five hundred in the morning," I told him. "Made out to the Police Relief Fund, if you want to. Because that's where it's going."

Copernik made the third page of the morning papers with two photos and a nice half-column. The little brown man in Apartment 31 didn't make the paper at all. The Apartment House Association has a good lobby too.

I went out after breakfast and the wind was all gone. It was soft, cool, a little foggy. The sky was close and comfortable and gray. I rode down to the boulevard and picked out the best jewelry store on it and laid a string of pearls on a black velvet mat under a daylight-blue lamp. A man in a wing collar and striped trousers looked down at them languidly.

"How good?" I asked.

"I'm sorry, sir. We don't make appraisals. I can give you the name of an appraiser."

"Don't kid me," I said. "They're Dutch."

He focused the light a little and leaned down and toyed with a few inches of the string.

"I want a string just like them, fitted to that clasp, and in a hurry," I added.

"How, like them?" He didn't look up. "And they're not Dutch. They're Bohemian."

"Okay, can you duplicate them?"

He shook his head and pushed the velvet pad away as if it soiled him. "In three months, perhaps. We don't blow glass like that in this country. If you wanted them matched – three

737

months at least. And this house would not do that sort of thing at all."

"It must be swell to be that snooty," I said. I put a card under his black sleeve. "Give me a name that will – and not in three months – and maybe not exactly like them."

He shrugged, went away with the card, came back in five minutes and handed it back to me. There was something written on the back.

The old Levantine had a shop on Melrose, a junk shop with everything in the window from a folding baby carriage to a French horn, from a mother-of-pearl lorgnette in a faded plush case to one of those .44 Special Single Action six-shooters they still make for Western peace officers whose grandfathers were tough.

The old Levantine wore a skull cap and two pairs of glasses and a full beard. He studied my pearls, shook his head sadly, and said: "For twenty dollars, almost so good. Not so good, you understand. Not so good glass."

"How alike will they look?"

He spread his firm strong hands. "I am telling you the truth," he said. "They would not fool a baby."

"Make them up," I said. "With this clasp. And I want the others back, too, of course."

"Yah. Two o'clock," he said.

Leon Valesanos, the little brown man from Uruguay, made the afternoon papers. He had been found hanging in an unnamed apartment. The police were investigating.

At four o'clock I walked into the long cool bar of the Club Esquire and prowled along the row of booths until I found one where a woman sat alone. She wore a hat like a shallow soup plate with a very wide edge, a brown tailor-made suit with a severe mannish shirt and tie.

I sat down beside her and slipped a parcel along the seat. "You don't open that," I said. "In fact you can slip it into the incinerator as is, if you want to."

She looked at me with dark tired eyes. Her fingers twisted a thin glass that smelled of peppermint. "Thanks." Her face was very pale.

I ordered a highball and the waiter went away. "Read the papers?"

"Yes."

"You understand now about this fellow Copernik who stole your act? That's why they won't change the story or bring you into it."

"It doesn't matter now," she said. "Thank you, all the same. Please – please show them to me."

I pulled the string of pearls out of the loosely wrapped tissue paper in my pocket and slid them across to her. The silver propeller clasp winked in the light of the wall bracket. The little diamond winked. The pearls were as dull as white soap. They didn't even match in size.

"You were right," she said tonelessly. "They are not my pearls."

The waiter came with my drink and she put her bag on them deftly. When he was gone she fingered them slowly once more, dropped them into the bag and gave me a dry mirthless smile.

I stood there a moment with a hand hard on the table.

"As you said – I'll keep the clasp."

I said slowly: "You don't know anything about me. You saved my life last night and we had a moment, but it was just a moment. You still don't know anything about me. There's a detective downtown named Ybarra, a Mexican of the nice sort, who was on the job when the pearls were found in Waldo's suitcase. That is in case you would like to make sure – "

She said: "Don't be silly. It's all finished. It was a memory. I'm too young to nurse memories. It may be for the best. I loved Stan Phillips – but he's gone – long gone."

I stared at her, didn't say anything.

She added quietly: "This morning my husband told me something I hadn't known. We are to separate. So I have very little to laugh about today."

"I'm sorry," I said lamely. "There's nothing to say. I may see you sometime. Maybe not. I don't move much in your circle. Good luck."

I stood up. We looked at each other for a moment. "You haven't touched your drink," she said.

"You drink it. That peppermint stuff will just make you sick."

I stood there a moment with a hand on the table.

"If anybody ever bothers you," I said, "let me know."

I went out of the bar without looking back at her, got into my car and drove west on Sunset and down all the way to the Coast Highway. Everywhere along the way gardens were full of withered and blackened leaves and flowers which the hot wind had burned.

But the ocean looked cool and languid and just the same as ever. I drove on almost to Malibu and then parked and went and sat on a big rock that was inside somebody's wire fence. It was about half-tide and coming in. The air smelled of kelp. I watched the water for a while and then I pulled a string of Bohemian glass imitation pearls out of my pocket and cut the knot at one end and slipped the pearls off one by one.

When I had them all loose in my left hand I held them like that for a while and thought. There wasn't really anything to think about. I was sure.

"To the memory of Mr. Stan Phillips," I said aloud. "Just another four-flusher."

I flipped her pearls out into the water one by one at the floating seagulls.

They made little splashes and the seagulls rose off the water and swooped at the splashes.

THE KING IN YELLOW

1

GEORGE MILLAR, NIGHT auditor at the Carlton Hotel, was a dapper wiry little man, with a soft deep voice like a torch singer's. He kept it low, but his eyes were sharp and angry, as he said into the PBX mouthpiece: "I'm very sorry. It won't happen again. I'll send up at once."

He tore off the headpiece, dropped it on the keys of the switchboard and marched swiftly from behind the pebbled screen and out into the entrance lobby. It was past one and the Carlton was two thirds residential. In the main lobby, down three shallow steps, lamps were dimmed and the night porter had finished tidying up. The place was deserted – a wide space of dim furniture, rich carpet. Faintly in the distance a radio sounded. Millar went down the steps and walked quickly towards the sound, turned through an archway and looked at a man stretched out on a pale green davenport and what looked like all the loose cushions in the hotel. He lay on his side dreamy-eyed and listened to the radio two yards away from him.

Millar barked: "Hey, you! Are you the house dick here or the house cat?"

Steve Grayce turned his head slowly and looked at Millar. He was a long black-haired man, about twenty-eight, with deep-set silent eyes and a rather gentle mouth. He jerked a thumb at the radio and smiled. "King Leopardi, George. Hear that trumpet tone. Smooth as an angel's wing, boy."

"Swell! Go on back upstairs and get him out of the corridor!"

Steve Grayce looked shocked. "What – again? I thought I had those birds put to bed long ago." He swung his feet to the floor and stood up. He was at least a foot taller than Millar.

"Well, Eight-sixteen says no. Eight-sixteen says he's out in the hall with two of his stooges. He's dressed in yellow satin shorts and a trombone and he and his pals are putting on a jam session. And one of those hustlers Quillan registered in Eight-eleven is out there truckin' for them. Now get on to it, Steve – and this time make it stick."

Steve Grayce smiled wryly. He said: "Leopardi doesn't belong here anyway. Can I use chloroform or just my blackjack?"

He stepped long legs over the pale-green carpet, through the arch and across the main lobby to the single elevator that was open and lighted. He slid the doors shut and ran it up to Eight, stopped it roughly and stepped out into the corridor.

The noise hit him like a sudden wind. The walls echoed with it. Half a dozen doors were open and angry guests in night robes stood in them peering.

"It's okay folks," Steve Grayce said rapidly. "This is absolutely the last act. Just relax."

He rounded a corner and the hot music almost took him off his feet. Three men were lined up against the wall, near an open door from which light streamed. The middle one, the one with the trombone, was six feet tall, powerful and graceful, with a hairline mustache. His face was flushed and his eyes had an alcoholic glitter. He wore yellow satin shorts with large initials embroidered in black on the left leg – nothing more. His torso was tanned and naked.

The two with him were in pajamas, the usual halfway-good-looking band boys, both drunk, but not staggering drunk. One jittered madly on a clarinet and the other on a tenor saxophone.

Back and forth in front of them, strutting, trucking, preening herself like a magpie, arching her arms and her eyebrows, bending her fingers back until the carmine nails almost touched her arms, a metallic blonde swayed and went to town on the music. Her voice was a throaty screech, without melody, as false as her eyebrows and as sharp as her nails. She wore high-heeled slippers and black pajamas with a long purple sash.

Steve Grayce stopped dead and made a sharp downward motion with his hand. "Wrap it up!" he snapped. "Can it. Put it on ice. Take it away and bury it. The show's out. Scram, now – scram!"

King Leopardi took the trombone from his lips and bellowed: "Fanfare to a house dick!"

The three drunks blew a stuttering note that shook the walls. The girl laughed foolishly and kicked out. Her slipper caught Steve Grayce in the chest. He picked it out of the air, jumped towards the girl and took hold of her wrist.

"Tough, eh?" he grinned. "I'll take you first."

"Get him!" Leopardi yelled. "Sock him low! Dance the gum-heel on his neck!"

Steve swept the girl off her feet, tucked her under his arm and ran. He carried her as easily as a parcel. She tried to kick his legs. He laughed and shot a glance through a lighted doorway. A man's brown brogues lay under a bureau. He went on past that to a second lighted doorway, slammed through and kicked the door shut, turned far enough to twist the tabbed key in the lock. Almost at once a fist hit the door. He paid no attention to it.

He pushed the girl along the short passage past the bathroom, and let her go. She reeled away from him and put her back to the bureau, panting, her eyes furious. A lock of damp gold-dipped hair swung down over one eye. She shook her head violently and bared her teeth.

"How would you like to get vagged, sister?"

"Go to hell!" she spit out. "The King's a friend of mine, see? You better keep your paws off me, copper."

"You run the circuit with the boys?"

745

She spit at him again.

"How'd you know they'd be here?"

Another girl was sprawled across the bed, her head to the wall, tousled black hair over a white face. There was a tear in the leg of her pajamas. She lay limp and groaned.

Steve said harshly: "Oh, oh, the torn-pajama act. It flops here, sister, it flops hard. Now listen, you kids. You can go to bed and stay till morning or you can take the bounce. Make up your minds."

The black-haired girl groaned. The blonde said: "You get out of my room, you damned gum-heel!"

She reached behind her and threw a hand mirror. Steve ducked. The mirror slammed against the wall and fell without breaking. The black-haired girl rolled over on the bed and said wearily: "Oh lay off. I'm sick."

She lay with her eyes closed, the lids fluttering.

The blonde swiveled her hips across the room to a desk by the window, poured herself a full half-glass of Scotch in a water glass and gurgled it down before Steve could get to her. She choked violently, dropped the glass and went down on her hands and knees.

Steve said grimly: "That's the one that kicks you in the face, sister."

The girl crouched, shaking her head. She gagged once, lifted the carmine nails to paw at her mouth. She tried to get up, and her foot skidded out from under her and she fell down on her side and went fast asleep.

Steve sighed, went over and shut the window and fastened it. He rolled the black-haired girl over and straightened her on the bed and got the bedclothes from under her, tucked a pillow under her head. He picked the blonde bodily off the floor and dumped her on the bed and covered both girls to the chin. He opened the transom, switched off the ceiling light and unlocked the door. He relocked it from the outside, with a master key on a chain.

"Hotel business," he said under his breath. "Phooey."

The corridor was empty now. One lighted door still stood open. Its number was 815, two doors from the room the girls were in. Trombone music came from it softly – but not softly enough for 1:25 A.M.

Steve Grayce turned into the room, crowded the door shut with his shoulder and went along past the bathroom. King Leopardi was alone in the room.

The bandleader was sprawled out in an easy chair, with a tall misted glass at his elbow. He swung the trombone in a tight circle as he played it and the lights danced on the horn.

Steve lit a cigarette, blew a plume of smoke and stared through it at Leopardi with a queer, half-admiring, half-contemptuous expression.

He said softly: "Lights out, yellow-pants. You play a sweet trumpet and your trombone don't hurt either. But we can't use it here. I already told you that once. Lay off. Put that thing away."

Leopardi smiled nastily and blew a stuttering raspberry that sounded like a devil laughing.

"Says you," he sneered. "Leopardi does what he likes, where he likes, when he likes. Nobody's stopped him yet, gum-shoe. Take the air."

Steve bunched his shoulders and went close to the tall dark man. He said patiently: "Put that bazooka down, big-stuff. People are trying to sleep. They're funny that way. You're a great guy on a band shell. Everywhere else you're just a guy with a lot of jack and a personal reputation that stinks from here to Miami and back. I've got a job to do and I'm doing it. Blow that thing again and I'll wrap it around your neck."

Leopardi lowered the trombone and took a long drink from the glass at his elbow. His eyes glinted nastily. He lifted the trombone to his lips again, filled his lungs with air and blew a blast that rocked the walls. Then he stood up very suddenly and smoothly and smashed the instrument down on Steve's head.

747

"I never did like house peepers," he sneered. "They smell like public toilets."

Steve took a short step back and shook his head. He leered, slid forward on one foot and smacked Leopardi open-handed. The blow looked light, but Leopardi reeled all the way across the room and sprawled at the foot of the bed, sitting on the floor, his right arm draped in an open suitcase.

For a moment neither man moved. Then Steve kicked the trombone away from him and squashed his cigarette in a glass tray. His black eyes were empty but his mouth grinned whitely.

"If you want trouble," he said, "I come from where they make it."

Leopard smiled thinly, tautly, and his right hand came up out of the suitcase with a gun in it. His thumb snicked the safety catch. He held the gun steady, pointing.

"Make some with this," he said, and fired.

The bitter roar of the gun seemed a tremendous sound in the closed room. The bureau mirror splintered and glass flew. A sliver cut Steve's cheek like a razor blade. Blood oozed in a small narrow line on his skin.

He left his feet in a dive. His right shoulder crushed against Leopardi's bare chest and his left hand brushed the gun away from him, under the bed. He rolled swiftly to his right and came up on his knees spinning.

He said thickly, harshly: "You picked the wrong gee, brother."

He swarmed on Leopardi and dragged him to his feet by his hair, by main strength. Leopardi yelled and hit him twice on the jaw and Steve grinned and kept his left hand twisted in the bandleader's long sleek black hair. He turned his hand and the head twisted with it and Leopardi's third punch landed on Steve's shoulder. Steve took hold of the wrist behind the punch and twisted that and the bandleader went down on his knees yowling. Steve lifted him by the hair again, let go of his wrist and punched him three times in the stomach, short terrific jabs. He let go of the hair then as he sank the fourth punch almost to his wrist.

Leopardi sagged blindly to his knees and vomited.

Steve stepped away from him and went into the bathroom and got a towel off the rack. He threw it at Leopardi, jerked the open suitcase onto the bed and started throwing things into it.

Leopardi wiped his face and got to his feet still gagging. He swayed, braced himself on the end of the bureau. He was white as a sheet.

Steve Grayce said: "Get dressed, Leopardi. Or go out the way you are. It's all one to me."

Leopardi stumbled into the bathroom, pawing the wall like a blind man.

2

MILLAR STOOD VERY still behind the desk as the elevator opened. His face was white and scared and his cropped black mustache was a smudge across his upper lip. Leopardi came out of the elevator first, a muffler around his neck, a lightweight coat tossed over his arm, a hat tilted on his head. He walked stiffly, bent forward a little, his eyes vacant. His face had a greenish pallor.

Steve Grayce stepped out behind him carrying a suitcase, and Carl, the night porter, came last with two more suitcases and two instrument cases in black leather. Steve marched over to the desk and said harshly: "Mr. Leopardi's bill – if any. He's checking out."

Millar goggled at him across the marble desk. "I – I don't think, Steve – "

"Okay, I thought not."

Leopardi smiled very thinly and unpleasantly and walked out through the brass-edged swing doors the porter held

749

open for him. There were two nighthawk cabs in the line. One of them came to life and pulled up to the canopy and the porter loaded Leopardi's stuff into it. Leopardi got into the cab and leaned forward to put his head to the open window. He said slowly and thickly: "I'm sorry for you, gum-heel. I mean sorry."

Steve Grayce stepped back and looked at him woodenly. The cab moved off down the street, rounded a corner and was gone. Steve turned on his heel, took a quarter from his pocket and tossed it up in the air. He slapped it into the night porter's hand.

"From the King," he said. "Keep it to show your grand-children."

He went back into the hotel, got into the elevator without looking at Millar, shot it up to Eight again and went along the corridor, master-keyed his way into Leopardi's room. He relocked it from the inside, pulled the bed out from the wall and went in behind it. He got a .32 automatic off the carpet, put it in his pocket and prowled the floor with his eyes look-ing for the ejected shell. He found it against the wastebasket, reached to pick it up, and stayed bent over, staring into the basket. His mouth tightened. He picked up the shell and dropped it absently into his pocket, then reached a questing finger into the basket and lifted out a torn scrap of paper on which a piece of newsprint had been pasted. Then he picked up the basket, pushed the bed back against the wall and dumped the contents of the basket out on it.

From the trash of torn papers and matches he separated a number of pieces with newsprint pasted to them. He went over to the desk with them and sat down. A few minutes later he had the torn scraps put together like a jigsaw puzzle and could read the message that had been made by cutting words and letters from magazines and pasting them on a sheet.

TEN GRAND BY TH U RS DAY NI GHT,
LEO PAR DI. DAY AFTER *YOU* OPEN AT
T HE CL U B SHAL OTTE. OR EL SE – CUR -
TAINS. FROM HER BROTHER.

Steve Grayce said: "Huh." He scooped the torn pieces into a hotel envelope, put that in his inside breast pocket and lit a cigarette. "The guy had guts," he said. "I'll grant him that – and his trumpet."

He locked the room, listened a moment in the now silent corridor, then went along to the room occupied by the two girls. He knocked softly and put his ear to the panel. A chair squeaked and feet came towards the door.

"What is it?" The girl's voice was cool, wide awake. It was not the blonde's voice.

"The house man. Can I speak to you a minute?"

"You're speaking to me."

"Without the door between, lady."

"You've got the passkey. Help yourself." The steps went away. He unlocked the door with his master key, stepped quietly inside, and shut it. There was a dim light in a lamp with a shirred shade on the desk. On the bed the blonde snored heavily, one hand clutched in her brilliant metallic hair. The black-haired girl sat in the chair by the window, her legs crossed at right angles like a man's and stared at Steve emptily.

He went close to her and pointed to the long tear in her pajama leg. He said softly: "You're not sick. You were not drunk. That tear was done a long time ago. What's the racket? A shakedown on the King?"

The girl stared at him coolly, puffed at a cigarette and said nothing.

"He checked out," Steve said. "Nothing doing in that direction now, sister." He watched her like a hawk, his black eyes hard and steady on her face.

"Aw, you house dicks make me sick!" the girl said with sudden anger. She surged to her feet and went past him into the bathroom, shut and locked the door.

Steve shrugged and felt the pulse of the girl asleep in the bed — a thumpy, draggy pulse, a liquor pulse.

"Poor damn hustlers," he said under his breath.

He looked at a large purple bag that lay on the bureau, lifted it idly and let it fall. His face stiffened again. The bag made a heavy sound on the glass top, as if there were a lump of lead inside it. He snapped it open quickly and plunged a hand in. His fingers touched the cold metal of a gun. He opened the bag wide and stared down into it at a small .25 automatic. A scrap of white paper caught his eye. He fished it out and held it to the light — a rent receipt with a name and address. He stuffed it into his pocket, closed the bag and was standing by the window when the girl came out of the bathroom.

"Hell, are you still haunting me?" she snapped. "You know what happens to hotel dicks that master-key their way into ladies' bedrooms at night?"

Steve said loosely: "Yeah. They get in trouble. They might even get shot at."

The girl's face became set, but her eyes crawled sideways and looked at the purple bag. Steve looked at her. "Know Leopardi in Frisco?" he asked. "He hasn't played here in two years. Then he was just a trumpet player in Vane Utigore's band — a cheap outfit."

The girl curled her lip, went past him and sat down by the window again. Her face was white, stiff. She said dully: "Blossom did. That's Blossom on the bed."

"Know he was coming to this hotel tonight?"

"What makes it your business?"

"I can't figure him coming here at all," Steve said. "This is a quiet place. So I can't figure anybody coming here to put the bite on him."

"Go somewhere else and figure. I need sleep."

Steve said: "Good night, sweetheart – and keep your door locked."

★

A thin man with thin blond hair and thin face was standing by the desk, tapping on the marble with thin fingers. Millar was still behind the desk and he still looked white and scared. The thin man wore a dark gray suit with a scarf inside the collar of the coat. He had a look of having just got up. He turned sea-green eyes slowly on Steve as he got out of the elevator, waited for him to come up to the desk and throw a tabbed key on it.

Steve said: "Leopardi's key, George. There's a busted mirror in his room and the carpet has his dinner on it – mostly Scotch." He turned to the thin man.

"You want to see me, Mr. Peters?"

"What happened, Grayce?" The thin man had a tight voice that expected to be lied to.

"Leopardi and two of his boys were on Eight, the rest of the gang on Five. The bunch on Five went to bed. A couple of obvious hustlers managed to get themselves registered just two rooms from Leopardi. They managed to contact him and everybody was having a lot of nice noisy fun in the hall. I could only stop it by getting a little tough."

"There's blood on your cheek," Peters said coldly. "Wipe it off."

Steve scratched at his cheek with a handkerchief. The thin thread of blood had dried. "I got the girls tucked away in their room," he said. "The two stooges took the hint and holed up, but Leopardi still thought the guests wanted to hear trombone music. I threatened to wrap it around his neck and he beaned me with it. I slapped him open-handed and he pulled a gun and took a shot at me. Here's the gun."

753

He took the .32 automatic out of his pocket and laid it on the desk. He put the used shell beside it. "So I beat some sense into him and threw him out," he added.

Peters tapped on the marble. "Your usual tact seems to have been well in evidence."

Steve stared at him. "He shot at me," he repeated quietly. "With a gun. This gun. I'm tender to bullets. He missed, but suppose he hadn't? I like my stomach the way it is, with just one way in and one way out."

Peters narrowed his tawny eyebrows. He said very politely: "We have you down on the payroll here as a night clerk, because we don't like the name house detective. But neither night clerks nor house detectives put guests out of the hotel without consulting me. Not ever, Mr. Grayce."

Steve said: "The guy shot at me, pal. With a gun. Catch on? I don't have to take that without a kickback, do I?" His face was a little white.

Peters said: "Another point for your consideration. The controlling interest in this hotel is owned by Mr. Halsey G. Walters. Mr. Walters also owns the Club Shalotte, where King Leopardi is opening on Wednesday night. And that, Mr. Grayce, is why Leopardi was good enough to give us his business. Can you think of anything else I should like to say to you?"

"Yeah. I'm canned," Steve said mirthlessly.

"Very correct, Mr. Grayce. Good night, Mr. Grayce."

The thin blond man moved to the elevator and the night porter took him up.

Steve looked at Millar.

"Jumbo Walters, huh?" he said softly. "A tough, smart guy. Much too smart to think this dump and the Club Shalotte belong to the same sort of customers. Did Peters write Leopardi to come here?"

"I guess he did, Steve." Millar's voice was low and gloomy.

"Then why wasn't he put in a tower suite with a private balcony to dance on, at twenty-eight bucks a day? Why was he put on a medium-priced transient floor? And why did Quillan let those girls get so close to him?"

Millar pulled at his black mustache. "Tight with money — as well as with Scotch, I suppose. As to the girls, I don't know."

Steve slapped the counter open-handed. "Well, I'm canned, for not letting a drunken heel make a parlor house and a shooting gallery out of the eighth floor. Nuts! Well, I'll miss the joint at that."

"I'll miss you too, Steve," Millar said gently. "But not for a week. I take a week off starting tomorrow. My brother has a cabin at Crestline."

"Didn't know you had a brother," Steve said absently. He opened and closed his fist on the marble desk top.

"He doesn't come into town much. A big guy. Used to be a fighter."

Steve nodded and straightened from the counter. "Well, I might as well finish out the night," he said. "On my back. Put this gun away somewhere, George."

He grinned coldly and walked away, down the steps into the dim main lobby and across to the room where the radio was. He punched the pillows into shape on the pale green davenport, then suddenly reached into his pocket and took out the scrap of white paper he had lifted from the black-haired girl's purple handbag. It was a receipt for a week's rent, to a Miss Marilyn Delorme, Apt. 211, Ridgeland Apartments, 118 Court Street.

He tucked it into his wallet and stood staring at the silent radio. "Steve, I think you got another job," he said under his breath. "Something about this set-up smells."

He slipped into a closetlike phone booth in the corner of the room, dropped a nickel and dialed an all-night radio station. He had to dial four times before he got a clear line to the Owl Program announcer.

"How's to play King Leopardi's record of 'Solitude' again?" he asked him.

"Got a lot of requests piled up. Played it twice already. Who's calling?"

"Steve Grayce, night man at the Carlton Hotel."

"Oh, a sober guy on his job. For you, pal, anything."

Steve went back to the davenport, snapped the radio on and lay down on his back, with his hands clasped behind his head.

Ten minutes later the high, pleasingly sweet trumpet notes of King Leopardi came softly from the radio, muted almost to a whisper, and sustaining E above high C for an almost incredible period of time.

"Shucks," Steve grumbled, when the record ended. "A guy that can play like that – maybe I was too tough with him."

3

COURT STREET WAS old town, wop town, cook town, arty town. It lay across the top of Bunker Hill and you could find anything there from down-at-heels ex-Greenwich-villagers to crooks on the lam, from ladies of anybody's evening to County Relief clients brawling with haggard landladies in grand old houses with scrolled porches, parquetry floors, and immense sweeping banisters of white oak, mahogany and Circassian walnut.

It had been a nice place once, had Bunker Hill, and from the days of its niceness there still remained the funny little funicular railway, called the Angel's Flight, which crawled up and down a yellow clay bank from Hill Street. It was afternoon when Steve Grayce got off the car at the top, its only passenger. He walked along in the sun, a tall, wide-shouldered, rangy-looking man in a well-cut blue suit.

He turned west at Court and began to read the numbers. The one he wanted was two from the corner, across the street from a red brick funeral parlor with a sign in gold over it: Paolo Perrugini Funeral Home. A swarthy iron-gray Italian in a cutaway coat stood in front of the curtained door of the red brick building, smoking a cigar and waiting for somebody to die.

One-eighteen was a three-storied frame apartment house. It had a glass door, well marked by a dirty net curtain, a hall runner eighteen inches wide, dim doors with numbers painted on them with dim-paint, a staircase halfway back. Brass stair rods glittered in the dimness of the hallway.

Steve Grayce went up the stairs and prowled back to the front. Apartment 211, Miss Marilyn Delorme, was on the right, a front apartment. He tapped lightly on the wood, waited, tapped again. Nothing moved beyond the silent door, or in the hallway. Behind another door across the hall somebody coughed and kept on coughing.

Standing there in the half-light Steve Grayce wondered why he had come. Miss Delorme had carried a gun. Leopardi had received some kind of a threat letter and torn it up and thrown it away. Miss Delorme had checked out of the Carlton about an hour after Steve told her Leopardi was gone. Even at that –

He took out a leather keyholder and studied the lock of the door. It looked as if it would listen to reason. He tried a pick on it, snicked the bolt back and stepped softly into the room. He shut the door, but the pick wouldn't lock it.

The room was dim with drawn shades across two front windows. The air smelled of face powder. There was light-painted furniture, a pull-down double bed which was pulled down but had been made up. There was a magazine on it, a glass tray full of cigarette butts, a pint bottle half full of whiskey, and a glass on a chair beside the bed. Two pillows had been used for a back rest and were still crushed in the middle.

On the dresser there was a composition toilet set, neither cheap nor expensive, a comb with black hair in it, a tray of manicuring stuff, plenty of spilled powder – in the bathroom, nothing. In a closet behind the bed a lot of clothes and two suitcases. The shoes were all one size.

Steve stood beside the bed and pinched his chin. "Blossom, the spitting blonde, doesn't live here," he said under his breath. "Just Marilyn the torn-pants brunette."

He went back to the dresser and pulled drawers out. In the bottom drawer, under the piece of wall paper that lined it, he found a box of .25 copper-nickel automatic shells. He poked at the butts in the ashtray. All had lipstick on them. He pinched his chin again, then feathered the air with the palm of his hand, like an oarsman with a scull.

"Bunk," he said softly. "Wasting your time, Stevie."

He walked over to the door and reached for the knob, then turned back to the bed and lifted it by the footrail.

Miss Marilyn Delorme was in.

She lay on her side on the floor under the bed, long legs scissored out as if in running. One mule was on, one off. Garters and skin showed at the tops of her stockings, and a blue rose on something pink. She wore a square-necked, short-sleeved dress that was not too clean. Her neck above the dress was blotched with purple bruises.

Her face was a dark plum color, her eyes had the faint stale glitter of death, and her mouth was open so far that it fore-shortened her face. She was colder than ice, and still quite limp. She had been dead two or three hours at least, six hours at most.

The purple bag was beside her, gaping like her mouth. Steve didn't touch any of the stuff that had been emptied out on the floor. There was no gun and there were no papers.

He let the bed down over her again, then made the rounds of the apartment, wiping everything he had touched and a lot of things he couldn't remember whether he had touched or not.

He listened at the door and stepped out. The hall was still empty. The man behind the opposite door still coughed. Steve went down the stairs, looked at the mailboxes and went back along the lower hall to a door.

Behind this door a chair creaked monotonously. He knocked and a woman's sharp voice called out. Steve opened the door with his handkerchief and stepped in.

In the middle of the room a woman rocked in an old Boston rocker, her body in the slack boneless attitude of exhaustion. She had a mud-colored face, stringy hair, gray cotton stockings – everything a Bunker Hill landlady should have. She looked at Steve with the interested eye of a dead goldfish.

"Are you the manager?"

The woman stopped rocking, screamed, "Hi, Jake! Company!" at the top of her voice, and started rocking again.

An icebox door thudded shut behind a partly open inner door and a very big man came into the room carrying a can of beer. He had a doughy mooncalf face, a tuft of fuzz on top of an otherwise bald head, a thick brutal neck and chin, and brown pig eyes about as expressionless as the woman's. He needed a shave – had needed one the day before – and his collarless shirt gaped over a big hard hairy chest. He wore scarlet suspenders with large gilt buckles on them.

He held the can of beer out to the woman. She clawed it out of his hand and said bitterly: "I'm so tired I ain't got no sense."

The man said: "Yah. You ain't done the halls so good at that."

The woman snarled: "I done 'em as good as I aim to." She sucked the beer thirstily.

Steve looked at the man and said: "Manager?"

"Yah. 'S me. Jake Stoyanoff. Two hun'erd eighty-six stripped, and still plenty tough."

Steve said: "Who lives in Two-eleven?"

The big man leaned forward a little from the waist and snapped his suspenders. Nothing changed in his eyes. The skin along his big jaw may have tightened a little. "A dame," he said.

759

"Alone?"

"Go on – ask me," the big man said. He stuck his hand out and lifted a cigar off the edge of a stained-wood table. The cigar was burning unevenly and it smelled as if somebody had set fire to the doormat. He pushed it into his mouth with a hard, thrusting motion, as if he expected his mouth wouldn't want it to go in.

"I'm asking you," Steve said.

"Ask me out in the kitchen," the big man drawled.

He turned and held the door open. Steve went past him.

The big man kicked the door shut against the squeak of the rocking chair, opened up the icebox and got out two cans of beer. He opened them and handed one to Steve.

"Dick?"

Steve drank some of the beer, put the can down on the sink, got a brand-new card out of his wallet – a business card printed that morning. He handed it to the man.

The man read it, put it down on the sink, picked it up and read it again. "One of them guys," he growled over his beer. "What's she pulled this time?"

Steve shrugged and said: "I guess it's the usual. The torn-pajama act. Only there's a kickback this time."

"How come? You handling it, huh? Must be a nice cozy one."

Steve nodded. The big man blew smoke from his mouth. "Go ahead and handle it," he said.

"You don't mind a pinch here?"

The big man laughed heartily. "Nuts to you, brother," he said pleasantly enough. "You're a private dick. So it's a hush. Okay. Go out and hush it. And if it *was* a pinch – that bothers me like a quart of milk. Go into your act. Take all the room you want. Cops don't bother Jake Stoyanoff."

Steve stared at the man. He didn't say anything. The big man talked it up some more, seemed to get more interested. "Besides," he went on, making motions with the cigar, "I'm softhearted. I never turn up a dame. I never put a frill in the middle." He finished his beer and threw the can in a basket under the sink, and pushed his hand out in front of him, revolving the large thumb slowly against the next two fingers. "Unless there's some of that," he added.

Steve said softly: "You've got big hands. You could have done it."

"Huh?" His small brown leathery eyes got silent and stared.

Steve said: "Yeah. You might be clean. But with those hands the cops'd go round and round with you just the same."

The big man moved a little to his left, away from the sink. He let his right hand hang down at his side, loosely. His mouth got so tight that the cigar almost touched his nose.

"What's the beef, huh?" he barked. "What you shovin' at me, guy? What − "

"Cut it," Steve drawled. "She's been croaked. Strangled. Upstairs, on the floor under her bed. About midmorning, I'd say. Big hands did it − hands like yours."

The big man did a nice job of getting the gun off his hip. It arrived so suddenly that it seemed to have grown in his hand and been there all the time.

Steve frowned at the gun and didn't move. The big man looked him over. "You're tough," he said. "I been in the ring long enough to size up a guy's meat. You're plenty hard, boy. But you ain't as hard as lead. Talk it up fast."

"I knocked at her door. No answer. The lock was a pushover. I went in. I almost missed her because the bed was pulled down and she had been sitting on it, reading a magazine. There was no sign of struggle. I lifted the bed just before I left − and there she was. Very dead, Mr. Stoyanoff. Put the gat away. Cops don't bother you, you said a minute ago."

The big man whispered: "Yes and no. They don't make me happy neither. I get a bump once'n a while. Mostly a Dutch. You said something about my hands, mister."

Steve shook his head. "That was a gag," he said. "Her neck has nail marks. You bite your nails down close. You're clean."

The big man didn't look at his fingers. He was very pale. There was sweat on his lower lip, in the black stubble of his beard. He was still leaning forward, still motionless, when there was a knocking beyond the kitchen door, the door from the living-room to the hallway. The creaking chair stopped and the woman's sharp voice screamed: "Hi, Jake! Company!"

The big man cocked his head. "That old slut wouldn't climb off'n her fanny if the house caught fire," he said thickly.

He stepped to the door and slipped through it, locking it behind him.

Steve ranged the kitchen swiftly with his eyes. There was a small high window beyond the sink, a trap low down for a garbage pail and parcels, but no other door. He reached for his card Stoyanoff had left lying on the drainboard and slipped it back into his pocket. Then he took a short-barreled Detective Special out of his left breast pocket where he wore it nose down, as in a holster.

He had got that far when the shots roared beyond the wall – muffled a little, but still loud – four of them blended in a blast of sound.

Steve stepped back and hit the kitchen door with his leg out straight. It held and jarred him to the top of his head and in his hip joint. He swore, took the whole width of the kitchen and slammed into it with his left shoulder. It gave this time. He pitched into the living-room. The mud-faced woman sat leaning forward in her rocker, her head to one side and a lock of mousy hair smeared down over her bony forehead.

"Backfire, huh?" she said stupidly. "Sounded kinda close. Musta been in the alley."

Steve jumped across the room, yanked the outer door open and plunged out into the hall.

The big man was still on his feet, a dozen feet down the hallway, in the direction of a screen door that opened flush on

762

an alley. He was clawing at the wall. His gun lay at his feet. His left knee buckled and he went down on it.

A door was flung open and a hard-looking woman peered out, and instantly slammed her door shut again. A radio suddenly gained in volume beyond her door.

The big man got up off his left knee and the leg shook violently inside his trousers. He went down on both knees and got the gun into his hand and began to crawl towards the screen door. Then, suddenly he went down flat on his face and tried to crawl that way, grinding his face into the narrow hall runner.

Then he stopped crawling and stopped moving altogether. His body went limp and the hand holding the gun opened and the gun rolled out of it.

Steve hit the screen door and was out in the alley. A gray sedan was speeding towards the far end of it. He stopped, steadied himself and brought his gun up level, and the sedan whisked out of sight around the corner.

A man boiled out of another apartment house across the alley. Steve ran on, gesticulating back at him and pointing ahead. As he ran he slipped the gun back into his pocket. When he reached the end of the alley, the gray sedan was out of sight. Steve skidded around the wall onto the sidewalk, slowed to a walk and then stopped.

Half a block down a man finished parking a car, got out and went across the sidewalk to a lunchroom. Steve watched him go in, then straightened his hat and walked along the wall to the lunchroom.

He went in, sat at the counter and ordered coffee. In a little while there were sirens.

Steve drank his coffee, asked for another cup and drank that. He lit a cigarette and walked down the long hill to Fifth, across to Hill, back to the foot of the Angel's Flight, and got his convertible out of a parking lot.

He drove out west, beyond Vermont, to the small hotel where he had taken a room that morning.

4

BILL DOCKERY, FLOOR manager of the Club Shalotte, teetered on his heels and yawned in the unlighted entrance to the dining room. It was a dead hour for business, late cocktail time, too early for dinner, and much too early for the real business of the club, which was high-class gambling.

Dockery was a handsome mug in a midnight-blue dinner jacket and a maroon carnation. He had a two-inch forehead under black lacquer hair, good features a little on the heavy side, alert brown eyes and very long curly eyelashes which he liked to let down over his eyes, to fool troublesome drunks into taking a swing at him.

The entrance door of the foyer was opened by the uniformed doorman and Steve Grayce came in.

Dockery said, "Ho, hum," tapped his teeth and leaned his weight forward. He walked across the lobby slowly to meet the guest. Steve stood just inside the doors and ranged his eyes over the high foyer walled with milky glass, lighted softly from behind. Molded in the glass were etchings of sailing ships, beasts of the jungle, Siamese pagodas, temples of Yucatan. The doors were square frames of chromium, like photo frames. The Club Shalotte had all the class there was, and the mutter of voices from the bar lounge on the left was not noisy. The faint Spanish music behind the voices was delicate as a carved fan.

Dockery came up and leaned his sleek head forward an inch. "May I help you?"

"King Leopardi around?"

Dockery leaned back again. He looked less interested. "The bandleader? He opens tomorrow night."

"I thought he might be around – rehearsing or something."

"Friend of his?"

"I know him. I'm not job-hunting, and I'm not a song plugger if that's what you mean."

Dockery teetered on his heels. He was tone-deaf and Leopardi meant no more to him than a bag of peanuts. He half smiled. "He was in the bar lounge a while ago." He pointed with his square rock-like chin. Steve Grayce went into the bar lounge.

It was about a third full, warm and comfortable and not too dark nor too light. The little Spanish orchestra was in an archway, playing with muted strings small seductive melodies that were more like memories than sounds. There was no dance floor. There was a long bar with comfortable seats, and there were small round composition-top tables, not too close together. A wall seat ran around three sides of the room. Waiters flitted among the tables like moths.

Steve Grayce saw Leopardi in the far corner, with a girl. There was an empty table on each side of him. The girl was a knockout.

She looked tall and her hair was the color of a brush fire seen through a dust cloud. On it, at the ultimate rakish angle, she wore a black velvet double-pointed beret with two artificial butterflies made of polka-dotted feathers and fastened on with tall silver pins. Her dress was burgundy-red wool and the blue fox draped over one shoulder was at least two feet wide. Her eyes were large, smoke-blue, and looked bored. She slowly turned a small glass on the table top with a gloved left hand.

Leopardi faced her, leaning forward, talking. His shoulders looked very big in a shaggy, cream-colored sports coat. Above the neck of it his hair made a point on his brown neck. He laughed across the table as Steve came up and his laugh had a confident, sneering sound.

Steve stopped, then moved behind the next table. The movement caught Leopardi's eye. His head turned, he looked annoyed, and then his eyes got very wide and brilliant and his whole body turned slowly, like a mechanical toy.

Leopardi put both his rather small well-shaped hands down on the table, on either side of a highball glass. He smiled. Then he pushed his chair back and stood up. He put one finger up and touched his hairline mustache, with theatrical delicacy. Then he said drawlingly, but distinctly: "You son of a bitch!"

A man at a nearby table turned his head and scowled. A waiter who had started to come over stopped in his tracks, then faded back among the tables. The girl looked at Steve Grayce and then leaned back against the cushions of the wall seat and moistened the end of one bare finger on her right hand and smoothed a chestnut eyebrow.

Steve stood quite still. There was a sudden high flush on his cheekbones. He said softly: "You left something at the hotel last night. I think you ought to do something about it. Here."

He reached a folded paper out of his pocket and held it out. Leopardi took it, still smiling, opened it and read it. It was a sheet of yellow paper with torn pieces of white paper pasted on it. Leopardi crumpled the sheet and let it drop at his feet.

He took a smooth step towards Steve and repeated more loudly: "You son of a bitch!"

The man who had first looked around stood up sharply and turned. He said clearly: "I don't like that sort of language in front of my wife."

Without even looking at the man Leopardi said: "To hell with you and your wife."

The man's face got a dusky red. The woman with him stood up and grabbed a bag and a coat and walked away. After a moment's indecision the man followed her. Everybody in the place was staring now. The waiter who had faded back among the tables went through the doorway into the entrance foyer, walking very quickly.

Leopardi took another, longer step and slammed Steve Grayce on the jaw. Steve rolled with the punch and stepped back and put his hand down on another table and upset a glass. He turned to apologize to the couple at the table. Leopardi jumped forward very fast and hit him behind the ear.

Dockery came through the doorway, split two waiters like a banana skin and started down the room showing all his teeth.

Steve gagged a little and ducked away. He turned and said thickly: "Wait a minute, you fool – that isn't all of it – there's – "

Leopardi closed in fast and smashed him full on the mouth. Blood oozed from Steve's lip and crawled down the line at the corner of his mouth and glistened on his chin. The girl with the red hair reached for her bag, white-faced with anger, and started to get up from behind her table.

Leopardi turned abruptly on his heel and walked away. Dockery put out a hand to stop him. Leopardi brushed it aside and went on, went out of the lounge.

The tall red-haired girl put her bag down on the table again and dropped her handkerchief on the floor. She looked at Steve quietly, spoke quietly. "Wipe the blood off your chin before it drips on your shirt." She had a soft, husky voice with a trill in it.

Dockery came up harsh-faced, took Steve by the arm and put weight on the arm. "All right, you! Let's go!"

Steve stood quite still, his feet planted, staring at the girl. He dabbed at his mouth with a handkerchief. He half smiled. Dockery couldn't move him an inch. Dockery dropped his hand, signaled two waiters and they jumped behind Steve, but didn't touch him.

Steve felt his lip carefully and looked at the blood on his handkerchief. He turned to the people at the table behind him and said: "I'm terribly sorry. I lost my balance."

The girl whose drink he had spilled was mopping her dress with a small fringed napkin. She smiled up at him and said: "It wasn't your fault."

The two waiters suddenly grabbed Steve's arms from behind. Dockery shook his head and they let go again. Dockery said tightly: "You hit him?"

"No."

"You say anything to make him hit you?"

"No."

The girl at the corner table bent down to get her fallen handkerchief. It took her quite a time. She finally got it and slid into the corner behind the table again. She spoke coldly.

"Quite right, Bill. It was just some more of the King's sweet way with his public."

Dockery said "Huh?" and swiveled his head on his thick hard neck. Then he grinned and looked back at Steve.

Steve said grimly: "He gave me three good punches, one from behind, without a return. You look pretty hard. See can you do it."

Dockery measured him with his eyes. He said evenly: "You win. I couldn't . . . Beat it!" he added sharply to the waiters. They went away. Dockery sniffed his carnation, and said quietly: "We don't go for brawls in here." He smiled at the girl again and went away, saying a word here and there at the tables. He went out through the foyer doors.

Steve tapped his lip, put his handkerchief in his pocket and stood searching the floor with his eyes.

The red-haired girl said calmly: "I think I have what you want – in my handkerchief. Won't you sit down?"

Her voice had a remembered quality, as if he had heard it before.

He sat down opposite her, in the chair where Leopardi had been sitting.

The red-haired girl said: "The drink's on me. I was with him."

Steve said, "Coke with a dash of bitters," to the waiter.

The waiter said: "Madame?"

"Brandy and soda. Light on the brandy, please." The waiter bowed and drifted away. The girl said amusedly: "Coke with a dash of bitters. That's what I love about Hollywood. You meet so many neurotics."

Steve stared into her eyes and said softly: "I'm an occasional drinker, the kind of guy who goes out for a beer and wakes up in Singapore with a full beard."

"I don't believe a word of it. Have you known the King long?"

"I met him last night. I didn't get along with him."

"I sort of noticed that." She laughed. She had a rich low laugh, too.

"Give me that paper, lady."

"Oh, one of these impatient men. Plenty of time." The handkerchief with the crumpled yellow sheet inside it was clasped tightly in her gloved hand. Her middle right finger played with an eyebrow. "You're not in pictures, are you?"

"Hell, no."

"Same here. Me, I'm too tall. The beautiful men have to wear stilts in order to clasp me to their bosoms."

The waiter set the drinks down in front of them, made a grace note in the air with his napkin and went away.

Steve said quietly, stubbornly: "Give me that paper, lady."

"I don't like that 'lady' stuff. It sounds like cop to me."

"I don't know your name."

"I don't know yours. Where did you meet Leopardi?"

Steve sighed. The music from the little Spanish orchestra had a melancholy minor sound now and the muffled clicking of gourds dominated it.

Steve listened to it with his head on one side. He said: "The E string is a half-tone flat. Rather cute effect."

The girl stared at him with new interest. "I'd never have noticed that," she said. "And I'm supposed to be a pretty good singer. But you haven't answered my question."

He said slowly: "Last night I was house dick at the Carlton Hotel. They called me night clerk, but house dick was what I was. Leopardi stayed there and cut up too rough. I threw him out and got canned."

The girl said: "Ah. I begin to get the idea. He was being the King and you were being – if I might guess – a pretty tough order of house detective."

"Something like that. Now will you please – "

"You still haven't told me your name."

He reached for his wallet, took one of the brand-new cards out of it and passed it across the table. He sipped his drink while she read it.

"A nice name," she said slowly. "But not a very good address. And *Private investigator* is bad. It should have been *Investigations*, very small, in the lower left-hand corner."

"They'll be small enough," Steve grinned. "Now will you please – "

She reached suddenly across the table and dropped the crumpled ball of paper in his hand.

"Of course I haven't read it – and of course I'd like to. You do give me that much credit, I hope" – she looked at the card again, and added – "Steve. Yes, and your office should be in a Georgian or very modernistic building in the Sunset Eighties. Suite Something-or-other. And your clothes should be very jazzy. Very jazzy indeed, Steve. To be inconspicuous in this town is to be a busted flush."

He grinned at her. His deep-set black eyes had lights in them. She put the card away in her bag, gave her fur piece a yank, and drank about half of her drink. "I have to go." She signaled the waiter and paid the check. The waiter went away and she stood up.

Steve said sharply: "Sit down."

She stared at him wonderingly. Then she sat down again and leaned against the wall, still staring at him. Steve leaned across the table, asked: "How well do *you* know Leopardi?"

"Off and on for years. If it's any of your business. Don't go masterful on me, for God's sake. I loathe masterful men. I once sang for him, but not for long. You can't just sing for Leopardi – if you get what I mean."

770

"You were having a drink with him."

She nodded slightly and shrugged. "He opens here tomorrow night. He was trying to talk me into singing for him again. I said no, but I may have to, for a week or two anyway. The man who owns the Club Shalotte also owns my contract – and the radio station where I work a good deal."

"Jumbo Walters," Steve said. "They say he's tough but square. I never met him, but I'd like to. After all I've got a living to get. Here."

He reached back across the table and dropped the crumpled paper. "The name was – "

"Dolores Chiozza."

Steve repeated it lingeringly. "I like it. I like your singing too. I've heard a lot of it. You don't oversell a song, like most of these high-money torchers." His eyes glistened.

The girl spread the paper on the table and read it slowly, without expression. Then she said quietly: "Who tore it up?"

"Leopardi, I guess. The pieces were in his wastebasket last night. I put them together, after he was gone. The guy has guts – or else he gets these things so often they don't register any more."

"Or else he thought it was a gag." She looked across the table levelly, then folded the paper and handed it back.

"Maybe. But if he's the kind of guy I hear he is – one of them is going to be on the level and the guy behind it is going to do more than just shake him down."

Dolores Chiozza said: "He's the kind of guy you hear he is."

"It wouldn't be hard for a woman to get to him then – would it – a woman with a gun?"

She went on staring at him. "No. And everybody would give her a big hand, if you ask me. If I were you, I'd just forget the whole thing. If he wants protection – Walters can throw more around him than the police. If he doesn't – who cares? I don't. I'm damn sure I don't."

771

"You're kind of tough yourself, Miss Chiozza – over some things."

She said nothing. Her face was a little white and more than a little hard.

Steve finished his drink, pushed his chair back and reached for his hat. He stood up. "Thank you very much for the drink, Miss Chiozza. Now that I've met you I'll look forward all the more to hearing you sing again."

"You're damn formal all of a sudden," she said.

He grinned. "So long, Dolores."

"So long, Steve. Good luck – in the sleuth racket. If I hear of anything – "

He turned and walked among the tables out of the bar lounge.

5

IN THE CRISP fall evening the lights of Hollywood and Los Angeles winked at him. Searchlight beams probed the cloudless sky as if searching for bombing-planes.

Steve got his convertible out of the parking lot and drove it east along Sunset. At Sunset and Fairfax he bought an evening paper and pulled over to the curb to look through it. There was nothing in the paper about 118 Court Street.

He drove on and ate dinner at the little coffee shop beside his hotel and went to a movie. When he came out he bought a Home Edition of the *Tribune*, a morning sheet. They were in that – both of them.

Police thought Jake Stoyanoff might have strangled the girl, but she had not been attacked. She was described as a stenographer, unemployed at the moment. There was no picture of her. There was a picture of Stoyanoff that looked like a touched-up police photo. Police were looking for a man who had been talking to Stoyanoff just before he was shot.

Several people said he was a tall man in a dark suit. That was all the description the police got – or gave out.

Steve grinned sourly, stopped at the coffee shop for a good-night cup of coffee and then went up to his room. It was a few minutes to eleven o'clock. As he unlocked his door the telephone started to ring.

He shut the door and stood in the darkness remembering where the phone was. Then he walked straight to it, catlike in the dark room, sat in an easy chair and reached the phone up from the lower shelf of a small table. He held the one piece to his ear and said: "Hello."

"Is this Steve?" It was a rich, husky voice, low, vibrant. It held a note of strain.

"Yeah, this is Steve. I can hear you. I know who you are."

There was a faint dry laugh. "You'll make a detective after all. And it seems I'm to give you your first case. Will you come over to my place at once? It's Twenty-four-twelve Renfrew – North, there isn't any South – just half a block below Fountain. It's a sort of bungalow court. My house is the last in line, at the back."

Steve said: "Yes. Sure. What's the matter?"

There was a pause. A horn blared in the street outside the hotel. A wave of white light went across the ceiling from some car rounding the corner uphill. The low voice said very slowly: "Leopardi. I can't get rid of him. He's – he's passed out in my bedroom." Then a tinny laugh that didn't go with the voice at all.

Steve held the phone so tight his hand ached. His teeth clicked in the darkness. He said flatly, in a dull, brittle voice: "Yeah. It'll cost you twenty bucks."

"Of course. Hurry, please."

He hung up, sat there in the dark room breathing hard. He pushed his hat back on his head, then yanked it forward again with a vicious jerk and laughed out loud. "Hell," he said. "*That* kind of a dame."

773

Twenty-four-twelve Renfrew was not strictly a bungalow court. It was a staggered row of six bungalows, all facing the same way, but so-arranged that no two of their front entrances overlooked each other. There was a brick wall at the back and beyond the brick wall a church. There was a long smooth lawn, moon-silvered.

The door was up two steps, with lanterns on each side and an iron-work grille over the peep hole. This opened to his knock and a girl's face looked out, a small oval face with a Cupid's-bow mouth, arched and plucked eyebrows, wavy brown hair. The eyes were like two fresh and shiny chestnuts.

Steve dropped a cigarette and put his foot on it. "Miss Chiozza. She's expecting me. Steve Grayce."

"Miss Chiozza has retired, sir," the girl said with a half-insolent twist to her lips.

"Break it up, kid. You heard me, I'm expected."

The wicket slammed shut. He waited, scowling back along the narrow moonlit lawn towards the street. Okay. So it was like that – well, twenty bucks was worth a ride in the moon-light anyway.

The lock clicked and the door opened wide. Steve went past the maid into a warm cheerful room, old-fashioned with chintz. The lamps were neither old nor new and there were enough of them – in the right places. There was a hearth behind a paneled copper screen, a davenport close to it, a bar-top radio in the corner.

The maid said stiffly: "I'm sorry, sir. Miss Chiozza forgot to tell me. Please have a chair." The voice was soft, and it might be cagey. The girl went off down the room – short skirts, sheer silk stockings, and four-inch spike heels.

Steve sat down and held his hat on his knee and scowled at the wall. A swing door creaked shut. He got a cigarette out and rolled it between his fingers and then deliberately squeezed it to a shapeless flatness of white paper and ragged tobacco. He threw it away from him, at the fire screen.

Dolores Chiozza came towards him. She wore green velvet lounging pajamas with a long gold-fringed sash. She spun the end of the sash as if she might be going to throw a loop with it. She smiled a slight artificial smile. Her face had a clean scrubbed look and her eyelids were bluish and they twitched.

Steve stood up and watched the green morocco slippers peep out under the pajamas as she walked. When she was close to him he lifted his eyes to her face and said dully: "Hello."

She looked at him very steadily, then spoke in a high, carrying voice. "I know it's late, but I knew you were used to being up all night. So I thought what we had to talk over – Won't you sit down?"

She turned her head very slightly, seemed to be listening for something.

Steve said: "I never go to bed before two. Quite all right."

She went over and pushed a bell beside the hearth. After a moment the maid came through the arch.

"Bring some ice cubes, Agatha. Then go along home. It's getting pretty late."

"Yes'm." The girl disappeared.

There was a silence then that almost howled till the tall girl took a cigarette absently out of a box, put it between her lips and Steve struck a match clumsily on his shoe. She pushed the end of the cigarette into the flame and her smoke-blue eyes were very steady on his black ones. She shook her head very slightly.

The maid came back with a copper ice bucket. She pulled a low Indian-brass tray-table between them before the davenport, put the ice bucket on it, then a siphon, glasses and spoons, and a triangular bottle that looked like good Scotch had come in it except that it was covered with silver filigree work and fitted with a stopper.

Dolores Chiozza said, "Will you mix a drink?" in a formal voice.

He mixed two drinks, stirred them, handed her one. She sipped it, shook her head. "Too light," she said. He put more whiskey in it and handed it back. She said, "Better," and leaned back against the corner of the davenport.

The maid came into the room again. She had a small rakish red hat on her wavy brown hair and was wearing a gray coat trimmed with nice fur. She carried a black brocade bag that could have cleaned out a fair-sized icebox. She said: "Good night, Miss Dolores."

"Good night, Agatha."

The girl went out the front door, closed it softly. Her heels clicked down the walk. A car door opened and shut distantly and a motor started. Its sound soon dwindled away. It was a very quiet neighborhood.

Steve put his drink down on the brass tray and looked levelly at the tall girl, said harshly: "That means she's out of the way?"

"Yes. She goes home in her own car. She drives me home from the studio in mine − when I go to the studio, which I did tonight. I don't like to drive a car myself."

"Well, what are you waiting for?"

The red-haired girl looked steadily at the paneled fire screen and the unlit log fire behind it. A muscle twitched in her cheek.

After a moment she said: "Funny that I called you instead of Walters. He'd have protected me better than you can. Only he wouldn't have believed me. I thought perhaps you would. I didn't invite Leopardi here. So far as I know − we two are the only people in the world who know he's here."

Something in her voice jerked Steve upright.

She took a small crisp handkerchief from the breast pocket of the green velvet pajama-suit, dropped it on the floor, picked it up swiftly and pressed it against her mouth. Suddenly, without making a sound, she began to shake like a leaf.

776

Steve said swiftly: "What the hell — I can handle that heel in my hip pocket. I did last night — and last night he had a gun and took a shot at me."

Her head turned. Her eyes were very wide and staring. "But it couldn't have been my gun," she said in a dead voice.

"Huh? Of course not — what — ?"

"It's my gun tonight," she said and stared at him. "You said a woman could get to him with a gun very easily."

He just stared at her. His face was white now and he made a vague sound in his throat.

"He's not drunk, Steve," she said gently. "He's dead. In yellow pajamas — in my bed. With my gun in his hand. You didn't think he was just drunk — did you, Steve?"

He stood up in a swift lunge, then became absolutely motionless, staring down at her. He moved his tongue on his lips and after a long time he formed words with it. "Let's go look at him," he said in a hushed voice.

6

THE ROOM WAS at the back of the house to the left. The girl took a key out of her pocket and unlocked the door. There was a low light on a table, and the venetian blinds were drawn. Steve went in past her silently, on cat feet.

Leopardi lay squarely in the middle of the bed, a large smooth silent man, waxy and artificial in death. Even his mustache looked phony. His half-open eyes, sightless as marbles, looked as if they had never seen. He lay on his back, on the sheet, and the bedclothes were thrown over the foot of the bed.

The King wore yellow silk pajamas, the slip-on kind, with a turned collar. They were loose and thin. Over his breast they were dark with blood that had seeped into the silk as if into blotting-paper. There was a little blood on his bare brown neck.

Steve stared at him and said tonelessly: "The King in Yellow. I read a book with that title once. He liked yellow, I guess. I packed some of his stuff last night. And he wasn't yellow either. Guys like him usually are – or are they?"

The girl went over to the corner and sat down in a slipper chair and looked at the floor. It was a nice room, as modernistic as the living-room was casual. It had a chenille rug, café-au-lait color, severely angled furniture in inlaid wood, and a trick dresser with a mirror for a top, a kneehole and drawers like a desk. It had a box mirror above and a semi-cylindrical frosted wall light set above the mirror. In the corner there was a glass table with a crystal greyhound on top of it, and a lamp with the deepest drum shade Steve had ever seen.

He stopped looking at all this and looked at Leopardi again. He pulled the King's pajamas up gently and examined the wound. It was directly over the heart and the skin was scorched and mottled there. There was not so very much blood. He had died in a fraction of a second.

A small Mauser automatic lay cuddled in his right hand, on top of the bed's second pillow.

"That's artistic," Steve said and pointed. "Yeah, that's a nice touch. Typical contact wound, I guess. He even pulled his pajama shirt up. I've heard they do that. A Mauser seven-six-three about. Sure it's your gun?"

"Yes." She kept on looking at the floor. "It was in a desk in the living-room – not loaded. But there were shells. I don't know why. Somebody gave it to me once. I didn't even know how to load it."

Steve smiled. Her eyes lifted suddenly and she saw his smile and shuddered. "I don't expect anybody to believe that," she said. "We may as well call the police, I suppose."

Steve nodded absently, put a cigarette in his mouth and flipped it up and down with his lips that were still puffy from Leopardi's punch. He lit a match on his thumbnail, puffed a small plume of smoke and said quietly: "No cops. Not yet. Just tell it."

The red-haired girl said: "I sing at KFQC, you know. Three nights a week – on a quarter-hour automobile program. This was one of the nights. Agatha and I got home – oh, close to half-past ten. At the door I remembered there was no fizzwater in the house, so I sent her back to the liquor store three blocks away, and came in alone. There was a queer smell in the house. I don't know what it was. As if several men had been in here, somehow. When I came in the bedroom   he was exactly as he is now. I saw the gun and I went and looked and then I knew I was sunk. I didn't know what to do. Even if the police cleared me, everywhere I went from now on – "

Steve said sharply: "He got in here – how?"

"I don't know."

"Go on," he said.

"I locked the door. Then I undressed – with that on my bed. I went into the bathroom to shower and collect my brains, if any. I locked the door when I left the room and took the key. Agatha was back then, but I don't think she saw me. Well, I took the shower and it braced me up a bit. Then I had a drink and then I came in here and called you."

She stopped and moistened the end of a finger and smoothed the end of her left eyebrow with it. "That's all, Steve – absolutely all."

"Domestic help can be pretty nosey. This Agatha's nosier than most – or I miss my guess." He walked over to the door and looked at the lock. "I bet there are three or four keys in the house that knock this over." He went to the windows and felt the catches, looked down at the screens through the glass. He said over his shoulder, casually: "Was the King in love with you?"

Her voice was sharp, almost angry. "He never was in love with any woman. A couple of years back in San Francisco, when I was with his band for a while, there was some slap-silly publicity about us. Nothing to it. It's been revived here in the hand-outs to the press, to build up his opening. I was telling him this afternoon I wouldn't stand for it, that I wouldn't be linked with him in anybody's mind. His private life was filthy. It reeked. Everybody in the business knows that. And it's not a business where daisies grow very often."

Steve said: "Yours was the only bedroom he couldn't make?"

The girl flushed to the roots of her dusky red hair.

"That sounds lousy," he said. "But I have to figure the angles. That's about true, isn't it?"

"Yes – I suppose so. I wouldn't say the only one."

"Go on out in the other room and buy yourself a drink."

She stood up and looked at him squarely across the bed. "I didn't kill him, Steve. I didn't let him into this house tonight. I didn't know he was coming here, or had any reason to come here. Believe that or not. But something about this is wrong. Leopardi was the last man in the world to take his lovely life himself."

Steve said: "He didn't, angel. Go buy that drink. He was murdered. The whole thing is a frame – to get a cover-up from Jumbo Walters. Go on out."

He stood silent, motionless, until sounds he heard from the living-room told him she was out there. Then he took out his handkerchief and loosened the gun from Leopardi's right hand and wiped it over carefully on the outside, broke out the magazine and wiped that off, spilled out all the shells and wiped every one, ejected the one in the breech and wiped that. He reloaded the gun and put it back in Leopardi's dead hand and closed his fingers around it and pushed his index finger against the trigger. Then he let the hand fall naturally back on the bed.

He pawed through the bedclothes and found an ejected shell and wiped that off, put it back where he had found it. He put the handkerchief to his nose, sniffed it wryly, went around the bed to a clothes closet and opened the door.

"Careless of your clothes, boy," he said softly.

The rough cream-colored coat hung in there, on a hook, over dark gray slacks with a lizard-skin belt. A yellow satin shirt and a wine-colored tie dangled alongside. A handkerchief to match the tie flowed loosely four inches from the breast pocket of the coat. On the floor lay a pair of gazelle-leather nutmeg-brown sports shoes, and socks without garters. And there were yellow satin shorts with heavy black initials on them lying close by.

Steve felt carefully in the gray slacks and got out a leather keyholder. He left the room, went along the cross-hall and into the kitchen. It had a solid door, a good spring lock with a key stuck in it. He took it out and tried keys from the bunch in the keyholder, found none that fitted, put the other key back and went into the living-room. He opened the front door, went outside and shut it again without looking at the girl huddled in a corner of the davenport. He tried keys in the lock, finally found the right one. He let himself back into the house, returned to the bedroom and put the keyholder back in the pocket of the gray slacks again. Then he went to the living-room.

The girl was still huddled motionless, staring at him.

He put his back to the mantel and puffed a cigarette. "Agatha with you all the time at the studio?"

She nodded. "I suppose so. So he had a key. That was what you were doing, wasn't it?"

"Yes. Had Agatha long?"

"About a year."

"She steal from you? Small stuff, I mean?"

Dolores Chiozza shrugged wearily. "What does it matter? Most of them do. A little face cream or powder, a handkerchief, a pair of stockings once in a while. Yes, I think she stole from me. They look on that sort of thing as more or less legitimate."

"Not the nice ones, angel."

"Well – the hours were a little trying. I work at night, often get home very late. She's a dresser as well as a maid."

"Anything else about her? She use cocaine or weed? Hit the bottle? Ever have laughing fits?"

"I don't think so. What has she got to do with it, Steve?"

"Lady, she sold somebody a key to your apartment. That's obvious. You didn't give him one, the landlord wouldn't give him one, but Agatha had one. Check?"

Her eyes had a stricken look. Her mouth trembled a little, not much. A drink was untasted at her elbow. Steve bent over and drank some of it.

She said slowly: "We're wasting time, Steve. We have to call the police. There's nothing anybody can do. I'm done for as a nice person, even if not as a lady at large. They'll think it was a lovers' quarrel and I shot him and that's that. If I could convince them I didn't, then he shot himself in my bed, and I'm still ruined. So I might as well make up my mind to face the music."

Steve said softly: "Watch this. My mother used to do it."

He put a finger to his mouth, bent down and touched her lips at the same spot with the same finger. He smiled, said: "We'll go to Walters – or you will. He'll pick his cops and the ones he picks won't go screaming through the night with reporters sitting in their laps. They'll sneak in quiet, like process servers. Walters can handle this. That was what was counted on. Me, I'm going to collect Agatha. Because I want a description of the guy she sold that key to – and I want it fast. And by the way, you owe me twenty bucks for coming over here. Don't let that slip your memory."

The tall girl stood up, smiling. "You're a kick, you are," she said. "What makes you so sure he was murdered?"

"He's not wearing his own pajamas. His have his initials on them. I packed his stuff last night – before I threw him out of the Carlton. Get dressed, angel – and get me Agatha's address."

He went into the bedroom and pulled a sheet over Leopardi's body, held it a moment above the still, waxen face before letting it fall.

"So long, guy," he said gently. "You were a louse – but you sure had music in you."

It was a small frame house on Brighton Avenue near Jefferson, in a block of small frame houses, all old-fashioned, with front porches. This one had a narrow concrete walk which the moon made whiter than it was.

Steve mounted the steps and looked at the light-edged shade of the wide front window. He knocked. There were shuffling steps and a woman opened the door and looked at him through the hooked screen – a dumpy elderly woman with frizzled gray hair. Her body was shapeless in a wrapper and her feet slithered in loose slippers. A man with a polished bald head and milky eyes sat in a wicker chair beside a table. He held his hands in his lap and twisted the knuckles aimlessly. He didn't look towards the door.

Steve said: "I'm from Miss Chiozza. Are you Agatha's mother?"

The woman said dully: "I reckon. But she ain't home, mister." The man in the chair got a handkerchief from somewhere and blew his nose. He snickered darkly.

Steve said: "Miss Chiozza's not feeling so well tonight. She was hoping Agatha would come back and stay the night with her."

The milky-eyed man snickered again, sharply. The woman said: "We dunno where she is. She don't come home. Pa 'n me waits up for her to come home. She stays out till we're sick."

The old man snapped in a reedy voice: "She'll stay out till the cops get her one of these times."

"Pa's half blind," the woman said. "Makes him kinda mean. Won't you step in?"

Steve shook his head and turned his hat around in his hands like a bashful cowpuncher in a horse opera. "I've got to find her," he said. "Where would she go?"

"Out drinkin' liquor with cheap spenders," Pa cackled. "Panty-waists with silk handkerchiefs 'stead of neckties. If

I had eyes, I'd strap her till she dropped." He grabbed the arms of his chair and the muscles knotted on the backs of his hands. Then he began to cry. Tears welled from his milky eyes and started through the white stubble on his cheeks. The woman went across and took the handkerchief out of his fist and wiped his face with it. Then she blew her nose on it and came back to the door.

"Might be anywhere," she said to Steve. "This is a big town, mister. I dunno where at to say."

Steve said dully: "I'll call back. If she comes in, will you hang onto her. What's your phone number?"

"What's the phone number, Pa?" the woman called back over her shoulder.

"I ain't sayin'," Pa snorted.

The woman said: "I remember now. South two-four-five-four. Call any time. Pa'n me ain't got nothing to do."

Steve thanked her and went back down the white walk to the street and along the walk half a block to where he had left his car. He glanced idly across the way and started to get into his car, then stopped moving suddenly with his hand gripping the car door. He let go of that, took three steps sideways and stood looking across the street tight-mouthed.

All the houses in the block were much the same, but the one opposite had a FOR RENT placard stuck in the front window and a real-estate sign spiked into the small patch of front lawn. The house itself looked neglected, utterly empty, but in its little driveway stood a small neat black coupe.

Steve said under his breath: "Hunch. Play it up, Stevie."

He walked almost delicately across the wide dusty street, his hand touching the hard metal of the gun in his pocket, and came up behind the little car, stood and listened. He moved silently along its left side, glanced back across the street, then looked in the car's open left-front window.

The girl sat almost as if driving, except that her head was tipped a little too much into the corner. The little red hat was still on her head, the gray coat, trimmed with fur, still around her body. In the reflected moonlight her mouth was strained open. Her tongue stuck out. And her chestnut eyes stared at the roof of the car.

Steve didn't touch her. He didn't have to touch her to look any closer to know there would be heavy bruises on her neck.

"Tough on women, these guys," he muttered.

The girl's big black brocade bag lay on the seat beside her, gaping open like her mouth – like Miss Marilyn Delorme's mouth, and Miss Marilyn Delorme's purple bag.

"Yeath – tough on women."

He backed away till he stood under a small palm tree by the entrance to the driveway. The street was as empty and deserted as a closed theater. He crossed silently to his car, got into it and drove away.

Nothing to it. A girl coming home alone late at night, stuck up and strangled a few doors from her own home by some tough guy. Very simple. The first prowl car that cruised that block – if the boys were half awake – would take a look the minute they spotted the FOR RENT sign. Steve tramped hard on the throttle and went away from there.

At Washington and Figueroa he went into an all-night drugstore and pulled shut the door of the phone booth at the back. He dropped his nickel and dialed the number of police headquarters.

He asked for the desk and said: "Write this down, will you, sergeant? Brighton Avenue, thirty-two-hundred block, west side, in driveway of empty house. Got that much?"

"Yeah. So what?"

"Car with dead woman in it," Steve said, and hung up.

7

QUILLAN, HEAD DAY clerk and assistant manager of the Carlton Hotel, was on night duty, because Millar, the night auditor, was off for a week. It was half-past one and things were dead and Quillan was bored. He had done everything there was to do long ago, because he had been a hotel man for twenty years and there was nothing to it.

The night porter had finished cleaning up and was in his room beside the elevator bank. One elevator was lighted and open, as usual. The main lobby had been tidied up and the lights had been properly dimmed. Everything was exactly as usual.

Quillan was a rather short, rather thick-set man with clear bright toadlike eyes that seemed to hold a friendly expression without really having any expression at all. He had pale sandy hair and not much of it. His pale hands were clasped in front of him on the marble top of the desk. He was just the right height to put his weight on the desk without looking as if he were sprawling. He was looking at the wall across the entrance lobby, but he wasn't seeing it. He was half asleep, even though his eyes were wide open, and if the night porter struck a match behind his door, Quillan would know it and bang on his bell.

The brass-trimmed swing doors at the street entrance pushed open and Steve Grayce came in, a summer-weight coat turned up around his neck, his hat yanked low and a cigarette wisping smoke at the corner of his mouth. He looked very casual, very alert, and very much at ease. He strolled over to the desk and rapped on it.

"Wake up!" he snorted.

Quillan moved his eyes an inch and said: "All outside rooms with bath. But positively no parties on the eighth floor. Hiyah, Steve. So you finally got the axe. And for the wrong thing. That's life."

Steve said: "Okay. Have you got a new night man here?"

"Don't need one, Steve. Never did, in my opinion."

"You'll need one as long as old hotel men like you register floozies on the same corridor with people like Leopardi."

Quillan half closed his eyes and then opened them to where they had been before. He said indifferently: "Not me, pal. But anybody can make a mistake. Millar's really an accountant – not a desk man."

Steve leaned back and his face became very still. The smoke almost hung at the tip of his cigarette. His eyes were like black glass now. He smiled a little dishonestly.

"And why was Leopardi put in an eight-dollar room on Eight instead of in a tower suite at twenty-eight per?"

Quillan smiled back at him. "I didn't register Leopardi, old sock. There were reservations in. I supposed they were what he wanted. Some guys don't spend. Any other questions, Mr. Grayce?"

"Yeah. Was Eight-fourteen empty last night?"

"It was on change, so it was empty. Something about the plumbing. Proceed."

"Who marked it on change?"

Quillan's bright fathomless eyes turned and became curiously fixed. He didn't answer.

Steve said: "Here's why. Leopardi was in Eight-fifteen and the two girls in Eight-eleven. Just Eight-thirteen between. A lad with a passkey could have gone into Eight-thirteen and turned both the bolt locks on the communicating doors. Then, if the folks in the two other rooms had done the same thing on their side, they'd have a suite set up."

"So what?" Quillan asked. "We got chiseled out of eight bucks, eh? Well, it happens, in better hotels than this." His eyes looked sleepy now.

Steve said: "Millar could have done that. But hell, it doesn't make sense. Millar's not that kind of a guy. Risk a job for a buck tip – phooey. Millar's no dollar pimp."

Quillan said: "All right, policeman. Tell me what's really on your mind."

"One of the girls in Eight-eleven had a gun. Leopardi got a threat letter yesterday – I don't know where or how. It didn't faze him, though. He tore it up. That's how I know. I collected the pieces from his basket. I suppose Leopardi's boys all checked out of here."

"Of course. They went to the Normandy."

"Call the Normandy, and ask to speak to Leopardi. If he's there, he'll still be at the bottle. Probably with a gang."

"Why?" Quillan asked gently.

"Because you're a nice guy. If Leopardi answers – just hang up." Steve paused and pinched his chin hard. "If he went out, try to find out where."

Quillan straightened, gave Steve another long quiet look and went behind the pebbled-glass screen. Steve stood very still, listening, one hand clenched at his side, the other tapping noiselessly on the marble desk.

In about three minutes Quillan came back and leaned on the desk again and said: "Not there. Party going on in his suite – they sold him a big one – and sounds loud. I talked to a guy who was fairly sober. He said Leopardi got a call around ten – some girl. He went out preening himself, as the fellow says. Hinting about a very juicy date. The guy was just lit enough to hand me all this."

Steve said: "You're a real pal. I hate not to tell you the rest. Well, I liked working here. Not much work at that."

He started towards the entrance doors again. Quillan let him get his hand on the brass handle before he called out. Steve turned and came back slowly.

Quillan said: "I heard Leopardi took a shot at you. I don't think it was noticed. It wasn't reported down here. And I don't think Peters fully realized that until he saw the mirror in Eight-fifteen. If you care to come back, Steve – "

Steve shook his head. "Thanks for the thought."

"And hearing about that shot," Quillan added, "made me remember something. Two years ago a girl shot herself in Eight-fifteen."

Steve straightened his back so sharply that he almost jumped. "What girl?"

Quillan looked surprised. "I don't know. I don't remember her real name. Some girl who had been kicked around all she could stand and wanted to die in a clean bed – alone."

Steve reached across and took hold of Quillan's arm. "The hotel files," he rasped. "The clippings, whatever there was in the papers will be in them. I want to see those clippings."

Quillan stared at him for a long moment. Then he said: "Whatever game you're playing, kid – you're playing it damn close to your vest. I will say that for you. And me bored stiff with a night to kill."

He reached along the desk and thumped the call bell. The door of the night porter's room opened and the porter came across the entrance lobby. He nodded and smiled at Steve.

Quillan said: "Take the board, Carl. I'll be in Mr. Peters' office for a little while."

He went to the safe and got keys out of it.

8

THE CABIN WAS high up on the side of the mountain, against a thick growth of digger pine, oak and incense cedar. It was solidly built, with a stone chimney, shingled all over and heavily braced against the slope of the hill. By daylight the roof was green and the sides dark reddish brown and the window frames and draw curtains red. In the uncanny brightness of an all-night mid-October moon in the mountains, it stood out sharply in every detail, except color.

It was at the end of a road, a quarter of a mile from any other cabin. Steve rounded the bend towards it without lights, at five in the morning. He stopped his car at once, when he was sure it was the right cabin, got out and walked soundlessly along the side of the gravel road, on a carpet of wild iris.

On the road level there was a rough pine board garage, and from this a path went up to the cabin porch. The garage was unlocked. Steve swung the door open carefully, groped in past the dark bulk of a car and felt the top of the radiator. It was still warmish. He got a small flash out of his pocket and played it over the car. A gray sedan, dusty, the gas gauge low. He snapped the flash off, shut the garage door carefully and slipped into place the piece of wood that served for a hasp. Then he climbed the path to the house.

There was light behind the drawn red curtains. The porch was high and juniper logs were piled on it, with the bark still on them. The front door had a thumb latch and a rustic door handle above.

He went up, neither too softly nor too noisily, lifted his hand, sighed deep in his throat, and knocked. His hand touched the butt of the gun in the inside pocket of his coat, once, then came away empty.

A chair creaked and steps padded across the floor and a voice called out softly: "What is it?" Millar's voice.

Steve put his lips close to the wood and said: "This is Steve, George. You up already?"

The key turned, and the door opened. George Millar, the dapper night auditor of the Carlton House, didn't look dapper now. He was dressed in old trousers and a thick blue sweater with a roll collar. His feet were in ribbed wool socks and fleece-lined slippers. His clipped black mustache was a curved smudge across his pale face. Two electric bulbs burned in their sockets in a low beam across the room, below the slope of the high roof. A table lamp was lit and its shade was tilted to throw light on a big Morris chair with a leather seat and back-cushion. A fire burned lazily in a heap of soft ash on the big open hearth.

Millar said in his low, husky voice: "Hell's sake, Steve. Glad to see you. How'd you find us anyway? Come on in, guy."

Steve stepped through the door and Millar locked it. "City habit," he said grinning. "Nobody locks anything in the mountains. Have a chair. Warm your toes. Cold out at this time of night."

Steve said: "Yeah. Plenty cold."

He sat down in the Morris chair and put his hat and coat on the end of the solid wood table behind it. He leaned forward and held his hands out to the fire.

Millar said: "How the hell did you find us, Steve?"

Steve didn't look at him. He said quietly: "Not so easy at that. You told me last night your brother had a cabin up here – remember? So I had nothing to do, so I thought I'd drive up and bum some breakfast. The guy in the inn at Crestline didn't know who had cabins where. His trade is with people passing through. I rang up a garage man and he didn't know any Millar cabin. Then I saw a light come on down the street in a coal-and-wood yard and a little guy who is forest ranger and deputy sheriff and wood-and-gas dealer and half a dozen other things was getting his car out to go down to San Bernardino for some tank gas. A very smart little guy. The minute I said your brother had been a fighter he wised up. So here I am."

Millar pawed at his mustache. Bedsprings creaked at the back of the cabin somewhere. "Sure, he still goes under his fighting name – Gaff Talley. I'll get him up and we'll have some coffee. I guess you and me are both in the same boat. Used to working at night and can't sleep. I haven't been to bed at all."

Steve looked at him slowly and looked away. A burly voice behind them said: "Gaff is up. Who's your pal, George?"

Steve stood up casually and turned. He looked at the man's hands first. He couldn't help himself. They were large hands, well kept as to cleanliness, but coarse and ugly. One knuckle had been broken badly. He was a big man with reddish hair. He wore a sloppy bathrobe over outing-flannel pajamas. He had a leathery expressionless face, scarred over the cheekbones. There were fine white scars over his eyebrows and at the corners of his mouth. His nose was spread and thick. His whole face looked as if it had caught a lot of gloves. His eyes alone looked vaguely like Millar's eyes.

Millar said: "Steve Grayce. Night man at the hotel – until last night." His grin was a little vague.

Gaff Talley came over and shook hands. "Glad to meet you," he said. "I'll get some duds on and we'll scrape a breakfast off the shelves. I slept enough. George ain't slept any, the poor sap."

He went back across the room towards the door through which he'd come. He stopped there and leaned on an old phonograph, put his big hand down behind a pile of records in paper envelopes. He stayed just like that, without moving.

Millar said: "Any luck on a job, Steve? Or did you try yet?"

"Yeah. In a way. I guess I'm a sap, but I'm going to have a shot at the private-agency racket. Not much in it unless I can land some publicity." He shrugged. Then he said very quietly: "King Leopardi's been bumped off."

Millar's mouth snapped wide open. He stayed like that for almost a minute – perfectly still, with his mouth open. Gaff Talley leaned against the wall and stared without showing anything in his face. Millar finally said: "Bumped off? Where? Don't tell me – "

"Not in the hotel, George. Too bad, wasn't it? In a girl's apartment. Nice girl too. She didn't entice him there. The old suicide gag – only it won't work. And the girl is my client."

Millar didn't move. Neither did the big man. Steve leaned his shoulders against the stone mantel. He said softly: "I went out to the Club Shalotte this afternoon to apologize to Leopardi. Silly idea, because I didn't owe him an apology. There was a girl there in the bar lounge with him. He took three socks at me and left. The girl didn't like that. We got rather clubby. Had a drink together. Then late tonight – last night – she called me up and said Leopardi was over at her place and – he was drunk and she couldn't get rid of him. I went there. Only he wasn't drunk. He was dead, in her bed, in yellow pajamas."

The big man lifted his left hand and roughed back his hair. Millar leaned slowly against the edge of the table, as if he were afraid the edge might be sharp enought to cut him. His mouth twitched under the clipped black mustache.

He said huskily: "That's lousy."

The big man said: "Well, for cryin' into a milk bottle."

Steve said: "Only they weren't Leopardi's pajamas. His had initials on them — big black initials. And his were satin, not silk. And although he had a gun in his hand — this girl's gun by the way — *he* didn't shoot himself in the heart. The cops will determine that. Maybe you birds never heard of the Lund test, with paraffin wax, to find out who did or didn't fire a gun recently. The kill ought to have been pulled in the hotel last night, in Room Eight-fifteen. I spoiled that by heaving him out on his neck before that black-haired girl in Eight-eleven could get to him. Didn't I, George?"

Milar said: "I guess you did — if I know what you're talking about."

Steve said slowly: "I think you know what I'm talking about, George. It would have been a kind of poetic justice if King Leopardi had been knocked off in Room Eight-fifteen. Because that was the room where a girl shot herself two years ago. A girl who registered as Mary Smith — but whose usual name was Eve Talley. And whose real name was Eve Millar."

The big man leaned heavily on the victrola and said thickly: "Maybe I ain't woke up yet. That sounds like it might grow up to be a dirty crack. We had a sister named Eve that shot herself in the Carlton. So what?"

Steve smiled a little crookedly. He said: "Listen, George. You told me Quillan registered those girls in Eight-eleven. You did. You told me Leopardi registered on Eight, instead of in a good suite because he was tight. He wasn't tight. He just didn't care where he was put, as long as female company was handy. And you saw to that. You planned the whole thing, George. You even got Peters to write Leopardi at the Raleigh in Frisco and ask him to use the Carlton when he came down – because the same man owned it who owned the Club Shalotte. As if a guy like Jumbo Walters would care where a bandleader registered."

Millar's face was dead white, expressionless. His voice cracked. "Steve – for God's take. Steve, what are you talking about? How the hell could I – "

"Sorry, kid. I liked working with you. I liked you a lot. I guess I still like you. But I don't like people who strangle women – or people who smear women in order to cover up a revenge murder."

His hand shot up – and stopped. The big man said: "Take it easy – and look at this one."

Gaff's hand had come up from behind the pile of records. A Colt .45 was in it. He said between his teeth: "I always thought house dicks were just a bunch of cheap grafters. I guess I missed out on you. You got a few brains. Hell, I bet you even run out to One-eighteen Court Street. Right?"

Steve let his hand fall empty and looked straight at the big Colt. "Right, I saw the girl – dead – with your fingers marked into her neck. They can measure those, fella. Killing Dolores Chiozza's maid the same way was a mistake. They'll match up the two sets of marks, find out that your black-haired gun girl was at the Carlton last night and piece the whole story together. With the information they get in the hotel they can't miss. I give you two weeks, if you beat it quick. And I mean quick."

Millar licked his dry lips and said softly: "There's no hurry, Steve. No hurry at all. Our job is done. Maybe not the best way, maybe not the nicest way, but it wasn't a nice job. And Leopardi was the worst kind of a louse. We loved our sister, and he made a tramp out of her. She was a wide-eyed kid that fell for a flashy greaseball, and the greaseball went up in the world and threw her out on her ear for a red-headed torcher who was more his kind. He threw her out and broke her heart and she killed herself."

Steve said harshly: "Yeah – and what were you doing all that time – manicuring your nails?"

"We weren't around when it happened. It took us a little time to find out the why of it."

Steve said: "So that was worth killing four people for, was it? And as for Dolores Chiozza, she wouldn't have wiped her feet on Leopardi – then, or any time since. But you had to put her in the middle too, with your mean little revenge murder. You make me sick, George. Tell your big tough brother to get on with his murder party."

The big man grinned and said: "Nuff talk, George. See has he a gat and don't get behind him or in front of him. This bean-shooter goes on through."

Steve stared at the big man's .45. His face was hard as white bone. There was a thin cold sneer on his lips and his eyes were cold and dark.

Millar moved softly in his fleece-lined slippers. He came around the end of the table and went close to Steve's side and reached out a hand to tap his pockets. He stepped back and pointed: "In there."

Steve said softly: "I must be nuts. I could have taken you then, George."

Gaff Talley barked: "Stand away from him."

He walked solidly across the room and put the big Colt against Steve's stomach hard. He reached up with his left hand and worked the Detective Special from the inside breast pocket. His eyes were sharp on Steve's eyes. He held Steve's gun out behind him. "Take this, George."

Millar took the gun and went over beyond the big table again and stood at the far corner of it. Gaff Talley backed away from Steve.

"You're through, wise guy," he said. "You got to know that. There's only two ways outa these mountains and we gotta have time. And maybe you didn't tell nobody. See?"

Steve stood like a rock, his face white, a twisted half-smile working at the corners of his lips. He stared hard at the big man's gun and his stare was faintly puzzled.

Millar said: "Does it have to be that way, Gaff?" His voice was a croak now, without tone, without its usual pleasant huskiness.

Steve turned his head a little and looked at Millar. "Sure it has, George. You're just a couple of cheap hoodlums after all. A couple of nasty-minded sadists playing at being revengers of wronged girlhood. Hillbilly stuff. And right this minute you're practically cold meat – cold, rotten meat."

Gaff Talley laughed and cocked the big revolver with his thumb. "Say your prayers, guy," he jeered.

Steve said grimly: "What makes you think you're going to bump me off with that thing? No shells in it, strangler. Better try to take me the way you handle women – with your hands."

The big man's eyes flicked down, clouded. Then he roared with laughter. "Geez, the dust on that one must be a foot thick," he chuckled. "Watch."

He pointed the big gun at the floor and squeezed the trigger. The firing pin clicked dryly – on an empty chamber. The big man's face convulsed.

For a short moment nobody moved. Then Gaff turned slowly on the balls of his feet and looked at his brother. He said almost gently: "You, George?"

Millar licked his lips and gulped. He had to move his mouth in and out before he could speak.

"Me, Gaff. I was standing by the window when Steve got out of his car down the road. I saw him go into the garage. I knew the car would still be warm. There's been enough killing, Gaff. Too much. So I took the shells out of your gun."

Millar's thumb moved back the hammer on the Detective Special. Gaff's eyes bulged. He stared fascinated at the snub-nosed gun. Then he lunged violently towards it, flailing with the empty Colt. Millar braced himself and stood very still and said dimly, like an old man: "Goodbye, Gaff."

The gun jumped three times in his small neat hand. Smoke curled lazily from its muzzle. A piece of burned log fell over in the fireplace.

Gaff Talley smiled queerly and stooped and stood perfectly still. The gun dropped at his feet. He put his big heavy hands against his stomach, said slowly, thickly: " 'S all right, kid. 'S all right, I guess . . . I guess I . . ."

His voice trailed off and his legs began to twist under him. Steve took three long quick silent steps, and slammed Millar hard on the angle of the jaw. The big man was still falling – as slowly as a tree falls.

Millar spun across the room and crashed against the end wall and a blue-and-white plate fell off the plate molding and broke. The gun sailed from his fingers. Steve dived for it and came up with it. Millar crouched and watched his brother.

Gaff Talley bent his head to the floor and braced his hands and then lay down quietly, on his stomach, like a man who was very tired. He made no sound of any kind.

Daylight showed at the windows, around the red glass-curtains. The piece of broken log smoked against the side of the hearth and the rest of the fire was a heap of soft gray ash with a glow at its heart.

Steve said dully: "You saved my life, George – or at least you saved a lot of shooting. I took the chance because what I wanted was evidence. Step over there to the desk and write it all out and sign it."

Millar said: "Is he dead?"

"He's dead, George. You killed him. Write that too."

Millar said quietly: "It's funny. I wanted to finish Leopardi myself, with my own hands, when he was at the top, when he had the farthest to fall. Just finish him and then take what came. But Gaff was the guy who wanted it done cute. Gaff, the tough mug who never had any education and never dodged a punch in his life, wanted to do it smart and figure angles. Well, maybe that's why he owned property, like that apartment house on Court Street that Jake Stoyanoff managed for him. I don't know how he got to Dolores Chiozza's maid. It doesn't matter much, does it?"

Steve said: "Go and write it. You were the one called Leopardi up and pretended to be the girl, huh?"

Millar said: "Yes, I'll write it all down, Steve. I'll sign it and then you'll let me go – just for an hour. Won't you, Steve? Just an hour's start. That's not much to ask of an old friend, is it, Steve?"

Millar smiled. It was a small, frail, ghostly smile. Steve bent beside the big sprawled man and felt his neck artery. He looked up, said: "Quite dead . . . Yes, you get an hour's start, George – if you write it all out."

Millar walked softly over to a tall oak highboy desk, studded with tarnished brass nails. He opened the flap and sat down and reached for a pen. He unscrewed the top from a bottle of ink and began to write in his neat, clear accountant's handwriting.

Steve Grayce sat down in front of the fire and lit a cigarette and stared at the ashes. He held the gun with his left hand on his knee. Outside the cabin, birds began to sing. Inside there was no sound but the scratching pen.

9

THE SUN WAS well up when Steve left the cabin, locked it up, walked down the steep path and along the narrow gravel road to his car. The garage was empty now. The gray sedan was gone. Smoke from another cabin floated lazily above the pines and oaks half a mile away. He started his car, drove it around a bend, past two old boxcars that had been converted into cabins, then on to a main road with a stripe down the middle and so up the hill to Crestline.

He parked on the main street before the Rim-of-the-World Inn, had a cup of coffee at the counter, then shut himself in a phone booth at the back of the empty lounge. He had the long distance operator get Jumbo Walters' number in Los Angeles, then called the owner of the Club Shalotte.

A voice said silkily: "This is Mr. Walters' residence."

"Steve Grayce. Put him on, if you please."

"One moment, please." A click, another voice, not so smooth and much harder. "Yeah?"

"Steve Grayce. I want to speak to Mr. Walters."

"Sorry. I don't seem to know you. It's a little early, amigo. What's your business?"

"Did he go to Miss Chiozza's place?"

"Oh." A pause. "The shamus. I get it. Hold the line, pal."

Another voice now – lazy, with the faintest color of Irish in it. "You can talk, son. This is Walters."

"I'm Steve Grayce. I'm the man – "

"I know all about that, son. The lady is okay, by the way. I think she's asleep upstairs. Go on."

"I'm at Crestline – top of the Arrowhead grade. Two men murdered Leopardi. One was George Millar, night auditor at the Carlton Hotel. The other his brother, an ex-fighter named Gaff Talley. Talley's dead – shot by his brother. Millar got away – but he left me a full confession signed, detailed, complete."

Walters said slowly: "You're a fast worker, son – unless you're just plain crazy. Better come in here fast. Why did they do it?"

"They had a sister."

Walters repeated quietly: "They had a sister . . . What about this fellow that got away? We don't want some hick sheriff or publicity-hungry county attorney to get ideas – "

Steve broke in quietly: "I don't think you'll have to worry about that, Mr. Walters. I think I know where he's gone."

He ate breakfast at the inn, not because he was hungry, but because he was weak. He got into his car again and started down the long smooth grade from Crestline to San Bernardino, a broad paved boulevard skirting the edge of a sheer drop into the deep valley. There were places where the road went close to the edge, white guard-fences alongside.

Two miles below Crestline was the place. The road made a sharp turn around a shoulder of the mountain. Cars were parked on the gravel off the pavement – several private cars, an official car, and a wrecking car. The white fence was broken through and men stood around the broken place looking down.

Eight hundred feet below, what was left of a gray sedan lay silent and crumpled in the morning sunshine.

BAY CITY BLUES

1 CINDERELLA SUICIDE

IT MUST HAVE been Friday because the fish smell from the Mansion House coffee-shop next door was strong enough to build a garage on. Apart from that it was a nice warm day in spring, the tail of the afternoon, and there hadn't been any business in a week. I had my heels in the groove on my desk and was sunning my ankles in a wedge of sunlight when the phone rang. I took my hat off it and made a yawning sound into the mouthpiece.

A voice said: "I heard that. You oughta be ashamed of yourself, Johnny Dalmas. Ever hear of the Austrian case?"

It was Violets M'Gee, a homicide dick in the sheriff's office and a very nice guy except for one bad habit – passing me cases where I got tossed around and didn't make enough money to buy a secondhand corset.

"No."

"One of those things down at the beach – Bay City. I hear the little burg went sour again the last time they elected themselves a mayor, but the sheriff lives down there and we like to be nice. We ain't tramped on it. They say the gambling boys put up thirty grand campaign money, so now you get a racing form with the bill of fare in the hash houses."

I yawned again.

"I heard that, too," M'Gee barked. "If you ain't interested I'll just bite my other thumbnail and let the whole thing go. The guy's got a little dough to spend, he says."

"What guy?"

"This Matson, the guy that found the stiff."

"What stiff?"

"You don't know nothing about the Austrian case, huh?"

"Didn't I say I didn't?"

"You ain't done nothing but yawn and say 'What.' Okay. We'll just let the poor guy get bumped off and City Homicide can worry about that one, now he's up here in town."

"This Matson? Who's going to bump him off?"

"Well, if he knew that, he wouldn't want to hire no shamus to find out, would he? And him in your own racket until they bust him a while back and now he can't go out hardly, on account of these guys with guns are bothering him."

"Come on over," I said. "My left arm is getting tired."

"I'm on duty."

"I was just going down to the drugstore for a quart of V.O. Scotch."

"That's me you hear knocking on the door," M'Gee said.

He arrived in less than half an hour – a large, pleasant-faced man with silvery hair and a dimpled chin and a tiny little mouth made to kiss babies with. He wore a well-pressed blue suit, polished square-toed shoes, and an elk's tooth on a gold chain hung across his stomach.

He sat down carefully, the way a fat man sits down, and unscrewed the top of the whiskey bottle and sniffed it carefully, to make sure I hadn't refilled a good bottle with ninety-eight-cent hooch, the way they do in the bars. Then he poured himself a big drink and rolled some of it around on his tongue and pawed my office with his eyes.

"No wonder you sit around waiting for jobs," he said. "You gotta have front these days."

"You could spare me a little," I said. "What about this Matson and this Austrian case?"

M'Gee finished his drink and poured another, not so large. He watched me play with a cigarette.

"A monoxide Dutch," he said. "A blonde bim named Austrian, wife of a doctor down at Bay City. A guy that runs around all night keeping movie hams from having pink elephants for breakfast. So the frill went around on her own. The night she croaked herself she was over to Vance Conried's club on the bluff north of there. Know it?"

"Yeah. It used to be a beach club, with a nice private beach down below and the swellest legs in Hollywood in front of the cabañas. She went there to play roulette, huh?"

"Well, if we had any gambling joints in this county," M'Gee said, "I'd say the Club Conried would be one of them and there would be roulette. Say she played roulette. They tell me she had more personal games she played with Conried, but say she played roulette on the side. She loses, which is what roulette is for. That night she loses her shirt and she gets sore and throws a wingding all over the house. Conried gets her into his private room and pages the doc, her husband, through the Physicians' Exchange. So then the doc – "

"Wait a minute," I said. "Don't tell me all this was in evidence – not with the gambling syndicate we would have in this county, if we had a gambling syndicate."

M'Gee looked at me pityingly. "My wife's got a kid brother works on a throw-away paper down there. They didn't have no inquest. Well, the doc steams over to Conried's joint and pokes his wife in the arm with a needle to quiet her down. But he can't take her home on account of he has a babe case in Brentwood Heights. So Vance Conried gets his personal car out and takes her home and meantime the doc has called up his office nurse and asked her to go over to the house and see that his wife is all right. Which is all done, and Conried goes back to his chips and the nurse sees her in bed and leaves, and the maid goes back to bed. This is maybe midnight, or just a little after.

"Well, along about 2 A.M. this Harry Matson happens by. He's running a night-watchman service down there and that night he's out making rounds himself. On the street where Austrian lives he hears a car engine running in a dark garage, and he goes in to investigate. He finds the blonde frail on the floor on her back, in peekaboo pajamas and slippers, with soot from the exhaust all over her hair."

M'Gee paused to sip a little more whiskey and stare around my office again. I watched the last of the sunlight sneak over my windowsill and drop into the dark slit of the alley.

"So what does the chump do?" M'Gee said, wiping his lips on a silk handkerchief. "He decides the bim is dead, which maybe she is, but you can't always be sure in a gas case, what with this new methylene-blue treatment – "

"For God's sake," I said. "What does he do?"

"He don't call no law," M'Gee said sternly. "He kills the car motor and douses his flash and beats it home to where he lives a few blocks away. He pages the doc from there and after a while they're both back at the garage. The doc says she's dead. He sends Matson in at a side door to call the local chief of police personal, at his home. Which Matson does, and after a while the chief buzzes over with a couple of stooges, and a little while after them the body snatcher from the undertaker, whose turn it is to be deputy coroner that week. They cart the stiff away and some lab man takes a blood sample and says it's full of monoxide. The coroner gives a release and the dame is cremated and the case is closed."

"Well, what's the matter with it?" I asked.

M'Gee finished his second drink and thought about having a third. He decided to have a cigar first. I didn't have any cigars and that annoyed him slightly, but he lit one of his own.

"I'm just a cop," he said, blinking at me calmly through the smoke. "I wouldn't know. All I know is, this Matson got bust loose from his license and run out of town and he's scared."

"The hell with it," I said. "The last time I muscled into a small-town setup I got a fractured skull. How do I contact Matson?"

"I give him your number. He'll contact you."

"How well do you know him?"

"Well enough to give him your name," M'Gee said. "Of course, if anything comes up I should look into – "

"Sure," I said. "I'll put it on your desk. Bourbon or rye?"

"Go to hell," M'Gee said. "Scotch."

"What does Matson look like?"

"He's medium heavy, five-seven, one-seventy, gray hair."

He had another short, quick drink and left.

I sat there for an hour and smoked too many cigarettes. It got dark and my throat felt dry. Nobody called me up. I went over and switched the lights on, washed my hands, tucked away a small drink and locked the bottle up. It was time to eat.

I had my hat on and was going through the door when the Green Feather messenger boy came along the hallway looking at numbers. He wanted mine. I signed for a small irregular-shaped parcel done up in the kind of flimsy yellowish paper laundries use. I put the parcel on my desk and cut the string. Inside there was tissue paper and an envelope with a sheet of paper and a flat key in it. The note began abruptly:

A friend in the sheriff's office gave me your name as a man I could trust. I have been a heel and am in a jam and all I want now is to get clear. Please come after dark to 524 Tennyson Arms Apartments, Harvard near Sixth, and use key to enter if I am out. Look out for Pat Reel, the manager, as I don't trust him. Please put the slipper in a safe place and keep it clean. P.S. They call him Violets, I never knew why.

I knew why. It was because he chewed violet-scented breath purifiers. The note was unsigned. It sounded a little jittery to me. I unwound the tissue paper. It contained a green velvet pump, size about 4A lined with white kid. The name *Verschoyle* was stamped in flowing gold script on the white kid insole. On the side a number was written very small in indelible ink – *S465* – where a size number would be, but

I knew it wasn't a size number because Verschoyle, Inc., on Cherokee Street in Hollywood made only custom shoes from individual lasts, and theatrical footwear and riding boots.

I leaned back and lit a cigarette and thought about it for a while. Finally I reached for the phone book and looked up the number of Verschoyle, Inc., and dialed it. The phone rang several times before a chirpy voice said: "Hello? Yes?"

"Verschoyle – in person," I said. "This is Peters, Identification Bureau." I didn't say what identification bureau.

"Oh, Mr. Verschoyle has gone home. We're closed, you know. We close at five-thirty. I'm Mr. Pringle, the book-keeper. Is there anything – "

"Yeah. We got a couple of your shoes in some stolen goods. The mark is S-Four-Six-Five. That mean anything to you?"

"Oh yes, of course. That's a last number. Shall I look it up for you?"

"By all means," I said.

He was back in no time at all. "Oh yes, indeed, that is Mrs. Leland Austrian's number. Seven-thirty-six Altair Street, Bay City. We made all her shoes. Very sad. Yes. About two months ago we made her two pairs of emerald velvet pumps."

"What do you mean, sad?"

"Oh, she's dead, you know. Committed suicide."

"The hell you say. Two pairs of pumps, huh?"

"Oh yes, both the same you know. People often order delicate colors in pairs like that. You know a spot or stain of any kind – and they might be made to match a certain dress – "

"Well, thanks a lot and take care of yourself," I said, and gave the phone back to him.

I picked up the slipper again and looked it over carefully. It hadn't been worn. There was no sign of rubbing on the buffed leather of the thin sole. I wondered what Harry Matson was doing with it. I put it in my office safe and went out to dinner.

2 MURDER ON THE CUFF

THE TENNYSON ARMS was an old-fashioned dump, about eight stories high, faced with dark red brick. It had a wide center court with palm trees and a concrete fountain and some prissy-looking flower beds. Lanterns hung beside the Gothic door and the lobby inside was paved with red plush. It was large and empty except for a bored canary in a gilt cage the size of a barrel. It looked like the sort of apartment house where widows would live on the life insurance – not very young widows. The elevator was the self-operating kind that opens both doors automatically when it stops.

I walked along the narrow maroon carpet of the fifth-floor hallway and didn't see anybody, hear anybody, or smell anybody's cooking. The place was as quiet as a minister's study. Apartment 524 must have opened on the center court because a stained-glass window was right beside its door. I knocked, not loud, and nobody came to the door so I used the flat key and went in, and shut the door behind me.

A mirror glistened in a wall bed across the room. Two windows in the same wall as the entrance door were shut and dark drapes were drawn half across them, but enough light from some apartment across the court drifted in to show the dark bulk of heavy, overstuffed furniture, ten years out of date, and the shine of two brass doorknobs. I went over to the windows and pulled the drapes closed, then used my pocket flash to find my way back to the door. The light switch there set off a big cluster of flame-colored candles in the ceiling fixture. They made the room look like a funeral-chapel annex. I put the light on in a red standing lamp, doused the ceiling light and started to give the place the camera eye.

In the narrow dressing room behind the wall bed there was a built-in bureau with a black brush and comb on it and gray hairs in the comb. There was a can of talcum, a flashlight, a crumpled man's handkerchief, a pad of writing paper, a bank pen and a bottle of ink on a blotter – about what one suitcase would hold in the drawers. The shirts had been bought in a Bay City men's furnishing store. There was a dark gray suit on a hanger and a pair of black brogues on the floor. In the bathroom there was a safety razor, a tube of brushless cream, some blades, three bamboo toothbrushes in a glass, a few other odds and ends. On the porcelain toilet tank there was a book bound in red cloth – Dorsey's *Why We Behave Like Human Beings*. It was marked at page 116 by a rubber band. I had it open and was reading about the Evolution of Earth, Life and Sex when the phone started to ring in the living-room.

I snicked off the bathroom light and padded across the carpet to the davenport. The phone was on a stand at one end. It kept on ringing and a horn tooted outside in the street, as if answering it. When it had rung eight times I shrugged and reached for it.

"Pat? Pat Reel?" the voice said.

I didn't know how Pat Reel would talk. I grunted. The voice at the other end was hard and hoarse at the same time. It sounded like a tough-guy voice.

"Pat?"

"Sure," I said.

There was silence. It hadn't gone over. Then the voice said: "This is Harry Matson. Sorry as all hell I can't make it back tonight. Just one of those things. That bother you much?"

"Sure," I said.

"What's that?"

"Sure."

"Is 'sure' all the words you know, for God's sake?"

"I'm a Greek."

The voice laughed. It seemed pleased with itself.

I said: "What kind of toothbrushes do you use, Harry?"

"Huh?"

This was a startled explosion of breath – not so pleased now.

"Toothbrushes – the little dinguses some people brush their teeth with. What kind do you use?"

"Aw, go to hell."

"Meet you on the step," I said.

The voice got mad now. "Listen, smart monkey! You ain't pulling nothin', see? We got your name, we got your number, and we got a place to put you if you don't keep your nose clean, see? And Harry don't live there any more, ha, ha."

"You picked him off, huh?"

"I'll say we picked him off. What do you think we done, took him to a picture show?"

"That's bad," I said. "The boss won't like that."

I hung up in his face and put the phone down on the table at the end of the davenport and rubbed the back of my neck. I took the door key out of my pocket and polished it on my handkerchief and laid it down carefully on the table. I got up and walked across to one of the windows and pulled the drapes aside far enough to look out into the court. Across its palm-dotted oblong, on the same floor level I was on, a bald-headed man sat in the middle of a room under a hard, bright light, and didn't move a muscle. He didn't look like a spy.

I let the drapes fall together again and settled my hat on my head and went over and put the lamp out. I put my pocket flash down on the floor and palmed my handkerchief on the doorknob and quietly opened the door.

Braced to the door frame by eight hooked fingers, all but one of which were white as wax, there hung what was left of a man.

He had eyes an eighth of an inch deep, china-blue, wide open. They looked at me but they didn't see me. He had coarse gray hair on which the smeared blood looked purple. One of his temples was a pulp, and the tracery of blood from it reached clear to the point of his chin. The one straining finger that wasn't white had been pounded to shreds as far as the second joint. Sharp splinters of bone stuck out of the mangled flesh. Something that might once have been a fingernail looked now like a ragged splinter of glass.

The man wore a brown suit with patch pockets, three of them. They had been torn off and hung at odd angles showing the dark alpaca lining beneath.

He breathed with a faraway unimportant sound, like distant footfalls on dead leaves. His mouth was strained open like a fish's mouth, and blood bubbled from it. Behind him the hallway was empty as a new-dug grave.

Rubber heels squeaked suddenly on the bare space of wood beside the hall runner. The man's straining fingers slipped from the door frame and his body started to wind up on his legs. The legs couldn't hold it. They scissored and the body turned in mid-air, like a swimmer in a wave, and then jumped at me.

I clamped my teeth hard and spread my feet and caught him from behind, after his torso had made a half turn. He weighed enough for two men. I took a step back and nearly went down, took two more and then I had his dragging heels clear of the doorway. I let him down on his side as slowly as I could, crouched over him panting. After a second I straightened, went over to the door and shut and locked it. Then I switched the ceiling light on and started for the telephone.

He died before I reached it. I heard the rattle, the spent sigh, then silence. An outflung hand, the good one, twitched once and the fingers spread out slowly into a loose curve and stayed like that. I went back and felt his carotid artery, digging my fingers in hard. Not a flicker of a pulse. I got a small steel mirror out of my wallet and held it against his open mouth for a long minute. There was no trace of mist on it when I took it away. Harry Matson had come home from his ride.

A key tickled at the outside of the door lock and I moved fast. I was in the bathroom when the door opened, with a gun in my hand and my eyes to the crack of the bathroom door.

This one came in quickly, the way a wise cat goes through a swing door. His eyes flicked up at the ceiling lights, then down at the floor. After that they didn't move at all. All his big body didn't move a muscle. He just stood and looked.

He was a big man in an unbuttoned overcoat, as if he had just come in or was just going out. He had a gray felt hat on the back of a thick creamy-white head. He had the heavy black eyebrows and broad pink face of a boss politician, and his mouth looked as if it usually had the smile – but not now. His face was all bone and his mouth jiggled a half-smoked cigar along his lips with a sucking noise.

He put a bunch of keys back in his pocket and said "God!" very softly, over and over again. Then he took a step forward and went down beside the dead man with a slow, clumsy motion. He put large fingers into the man's neck, took them away again, shook his head, looked slowly around the room. He looked at the bathroom door behind which I was hiding, but nothing changed in his eyes.

"Fresh dead," he said, a little louder. "Beat to a pulp."

He straightened up slowly and rocked on his heels. He didn't like the ceiling light any better than I had. He put the standing lamp on and switched the ceiling light off, rocked on his heels some more. His shadow crawled up the end wall, started across the ceiling, paused and dropped back again. He worked the cigar around in his mouth, dug a match out of his pocket and relit the butt carefully, turning it around and around in the flame. When he blew the match out he put it in his pocket. He did all this without once taking his eyes off the dead man on the floor.

He moved sideways over to the davenport and let himself down on the end of it. The springs squeaked dismally. He reached for the phone without looking at it, eyes still on the dead man.

He had the phone in his hand when it started to ring again. That jarred him. His eyes rolled and his elbows jerked against the sides of his thick overcoated body. Then he grinned very carefully and lifted the phone off the cradle and said in a rich, fruity voice: "Hello. . . . Yeah, this is Pat."

I heard a dry, inarticulate croaking noise on the wire, and I saw Pat Reel's face slowly congest with blood until it was the color of fresh beef liver. His big hand shook the phone savagely.

"So it's Mister Big Chin!" he blared. "Well, listen here, saphead, you know something? Your stiff is right here on my carpet, that's where he is. . . . How did he get here? How the hell would I know? Ask me, you croaked him here, and lemme tell you something. It's costing you plenty, see, plenty. No murder on the cuff in my house. I spot a guy for you and you knock him off in my lap, damn you! I'll take a grand and not a cent less, and you come and get what's here and I mean get it, see?"

There was more croaking on the wire. Pat Reel listened. His eyes got almost sleepy and the purple died out of his face. He said more steadily: "Okay. Okay. I was only kidding. . . . Call me in half an hour downstairs."

He put down the phone and stood up. He didn't look towards the bathroom door, he didn't look anywhere. He began to whistle. Then he scratched his chin and took a step towards the door, stopped to scratch his chin again. He didn't know there was anybody in the apartment, he didn't know there *wasn't* anybody in the apartment – and he didn't have a gun. He took another step towards the door. Big Chin had told him something and the idea was to get out. He took a third step, then he changed his mind.

"Aw hell," he said out loud. "That screwy mug." Then his eyes ranged round the apartment swiftly. "Tryin' to kid me, huh?"

His hand raised to the chain switch. Suddenly he let it fall and knelt beside the dead man again. He moved the body a little, rolling it without effort on the carpet, and put his face down close to squint at the spot where the head had lain. Pat

Reel shook his head in displeasure, got to his feet and put his hands under the dead man's armpits. He threw a glance over his shoulder at the dark bathroom and started to back towards me, dragging the body, grunting, the cigar butt still clamped in his mouth. His creamy-white hair glistened cleanly in the lamplight.

He was still bent over with his big legs spraddled when I stepped out behind him. He may have heard me at the last second but it didn't matter. I had shifted the gun to my left hand and I had a small pocket sap in my right. I laid the sap against the side of his head, just behind his right ear, and I laid it as though I loved it.

Pat Reel collapsed forward across the sprawled body he was dragging, his head down between the dead man's legs. His hat rolled gently off to the side. He didn't move. I stepped past him to the door and left.

3 GENTLEMAN OF THE PRESS

OVER ON WESTERN Avenue I found a phone booth and called the sheriff's office. Violets M'Gee was still there, just ready to go home.

I said: "What was the name of your kid brother-in-law that works on the throw-away paper down at Bay City?"

"Kincaid. They call him Dolly Kincaid. A little feller."

"Where would he be about now?"

"He hangs around the city hall. Thinks he's got a police beat. Why?"

"I saw Matson," I said. "Do you know where he's staying?"

"Naw. He just called me on the phone. What you think of him?"

"I'll do what I can for him. Will you be home tonight?"

"I don't know why not. Why?"

I didn't tell him why. I got into my car and pointed it towards Bay City. I got down there about nine. The police department was half a dozen rooms in a city hall that belonged in the hook-worm-and-Bible belt. I pushed past a knot of smoothies into an open doorway where there was light and a counter. There was a PBX board in the corner and a uniformed man behind it.

I put an arm on the counter and a plainclothes man with his coat off and an under-arm holster looking the size of a wooden leg against his ribs took one eye off his paper and said, "Yeah?" and bonged a spittoon without moving his head more than an inch.

I said: "I'm looking for a fellow named Dolly Kincaid."

"Out to eat. I'm holdin' down his beat," he said in a solid, unemotional voice.

"Thanks. You got a pressroom here?"

"Yeah. Got a toilet, too. Wanta see?"

"Take it easy," I said. "I'm not trying to get fresh with your town."

He bonged the spittoon again. "Pressroom's down the hall. Nobody in it. Dolly's due back, if he don't get drowned in a pop bottle."

A small-boned, delicate-faced young man with a pink complexion and innocent eyes strolled into the room with a half-eaten hamburger sandwich in his left hand. His hat, which looked like a reporter's hat in a movie, was smashed on the back of his small blond head. His shirt collar was unbuttoned at the neck and his tie was pulled to one side. The ends of it hung out over his coat. The only thing the matter with him for a movie newshawk was that he wasn't drunk. He said casually: "Anything stirring, boys?"

The big black-haired plainclothes man bonged his private spittoon again and said: "I hear the mayor changed his underpants, but it's just a rumor."

The small young man smiled mechanically and turned away. The cop said: "This guy wants to see you, Dolly."

Kincaid munched his hamburger and looked at me hopefully. I said: "I'm a friend of Violets. Where can we talk?"

"Let's go into the pressroom," he said. The black-haired cop studied me as we went out. He had a look in his eyes as if he wanted to pick a fight with somebody, and he thought I would do.

We went along the hall towards the back and turned into a room with a long, bare, scarred table, three or four wooden chairs and a lot of newspapers on the floor. There were two telephones on one end of the table, and a flyblown framed picture in the exact center of each wall – Washington, Lincoln, Horace Greeley, and the other one somebody I didn't recognize. Kincaid shut the door and sat on one end of the table and swung his leg and bit into the last of his sandwich.

I said: "I'm John Dalmas, a private dick from L.A. How's to take a ride over to Seven thirty-six Altair Street and tell me what you know about the Austrian case? Maybe you better call M'Gee up and get him to introduce us." I pushed a card at him.

The pink young man slid down off the table very rapidly and stuffed the card into his pocket without looking at it and spoke close to my ear. "Hold it."

Then he walked softly over to the framed picture of Horace Greeley and lifted it off the wall and pressed on a square of paint behind it. The paint gave – it was painted over fabric. Kincaid looked at me and raised his eyebrows. I nodded. He hung the picture back on the wall and came back to me. "Mike," he said under his breath. "Of course I don't know who listens or when, or even whether the damn thing still works."

"Horace Greeley would have loved it," I said.

"Yeah. The beat's pretty dead tonight. I guess I could go out. Al De Spain will cover for me anyway." He was talking loud now.

"The big black-haired cop?"

"Yeah."

"What makes him sore?"

"He's been reduced to acting patrolman. He ain't even working tonight. Just hangs around and he's so tough it would take the whole damn police force to throw him out."

I looked towards the microphone and raised my eyebrows. "That's okay," Kincaid said. "I gotta feed 'em something to chew on."

He went over to a dirty washbowl in the corner and washed his hands on a scrap of lava soap and dried them on his pocket handkerchief. He was just putting the handkerchief away when the door opened. A small, middle-aged, gray-haired man stood in it, looking at us expressionlessly.

Dolly Kincaid said: "Evening, Chief, anything I can do for you?"

The chief looked at me silently and without pleasure. He had sea-green eyes, a tight, stubborn mouth, a ferret-shaped nose, and an unhealthy skin. He didn't look big enough to be a cop. He nodded very slightly and said: "Who's your friend?"

"He's a friend of my brother-in-law. He's a private dick from L.A. Let's see — " Kincaid gripped desperately in his pocket for my card. He didn't even remember my name.

The chief said sharply: "What's that? A private detective? What's your business here?"

"I didn't say I was here on business," I told him.

"Glad to hear it," he said. "Very glad to hear it. Good night."

He opened the door and went out quickly and snapped it shut behind him.

"Chief Anders — one swell guy," Kincaid said loudly. "They don't come any better." He was looking at me like a scared rabbit.

"They never have," I said just as loudly. "In Bay City."

I thought for a moment he was going to faint, but he didn't. We went out in the front of the city hall and got into my car and drove away.

I stopped the car on Altair Street across the way from the residence of Dr. Leland Austrian. The night was windless and there was a little fog under the moon. A faint pleasant smell of brackish water and kelp came up the side of the bluff from the beach. Small riding lights pinpointed the yacht harbor and the shimmering lines of three piers. Quite far out to sea a big-masted fishing barge had lights strung between its masts and from the mastheads down to the bow and stern. Other things than fishing probably happened on it.

Altair Street in that block was a dead-end, cut off by a tall, ornamental iron fence that walled a big estate. The houses were on the inland side of the street only, on eighty- or hundred-foot lots, well spaced. On the seaward side there was a narrow sidewalk and a low wall, beyond which the bluff dropped almost straight down.

Dolly Kincaid was pressed back into the corner of the seat, the red tip of a cigarette glowing at intervals in front of his small blurred face. The Austrian house was dark except for a small light over the embrasure in which the front door was set. It was stucco, with a wall across the front yard, iron gates, the garage outside the wall. A cement walk went from a side door of the garage to a side door of the house. There was a bronze plate set into the wall beside the gates and I knew it would read *Leland M. Austrian, M.D.*

"All right," I said. "Now what was the matter with the Austrian case?"

"Nothing was the matter with it," Kincaid said slowly. "Except you're going to get me in a jam."

"Why?"

"Somebody must have heard you mention Austrian's address over that mike. That's why Chief Anders came in to look at you."

"De Spain might have figured me for a dick – just on looks. He might have tipped him off."

"No. De Spain hates the chief's guts. Hell, he was a detective lieutenant up to a week ago. Anders don't want the Austrian case monkeyed with. He wouldn't let us write it up."

"Swell press you got in Bay City."

"We got a swell climate — and the press is a bunch of stooges."

"Okay," I said. "You got a brother-in-law who's a homicide dick in the sheriff's office. All the L.A. papers but one are strong for the sheriff. This town is where he lives, though, and like a lot of other guys he don't keep his own yard clean. So you're scared, huh?"

Dolly Kincaid threw his cigarette out of the window. I watched it fall in a small red arc and lie faintly pink on the narrow sidewalk. I leaned forward and pressed on the starter button. "Excuse it, please," I said. "I won't bother you any more."

I meshed the gears and the car crawled forward a couple of yards before Kincaid leaned over and jerked the parking brake on. "I'm not yellow," he said sharply. "What do you wanta know?"

I cut the motor again and leaned back with my hands on the wheel. "First off, why did Matson lose his license? He's my client."

"Oh — Matson. They said he tried to put the bite on Dr. Austrian. And they not only took his license, they run him out of town. A couple of guys with guns shoved him into a car one night and roughed him around and told him to skip the burg or else. He reported it down at headquarters and you could have heard them laugh for blocks. But I don't think it was cops."

"Do you know anybody called Big Chin?"

Dolly Kincaid thought. "No. The mayor's driver, a goof called Moss Lorenz, has a chin you could balance a piano on. But I never heard him called Big Chin. He used to work for Vance Conried. Ever hear of Conried?"

"I'm all caught up on that angle," I said. "Then if this Conried wanted to bump somebody off that was bothering him, and especially somebody that had made a little trouble here in Bay City, this Lorenz would be just the guy. Because the mayor would have to cover for him – up to a point, anyway."

Dolly Kincaid said, "Bump who off?" and his voice was suddenly thick and tense.

"They didn't only run Matson out of town," I told him. "They traced him to an apartment house in L.A. and some guy called Big Chin gave him the works. Matson must have been working still on whatever it was he was working on."

"Geez," Dolly Kincaid whispered. "I didn't get a word on that."

"The L.A. cops neither – when I left. Did you know Matson?"

"A little. Not well."

"Would you call him honest?"

"Well, as honest as – well, yeah, I guess he was all right. Geez, bumped off, huh?"

"As honest as a private dick usually is?" I said.

He giggled, from sudden strain and nervousness and shock – very little from amusement. A car turned into the end of the street and stopped by the curb and its lights went out. Nobody got out.

"How about Dr. Austrian," I said. "Where was he when his wife was murdered?"

Dolly Kincaid jumped. "Jeepers, who said she was murdered?" he gasped.

"I think Matson was trying to say so. But he was trying to get paid for not saying it even harder than he was trying to say it. Either way would have got him disliked, but his way got him chilled with a piece of lead pipe. My hunch is that Conried would have that done because he would not like to have anybody make the pay sign at him, except in the way of legitimate graft. But on the other hand it would be a little better for Conried's club to have Dr. Austrian murder his wife than for her to do a Dutch on account of losing all her dough at Conried's roulette tables. Maybe not a lot better, but some better. So I can't figure why Conried would have Matson bumped off for talking about murder. I figure he could have been talking about something else as well."

"Does all this figuring ever get you anywhere?" Dolly Kincaid asked politely.

"No. It's just something to do while I'm patting the cold cream into my face at night. Now about this lab man that made the blood sample. Who was he?"

Kincaid lit another cigarette and looked down the block at the car that had stopped in front of the end house. Its lights had gone on again now and it was moving forward slowly.

"A guy named Greb," he said. "He has a small place in the Physicians and Surgeons Building and works for the doctors."

"Not official, huh?"

"No, but they don't run to lab men down here. And the undertakers all take turns being coroner for a week, so what the hell. The chief handles it the way he likes."

"Why would he want to handle it at all?"

"I guess maybe he might get orders from the mayor, who might get a hint from the gambling boys that Vance Conried works for, or from Vance Conried direct. Conried might not like his bosses to know he was mixed up with a dead frill in a way to make a kickback on the club."

"Right," I said. "That guy down the block don't know where he lives."

The car was still crawling forward along the curb. Its lights were out again, but it was still moving.

"And while I'm still healthy," Dolly Kincaid said, "you might as well know that Doc Austrian's office nurse used to be Matson's wife. She's a redheaded man-eater with no looks but a lot of outside curve."

"I like a well-crowded stocking myself," I said. "Get out of that door and in the back of the car and lie down and make it fast."

"Geez – "

"Do what I say!" I snapped. "Fast!"

The door on the right clicked open and the little man slid out like a wisp of smoke. The door clicked shut. I heard the rear door open and sneaked a look back and saw a dark shape haunched on the floor of the car. I slid over to the right side myself and opened the door again and stepped out on the narrow sidewalk that ran along the rim of the bluff.

The other car was close now. Its lights flared up again and I ducked. The lights swerved so that they swept my car, then swerved back and the car stopped opposite and went quietly dark. It was a small black coupe. Nothing happened for a minute, then its left door opened and a chunky man stepped out and started to stroll over towards my side of the side-paved street. I took my gun from under my arm and tucked it in my belt and buttoned the bottom button of my coat. Then I walked around the rear end of my car to meet him.

He stopped dead when he saw me. His hands hung empty at his sides. There was a cigar in his mouth. "Police," he said briefly. His right hand shaded back slowly towards his right hip. "Nice night ain't it?"

"Swell," I said. "A little foggy, but I like fog. It softens the air up and – "

He cut in on me sharply: "Where's the other guy?"

"Huh?"

"Don't kid me, stranger. I saw a cigarette on the right side of your car."

"That was me," I said. "I didn't know it was against the law to smoke on the right side of a car."

"Oh, a smart monkey. Who are you and what's your business here?" His heavy, greasy face reflected the sifted light in the soft misty air.

"The name's O'Brien," I said. "Just down from San Mateo on a little pleasure trip."

His hand was very close to his hip now. "I'll look at your driver's license," he said. He came close enough to reach it, if we both stretched out our arms to each other.

"I'll look at what gives you the right to look at it," I said.

His right hand made an abrupt movement. Mine flicked the gun out of my belt and pointed it at his stomach. His hand stopped as though it had been frozen in a block of ice.

"Maybe you're a stick-up," I said. "It's still being done with nickel badges."

He stood there, paralyzed, hardly breathing. He said thickly: "Got a license for that heater?"

"Every day in the week," I said. "Let's see your badge and I'll put it away. You don't wear the buzzer where you sit down, do you?"

He stood for another frozen minute. Then he looked along the block as if he hoped another car might arrive. Behind me, in the back of my car, there was a soft, sibilant breathing. I didn't know whether the chunky man heard it or not. His own breathing was heavy enough to iron a shirt with.

"Aw, quit your kiddin'," he snarled out with sudden ferocity. "You're nothin' but a lousy two-bit shamus from L.A."

"I upped the rate," I said. "I get thirty cents now."

"Go to hell. We don't want you nosin' around here, see. This time I'm just tellin' you."

He turned on his heel and walked back to his coupe and put a foot on the running board. His thick neck turned slowly and his greasy skin showed again. "Go to hell," he said, "before we send you there in a basket."

"So long, Greasy-Puss," I said. "Nice to have met you with your pants down."

He slammed into his car, started it with a jerk and lurched it around. He was gone down the block in a flash.

I jumped into mine and was only a block behind him when he made the stop for Arguello Boulevard. He turned right. I turned left. Dolly Kincaid came up and put his chin on the back of the seat beside my shoulder.

"Know who that was?" he croaked. "That was Trigger Weems, the chief's right bower. He might have shot you."

"Fanny Brice might have had a pug nose," I said. "It was that close."

I rode around a few blocks and stopped to let him get in beside me. "Where's your car?" I said.

He took his crumpled reporter's hat off and smacked it on his knee and put it back on again. "Why, down at the city hall. In the police yard."

"Too bad," I said. "You'll have to take the bus to L.A. You ought to spend a night with your sister once in a while. Especially tonight."

4 REDHEADED WOMAN

THE ROAD TWISTED, dipped, soared along the flank of the foothills, a scatter of lights to the northwest and a carpet of them to the south. The three piers seemed remote from this point, thin pencils of light laid out on a pad of black velvet. There was fog in the canyons and a smell of wild growth, but no fog on the high ground between the canyons.

I swung past a small, dim service station, closed up for the night, down into another wide canyon, up past half a mile of expensive wire fence walling in some invisible estate. Then the scattered houses got still more scattered along the hills and the air smelled strongly of the sea. I turned left past a house with a round white turret and drove out between the only electroliers in miles to a big stucco building on a point above the coast highway. Light leaked from draped windows and along an arched stucco colonnade, and shone dimly on a thick cluster of cars parked in diagonal slots around an oval lawn.

This was the Club Conried. I didn't know exactly what I was going to do there, but it seemed to be one of the places where I had to go. Dr. Austrian was still wandering in unknown parts of the town visiting unnamed patients. The Physicians' Exchange said he usually called in about eleven. It was now about ten-fifteen.

I parked in a vacant slot and walked along the arched colonnade. A six-foot-six Negro, in the uniform of a comic-opera South American field marshal, opened one half of a wide grilled door from the inside and said: "Card, please, suh."

I tucked a dollar's worth of folding money into his lilac-colored palm. Enormous ebony knuckles closed over it like a dragline over a bucketful of gravel. His other hand picked a piece of lint off my left shoulder and left a metal tag down behind my show handkerchief in the outside breast pocket of my jacket.

"New floor boss kinda tough," he whispered. "I thank you, suh."

"You mean sucker," I said, and went in past him.

The lobby – they called it a foyer – looked like an MGM set for a night club in the Broadway Melody of 1980. Under the artificial light, it looked as if it had cost about a million dollars and took up enough space for a polo field. The carpet didn't quite tickle my ankles. At the back there was a chromium gangway like a ship's gangway going up to the dining-room entrance, and at the top of this a chubby Italian captain of waiters stood with a set smile and a two-inch satin stripe on his pants and a bunch of gold-plated menus under his arm.

There was a free-arched stairway with banisters like white-enameled sleigh rails. This would go up to the second-floor gambling rooms. The ceiling had stars in it and they twinkled. Beside the bar entrance, which was dark and vaguely purple, like a half-remembered nightmare, there was a huge round mirror set back in a white tunnel with an Egyptian headdress over the top of it. In front of this a lady in green was preening her metallic blond hair. Her evening gown was cut so low at the back that she was wearing a black beauty patch on her lumbar muscle, about an inch below where her pants would have been, if she had been wearing any pants.

A check girl in peach-bloom pajamas with small black dragons on them came over to take my hat and disapprove of my clothes. She had eyes as black and shiny and expressionless as the toes of patent-leather pumps. I gave her a quarter and kept my hat. A cigarette girl with a tray the size of a five-pound candy box came down the gangway. She wore feathers in her hair, enough clothes to hide behind a three-cent stamp, and one of her long, beautiful, naked legs was gilded and the other was silvered. She had the cold, disdainful expression of a dame who is dated so far ahead that she would have to think twice before accepting a knockdown to a maharajah with a basket of rubies under his arm.

I went into the soft purple twilight of the bar. Glasses tinkled gently. There were quiet voices, chords on a piano off in a corner, and a pansy tenor singing "My Little Buckeroo" as confidentially as a bartender mixing a Mickey Finn. Little by little the purple light got to be something I could see by. The bar was fairly full but not crowded. A man laughed off-key and the pianist expressed his annoyance by doing an Eddie Duchin ripple down the keyboard with his thumbnail.

I spotted an empty table and went and sat behind it, against the cushioned wall. The light grew still brighter for me. I could even see the buckeroo singer now. He had wavy red hair that looked hennaed. The girl at the table next to me had red hair too. It was parted in the middle and strained back as if she hated it. She had large, dark, hungry eyes, awkward features and no make-up except a mouth that glared like a neon sign. Her street suit had too-wide shoulders, too-flaring lapels. An orange undersweater snuggled her neck and there was a black-and-orange quill in her Robin Hood hat, crooked on the back of her head. She smiled at me and her teeth were as thin and sharp as a pauper's Christmas. I didn't smile back.

She emptied her glass and rattled it on the tabletop. A waiter in a neat mess jacket slipped out of nowhere and stood in front of me.

"Scotch and soda," the girl snapped. She had a hard, angular voice with a liquor slur in it.

The waiter looked at her, barely moved his chin and looked back at me. I said: "Bacardi and grenadine."

He went away. The girl said: "That'll make you sicky, big boy."

I didn't look at her. "So you don't want to play," she said loosely. I lit a cigarette and blew a ring in the soft purplish air. "Go chase yourself," the girl said. "I could pick up a dozen gorillas like you on every block on Hollywood Boulevard. Hollywood Boulevard, my foot. A lot of bit players out of work and fish-faced blondes trying to shake a hangover out of their teeth."

"Who said anything about Hollywood Boulevard?" I asked.

"You did. Nobody but a guy from Hollywood Boulevard wouldn't talk back to a girl that insulted him civilly."

A man and a girl at a nearby table turned their heads and stared. The man gave me a short, sympathetic grin. "That goes for you, too," the girl said to him.

"You didn't insult me yet," he said.

"Nature beat me to it, handsome."

The waiter came back with the drinks. He gave me mine first. The girl said loudly: "I guess you're not used to waiting on ladies."

The waiter gave her her Scotch and soda. "I beg your pardon, madam," he said in an icy tone.

"Sure. Come around sometime and I'll give you a manicure, if I can borrow a hoe. Boy friend's paying the ticket on this."

The waiter looked at me. I gave him a bill and a lift of my right shoulder. He made change, took his tip, and faded off among the tables.

The girl picked her drink up and came over to my table. She put her elbows on the table and cupped her chin in her hands. "Well, well, a spender," she said. "I didn't know they made them any more. How do you like me?"

"I'm thinking it over," I said. "Keep your voice down or they'll throw you out."

"I doubt it," she said. "As long as I don't break any mirrors. Besides, me and their boss are like that." She held up two fingers close together. "That is we would be if I could meet him." She laughed tinnily, drank a little of her drink. "Where've I seen you around?"

"Most anywhere."

"Where've you seen me?"

"Hundreds of places."

"Yes," she said. "Just like that. A girl can't hang on to her individuality any more."

"She can't get it back out of a bottle," I said.

"The heck you say. I could name you plenty of big names that go to sleep with a bottle in each hand. And have to get pushed in the arm so they won't wake up yelling."

"Yeah?" I said. "Movie soaks, huh?"

"Yeah. I work for a guy that pushes them in the arm — at ten bucks a push. Sometimes twenty-five or fifty."

"Sounds like a nice racket," I said.

"If it lasts. You think it'll last?"

"You can always go to Palm Springs when they run you out of here."

"Who's going to run who out of where?"

"I don't know," I said. "What were we talking about?"

She had red hair. She was not good-looking, but she had curves. And she worked for a man who pushed people in the arm. I licked my lips.

A big dark man came through the entrance door and stood just inside it, waiting for his eyes to get used to the light. Then he started to look the place over without haste. His glance traveled to the table where I was sitting. He leaned his big body forward and started to walk our way.

"Oh, oh," the girl said. "The bouncer. Can you take it?"

I didn't answer. She stroked her colorless cheek with a strong pale hand and leered at me. The man at the piano struck some chords and began to whine about "We Can Still Dream, Can't We?"

The big, dark man stopped with his hand on the chair across the table from me. He pulled his eyes off the girl and smiled at me. She was the one he had been looking at. She was the one he had come down the room to get near. But I was the one he looked at from now on. His hair was smooth and dark and shiny above cold gray eyes and eyebrows that looked as if they were penciled, and a handsome actorish mouth and a nose that had been broken but well set. He spoke liplessly.

"Haven't seen you around for some time — or is my memory bad?"

"I don't know," I said. "What are you trying to remember?"

"Your name, doc."

I said: "Quit trying. We never met." I fished the metal tag out of my breast pocket and tossed it down. "Here's my ticket in from the drum major on the wicket." I got a card out of my wallet and tossed that down. "Here's my name, age, height, weight, scars if any, and how many times convicted. And my business is to see Conried."

He ignored the tag and read the card twice, turned it over and looked at the back, then looked at the front again, hooked an arm over the chairback and gave me a mealy smile. He didn't look at the girl then or ever. He racked the card edge across the tabletop and made a faint squeak, like a very young mouse. The girl stared at the ceiling and pretended to yawn.

He said dryly: "So you're one of those guys. So sorry. Mr. Conried had to go north on a little business trip. Caught an early plane."

The girl said: "That must have been his stand-in I saw this afternoon at Sunset and Vine, in a gray Cord sedan."

He didn't look at her. He smiled faintly. "Mr. Conried doesn't have a gray Cord sedan."

The girl said: "Don't let him kid you. I bet he's upstairs crooking a roulette wheel right this minute."

The dark man didn't look at her. His not looking at her was more emphatic than if he had slapped her face. I saw her whiten a little, very slowly, and stay white.

I said: "He's not here, he's not here. Thanks for listening. Maybe some other time."

"Oh sure. But we don't use any private eyes in here. So sorry."

"Say that 'so sorry' again and I'll scream. So help me," the red-haired girl said.

The black-haired man put my card in the casual outer pocket of his dinner jacket. He pushed his chair back and stood up.

"You know how it is," he said. "So – "

The girl cackled and threw her drink in his face.

The dark man stepped back jarringly and swept a crisp white handkerchief from his pocket. He mopped his face swiftly, shaking his head. When he lowered the handkerchief there was a big soaked spot on his shirt, limp above the black pearl stud. His collar was a ruin.

"So sorry," the girl said. "Thought you were a spittoon."

He dropped his hand and his teeth glinted edgily. "Get her out," he purred. "Get her out fast."

He turned and walked off very quickly among the tables, holding his handkerchief against his mouth. Two waiters in mess jackets came up close and stood looking at us. Everybody in the place was looking at us.

"Round one," the girl said. "A little slow. Both fighters were cautious."

"I'd hate to be with you when you'd take a chance," I said.

Her head jerked. In that queer purple light the extreme whiteness of her face seemed to leap at me. Even her rouged lips had a drained look. Her hand went up to her mouth, stiff and clawlike. She coughed dryly like a consumptive and reached for my glass. She gulped the bacardi and grenadine down in bubbling swallows. Then she began to shake. She reached for her bag and pushed it over the edge of the table to the floor. It fell open and some stuff came out. A gilt-metal cigarette case slid under my chair. I had to get up and move the chair to reach it. One of the waiters was behind me.

"Can I help?" he asked suavely.

I was stooped over when the glass the girl had drunk from rolled over the edge of the table and hit the floor beside my hand. I picked up the cigarette case, looked at it casually, and saw that a hand-tinted photo of a big-boned, dark man decorated the front of it. I put it back in her bag and took hold of the girl's arm and the waiter who had spoken to me slid around and took her other arm. She looked at us blankly, moving her head from side to side as if trying to limber up a stiff neck.

"Mama's about to pass out," she croaked, and we started down the room with her. She put her feet out crazily, threw her weight from one side to the other as if trying to upset us. The waiter swore steadily to himself in a monotonous whisper. We came out of the purple light into the bright lobby.

"Ladies' Room," the waiter grunted, and pointed with his chin at a door which looked like the side entrance to the Taj Mahal. "There's a colored heavyweight in there can handle anything."

"Nuts to the Ladies' Room," the girl said nastily. "And leggo of my arm, steward. Boy friend's all the transportation I need."

"He's not your boy friend, madam. He don't even know you."

"Beat it, wop. You're either too polite or not polite enough. Beat it before I lose my culture and bong you."

"Okay," I told him. "I'll set her out to cool. She come in alone?"

"I couldn't think of any reason why not," he said, and stepped away. The captain of waiters came halfway down his gangplank and stood glowering, and the vision at the checkroom looked as bored as the referee of a four-round opener.

I pushed my new friend out into the cold, misty air, walked her along the colonnade and felt her body come controlled and steady on my arm.

"You're a nice guy," she said dully. "I played that about as smooth as a handful of tacks. You're a nice guy, mister. I didn't think I'd ever get out of there alive."

"Why?"

"I had a wrong idea about making some money. Forget it. Let it lay with all the other wrong ideas I've been having all my life. Do I get a ride? I came in a cab."

"Sure. Do I get told your name?"

"Helen Matson," she said.

I didn't get any kick out of that now. I had guessed it long ago.

She still leaned on me a little as we walked down the strip of paved road past the parked cars. When we came to mine I unlocked it and held the door for her and she climbed in and fell back in the corner with her head on the cushion.

I shut the door and then I opened it again and said: "Would you tell me something else? Who's that mug on the cigarette case you carry? Seems to me I've seen him somewhere."

She opened her eyes. "An old sweet," she said, "that wore out. He – " Her eyes widened and her mouth snapped open and I barely heard the faint rustle behind me as something hard dug into my back and a muffled voice said: "Hold it, buddy. This is a heist."

Then a naval gun went off in my ear and my head was a large pink firework exploding into the vault of the sky and scattering and falling slow and pale, and then dark, into the waves. Blackness ate me up.

5 MY DEAD NEIGHBOR

I SMELLED OF gin. Not just casually, as if I had taken a few drinks, but as if the Pacific Ocean was pure gin and I had been swimming in it with my clothes on. The gin was on my hair, on my eyebrows, on my face and under my chin on my shirt. My coat was off and I was lying flat on somebody's carpet and I was looking up at a framed photograph on the end of a plaster mantel. The frame was some kind of grained wood and the photo was intended to be arty, with a highlight on a long, thin, unhappy face, but all the highlight did was make the face look just that – long and thin and unhappy under some kind of flat, pale hair that might have been paint on a dried skull. There was writing across the corner of the photo behind the glass, but I couldn't read that.

I reached up and pressed the side of my head and I could feel a shoot of pain clear to the soles of my feet. I groaned and made a grunt out of the groan, from professional pride, and then I rolled over slowly and carefully and looked at the foot of a pulled-down twin wall bed. The other twin was still up in the wall with a flourish of design painted on the enameled wood. When I rolled, a gin bottle rolled off my chest and hit the floor. It was water-white, empty. I thought there couldn't have been that much gin in just one bottle.

I got my knees under me and stayed on all fours for a while, sniffing like a dog who can't finish his dinner and yet hates to leave it. I moved my head around on my neck. It hurt.

I moved it some more and it still hurt, so I got up on my feet and discovered that I didn't have any shoes on.

It seemed like a nice apartment, not too cheap and not too expensive – the usual furniture, the usual drum lamp, the usual durable carpet. On the bed, which was down, a girl was lying, clothed in a pair of tan silk stockings. There were deep scratches that had bled and there was a thick bath towel across her middle, wadded up almost into a roll. Her eyes were open. The red hair that had been parted and strained back as if she hated it was still that way. But she didn't hate it any more.

She was dead.

Above and inside her left breast there was a scorched place the size of the palm of a man's hand, and in the middle of that there was a thimbleful of blazed blood. Blood had run down her side, but it had dried now.

I saw clothes on a davenport, mostly hers, but including my coat. There were shoes on the floor – mine and hers. I went over, stepping on the balls of my feet as though on very thin ice, and picked up my coat and felt through the pockets. They still held everything I could remember having put in them. The holster that was still strapped around my body was empty, of course. I put my shoes and coat on, pushed the empty holster around under my arm and went over to the bed and lifted the heavy bath towel. A gun fell out of it – my gun. I wiped some blood off the barrel, sniffed the muzzle for no reason at all, and quietly put the gun back under my arm.

Heavy feet came along the corridor outside the apartment door and stopped. There was a mutter of voices, then some-body knocked, a quick, hard, impatient rapping. I looked at the door and wondered how long it would be before they tried it, and if the spring lock would be set so they could walk in, and if it wasn't set how long it would take to get the man-ager up with a passkey if he wasn't there already. I was still wondering when a hand tried the door. It was locked.

That was very funny. I almost laughed out loud.

I stepped over to another door and glanced into a bathroom. There were two wash rugs on the floor, a bath mat folded neatly over the edge of the tub, a pebbled glass window above it. I eased the bathroom door shut quietly and stood on the edge of the bathtub and pushed up the lower sash of the bathroom window. I put my head out and looked down about six floors to the darkness of a side street lined with trees. To do this I had to look out through a slot formed by two short blank walls, hardly more than an air shaft. The windows were in pairs, all in the same end wall opposite the open end of the slot. I leaned farther out and decided I could make the next window if I tried. I wondered if it was unlocked, and if it would do me any good, and if I'd have time before they could get the door open.

Behind me, beyond the closed bathroom door, the pounding was a little louder and harder and a voice was growling out: "Open it up or we'll bust it in."

That didn't mean anything. That was just routine cop stuff. They wouldn't break it down because they could get a key, and kicking that kind of door in without a fire axe is a lot of work and tough on the feet.

I shut the lower half of the window and pulled down the upper half and took a towel off the rack. Then I opened the bathroom door again and my eyes were looking straight at the face in the photo frame on the mantel. I had to read the inscription on that photo before I left. I went over and scanned it while the pounding on the door went on angrily. The inscription said – *With all my love – Leland*.

That made a sap out of Dr. Austrian, without anything else. I grabbed the photo and went back into the bathroom and shut the door again. Then I shoved the photo under the dirty towels and linen in the cupboard under the bathroom closet. It would take them a little while to find it, if they were good cops. If we were in Bay City, they probably wouldn't find it at all. I didn't know of any reason why we should be in Bay City, except that Helen Matson would very likely live there and the air outside the bathroom window seemed to be beach air.

I squeezed out through the upper half of the window with the towel in my hand and swung my body across to the next window, holding on to the sash of the one I had left. I could reach just far enough to push the next window up, if it was unlocked. It wasn't unlocked. I swung my foot and kicked the glass in just over the catch. It made a noise that ought to have been heard a mile. The distant pounding went on monotonously.

I wrapped the towel around my left hand and stretched my arms for all they had in them and shoved my hand in through the broken place and turned the window catch. Then I swung over to the other sill and reached back to push up the window I had come out of. They could have the fingerprints. I didn't expect to be able to prove I hadn't been in Helen Matson's apartment. All I wanted was a chance to prove how I had got there.

I looked down at the street. A man was getting into a car. He didn't even look up at me. No light had gone on in the apartment I was breaking into. I got the window down and climbed in. There was a lot of broken glass in the bathtub. I got down to the floor and switched the light on and picked the glass out of the bathtub and wrapped it in my towel and hid it. I used somebody else's towel to wipe off the sill and the edge of the bathtub where I'd stood. Then I took my gun out and opened the bathroom door.

This was a larger apartment. The room I was looking at had twin beds with pink dust covers. They were made up nicely and they were empty. Beyond the bedroom there was a living-room. All the windows were shut and the place had a close, dusty smell. I lit a floor lamp, then I ran a finger along the arm of a chair and looked at dust on it. There was an armchair radio, a book rack built like a hod, a big bookcase full of novels with the jackets still on them, a dark wood highboy with a siphon and a decanter of liquor on it, and four striped glasses upside down. I sniffed the liquor, which was Scotch, and used a little of it. It made my head feel worse but it made me feel better.

I left the light on and went back to the bedroom and poked into bureau and closets. There were male clothes in one closet, tailor-made, and the name written on the label by the tailor was George Talbot. George's clothes looked a little small for me. I tried the bureau and found a pair of pajamas I thought would do. The closet gave me a bathrobe and slippers. I stripped to the skin.

When I came out of the shower I smelled only faintly of gin. There was no noise or pounding going on anywhere now, so I knew they were in Helen Matson's apartment with their little pieces of chalk and string. I put Mr. Talbot's pajamas and slippers and bathrobe on, used some of Mr. Talbot's tonic on my hair and his brush and comb to tidy up. I hoped Mr. and Mrs. Talbot were having a good time wherever they were and that they would not have to hurry home.

I went back to the living-room, used some more Talbot Scotch and lit one of his cigarettes. Then I unlocked the entrance door. A man coughed close by in the hall. I opened the door and leaned against the jamb and looked out. A uniformed man was leaning against the opposite wall – a small-ish, blond, sharp-eyed man. His blue trousers were edged like a knife and he looked neat, clean, competent and nosey.

I yawned and said: "What goes on, officer?"

He stared at me with sharp reddish-brown eyes flecked with gold, a color you seldom see with blond hair. "A little trouble next door to you. Hear anything?" His voice was mildly sarcastic.

"The carrot-top?" I said. "Haw, haw. Just the usual big-game hunt. Drink?"

The cop went on with his careful stare. Then he called down the hallway: "Hey, Al!"

A man stepped out of an open door. He was about six feet, weighed around two hundred, and he had coarse black hair and deep-set expressionless eyes. It was Al De Spain whom I had met that evening at Bay City headquarters.

He came down the hall without haste. The uniformed cop said: "Here's the guy lives next door."

De Spain came close to me and looked into my eyes. His own held no more expression than pieces of black slate. He spoke almost softly.

"Name?"

"George Talbot," I said. I didn't quite squeak.

"Hear any noises? I mean, before we got here?"

"Oh, a brawl, I guess. Around midnight. That's nothing new in there." I jerked a thumb towards the dead girl's apartment.

"That so? Acquainted with the dame?"

"No. Doubt if I'd want to know her."

"You won't have to," De Spain said. "She's croaked."

He put a big, hard hand against my chest and pushed me back very gently through the door into the apartment. He kept his hand against my chest and his eyes flicked down sharply to the side pockets of the bathrobe, then back to my face again. When he had me eight feet from the door he said over his shoulder: "Come in and shut the door, Shorty."

Shorty came and shut the door, small, sharp eyes gleaming. "Quite a gag," De Spain said, very casually. "Put a gun on him, Shorty."

Shorty flicked his black belt holster open and had a police gun in his hand like lightning. He licked his lips. "Oh boy," he said softly. "Oh boy." He snapped his handcuff holder open and half drew the cuffs out. "How'd you know, Al?"

"Know what?" De Spain kept his eyes on my eyes. He spoke to me gently. "What was you goin' to do – go down and buy a paper?"

"Yah," Shorty said. "He's the killer, sure. He come in through the bathroom window and put on clothes belonging

839

to the guy that lives here. The folks are away. Look at the dust. No windows open. Dead air in the place."

De Spain said softly: "Shorty's a scientific cop. Don't let him get you down. He's got to be wrong some day."

I said: "What for is he in uniform, if he's so hot?"

Shorty reddened. De Spain said: "Find his clothes, Shorty. And his gun. And make it fast. This is our pinch, if we make it fast."

"You ain't detailed on the case even," Shorty said.

"What can I lose?"

"*I* can lose this here uniform."

"Take a chance, boy. That lug Reed next door couldn't catch a moth in a shoe box."

Shorty scuttled into the bedroom. De Spain and I stood motionless, except that he took his hand off my chest and dropped it to his side. "Don't tell me," he drawled. "Just let me guess."

We heard Shorty fussing around opening doors. Then we heard a yelp like a terrier's yelp when he smells a rathole. Shorty came back into the room with my gun in his right hand and my wallet in his left. He held the gun by the fore sight, with a handkerchief. "The gat's been fired," he said. "And this guy ain't called Talbot."

De Spain didn't turn his head or change expression. He smiled at me thinly, moving only the extreme corners of his wide, rather brutal mouth.

"You don't say," he said. "You don't say." He pushed me away from him with a hand as hard as a piece of tool steel. "Get dressed, sweetheart – and don't fuss with your necktie. Places want us to go to them."

6 I GET MY GUN BACK

WE WENT OUT of the apartment and along the hall. Light still came from the open door of Helen Matson's apartment. Two men with a basket stood outside it smoking. There was a sound of wrangling voices inside the dead woman's place.

We went around a bend of the hall and started down the stairs, floor after floor, until we came out in the lobby. Half a dozen people stood around bug-eyed – three women in bathrobes, a bald-headed man with a green eyeshade, like a city editor, two more who hung back in the shadows. Another uniformed man walked up and down just inside the front door, whistling under his breath. We went out past him. He looked completely uninterested. A knot of people clustered on the sidewalk outside.

De Spain said: "This is a big night in our little town."

We walked along to a black sedan that had no police insignia on it and De Spain slid in behind the wheel and motioned me to get in beside him. Shorty got in the back. He'd had his gun back in his holster long since, but he left the flap unbuttoned, and kept his hand close to it.

De Spain put the car into motion with a jerk that threw me back against the cushions. We made the nearest corner on two wheels, going east. A big black car with twin red spot-lights was only half a block away and coming fast as we made the turn.

De Spain spat out of the window and drawled: "That's the chief. He'll be late for his own funeral. Boy, did we skin his nose on this one."

Shorty said disgustedly from the back seat: "Yeah – for a thirty-day lay-off."

De Spain said: "Keep that mush of yours in low and you might get back on Homicide."

"I'd rather wear buttons and eat," Shorty said.

De Spain drove the car hard for ten blocks, then slowed a little. Shorty said: "This ain't the way to headquarters."

De Spain said: "Don't be an ass."

He let the car slow to a crawl, turned it left into a quiet, dark, residential street lined with coniferous trees and small exact houses set back from small exact lawns. He braked the car gently, coasted it over to the curb and switched the motor off. Then he threw an arm over the back of the seat and turned to look at the small "sharp-eyed" uniformed man.

"You think this guy plugged her, Shorty?"

"His gun went off."

"Get that big flash outa the pocket and look at the back of his head."

Shorty snorted, fussed around in the back of the car, and then metal clicked and the blinding white beam of a large bell-topped flashlight sprayed over my head. I heard the little man's close breathing. He reached out and pressed the sore place on the back of my head. I yelped. The light went off and the blackness of the dark street jumped at us again.

Shorty said: "I guess he was sapped."

De Spain said without emotion: "So was the girl. It didn't show much but it's there. She was sapped so she could have her clothes pulled off and be clawed up before she was shot, so the scratches would bleed and look like you know what. Then she was shot with a bath towel around the gun. Nobody heard the shot. Who reported it, Shorty?"

"How the hell would I know? A guy called up two-three minutes before you came into the Hall, while Reed was still looking for a cameraman. A guy with a thick voice, the operator said."

"Okay. If you done it, Shorty, how would you get out of there?"

"I'd walk out," Shorty said. "Why not? Hey," he barked at me, "why didn't you?"

I said: "I have to have my little secrets."

De Spain said tonelessly: "You wouldn't climb across no air shaft, would you, Shorty? You wouldn't crash into the next apartment and pretend to be the guy that lived there, would you? And you wouldn't call no law and tell them to take it up there in high and they'd catch the killer, would you?"

"Hell," Shorty said, "this guy call up? No, I wouldn't do any of them things."

"Neither did the killer," De Spain said, "except the last one. He called up."

"Them sex fiends do funny things," Shorty said. "This guy could have had help and the other guy tried to put him in the middle after knocking him out with a sap."

De Spain laughed harshly. "Hello, sex fiend," he said, and poked me in the ribs with a finger as hard as a gun barrel. "Look at us saps, just sitting here and throwing our jobs away – that is, the one of us that has a job – and arguing it out when you, the guy that knows all the answers, ain't told us a damn thing. We don't even know who the dame was."

"A redhead I picked up in the bar of the Club Conried," I said. "No, she picked me up."

"No name or anything?"

"No. She was tight. I helped her out into the air and she asked me to take her away from there and while I was putting her into my car somebody sapped me. I came to on the floor of the apartment and the girl was dead."

De Spain said: "What was you doing in the bar of the Club Conried?"

"Getting my hair cut," I said. "What do you do in a bar? This redhead was tight and seemed scared about something and she threw a drink in the floor boss's face. I felt a little sorry for her."

"I always feel sorry for a redhead, too," De Spain said. "This guy that sapped you must have been an elephant, if he carried you up to that apartment."

I said: "Have you ever been sapped?"

"No," De Spain said. "Have you, Shorty?"

Shorty said he had never been sapped either. He said it unpleasantly.

"All right," I said. "It's like an alcohol drunk. I probably came to in the car and the fellow would have a gun and that

843

would keep me quiet. He would walk me up to the apartment with the girl. The girl may have known him. And when he had me up there he would sap me again and I wouldn't remember anything that happened in between the two sappings."

"I've heard of it," De Spain said. "But I never believed it."

"Well, it's true," I said. "It's got to be true. Because I don't remember and the guy couldn't have carried me up there without help."

"I could," De Spain said. "I've carried heavier guys than you."

"All right," I said. "He carried me up. Now what do we do?"

Shorty said: "I don't get why he went to all that trouble."

"Sapping a guy ain't trouble," De Spain said. "Pass over that heater and wallet."

Shorty hesitated, then passed them over. De Spain smelled the gun and dropped it carelessly into his side pocket, the one next to me. He flipped the wallet open and held it down under the dashlight and then put it away. He started the car, turned it in the middle of the block, and shot back up Arguello Boulevard, turned east on that and pulled up in front of a liquor store with a red neon sign. The place was wide open, even at that hour of the night.

De Spain said over his shoulder: "Run inside and phone the desk, Shorty. Tell the sarge we got a hot lead and we're on our way to pick up a suspect in the Brayton Avenue killing. Tell him to tell the chief his shirt is out."

Shorty got out of the car, slammed the rear door, started to say something, then walked fast across the sidewalk into the store.

De Spain jerked the car into motion and hit forty in the first block. He laughed deep down in his chest. He made it fifty in the next block and then began to turn in and out of streets and finally he pulled to a stop again under a pepper tree outside a schoolhouse.

I got the gun when he reached forward for the parking brake. He laughed dryly and spat out of the open window.

"Okay," he said. "That's why I put it there. I talked to Violets M'Gee. That kid reporter called me up from L.A. They've found Matson. They're sweating some apartment house guy right now."

I slid away from him over to my corner of the car and held the gun loosely between my knees. "We're outside the limits of Bay City, copper," I told him. "What did M'Gee say?"

"He said he gave you a lead to Matson, but he didn't know whether you had contacted him or not. This apartment house guy – I didn't hear his name – was trying to dump a stiff in the alley when a couple of prowlies jumped him. M'Gee said if you had contacted Matson and heard his story you would be down here getting in a jam, and would likely wake up sapped beside some stiff."

"I didn't contact Matson," I said.

I could feel De Spain staring at me under his dark craggy brows. "But you're down here in a jam," he said.

I got a cigarette out of my pocket with my left hand and lit it with the dash lighter. I kept my right hand on the gun. I said: "I got the idea you were on the way out down here. That you weren't even detailed on this killing. Now you've taken a prisoner across the city line. What does that make you?"

"A bucket of mud – unless I deliver something good."

"That's what I am," I said. "I guess we ought to team up and break these three killings."

"Three?"

"Yeah. Helen Matson, Harry Matson and Doc Austrian's wife. They all go together."

"I ditched Shorty," De Spain said quietly, "because he's a little guy and the chief likes little guys and Shorty can put the blame on me. Where do we start?"

"We might start by finding a man named Greb who runs a laboratory in the Physicians and Surgeons Building. I think he turned in a phony report on the Austrian death. Suppose they put out an alarm for you?"

"They use the L.A. air. They won't use that to pick up one of their own cops."

He leaned forward and started the car again.

"You might give me my wallet," I said. "So I can put this gun away."

He laughed harshly and gave it to me.

7 BIG CHIN

THE LAB MAN lived on Ninth Street, on the wrong side of town. The house was a shapeless frame bungalow. A large dusty hydrangea bush and some small undernourished plants along the path looked like the work of a man who had spent his life trying to make something out of nothing.

De Spain doused the lights as we glided up front and said: "Whistle, if you need help. If any cops should crowd us, skin over to Tenth and I'll circle the block and pick you up. I don't think they will, though. All they're thinking of tonight is that dame on Brayton Avenue."

I looked up and down the quiet block, walked across the street in foggy moonlight and up the walk to the house. The front door was set at right angles to the street in a front projection that looked like a room which had been added as an afterthought to the rest of the house. I pushed a bell and heard it ring somewhere in the back. No answer. I rang it twice more and tried the front door. It was locked.

I went down off the little porch and around the north side of the house towards a small garage on the back lot. Its doors were shut and locked with a padlock you could break with a strong breath. I bent over and shot my pocket flash under the loose doors. The wheels of a car showed. I went back to the front door of the house and knocked this time – plenty loud.

The window in the front room creaked and came down slowly from the top, about halfway. There was a shade pulled down behind the window and darkness behind the shade. A thick, hoarse voice said: "Yeah?"

"Mr. Greb?"

"Yeah."

"I'd like to speak to you – on important business."

"I gotta get my sleep, mister. Come back tomorrow."

The voice didn't sound like the voice of a laboratory technician. It sounded like a voice I had heard over the telephone once, a long time ago, early in the evening at the Tennyson Arms Apartments.

I said: "Well, I'll come to your office then, Mr. Greb. What's the address again?"

The voice didn't speak for a moment. Then it said: "Aw, go on, beat it before I come out there and paste you one."

"That's no way to get business, Mr. Greb," I said. "Are you sure you couldn't give me just a few moments, now you're up?"

"Pipe down. You'll wake the wife. She's sick. If I gotta come out there – "

"Good night, Mr. Greb," I said.

I went back down the walk in the soft, foggy moonlight. When I got across to the far side of the dark parked car I said: "It's a two-man job. Some tough guy is in there. I think it's the man I heard called Big Chin over the phone in L.A."

"Geez. The guy that killed Matson, huh?" De Spain came over to my side of the car and stuck his head out and spit clear over a fireplug that must have been eight feet away. I didn't say anything.

De Spain said: "If this guy you call Big Chin is Moss Lorenz, I'll know him. We might get in. Or maybe we walk ourselves into some hot lead."

"Just like the coppers do on the radio," I said.

"You scared?"

"Me?" I said. "Sure I'm scared. The car's in the garage, so either he's got Greb in there and is trying to make up his mind what to do with him – "

"If it's Moss Lorenz, he don't have a mind," De Spain growled. "That guy is screwy except in two places – behind a gun and behind the wheel of a car."

"And behind a piece of lead pipe," I said. "What I was saying was, Greb might be out without his car and this Big Chin – "

De Spain bent over to look at the clock on the dash. "My guess would be he's skipped. He'd be home by now. He's got a tip to scram out of some trouble."

"Will you go in there or won't you?" I snapped. "Who would tip him?"

"Whoever fixed him in the first place, if he was fixed." De Spain clicked the door open and slid out of the car, stood looking over it across the street. He opened his coat and loosened the gun in his shoulder clip. "Maybe I could kid him," he said. "Keep your hands showing and empty. It's our best chance."

We went back across the street and up the walk, up on the porch. De Spain leaned on the bell.

The voice came growling at us again from the half-open window, behind the frayed dark green shade.

"Yeah?"

"Hello, Moss," De Spain said.

"Huh?"

"This is Al De Spain, Moss. I'm in on the play."

Silence – a long, murderous silence. Then the thick, hoarse voice said: "Who's that with you?"

"A pal from L.A. He's okay."

More silence, then, "What's the angle?"

"You alone in there?"

"Except for a dame. She can't hear you."

"Where's Greb?"

"Yeah — where is he? What's the angle, copper? Snap it up!"

De Spain spoke as calmly as though he had been at home in an armchair, beside the radio. "We're workin' for the same guy, Moss."

"Haw, haw," Big Chin said.

"Matson's been found dead in L.A., and those city dicks have already connected him with the Austrian dame. We gotta step fast. The big shot's up north alibi-ing himself, but what does that do for us?"

The voice said, "Aw, baloney," but there was a note of doubt in it.

"It looks like a stink," De Spain said. "Come on, open up. You can see we don't have anything to hold on you."

"By the time I got around to the door you would have," Big Chin said.

"You ain't that yellow," De Spain sneered.

The shade rustled at the window as if a hand had let go of it and the sash moved up into place. My hand started up.

De Spain growled: "Don't be a sap. This guy is our case. We want him all in one piece."

Faint steps sounded inside the house. A lock turned in the front door and it opened and a figure stood there, shadowed, a big Colt in his hand. Big Chin was a good name for him. His big, broad jaw stuck out from his face like a cowcatcher. He was a bigger man than De Spain — a good deal bigger.

"Snap it up," he said, and started to move back.

De Spain, his hands hanging loose and empty, palms turned out, took a quiet step forward on his left foot and kicked Big Chin in the groin — just like that — without the slightest hesitation, and against a gun.

Big Chin was still fighting — inside himself — when we got our guns out. His right hand was fighting to press the trigger and hold the gun up. His sense of pain was fighting down everything else but the desire to double up and yell. That

849

internal struggle of his wasted a split second and he had neither shot nor yelled when we slammed him. De Spain hit him
on the head and I hit him on the right wrist. I wanted to hit
his chin – it fascinated me – but his wrist was nearest the gun.
The gun dropped and Big Chin dropped, almost as suddenly,
then plunged forward against us. We caught and held him and
his breath blew hot and rank in our faces, then his knees went
to pieces and we fell into the hallway on top of him.

De Spain grunted and struggled to his feet and shut the
door. Then he rolled the big, groaning, half-conscious man
over and dragged his hands behind him and snapped cuffs on
his wrists.

We went down the hall. There was a dim light in the room
to the left, from a small table lamp with a newspaper over it.
De Spain lifted the paper off and we looked at the woman on
the bed. At least he hadn't murdered her. She lay in sleazy
pajamas with her eyes wide open and staring and half mad
with fear. Mouth, wrists, ankles and knees were taped and the
ends of thick wads of cotton stuck out of her ears. A vague
bubbling sound came from behind the slab of two-inch
adhesive that plastered her mouth shut. De Spain bent the
lampshade a little. Her face was mottled. She had bleached
hair, dark at the roots, and a thin, scraped look about the
bones of her face.

De Spain said: "I'm a police officer. Are you Mrs. Greb?"

The woman jerked and stared at him agonizingly. I pulled
the cotton out of her ears and said: "Try again."

"Are you Mrs. Greb?"

She nodded.

De Spain took hold of the tape at the side of her mouth.
Her eyes winced and he jerked it hard and capped a hand
down over her mouth at once. He stood there, bending over,
the tape in his left hand – a big, dark, dead-pan copper who
didn't seem to have any more nerves than a cement mixer.

"Promise not to scream?" he said.

The woman forced a nod and he took his hand away. "Where's Greb?" he asked.

He pulled the rest of the tape off her.

She swallowed and took hold of her forehead with her red-nailed hand and shook her head. "I don't know. He hasn't been home."

"What talk was there when the gorilla came in?"

"There wasn't any," she said dully. "The bell rang and I opened the door and he walked in and grabbed me. Then the big brute tied me up and asked me where my husband was and I said I didn't know and he slapped my face a few times, but after a while he seemed to believe me. He asked me why my husband didn't have the car and I said he always walked to work and never took the car. Then he just sat in the corner and didn't move or speak. He didn't even smoke."

"Did he use the telephone?" De Spain asked.

"No."

"You ever seen him before?"

"No."

"Get dressed," De Spain said. "You gotta find some friends you can go to for the rest of the night."

She stared at him and sat up slowly on the bed and rumpled her hair. Then her mouth opened and De Spain clapped his hand over it again, hard.

"Hold it," he said sharply. "Nothing's happened to him that we know of. But I guess you wouldn't be too damn surprised if it did."

The woman pushed his hand away and stood up off the bed and walked around it to a bureau and took out a pint of whiskey. She unscrewed the top and drank from the bottle. "Yeah," she said in a strong, coarse voice. "What would you do, if you had to soap a bunch of doctors for every nickel you made and there was damn few nickels to be made at that?" She took another drink.

De Spain said: "I might switch blood samples."

The woman stared at him blankly. He looked at me and shrugged. "Maybe it's happy powder," he said. "Maybe he peddles a little of that. It must be damn little, to go by how he lives." He looked around the room contemptuously. "Get dressed, lady."

We went out of the room and shut the door. De Spain bent down over Big Chin, lying on his back and half on his side on the floor. The big man groaned steadily with his mouth open, neither completely out nor fully aware of what was going on around him. De Spain, still bending down in the dim light he'd put on in the hall, looked at the piece of adhesive in the palm of his hand and laughed suddenly. He slammed the tape hard over Big Chin's mouth.

"Think we can make him walk?" he asked. "I'd hate like hell to have to carry him."

"I don't know," I said. "I'm just the swamper on this route. Walk to where?"

"Up in the hills where it's quiet and the birds sing," De Spain said grimly.

I sat on the running board of the car with the big bell-shaped flashlight hanging down between my knees. The light wasn't too good, but it seemed to be good enough for what De Spain was doing to Big Chin. A roofed reservoir was just above us and the ground sloped away from that into a deep canyon. There were two hilltop houses about half a mile away, both dark, with a glisten of moonlight on their stucco walls. It was cold up there in the hills, but the air was clear and the stars were like pieces of polished chromium. The light haze over Bay City seemed to be far off, as if in another country, but it was only a fast ten-minute drive.

De Spain had his coat off. His shirt-sleeves were rolled up and his wrists and his big hairless arms looked enormous in the faint hard light. His coat lay on the ground between him and Big Chin. His gun holster lay on the coat, with the gun in the holster, and the butt towards Big Chin. The coat was a little to one side so that between De Spain and Big Chin there was a small space of scuffed moonlit gravel. The gun was to Big Chin's right and to De Spain's left.

After a long silence thick with breathing De Spain said: "Try again." He spoke casually, as if he were talking to a man playing a pinball game.

Big Chin's face was a mass of blood. I couldn't see it as red, but I had put the flash on it a time or two and I knew it was there. His hands were free and what the kick in the groin had done to him was long ago, on the far side of oceans of pain. He made a croaking noise and turned his left hip suddenly against De Spain and went down on his right knee and lunged for the gun.

De Spain kicked him in the face.

Big Chin rolled back on the gravel and clawed at his face with both hands and a wailing sound came through his fingers. De Spain stepped over and kicked him on the ankle. Big Chin howled. De Spain stepped back to his original position beyond the coat and the holstered gun. Big Chin rolled a little and came up on his knees and shook his head. Big dark drops fell from his face to the gravelly ground. He got up to his feet slowly and stayed hunched over a little.

De Spain said: "Come on up. You're a tough guy. You got Vance Conried behind you and he's got the syndicate behind him. You maybe got Chief Anders behind you. I'm a lousy flatfoot with a ticket to nowhere in my pants. Come up. Let's put on a show."

Big Chin shot out in a diving lunge for the gun. His hand touched the butt but only slewed it around. De Spain came down hard on the hand with his heel and screwed his heel. Big Chin yelled. De Spain jumped back and said wearily: "You ain't overmatched, are you, sweetheart?"

I said thickly: "For God's sake, why don't you let him talk?"

"He don't want to talk," De Spain said. "He ain't the talking kind. He's a tough guy."

"Well, let's shoot the poor devil then."

"Not a chance. I'm not that kind of cop. Hey, Moss, this guy thinks I'm just one of those sadistic cops that has to smack a head with a piece of lead pipe every so often to keep from getting nervous indigestion. You ain't going to let him think that, are you? This is a square fight. You got me shaded twenty pounds and look where the gun is."

Big Chin mumbled: "Suppose I got it. Your pal would blast me."

"Not a chance. Come on, big boy. Just once more. You got a lot of stuff left."

Big Chin got up on his feet again. He got up so slowly that he seemed like a man climbing up a wall. He swayed and wiped blood off his face with his hand. My head ached. I felt sick at my stomach.

Big Chin swung his right foot very suddenly. It looked like something for a fraction of a second, then De Spain picked the foot out of the air and stepped back, pulled on it. He held the leg taut and the big bruiser swayed on his other foot trying to hold his balance.

De Spain said conversationally: "That was okay when I did it because you had plenty of gun in your mitt and I didn't have any gun and you didn't figure on me taking a chance like that. Now you see how wrong the play is in this spot."

He twisted the foot quickly, with both hands. Big Chin's body seemed to leap into the air and dive sideways, and his shoulder and face smashed into the ground, but De Spain held on to the foot. He kept on turning it. Big Chin began to thresh around on the ground and make harsh animal sounds, half stifled in the gravel. De Spain gave the foot a sudden hard wrench. Big Chin screamed like a dozen sheets tearing.

De Spain lunged forward and stepped on the ankle of Big Chin's other foot. He put his weight against the foot he held in his hands and spread Big Chin's legs. Big Chin tried to gasp and yell at the same time and made a sound something like a very large and very old dog barking.

De Spain said: "Guys get paid money for what I'm doing. Not nickels – real dough. I oughta look into it."

Big Chin yelled: "Lemme up! I'll talk! I'll talk!"

De Spain spread the legs some more. He did something to the foot and Big Chin suddenly went limp. It was like a sea lion fainting. It staggered De Spain and he reeled to one side as the leg smacked the ground. Then he reached a handkerchief out of his pocket and slowly mopped his face and hands.

"Soft," he said. "Too much beer. The guy looked healthy. Maybe it's always having his fanny under a wheel."

"And his hand under a gun," I said.

"That's an idea," De Spain said. "We don't want to lose him his self-respect."

He stepped over and kicked Big Chin in the ribs. After the third kick there was a grunt and a glistening where the blankness of Big Chin's eyelids had been.

"Get up," De Spain said. "I ain't goin' to hurt you no more."

Big Chin got up. It took him a whole minute to get up. His mouth – what was left of it – was strained wide open. It made me think of another man's mouth and I stopped having pity for him. He pawed the air with his hands, looking for something to lean against.

De Spain said: "My pal here says you're soft without a gun in your hand. I wouldn't want a strong guy like you to be soft. Help yourself to my gat." He kicked the holster lightly so that it slid off the coat and close to Big Chin's foot. Big Chin bowed his shoulders to look down at it. He couldn't bend his neck any more.

"I'll talk," he grunted.

"Nobody asked you to talk. I asked you to get that gun in your hand. Don't make me cave you in again to make you do it. See – the gun in your hand."

855

Big Chin staggered down to his knees and his hand folded slowly over the butt of the gun. De Spain watched without moving a muscle.

"Attaboy. Now you got a gun. Now you're tough again. Now you can bump off some more women. Pull it outa the clip."

Very slowly, with what seemed to be enormous effort, Big Chin drew the gun out of the holster and knelt there with it dangling down between his legs.

"What, ain't you going to bump anybody off?" De Spain taunted him.

Big Chin dropped the gun out of his hand and sobbed.

"Hey, you!" De Spain barked. "Put that gun back where you got it, I want that gun clean, like I always keep it myself."

Big Chin's hand fumbled for the gun and got hold of it and slowly pushed it home in the leather sheath. The effort took all his remaining strength. He fell flat on his face over the holster.

De Spain lifted him by an arm and rolled him over on his back and picked the holster up off the ground. He rubbed the butt of the gun with his hand and strapped the holster around his chest. Then he picked up his coat and put that on.

"Now we'll let him spill his guts," he said. "I don't believe in makin' a guy talk when he don't want to talk. Got a cigarette?"

I reached a pack out of my pocket with my left hand and shook a cigarette loose and held the pack out. I clicked the big flash on and held it on the projecting cigarette and on his big fingers as they came forward to take it.

"I don't need that," he said. He fumbled for a match and struck it and drew smoke slowly into his lungs. I doused the flash again. De Spain looked down the hill towards the sea and the curve of the shore and the lighted piers. "Kind of nice up here," he added.

"Cold," I said. "Even in summer. I could use a drink."

"Me too," De Spain said. "Only I can't work on the stuff."

8 NEEDLE-PUSHER

DE SPAIN STOPPED the car in front of the Physicians and Surgeons Building and looked up at a lighted window on the sixth floor. The building was designed in a series of radiating wings so that all the offices had an outside exposure.

"Good grief," De Spain said. "He's up there right now. That guy don't never sleep at all, I guess. Take a look at that heap down the line."

I got up and walked down in front of the dark drugstore that flanked the lobby entrance of the building on one side. There was a long black sedan parked diagonally and correctly in one of the ruled spaces, as though it had been high noon instead of almost three in the morning. The sedan had a doctor's emblem beside the front license plate, the staff of Hippocrates and the serpents twisted around it. I put my flash into the car and read part of the name on the license holder and snapped the light off again. I went back to De Spain.

"Check," I said. "How did you know that was his window and what would he be doing here at this time of night?"

"Loading up his little needles," he said. "I've watched the guy some is how I know."

"Watched him why?"

He looked at me and said nothing. Then he looked back over his shoulder into the back part of the car. "How you doin', pal?"

A thick sound that might be trying to be a voice came from under a rug on the floor of the car. "He likes riding," De Spain said. "All these hard guys like riding around in cars. Okay. I'll tuck the heap in the alley and we'll go up."

He slid around the corner of the building without lights and the car sound died in the moonlit darkness. Across the street a row of enormous eucalyptus trees fringed a set of public tennis courts. The smell of kelp came up along the boulevard from the ocean.

De Spain came back around the corner of the building and we went up to the locked lobby door and knocked on the heavy plate glass. Far back there was light from an open elevator beyond a big bronze mailbox. An old man came out of the elevator and along the corridor to the door and stood looking out at us with keys in his hand. De Spain held up his police shield. The old man squinted at it and unlocked the door and locked it after us without saying a word. He went back along the hall to the elevator and rearranged the homemade cushion on the stool and moved his false teeth around with his tongue and said: "What you want?"

He had a long gray face that grumbled even when it didn't say anything. His trousers were frayed at the cuffs and one of his heelworn black shoes contained an obvious bunion. His blue uniform coat fitted him the way a stall fits a horse.

De Spain said: "Doc Austrian is upstairs, ain't he?"

"I wouldn't be surprised."

"I ain't trying to surprise you," De Spain said. "I'd have worn my pink tights."

"Yeah, he's up there," the old man said sourly.

"What time you last see Greb, the laboratory man on Four?"

"Didn't see him."

"What time you come on, Pop?"

"Seven."

"Okay. Take us up to Six."

The old man whooshed the doors shut and rode us up slowly and gingerly and whooshed the doors open again and sat like a piece of gray driftwood carved to look like a man.

De Spain reached up and lifted down the passkey that hung over the old man's head.

"Hey, you can't do that," the old man said.

"Who says I can't?"

The old man shook his head angrily, said nothing.

"How old are you, Pop?" De Spain said.

"Goin' on sixty."

"Goin' on sixty hell. You're a good juicy seventy. How come you got an elevator license?"

The old man didn't say anything. He clicked his false teeth.

"That's better," De Spain said. "Just keep the old trap buttoned that way and everything will be wicky-wacky. Take her down, Pop."

We got out of the elevator and it dropped quietly in the enclosed shaft and De Spain stood looking down the hallway, jiggling the loose passkey on the ring. "Now listen," he said. "His suite is at the end, four rooms. There's a reception room made out of an office cut in half to make two reception rooms for adjoining suites. Out of that there's a narrow hall inside the wall of this hall, a couple small rooms and the doc's room. Got that?"

"Yeah," I said. "What did you plan to do – burgle it?"

"I kept an eye on the guy for a while, after his wife died."

"Too bad you didn't keep an eye on the redheaded office nurse," I said. "The one that got bumped off tonight."

He looked at me slowly, out of his deep black eyes, out of his dead-pan face.

"Maybe I did," he said. "As much as I had a chance."

"Hell, you didn't even know her name," I said, and stared at him. "I had to tell you."

He thought that over. "Well, seeing her in a white office uniform and seeing her naked and dead on a bed is kind of different, I guess."

"Sure," I said, and kept on looking at him.

"Okay. Now – you knock at the doc's office, which is the third door from the end, and when he opens up I'll sneak in at the reception room and come along inside and get an earful of whatever he says."

"It sounds all right," I said. "But I don't feel lucky."

We went down the corridor. The doors were solid wood and well fitted and no light showed behind any of them. I put my ear against the one De Spain indicated and heard faint movement inside. I nodded to De Spain down at the end of the hall. He fitted the passkey slowly into the lock and I rapped hard on the door and saw him go in out of the tail of my eye. The door shut behind him almost at once. I rapped on my door again.

It opened almost suddenly then, and a tall man was standing about a foot away from me with the ceiling light glinting on his pale sand-colored hair. He was in his shirt-sleeves and he held a flat leather case in his hand. He was rail-thin, with dun eyebrows and unhappy eyes. He had beautiful hands, long and slim, with square but not blunt fingertips. The nails were highly polished and cut very close.

I said: "Dr. Austrian?"

He nodded. His Adam's apple moved vaguely in his lean throat.

"This is a funny hour for me to come calling," I said, "but you're a hard man to catch up with. I'm a private detective from Los Angeles. I have a client named Harry Matson."

He was either not startled or so used to hiding his feelings that it didn't make any difference. His Adam's apple moved around again and his hand moved the leather case he was holding, and he looked at it in a puzzled sort of way and then stepped back.

"I have no time to talk to you now," he said. "Come back tomorrow."

"That's what Greb told me," I said.

He got a jolt out of that. He didn't scream or fall down in a fit but I could see it jarred him. "Come in," he said thickly.

I went in and he shut the door. There was a desk that seemed to be made of black glass. The chairs were chromium tubing with rough wool upholstery. The door to the next room was half open and the room was dark. I could see the stretched white sheet on an examination table and the stirrup-like things at the foot of it. I didn't hear any sound from that direction.

On top of the black glass desk a clean towel was laid out and on the towel a dozen or so hypodermic syringes lay with needles separate. There was an electric sterilizing cabinet on the wall and inside there must have been another dozen needles and syringes. The juice was turned on. I went over and looked at the thing while the tall, rail-thin man walked around behind his desk and sat down.

"That's a lot of needles working," I said, and pulled one of the chairs near the desk.

"What's your business with me?" His voice was still thick.

"Maybe I could do you some good about your wife's death," I said.

"That's very kind of you," he said calmly. "What kind of good?"

"I might be able to tell you who murdered her," I said.

His teeth glinted in a queer, unnatural half-smile. Then he shrugged and when he spoke his voice was no more dramatic than if we had been discussing the weather. "That *would* be kind of you. I had thought she committed suicide. The coroner and the police seemed to agree with me. But of course a private detective – "

"Greb didn't think so," I said, without any particular attempt at the truth. "The lab man who switched a sample of your wife's blood for a sample from a real monoxide case."

He stared at me levelly, out of deep, sad, remote eyes under the dun-colored eyebrows. "You haven't seen Greb," he said, almost with an inner amusement. "I happen to know he went East this noon. His father died in Ohio." He got up and went to the electric sterilizer and looked at his strap watch and then switched the juice off. He came back to the desk then and opened a flat box of cigarettes and put one in his mouth and pushed the box across the desk. I reached and took one. I half glanced at the dark examination room, but I saw nothing that I hadn't seen the last time I looked at it.

"That's funny," I said. "His wife didn't know that. Big Chin didn't know it. He was sitting there with her all tied up on the bed tonight, waiting for Greb to come back home, so he could bump him off."

Dr. Austrian looked at me vaguely now. He pawed around on his desk for a match and then opened a side drawer and took out a small white-handled automatic, and held it on the flat of his hand. Then he tossed a packet of matches at me with his other hand.

"You won't need the gun," I said. "This is a business talk which I'm going to show you it will pay to keep a business talk."

He took the cigarette out of his mouth and dropped it on the desk. "I don't smoke," he said. "That was just what one might call the necessary gesture. I'm glad to hear I won't need the gun. But I'd rather be holding it and not need it than be needing it and not hold it. Now, who is Big Chin, and what else important have you to say before I call the police?"

"Let me tell you," I said. "That's what I'm here for. Your wife played a lot of roulette at Vance Conried's club and lost the money you made with your little needles almost as fast as you made it. There's some talk she was going around with Conried in an intimate way also. You maybe didn't care about that, being out all night and too busy to bother being much of a husband to her. But you probably did care about the money, because you were risking a lot to get it. I'll come to that later.

"On the night your wife died she got hysterical over at Conried's and you were sent for and went over and needled her in the arm to quiet her. Conried took her home. You phoned your office nurse, Helen Matson — Matson's ex-wife — to go into your house and see if she was all right. Then later on Matson found her dead under the car in the garage and got hold of you, and you got hold of the chief of police, and there was a hush put on it that would have made a Southern senator sound like a deaf mute asking for a second plate of mush. But Matson, the first guy on the scene, had something. He didn't have any luck trying to peddle it to you, because you in your quiet way have a lot of guts. And perhaps your friend, Chief Anders, told you it wasn't evidence. So Matson tried to put the bite on Conried, figuring that if the case got opened up before the tough grand jury that's sitting now it would all bounce back on Conried's gambling joint, and he would be closed up tighter than a frozen piston, and the people behind him might get sore at him and take his polo ponies away from him.

"So Conried didn't like that idea and he told a mug named Moss Lorenz, the mayor's chauffeur now but formerly a strong-arm for Conried – he's the fellow I called Big Chin – to take care of Matson. And Matson lost his license and was run out of Bay City. But he had his own brand of guts too, and he holed up in an apartment house in L.A. and kept on trying. The apartment house manager got wise to him some-how – I don't know how but the L.A. police will find out – and put him on the spot, and tonight Big Chin went up to town and bumped Matson off."

I stopped talking and looked at the thin, tall man. Nothing had changed in his face. His eyes flicked a couple of times and he turned the gun over on his hand. The office was very silent. I listened for breathing from the next room but I didn't hear anything.

"Matson is dead?" Dr. Austrian said very slowly. "I hope you don't think I had anything to do with that." His face glistened a little.

"Well, I don't know," I said. "Greb was the weak link in your setup and somebody got him to leave town today – fast – before Matson was killed, if it was at noon. And probably somebody gave him money, because I saw where he lived and it didn't look like the home of a fellow who was taking in any dough."

Dr. Austrian said very swiftly: "Conried, damn him! He called me up early this morning and told me to get Greb out of town. I gave him the money to go, but – " he stopped talking and looked mad at himself and then looked down at the gun again.

"But you didn't know what was up. I believe you, Doc. I really do. Put that gun down, won't you, just for a little while?"

"Go on," he said tensely. "Go on with your story."

"Okay," I said. "There's plenty more. First off the L.A. police have found Matson's body but they won't be down here before tomorrow; first, because it's too late, and second, because when they put the story together they won't want to bust the case. The Club Conried is within the L.A. city limits and the grand jury I was telling you about would just love that. They'll get Moss Lorenz and Moss will cop a plea and take a few years up in Quentin. That's the way those things are handled when the law wants to handle them. Next point is how I know what Big Chin did. He told us. A pal and I went around to see Greb and Big Chin was squatting there in the dark with Mrs. Greb all taped up on the bed and we took him. We took him up in the hills and gave him the boot and he talked. I felt kind of sorry for the poor guy. Two murders and he didn't even get paid."

"Two murders?" Dr. Austrian said queerly.

"I'll get to that after a while. Now you see where you stand. In a little while you are going to tell me who murdered your wife. And the funny thing is I am not going to believe you."

"My God!" he whispered. "My God!" He pointed the gun at me and immediately dropped it again, before I had time to start dodging.

"I'm a miracle man," I said. "I'm the great American detective – unpaid. I never talked to Matson, although he was trying to hire me. Now I'm going to tell you what he had on you, and how your wife was murdered, and why you didn't do it. All from a pinch of dust, just like the Vienna police."

He was not amused. He sighed between still lips and his face was old and gray and drawn under the pale sand-colored hair that painted his bony skull.

"Matson had a green velvet slipper on you," I said. "It was made for your wife by Verschoyle of Hollywood – custom-made, with her last number on it. It was brand-new and had never been worn. They made her two pairs exactly the same. She had it on one of her feet when Matson found her. And you know where he found her – on the floor of a garage to get to which she had to go along a concrete path from a side door of the house. So she couldn't have walked in that slipper. So she was carried. So she was murdered. Whoever put the slippers on her got one that had been worn and one that had not. And Matson spotted it and swiped the slipper. And when you sent him into the house to phone the chief you sneaked up and got the other worn slipper and put it on her bare foot. You knew Matson must have swiped that slipper. I don't know whether you told anybody or not. Okay?"

He moved his head half an inch downward. He shivered slightly, but the hand holding the bone-handled automatic didn't shiver.

"This is how she was murdered. Greb was dangerous to somebody, which proves she did *not* die of monoxide poisoning. She was dead when she was put under the car. She died of morphine. That's guessing. I admit, but it's a swell guess, because that would be the only way to kill her which would force you to cover up for the killer. And it was easy, to somebody who had the morphine and got a chance to use it. All they had to do was give her a second fatal dose in the same spot where you had shot her earlier in the evening. Then you came home and found her dead. And you had to cover up because you knew how she had died and you couldn't have that come out. You're in the morphine business."

He smiled now. The smile hung at the corners of his mouth like cobwebs in the corners of an old ceiling. He didn't even know it was there. "You interest me," he said. "I am going to kill you, I think, but you interest me."

I pointed to the electric sterilizer. "There are a couple dozen medicos like you around Hollywood – needle-pushers. They run around at night with leather cases full of loaded hypodermics. They keep dopes and drunks from going screwy – for a while. Once in a while one of them becomes an addict and then there's trouble. Maybe most of the people you fix up would land in the hoosegow or the psycho ward, if you didn't take care of them. It's a cinch they would lose their jobs, if they have jobs. And some of them have pretty big jobs. But it's dangerous because any sorehead can stick the Feds onto you and once they start checking your patients they'll find one that will talk. You try to protect yourself part of the way by not getting all of your dope through legitimate channels. I'd say Conried got some of it for you, and that was why you had to let him take your wife and your money."

Dr. Austrian said almost politely: "You don't hold very much back, do you?"

"Why should I? This is just a man-to-man talk. I can't prove any of it. That slipper Matson stole is good for a buildup, but it wouldn't be worth a nickel in court. And any defense attorney would make a monkey out of a little squirt like this Greb, even if they ever brought him back to testify. But it might cost you a lot of money to keep your medical license."

"So it would be better for me to give you part of it now. Is that it?" he asked softly.

"No. Keep your money to buy life insurance. I have one more point to make. Will you admit, just man to man, that you killed your wife?"

"Yes," he said. He said it simply and directly, as though I had asked him if he had a cigarette.

"I thought you would," I said. "But you don't have to. You see the party that did kill your wife, because your wife was wasting money somebody else could have fun spending, also knew what Matson knew and was trying to shake Conried down herself. So she got bumped off – last night, on Brayton Avenue, and you don't have to cover up for her any more. I saw your photo on her mantel – *With all my love – Leland –* and I hid it. But you don't have to cover up for her any more. Helen Matson is dead."

I went sideways out of the chair as the gun went off. I had kidded myself by this time that he wouldn't try to shoot me, but there must have been part of me that wasn't sold on the idea. The chair tipped over and I was on my hands and knees on the floor, and then another much louder gun went off from the dark room with the examination table in it.

De Spain stepped through the door with the smoking police gun in his big right hand. "Boy, was that a shot," he said, and stood there grinning.

I came up on my feet and looked across the desk. Dr. Austrian sat there perfectly still, holding his right hand with his left, shaking it gently. There was no gun in his hand. I looked along the floor and saw it at the corner of the desk.

"Geez, I didn't even hit him," De Spain said. "All I hit was the gun."

"That's perfectly lovely," I said. "Suppose all he had hit was my head?"

De Spain looked at me levelly and the grin left his face. "You put him through it, I will say that for you," he growled. "But what was the idea of holding out on me on that green-slipper angle?"

"I got tired of being your stooge," I said. "I wanted a little play out of my own hand."

"How much of it was true?"

"Matson had the slipper. It must have meant something. Now that I've made it up I think it's all true."

Dr. Austrian got up slowly out of his chair and De Spain swung the gun on him. The thin, haggard man shook his head slowly and walked over to the wall and leaned against it.

"I killed her," he said in a dead voice to nobody at all. "Not Helen. I killed her. Call the police."

De Spain's face twisted and he stooped down and picked up the gun with the bone handle and dropped it into his pocket. He put his police gun back under his arm and sat down at the desk and pulled the phone towards him.

"Watch me get Chief of Homicide out of this," he drawled.

9 A GUY WITH GUTS

THE LITTLE CHIEF of police came in springily, with his hat on the back of his head and his hands in the pockets of a thin dark overcoat. There was something in the right-hand over-coat pocket that he was holding on to, something large and heavy. There were two plainclothes men behind him and one of them was Weems, the chunky fat-faced man who had fol-lowed me over to Altair Street. Shorty, the uniformed cop we had ditched on Arguello Boulevard, brought up the rear.

Chief Anders stopped a little way inside the door and smiled at me unpleasantly. "So you've had a lot of fun in our town, I hear. Put the cuffs on him, Weems."

The fat-faced man stepped around him and pulled hand-cuffs out of his left hip pocket. "Nice to meet you again – with your pants down," he told me in an oily voice.

De Spain leaned against the wall beyond the door of the examination room. He rolled a match across his lips and stared silently. Dr. Austrian was in his desk chair again, holding his head in his hands, staring at the polished black top of the desk and the towel of hypodermic needles and the small black perpetual calendar and the pen set and the hero doodads that were on the desk. His face was stone pale and he sat without moving, without even seeming to breathe.

De Spain said: "Don't be in too much of a hurry, Chief. This lad has friends in L.A. who are working on the Matson kill right now. And that kid reporter has a brother-in-law who is a cop. You didn't know that."

The chief made a vague motion with his chin. "Wait a minute, Weems." He turned to De Spain. "You mean they know in town that Helen Matson has been murdered?"

Dr. Austrian's face jerked up, haggard and drawn. Then he dropped it into his hands and covered his whole face with his long fingers.

De Spain said: "I meant Harry Matson, Chief. He was bumped off in L.A. tonight – last night – now – by Moss Lorenz."

The chief seemed to pull his thin lips back into his mouth, almost out of sight. He spoke with them like that. "How do you know that?"

"The shamus and me picked off Moss. He was hiding out in the house of a man named Greb, the lab man who did a job on the Austrian death. He was hiding there because it looked like somebody was going to open up the Austrian case wide enough for the mayor to think it was a new boulevard and come out with a bunch of flowers and make a speech. That is, if Greb and the Matsons didn't get took care of. It seems the Matsons were workin' together, in spite of being divorced, shaking Conried down, and Conried put the pencil on them."

The chief turned his head and snarled at his stooges. "Get out in the hall and wait."

The plainclothes man I didn't know opened the door and went out, and after a slight hesitation Weems followed him. Shorty had his hand on the door when De Spain said: "I want Shorty to stay. Shorty's a decent cop – not like them two vice squad grafters you been sleepin' with lately."

869

Shorty let go of the door and went and leaned against the wall and smiled behind his hand. The chief's face colored. "Who detailed you to the Brayton Avenue death?" he barked.

"I detailed myself, Chief. I was in the dicks' room a minute or so after the call come in and I went over with Reed. He picked Shorty up too. Shorty and me was both off duty."

De Spain grinned, a hard, lazy grin that was neither amused nor triumphant. It was just a grin.

The chief jerked a gun out of his overcoat pocket. It was a foot long, a regular hogleg, but he seemed to know how to hold it. He said tightly: "Where's Lorenz?"

"He's hid. We got him all ready for you. I had to bruise him a little, but he talked. That right, shamus?"

I said: "He says something that might be yes or no, but he makes the sounds in the right places."

"That's the way I like to hear a guy talk," De Spain said. "You oughtn't to be wasting your strength on that homicide stuff, Chief. And them toy dicks you run around with don't know nothing about police work except to go through apartment houses and shake down all the women that live alone. Now, you give me back my job and eight men and I'll show you some homicide work."

The chief looked down at his big gun and then he looked at Dr. Austrian's bowed head. "So he killed his wife," he said softly. "I knew there was a chance of it, but I didn't believe it."

"Don't believe it now," I said. "Helen Matson killed her. Dr. Austrian knows that. He covered up for her, and you covered up for him, and he's still willing to cover up for her. Love is like that with some people. And this is some town, Chief, where a gal can commit a murder, get her friends and the police to cover it, and then start out to blackmail the very people that kept her out of trouble."

The chief bit his lip. His eyes were nasty, but he was thinking – thinking hard. "No wonder she got rubbed out," he said quietly. "Lorenz – "

I said: "Take a minute to think. Lorenz didn't kill Helen Matson. He said he did, but De Spain beat him up to the point where he would have confessed shooting McKinley."

De Spain straightened from the wall. He had both hands lazily in the pockets of his suit coat. He kept them there. He stood straight on wide-planted feet, a wick of black hair showing under the side of his hat.

"Huh?" he said almost gently. "What was that?"

I said: "Lorenz didn't kill Helen Matson for several reasons. It was too fussy a job for his type of mind. He'd have knocked her off and let her lay. Second, he didn't know Greb was leaving town, tipped off by Dr. Austrian who was tipped off, in turn, by Vance Conried, who is now up north providing himself with all the necessary alibis. And if Lorenz didn't know that much, he didn't know anything about Helen Matson. Especially as Helen Matson had never really got to Conried at all. She had just tried to. She told me that and she was drunk enough to be telling the truth. So Conried wouldn't have taken the silly risk of having her knocked off in her own apartment by the sort of man anybody would remember seeing if they saw him anywhere near that apartment. Knocking off Matson up in L.A. was something else again. That was way off the home grounds."

The chief said tightly: "The Club Conried is in L.A."

"Legally," I admitted. "But by position and clientele it's just outside Bay City. It's part of Bay City — and it helps to run Bay City."

Shorty said: "That ain't no way to talk to the chief."

"Let him alone," the chief said. "It's so long since I heard a guy think I didn't know they did it any more."

I said: "Ask De Spain who killed Helen Matson."

De Spain laughed harshly. He said: "Sure. I killed her."

Dr. Austrian lifted his face off his hands and turned his head slowly and looked at De Spain. His face was as dead, as expressionless as the big dead-pan copper's. Then he reached over and opened the right-hand drawer of his desk. Shorty flipped his gun out and said: "Hold it, Doc."

Dr. Austrian shrugged and quietly took a wide-mouthed bottle with a glass stopper out of the drawer. He loosened the stopper and held the bottle close to his nose. "Just smelling salts," he said dully.

Shorty relaxed and dropped the gun to his side. The chief stared at me and chewed his lip. De Spain stared at nothing, at nobody. He grinned loosely, kept on grinning.

I said: "He thinks I'm kidding. You think I'm kidding. I'm not kidding. He knew Helen – well enough to give her a gilt cigarette case with his photo on it. I saw it. It was a small hand-tinted photo and not very good and I had only seen him once. She told me it was an old sweet that wore out. Afterwards it came back to me who that photo was. But he concealed the fact that he knew her and he didn't act very much like a copper tonight, in a lot of ways. He didn't get me out of a jam and run around with me in order to be nice. He did it to find out what I knew before I was put under the lamps down at headquarters. He didn't beat Lorenz half to death just in order to make Lorenz tell the truth. He did it to make Lorenz tell anything De Spain wanted him to tell, including confessing to the murder of the Matson girl whom Lorenz probably didn't even know.

"Who called up headquarters and tipped the boys about the murder? De Spain. Who walked in there immediately afterwards and horned in on the investigation? De Spain. Who scratched the girl's body up in a fit of jealous rage because she had ditched him for a better prospect? De Spain. Who still has blood and cuticle under the nails of his right hand which a good police chemist can do a lot with? De Spain. Take a look. I took several."

The chief turned his head very slowly, as if it were on a pivot. He whistled and the door opened and the other men came back into the room. De Spain didn't move. The grin stayed on his face, carved there, a meaningless hollow grin that meant and looked as if it would never go away again.

He said quietly: "And you the guy I thought was my pal. Well, you have some wild ideas, shamus. I will say that for you."

The chief said sharply: "It doesn't make sense. If De Spain did kill her, then he was the one who tried to put you in a frame and the one that got you out of it. How come?"

I said: "Listen. You can find out if De Spain knew the girl and how well. You can find out how much of his time tonight is not accounted for and make him account for it. You can find out if there is blood and cuticle under his nails and, within limits, whether it is or could be the girl's blood and the girl's skin. And whether it was there before De Spain hit Moss Lorenz, before he hit anybody. And he didn't scratch Lorenz. That's all you need and all you can use — except a confession. And I don't think you'll get that.

"As to the frame, I would say De Spain followed the girl over to the Club Conried, or knew she had gone there and went over himself. He saw her come out with me and he saw me put her in my car. That made him mad. He sapped me and the girl was too scared not to help him get me to her apartment and up into it. I don't remember any of that. It would be nice if I did, but I don't. They got me up there somehow, and they had a fight, and De Spain knocked her out and then he deliberately murdered her. He had some clumsy idea of making it look like a rape murder and making me the fall guy. Then he beat it, turned in an alarm, horned in on the investigation, and I got out of the apartment before I was caught there.

"He realized by this time that he had done a foolish thing. He knew I was a private dick from L.A., that I had talked to Dolly Kincaid, and from the girl he probably knew that I had gone to see Conried. And he may easily have known I was interested in the Austrian case. Okay. He turned a foolish play into a smart one by stringing along with me on the investigation I was trying to make, helping me on it, getting my story, and then finding himself another and much better fall guy for the murder of the Matson girl."

De Spain said tonelessly: "I'm goin' to start climbing on this guy in a minute, Chief. Okay?"

The chief said: "Just a minute. What made you suspect De Spain at all?"

"The blood and skin under his nails, and the brutal way he handled Lorenz, and the fact that the girl told me he had been her sweet and he pretended not to know who she was. What the hell more would I want?"

De Spain said: "This."

He shot from his pocket with the white-handled gun he had taken from Dr. Austrian. Shooting from the pocket takes a lot of practice of a kind cops don't get. The slug went a foot over my head and I sat down on the floor and Dr. Austrian stood up very quickly and swung his right hand into De Spain's face, the hand that held the wide-mouthed brown bottle. A colorless liquid splashed into his eyes and smoked down his face. Any other man would have screamed. De Spain pawed the air with his left hand and the gun in his pocket banged three times more and Dr. Austrian fell sideways across the end of the desk and then collapsed to the floor, out of range. The gun went on banging.

The other men in the room had all dropped to their knees. The chief jerked his hogleg up and shot De Spain twice in the body. Once would have been enough with that gun. De Spain's body twisted in the air and hit the floor like a safe. The chief went over and knelt beside him and looked at him silently. He stood up and came back around the desk, then went back and stooped over Dr. Austrian.

"This one's alive," he snapped. "Get on the phone, Weems."

The chunky, fat-faced man went around the far side of the desk and scooped the telephone towards him and started to dial. There was a sharp smell of acid and scorched flesh in the air, a nasty smell. We were standing up again now, and the little police chief was looking at me bleakly.

"He oughtn't to have shot at you," he said. "You couldn't have proved a thing. We wouldn't have let you."

I didn't say anything. Weems put the phone down and looked at Dr. Austrian again.

"I think he's croaked," he said, from behind the desk.

The chief kept on looking at me. "You take some awful chances, Mr. Dalmas. I don't know what your game is, but I hope you like your chips."

"I'm satisfied," I said. "I'd like to have had a chance to talk to my client before he was bumped off, but I guess I've done all I could for him. The hell of it is I liked De Spain. He had all the guts they ever made."

The chief said: "If you want to know about guts, try being a small-town chief of police some day."

I said: "Yeah. Tell somebody to tie a handkerchief around De Spain's right hand, Chief. You kind of need the evidence yourself now."

A siren wailed distantly on Arguello Boulevard. The sound came faintly through the closed windows, like a coyote howling in the hills.

THE LADY IN THE LAKE

1 NOT FOR MISSING PERSONS

I WAS BREAKING a new pair of shoes in on my desk that morning when Violets M'Gee called me up. It was a dull, hot, damp August day and you couldn't keep your neck dry with a bath towel.

"How's the boy?" Violets began, as usual. "No business in a week, huh? There's a guy named Howard Melton over in the Avenant Building lost track of his wife. He's district manager for the Doreme Cosmetic Company. He don't want to give it to Missing Persons for some reason. The boss knows him a little. Better get over there, and take your shoes off before you go in. It's a pretty snooty outfit."

Violets M'Gee is a homicide dick in the sheriff's office, and if it wasn't for all the charity jobs he gives me, I might be able to make a living. This looked a little different, so I put my feet on the floor and swabbed the back of my neck again and went over there.

The Avenant Building is on Olive near Sixth and has a black-and-white rubber sidewalk out in front. The elevator girls wear gray silk Russian blouses and the kind of flop-over berets artists used to wear to keep the paint out of their hair. The Doreme Cosmetic Company was on the seventh floor and had a good piece of it. There was a big glass-walled reception room with flowers and Persian rugs and bits of nutty sculpture in glazed ware. A neat little blonde sat in a built-in switchboard at a big desk with flowers on it and a tilted sign reading: MISS VAN DE GRAAF. She wore Harold Lloyd cheaters and her hair was dragged back to where her forehead looked high enough to have snow on it.

She said Mr. Howard Melton was in conference, but she would take my card in to him when she had an opportunity, and what was my business, please? I said I didn't have a card, but the name was John Dalmas, from Mr. West.

"Who is Mr. West?" she inquired coldly. "Does Mr. Melton know him?"

"That's past me, sister. Not knowing Mr. Melton I would not know his friends."

"What is the nature of your business?"

"Personal."

"I see." She initialed three papers on her desk quickly, to keep from throwing her pen set at me. I went and sat in a blue leather chair with chromium arms. It felt, looked and smelled very much like a barber's chair.

In about half an hour a door opened beyond a bronze railing and two men came out backwards laughing. A third man held the door and echoed their laughter. They shook hands and the two men went away and the third man wiped the grin off his face in nothing flat and looked at Miss Van De Graaf. "Any calls?" he asked in a bossy voice.

She fluttered papers and said: "No, sir. A Mr. – Dalmas to see you – from a Mr. – West. His business is personal."

"Don't know him," the man barked. "I've got more insurance than I can pay for." He gave me a swift, hard look and went into his room and slammed the door. Miss Van De Graaf smiled at me with delicate regret. I lit a cigarette and crossed my legs the other way. In another five minutes the door beyond the railing opened again and he came out with his hat on and sneered that he was going out for half an hour.

He came through a gate in the railing and started for the entrance and then did a nice cutback and came striding over to me. He stood looking down at me – a big man, two inches over six feet and built to proportion. He had a well-massaged face that didn't hide the lines of dissipation. His eyes were black, hard, and tricky.

"You want to see me?"

I stood up, got out my billfold and gave him a card. He stared at the card and palmed it. His eyes became thoughtful.

"Who's Mr. West?"

"Search me."

He gave me a hard, direct, interested look. "You have the right idea," he said. "Let's go into my office."

The receptionist was so mad she was trying to initial three papers at once when we went past her through the railing.

The office beyond was long, dim and quiet, but not cool. There was a large photo on the wall of a tough-looking old bird who had held lots of noses to lots of grindstones in his time. The big man went behind about eight hundred dollars' worth of desk and tilted himself back in a padded high-backed director's chair. He pushed a cigar humidor at me. I lit a cigar and he watched me light it with cool, steady eyes.

"This is very confidential," he said.

"Uh-huh."

He read my card again and put it away in a gold-plated wallet. "Who sent you?"

"A friend in the sheriff's office."

"I'd have to know a little more about you than that."

I gave him a couple of names and numbers. He reached for his phone, asked for a line and dialed them himself. He got both the parties I had mentioned and talked. In four minutes he had hung up and tilted his chair again. We both wiped the backs of our necks.

"So far, so good," he said. "Now show me you're the man you say you are."

I got my billfold out and showed him a small photostat of my license. He seemed pleased. "How much do you charge?"

"Twenty-five bucks a day and expenses."

"That's too much. What is the nature of the expenses?"

"Gas and oil, maybe a bribe or two, meals and whiskey. Mostly whiskey."

"Don't you eat when you're not working?"

"Yeah – but not so well."

He grinned. His grin like his eyes had a stony cast to it. "I think maybe we'll get along," he said.

He opened a drawer and brought out a Scotch bottle. We had a drink. He put the bottle on the floor, wiped his lips, lit a monogrammed cigarette and inhaled comfortably. "Better make it fifteen a day," he said. "In times like these. And go easy on the liquor."

"I was just kidding you," I said. "A man you can't kid is a man you can't trust."

He grinned again. "It's a deal. First off though, your promise that in no circumstances you have anything to do with any cop friends you may happen to have."

"As long as you haven't murdered anybody, it suits me."

He laughed. "Not yet. But I'm a pretty tough guy still. I want you to trace my wife and find out where she is and what she's doing, and without her knowing it.

"She disappeared eleven days ago – August twelfth – from a cabin we have at Little Fawn Lake. That's a small lake owned by myself and two other men. It's three miles from Puma Point. Of course you know where that is."

"In the San Bernardino Mountains, about forty miles from San Bernardino."

"Yes." He flicked ash from his cigarette on the desk top and leaned over to blow it off. "Little Fawn Lake is only about three-eighths of a mile long. It has a small dam we built for real estate development – just at the wrong time. There are four cabins up there. Mine, two belonging to my friends, neither of them occupied this summer, and a fourth on the near side of the lake as you come in. That one is occupied by a man named William Haines and his wife. He's a disabled veteran with a pension. He lives there rent free and looks after the place. My wife has been spending the summer up there and was to leave on the twelfth to come in to town for some social activity over the weekend. She never came."

I nodded. He opened a locked drawer and took out an envelope. He took a photo and a telegram from the envelope, and passed the telegram across the desk. It had been sent from El Paso, Texas, on August 15th at 9:18 A.M. It was addressed to Howard Melton, 715 Avenant Building, Los Angeles. It read: *Am crossing to get Mexican divorce. Will marry Lance. Good luck and goodbye. Julia.*

I put the yellow form down on the desk. "Julia is my wife's name," Melton said.

"Who's Lance?"

"Lancelot Goodwin. He used to be my confidential secretary up to a year ago. Then he came into some money and quit. I have known for a long time that Julia and he were a bit soft on each other, if I may put it that way."

"It's all right with me," I said.

He pushed the photo across the desk. It was a snapshot on glazed paper showing a slim, small blonde and a tall, lean, dark, handsome guy, about thirty-five, a shade too handsome. The blonde could have been anything from eighteen to forty. She was that type. She had a figure and didn't act stingy with it. She wore a swimsuit which didn't strain the imagination and the man wore trunks. They sat against a striped beach umbrella on the sand. I put the snapshot down on top of the telegram.

"That's all the exhibits," Melton said, "but not all the facts. Another drink?" He poured it and we drank it. He put the bottle down on the floor again and his telephone rang. He talked a moment, then juggled the hood and told the operator to hold his calls for a while.

"So far there would be nothing much to it," he said. "But I met Lance Goodwin on the street last Friday. He said he hadn't seen Julia in months. I believed him, because Lance is a fellow without many inhibitions, and he doesn't scare. He'd be apt to tell me the truth about a thing like that. And I think he'll keep his mouth shut."

"Were there other fellows you thought of?"

"No. If there are any, I don't know them. My hunch is, Julia has been arrested and is in jail somewhere and has managed, by bribery or otherwise, to hide her identity."

"In jail for what?"

He hesitated a moment and then said very quietly: "Julia is a kleptomaniac. Not bad, and not all the time. Mostly when she is drinking too much. She has spells of that, too. Most of her tricks have been here in Los Angeles in the big stores where we have accounts. She's been caught a few times and been able to bluff out and have the stuff put on the bill. No scandal so far that I couldn't take care of. But in a strange town – " He stopped and frowned hard. "I have my job with the Doreme people to worry about," he said.

"She ever been printed?"

"How?"

"Had her fingerprints taken and filed?"

"Not that I know of." He looked worried at that.

"This Goodwin know about the sideline she worked?"

"I couldn't say. I hope not. He's never mentioned it, of course."

"I'd like his address."

"He's in the book. Has a bungalow over in the Chevy Chase district, near Glendale. Very secluded place. I've a hunch Lance is quite a chaser."

It looked like a very nice setup, but I didn't say so out loud. I could see a little honest money coming my way for a change. "You've been up to this Little Fawn Lake since your wife disappeared, of course."

He looked surprised. "Well, no. I've had no reason to. Until I met Lance in front of the Athletic Club I supposed he and Julia were together somewhere – perhaps even married already. Mexican divorces are quick."

"How about money? She have much with her?"

"I don't know. She has quite a lot of money of her own, inherited from her father. I guess she can get plenty of money."

"I see. How was she dressed – or would you know?"

He shook his head. "I hadn't seen her in two weeks. She wore rather dark clothes as a rule. Haines might be able to tell you. I suppose he'll have to know she disappeared. I think he can be trusted to keep his mouth shut." Melton smiled wryly. "She had a small octagonal platinum wrist watch with a chain of large links. A birthday present. It had her name inside. She had a diamond and emerald ring and a platinum wedding ring engraved inside: *Howard and Julia Melton. July 27th, 1926.*"

"But you don't suspect foul play, do you?"

"No." His large cheekbones reddened a little. "I told you what I suspected."

"If she's in somebody's jailhouse, what do I do? Just report back and wait?"

"Of course. If she's not, keep her in sight until I can get there, wherever it is. I think I can handle the situation."

"Uh-huh. You look big enough. You said she left Little Fawn Lake on August twelfth. But you haven't been up there. You mean she did – or she was just supposed to – or you guess it from the date of the telegram?"

"Right. There's one more thing I forgot. She did leave on the twelfth. She never drove at night, so she drove down the mountain in the afternoon and stopped at the Olympia Hotel until train time. I know that because they called me up a week later and said her car was in their garage and did I want to call for it. I said I'd be over and get it when I had time."

"Okay, Mr. Melton. I think I'll run around and check over this Lancelot Goodwin a little first. He might happen not to have told you the truth."

He handed me the Other Cities phone book and I looked it up. Lancelot Goodwin lived at 3416 Chester Lane. I didn't know where that was, but I had a map in the car.

I said: "I'm going out there and snoop around. I'd better have a little money on account. Say a hundred bucks."

"Fifty should do to start," he said. He took out his gold-plated wallet and gave me two twenties and a ten. "I'll get you to sign a receipt – just as a matter of form."

He had a receipt book in his desk and wrote out what he wanted and I signed it. I put the two exhibits in my pocket and stood up. We shook hands.

I left him with the feeling that he was a guy who would not make many small mistakes, especially about money. As I went out the receptionist gave me the nasty eye. I worried about it almost as far as the elevator.

2 THE SILENT HOUSE

MY CAR WAS in a lot across the street, so I took it north to Fifth and west to Flower and from there down to Glendale Boulevard and so on into Glendale. That made it about lunch time, so I stopped and ate a sandwich.

Chevy Chase is a deep canyon in the foothills that separate Glendale from Pasadena. It is heavily wooded, and the streets branching off the main drag are apt to be pretty shut-in and dark. Chester Lane was one of them, and was dark enough to be in the middle of a redwood forest. Goodwin's house was at the deep end, a small English bungalow with a peaked roof and leaded windowpanes that wouldn't have let much light in, even if there had been any to let in. The house was set back in a fold of the hills, with a big oak tree practically on the front porch. It was a nice little place to have fun.

The garage at the side was shut up. I walked along a twisted path made of steppingstones and pushed the bell. I could hear it ring somewhere in the rear with that sound bells seem to have in an empty house. I rang it twice more. Nobody came to the door. A mockingbird flew down on the small, neat front lawn and poked a worm out of the sod and went away with it. Somebody started a car out of sight down the curve of the street. There was a brand-new house across the street with a *For Sale* sign stuck into the manure and grass seed in front of it. No other house was in sight.

I tried the bell one more time and did a snappy tattoo with the knocker, which was a ring held in the mouth of a lion. Then I left the front door and put an eye to the crack between the garage doors. There was a car in there, shining dimly in the faint light. I prowled around to the back yard and saw two more oak trees and a rubbish burner and three chairs around a green garden table under one of the trees. It looked so shady and cool and pleasant back there, I would have liked to stay. I went to the back door, which was half glass but had a spring lock. I tried turning the knob, which was silly. It opened and I took a deep breath and walked in.

This Lancelot Goodwin ought to be willing to listen to a little reason, if he caught me. If he didn't, I wanted to glance around his effects. There was something about him – maybe just his first name – that worried me.

The back door opened on a porch with high, narrow screens. From that another unlocked door, also with a spring lock, opened into a kitchen with gaudy tiles and an enclosed gas stove. There were a lot of empty bottles on the sink. There were two swing doors. I pushed the one towards the front of the house. It gave on an alcove dining room with a buffet on which there were more liquor bottles but not empty.

The living-room was to my right under an arch. It was dark even in the middle of the day. It was nicely furnished, with built-in bookshelves and books that hadn't been bought in sets. There was a highboy radio in the corner, with a half-empty glass of amber fluid on top of it. And there was ice in the amber fluid. The radio made a faint humming sound and light glowed behind the dial. It was on, but the volume was down to nothing.

That was funny. I turned around and looked at the back corner of the room and saw something funnier.

A man was sitting in a deep brocade chair with slippered feet on a footstool that matched the chair. He wore an open-neck polo shirt and ice-cream pants and a white belt. His left hand rested easily on the wide arm of the chair and his right hand drooped languidly outside the other arm to the carpet, which was a solid dull rose. He was a lean, dark, handsome guy, rangily built. One of those lads who move fast and are much stronger than they look. His mouth was slightly open showing the edges of his teeth. His head was a little sideways, as though he had dozed off as he sat there, having himself a few drinks and listening to the radio.

There was a gun on the floor beside his right hand and there was a scorched red hole in the middle of his forehead.

Blood dripped very quietly from the end of his chin and fell on his white polo shirt.

For all of a minute – which in a spot like that can be as long as a chiropractor's thumb – I didn't move a muscle. If I drew a full breath, it was a secret. I just hung there, empty as a busted flush, and watched Mr. Lancelot Goodwin's blood form small pear-shaped globules on the end of his chin and then very slowly and casually drop and add themselves to the large patch of crimson that changed the whiteness of his polo shirt. It seemed to me that even in that time the blood dripped slower. I lifted a foot at last, dragged it out of the cement it was stuck in, took a step, and then hauled the other foot after it like a ball and chain. I moved across the dark and silent room.

His eyes glittered as I got close. I bent over to stare into them, to try and meet their look. It couldn't be done. It never can, with dead eyes. They are always pointed a little to one side or up or down. I touched his face. It was warm and slightly moist. That would be from his drink. He hadn't been dead more than twenty minutes.

I swung around hard, as if somebody were trying to sneak up behind me with a blackjack, but nobody was. The silence held. The room was full of it, brimming over with it. A bird chirped outdoors in a tree, but that only made the silence thicker. You could have cut slices of it and buttered them.

I started looking at other things in the room. There was a silver-framed photo lying on the floor, back up, in front of the plaster mantel. I went over and lifted it with a handkerchief and turned it. The glass was cracked neatly from corner to corner. The photo showed a slim, light haired lady with a dangerous smile. I took out the snapshot Howard Melton had given me and held it beside the photo. I was sure it was the same face, but the expression was different, and it was a very common type of face.

I took the photograph carefully into a nicely furnished bedroom and opened a drawer in a long-legged chest. I removed the photo from the frame, polished the frame off nicely with my handkerchief and tucked it under some shirts. Not very clever, but as clever as I felt.

Nothing seemed very pressing now. If the shot had been heard, and recognized as a shot, radio cops would have been there long ago. I took my photo into the bathroom and trimmed it close with my pocketknife and flushed the scraps down the toilet. I added the photo to what I had in my breast pocket, and went back to the living-room.

There was an empty glass on the low table beside the dead man's left hand. It would have his prints. On the other hand somebody else might have taken a sip out of it and left other prints. A woman, of course. She would have been sitting on the arm of the chair, with a soft, sweet smile on her face, and the gun down behind her back. It had to be a woman. A man couldn't have shot him in just that perfectly relaxed position. I gave a guess what woman it was – but I didn't like her leaving her photo on the floor. That was bad publicity.

I couldn't risk the glass. I wiped it off and did something I didn't enjoy. I made his hand hold it again, then put it back on the table. I did the same thing with the gun. When I let his hand fall – the trailing hand this time – it swung and swung, like a pendulum on a grandfather's clock. I went to the glass on the radio and wiped it off. That would make them think she was pretty wise, a different kind of woman altogether – if there are different kinds. I collected four cigarette stubs with lipstick about the shade called "Carmen," a blond shade. I took them to the bathroom and gave them to the city. I wiped off a few shiny fixtures with a towel, did the same for the front doorknob, and called it a day. I couldn't wipe over the whole damn house.

I stood and looked at Lancelot Goodwin a moment longer. The blood had stopped flowing. The last drop on his chin wasn't going to fall. It was going to hang there and get dark and shiny and as permanent as a wart.

I went back through the kitchen and porch, wiping a couple more doorknobs as I went, strolled around the side of the house and took a quick gander up and down the street. Nobody being in sight, I tied the job up with ribbon by ringing the front doorbell again and smearing the button and knob well while I did it. I went to my car, got in and drove away. This had all taken less than half an hour. I felt as if I had fought all the way through the Civil War.

Two-thirds of the way back to town I stopped at the foot of Alessandro Street and tucked myself into a drugstore phone booth. I dialed Howard Melton's office number.

A chirpy voice said: "Doreme Cosmetic Company. Good afternoowun."

"Mr. Melton."

"I'll connect you with his secretary," sang the voice of the little blonde who had been off in the corner, out of harm's way.

"Miss Van De Graaf speaking." It was a nice drawl that could get charming or snooty with the change of a quarter-tone. "Who is calling Mr. Melton, please?"

"John Dalmas."

"Ah – does Mr. Melton know you, Mr. – ah – Dalmas?"

"Don't start that again," I said. "Ask him, girlie. I can get all the ritzing I need at the stamp window."

Her intaken breath almost hurt my eardrum.

There was a wait, a click, and Melton's burly businesslike voice said: "Yes? Melton talking. Yes?"

"I have to see you quick."

"What's that?" he barked.

"I said what you heard. There have been what the boys call developments. You know who you're talking to, don't you?"

"Oh – yes. Yes. Well, let me see. Let me look at my desk calendar."

"To hell with your desk calendar," I said. "This is serious. I have enough sense not to break in on your day, if it wasn't."

"Athletic Club – ten minutes," he said crisply. "Have me paged in the reading room."

"I'll be a little longer than that." I hung up before he could argue.

I was twenty minutes as a matter of fact.

The hop in the lobby of the Athletic Club scooted neatly into one of the old open-cage elevators they have there and was back in no time at all with a nod. He took me up to the fourth floor and showed me the reading room.

"Around to the left, sir."

The reading room was not built principally for reading. There were papers and magazines on a long mahogany table and leather bindings behind glass on the walls and a portrait of the club's founder in oil, with a hooded light over it. But mostly the place was little nooks and corners with enormous sloping high-backed leather chairs, and old boys snoozing in them peacefully, their faces violet with old age and high blood pressure.

I sneaked quietly around to the left. Melton sat there, in a private nook between shelves, with his back to the room, and the chair, high as it was, not high enough to hide his big dark head. He had another chair drawn up beside him. I slipped into it and gave him the eye.

"Keep your voice down," he said. "This place is for after-luncheon naps. Now, what is it? When I employed you, it was to save me bother, not to add bother to what I already have."

"Yeah," I said, and put my face close to his. He smelled of highballs, but nicely. "She shot him."

His stiff eyebrows went up a little. His eyes got the stony look. His teeth clamped. He breathed softly and twisted one large hand on his knee and looked down at it.

"Go on," he said, in a voice the size of a marble.

I craned back over the top of the chair. The nearest old geezer was snoozling lightly and blowing the fuzz in his nostrils back and forth with each breath.

"I went out there to Goodwin's place. No answer. Tried the back door. Open. Walked in. Radio turned on, but muted. Two glasses with drinks. Smashed photo on floor below mantel. Goodwin in chair shot dead at close range. Contact wound. Gun on floor by his right hand. Twenty-five automatic – a woman's gun. He sat there as if he had never known it. I wiped glasses, gun, doorknobs, put his prints where they should be, left."

Melton opened and shut his mouth. His teeth made a grating noise. He made fists of both hands. Then he looked steadily at me with hard black eyes.

"Photo," he said thickly.

I reached it out of my pocket and showed it to him, but I held on to it.

"Julia," he said. His breath made a queer, sharp keening sound and his hand went limp. I slipped the photo back into my pocket. "What then?" he whispered.

"All. I may have been seen, but not going in or coming out. Trees in back. The place is well shaded. She have a gun like that?"

His head drooped and he held it in his hands. He held still for a while, then pushed it up and spread his fingers on his face and spoke through them at the wall we were facing.

"Yes. But I never knew her to carry it. I suppose he ditched her, the dirty rat." He said it quietly without heat.

"You're quite a guy," he said. "It's a suicide now, eh?"

"Can't tell. Without a suspect they're apt to handle it that way. They'll test his hand with paraffin to see if he fired the gun. That's routine now. But it sometimes doesn't work, and without a suspect they may let it ride anyway. I don't get the photo angle."

"I don't either," he whispered, still talking between his fingers. "She must have got panicked up very suddenly."

"Uh-huh. You realize I've put my head in a bag, don't you? It's my license if I'm caught. Of course there's a bare chance it was suicide. But he doesn't seem the type. You've got to play ball, Melton."

He laughed grimly. Then he turned his head enough to look at me, but still kept his hands on his face. The gleam of his eyes shot through his fingers.

"Why did you fix it up?" he asked quietly.

"Damned if I know. I guess I took a dislike to him – from that photo. He didn't look worth what they'd do to her – and to you."

"Five hundred, as a bonus," he said.

I leaned back and gave him a stony stare. "I'm not trying to pressure you. I'm a fairly tough guy – but not in spots like this. Did you give me everything you had?"

He said nothing for a long minute. He stood up and looked along the room, put his hands in his pockets, jingled something, and sat down again.

"That's the wrong approach – both ways," he said. "I wasn't thinking of blackmail – or offering to pay it. It isn't enough money. These are hard times. You take an extra risk,

I offer you an extra compensation. Suppose Julia had nothing to do with it. That might explain the photo being left. There were plenty of other women in Goodwin's life. But if the story comes out and I'm connected with it at all, the home offices will bounce me. I'm in a sensitive business, and it hasn't been doing too well. They might be glad of the excuse."

"That's different," I said. "I asked you, did you give me everything you had."

He looked at the floor. "No. I suppressed something. It didn't seem important then. And it hurts the position badly now. A few days ago, just after I met Goodwin downtown, the bank called me and said a Mr. Lancelot Goodwin was there to cash a check for one thousand dollars made out to cash by Julia Melton. I told them Mrs. Melton was out of town, but that I knew Mr. Goodwin very well and I saw no objection to cashing the check, if it was in order and he was properly identified. I couldn't say anything else – in the circumstances. I suppose they cashed it. I don't know."

"I thought Goodwin had dough."

Melton shrugged stiffly.

"A blackmailer of women, huh? And a sappy one at that, to be taking checks. I think I'll play with you on it, Melton. I hate like hell to see these newspaper ghouls go to town on a yarn like that. But if they get to you, I'm out – if I can get out."

He smiled for the first time. "I'll give you the five hundred right now," he said.

"Nothing doing. I'm hired to find her. If I find her I get five hundred flat – all other bets off."

"You'll find me a good man to trust," he said.

"I want a note to this Haines up at your place at Little Fawn Lake. I want into your cabin. My only way to go at it is as if I'd never been to Chevy Chase."

He nodded and stood up. He went over to a desk and came back with a note on the club stationery.

Mr. William Haines,
Little Fawn Lake.

Dear Bill

Please allow bearer, Mr. John Dalmas, to view my cabin and assist him in all ways to look over the property.

Sincerely

HOWARD MELTON

I folded the note and put it away with my other gatherings from the day. Melton put a hand on my shoulder. "I'll never forget this," he said. "Are you going up there now?"

"I think so."

"What do you expect to find?"

"Nothing. But I'd be a sap not to start where the trail starts."

"Of course. Haines is a good fellow, but a little surly. He has a pretty blonde wife that rides him a lot. Good luck."

We shook hands. His hand felt clammy as a pickled fish.

3 THE MAN WITH THE PEG LEG

I MADE SAN Bernardino in less than two hours and for once in its life it was almost as cool as Los Angeles, and not nearly as sticky. I took on a cup of coffee and bought a pint of rye and gassed up and started up the grade. It was overcast all the way to Bubbling Springs. Then it suddenly got dry and bright and cool air blew down the gorges, and I finally came to the big dam and looked along the level blue reaches of Puma Lake. Canoes paddled on it, and rowboats with outboard motors and speedboats churned up the water and made a lot of fuss over nothing. Jounced around in their wake, people who had paid two dollars for a fishing license wasted their time trying to catch a dime's worth of fish.

The road turned two ways from the dam. My way was the south shore. It skimmed along high among piled-up masses of granite. Hundred-foot yellow pines probed at the clear blue sky. In the open spaces grew bright green manzanita and what was left of the wild irises and white and purple lupine and bugle flowers and desert paintbrush. The road dropped to the lake level and I began to pass flocks of camps and flocks of girls in shorts on bicycles, on motor scooters, walking all over the highway, or just sitting under trees showing off their legs. I saw enough beef on the hoof to stock a cattle ranch.

Howard Melton had said to turn away from the lake at the old Redlands road, a mile short of Puma Point. It was a frayed asphalt ribbon that climbed into the surrounding mountains. Cabins were perched here and there on the slopes. The asphalt gave out and after a while a small, narrow dirt road sneaked off to my right. A sign at its entrance said: *Private Road to Little Fawn Lake. No Trespassing.* I took it and crawled around big bare stones and past a little waterfall and through yellow pines and black oaks and silence. A squirrel sat on a branch and tore a fresh pine cone to pieces and sent the pieces fluttering down like confetti. He scolded at me and beat one paw angrily on the cone.

The narrow road swerved sharply around a big tree trunk and then there was a five-barred gate across it with another sign. This one said: *Private – No Admittance.*

I got out and opened the gate and drove through and closed it again. I wound through trees for another couple of hundred yards. Suddenly below me was a small oval lake that lay deep in trees and rocks and wild grass, like a drop of dew caught in a furled leaf. At the near end there was a yellow concrete dam with a rope handrail across the top and an old mill wheel at the side. Near that stood a small cabin of native wood covered with rough bark. It had two sheet-metal chimneys and smoke lisped from one of them. Somewhere an axe thudded.

Across the lake, a long way by the road and the short way over the dam, there was a large cabin close to the water and two others not so large, spaced at wide intervals. At the far end, opposite the dam, was what looked like a small pier and band pavilion. A warped wooden sign on it read: *Camp Kilkare*. I couldn't see any sense in that, so I walked down a path to the bark-covered cabin and pounded on the door.

The sound of the axe stopped. A man's voice yelled from somewhere behind. I sat down on a big stone and rolled an unlit cigarette around in my fingers. The owner of the cabin came around its side with an axe in his hands. He was a thick-bodied man, not very tall, with a dark, rough, unshaven chin, steady brown eyes and grizzled hair that curled. He wore blue denim pants and a blue shirt open on a muscular brown neck. When he walked he seemed to give his right foot a little kick outwards with each step. It swung out from his body in a shallow arc. He walked slowly and came up to me, a cigarette dangling from his thick lips. He had a city voice.

"Yeah?"

"Mr. Haines?"

"That's me."

"I have a note for you." I took it out and gave it to him. He threw the axe to one side and looked squintingly at the note, then turned and went into the cabin. He came out wearing glasses, reading the note as he came.

"Oh, yeah," he said. "From the boss." He studied the note again. "Mr. John Dalmas, huh? I'm Bill Haines. Glad to know you." We shook hands. He had a hand like a steel trap.

"You want to look around and see Melton's cabin, huh? What's the matter? He ain't selling, for God's sake?"

I lit my cigarette and flipped the match into the lake. "He has more than he needs here," I said.

"Land sure. But it says the cabin — "

"He wanted me to look it over. It's a pretty nice cabin, he says."

897

He pointed. "That one over there, the big one. Milled red-wood walls, celarex lined and then knotty pine inside. Composition shingle roof, stone foundations and porches, bathroom, shower and toilet. He's got a spring-filled reservoir back in the hill behind. I'll say it's a nice cabin."

I looked at the cabin, but I looked at Bill Haines more. His eyes had a glitter and there were pouches under his eyes, for all his weathered look.

"You wanta go over now? I'll get the keys."

"I'm kind of tired after that long drive up. I sure could use a drink, Haines."

He looked interested, but shook his head. "I'm sorry, Mr. Dalmas, I just finished up a quart." He licked his broad lips and smiled at me.

"What's the mill wheel for?"

"Movie stuff. They make a picture up here once in a while. That's another set down at the end. They made *Love Among the Pines* with that. The rest of the sets are tore down. I heard the picture flopped."

"Is that so? Would you join me in a drink?" I brought out my pint of rye.

"Never been heard to say no. Wait'll I get some glasses."

"Mrs. Haines away?"

He stared at me with sudden coldness. "Yeah," he said very slowly. "Why?"

"On account of the liquor."

He relaxed, but kept an eye on me for a moment longer. Then he turned and walked his stiff-legged walk back into the cabin. He came out with a couple of the little glasses they pack fancy cheese in. I opened my bottle and poured a couple of stiff ones and we sat holding them, Haines with his right leg almost straight out in front of him, the foot twisted a little outwards.

"I copped that in France," he said, and drank. "Old Pegleg Haines. Well, it got me a pension and it ain't hurt me with the ladies. Here's to crime." He finished his drink.

We set our glasses down and watched a bluejay go up a big pine, hopping from branch to branch without pausing to balance, like a man running upstairs.

"Cold and nice here, but lonely," Haines said. "Too damn lonely." He watched me with the corners of his eyes. He had something on his mind.

"Some people like that." I reached for the glasses and did my duty with them.

"Gets me. I been drinkin' too much account of it gets me. It gets me at night."

I didn't say anything. He put his second drink down in a swift, hard gulp. I passed the bottle to him silently. He sipped his third drink, cocked his head on one side, and licked at his lip.

"Kind of funny what you said there – about Mrs. Haines bein' away."

"I just thought maybe we ought to take our bottle out of sight of the cabin."

"Uh-huh. You a friend of Melton's?"

"I know him. Not intimately."

Haines looked across at the big cabin.

"That damn floozie!" he snarled suddenly, his face twisted.

I stared at him. "Lost me Beryl, the damn tart," he said bitterly. "Had to have even one-legged guys like me. Had to get me drunk and make me forget I had as cute a little wife as ever a guy had."

I waited, nerves taut.

"The hell with him, too! Leavin' that tramp up here all alone. I don't have to live in his goddam cabin. I can live anywheres I like. I got a pension. War pension."

"It's a nice place to live," I said. "Have a drink."

He did that, turned angry eyes on me. "It's a lousy place to live," he snarled. "When a guy's wife moves out on him and he don't know where she's at – maybe with some other guy." He clenched an iron left fist.

899

After a moment he unclenched it slowly and poured his glass half full. The bottle was looking pretty peaked by this time. He put his big drink down in a lump.

"I don't know you from a mule's hind leg," he growled, "but what the hell! I'm sick of bein' alone. I been a sucker – but I ain't just human. She has looks – like Beryl. Same size, same hair, same walk as Beryl. Hell, they coulda been sisters. Only just enough different – if you get what I mean." He leered at me, a little drunk now.

I looked sympathetic.

"I'm over there to burn trash," he scowled, waving an arm. "She comes out on the back porch in pajamas like they was made of cellophane. With two drinks in her hands. Smiling at me, with them bedroom eyes. 'Have a drink, Bill.' Yeah. I had a drink. I had nineteen drinks. I guess you know what happened."

"It's happened to a lot of good men."

"Leaves her alone up here, the ——— ——— ——— ! While he plays around in L.A. And Beryl walks out on me – two weeks come Friday."

I stiffened. I stiffened so hard that I could feel my muscles strain all over my body. Two weeks come Friday would be a week ago last Friday. That would be August twelfth – the day Mrs. Julia Melton was supposed to have left for El Paso, the day she had stopped over at the Olympia Hotel down at the foot of the mountains.

Haines put his empty glass down and reached into his buttoned shirt pocket. He passed me a dog-eared piece of paper. I unfolded it carefully. It was written in pencil.

I'd rather be dead than live with you any longer, you lousy cheater – Beryl. That was what it said.

"Wasn't the first time," Haines said, with a rough chuckle. "Just the first time I got caught." He laughed. Then he scowled again. I gave him back his note and he buttoned it up in the pocket. "What the hell am I tellin' you for?" he growled at me.

900

A bluejay scolded at a big speckled woodpecker and the woodpecker said "Cr-racker!" just like a parrot.

"You're lonely," I said. "You need to get it off your chest. Have another drink. I've had my share. You were away that afternoon – when she left you?"

He nodded moodily and sat holding the bottle between his legs. "We had a spat and I drove on over to the north shore to a guy I know. I felt meaner than flea dirt. I had to get good and soused. I done that. I got home maybe two A.M. – plenty stinko. But I drive slow account of this trick pin. She's gone. Just the note left."

"That was a week ago last Friday, huh? And you haven't heard from her since?"

I was being a little too exact. He gave me a hard questioning glance, but it went away. He lifted the bottle and drank moodily and held it against the sun. "Boy, this is damn near a dead soldier," he said. "*She* scrammed too." He jerked a thumb towards the other side of the lake.

"Maybe they had a fight."

"Maybe they went together."

He laughed raucously. "Mister, you don't know my little Beryl. She's a hell cat when she starts."

"Sounds as if they both are. Did Mrs. Haines have a car? I mean, you drove yours that day, didn't you?"

"We got two Fords. Mine has to have the foot throttle and brake pedal over on the left, under the good leg. She took her own."

I stood up and walked to the water and threw my cigarette stub into it. The water was dark blue and looked deep. The level was high from the spring flood and in a couple of places the water licked across the top of the dam.

I went back to Haines. He was draining the last of my whisky down his throat. "Gotta get some more hooch," he said thickly. "Owe you a pint. You ain't drunk nothing."

"Plenty more where it came from," I said. "When you feel like it I'll go over and look at that cabin."

"Sure. We'll walk around the lake. You don't mind me soundin' off that way at you – about Beryl?"

"A guy sometimes has to talk his troubles to somebody," I said. "We could go across the dam. You wouldn't have to walk so far."

"Hell, no. I walk good, even if it don't look good. I ain't been around the lake in a month." He stood up and went into the cabin and came out with some keys. "Let's go."

We started towards the little wooden pier and pavilion at the far end of the lake. There was a path close to the water, winding in and out among big rough granite boulders. The dirt road was farther back and higher up. Haines walked slowly, kicking his right foot. He was moody, just drunk enough to be living in his own world. He hardly spoke. We reached the little pier and I walked out on it. Haines followed me, his foot thumping heavily on the planks. We reached the end, beyond the little open band pavilion, and leaned against a weathered dark green railing.

"Any fish in here?" I asked.

"Sure. Rainbow trout, black bass. I ain't no fish-eater myself. I guess there's too many of them."

I leaned out and looked down into the deep still water. There was swirl down there and a greenish form moved under the pier. Haines leaned beside me. His eyes stared down into the depths of the water. The pier was solidly built and had an underwater flooring – wider than the pier itself – as if the lake had once been at a much lower level, and this underwater flooring had been a boat landing. A flat-bottomed boat dangled in the water on a frayed rope.

Haines took hold of my arm. I almost yelled. His fingers bit into my muscles like iron claws. I looked at him. He was bent over, staring like a loon, his face suddenly white and glistening. I looked down into the water.

Languidly, at the edge of the underwater flooring, something that looked vaguely like a human arm and hand in a dark sleeve waved out from under the submerged boarding, hesitated, waved back out of sight.

Haines straightened his body slowly and his eyes were suddenly sober and frightful. He turned from me without a word and walked back along the pier. He went to a pile of rocks and bent down and heaved. His panting breath came to me. He got a rock loose and his thick back straightened. He lifted the rock breast high. It must have weighed a hundred pounds. He walked steadily back out on the pier with it, game leg and all, reached the end railing and lifted the rock high above his head. He stood there a moment holding it, his neck muscles bulging above his blue shirt. His mouth made some vague distressful sound. Then his whole body gave a hard lurch and the big stone smashed down into the water.

It made a huge splash that went over both of us. It fell straight and true through the water and crashed on the edge of the submerged planking. The ripples widened swiftly and the water boiled. There was a dim sound of boards breaking underwater. Waves rippled off into the distance and the water down there under our eyes began to clear. An old rotten plank suddenly popped up above the surface and sank back with a flat slap and floated off.

The depths cleared still more. In them something moved. It rose slowly, a long, dark, twisted something that rolled as it came up. It broke surface. I saw wool, sodden black now – a sweater, a pair of slacks. I saw shoes, and something that bulged shapeless and swollen over the edges of the shoes. I saw a wave of blond hair straighten out in the water and lie still for an instant.

The thing rolled then and an arm flapped in the water and the hand at the end of the arm was no decent human hand. The face came rolling up. A swollen, pulpy, gray-white mass of bloated flesh, without features, without eyes, without

903

mouth. A thing that had once been a face. Haines looked down at it. Green stones showed below the neck that belonged to the face. Haines' right hand took hold of the railing and his knuckles went as white as snow under the hard brown skin.

"Beryl!" His voice seemed to come to me from a long way off, over a hill, through a thick growth of trees.

4 THE LADY IN THE LAKE

A LARGE WHITE card in the window, printed in heavy block capitals, said: KEEP TINCHFIELD CONSTABLE. Behind the window was a narrow counter with piles of dusty folders on it. The door was glass and lettered in black paint: *Chief of Police. Fire Chief. Town Constable. Chamber of Commerce. Enter.*

I entered and was in what was nothing but a small one-room pineboard shack with a potbellied stove in the corner, a littered roll-top desk, two hard chairs, and the counter. On the wall hung a large blueprint map of the district, a calendar, a thermometer. Beside the desk telephone numbers had been written laboriously on the wood in large deeply bitten figures.

A man sat tilted back at the desk in an antique swivel chair, with a flat-brimmed Stetson on the back of his head and a huge spittoon beside his right foot. His large hairless hands were clasped comfortably on his stomach. He wore a pair of brown pants held by suspenders, a faded and much washed tan shirt buttoned tight to his fat neck, no tie. What I could see of his hair was mousy-brown except the temples, which were snow-white. On his left breast there was a star. He sat more on his left hip than his right, because he wore a leather hip holster with a big black gun in it down inside his hip pocket.

I leaned on the counter and looked at him. He had large ears and friendly gray eyes and he looked as if a child could pick his pocket.

"Are you Mr. Tinchfield?"

"Yep. What law we got to have, I'm it – come election anyways. There's a couple good boys running against me and they might up and whip me." He sighed.

"Does your jurisdiction extend to Little Fawn Lake?"

"What was that, son?"

"Little Fawn Lake, back in the mountains. You cover that?"

"Yep. Guess I do. I'm deppity sheriff. Wasn't no more room on the door." He eyed the door, without displeasure. "I'm all them things there. Melton's place, eh? Something botherin' there, son?"

"There's a dead woman in the lake."

"Well, I swan." He unclasped his hands and scratched his ear and stood up heavily. Standing up he was a big, powerful man. His fat was just cheerfulness. "Dead, you said? Who is it?"

"Bill Haines' wife, Beryl. Looks like suicide. She's been in the water a long time, Sheriff. Not nice to look at. She left him ten days ago, he said. I guess that's when she did it."

Tinchfield bent over the spittoon and discharged a tangled mass of brown fiber into it. It fell with a soft plop. He worked his lips and wiped them with the back of his hand.

"Who are you, son?"

"My name is John Dalmas. I came up from Los Angeles with a note to Haines from Mr. Melton – to look at the property. Haines and I were walking around the lake and we went out on the little pier the movie people built there once. We saw something down in the water underneath. Haines threw a large rock in and the body came up. It's not nice to look at, Sheriff."

"Haines up there?"

"Yeah. I came down because he's pretty badly shaken."

"Ain't surprised at that, son." Tinchfield opened a drawer in his desk and took out a full pint of whiskey. He slipped it inside his shirt and buttoned the shirt again. "We'll get Doc

Menzies," he said. "And Paul Loomis." He moved calmly around the end of the counter. The situation seemed to bother him slightly less than a fly.

We went out. Before going out he adjusted a clock card hanging inside the glass to read – *Back at 6 p.m.* He locked the door and got into a car that had a siren on it, two red spotlights, two amber foglights, a red-and-white fire plate, and various legends on the side which I didn't bother to read.

"You wait here, son. I'll be back in a frog squawk."

He swirled the car around in the street and went off down the road towards the lake and pulled up at a frame building opposite the stage depot. He went into this and came out with a tall, thin man. The car came slowly swirling back and I fell in behind it. We went through the village, dodging girls in shorts and men in trunks, shorts and pants, most of them naked and brown from the waist up. Tinchfield stood on his horn, but didn't use his siren. That would have started a mob of cars after him. We went up a dusty hill and stopped at a cabin. Tinchfield honked his horn and yelled. A man in blue overalls opened the door.

"Get in, Paul."

The man in overalls nodded and ducked back into the cabin and came out with a dirty lion hunter's hat on his head. We went back to the highway and along to the branch road and so over to the gate on the private road. The man in overalls got out and opened it and closed it after our cars had gone through.

When we came to the lake, smoke was no longer rising from the small cabin. We got out.

Doc Menzies was an angular yellow-faced man with bug eyes and nicotine-stained fingers. The man in blue overalls and the lion hunter's hat was about thirty, dark, swarthy, lithe, and looked underfed.

We went to the edge of the lake and looked towards the pier. Bill Haines was sitting on the floor of the pier, stark naked, with his head in his hands. There was something beside him on the pier.

"We can ride a ways more," Tinchfield said. We got back into the cars and went on, stopped again, and all trooped down to the pier.

The thing that had been a woman lay on its face on the pier with a rope under the arms. Haines' clothes lay to one side. His artificial leg, gleaming with leather and metal, lay beside them. Without a word spoken Tinchfield slipped the bottle of whiskey out of his shirt and uncorked it and handed it to Haines.

"Drink hearty, Bill," he said casually. There was a sickening, horrible smell on the air. Haines didn't seem to notice it, nor Tinchfield and Menzies. Loomis got a blanket from the car and threw it over the body, then he and I backed away from it.

Haines drank from the bottle and looked up with dead eyes. He held the bottle down between his bare knee and his stump and began to talk. He spoke in a dead voice, without looking at anybody or anything. He spoke slowly and told everything he had told me. He said that after I went he had got the rope and stripped and gone into the water and got the thing out. When he had finished he stared at the wooden planks and became as motionless as a statue.

Tinchfield put a cut of tobacco in his mouth and chewed on it for a moment. Then he shut his teeth tight and leaned down and turned the body over carefully, as if he was afraid it would come apart in his hands. The late sun shone on the loose necklace of green stones I had noticed in the water. They were roughly carved and lusterless, like soapstone. A gilt chain joined them. Tinchfield straightened his broad back and blew his nose hard on a tan handkerchief.

"What you say, Doc?"

Menzies spoke in a tight, high, irritable voice. "What the hell do you want me to say?"

"Cause and time of death," Tinchfield said mildly.

"Don't be a damn fool, Jim," the doctor said nastily.

"Can't tell nothing, eh?"

"By looking at that? Good God!"

Tinchfield sighed and turned to me. "Where was it when you first seen it?"

I told him. He listened with his mouth motionless and his eyes blank. Then he began to chew again. "Funny place to be. No current here. If there was any, 'twould be towards the dam."

Bill Haines got to his foot, hopped over to his clothes and strapped his leg on. He dressed slowly, awkwardly, dragging his shirt over his wet skin. He spoke again without looking at anybody.

"She done it herself. Had to. Swum under the boards there and breathed water in. Maybe got stuck. Had to. No other way."

"One other way, Bill," Tinchfield said mildly, looking at the sky.

Haines rummaged in his shirt and got out his dog-eared note. He gave it to Tinchfield. By mutual consent everybody moved some distance away from the body. Then Tinchfield went back to get his bottle of whiskey and put it away under his shirt. He joined us and read the note over and over.

"It don't have a date. You say this was a couple of weeks ago?"

"Two weeks come Friday."

"She left you once before, didn't she?"

"Yeah." Haines didn't look at him. "Two years ago. I got drunk and stayed with a chippy." He laughed wildly.

The sheriff calmly read the note once more. "Note left that time?" he inquired.

"I get it," Haines snarled. "I get it. You don't have to draw me pictures."

"Note looks middlin' old," Tinchfield said gently.

"I had it in my shirt ten days," Haines yelled. He laughed wildly again.

"What's amusing you, Bill?"

"You ever try to drag a person six feet under water?"

"Never did, Bill."

"I swim pretty good – for a guy with one leg. I don't swim that good."

Tinchfield sighed. "Now that don't mean anything, Bill. Could have been a rope used. She could have been weighted down with a stone, maybe two stones, head and foot. Then after she's under them boards the rope could be cut loose. Could be done, son."

"Sure. I done it," Haines said and roared laughing. "Me – I done it to Beryl. Take me in, you —— s —— s!"

"I aim to," Tinchfield said mildly. "For investigation. No charges yet, Bill. You could have done it. Don't tell me different. I ain't saying you did, though. I'm just sayin' you could."

Haines sobered as quickly as he had gone to pieces.

"Any insurance?" Tinchfield asked, looking at the sky.

Haines started. "Five thousand. That does it. That hangs me. Okay. Let's go."

Tinchfield turned slowly to Loomis. "Go back there in the cabin, Paul, and get a couple of blankets. Then we better all get some whiskey inside our nose."

Loomis turned and walked back along the path that skirted the lake towards the Haines cabin. The rest of us just stood. Haines looked down at his hard brown hands and clenched them. Without a word he swept his right fist up and hit himself a terrible blow in the face.

"You —— ——!" he said in a harsh whisper.

His nose began to bleed. He stood lax. The blood ran down his lip, down the side of his mouth to the point of his chin. It began to drip off his chin.

That reminded me of something I had almost forgotten.

5 THE GOLDEN ANKLET

I TELEPHONED HOWARD Melton at his Beverly Hills home an hour after dark. I called from the telephone company's little log-cabin office half a block from the main street of Puma Point, almost out of hearing of the .22's at the shooting gallery, the rattle of the ski balls, the tooting of fancy auto horns, and the whine of hillbilly music from the dining room of the Indian Head Hotel.

When the operator got him she told me to take the call in the manager's office. I went in and shut the door and sat down at a small desk and answered the phone.

"Find anything up there?" Melton's voice asked. It had a thickish edge to it, a three-highball edge.

"Nothing I expected. But something has happened up here you won't like. Want it straight – or wrapped in Christmas paper?"

I could hear him cough. I didn't hear any other sounds from the room in which he was talking. "I'll take it straight," he said steadily.

"Bill Haines claims your wife made passes at him – and they scored. They got drunk together the very morning of the day she went away. Haines had a row with his wife about it afterwards, and then he went over to the north shore of Puma Lake to get drunk some more. He was gone until two A.M. I'm just telling you what he says, you understand."

I waited. Melton's voice said finally: "I heard you. Go on, Dalmas." It was a toneless voice, as flat as a piece of slate.

"When he got home both the women had gone. His wife Beryl had left a note saying she'd rather be dead than live with a lousy cheater any more. He hasn't seen her since – until today."

Melton coughed again. The sound made a sharp noise in my ear. There were buzzes and crackles on the wire. An operator broke in and I asked her to go brush her hair. After the interruption Melton said: "Haines told all this to you, a complete stranger?"

"I brought some liquor with me. He likes to drink and he was aching to talk to somebody. The liquor broke down the barriers. There's more. I said he didn't see his wife again until today. Today she came up out of your little lake. I'll let you guess what she looked like."

"Good God!" Melton cried.

"She was stuck down under the underwater boarding below the pier the movie people built. The constable here, Jim Tinchfield, didn't like it too well. He's taken Haines in. I think they've gone down to see the D.A. in San Bernardino and have an autopsy and so on."

"Tinchfield thinks Haines killed her?"

"He thinks it could have happened that way. He's not saying everything he thinks. Haines put on a swell broken-hearted act, but this Tinchfield is no fool. He may know a lot of things about Haines that I don't know."

"Did they search Haines' cabin?"

"Not while I was around. Maybe later."

"I see." He sounded tired now, spent.

"It's a nice dish for a county prosecutor close to election time," I said. "But it's not a nice dish for us. If I have to appear at an inquest, I'll have to state my business, on oath. That means telling what I was doing up there, to some extent, at least. And that means pulling you in."

"It seems," Melton's voice said flatly, "that I'm pulled in already. If my wife – " He broke off and swore. He didn't speak again for a long time. Wire noises came to me and a sharper crackling, thunder somewhere in the mountains along the lines.

I said at last: "Beryl Haines had a Ford of her own. Not Bill's. His was fixed up for his left leg to do the heavy work. The car is gone. And that note didn't sound like a suicide note to me."

"What do you plan to do now?"

"It looks as though I'm always being sidetracked on this job. I may come down tonight. Can I call you at your home?"

"Any time," he said. "I'll be home all evening and all night. Call me any time. I didn't think Haines was that sort of a guy at all."

"But you knew your wife had drinking spells and you left her up here alone."

"My God," he said, as if he hadn't heard me. "A man with a wooden – "

"Oh let's skip that part of it," I growled. "It's dirty enough without. Goodbye."

I hung up and went back to the outer office and paid the girl for the call. Then I walked back to the main street and got into my car parked in front of the drugstore. The street was full of gaudy neon signs and noise and glitter. On the dry mountain air every sound seemed to carry a mile. I could hear people talking a block away. I got out of my car again and bought another pint at the drugstore and drove away from there.

When I got to the place back along the highway where the road turned off to Little Fawn Lake, I pulled over to the side and thought. Then I started up the road into the mountains towards Melton's place.

The gate across the private road was shut and padlocked now. I tucked my car off to the side in some bushes and climbed over the gate and pussyfooted along the side of the road until the starlit glimmer of the lake suddenly bloomed at my feet. Haines' cabin was dark. The cabins on the other side of the lake were vague shadows against the slope. The old mill wheel beside the dam looked funny as hell up there all alone. I listened – didn't hear a sound. There are no night birds in the mountains.

I padded along to Haines' cabin and tried the door – locked. I went around to the back and found another locked door. I prowled around the cabin walking like a cat on a wet floor. I pushed on the one screenless window. That was locked also. I stopped and listened some more. The window was not very tight. Wood dries out in that air and shrinks. I tried my knife between the two sashes, which opened inward, like small cottage windows. No dice. I leaned against the wall and looked at the hard shimmer of the lake and took a drink from my pint. That made me tough. I put the bottle away and picked up a big stone and smacked the window frame in without breaking the glass. I heaved up on the sill and climbed into the cabin.

A flash hit me in the face.

A calm voice said: "I'd rest right there, son. You must be all tired out."

The flash pinned me against the wall for a moment and then a light switch clicked and a lamp went on. The flash died. Tinchfield sat there peacefully in a leather Morris chair beside a table over the edge of which a brown-fringed shawl dangled foolishly. Tinchfield wore the same clothes as he had worn that afternoon, and the addition of a brown wool windbreaker over his shirt. His jaws moved quietly.

"That movie outfit strung two miles of wire up here," he said reflectively. "Kind of nice for the folks. Well, what's on your mind, son – besides breakin' and enterin'?"

I picked out a chair and sat down and looked around the cabin. The room was a small square room with a double bed and a rag rug and a few modest pieces of furniture. An open door at the back showed the corner of a cookstove.

"I had an idea," I said. "From where I sit now it looks lousy."

Tinchfield nodded and his eyes studied me without rancor. "I heard your car," he said. "I knew you was on the private road and comin' this way. You walk right nice, though. I didn't hear you walk worth a darn. I've been mighty curious about you, son."

"Why?"

"Ain't you kind of heavy under the left arm, son?"

I grinned at him. "Maybe I better talk," I said.

"Well, you don't have to bother a lot about pushin' in that winder. I'm a tolerant man. I figure you got a proper right to carry that six-gun, eh?"

I reached into my pocket and laid my open billfold on his thick knee. He lifted it and held it carefully to the lamplight, looking at the photostat license behind the celluloid window. He handed the billfold back to me.

"I kind of figured you was interested in Bill Haines," he said. "A private dective, eh? Well, you got a good hard build on you and your face don't tell a lot of stories. I'm kind of worried about Bill myself. You aim to search the cabin?"

"I did have the idea."

"It's all right by me, but there ain't really no necessity. I already pawed around considerable. Who hired you?"

"Howard Melton."

He chewed a moment in silence. "Might I ask to do what?"

"To find his wife. She skipped out on him a couple of weeks back."

Tinchfield took his flat-crowned Stetson off and rumpled his mousy hair. He stood up and unlocked and opened the door. He sat down again and looked at me in silence.

"He's very anxious to avoid publicity," I said. "On account of a certain failing his wife has which might lose him his job." Tinchfield eyed me unblinkingly. The yellow lamplight made bronze out of one side of his face. "I don't mean liquor or Bill Haines," I added.

"None of that don't hardly explain your wantin' to search Bill's cabin," he said mildly.

"I'm just a great guy to poke around."

He didn't budge for a long minute, during which he was probably deciding whether or not I was kidding him, and if I was, whether he cared.

He said at length: "Would this interest you at all, son?" He took a folded piece of newspaper from the slanting pocket of his windbreaker and opened it up on the table under the lamp. I went over and looked. On the newspaper lay a thin gold chain with a tiny lock. The chain had been snipped through neatly by a pair of cutting pliers. The lock was not unlocked. The chain was short, not more than four or five inches long and the lock was tiny and hardly any larger around than the chain itself. There was a little white powder on both chain and newspaper.

"Where would you guess I found that?" Tinchfield asked.

I moistened a finger and touched the white powder and tasted it. "In a sack of flour. That is, in the kitchen here. It's an anklet. Some women wear them and never take them off. Whoever took this one off didn't have the key."

Tinchfield looked at me benignly. He leaned back and patted one knee with a large hand and smiled remotely at the pineboard ceiling. I rolled a cigarette around in my fingers and sat down again.

Tinchfield refolded the piece of newspaper and put it back in his pocket. "Well, I guess that's all — unless you care to make a search in my presence."

"No," I said.

"It looks like me and you are goin' to do our thinkin' separate."

"Mrs. Haines had a car, Bill said. A Ford."

"Yep. A blue coupe. It's down the road a piece, hid in some rocks."

"That doesn't sound much like a planned murder."

"I don't figure anything was planned, son. Just come over him sudden. Maybe choked her, and he has awful powerful hands. There he is — stuck with a body to dispose of. He done it the best way he could think of and for a pegleg he done pretty damn well."

"The car sounds more like a suicide," I said. "A planned suicide. People have been known to commit suicide in such a way as to make a murder case stick against somebody they were mad at. She wouldn't take the car far away, because she had to walk back."

Tinchfield said: "Bill wouldn't neither. That car would be mighty awkward for him to drive, him being used to use his left foot."

"He showed me that note from Beryl before we found the body," I said. "And I was the one that walked out on the pier first."

"You and me could get along, son. Well, we'll see. Bill's a good feller at heart – except these veterans give themselves too many privileges in my opinion. Some of 'em did three weeks in a camp and act like they was wounded nine times. Bill must have been mighty sentimental about this piece of chain I found."

He got up and went to the open door. He spit his chaw out into the dark. "I'm a man sixty-two years of age," he said over his shoulder. "I've known folks to do all manner of funny things. I would say offhand that jumpin' into a cold lake with all your clothes on, and swimmin' hard to get down under that board, and then just dyin' there was a funny thing to do. On the other hand, since I'm tellin' you all my secrets and you ain't tellin' me nothing, I've had to speak to Bill a number of times for slapping his wife around when he was drunk. That ain't goin' to sound good to a jury. And if this here little chain come off Beryl Haines' leg, it's just about enough to set him in that nice new gas chamber they got up north. And you and me might as well mosey on home, son."

I stood up.

"And don't go smokin' that cigarette on the highway," he added. "It's contrary to the law up here."

I put the unlit cigarette back in my pocket and stepped out into the night. Tinchfield switched the lamp off and locked up the cabin and put the key in his pocket. "Where at are you stayin', son?"

"I'm going down to the Olympia in San Bernardino."

"It's a nice place, but they don't have the climate we have up here. Too hot."

"I like it hot," I said.

We walked back to the road and Tinchfield turned to the right. "My car's up a piece towards the end of the lake. I'll say good night to you, son."

"Good night, Sheriff. I don't think he murdered her."

He was already walking off. He didn't turn. "Well, we'll see," he said quietly.

I went back to the gate and climbed it and found my car and started back down the narrow road past the waterfall. At the highway I turned west towards the dam and the grade to the valley.

On the way I decided that if the citizens around Puma Lake didn't keep Tinchfield constable, they would be making a very bad mistake.

6 MELTON UPS THE ANTE

IT WAS PAST ten-thirty when I got to the bottom of the grade and parked in one of the diagonal slots in front of the Hotel Olympia in San Bernardino. I pulled an overnight bag out of the back of my car and had taken about four steps with it when a bellhop in braided pants and a white shirt and black bow tie had it out of my hand.

The clerk on duty was an egg-headed man with no interest in me. I signed the register.

The hop and I rode a four-by-four elevator to the second floor and walked a couple of blocks around corners. As we walked it got hotter and hotter. The hop unlocked a door into a boy's-size room with one window on an air-shaft.

The hop, who was tall, thin, yellow, and as cool as a slice of chicken in aspic, moved his gum around in his face, put my bag on a chair, opened the window and stood looking at me. He had eyes the color of a drink of water.

"Bring us up some ginger ale and glasses and ice," I said.

"Us?"

"That is, if you happen to be a drinking man."

"After eleven I reckon I might take a chance."

"It's now ten-thirty-nine," I said. "If I give you a dime, will you say 'I sho'ly do thank you'?"

He grinned and snapped his gum.

He went out, leaving the door open. I took off my coat and unstrapped my holster. It was wearing grooves in my hide. I removed my tie, shirt, undershirt and walked around the room in the draft from the open door. The draft smelled of hot iron. I went into the bathroom sideways — it was that kind of bathroom — doused myself with cold water and was breathing more freely, when the tall, languid hop returned with a tray. He shut the door and I brought out my bottle. He mixed a couple of drinks and we drank. The perspiration started from the back of my neck down my spine, but I felt better all the same. I sat on the bed holding my glass and looking at the hop.

"How long can you stay?"

"Doing what?"

"Remembering."

"I ain't a damn bit of use at it."

"I have money to spend," I said, "in my own peculiar way." I took my wallet from my coat and spread bills along the bed.

"I beg yore pardon," the hop said. "You're a copper?"

"Private."

"I'm interested. This likker makes my mind work."

I gave him a dollar bill. "Try that on your mind. Can I call you Tex?"

"You done guessed it," he drawled, tucking the bill neatly into the watch pocket of his pants.

"Where were you on Friday the twelfth of August, in the late afternoon?"

He sipped his drink and thought, shaking the ice very gently and drinking past his gum. "Here. Four-to-twelve shift," he answered finally.

"A lady named Mrs. George Atkins, a small, slim, pretty blonde, checked in and stayed until time for the night train east. She put her car in the hotel garage and I believe it is still there. I want the lad that checked her in. That wins another dollar." I separated it from my stake and laid it by itself on the bed.

"I sho'ly do thank you," the hop said, grinning. He finished his drink and left the room, closing the door quietly. I finished my drink and made another. Time passed. Finally the wall telephone rang. I wedged myself into a small space between the bathroom door and the bed and answered it.

"That was Sonny. Off at eight tonight. He can be reached, I reckon."

"How soon?"

"You want him over?"

"Yeah."

"Half an hour, if he's home. Another boy checked her out. A fellow we call Les. He's here."

"Okay. Shoot him up."

I finished my second drink and thought well enough of it to mix a third before the ice melted. I was stirring it when the knock came, and I opened to a small, wiry, carrot-headed, green-eyed rat with a tight little girlish mouth.

"Drink?"

"Sure," he said. He poured himself a large one and added a whisper of mixer. He put the mixture down in one swallow, tucked a cigarette between his lips and snapped a match alight while it was still coming up from his pocket. He blew smoke, fanned it with his hand, and stared at me coldly. I noticed, stitched over his pocket instead of a number, the word *Captain*.

"Thanks," I said. "That will be all."

"Huh?" His mouth twisted unpleasantly.

"Beat it."

"I thought you wanted to see me," he snarled.

"You're the night bell captain?"

"Check."

"I wanted to buy you a drink. I wanted to give you a buck. Here. Thanks for coming up."

He took the dollar and hung there, smoke trailing from his nose, his eyes beady and mean. He turned then with a swift, tight shrug and slipped out of the room soundlessly.

Ten minutes passed, then another knock, very light. When I opened the lanky lad stood there grinning. I walked away from him and he slipped inside and came over beside the bed. He was still grinning.

"You didn't take to Les, huh?"

"No. Is he satisfied?"

"I reckon so. You know what captains are. Have to have their cut. Maybe you better call me Les, Mr. Dalmas."

"So you checked her out."

"Not if Mrs. George Atkins was her name, I didn't."

I took the photo of Julia from my pocket and showed it to him. He looked at it carefully, for a long time. "She looked like that," he said. "She gave me four bits, and in this little town that gets you remembered. Mrs. Howard Melton was the name. There's been talk about her car. I guess we just don't have much to talk about here."

"Uh-huh. Where did she go from here?"

"She took a hack to the depot. You use nice likker, Mr. Dalmas."

"Excuse me. Help yourself." When he had I said: "Remember anything about her? She have any visitors?"

"No, sir. But I do recall something. She was addressed by a gentleman in the lobby. A tall, good-lookin' jasper. She didn't seem pleased to see him."

"Ah." I took the other photo out of my pocket and showed it to him. He studied that carefully also.

"This don't look quite so much like her. But I'm sure it's the gentleman I spoke of."

"Ah."

He picked up both photos again and held them side by side. He looked a little puzzled. "Yes, sir. That's him all right," he said.

"You're an accommodating guy," I said. "You'd remember almost anything, wouldn't you?"

"I don't get you, sir."

"Take another drink. I owe you four bucks. That's five in all. It's not worth it. You hops are always trying to pull some gag."

He took a very small one and balanced it in his hand, his yellow face puckered. "I do the best I can," he said stiffly. He drank his drink, put the glass down silently and moved to the door. "You can keep your goddam money," he said. He took the dollar out of his watch pocket and threw it on the floor. "To hell with you, you —— " he said softly.

He went out.

I picked up the two photos and held them side by side and scowled at them. After a long moment an icy finger touched my spine. It had touched it once before, very briefly, but I had shaken off the feeling. It came back now to stay.

I went to the tiny desk and got an envelope and put a five-dollar bill in it and sealed it and wrote "Les" on it. I put my clothes on and my bottle on my hip and picked up my overnight bag and left the room.

Down in the lobby the redhead jumped at me. Les stayed back by a pillar, his arms folded, silent. I went to the desk and asked for my bill.

"Anything wrong, sir?" The clerk looked troubled.

I paid the bill and walked out to my car and then turned and went back to the desk. I gave the clerk the envelope with the five in it. "Give this to the Texas boy, Les. He's mad at me, but he'll get over it."

I made Glendale before 2 A.M. and looked around for a place where I could phone. I found an all-night garage.

I got out dimes and nickels and dialed the operator and got Melton's number in Beverly Hills. His voice, when it finally came over the wire, didn't sound very sleepy.

"Sorry to call at this hour," I said, "but you told me to. I traced Mrs. Melton to San Bernardino and to the depot there."

"We knew that already," he said crossly.

"Well, it pays to be sure. Haines' cabin has been searched. Nothing much was found. If you thought he knew where Mrs. Melton – "

"I don't know what I thought," he broke in sharply. "After what you told me I thought the place ought to be searched. Is that all you have to report?"

"No." I hesitated a little. "I've had a bad dream. I dreamed there was a woman's bag in a chair in that Chester Lane house this morning. It was pretty dark in there from the trees and I forgot to remove it."

"What color bag?" His voice was as stiff as a clam shell.

"Dark blue – maybe black. The light was bad."

"You'd better go back and get it," he snapped.

"Why?"

"That's what I'm paying you five hundred dollars for – among other things."

"There's a limit to what I have to do for five hundred bucks – even if I had them."

He swore. "Listen, fella. I owe you a lot, but this is up to you and you can't let me down."

"Well, there might be a flock of cops on the front step. And then again the place might be as quiet as a pet flea. Either way I don't like it. I've had enough of that house."

There was a deep silence from Melton's end. I took a long breath and gave him some more: "What's more, I think you know where your wife is, Melton. Goodwin ran into her in the hotel in San Bernardino. He had a check of hers a few days ago. You met Goodwin on the street. You helped him get the check cashed, indirectly. I think you know. I think you just hired me to backtrack over her trail and see that it was properly covered."

There was more heavy silence from him. When he spoke again it was in a small, chastened voice. "You win, Dalmas. Yeah — it was blackmail all right, on that check business. But I don't know where she is. That's straight. And that bag has to be got. How would seven hundred and fifty sound to you?"

"Better. When do I get it?"

"Tonight, if you'll take a check. I can't make better than eighty dollars in cash before tomorrow."

I hesitated again. I knew by the feel of my face that I was grinning. "Okay," I said at last. "It's a deal. I'll get the bag unless there's a flock of johns there."

"Where are you now?" He almost whistled with relief.

"Azusa. It'll take me about an hour to get there," I lied.

"Step on it," he said. "You'll find me a good guy to play ball with. You're in this pretty deep yourself, fella."

"I'm used to jams," I said, and hung up.

7 A PAIR OF FALL GUYS

I DROVE BACK to Chevy Chase Boulevard and along it to the foot of Chester Lane where I dimmed my lights and turned in. I drove quickly up around the curve to the new house across from Goodwin's place. There was no sign of life around it, no cars in front, no sign of a stakeout that I could spot. That was a chance I had to take, like another and worse one I was taking.

I drove into the driveway of the house and got out and lifted up the unlocked swing-up garage door. I put my car inside, lowered the door and snaked back across the street as if Indians were after me. I used all the cover of Goodwin's trees to the back yard and put myself behind the biggest of them there. I sat down on the ground and allowed myself a sip from my pint of rye.

Time passed, with a deadly slowness. I expected company, but I didn't know how soon. It came sooner than I expected.

In about fifteen minutes a car came up Chester Lane and I caught a faint glisten of it between the trees, along the side of the house. It was running without lights. I liked that. It stopped somewhere near and a door closed softly. A shadow moved without sound at the corner of the house. It was a small shadow, a foot shorter than Melton's would have been. He couldn't have driven from Beverly Hills in that time anyway.

Then the shadow was at the back door, the back door opened, and the shadow vanished through it into deeper darkness. The door closed silently. I got up on my feet and sneaked across the soft, moist grass. I stepped silently into Mr. Goodwin's porch and from there into his kitchen. I stood still, listening hard. There was no sound, no light beyond me. I took the gun out from under my arm and squeezed the butt down at my side. I breathed shallowly, from the top of my lungs. Then a funny thing happened. A crack of light appeared suddenly under the swing door to the dining room. The shadow had turned the lights up. Careless shadow! I walked across the kitchen and pushed the swing door open and left it that way. The light poured into the alcove dining room from beyond the living-room arch. I went that way, carelessly — much too carelessly. I stepped past the arch.

A voice at my elbow said: "Drop it — and keep on walking."

I looked at her. She was small, pretty after a fashion, and her gun pointed at my side very steadily.

"You're not clever," she said. "Are you?"

I opened my hand and let the gun fall. I walked four steps beyond it and turned.

"No," I said.

The woman said nothing more. She moved away, circling a little, leaving the gun on the floor. She circled until she faced me. I looked past her at the corner chair with the footstool. White buck shoes still rested on the footstool. Mr. Lance Goodwin still sat negligently in the chair, with his left hand on the wide brocaded arm and his right trailing to the small gun on the floor. The last blood drop had frozen on his chin. It looked black and hard and permanent. His face had a waxy look now.

I looked at the woman again. She wore well-pressed blue slacks and a double-breasted jacket and a small tilted hat. Her hair was long and curled in at the ends and it was a dark red color with glints of blue in the shadows – dyed. Red spots of hastily applied rouge burned on her cheeks too high up. She pointed her gun and smiled at me. It wasn't the nicest smile I had ever seen.

I said: "Good evening, Mrs. Melton. What a lot of guns you must own."

"Sit down in the chair behind you and clasp your hands behind your neck and keep them there. That's important. Don't get careless about it." She showed me her teeth to her gums.

I did as she suggested. The smile dropped from her face – a hard little face, even though pretty in a conventional sort of way. "Just wait," she said. "That's important, too. Maybe you could guess how important that is."

"This room smells of death," I said. "I suppose that's important, too."

"Just wait, smart boy."

"They don't hang women any more in this state," I said. "But two cost more than one. A lot more. About fifteen years more. Think it over."

925

She said nothing. She stood firmly, pointing the gun. This was a heavier gun, but it didn't seem to bother her. Her ears were busy with the distance. She hardly heard me. The time passed, as it does, in spite of everything. My arms began to ache.

At last he came. Another car drifted quietly up the street outside and stopped and its door closed quietly. Silence for a moment, then the house door at the back opened. His steps were heavy. He came through the open swing door and into the lighted room. He stood silent, looking around it, a hard frown on his big face. He looked at the dead man in the chair, at the woman with her gun, last of all at me. He stopped and picked up my gun and dropped it into his side pocket. He came to me quietly, almost without recognition in his eyes, stepped behind me and felt my pockets. He took out the two photos and the telegram. He stepped away from me, near the woman. I put my arms down and rubbed them. They both stared at me quietly.

At last he said softly: "A gag, eh? First off I checked your call and found out it came from Glendale – not from Azusa. I don't know just why I did that, but I did. Then I made another call. The second call told me there wasn't any bag left in this room. Well?"

"What do you want me to say?"

"Why the trick-work? What's it all about?" His voice was heavy, cold, but more thoughtful than menacing. The woman stood beside him, motionless, holding her gun.

"I took a chance," I said. "You took one too – coming here. I hardly thought it would work. The idea, such as it was, that you would call her quickly about the bag. She would know there wasn't one. You would both know then that I was trying to pull something. You'd be very anxious to know what it was. You'd be pretty sure I wasn't working with any law, because I knew where you were and you could have been jumped there without any trouble at all. I wanted to bring the lady out of hiding – that's all. I took a long chance. If it didn't work, I had to think up a better way."

The woman made a contemptuous sound and said: "I'd like to know why you hired this snooper in the first place, Howie."

He ignored her. He looked at me steadily out of stony black eyes. I turned my head and gave him a quick, hard wink. His mouth got rigid at once. The woman didn't see it. She was too far to the side.

"You need a fall guy, Melton," I said. "Bad."

He turned his body a little so that his back was partly to the woman. His eyes ate my face. He lifted his eyebrows a little and half nodded. He still thought I was for sale.

He did it nicely. He put a smile on his face and turned towards her and said, "How about getting out of here and talking it over in a safer place?" and while she was listening and her mind was on the question his big hand struck down sharply at her wrist. She yelped and the gun dropped. She reeled back and clenched both her fists and spit at him.

"Aw, go sit down and get wise to yourself," he said dryly.

He stooped and picked up her gun and dropped it into his other pocket. He smiled then, a large confident smile. He had forgotten something completely. I almost laughed – in spite of the spot I was in. The woman sat down in a chair behind him and leaned her head in her hands broodingly.

"You can tell me about it now," Melton said cheerfully. "Why I need a fall guy, as you say."

"I lied to you over the phone a little. About Haines' cabin. There's a wise old country cop up there who went through it with a sifter. He found a gold anklet in the flour bag, cut through with pliers."

The woman let out a queer yelp. Melton didn't even bother to look at her. She was staring at me with all her eyes now.

"He might figure it out," I said, "and he might not. He doesn't know Mrs. Melton stayed over at the Hotel Olympia, for one thing, and that she met Goodwin there. If he knew that, he'd be wise in a second. That is, if he had photos to show the bellhops, the way I had. The hop who checked Mrs. Melton out and remembered her on account of her leaving her car there without any instructions remembered Goodwin, remembered him speaking to her. He said she was startled. He wasn't so sure about Mrs. Melton from the photos. He knew Mrs. Melton."

Melton opened his mouth a little in a queer grimace and grated the edges of his teeth together. The woman stood up noiselessly behind him and drifted back, inch by inch, into the dark back part of the room. I didn't look at her. Melton didn't seem to hear her move.

I said: "Goodwin trailed her into town. She must have come by bus or in a rent car, because she left the other in San Bernardino. He trailed her to her hideout without her knowing it, which was pretty smart, since she must have been on her guard, and then he jumped her. She stalled him for a while – I don't know with what story – and he must have had her watched every minute, because she didn't slip away from him. Then she couldn't stall him any longer and she gave him that check. That was just a retainer. He came back for more and she fixed him up permanently – over there the chair. You didn't know that, or you would never have let me come out here this morning."

Melton smiled grimly. "Right, I didn't know that," he said. "Is that what I need a fall guy for?"

I shook my head. "You don't seem to want to understand me," I said. "I told you Goodwin knew Mrs. Melton personally. That's not news, is it? What would Goodwin have on Mrs. Melton to blackmail her for? Nothing. He wasn't blackmailing Mrs. Melton. Mrs. Melton is dead. She has been dead for eleven days. She came up out of Little Fawn Lake today – in Beryl Haines' clothes. That's what you need a fall guy for – and you have one, two of them, made to order."

The woman in the shadows of the room stooped and picked something up and rushed. She panted as she rushed. Melton turned hard and his hands jerked at his pockets, but he hesitated just too long, looking at the gun she had snatched up from the floor beside Goodwin's dead hand, the gun that was the thing he had forgotten about.

"You —— —— !" she said.

He still wasn't very scared. He made placating movements with his empty hands. "Okay, honey, we'll play it your way," he said softly. He had a long arm. He could reach her now. He had done it already when she held a gun. He tried it once more. He leaned towards her quickly and swept his hand. I put my feet under me and dived for his legs. It was a long dive – too long.

"I'd make a swell fall guy, wouldn't I?" she said raspingly, and stepped back. The gun banged three times.

He jumped at her with the slugs in him, and fell hard against her and carried her to the floor. She ought to have thought of that too. They crashed together, his big body pinning her down. She wailed and an arm waved up towards me holding the gun. I smacked it out of her hand. I grabbed at his pockets and got my gun out and jumped away from them. I sat down. The back of my neck felt like a piece of ice. I sat down and held the gun on my knee and waited.

His big hand reached out and took hold of the claw-shaped leg of a davenport and whitened on the wood. His body arched and rolled and the woman wailed again. His body rolled back and sagged and the hand let go of the davenport leg. The fingers uncurled quietly and lay limp on the nap of the carpet. There was a choking rattle – and silence.

She fought her way out from under him and got to her feet panting, glaring like an animal. She turned without a sound and ran. I didn't move. I just let her go.

I went over and bent down above the big, sprawled man and held a finger hard against the side of his neck. I stood there silently, leaning down, feeling for a pulse, and listening. I straightened up slowly and listened some more. No sirens, no car, no noise. Just the dead stillness of the room. I put my gun back under my arm and put the light out and opened the front door and walked down the path to the sidewalk. Nothing moved on the street. A big car stood at the curb, beside the fireplug, up at the dead-end beyond Goodwin's place. I crossed the street to the new house and got my car out of its garage and shut the garage up again and started for Puma Lake again.

8 KEEP TINCHFIELD CONSTABLE

THE CABIN STOOD in a hollow, in front of a growth of jack-pines. A big barnlike garage with cordwood piled on one side was open to the morning sun and Tinchfield's car glistened inside it. There was a cleated walk down to the front door and smoke lisped from the chimney.

Tinchfield opened the door himself. He wore an old gray roll-collar sweater and his khaki pants. He was fresh-shaved and as smooth as a baby.

"Well, step in, son," he said peacefully. "I see you go to work bright and early. So you didn't go down the hill last night, eh?"

I went past him into the cabin and sat in an old Boston rocker with a crocheted antimacassar over its back. I rocked in it and it gave out a homey squeak.

"Coffee's just about ready to pour," Tinchfield said genially. "Emma'll lay a plate for you. You got a kind of tuckered-out look, son."

"I went back down the hill," I said. "I just came back up. That wasn't Beryl Haines in the lake yesterday."

Tinchfield said: "Well, I swan."

"You don't seem a hell of a lot surprised," I growled.

"I don't surprise right easy, son. Particularly before breakfast."

"It was Julia Melton," I said. "She was murdered – by Howard Melton and Beryl Haines. She was dressed in Beryl's clothes and put down under those boards, six feet under water, so that she would stay long enough not to look like Julia Melton. Both the women were blondes, of the same size and general appearance. Bill said they were enough alike to be sisters. Not twin sisters, probably."

"They were some alike," Tinchfield said, staring at me gravely. He raised his voice. "Emma!"

A stout woman in a print dress opened the inner door of the cabin. An enormous white apron was tied around what had once been her waist. A smell of coffee and frying bacon rushed out.

"Emma, this is Detective Dalmas from Los Angeles. Lay another plate and I'll pull the table out from the wall a ways. He's a mite tired and hungry."

The stout woman ducked her head and smiled and put silver on the table.

We sat down and ate bacon and eggs and hot cakes and drank coffee by the quart. Tinchfield ate like four men and his wife ate like a bird and kept hopping up and down like a bird to get more food.

We finished at last and Mrs. Tinchfield gathered up the dishes and shut herself in the kitchen. Tinchfield cut a large slice of plug and tucked it carefully into his face and I sat down in the Boston rocker again.

"Well, son," he said, "I guess I'm ready for the word. I was a mite anxious about that there piece of gold chain bein' hid where it was, what with the lake so handy. But I'm a slow thinker. What makes you think Melton murdered his wife?"

"Because Beryl Haines is still alive, with her hair dyed red."

I told him my story, all of it, fact by fact, concealing nothing. He said nothing until I had finished.

"Well, son," he said then, "you done a mighty smart piece of detectin' work there – what with a little luck in a couple

of places, like we all have to have. But you didn't have no business to be doin' it at all, did you?"

"No. But Melton took me for a ride and played me for a
sucker. I'm a stubborn sort of guy."

"What for do you reckon Melton hired you?"

"He had to. It was a necessary part of his plan to have the
body correctly identified in the end; perhaps not for some
time, perhaps not until after it had been buried and the case
closed. But he had to have it identified in the end in order to
get his wife's money. That or wait for years to have the courts
declare her legally dead. When it was correctly identified, he
would have to show that he had made an effort to find her. If
his wife was a kleptomaniac, as he said, he had a good excuse
for hiring a private dick instead of going to the police. But he
had to do something. Also there was the meance of Goodwin.
He might have planned to kill Goodwin and frame me for it.
He certainly didn't know Beryl had beat him to it, or he
wouldn't have let me go to Goodwin's house.

"After that – and I was foolish enough to come up here
before I had reported Goodwin's death to the Glendale police
– he probably thought I could be handled with money. The
murder itself was fairly simple, and there was an angle to it
that Beryl didn't know or think about. She was probably in
love with him. An underprivileged woman like that, with a
drunken husband, would be apt to go for a guy like Melton.

"Melton couldn't have known the body would be found
yesterday, because that was pure accident, but he would have
kept me on the job and kept hinting around until it was
found. He knew Haines would be suspected of murdering his
wife and the note she left was worded to sound a bit unlike a
real suicide note. Melton knew his wife and Haines were getting tight together up here and playing games.

"He and Beryl just waited for the right time, when Haines
had gone off to the north shore on a big drunk. Beryl must
have telephoned him from somewhere. You'll be able to check

that. He could make it up here in three hours' hard driving. Julia was probably still drinking. Melton knocked her out, dressed her in Beryl's clothes and put her down in the lake. He was a big man and could do it alone, without much trouble. Beryl would be acting as lookout down the only road into the property. That gave him a chance to plant the anklet in the Haines cabin. Then he rushed back to town and Beryl put on Julia's clothes and took Julia's car and luggage and went to the hotel in San Bernardino.

"There she was unlucky enough to be seen and spoken to by Goodwin, who must have known something was wrong, by her clothes or her bags or perhaps hearing her spoken to as Mrs. Melton. So he followed her into town and you know the rest. The fact that Melton had her lay this trail shows two things, as I see it. One, that he intended to wait some time before having the body properly identified. It would be almost certain to be accepted as the body of Beryl Haines on Bill's say-so, especially as that put Bill in a very bad spot.

"The other thing is that when the body was identified as Julia Melton, then the false trail laid by Beryl would make it look as though she and Bill had committed the murder to collect her insurance. I think Melton made a bad mistake by planting that anklet where he did. He should have dropped it into the lake, tied to a bolt or something, and later on, accidentally on purpose, fished it out. Putting it in Haines' cabin and then asking me if Haines' cabin had been searched was a little too sloppy. But planned murders are always like that."

Tinchfield switched his chaw to the other side of his face and went to the door to spit. He stood in the open door with his big hands clasped behind him.

"He couldn't have pinned nothing on Beryl," he said over his shoulder. "Not without her talkin' a great deal, son. Did you think of that?"

"Sure. Once the police were looking for her and the case broke wide open in the papers – I mean the real case – he would have had to bump Beryl off and make it look like a suicide. I think it might have worked."

"You hadn't ought to have let that there murderin' woman get away, son. There's other things you hadn't ought to have done, but that one was bad."

"Whose case is this?" I growled. "Yours – or the Glendale police's? Beryl will be caught all right. She's killed two men and she'll flop on the next trick she tries to pull. They always do. And there's collateral evidence to be dug up. That's police work – not mine. I thought you were running for re-election, against a couple of younger men. I didn't come back up here just for the mountain air."

He turned and looked at me slyly. "I kind of figured you thought old man Tinchfield might be soft enough to keep you out of jail, son." Then he laughed and slapped his leg. "Keep Tinchfield Constable," he boomed at the big outdoors. "You're darn right they will. They'd be dum fools not to – after this. Let's mosey on over to the office and call the 'cutor down in Berdoo." He sighed. "Just too dum smart that Melton was," he said. "I like simple folks."

"Me too," I said. "That's why I'm here."

They caught Beryl Haines on the California–Oregon line, doubling back south to Yreka in a rent car. The highway patrol stopped her for a routine border fruit inspection, but she didn't know that. She pulled another gun. She still had Julia Melton's luggage and Julia Melton's clothes and Julia Melton's checkbook, with nine blank checks in it traced from one of Julia Melton's genuine signatures. The check cashed by Goodwin proved to be another forgery.

Tinchfield and the county prosecutor went to bat for me with the Glendale police, but I got hell from them just the same. From Violets M'Gee I got the large and succulent razzberry, and from the late Howard Melton I got what was left of the fifty dollars he had advanced me. They kept Tinchfield constable, by a landslide.

PEARLS ARE A NUISANCE

1

IT IS QUITE true that I wasn't doing anything that morning except looking at a blank sheet of paper in my typewriter and thinking about writing a letter. It is also quite true that I don't have a great deal to do any morning. But that is no reason why I should have to go out hunting for old Mrs. Penruddock's pearl necklace. I don't happen to be a policeman.

It was Ellen Macintosh who called me up, which made a difference, of course. "How are you, darling?" she asked. "Busy?"

"Yes and no," I said. "Mostly no. I am very well. What is it now?"

"I don't think you love me, Walter. And anyway you ought to get some work to do. You have too much money. Somebody has stolen Mrs. Penruddock's pearls and I want you to find them."

"Possibly you think you have the police department on the line," I said coldly. "This is the residence of Walter Gage. Mr. Gage talking."

"Well, you can tell Mr. Gage from Miss Ellen Macintosh," she said, "that if he is not out here in half an hour, he will receive a small parcel by registered mail containing one diamond engagement ring."

"And a lot of good it did me," I said. "That old crow will live for another fifty years."

But she had already hung up so I put my hat on and went down and drove off in the Packard. It was a nice late April morning, if you care for that sort of thing. Mrs. Penruddock lived on a wide quiet street in Carondelet Park. The house had probably looked exactly the same for the last fifty years, but that didn't make me any better pleased that Ellen Macintosh might live in it another fifty years, unless old Mrs. Penruddock died and didn't need a nurse any more. Mr. Penruddock had died a few years before, leaving no will, a thoroughly tangled-up estate, and a list of pensioners as long as a star boarder's arm.

I rang the front doorbell and the door was opened, not very soon, by a little old woman with a maid's apron and a strangled knot of gray hair on the top of her head. She looked at me as if she had never seen me before and didn't want to see me now.

"Miss Ellen Macintosh, please," I said. "Mr. Walter Gage calling."

She sniffed, turned without a word and we went back into the musty recesses of the house and came to a glassed-in porch full of wicker furniture and the smell of Egyptian tombs. She went away, with another sniff.

In a moment the door opened again and Ellen Macintosh came in. Maybe you don't like tall girls with honey-colored hair and skin like the first strawberry peach the grocer sneaks out of the box for himself. If you don't, I'm sorry for you.

"Darling, so you did come," she cried. "That was nice of you, Walter. Now sit down and I'll tell you all about it."

We sat down.

"Mrs. Penruddock's pearl necklace has been stolen, Walter."

"You told me that over the telephone. My temperature is still normal."

"If you will excuse a professional guess," she said, "it is probably subnormal – permanently. The pearls are a string of forty-nine matched pink ones which Mr. Penruddock gave to Mrs. Penruddock for her golden wedding present. She hardly ever wore them lately, except perhaps on Christmas or when she had a couple of very old friends in to dinner and was well enough to sit up. And every Thanksgiving she gives a dinner to all the pensioners and friends and old employees Mr. Penruddock left on her hands, and she wore them then."

"You are getting your verb tenses a little mixed," I said, "but the general idea is clear. Go on."

"Well, Walter," Ellen said, with what some people call an arch look, "the pearls have been stolen. Yes, I know that is the third time I told you that, but there's a strange mystery about it. They were kept in a leather case in an old safe which was open half the time and which I should judge a strong man could open with his fingers even when it was locked. I had to go there for a paper this morning and I looked in at the pearls just to say hello – "

"I hope your idea in hanging on to Mrs. Penruddock has not been that she might leave you that necklace," I said stiffly. "Pearls are all very well for old people and fat blondes, but for tall willowy – "

"Oh shut up, darling," Ellen broke in. "I should certainly not have been waiting for these pearls – because they were false."

I swallowed hard and stared at her. "Well," I said, with a leer, "I have heard that old Penruddock pulled some cross-eyed rabbits out of the hat occasionally, but giving his own wife a string of phony pearls on her golden wedding gets my money."

"Oh, don't be such a fool, Walter! They were real enough then. The fact is Mrs. Penruddock sold them and had imitations made. One of her old friends, Mr. Lansing Gallemore of the Gallemore Jewelry Company, handled it all for her very quietly, because of course she didn't want anyone to know. And that is why the police have not been called in. You *will* find them for her, won't you, Walter?"

"How? And what did she sell them for?"

"Because Mr. Penruddock died suddenly without making any provision for all these people he had been supporting.

Then the depression came, and there was hardly any money at all. Only just enough to carry on the household and pay the servants, all of whom have been with Mrs. Penruddock so long that she would rather starve than let any of them go."

"That's different," I said. "I take my hat off to her. But how the dickens am I going to find them, and what does it matter anyway – if they were false?"

"Well, the pearls – imitations, I mean – cost two hundred dollars and were specially made in Bohemia and it took several months and the way things are over there now she might never be able to get another set of really good imitations. And she is terrified somebody will find out they were false, or that the thief will blackmail her, when he finds out they were false. You see, darling, I know who stole them."

I said, "Huh?" a word I very seldom use as I do not think it part of the vocabulary of a gentleman.

"The chauffeur we had here a few months, Walter – a horrid big brute named Henry Eichelberger. He left suddenly the day before yesterday, for no reason at all. Nobody ever leaves Mrs. Penruddock. Her last chauffeur was a very old man and he died. But Henry Eichelberger left without a word and I'm sure he had stolen the pearls. He tried to kiss me once, Walter."

"Oh, he did," I said in a different voice. "Tried to kiss you, eh? Where is this big slab of meat, darling? Have you any idea at all? It seems hardly likely he would be hanging around on the street corner for me to punch his nose for him."

Ellen lowered her long silky eyelashes at me – and when she does that I go limp as a scrubwoman's back hair.

"He didn't run away. He must have known the pearls were false and that he was safe enough to blackmail Mrs. Penruddock. I called up the agency he came from and he has been back there and registered again for employment. But they said it was against their rules to give his address."

"Why couldn't somebody else have taken the pearls? A burglar, for instance?"

"There is no one else. The servants are beyond suspicion and the house is locked up as tight as an icebox every night and there were no signs of anybody having broken in. Besides, Henry Eichelberger knew where the pearls were kept, because he saw me putting them away after the last time she wore them – which was when she had two very dear friends in to dinner on the occasion of the anniversary of Mr. Penruddock's death."

"That must have been a pretty wild party," I said. "All right, I'll go down to the agency and make them give me his address. Where is it?"

"It is called the Ada Twomey Domestic Employment Agency, and it is in the two-hundred block on East Second, a very unpleasant neighborhood."

"Not half as unpleasant as my neighborhood will be to Henry Eichelberger," I said. "So he tried to kiss you, eh?"

"The pearls, Walter," Ellen said gently, "are the important thing. I do hope he hasn't already found out they are false and thrown them in the ocean."

"If he has, I'll make him dive for them."

"He is six feet three and very big and strong, Walter," Ellen said coyly. "But not handsome like you, of course."

"Just my size," I said. "It will be a pleasure. Goodbye, darling."

She took hold of my sleeve. "There is just one thing, Walter. I don't mind a little fighting because it is manly. But you mustn't cause a disturbance that would bring the police in, you know. And although you are very big and strong and played right tackle at college, you are a little weak about one thing. Will you promise me not to drink any whiskey?"

"This Eichelberger," I said, "is all the drink I want."

2

THE ADA TWOMEY Domestic Employment Agency on East Second Street proved to be all that the name and location implied. The odor of the anteroom, in which I was compelled to wait for a short time, was not at all pleasant. The agency was presided over by a hard-faced middle-aged woman who said that Henry Eichelberger was registered with them for employment as a chauffeur, and that she could arrange to have him call upon me, or could bring him there to the office for an interview. But when I placed a ten-dollar bill on her desk and indicated that it was merely an earnest of good faith, without prejudice to any commission which might become due to her agency, she relented and gave me his address, which was out west on Santa Monica Boulevard, near the part of the city which used to be called Sherman.

I drove out there without delay, for fear that Henry Eichelberger might telephone in and be informed that I was coming. The address proved to be a seedy hotel, conveniently close to the interurban car tracks and having its entrance adjoining a Chinese laundry. The hotel was upstairs, the steps being covered – in places – with strips of decayed rubber matting to which were screwed irregular fragments of unpolished brass. The smell of the Chinese laundry ceased about halfway up the stairs and was replaced by a smell of kerosene, cigar butts, slept-in air and greasy paper bags. There was a register at the head of the stairs on a wooden shelf. The last entry was in pencil, three weeks previous as to date, and had been written by someone with a very unsteady hand. I deduced from this that the management was not over-particular.

There was a bell beside the book and a sign reading: MAN-AGER. I rang the bell and waited. Presently a door opened down the hall and feet shuffled towards me without haste. A man appeared wearing frayed leather slippers and trousers of a nameless color, which had the two top buttons unlatched to permit more freedom to the suburbs of his extensive stomach. He also wore red suspenders, his shirt was darkened under the arms, and elsewhere, and his face badly needed a thorough laundering and trimming.

He said, "Full-up, bud," and sneered.

I said: "I am not looking for a room. I am looking for one Eichelberger, who, I am informed, lives here, but who, I observe, has not registered in your book. And this, as of course you know, is contrary to the law."

"A wise guy," the fat man sneered again. "Down the hall, bud. Two-eighteen." He waved a thumb the color and almost the size of a burnt baked potato.

"Have the kindness to show me the way," I said.

"Geez, the lootenant-governor," he said, and began to shake his stomach. His small eyes disappeared in folds of yellow fat. "Okay, bud. Follow on."

We went into the gloomy depths of the back hall and came to a wooden door at the end with a closed wooden transom above it. The fat man smote the door with a fat hand. Nothing happened.

"Out," he said.

"Have the kindness to unlock the door," I said. "I wish to go in and wait for Eichelberger."

"In a pig's valise," the fat man said nastily. "Who the hell you think you are, bum?"

This angered me. He was a fair-sized man, about six feet tall, but too full of the memories of beer. I looked up and down the dark hall. The place seemed utterly deserted.

I hit the fat man in the stomach.

He sat down on the floor and belched and his right knee-cap came into sharp contact with his jaw. He coughed and tears welled up in his eyes.

"Cripes, bud," he whined. "You got twenty years on me. That ain't fair."

"Open the door," I said. "I have no time to argue with you."

"A buck," he said, wiping his eyes on his shirt. "Two bucks and no tip-off."

943

I took two dollars out of my pocket and helped the man to his feet. He folded the two dollars and produced an ordinary passkey which I could have purchased for five cents.

"Brother, you sock," he said. "Where you learn it? Most big guys are muscle-bound." He unlocked the door.

"If you hear any noises later on," I said, "ignore them. If there is any damage, it will be paid for generously."

He nodded and I went into the room. He locked the door behind me and his steps receded. There was silence.

The room was small, mean and tawdry. It contained a brown chest of drawers with a small mirror hanging over it, a straight wooden chair, a wooden rocking chair, a single bed of chipped enamel, with a much mended cotton counterpane. The curtains at the single window had fly marks on them and the green shade was without a slat at the bottom. There was a washbowl in the corner with two paper-thin towels hanging beside it. There was, of course, no bathroom, and there was no closet. A piece of dark figured material hanging from a shelf made a substitute for the latter. Behind this I found a gray business suit of the largest size made, which would be my size, if I wore ready-made clothes, which I do not. There was a pair of black brogues on the floor, size number twelve at least. There was also a cheap fiber suitcase, which of course I searched, as it was not locked.

I also searched the bureau and was surprised to find that everything in it was neat and clean and decent. But there was not much in it. Particularly there were no pearls in it. I searched in all other likely and unlikely places in the room but I found nothing of interest.

I sat on the side of the bed and lit a cigarette and waited. It was now apparent to me that Henry Eichelberger was either a very great fool or entirely innocent. The room and the open trail he had left behind him did not suggest a man dealing in operations like stealing pearl necklaces.

I had smoked four cigarettes, more than I usually smoke in an entire day, when approaching steps sounded. They were light quick steps but not at all clandestine. A key was thrust into the door and turned and the door swung carelessly open. A man stepped through it and looked at me.

I am six feet three inches in height and weigh over two hundred pounds. This man was tall, but he seemed lighter. He wore a blue serge suit of the kind which is called neat for lack of anything better to say about it. He had thick wiry blond hair, a neck like a Prussian corporal in a cartoon, very wide shoulders and large hard hands, and he had a face that had taken much battering in its time. His small greenish eyes glinted at me with what I then took to be evil humor. I saw at once that he was not a man to trifle with, but I was not afraid of him. I was his equal in size and strength, and, I had small doubt, his superior in intelligence.

I stood up off the bed calmly and said: "I am looking for one Eichelberger."

"How you get in here, bud?" It was a cheerful voice, rather heavy, but not unpleasant to the ear.

"The explanation of that can wait," I said stiffly. "I am looking for one Eichelberger. Are you he?"

"Haw," the man said. "A gut-buster. A comedian. Wait'll I loosen my belt." He took a couple of steps farther into the room and I took the same number towards him.

"My name is Walter Gage," I said. "Are you Eichelberger?"

"Gimme a nickel," he said, "and I'll tell you."

I ignored that. "I am the fiancé of Miss Ellen Macintosh," I told him coldly. "I am informed that you tried to kiss her."

He took another step towards me and I another towards him. "Whaddaya mean – tried?" he sneered.

I led sharply with my right and it landed flush on his chin. It seemed to me a good solid punch, but it scarcely moved him. I then put two hard left jabs into his neck and landed a second hard right at the side of his rather wide nose. He snorted and hit me in the solar plexus.

I bent over and took hold of the room with both hands and spun it. When I had it nicely spinning I gave it a full swing and hit myself on the back of the head with the floor. This made me lose my balance temporarily and while I was thinking about how to regain it a wet towel began to slap at my face and I opened my eyes. The face of Henry Eichelberger was close to mine and bore a certain appearance of solicitude.

"Bud," his voice said, "your stomach is as weak as a Chinaman's tea."

"Brandy!" I croaked. "What happened?"

"You tripped on a little tear in the carpet, bud. You really got to have liquor?"

"Brandy," I croaked again, and closed my eyes.

"I hope it don't get me started," his voice said.

A door opened and closed. I lay motionless and tried to avoid being sick at my stomach. The time passed slowly, in a long gray veil. Then the door of the room opened and closed once more and a moment later something hard was being pressed against my lips. I opened my mouth and liquor poured down my throat. I coughed, but the fiery liquid coursed through my veins and strengthened me at once. I sat up.

"Thank you, Henry," I said. "May I call you Henry?"

"No tax on it, bud."

I got to my feet and stood before him. He stared at me curiously. "You look okay," he said. "Why'n't you told me you was sick?"

"Damn you, Eichelberger!" I said and hit with all my strength on the side of his jaw. He shook his head and his eyes seemed annoyed. I delivered three more punches to his face and jaw while he was still shaking his head.

"So you wanta play for keeps!" he yelled and took hold of the bed and threw it at me.

I dodged the corner of the bed, but in doing so I moved a little too quickly and lost my balance and pushed my head about four inches into the baseboard under the window.

A wet towel began to slap at my face. I opened my eyes.

"Listen, kid. You got two strikes and no balls on you. Maybe you oughta try a lighter bat."

"Brandy," I croaked.

"You'll take rye." He pressed a glass against my lips and I drank thirstily. Then I climbed to my feet again.

The bed, to my astonishment, had not moved. I sat down on it and Henry Eichelberger sat down beside me and patted my shoulder.

"You and me could get along," he said. "I never kissed your girl, although I ain't saying I wouldn't like to. Is that all is worrying at you?"

He poured himself half a waterglassful of the whiskey out of the pint bottle which he had gone out to buy. He swallowed the liquor thoughtfully.

"No, there is another matter," I said.

"Shoot. But no more haymakers. Promise?"

I promised him rather reluctantly. "Why did you leave the employ of Mrs. Penruddock?" I asked him.

He looked at me from under his shaggy blond eyebrows. Then he looked at the bottle he was holding in his hand. "Would you call me a looker?" he asked.

"Well, Henry – "

"Don't pansy up on me," he snarled.

"No, Henry, I should not call you very handsome. But unquestionably you are virile."

He poured another half-waterglassful of whiskey and handed it to me. "Your turn," he said. I drank it down without fully realizing what I was doing. When I had stopped coughing Henry took the glass out of my hand and refilled it. He took his own drink moodily. The bottle was now nearly empty.

947

"Suppose you fell for a dame with all the looks this side of heaven. With a map like mine. A guy like me, a guy from the stockyards that played himself a lot of very tough left end at a cow college and left his looks and education on the scoreboard. A guy that has fought everything but whales and freight hogs – engines to you – and licked 'em all, but naturally had to take a sock now and then. Then I get a job where I see this lovely all the time and every day and know it's no dice. What would you do, pal? Me, I just quit the job."

"Henry, I'd like to shake your hand," I said.

He shook hands with me listlessly. "So I ask for my time," he said. "What else would I do?" He held the bottle up and looked at it against the light. "Bo, you made an error when you had me get this. When I start drinking it's a world cruise. You got plenty dough?"

"Certainly," I said. "If whiskey is what you want, Henry, whiskey is what you shall have. I have a very nice apartment on Franklin Avenue in Hollywood and while I cast no aspersions on your own humble and of course quite temporary abode, I now suggest we repair to my apartment, which is a good deal larger and gives one more room to extend one's elbow." I waved my hand airily.

"Say, you're drunk," Henry said, with admiration in his small green eyes.

"I am not yet drunk, Henry, although I do in fact feel the effect of that whiskey and very pleasantly. You must not mind my way of talking which is a personal matter, like your own clipped and concise method of speech. But before we depart there is one other rather insignificant detail I wish to discuss with you. I am empowered to arrange for the return of Mrs. Penruddock's pearls. I understand there is some possibility that you may have stolen them."

"Son, you take some awful chances," Henry said softly.

"This is a business matter, Henry, and plain talk is the best way to settle it. The pearls are only false pearls, so we should

948

very easily be able to come to an agreement. I mean you no ill will, Henry, and I am obliged to you for procuring the whiskey, but business is business. Will you take fifty dollars and return the pearls and no questions asked?"

Henry laughed shortly and mirthlessly, but he seemed to have no animosity in his voice when he said: "So you think I stole some marbles and am sitting around here waiting for a flock of dicks to swarm me?"

"No police have been told, Henry, and you may not have known the pearls were false. Pass the liquor, Henry."

He poured me most of what was left in the bottle, and I drank it down with the greatest good humor. I threw the glass at the mirror, but unfortunately missed. The glass, which was of heavy and cheap construction, fell on the floor and did not break. Henry Eichelberger laughed heartily.

"What are you laughing at, Henry?"

"Nothing," he said. "I was just thinking what a sucker some guy is finding out he is – about them marbles."

"You mean you did not steal the pearls, Henry?"

He laughed again, a little gloomily. "Yeah," he said, "meaning no. I oughta sock you, but what the hell? Any guy can get a bum idea. No, I didn't steal no pearls, bud. If they was ringers, I wouldn't be bothered, and if they was what they looked like the one time I saw them on the old lady's neck, I wouldn't decidedly be holed up in no cheap flot in L. A. waiting for a couple carloads of johns to put the sneeze on me."

I reached for his hand again and shook it.

"That is all I required to know," I said happily. "Now I am at peace. We shall now go to my apartment and consider ways and means to recover these pearls. You and I together should make a team that can conquer any opposition, Henry."

"You ain't kidding me, huh?"

I stood up and put my hat on – upside down. "No, Henry. I am making you an offer of employment which I understand you need, and all the whiskey you can drink. Let us go. Can you drive a car in your condition?"

"Hell, I ain't drunk," Henry said, looking surprised.

We left the room and walked down the dark hallway. The fat manager very suddenly appeared from some nebulous shade and stood in front of us rubbing his stomach and looking at me with small greedy expectant eyes. "Everything okay?" he inquired, chewing on a time-darkened toothpick.

"Give him a buck," Henry said.

"What for, Henry?"

"Oh, I dunno. Just give him a buck."

I withdrew a dollar bill from my pocket and gave it to the fat man.

"Thanks, pal," Henry said. He chucked the fat man under the Adam's apple, and removed the dollar bill deftly from between his fingers. "That pays for the hooch," he added. "I hate to have to bum dough."

We went down the stairs arm in arm, leaving the manager trying to cough the toothpick up from his esophagus.

3

AT FIVE O CLOCK that afternoon I awoke from slumber and found that I was lying on my bed in my apartment in the Chateau Moraine, on Franklin Avenue near Ivar Street, in Hollywood. I turned my head, which ached, and saw that Henry Eichelberger was lying beside me in his undershirt and trousers. I then perceived that I also was as lightly attired. On the table near by there stood an almost full bottle of Old Plantation rye whiskey, the full quart size, and on the floor lay an entirely empty bottle of the same excellent brand. There were garments lying here and there on the floor, and a cigarette had burned a hole in the brocaded arm of one of my easy chairs.

I felt myself over carefully. My stomach was stiff and sore and my jaw seemed a little swollen on one side. Otherwise I was none the worse for wear. A sharp pain darted through my temples as I stood up off the bed, but I ignored it and walked steadily to the bottle on the table and raised it to my lips. After a steady draught of the fiery liquid I suddenly felt much better. A hearty and cheerful mood came over me and I was ready for any adventure. I went back to the bed and shook Henry firmly by the shoulder.

"Wake up, Henry," I said. "The sunset hour is nigh. The robins are calling and the squirrels are scolding and the morning glories furl themselves in sleep."

Like all men of action Henry Eichelberger came awake with his fist doubled. "What was that crack?" he snarled. "Oh, yeah. Hi, Walter. How you feel?"

"I feel splendid. Are you rested?"

"Sure." He swung his shoeless feet to the floor and rumpled his thick blond hair with his fingers. "We was going swell until you passed out," he said. "So I had me a nap. I never drink solo. You Okay?"

"Yes, Henry, I feel very well indeed. And we have work to do."

"Swell." He went to the whiskey bottle and quaffed from it freely. He rubbed his stomach with the flat of his hand. His green eyes shone peacefully. "I'm a sick man," he said, "and I got to take my medicine." He put the bottle down on the table and surveyed the apartment. "Geez," he said, "we thrown it into us so fast I ain't hardly looked at the dump. You got a nice little place here, Walter. Geez, a white typewriter and a white telephone. What's the matter, kid – you just been confirmed?"

"Just a foolish fancy, Henry," I said, waving an airy hand.

Henry went over and looked at the typewriter and the telephone side by side on my writing desk, and the silver-mounted desk set, each piece chased with my initials.

"Well fixed, huh?" Henry said, turning his green gaze on me.

"Tolerably so, Henry," I said modestly.

"Well, what next pal? You got any ideas or do we just drink some?"

"Yes, Henry, I do have an idea. With a man like you to help me I think it can be put into practice. I feel that we must, as they say, tap the grapevine. When a string of pearls is stolen, all the underworld knows it at once. Pearls are hard to sell, Henry, inasmuch as they cannot be cut and can be identified by experts, I have read. The underworld will be seething with activity. It should not be too difficult for us to find someone who would send a message to the proper quarter that we are willing to pay a reasonable sum for their return."

"You talk nice – for a drunk guy," Henry said, reaching for the bottle. "But ain't you forgot these marbles are phonies?"

"For sentimental reasons I am quite willing to pay for their return, just the same."

Henry drank some whiskey, appeared to enjoy the flavor of it and drank some more. He waved the bottle at me politely.

"That's okay – as far as it goes," he said. "But this under-world that's doing all this here seething you spoke of ain't going to seethe a hell of a lot over a string of glass beads. Or am I screwy?"

"I was thinking, Henry, that the underworld probably has a sense of humor and the laugh that would go around would be quite emphatic."

"There's an idea in that," Henry said. "Here's some mug finds out lady Penruddock has a string of oyster fruit worth oodles of kale, and he does hisself a neat little box job and trots down to the fence. And the fence gives him the belly laugh. I would say something like that could get around the poolrooms and start a little idle chatter. So far, so nutty. But this box man is going to dump them beads in a hurry, because he has a three-to-ten on him even if they are only worth a nickel plus sales tax. Breaking and entering is the rap, Walter."

"However, Henry," I said, "there is another element in the situation. If this thief is very stupid, it will not, of course, have much weight. But if he is even moderately intelligent, it will. Mrs. Penruddock is a very proud woman and lives in a very exclusive section of the city. If it should become known that she wore imitation pearls, and above all, if it should be even hinted in the public press that these were the very pearls her own husband had given her for her golden wedding present – well, I am sure you see the point, Henry."

"Box guys ain't too bright," he said and rubbed his stony chin. Then he lifted his right thumb and bit it thoughtfully. He looked at the windows, at the corner of the room, at the floor. He looked at me from the corners of his eyes.

"Blackmail, huh?" he said. "Maybe. But crooks don't mix their rackets much. Still, the guy might pass the word along. There's a chance, Walter. I wouldn't care to hock my gold fillings to buy me a piece of it, but there's a chance. How much you figure to put out?"

"A hundred dollars should be ample, but I am willing to go as high as two hundred, which is the actual cost of the imitations."

Henry shook his head and patronized the bottle. "Nope. The guy wouldn't uncover hisself for that kind of money. Wouldn't be worth the chance he takes. He'd dump the marbles and keep his nose clean."

"We can at least try, Henry."

"Yeah, but where? And we're getting low on liquor. Maybe I better put my shoes on and run out, huh?"

At that very moment, as if in answer to my unspoken prayer, a soft dull thump sounded on the door of my apartment. I opened it and picked up the final edition of the evening paper. I closed the door again and carried the paper back across the room, opening it up as I went. I touched it with my right forefinger and smiled confidently at Henry Eichelberger.

"Here. I will wager you a full quart of Old Plantation that the answer will be on the crime page of this paper."

"There ain't any crime page," Henry chortled. "This is Los Angeles. I'll fade you."

I opened the paper to page three with some trepidation, for, although I had already seen the item I was looking for in an early edition of the paper while waiting in Ada Twomey's Domestic Employment Agency, I was not certain it would appear intact in the later editions. But my faith was rewarded. It had not been removed, but appeared midway of column three exactly as before. The paragraph, which was quite short, was headed: LOU GANDESI QUESTIONED IN GEM THEFTS. "Listen to this, Henry," I said, and began to read.

Acting on an anonymous tip police late last night picked up Louis G. (Lou) Gandesi, proprietor of a well-known Spring Street tavern, and quizzed him intensively concerning the recent wave of dinner-party hold-ups in an exclusive western section of this city, hold-ups during which, it is alleged, more than two hundred thousand dollars' worth of valuable jewels have been torn at gun's point from women guests in fashionable homes. Gandesi was released at a late hour and refused to make any statement to reporters. "I never kibitz the cops," he said modestly. Captain William Norgaard, of the General Robbery Detail, announced himself as satisfied that Gandesi had no connection with the robberies, and that the tip was merely an act of personal spite.

I folded the paper and threw it on the bed.

"You win, bo," Henry said, and handed me the bottle. I took a long drink and returned it to him. "Now what? Brace this Gandesi and take him through the hoops?"

"He may be a dangerous man, Henry. Do you think we are equal to it?"

Henry snorted contemptuously. "Yah, a Spring Street punk. Some fat slob with a phony ruby on his mitt. Lead me to him. We'll turn the slob inside out and drain his liver. But we're just about fresh out of liquor. All we got is maybe a pint." He examined the bottle against the light.

"We have had enough for the moment, Henry."

"We ain't drunk, are we? I only had seven drinks since I got here, maybe nine."

"Certainly we are not drunk, Henry, but you take very large drinks, and we have a difficult evening before us. I think we should now get shaved and dressed, and I further think that we should wear dinner clothes. I have an extra suit which will fit you admirably, as we are almost exactly the same size. It is certainly a remarkable omen that two such large men should be associated in the same enterprise. Evening clothes impress these low characters, Henry."

"Swell," Henry said. "They'll think we're mugs workin' for some big shot. This Gandesi will be scared enough to swallow his necktie."

We decided to do as I had suggested and I laid out clothes for Henry, and while he was bathing and shaving I telephoned to Ellen Macintosh.

"Oh, Walter, I am so glad you called up," she cried. "Have you found anything?"

"Not yet, darling," I said. "But we have an idea. Henry and I are just about to put it into execution."

"Henry, Walter? Henry who?"

"Why, Henry Eichelberger, of course, darling. Have you forgotten him so soon? Henry and I are warm friends and we – "

She interrupted me coldly. "Are you drinking, Walter?" she demanded in a very distant voice.

"Certainly not, darling. Henry is a teetotaler."

She sniffed sharply. I could hear the sound distinctly over the telephone. "But didn't Henry take the pearls?" she asked, after quite a long pause.

"Henry, angel? Of course not. Henry left because he was in love with you."

"Oh, Walter. That ape? I'm sure you're drinking terribly. I don't ever want to speak to you again. Goodbye." And she hung the phone up very sharply so that a painful sensation made itself felt in my ear.

I sat down in a chair with a bottle of Old Plantation in my hand wondering what I had said that could be construed as offensive or indiscreet. As I was unable to think of anything, I consoled myself with the bottle until Henry came out of the bathroom looking extremely personable in one of my pleated shirts and a wing collar and black bow tie.

It was dark when we left the apartment and I, at least, was full of hope and confidence, although a little depressed by the way Ellen Macintosh had spoken to me over the telephone.

4

MR. GANDESI'S ESTABLISHMENT was not difficult to find, inasmuch as the first taxicab driver Henry yelled at on Spring Street directed us to it. It was called the Blue Lagoon and its interior was bathed in an unpleasant blue light. Henry and I entered it steadily, since we had consumed a partly solid meal at Mandy's Caribbean Grotto before starting out to find Mr. Gandesi. Henry looked almost handsome in my second-best dinner suit, with a fringed white scarf hanging over his shoulder, a lightweight black felt hat on the back of his head (which was only a little larger than mine), and a bottle of whiskey in each of the side pockets of the summer overcoat he was wearing.

The bar of the Blue Lagoon was crowded, but Henry and I went on back to the small dim dining room behind it. A man in a dirty dinner suit came up to us and Henry asked him for Gandesi, and he pointed out a fat man who sat alone at a small table in the far corner of the room. We went that way.

The man sat with a small glass of red wine in front of him and slowly twisted a large green stone on his finger. He did not look up. There were no other chairs at the table, so Henry leaned on it with both elbows.

"You Gandesi?" he said.

The man did not look up even then. He moved his thick black eyebrows together and said in an absent voice: "Si. Yes."

"We got to talk to you in private," Henry told him. "Where we won't be disturbed."

Gandesi looked up now and there was extreme boredom in his flat black almond-shaped eyes. "So?" he asked and shrugged. "Eet ees about what?"

"About some pearls," Henry said. "Forty-nine on the string, matched and pink."

"You sell – or you buy?" Gandesi inquired and his chin began to shake up and down as if with amusement.

"Buy," Henry said.

The man at the table crooked his finger quietly and a very large waiter appeared at his side. "Ees dronk," he said lifelessly. "Put dees men out."

The waiter took hold of Henry's shoulder. Henry reached up carelessly and took hold of the waiter's hand and twisted it. The waiter's face in that bluish light turned some color I could not describe, but which was not at all healthy. He let out a low moan. Henry dropped the hand and said to me: "Put a C-note on the table."

I took my wallet out and extracted from it one of the two hundred-dollar bills I had taken the precaution to obtain from the cashier at the Chateau Moraine. Gandesi stared at the bill and made a gesture to the large waiter, who went away rubbing his hand and holding it tight against his chest.

"What for?" Gandesi asked.

"Five minutes of your time alone."

"Ees very fonny. Okay, I bite." Gandesi took the bill and folded it neatly and put it in his vest pocket. Then he put both hands on the table and pushed himself heavily to his feet. He started to waddle away without looking at us.

Henry and I followed him among the crowded tables to the far side of the dining room and through a door in the wainscoting and then down a narrow dim hallway. At the end of this Gandesi opened a door into a lighted room and stood holding it for us, with a grave smile on his olive face. I went in first.

As Henry passed in front of Gandesi into the room the latter, with surprising agility, took a small shiny black leather club from his clothes and hit Henry on the head with it very hard. Henry sprawled forward on his hands and knees. Gandesi shut the door of the room very quickly for a man of his build and leaned against it with the small club in his left hand. Now, very suddenly, in his right hand appeared a short but heavy black revolver.

"Ees very fonny," he said politely, and chuckled to himself.

Exactly what happened then I did not see clearly. Henry was at one instant on his hands and knees with his back to Gandesi. In the next, or possibly even in the same instant, something swirled like a big fish in water and Gandesi grunted. I then saw that Henry's hard blond head was buried in Gandesi's stomach and that Henry's large hands held both of Gandesi's hairy wrists. Then Henry straightened his body to its full height and Gandesi was high up in the air balanced on top of Henry's head, his mouth strained wide open and his face a dark purple color. Then Henry shook himself, as it seemed, quite lightly, and Gandesi landed on his back on the floor with a terrible thud and lay gasping. Then a key turned in the door and Henry stood with his back to it, holding both the club and the revolver in his left hand, and solicitously feeling the pockets which contained our supply of whiskey. All this happened with such rapidity that I leaned against the side wall and felt a little sick at my stomach.

"A gut-buster," Henry drawled. "A comedian. Wait'll I loosen my belt."

Gandesi rolled over and got to his feet very slowly and painfully and stood swaying and passing his hand up and down his face. His clothes were covered with dust.

"This here's a sap," Henry said, showing me the small black club. "He hit me with it, didn't he?"

"Why, Henry, don't you know?" I inquired.

"I just wanted to be sure," Henry said. "You don't do that to the Eichelbergers."

"Okay, what you boys want?" Gandesi asked abruptly, with no trace whatever of his Italian accent.

"I told you what we wanted, dough-face."

"I don't think I know you boys," Gandesi said and lowered his body with care into a wooden chair beside a shabby office desk. He mopped his face and neck and felt himself in various places.

"You got the wrong idea, Gandesi. A lady living in Carondelet Park lost a forty-nine-bead pearl necklace a couple of days back. A box job, but a pushover. Our outfit's carrying a little insurance on those marbles. And I'll take that C note."

He walked over to Gandesi and Gandesi quickly reached the folded bill from his pocket and handed it to him. Henry gave me the bill and I put it back in my wallet.

"I don't think I hear about it," Gandesi said carefully.

"You hit me with a sap," Henry said. "Listen kind of hard."

Gandesi shook his head and then winced. "I don't back no petermen," he said, "nor no heist guys. You got me wrong."

"Listen hard," Henry said in a low voice. "You might hear something." He swung the small black club lightly in front of his body with two fingers of his right hand. The slightly too-small hat was still on the back of his head, although a little crumpled.

"Henry," I said, "you seem to be doing all the work this evening. Do you think that is quite fair?"

"Okay, work him over," Henry said. "These fat guys bruise something lovely."

By this time Gandesi had become a more natural color and was gazing at us steadily. "Insurance guys, huh?" he inquired dubiously.

"You said it, dough-face."

"You try Melachrino?" Gandesi asked.

"Haw," Henry began raucously, "a gut-buster. A — " but I interrupted him sharply.

"One moment, Henry," I said. Then turning to Gandesi, "Is this Melachrino a person?" I asked him.

Gandesi's eyes rounded in surprise. "Sure — a guy. You don't know him, huh?" A look of dark suspicion was born in his sloe-black eyes, but vanished almost as soon as it appeared.

"Phone him," Henry said, pointing to the instrument which stood on the shabby office desk.

"Phone is bad," Gandesi objected thoughtfully.

"So is sap poison," Henry said.

Gandesi sighed and turned his thick body in the chair and drew the telephone towards him. He dialed a number with an inky nail and listened. After an interval he said: "Joe? . . . Lou. Couple insurance guys tryin' to deal on a Carondelet Park job . . . Yeah . . . No, marbles . . . You ain't heard a whisper, huh? . . . Okay, Joe."

Gandesi replaced the phone and swung around in the chair again. He studied us with sleepy eyes. "No soap. What insurance outfit you boys work for?"

"Give him a card," Henry said to me.

I took my wallet out once more and withdrew one of my cards from it. It was an engraved calling card and contained nothing but my name. So I used my pocket pencil to write, Chateau Moraine Apartments, Franklin near Ivar, below the name. I showed the card to Henry and then gave it to Gandesi.

Gandesi read the card and quietly bit his finger. His face brightened suddenly. "You boys better see Jack Lawler," he said.

Henry stared at him closely. Gandesi's eyes were now bright and unblinking and guileless.

"Who's he?" Henry asked.

"Runs the Penguin Club. Out on the Strip — Eighty-six Forty-four Sunset or some number like that. He can find out, if any guy can."

"Thanks," Henry said quietly. He glanced at me. "You believe him?"

"Well, Henry," I said, "I don't really think he would be above telling us an untruth."

"Haw!" Gandesi began suddenly. "A gut-buster! A — "

"Can it!" Henry snarled. "That's my line. Straight goods, is it, Gandesi? About this Jack Lawler?"

Gandesi nodded vigorously. "Straight goods, absolute. Jack Lawler got a finger in everything high class that's touched. But he ain't easy to see."

"Don't worry none about that. Thanks, Gandesi."

Henry tossed the black club into the corner of the room and broke open the breech of the revolver he had been holding all this time in his left hand. He ejected the shells and then bent down and slid the gun along the floor until it disappeared under the desk. He tossed the cartridges idly in his hand for a moment and then let them spill on the floor.

"So long, Gandesi," he said coldly. "And keep that schnozzle of yours clean, if you don't want to be looking for it under the bed."

He opened the door then and we both went out quickly and left the Blue Lagoon without interference from any of the employees.

5

MY CAR WAS parked a short distance away down the block. We entered it and Henry leaned his arms on the wheel and stared moodily through the windshield.

"Well, what you think, Walter?" he inquired at length.

"If you ask my opinion, Henry, I think Mr. Gandesi told us a cock-and-bull story merely to get rid of us. Furthermore I do not believe he thought we were insurance agents."

"Me too, and an extra helping," Henry said. "I don't figure there's any such guy as this Melachrino or this Jack Lawler and this Gandesi called up some dead number and had himself a phony chin with it. I oughta go back there and pull his arms and legs off. The hell with the fat slob."

"We had the best idea we could think of, Henry, and we executed it to the best of our ability. I now suggest that we return to my apartment and try to think of something else."

"And get drunk," Henry said, starting the car and guiding it away from the curb.

"We could perhaps have a small allowance of liquor, Henry."

"Yah!" Henry snorted. "A stall. I oughta go back there and wreck the joint."

He stopped at the intersection, although no traffic signal was in operation at the time, and raised a bottle of whiskey to his lips. He was in the act of drinking when a car came up behind us and collided with our car, but not very severely. Henry choked and lowered his bottle, spilling some of the liquor on his garments.

"This town's getting too crowded," he snarled. "A guy can't take hisself a drink without some smart monkey bumps his elbow."

Whoever it was in the car behind us blew a horn with some insistence, inasmuch as our car had not yet moved forward. Henry wrenched the door open and got out and went back. I heard voices of considerable loudness, the louder being Henry's voice. He came back after a moment and got into the car and drove on.

"I oughta have pulled his mush off," he said, "but I went soft." He drove rapidly the rest of the way to Hollywood and the Chateau Moraine and we went up to my apartment and sat down with large glasses in our hands.

"We got better than a quart and a half of hooch," Henry said, looking at the two bottles which he had placed on the table beside others which had long since been emptied. "That oughta be good for an idea."

"If it isn't enough, Henry, there is an abundant further supply where it came from." I drained my glass cheerfully.

"You seem a right guy," Henry said. "What makes you always talk so funny?"

"I cannot seem to change my speech, Henry. My father and mother were both severe purists in the New England tradition, and the vernacular has never come naturally to my lips, even while I was in college."

Henry made an attempt to digest this remark, but I could see that it lay somewhat heavily on his stomach.

We talked for a time concerning Gandesi and the doubtful quality of his advice, and thus passed perhaps half an hour. Then rather suddenly the white telephone on my desk began to ring. I hurried over to it, hoping that it was Ellen Macintosh and that she had recovered from her ill humor. But it proved to be a male voice and a strange one to me. It spoke crisply with an unpleasant metallic quality of tone.

"You Walter Gage?"

"This is Mister Gage speaking."

"Well, *Mister* Gage, I understand you're in the market for some jewelry."

I held the phone very tightly and turned my body and made grimaces to Henry over the top of the instrument. But he was moodily pouring himself another large portion of Old Plantation.

"That is so," I said into the telephone, trying to keep my voice steady although my excitement was almost too much for me. "If by jewelry you mean pearls."

"Forty-nine in a rope, brother. And five grand is the price."

"Why that is entirely absurd," I gasped. "Five thousand dollars for those – "

The voice broke in on me rudely. "You heard me, brother. Five grand. Just hold up the hand and count the fingers. No more, no less. Think it over. I'll call you later."

The phone clicked dryly and I replaced the instrument back in its cradle. I was trembling. I walked back to my chair and sat down and wiped my face with my handkerchief.

"Henry," I said in a low tense voice, "it worked. But how strangely."

Henry put his empty glass down on the floor. It was the first time that I had ever seen him put an empty glass down and leave it empty. He stared at me closely with his tight unblinking green eyes.

"Yeah?" he said gently. "What worked, lad?" He licked his lips slowly with the tip of his tongue.

"What we accomplished down at Gandesi's place, Henry. A man just called me on the telephone and asked me if I was in the market for pearls."

"Geez." Henry pursed his lips and whistled gently. "That damn dago had something after all."

"But the price is five thousand dollars, Henry. That seems beyond reasonable explanation."

"Huh?" Henry's eyes seemed to bulge as if they were about to depart from their orbits. "Five grand for them ringers? The guy's nuts. They cost two C's, you said. Bugs completely is what the guy is. Five grand? Why, for five grand I could buy me enough phony pearls to cover an elephant's caboose."

I could see that Henry seemed puzzled. He refilled our glasses silently and we stared at each other over them. "Well, what the heck can you do with that, Walter?" he asked after a long silence.

"Henry," I said firmly, "there is only one thing to do. It is true that Ellen Macintosh spoke to me in confidence, and as she did not have Mrs. Penruddock's express permission to tell me about the pearls, I suppose I should respect that confidence. But Ellen is now angry with me and does not wish to speak to me, for the reason that I am drinking whiskey in considerable quantities, although my speech and brain are still reasonably clear. This last is a very strange development and I think, in spite of everything, some close friend of the family should be consulted. Preferably of course, a man, someone of large business experience, and in addition to that a man who understands about jewels. There *is* such a man, Henry, and tomorrow morning I shall call upon him."

"Geez," Henry said. "You coulda said all that in nine words, bo. Who is this guy?"

"His name is Mr. Lansing Gallemore, and he is president of the Gallemore Jewelry Company on Seventh Street. He is a very old friend of Mrs. Penruddock — Ellen has often mentioned him — and is, in fact, the very man who procured for her the imitation pearls."

"But this guy will tip the bulls," Henry objected.

"I do not think so, Henry. I do not think he will do anything to embarrass Mrs. Penruddock in any way."

Henry shrugged. "Phonies are phonies," he said. "You can't make nothing else outa them. Not even no president of no jewlery store can't."

"Nevertheless, there must be a reason why so large a sum is demanded, Henry. The only reason that occurs to me is blackmail and, frankly, that is a little too much for me to handle alone, because I do not know enough about the background of the Penruddock family."

"Okay," Henry said, sighing. "If that's your hunch, you better follow it, Walter. And I better breeze on home and flop so as to be in good shape for the rough work, if any."

"You would not care to pass the night here, Henry?"

"Thanks, pal, but I'm okay back at the hotel. I'll just take this spare bottle of the tiger sweat to put me to sleep. I might happen to get a call from the agency in the A.M. and would have to brush my teeth and go after it. And I guess I better change my duds back to where I can mix with the common people."

So saying he went into the bathroom and in a short time emerged wearing his own blue serge suite. I urged him to take my car, but he said it would not be safe in his neighborhood. He did, however, consent to use the topcoat he had been wearing and, placing in it carefully the unopened quart of whiskey, he shook me warmly by the hand.

"One moment, Henry," I said and took out my wallet. I extended a twenty-dollar bill to him.

"What's that in favor of?" he growled.

"You are temporarily out of employment, Henry, and you have done a noble piece of work this evening, puzzling as are the results. You should be rewarded and I can well afford this small token."

"Well, thanks, pal," Henry said. "But it's just a loan." His voice was gruff with emotion. "Should I give you a buzz in the A.M.?"

"By all means. And there is one thing more that has occurred to me. Would it not be advisable for you to change your hotel? Suppose, through no fault of mine, the police learn of this theft. Would they not at least suspect you?"

"Hell, they'd bounce me up and down for hours," Henry said. "But what'll it get them? I ain't no ripe peach."

"It is for you to decide, of course, Henry."

"Yeah. Good night, pal, and don't have no nightmares."

He left me then and I felt suddenly very depressed and lonely. Henry's company had been very stimulating to me, in spite of his rough way of talking. He was very much of a man. I poured myself a rather large drink of whiskey from the remaining bottle and drank it quickly but gloomily.

The effect was such that I had an overmastering desire to speak to Ellen Macintosh at all costs. I went to the telephone and called her number. After a long wait a sleepy maid answered. But Ellen, upon hearing my name, refused to come to the telephone. That depressed me still further and I finished the rest of the whiskey almost without noticing what I was doing. I then lay down on the bed and fell into fitful slumber.

6

THE BUSY RINGING of the telephone awoke me and I saw that the morning sunlight was streaming into the room. It was nine o'clock and all the lamps were still burning. I arose feeling a little stiff and dissipated, for I was still wearing my dinner suit. But I am a healthy man with very steady nerves and I did not feel as badly as I expected. I went to the telephone and answered it.

Henry's voice said: "How you feel, pal? I got a hangover like twelve Swedes."

"Not too badly, Henry."

"I got a call from the agency about a job. I better go down and take a gander at it. Should I drop around later?"

"Yes, Henry, by all means do that. By eleven o'clock I should be back from the errand about which I spoke to you last night."

"Any more calls from you know?"

"Not yet, Henry."

"Check. Abyssinia." He hung up and I took a cold shower and shaved and dressed. I donned a quiet brown business suit and had some coffee sent up from the coffee shop downstairs. I also had the waiter remove the empty bottles from my apartment and gave him a dollar for his trouble. After drinking two cups of black coffee I felt my own man once more and drove downtown to the Gallemore Jewelry Company's large and brilliant store on West Seventh Street.

It was another bright, golden morning and it seemed that somehow things should adjust themselves on so pleasant a day.

Mr. Lansing Gallemore proved to be a little difficult to see, so that I was compelled to tell his secretary that it was a matter concerning Mrs. Penruddock and of a confidential nature. Upon this message being carried in to him I was at once ushered into a long paneled office, at the far end of which Mr. Gallemore stood behind a massive desk. He extended a thin pink hand to me.

"Mr. Gage? I don't believe we have met, have we?"

"No, Mr. Gallemore, I do not believe we have. I am the fiancé – or was until last night – of Miss Ellen Macintosh, who, as you probably know, is Mrs. Penruddock's nurse. I am come to you upon a very delicate matter and it is necessary that I ask for your confidence before I speak."

He was a man of perhaps seventy-five years of age, and very thin and tall and correct and well preserved. He had cold blue eyes but a warming smile. He was attired youthfully enough in a gray flannel suit with a red carnation at his lapel.

"That is something I make it a rule never to promise, Mr. Gage," he said. "I think it is almost always a very unfair request. But if you assure me the matter concerns Mrs. Penruddock and is really of a delicate and confidential nature, I will make an exception."

"It is indeed, Mr. Gallemore," I said, and thereupon told him the entire story, concealing nothing, not even the fact that I had consumed far too much whiskey the day before.

He stared at me curiously at the end of my story. His finely shaped hand picked up an old-fashioned white quill pen and he slowly tickled his right ear with the feather of it.

"Mr. Gage," he said, "can't you guess why they ask five thousand dollars for that string of pearls?"

"If you permit me to guess, in a matter of so personal a nature, I could perhaps hazard an explanation, Mr. Gallemore."

He moved the white feather around to his left ear and nodded. "Go ahead, son."

"The pearls are in fact real, Mr. Gallemore. You are a very old friend of Mrs. Penruddock – perhaps even a childhood sweetheart. When she gave you her pearls, her golden wedding present, to sell because she was in sore need of money for a generous purpose, you did not sell them, Mr. Gallemore. You only pretended to sell them. You gave her twenty thousand dollars of your own money, and you returned the real pearls to her, pretending that they were an imitation made in Czechoslovakia."

"Son, you think a lot smarter than you talk," Mr. Gallemore said. He arose and walked to a window, pulled aside a fine net curtain and looked down on the bustle of Seventh Street. He came back to his desk and seated himself and smiled a little wistfully.

"You are almost embarrassingly correct, Mr. Gage," he said, and sighed. "Mrs. Penruddock is a very proud woman, or I should simply have offered her the twenty thousand dollars as an unsecured loan. I happened to be the coadministrator of Mr. Penruddock's estate and I knew that in the condition of the financial market at that time it would be out of the question to raise enough cash, without damaging the corpus of the estate beyond reason, to care for all those relatives and pensioners. So Mrs. Penruddock sold her pearls – as she thought – but she insisted that no one should know about it. And I did what you have guessed. It was unimportant. I could afford the gesture. I have never married, Gage, and I am rated a wealthy man. As a matter of fact, at that time, the pearls would not have fetched more than half of what I gave her, or of what they should bring today."

I lowered my eyes for fear this kindly old gentleman might be troubled by my direct gaze.

"So I think we had better raise that five thousand, son," Mr. Gallemore at once added in a brisk voice. "The price is pretty low, although stolen pearls are a great deal more difficult to deal in than cut stones. If I should care to trust you that far on your face, do you think you could handle the assignment?"

"Mr. Gallemore," I said firmly but quietly, "I am a total stranger to you and I am only flesh and blood. But I promise you by the memories of my dead and revered parents that there will be no cowardice."

"Well, there is a good deal of the flesh and blood, son," Mr. Gallemore said kindly. "And I am not afraid of your stealing the money, because possibly I know a little more about Miss Ellen Macintosh and her boy friend than you might suspect. Furthermore, the pearls are insured, in my name, of course, and the insurance company should really handle this affair. But you and your funny friend seem to have got along very nicely so far, and I believe in playing out a hand. This Henry must be quite a man."

"I have grown very attached to him, in spite of his uncouth ways," I said.

Mr. Gallemore played with his white quill pen a little longer and then he brought out a large checkbook and wrote a check, which he carefully blotted and passed across the desk.

"If you get the pearls, I'll see that the insurance people refund this to me," he said. "If they like my business, there will be no difficulty about that. The bank is down at the corner and I will be waiting for their call. They won't cash the check without telephoning me, probably. Be careful, son, and don't get hurt."

He shook hands with me once more and I hesitated. "Mr. Gallemore, you are placing a greater trust in me than any man ever has," I said. "With the exception, of course, of my own father."

"I am acting like a damn fool," he said with a peculiar smile. "It is so long since I heard anyone talk the way Jane Austen writes that it is making a sucker out of me."

"Thank you, sir. I know my language is a bit stilted. Dare I ask you to do me a small favor, sir?"

"What is it, Gage?"

"To telephone Miss Ellen Macintosh, from whom I am now a little estranged, and tell her that I am not drinking today, and that you have entrusted me with a very delicate mission."

He laughed aloud. "I'll be glad to, Walter. And as I know she can be trusted, I'll give her an idea of what's going on."

I left him then and went down to the bank with the check, and the teller, after looking at me suspiciously, then absenting himself from his cage for a long time, finally counted out the money in hundred-dollar bills with the reluctance one might have expected, if it had been his own money.

I placed the flat packet of bills in my pocket and said: "Now give me a roll of quarters, please."

"A roll of quarters, sir?" His eyebrows lifted.

"Exactly. I use them for tips. And naturally I should prefer to carry them home in the wrappings."

"Oh, I see. Ten dollars, please."

I took the fat hard roll of coins and dropped it into my pocket and drove back to Hollywood.

Henry was waiting for me in the lobby of the Chateau Moraine, twirling his hat between his rough hard hands. His face looked a little more deeply lined than it had the day before and I noticed that his breath smelled of whiskey. We went up to my apartment and he turned to me eagerly.

"Any luck, pal?"

"Henry," I said, "before we proceed further into this day I wish it clearly understood that I am not drinking. I see that already you have been at the bottle."

"Just a pick-up, Walter," he said a little contritely. "That job I went out for was gone before I got there. What's the good word?"

I sat down and lit a cigarette and stared at him evenly. "Well, Henry, I don't really know whether I should tell you or not. But it seems a little petty not to do so after all you did last night to Gandesi." I hesitated a moment longer while Henry stared at me and pinched the muscles of his left arm. "The pearls are real, Henry. And I have instructions to proceed with the business and I have five thousand dollars in cash in my pocket at this moment."

I told him briefly what had happened.

He was more amazed than words could tell. "Cripes!" he exclaimed, his mouth hanging wide open. "You mean you got the five grand from this Gallemore – just like that?"

"Precisely that, Henry."

"Kid," he said earnestly, "you got something with that daisy pan and that fluff talk that a lot of guys would give important dough to cop. Five grand – out of a business guy – just like that. Why, I'll be a monkey's uncle. I'll be a snake's daddy. I'll be a mickey finn at a woman's-club lunch."

At that exact moment, as if my entrance to the building had been observed, the telephone rang again and I sprang to answer it.

It was one of the voices I was awaiting, but not the one I wanted to hear with the greater longing. "How's it looking to you this morning, Gage?"

"It is looking better," I said. "If I can have any assurance of honorable treatment, I am prepared to go through with it."

"You mean you got the dough?"

"In my pocket at this exact moment."

The voice seemed to exhale a slow breath. "You'll get your marbles okay – if we get the price, Gage. We're in this business for a long time and we don't welsh. If we did, it would soon get around and nobody would play with us any more."

"Yes, I can readily understand that," I said. "Proceed with your instructions," I added coldly.

"Listen close, Gage. Tonight at eight sharp you be in Pacific Palisades. Know where that is?"

"Certainly. It is a small residential section west of the polo fields on Sunset Boulevard."

"Right. Sunset goes slap through it. There's one drugstore there – open till nine. Be there waiting a call at eight sharp tonight. Alone. And I mean alone, Gage. No cops and no strong-arm guys. It's rough country down there and we got a way to get you to where we want you and know if you're alone. Get all this?"

"I am not entirely an idiot," I retorted.

"No dummy packages, Gage. The dough will be checked. No guns. You'll be searched and there's enough of us to cover you from all angles. We know your car. No funny business, no smart work, no slip-up and nobody hurt. That's the way we do business. How's the dough fixed?"

"One-hundred-dollar bills," I said. "And only a few of them are new."

"Attaboy. Eight o'clock then. Be smart, Gage."

The phone clicked in my ear and I hung up. It rang again almost instantly. This time it was the *one* voice.

"Oh, Walter," Ellen cried, "I was so mean to you! Please forgive me, Walter. Mr. Gallemore has told me everything and I'm so frightened."

"There is nothing of which to be frightened," I told her warmly. "Does Mrs. Penruddock know, darling?"

"No, darling. Mr. Gallemore told me not to tell her. I am phoning from a store down on Sixth Street. Oh, Walter, I really am frightened. Will Henry go with you?"

"I am afraid not, darling. The arrangements are all made and they will not permit it. I must go alone."

"Oh, Walter! I'm terrified. I can't bear the suspense."

"There is nothing to fear," I assured her. "It is a simple business transaction. And I am not exactly a midget."

"But, Walter — oh, I *will* try to be brave, Walter. Will you promise me just one teensy-weensy little thing?"

"Not a drop, darling," I said firmly. "Not a single solitary drop."

"Oh, Walter!"

There was a little more of that sort of thing, very pleasant to me in the circumstances, although possibly not of great interest to others. We finally parted with my promise to telephone as soon as the meeting between the crooks and myself had been consummated.

I turned from the telephone to find Henry drinking deeply from a bottle he had taken from his hip pocket.

"Henry!" I cried sharply.

He looked at me over the bottle with a shaggy determined look. "Listen, pal," he said in a low hard voice. "I got enough of your end of the talk to figure the set-up. Some place out in the tall weeds and you go alone and they feed you the old sap poison and take your dough and leave you lying — with the marbles still in their kitty. Nothing doing, pal. I said — nothing doing!" He almost shouted the last words.

"Henry, it is my duty and I must do it," I said quietly.

"Haw!" Henry snorted. "I say no. You're a nut, but you're a sweet guy on the side. I say no. Henry Eichelberger of the Wisconsin Eichelbergers — in fact, I might just as leave say of the Milwaukee Eichelbergers — says no. And he says it with both hands working." He drank again from his bottle.

"You certainly will not help matters by becoming intoxicated," I told him rather bitterly.

He lowered the bottle and looked at me with amazement written all over his rugged features. "Drunk, Walter?" he boomed. "Did I hear you say drunk? An Eichelberger drunk? Listen, son. We ain't got a lot of time now. It would take

974

maybe three months. Some day when you got three months and maybe five thousand gallons of whiskey and a funnel, I would be glad to take my own time and show you what an Eichelberger looks like when drunk. You wouldn't believe it. Son, there wouldn't be nothing left of this town but a few sprung girders and a lot of busted bricks, in the middle of which – Geez, I'll get talking English myself if I hang around you much longer – in the middle of which, peaceful, with no human life nearer than maybe fifty miles, Henry Eichelberger will be on his back smiling at the sun. Drunk, Walter. Not stinking drunk, not even country-club drunk. But you could use the word drunk and I wouldn't take no offense."

He sat down and drank again. I stared moodily at the floor. There was nothing for me to say.

"But that," Henry said, "is some other time. Right now I am just taking my medicine. I ain't myself without a slight touch of delirium tremens, as the guy says. I was brought up on it. And I'm going with you, Walter. Where is this place at?"

"It's down near the beach, Henry, and you are not going with me. If you must get drunk – get drunk, but you are not going with me."

"You got a big car, Walter. I'll hide in back on the floor under a rug. It's a cinch."

"No, Henry."

"Walter, you are a sweet guy," Henry said, "and I am going with you into this frame. Have a smell from the barrel, Walter. You look to me kind of frail."

We argued for an hour and my head ached and I began to feel very nervous and tired. It was then that I made what might have been a fatal mistake. I succumbed to Henry's blandishments and took a small portion of whiskey, purely for medicinal purposes. This made me feel so much more relaxed that I took another and larger portion. I had had no food except coffee that morning and only a very light dinner the evening before. At the end of another hour Henry had been out for two more bottles of whiskey and I was as bright as a bird. All difficulties had now disappeared and I had agreed heartily that Henry should lie in the back of my car hidden by a rug and accompany me to the rendezvous.

We had passed the time very pleasantly until two o'clock, at which hour I began to feel sleepy and lay down on the bed, and fell into a deep slumber.

7

WHEN I AWOKE again it was almost dark. I rose from the bed with panic in my heart, and also a sharp shoot of pain through my temples. It was only six-thirty, however. I was alone in the apartment and lengthening shadows were stealing across the floor. The display of empty whiskey bottles on the table was very disgusting. Henry Eichelberger was nowhere to be seen. With an instinctive pang, of which I was almost immediately ashamed, I hurried to my jacket hanging on the back of a chair and plunged my hand into the inner breast pocket. The packet of bills was there intact. After a brief hesitation, and with a feeling of secret guilt, I drew them out and slowly counted them over. Not a bill was missing. I replaced the money and tried to smile at myself for this lack of trust, and then switched on a light and went into the bathroom to take alternate hot and cold showers until my brain was once more comparatively clear.

I had done this and was dressing in fresh linen when a key turned in the lock and Henry Eichelberger entered with two wrapped bottles under his arm. He looked at me with what I thought was genuine affection.

"A guy that can sleep it off like you is a real champ, Walter," he said admiringly. "I snuck your keys so as not to wake you. I had to get some eats and some more hooch. I done a little solo drinking, which as I told you is against my principles, but this is a big day. However, we take it easy from now on as to the hooch. We can't afford no jitters till it's all over."

He had unwrapped a bottle while he was speaking and poured me a small drink. I drank it gratefully and immediately felt a warm glow in my veins.

"I bet you looked in your poke for that deck of mazuma," Henry said, grinning at me.

I felt myself reddening, but I said nothing. "Okay, pal, you done right. What the heck do you know about Henry Eichelberger anyways? I done something else." He reached behind him and drew a short automatic from his hip pocket. "If these boys wanta play rough," he said, "I got me five bucks' worth of iron that don't mind playin' rough a little itself. And the Eichelbergers ain't missed a whole lot of the guys they shot at."

"I don't like that, Henry," I said severely. "That is contrary to the agreement."

"Nuts to the agreement," Henry said. "The boys get their dough and no cops. I'm out to see that they hand over them marbles and don't pull any fast footwork."

I saw there was no use arguing with him, so I completed my dressing and prepared to leave the apartment. We each took one more drink and then Henry put a full bottle in his pocket and we left.

On the way down the hall to the elevator he explained in a low voice: "I got a hack out front to tail you, just in case these boys got the same idea. You might circle a few quiet blocks so as I can find out. More like they don't pick you up till down close to the beach."

"All this must be costing you a great deal of money, Henry," I told him, and while we were waiting for the elevator to come up I took another twenty-dollar bill from my wallet and offered it to him. He took the money reluctantly, but finally folded it and placed it in his pocket.

I did as Henry had suggested, driving up and down a number of the hilly streets north of Hollywood Boulevard, and presently I heard the unmistakable hoot of a taxicab horn behind me. I pulled over to the side of the road. Henry got out of the cab and paid off the driver and got into my car beside me.

"All clear," he said. "No tail. I'll just keep kind of slumped down and you better stop somewhere for some groceries on account of if we have to get rough with these mugs, a full head of steam will help."

So I drove westward and dropped down to Sunset Boulevard and presently stopped at a crowded drive-in restaurant where we sat at the counter and ate a light meal of omelette and black coffee. We then proceeded on our way. When we reached Beverly Hills, Henry again made me wind in and out through a number of residential streets where he observed very carefully through the rear window of the car.

Fully satisfied at last we drove back to Sunset, and without incident onwards through Bel-Air and the fringes of Westwood, almost as far as the Riviera Polo field. At this point, down in the hollow, there is a canyon called Mandeville Canyon, a very quiet place. Henry had me drive up this for a short distance. We then stopped and had a little whiskey from his bottle and he climbed into the back of the car and curled his big body up on the floor, with the rug over him and his automatic pistol and his bottle down on the floor conveniently to his hand. That done I once more resumed my journey.

Pacific Palisades is a district whose inhabitants seem to retire rather early. When I reached what might be called the business center nothing was open but the drugstore beside the bank. I parked the car, with Henry remaining silent under the rug in the back, except for a slight gurgling noise I noticed as I stood on the dark sidewalk. Then I went into the drugstore and saw by its clock that it was now fifteen minutes to eight. I bought a package of cigarettes and lit one and took up my position near the open telephone booth.

The druggist, a heavy-set red-faced man of uncertain age, had a small radio up very loud and was listening to some foolish serial. I asked him to turn it down, as I was expecting an important telephone call. This he did, but not with any good grace, and immediately retired to the back part of his store whence I saw him looking out at me malignantly through a small glass window.

At precisely one minute to eight by the drugstore clock the phone rang sharply in the booth. I hastened into it and pulled the door tight shut. I lifted the receiver, trembling a little in spite of myself.

It was the same cool metallic voice. "Gage?"

"This is Mr. Gage."

"You done just what I told you?"

"Yes," I said. "I have the money in my pocket and I am entirely alone." I did not like the feeling of lying so brazenly, even to a thief, but I steeled myself to it.

"Listen, then. Go back about three hundred feet the way you come. Beside the firehouse there's a service station, closed up, painted green and red and white. Beside that, going south, is a dirt road. Follow it three-quarters of a mile and you come to a white fence of four-by-four built almost across the road. You can just squeeze your car by at the left side. Dim your lights and get through there and keep going down the little hill into a hollow with sage all around. Park there, cut your lights, and wait. Get it?"

"Perfectly," I said coldly, "and it shall be done exactly that way."

"And listen, pal. There ain't a house in half a mile, and there ain't any folks around at all. You got ten minutes to get there. You're watched right this minute. You get there fast and you get there alone – or you got a trip for biscuits. And don't light no matches or pills nor use no flashlights. On your way."

The phone went dead and I left the booth. I was scarcely outside the drugstore before the druggist rushed at his radio

979

and turned it up to a booming blare. I got into my car and turned it and drove back along Sunset Boulevard, as directed. Henry was as still as the grave on the floor behind me.

I was now very nervous and Henry had all the liquor which we had brought with us. I reached the firehouse in no time at all and through its front window I could see four firemen playing cards. I turned to the right down the dirt road past the red-and-green-and-white service station and almost at once the night was so still, in spite of the quiet sound of my car, that I could hear the crickets and treefrogs chirping and trilling in all directions, and from some nearby watery spot came the hoarse croak of a solitary bullfrog.

The road dipped and rose again and far off there was a yellow window. Then ahead of me, ghostly in the blackness of the moonless night, appeared the dim white barrier across the road. I noted the gap at the side and then dimmed my headlamps and steered carefully through it and so on down a rough short hill into an oval-shaped hollow space surrounded by low brush and plentifully littered with empty bottles and cans and pieces of paper. It was entirely deserted, however, at this dark hour. I stopped my car and shut off the ignition, and the lights, and sat there motionless, hands on the wheel.

Behind me I heard no murmur of sound from Henry. I waited possibly five minutes, although it seemed much longer, but nothing happened. It was very still, very lonely, and I did not feel happy.

Finally there was a faint sound of movement behind me and I looked back to see the pale blur of Henry's face peering at me from under the rug.

His voice whispered huskily, "Anything stirring, Walter?"

I shook my head at him vigorously and he once more pulled the rug over his face. I heard a faint sound of gurgling.

Fully fifteen minutes passed before I dared to move again. By this time the tensity of waiting had made me stiff. I therefore boldly unlatched the door of the car and stepped out upon the rough ground. Nothing happened. I walked slowly back and forth with my hands in my pockets. More and more time dragged by. More than half an hour had now elapsed and I became impatient. I went to the rear window of the car and spoke softly into the interior.

"Henry, I fear we have been victimized in a very cheap way. I fear very much that this is nothing but a low practical joke on the part of Mr. Gandesi in retaliation for the way you handled him last night. There is no one here and only one possible way of arriving. It looks to me like a very unlikely place for the sort of meeting we have been expecting."

"The son of a bitch!" Henry whispered back, and the gurgling sound was repeated in the darkness of the car. Then there was movement and he appeared free of the rug. The door opened against my body. Henry's head emerged. He looked in all directions his eyes could command. "Sit down on the running board," he whispered. "I'm getting out. If they got a bead on us from them bushes, they'll only see one head."

I did what Henry suggested and turned my collar up high and pulled my hat down over my eyes. As noiselessly as a shadow Henry stepped out of the car and shut the door without sound and stood before me ranging the limited horizon with his eyes. I could see the dim reflection of light on the gun in his hand. We remained thus for ten more minutes.

Henry then got angry and threw discretion to the winds. "Suckered!" he snarled. "You know what happened, Walter?"

"No, Henry. I do not."

"It was just a tryout, that's what it was. Somewhere along the line these dirty so-and-so's checked on you to see did you play ball, and then again they checked on you at that drugstore back there. I bet you a pair of solid platinum bicycle wheels that was a long-distance call you caught back there."

"Yes, Henry, now that you mention it, I am sure it was," I said sadly.

"There you are, kid. The bums ain't even left town. They are sitting back there beside their plush-lined spittoons giving you the big razzoo. And tomorrow this guy calls you again on the phone and says okay so far, but they had to be careful and they will try again tonight maybe out in San Fernando Valley and the price will be upped to ten grand, on account of their extra trouble. I oughta go back there and twist that Gandesi so he would be lookin' up his left pants leg."

"Well, Henry," I said, "after all, I did not do exactly what they told me to, because you insisted on coming with me. And perhaps they are more clever than you think. So I think the best thing now is to go back to town and hope there will be a chance tomorrow to try again. And you must promise me faithfully not to interfere."

"Nuts!" Henry said angrily. "Without me along they would take you the way the cat took the canary. You are a sweet guy, Walter, but you don't know as many answers as Baby Leroy. These guys are thieves and they have a string of marbles that might probably bring them twenty grand with careful handling. They are out for a quick touch, but they will squeeze all they can just the same. I oughta go back to that fat wop Gandesi right now. I could do things to that slob that ain't been invented yet."

"Now, Henry, don't get violent," I said.

"Haw," Henry snarled. "Them guys give me an ache in the back of my lap." He raised his bottle to his lips with his left hand and drank thirstily. His voice came down a few tones and sounded more peaceful. "Better dip the bill, Walter. The party's a flop."

"Perhaps you are right, Henry," I sighed. "I will admit that my stomach has been trembling like an autumn leaf for all of half an hour."

So I stood up boldly beside him and poured a liberal portion of the fiery liquid down my throat. At once my courage revived. I handed the bottle back to Henry and he placed it carefully down on the running board. He stood beside me dancing the short automatic pistol up and down on the broad palm of his hand.

"I don't need no tools to handle that bunch. The hell with it." And with a sweep of his arm he hurled the pistol off among the bushes, where it fell to the ground with a muffled thud. He walked away from the car and stood with his arms akimbo, looking up at the sky.

I moved over beside him and watched his averted face, insofar as I was able to see it in that dim light. A strange melancholy came over me. In the brief time I had known Henry I had grown very fond of him.

"Well, Henry," I said at last, "what is the next move?"

"Beat it on home, I guess," he said slowly and mournfully. "And get good and drunk." He doubled his hands into fists and shook them slowly. Then he turned to face me. "Yeah," he said. "Nothing else to do. Beat it on home, kid, is all that is left to us."

"Not quite yet, Henry," I said softly.

I took my right hand out of my pocket. I have large hands. In my right hand nestled the roll of wrapped quarters which I had obtained at the bank that morning. My hand made a large fist around them.

"Good night, Henry," I said quietly, and swung my fist with all the weight of my arm and body. "You had two strikes on me, Henry," I said. "The big one is still left."

But Henry was not listening to me. My fist with the wrapped weight of metal inside it had caught him fairly and squarely on the point of his jaw. His legs became boneless and he pitched straight forward, brushing my sleeve as he fell. I stepped quickly out of his way.

Henry Eichelberger lay motionless on the ground, as limp as a rubber glove.

I looked down at him a little sadly, waiting for him to stir, but he did not move a muscle. He lay inert, completely unconscious. I dropped the roll of quarters back into my pocket, bent over him, searched him thoroughly, moving him around like a sack of meal, but it was a long time before I found the pearls. They were twined around his ankle inside his left sock.

"Well, Henry," I said, speaking to him for the last time, although he could not hear me, "you are a gentleman, even if you are a thief. You could have taken the money a dozen times this afternoon and given me nothing. You could have taken it a little while ago when you had the gun in your hand, but even that repelled you. You threw the gun away and we were man to man, far from help, far from interference. And even then you hesitated, Henry. In fact, Henry, I think for a successful thief you hesitated just a little too long. But as a man of sporting feelings I can only think the more highly of you. Goodbye, Henry, and good luck."

I took my wallet out and withdrew a one-hundred-dollar bill and placed it carefully in the pocket where I had seen Henry put his money. Then I went back to the car and took a drink out of the whiskey bottle and corked it firmly and laid it beside him, convenient to his right hand.

I felt sure that when he awakened he would need it.

8

IT WAS PAST ten o'clock when I returned home to my apartment, but I at once went to the telephone and called Ellen Macintosh. "Darling!" I cried. "I have the pearls."

I caught the sound of her indrawn breath over the wire. "Oh darling," she said tensely and excitedly, "and you are not hurt? They did not hurt you, darling? They just took the money and let you go?"

"There were no 'they,' darling," I said proudly. "I still have Mr. Gallemore's money intact. There was only Henry."

"Henry!" she cried in a very strange voice. "But I thought – Come over here at once, Walter Gage, and tell me – "

984

"I have whiskey on my breath, Ellen."

"Darling! I'm sure you needed it. Come at once."

So once more I went down to the street and hurried to Carondelet Park and in no time at all was at the Penruddock residence. Ellen came out on the porch to meet me and we talked there quietly in the dark, holding hands, for the household had gone to bed. As simply as I could I told her my story.

"But darling," she said at last, "how did you know it was Henry? I thought Henry was your friend. And this other voice on the telephone – "

"Henry *was* my friend," I said a little sadly, "and that is what destroyed him. As to the voice on the telephone, that was a small matter and easily arranged. Henry was away from me a number of times to arrange it. There was just one small point that gave me thought. After I gave Gandesi my private card with the name of my apartment house scribbled upon it, it was necessary for Henry to communicate to his confederate that we had seen Gandesi and given him my name and address. For of course when I had this foolish, or perhaps not so very foolish idea of visiting some well-known underworld character in order to send a message that we would buy back the pearls, this was Henry's opportunity to make me think the telephone message came as a result of our talking to Gandesi, and telling him our difficulty. But since the first call came to me at my apartment before Henry had had a chance to inform his confederate of our meeting with Gandesi, it was obvious that a trick had been employed.

"Then I recalled that a car had bumped into us from behind and Henry had gone back to abuse the driver. And of course the bumping was deliberate, and Henry had made the opportunity for it on purpose, and his confederate was in the car. So Henry, while pretending to shout at him, was able to convey the necessary information."

"But, Walter," Ellen said, having listened to this explanation a little impatiently, "that is a very small matter. What I really want to know is how you decided that Henry had the pearls at all."

"But you told me he had them," I said. "You were quite sure of it. Henry is a very durable character. It would be just like him to hide the pearls somewhere, having no fear of what the police might do to him, and get another position and then after perhaps quite a long time, retrieve the pearls and quietly leave this part of the country."

Ellen shook her head impatiently in the darkness of the porch. "Walter," she said sharply, "you are hiding something. You could not have been sure and you would not have hit Henry in that brutal way, unless you had been sure. I know you well enough to know that."

"Well, darling," I said modestly, "there was indeed another small indication, one of those foolish trifles which the cleverest men overlook. As you know, I do not use the regular apartment-house telephone, not wishing to be annoyed by solicitors and such people. The phone which I use is a private line and its number is unlisted. But the calls I received from Henry's confederate came over that phone, and Henry had been in my apartment a great deal, and I had been careful not to give Mr. Gandesi that number, because of course I did not expect anything from Mr. Gandesi, as I was perfectly sure from the beginning that Henry had the pearls, if only I could get him to bring them out of hiding."

"Oh, darling," Ellen cried, and threw her arms around me. "How brave you are, and I really think that you are actually clever in your own peculiar way. Do you believe that Henry was in love with me?"

But that was a subject in which I had no interest whatever. I left the pearls in Ellen's keeping and late as the hour now was I drove at once to the residence of Mr. Lansing Gallemore and told him my story and gave him back his money.

A few months later I was happy to receive a letter post-marked in Honolulu and written on a very inferior brand of paper.

Well, pal, that Sunday punch of yours was the money and I did not think you had it in you, altho of course I was not set for it. But it was a pip and made me think of you for a week every time I brushed my teeth. It was too bad I had to scram because you are a sweet guy altho a little on the goofy side and I'd like to be getting plastered with you right now instead of wiping oil valves where I am at which is not where this letter is mailed by several thousand miles. There is just two things I would like you to know and they are both kosher. I did fall hard for that tall blonde and this was the main reason I took my time from the old lady. Glomming the pearls was just one of those screwy ideas a guy can get when he is dizzy with a dame. It was a crime the way they left them marbles lying around in that bread box and I worked for a Frenchy once in Djibouty and got to know pearls enough to tell them from snowballs. But when it came to the clinch down there in that brush with us two alone and no holds barred I just was too soft to go through with the deal. Tell that blonde you got a loop on I was asking for her.

 YRS. *as ever,*

   HENRY EICHELBERGER (*Alias*)

P.S. What do you know, that punk that did the phone work on you tried to take me for a fifty cut on that C note you tucked in my vest. I had to twist the sucker plenty.

   Yrs. H. E. (*Alias*)

TROUBLE IS MY BUSINESS

1

ANNA HALSEY WAS about two hundred and forty pounds of middle-aged putty-faced woman in a black tailor-made suit. Her eyes were shiny black shoe buttons, her cheeks were as soft as suet and about the same color. She was sitting behind a black glass desk that looked like Napoleon's tomb and she was smoking a cigarette in a black holder that was not quite as long as a rolled umbrella. She said: "I need a man."

I watched her shake ash from the cigarette to the shiny top of the desk where flakes of it curled and crawled in the draft from an open window.

"I need a man good-looking enough to pick up a dame who has a sense of class, but he's got to be tough enough to swap punches with a power shovel. I need a guy who can act like a bar lizard and backchat like Fred Allen, only better, and get hit on the head with a beer truck and think some cutie in the leg-line topped him with a breadstick."

"It's a cinch," I said. "You need the New York Yankees, Robert Donat, and the Yacht Club Boys."

"You might do," Anna said, "cleaned up a little. Twenty bucks a day and ex's. I haven't brokered a job in years, but this one is out of my line. I'm in the smooth-angles of the detecting business and I make money without getting my can knocked off. Let's see how Gladys likes you."

She reversed the cigarette holder and tipped a key on a large black-and-chromium annunciator box. "Come in and empty Anna's ashtray, honey."

We waited.

The door opened and a tall blonde dressed better than the Duchess of Windsor strolled in.

She swayed elegantly across the room, emptied Anna's ashtray, patted her fat cheek, gave me a smooth rippling glance and went out again.

"I think she blushed," Anna said when the door closed. "I guess you still have It."

"She blushed — and I have a dinner date with Darryl Zanuck," I said. "Quit horsing around. What's the story?"

"It's to smear a girl. A redheaded number with bedroom eyes. She's shill for a gambler and she's got her hooks into a rich man's pup."

"What do I do to her?"

Anna sighed. "It's kind of a mean job, Philip, I guess. If she's got a record of any sort you dig it up and toss it in her face. If she hasn't, which is more likely as she comes from good people, it's kind of up to you. You get an idea once in a while, don't you?"

"I can't remember the last one I had. What gambler and what rich man?"

"Marty Estel."

I started to get up from my chair, then remembered that business had been bad for a month and that I needed the money.

I sat down again.

"You might get into trouble, of course," Anna said. "I never heard of Marty bumping anybody off in the public square at high noon, but he don't play with cigar coupons."

"Trouble is my business," I said. "Twenty-five a day and guarantee of two-fifty, if I pull the job."

"I gotta make a little something for myself," Anna whined.

"Okay. There's plenty of coolie labor around town. Nice to have seen you looking so well. So long, Anna."

I stood up this time. My life wasn't worth much, but it was worth that much. Marty Estel was supposed to be pretty tough people, with the right helpers and the right protection behind him. His place was out in West Hollywood, on the Strip. He wouldn't pull anything crude, but if he pulled at all, something would pop.

"Sit down, it's a deal," Anna sneered. "I'm a poor old broken-down woman trying to run a high-class detective agency on nothing but fat and bad health, so take my last nickel and laugh at me."

"Who's the girl?" I had sat down again.

"Her name is Harriet Huntress — a swell name for the part too. She lives in the El Milano, nineteen-hundred block on North Sycamore, very high-class. Father went broke back in thirty-one and jumped out of his office window. Mother dead. Kid sister in boarding school back in Connecticut. That might make an angle."

"Who dug up all this?"

"The client got a bunch of photostats of notes the pup had given to Marty. Fifty grand worth. The pup — he's an adopted son to the old man — denied the notes, as kids will. So the client had the photostats experted by a guy named Arbogast, who pretends to be good at that sort of thing. He said okay and dug around a bit, but he's too fat to do legwork, like me, and he's off the case now."

"But I could talk to him?"

"I don't know why not." Anna nodded several of her chins.

"This client — does he have a name?"

"Son, you have a treat coming. You can meet him in person — right now."

She tipped the key of her call box again. "Have Mr. Jeeter come in, honey."

"That Gladys," I said, "does she have a steady?"

"You lay off Gladys!" Anna almost screamed at me. "She's worth eighteen grand a year in divorce business to me. Any guy that lays a finger on her, Philip Marlowe, is practically cremated."

"She's got to fall some day," I said. "Why couldn't I catch her?"

The opening door stopped that.

I hadn't seen him in the paneled reception room, so he must have been waiting in a private office. He hadn't enjoyed it. He came in quickly, shut the door quickly, and yanked a thin octagonal platinum watch from his vest and glared at it. He was a tall white-blond type in pin-striped flannel of youthful cut. There was a small pink rosebud in his lapel. He had a keen frozen face, a little pouchy under the eyes, a little thick in the lips. He carried an ebony cane with a silver knob, wore spats and looked a smart sixty, but I gave him close to ten years more. I didn't like him.

"Twenty-six minutes, Miss Halsey," he said icily. "My time happens to be valuable. By regarding it as valuable I have managed to make a great deal of money."

"Well, we're trying to save you some of the money," Anna drawled. She didn't like him either. "Sorry to keep you waiting, Mr. Jeeter, but you wanted to see the operative I selected and I had to send for him."

"He doesn't look the type to me," Mr. Jeeter said, giving me a nasty glance. "I think more of a gentleman – "

"You're not the Jeeter of *Tobacco Road*, are you?" I asked him.

He came slowly towards me and half lifted the stick. His icy eyes tore at me like claws. "So you insult me," he said. "Me – a man in my position."

"Now wait a minute," Anna began.

"Wait a minute nothing," I said. "This party said I was not a gentleman. Maybe that's okay for a man in his position, whatever it is – but a man in my position doesn't take a dirty crack from anybody. He can't afford to. Unless, of course, it wasn't intended."

Mr. Jeeter stiffened and glared at me. He took his watch out again and looked at it. "Twenty-eight minutes," he said. "I apologize, young man. I had no desire to be rude."

994

"That's swell," I said. "I knew you weren't the Jeeter in *Tobacco Road* all along."

That almost started him again, but he let it go. He wasn't sure how I meant it.

"A question or two while we are together," I said. "Are you willing to give this Huntress girl a little money – for expenses?"

"Not one cent," he barked. "Why should I?"

"It's got to be a sort of custom. Suppose she married him. What would he have?"

"At the moment a thousand dollars a month from a trust fund established by his mother, my late wife." He dipped his head. "When he is twenty-eight years old, far too much money."

"You can't blame the girl for trying," I said. "Not these days. How about Marty Estel? Any settlement there?"

He crumpled his gray gloves with a purple-veined hand. "The debt is uncollectible. It is a gambling debt."

Anna sighed wearily and flicked ash around on her desk.

"Sure," I said. "But gamblers can't afford to let people welsh on them. After all, if your son had won, Marty would have paid *him*."

"I'm not interested in that," the tall thin man said coldly.

"Yeah, but think of Marty sitting there with fifty grand in notes. Not worth a nickel. How will he sleep nights?"

Mr. Jeeter looked thoughtful. "You mean there is danger of violence?" he suggested, almost suavely.

"That's hard to say. He runs an exclusive place, gets a good movie crowd. He has his own reputation to think of. But he's in a racket and he knows people. Things can happen – a long way off from where Marty is. And Marty is no bathmat. He gets up and walks."

Mr. Jeeter looked at his watch again and it annoyed him. He slammed it back into his vest. "All that is your affair," he snapped. "The district attorney is a personal friend of mine. If this matter seems to be beyond your powers – "

"Yeah," I told him. "But you came slumming down our street just the same. Even if the D.A. is in your vest pocket – along with that watch."

He put his hat on, drew on one glove, tapped the edge of his shoe with his stick, walked to the door and opened it.

"I ask results and I pay for them," he said coldly. "I pay promptly. I even pay generously sometimes, although I am not considered a generous man. I think we all understand one another."

He almost winked then and went on out. The door closed softly against the cushion of air in the door-closer. I looked at Anna and grinned.

"Sweet, isn't he?" she said. "I'd like eight of him for my cocktail set."

I gouged twenty dollars out of her – for expenses.

2

THE ARBOGAST I wanted was John D. Arbogast and he had an office on Sunset near Ivar. I called him up from a phone booth. The voice that answered was fat. It wheezed softly, like the voice of a man who had just won a pie-eating contest.

"Mr. John D. Arbogast?"

"Yeah."

"This is Philip Marlowe, a private detective working on a case you did some experting on. Party named Jeeter."

"Yeah?"

"Can I come up and talk to you about it – after I eat lunch?"

"Yeah." He hung up. I decided he was not a talkative man.

I had lunch and drove out there. It was east of Ivar, an old two-story building faced with brick which had been painted recently. The street floor was stores and a restaurant. The building entrance was the foot of a wide straight stairway to the second floor. On the directory at the bottom I read: John

D. Arbogast, Suite 212. I went up the stairs and found myself in a wide straight hall that ran parallel with the street. A man in a smock was standing in an open doorway down to my right. He wore a round mirror strapped to his forehead and pushed back, and his face had a puzzled expression. He went back to his office and shut the door.

I went the other way, about half the distance along the hall. A door on the side away from Sunset was lettered: JOHN D. ARBOGAST, EXAMINER OF QUESTIONED DOCUMENTS. PRIVATE INVESTIGATOR. ENTER. The door opened without resistance onto a small windowless anteroom with a couple of easy chairs, some magazines, two chromium smoking stands. There were two floor lamps and a ceiling fixture, all lighted. A door on the other side of the cheap but thick new rug was lettered: JOHN D. ARBOGAST, EXAMINER OF QUESTIONED DOCUMENTS. PRIVATE.

A buzzer had rung when I opened the outer door and gone on ringing until it closed. Nothing happened. Nobody was in the waiting room. The inner door didn't open. I went over and listened at the panel – no sound of conversation inside. I knocked. That didn't buy me anything either. I tried the knob. It turned, so I opened the door and went in.

This room had two north windows, both curtained at the sides and both shut tight. There was dust on the sills. There was a desk, two filing cases, a carpet which was just a carpet, and walls which were just walls. To the left another door with a glass panel was lettered: JOHN D. ARBOGAST. LABORATORY. PRIVATE.

I had an idea I might be able to remember the name.

The room in which I stood was small. It seemed almost too small even for the pudgy hand that rested on the edge of the desk, motionless, holding a fat pencil like a carpenter's pencil. The hand had a wrist, hairless as a plate. A buttoned shirt cuff, not too clean, came down out of a coat sleeve. The rest of the sleeve dropped over the far edge of the desk out of sight. The desk was less than six feet long, so he couldn't have been a very tall man. The hand and the ends of the sleeves were all I saw of him from where I stood. I went quietly back through the anteroom and fixed its door so that it couldn't be opened from the outside and put out the three lights and went back to the private office. I went around an end of the desk.

He was fat all right, enormously fat, fatter by far than Anna Halsey. His face, what I could see of it, looked about the size of a basket ball. It had a pleasant pinkness, even now. He was kneeling on the floor. He had his large head against the sharp inner corner of the kneehole of the desk, and his left hand was flat on the floor with a piece of yellow paper under it. The fingers were outspread as much as such fat fingers could be, and the yellow paper showed between. He looked as if he were pushing hard on the floor, but he wasn't really. What was holding him up was his own fat. His body was folded down against his enormous thighs, and the thickness and fatness of them held him that way, kneeling, poised solid. It would have taken a couple of good blocking backs to knock him over. That wasn't a very nice idea at the moment, but I had it just the same. I took time out and wiped the back of my neck, although it was not a warm day.

His hair was gray and clipped short and his neck had as many folds as a concertina. His feet were small, as the feet of fat men often are, and they were in black shiny shoes which were sideways on the carpet and close together and neat and nasty. He wore a dark suit that needed cleaning. I leaned down and buried my fingers in the bottomless fat of his neck. He had an artery in there somewhere, probably, but I couldn't find it and he didn't need it any more anyway. Between his bloated knees on the carpet a dark stain had spread and spread –

I knelt in another place and lifted the pudgy fingers that were holding down the piece of yellow paper. They were cool, but not cold, and soft and a little sticky. The paper was from a scratch pad. It would have been very nice if it had had a message on it, but it hadn't. There were vague meaningless marks, not words, not even letters. He had tried to write something after he was shot – perhaps even thought he *was* writing something – but all he managed was some hen scratches.

He had slumped down then, still holding the paper, pinned it to the floor with his fat hand, held on to the fat pencil with his other hand, wedged his torso against his huge thighs, and so died. John D. Arbogast. Examiner of Questioned Documents. Private. Very damned private. He had said "yeah" to me three times over the phone.

And here he was.

I wiped doorknobs with my handkerchief, put off the lights in the anteroom, left the outer door so that it was locked from the outside, left the hallway, left the building and left the neighborhood. So far as I could tell nobody saw me go. So far as I could tell.

3

THE EL MILANO was, as Anna had told me, in the 1900 block on North Sycamore. It was most of the block. I parked fairly near the ornamental forecourt and went along to the pale blue neon sign over the entrance to the basement garage. I walked down a railed ramp into a bright space of glistening cars and cold air. A trim light-colored Negro in a spotless coverall suit with blue cuffs came out of a glass office. His black hair was as smooth as a bandleader's.

"Busy?" I asked him.

"Yes and no, sir."

"I've got a car outside that needs a dusting. About five bucks' worth of dusting."

It didn't work. He wasn't the type. His chestnut eyes became thoughtful and remote. "That is a good deal of dusting, sir. May I ask if anything else would be included?"

"A little. Is Miss Harriet Huntress' car in?"

He looked. I saw him look along the glistening row at a canary-yellow convertible which was about as inconspicuous as a privy on the front lawn.

"Yes, sir. It is in."

"I'd like her apartment number and a way to get up there without going through the lobby. I'm a private detective." I showed him a buzzer. He looked at the buzzer. It failed to amuse him.

He smiled the faintest smile I ever saw. "Five dollars is nice money, sir, to a working man. It falls a little short of being nice enough to make me risk my position. About from here to Chicago short, sir. I suggest that you save your five dollars, sir, and try the customary mode of entry."

"You're quite a guy," I said. "What are you going to be when you grow up – a five-foot shelf?"

"I am already grown up, sir. I am thirty-four years old, married happily, and have two children. Good afternoon, sir."

He turned on his heel. "Well, goodbye," I said. "And pardon my whiskey breath. I just got in from Butte."

I went back up along the ramp and wandered along the street to where I should have gone in the first place. I might have known that five bucks and a buzzer wouldn't buy me anything in a place like the El Milano.

The Negro was probably telephoning the office right now.

The building was a huge white stucco affair, Moorish in style, with great fretted lanterns in the forecourt and huge date palms. The entrance was at the inside corner of an L, up marble steps, through an arch framed in California or dishpan mosaic.

A doorman opened the door for me and I went in. The lobby was not quite as big as the Yankee Stadium. It was floored with a pale blue carpet with sponge rubber underneath. It was so soft it made me want to lie down and roll. I waded over to the desk and put an elbow on it and was stared at by a pale thin clerk with one of those mustaches that get stuck under your fingernail. He toyed with it and looked past my shoulder at an Ali Baba oil jar big enough to keep a tiger in.

"Miss Huntress in?"

"Who shall I announce?"

"Mr. Marty Estel."

That didn't take any better than my play in the garage. He leaned on something with his left foot. A blue-and-gilt door opened at the end of the desk and a large sandy-haired man with cigar ash on his vest came out and leaned absently on the end of the desk and stared at the Ali Baba oil jar, as if trying to make up his mind whether it was a spittoon.

The clerk raised his voice. "You are Mr. Marty Estel?"

"From him."

"Isn't that a little different? And what is your name, sir, if one may ask?"

"One may ask," I said. "One may not be told. Such are my orders. Sorry to be stubborn and all that rot."

He didn't like my manner. He didn't like anything about me. "I'm afraid I can't announce you," he said coldly. "Mr. Hawkins, might I have your advice on a matter?"

The sandy-haired man took his eyes off the oil jar and slid along the desk until he was within blackjack range of me.

"Yes, Mr. Gregory?" he yawned.

"Nuts to both of you," I said. "And that includes your lady friends."

Hawkins grinned. "Come into my office, bo. We'll kind of see if we can get you straightened out."

I followed him into the doghole he had come out of. It was large enough for a pint-sized desk, two chairs, a knee-high cuspidor, and an open box of cigars. He placed his rear end against the desk and grinned at me sociably.

"Didn't play it very smooth, did you, bo? I'm the house man here. Spill it."

"Some days I feel like playing smooth," I said, "and some days I feel like playing it like a waffle iron." I got my wallet out and showed him the buzzer and the small photostat of my license behind a celluloid window.

"One of the boys, huh?" He nodded. "You ought to of asked for me in the first place."

"Sure. Only I never heard of you. I want to see this Huntress frail. She doesn't know me, but I have business with her, and it's not noisy business."

He made a yard and half sideways and cocked his cigar in the other corner of his mouth. He looked at my right eyebrow.

"What's the gag? Why try to apple-polish the dinge downstairs? You gettin' any expense money?"

"Could be."

"I'm nice people," he said. "But I gotta protect the guests."

"You're almost out of cigars," I said, looking at the ninety or so in the box. I lifted a couple, smelled them, tucked a folded ten-dollar bill below them and put them back.

"That's cute," he said. "You and me could get along. What you want done?"

"Tell her I'm from Marty Estel. She'll see me."

"It's the job if I get a kickback."

"You won't. I've got important people behind me." I started to reach for my ten, but he pushed my hand away. "I'll take a chance," he said. He reached for his phone and asked for Suite 814 and began to hum. His humming sounded like a cow being sick. He leaned forward suddenly and his face became a honeyed smile. His voice dripped.

"Miss Huntress? This is Hawkins, the house man. Hawkins. Yeah . . . Hawkins. Sure, you meet a lot of people, Miss Huntress. Say, there's a gentleman in my office wanting to see you with a message from Mr. Estel. We can't let him up without your say so, because he don't want to give us no name . . . Yeah, Hawkins, the house detective, Miss Huntress. Yeah, he says you don't know him personal, but he looks okay to me . . . okay. Thanks a lot, Miss Huntress. Serve him right up."

He put the phone down and patted it gently.

"All you needed was some background music," I said.

"You can ride up," he said dreamily. He reached absently into his cigar box and removed the folded bill. "A darb," he said softly. "Every time I think of that dame I have to go out and walk around the block. Let's go."

We went out to the lobby again and Hawkins took me to the elevator and highsigned me in.

As the elevator doors closed I saw him on his way to the entrance, probably for his walk around the block.

The elevator had a carpeted floor and mirrors and indirect lighting. It rose as softly as the mercury in a thermometer. The doors whispered open, I wandered over the moss they used for a hall carpet and came to a door marked 814. I pushed a little button beside it, chimes rang inside and the door opened.

She wore a street dress of pale green wool and a small cockeyed hat that hung on her ear like a butterfly. Her eyes were wide-set and there was thinking room between them. Their color was lapis-lazuli blue and the color of her hair was dusky red, like a fire under control but still dangerous. She was too tall to be cute. She wore plenty of make-up in the right places and the cigarette she was poking at me had a built-on mouthpiece about three inches long. She didn't look hard, but she looked as if she had heard all the answers and remembered the ones she thought she might be able to use sometime.

She looked me over coolly. "Well, what's the message, brown-eyes?"

"I'd have to come in," I said. "I never could talk on my feet."

She laughed disinterestedly and I slid past the end of her cigarette into a long rather narrow room with plenty of nice furniture, plenty of windows, plenty of drapes, plenty of everything. A fire blazed behind a screen, a big log on top of a gas teaser. There was a silk Oriental rug in front of a nice rose davenport in front of the nice fire, and beside that there was Scotch and swish on a tabouret, ice in a bucket, everything to make a man feel at home.

"You'd better have a drink," she said. "You probably can't talk without a glass in your hand."

I sat down and reached for the Scotch. The girl sat in a deep chair and crossed her knees. I thought of Hawkins walking around the block. I could see a little something in his point of view.

"So you're from Marty Estel," she said, refusing a drink.

"Never met him."

"I had an idea to that effect. What's the racket, bum? Marty will love to hear how you used his name."

"I'm shaking in my shoes. What made you let me up?"

"Curiosity. I've been expecting lads like you any day. I never dodge trouble. Some kind of a dick, aren't you?"

I lit a cigarette and nodded. "Private. I have a little deal to propose."

"Propose it." She yawned.

"How much will you take to lay off young Jeeter?"

She yawned again. "You interest me – so little I could hardly tell you."

"Don't scare me to death. Honest, how much are you asking? Or is that an insult?"

She smiled. She had a nice smile. She had lovely teeth. "I'm a bad girl now," she said. "I don't have to ask. They bring it to me, tied up with ribbon."

"The old man's a little tough. They say he draws a lot of water."

"Water doesn't cost much."

I nodded and drank some more of my drink. It was good Scotch. In fact it was perfect. "His idea is you get nothing. You get smeared. You get put in the middle. I can't see it that way."

"But you're working for him."

"Sounds funny, doesn't it? There's probably a smart way to play this, but I just can't think of it at the moment. How much would you take – or would you?"

"How about fifty grand?"

"Fifty grand for you and another fifty for Marty?"

She laughed. "Now, you ought to know Marty wouldn't like me to mix in his business. I was just thinking of my end."

She crossed her legs the other way. I put another lump of ice in my drink.

"I was thinking of five hundred," I said.

"Five hundred what?" She looked puzzled.

"Dollars – not Rolls-Royces."

She laughed heartily. "You amuse me. I ought to tell you to go to hell, but I like brown eyes. Warm brown eyes with flecks of gold in them."

"You're throwing it away. I don't have a nickel."

She smiled and fitted a fresh cigarette between her lips. I went over to light it for her. Her eyes came up and looked into mine. Hers had sparks in them.

"Maybe I have a nickel already," she said softly.

"Maybe that's why he hired the fat boy – so you couldn't make him dance." I sat down again.

"Who hired what fat boy?"

"Old Jeeter hired a fat boy named Arbogast. He was on the case before me. Didn't you know? He got bumped off this afternoon."

I said it quite casually for the shock effect, but she didn't move. The provocative smile didn't leave the corners of her lips. Her eyes didn't change. She made a dim sound with her breath.

"Does it have to have something to do with me?" she asked quietly.

"I don't know. I don't know who murdered him. It was done in his office, around noon or a little later. It may not have anything to do with the Jeeter case. But it happened pretty pat – just after I had been put on the job and before I got a chance to talk to him."

She nodded. "I see. And you think Marty does things like that. And of course you told the police?"

"Of course I did not."

"You're giving away a little weight there, brother."

"Yeah. But let's get together on a price and it had better be low. Because whatever the cops do to me they'll do plenty to Marty Estel and you when they get the story – if they get it."

"A little spot of blackmail," the girl said coolly. "I think I might call it that. Don't go too far with me, brown-eyes. By the way, do I know your name?"

"Philip Marlowe."

"Then listen, Philip. I was in the Social Register once. My family were nice people. Old man Jeeter ruined my father – all proper and legitimate, the way that kind of heel ruins people – but he ruined him, and my father committed sui-cide, and my mother died and I've got a kid sister back East in school and perhaps I'm not too damn particular how I get the money to take care of her. And maybe I'm going to take care of old Jeeter one of these days, too – even if I have to marry his son to do it."

"Stepson, adopted son," I said. "No relation at all."

"It'll hurt him just as hard, brother. And the boy will have plenty of the long green in a couple of years. I could do worse – even if he does drink too much."

"You wouldn't say that in front of him, lady."

"No? Take a look behind you, gumshoe. You ought to have the wax taken out of your ears."

I stood up and turned fast. He stood about four feet from me. He had come out of some door and sneaked across the carpet and I had been too busy being clever with nothing on the ball to hear him. He was big, blond, dressed in a rough sporty suit, with a scarf and open-necked shirt. He was red–faced and his eyes glittered and they were not focusing any too well. He was a bit drunk for that early in the day.

"Beat it while you can still walk," he sneered at me. "I heard it. Harry can say anything she likes about me. I like it. Dangle, before I knock your teeth down your throat!"

The girl laughed behind me. I didn't like that. I took a step towards the big blond boy. His eyes blinked. Big as he was, he was a pushover.

"Ruin him, baby," the girl said coldly behind my back. "I love to see these hard numbers bend at the knees."

I looked back at her with a leer. That was a mistake. He was wild, probably, but he could still hit a wall that didn't jump. He hit me while I was looking back over my shoulder. It hurts to be hit that way. He hit me plenty hard, on the back end of the jawbone.

I went over sideways, tried to spread my legs, and slid on the silk rug. I did a nose dive somewhere or other and my head was not as hard as the piece of furniture it smashed into.

For a brief blurred moment I saw his red face sneering down at me in triumph. I think I was a little sorry for him – even then.

Darkness folded down and I went out.

4

WHEN I CAME to, the light from the windows across the room was hitting me square in the eyes. The back of my head ached. I felt it and it was sticky. I moved around slowly, like a cat in a strange house, got up on my knees and reached for the bottle of Scotch on the tabouret at the end of the davenport. By some miracle I hadn't knocked it over. Falling I had hit my head on the clawlike leg of a chair. That had hurt me a lot more than young Jeeter's haymaker. I could feel the sore place on my jaw all right, but it wasn't important enough to write in my diary.

I got up on my feet, took a swig of the Scotch and looked around. There wasn't anything to see. The room was empty. It was full of silence and the memory of a nice perfume. One of those perfumes you don't notice until they are almost gone, like the last leaf on a tree. I felt my head again, touched the sticky place with my handkerchief, decided it wasn't worth yelling about, and took another drink.

I sat down with the bottle on my knees, listening to traffic noise somewhere, far off. It was a nice room. Miss Harriet Huntress was a nice girl. She knew a few wrong numbers, but who didn't? I should criticize a little thing like that. I took another drink. The level in the bottle was a lot lower now. It was smooth and you hardly noticed it going down. It didn't take half your tonsils with it, like some of the stuff I had to drink. I took some more. My head felt all right now. I felt fine. I felt like singing the Prologue to *Pagliacci*. Yes, she was a nice girl. If she was paying her own rent, she was doing right well. I was for her. She was swell. I used some more of her Scotch.

The bottle was still half full. I shook it gently, stuffed it in my overcoat pocket, put my hat somewhere on my head and left. I made the elevator without hitting the walls on either side of the corridor, floated downstairs, strolled out into the lobby.

Hawkins, the house dick, was leaning on the end of the desk again, staring at the Ali Baba oil jar. The same clerk was nuzzling at the same itsy-bitsy mustache. I smiled at him. He smiled back. Hawkins smiled at me. I smiled back. Everybody was swell.

I made the front door the first time and gave the doorman two bits and floated down the steps and along the walk to the street and my car. The swift California twilight was falling. It was a lovely night. Venus in the west was as bright as a street lamp, as bright as life, as bright as Miss Huntress' eyes, as bright as a bottle of Scotch. That reminded me. I got the square bottle out and tapped it with discretion, corked it, and tucked it away again. There was still enough to get home on.

I crashed five red lights on the way back but my luck was in and nobody pinched me. I parked more or less in front of my apartment house and more or less near the curb. I rode to my floor in the elevator, had a little trouble opening the doors and helped myself out with my bottle. I got the key into my door and unlocked it and stepped inside and found the light switch. I took a little more of my medicine before exhausting myself any further. Then I started for the kitchen to get some ice and ginger ale for a real drink.

I thought there was a funny smell in the apartment – nothing I could put a name to offhand – a sort of medicinal smell. I hadn't put it there and it hadn't been there when I went out. But I felt too well to argue about it. I started for the kitchen, got about halfway there.

They came out at me, almost side by side, from the dressing room beside the wall bed – two of them – with guns. The tall one was grinning. He had his hat low on his forehead and he had a wedge-shaped face that ended in a point, like the bottom half of the ace of diamonds. He had dark moist eyes and a nose so bloodless that it might have been made of white wax. His gun was a Colt Woodsman with a long barrel and the front sight filed off. That meant he thought he was good.

The other was a little terrierlike punk with bristly reddish hair and no hat and watery blank eyes and bat ears and small feet in dirty white sneakers. He had an automatic that looked too heavy for him to hold up, but he seemed to like holding it. He breathed open-mouthed and noisily and the smell I had noticed came from him in waves – menthol.

"Reach, you bastard," he said.

I put my hands up. There was nothing else to do.

The little one circled around to the side and came at me from the side. "Tell us we can't get away with it," he sneered.

"You can't get away with it," I said.

The tall one kept on grinning loosely and his nose kept on looking as if it was made of white wax. The little one spat on my carpet. "Yah!" He came close to me, leering, and made a pass at my chin with the big gun.

I dodged. Ordinarily that would have been just something which, in the circumstances, I had to take and like. But I was feeling better than ordinary. I was a world-beater. I took them in sets, guns and all. I took the little man around the throat and jerked him hard against my stomach, put a hand over his little gun hand and knocked the gun to the floor. It was easy. Nothing was bad about it but his breath. Blobs of saliva came out on his lips. He spit curses.

The tall man stood and leered and didn't shoot. He didn't move. His eyes looked a little anxious, I thought, but I was too busy to make sure. I went down behind the little punk, still holding him, and got hold of his gun. That was wrong. I ought to have pulled my own.

I threw him away from me and he reeled against a chair and fell down and began to kick the chair savagely. The tall man laughed.

"It ain't got any firing pin in it," he said.

"Listen," I told him earnestly, "I'm half full of good Scotch and ready to go places and get things done. Don't waste much of my time. What do you boys want?"

"It still ain't got any firing pin in it," Waxnose said. "Try and see. I don't never let Frisky carry a loaded rod. He's too impulsive. You got a nice arm action there, pal. I will say that for you."

Frisky sat up on the floor and spit on the carpet again and laughed. I pointed the muzzle of the big automatic at the floor and squeezed the trigger. It clicked dryly, but from the balance it felt as if it had cartridges in it.

"We don't mean no harm," Waxnose said. "Not this trip. Maybe next trip? Who knows? Maybe you're a guy that will take a hint. Lay off the Jeeter kid is the word. See?"

"No."

"You won't do it?"

"No, I don't see. Who's the Jeeter kid?"

Waxnose was not amused. He waved his long .22 gently. "You oughta get your memory fixed, pal, about the same time you get your door fixed. A pushover that was. Frisky just blew it in with his breath."

"I can understand that," I said.

"Gimme my gat," Frisky yelped. He was up off the floor again, but this time he rushed his partner instead of me.

"Lay off, dummy," the tall one said. "We just got a message for a guy. We don't blast him. Not today."

"Says you!" Frisky snarled and tried to grab the .22 out of Waxnose's hand. Waxnose threw him to one side without trouble but the interlude allowed me to switch the big automatic to my left hand and jerk out my Luger. I showed it to Waxnose. He nodded, but did not seem impressed.

"He ain't got no parents," he said sadly. "I just let him run around with me. Don't pay him no attention unless he bites you. We'll be on our way now. You get the idea. Lay off the Jeeter kid."

"You're looking at a Luger," I said. "Who is the Jeeter kid? And maybe we'll have some cops before you leave."

He smiled wearily. "Mister, I pack this small-bore because I can shoot. If you think you can take me, go to it."

"Okay," I said. "Do you know anybody named Arbogast?"

"I meet such a lot of people," he said, with another weary smile. "Maybe yes, maybe no. So long, pal. Be pure."

He strolled over to the door, moving a little sideways, so that he had me covered all the time, and I had him covered, and it was just a case of who shot first and straightest, or whether it was worthwhile to shoot at all, or whether I could hit anything with so much nice warm Scotch in me. I let him go. He didn't look like a killer to me, but I could have been wrong.

The little man rushed me again while I wasn't thinking about him. He clawed his big automatic out of my left hand, skipped over to the door, spit on the carpet again, and slipped out. Waxnose backed after him – long sharp face, white nose, pointed chin, weary expression. I wouldn't forget him.

He closed the door softly and I stood there, foolish, holding my gun. I heard the elevator come up and go down again and stop. I still stood there. Marty Estel wouldn't be very likely to hire a couple of comics like that to throw a scare into anybody. I thought about that, but thinking got me nowhere. I remembered the half-bottle of Scotch I had left and went into executive session with it.

An hour and a half later I felt fine, but I still didn't have any ideas. I just felt sleepy.

The jarring of the telephone bell woke me. I had dozed off in the chair, which was a bad mistake, because I woke up with two flannel blankets in my mouth, a splitting headache, a bruise on the back of my head and another on my jaw, neither of them larger than a Yakima apple, but sore for all that. I felt terrible. I felt like an amputated leg.

I crawled over to the telephone and humped myself in a chair beside it and answered it. The voice dripped icicles.

"Mr. Marlowe? This is Mr. Jeeter. I believe we met this morning. I'm afraid I was a little stiff with you."

"I'm a little stiff myself. Your son poked me in the jaw. I mean your stepson, or your adopted son – or whatever he is."

"He is both my stepson and my adopted son. Indeed?" He sounded interested. "And where did you meet him?"

"In Miss Huntress' apartment."

"Oh I see." There had been a sudden thaw. The icicles had melted. "Very interesting. What did Miss Huntress have to say?"

"She liked it. She liked him poking me in the jaw."

"I see. And why did he do that?"

"She had him hid out. He overheard some of our talk. He didn't like it."

"I see. I have been thinking that perhaps some consideration – not large, of course – should be granted to her for her co-operation. That is, if we can secure it."

"Fifty grand is the price."

"I'm afraid I don't – "

"Don't kid me," I snarled. "Fifty thousand dollars. Fifty grand. I offered her five hundred – just for a gag."

"You seem to treat this whole business in a spirit of considerable levity," he snarled back. "I am not accustomed to that sort of thing and I don't like it."

I yawned. I didn't give a damn if school kept in or not. "Listen, Mr. Jeeter, I'm a great guy to horse around, but I have my mind on the job just the same. And there are some very unusual angles to this case. For instance a couple of gunmen just stuck me up in my apartment here and told me to lay off the Jeeter case. I don't see why it should get so tough."

"Good heavens!" He sounded shocked. "I think you had better come to my house at once and we will discuss matters. I'll send my car for you. Can you come right away?"

"Yeah. But I can drive myself. I – "

"No. I'm sending my car and chauffeur. His name is George; you may rely upon him absolutely. He should be there in about twenty minutes."

"Okay," I said. "That just gives me time to drink my dinner. Have him park around the corner of Kenmore, facing towards Franklin." I hung up.

When I'd had a hot-and-cold shower and put on some clean clothes I felt more respectable. I had a couple of drinks, small ones for a change, and put a light overcoat on and went down to the street.

The car was there already. I could see it half a block down the side street. It looked like a new market opening. It had a couple of headlamps like the one on the front end of a streamliner, two amber foglights hooked to the front fender, and a couple of sidelights as big as ordinary headlights. I came up beside it and stopped and a man stepped out of the shadows, tossing a cigarette over his shoulder with a neat flip of the wrist. He was tall, broad, dark, wore a peaked cap, a Russian tunic with a Sam Browne belt, shiny leggings and breeches that flared like an English staff major's whipcords.

"Mr. Marlowe?" He touched the peak of his cap with a gloved forefinger.

"Yeah," I said. "At ease. Don't tell me that's old man Jeeter's car."

"One of them." It was a cool voice that could get fresh.

He opened the rear door and I got in and sank down into the cushions and George slid under the wheel and started the big car. It moved away from the curb and around the corner with as much noise as a bill makes in a wallet. We went west. We seemed to be drifting with the current, but we passed everything. We slid through the heart of Hollywood, the west end of it, down to the Strip and along the glitter of that to the cool quiet of Beverly Hills where the bridle path divides the boulevard.

We gave Beverly Hills the swift and climbed along the foothills, saw the distant lights of the university buildings and swung north into Bel-Air. We began to slide up long narrow streets with high walls and no sidewalks and big gates. Lights on mansions glowed politely through the early night. Nothing stirred. There was no sound but the soft purr of the tires on concrete. We swung left again and I caught a sign which read Calvello Drive. Halfway up this George started to swing the car wide to make a left turn in at a pair of twelve-foot wrought-iron gates. Then something happened.

A pair of lights flared suddenly just beyond the gates and a horn screeched and a motor raced. A car charged at us fast. George straightened out with a flick of the wrist, braked the car and slipped off his right glove, all in one motion.

The car came on, the lights swaying. "Damn drunk," George swore over his shoulder.

It could be. Drunks in cars go all kinds of places to drink. It could be. I slid down onto the floor of the car and yanked the Luger from under my arm and reached up to open the catch. I opened the door a little and held it that way, looking over the sill. The headlights hit me in the face and I ducked, then came up again as the beam passed.

The other car jammed to a stop. Its door slammed open and a figure jumped out of it, waving a gun and shouting. I heard the voice and knew.

"Reach, you bastards!" Frisky screamed at us.

George put his left hand on the wheel and I opened my door a little more. The little man in the street was bouncing up and down and yelling. Out of the small dark car from which he had jumped came no sound except the noise of its motor.

"This is a heist!" Frisky yelled. "Out of there and line up, you sons of bitches!"

I kicked my door open and started to get out, the Luger down at my side.

"You asked for it!" the little man yelled.

I dropped — fast. The gun in his hand belched flame. Somebody must have put a firing pin in it. Glass smashed behind my head. Out of the corner of my eye, which oughtn't to have had any corners at that particular moment, I saw George make a movement as smooth as a ripple of water. I brought the Luger up and started to squeeze the trigger, but a shot crashed beside me — George.

I held my fire. It wasn't needed now.

The dark car lurched forward and started down the hill furiously. It roared into the distance while the little man out in the middle of the pavement was still reeling grotesquely in the light reflected from the walls.

There was something dark on his face that spread. His gun bounded along the concrete. His little legs buckled and he plunged sideways and rolled and then, very suddenly, became still.

George said, "Yah!" and sniffed at the muzzle of his revolver.

"Nice shooting." I got out of the car, stood there looking at the little man — a crumpled nothing. The dirty white of his sneakers gleamed a little in the side glare of the car's lights.

George got out beside me. "Why me, brother?"

"I didn't fire. I was watching that pretty hip draw of yours. It was sweeter than honey."

"Thanks, pal. They were after Mister Gerald, of course. I usually ferry him home from the club about this time, full of liquor and bridge losses."

We went over to the little man and looked down at him. He wasn't anything to see. He was just a little man who was dead, with a big slug in his face and blood on him.

"Turn some of those damn lights off," I growled. "And let's get away from here fast."

"The house is just across the street." George sounded as casual as if he had just shot a nickel in a slot machine instead of a man.

"The Jeeters are out of this, if you like your job. You ought to know that. We'll go back to my place and start all over."

"I get it," he snapped, and jumped back into the big car. He cut the foglights and the sidelights and I got in beside him in the front seat.

We straightened out and started up the hill, over the brow. I looked back at the broken window. It was the small one at the extreme back of the car and it wasn't shatterproof. A large piece was gone from it. They could fit that, if they got around to it, and make some evidence. I didn't think it would matter, but it might.

At the crest of the hill a large limousine passed us going down. Its dome light was on and in the interior, as in a lighted showcase, an elderly couple sat stiffly, taking the royal salute. The man was in evening clothes, with a white scarf and a crush hat. The woman was in furs and diamonds.

George passed them casually, gunned the car and we made a fast right turn into a dark street. "There's a couple of good dinners all shot to hell," he drawled, "and I bet they don't even report it."

"Yeah. Let's get back home and have a drink," I said. "I never really got to like killing people."

5

WE SAT WITH some of Miss Harriet Huntress' Scotch in our glasses and looked at each other across the rims. George looked nice with his cap off. His head was clustered over with wavy dark-brown hair and his teeth were very white and clean. He sipped his drink and nibbled a cigarette at the same time. His snappy black eyes had a cool glitter in them.

"Yale?" I asked.

"Dartmouth, if it's any of your business."

"Everything's my business. What's a college education worth these days?"

"Three squares and a uniform," he drawled.

"What kind of guy is young Jeeter?"

"Big blond bruiser, plays a fair game of golf, thinks he's hell with the women, drinks heavy but hasn't sicked up on the rugs so far."

"What kind of guy is old Jeeter?"

"He'd probably give you a dime – if he didn't have a nickel with him."

"Tsk, tsk, you're talking about your boss."

George grinned. "He's so tight his head squeaks when he takes his hat off. I always took chances. Maybe that's why I'm just somebody's driver. This is good Scotch."

I made another drink, which finished the bottle. I sat down again.

"You think those two gunnies were stashed out for Mister Gerald?"

"Why not? I usually drive him home about that time. Didn't today. He had a bad hangover and didn't go out until late. You're a dick, you know what it's all about, don't you?"

"Who told you I was a dick?"

"Nobody but a dick ever asked so goddam many questions."

I shook my head. "Uh-uh. I've asked you just six questions. Your boss has a lot of confidence in you. He must have told you."

The dark man nodded, grinned faintly and sipped. "The whole set-up is pretty obvious," he said. "When the car started to swing for the turn into the driveway these boys went to work. I don't figure they meant to kill anybody, somehow. It was just a scare. Only that little guy was nuts."

I looked at George's eyebrows. They were nice black eyebrows, with a gloss on them like horsehair.

"It doesn't sound like Marty Estel to pick that sort of helpers."

"Sure. Maybe that's why he picked that sort of helpers."

"You're smart. You and I can get along. But shooting that little punk makes it tougher. What will you do about that?"

"Nothing."

"Okay. If they get to you and tie it to your gun, if you still have the gun, which you probably won't, I suppose it will be passed off as an attempted stick-up. There's just one thing."

"What?" George finished his second drink, laid the glass aside, lit a fresh cigarette and smiled.

"It's pretty hard to tell a car from in front – at night. Even with all those lights. It might have been a visitor."

He shrugged and nodded. "But if it's a scare, that would do just as well. Because the family would hear about it and the old man would guess whose boys they were – and why."

"Hell, you really are smart," I said admiringly, and the phone rang.

It was an English-butler voice, very clipped and precise, and it said that if I was Mr. Philip Marlowe, Mr. Jeeter would like to speak to me. He came on at once, with plenty of frost.

"I must say that you take your time about obeying orders," he barked. "Or hasn't that chauffeur of mine – "

"Yeah, he got here, Mr. Jeeter," I said. "But we ran into a little trouble. George will tell you."

"Young man, when I want something done – "

"Listen, Mr. Jeeter, I've had a hard day. Your son punched me on the jaw and I fell and cut my head open. When I staggered back to my apartment, more dead than alive, I was stuck up by a couple of hard guys with guns who told me to lay off the Jeeter case. I'm doing my best but I'm feeling a little frail, so don't scare me."

"Young man – "

"Listen," I told him earnestly, "if you want to call all the plays in this game, you can carry the ball yourself. Or you can save yourself a lot of money and hire an order taker. I have to do things my way. Any cops visit you tonight?"

"Cops?" he echoed in a sour voice. "You mean policemen?"

"By all means – I mean policemen."

"And why should I see any policemen?" he almost snarled.

"There was a stiff in front of your gates half an hour ago. Stiff meaning dead man. He's quite small. You could sweep him up in a dustpan, if he bothers you."

"My God! Are you serious?"

"Yes. What's more he took a shot at George and me. He recognized the car. He must have been all set for your son, Mr. Jeeter."

A silence with barbs on it. "I thought you said a dead man," Mr. Jeeter's voice said very coldly. "Now you say he shot at you."

"That was while he wasn't dead," I said. "George will tell you. George – "

"You come out here at once!" he yelled at me over the phone. "At once, do you hear? At once!"

"George will tell you," I said softly and hung up.

George looked at me coldly. He stood up and put his cap on. "Okay, pal," he said. "Maybe some day I can put you on to a soft thing." He started for the door.

"It had to be that way. It's up to him. He'll have to decide."

"Nuts," George said, looking back over his shoulder. "Save your breath, shamus. Anything you say to me is just so much noise in the wrong place."

He opened the door, went out, shut it, and I sat there still holding the telephone, with my mouth open and nothing in it but my tongue and a bad taste on that.

I went out to the kitchen and shook the Scotch bottle, but it was still empty. I opened some rye and swallowed a drink and it tasted sour. Something was bothering me. I had a feeling it was going to bother me a lot more before I was through.

They must have missed George by a whisker. I heard the elevator come up again almost as soon as it had stopped going down. Solid steps grew louder along the hallway. A fist hit the door. I went over and opened it.

One was in brown, one in blue, both large, hefty and bored.

The one in brown pushed his hat back on his head with a freckled hand and said: "You Philip Marlowe?"

"Me," I said.

They rode me back into the room without seeming to. The one in blue shut the door. The one in brown palmed a shield and let me catch a glint of the gold and enamel.

"Finlayson, Detective Lieutenant working out of Central Homicide," he said. "This is Sebold, my partner. We're a couple of swell guys not to get funny with. We hear you're kind of sharp with a gun."

Sebold took his hat off and dusted his salt-and-pepper hair back with the flat of his hand. He drifted noiselessly out to the kitchen.

Finlayson sat down on the edge of a chair and flicked his chin with a thumbnail as square as an ice cube and yellow as a mustard plaster. He was older than Sebold, but not so good-looking. He had the frowsy expression of a veteran cop who hadn't got very far.

I sat down. I said: "How do you mean, sharp with a gun?"

"Shooting people is how I mean."

I lit a cigarette. Sebold came out of the kitchen and went into the dressing room behind the wall bed.

"We understand you're a private-license guy," Finlayson said heavily.

"That's right."

"Give." He held his hand out. I gave him my wallet. He chewed it over and handed it back. "Carry a gun?"

I nodded. He held out his hand for it. Sebold came out of the dressing room. Finlayson sniffed at the Luger, snapped the magazine out, cleared the breech and held the gun so that a little light shone up through the magazine opening into the breech end of the barrel. He looked down the muzzle, squinting. He handed the gun to Sebold. Sebold did the same thing.

"Don't think so," Sebold said. "Clean, but not that clean. Couldn't have been cleaned within the hour. A little dust."

"Right."

Finlayson picked the ejected shell off the carpet, pressed it into the magazine and snapped the magazine back in place. He handed me the gun. I put it back under my arm.

"Been out anywhere tonight?" he asked tersely.

"Don't tell me the plot," I said. "I'm just a bit-player."

"Smart guy," Sebold said dispassionately. He dusted his hair again and opened a desk drawer. "Funny stuff. Good for a column. I like 'em that way – with my blackjack."

Finlayson sighed. "Been out tonight, shamus?"

"Sure. In and out all the time. Why?"

He ignored the question. "Where you been?"

"Out to dinner. Business call or two."

"Where at?"

"I'm sorry, boys. Every business has its private files."

"Had company, too," Sebold said, picking up George's glass and sniffing it. "Recent – within the hour."

"You're not that good," I told him sourly.

"Had a ride in a big Caddy?" Finlayson bored on, taking a deep breath. "Over West L. A. direction?"

"Had a ride in a Chrysler – over Vine Street direction."

"Maybe we better just take him down," Sebold said, looking at his fingernails.

"Maybe you better skip the gang-buster stuff and tell me what's stuck in your nose. I get along with cops – except when they act as if the law is only for citizens."

Finlayson studied me. Nothing I had said made an impression on him. Nothing Sebold said made any impression on him. He had an idea and he was holding it like a sick baby.

"You know a little rat named Frisky Lavon?" he sighed. "Used to be a dummy-chucker, then found out he could bug his way outa raps. Been doing that for say twelve years. Totes a gun and acts simple. But he quit acting tonight at seventhirty about. Quit cold – with a slug in his head."

"Never heard of him," I said.

"You bumped anybody off tonight?"

"I'd have to look at my notebook."

Sebold leaned forward politely. "Would you care for a smack in the kisser?" he inquired.

Finlayson held his hand out sharply. "Cut it, Ben. Cut it. Listen, Marlowe. Maybe we're going at this wrong. We're not talking about murder. Could have been legitimate. This Frisky Lavon got froze off tonight on Calvello Drive in Bel-Air. Out in the middle of the street. Nobody seen or heard anything. So we kind of want to know."

"All right," I growled. "What makes it my business? And keep that piano tuner out of my hair. He has a nice suit and his nails are clean, but he bears down on his shield too hard."

"Nuts to you," Sebold said.

"We got a funny phone call," Finlayson said. "Which is where you come in. We ain't just throwing our weight around. And we want a forty-five. They ain't sure what kind yet."

"He's smart. He threw it under the bar at Levy's," Sebold sneered.

"I never had a forty-five," I said. "A guy who needs that much gun ought to use a pick."

Finlayson scowled at me and counted his thumbs. Then he took a deep breath and suddenly went human on me. "Sure, I'm just a dumb flatheel," he said. "Anybody could pull my ears off and I wouldn't even notice it. Let's all quit horsing around and talk sense.

"This Frisky was found dead after a no-name phone call to West L. A. police. Found dead outside a big house belonging to a man named Jeeter who owns a string of investment companies. He wouldn't use a guy like Frisky for a penwiper, so there's nothing in that. The servants didn't hear nothing, nor the servants at any of the four houses on the block. Frisky is lying in the street and somebody run over his foot, but what killed him was a forty-five slug smack in his face. West L. A. ain't hardly started the routine when some guy calls up Central and says to tell Homicide if they want to know who got Frisky Lavon, ask a private eye named Philip Marlowe, complete with address and everything, then a quick hang-up.

"Okay. The guy on the board gives me the dope and I don't know Frisky from a hole in my sock, but I ask Identification and sure enough they have him and just about the time I'm looking it over the flash comes from West L. A. and the description seems to check pretty close. So we get together and it's the same guy all right and the chief of detectives has us drop around here. So we drop around."

"So here you are," I said. "Will you have a drink?"

"Can we search the joint, if we do?"

"Sure. It's a good lead — that phone call, I mean — if you put in about six months on it."

"We already got that idea," Finlayson growled. "A hundred guys could have chilled this little wart, and two-three of them maybe could have thought it was a smart rib to pin it on you. Them two-three is what interests us."

I shook my head.

"No ideas at all, huh?"

"Just for wisecracks," Sebold said.

Finlayson lumbered to his feet. "Well, we gotta look around."

"Maybe we had ought to have brought a search warrant," Sebold said, tickling his upper lip with the end of his tongue.

"I don't *have* to fight this guy, do I?" I asked Finlayson. "I mean, is it all right if I leave him his gag lines and just keep my temper?"

Finlayson looked at the ceiling and said dryly: "His wife left him day before yesterday. He's just trying to compensate, as the fellow says."

Sebold turned white and twisted his knuckles savagely. Then he laughed shortly and got to his feet.

They went at it. Ten minutes of opening and shutting drawers and looking at the backs of shelves and under seat cushions and letting the bed down and peering into the electric refrigerator and the garbage pail fed them up.

They came back and sat down again. "Just a nut," Finlayson said wearily. "Some guy that picked your name outa the directory maybe. Could be anything."

"Now I'll get that drink."

"I don't drink," Sebold snarled.

Finlayson crossed his hands on his stomach. "That don't mean any liquor gets poured in the flowerpot, son."

I got three drinks and put two of them beside Finlayson. He drank half of one of them and looked at the ceiling. "I got another killing, too," he said thoughtfully. "A guy in your racket, Marlowe. A fat guy on Sunset. Name of Arbogast. Ever hear of him?"

"I thought he was a handwriting expert," I said.

"You're talking about police business," Sebold told his partner coldly.

"Sure. Police business that's already in the morning paper. This Arbogast was shot three times with a twenty-two. Target gun. You know any crooks that pack that kind of heat?"

I held my glass tightly and took a long slow swallow. I hadn't thought Waxnose looked dangerous enough, but you never knew.

"I did," I said slowly. "A killer named Al Tessilore. But he's in Folsom. He used a Colt Woodsman."

Finlayson finished the first drink, used the second in about the same time, and stood up. Sebold stood up, still mad.

Finlayson opened the door. "Come on, Ben." They went out.

I heard their steps along the hall, the clang of the elevator once more. A car started just below in the street and growled off into the night.

"Clowns like that don't kill," I said out loud. But it looked as if they did.

I waited fifteen minutes before I went out again. The phone rang while I was waiting, but I didn't answer it.

I drove towards the El Milano and circled around enough to make sure I wasn't followed.

6

THE LOBBY HADN'T changed any. The blue carpet still tickled my ankles while I ambled over to the desk, the same pale clerk was handing a key to a couple of horse-faced females in tweeds, and when he saw me he put his weight on his left foot again and the door at the end of the desk popped open and out popped the fat and erotic Hawkins, with what looked like the same cigar stub in his face.

He hustled over and gave me a big warm smile this time, took hold of my arm. "Just the guy I was hoping to see," he chuckled. "Let's us go upstairs a minute."

"What's the matter?"

"Matter?" His smile became broad as the door to a two-car garage. "Nothing ain't the matter. This way."

He pushed me into the elevator and said "Eight" in a fat cheerful voice and up we sailed and out we got and slid along the corridor. Hawkins had a hard hand and knew where to hold an arm. I was interested enough to let him get away with it. He pushed the buzzer beside Miss Huntress' door and Big Ben chimed inside and the door opened and I was looking at a deadpan in a derby hat and a dinner coat. He had his right hand in the side pocket of the coat, and under the derby a pair of scarred eyebrows and under the eyebrows a pair of eyes that had as much expression as the cap on a gas tank.

The mouth moved enough to say: "Yeah?"

"Company for the boss," Hawkins said expansively.

"What company?"

"Let me play too," I said. "Limited Liability Company. Gimme the apple."

"Huh?" The eyebrows went this way and that and the jaw came out. "Nobody ain't kiddin' anybody, I hope."

"Now, now, gents — " Hawkins began.

A voice behind the derby-hatted man interrupted him. "What's the matter, Beef?"

"He's in a stew," I said.

"Listen, mug — "

"Now, now, gents — " as before.

"Ain't nothing the matter," Beef said, throwing his voice over his shoulder as if it were a coil of rope. "The hotel dick got a guy up here and he says he's company."

"Show the company in, Beef." I liked this voice. It was smooth quiet, and you could have cut your name in it with a thirty-pound sledge and a cold chisel.

"Lift the dogs," Beef said, and stood to one side.

We went in. I went first, then Hawkins, then Beef wheeled neatly behind us like a door. We went in so close together that we must have looked like a three-decker sandwich.

Miss Huntress was not in the room. The log in the fireplace had almost stopped smoldering. There was still that smell of sandalwood on the air. With it cigarette smoke blended.

A man stood at the end of the davenport, both hands in the pockets of a blue camel's hair coat with the collar high to a black snap-brim hat. A loose scarf hung outside his coat. He stood motionless, the cigarette in his mouth lisping smoke. He was tall, black-haired, suave, dangerous. He said nothing.

Hawkins ambled over to him. "This is the guy I was telling you about, Mr. Estel," the fat man burbled. "Come in earlier today and said he was from you. Kinda fooled me."

"Give him a ten, Beef."

The derby hat took its left hand from somewhere and there was a bill in it. It pushed the bill at Hawkins. Hawkins took the bill, blushing.

"This ain't necessary, Mr. Estel. Thanks a lot just the same."

"Scram."

"Huh?" Hawkins looked shocked.

"You heard him," Beef said truculently. "Want your fanny out the door first, huh?"

Hawkins drew himself up. "I gotta protect the tenants. You gentlemen know how it is. A man in a job like this."

"Yeah. Scram," Estel said without moving his lips.

Hawkins turned and went out quickly, softly. The door clicked gently shut behind him. Beef looked back at it, then moved behind me.

"See if he's rodded, Beef."

The derby hat saw if I was rodded. He took the Luger and went away from me. Estel looked casually at the Luger, back at me. His eyes held an expression of indifferent dislike.

"Name's Philip Marlowe, eh? A private dick."

"So what?" I said.

"Somebody's goin' to get somebody's face pushed into somebody's floor," Beef said coldly.

"Aw, keep that crap for the boiler room," I told him. "I'm sick of hard guys for this evening. I said 'so what,' and 'so what' is what I said."

Marty Estel looked mildly amused. "Hell, keep your shirt in. I've got to look after my friends, don't I? You know who I am. Okay, I know what you talked to Miss Huntress about. And I know something about you that you don't know I know."

"All right," I said. "This fat slob Hawkins collected ten from me for letting me up here this afternoon – knowing perfectly well who I was – and he has just collected ten from your iron man for slipping me the nasty. Give me back my gun and tell me what makes my business your business."

"Plenty. First off, Harriet's not home. We're waiting for her on account of a thing that happened. I can't wait any longer. Got to go to work at the club. So what did you come after this time?"

"Looking for the Jeeter boy. Somebody shot at his car tonight. From now on he needs somebody to walk behind him."

"You think I play games like that?" Estel asked me coldly.

I walked over to a cabinet and opened it and found a bottle of Scotch. I twisted the cap off, lifted a glass from the tabouret and poured some out. I tasted it. It tasted all right.

I looked around for ice, but there wasn't any. It had all melted long since in the bucket.

"I asked you a question," Estel said gravely.

"I heard it. I'm making my mind up. The answer is, I wouldn't have thought it – no. But it happened, I was there. I was in the car instead of young Jeeter. His father had sent for me to come to the house to talk things over."

"What things?"

I didn't bother to look surprised. "You hold fifty grand of the boy's paper. That looks bad for you, if anything happens to him."

"I don't figure it that way. Because that way I would lose my dough. The old man won't pay – granted. But I wait a couple of years and I collect from the kid. He gets his estate out of trust when he's twenty-eight. Right now he gets a grand a month and he can't even will anything, because it's still in trust. Savvy?"

"So you wouldn't knock him off," I said, using my Scotch. "But you might throw a scare into him."

Estel frowned. He discarded his cigarette into a tray and watched it smoke a moment before he picked it up again and snubbed it out. He shook his head.

"If you're going to bodyguard him, it would almost pay me to stand part of your salary, wouldn't it? Almost. A man in my racket can't take care of everything. He's of age and it's his business who he runs around with. For instance, women. Any reason why a nice girl shouldn't cut herself a piece of five million bucks?"

I said: "I think it's a swell idea. What was it you knew about me that I didn't know you knew?"

He smiled, faintly. "What was it you were waiting to tell Miss Huntress – the thing that happened?"

He smiled faintly again.

"Listen, Marlowe, there are lots of ways to play any game. I play mine on the house percentage, because that's all I need to win. What makes me get tough?"

I rolled a fresh cigarette around in my fingers and tried to roll it around my glass with two fingers. "Who said you were tough? I always heard the nicest things about you."

Marty Estel nodded and looked faintly amused. "I have sources of information," he said quietly. "When I have fifty grand invested in a guy, I'm apt to find out a little about him. Jeeter hired a man named Arbogast to do a little work. Arbogast was killed in his office today — with a twenty-two. That could have nothing to do with Jeeter's business. But there was a tail on you when you went there and you didn't give it to the law. Does that make you and me friends?"

I licked the edge of my glass, nodded. "It seems it does."

"From now on just forget about bothering Harriet, see?"

"Okay."

"So we understand each other real good, now."

"Yeah."

"Well, I'll be going. Give the guy back his Luger, Beef."

The derby hat came over and smacked my gun into my hand hard enough to break a bone.

"Staying?" Estel asked, moving towards the door.

"I guess I'll wait a little while. Until Hawkins comes up to touch me for another ten."

Estel grinned. Beef walked in front of him wooden-faced to the door and opened it. Estel went out. The door closed. The room was silent. I sniffed at the dying perfume of sandalwood and stood motionless, looking around.

Somebody was nuts. I was nuts. Everybody was nuts. None of it fitted together worth a nickel. Marty Estel, as he said, had no good motive for murdering anybody, because that would be the surest way to kill chances to collect his money. Even if he had a motive for murdering anybody, Waxnose and Frisky didn't seem like the team he would select for the job. I was in bad with the police, I had spent ten dollars of my twenty expense money, and I didn't have enough leverage anywhere to lift a dime off a cigar counter.

I finished my drink, put the glass down, walked up and down the room, smoked a third cigarette, looked at my watch, shrugged and felt disgusted. The inner doors of the suite were closed. I went across to the one out of which young Jeeter must have sneaked that afternoon. Opening it I looked into a bedroom done in ivory and ashes of roses. There was a big double bed with no footboard, covered with figured brocade. Toilet articles glistened on a built-in dressing table with a panel light. The light was lit. A small lamp on a table beside the door was lit also. A door near the dressing table showed the cool green of bathroom tiles.

I went over and looked in there. Chromium, a glass stall shower, monogrammed towels on a rack, a glass shelf for perfume and bath salts at the foot of the tub, everything nice and refined. Miss Huntress did herself well. I hoped she was paying her own rent. It didn't make any difference to me – I just liked it that way.

I went back towards the living-room, stopped in the doorway to take another pleasant look around, and noticed something I ought to have noticed the instant I stepped into the room. I noticed the sharp tang of cordite on the air, almost, but not quite gone. And then I noticed something else.

The bed had been moved over until its head overlapped the edge of a closet door which was not quite closed. The weight of the bed was holding it from opening. I went over there to find out why it wanted to open. I went slowly and about halfway there I noticed that I was holding a gun in my hand.

I leaned against the closet door. It didn't move. I threw more weight against it. It still didn't move. Braced against it I pushed the bed away with my foot, gave ground slowly.

A weight pushed against me hard. I had gone back a foot or so before anything else happened. Then it happened suddenly. He came out – sideways, in a sort of roll. I put some more weight back on the door and held him like that a moment, looking at him.

He was still big, still blond, still dressed in rough sporty material, with scarf and open-necked shirt. But his face wasn't red any more.

I gave ground again and he rolled down the back of the door, turning a little like a swimmer in the surf, thumped the floor and lay there, almost on his back, still looking at me. Light from the bedside lamp glittered on his head. There was a scorched and soggy stain on the rough coat – about where his heart would be. So he wouldn't get that five million after all. And nobody would get anything and Marty Estel wouldn't get his fifty grand. Because young Mister Gerald was dead.

I looked back into the closet where he had been. Its door hung wide open now. There were clothes on racks, feminine clothes, nice clothes. He had been backed in among them, probably with his hands in the air and a gun against his chest. And then he had been shot dead, and whoever did it hadn't been quite quick enough or quite strong enough to get the door shut. Or had been scared and had just yanked the bed over against the door and left it that way.

Something glittered down on the floor. I picked it up. A small automatic, .25 caliber, a woman's purse gun with a beautifully engraved butt inlaid with silver and ivory. I put the gun in my pocket. That seemed a funny thing to do, too.

I didn't touch him. He was as dead as John D. Arbogast and looked a whole lot deader. I left the door open and listened, walked quickly back across the room and into the living-room and shut the bedroom door, smearing the knob as I did it.

A lock was being tinkled at with a key. Hawkins was back again, to see what delayed me. He was letting himself in with his passkey.

I was pouring a drink when he came in.

He came well into the room, stopped with his feet planted and surveyed me coldly.

"I seen Estel and his boy leave," he said. "I didn't see you leave. So I come up. I gotta – "

"You gotta protect the guests," I said.

"Yeah. I gotta protect the guests. You can't stay up here, pal. Not without the lady of the house home."

"But Marty Estel and his hard boy can."

He came a little closer to me. He had a mean look in his eye. He had always had it, probably, but I noticed it more now.

"You don't want to make nothing of that, do you?" he asked me.

"No. Every man to his own chisel. Have a drink."

"That ain't your liquor."

"Miss Huntress gave me a bottle. We're pals. Marty Estel and I are pals. Everybody is pals. Don't you want to be pals?"

"You ain't trying to kid me, are you?"

"Have a drink and forget it."

I found a glass and poured him one. He took it.

"It's the job if anybody smells it on me," he said.

"Uh-huh."

He drank slowly, rolling it around on his tongue. "Good Scotch."

"Won't be the first time you tasted it, will it?"

He started to get hard again, then relaxed. "Hell, I guess you're just a kidder." He finished the drink, put the glass down, patted his lips with a large and very crumpled handkerchief and sighed.

"Okay," he said. "But we'll have to leave now."

"All set. I guess she won't be home for a while. You see them go out?"

"Her and the boy friend. Yeah, long time ago."

I nodded. We went towards the door and Hawkins saw me out. He saw me downstairs and off the premises. But he didn't see what was in Miss Huntress' bedroom. I wondered if he would go back up. If he did, the Scotch bottle would probably stop him.

I got into my car and drove off home — to talk to Anna Halsey on the phone. There wasn't any case any more — for us. I parked close to the curb this time. I wasn't feeling gay any more. I rode up in the elevator and unlocked the door and clicked the light on.

Waxnose sat in my best chair, an unlit hand-rolled brown cigarette between his fingers, his bony knees crossed, and his long Woodsman resting solidly on his leg. He was smiling. It wasn't the nicest smile I ever saw.

"Hi, pal," he drawled. "You still ain't had that door fixed. Kind of shut it, huh?" His voice, for all the drawl, was deadly.

I shut the door, stood looking across the room at him.

"So you killed my pal," he said.

He stood up slowly, came across the room slowly and leaned the .22 against my throat. His smiling thin-lipped mouth seemed as expressionless, for all its smile, as his wax-white nose. He reached quietly under my coat and took the Luger. I might as well leave it home from now on. Everybody in town seemed to be able to take it away from me.

He stepped back across the room and sat down again in the chair.

"Steady does it," he said almost gently. "Park the body, friend. No false moves. No moves at all. You and me are at the jumping-off place. The clock's tickin' and we're waiting to go."

I sat down and stared at him. A curious bird. I moistened my dry lips. "You told me his gun had no firing pin," I said.

"Yeah. He fooled me on that, the little so-and-so. And I told you to lay off the Jeeter kid. That's cold now. It's Frisky I'm thinking about. Crazy, ain't it? Me bothering about a dimwit like that, packin' him around with me, and letting him get hisself bumped off." He sighed and added simply, "He was my kid brother."

"I didn't kill him," I said.

He smiled a little more. He had never stopped smiling. The corners of his mouth just tucked in a little deeper.

"Yeah?"

He slid the safety catch off the Luger, laid it carefully on the arm of the chair at his right, and reached into his pocket. What he brought out made me as cold as an ice bucket.

It was a metal tube, dark and rough-looking, about four inches long and drilled with a lot of small holes. He held his Woodsman in his left hand and began to screw the tube casually on the end of it.

"Silencer," he said. "They're the bunk, I guess you smart guys think. This one ain't the bunk — not for three shots. I oughta know. I made it myself."

I moistened my lips again. "It'll work for one shot," I said. "Then it jams your action. That one looks like cast-iron. It will probably blow your hand off."

He smiled his waxy smile, screwed it on, slowly, lovingly, gave it a last hard turn and sat back relaxed. "Not this baby. She's packed with steel wool and that's good for three shots, like I said. Then you got to repack it. And there ain't enough back pressure to jam the action on this gun. You feel good? I'd like you to feel good."

"I feel swell, you sadistic son of a bitch," I said.

"I'm having you lie down on the bed after a while. You won't feel nothing. I'm kind of fussy about my killings. Frisky didn't feel nothing, I guess. You got him neat."

"You don't see good," I sneered. "The chauffeur got him with a Smith & Wesson forty-four. I didn't even fire."

"Uh-huh."

"Okay, you don't believe me," I said. "What did you kill Arbogast for? There was nothing fussy about that killing. He was just shot at his desk, three times with a twenty-two and he fell down on the floor. What did he ever do to your filthy little brother?"

He jerked the gun up, but his smile held. "You got guts," he said. "Who is this here Arbogast?"

I told him. I told him slowly and carefully, in detail. I told him a lot of things. And he began in some vague way to look worried. His eyes flickered at me, away, back again, restlessly, like a hummingbird.

"I don't know any party named Arbogast, pal," he said

slowly. "Never heard of him. And I ain't shot any fat guys today."

"You killed him," I said. "And you killed young Jeeter – in the girl's apartment at the El Milano. He's lying there dead right now. You're working for Marty Estel. He's going to be awfully damn sorry about that kill. Go ahead and make it three in a row."

His face froze. The smile went away at last. His whole face looked waxy now. He opened his mouth and breathed through it, and his breath made a restless worrying sound. I could see the faint glitter of sweat on his forehead, and I could feel the cold from the evaporation of sweat on mine.

Waxnose said very gently: "I ain't killed anybody at all, friend. Not anybody. I wasn't hired to kill people. Until Frisky stopped that slug I didn't have no such ideas. That's straight."

I tried not to stare at the metal tube on the end of the Woodsman.

A flame flickered at the back of his eyes, a small, weak, smoky flame. It seemed to grow larger and clearer. He looked down at the floor between his feet. I looked around at the light switch, but it was too far away. He looked up again. Very slowly he began to unscrew the silencer. He had it loose in his hand. He dropped it back into his pocket, stood up, holding the two guns, one in each hand. Then he had another idea. He sat down again, took all the shells out of the Luger quickly and threw it on the floor after them.

He came towards me softly across the room. "I guess this is your lucky day," he said. "I got to go a place and see a guy."

"I knew all along it was my lucky day. I've been feeling so good."

He moved delicately around me to the door and opened it a foot and started through the narrow opening, smiling again.

"I gotta see a guy," he said very gently, and his tongue moved along his lips.

"Not yet," I said, and jumped.

His gun hand was at the edge of the door, almost beyond the edge. I hit the door hard and he couldn't bring it in quickly enough. He couldn't get out of the way. I pinned him in the doorway, and used all the strength I had. It was a crazy thing. He had given me a break and all I had to do was to stand still and let him go. But I had a guy to see too – and I wanted to see him first.

Waxnose leered at me. He grunted. He fought with his hand beyond the door edge. I shifted and hit his jaw with all I had. It was enough. He went limp. I hit him again. His head bounced against the wood. I heard a light thud beyond the door edge. I hit him a third time. I never hit anything any harder.

I took my weight back from the door then and he slid towards me, blank-eyed, rubber-kneed and I caught him and twisted his empty hands behind him and let him fall. I stood over him panting. I went to the door. His Woodsman lay almost on the sill. I picked it up, dropped it into my pocket – not the pocket that held Miss Huntress' gun. He hadn't even found that.

There he lay on the floor. He was thin, he had no weight, but I panted just the same. In a little while his eyes flickered open and looked up at me.

"Greedy guy," he whispered wearily. "Why did I ever leave Saint Looey?"

I snapped handcuffs on his wrists and pulled him by the shoulders into the dressing room and tied his ankles with a piece of rope. I left him laying on his back, a little sideways, his nose as white as ever, his eyes empty now, his lips moving a little as if he were talking to himself. A funny lad, not all bad, but not so pure I had to weep over him either.

I put my Luger together and left with my three guns. There was nobody outside the apartment house.

7

THE JEETER MANSION was on a nine- or ten-acre knoll, a big colonial pile with fat white columns and dormer windows and magnolias and a four-car garage. There was a circular parking space at the top of the driveway with two cars parked in it – one was the big dreadnought in which I'd ridden and the other a canary-yellow sports convertible I had seen before.

I rang a bell the size of a silver dollar. The door opened and a tall narrow cold-eyed bird in dark clothes looked out at me.

"Mr. Jeeter home? Mr. Jeeter, Senior?"

"May I arsk who is calling?" The accent was a little too thick, like cut Scotch.

"Philip Marlowe. I'm working for him. Maybe I had ought to of gone to the servants' entrance."

He hitched a finger at a wing collar and looked at me without pleasure. "Aw, possibly. You may step in. I shall inform Mr. Jeeter. I believe he is engaged at the moment. Kindly wait 'ere in the 'all."

"The act stinks," I said. "English butlers aren't dropping their h's this year."

"Smart guy, huh?" he snarled, in a voice from not any farther across the Atlantic than Hoboken. "Wait here." He slid away.

I sat down in a carved chair and felt thirsty. After a while the butler came cat-footing back along the hall and jerked his chin at me unpleasantly.

We went along a mile of hallway. At the end it broadened without any doors into a huge sunroom. On the far side of the sunroom the butler opened a wide door and I stepped past him into an oval room with a black-and-silver oval rug, a black marble table in the middle of the rug, stiff high-backed carved chairs against the walls, a huge oval mirror with a rounded surface that made me look like a pygmy with water on the brain, and in the room three people.

By the door opposite where I came in, George the chauffeur stood stiffly in his neat dark uniform, with his peaked cap in his hand. In the least uncomfortable of the chairs sat Miss Harriet Huntress holding a glass in which there was half a drink. And around the silver margin of the oval rug, Mr. Jeeter, Senior, was trying his legs out in a brisk canter, still under wraps, but mad inside. His face was red and the veins on his nose were distended. His hands were in the pockets of a velvet smoking jacket. He wore a pleated shirt with a black pearl in the bosom, a batwing black tie and one of his patent-leather oxfords was unlaced.

He whirled and yelled at the butler behind me: "Get out and keep those doors shut! And I'm not at home to anybody, understand? Nobody!"

The butler closed the doors. Presumably, he went away. I didn't hear him go.

George gave me a cool one-sided smile and Miss Huntress gave me a bland stare over her glass. "You made a nice comeback," she said demurely.

"You took a chance leaving me alone in your apartment," I told her. "I might have sneaked some of your perfume."

"Well, what do you want?" Jeeter yelled at me. "A nice sort of detective you turned out to be. I put you on a confidential job and you walk right in on Miss Huntress and explain the whole thing to her."

"It worked, didn't it?"

He stared. They all stared. "How do you know that?" he barked.

"I know a nice girl when I see one. She's here telling you she had an idea she got not to like, and for you to quit worrying about it. Where's Mister Gerald?"

Old man Jeeter stopped and gave me a hard level stare. "I still regard you as incompetent," he said. "My son is missing."

"I'm not working for you. I'm working for Anna Halsey. Any complaints you have to make should be addressed to her. Do I pour my own drink or do you have a flunky in a purple suit to do it? And what do you mean, your son is missing?"

"Should I give him the heave, sir?" George asked quietly.

Jeeter waved his hand at a decanter and siphon and glasses on the black marble table and started around the rug again. "Don't be silly," he snapped at George.

George flushed a little, high on his cheekbones. His mouth looked tough.

I mixed myself a drink and sat down with it and tasted it and asked again: "What do you mean your son is missing, Mr. Jeeter?"

"I'm paying you good money," he started to yell at me, still mad.

"When?"

He stopped dead in his canter and looked at me again. Miss Huntress laughed lightly. George scowled.

"What do you suppose I mean – my son is missing?" he snapped. "I should have thought that would be clear enough even to you. Nobody knows where he is. Miss Huntress doesn't know. I don't know. No one at any of the places where he might be knows."

"But I'm smarter than they are," I said. "*I* know."

Nobody moved for a long minute. Jeeter stared at me fish-eyed. George stared at me. The girl stared at me. She looked puzzled. The other two just stared.

I looked at her. "Where did you go when you went out, if you're telling?"

Her dark blue eyes were water-clear. "There's no secret about it. We went out together – in a taxi. Gerald had had his driving license suspended for a month. Too many tickets. We went down towards the beach and I had a change of heart, as you guessed. I decided I was just being a chiseler after all.

I didn't want Gerald's money really. What I wanted was revenge. On Mr. Jeeter here for ruining my father. Done all legally of course, but done just the same. But I got myself in a spot where I couldn't have my revenge and not look like a cheap chiseler. So I told Gerald to find some other girl to play with. He was sore and we quarreled. I stopped the taxi and got out in Beverly Hills. He went on. I don't know where. Later I went back to the El Milano and got my car out of the garage and came here. To tell Mr. Jeeter to forget the whole thing and not bother to sic sleuths on to me."

"You say you went with him in a taxi," I said. "Why wasn't George driving him, if he couldn't drive himself?"

I stared at her, but I wasn't talking to her. Jeeter answered me, frostily. "George drove me home from the office, of course. At that time Gerald had already gone out. Is there anything important about that?"

I turned to him. "Yeah. There's going to be. Mister Gerald is at the El Milano. Hawkins the house dick told me. He went back there to wait for Miss Huntress and Hawkins let him into her apartment. Hawkins will do you those little favors – for ten bucks. He may be there still and he may not."

I kept on watching them. It was hard to watch all three of them. But they didn't move. They just looked at me.

"Well – I'm glad to hear it," old man Jeeter said. "I was afraid he was off somewhere getting drunk."

"No. He's not off anywhere getting drunk," I said. "By the way, among these places you called to see if he was there, you didn't call the El Milano?"

George nodded. "Yes, I did. They said he wasn't there. Looks like this house peeper tipped the phone girl off not to say anything."

"He wouldn't have to do that. She'd just ring the apartment and he wouldn't answer – naturally." I watched old man Jeeter hard then, with a lot of interest. It was going to be hard for him to take that up, but he was going to have to do it.

He did. He licked his lips first. "Why – naturally, if I may ask?" he said coldly.

I put my glass down on the marble table and stood against the wall, with my hands hanging free. I still tried to watch them – all three of them.

"Let's go back over this thing a little," I said. "We're all wise to the situation. I know George is, although he shouldn't be, being just a servant. I know Miss Huntress is. And of course *you* are, Mr. Jeeter. So let's see what we have got. We have a lot of things that don't add up, but I'm smart. I'm going to add them up anyhow. First-off a handful of photostats of notes from Marty Estel. Gerald denies having given these and Mr. Jeeter won't pay them, but he has a handwriting man named Arbogast check the signatures, to see if they look genuine. They do. They are. This Arbogast may have done other things. I don't know. I couldn't ask him. When I went to see him, he was dead – shot three times – as I've since heard – with a twenty-two. No, I didn't tell the police, Mr. Jeeter."

The tall silver-haired man looked horribly shocked. His lean body shook like a bulrush. "Dead?" he whispered. "Murdered?"

I looked at George. George didn't move a muscle. I looked at the girl. She sat quietly, waiting, tight-lipped.

I said: "There's only one reason to suppose his killing had anything to do with Mr. Jeeter's affairs. He was shot with a twenty-two – and there is a man in this case who wears a twenty-two."

I still had their attention. And their silence.

"Why he was shot I haven't the faintest idea. He was not a dangerous man to Miss Huntress or Marty Estel. He was too fat to get around much. My guess is he was a little too smart. He got a simple case of signature identification and he went on from there to find out more than he should. And after he had found out more than he should – he guessed more than he ought – and maybe he even tried a little blackmail. And somebody rubbed him out this afternoon with a twenty-two. Okay, I can stand it. I never knew him.

"So I went over to see Miss Huntress and after a lot of finagling around with this itchy-handed house dick I got to see her and we had a chat, and then Mister Gerald stepped neatly out of hiding and bopped me a nice one on the chin and over I went and hit my head on a chair leg. And when I came out of that the joint was empty. So I went on home.

"And home I found the man with the twenty-two and with him a dimwit called Frisky Lavon, with bad breath and a very large gun, neither of which matters now as he was shot dead in front of your house tonight, Mr. Jeeter — shot trying to stick up your car. The cops know about that one — they came to see me about it — because the other guy, the one that packs the twenty-two, is the little dimwit's brother and he thought I shot Dimwit and tried to put the bee on me. But it didn't work. That's two killings.

"We now come to the third and most important. I went back to the El Milano because it no longer seemed a good idea for Mister Gerald to be running around casually. He seemed to have a few enemies. It even seemed that he was supposed to be in the car this evening when Frisky Lavon shot at it — but of course that was just a plant."

Old Jeeter drew his white eyebrows together in an expression of puzzlement. George didn't look puzzled. He didn't look anything. He was as wooden-faced as a cigar-store Indian. The girl looked a little white now, a little tense. I plowed on.

"Back at the El Milano I found that Hawkins had let Marty Estel and his bodyguard into Miss Huntress' apartment to wait for her. Marty had something to tell her — that Arbogast had been killed. That made it a good idea for her to lay off young Jeeter for a while — until the cops quieted down anyhow. A thoughtful guy, Marty. A much more thoughtful guy than you would suppose. For instance, he knew about

Arbogast and he knew Mr. Jeeter went to Anna Halsey's office this morning and he knew somehow – Anna might have told him herself, I wouldn't put it past her – that I was working on the case now. So he had me tailed to Arbogast's place and away, and he found out later from his cop friends that Arbogast had been murdered, and he knew I hadn't given it out. So he had me there and that made us pals. He went away after telling me this and once more I was left alone in Miss Huntress' apartment. But this time for no reason at all I poked around. And I found young Mister Gerald, in the bedroom, in a closet."

I stepped quickly over to the girl and reached into my pocket and took out the small fancy .25 automatic and laid it down on her knee.

"Ever see this before?"

Her voice had a curious tight sound, but her dark blue eyes looked at me levelly.

"Yes. It's mine."

"You kept it where?"

"In the drawer of a small table beside the bed."

"Sure about that?"

She thought. Neither of the two men stirred.

George began to twitch the corner of his mouth. She shook her head suddenly, sideways.

"No. I have an idea now I took it out to show somebody – because I don't know much about guns – and left it lying on the mantel in the living-room. In fact, I'm almost sure I did. It was Gerald I showed it to."

"So he might have reached for it there, if anybody tried to make a wrong play at him?"

She nodded, troubled. "What do you mean – he's in the closet?" she asked in a small quick voice.

"You know. Everybody in this room knows what I mean. They know that I showed you that gun for a purpose." I stepped away from her and faced George and his boss. "He's dead, of course. Shot through the heart – probably with this gun. It was left there with him. That's why it would be left."

The old man took a step and stopped and braced himself against the table. I wasn't sure whether he had turned white or whether he had been white already. He stared stonily at the girl. He said very slowly, between his teeth: "You damned murderess!"

"Couldn't it have been suicide?" I sneered.

He turned his head enough to look at me. I could see that the idea interested him. He half nodded.

"No," I said. "It couldn't have been suicide."

He didn't like that so well. His face congested with blood and the veins on his nose thickened. The girl touched the gun lying on her knee, then put her hand loosely around the butt. I saw her thumb slide very gently towards the safety catch. She didn't know much about guns, but she knew that much.

"It couldn't be suicide," I said again, very slowly. "As an isolated event – maybe. But not with all the other stuff that's been happening. Arbogast, the stick-up down on Calvello Drive outside this house, the thugs planted in my apartment, the job with the twenty-two."

I reached into my pocket again and pulled out Waxnose's Woodsman. I held it carelessly on the flat of my left hand. "And curiously enough, I don't think it was *this* twenty-two – although this happens to be the gunman's twenty-two. Yeah, I have the gunman, too. He's tied up in my apartment. He came back to knock me off, but I talked him out of it. I'm a swell talker."

"Except that you overdo it," the girl said coolly, and lifted the gun a little.

"It's obvious who killed him, Miss Huntress," I said. "It's simply a matter of motive and opportunity. Marty Estel didn't, and didn't have it done. That would spoil his chances to get his fifty grand. Frisky Lavon's pal didn't, regardless of who he was working for, and I don't think he was working for Marty

Estel. He couldn't have got into the El Milano to do the job, and certainly not into Miss Huntress' apartment. Whoever did it had something to gain by it and an opportunity to get to the place where it was done. Well, who had something to gain? Gerald had five million coming to him in two years out of a trust fund. He couldn't will it until he got it. So if he died, his natural heir got it. Who's his natural heir? You'd be surprised. Did you know that in the state of California and some others, but not in all, a man can by his own act become a natural heir? Just by adopting somebody who has money and no heirs!"

George moved then. His movement was once more as smooth as a ripple of water. The Smith & Wesson gleamed dully in his hand, but he didn't fire it. The small automatic in the girl's hand cracked. Blood spurted from George's brown hard hand. The Smith & Wesson dropped to the floor. He cursed. She didn't know much about guns – not very much.

"Of course!" she said grimly. "George could get into the apartment without any trouble, if Gerald was there. He would go in through the garage, a chauffeur in uniform, ride up in the elevator and knock at the door. And when Gerald opened it, George would back him in with that Smith & Wesson. But how did he know Gerald was there?"

I said: "He must have followed your taxi. We don't know where he has been all evening since he left me. He had a car with him. The cops will find out. How much was in it for you, George?"

George held his right wrist with his left hand, held it tightly, and his face was twisted, savage. He said nothing.

"George would back him in with the Smith & Wesson," the girl said wearily. "Then he would see my gun on the mantelpiece. That would be better. He would use that. He would back Gerald into the bedroom, away from the corridor, into the closet, and there, quietly, calmly, he would kill him and drop the gun on the floor."

"George killed Arbogast, too. He killed him with a twenty-two because he knew that Frisky Lavon's brother had a twenty-two, and he knew that because he had hired Frisky and his brother to put over a big scare on Gerald – so that when he was murdered it would look as if Marty Estel had had it done. That was why I was brought out here tonight in the Jeeter car – so that the two thugs who had been warned and planted could pull their act and maybe knock me off, if I got too tough. Only George likes to kill people. He made a neat shot at Frisky. He hit him in the face. It was so good a shot I think he meant it to be a miss. How about it, George?"

Silence.

I looked at old Jeeter at last. I had been expecting him to pull a gun himself, but he hadn't. He just stood there, open-mouthed, appalled, leaning against the black marble table, shaking.

"My God!" he whispered. "My God!"

"You don't have one – except money."

A door squeaked behind me. I whirled, but I needn't have bothered. A hard voice, about as English as Amos and Andy, said: "Put 'em up, bud."

The butler, the very English butler, stood there in the doorway, a gun in his hand, tight-lipped. The girl turned her wrist and shot him just kind of casually, in the shoulder or something. He squealed like a stuck pig.

"Go away, you're intruding," she said coldly.

He ran. We heard his steps running.

"He's going to fall," she said.

I was wearing my Luger in my right hand now, a little late in the season, as usual. I came around with it. Old man Jeeter was holding on to the table, his face gray as a paving block. His knees were giving. George stood cynically, holding a handkerchief around his bleeding wrist, watching him.

"Let him fall," I said. "Down is where he belongs."

He fell. His head twisted. His mouth went slack. He hit the carpet on his side and rolled a little and his knees came up. His mouth drooled a little. His skin turned violet.

"Go call the law, angel," I said. "I'll watch them now."

"All right," she said standing up. "But you certainly need a lot of help in your private-detecting business, Mr. Marlowe."

8

I HAD BEEN in there for a solid hour, alone. There was the scarred desk in the middle, another against the wall, a brass spittoon on a mat, a police loudspeaker box on the wall, three squashed flies, a smell of cold cigars and old clothes. There were two hard armchairs with felt pads and two hard straight chairs without pads. The electric-light fixture had been dusted about Coolidge's first term.

The door opened with a jerk and Finlayson and Sebold came in. Sebold looked as spruce and nasty as ever, but Finlayson looked older, more worn, mousier. He held a sheaf of papers in his hand. He sat down across the desk from me and gave me a hard bleak stare.

"Guys like you get in a lot of trouble," Finlayson said sourly. Sebold sat down against the wall and tilted his hat over his eyes and yawned and looked at his new stainless-steel wrist watch.

"Trouble is my business," I said. "How else would I make a nickel?"

"We oughta throw you in the can for all this cover-up stuff. How much you making on this one?"

"I was working for Anna Halsey who was working for old man Jeeter. I guess I made a bad debt."

Sebold smiled his blackjack smile at me. Finlayson lit a cigar and licked at a tear on the side of it and pasted it down, but it leaked smoke just the same when he drew on it. He pushed papers across the desk at me.

"Sign three copies."

I signed three copies.

He took them back, yawned and rumpled his old gray head. "The old man's had a stroke," he said. "No dice there. Probably won't know what time it is when he comes out. This George Hasterman, this chauffeur guy, he just laughs at us. Too bad he got pinked. I'd like to wrastle him a bit."

"He's tough," I said.

"Yeah. Okay, you can beat it for now."

I got up and nodded to them and went to the door. "Well, good night, boys."

Neither of them spoke to me.

I went out, along the corridor and down in the night elevator to the City Hall lobby. I went out the Spring Street side and down the long flight of empty steps and the wind blew cold. I lit a cigarette at the bottom. My car was still out at the Jeeter place. I lifted a foot to start walking to a taxi half a block down across the street. A voice spoke sharply from a parked car.

"Come here a minute."

It was a man's voice, tight, hard. It was Marty Estel's voice. It came from a big sedan with two men in the front seat. I went over there. The rear window was down and Marty Estel leaned a gloved hand on it.

"Get in." He pushed the door open. I got in. I was too tired to argue. "Take it away, Skin."

The car drove west through dark, almost quiet streets, almost clean streets. The night air was not pure but it was cool. We went up over a hill and began to pick up speed.

"What they get?" Estel asked coolly.

"They didn't tell me. They didn't break the chauffeur yet."

"You can't convict a couple million bucks of murder in this man's town." The driver called Skin laughed without turning his head. "Maybe I don't even touch my fifty grand now . . . she likes you."

"Uh–huh. So what?"

"Lay off her."

"What will it get me?"

"It's what it'll get you if you don't."

"Yeah, sure," I said. "Go to hell, will you please. I'm tired."
I shut my eyes and leaned in the corner of the car and just like
that went to sleep. I can do that sometimes, after a strain.

A hand shaking my shoulder woke me. The car had
stopped. I looked out at the front of my apartment house.

"Home," Marty Estel said. "And remember. Lay off her."

"Why the ride home? Just to tell me that?"

"She asked me to look out for you. That's why you're
loose. She likes you. I like her. See? You don't want any more
trouble."

"Trouble – " I started to say, and stopped. I was tired of that
gag for that night. "Thanks for the ride, and apart from that,
nuts to you." I turned away and went into the apartment
house and up.

The door lock was still loose but nobody waited for me
this time. They had taken Waxnose away long since. I left the
door open and threw the windows up and I was still sniffing
at policemen's cigar butts when the phone rang. It was her
voice, cool, a little hard, not touched by anything, almost
amused. Well, she'd been through enough to make her that
way, probably.

"Hello, brown-eyes. Make it home all right?"

"Your pal Marty brought me home. He told me to lay off
you. Thanks with all my heart, if I have any, but don't call me
up any more."

"A little scared, Mr. Marlowe?"

"No. Wait for me to call you," I said. "Good night, angel."

"Good night, brown-eyes."

The phone clicked. I put it away and shut the door and
pulled the bed down. I undressed and lay on it for a while in
the cold air.

Then I got up and had a drink and a shower and went to sleep.

They broke George at last, but not enough. He said there had been a fight over the girl and young Jeeter had grabbed the gun off the mantel and George had fought with him and it had gone off. All of which, of course, looked possible – in the papers. They never pinned the Arbogast killing on him or on anybody. They never found the gun that did it, but it was not Waxnose's gun. Waxnose disappeared – I never heard where. They didn't touch old man Jeeter, because he never came out of his stroke, except to lie on his back and have nurses and tell people how he hadn't lost a nickel in the depression.

Marty Estel called me up four times to tell me to lay off Harriet Huntress. I felt kind of sorry for the poor guy. He had it bad. I went out with her twice and sat with her twice more at home, drinking her Scotch. It was nice, but I didn't have the money, the clothes, the time or the manners. Then she stopped being at the El Milano and I heard she had gone to New York.

I was glad when she left – even though she didn't bother to tell me goodbye.

I'LL BE WAITING

AT ONE O'CLOCK in the morning, Carl, the night porter, turned down the last of three table lamps in the main lobby of the Windermere Hotel. The blue carpet darkened a shade or two and the walls drew back into remoteness. The chairs filled with shadowy loungers. In the corners were memories like cobwebs.

Tony Reseck yawned. He put his head on one side and listened to the frail, twittery music from the radio room beyond a dim arch at the far side of the lobby. He frowned. That should be his radio room after one A.M. Nobody should be in it. That red-haired girl was spoiling his nights.

The frown passed and a miniature of a smile quirked at the corners of his lips. He sat relaxed, a short, pale, paunchy, middle-aged man with long, delicate fingers clasped on the elk's tooth on his watch chain; the long delicate fingers of a sleight-of-hand artist, fingers with shiny, molded nails and tapering first joints, fingers a little spatulate at the ends. Handsome fingers. Tony Reseck rubbed them gently together and there was peace in his quiet sea-gray eyes.

The frown came back on his face. The music annoyed him. He got up with a curious litheness, all in one piece, without moving his clasped hands from the watch chain. At one moment he was leaning back relaxed, and the next he was standing balanced on his feet, perfectly still, so that the movement of rising seemed to be a thing perfectly perceived, an error of vision. . . .

He walked with small, polished shoes delicately across the blue carpet and under the arch. The music was louder. It contained the hot, acid blare, the frenetic, jittering runs of a jam session. It was too loud. The red-haired girl sat there and stared silently at the fretted part of the big radio cabinet as though she could see the band with its fixed professional grin and the sweat running down its back. She was curled up with her feet under her on a davenport which seemed to contain most of the cushions in the room. She was tucked among them carefully, like a corsage in the florist's tissue paper.

She didn't turn her head. She leaned there, one hand in a small fist on her peach-colored knee. She was wearing lounging pajamas of heavy ribbed silk embroidered with black lotus buds.

"You like Goodman, Miss Cressy?" Tony Reseck asked.

The girl moved her eyes slowly. The light in there was dim, but the violet of her eyes almost hurt. They were large, deep eyes without a trace of thought in them. Her face was classical and without expression.

She said nothing.

Tony smiled and moved his fingers at his sides, one by one, feeling them move. "You like Goodman, Miss Cressy?" he repeated gently.

"Not to cry over," the girl said tonelessly.

Tony rocked back on his heels and looked at her eyes. Large, deep, empty eyes. Or were they? He reached down and muted the radio.

"Don't get me wrong," the girl said. "Goodman makes money, and a lad that makes legitimate money these days is a lad you have to respect. But this jitterbug music gives me the backdrop of a beer flat. I like something with roses in it."

"Maybe you like Mozart," Tony said.

"Go on, kid me," the girl said.

"I wasn't kidding you, Miss Cressy. I think Mozart was the greatest man that ever lived — and Toscanini is his prophet."

"I thought you were the house dick." She put her head back on a pillow and stared at him through her lashes.

"Make me some of that Mozart," she added.

"It's too late," Tony sighed. "You can't get it now."

She gave him another long lucid glance. "Got the eye on me, haven't you, flatfoot?" She laughed a little, almost under her breath. "What did I do wrong?"

Tony smiled his toy smile. "Nothing, Miss Cressy. Nothing at all. But you need some fresh air. You've been five days in this hotel and you haven't been outdoors. And you have a tower room."

She laughed again. "Make me a story about it. I'm bored."

"There was a girl here once had your suite. She stayed in the hotel a whole week, like you. Without going out at all, I mean. She didn't speak to anybody hardly. What do you think she did then?"

The girl eyed him gravely. "She jumped her bill."

He put his long delicate hand out and turned it slowly, fluttering the fingers, with an effect almost like a lazy wave breaking. "Unh-uh. She sent down for her bill and paid it. Then she told the hop to be back in half an hour for her suitcases. Then she went out on her balcony."

The girl leaned forward a little, her eyes still grave, one hand capping her peach-colored knee. "What did you say your name was?"

"Tony Reseck."

"Sounds like a hunky."

"Yeah," Tony said. "Polish."

"Go on, Tony."

"All the tower suites have private balconies, Miss Cressy. The walls of them are too low for fourteen stories above the street. It was a dark night, that night, high clouds." He dropped his hand with a final gesture, a farewell gesture. "Nobody saw her jump. But when she hit, it was like a big gun going off."

"You're making it up, Tony." Her voice was a clean dry whisper of sound.

He smiled his toy smile. His quiet sea-gray eyes seemed almost to be smoothing the long waves of her hair. "Eve Cressy," he said musingly. "A name waiting for lights to be in."

"Waiting for a tall dark guy that's no good, Tony. You wouldn't care why. I was married to him once. I might be married to him again. You can make a lot of mistakes in just one lifetime." The hand on her knee opened slowly until the fingers were strained back as far as they would go. Then they closed quickly and tightly, and even in that dim light the knuckles shone like the little polished bones. "I played him a low trick once. I put him in a bad place – without meaning to. You wouldn't care about that either. It's just that I owe him something."

He leaned over softly and turned the knob on the radio. A waltz formed itself dimly on the warm air. A tinsel waltz, but a waltz. He turned the volume up. The music gushed from the loudspeaker in a swirl of shadowed melody. Since Vienna died, all waltzes are shadowed.

The girl put her hand on one side and hummed three or four bars and stopped with a sudden tightening of her mouth.

"Eve Cressy," she said. "It was in lights once. At a bum night club. A dive. They raided it and the lights went out."

He smiled at her almost mockingly. "It was no dive while you were there, Miss Cressy . . . That's the waltz the orchestra always played when the old porter walked up and down in front of the hotel entrance, all swelled up with his medals on his chest. *The Last Laugh*. Emil Jannings. You wouldn't remember that one, Miss Cressy."

" 'Spring, Beautiful Spring,' " she said. "No, I never saw it."

He walked three steps away from her and turned. "I have to go upstairs and palm doorknobs. I hope I didn't bother you. You ought to go to bed now. It's pretty late."

The tinsel waltz stopped and a voice began to talk. The girl spoke through the voice. "You really thought something like that – about the balcony?"

He nodded. "I might have," he said softly. "I don't any more."

"No chance, Tony." Her smile was a dim lost leaf. "Come and talk to me some more. Redheads don't jump, Tony. They hang on — and wither."

He looked at her gravely for a moment and then moved away over the carpet. The porter was standing in the archway that led to the main lobby. Tony hadn't looked that way yet, but he knew somebody was there. He always knew if anybody was close to him. He could hear the grass grow, like the donkey in *The Blue Bird*.

The porter jerked his chin at him urgently. His broad face above the uniform collar looked sweaty and excited. Tony stepped up close to him and they went together through the arch and out to the middle of the dim lobby.

"Trouble?" Tony asked wearily.

"There's a guy outside to see you, Tony. He won't come in. I'm doing a wipe-off on the plate glass of the doors and he comes up beside me, a tall guy. 'Get Tony,' he says, out of the side of his mouth."

Tony said: "Uh-huh," and looked at the porter's pale blue eyes. "Who was it?"

"Al, he said to say he was."

Tony's face became as expressionless as dough. "Okay." He started to move off.

The porter caught his sleeve. "Listen, Tony. You got any enemies?"

Tony laughed politely, his face still like dough.

"Listen, Tony." The porter held his sleeve tightly. "There's a big black car down the block, the other way from the hacks. There's a guy standing beside it with his foot on the running board. This guy that spoke to me, he wears a dark-colored, wrap-around overcoat with a high collar turned up against his ears. His hat's way low. You can't hardly see his face. He says, 'Get Tony,' out of the side of his mouth. You ain't got any enemies, have you, Tony?"

"Only the finance company," Tony said. "Beat it."

He walked slowly and a little stiffly across the blue carpet, up the three shallow steps to the entrance lobby with the three elevators on one side and the desk on the other. Only one elevator was working. Beside the open doors, his arms folded, the night operator stood silent in a neat blue uniform with silver facings. A lean, dark Mexican named Gomez. A new boy, breaking in on the night shift.

The other side was the desk, rose marble, with the night clerk leaning on it delicately. A small neat man with a wispy reddish mustache and cheeks so rosy they looked rouged. He stared at Tony and poked a nail at his mustache.

Tony pointed a stiff index finger at him, folded the other three fingers tight to his palm, and flicked his thumb up and down on the stiff finger. The clerk touched the other side of his mustache and looked bored.

Tony went on past the closed and darkened newsstand and the side entrance to the drugstore, out to the brassbound plate-glass doors. He stopped just inside them and took a deep, hard breath. He squared his shoulders, pushed the doors open and stepped out into the cold damp night air.

The street was dark, silent. The rumble of traffic on Wilshire, two blocks away, had no body, no meaning. To the left were two taxis. Their drivers leaned against a fender, side by side, smoking. Tony walked the other way. The big dark car was a third of a block from the hotel entrance. Its lights were dimmed and it was only when he was almost up to it that he heard the gentle sound of its engine turning over.

A tall figure detached itself from the body of the car and strolled toward him, both hands in the pockets of the dark overcoat with the high collar. From the man's mouth a cigarette tip glowed faintly, a rusty pearl.

They stopped two feet from each other.

The tall man said, "Hi, Tony. Long time no see."

"Hello, Al. How's it going?"

"Can't complain." The tall man started to take his right hand out of his overcoat pocket, then stopped and laughed quietly. "I forgot. Guess you don't want to shake hands."

"That don't mean anything," Tony said. "Shaking hands. Monkeys can shake hands. What's on your mind, Al?"

"Still the funny little fat guy, eh, Tony?"

"I guess." Tony winked his eyes tight. His throat felt tight.

"You like your job back there?"

"It's a job."

Al laughed his quiet laugh again. "You take it slow, Tony. I'll take it fast. So it's a job and you want to hold it. Okay. There's a girl named Eve Cressy flopping in your quiet hotel. Get her out. Fast and right now."

"What's the trouble?"

The tall man looked up and down the street. A man behind in the car coughed lightly. "She's hooked with a wrong number. Nothing against her personal, but she'll lead trouble to you. Get her out, Tony. You got maybe an hour."

"Sure," Tony said aimlessly, without meaning.

Al took his hand out of his pocket and stretched it against Tony's chest. He gave him a light lazy push. "I wouldn't be telling you just for the hell of it, little fat brother. Get her out of there."

"Okay," Tony said, without any tone in his voice.

The tall man took back his hand and reached for the car door. He opened it and started to slip in like a lean black shadow.

Then he stopped and said something to the men in the car and got out again. He came back to where Tony stood silent, his pale eyes catching a little dim light from the street.

"Listen, Tony. You always kept your nose clean. You're a good brother, Tony."

Tony didn't speak.

Al leaned toward him, a long urgent shadow, the high collar almost touching his ears. "It's trouble business, Tony. The boys won't like it, but I'm telling you just the same. This Cressy was married to a lad named Johnny Ralls. Ralls is out of Quentin two, three days, or a week. He did a three-spot for manslaughter. The girl put him there. He ran down an old man one night when he was drunk, and she was with him. He wouldn't stop. She told him to go in and tell it, or else. He didn't go in. So the Johns come for him."

Tony said, "That's too bad."

"It's kosher, kid. It's my business to know. This Ralls flapped his mouth in stir about how the girl would be waiting for him when he got out, all set to forgive and forget, and he was going straight to her."

Tony said, "What's he to you?" His voice had a dry, stiff crackle, like thick paper.

Al laughed. "The trouble boys want to see him. He ran a table at a spot on the Strip and figured out a scheme. He and another guy took the house for fifty grand. The other lad coughed up, but we still need Johnny's twenty-five. The trouble boys don't get paid to forget."

Tony looked up and down the dark street. One of the taxi drivers flicked a cigarette stub in a long arc over the top of one of the cabs. Tony watched it fall and spark on the pavement. He listened to the quiet sound of the big car's motor.

"I don't want any part of it," he said. "I'll get her out."

Al backed away from him, nodding. "Wise kid. How's mom these days?"

"Okay," Tony said.

"Tell her I was asking for her."

"Asking for her isn't anything," Tony said.

Al turned quickly and got into the car. The car curved lazily in the middle of the block and drifted back toward the corner. Its lights went up and sprayed on a wall. It turned a corner and was gone. The lingering smell of its exhaust drifted past Tony's nose. He turned and walked back to the hotel and into it. He went along to the radio room.

The radio still muttered, but the girl was gone from the davenport in front of it. The pressed cushions were hollowed out by her body. Tony reached down and touched them. He thought they were still warm. He turned the radio off and stood there, turning a thumb slowly in front of his body, his hand flat against his stomach. Then he went back through the lobby toward the elevator bank and stood beside a majolica jar of white sand. The clerk fussed behind a pebbled-glass screen at one end of the desk. The air was dead.

The elevator bank was dark. Tony looked at the indicator of the middle car and saw that it was at 14.

"Gone to bed," he said under his breath.

The door of the porter's room beside the elevators opened and the little Mexican night operator came out in street clothes. He looked at Tony with a quiet sidewise look out of eyes the color of dried-out chestnuts.

"Good night, boss."

"Yeah," Tony said absently.

He took a thin dappled cigar out of his vest pocket and smelled it. He examined it slowly, turning it around in his neat fingers. There was a small tear along the side. He frowned at that and put the cigar away.

There was a distant sound and the hand on the indicator began to steal around the bronze dial. Light glittered up in the shaft and the straight line of the car floor dissolved the darkness below. The car stopped and the doors opened, and Carl came out of it.

His eyes caught Tony's with a kind of jump and he walked over to him, his head on one side, a thin shine along his pink upper lip.

"Listen, Tony."

Tony took his arm in a hard swift hand and turned him. He pushed him quickly, yet somehow casually, down the steps to the dim main lobby and steered him into a corner. He let go of the arm. His throat tightened again, for no reason he could think of.

"Well?" he said darkly. "Listen to what?"

The porter reached into a pocket and hauled out a dollar bill. "He gimme this," he said loosely. His glittering eyes looked past Tony's shoulder at nothing. They winked rapidly. "Ice and ginger ale."

"Don't stall," Tony growled.

"Guy in Fourteen-B," the porter said.

"Lemme smell your breath."

The porter leaned toward him obediently.

"Liquor," Tony said harshly.

"He gimme a drink."

Tony looked down at the dollar bill. "Nobody's in Fourteen-B. Not on my list," he said.

"Yeah. There is." The porter licked his lips and his eyes opened and shut several times. "Tall dark guy."

"All right," Tony said crossly. "All right. There's a tall dark guy in Fourteen-B and he gave you a buck and a drink. Then what?"

"Gat under his arm," Carl said, and blinked.

Tony smiled, but his eyes had taken on the lifeless glitter of thick ice. "You take Miss Cressy up to her room?"

Carl shook his head. "Gomez. I saw her go up."

"Get away from me," Tony said between his teeth. "And don't accept any more drinks from the guests."

He didn't move until Carl had gone back into his cubby-hole by the elevators and shut the door. Then he moved silently up the three steps and stood in front of the desk, looking at the veined rose marble, the onyx pen set, the fresh registration card in its leather frame. He lifted a hand and smacked it down hard on the marble. The clerk popped out from behind the glass screen like a chipmunk coming out of its hole.

Tony took a flimsy out of his breast pocket and spread it on the desk. "No Fourteen-B on this," he said in a bitter voice.

The clerk wisped politely at his mustache. "So sorry. You must have been out to supper when he checked in."

"Who?"

"Registered as James Watterson, San Diego." The clerk yawned.

"Ask for anybody?"

The clerk stopped in the middle of the yawn and looked at the top of Tony's head. "Why yes. He asked for a swing band. Why?"

"Smart, fast and funny," Tony said. "If you like 'em that way." He wrote on his flimsy and stuffed it back into his pocket. "I'm going upstairs and palm doorknobs. There's four tower rooms you ain't rented yet. Get up on your toes, son. You're slipping."

"I made out," the clerk drawled, and completed his yawn. "Hurry back, pop. I don't know how I'll get through the time."

"You could shave that pink fuzz off your lip," Tony said, and went across to the elevators.

He opened up a dark one and lit the dome light and shot the car up to fourteen. He darkened it again, stepped out and closed the doors. This lobby was smaller than any other, except the one immediately below it. It had a single blue-paneled door in each of the walls other than the elevator wall. On each door was a gold number and letter with a gold wreath around it. Tony walked over to 14A and put his ear to the panel. He heard nothing. Eve Cressy might be in bed asleep, or in the bathroom, or out on the balcony. Or she might be sitting there in the room, a few feet from the door, looking at the wall. Well, he wouldn't expect to be able to hear her sit and look at the wall. He went over to 14B and put his ear to that panel. This was different. There was a sound in there. A man coughed. It sounded somehow like a solitary cough. There were no voices. Tony pressed the small nacre button beside the door.

Steps came without hurry. A thickened voice spoke through the panel. Tony made no answer, no sound. The thickened voice repeated the question. Lightly, maliciously, Tony pressed the bell again.

Mr. James Watterson, of San Diego, should now open the door and give forth noise. He didn't. A silence fell beyond that door that was like the silence of a glacier. Once more Tony put his ear to the wood. Silence utterly.

He got out a master key on a chain and pushed it delicately into the lock of the door. He turned it, pushed the door inward three inches and withdrew the key. Then he waited.

"All right," the voice said harshly. "Come in and get it."

Tony pushed the door wide and stood there, framed against the light from the lobby. The man was tall, black-haired, angular and white-faced. He held a gun. He held it as though he knew about guns.

"Step right in," he drawled.

Tony went in through the door and pushed it shut with his shoulder. He kept his hands a little out from his sides, the clever fingers curled and slack. He smiled his quiet little smile.

"Mr. Watterson?"

"And after that what?"

"I'm the house detective here."

"It slays me."

The tall, white-faced, somehow handsome and somehow not handsome man backed slowly into the room. It was a large room with a low balcony around two sides of it. French doors opened out on the little private open-air balcony that each of the tower rooms had. There was a grate set for a log fire behind a paneled screen in front of a cheerful davenport. A tall misted glass stood on a hotel tray beside a deep, cozy chair. The man backed toward this and stood in front of it. The large, glistening gun drooped and pointed at the floor.

"It slays me," he said. "I'm in the dump an hour and the house copper gives me the bus. Okay, sweetheart, look in the closet and bathroom. But she just left."

"You didn't see her yet," Tony said.

The man's bleached face filled with unexpected lines. His thickened voice edged toward a snarl. "Yeah? Who didn't I see yet?"

"A girl named Eve Cressy."

The man swallowed. He put his gun down on the table beside the tray. He let himself down into the chair backwards, stiffly, like a man with a touch of lumbago. Then he leaned forward and put his hands on his kneecaps and smiled brightly between his teeth. "So she got here, huh? I didn't ask about her yet. I'm a careful guy. I didn't ask yet."

"She's been here five days," Tony said. "Waiting for you. She hasn't left the hotel a minute."

The man's mouth worked a little. His smile had a knowing tilt to it. "I got delayed a little up north," he said smoothly. "You know how it is. Visiting old friends. You seem to know a lot about my business, copper."

"That's right, Mr. Ralls."

The man lunged to his feet and his hand snapped at the gun. He stood leaning over, holding it on the table, staring. "Dames talk too much," he said with a muffled sound in his voice as though he held something soft between his teeth and talked through it.

"Not dames, Mr. Ralls."

"Huh?" The gun slithered on the hard wood of the table. "Talk it up, copper. My mind reader just quit."

"Not dames, guys. Guys with guns."

The glacier silence fell between them again. The man straightened his body out slowly. His face was washed clean of expression, but his eyes were haunted. Tony leaned in front of him, a shortish plump man with a quiet, pale, friendly face and eyes as simple as forest water.

"They never run out of gas – those boys," Johnny Ralls said, and licked at his lip. "Early and late, they work. The old firm never sleeps."

"You know who they are?" Tony said softly.

"I could maybe give nine guesses. And twelve of them would be right."

"The trouble boys," Tony said, and smiled a brittle smile.

"Where is she?" Johnny Ralls asked harshly.

"Right next door to you."

The man walked to the wall and left his gun lying on the table. He stood in front of the wall, studying it. He reached up and gripped the grillwork of the balcony railing. When he dropped his hand and turned, his face had lost some of its lines. His eyes had a quieter glint. He moved back to Tony and stood over him.

"I've got a stake," he said. "Eve sent me some dough and I built it up with a touch I made up north. Case dough, what I mean. The trouble boys talk about twenty-five grand." He smiled crookedly. "Five C's I can count. I'd have a lot of fun making them believe that, I would."

"What did you do with it?" Tony asked indifferently.

"I never had it, copper. Leave that lay. I'm the only guy in the world that believes it. It was a little deal that I got suckered on."

"I'll believe it," Tony said.

"They don't kill often. But they can be awful tough."

"Mugs," Tony said with a sudden bitter contempt. "Guys with guns. Just mugs."

Johnny Ralls reached for his glass and drained it empty. The ice cubes tinkled softly as he put it down. He picked his gun up, danced it on his palm, then tucked it, nose down, into an inner breast pocket. He stared at the carpet.

"How come you're telling me this, copper?"

"I thought maybe you'd give her a break."

"And if I wouldn't?"

"I kind of think you will," Tony said.

Johnny Ralls nodded quietly. "Can I get out of here?"

"You could take the service elevator to the garage. You could rent a car. I can give you a card to the garage man."

"You're a funny little guy," Johnny Ralls said.

Tony took out a worn ostrich-skin billfold and scribbled on a printed card. Johnny Ralls read it, and stood holding it, tapping it against a thumbnail.

"I could take her with me," he said, his eyes narrow.

"You could take a ride in a basket too," Tony said. "She's been here five days, I told you. She's been spotted. A guy I know called me up and told me to get her out of here. Told me what it was all about. So I'm getting you out instead."

"They'll love that," Johnny Ralls said. "They'll send you violets."

"I'll weep about it on my day off."

Johnny Ralls turned his hand over and stared at the palm. "I could see her, anyway. Before I blow. Next door to here, you said?"

Tony turned on his heel and started for the door. He said over his shoulder, "Don't waste a lot of time, handsome. I might change my mind."

The man said, almost gently: "You might be spotting me right now, for all I know."

Tony didn't turn his head. "That's a chance you have to take."

He went on to the door and passed out of the room. He shut it carefully, silently, looked once at the door of 14A and got into his dark elevator. He rode it down to the linen-room floor and got out to remove the basket that held the service elevator open at that floor. The door slid quietly shut. He held it so that it made no noise. Down the corridor, light came from the open door of the housekeeper's office. Tony got back into his elevator and went on down to the lobby.

The little clerk was out of sight behind his pebbled-glass screen, auditing accounts. Tony went through the main lobby and turned into the radio room. The radio was on again, soft. She was there, curled on the davenport again. The speaker hummed to her, a vague sound so low that what it said was as wordless as the murmur of trees. She turned her head slowly and smiled at him.

"Finished palming doorknobs? I couldn't sleep worth a nickel. So I came down again. Okay?"

He smiled and nodded. He sat down in a green chair and patted the plump brocade arms of it. "Sure, Miss Cressy."

"Waiting is the hardest kind of work, isn't it? I wish you'd talk to that radio. It sounds like a pretzel being bent."

Tony fiddled with it, got nothing he liked, set it back where it had been.

"Beer-parlor drunks are all the customers now."

She smiled at him again.

"I don't bother you being here, Miss Cressy?"

"I like it. You're a sweet little guy, Tony."

He looked stiffly at the floor and a ripple touched his spine. He waited for it to go away. It went slowly. Then he sat back, relaxed again, his neat fingers clasped on his elk's tooth. He listened. Not to the radio – to far-off, uncertain things, menacing things. And perhaps to just the safe whir of wheels going away into a strange night.

"Nobody's all bad," he said out loud.

The girl looked at him lazily. "I've met two or three I was wrong on, then."

He nodded. "Yeah," he admitted judiciously. "I guess there's some that are."

The girl yawned and her deep violet eyes half closed. She nestled back into the cushions. "Sit there for a while, Tony. Maybe I could nap."

"Sure. Not a thing for me to do. Don't know why they pay me."

She slept quickly and with complete stillness, like a child. Tony hardly breathed for ten minutes. He just watched her, his mouth a little open. There was a quiet fascination in his limpid eyes, as if he was looking at an altar.

Then he stood up with infinite care and padded away under the arch to the entrance lobby and the desk. He stood at the desk listening for a little while. He heard a pen rustling out of sight. He went around the corner to the row of house phones in little glass cubbyholes. He lifted one and asked the night operator for the garage.

It rang three or four times and then a boyish voice answered: "Windermere Hotel. Garage speaking."

"This is Tony Reseck. That guy Watterson I gave a card to. He leave?"

"Sure, Tony. Half an hour almost. Is it your charge?"

"Yeah," Tony said. "My party. Thanks. Be seein' you."

He hung up and scratched his neck. He went back to the desk and slapped a hand on it. The clerk wafted himself around the screen with his greeter's smile in place. It dropped when he saw Tony.

"Can't a guy catch up on his work?" he grumbled.

"What's the professional rate on Fourteen-B?"

The clerk stared morosely. "There's no professional rate in the tower."

"Make one. The fellow left already. Was there only an hour."

"Well, well," the clerk said airily. "So the personality didn't click tonight. We get a skip-out."

"Will five bucks satisfy you?"

"Friend of yours?"

"No. Just a drunk with delusions of grandeur and no dough."

"Guess we'll have to let it ride, Tony. How did he get out?"

"I took him down the service elevator. You was asleep. Will five bucks satisfy you?"

"Why?"

The worn ostrich-skin wallet came out and a weedy five slipped across the marble. "All I could shake him for," Tony said loosely.

The clerk took the five and looked puzzled. "You're the boss," he said, and shrugged. The phone shrilled on the desk and he reached for it. He listened and then pushed it toward Tony. "For you."

Tony took the phone and cuddled it close to his chest. He put his mouth close to the transmitter. The voice was strange to him. It had a metallic sound. Its syllables meticulously anonymous.

"Tony? Tony Reseck?"

"Talking."

"A message from Al. Shoot?"

Tony looked at the clerk. "Be a pal," he said over the mouthpiece. The clerk flicked a narrow smile at him and went away. "Shoot," Tony said into the phone.

"We had a little business with a guy in your place. Picked him up scramming. Al had a hunch you'd run him out. Tailed him and took him to the curb. Not so good. Backfire."

Tony held the phone very tight and his temples chilled with the evaporation of moisture. "Go on," he said. "I guess there's more."

"A little. The guy stopped the big one. Cold. Al – Al said to tell you goodbye."

Tony leaned hard against the desk. His mouth made a sound that was not speech.

"Get it?" The metallic voice sounded impatient, a little bored. "This guy had him a rod. He used it. Al won't be phoning anybody any more."

Tony lurched at the phone, and the base of it shook on the rose marble. His mouth was a hard dry knot.

The voice said: "That's as far as we go, bub. G'night." The phone clicked dryly, like a pebble hitting a wall.

Tony put the phone down in its cradle very carefully, so as not to make any sound. He looked at the clenched palm of his left hand. He took a handkerchief out and rubbed the palm softly and straightened the fingers out with his other hand. Then he wiped his forehead. The clerk came around the screen again and looked at him with glinting eyes.

"I'm off Friday. How about lending me that phone number?"

Tony nodded at the clerk and smiled a minute frail smile. He put his handkerchief away and patted the pocket he had put it in. He turned and walked away from the desk, across the entrance lobby, down the three shallow steps, along the shadowy reaches of the main lobby, and so in through the arch to the radio room once more. He walked softly, like a man moving in a room where somebody is very sick. He reached the chair he had sat in before and lowered himself into it inch by inch. The girl slept on, motionless, in that curled-up looseness achieved by some women and all cats. Her breath made no slightest sound against the vague murmur of the radio.

Tony Reseck leaned back in the chair and clasped his hands on his elk's tooth and quietly closed his eyes.

THE BRONZE DOOR

1

THE LITTLE MAN was from the Calabar coast or from Papua or Tongatabu, some such remote place like that. An empire-builder frayed at the temples, thin and yellow, and slightly drunk at the club bar. And he was wearing a faded school tie he had probably kept year after year in a tin box so the centipedes wouldn't eat it.

Mr. Sutton-Cornish didn't know him, at least not then, but he knew the tie because it was his own school tie. So he spoke to the man timidly, and the man talked to him, being a little drunk and not knowing anybody. They had drinks and talked of the old school, in that peculiar, remote way the English have, without even exchanging names, but quite friendly underneath.

It was a big thrill for Mr. Sutton-Cornish, because nobody ever talked to him at the club except the servants. He was too defeated, too ingrowing, and you don't have to talk to people in London clubs. That's what they're for.

Mr. Sutton-Cornish got home to tea a little thick-tongued, for the first time in fifteen years. He sat there blankly in the upstairs drawing room, holding his cup of tepid tea and going over the man's face in his mind, making it younger and chubbier, a face that would go over an Eton collar or under a school cricket cap.

Suddenly he got it, and chuckled. That was something he hadn't done in a good few years either.

"Llewellyn, m'dear," he said. "Llewellyn Minor. Had an elder brother. Killed in the War, in the horse artillery."

Mrs. Sutton-Cornish stared at him bleakly across the heav-ily embroidered tea cozy. Her chestnut-colored eyes were dull with disdain – dried-out chestnuts, not fresh ones. The rest of her large face looked gray. The late October afternoon was gray, and the heavy, full-bottomed, monogrammed curtains across the windows. Even the ancestors on the walls were gray – all except the bad one, the general.

The chuckle died in Mr. Sutton-Cornish's throat. The long gray stare took care of that. Then he shivered a little, and as he wasn't very steady, his hand jerked. He emptied his tea on the rug, almost delicately, cup and all.

"Oh, rot," he said thickly. "Sorry, m'dear. Missed me trousers, though. Awfully sorry, m'dear."

For a full minute Mrs. Sutton-Cornish made only the sound of a large woman breathing. Then suddenly things began to tinkle on her – to tinkle and rustle and squeak. She was full of quaint noises, like a haunted house, but Mr. Sutton-Cornish shuddered, because he knew she was trembling with rage.

"Ah-h-h," she breathed out very, very slowly, after a long time, in her firing-squad manner. "Ah-h-h. Intoxicated, James?"

Something stirred suddenly at her feet. Teddy, the Pomeranian, stopped snoring and lifted his head and smelled blood. He let out a short snapping bark, merely a ranging shot, and waddled to his feet. His protuberant brown eyes stared malignantly at Mr. Sutton-Cornish.

"I'd better ring the bell, m'dear," Mr. Sutton-Cornish said humbly, and stood up. "Hadn't I?"

She didn't answer him. She spoke to Teddy instead, softly. A sort of doughy softness, with something sadistic in it.

"Teddy," she said softly, "look at that man. Look at that man, Teddy."

Mr. Sutton-Cornish said thickly: "Now don't let him snap at me, m'dear. D-don't let him snap at me, please, m'dear."

No answer. Teddy braced himself and leered. Mr. Sutton-Cornish tore his eyes away and looked up at the bad ancestor, the general. The general wore a scarlet coat with a diagonal blue sash across it, rather like a bar sinister. He had the winy complexion generals used to have in his day. He had a lot of very fruity-looking decorations and a bold stare, the stare of an unrepentant sinner. The general was no violet. He had broken up more homes than he had fought duels and he had fought more duels than he had won battles, and he had won plenty of battles.

Looking up at the bold-veined face, Mr. Sutton-Cornish braced himself, leaned down and took a small triangular sandwich from the tea table.

"Here, Teddy," he gulped. "Catch, boy, catch!"

He threw the sandwich. It fell in front of Teddy's little, brown paws. Teddy snuffled it languidly and yawned. He had his meals served to him on china, not thrown at him. He sidled innocently over to the edge of the rug and suddenly pounced on it, snarling.

"At table, James?" Mrs. Sutton-Cornish said slowly and dreadfully.

Mr. Sutton-Cornish stood on his teacup. It broke into thin light slivers of fine china. He shuddered again.

But now was the time. He started quickly toward the bell. Teddy let him get almost there, still pretending to worry the fringe of the rug. Then he spit out a piece of fringe, and charged low and soundlessly, his small feet like feathers in the nap of the rug. Mr. Sutton-Cornish was just reaching for the bell.

Small bright teeth tore rapidly and expertly at a pearl-gray spat.

Mr. Sutton-Cornish yelped, pivoted swiftly – and kicked. His neat shoe flashed in the gray light. A silky brown object sailed through the air and landed gobbling.

Then there was a quite indescribable stillness in the room, like the silence in the innermost room of a cold-storage warehouse, at midnight.

Teddy whimpered once, artfully, crept along the floor with his body close to it, crept under Mrs. Sutton-Cornish's chair. Her purplish-brown skirts moved and Teddy's face emerged slowly, framed in silk, the face of a nasty old woman with a shawl over her head.

"Caught me off balance," Mr. Sutton-Cornish mumbled, leaning against the mantelpiece. "Didn't mean . . . never intended – "

Mrs. Sutton-Cornish rose. She rose with the air of gathering a retinue about her. Her voice was the cold bleat of a foghorn on an icy river.

"Chinverly," she said. "I shall leave at once for Chinverly. At once. This hour . . . Drunk! Filthily drunk in the middle of the afternoon. Kicking little inoffensive animals. Vile! Utterly vile! *Open the door!* "

Mr. Sutton-Cornish staggered across the room and opened the door. She went out. Teddy trotted beside her, on the side away from Mr. Sutton-Cornish, and for once he didn't try to trip her in the doorway.

Outside she turned, slowly, as a liner turns.

"James," she said, "have you anything to say to me?"

He giggled – from pure nervous strain.

She looked at him horribly, turned again, said over her shoulder: "This is the end, James. The end of our marriage."

Mr. Sutton-Cornish said appallingly: "Goodness, m'dear – are we married?"

She started to turn again, but didn't. A sound like somebody being strangled in a dungeon came from her. Then she went on.

The door of the room hung open like a paralyzed mouth. Mr. Sutton-Cornish stood just inside it, listening. He didn't move until he heard steps on the floor above – heavy steps – hers. He sighed and looked down at his torn spat. Then he crept downstairs, into his long, narrow study beside the entrance hall, and got at the whiskey.

He hardly noticed the sounds of departure, luggage being descended, voices, the throbbing of the big car out in front, voices, the last bark from Teddy's iron-old throat. The house grew utterly silent. The furniture waited with its tongue in its cheek. Outside the lamps were lit in a light fog. Taxis hooted along the wet street. The fire died low in the grate.

Mr. Sutton-Cornish stood in front of it, swaying a little, looking at his long gray face in the wall mirror.

"Take a little stroll," he whispered wryly. "You and me. Never was anyone else, was there?"

He sneaked out into the hall without Collins, the butler, hearing him. He got his scarf and overcoat and hat on, grasped his stick and gloves, let himself out silently into the dusk.

He stood a little while at the bottom of the steps and looked up at the house. No. 14 Grinling Crescent. His father's house, his grandfather's house, his great-grandfather's house. All he had left. The rest was hers. Even the clothes he wore, the money in his bank account. But the house was still his – at least in name.

Four white steps, as spotless as the souls of virgins, leading up to an apple-green, deep paneled door, painted as things used to be painted long ago, in the age of leisure. It had a brass knocker and a thumb latch above the handle and one of those bells you twisted, instead of pushing or pulling them, and it rang just on the other side of the door, rather ridiculously, if you were not used to it.

He turned and looked across the street at the little railed-in park always kept locked, where on sunny days the small, prim children of Grinling Crescent walked along the smooth paths, around the little ornamental lake, beside rhododendron bushes, holding the hands of their nursemaids.

He looked at all this a little wanly, then he squared his thin shoulders and marched off into the dusk, thinking of Nairobi and Papua and Tongatabu, thinking of the man in the faded school tie who would go back there presently, wherever it was he came from, and lie awake in the jungle, thinking of London.

2

"KEB, SIR?"

Mr. Sutton-Cornish halted, stood on the edge of the curb and stared. The voice came from above, one of those wind-husked, beery voices you don't hear very often any more. It came from the driver's seat of a hansom cab.

The hansom cab had come out of the darkness, sliding oilily along the street on high rubber-tired wheels, the horse's hoofs making a slow, even *clop-clop* that Mr. Sutton-Cornish hadn't noticed until the driver called down to him.

It looked real enough. The horse had time-worn black blinkers and the characteristic well-fed and yet somehow dilapidated look that cab horses used to have. The half doors of the hansom were folded back and Mr. Sutton-Cornish could see the quilted gray upholstery inside. The long reins were riddled with cracks and following them upward he saw the beefy driver, the wide-brimmed coachman's "topper" he wore, the huge buttons on the upper part of his greatcoat, and the well-worn blanket that swathed the lower part of him round and round. He held his long whip lightly and delicately, as a hansom driver should hold his whip.

The trouble was that there weren't any more hansom cabs.

Mr. Sutton-Cornish gulped, slipped a glove off and reached out to touch the wheel. It was cold, very solid, wet with the muddy slime of the city streets.

"Doubt if I've ever seen one of these since the War," he said out loud, very steadily.

"Wot war, guv'nor?"

Mr. Sutton-Cornish started. He touched the wheel again. Then he smiled, slowly and carefully drew his glove on again.

"I'm getting in," he said.

"Steady there, Prince," the driver wheezed.

The horse switched his long tail contemptuously. Telling *him* to be steady. Mr. Sutton-Cornish climbed in over the wheel, rather clumsily, because one had lost the knack of that art these many years. He closed the half doors around in front of him, leaned back against the seat in the pleasant harness-room smell.

The trap opened over his head and the driver's large nose and alcoholic eyes made an improbable picture in the opening, like a deep-sea fish staring you down through the glass wall of an aquarium.

"Where to, guv'nor?"

"Well . . . Soho." It was the most foreign place he could think of — for a hansom cab to go to.

The cabman's eyes stared down at him.

"Won't like it there, guv'nor. Too many dagoes."

"I don't have to like it," Mr. Sutton-Cornish said bitterly.

The cabman stared down at him a little longer. "Yus," he said. "Soho. Wardour Street like. Right you are, guv'nor."

The trap slammed shut, the whip flicked delicately beside the horse's right ear, and motion came to the hansom cab.

Mr. Sutton-Cornish sat perfectly still, his scarf tight around his thin neck and his stick between his knees and his gloved hands clasped on the crook of the stick. He stared mutely out into the mist, like an admiral on the bridge. The horse *clop-clopped* out of Grinling Crescent, through Belgrave Square, over to Whitehall, up to Trafalgar Square, across that to St. Martin's Lane.

It went neither fast nor slow, and yet it went as fast as anything else went. It moved without sound, except for the *clop-clop*, across a world that stank of gasoline fumes and charred oil, that shrilled with whistles and hooted with horns.

And nobody seemed to notice it and nothing seemed to get in its way. That was rather amazing, Mr. Sutton-Cornish thought. But after all a hansom cab had nothing to do with that world. It was a ghost, an underlayer of time, the first writing on a palimpsest, brought out by ultra-violet light in a darkened room.

"Y'know," he said, speaking to the horse's rump, because there wasn't anything else there to speak to, "things might happen to a man, if a man would just let them happen."

The long whip flicked by Prince's ear as lightly as a trout fly flicking at a small dark pool under a rock.

"They already have," he added glumly.

The cab slowed along a curb, and the trap snapped open again.

"Well, 'ere we are, guv'nor. 'Ow about one of them little French dinners for eighteen pence? You know, guv'nor. Six courses of nothink at all. You 'ave one on me and then I 'ave one on you and we're still 'ungry. 'Ow about it?"

A very chill hand clutched at Mr. Sutton-Cornish's heart. Six-course dinners for eighteen pence? A hansom cab driver who said: "Wot war, guv'nor?" Twenty years ago, perhaps –

"Let me out here!" he said shrilly.

He threw the doors open, thrust money up at the face in the trap, hopped over the wheel to the sidewalk.

He didn't quite run, but he walked pretty fast and close to a dark wall and a little slinkingly. But nothing followed him, not even the *clop-clop* of the horse's hoofs. He swung around a corner into a narrow crowded street.

The light came from the open door of a shop. "Curios and Antiques" it said on the facade, in letters once gold, heavily Gothic in style. There was a flare on the sidewalk to attract attention and by this light he read the sign. The voice came from inside, from a little, plump man standing on a box who chanted over the heads of a listless crowd of silent, bored, foreign-looking men. The chanting voice held a note of exhaustion and futility.

"Now what am I bid, gents? Now what am I bid on this magnificent example of Oriental art? One pound starts the ball rolling, gents. One pound note coin of the realm. Now 'oo says a pound, gents? 'Oo says a pound?"

Nobody said anything. The little plump man on the box shook his head, wiped his face with a dirty handkerchief and drew a long breath. Then he saw Mr. Sutton-Cornish standing on the fringe of the little crowd.

" 'Ow about you, sir?" he pounced. "You look as if you'd a country 'ouse. Now that door's made for a country 'ouse. 'Ow about you, sir? Just give me a start like."

Mr. Sutton-Cornish blinked at him. "Eh? What's that?" he snapped.

The listless men smiled faintly and spoke among themselves without moving their thick lips.

"No offense, sir," the auctioneer chirped. "If you did 'ave a country 'ouse, that there door might be just what you could use."

Mr. Sutton-Cornish turned his head slowly, following the auctioneer's pointing hand, and looked for the first time at the bronze door.

3

IT STOOD ALL by itself over against the left-hand wall of the nearly stripped shop. It stood about two feet out from the side wall, on its own base. It was a double door, apparently of cast bronze, although from its size that seemed impossible. It was heavily scrolled over with a welter of Arabic script in relief, an endless story that here found no listener, a procession of curves and dots that might have expressed anything from an anthology of the Koran to the by-laws of a well-organized harem.

The two leaves of the door were only part of the thing. It had a wide, heavy base below and a superstructure topped by a Moorish arch. From the meeting edge of the two leaves a huge key stuck out of a huge keyhole, the sort of key a medieval jailer used to wear in enormous clanking bunches on a leather belt around his waist. A key from "The Yeomen of the Guard" – a comic-opera key.

"Oh . . . that," Mr. Sutton-Cornish said in the stillness. "Well, really, you know. I'm afraid not that, you know."

The auctioneer sighed. No hope had ever been smaller, probably, but at least it was worth a sigh. Then he picked up something which might have been carved ivory, but wasn't, stared at it pessimistically, and burst out again:

"Now 'ere, gents, I 'old in my 'and one of the finest examples – "

Mr. Sutton-Cornish smiled faintly and skimmed along the cluster of men until he came close to the bronze door.

He stood in front of it leaning on his stick, which was a section of polished rhinoceros hide over a steel core, dull mahogany in color, and a stick even a heavy man could have leaned on. After a while he reached forward idly and twisted the great key. It turned stubbornly, but it turned. A ring beside it was the doorknob. He twisted that, too, and tugged one half of the door open.

He straightened, and with a pleasantly idle gesture thrust his stick forward through the opening. And then, for the second time that evening, something incredible happened to him.

He wheeled sharply. Nobody was paying any attention. The auction was dead on its feet. The silent men were drifting out into the night. In a pause, hammering sounded at the back of the shop. The plump little auctioneer looked more and more as if he were eating a bad egg.

Mr. Sutton-Cornish looked down at his gloved right hand. There was no stick in it. There was nothing in it. He stepped to one side and looked behind the door. There was no stick there, on the dusty floor.

He had felt nothing. Nothing had jerked at him. The stick had merely passed part way through the door and then – it had merely ceased to exist.

He leaned down and picked up a piece of torn paper, wadded it swiftly into a ball, glanced behind him again and tossed the ball through the open part of the door.

Then he let out a slow sigh in which some neolithic rapture struggled with his civilized amazement. The ball of paper didn't fall to the floor behind the door. It fell, in midair, clean out of the visible world.

Mr. Sutton-Cornish reached his empty right hand forward and very slowly and carefully pushed the door shut. Then he just stood there, and licked his lips.

After a while: "Harem door," he said very softly. "Exit door of a harem. Now, that's an idea."

A very charming idea, too. The silken lady, her night of pleasure with the sultan over, would be conducted politely to that door and would casually step through it. Then nothing. No sobbing in the night, no broken hearts, no blackamoor with cruel eyes and a large scimitar, no knotted silk cord, no blood, no dull splash in the midnight Bosphorus. Merely nothing. A cool, clean, perfectly timed, and perfectly irrevocable absence of existence. Someone would close the door and lock it and take the key out, and for the time being that would be that.

Mr. Sutton-Cornish didn't notice the emptying of the shop. Faintly he heard its street door close, but without giving it any meaning. The hammering at the back stopped for a moment, voices spoke. Then steps came near. They were weary steps in the silence, the steps of a man who had had enough of that day, and of many such days. A voice spoke at Mr. Sutton-Cornish's elbow, an end-of-the-day voice.

"A very fine piece of work, sir. A bit out of my line – to be frank with you."

Mr. Sutton-Cornish didn't look at him, not yet. "Quite a bit out of anybody's line," he said gravely.

"I see it interests you, sir, after all."

Mr. Sutton-Cornish turned his head slowly. Down on the floor, off his box, the auctioneer was a mere wisp of a man.

A shabby, unpressed red-eyed little man who had found life no picnic.

"Yes, but what would one *do* with it?" Mr. Sutton-Cornish asked throatily.

"Well – it's a door like any other, sir. Bit 'eavy. Bit queer-like. But still a door like any other."

"I wonder," Mr. Sutton-Cornish said, still throatily.

The auctioneer gave him a swift appraising glance, shrugged and gave it up. He sat down on an empty box, lit a cigarette and relaxed sloppily into private life.

"What are you asking for it?" Mr. Sutton-Cornish inquired, quite suddenly. "What are you asking for it, Mr. – "

"Skimp, sir. Josiah Skimp. Well, a twenty-pound note, sir? Bronze alone ought to be worth that for art work." The little man's eyes were glittering again.

Mr. Sutton-Cornish nodded absently. "I don't know much about that," he said.

" 'Ell of a lot of it, sir." Mr. Skimp hopped off his box, patted over and heaved the leaf of the door open, grunting. "Beats me 'ow it ever got 'ere. For seven footers. No door for shrimps like me. Look, sir."

Mr. Sutton-Cornish had a rather ghastly presentiment, of course. But he didn't do anything about it. He couldn't. His tongue stuck in his throat and his legs were like ice. The comical contrast between the massiveness of the door and his own wisp of a body seemed to amuse Mr. Skimp. His little, round face threw back the shadow of a grin. Then he lifted his foot and hopped.

Mr. Sutton-Cornish watched him – as long as there was anything to watch. In fact he watched much longer. The hammering at the back of the shop seemed to get quite thunderous in the silence.

Once more, after a long time, Mr. Sutton-Cornish bent forward and closed the door. This time he twisted the key and dragged it out and put it in his overcoat pocket.

"Got to do something," he mumbled. "Got to do – Can't let this sort of thing – " His voice trailed off and then he jerked violently, as though a sharp pain had shot through him. Then he laughed out loud, off key. Not a natural laugh. Not a very nice laugh.

"That was beastly," he said under his breath. "But amazingly funny."

He was still standing there rooted when a pale young man with a hammer appeared at his elbow.

"Mr. Skimp step out, sir – or did you notice? We're supposed to be closed up, sir."

Mr. Sutton-Cornish didn't look up at the pale young man with the hammer. Moving a clammy tongue he said:

"Yes . . . Mr. Skimp . . . stepped out."

The young man started to turn away. Mr. Sutton-Cornish made a gesture. "I've bought this door – from Mr. Skimp," he said. "Twenty pounds. Will you take the money – and my card?"

The pale young man beamed, delighted at personal contact with a sale. Mr. Sutton-Cornish drew out a note case, extracted four five-pound notes from it, also a formal calling card. He wrote on the card with a small, gold pencil. His hand seemed surprisingly steady.

"No. 14 Grinling Crescent," he said. "Have it sent tomorrow without fail. It's . . . it's very heavy. I shall pay the drayage, of course. Mr. Skimp will – " His voice trailed off again. Mr. Skimp wouldn't.

"Oh, that's all right, sir. Mr. Skimp is my uncle."

"Ah, that's too – I mean, well, take this ten-shilling note for yourself, won't you?"

Mr. Sutton-Cornish left the shop rather rapidly, his right hand clutching the big key down in his pocket.

An ordinary taxi took him home to dinner. He dined alone – after three whiskeys. But he wasn't as much alone as he looked. He never would be any more.

4

IT CAME THE next day, swathed in sacking and bound about with cords, looking like nothing on earth and conducting itself with rather less agility than a concert grand.

Four large men in leather aprons perspired it up the four front steps and into the hall, with a good deal of sharp language back and forth. They had a light hoist to help them get it off their dray, but the steps almost beat them. Once inside the hall they got it on two dollies and after that it was just an average heavy, grunting job. They set it up at the back of Mr. Sutton-Cornish's study, across a sort of alcove he had an idea about.

He tipped them liberally, they went away, and Collins, the butler, left the front door open for a while to air the place through.

Carpenters came. The sacking was stripped off, and a framework was built around the door, so that it became part of a partition wall across the alcove. A small door was set in the partition. When the work was done and the mess cleared up Mr. Sutton-Cornish asked for an oil-can, and locked himself into his study. Then and only then he got out the big bronze key and fitted it again into the huge lock and opened the bronze door wide, both sides of it.

He oiled the hinges from the rear, just in case. Then he shut it again and oiled the lock, removed the key and went for a good long walk, in Kensington Gardens, and back. Collins and the first parlormaid had a look at it while he was out. Cook hadn't been upstairs yet.

"Beats me what the old fool's after," the butler said stonily. "I give him another week, Bruggs. If *she's* not back by then, I give him my notice. How about you, Bruggs?"

"Let him have his fun," Bruggs said, tossing her head. "That old sow he's married to – "

"Bruggs!"

"Tit-tat to you, Mr. Collins," Bruggs said and flounced out of the room.

Mr. Collins remained long enough to sample the whiskey in the big square decanter on Mr. Sutton-Cornish's smoking table.

In a shallow, tall cabinet in the alcove behind the bronze door, Mr. Sutton-Cornish arranged a few odds and ends of old china and bric-a-brac and carved ivory and some idols in shiny black wood, very old and unnecessary. It wasn't much of an excuse for so massive a door. He added three statuettes in pink marble. The alcove still had an air of not being quite on to itself. Naturally the bronze door was never open unless the room door was locked.

In the morning Bruggs, or Mary the housemaid, dusted in the alcove, having entered, of course, by the partition door. That amused Mr. Sutton-Cornish slightly, but the amusement began to wear thin. It was about three weeks after his wife and Teddy left that something happened to brighten him up.

A large, tawny man with a waxed mustache and steady gray eyes called on him and presented a card that indicated he was Detective-sergeant Thomas Lloyd of Scotland Yard. He said that one Josiah Skimp, an auctioneer, living in Kennington, was missing from his home to the great concern of his family, and that his nephew, one George William Hawkins, also of Kennington, had happened to mention that Mr. Sutton-Cornish was present in a shop in Soho on the very night when Mr. Skimp vanished. In fact, Mr. Sutton-Cornish might even have been the last person known to have spoken to Mr. Skimp.

Mr. Sutton-Cornish laid out the whiskey and cigars, placed his fingertips together and nodded gravely.

"I recall him perfectly, sergeant. In fact I bought that funny door over there from him. Quaint, isn't it?"

The detective glanced at the bronze door, a brief and empty glance.

"Out of my line, sir, I'm afraid. I do recall now something was said about the door. They had quite a job moving it. Very smooth whiskey, sir. Very smooth indeed."

"Help yourself, sergeant. So Mr. Skimp has run off and lost himself. Sorry I can't help you. I really didn't know him, you know."

The detective nodded his large tawny head. "I didn't think you did, sir. The Yard only got the case a couple of days ago. Routine call, you know. Did he seem excited, for instance?"

"He seemed tired," Mr. Sutton-Cornish mused. "Very fed up – with the whole business of auctioneering, perhaps. I only spoke to him a moment. About that door, you know. A nice little man – but tired."

The detective didn't bother to look at the door again. He finished his whiskey and allowed himself a little more.

"No family trouble," he said. "Not much money, but who has these days? No scandal. Not a melancholy type, they say. Odd."

"Some very queer types in Soho," Mr. Sutton-Cornish said mildly.

The detective thought it over. "Harmless, though. A rough district once, but not in our time. Might I ask you what you was doing over there, sir?"

"Wandering," Mr. Sutton-Cornish said. "Just wandering. A little more of this?"

"Well, now, really, sir, three whiskeys in a morning . . . well, just this once and many thanks to you, sir."

Detective-sergeant Lloyd left – rather regretfully.

After he had been gone ten minutes or so, Mr. Sutton-Cornish got up and locked the study door. He walked softly down the long, narrow room and got the big bronze key out of his inside breast pocket, where he always carried it now.

The door opened noiselessly and easily now. It was well-balanced for its weight. He opened it wide, both sides of it.

"Mr. Skimp," he said very gently into the emptiness, "you are wanted by the police, Mr. Skimp."

The fun of that lasted him well on to lunch time.

5

IN THE AFTERNOON Mrs. Sutton-Cornish came back. She appeared quite suddenly before him in the study, sniffed harshly at the smell of tobacco and Scotch, refused a chair, and stood very solid and lowering just inside the closed door. Teddy stood beside her for a moment, then hurled himself at the edge of the rug.

"Stop that, you little beast. Stop that at once, darling," Mrs. Sutton-Cornish said. She picked Teddy up and stroked him. He lay in her arms and licked her nose and sneered at Mr. Sutton-Cornish.

"I find," Mrs. Sutton-Cornish said, in a voice that had the brittleness of dry suet, "after numerous very boring interviews with my solicitor, that I can do nothing without your help. Naturally I dislike asking for that."

Mr. Sutton-Cornish made ineffectual motions towards a chair and when they were ignored he leaned resignedly against the mantelpiece. He said he supposed that was so.

"Perhaps it has escaped your attention that I am still comparatively a young woman. And these are modern days, James."

Mr. Sutton-Cornish smiled wanly and glanced at the bronze door. She hadn't noticed it yet. Then he put his head on one side and wrinkled his nose and said mildly, without much interest:

"You're thinking of a divorce?"

"I'm thinking of very little else," she said brutally.

"And you wish me to compromise myself in the usual manner, at Brighton, with a lady who will be described in court as an actress?"

She glared at him. Teddy helped her glare. Their combined glare failed even to perturb Mr. Sutton-Cornish. He had other resources now.

"Not with that dog," he said carelessly, when she didn't answer.

She made some kind of furious noise, a snort with a touch of snarl in it. She sat down then, very slowly and heavily, a little puzzled. She let Teddy jump to the floor.

"Just what are you talking about, James?" she asked witheringly.

He strolled over to the bronze door, leaned his back against it and explored its rich protuberances with a fingertip. Even then she didn't see the door.

"You want a divorce, my dear Louella," he said slowly, "so that you may marry another man. There's absolutely no point in it — with that dog. I shouldn't be asked to humiliate myself. Too useless. No man would marry that dog."

"James — are you attempting to blackmail me?" Her voice was rather dreadful. She almost bugled. Teddy sneaked across to the window curtains and pretended to lie down.

"And even if he would," Mr. Sutton-Cornish said with a peculiar quiet in his tone, "I oughtn't to make it possible. I ought to have enough human compassion — "

"James! How dare you! You make me physically sick with your insincerity!"

For the first time in his life James Sutton-Cornish laughed in his wife's face.

"Those are two or three of the silliest speeches I ever had to listen to," he said. "You're an elderly, ponderous and damn dull woman. Go out and buy yourself a gigolo, if you want someone to fawn on you. But don't ask me to make a beast of myself so that he can marry you and throw me out of my father's house. Now run along and take your miserable brown beetle with you."

She got up quickly, very quickly for her, and stood a moment almost swaying. Her eyes were as blank as a blind man's eyes. In the silence Teddy tore fretfully at a curtain, with bitter, preoccupied growls that neither of them noticed.

She said very slowly and almost gently: "We'll see how long you stay in your father's house, James Sutton-Cornish – *pauper.*"

She moved very quickly the short distance to the door, went through and slammed it behind her.

The slamming of the door, an unusual event in that household, seemed to awaken a lot of echoes that had not been called upon to perform for a long time. So that Mr. Sutton-Cornish was not instantly aware of the small peculiar sound at his own side of the door, a mixture of sniffing and whimpering, with just a dash of growl.

Teddy. Teddy hadn't made the door. The sudden, bitter exit had for once caught him napping. Teddy was shut in – with Mr. Sutton-Cornish.

For a little while Mr. Sutton-Cornish watched him rather absently, still shaken by the interview, not fully realizing what had happened. The small, wet, black snout explored the crack at the bottom of the closed door. At moments, while the whimpering and sniffing went on, Teddy turned a reddish brown outjutting eye, like a fat wet marble, toward the man he hated.

Mr. Sutton-Cornish snapped out of it rather suddenly. He straightened and beamed. "Well, well, old man," he purred. "Here we are, and for once without the ladies."

Cunning dawned in his beaming eye. Teddy read it and slipped off under a chair. He was silent now, very silent. And Mr. Sutton-Cornish was silent as he moved swiftly along the wall and turned the key in the study door. Then he sped back toward the alcove, dug the key of the bronze door out of his pocket, unlocked and opened that – wide.

He sauntered back toward Teddy, beyond Teddy, as far as the window. He grinned at Teddy.

"Here we are, old man. Jolly, eh? Have a shot of whiskey, old man?"

Teddy made a small sound under the chair, and Mr. Sutton-Cornish sidled toward him delicately, bent down suddenly and lunged. Teddy made another chair, farther up the room. He breathed hard and his eyes stuck out rounder and wetter than ever, but he was silent, except for his breathing. And Mr. Sutton-Cornish, stalking him patiently from chair to chair, was as silent as the last leaf of autumn falling in slow eddies in a windless copse.

At about that time the doorknob turned sharply. Mr. Sutton-Cornish paused to smile and click his tongue. A sharp knock followed. He ignored it. The knocking went on sharper and sharper and an angry voice accompanied it.

Mr. Sutton-Cornish went on stalking Teddy. Teddy did the best he could, but the room was narrow and Mr. Sutton-Cornish was patient and rather agile when he wanted to be. In the interests of agility he was quite willing to be undignified.

The knocking and calling out beyond the door went on, but inside the room things could only end one way. Teddy reached the sill of the bronze door, sniffed at it rapidly, almost lifted a contemptuous hind leg, but didn't because Mr. Sutton-Cornish was too close to him. He sent a low snarl back over his shoulder and hopped that disastrous sill.

Mr. Sutton-Cornish raced back to the room door, turned the key swiftly and silently, crept over to a chair and sprawled in it laughing. He was still laughing when Mrs. Sutton-Cornish thought to try the knob again, found the door yielded this time, and stormed into the room. Through the mist of his grisly, solitary laughter he saw her cold stare, then he heard her rustling about the room, heard her calling Teddy.

Then, "What's that thing?" he heard her snap suddenly. "What utter foolishness – Teddy! Come; mother's little lamb! Come, Teddy!"

Even in his laughter Mr. Sutton-Cornish felt the wing of a regret brush his cheek. Poor little Teddy. He stopped laughing and sat up, stiff and alert. The room was too quiet.

"Louella!" he called sharply.

No sound answered him.

He closed his eyes, gulped, opened them again, crept along the room staring. He stood in front of his little alcove for a long time, peering, peering through that bronze portal at the innocent little collection of trivia beyond.

He locked the door with quivering hands, stuffed the key down in his pocket, poured himself a stiff peg of whiskey.

A ghostly voice that sounded something like his own, and yet unlike it, said out loud, very close to his ear:

"I didn't really intend anything like that . . . never . . . never . . . oh, never . . . or . . ." – after a long pause – "did I?"

Braced by the Scotch he sneaked out into the hall and out of the front door without Collins seeing him. No car waited outside. As luck would have it she had evidently come up from Chinverly by train and taken a taxi. Of course they could trace the taxi – later on, when they tried. A lot of good that would do them.

Collins was next. He thought about Collins for some time, glancing at the bronze door, tempted a good deal, but finally shaking his head negatively.

"Not that way," he muttered. "Have to draw the line some-where. Can't have a procession – "

He drank some more whiskey and rang the bell. Collins made it rather easy for him.

"You rang, sir?"

"What did it sound like?" Mr. Sutton-Cornish asked, a little thick-tongued. "Canaries?"

Collins' chin snapped back a full two inches.

"The dowager won't be here to dinner, Collins. I think I'll dine out. That's all."

Collins stared at him. A grayness spread over Collins' face, with a little flush at the cheekbones.

"You allude to Mrs. Sutton-Cornish, sir?"

Mr. Sutton-Cornish hiccuped. "Who d'you suppose? Gone back to Chinverly to stew in her own juice some more. Ought to be plenty of it."

With deadly politeness Collins said: "I had meant to ask you, sir, whether Mrs. Sutton-Cornish would return here – permanently. Otherwise – "

"Carry on." Another hiccup.

"Otherwise I should not care to remain myself, sir."

Mr. Sutton-Cornish stood up and went close to Collins and breathed in his face. Haig & Haig. A good breath, of the type.

"Get out!" he rasped. "Get out now! Upstairs with you and pack your things. Your check will be ready for you. A full month. Thirty-two pounds in all, I believe?"

Collins stepped back and moved towards the door. "That will suit me perfectly, sir. Thirty-two pounds is the correct amount." He reached the door, spoke again before he opened it. "A reference from *you*, sir, will not be desired."

He went out, closing the door softly.

"Ha!" Mr. Sutton-Cornish said.

Then he grinned slyly, stopped pretending to be angry or drunk, and sat down to write the check.

He dined out that night, and the next night, and the next. Cook left on the third day, taking the kitchenmaid with her. That left Bruggs and Mary, the housemaid. On the fifth day Bruggs wept when she gave her notice.

"I'd rather go at once, sir, if you'll let me," she sobbed. "There's something creepylike about the house since cook and Mr. Collins and Teddy and Mrs. Sutton-Cornish left."

Mr. Sutton-Cornish patted her arm. "Cook and Mr. Collins and Teddy and Mrs. Sutton-Cornish," he repeated. "If only she could hear *that* order of precedence."

Bruggs stared at him, red-eyed. He patted her arm again. "Quite all right, Bruggs. I'll give you your month. And tell Mary to go, too. Think I'll close the house up and live in the south of France for a while. Now don't cry, Bruggs."

"No, sir." She bawled her way out of the room.

He didn't get to the south of France, of course. Too much fun being right where he was – alone at last in the home of his fathers. Not quite what they would have approved of, perhaps, except possibly the general. But the best he could do.

Almost overnight the house began to have the murmurs of an empty place. He kept the windows closed and the shades down. That seemed to be a gesture of respect he could hardly afford to omit.

6

SCOTLAND YARD MOVES with the deadly dependability of a glacier, and at times almost as slowly. So it was a full month and nine days before Detective-sergeant Lloyd came back to No. 14 Grinling Crescent.

By that time the front steps had long since lost their white serenity. The apple-green door had acquired a sinister shade of gray. The brass saucer around the bell, the knocker, the big latch, all these were tarnished and stained, like the brass work of an old freighter limping around the Horn. Those who rang the bell departed slowly, with backward glances, and Mr. Sutton-Cornish would be peeping out at them from the side of a drawn window shade.

He concocted himself weird meals in the echoing kitchen, creeping in after dark with ragged-looking parcels of food. Later he would slink out again with his hat pulled low and his overcoat collar up, give a quick glance up and down the street, then scramble off around the corner. The police constable on duty saw him occasionally at these maneuvers and rubbed his chin a good deal over the situation.

No longer a study even in withered elegance, Mr. Sutton-Cornish became a customer in obscure eating houses where draymen blew on their soup on naked tables in compartments like horse stalls; in foreign cafes where men with blue-black hair and pointed shoes dined interminably over minute bottles of wine; in crowded, anonymous tea shops where the food looked and tasted as tired as the people who ate it.

He was no longer a perfectly sane man. In his dry, solitary, poisoned laughter there was the sound of crumbling walls. Even the pinched loafers under the arches of the Thames Embankment, who listened to him because he had sixpences, even these were glad when he passed on, stepping carefully in unshined shoes and lightly swinging the stick he no longer carried.

Then, late one night, returning softly out of the dull-gray darkness, he found the man from Scotland Yard lurking near the dirty front steps with an air of thinking himself hidden behind the lamp-post.

"I'd like a few words with you, sir," he said, stepping forth briskly and holding his hands as though he might have to use them suddenly.

"Charmed, I'm sure," Mr. Sutton-Cornish chuckled. "Trot right in."

He opened the door with his latchkey, switched the light on, and stepped with accustomed ease over a pile of dusty letters on the floor.

"Got rid of the servants," he explained to the detective. "Always did want to be alone some day."

The carpet was covered with burned matches, pipe ash, torn paper, and the corners of the hall had cobwebs in them. Mr. Sutton-Cornish opened his study door, switched the light on in there and stood aside. The detective passed him warily, staring hard at the condition of the house.

Mr. Sutton-Cornish pushed him into a dusty chair, thrust a cigar at him, reached for the whiskey decanter.

"Business or pleasure this time?" he inquired archly.

Detective-sergeant Lloyd held his hard hat on one knee and looked the cigar over dubiously. "Smoke it later, thank you, sir. . . . Business, I take it. I'm instructed to make inquiries as to the whereabouts of Mrs. Sutton-Cornish."

Mr. Sutton-Cornish sipped whiskey amiably and pointed at the decanter. He took his whiskey straight now. "Haven't the least idea," he said. "Why? Down at Chinverly, I suppose. Country place. She owns it."

"It so 'appens she ain't," Detective-sergeant Lloyd said, slipping on an "h," which he seldom did any more. "Been a separation, I'm told," he added grimly.

"That's *our* business, old man."

"Up to a point, yes, sir. Granted. Not after her solicitor can't find her and she ain't anywhere anybody can find her. Not *then*, it ain't just your business."

Mr. Sutton-Cornish thought it over. "You might have something there – as the Americans say," he conceded.

The detective passed a large pale hand across his forehead and leaned forward.

"Let's 'ave it, sir," he said quietly. "Best in the long run. Best for all. Nothing to gain by foolishness. The law's the law."

"Have some whiskey," Mr. Sutton-Cornish said.

"Not tonight I won't," Detective-sergeant Lloyd said grimly.

"She left me," Mr. Sutton-Cornish shrugged. "And because of that the servants left me. You know what servants are nowadays. Beyond that I haven't an idea."

"Oh yus I think you 'ave," the detective said, losing a little more of his West End manner. "No charges have been preferred, but I think you know all right, all right."

Mr. Sutton-Cornish smiled airily. The detective scowled at him and went on:

"We've taken the liberty of watching you, and for a gentleman of your position – you've been living a damn queer life, if I may say so."

"You may say so, and then you may get to hell out of my house," Mr. Sutton-Cornish said suddenly.

"Not so farst. Not yet I won't."

"Perhaps you would like to search the house."

"Per'aps I should. Per'aps I shall. No hurry there. Takes time. Sometimes takes shovels." Detective-sergeant Lloyd permitted himself to leer rather nastily. "Seems to me like people does a bit of disappearin' when you 'appen to be around. Take that Skimp. Now take Mrs. Sutton-Cornish."

Mr. Sutton-Cornish stared at him with lingering malice. "And in your experience, sergeant, where do people go when they disappear?"

"Sometimes they don't disappear. Sometimes somebody disappears them." The detective licked his strong lips, with a slightly cat-like expression.

Mr. Sutton-Cornish slowly raised his arm and pointed to the bronze door. "You wanted it, sergeant," he said suavely. "You shall have it. There is where you should look for Mr. Skimp, for Teddy the Pomeranian, and for my wife. There – behind that ancient door of bronze."

The detective didn't shift his gaze. For a long moment he didn't change expression. Then, quite amiably, he grinned. There was something else behind his eyes, but it was behind them.

"Let's you and me take a nice little walk," he said breezily. "The fresh air would do you a lot of good, sir. Let's – "

"There," Mr. Sutton-Cornish announced, still pointing with his arm rigid, "behind that door."

"Ah-ah." Detective-sergeant Lloyd waggled a large finger roguishly. "Been alone too much, you 'ave, sir. Thinkin' about things. Do it myself once in a while. Gets a fellow balmy in the crumpet like. Take a nice little walk with me, sir. We could stop somewhere for a nice – " The big, tawny man planted a forefinger on the end of his nose and pushed his head back and wiggled his little finger in the air at the same time. But his steady gray eyes remained in another mood.

"We'll look at my bronze door first."

Mr. Sutton-Cornish skipped out of his chair. The detective had him by the arm in a flash. "None of that," he said in a frosty voice. "Hold still, you."

"Key in here," Mr. Sutton-Cornish said, pointing at his breast pocket, but not trying to get his hand into it.

The detective got it out for him, stared at it heavily.

"All behind the door – on meathooks," Mr. Sutton-Cornish said. "All three. Little meathook for Teddy. Very large meathook for my wife. *Very* large meathook."

Holding him with his left hand, Detective-sergeant Lloyd thought it over. His pale brows were drawn tight. His large weathered face was grim – but skeptical.

"No harm to look," he said finally.

He marched Mr. Sutton-Cornish across the floor, pushed the bronze key into the huge antique lock, twisted the ring, and opened the door. He opened both sides of it. He stood looking into that very innocent alcove with its cabinet of knickknacks and absolutely nothing else. He became genial again.

"Meathooks, did you say, sir? Very cute, if I may say so."

He laughed, released Mr. Sutton-Cornish's arm and teetered on his heels.

"What the hell's it for?" he asked.

Mr. Sutton-Cornish doubled over very swiftly and launched his thin body with furious speed at the big detective.

"Take a little walk yourself – and find out!" he screamed.

Detective-sergeant Lloyd was a big and solid man and probably used to being butted. Mr. Sutton-Cornish could hardly have moved him six inches, even with a running start. But the bronze door had a high sill. The detective moved with the deceptive quickness of his trade, swayed his body just enough, and jarred his foot against the bronze sill.

If it hadn't been for that he would have plucked Mr. Sutton-Cornish neatly out of the air and held him squirming like a kitten, between his large thumb and fore-finger. But the sill jarred him off balance. He stumbled a little, and swayed his body completely out of Mr. Sutton-Cornish's way.

Mr. Sutton-Cornish butted empty space – the empty space framed by that majestic door of bronze. He sprawled forward clutching – falling – clutching – across the sill –

Detective-sergeant Lloyd straightened up slowly, twisted his thick neck and stared. He moved back a little from the sill so that he could be perfectly certain the side of the door hid nothing from him. It didn't. He saw a cabinet of odd pieces of china, odds and ends of carved ivory and shiny black wood, and on top of the cabinet three little statuettes of pink marble.

He saw nothing else. There was nothing else in there to see.

"Gorblimey!" he said at last, violently. At least he thought he said it. Somebody said it. He wasn't quite sure. He was never absolutely sure about anything – after that night.

7

THE WHISKEY LOOKED all right. It smelled all right, too. Shaking so that he could hardly hold the decanter Detective-sergeant Lloyd poured a little into a glass and took a sip in his dry mouth and waited.

After a little while he drank another spoonful. He waited again. Then he drank a stiff drink – a very stiff drink.

He sat down in the chair beside the whiskey and took his large folded cotton handkerchief out of his pocket and unfolded it slowly and mopped his face and neck and behind his ears.

In a little while he wasn't shaking quite so much. Warmth began to flow through him. He stood up, drank some more whiskey, then slowly and bitterly moved back down the room.

He swung the bronze door shut, locked it, put the key down in his own pocket. He opened the partition door at the side, braced himself and stepped through into the alcove. He looked at the back of the bronze door. He touched it. It wasn't very light in there, but he could see that the place was empty, except for the silly-looking cabinet. He came out again shaking his head.

"Can't be," he said out loud. "Not a chance. Not 'arf a chance."

Then, with the sudden unreasonableness of the reasonable man, he flew into a rage.

"If I get 'ooked for this," he said between his teeth, "I get 'ooked."

He went down to the dark cellar, rummaged around until he found a hand axe and carried it back upstairs.

He hacked the woodwork to ribbons. When he was done the bronze door stood alone on its base, jagged wood all around it, but not holding it any longer. Detective-sergeant Lloyd put the hand axe down, wiped his hands and face on his big handkerchief, and went in behind the door. He put his shoulder to it and set his strong, yellow teeth.

Only a brutally determined man of immense strength could have done it. The door fell forward with a heavy rumbling crash that seemed to shake the whole house. The echoes of that crash died away slowly, along infinite corridors of unbelief.

Then the house was silent again. The big man went out into the hall and had another look out of the front door.

He put his coat on, adjusted his hard hat, folded his damp handkerchief carefully and put it in his hip pocket, lit the cigar Mr. Sutton-Cornish had given him, took a drink of whiskey and swaggered to the door.

At the door he turned and deliberately sneered at the bronze door, lying fallen but still huge in the welter of splintered wood.

"To 'ell with you, 'ooever you are," Detective-sergeant Lloyd said. "I ain't no bloody primrose."

He shut the house door behind him. A little high fog outside, a few dim stars, a quiet street with lighted windows. Two or three cars of expensive appearance, very likely chauffeurs lounging in them, but no one in sight.

He crossed the street at an angle and walked along beside the tall iron railing of the park. Faintly through the rhododendron bushes he could see the dull glimmer of the little ornamental lake. He looked up and down the street and took the big bronze key out of his pocket.

"Make it a good 'un," he told himself softly.

His arm swept up and over. There was a minute splash in the ornamental lake, then silence. Detective-sergeant Lloyd walked on calmly, puffing at his cigar.

Back at the C.I.D. he gave his report steadily, and for the first and last time in his life, there was something besides truth in it. Couldn't raise anybody at the house. All dark. Waited three hours. Must all be away.

The inspector nodded and yawned.

The Sutton-Cornish heirs eventually pried the estate out of Chancery and opened up No. 14 Grinling Crescent and found the bronze door lying in a welter of dust and splintered wood and matted cobwebs. They stared at it goggle-eyed, and when they found out what it was, sent for dealers, thinking there might be a little money in it. But the dealers sighed and said no, no money in that sort of thing now. Better ship it off to a foundry and have it melted down for the metal. Get so much a pound. The dealers departed noiselessly with wry smiles.

Sometimes when things are a little dull in the Missing Persons section of the C.I.D. they take the Sutton-Cornish file out and dust it off and look through it sourly and put it away again.

Sometimes when Inspector – formerly Detective-sergeant – Thomas Lloyd is walking along an unusually dark and quiet street he will whirl suddenly, for no reason at all, and jump to one side with a swift anguished agility.

But there isn't really anybody there, trying to butt him.

NO CRIME IN THE MOUNTAINS

1

THE LETTER CAME just before noon, special delivery, a dime-store envelope with the return address F. S. Lacey, Puma Point, California. Inside was a check for a hundred dollars, made out to cash and signed Frederick S. Lacey, and a sheet of plain white bond paper typed with a number of strikeovers. It said:

Mr. John Evans.
Dear Sir:

I have your name from Len Esterwald. My business is urgent and extremely confidential. I enclose a retainer. Please come to Puma Point Thursday afternoon or evening, if at all possible, register at the Indian Head Hotel, and call me at 2306.

Yours,

FRED LACEY

There hadn't been any business in a week, but this made it a nice day. The bank on which the check was drawn was about six blocks away. I went over and cashed it, ate lunch, and got the car out and started off.

It was hot in the valley, hotter still in San Bernardino, and it was still hot at five thousand feet, fifteen miles up the high-gear road to Puma Lake. I had done forty of the fifty miles of curving, twisting highway before it started to cool off, but it didn't get really cool until I reached the dam and started along the south shore of the lake past the piled-up granite boulders and the sprawled camps in the flats beyond. It was early evening when I reached Puma Point and I was as empty as a gutted fish.

The Indian Head Hotel was a brown building on a corner, opposite a dance hall. I registered, carried my suitcase upstairs and dropped it in a bleak, hard-looking room with an oval rug on the floor, a double bed in the corner, and nothing on the bare pine wall but a hardware-store calendar all curled up from the dry mountain summer. I washed my face and hands and went downstairs to eat.

The dining-drinking parlor that adjoined the lobby was full to overflowing with males in sports clothes and liquor breaths and females in slacks and shorts with blood-red fingernails and dirty knuckles. A fellow with eyebrows like John L. Lewis was prowling around with a cigar screwed into his face. A lean, pale-eyed cashier in shirt-sleeves was fighting to get the race results from Hollywood Park on a small radio that was as full of static as the mashed potato was full of water. In the deep, black corner of the room a hillbilly symphony of five defeatists in white coats and purple shirts was trying to make itself heard above the brawl at the bar.

I gobbled what they called the regular dinner, drank a brandy to sit on it, and went out on to the main stem. It was still broad daylight, but the neon lights were turned on and the evening was full of the noise of auto horns, shrill voices, the rattle of bowls, the snap of .22's at the shooting gallery, jukebox music, and behind all this the hoarse, hard mutter of speedboats on the lake. At a corner opposite the post office a blue-and-white arrow said *Telephone*. I went down a dusty side road that suddenly became quiet and cool and piny. A tame doe deer with a leather collar on its neck wandered across the road in front of me. The phone office was a log cabin, and there was a booth in the corner with a coin-in-the-slot telephone. I shut myself inside and dropped my nickel and dialed 2306. A woman's voice answered.

I said: "Is Mr. Fred Lacey there?"

"Who is calling, please?"

"Evans is the name."

"Mr. Lacey is not here right now, Mr. Evans. Is he expecting you?"

That gave her two questions to my one. I didn't like it. I said: "Are you Mrs. Lacey?"

"Yes. I am Mrs. Lacey." I thought her voice was taut and overstrung; but some voices are like that all the time.

"It's a business matter," I said. "When will he be back?"

"I don't know exactly. Some time this evening, I suppose. What did you – "

"Where is your cabin, Mrs. Lacey?"

"It's . . . it's on Ball Sage Point, about two miles west of the village. Are you calling from the village? Did you – "

"I'll call back in an hour, Mrs. Lacey," I said, and hung up. I stepped out of the booth. In the other corner of the room a dark girl in slacks was writing in some kind of account book at a little desk. She looked up and smiled and said: "How do you like the mountains?"

I said: "Fine."

"It's very quiet up here," she said. "Very restful."

"Yeah. Do you know anybody named Fred Lacey?"

"Lacey? Oh, yes, they just had a phone put in. They bought the Baldwin cabin. It was vacant for two years, and they just bought it. It's out at the end of Ball Sage Point, a big cabin on high ground, looking out over the lake. It has a marvelous view. Do you know Mr. Lacey?"

"No," I said, and went out of there.

The tame doe was in the gap of the fence at the end of the walk. I tried to push her out of the way. She wouldn't move, so I stepped over the fence and walked back to the Indian Head and got into my car.

There was a gas station at the east end of the village. I pulled up for some gas and asked the leathery man who poured it where Ball Sage Point was.

"Well," he said. "That's easy. That ain't hard at all. You won't have no trouble finding Ball Sage Point. You go down here about a mile and a half past the Catholic church and Kincaid's Camp, and at the bakery you turn right and then you keep on the road to Willerton Boys' Camp, and it's the first road to the left after you pass on by. It's a dirt road, kind of rough. They don't sweep the snow off in winter, but it ain't winter now. You know somebody out there?"

"No." I gave him money. He went for the change and came back.

"It's quiet out there," he said. "Restful. What was the name?"

"Murphy," I said.

"Glad to know you, Mr. Murphy," he said, and reached for my hand. "Drop in any time. Glad to have the pleasure of serving you. Now, for Ball Sage Point you just keep straight on down this road – "

"Yeah," I said, and left his mouth flapping.

I figured I knew how to find Ball Sage Point now, so I turned around and drove the other way. It was just possible Fred Lacey would not want me to go to his cabin.

Half a block beyond the hotel the paved road turned down towards a boat landing, then east again along the shore of the lake. The water was low. Cattle were grazing in the sour-looking grass that had been under water in the spring. A few patient visitors were fishing for bass or blue-gill from boats with outboard motors. About a mile or so beyond the meadows a dirt road wound out towards a long point covered with junipers. Close inshore there was a lighted dance pavilion. The music was going already, although it still looked like late afternoon at that altitude. The band sounded as if it was in my pocket. I could hear a girl with a throaty voice singing "The Woodpecker's Song." I drove on past and the music faded and the road got rough and stony. A cabin on the shore slid past me, and there was nothing beyond it but pines and junipers and the shine of the water. I stopped the car out near the tip of the point and walked over to a huge tree fallen with its roots twelve feet in the air. I sat down against it on the bone-dry ground and lit a pipe. It was peaceful and quiet and far from everything. On the far side of the lake a couple of speedboats played tag, but on my side there was nothing but silent water, very slowly getting dark in the mountain dusk. I wondered who the hell Fred Lacey was and what he wanted and why he didn't stay home or leave a message if his business was so urgent. I didn't wonder about it very long. The evening was too peaceful. I smoked and looked at the lake and the sky, and at a robin waiting on the bare spike at the top of a tall pine for it to get dark enough so he could sing his good-night song.

At the end of half an hour I got up and dug a hole in the soft ground with my heel and knocked my pipe out and stamped down the dirt over the ashes. For no reason at all, I walked a few steps towards the lake, and that brought me to the end of the tree. So I saw the foot.

It was in a white duck shoe, about size nine. I walked around the roots of the tree.

There was another foot in another white duck shoe. There were pinstriped white pants with legs in them, and there was a torso in a pale-green sport shirt of the kind that hangs outside and has pockets like a sweater. It had a buttonless V-neck and chest hair showed through the V. The man was middle-aged, half bald, had a good coat of tan and a line mustache shaved up from the lip. His lips were thick, and his mouth, a little open as they usually are, showed big strong teeth. He had the kind of face that goes with plenty of food and not too much worry. His eyes were looking at the sky. I couldn't seem to meet them.

The left side of the green sport shirt was sodden with blood in a patch as big as a dinner plate. In the middle of the patch there might have been a scorched hole. I couldn't be sure. The light was getting a little tricky.

I bent down and felt matches and cigarettes in the pockets of the shirt, a couple of rough lumps like keys and silver in his pants pockets at the sides. I rolled him a little to get at his hip. He was still limp and only a little cooled off. A wallet of rough leather made a tight fit in his right hip pocket. I dragged it out, bracing my knee against his back.

There was twelve dollars in the wallet and some cards, but what interested me was the name on his photostat driver's license. I lit a match to make sure I read it right in the fading daylight.

The name on the license was Frederick Shield Lacey.

2

I PUT THE wallet back and stood up and made a full circle, staring hard. Nobody was in sight, on land or on the water. In that light, nobody could have seen what I was doing unless he was close.

I walked a few steps and looked down to see if I was making tracks. No. The ground was half pine needles of many years past, and the other half pulverized rotten wood.

The gun was about four feet away, almost under the fallen tree. I didn't touch it. I bent down and looked at it. It was a .22 automatic, a Colt with a bone grip. It was half buried in a small pile of the powdery, brown, rotted wood. There were large black ants on the pile, and one of them was crawling along the barrel of the gun.

I straightened up and took another quick look around. A boat idled offshore out of sight around the point. I could hear an uneven stutter from the throttled-down motor, but I couldn't see it. I started back toward the car. I was almost up to it. A small figure rose silently behind a heavy manzanita bush. The light winked on glasses and on something else, lower down in a hand.

A voice said hissingly: "Placing the hands up, please."

It was a nice spot for a very fast draw. I didn't think mine would be fast enough. I placed the hands up.

The small figure came around the manzanita bush. The shining thing below the glasses was a gun. The gun was large enough. It came towards me.

A gold tooth winked out of a small mouth below a black mustache.

"Turning around, please," the nice little voice said soothingly. "You seeing man lie on ground?"

"Look," I said, "I'm a stranger here. I – "

"Turning around very soon," the man said coldly.

I turned around.

The end of the gun made a nest against my spine. A light, deft hand prodded me here and there, rested on the gun under my arm. The voice cooed. The hand went to my hip. The pressure of my wallet went away. A very neat pickpocket. I could hardly feel him touch me.

"I look at wallet now. You very still," the voice said. The gun went away.

A good man had a chance now. He would fall quickly to the ground, do a back flip from a kneeling position, and come up with his gun blazing in his hand. It would happen very fast. The good man would take the little man with glasses the way a dowager takes her teeth out, in one smooth motion. I somehow didn't think I was that good.

The wallet went back on my hip, the gun barrel back into my back.

"So," the voice said softly. "You coming here you making mistake."

"Brother, you said it," I told him.

"Not matter," the voice said. "Go away now, go home. Five hundred dollars. Nothing being said five hundred dollars arriving one week from today."

"Fine," I said. "You having my address?"

"Very funny," the voice cooed. "Ha, ha."

Something hit the back of my right knee, and the leg folded suddenly the way it will when hit at that point. My head began to ache from where it was going to get a crack from the gun, but he fooled me. It was the old rabbit punch, and it was a honey of its type. Done with the heel of a very hard little hand. My head came off and went half-way across the lake and did a boomerang turn and came back and slammed on top of my spine with a sickening jar. Somehow on the way it got a mouthful of pine needles.

There was an interval of midnight in a small room with the windows shut and no air. My chest labored against the ground. They put a ton of coal on my back. One of the hard lumps pressed into the middle of my back. I made some noises, but they must have been unimportant. Nobody bothered about them. I heard the sound of a boat motor get louder, and a soft thud of feet walking on the pine needles, making a dry, slithering sound. Then a couple of heavy grunts and steps going away. Then steps coming back and a burry voice, with a sort of accent.

"What did you get there, Charlie?"

"Oh nothing," Charlie said cooingly. "Smoking pipe, not doing anything. Summer visitor, ha, ha."

"Did he see the stiff?"

"Not seeing," Charlie said. I wondered why.

"Okay, let's go."

"Ah, too bad," Charlie said. "Too bad." The weight got off my back and the lumps of hard coal went away from my spine. "Too bad," Charlie said again. "But must do."

He didn't fool this time. He hit me with the gun. Come around and I'll let you feel the lump under my scalp. I've got several of them.

Time passed and I was up on my knees, whining. I put a foot on the ground and hoisted myself on it and wiped my face off with the back of my hand and put the other foot on the ground and climbed out of the hole it felt like I was in.

The shine of water, dark now from the sun but silvered by the moon, was directly in front of me. To the right was the big fallen tree. That brought it back. I moved cautiously towards it, rubbing my head with careful fingertips. It was swollen and soft, but not bleeding. I stopped and looked back for my hat, and then remembered I had left it in the car.

I went around the tree. The moon was bright as it can only be in the mountains or in the desert. You could almost have read the paper by its light. It was very easy to see that there was no body on the ground now and no gun lying against the tree with ants crawling on it. The ground had a sort of smoothed-out, raked look.

I stood there and listened, and all I heard was the blood pounding in my head, and all I felt was my head aching. Then my hand jumped for the gun and the gun was there. And the hand jumped again for my wallet and the wallet was there. I hauled it out and looked at my money. That seemed to be there, too.

I turned around and plowed back to the car. I wanted to go back to the hotel and get a couple of drinks and lie down. I wanted to meet Charlie after a while, but not right away. First I wanted to lie down for a while. I was a growing boy and I needed rest.

I got into the car and started it and tooled it around on the soft ground and back on to the dirt road and back along that to the highway. I didn't meet any cars. The music was still going well in the dancing pavilion off to the side, and the throaty-voiced singer was giving out "I'll Never Smile Again."

When I reached the highway I put the lights on and drove back to the village. The local law hung out in a one-room pine-board shack halfway up the block from the boat landing, across the street from the firehouse. There was a naked light burning inside, behind a glass-paneled door.

I stopped the car on the other side of the street and sat there for a minute looking into the shack. There was a man inside, sitting bareheaded in a swivel chair at an old roll-top desk. I opened the car door and moved to get out, then stopped and shut the door again and started the motor and drove on.

I had a hundred dollars to earn, after all.

3

I DROVE TWO miles past the village and came to the bakery and turned on a newly oiled road towards the lake. I passed a couple of camps and then saw the brownish tents of the boys' camp with lights strung between them and a clatter coming from a big tent where they were washing dishes. A little beyond that the road curved around an inlet and a dirt road branched off. It was deeply rutted and full of stones half embedded in the dirt, and the trees barely gave it room to pass. I went by a couple of lighted cabins, old ones built of pine with the bark left on. Then the road climbed and the place got emptier, and after a while a big cabin hung over the edge of the bluff looking down on the lake at its feet. The cabin had two chimneys and a rustic fence, and a double garage outside the fence. There was a long porch on the lake side, and steps going down to the water. Light came from the windows. My headlights tilted up enough to catch the name Baldwin painted on a wooden board nailed to a tree. This was the cabin, all right.

The garage was open and a sedan was parked in it. I stopped a little beyond and went far enough into the garage to feel the exhaust pipe of the car. It was cold. I went through a rustic gate up a path outlined in stones to the porch. The door opened as I got there. A tall woman stood there, framed against the light. A little silky dog rushed out past her, tumbled down the steps and hit me in the stomach with two front paws, then dropped to the ground and ran in circles making noises of approval.

"Down, Shiny!" the woman called. "Down! Isn't she a funny little dog? Funny itty doggie. She's half coyote."

The dog ran back into the house. I said: "Are you Mrs. Lacey? I'm Evans. I called you up about an hour ago."

"Yes, I'm Mrs. Lacey," she said. "My husband hasn't come in yet. I – well, come in, won't you?" Her voice had a remote sound, like a voice in the mist.

She closed the door behind me after I went in and stood there looking at me, then shrugged a little and sat down in a wicker chair. I sat down in another just like it. The dog appeared from nowhere, jumped in my lap, wiped a neat tongue across the end of my nose and jumped down again. It was a small grayish dog with a sharp nose and a long, feathery tail.

It was a long room with a lot of windows and not very fresh curtains at them. There was a big fireplace, Indian rugs, two davenports with faded cretonne slips over them, more wicker furniture, not too comfortable. There were some antlers on the wall, one pair with six points.

"Fred isn't home yet," Mrs. Lacey said again. "I don't know what's keeping him."

I nodded. She had a pale face, rather taut, dark hair that was a little wild. She was wearing a double-breasted scarlet coat with brass buttons, gray flannel slacks, pigskin clog sandals, and no stockings. There was a necklace of cloudy amber around her throat and a bandeau of old-rose material in her hair. She was in her middle thirties, so it was too late for her to learn how to dress herself.

"You wanted to see my husband on business?"

"Yes. He wrote me to come up and stay at the Indian Head and phone him."

"Oh – at the Indian Head," she said, as if that meant something. She crossed her legs, didn't like them that way, and uncrossed them again. She leaned forward and cupped a long chin in her hand. "What kind of business are you in, Mr. Evans?"

"I'm a private detective."

"It's . . . it's about the money?" she asked quickly.

I nodded. That seemed safe. It was usually about money. It was about a hundred dollars that I had in my pocket, anyhow.

"Of course," she said. "Naturally. Would you care for a drink?"

"Very much."

She went over to a little wooden bar and came back with two glasses. We drank. We looked at each other over the rims of our glasses.

"The Indian Head," she said. "We stayed there two nights when we came up. While the cabin was being cleaned up. It had been empty for two years before we bought it. They get so dirty."

"I guess so," I said.

"You say my husband wrote to you?" She was looking down into her glass now. "I suppose he told you the story."

I offered her a cigarette. She started to reach, then shook her head and put her hand on her kneecap and twisted it. She gave me the careful up-from-under look.

"He was a little vague," I said. "In spots."

She looked at me steadily and I looked at her steadily. I breathed gently into my glass until it misted.

"Well, I don't think we need be mysterious about it," she said. "Although as a matter of fact I know more about it than Fred thinks I do. He doesn't know, for example, that I saw that letter."

"The letter he sent me?"

"No. The letter he got from Los Angeles with the report on the ten-dollar bill."

"How did you get to see it?" I asked.

She laughed without much amusement. "Fred's too secretive. It's a mistake to be too secretive with a woman. I sneaked a look at it while he was in the bathroom. I got it out of his pocket."

I nodded and drank some more of my drink. I said: "Uh-huh." That didn't commit me very far, which was a good idea as long as I didn't know what we were talking about. "But how did you know it was in his pocket?" I asked.

"He'd just got it at the post office. I was with him." She laughed, with a little more amusement this time. "I saw that there was a bill in it and that it came from Los Angeles. I knew he had sent one of the bills to a friend there who is an expert on such things. So of course I knew this letter was a report. It was."

"Seems like Fred doesn't cover up very well," I said. "What did the letter say?"

She flushed slightly. "I don't know that I should tell you. I don't really know that you are a detective or that your name is Evans."

"Well, that's something that can be settled without violence," I said. I got up and showed her enough to prove it. When I sat down again the little dog came over and sniffed at the cuffs on my trousers. I bent down to pat her head and got a handful of spit.

"It said that the bill was beautiful work. The paper, in particular, was just about perfect. But under a comparison microscope there were very small differences of registration. What does that mean?"

"It means that the bill he sent hadn't been made from a government plate. Anything else wrong?"

"Yes. Under black light – whatever that is – there appeared to be slight differences in the composition of the inks. But the letter added that to the naked eye the counterfeit was practically perfect. It would fool any bank teller."

I nodded. This was something I hadn't expected. "Who wrote the letter, Mrs. Lacey?"

"He signed himself Bill. It was on a plain sheet of paper. I don't know who wrote it. Oh, there was something else. Bill said that Fred ought to turn it in to the Federal people right away, because the money was good enough to make a lot of trouble if much of it got into circulation. But, of course, Fred wouldn't want to do that if he could help it. That would be why he sent for you."

"Well, no, of course not," I said. This was a shot in the dark, but it wasn't likely to hit anything. Not with the amount of dark I had to shoot into.

She nodded, as if I had said something.

"What is Fred doing now, mostly?" I asked.

"Bridge and poker, like he's done for years. He plays bridge almost every afternoon at the athletic club and poker at night a good deal. You can see that he couldn't afford to be connected with counterfeit money, even in the most innocent way. There would always be someone who wouldn't believe it *was* innocent. He plays the races, too, but that's just fun. That's how he got the five hundred dollars he put in my shoe for a present for me. At the Indian Head."

I wanted to go out in the yard and do a little yelling and breast beating, just to let off steam. But all I could do was sit there and look wise and guzzle my drink. I guzzled it empty and made a lonely noise with the ice cubes and she went and got me another one. I took a slug of that and breathed deeply and said: "If the bill was so good, how did he know it was bad, if you get what I mean?"

Her eyes widened a little. "Oh – I see. He didn't, of course. Not that one. But there were fifty of them, all ten-dollar bills, all new. And the money hadn't been that way when he put it in the shoe."

I wondered if tearing my hair would do me any good. I didn't think – my head was too sore. Charlie. Good old Charlie! Okay, Charlie, after a while I'll be around with my gang.

"Look," I said. "Look, Mrs. Lacey. He didn't tell me about the shoe. Does he always keep his money in a shoe, or was this something special on account of he won it at the races and horses wear shoes?"

"I told you it was a surprise present for me. When I put the shoe on I would find it, of course."

"Oh." I gnawed about half an inch off my upper lip. "But you didn't find it?"

"How could I when I sent the maid to take the shoes to the shoemaker in the village to have lifts put on them? I didn't look inside. I didn't know Fred had put anything in the shoe."

A little light was coming. It was very far off and coming very slowly. It was a very little light, about half a firefly's worth.

I said: "And Fred didn't know that. And this maid took the shoes to the shoemaker. What then?"

"Well, Gertrude – that's the maid's name – said she had-n't noticed the money, either. So when Fred found out about it and had asked her, he went over to the shoemak-er's place, and he hadn't worked on the shoes and the roll of money was still stuffed down into the toe of the shoe. So Fred laughed and took the money out and put it in his pocket and gave the shoemaker five dollars because he was lucky."

I finished my second drink and leaned back. "I get it now. Then Fred took the roll out and looked it over and he saw it wasn't the same money. It was all new ten-dollar bills, and before it had probably been various sizes of bills and not new or not all new."

She looked surprised that I had to reason it out. I won-dered how long a letter she thought Fred had written me. I said: "Then Fred would have to assume that there was some reason for changing the money. He thought of one and sent a bill to a friend of his to be tested. And the report came back that it was very good counterfeit, but still counterfeit. Who did he ask about it at the hotel?"

"Nobody except Gertrude, I guess. He didn't want to start anything. I guess he just sent for you."

I snubbed my cigarette out and looked out of the open front windows at the moonlit lake. A speedboat with a hard white headlight slid muttering along in the water, far off over the water, and disappeared behind a wooded point.

I looked back at Mrs. Lacey. She was still sitting with her chin propped in a thin hand. Her eyes seemed far away.

"I wish Fred would come home," she said.

"Where is he?"

"I don't know. He went out with a man named Frank Luders, who is staying at the Woodland Club, down at the far end of the lake. Fred said he owned an interest in it. But I called Mr. Luders up a while ago and he said Fred had just ridden uptown with him and got off at the post office. I've been expecting Fred to phone and ask me to pick him up somewhere. He left hours ago."

"They probably have some card games down at the Woodland Club. Maybe he went there."

She nodded. "He usually calls me, though."

I stared at the floor for a while and tried not to feel like a heel. Then I stood up. "I guess I'll go on back to the hotel. I'll be there if you want to phone me. I think I've met Mr. Lacey somewhere. Isn't he a thick-set man about forty-five, going a little bald, with a small mustache?"

She went to the door with me. "Yes," she said. "That's Fred, all right."

She had shut the dog in the house and was standing outside herself as I turned the car and drove away. God, she looked lonely.

4

I WAS LYING on my back on the bed, wobbling a cigarette around and trying to make up my mind just why I had to play cute with this affair, when the knock came at the door. I called out. A girl in a working uniform came in with some towels. She had dark, reddish hair and a pert, nicely made-up face and long legs. She excused herself and slung some towels on the rack and started back to the door and gave me a side-long look with a good deal of fluttering eyelash in it.

I said, "Hello, Gertrude," just for the hell of it.

She stopped, and the dark-red head came around and the mouth was ready to smile.

"How'd you know my name?"

"I didn't. But one of the maids is Gertrude. I wanted to talk to her."

She leaned against the door frame, towels over her arm. Her eyes were lazy. "Yeah?"

"Live up here, or just up here for the summer?" I asked.

Her lip curled. "I should say I don't live up here. With these mountain screwballs? I should say not."

"You doing all right?"

She nodded. "And I don't need any company, mister." She sounded as if she could be talked out of that.

I looked at her for a minute and said: "Tell about that money somebody hid in a shoe."

"Who are you?" she asked coolly.

"The name is Evans. I'm a Los Angeles detective." I grinned at her, very wise.

Her face stiffened a little. The hand holding the towels clutched and her nails made a scratching sound on the cloth. She moved back from the door and sat down in a straight chair against the wall. Trouble dwelt in her eyes.

"A dick," she breathed. "What goes on?"

"Don't you know?"

"All I heard was Mrs. Lacey left some money in a shoe she wanted a lift put on the heel, and I took it over to the shoe-maker and he didn't steal the money. And I didn't, either. She got the money back, didn't she?"

"Don't like cops, do you? Seems to me I know your face," I said.

The face hardened. "Look, copper, I got a job and I work at it. I don't need any help from any copper. I don't owe anybody a nickel."

"Sure," I said. "When you took those shoes from the room did you go right over to the shoemaker with them?"

She nodded shortly.

"Didn't stop on the way at all?"

"Why would I?"

"I wasn't around then. I wouldn't know."

"Well, I didn't. Except to tell Weber I was going out for a guest."

"Who's Mr. Weber?"

"He's the assistant manager. He's down in the dining room a lot."

"Tall, pale guy that writes down all the race results?"

She nodded. "That would be him."

"I see," I said. I struck a match and lit my cigarette. I stared at her through smoke. "Thanks very much," I said.

She stood up and opened the door. "I don't think I remember you," she said, looking back at me.

"There must be a few of us you didn't meet," I said.

She flushed and stood there glaring at me.

"They always change the towels this late in your hotel?" I asked her, just to be saying something.

"Smart guy, ain't you?"

"Well, I try to give that impression," I said with a modest smirk.

"You don't put it over," she said, with a sudden trace of thick accent.

"Anybody handle those shoes except you – after you took them?"

"No. I told you I just stopped to tell Mr. Weber – " She stopped dead and thought a minute. "I went to get him a cup of coffee," she said. "I left them on his desk by the cash register. How the hell would I know anybody handled them? And what difference does it make if they got their dough back all right?"

"Well, I see you're anxious to make me feel good about it. Tell me about this guy, Weber. He been here long?"

"Too long," she said nastily. "A girl don't want to walk too close to him if you get what I mean. What am I talking about?"

"About Mr. Weber."

"Well, to hell with Mr. Weber — if you get what I mean."

"You been having any trouble getting it across?"

She flushed again. "And strictly off the record," she said, "to hell with you."

"If I get what you mean," I said.

She opened the door and gave me a quick, half-angry smile and went out.

Her steps made a tapping sound going along the hall. I didn't hear her stop at any other doors. I looked at my watch. It was after half past nine.

Somebody came along the hall with heavy feet, went into the room next to me and banged the door. The man started hawking and throwing shoes around. A weight flopped on the bed springs and started bounding around. Five minutes of this and he got up again. Two big, unshod feet thudded on the floor, a bottle tinkled against a glass. The man had himself a drink, lay down on the bed again, and began to snore almost at once.

Except for that and the confused racket from downstairs in the dining room and the bar there was the nearest thing you get to silence in a mountain resort. Speedboats stuttered out on the lake, dance music murmured here and there, cars went by blowing horns, the .22's snapped in the shooting gallery, and kids yelled at each other across the main drag.

It was so quiet that I didn't hear my door open. It was half open before I noticed it. A man came in quietly, half closed the door, moved a couple of steps farther into the room and stood looking at me. He was tall, thin, pale, quiet, and his eyes had a flat look of menace.

"Okay, sport," he said. "Let's see it."

I rolled around and sat up. I yawned. "See what?"

"The buzzer."

"What buzzer?"

"Shake it up, half-smart. Let's see the buzzer that gives you the right to ask questions of the help."

"Oh, that," I said, smiling weakly. "I don't have any buzzer, Mr. Weber."

"Well, that is very lovely," Mr. Weber said. He came across the room, his long arms swinging. When he was about three feet from me he leaned forward a little and made a very sudden movement. An open palm slapped the side of my face hard. It rocked my head and made the back of it shoot pain in all directions.

"Just for that," I said, "you don't go to the movies tonight."

He twisted his face into a sneer and cocked his right fist. He telegraphed his punch well ahead. I would almost have had time to run out and buy a catcher's mask. I came up under the fist and stuck a gun in his stomach. He grunted unpleasantly. I said: "Putting the hands up, please."

He grunted again and his eyes went out of focus, but he didn't move his hands. I went around him and backed towards the far side of the room. He turned slowly, eyeing me. I said: "Just a moment until I close the door. Then we will go into the case of the money in the shoe, otherwise known as the Clue of the Substituted Lettuce."

"Go to hell," he said.

"A right snappy comeback," I said. "And full of originality."

I reached back for the knob of the door, keeping my eyes on him. A board creaked behind me. I swung around, adding a little power to the large, heavy, hard and business-like hunk of concrete which landed on the side of my jaw. I spun off into the distance, trailing flashes of lightning, and did a nose dive out into space. A couple of thousand years passed. Then I stopped a planet with my back, opened my eyes fuzzily and looked at a pair of feet.

They were sprawled out at a loose angle, and legs came towards me from them. The legs were splayed out on the floor of the room. A hand hung down limp, and a gun lay just out of its reach. I moved one of the feet and was surprised to find it belonged to me. The lax hand twitched and reached automatically for the gun, missed it, reached again and grabbed the smooth grip. I lifted it. Somebody had tied a fifty-pound weight to it, but I lifted it anyway. There was nothing in the room but silence. I looked across and was staring straight at the closed door. I shifted a little and ached all over. My head ached. My jaw ached. I lifted the gun some more and then put it down again. The hell with it. I should be lifting guns around for what. The room was empty. All visitors departed. The droplight from the ceiling burned with an empty glare. I rolled a little and ached some more and got a leg bent and a knee under me. I came up grunting hard, grabbed the gun again and climbed the rest of the way. There was a taste of ashes in my mouth.

"Ah, too bad," I said out loud. "Too bad. Must do. Okay, Charlie. I'll be seeing you."

I swayed a little, still groggy as a three-day drunk, swiveled slowly and prowled the room with my eyes.

A man was kneeling in prayer against the side of the bed. He wore a gray suit and his hair was a dusty blond color. His legs were spread out, and his body was bent forward on the bed and his arms were flung out. His head rested sideways on his left arm.

He looked quite comfortable. The rough deer-horn grip of the hunting knife under his left shoulder-blade didn't seem to bother him at all.

I went over to bend down and look at his face. It was the face of Mr. Weber. Poor Mr. Weber! From under the handle of the hunting knife, down the back of his jacket, a dark streak extended.

It was not mercurochrome.

I found my hat somewhere and put it on carefully, and put the gun under my arm and waded over to the door. I reversed the key, switched the light off, went out and locked the door after me and dropped the key into my pocket.

I went along the silent hallway and down the stairs to the office. An old wasted-looking night clerk was reading the paper behind the desk. He didn't even look at me. I glanced through the archway into the dining room. The same noisy crowd was brawling at the bar. The same hillbilly symphony was fighting for life in the corner. The guy with the cigar and the John L. Lewis eyebrows was minding the cash register. Business seemed good. A couple of summer visitors were dancing in the middle of the floor, holding glasses over each other's shoulders.

5

I WENT OUT of the lobby door and turned left along the street to where my car was parked, but I didn't go very far before I stopped and turned back into the lobby of the hotel. I leaned on the counter and asked the clerk: "May I speak to the maid called Gertrude?"

He blinked at me thoughtfully over his glasses.

"She's off at nine-thirty. She's gone home."

"Where does she live?"

He stared at me without blinking this time.

"I think maybe you've got the wrong idea," he said.

"If I have, it's not the idea you have."

He rubbed the end of his chin and washed my face with his stare. "Something wrong?"

"I'm a detective from L.A. I work very quietly when people let me work quietly."

"You'd better see Mr. Holmes," he said. "The manager."

"Look, pardner, this is a very small place. I wouldn't have to do more than wander down the row and ask in the bars and eating places for Gertrude. I could think up a reason. I could find out. You would save me a little time and maybe save somebody from getting hurt. Very badly hurt."

He shrugged. "Let me see your credentials, Mr. – "

"Evans." I showed him my credentials. He stared at them a long time after he had read them, then handed the wallet back and stared at the ends of his fingertips.

"I believe she's stopping at the Whitewater Cabins," he said.

"What's her last name?"

"Smith," he said, and smiled a faint, old, and very weary smile, the smile of a man who has seen too much of one world. "Or possibly Schmidt."

I thanked him and went back out on the sidewalk. I walked half a block, then turned into a noisy little bar for a drink. A three-piece orchestra was swinging it on a tiny stage at the back. In front of the stage there was a small dance floor, and a few fuzzy-eyed couples were shagging around flat-footed with their mouths open and their faces full of nothing.

I drank a jigger of rye and asked the barman where the Whitewater Cabins were. He said at the east end of the town, half a block back, on a road that started at the gas station.

I went back for my car and drove through the village and found the road. A pale blue neon sign with an arrow on it pointed the way. The Whitewater Cabins were a cluster of shacks on the side of the hill with an office down front. I stopped in front of the office. People were sitting out on their tiny front porches with portable radios. The night seemed peaceful and homey. There was a bell in the office.

I rang it and a girl in slacks came in and told me Miss Smith and Miss Hoffman had a cabin kind of off by itself because the girls slept late and wanted quiet. Of course, it was

1133

always kind of busy in the season, but the cabin where they were — it was called Tuck-Me-Inn — was quiet and it was at the back, way off to the left, and I wouldn't have any trouble finding it. Was I a friend of theirs?

I said I was Miss Smith's grandfather, thanked her and went out and up the slope between the clustered cabins to the edge of the pines at the back. There was a long woodpile at the back, and at each end of the cleared space there was a small cabin. In front of the one to the left there was a coupe standing with its lights dim. A tall blonde girl was putting a suitcase into the boot. Her hair was tied in a blue handkerchief, and she wore a blue sweater and blue pants. Or dark enough to be blue, anyhow. The cabin behind her was lighted, and the little sign hanging from the roof said *Tuck-Me-Inn*.

The blonde girl went back into the cabin, leaving the boot of the car open. Dim light oozed out through the open door. I went very softly up on the steps and walked inside.

Gertrude was snapping down the top of a suitcase on a bed. The blonde girl was out of sight, but I could hear her out in the kitchen of the little white cabin.

I couldn't have made very much noise. Gertrude snapped down the lid of the suitcase, hefted it and started to carry it out. It was only then that she saw me. Her face went very white, and she stopped dead, holding the suitcase at her side. Her mouth opened, and she spoke quickly back over her shoulder: "Anna — *achtung!*"

The noise stopped in the kitchen. Gertrude and I stared at each other.

"Leaving?" I asked.

She moistened her lips. "Going to stop me, copper?"

"I don't guess. What you leaving for?"

"I don't like it up here. The altitude is bad for my nerves."

"Made up your mind rather suddenly, didn't you?"

"Any law against it?"

"I don't guess. You're not afraid of Weber, are you?"

She didn't answer me. She looked past my shoulder. It was an old gag, and I didn't pay any attention to it. Behind me, the cabin door closed. I turned, then. The blonde girl was behind me. She had a gun in her hand. She looked at me thoughtfully, without any expression much. She was a big girl, and looked very strong.

"What is it?" she asked, speaking a little heavily, in a voice almost like a man's voice.

"A Los Angeles dick," replied Gertrude.

"So," Anna said. "What does he want?"

"I don't know," Gertrude said. "I don't think he's a real dick. He don't seem to throw his weight enough."

"So," Anna said. She moved to the side and away from the door. She kept the gun pointed at me. She held it as if guns didn't make her nervous – not the least bit nervous. "What do you want?" she asked throatily.

"Practically everything," I said. "Why are you taking a powder?"

"That has been explained," the blonde girl said calmly. "It is the altitude. It is making Gertrude sick."

"You both work at the Indian Head?"

The blonde girl said: "Of no consequence."

"What the hell," Gertrude said. "Yeah, we both worked at the hotel until tonight. Now we're leaving. Any objection?"

"We waste time," the blonde girl said. "See if he has a gun."

Gertrude put her suitcase down and felt me over. She found the gun and I let her take it, big-hearted. She stood there looking at it with a pale, worried expression. The blonde girl said: "Put the gun down outside and put the suitcase in the car. Start the engine of the car and wait for me."

Gertrude picked her suitcase up again and started around me to the door.

"That won't get you anywhere," I said. "They'll telephone ahead and block you on the road. There are only two roads out of here, both easy to block."

The blonde girl raised her fine, tawny eyebrows a little. "Why should anyone wish to stop us?"

"Yeah, why are you holding that gun?"

"I did not know who you were," the blonde girl said. "I do not know even now. Go on, Gertrude."

Gertrude opened the door, then looked back at me and moved her lips one over the other. "Take a tip, shamus, and beat it out of this place while you're able," she said quietly.

"Which of you saw the hunting knife?"

They glanced at each other quickly, then back at me. Gertrude had a fixed stare, but it didn't look like a guilty kind of stare. "I pass," she said. "You're over my head."

"Okay," I said. "I know you didn't put it where it was. One more question: How long were you getting that cup of coffee for Mr. Weber the morning you took the shoes out?"

"You are wasting time, Gertrude," the blonde girl said impatiently, or as impatiently as she would ever say anything. She didn't seem an impatient type.

Gertrude didn't pay any attention to her. Her eyes held a tight speculation. "Long enough to get him a cup of coffee."

"They have that right in the dining room."

"It was stale in the dining room. I went out to the kitchen for it. I got him some toast, also."

"Five minutes?"

She nodded. "About that."

"Who else was in the dining room besides Weber?"

She stared at me very steadily. "At that time I don't think anybody. I'm not sure. Maybe someone was having a late breakfast."

"Thanks very much," I said. "Put the gun down carefully on the porch and don't drop it. You can empty it if you like. I don't plan to shoot anyone."

She smiled a very small smile and opened the door with the hand holding the gun and went out. I heard her go down the steps and then heard the boot of the car slammed shut. I heard the starter, then the motor caught and purred quietly.

The blonde girl moved around to the door and took the key from the inside and put it on the outside. "I would not care to shoot anybody," she said. "But I could do it if I had to. Please do not make me."

She shut the door and the key turned in the lock. Her steps went down off the porch. The car door slammed and the motor took hold. The tires made a soft whisper going down between the cabins. Then the noise of the portable radios swallowed that sound.

I stood there looking around the cabin, then walked through it. There was nothing in it that didn't belong there. There was some garbage in a can, coffee cups not washed, a saucepan full of grounds. There were no papers, and nobody had left the story of his life written on a paper match.

The back door was locked, too. This was on the side away from the camp, against the dark wilderness of the trees. I shook the door and bent down to look at the lock. A straight bolt lock. I opened a window. A screen was nailed over it against the wall outside. I went back to the door and gave it the shoulder. It held without any trouble at all. It also started my head blazing again. I felt in my pockets and was disgusted. I didn't even have a five-cent skeleton key.

I got the can opener out of the kitchen drawer and worked a corner of the screen loose and bent it back. Then I got up on the sink and reached down to the outside knob of the door and groped around. The key was in the lock. I turned it and drew my hand in again and went out of the door. Then I went back and put the lights out. My gun was lying on the front porch behind a post of the little railing. I tucked it under my arm and walked downhill to the place where I had left my car.

6

THERE WAS A wooden counter leading back from beside the door and a potbellied stove in the corner, and a large blueprint map of the district and some curled-up calendars on the wall. On the counter were piles of dusty-looking folders, a rusty pen, a bottle of ink, and somebody's sweat-darkened Stetson.

Behind the counter there was an old golden-oak roll-top desk, and at the desk sat a man, with a tall corroded brass spittoon leaning against his leg. He was a heavy, calm man, and he sat tilted back in his chair with large, hairless hands clasped on his stomach. He wore scuffed brown army shoes, white socks, brown wash pants held up by faded suspenders, a khaki shirt buttoned to the neck. His hair was mousy-brown except at the temples, where it was the color of dirty snow. On his left breast there was a star. He sat a little more on his left hip than on his right, because there was a brown leather hip holster inside his right hip pocket, and about a foot of .45 gun in the holster.

He had large ears, and friendly eyes, and he looked about as dangerous as a squirrel, but much less nervous. I leaned on the counter and looked at him, and he nodded at me and loosed a half-pint of brown juice into the spittoon. I lit a cigarette and looked around for some place to throw the match.

"Try the floor," he said. "What can I do for you, son?"

I dropped the match on the floor and pointed with my chin at the map on the wall. "I was looking for a map of the district. Sometimes chambers of commerce have them to give away. But I guess you wouldn't be the chamber of commerce."

"We ain't got no maps," the man said. "We had a mess of them a couple of years back, but we run out. I was hearing that Sid Young had some down at the camera store by the post office. He's the justice of the peace here, besides running the camera store, and he gives them out to show them whereat they can smoke and where not. We got a bad fire hazard up here. Got a good map of the district up there on the wall. Be glad to direct you any place you'd care to go. We aim to make the summer visitors at home."

He took a slow breath and dropped another load of juice.

"What was the name?" he asked.

"Evans. Are you the law around here?"

"Yep. I'm Puma Point constable and San Berdoo deppity sheriff. What law we gotta have, me and Sid Young is it. Barron is the name. I come from L.A. Eighteen years in the fire department. I come up here quite a while back. Nice and quiet up here. You up on business?"

I didn't think he could do it again so soon, but he did. That spittoon took an awful beating.

"Business?" I asked.

The big man took one hand off his stomach and hooked a finger inside his collar and tried to loosen it. "Business," he said calmly. "Meaning, you got a permit for that gun, I guess?"

"Hell, does it stick out that much?"

"Depends what a man's lookin' for," he said, and put his feet on the floor. "Maybe you 'n' me better get straightened out."

He got to his feet and came over to the counter and I put my wallet on it, opened out so that he could see the photostat of the license behind the celluloid window. I drew out the L.A. sheriff's gun permit and laid it beside the license.

He looked them over. "I better kind of check the number," he said.

I pulled the gun out and laid it on the counter beside his hand. He picked it up and compared the numbers. "I see you got three of them. Don't wear them all to onst, I hope. Nice gun, son. Can't shoot like mine, though." He pulled his cannon off his hip and laid it on the counter. A Frontier Colt that would weigh as much as a suitcase. He balanced it, tossed it into the air and caught it spinning, then put it back on his hip. He pushed my .38 back across the counter.

"Up here on business, Mr. Evans?"

"I'm not sure. I got a call, but I haven't made a contact yet. A confidential matter."

He nodded. His eyes were thoughtful. They were deeper, colder, darker than they had been.

"I'm stopping at the Indian Head," I said.

"I don't aim to pry into your affairs, son," he said. "We don't have no crime here. Onst in a while a fight or a drunk driver in summertime. Or maybe a couple hard-boiled kids on a motorcycle will break into a cabin just to sleep and steal food. No real crime, though. Mighty little inducement to crime in the mountains. Mountain folks are mighty peaceable."

"Yeah," I said. "And again, no."

He leaned forward a little and looked into my eyes.

"Right now," I said, "you've got a murder."

Nothing much changed in his face. He looked me over feature by feature. He reached for his hat and put it on the back of his head.

"What was that, son?" he asked calmly.

"On the point east of the village out past the dancing pavilion. A man shot, lying behind a big fallen tree. Shot through the heart. I was down there smoking for half an hour before I noticed him."

"Is that so?" he drawled. "Out Speaker Point, eh? Past Speaker's Tavern. That the place?"

"That's right," I said.

"You taken a longish while to get around to telling me, didn't you?" The eyes were not friendly.

"I got a shock," I said. "It took me a while to get myself straightened out."

He nodded. "You and me will now drive out that way. In your car."

"That won't do any good," I said. "The body has been moved. After I found the body I was going back to my car and a Japanese gunman popped up from behind a bush and knocked me down. A couple of men carried the body away and they went off in a boat. There's no sign of it there at all now."

The sheriff went over and spat in his gobboon. Then he made a small spit on the stove and waited as if for it to sizzle, but it was summer and the stove was out. He turned around and cleared his throat and said: "You'd kind of better go on home and lie down a little while, maybe." He clenched a fist at his side. "We aim for the summer visitors to enjoy their-selves up here." He clenched both his hands, then pushed them hard down into the shallow pockets in the front of his pants.

"Okay," I said.

"We don't have no Japanese gunmen up here," the sheriff said thickly. "We are plumb out of Japanese gunmen."

"I can see you don't like that one," I said. "How about this one? A man named Weber was knifed in the back at the Indian Head a while back. In my room. Somebody I didn't see knocked me out with a brick, and while I was out this Weber was knifed. He and I had been talking together. Weber worked at the hotel. As cashier."

"You said this happened in your room?"

"Yeah."

"Seems like," Barron said thoughtfully, "you could turn out to be a bad influence in this town."

"You don't like that one, either?"

He shook his head. "Nope. Don't like this one, neither. Unless, of course, you got a body to go with it."

"I don't have it with me," I said, "but I can run over and get it for you."

He reached and took hold of my arm with some of the hardest fingers I ever felt. "I'd hate for you to be in your right mind, son," he said. "But I'll kind of go over with you. It's a nice night."

"Sure," I said, not moving. "The man I came up here to work for is called Fred Lacey. He just bought a cabin out on Ball Sage Point. The Baldwin cabin. The man I found dead on Speaker Point was named Frederick Lacey, according to the driver's license in his pocket. There's a lot more to it, but you wouldn't want to be bothered with the details, would you?"

"You and me," the sheriff said, "will now run over to the hotel. You got a car?"

I said I had.

"That's fine," the sheriff said. "We won't use it, but give me the keys."

7

THE MAN WITH the heavy, furled eyebrows and the screwed-in cigar leaned against the closed door of the room and didn't say anything or look as if he wanted to say anything. Sheriff Barron sat straddling a straight chair and watching the doctor, whose name was Menzies, examine the body. I stood in the corner where I belonged. The doctor was an angular, bug-eyed man with a yellow face relieved by bright red patches on his cheeks. His fingers were brown with nicotine stains, and he didn't look very clean.

He puffed cigarette smoke into the dead man's hair and rolled him around on the bed and felt him here and there. He looked as if he was trying to act as if he knew what he was doing. The knife had been pulled out of Weber's back. It lay on the bed beside him. It was a short, wide-bladed knife of the kind that is worn in a leather scabbard attached to the belt. It had a heavy guard which would seal the wound as the blow was struck and keep blood from getting back on the handle. There was plenty of blood on the blade.

"Sears Sawbuck Hunter's Special No. 2438," the sheriff said, looking at it. "There's a thousand of them around the lake. They ain't bad and they ain't good. What do you say, Doc?"

The doctor straightened up and took a handkerchief out.

He coughed hackingly into the handkerchief, looked at it, shook his head sadly and lit another cigarette.

"About what?" he asked.

"Cause and time of death."

"Dead very recently," the doctor said. "Not more than two hours. There's no beginning of rigor yet."

"Would you say the knife killed him?"

"Don't be a damn fool, Jim Barron."

"There's been cases," the sheriff said, "where a man would be poisoned or something and they would stick a knife into him to make it look different."

"That would be very clever," the doctor said nastily. "You had many like that up here?"

"Only murder I had up here," the sheriff said peacefully, "was old Dad Meacham over to the other side. Had a shack in Sheedy Canyon. Folks didn't see him around for a while, but it was kinda cold weather and they figured he was in there with his oil stove resting up. Then when he didn't show up they knocked and found the cabin was locked up, so they figured he had gone down for the winter. Then come a heavy snow and the roof caved in. We was over there a-trying to prop her up so he wouldn't lose all his stuff, and, by gum, there was Dad in bed with an axe in the back of his head. Had a little gold he'd panned in summer – I guess that was what he was killed for. We never did find out who done it."

"You want to send him down in my ambulance?" the doctor asked, pointing at the bed with his cigarette.

The sheriff shook his head. "Nope. This is a poor county, Doc. I figure he could ride cheaper than that."

The doctor put his hat on and went to the door. The man with the eyebrows moved out of the way. The doctor opened the door. "Let me know if you want me to pay for the funeral," he said, and went out.

"That ain't no way to talk," the sheriff said.

The man with the eyebrows said: "Let's get this over with and get him out of here so I can go back to work. I got a movie outfit coming up Monday and I'll be busy. I got to find me a new cashier, too, and that ain't so easy."

"Where you find Weber?" the sheriff asked. "Did he have any enemies?"

"I'd say he had at least one," the man with the eyebrows said. "I got him through Frank Luders over at the Woodland Club. All I know about him is he knew his job and he was able to make a ten-thousand-dollar bond without no trouble. That's all I needed to know."

"Frank Luders," the sheriff said. "That would be the man that's bought in over there. I don't think I met him. What does he do?"

"Ha, ha," the man with the eyebrows said.

The sheriff looked at him peacefully. "Well, that ain't the only place where they run a nice poker game, Mr. Holmes."

Mr. Holmes looked blank. "Well, I got to go back to work," he said. "You need any help to move him?"

"Nope. Ain't going to move him right now. Move him before daylight. But not right now. That will be all for now, Mr. Holmes."

The man with the eyebrows looked at him thoughtfully for a moment, then reached for the doorknob.

I said: "You have a couple of German girls working here, Mr. Holmes. Who hired them?"

The man with the eyebrows dragged his cigar out of his mouth, looked at it, put it back and screwed it firmly in place. He said: "Would that be your business?"

"Their names are Anna Hoffman and Gertrude Smith, or maybe Schmidt," I said. "They had a cabin together over at the Whitewater Cabins. They packed up and went down the hill tonight. Gertrude is the girl that took Mrs. Lacey's shoes to the shoemaker."

The man with the eyebrows looked at me very steadily.

I said: "When Gertrude was taking the shoes, she left them on Weber's desk for a short time. There was five hundred dollars in one of the shoes. Mr. Lacey had put it in there for a joke, so his wife would find it."

"First I heard of it," the man with the eyebrows said. The sheriff didn't say anything at all.

"The money wasn't stolen," I said. "The Laceys found it still in the shoe over at the shoemaker's place."

The man with the eyebrows said: "I'm certainly glad that got straightened out all right." He pulled the door open and went out and shut it behind him. The sheriff didn't say anything to stop him.

He went over into the corner of the room and spit in the wastebasket. Then he got a large khaki-colored handkerchief out and wrapped the bloodstained knife in it and slipped it down inside his belt, at the side. He went over and stood looking down at the dead man on the bed. He straightened his hat and started towards the door. He opened the door and looked back at me. "This is a little tricky," he said. "But it probably ain't as tricky as you would like for it to be. Let's go over to Lacey's place."

I went out and he locked the door and put the key in his pocket. We went downstairs and out through the lobby and crossed the street to where a small, dusty, tan-colored sedan was parked against the fireplug. A leathery young man was at the wheel. He looked underfed and a little dirty, like most of the natives. The sheriff and I got in the back of the car. The sheriff said: "You know the Baldwin place out to the end of Ball Sage, Andy?"

"Yup."

"We'll go out there," the sheriff said. "Stop a little to this side." He looked up at the sky. "Full moon all night, tonight," he said. "And it's sure a dandy."

8

THE CABIN ON the point looked the same as when I had seen it last. The same windows were lighted, the same car stood in the open double garage, and the same wild, screaming bark burst on the night.

"What in heck's that?" the sheriff asked as the car slowed. "Sounds like a coyote."

"It's half a coyote," I said.

The leathery lad in front said over his shoulder, "You want to stop in front, Jim?"

"Drive her down a piece. Under them old pines."

The car stopped softly in black shadow at the roadside. The sheriff and I got out. "You stay here, Andy, and don't let nobody see you," the sheriff said. "I got my reasons."

We went back along the road and through the rustic gate. The barking started again. The front door opened. The sheriff went up on the steps and took his hat off.

"Mrs. Lacey? I'm Jim Barron, constable at Puma Point. This here is Mr. Evans, from Los Angeles. I guess you know him. Could we come in a minute?"

The woman looked at him with a face so completely shadowed that no expression showed on it. She turned her head a little and looked at me. She said, "Yes, come in," in a lifeless voice.

We went in. The woman shut the door behind us. A big gray-haired man sitting in an easy chair let go of the dog he was holding on the floor and straightened up. The dog tore across the room, did a flying tackle on the sheriff's stomach, turned in the air and was already running in circles when she hit the floor.

"Well, that's a right nice little dog," the sheriff said, tucking his shirt in.

The gray-haired man was smiling pleasantly. He said: "Good evening." His white, strong teeth gleamed with friendliness.

Mrs. Lacey was still wearing the scarlet double-breasted coat and the gray slacks. Her face looked older and more drawn. She looked at the floor and said: "This is Mr. Frank Luders from the Woodland Club. Mr. Bannon and" — she stopped and raised her eyes to look at a point over my left shoulder — "I didn't catch the other gentleman's name," she said.

"Evans," the sheriff said, and didn't look at me at all. "And mine is Barron, not Bannon." He nodded at Luders. I nodded at Luders. Luders smiled at both of us. He was big, meaty, powerful-looking, well kept and cheerful. He didn't have a care in the world. Big, breezy Frank Luders, everybody's pal.

He said: "I've known Fred Lacey for a long time. I just dropped by to say hello. He's not home, so I am waiting a little while until a friend comes by in a car to pick me up."

"Pleased to know you, Mr. Luders," the sheriff said. "I heard you had bought in at the club. Didn't have the pleasure of meeting you yet."

The woman sat down very slowly on the edge of a chair. I sat down. The little dog, Shiny, jumped in my lap, washed my right ear for me, squirmed down again and went under my chair. She lay there breathing out loud and thumping the floor with her feathery tail.

The room was still for a moment. Outside the windows on the lake side there was a very faint throbbing sound. The sheriff heard it. He cocked his head slightly, but nothing changed in his face.

He said: "Mr. Evans here come to me and told me a queer story. I guess it ain't no harm to mention it here, seeing Mr. Luders is a friend of the family."

He looked at Mrs. Lacey and waited. She lifted her eyes slowly, but not enough to meet his. She swallowed a couple of times and nodded her head. One of her hands began to slide slowly up and down the arm of her chair, back and forth, back and forth. Luders smiled.

"I'da liked to have Mr. Lacey here," the sheriff said. "You think he'll be in pretty soon?"

The woman nodded again. "I suppose so," she said in a drained voice. "He's been gone since midafternoon. I don't know where he is. I hardly think he would go down the hill without telling me, but he has had time to do that. Something might have come up."

"Seems like something did," the sheriff said. "Seems like Mr. Lacey wrote a letter to Mr. Evans, asking him to come up here quickly. Mr. Evans is a detective from L.A."

The woman moved restlessly. "A detective?" she breathed.

Luders said brightly: "Now why in the world would Fred do that?"

"On account of some money that was hid in a shoe," the sheriff said.

Luders raised his eyebrows and looked at Mrs. Lacey. Mrs. Lacey moved her lips together and then said very shortly: "But we got that back, Mr. Bannon. Fred was having a joke. He won a little money at the races and hid it in one of my shoes. He meant it for a surprise. I sent the shoe out to be repaired with the money still in it, but the money was still in it when we went over to the shoemaker's place."

"Barron is the name, not Bannon," the sheriff said. "So you got your money back all intact, Mrs. Lacey?"

"Why – of course. Of course, we thought at first, it being a hotel and one of the maids having taken the shoe – well, I don't know just what we thought, but it was a silly place to hide money – but we got it back, every cent of it."

"And it was the same money?" I said, beginning to get the idea and not liking it.

She didn't quite look at me. "Why, of course. Why not?"

"That ain't the way I heard it from Mr. Evans," the sheriff said peacefully, and folded his hands across his stomach.

"There was a slight difference, seems like, in the way you told it to Evans."

Luders leaned forward suddenly in his chair, but his smile stayed put. I didn't even get tight. The woman made a vague gesture and her hand kept moving on the chair arm. "I . . . told it . . . told what to Mr Evans?"

The sheriff turned his head very slowly and gave me a straight, hard stare. He turned his head back. One hand patted the other on his stomach.

"I understand Mr. Evans was over here earlier in the evening and you told him about it, Mrs. Lacey. About the money being changed?"

"Changed?" Her voice had a curiously hollow sound. "Mr. Evans told you he was here earlier in the evening? I . . . I never saw Mr. Evans before in my life."

I didn't even bother to look at her. Luders was my man. I looked at Luders. It got me what the nickel gets you from the slot machine. He chuckled and put a fresh match to his cigar.

The sheriff closed his eyes. His face had a sort of sad expression. The dog came out from under my chair and stood in the middle of the room looking at Luders. Then she went over in the corner and slid under the fringe of a daybed cover. A snuffling sound came from her a moment, then silence.

"Hum, hum, dummy," the sheriff said, talking to himself. "I ain't really equipped to handle this sort of a deal. I don't have the experience. We don't have no fast work like that up here. No crime at all in the mountains. Hardly." He made a wry face.

He opened his eyes. "How much money was that in the shoe, Mrs. Lacey?"

"Five hundred dollars." Her voice was hushed.

"Where at is this money, Mrs. Lacey?"

"I suppose Fred has it."

"I thought he was goin' to give it to you, Mrs. Lacey."

"He was," she said sharply. "He is. But I don't need it at the moment. Not up here. He'll probably give me a check later on."

"Would he have it in his pocket or would it be in the cabin here, Mrs. Lacey?"

She shook her head. "In his pocket, probably. I don't know. Do you want to search the cabin?"

The sheriff shrugged his fat shoulders. "Why, no, I guess not, Mrs. Lacey. It wouldn't do me no good if I found it. Especially if it wasn't changed."

Luders said: "Just how do you mean changed, Mr. Barron?"

"Changed for counterfeit money," the sheriff said.

Luders laughed quietly. "That's really amusing, don't you think? Counterfeit money at Puma Point? There's no opportunity for that sort of thing up here, is there?"

The sheriff nodded at him sadly. "Don't sound reasonable, does it?"

Luders said: "And your only source of information on the point is Mr. Evans here – who claims to be a detective? A private detective, no doubt?"

"I thought of that," the sheriff said.

Luders leaned forward a little more. "Have you any knowledge other than Mr. Evans' statement that Fred Lacey sent for him?"

"He'd have to know something to come up here, wouldn't he?" the sheriff said in a worried voice. "And he knew about that money in Mrs. Lacey's slipper."

"I was just asking a question," Luders said softly.

The sheriff swung around on me. I was already wearing my frozen smile. Since the incident in the hotel I hadn't looked for Lacey's letter. I knew I wouldn't have to look, now.

"You got a letter from Lacey?" he asked me in a hard voice.

I lifted my hand towards my inside breast pocket. Barron threw his right hand down and up. When it came up it held the Frontier Colt. "I'll take that gun of yours first," he said between his teeth. He stood up.

I pulled my coat open and held it open. He leaned down over me and jerked the automatic from the holster. He looked at it sourly a moment and dropped it into his left hip pocket. He sat down again. "*Now* look," he said easily.

Luders watched me with bland interest. Mrs. Lacey put her hands together and squeezed them hard and stared at the floor between her shoes.

I took the stuff out of my breast pocket. A couple of letters, some plain cards for casual notes, a packet of pipe cleaners, a spare handkerchief. Neither of the letters was the one. I put the stuff back and got a cigarette out and put it between my lips. I struck the match and held the flame to the tobacco. Nonchalant.

"You win," I said, smiling. "Both of you."

There was a slow flush on Barron's face and his eyes glittered. His lips twitched as he turned away from me.

"Why not," Luders asked gently, "see also if he really is a detective?"

Barron barely glanced at him. "The small things don't bother me," he said. "Right now I'm investigatin' a murder."

He didn't seem to be looking at either Luders or Mrs. Lacey. He seemed to be looking at a corner of the ceiling. Mrs. Lacey shook, and her hands tightened so that the knuckles gleamed hard and shiny and white in the lamplight. Her mouth opened very slowly, and her eyes turned up in her head. A dry sob half died in her throat.

Luders took the cigar out of his mouth and laid it carefully in the brass dip on the smoking stand beside him. He stopped smiling. His mouth was grim. He said nothing.

It was beautifully timed. Barron gave them all they needed for the reaction and not a second for a comeback. He said, in the same almost indifferent voice: "A man named Weber, cashier in the Indian Head Hotel. He was knifed in

Evans' room. Evans was there, but he was knocked out before it happened, so he is one of them boys we hear so much about and don't often meet – the boys that get there first."

"Not me," I said. "They bring their murders and drop them right at my feet."

The woman's head jerked. Then she looked up, and for the first time she looked straight at me. There was a queer light in her eyes, shining far back, remote and miserable.

Barron stood up slowly. "I don't get it," he said. "I don't get it at all. But I guess I ain't making any mistake in takin' this feller in." He turned to me. "Don't run too fast, not at first, bud. I always give a man forty yards."

I didn't say anything. Nobody said anything.

Barron said slowly: "I'll have to ask you to wait here till I come back, Mr. Luders. If your friend comes for you, you could let him go on. I'd be glad to drive you back to the club later."

Luders nodded. Barron looked at a clock on the mantel. It was a quarter to twelve. "Kinda late for a old fuddy-duddy like me. You think Mr. Lacey will be home pretty soon, ma'am?"

"I . . . I hope so," she said, and made a gesture that meant nothing unless it meant hopelessness.

Barron moved over to open the door. He jerked his chin at me. I went out on the porch. The little dog came halfway out from under the couch and made a whining sound. Barron looked down at her.

"That sure is a nice little dog," he said. "I heard she was half coyote. What did you say the other half was?"

"We don't know," Mrs. Lacey murmured.

"Kind of like this case I'm working on," Barron said, and came out on to the porch after me.

9

WE WALKED DOWN the road without speaking and came to the car. Andy was leaning back in the corner, a dead half cigarette between his lips.

We got into the car. "Drive down a piece, about two hundred yards," Barron said. "Make plenty of noise."

Andy started the car, raced the motor, clashed the gears, and the car slid down through the moonlight and around a curve of the road and up a moonlit hill sparred with the shadows of tree trunks.

"Turn her at the top and coast back, but not close," Barron said. "Stay out of sight of that cabin. Turn your lights off before you turn."

"Yup," Andy said.

He turned the car just short of the top, going around a tree to do it. He cut the lights off and started back down the little hill, then killed the motor. Just beyond the bottom of the slope there was a heavy clump of manzanita, almost as tall as ironwood. The car stopped there. Andy pulled the brake back very slowly to smooth out the noise of the ratchet.

Barron leaned forward over the back seat. "We're goin' across the road and get near the water," he said. "I don't want no noise and nobody walkin' in no moonlight."

Andy said: "Yup."

We got out. We walked carefully on the dirt of the road, then on the pine needles. We filtered through the trees, behind fallen logs, until the water was down below where we stood. Barron sat down on the ground and then lay down. Andy and I did the same. Barron put his face close to Andy.

"Hear anything?"

Andy said: "Eight cylinders, kinda rough."

I listened. I could tell myself I heard it, but I couldn't be sure. Barron nodded in the dark. "Watch the lights in the cabin," he whispered.

We watched. Five minutes passed, or enough time to seem like five minutes. The lights in the cabin didn't change. Then there was a remote, half-imagined sound of a door closing. There were shoes on wooden steps.

"Smart. They left the light on," Barron said in Andy's ear.

We waited another short minute. The idling motor burst into a roar of throbbing sound, a stuttering, confused racket, with a sort of hop, skip and jump in it. The sound sank to a heavy purring roar and then quickly began to fade. A dark shape slid out on the moonlit water, curved with a beautiful line of froth and swept past the point out of sight.

Barron got a plug of tobacco out and bit. He chewed comfortably and spat four feet beyond his feet. Then he got up on his feet and dusted off the pine needles. Andy and I got up.

"Man ain't got good sense chewin' tobacco these days," he said. "Things ain't fixed for him. I near went to sleep back there in the cabin." He lifted the Colt he was still holding in his left hand, changed hands and packed the gun away on his hip.

"Well?" he said, looking at Andy.

"Ted Rooney's boat," Andy said. "She's got two sticky valves and a big crack in the muffler. You hear it best when you throttle her up, like they did just before they started."

It was a lot of words for Andy, but the sheriff liked them.

"Couldn't be wrong, Andy? Lots of boats get sticky valves."

Andy said: "What the hell you ask me for?" in a nasty voice.

"Okay, Andy, don't get sore."

Andy grunted. We crossed the road and got into the car again. Andy started it up, backed and turned and said: "Lights?"

Barron nodded. Andy put the lights on. "Where to now?"

"Ted Rooney's place," Barron said peacefully. "And make it fast. We got ten miles to there."

"Can't make it in less'n twenty minutes," Andy said sourly. "Got to go through the Point."

The car hit the paved lake road and started back past the dark boys' camp and the other camps, and turned left on the highway. Barron didn't speak until we were beyond the village and the road out to Speaker Point. The dance band was still going strong in the pavilion.

"I fool you any?" he asked me then.

"Enough."

"Did I do something wrong?"

"The job was perfect," I said, "but I don't suppose you fooled Luders."

"That lady was mighty uncomfortable," Barron said. "That Luders is a good man. Hard, quiet, full of eyesight. But I fooled him some. He made mistakes."

"I can think of a couple," I said. "One was being there at all. Another was telling us a friend was coming to pick him up, to explain why he had no car. It didn't need explaining. There was a car in the garage, but you didn't know whose car it was. Another was keeping that boat idling."

"That wasn't no mistake," Andy said from the front seat. "Not if you ever tried to start her up cold."

Barron said: "You don't leave your car in the garage when you come callin' up here. Ain't no moisture to hurt it. The boat could have been anybody's boat. A couple of young folks could have been in it getting acquainted. I ain't got anything on him, anyways, so far as he knows. He just worked too hard tryin' to head me off."

He spit out of the car. I heard it smack the rear fender like a wet rag. The car swept through the moonlit night, around curves, up and down hills, through fairly thick pines and along open flats where cattle lay.

I said: "He knew I didn't have the letter Lacey wrote me. Because he took it away from me himself, up in my room at the hotel. It was Luders that knocked me out and knifed

Weber. Luders knows that Lacey is dead, even if he didn't kill him. That's what he's got on Mrs. Lacey. She thinks her husband is alive and that Luders has him."

"You make this Luders out a pretty bad guy," Barron said calmly. "Why would Luders knife Weber?"

"Because Weber started all the trouble. This is an organization. Its object is to unload some very good counterfeit ten-dollar bills, a great many of them. You don't advance the cause by unloading them in five-hundred-dollar lots, all brand-new, in circumstances that would make anybody suspicious, would make a much less careful man than Fred Lacey suspicious."

"You're doing some nice guessin', son," the sheriff said, grabbing the door handle as we took a fast turn, "but the neighbors ain't watchin' you. I got to be more careful. I'm in my own back yard. Puma Lake don't strike me as a very good place to go into the counterfeit money business."

"Okay," I said.

"On the other hand, if Luders is the man I want, he might be kind of hard to catch. There's three roads out of the valley, and there's half a dozen planes down to the east end of the Woodland Club golf course. Always is in summer."

"You don't seem to be doing very much worrying about it," I said.

"A mountain sheriff don't have to worry a lot," Barron said calmly. "Nobody expects him to have any brains. Especially guys like Mr. Luders don't."

10

THE BOAT LAY in the water at the end of a short painter, moving as boats move even in the stillest water. A canvas tarpaulin covered most of it and was tied down here and there, but not everywhere it should have been tied. Behind the short rickety pier a road twisted back through juniper trees to the highway. There was a camp off to one side, with a miniature white lighthouse for its trademark. A sound of dance music came from one of the cabins, but most of the camp had gone to bed.

We came down there walking, leaving the car on the shoulder of the highway. Barron had a big flash in his hand and kept throwing it this way and that, snapping it on and off. When we came to the edge of the water and the end of the road to the pier, he put his flashlight on the road and studied it carefully. There were fresh-looking tire tracks.

"What do you think?" he asked me.

"Looks like tire tracks," I said.

"What do you think, Andy?" Barron said. "This man is cute, but he don't give me no ideas."

Andy bent over and studied the tracks. "New tires and big ones," he said, and walked towards the pier. He stooped down again and pointed. The sheriff threw the light where he pointed. "Yup, turned around here," Andy said. "So what? The place is full of new cars right now. Come October and they'd mean something. Folks that live up here buy one tire at a time, and cheap ones, at that. These here are heavy-duty all-weather treads."

"Might see about the boat," the sheriff said.

"What about it?"

"Might see if it was used recent," Barron said.

"Hell," Andy said, "we know it was used recent, don't we?"

"Always supposin' you guessed right," Barron said mildly.

Andy looked at him in silence for a moment. Then he spit on the ground and started back to where we had left the car. When he had gone a dozen feet he said over his shoulder: "I wasn't guessin'." He turned his head again and went on, plowing through the trees.

"Kind of touchy," Barron said. "But a good man." He went down on the boat landing and bent over it, passing his hand along the forward part of the side, below the tarpaulin. He came back slowly and nodded. "Andy's right. Always is, durn him. What kind of tires would you say those marks were, Mr. Evans? They tell you anything?"

"Cadillac V-12," I said. "A club coupe with red leather seats and two suitcases in the back. The clock on the dash is twelve and one-half minutes slow."

He stood there, thinking about it. Then he nodded his big head. He sighed. "Well, I hope it makes money for you," he said, and turned away.

We went back to the car. Andy was in the front seat behind the wheel again. He had a cigarette going. He looked straight ahead of him through the dusty windshield.

"Where's Rooney live now?" Barron asked.

"Where he always lived," Andy said.

"Why, that's just a piece up the Bascomb road."

"I ain't said different," Andy growled.

"Let's go there," the sheriff said, getting in. I got in beside him.

Andy turned the car and went back half a mile and then started to turn. The sheriff snapped to him: "Hold it a minute."

He got out and used his flash on the road surface. He got back into the car. "I think we got something. Them tracks down by the pier don't mean a lot. But the same tracks up here might turn out to mean more. If they go on in to Bascomb, they're goin' to mean plenty. Them old gold camps over there is made to order for monkey business."

The car went into the side road and climbed slowly into a gap. Big boulders crowded the road, and the hillside was studded with them. They glistened pure white in the moonlight. The car growled on for half a mile and then Andy stopped again.

"Okay, Hawkshaw, this is the cabin," he said. Barron got out again and walked around with his flash. There was no light in the cabin. He came back to the car.

"They come by here," he said. "Bringing Ted home. When they left they turned towards Bascomb. You figure Ted Rooney would be mixed up in something crooked, Andy?"

"Not unless they paid him for it," Andy said.

I got out of the car and Barron and I went up towards the cabin. It was small, rough, covered with native pine. It had a wooden porch, a tin chimney guyed with wires, and a sagging privy behind the cabin at the edge of the trees. It was dark. We walked up on the porch and Barron hammered on the door. Nothing happened. He tried the knob. The door was locked. We went down off the porch and around the back, looking at the windows. They were all shut. Barron tried the back door, which was level with the ground. That was locked, too. He pounded. The echoes of the sound wandered off through the trees and echoed high up on the rise among the boulders.

"He's gone with them," Barron said. "I guess they wouldn't dast leave him now. Prob'ly stopped here just to let him get his stuff – some of it. Yep."

I said: "I don't think so. All they wanted of Rooney was his boat. That boat picked up Fred Lacey's body out at the end of Speaker Point early this evening. The body was probably weighted and dropped out in the lake. They waited for dark to do that. Rooney was in on it, and he got paid. Tonight they wanted the boat again. But they got to thinking they didn't need Rooney along. And if they're over in Bascomb Valley in some quiet little place, making or storing counterfeit money, they wouldn't at all want Rooney to go over there with them."

"You're guessing again, son," the sheriff said kindly. "Anyways, I don't have no search warrant. But I can look over Rooney's dollhouse a minute. Wait for me."

He walked away towards the privy. I took six feet and hit the door of the cabin. It shivered and split diagonally across the upper panel. Behind me, the sheriff called out, "Hey," weakly, as if he didn't mean it.

I took another six feet and hit the door again. I went in with it and landed on my hands and knees on a piece of linoleum that smelled like a fish skillet. I got up to my feet and reached up and turned the key switch of a hanging bulb. Barron was right behind me, making clucking noises of disapproval.

There was a kitchen with a wood stove, some dirty wooden shelves with dishes on them. The stove gave out a faint warmth. Unwashed pots sat on top of it and smelled. I went across the kitchen and into the front room. I turned on another hanging bulb. There was a narrow bed to one side, made up roughly, with a slimy quilt on it. There was a wooden table, some wooden chairs, an old cabinet radio, hooks on the wall, an ashtray with four burned pipes in it, a pile of pulp magazines in the corner on the floor.

The ceiling was low to keep the heat in. In the corner there was a trap to get up to the attic. The trap was open and a stepladder stood under the opening. An old water-stained canvas suitcase lay open on a wooden box, and there were odds and ends of clothing in it.

Barron went over and looked at the suitcase. "Looks like Rooney was getting ready to move out or go for a trip. Then these boys come along and picked him up. He ain't finished his packing, but he got his suit in. A man like Rooney don't have but one suit and don't wear that 'less he goes down the hill."

"He's not here," I said. "He ate dinner here, though. The stove is still warm."

The sheriff cast a speculative eye at the stepladder. He went over and climbed up it and pushed the trap up with his head. He raised his torch and shone it around overhead. He let the trap close and came down the stepladder again.

"Likely he kept the suitcase up there," he said. "I see there's a old steamer trunk up there, too. You ready to leave?"

"I didn't see a car around," I said. "He must have had a car."

"Yep. Had a old Plymouth. Douse the light."

He walked back into the kitchen and looked around that and then we put both the lights out and went out of the house. I shut what was left of the back door. Barron was examining tire tracks in the soft decomposed granite, trailing them back over to a space under a big oak tree where a couple of large darkened areas showed where a car had stood many times and dripped oil.

He came back swinging his flash, then looked towards the privy and said: "You could go on back to Andy. I still gotta look over that dollhouse."

I didn't say anything. I watched him go along the path to the privy and unlatch the door, and open it. I saw his flash go inside and the light leaked out of a dozen cracks and from the ramshackle roof. I walked back along the side of the cabin and got into the car. The sheriff was gone a long time. He came back slowly, stopped beside the car and bit off another chew from his plug. He rolled it around in his mouth and then got to work on it.

"Rooney," he said, "is in the privy. Shot twice in the head." He got into the car. "Shot with a big gun, and shot very dead. Judgin' from the circumstances I would say somebody was in a hell of a hurry."

11

THE ROAD CLIMBED steeply for a while following the meanderings of a dried mountain stream the bed of which was full of boulders. Then it leveled off about a thousand or fifteen hundred feet above the level of the lake. We crossed a cattle stop of spaced narrow rails that clanked under the car wheels. The road began to go down. A wide undulating flat appeared with a few browsing cattle in it. A lightless farmhouse showed up against the moonlit sky. We reached a wider road that ran at right angles. Andy stopped the car and Barron got out with his big flashlight again and ran the spot slowly over the road surface.

"Turned left," he said, straightening. "Thanks be there ain't been another car past since them tracks were made." He got back into the car.

"Left don't go to no old mines," Andy said. "Left goes to Worden's place and then back down to the lake at the dam."

Barron sat silent a moment and then got out of the car and used his flash again. He made a surprised sound over to the right of the T intersection. He came back again, snapping the light off.

"Goes right, too," he said. "But goes left first. They doubled back, but they been somewhere off west of here before they done it. We go like they went."

Andy said: "You sure they went left first and not last? Left would be a way out to the highway."

"Yep. Right marks overlays left marks," Barron said.

We turned left. The knolls that dotted the valley were covered with ironwood trees, some of them half dead. Ironwood grows to about eighteen or twenty feet high and then dies. When it dies the limbs strip themselves and get a gray-white color and shine in the moonlight.

We went about a mile and then a narrow road shot off towards the north, a mere track. Andy stopped. Barron got out again and used his flash. He jerked his thumb and Andy swung the car. The sheriff got in.

"Them boys ain't too careful," he said. "Nope. I'd say they ain't careful at all. But they never figured Andy could tell where that boat come from, just by listenin' to it."

The road went into a fold of the mountains and the growth got so close to it that the car barely passed without scratching. Then it doubled back at a sharp angle and rose again and went around a spur of hill and a small cabin showed up, pressed back against a slope with trees on all sides of it.

And suddenly, from the house or very close to it, came a long, shrieking yell which ended in a snapping bark. The bark was choked off suddenly.

Barron started to say: "Kill them – " but Andy had already cut the lights and pulled off the road. "Too late, I guess," he said dryly. "Must've seen us, if anybody's watchin'."

Barron got out of the car. "That sounded mighty like a coyote, Andy."

"Yup."

"Awful close to the house for a coyote, don't you think, Andy?"

"Nope," Andy said. "Light's out, a coyote would come right up to the cabin lookin' for buried garbage."

"And then again it could be that little dog," Barron said.

"Or a hen laying a square egg," I said. "What are we waiting for? And how about giving me back my gun? And are we trying to catch up with anybody, or do we just like to get things all figured out as we go along?"

The sheriff took my gun off his left hip and handed it to me. "I ain't in no hurry," he said. "Because Luders ain't in no hurry. He coulda been long gone, if he was. They was in a hurry to get Rooney, because Rooney knew something about them. But Rooney don't know nothing about them now because he's dead and his house locked up and his car driven away. If you hadn't bust in his back door, he could be there in his privy a couple of weeks before anybody would get curious. Them tire tracks looks kind of obvious, but that's only because we know where they started. They don't have any reason to think we could find that out. So where would we start? No, I ain't in any hurry."

Andy stooped over and came up with a deer rifle. He opened the left-hand door and got out of the car.

"The little dog's in there," Barron said peacefully. "That means Mrs. Lacey is in there, too. And there would be somebody to watch her. Yep, I guess we better go up and look, Andy."

"I hope you're scared," Andy said. "I am."

We started through the trees. It was about two hundred yards to the cabin. The night was very still. Even at that distance I heard a window open. We walked about fifty feet apart. Andy stayed back long enough to lock the car. Then he started to make a wide circle, far out to the right.

Nothing moved in the cabin as we got close to it, no light showed. The coyote or Shiny, the dog, whichever it was, didn't bark again.

We got very close to the house, not more than twenty yards. Barron and I were about the same distance apart. It was a small rough cabin, built like Rooney's place, but larger. There was an open garage at the back, but it was empty. The cabin had a small porch of fieldstone.

Then there was the sound of a short, sharp struggle in the cabin and the beginning of a bark, suddenly choked off. Barron fell down flat on the ground. I did the same. Nothing happened.

Barron stood up slowly and began to move forward a step at a time and a pause between each step. I stayed out. Barron reached the cleared space in front of the house and started to go up the steps to the porch. He stood there, bulky, clearly outlined in the moonlight, the Colt hanging at his side. It looked like a swell way to commit suicide.

Nothing happened. Barron reached the top of the steps, moved over tight against the wall. There was a window to his left, the door to his right. He changed his gun in his hand and reached out to bang on the door with the butt, then swiftly reversed it again, and flattened to the wall.

The dog screamed inside the house. A hand holding a gun came out at the bottom of the opened window and turned.

It was a tough shot at the range. I had to make it. I shot. The bark of the automatic was drowned in the duller boom of a rifle. The hand drooped and the gun dropped to the porch. The hand came out a little farther and the fingers twitched, then began to scratch at the sill. Then they went back in through the window and the dog howled. Barron was at the door, jerking at it. And Andy and I were running hard for the cabin, from different angles.

Barron got the door open and light framed him suddenly as someone inside lit a lamp and turned it up.

I made the porch as Barron went in, Andy close behind me. We went into the living-room of the cabin.

Mrs. Fred Lacey stood in the middle of the floor beside a table with a lamp on it, holding the little dog in her arms. A thick-set, blondish man lay on his side under the window, breathing heavily, his hand groping around aimlessly for the gun that had fallen outside the window.

Mrs. Lacey opened her arms and let the dog down. It leaped and hit the sheriff in the stomach with its small, sharp nose and pushed inside his coat at his shirt. Then it dropped to the floor again and ran around in circles, silently, weaving its hind end with delight.

Mrs. Lacey stood frozen, her face as empty as death. The man on the floor groaned a little in the middle of his heavy breathing. His eyes opened and shut rapidly. His lips moved and bubbled pink froth.

"That sure is a nice little dog, Mrs. Lacey," Barron said, tucking his shirt in. "But it don't seem a right handy time to have him around – not for some people."

He looked at the blond man on the floor. The blond man's eyes opened and became fixed on nothing.

"I lied to you," Mrs. Lacey said quickly. "I had to. My husband's life depended on it. Luders has him. He has him somewhere over here. I don't know where, but it isn't far off, he said. He went to bring him back to me, but he left this man to guard me. I couldn't do anything about it, sheriff. I'm – I'm sorry."

"I knew you lied, Mrs. Lacey," Barron said quietly. He looked down at his Colt and put it back on his hip. "I knew why. But your husband is dead, Mrs. Lacey. He was dead long ago. Mr. Evans here saw him. It's hard to take, ma'am, but you better know it now."

She didn't move or seem to breathe. Then she went very slowly to a chair and sat down and leaned her face in her hands. She sat there without motion, without sound. The little dog whined and crept under her chair.

The man on the floor started to raise the upper part of his body. He raised it very slowly, stiffly. His eyes were blank. Barron moved over to him and bent down.

"You hit bad, son?"

The man pressed his left hand against his chest. Blood oozed between his fingers. He lifted his right hand slowly, until the arm was rigid and pointing to the corner of the ceiling. His lips quivered, stiffened, spoke.

"Heil Hitler!" he said thickly.

He fell back and lay motionless. His throat rattled a little and then that, too, was still, and everything in the room was still, even the dog.

"This man must be one of them Nazis," the sheriff said. "You hear what he said?"

"Yeah," I said.

I turned and walked out of the house, down the steps and down through the trees again to the car. I sat on the running board and lit a cigarette, and sat there smoking and thinking hard.

After a little while they all came down through the trees. Barron was carrying the dog. Andy was carrying his rifle in his left hand. His leathery young face looked shocked.

Mrs. Lacey got into the car and Barron handed the dog in to her. He looked at me and said: "It's against the law to smoke out here, son, more than fifty feet from a cabin."

I dropped the cigarette and ground it hard into the powdery gray soil. I got into the car, in front beside Andy.

The car started again and we went back to what they probably called the main road over there. Nobody said anything for a long time, then Mrs. Lacey said in a low voice: "Luders mentioned a name that sounded like Sloat. He said it to the man you shot. They called him Kurt. They spoke German. I understand a little German, but they talked too fast. Sloat didn't sound like German. Does it mean anything to you?"

"It's the name of an old gold mine not far from here," Barron said. "Sloat's Mine. You know where it is, don't you, Andy?"

"Yup. I guess I killed that feller, didn't I?"

"I guess you did, Andy."

"I never killed nobody before," Andy said.

"Maybe I got him," I said. "I fired at him."

"Nope," Andy said. "You wasn't high enough to get him in the chest. I was."

Barron said: "How many brought you to that cabin, Mrs. Lacey? I hate to be asking you questions at a time like this, ma'am, but I just got to."

The dead voice said: "Two. Luders and the man you killed. He ran the boat."

"Did they stop anywhere – on this side of the lake, ma'am?"

"Yes. They stopped at a small cabin near the lake. Luders was driving. The other man, Kurt, got out, and we drove on. After a while Luders stopped and Kurt came up with us in an old car. He drove the car into a gully behind some willows and then came on with us."

"That's all we need," Barron said. "If we get Luders, the job's all done. Except I can't figure what it's all about."

I didn't say anything. We drove on to where the T intersection was and the road went back to the lake. We kept on across this for about four miles.

"Better stop here, Andy. We'll go the rest of the way on foot. You stay here."

"Nope. I ain't going to," Andy said.

"You stay here," Barron said in a voice suddenly harsh. "You got a lady to look after and you done your killin' for tonight. All I ask is you keep that little dog quiet."

The car stopped. Barron and I got out. The little dog whined and then was still. We went off the road and started across country through a grove of young pines and manzanita and ironwood. We walked silently, without speaking. The noise our shoes made couldn't have been heard thirty feet away except by an Indian.

12

WE REACHED THE far edge of the thicket in a few minutes. Beyond that the ground was level and open. There was a spidery something against the sky, a few low piles of waste dirt, a set of sluice boxes built one on top of the other like a miniature cooling tower, an endless belt going towards it from a cut. Barron put his mouth against my ear.

"Ain't been worked for a couple of years," he said. "Ain't worth it. Day's hard work for two men might get you a pennyweight of gold. This country was worked to death sixty years ago. That low hut over yonder's a old refrigerator car. She's thick and damn near bullet-proof. I don't see no car, but maybe it's behind. Or hidden. Most like hidden. You ready to go?"

I nodded. We started across the open space. The moon was almost as bright as daylight. I felt swell, like a clay pipe in a shooting gallery. Barron seemed quite at ease. He held the big Colt down at his side, with his thumb over the hammer.

Suddenly light showed in the side of the refrigerator car and we went down on the ground. The light came from a partly opened door, a yellow panel and a yellow spearhead on the ground. There was a movement in the moonlight and the noise of water striking the ground. We waited a little, then got up again and went on.

There wasn't much use playing Indian. They would come out of the door or they wouldn't. If they did, they would see us, walking, crawling or lying. The ground was that bare and the moon was that bright. Our shoes scuffed a little, but this was hard dirt, much walked on and tight packed. We reached a pile of sand and stopped beside it. I listened to myself breathing. I wasn't panting, and Barron wasn't panting either. But I took a lot of interest in my breathing. It was something

I had taken for granted for a long time, but right now I was interested in it. I hoped it would go on for a long time, but I wasn't sure.

I wasn't scared. I was a full-sized man and I had a gun in my hand. But the blond man back in the other cabin had been a full-sized man with a gun in his hand, too. And he had a wall to hide behind. I wasn't scared though. I was just thoughtful about little things. I thought Barron was breathing too loud, but I thought I would make more noise telling him he was breathing too loud than he was making breathing. That's the way I was, very thoughtful about the little things.

Then the door opened again. This time there was no light behind it. A small man, very small, came out of the doorway carrying what looked like a heavy suitcase. He carried it along the side of the car, grunting hard. Barron held my arm in a vise. His breath hissed faintly.

The small man with the heavy suitcase, or whatever it was, reached the end of the car and went around the corner. Then I thought that although the pile of sand didn't look very high it was probably high enough so that we didn't show above it. And if the small man wasn't expecting visitors, he might not see us. We waited for him to come back. We waited too long.

A clear voice behind us said: "I am holding a machine gun, Mr. Barron. Put your hands up, please. If you move to do anything else, I fire."

I put my hands up fast. Barron hesitated a little longer. Then he put his hands up. We turned slowly. Frank Luders stood about four feet away from us, with a tommy gun held waist-high. Its muzzle looked as big as the Second Street tunnel in L.A.

Luders said quietly: "I prefer that you face the other way. When Charlie comes back from the car, he will light the lamps inside. Then we shall all go in."

We faced the long, low car again. Luders whistled sharply. The small man came back around the corner of the car, stopped a moment, then went towards the door. Luders called out: "Light the lamps, Charlie. We have visitors."

The small man went quietly into the cabin and a match scratched and there was light inside.

"Now, gentlemen, you may walk," Luders said. "Observing, of course, that death walks close behind you and conducting yourselves accordingly."

We walked.

13

"TAKE THEIR GUNS and see if they have any more of them, Charlie."

We stood backed against a wall near a long wooden table. There were wooden benches on either side of the table. On it was a tray with a bottle of whiskey and a couple of glasses, a hurricane lamp and an old-fashioned farmhouse oil lamp of thick glass, both lit, a saucer full of matches and another full of ashes and stubs. In the end of the cabin, away from the table, there was a small stove and two cots, one tumbled, one made up as neat as a pin.

The little Japanese came towards us with the light shining on his glasses.

"Oh having guns," he purred. "Oh too bad."

He took the guns and pushed them backwards across the table to Luders. His small hands felt us over deftly. Barron winced and his face reddened, but he said nothing. Charlie said: "No more guns. Pleased to see, gentlemen. Very nice night, I think so. You having picnic in moonlight?"

Barron made an angry sound in his throat. Luders said: "Sit down, please, gentlemen, and tell me what I can do for you."

We sat down. Luders sat down opposite. The two guns were on the table in front of him and the tommy gun rested on it, his left hand holding it steady, his eyes quiet and hard.

His was no longer a pleasant face, but it was still an intelligent face. Intelligent as they ever are.

Barron said: "Guess I'll chew. I think better that way." He got his plug out and bit into it and put it away. He chewed silently and then spit on the floor.

"Guess I might mess up your floor some," he said. "Hope you don't mind."

The Jap was sitting on the end of the neat bed, his shoes not touching the floor. "Not liking much," he said hissingly, "very bad smell."

Barron didn't look at him. He said quietly: "You aim to shoot us and make your getaway, Mr. Luders?"

Luders shrugged and took his hand off the machine gun and leaned back against the wall.

Barron said: "You left a pretty broad trail here except for one thing. How we would know where to pick it up. You didn't figure that out because you wouldn't have acted the way you did. But you was all staked out for us when we got here. I don't follow that."

Luders said: "That is because we Germans are fatalists. When things go very easily, as they did tonight – except for that fool, Weber – we become suspicious. I said to myself, 'I have left no trail, no way they could follow me across the lake quickly enough. They had no boat, and no boat followed me. It would be impossible for them to find me. Quite impossible.' So I said, 'They will find me just because to me it appears impossible. Therefore, I shall be waiting for them.'"

"While Charlie toted the suitcases full of money out to the car," I said.

"What money?" Luders asked, and didn't seem to look at either of us. He seemed to be looking inward, searching.

I said: "Those very fine new ten-dollar bills you have been bringing in from Mexico by plane."

Luders looked at me then, but indifferently. "My dear friend, you could not possibly be serious?" he suggested.

"Phooey. Easiest thing in the world. The border patrol has no planes now. They had a few coast-guard planes a while back, but nothing came over, so they were taken off. A plane flying high over the border from Mexico lands on the field down by the Woodland Club golf course. It's Mr. Luders' plane and Mr. Luders owns an interest in the club and lives there. Why should anybody get curious about that? But Mr. Luders doesn't want half a million dollars' worth of queer money in his cabin at the club, so he finds himself an old mine over here and keeps the money in this refrigerator car. It's almost as strong as a safe and it doesn't look like a safe."

"You interest me," Luders said calmly. "Continue."

I said: "The money is very good stuff. We've had a report on it. That means organization – to get the inks and the right paper and the plates. It means an organization much more complete than any gang of crooks could manage. A government organization. The organization of the Nazi government."

The little Jap jumped up off the bed and hissed, but Luders didn't change expression. "I'm still interested," he said laconically.

"I ain't," Barron said. "Sounds to me like you're tryin' to talk yourself into a vestful of lead."

I went on: "A few years ago the Russians tried the same stunt. Planting a lot of queer money over here to raise funds for espionage work and, incidentally, they hoped, to damage our currency. The Nazis are too smart to gamble on that angle. All they want is good American dollars to work with in Central and South America. Nice mixed-up money that's been used. You can't go into a bank and deposit a hundred thousand dollars in brand-new ten-dollar bills. What's bothering the sheriff is why you picked this particular place, a mountain resort full of rather poor people."

"But that does not bother you with your superior brain, does it?" Luders sneered.

"It don't bother me a whole lot either," Barron said. "What bothers me is folks getting killed in my territory. I ain't used to it."

I said: "You picked the place primarily because it's a swell place to bring the money into. It's probably one of hundreds all over the country, places where there is very little law enforcement to dodge but places where in the summertime a lot of strange people come and go all the time. And places where planes set down and nobody checks them in or out. But that isn't the only reason. It's also a swell place to unload some of the money, quite a lot of it, if you're lucky. But you weren't lucky. Your man Weber pulled a dumb trick and made you unlucky. Should I tell you just why it's a good place to spread queer money if you have enough people working for you?"

"Please do," Luders said, and patted the side of the machine gun.

"Because for three months in the year this district has a floating population of anywhere from twenty to fifty thousand people, depending on the holidays and weekends. That means a lot of money brought in and a lot of business done. And there's no bank here. The result of that is that the hotels and bars and merchants have to cash checks all the time. The result of that is that the deposits they send out during the season are almost all checks and the money stays in circulation. Until the end of the season, of course."

"I think that is very interesting," Luders said. "But if this operation were under my control, I would not think of passing very much money up here. I would pass a little here and there, but not much. I would test the money out, to see how well it was accepted. And for a reason that you have thought of. Because most of it would change hands rapidly and, if it was discovered to be queer money, as you say, it would be very difficult to trace the source of it."

"Yeah," I said. "That would be smarter. You're nice and frank about it."

"To you," Luders said, "it naturally does not matter how frank I am."

Barron leaned forward suddenly. "Look here, Luders, killin' us ain't going to help you any. If you come right down to it, we don't have a thing on you. Likely you killed this man Weber, but the way things are up here, it's going to be mighty hard to prove it. If you been spreading bad money, they'll get you for it, sure, but that ain't a hangin' matter. Now I've got a couple pair handcuffs in my belt, so happens, and my proposition is you walk out of here with them on, you and your Japanese pal."

Charlie the Jap said: "Ha, ha. Very funny man. Some boob I guess yes."

Luders smiled faintly. "You put all the stuff in the car, Charlie?"

"One more suitcase coming right up," Charlie said.

"Better take it on out, and start the engine, Charlie."

"Listen, it won't work, Luders," Barron said urgently. "I got a man back in the woods with a deer rifle. It's bright moonlight. You got a fair weapon there, but you got no more chance against a deer rifle than Evans and me got against you. You'll never get out of here unless we go with you. He seen us come in here and how we come. He'll give us twenty minutes. Then he'll send for some boys to dynamite you out. Them were my orders."

Luders said quietly: "This work is very difficult. Even we Germans find it difficult. I am tired. I made a bad mistake. I used a man who was a fool, who did a foolish thing, and then he killed a man because he had done it and the man knew he had done it. But it was my mistake also. I shall not be forgiven. My life is no longer of great importance. Take the suitcase to the car, Charlie."

Charlie moved swiftly towards him. "Not liking, no," he said sharply. "That damn heavy suitcase. Man with rifle shooting. To hell."

Luders smiled slowly. "That's all a lot of nonsense, Charlie. If they had men with them, they would have been here long ago. That is why I let these men talk. To see if they were alone. They are alone. Go, Charlie."

Charlie said hissingly: "I going, but I still not liking."

He went over to the corner and hefted the suitcase that stood there. He could hardly carry it. He moved slowly to the door and put the suitcase down and sighed. He opened the door a crack and looked out. "Not see anybody," he said. "Maybe all lies, too."

Luders said musingly: "I should have killed the dog and the woman too. I was weak. The man Kurt, what of him?"

"Never heard of him," I said. "Where was he?"

Luders stared at me. "Get up on your feet, both of you."

I got up. An icicle was crawling around on my back. Barron got up. His face was gray. The whitening hair at the side of his head glistened with sweat. There was sweat all over his face, but his jaws went on chewing.

He said softly: "How much you get for this job, son?"

I said thickly: "A hundred bucks but I spent some of it."

Barron said in the same soft tone: "I been married forty years. They pay me eighty dollars a month, house and firewood. It ain't enough. By gum, I ought to get a hundred." He grinned wryly and spit and looked at Luders. "To hell with you, you Nazi bastard," he said.

Luders lifted the machine gun slowly and his lips drew back over his teeth. His breath made a hissing noise. Then very slowly he laid the gun down and reached inside his coat. He took out a Luger and moved the safety catch with his thumb. He shifted the gun to his left hand and stood looking at us quietly. Very slowly his face drained of all expression and became a dead gray mask. He lifted the gun, and at the same time he lifted his right arm stiffly above shoulder height. The arm was as rigid as a rod.

"Heil Hitler!" he said sharply.

He turned the gun quickly, put the muzzle in his mouth and fired.

14

THE JAP SCREAMED and streaked out of the door. Barron and I lunged hard across the table. We got our guns. Blood fell on the back of my hand and then Luders crumpled slowly against the wall.

Barron was already out of the door. When I got out behind him, I saw that the little Jap was running hard down the hill towards a clump of brush.

Barron steadied himself, brought the Colt up, then lowered it again.

"He ain't far enough," he said. "I always give a man forty yards."

He raised the big Colt again and turned his body a little and, as the gun reached firing position, it moved very slowly and Barron's head went down a little until his arm and shoulder and right eye were all in a line.

He stayed like that, perfectly rigid for a long moment, then the gun roared and jumped back in his hand and a lean thread of smoke showed faint in the moonlight and disappeared.

The Jap kept on running. Barron lowered his Colt and watched him plunge into a clump of brush.

"Hell," he said. "I missed him." He looked at me quickly and looked away again. "But he won't get nowhere. Ain't got nothing to get with. Them little legs of his ain't hardly long enough to jump him over a pine cone."

"He had a gun," I said. "Under his left arm."

Barron shook his head. "Nope. I noticed the holster was empty. I figure Luders got it away from him. I figure Luders meant to shoot him before he left."

Car lights showed in the distance, coming dustily along the road.

"What made Luders go soft?"

"I figure his pride was hurt," Barron said thoughtfully. "A big organizer like him gettin' hisself all balled to hell by a couple of little fellows like us."

We went around the end of the refrigerator car. A big new coupe was parked there. Barron marched over to it and opened the door. The car on the road was near now. It turned off and its headlights raked the big coupe. Barron stared into the car for a moment, then slammed the door viciously and spit on the ground.

"Caddy V-12," he said. "Red leather cushions and suitcases in the back." He reached in again and snapped on the dash-light. "What time is it?"

"Twelve minutes to two," I said.

"This clock ain't no twelve and a half minutes slow," Barron said angrily. "You slipped on that." He turned and faced me, pushing his hat back on his head. "Hell, you seen it parked in front of the Indian Head," he said.

"Right."

"I thought you was just a smart guy."

"Right," I said.

"Son, next time I got to get almost shot, could you plan to be around?"

The car that was coming stopped a few yards away and a dog whined. Andy called out: "Anybody hurt?"

Barron and I walked over to the car. The door opened and the little silky dog jumped out and rushed at Barron. She took off about four feet away and sailed through the air and planted her front paws hard against Barron's stomach, then dropped back to the ground and ran in circles.

Barron said: "Luders shot hisself inside there. There's a little Jap down in the bushes we got to round up. And there's three, four suitcases full of counterfeit money we got to take care of."

He looked off into the distance, a solid, heavy man like a rock. "A night like this," he said, "and it's got to be full of death."

PROFESSOR BINGO'S SNUFF

AT TEN O'CLOCK in the morning already the dance music. Loud. Boom, boom. Boom, boom, boom. The tone control way down in the bass. It almost made the floor vibrate. Behind the purring of the electric razor which Joe Pettigrew was running up and down his face it vibrated in the floors and walls. He seemed to feel it with his toes. It seemed to run up his legs. The neighbors must love it.

Already at ten o'clock in the morning the ice cubes in the glass, the flushed cheek, the slightly glazed eye, the silly smile, the loud laughter about nothing at all.

He pulled the plug loose and the purring of the razor stopped. As he ran his fingertips along the angle of his jaw his eyes met the eyes in the mirror with a somber stare. "Washed up," he said between his teeth. "At fifty-two you're senile. I'm surprised you're there at all. I'm surprised I can see you."

He blew the fluff out of the shaving head of the razor, put the protective cap back on it, wound the cord around it carefully and put it away in the drawer. He got out the after-shaving lotion, rubbed it into his face, dusted it with powder and carefully wiped the powder off with a hand towel.

He scowled at the rather gaunt face in the glass and turned and looked out of the bathroom window. Not much smog this morning. Quite sunny and clear. You could see the city hall. Who the hell wants to see the city hall? The heck with the city hall. He went out of the bathroom, putting his coat on as he started down the stairs. Boom, boom. Boom, boom, boom. Like back in a cheap dive where you could smell smoke and sweat, and perfume of a sort. The living-room door was half open. He moved in through it and stood looking at the two of them, cheek-to-cheek, drifting slowly around the room. They danced close together, dreamy-eyed, in a world of their own. Not drunk. Just lit enough to like the music loud. He stood there and watched them. As they turned and saw him they hardly looked at him. Gladys' lips curled a little in a faint sneer, very faint. Porter Green had a cigarette in the corner of his mouth, and his eyes half closed against the smoke. A tall, dark fellow, with a sprinkling of gray in his hair. Well dressed. A bit shifty-eyed. Might be a used car salesman. Might be anything that didn't take too much work or too much honesty. The music stopped and somebody started to spiel a commercial. The dancing couple broke apart. Porter Green stepped over and turned the volume control down. Gladys stood in the middle of the floor looking at Joe Pettigrew.

"Any little thing we can do for you, sweetheart?" she asked him in a clear contemptuous voice.

He shook his head without answering.

"Then you can do something for me. Drop dead." She opened her mouth wide and went off into a peal of laughter.

"Cut it," Porter Green said. "Stop picking on him, Glad. So he doesn't like dance music. So what? There are things you don't like, aren't there?"

"Sure there are," Gladys said. "Him."

Porter Green moved over and picked up a whiskey bottle, began to load the two highball glasses on the coffee table.

"How about a drink, Joe?" he asked, without looking up.

Joe Pettigrew again shook his head slightly and said nothing. "He can do tricks," Gladys said. "He's almost human. But he can't talk."

"Aw, shut up," Porter Green said, wearily. He stood up with the two full glasses in his hand. "Listen, Joe, I'm buying the liquor. You're not worrying about that, are you? No? Well, that's fine." He handed a glass to Gladys. They both drank, looking across the glasses at Joe Pettigrew standing silent in the doorway.

"You know I married that," Gladys said thoughtfully. "I really did. I wonder what kind of sleep medicine I'd been taking."

Joe Pettigrew stepped back into the hallway and half closed the door. Gladys stared at it. In a changed tone, she said, "Just the same, he scares me. He just stands there and don't say anything. Never complains. Never gets mad. What do you suppose goes on inside his head?"

The commercial spieler ended his stint and put on a new record. Porter Green stepped across and turned the volume up again, then turned it down. "I think I could guess," he said. "After all, it's a pretty old story." He turned the volume up again and held his arms out.

JOE PETTIGREW STEPPED out on the front porch, put the heavy old-fashioned front door on the latch, and closed it behind him to muffle the boom of the radio. Looking along the front of the house he saw that the front windows were closed. It wasn't so loud out here. These old frame houses were pretty solidly built. He was just starting to think whether the grass needed cutting when a funny-looking man turned up the concrete walk toward him. Once in a while you see a man in an opera cloak. But not on Lexington Avenue in that block. Not in the middle of the morning. And not wearing a top hat. Joe Pettigrew stared at the top hat. It was definitely not new, definitely on the rusty side. A bit rough in the nap like a cat's fur when the cat isn't feeling too well. And the opera cloak wasn't anything Adrian would have wanted to autograph. The man had a sharp nose and deep-set black eyes. He was pale but he didn't look sick. He stopped at the foot of the steps and looked up at Joe Pettigrew.

"Good morning," he said, touching the edge of the topper.

"Morning," Joe Pettigrew said. "What are you selling today?"

"I'm not selling magazines," the man in the opera cloak said.

"Not at this address, friend."

"Nor am I about to enquire if you have a photograph of yourself that would tint up in beautiful watercolors as transparent as moonlight on the Matterhorn." The man put a hand under his opera cloak.

"Don't tell me you've got a vacuum cleaner under that cloak," Joe Pettigrew said.

"Nor," went on the man in the opera cloak, "do I have an all-stainless-steel kitchen in my hip pocket. Not that I couldn't have, if I chose."

"But you *are* selling something," Joe Pettigrew said dryly.

"I am bestowing something," the man in the opera cloak said. "On the right persons. A carefully selected . . . "

"A suit club," Joe Pettigrew said disgustedly. "I didn't know they had them any more."

The tall skinny man brought his hand out from under the cloak with a card in it.

"A carefully selected few," he repeated. "I don't know. I'm lazy this morning. Perhaps I shall only select one."

"The jackpot," Joe Pettigrew said. "Me."

The man held the card out. Joe Pettigrew took it and read "Professor Augustus Bingo." Then in smaller letters in the corner "White Eagle Depilatory Powder." There was a telephone number and an address on North Wilcox. Joe Pettigrew flicked the card with a fingernail and shook his head. "Never use it, friend."

Professor Augustus Bingo smiled very faintly. Or rather his lips pulled back a fraction of an inch and his eyes crinkled at the corners. Call it a smile. It wasn't big enough to argue about. He put his hand under his cloak again, came out with a small round box about the size of a typewriter ribbon box. He held it up and sure enough it said on it "White Eagle Depilatory Powder."

"I presume you know what depilatory powder is, Mister . . ."

"Pettigrew," Joe Pettigrew said amiably. "Joe Pettigrew."

"Ah, my instinct was right," Professor Bingo remarked. "You are in trouble." He tapped on the round box with his long pointed finger. "This, Mr. Pettigrew, is not depilatory powder."

"Wait a minute," Joe Pettigrew said. "First it's depilatory powder, then it isn't. And I'm in trouble. Why? Because my name is Pettigrew?"

"All in good time, Mr. Pettigrew. Let me establish the background. This is a run-down neighborhood. No longer desirable. But your house is not run-down. It is old but well kept. Therefore, you own it."

"Say I own a piece of it," Joe Pettigrew said.

The Professor held up his left hand, palm outwards. "Quiet, please. I continue with my analysis. The taxes are high and you own the house. If you were able, you would have moved away. Why have you not? Because you can't sell this property. But it is a large house. Therefore you have roomers."

"One roomer," Joe Pettigrew said. "Just one." He sighed.

"You are about forty-eight years of age," the Professor suggested.

"Give or take four years," Joe Pettigrew said.

"You are shaved and neatly dressed. Yet you have an unhappy expression. Therefore I postulate a young wife. Spoiled, exacting. I also postulate . . . " He broke off abruptly and began to pull the lid off the box of something that was no depilatory powder. "I have ceased to postulate," he said calmly. "This," he held out the uncovered box, and Joe Pettigrew could see that it was half full of a white powder, "is not Copenhagen snuff."

"I'm a patient man," Joe Pettigrew said. "But just lay off telling me what it isn't and tell me what it is."

"It is snuff," the Professor said coldly. "Professor Bingo's snuff. *My* snuff."

"Never use snuff either," Joe Pettigrew said. "But I'll tell you. Down the end of the street there's a Tudor court called the Lexington Towers. Full of bit players and extras and so on. When they're not working, which is most of the time, and when they're not hitting the sixty-five-percent neutral spirits, which is hardly any of the time, a sniff of what you have there might be right down the middle for them. If you can collect for it, that is. And that's a point you want to watch."

"Professor Bingo's snuff," the Professor said with icy dignity, "is not cocaine." He folded his cloak around him with a gesture and touched the brim of his hat. He was still holding the small box in his left hand as he turned away.

"Cocaine, my friend?" he said. "Bah! Compared with Bingo's snuff cocaine is baby powder."

Joe Pettigrew watched him move down the concrete walk and turn along the sidewalk. Old streets have old trees along them. Lexington Avenue was lined with camphor trees. They had their new coats of leaves and the leaves were still tinged with pink here and there. The Professor moved off under the trees. From the house the boom boom sounded still. They would be on their third or fourth drink by now. They would be humming the music, cheek-to-cheek. After awhile they would start flopping around on the furniture. Mauling each other. Well, what difference did it make? He wondered what Gladys would be like when she was fifty-two years old. The way she was going now she wouldn't look like she sang in the choir.

He stopped thinking about this and watched Professor Bingo, who had now stopped under one of the camphor trees and turned to look back. He put his hand up to the brim of his rusty topper and lifted the hat clear off his head and bowed. Joe Pettigrew waved at him politely. The Professor put the hat back on and very slowly, so that Joe Pettigrew could see exactly what he was doing, he took a pinch of powder from the still open small round box and pushed it against his nostrils. Joe Pettigrew could almost hear him sniff it up with that long indrawn breath snuff takers use in order to get the stuff high up on the membranes.

He didn't actually hear this, of course, he just imagined it. But he saw it clearly enough. The hat, the opera cloak, the long thin legs, the white indoor face, the deep dark eyes, the arm raised, the round box in the left hand. He couldn't have been more than fifty feet away at most. Right in front of the fourth camphor tree from the foot of the walk.

But that couldn't have been right because if he had been standing in front of the tree Joe Pettigrew wouldn't have been able to see the entire trunk of the tree, the grass, the edge of the curbing, the street. Some of this would have been hidden behind the lean, fantastic body of Professor Bingo. Only it wasn't. Because Professor Augustus Bingo wasn't there any more. Nobody was there. Nobody at all.

Joe Pettigrew put his head on one side, staring down the street. He stood very still. He hardly heard the radio inside the house. A car turned the corner and went by along the block. Dust rose behind it. The leaves of the trees didn't quite rustle but they made a faint, barely audible sound. Then something else rustled.

Slow steps were coming towards Joe Pettigrew. No sound of heels. Just shoe leather slithering along the concrete of the walk. The muscles in the back of his neck began to ache. He could feel his teeth biting hard together. The steps came on slowly. They came very close. Then there was a moment of complete silence. Then the rustling steps moved away from Joe Pettigrew again. And then the voice of Professor Bingo said out of nowhere:

"A free sample with my compliments, Mr. Pettigrew. But, of course, I shall be available for further supplies on a more professional basis."

The steps rustled again going away. In a little while Joe Pettigrew didn't hear them at all. Exactly why he looked down at the top of the steps he was not quite clear; but he did. And there, where no hand had put it, beside the toe of his right shoe, was a small round box like a typewriter ribbon box. On the cover of it was written in ink, in a clear Spencerian hand, "Professor Bingo's Snuff."

Very slowly, like a man very old or in a dream, Joe Pettigrew leaned down and picked up the box, covered it with his hand and put it in his pocket.

Boom, boom. Boom, boom, boom, went the radio. Gladys and Porter Green were not paying any attention to it. They were locked in each other's arms in a corner of the davenport, lips on lips. With a long sigh, Gladys opened her eyes and looked across the room. Then she stiffened and jerked away. Very slowly the door of the room was opening.

"What's the matter, baby?"

"The door. What's he up to now?"

Porter Green turned his head. The door was wide open now. But nobody stood in it. "Okay the door's open," he said a little thickly. "So what?"

"It's Joe."

"It's Joe and still so what?" Porter Green said irritably.

"He's hiding out there. He's up to something."

"Phooey," Porter Green said. He stood up and walked across the room. He put his head out into the hall. "Nobody here," he said over his shoulder. "Must have been the draft."

"There isn't any draft," Gladys said. Porter Green shut the door, felt that it was firmly closed, shook it. It was closed all right. He started back across the room. When he was halfway to the davenport the door clicked behind him and slowly swung open again. Shrilly, against the heavy beat of the radio, Gladys yelled.

Porter Green lunged across and snapped off the radio, then turned angrily.

"Don't go loopy on me," he said between his teeth. "I don't like loopy dames."

Gladys just sat there with her mouth open staring at the open door. Porter Green went across to it and stepped out into the hall. There was nobody there. There was no sound. For a long moment the house was perfectly still.

Then, upstairs from the back of the house somebody began to whistle.

When Porter Green again shut the door he fixed it so that it was not on the latch. He would have been wiser to turn the knob of the bolt as well. He might just possibly have saved a lot of trouble. But he was not a very sensitive man and he had other things on his mind.

It might not have made any difference anyway.

THERE WERE THINGS to think about carefully. The noise – but that could be blanketed by turning up the radio. Wouldn't have to turn it up much either. Maybe not at all. Darn near shook the floor the way it was. Joe Pettigrew sneered at his reflection in the bathroom mirror.

"You and me spend such a lot of time together," he said to his reflection. "We're such little pals. From now on you ought to have a name. I'll call you Joseph."

"Don't go whimsical on me," Joseph said. "I don't go for the light touch. I'm the moody type."

"I need your advice," Joe said. "Not that it ever was worth anything. I'm serious enough. Take the question of the snuff the Professor gave me. It works. Gladys and her boy friend didn't see me. Twice I stood right in the open door and they looked straight at me. They didn't see a thing. That's why she yelled. Seeing me wouldn't have scared her worth a nickel."

"It would have made her laugh," Joseph said.

"But I can see you, Joseph. And you can see me. So suppose the effect of the snuff wears off after awhile? It's got to, because otherwise how would the Professor make any money? So I need to know how long."

"You'll know all right," Joseph said, "if anyone is looking your way when it wears off."

"That," Joe Pettigrew said, "could be very inconvenient, if you know what I'm thinking."

Joseph nodded. He knew that all right. "Maybe it doesn't wear off," he suggested. "Maybe the Professor has another powder that cancels this one out. Maybe that's the hook. He gives you what takes you out but when you want back in again you have to see him with folding money."

Joe Pettigrew thought about it, but he said no, he didn't think that could be right, because the Professor's card gave an address on Wilcox which would be in an office building. It would have elevators, and if the Professor was waiting around for customers that nobody could see, but that presumably they could feel if they touched them – well, having his place of business in an office building wouldn't be practical unless the effect did wear off.

"All right," Joseph said a little sourly. "I won't be stubborn."

"The next point," Joe Pettigrew said, "is where this being invisible leaves off. What I mean is, Gladys and Porter Green can't see me. Therefore they can't see the clothes I'm wearing because an empty suit of clothes standing in the doorway would scare them a lot worse than nothing standing there. But there's got to be some kind of system to it. Is it anything I touch?"

"That could be it," Joseph said. "Why not? Anything you touch fades out just the same as you do."

"But I touched the door," Joe said. "And I don't think that faded out. And I don't touch – I mean actually touch – all of my clothes. My feet touch my socks and my socks touch my shoes. I touch my shirt and I don't touch my jacket. And what about the things in pockets?"

"Maybe it's your aura," Joseph said. "Or your magnetic field or just your personality – what there is of it – anything that falls in that field goes with you. Cigarettes, money, anything that's properly yours, but not things like doors and walls and floors."

"I don't think that's very logical," Joe Pettigrew said severely.

"Would a logical guy be where you are?" Joseph inquired coldly. "Would that screwy Professor want to do business with a logical guy? What's logical about any part of this deal? He picks a complete stranger, a guy he never saw or heard of before, and gives him a batch of that stuff for free, and the guy he gives it to is maybe the one guy in the whole block that has a good quick use for it. Is any of that logical? In a pig's eye it's logical."

"So that," Joe Pettigrew said slowly, "brings me to what I'll be taking downstairs with me. They won't see that either. Chances are they won't even hear it."

"Of course you could try out with a highball glass," Joseph said. "You could pick one up just as somebody started to reach for it. You'd know quick enough whether it disappeared when you touched it."

"I could do that," Joe Pettigrew said. He paused and looked very thoughtful. "I wonder if you come back gradually," he added, "or all of a sudden. Bang."

"I vote for bang," Joseph said. "The old gentleman doesn't call himself Bingo for nothing. I say it's fast both ways – out and in. The thing you have to find out is when."

"I'll do that," Joe Pettigrew said. "I'll be very careful about it. It's important." He nodded at his reflection and Joseph nodded back. As he moved to turn away he added:

"I'm just a little sorry for Porter Green. All the time and money he's spent on her. And if I know a club chair from a catcher's mitt, all he's got out of it is a tease."

"That's something you can't be sure about," Joseph said. "He looks to me like a type that gets what he pays for or else."

That ended that. Joe Pettigrew went into the bedroom and got an old suitcase off a closet shelf. Inside was a scuffed brief-case with a broken strap. He unlocked it with a small key. There was a hard bundle in the briefcase, wrapped in a flannel duster. Inside the duster was an old woolen sock. And inside the sock, well oiled and clean, was a loaded .32 caliber automatic. Joe Pettigrew put this in his right hip pocket, where it felt heavier than sin. He replaced the briefcase in the closet and went downstairs, walking softly and stepping on the treads towards the side. Then he thought that was silly because if they creaked nobody could hear such a small sound with the radio going.

He reached the bottom of the stairs and moved across to the door of the living-room. He tried the knob gently. The door was locked. It was a spring lock which had been put on when most of the lower floor had been converted into a bachelor apartment for renting purposes. Joe got his keyholder out and pushed a key slowly into the lock. He turned it. He could feel the bolt coming back. The deadlatch wasn't on. Why should it be? You only do that at night, when you're the nervous type. He held the doorknob with his left hand and gently eased the door open enough for the lock to clear. This was the tricky bit – one of the tricky bits. When the bolt was clear he let the knob return to its original position and withdrew the key. Holding the knob tightly he pushed the door open until he could look around it. There was no sound from inside except the booming radio. Nobody yelled. Therefore nobody was looking at the door. So far, so good.

Joe Pettigrew put his head around the door and looked in. The room was warm and smelled of cigarette smoke and humanity and ever so lightly of liquor. But there was nobody in it. Joe pushed the door wide open and stepped inside, a frown of disappointment on his face. Then the frown of disappointment changed to a grimace of disgust.

At the back of the living-room sliding doors had once given on to the dining room. The dining room was now a bedroom, but the sliding doors had been left much as they had always been. Now they were closed tight together. Joe Pettigrew stood quite motionless staring at the sliding doors. His hand went up aimlessly and smoothed his thinning hair back. His face was completely expressionless for a long moment, then a faint smile that might have meant anything lifted the corners of his mouth. He turned back and closed the door. He moved across to the davenport and looked down at half-melted ice in the bottoms of two tall striped glasses, and the ice cubes swimming in water in a glass bowl beside the uncorked whiskey bottle, at the smeared cigarette stubs in a tray, one of them still wisping a tiny thread of smoke into the still air.

Joe sat down quietly on the corner of the davenport and looked at his watch. It seemed like a long, long time since he had made the acquaintance of Professor Bingo. A long, long time and a world away. Now if he could only remember at exactly what time he had taken the pinch of snuff. It would be about ten-twenty, he thought. It would be better to be sure, better to wait, better to experiment. Much better. But when had he ever done the better thing?

Not ever that he could recall. And certainly not since he had met Gladys.

He took the automatic out of his hip pocket and laid it down on the cocktail table in front of him. He sat looking at it absently, listening to the growl of the radio. Then he reached down and almost daintily he released the safety catch. That done he leaned back again and waited. And as he waited, with no particular emotion his mind remembered. It was the sort of thing many minds have to remember. Behind the closed double doors he half heard a series of noises which never quite registered on his mind, partly because of the radio and partly because of the intensity of his remembering.

WHEN THE SLIDING doors began to open Joe Pettigrew reached his hand out and took the gun off the cocktail table. He rested it on his knee. That was the only movement he made. He didn't even look at the doors.

When the doors were open enough for a man's body to pass through Porter Green's body appeared in the opening. His hands held on to the doors high up, the fingers glistening with strain. He swayed a little holding on to the doors like a man very drunk. But he was not drunk. His eyes were wide open in a fixed stare and his mouth had the beginnings of a silly grin on it. Sweat glistened on his face and on his puffy white belly. He was naked except for a pair of slacks. His feet were bare, his head was dank with sweat and tousled. On his face was something else that Joe Pettigrew didn't see because Joe Pettigrew kept on staring at the carpet between his feet, holding the gun on his knee, sideways, pointing at nothing.

Porter Green took a deep hard breath and let it out in a long sigh. He let go of the doors and took a couple of ragged steps forward into the room. His eyes came around to the whiskey bottle on the table in front of the davenport, in front of Joe Pettigrew. They focused on the bottle and his body turned a little and he leaned towards it even before he was near enough to reach it. The bottle rattled on the glass top of the cocktail table. Even then Joe Pettigrew didn't look up. He smelled the man so near him, so unaware of him and his gaunt face twisted suddenly with pain.

The bottle went up, the hand with the fine black hairs on the back of it disappeared from Joe Pettigrew's field of vision. The gurgling of the liquid was audible even against the radio.

"Bitch!" Porter Green said harshly between his teeth. "God damn rotten lousy filthy bitch." There was a puking horror and disgust in his voice.

Joe Pettigrew moved his head slightly and tensed. There was just room for him to stand up between the davenport and the cocktail table without squirming around. He stood up. The gun came up in his hand. As it came up his eyes came with it slowly, slowly. He saw the naked soft flesh above the waistband of Porter Green's slacks. He saw the sweat glistening on the bulge above his navel. His eyes moved to the right and crawled up the ribs. His hand steadied. The heart is higher up than most people think it is. Joe Pettigrew knew that. The muzzle of the automatic knew it also. The muzzle pointed straight at that heart and with a steady squeeze that was almost indifferent Joe Pettigrew pulled the trigger.

It was louder than the radio and a different kind of sound. There was a feeling of concussion about it, a hint of power. If you haven't fired a gun for a long time that always takes you by surprise – the sudden pulsing life in the instrument of death, the swift way it moves in your hand like a lizard on a rock.

Shot men fall in all sorts of ways. Porter Green fell sideways, one knee giving way before the other. He fell with a boneless leisure, as if his knees were hinged in all directions. In the second it took him to fall Joe Pettigrew remembered a vaudeville act he had seen long ago when he was in show business himself. An act with a tall thin boneless man and a girl. In the middle of their foolishness the tall man would start to fall sideways very slowly, his body curving like a hoop so that at no moment could you say he hit the floor of the stage. He seemed to melt into it without effort or shock. He did this six times. The first time it was just funny, the second time it was exciting to watch him do it and wonder how he did it. The fourth time women in the audience began to scream: "Don't let him do it! Don't let him do it!" He did it. And by the end of the act he had all the impressionable people in rags, dreading what he was going to do, because it was inhuman and unnatural, and no man built along the usual lines could possibly have done it.

Joe Pettigrew stopped remembering this and came back to where he was and there was Porter Green lying on the floor with his head against the carpet and no blood at all, and for the first time Joe Pettigrew looked at his face and saw that it was ripped and torn with deep scratches from a woman's long sharp frantic fingernails. That did it. Joe Pettigrew opened his mouth and screamed like a gored horse.

IN HIS OWN ears the scream sounded far off, like something in another house. A thin tearing sound that had nothing to do with him. Perhaps he hadn't screamed at all. It might have been tires taking a corner too fast. Or a lost soul on its headlong rush down to hell. He had no physical sensation at all. He seemed to float around the end of the table and around the cadaver of Porter Green. But his floating or whatever it was had a purpose. He was at the door now. He turned the deadlatch. He was at the windows. They were closed but one was not locked; he locked it. He was at the radio. He twisted that off. No more boom boom. A silence like interstellar space swathed him in a long white shroud. He moved back across the room to the sliding doors.

He moved through them into Porter Green's bedroom, which had been the dining room of the house long ago, when Los Angeles was young and hot and dry and dusty and belonged still to the desert and the rustling lines of eucalyptus trees and the fat palm trees that lined its streets.

All that remained of the dining room was a built-in china closet between the two north windows. There were books behind its fretted doors. Not many books. Porter Green wasn't what you would call a reading man. The bed was against the east wall, beyond which was the breakfast room and kitchen. It was very untidy, the bed was, and there was something on it, but Joe Pettigrew wasn't in the mood to look at what was on it. Beyond the bed was what had been a swing door but that had been changed for a solid door, that fitted tightly in its frame and had a turn bolt on it. The bolt was shot. Joe Pettigrew thought he could see dust in the cracks of the door. He knew it was seldom opened. But the bolt was shot, that was the important thing.

He passed on into a short hall that passed across the main hall under the stairs. This had been necessary to give access to the bathroom, once a sewing room, on the other side of the house. There was a closet under the stairs. Joe Pettigrew opened the door and switched on the light. A couple of suitcases in the corners, suits on hangers, an overcoat and a raincoat. A pair of dingy white buck shoes tossed in the corner. He switched the light off again and closed the door. He went on into the bathroom. It was pretty large for a bathroom and the tub was old-fashioned. Joe Pettigrew passed the mirror over the washbasin without looking into it. He didn't feel like talking to Joseph just now. Detail, that was the main thing, careful attention to detail. The bathroom windows were open and the gauze curtains fluttered. He shut them tight and turned the catches in the side of the frame. There was no door out of the bathroom except the one by which he had entered. There had been one towards the front of the house, but it had been filled in and papered over with waterproof paper, like the rest of the hall.

The room in front was practically a junk room. It had some old furniture and stuff and a roll-top desk in that hideous light oak people used to like. Joe Pettigrew never used it, never went in there at all. So that was that.

He turned back and stopped in front of the bathroom mirror. He didn't want to at all. But Joseph might have thought of something he ought to know, so he looked at Joseph. Joseph looked back at him with an unpleasant fixed stare.

"Radio," Joseph said curtly. "You turned it off. Wrong. Turn it down, yes. Off, no."

"Oh," Joe Pettigrew said to Joseph. "Yes, I guess you're right. Then there's the gun. But I hadn't forgotten that." He patted his pocket.

"And the bedroom windows," Joseph said, almost contemptuous. "And you're going to have to look at Gladys."

"The bedroom windows, check," Joe Pettigrew said and paused. "I don't want to look at her. She's dead. She's got to be dead. All you had to do was see him."

"Teased the wrong guy this time, didn't she?" Joseph said coldly. "Or were you expecting something like that?"

"I don't know," Joe said. "No, I don't think I went that far. But I messed it up good. I didn't have to shoot him at all."

Joseph looked at him with a peculiar expression. "And waste the Professor's time and material? You don't think he came by here just for the exercise, do you?"

"Goodbye, Joseph," Joe Pettigrew said.

"What for are you saying goodbye?" Joseph snapped.

"I have a feeling that way," Joe Pettigrew replied. He went out of the bathroom.

He went around the bed and closed and locked the windows. He did finally look at Gladys, although he didn't want to. He needn't have. His hunch had been right. If ever a bed looked like a battlefield this was it. If ever a face looked livid and twisted and dead, it was the face of Gladys. There were a few shreds of clothing on her, that's all. Just a few shreds. She looked battered. She looked awful.

Joe Pettigrew's diaphragm convulsed and his mouth tasted bile. He went out of there quickly and leaned against the doors on the other side, but was careful not to touch them with his hands.

"Radio on but not loud," he said in the silence, when he had his stomach back in place. "Gun in his hand. I'm not going to like doing that." His eyes went towards the outer door. "I'd better use the upstairs phone. Plenty of time to come back."

He let out a slow sigh and went about it. But when it came time to fix the gun in Porter Green's hand he found he couldn't look at Porter Green's face. He had a feeling, a certainty that Porter Green's eyes were open and looking at him, but he couldn't meet them, even dead. He felt that Porter Green would forgive him and hadn't really minded being shot. It was quick and probably much less unpleasant than what he had coming in the legal way.

It wasn't that which made him ashamed. And he wasn't ashamed because Porter Green had taken Gladys from him, for that would be silly. Porter Green hadn't done anything that hadn't been done already, years ago. He guessed maybe it was the awful bloody-looking scratches that made him ashamed. Up to then Porter Green had at least looked like a man. The scratches somehow or other made a damn fool out of him. Even dead. A man who looked and acted like Porter Green, who had been around as much as he must have been, known women too often and too well, and all the rest of it – a man like that ought to be above getting into a cat fight with a slut like Gladys, an empty paper bag of a woman who had nothing to give any man, not even herself.

Joe Pettigrew didn't think very highly of himself as a dominating male. But at least he had never had his face clawed.

He arranged the gun very nearly in Porter Green's hand, without once looking at his face. A shade too neatly, perhaps. With the same neatness and with no undue haste he arranged what other matters required to be arranged.

THE BLACK AND white radio car turned the corner and coasted down the block. There was no fuss or urgency about it. It stopped quietly in front of the house and for a moment both the uniformed officers looked up at the deep porch and the closed door and windows without saying anything, hearing the steady stream of talk from the squawk box and sorting it out in their minds without consciously paying any attention to it.

Then the one nearest the curb said: "I don't hear anybody screaming and I don't see any neighbors out front. Looks like somebody shot a blank."

The policeman behind the wheel nodded and said absently: "Better ring the bell anyway." He made a note of the time on his report sheet, reported the car out of service to the dispatcher. The one next to the curb got out and went up the concrete walk and onto the porch. He rang the bell. He could hear it ring somewhere in the house. He could also hear a radio or record player going quietly but distinctly to his left in the room with the closed windows. He rang again. No answer. He walked along the porch and tapped on the window glass above the screen. Then harder. The music went on but that was all. He went down off the porch and around the side of the house to the back door. The screen was hooked, the door inside shut. There was another bell here. He rang that. It buzzed close to him, quite loud, but no one answered it. He banged hard on the screen and then gave it a yank. The hook held. He went around the house the other way. The windows on the north side were too high to look into from the ground. He reached the front lawn and walked diagonally back across the lawn to the radio car. It was a well-kept lawn and had been watered the night before. At one point he looked back to see if his heels had marked it. They hadn't. He was glad they hadn't. He was just a young policeman and not tough at all.

"No answer, but there's music going," he told his partner, leaning into the car.

The driver listened to the squawk box a moment and then got out of the car. "You take that side," he answered, pointing south with his thumb. "I'll try the other house. Maybe the neighbors heard something."

"Couldn't have been much or they'd be breathing down our necks by now," the first policeman said.

"Better ask just the same."

An elderly man was cultivating with a one-prong cultivator around some rose bushes behind the house south of the Pettigrew house. The young cop asked him what he knew to cause a police call about next door. Nothing. See the people go out? No, he hadn't noticed anyone leave. Pettigrews had no car. Roomer had a car, but garage looked locked. You could see the padlock. What kind of people? Ordinary. Never

bothered anybody. Radio seemed a bit loud lately? Like now?
The old man shook his head. Wasn't loud now. Had been earlier. What time they turn it down? He didn't know. Heck, why
would he? An hour, half an hour. Nothing been happening
around here, officer. I been out pottering all morning.
Somebody called in, the officer said. Must be a mistake, the
old man said. Anybody else in his house? His house? The old
man shook his head. Nope, not now. The wife had gone to the
beauty parlor. She went for that purple stuff they were putting on white hair nowadays. He chuckled. The young cop
hadn't thought he had a chuckle in him, the way he kept
pecking at those roses, kind of short and cross.

On the other side of the Pettigrew house where the driver
of the radio car went nobody answered the front door. The
policeman went around back and saw a child of indeterminate
age and sex trying to kick the slats out of a play pen. The child
needed its nose wiped and looked as if it preferred it that way.
The officer banged at the back door and got a lank-haired slattern of a woman. When she opened the door some damn-fool
soap opera poured out of the kitchen and he could see that she
was listening to it with the passionate attention of an engineer
squad clearing a minefield. She hadn't heard a darn thing, she
screamed at him, timing her answer neatly between two lines of
dopey dialogue. She didn't have no time to bother with what
went on anywheres else. Radio next door? Yes, she guessed they
had one. Might have heard it once in a while. Could she turn
that thing down a little, the cop asked her, scowling at the table
radio on the kitchen sink. She said she could, but didn't aim to.
A thin dark girl with hair as lank as her mother's appeared suddenly from nowhere and stood about six inches from the officer's stomach and stared up his shirt front at him. He moved
back and she stayed right with him. He decided he was going
to get mad in a minute. Didn't hear anything at all, huh? he
yelled at the woman. She held up her hand for silence, listened
to a brief interchange of sparkling slop from the radio and then

shook her head. She started to close the door before he was half through it. The little girl speeded him on his way with a short sharp and efficient raspberry.

His face felt a little hot when he met the other policeman beside the radio car. They both looked across the street and then looked at each other and shrugged. The driver started around the back of the car to get back in, then changed his mind and went back up the walk to the front porch of Pettigrew's house. He listened to the radio and noted that there was lamplight around the blinds. He stopped and angled himself from window to window until he found a small chink he could see through with one eye.

After straining this way and that he finally saw what looked like a man's body lying on its back on the floor beside the leg of a low table. He straightened and made a sharp gesture to the other cop. The other came running.

"We go in," the driver said. "You don't see so good this shift. There's a guy in there and he ain't dancing. Radio on, lights on, all doors and windows locked, nobody answers the door and a guy is lying on the carpet. Don't that add to anything in your book?"

It was at that moment that Joe Pettigrew took his second pinch of Professor Bingo's snuff.

They got into the kitchen by forcing a window up with a screwdriver, without breaking the glass. The old man next door saw them and went right on pecking at his roses. It was a clean neat kitchen, because Joe Pettigrew kept it that way. Being in the kitchen they found they could as easily have stayed outside. There was no possible way into the lighted front room without breaking down a door. Which finally brought them back to the front porch. The driver of the radio car cracked a window with the heavy screwdriver, unlatched it, pulled it up far enough to lean in and knock the screen hook loose with the end of the screwdriver. They got both sashes of the window up and so got into the room without touching anything with their hands except the window catch.

The room was warm and oppressive. With a brief glance at Porter Green the driver went towards the bedroom, unbuttoning the flap of his holster as he went.

"Better put your hands in your pockets," he told the young policeman over his shoulder. "Could be this isn't your day." He said it without sarcasm or anything in his voice but the meaning of the words, but the young officer flushed just the same and bit his lip. He stood looking down at Porter Green. He had no need to touch him or even bend down. He had seen far more dead men than his partner. He stood perfectly still because he knew there was nothing for him to do and that anything he did, even walking around on the carpet, might happen to spoil something the lab boys could use.

Standing there quietly, and even with the radio still going in the corner, he seemed to hear a sound like a faint clink and then the rustle of a step outside on the porch. He turned swiftly and went to the window. He pushed the glass curtain aside and looked out.

No. Nothing. He looked faintly puzzled because he had very keen hearing. Then he looked disgusted.

"Watch yourself, kid," he told himself. "No Japs near this foxhole."

YOU COULD STAND in a recessed doorway and take a wallet out of your pocket and a card from the wallet and read it and nobody could see the wallet or the card or the hand holding it. People passed up and down the street idly or busily, the usual early afternoon mob, and nobody even glanced towards you. If they did, all they would see would be an empty doorway. In other circumstances it might have been amusing. It wasn't amusing now, for obvious reasons. Joe Pettigrew's feet were tired. He hadn't done so much walking in ten years. He pretty well had to walk. He couldn't very well have got Porter Green's car out. The sight of a perfectly empty car driving along in traffic would be apt to unhinge the traffic police. Somebody would start yelling. You never knew what would happen.

He might have risked crowding on to a bus or street car in a group of people. It looked feasible. They probably wouldn't look around to see who was jostling them but there was always the chance that some big strong character might make a grab at nothing and get hold of an arm and be just stubborn enough to hang on even if he couldn't see what it was he was hanging on to. No; much better walk. Joseph would certainly approve of that.

"Wouldn't you, Joseph?" he asked, looking into the dusty glass of the doorway behind him.

Joseph didn't say. He was there all right, but he wasn't sharp and well defined. He was foggy. He didn't have the clean-cut personality you expected from Joseph.

"All right Joseph. Some other time." Joe Pettigrew looked down at the card he was still holding. He would be about eight blocks to the building where, in Room 311, Professor Augustus Bingo maintained an office. There was a telephone number too. Joe Pettigrew wondered if it would be wiser to make an appointment. Yes, it would be wiser. There was probably an elevator and once in that he would be too much at the mercy of chance. A lot of these old buildings – and he knew Professor Bingo would be almost certain to have his office in a building that went with his rusty old hat – didn't have any fire stairs. They had outside fire escapes and a freight elevator you couldn't get to from the lobby. Much better make an appointment.

There was also the question of payment. Joe Pettigrew had thirty-seven dollars in his wallet, but he didn't suppose that thirty-seven dollars would cause Professor Bingo's heart to bulge with excitement. Professor Bingo undoubtedly selected his prospects with care and would be apt to demand a large slice of their available funds. This was not easy to manage. You could hardly cash a check if nobody could see the check.

Even if the teller could see the check, which Joe Pettigrew supposed would be possible if he put it down on the counter and took his hand away — after all there would *be* a check — the teller would hardly hold the money out to empty space. The bank was out. Of course, he might wait around for someone else to cash a check and then grab the money. But a bank was a bad place for that kind of operation. The person grabbed from would probably make a great deal of fuss and noise and Joe Pettigrew knew that the first thing a bank did in a case like that was block the doors and ring an alarm bell. It would be better to let the person with the money leave the bank first. But this had disadvantages. If it was a man, he would put the money where it would be difficult for an inexperienced pickpocket to lift it, even if he had a certain technical advantage over the most experienced pickpocket. It would have to be a woman. But women very seldom cashed large checks and Joe Pettigrew had scruples about snatching a woman's bag. Even if she could spare the money, the loss of her bag would make her so helpless.

"I'm not the right type," Joe Pettigrew said more or less out loud, still standing in the doorway, "to really get the value out of a situation like this."

That was the truth and the whole trouble. In spite of having put a neat slug into Porter Green, Joe Pettigrew was fundamentally a decent man. He had been a little carried away at first, but he could see now that being invisible had its drawbacks. Well, perhaps he didn't need any more snuff. There was a way to find out. But if he did need it, he would need it awfully fast.

There was nothing sensible except to telephone Professor Bingo and make an appointment.

He left the doorway and edged along the outside of the sidewalk to the next intersection. There was a dim-looking bar across the way. It might well have a secluded telephone booth. Of course even a secluded telephone booth could be a rat trap now. Suppose somebody came along and saw it was apparently empty and came in – no, better not think of that.

He went into the bar. It was secluded enough. There were two men on the stools and a couple in a booth. It was that time of day when almost no one drinks except a few loafers and alcoholics and an occasional pair of clandestine lovers. The pair in the booth looked like that. They were very close together and had eyes for themselves and no one else. The woman had an awful hat and a dirty white baby lamb jacket and she looked puffy and spoiled. The man looked a bit like Porter Green. He had that same sharp competent unscrupulous air. Joe Pettigrew stopped beside the booth and looked down at them with distaste. There was a pony of whiskey in front of the man with a chaser beside it. The woman had some godawful mess in layers of different colors. Joe Pettigrew looked down at the whiskey.

It probably wasn't wise, but he felt like it. He reached quickly for the small glass and poured the whiskey down his throat. It had an awful taste. He choked violently. The man in the booth straightened up and swung his head around. He stared straight at Joe Pettigrew.

"What the hell . . . " he said sharply.

JOE PETTIGREW WAS frozen. He stood there holding the glass and the man looked him straight in the eye. The man's eyes went down, down to the empty glass Joe Pettigrew was holding. The man put his hands on the edge of the table and started to move sideways. He didn't say another word, but Joe Pettigrew didn't have to be told. He turned and ran towards the back of the bar. The bartender and the two men on the stools both turned to look. The man from the booth was standing up now.

Just in time Joe Pettigrew found it. It said *Men* on the door. He went in quickly and swung around. There was no lock on the door. His hand gripped frantically for the box in his pocket and he was only just getting it out when the door started to open. He stepped behind it and wrenched the lid off the box and grabbed a big pinch. He got it to his nose a mere second before the man in the booth was in the men's room with him.

Joe Pettigrew's hand shook so violently that he dropped half the snuff on the floor. He also dropped the cover of the box. With a diabolical precision the cover rolled straight along the concrete floor and came to rest practically touching the tip of the right shoe of the man from the booth.

The man stood inside the door and looked around. He really looked around. And he looked straight at Joe Pettigrew. But his expression was quite different this time. He looked away. He stepped across to the two stalls. He pushed first one door open, then another. Both stalls were empty. The man stood there looking into them. A peculiar sound came from his throat. With an absent gesture he got out a pack of cigarettes and stuck a cigarette in his mouth. A neat small silver lighter came out next and snapped a neat small flame to the cigarette.

The man blew a long plume of smoke. He turned slowly and moved towards the door like a man in a dream. He went out. Then with appalling suddenness he came back in again, hurling the door in front of him. Joe Pettigrew got out of the way just in time. The man gave the room another raking glance. Here was a badly puzzled man, Joe Pettigrew thought. A very annoyed man, a man into whose morning a large drop of gall had been dropped. The man went out again.

Joe Pettigrew moved once more. There was a frosted window in the wall, small, but adequate. He unlatched it and tried to push it up. It stuck. He tried harder. The wrench of the effort hurt his back. The window came free at last and slid up jerkily as far as it would go.

As he dropped his hands and wiped them on his pants a voice behind him said: "That wasn't open."

Another voice said: "What wasn't open, mister?"

"The window, chump."

Joe looked around carefully. He sidled away from the window. The barkeep and the man from the booth were both looking at the window.

"Must of been," the barkeep said tersely. "And skip the chump."

"I say it wasn't." The man from the booth was more than emphatic, and less than polite.

"You callin' me a liar?" the barkeep enquired.

"How would you know whether it was open?" The man from the booth started to get aggressive again.

"Why you come back in here, if you was so sure?"

"Because I couldn't believe my eyes," the man from the booth almost yelled.

The barkeep grinned. "But you expect me to believe 'em. That the picture?"

"Oh, go to hell," the man from the booth said. He turned and banged out of the men's room. In so doing he stepped square on the top of Professor Bingo's snuff box. It crunched flat under his shoe. Nobody looked at it, except Joe Pettigrew. He looked at it all right.

The barkeep went across to the window and shut it and turned the catch.

"That takes care of that jerk," he said, and went on out. Joe Pettigrew moved carefully to the crushed box top and stooped for it. He straightened it out as best he could and put it back on the bottom half. It didn't look very safe any more. He wrapped it in a paper towel just to be a little safer.

Another man came into the men's room, but he was on business. Joe Pettigrew caught the door as it swung shut and slipped out. The barkeep was behind the bar again. The man from the booth and the woman with the dirty white lambswool were starting out.

"Come again soon," the barkeep said, in a voice that meant

exactly the opposite. The man from the booth almost stopped but the woman said something to him and they went on out.

"What's the beef?" the man on the stool asked, the one who had not gone to the men's room.

"I could pick a better-looking skirt than that over on North Broadway at one in the A.M.," the barkeep said contemptuously. "The guy not only ain't got no manners and no brains, he ain't got no taste."

"But you know what he has got," the man on the stool said laconically as Joe Pettigrew went quietly out of the door.

THE BUS STATION on Cahuenga was the place. People coming and going all the time, people intent on one thing, people who would never look to see who jostled them, people with no time to think and most of them nothing to think with if they had the time. There was plenty of noise. Dialing in an empty phone booth would attract no attention. He reached up and loosened the bulb so the light would not go on when he closed the door. He was a little worried now. The snuff couldn't be trusted for much more than an hour. He figured back from the time he had left the young policeman in the living-room at the house to when the man in the booth had looked up and seen him.

Just about an hour. This took thought. Much thought. He peered at the telephone number. Gladstone 7-4963. He dropped his nickel and dialed it. At first it didn't ring, then a wavy high-pitched whine reached his ears, then a click and then he heard his nickel drop down into the return slot. Then an operator's voice said: "What number are you calling, please?"

Joe Pettigrew told her. She said: "One moment, please." There was a pause. Joe Pettigrew kept looking out through the glass panel of the booth. He wondered how long it would be before somebody tried the door of the booth and how much longer before someone noticed what would seem to him or her a very curious position for the telephone receiver – at the ear of a someone who wasn't there. He supposed it was that way. The whole damn telephone system could hardly disappear just because he was using one instrument.

The operator's voice came back, "I'm sorry, sir, but there is no such telephone number listed."

"There must be," Joe Pettigrew said violently and repeated the number. The operator also repeated her remark, and added: "One moment, please, I will give you Information." The booth was hot and Joe Pettigrew was beginning to sweat. Information came and heard and went away and came back.

"I'm sorry, sir. There is no telephone listed under that name."

Joe Pettigrew stepped out of the booth just in time to avoid a woman with a string bag and an appearance of great hurry. He just slid away from her in time. He got out of there fast.

It could be an unlisted number. He should have thought of that long ago. The way Professor Bingo operated, he would certainly have an unlisted phone. Joe Pettigrew stopped dead and somebody kicked his heel. He skipped out of the way just in time.

No, he was being silly. He had dialed the number. And even if it was an unlisted number, the operator, knowing he had the number and that it was a correct number, would simply have told him to dial it again. She would think he had made a mistake in dialing. So Bingo had no telephone at all.

"All right," Joe Pettigrew said. "All right, Bingo. Maybe I'll just drop over and tell you about it. Maybe I won't need any money at all. A man your age ought to have more sense than to put a phony telephone number on a business card. How can you expect to sell the product if the customer can't get to talk to you?"

He said all this in his mind. Then he told himself he was probably doing Professor Bingo an injustice. The Professor looked like a pretty smooth operator. He would have a reason for what he did. Joe Pettigrew got the card out and looked at it again. 311 Blankey Building, on North Wilcox. Joe Pettigrew had never heard of the Blankey Building, but that didn't mean anything. Any big city is full of ratholes like that. It couldn't be more than half a mile. That would be about all there would be to the business part of Wilcox.

He walked south. The building had an even number, which would put it on the east side. He ought to have asked the telephone operator to check the address when she couldn't find the name. Maybe she would and maybe she would tell him to go fishing.

He found the block easily enough and he found the number not quite so easily, but by a process of elimination. It wasn't called the Blankey Building, though. He read the card again and made sure. No, he hadn't made a mistake. That was the right address, but it wasn't an office building. Nor was it a private home, nor a store.

Quite a sense of humor, Professor Augustus Bingo had. His business address turned out to be the Hollywood Police Station.

BESIDES THE LAB men and photographers and the fellow who did the block sketch to scale, showing the position of the furniture and windows and things, there was a lieutenant of detectives and a sergeant. Being from the Hollywood division they both looked a bit more sporty than you expect plainclothes cops to look. One had his sport shirt collar outside the collar of his shepherd's plaid jacket. He wore sky-blue slacks and shoes with gilt buckles on them. His argyle socks gleamed in the darkness of the clothes closet that opened under the stairs between the bedroom and the bathroom. He had the square of carpet rolled back. Underneath was a trap door with a sunken ring in it. The man in the blue slacks – he happened to be the sergeant although he looked older than the lieutenant – pulled at the ring and got the trap door up against the back wall of the closet. The space down below was half lit from the ventilating screens in the foundation walls. There was a rough wooden ladder leaning against the concrete wall of the basement. The sergeant, whose name was Rehder, got the ladder into position and backed down far enough to see what was under the floor.

"Big place," he said speaking up. "Must have been stairs down here once before they floored the space in hardwood to make the closet. They put the trap in to get at the gas and water pipes and the outfall. Think it's worth looking in the trunks?"

The lieutenant was a big handsome man built like a blocking back. He had sad dark eyes. His name was Waldman. He nodded vaguely.

"There's the bottom of the floor furnace," Rehder said. He reached out and rapped on it. The sheet iron rang. "That's all the furnace there is. And that would be installed from the top. Anybody check the air vents?"

"Yes," Waldman said. "They're big enough all right, but three of them are nailed shut and painted over. The one in back of the house is loose but the gas meter is just inside it. Nobody could get past that."

Rehder came back up the ladder and lowered the trap to the closet floor. "Also there's this carpet," he said. "Pretty hard to get that to fall in place without a wrinkle."

He dusted his hands off on the piece of carpet and they went out of the closet and shut the door. They went into the living-room and watched the lab men fussing around.

"Prints aren't going to mean anything," the lieutenant said moving a finger along the edge of his chin against the dark close-shaven bristles. "Unless we happen to get a clear overlay. Or something on a door or window. Even that wouldn't be too conclusive. After all Pettigrew lives here. It's his house."

"I'd sure like to know who reported that shot," Rehder said.

"Pettigrew. Who else?" Waldman kept on rubbing his chin. His eyes were sad and sleepy. "I can't go for suicide. I've seen too many and I never once saw one where a guy shot himself through the heart from a distance of not less than three feet and more likely four or five."

Rehder nodded. He was looking down at the floor furnace. It had a big grating partly in the floor, partly in the wall.

"But assume it *could* be suicide," Waldman went on. "The place is locked up tight – all except the window the prowl boys got in at, and one of them stayed right beside it until we got here. The door's not only locked but bolted with a dead-latch that is not connected with the lock. Every window is locked and the only other door, the one that connects with the breakfast room at the back of the house, has a deadlatch on this side which can't be opened from the breakfast room and a spring lock on the other side which can't be opened from in here. So the physical evidence proves Pettigrew couldn't have had access to these rooms when the shot was fired."

"So far," Rehder said.

"So far, sure. But somebody heard that shot and somebody reported it. None of the neighbors heard it."

"They say," Rehder put in.

"But why lie about it *after* we found the bodies? Before that maybe, just not to be involved. You could say whoever heard it doesn't want to be a witness at an inquest or a trial. Some people don't, sure. But they're likely to be bothered a lot more, if they didn't hear anything – or think they didn't – than if they did. The investigators are going to keep trying to make them remember something they think they've forgotten. You know how often that works out."

Rehder said: "Let's get back to Pettigrew." His eyes were on his partner now, very watchful and faintly triumphant, as if at some secret thought.

"We have to suspect him," Waldman said. "We always have to suspect the husband. He must have known his wife was playing around with this Porter Green. Pettigrew's not out of town or anything. The mailman saw him this morning. He either left before or after the shot. If he left before, he's clear. If he left after he still might not have heard it. But I'm saying he did because he had a better chance than anyone else. And if he did, what would he do?"

Rehder frowned. "They never do the obvious thing, do they? No. You'd say he'd try to get in and he'd find out he couldn't without breaking in. Then he'd call the law. But this guy is living right in the house where his wife is playing footie with the roomer. Either he's an awful cold fish and doesn't give a damn . . . "

"That's happened," Waldman put in.

" . . . or he'd be humiliated and pretty savage inside. When he hears that shot, he knows damn well he'd like to have fired it. And he knows we're likely to think the same. So he goes out and calls us from a pay station and then disappears. When he comes home he'll be the most surprised guy in the world."

Waldman nodded. "But until we get a chance to size him up, it doesn't mean a thing. It was pure chance nobody saw him leave, pure chance nobody reported the shot. He couldn't rely on any of that, therefore he couldn't rely on pretending not to know. If it's suicide I say he didn't hear the shot and didn't call in. He left either before or after and he doesn't know a thing about anybody being dead."

'So again it's not suicide," Rehder said. "So he had to get out of here and leave the place locked up. Fine. How did he do it?"

"Yes. How?"

"Floor furnace. It heats the hall too. Didn't you notice?" Rehder asked triumphantly.

Waldman's eyes went to the floor furnace and back to Rehder. "What size man is he?" he asked.

"One of the boys looked at his clothes upstairs. Five-ten, one-sixty, wears an eight and a half shoe, a thirty-eight shirt, a thirty-nine suit. Just small enough. That piece behind the upright grating just hangs on a rod. We'll print it and then try it out."

"Not trying to make a chump out of me, are you Max?"

"You know better than that, Lieutenant. If it's homicide, the guy had to get out of the room. There's no such thing as a locked room murder. Never has been."

Waldman sighed and looked towards the stain on the carpet by the corner of the cocktail table.

"I suppose not," he said. "But it does seem a pity we can't have just one."

AT SIXTEEN MINUTES to three Joe Pettigrew walked down a path in a quiet part of Hollywood Cemetery. Not that it wasn't all quiet. But here it was remote and forgotten. The grass was green and cool. There was a small stone bench. He sat down on it and looked across at a marble monument with angels on it. It looked expensive. He could see that the lettering had once been in gold. He read the name. It went back a long time, to a lost glamor, to the days when a star of the flickering screen lived like an Eastern caliph and died like a prince of the blood. It was a simple place for a man who had once been so famous. Not much like that hoked up demi-paradise over on the far side of the river.

A long time ago, in a lost and dingy world. Bathtub gin, gang wars, ten percent margin accounts, parties where everyone got paralyzed as a matter of course. Cigar smoke in the theater. Everybody smoked cigars in those days. A heavy pall of it always hung over the mezzanine boxes. The draft sucked it across on to the stage. He could smell it as he teetered fifteen feet in the air on a bike with wheels like watermelons. Joe Meredith – Clown Cyclist. Good too. Never quite a headliner – you couldn't be with that kind of act – but a hell of a long way from the acrobats. A solo. One of the best falls in the business. Looks easy, doesn't it? Try it some time and find out how easy – fifteen feet and land on the back of your neck on a hard stage and roll gently to your feet with the hat still on your head and nine inches of lighted cigar stuck in the corner of a huge painted mouth.

He wondered what would happen if he tried it now. Probably break four ribs and get a punctured lung.

A man came along the path. One of these young hard-looking kids that go coatless in any kind of weather. About twenty or twenty-one, too much black hair not clean enough, narrow flat black eyes, dark olive skin, shirt open on a hard hairless chest.

He stopped in front of the bench and measured Joe Pettigrew with a quick sweep of the eyes.

"Got a match?"

Joe Pettigrew stood up. It was time to go home now. He took a paper match folder out of his pocker and held it out.

"Thanks." The kid picked a loose cigarette out of his shirt pocket and lit the cigarette slowly, moving his eyes this way and that. As he handed the matches back with his left hand he looked over his shoulder, a quick glance. Joe Pettigrew reached for the matches. The kid dropped his right hand swiftly inside the shirt and jerked out a short gun.

"Now the wallet, chum, and take it s—— "

Joe Pettigrew kicked him in the groin. The kid doubled over and began to sweat. Not a sound came from him. His hand still held the gun, but not pointed. Tough kid all right. Joe Pettigrew took a step and kicked the gun out of his hand. He had it before the kid moved.

The kid was breathing in harsh gasps now. He looked pretty sick. Joe Pettigrew felt a little sad. He had the floor. He could say anything he liked. He had nothing to say. The world was full of tough kids. It was their world, the world of Porter Green.

Time to go home now. He walked away along the sunlit path and didn't look back. When he came to a neat green trash barrel he dropped the gun into it. He looked back then but the kid was nowhere in sight. Probably walking fast to get away and groaning as he walked. Perhaps even running. Where do you run to when you have killed a man? Nowhere. You go home. Running away is a very complicated business. It takes thought and preparation. It takes time, money and clothes.

His legs ached. He was tired. But he could buy coffee now and take the bus. He ought to have waited and thought it out. That was Professor Augustus Bingo's fault. He made it much too easy, like a short cut that wasn't on the map. You took it, and then you found that the short cut didn't go anywhere, just ended in a yard with a vicious dog. So, if you were very quick and very lucky, you kicked the vicious dog in the right place and went back the way you came.

His hand went into his pocket and his fingers touched the packet of Professor Bingo's product – a little crumpled and partly spilled, but still usable, if he could think of any use for it, which was now unlikely.

Too bad Professor Bingo didn't have a real address on his card. Joe Pettigrew would have liked to call on him and twist his neck. A fellow like that could do a lot of harm in the world. More harm than a hundred Porter Greens.

But a character as resourceful as Professor Bingo would know all that in advance. Even if he had an office, you wouldn't find him there unless he wanted you to.

Joe Pettigrew walked.

LIEUTENANT WALDMAN SAW him and knew him three houses away, long before he turned up the walk. He looked exactly like what Waldman had expected, gaunt face, neat gray suit, precise and exact way of moving. Right weight and build.

"Okay," he said, standing up from a chair by the window. "Nothing rough, Max. Feel him out slowly."

They had sent the police car off around the corner. The street was quiet again. Nothing looked sensational. Joe Pettigrew turned into the walk and came towards the porch. He stopped halfway, stepped over on the lawn and got out a pocket knife. He bent down and cut a dandelion off just below the surface. He folded the knife carefully after wiping it off on the grass and put it back in his pocket. He threw the dandelion off towards the corner of the house out of sight of the men watching.

"I don't buy it," Rehder said in a harsh whisper. "It just ain't possible that guy cooled anybody today."

"He sees the window," Waldman said, pulling back into shadow without moving too quickly. The lights were off in the room now and the radio had long since been stilled. Joe Pettigrew was looking up at the broken window right in front of him from where he stood on the lawn. He moved a little more quickly up on the porch and stopped. His hand went out and pulled at the screen enough to show that it was loose. He let go of the screen and straightened up. His face had an odd expression. Then he turned quickly towards the door.

The door opened as he reached it. Waldman stood inside looking out gravely.

"I think you would be Mr. Pettigrew," he said politely.

"Yes, I'm Pettigrew," the gaunt expressionless face told him. "Who are you?"

"A police officer, Mr. Pettigrew. The name is Waldman, Lieutenant Waldman. Come in, please."

"Police? Somebody break in here? The window . . . "

"No, it's not a burglary, Mr. Pettigrew. We'll explain it all to you." He stood back from the door and Joe Pettigrew stepped in past him. He took off his hat and hung it up, just as he always did.

Waldman stepped close to him and ran his hands rapidly over his body.

"Sorry, Mr. Pettigrew. Part of my job. This is Sergeant Rehder. We're from the Hollywood Division. Let's go into the living-room."

"That's not our living-room," Joe Pettigrew said. "This part of the house is rented."

"We know that, Mr. Pettigrew. Just sit down and take it easy."

Joe Pettigrew sat down and leaned back. His eyes searched the room. They saw the chalk marks and the dusting powder. He leaned forward again.

"What's that?" he asked sharply.

Waldman and Rehder looked at him with level unsmiling expressions. "What time did you go out today?" Waldman asked, and leaned back casually and lit a cigarette. Rehder sat hunched forward on the front half of a chair, his right hand loose on his knee. His gun was in a short leather holster inside his right hip pocket. He'd never liked an under-arm clip. This guy Pettigrew didn't look like it would take a gun to knock him over, but you never knew.

"What time? I don't remember. Somewhere around noon."

"To go where?"

"Just walking. I went over to Hollywood Cemetery for a while. My first wife is buried there."

"Oh, your first wife," Waldman said easily. "Any idea where your present wife is?"

"Probably out with the roomer. Fellow named Porter Green," Joe Pettigrew said calmly.

"Like that, eh?" Waldman said.

"Just like that." Pettigrew's eyes went to the floor again, over where the chalk marks were and the dark stain in the carpet. "Suppose you men tell me . . . "

"In a moment," Waldman cut in, rather more sharply. "Did you have any reason to call the police? From here or while you were out?"

Joe Pettigrew shook his head. "As long as the neighbors didn't complain, why should I?"

"I don't get it," Rehder said. "What's he talking about?"

"Pretty noisy, were they?" Waldman asked. He got it all right.

Pettigrew nodded again. "But they had all the windows shut."

"And locked?" Waldman asked casually.

"When a cop starts being subtle," Joe Pettigrew answered just as casually, "it's for laughs. How would I know if the windows were locked?"

"I'll stop being subtle, if it bothers you, Mr. Pettigrew." Waldman had a sweet sad smile on his face now. "The windows *were* locked. That's why the radio officers had to break the glass to get in. Now as to why they had to get in, Mr. Pettigrew."

Joe Pettigrew just looked at him steadily. Don't answer them, he thought, and they'll start telling you. One thing they won't do – they won't stop talking. They love to hear themselves talk. He didn't speak. Waldman went on:

"Somebody called in and said he'd heard a shot in this house. We thought it might have been you. We don't know that it was. The neighbors deny having heard anything."

Now is when you can make the mistake, Joe Pettigrew said in his mind. I wish I had Joseph to talk to. I feel clear in my mind. I feel okay, but these boys aren't dumb. Especially the one with the soft voice and the Jewish eyes. Nothing that dumb ever carried a badge. Nice guy, but he won't fool. I come home and the cops have the house and somebody's called in about a gun and the front window's broken and the room's been gone over until it looks all tired out. And there's a stain there that could be blood. And those chalk marks could be the outline of a body. And Gladys isn't around and Porter Green isn't around. Well, how would I act if I didn't know anything about it? Perhaps I don't care. I guess that's it. I just don't care what these birds think. Because any time I change my mind about being here I don't have to be here. Wait a minute though. It doesn't settle anything. It's murder and suicide. It has to be, because it couldn't be anything else. I'm not going to think that away. If it's murder and suicide, then I don't mind being here. I'm fine.

"A suicide pact," he said out loud, as if thoughtfully. "Porter Green didn't seem the type. Nor my wife – Gladys. Too shallow and too selfish."

"Nobody said anything about anybody being dead," Rehder said harshly.

That's a real cop, Joe Pettigrew thought. Like in the movies. Him I don't mind. Doesn't like anybody to have an idea or make an obvious deduction. That's a fat-headed remark he made, if ever I heard one. Out loud he said:

"How obvious does it have to get?"

Waldman smiled faintly. "Only one shot was heard, Mr. Pettigrew. If the informant heard correctly. And frankly, since we don't know the informant, we haven't been able to question him. But it was not a suicide pact. I can assure you of that. And since I have stopped being subtle – although I don't think you have – let me say at once that the radio officers found Porter Green dead where you see those marks. His chest was where you see that bloodstain. He bled very little. He was shot through the heart – quite accurately – at a distance that makes suicide very unlikely. Previous to that he had strangled your wife, after a rather violent struggle."

"He didn't know women as well as he thought he did," Joe Pettigrew said.

"This guy is shaking with excitement", Rehder put in nastily. "Just like an iron deer on somebody's front lawn."

Waldman waved his hand and kept the smile on his face. "This isn't a performance, Max," he said without looking at his partner. "Although I know you give a very good one.

Mr. Pettigrew is a very intelligent level-headed man. We don't know too much about his home life, but we know enough to suspect that it was not happy. He pretends to no false grief. Right, Mr. Pettigrew?"

"Exact."

"I thought so. Also, not being an idiot, Max, Mr. Pettigrew knows perfectly well from the appearance of this room, from our being here, and from our manner, that something serious has happened. He may even have expected something of the sort to happen."

Joe Pettigrew shook his head. "One of her boy friends beat her up once," he said calmly. "She disappointed him. She disappointed all of them. He even wanted to beat me up."

"Why didn't he?" Waldman asked, as if the situation was the most natural thing in the world – a wife like Gladys, a husband like Joe Pettigrew, and a roomer like Porter Green or a reasonable facsimile of Porter Green.

Joe Pettigrew smiled even more faintly than Waldman had smiled. This was something they were not going to know. His physical skills, which he seldom used, and then only at climacteric moments. Something in reserve, like what was left of Professor Bingo's sample of snuff.

"Probably didn't think it worth while," he answered.

"Quite a man, ain't you, Pettigrew?" Rehder sneered. A little taste of male disgust was rising in him, like bile.

"As I said," Waldman went on peacefully, "from the appearance of things when we got here we could assume a rather violent scene. The man's face was badly scratched and the woman was badly bruised up – in addition to the usual signs of strangulation – never too pleasant to a sensitive man. Are you a sensitive man, Mr. Pettigrew? You'll have to identify her body, even if you are."

"That's the first snide remark you've made, Lieutenant."

Waldman flushed. He bit his lip. He was himself a very sensitive man. Pettigrew was right. "I'm sorry," he said and as if he meant it sincerely. "You now understand what we found here. Since you're the husband – and since so far as we know now it's uncertain when you left the house – you would normally be a suspect for one of these deaths, and possibly both."

"Both?" Joe Pettigrew asked. He showed real surprise this time, and he instantly knew it was a mistake. He tried to retrieve it. "Oh, I see what you mean. The scratches on Porter Green – and the blows on my wife's body like you said – don't prove he strangled her. I might have shot him and then strangled her – while she was unconscious or helpless from the beating."

"This guy's got no emotions at all," Rehder said with a kind of wonder.

Waldman said gently: "He has emotions, Max. But he has lived with them a long time. They are pretty deep. Right, Mr. Pettigrew?"

Joe Pettigrew said he was right. He didn't think he had quite retrieved the mistake, but he might have.

"The wound on Porter Green was definitely not a typical suicide wound," Waldman went on. "It wouldn't be, even if you picture a man coolly and quietly deciding to kill himself for what seem to him good reasons – if a suicide ever is cool and quiet. Some of them do seem to be. But a man who had just passed through a violent scene – for such a man in such a mental state to hold a gun as far from his body as he could reach and deliberately and accurately aim it at his heart and pull the trigger – nobody could really believe that, Mr. Pettigrew. Nobody."

"So I did it," Pettigrew said and looked straight at Waldman's eyes.

Waldman stared at him and then turned to put his cigarette out in an amber glass tray. He ground it back and forth until the stub was shapeless. He spoke without looking at Pettigrew, a man thinking out loud, perfectly relaxed in his thinking.

"There are two objections to that. That is, there were. First, the windows were locked – all the windows. The door of this room was locked and although you would have a key, being the landlord – oh, by the way, I suppose you are the landlord?"

"I own the house," Pettigrew said.

"Your key would not open this door because of a dead-latch which is separate from the lock. The door into your kitchen can't be opened from the other side until a bolt on this side is turned. There's a trap door to the cellar, but it leads nowhere outside the house. We've determined that. So we thought at first that no one but himself could have killed Porter Green, because no one could have left the room after killing him and left it locked up as it *was* locked up. We found an answer to that."

Joe Pettigrew felt a slight tingling on the skin of his temples. His mouth seemed to feel dry and his tongue seemed large and stiff in it. He almost lost control. He almost said, there isn't any way. There just isn't. If there was, the whole thing would be a laugh. Professor Bingo would be a laugh. Why the hell would I stand inside the window and wait for the cop to break the glass and climb in and then right behind his back, not ten feet from him, step out onto that porch and soft shoe away and away and away? Why would I bother with all that and the rest of it and the dodging people on the streets and the not having any coffee or any way to get anywhere and not being able to speak to anybody, why would I do all that if there was a way out of the room that a couple of flatfeet would find?

He didn't say it. But his saying it in his mind did something to his face. Rehder leaned forward a little further and his tongue showed its tip between his lips. Waldman sighed. Funny neither he nor Max had thought of the killer having killed both of them.

"The furnace," he said in a cool detached voice.

Pettigrew stared and slowly his head went around and he was looking at the grating of the floor furnace, the two gratings, one horizontal and one upright where it cut into the wall between this room and the hall. "The furnace," he said and looked back at Waldman. "Why the furnace?"

"It was intended to send heat into the hall as well as this room, probably with the idea the heat would rise to the upper part of the house. Between the two parts of the furnace – that is, between the two rooms, there is a sheet iron screen hanging on a rod. It is intended to divert the heat where you want it. It will blank either of the upright gratings and put most of the heat into one outlet, or if it hangs straight up and down as we found it, the heat goes in both directions."

"A man could get through that?" Pettigrew asked wonderingly.

"Not every man. You could. The screen moves easily. We've tried it. One of our technical men went through. The available space is about twelve by twenty inches. Ample for you, Mr. Pettigrew."

"So I killed them and got out that way," Joe Pettigrew said. "I'm brilliant. Really brilliant. And put the gratings back afterwards".

"Nothing to that. They are not screwed down, just held in position by their weight. We tried it, Mr. Pettigrew. We know." He rumpled his dark wavy hair. "Unfortunately that's not a complete solution."

"No?" A pulse was beating in Joe Pettigrew's temple. A hard little angry hammer of a pulse. He was tired. The long accumulated tiredness of many small tirednesses. Yes, he was very tired now. He put his hand in his pocket and felt the crumpled box of snuff wrapped in the paper towel.

Both the detectives tensed. Rehder's hand went to his hip. He leaned his weight forward on his feet.

"Just snuff," Joe Pettigrew said.

Waldman stood up. "I'll take that," he said sharply, and stood over Joe Pettigrew.

"Just snuff. Quite harmless." Joe Pettigrew opened the package and dropped the piece of paper towel on the floor. He lifted off the crumpled lid of the box. He touched his finger to the spoonful of white powder that was all that was left. Two good pinches, no more. Two reprieves.

HE TURNED HIS hand and emptied the powder on to the floor.

"I never saw snuff that colour," Waldman said. He took the emptied box. The writing on the smashed cover was blurred with dirt. It could be read, but not quickly.

"It's snuff all right," Joe Pettigrew said. "It's not poison. At least not the kind you're thinking of. I don't want it any more. What's the rest of your analysis, Lieutenant?"

Waldman moved back and away from him, but he didn't sit down again.

"The other objection to the idea of murder is that there was no point in it – if it was Green that strangled your wife. Until you mentioned it, I hadn't thought of anything else. That makes you a reasonably sharp man, Mr. Pettigrew. If the finger marks on her throat – which are very clear and will be clearer still – come from your hands, there's no more to say."

"They didn't," Joe Pettigrew said. He held his hands out, palms up. "You ought to be able to tell. Porter Green's hands are twice as big as mine."

"If that is so, Mr. Pettigrew," and Waldman's voice began to rise in tone and volume as he spoke, "and your wife was already dead and you shot Porter Green, not only was it silly of you to run away and make an anonymous telephone call, because even if this could have been a deliberate murder on your part, no jury would convict you of as much as manslaughter – you had a perfect defense – self-defense . . . " Waldman was now speaking very loudly and clearly, although not shouting, and Rehder was watching him with a reluctant admiration. "If you had simply picked up the telephone and called the police and said you shot him because you heard a scream and had come downstairs with a gun and this man was half naked and had blood all over his face from the scratches and he had rushed at you and you . . . " Waldman's voice faded – "shot at him, by pure instinct. Anybody would believe that," he ended quietly.

"I didn't see the scratches until after I shot him," Joe Pettigrew said.

A dead silence fell into the room. Waldman stood with his mouth open, the final words hanging on his lips. Rehder laughed. He reached his hand back again and took the gun from his hip holster.

"I was ashamed," Joe Pettigrew said. "Ashamed to look at his face. Ashamed for him. You wouldn't understand. You hadn't lived with her."

Waldman stood silent, his chin down, his eyes brooding. He moved forward. "I'm afraid that's all, Mr. Pettigrew," he said quietly. "It's been interesting, and a little painful. Now we'll go where we have to go."

Joe Pettigrew laughed sharply. Just for a moment Waldman masked Rehder with his body. Joe Pettigrew went sideways out of the chair and seemed to twist in mid-air like a dropped cat. He was in the doorway.

Rehder yelled at him to stop. Then, too quickly, he fired. The shot knocked Joe Pettigrew clear across the hall. He hit the far wall, flopped his arms and half turned. He sat down with his back against the wall and his mouth and eyes open.

"Some boy," Rehder said, walking stiff-legged out past Waldman. "Betcha he did them both in, Lieutenant".

He bent down, then straightened and turned putting his gun away. "No ambulance," he said tersely. "Not that I meant it that way. You made it tough for me." Waldman stood in the doorway. He lit another cigarette. His hand shook a little. He looked at it waving the match out.

"Ever occur to you that he might be perfectly innocent after all?"

"Not a chance, Lieutenant. Not a shadow. I've seen too many."

"Too many of something," Waldman said distantly. His dark eyes were cold and angry. "You saw me frisk him. You knew he was not armed. How far could he have run? So you killed him because you like to show off. For no other reason."

He went past Rehder into the hall and bent down over Joe Pettigrew. He put a hand inside his jacket and felt his heart. He straightened and turned.

Rehder was sweating. His eyes were narrow and his whole face looked unnatural. He still had the gun in his hand.

"I didn't see you frisk him," he said thickly.

"So you think I'm a damn fool," Waldman said coldly. "Even if you're not lying – and you *are* lying."

"You rank me," Rehder said with a harsh rustle in his voice. "But you can't call me a liar, bud." He lifted the gun a little. Waldman's lip curled with contempt. He didn't say anything. After a moment, slowly, Rehder swung the gate of his gun out and blew through the barrel, and then put the gun away. "I made a mistake," he said, in a strained voice. "You tell it any way you like. And you better get you another partner. Yeah – I shot too quick. And the guy could of been innocent like you say. Crazy, anyway. Most they'd have done would be to commit him. Say a year, nine months. And he comes out to a happy life without Gladys. I spoiled all that."

Waldman said almost gently, "Crazy in a sense, no doubt. But he meant to kill both of them. The whole set-up points to that. We both know it. And he didn't get out through the floor furnace."

"Huh." Rehder's eyes jumped and his mouth fell open.

"I was watching him when I told him about it. That, Max, was the only thing we told him that really surprised him."

"He had to. Wasn't any other way."

Waldman nodded, then shrugged. "Say we haven't found any other way – and we don't have to now. I'll call in."

He went past Rehder into the living-room and sat down at the telephone.

The front door bell rang. Rehder looked down at Joe Pettigrew and then at the door. He stepped softly along the hall. He stepped to the door and opened it about six inches, holding it that way. He looked out at a tall angular wasted-looking man who wore a top hat and an opera cloak, although Rehder didn't know exactly what an opera cloak was. The man was pale and had deep-set black eyes. He took the hat off and bowed a little.

"Mr. Pettigrew?"

"He's busy. Who wants him?"

"I left him a small sample of a new kind of snuff this morning. I wondered if he liked it."

"He don't want no snuff," Rehder said. Funny-looking bird. Where did they dig them up? Better test that powder for coke, maybe.

"Well, if he does, he knows where to reach me," Professor Bingo said politely. "Good afternoon to you." He touched the brim of the hat, and turned away. He walked slowly, with great dignity. When he had taken three steps Rehder said in his harsh cop voice, which he didn't use as much as he had once: "Come here a minute, Doc. We might want to talk to you about that snuff. It don't look like no snuff to me."

Professor Bingo stopped and turned. His arms were under his opera cloak now. "And just who are you?" he asked Rehder with detached insolence.

"Police officer. There's been a homicide in this house. It could be that snuff . . . "

Professor Bingo smiled. "My business is with Mr. Pettigrew, officer."

"You come back here!" Rehder barked, jerking the door wide. Professor Bingo looked into the hall. He pursed his lips. Otherwise he didn't move.

"Why, that looks like Mr. Pettigrew on the floor," he said. "Is he ill?"

"Worse. He's dead. And like I said – you come back here."

Professor Bingo took a hand out from under his cloak. There was no weapon in it. Rehder had made a motion towards his hip. He relaxed and let his hand drop.

"Dead, eh?" Professor Bingo smiled almost gaily. "Well you mustn't let that disturb you, officer. I presume someone shot him as he tried to escape?"

"Come here, you!" Rehder started down the steps.

Professor Bingo waved a long white left hand. "Poor Mr. Pettigrew, he has really been dead for all of ten years. He just didn't know it, officer."

Rehder was at the bottom of the steps now. His hand was itching to go for his gun again. Something in Professor Bingo's eyes made him feel cold all over.

"I imagine you had quite a problem in there," Professor Bingo said politely. "Quite a problem. But it's very simple really."

His right hand came delicately out from under his cloak. His thumb and forefinger were pressed together. They went up towards his face.

Professor Bingo took a pinch of snuff.

THE PENCIL

INTRODUCTORY NOTE

This is the first Marlowe short story in twenty years and was written especially for England. I have persistently refused to write short stories, because I think books are my natural element, but was persuaded to do this because people for whom I have a high regard seemed to want me to do it, and I have always wanted to write a story about the technique of the Syndicate's murders.
1959.   *Raymond Chandler*

1

HE WAS A slightly fat man with a dishonest smile that pulled the corners of his mouth out half an inch leaving the thick lips tight and his eyes bleak. For a fattish man he had a slow walk. Most fat men are brisk and light on their feet. He wore a grey herringbone suit and a hand–painted tie with part of a diving girl visible on it. His shirt was clean, which comforted me, and his brown loafers, as wrong as the tie for his suit, shone from a recent polishing.

He sidled past me as I held the door between the waiting room and my thinking parlor. Once inside, he took a quick look around. I'd have placed him as a mobster, second grade, if I had been asked. For once I was right. If he carried a gun, it was inside his pants. His coat was too tight to hide the bulge of an under–arm holster.

He sat down carefully and I sat opposite and we looked at each other. His face had a sort of foxy eagerness. He was sweating a little. The expression on my face was meant to be interested but not clubby. I reached for a pipe and the leather humidor in which I kept my Pearce's tobacco. I pushed cigarettes at him.

"I don't smoke." He had a rusty voice. I didn't like it any more than I liked his clothes, or his face. While I filled the pipe he reached inside his coat, prowled in a pocket, came out with a bill, glanced at it and dropped it across the desk in front of me. It was a nice bill and clean and new. One thousand dollars.

"Ever save a guy's life?"

"Once in a while, maybe."

"Save mine."

"What goes?"

"I heard you leveled with the customers, Marlowe."

"That's why I stay poor."

"I still got two friends. You make it three and you'll be out of the red. You got five grand coming if you pry me loose."

"From what?"

"You're talkative as hell this morning. Don't you pipe who I am?"

"Nope."

"Never been east, huh?"

"Sure — but I wasn't in your set."

"What set would that be?"

I was getting tired of it. "Stop being so goddam cagey or pick up your grand and be missing."

"I'm Ikky Rosenstein. I'll be missing but good unless you can figure some out. Guess."

"I've already guessed. You tell me and tell me quick. I don't have all day to watch you feeding me with an eye-dropper."

"I ran out on the Outfit. The high boys don't go for that. To them it means you got info you figure you can peddle, or you got independent ideas, or you lost your moxie. Me, I lost my moxie. I had it up to here." He touched his Adam's apple with the forefinger of a stretched hand. "I done bad things. I scared and hurt guys. I never killed nobody. That's nothing to the Outfit. I'm out of line. So they pick up the pencil and they draw a line. I got the word. The operators are on the way. I made a bad mistake. I tried to hole up in Vegas. I figured they'd never expect me to lie up in their own joint. They out-figured me. What I did's been done before, but I didn't know it. When I took the plane to L.A. there must have been some-body on it. They know where I live."

"Move."

"No good now. I'm covered." I knew he was right.

"Why haven't they taken care of you already?"

"They don't do it that way. Always specialists. Don't you know how it works?"

"More or less. A guy with a nice hardware store in Buffalo. A guy with a small dairy in K.C. Always a good front. They report back to New York or somewhere. When they mount the plane west or wherever they're going, they have guns in their briefcases. They're quiet and well-dressed and they don't sit together. They could be a couple of lawyers or income tax sharpies – anything at all that's well-mannered and inconspicu-ous. All sorts of people carry briefcases. Including women."

"Correct as hell. And when they land they'll be steered to me, but not from the airfield. They got ways. If I go to the cops, somebody will know about me. They could have a couple Mafia boys right on the City Council for all I know. It's been done. The cops will give me twenty-four hours to leave town. No use. Mexico? Worse than here. Canada? Better but still no good. Connections there too."

"Australia?"

"Can't get a passport. I been here twenty-five years – illegal. They can't deport me unless they can prove a crime on me. The Outfit would see they didn't. Suppose I got tossed into the freezer. I'm out on a writ in twenty-four hours. And my nice friends got a car waiting to take me home – only not home."

I had my pipe lit and going well. I frowned down at the grand note. I could use it very nicely. My checking account could kiss the sidewalk without stooping.

"Let's stop horsing," I said. "Suppose – just suppose – I could figure an out for you. What's your next move?"

"I know a place – if I could get there without bein' tailed. I'd leave my car here and take a rent car. I'd turn it in just short of the county line and buy a secondhand job. Halfway to where I'm going I trade it on a new last's model, a leftover. This is just the right time of year. Good discount, new models out soon. Not to save money – less show off. Where I'd go is a good-sized place but still pretty clean."

"Uh-huh," I said. "Wichita, last I heard. But it may have changed."

He scowled at me. "Get smart, Marlowe, but not too damn smart."

"I'll get as smart as I want to. Don't try to make rules for me. If I take this on, there aren't any rules. I take it for this grand and the rest if I bring it off. Don't cross me. I might leak information. If I get knocked off, put just one red rose on my grave. I don't like cut flowers. I like to see them growing. But I could take one, because you're such a sweet character. When's the plane in?"

"Sometime today. It's nine hours from New York. Probably come in about 5.30 P.M."

"Might come by San Diego and switch or by San Francisco and switch. A lot of planes from Dago and Frisco. I need a helper."

"Goddam you, Marlowe – "

"Hold it. I know a girl. Daughter of a chief of police who got broken for honesty. She wouldn't leak under torture."

"You got no right to risk her," Ikky said angrily.

I was so astonished my jaw hung halfway to my waist. I closed it slowly and swallowed.

"Good God, the man's got a heart."

"Women ain't built for the rough stuff," he said grudgingly.
I picked up the thousand-dollar note and snapped it.
"Sorry. No receipt," I said. "I can't have my name in your
pocket. And there won't be any rough stuff if I'm lucky.
They'd have me outclassed. There's only one way to work it.
Now give me your address and all the dope you can think of,
names, descriptions of any operators you have ever seen in
the flesh."

He did. He was a pretty good observer. Trouble was the
Outfit would know what he had seen. The operators would
be strangers to him.

He got up silently and put his hand out. I had to shake it,
but what he had said about women made it easier. His hand
was moist. Mine would have been in his spot. He nodded and
went out silently.

2

IT WAS A quiet street in Bay City, if there are any quiet streets
in this beatnik generation when you can't get through a meal
without some male or female stomach singer belching out a
kind of love that is as old-fashioned as a bustle or some
Hammond organ jazzing it up in the customer's soup.

The little one-story house was as neat as a fresh pinafore.
The front lawn was cut lovingly and very green. The smooth
composition driveway was free of grease spots from standing
cars, and the hedge that bordered it looked as though the
barber came every day.

The white door had a knocker with a tiger's head, a go-
to-hell window and a dingus that let someone inside talk to
someone outside without even opening the little window.

I'd have given a mortgage on my left leg to live in a house
like that. I didn't think I ever would.

The bell chimed inside and after a while she opened the
door in a pale blue sports shirt and white shorts that were

short enough to be friendly. She had gray-blue eyes, dark red hair and fine bones in her face. There was usually a trace of bitterness in the gray-blue eyes. She couldn't forget that her father's life had been destroyed by the crooked power of a gambling ship mobster, that her mother had died too. She was able to suppress the bitterness when she wrote nonsense about young love for the shiny magazines, but this wasn't her life. She didn't really have a life. She had an existence without much pain and enough oil money to make it safe. But in a tight spot she was as cool and resourceful as a good cop. Her name was Anne Riordan.

She stood to one side and I passed her pretty close. But I have rules too. She shut the door and parked herself on a davenport and went through the cigarette routine, and here was one doll who had the strength to light her own cigarette.

I stood looking around. There were a few changes, not many.

"I need your help," I said.

"That's the only time I ever see you."

"I've got a client who is an ex-hood; used to be a trouble-shooter for the Outfit, the Syndicate, the big mob, or whatever name you want to use for it. You know damn well it exists and is as rich as Rockefeller. You can't beat it because not enough people want to, especially the million-a-year lawyers that work for it, and the bar associations that seem more anxious to protect other lawyers than their own country."

"My God, are you running for office somewhere? I never knew you to sound so pure."

She moved her legs around, not provocatively – she wasn't the type – but it made it difficult for me to think straight just the same.

"Stop moving your legs around," I said. "Or else put a pair of slacks on."

"Damn you, Marlowe. Can't you think of anything else?"

"I'll try. I like to think that I know at least one pretty and charming female who doesn't have round heels." I swallowed and went on. "The man's name is Ikky Rosenstein. He's not beautiful and he's not anything that I like – except one. He got mad when I said I needed a girl helper. He said women were not made for the rough stuff. That's why I took the job. To a real mobster, a woman means no more than a sack of flour. They use women in the usual way, but if it's advisable to get rid of them, they do it without a second thought."

"So far you've told me a whole lot of nothing. Perhaps you need a cup of coffee or a drink."

"You're sweet but I don't in the morning – except sometimes and this isn't one of them. Coffee later. Ikky has been penciled."

"Now what's that?"

"You have a list. You draw a line through a name with a pencil. The guy is as good as dead. The Outfit has reasons. They don't do it just for kicks any more. They don't get any kick. It's bookkeeping to them."

"What on earth can I do? I might even have said, what can *you* do?"

"I can try. What you can do is help me spot their plane and see where they go – the operators assigned to the job."

"Yes, but how can you do anything?"

"I said I could try. If they took a night plane they are already here. If they took a morning plane they can't be here before five or so. Plenty of time to get set. You know what they look like."

"Oh, sure. I meet killers every day. I have them in for whiskey sours and caviare on hot toast." She grinned. While she was grinning I took four long steps across the tan figured rug and lifted her and put a kiss on her mouth. She didn't fight me but she didn't go all trembly either. I went back and sat down.

"They'll look like anybody who's in a quiet well-run business or profession. They'll have quiet clothes and they'll be polite – when they want to be. They'll have briefcases with guns in them that have changed hands so often they can't possibly be traced. When and if they do the job, they'll drop the guns. They'll probably use revolvers, but they could use automatics. They won't use silencers because silencers can jam a gun and the weight makes it hard to shoot accurately. They won't sit together on the plane, but once off of it they may pretend to know each other and simply not have noticed during the flight. They may shake hands with appropriate smiles and walk away and get in the same taxi. I think they'll go to a hotel first. But very soon they will move into something from which they can watch Ikky's movements and get used to his schedule. They won't be in any hurry unless Ikky makes a move. That would tip them off that Ikky has been tipped off. He has a couple of friends left – he says."

"Will they shoot him from this room or apartment across the street – assuming there is one?"

"No. They'll shoot him from three feet away. They'll walk up behind him and say, 'Hello, Ikky.' He'll either freeze or turn. They'll fill him with lead, drop the guns, and hop into the car they have waiting. Then they'll follow the crash car off the scene."

"Who'll drive the crash car?"

"Some well-fixed and blameless citizen who hasn't been rapped. He'll drive his own car. He'll clear the way, even if he has to accidentally on purpose crash somebody, even a police car. He'll be so goddam sorry he'll cry all the way down his monogrammed shirt. And the killers will be long gone."

"Good heavens," Anne said. "How can you stand your life? If you did bring it off, they'll send operators to you."

"I don't think so. They don't kill a legit. The blame will go to the operators. Remember, these top mobsters are businessmen. They want lots and lots of money. They only get really tough when they figure they have to get rid of somebody, and they don't crave that. There's always a chance of a slip-up. Not much of a chance. No gang killing has ever been solved here or anywhere else except two or three times. Lepke Buchalter fried. Remember Anastasia? He was awful big and awful tough. Too big, too tough. Pencil."

She shuddered a little. "I think I need a drink myself."

I grinned at her. "You're right in the atmosphere, darling. I'll weaken."

She brought a couple of Scotch highballs. When we were drinking them I said: "If you spot them or think you spot them, follow to where they go – if you can do it safely. Not otherwise. If it's a hotel – and ten to one it will be – check in and keep calling me until you get me."

She knew my office number and I was still on Yucca Avenue. She knew that too.

"You're the damnedest guy," she said. "Women do anything you want them to. How come I'm still a virgin at twenty-eight?"

"We need a few like you. Why don't you get married?"

"To what? Some cynical chaser who has nothing left but technique? I don't know any really nice men – except you. I'm no pushover for white teeth and a gaudy smile."

I went over and pulled her to her feet. I kissed her long and hard. "I'm honest," I almost whispered. "That's something. But I'm too shop-soiled for a girl like you. I've thought of you, I've wanted you, but that sweet clear look in your eyes tells me to lay off."

"Take me," she said softly. "I have dreams too."

"I couldn't. It's not the first time it's happened to me. I've had too many women to deserve one like you. We have to save a man's life. I'm going."

She stood up and watched me leave with a grave face.

The women you get and the women you don't get – they live in different worlds. I don't sneer at either world. I live in both myself.

3

AT LOS ANGELES International Airport you can't get close to the planes unless you're leaving on one. You see them land, if you happen to be in the right place, but you have to wait at a barrier to get a look at the passengers. The airport buildings don't make it any easier. They are strung out from here to breakfast time, and you can get calluses walking from TWA to American.

I copied an arrival schedule off the boards and prowled around like a dog that has forgotten where he put his bone. Planes came in, planes took off, porters carried luggage, passengers sweated and scurried, children whined, the loud-speaker overrode all the other noises.

I passed Anne a number of times. She took no notice of me.

At 5.45 they must have come. Anne disappeared. I gave it half an hour, just in case she had some other reason for fading. No. She was gone for good. I went out to my car and drove some long crowded miles to Hollywood and my office. I had a drink and sat. At 6.45 the phone rang.

"I think so," she said. "Beverly-Western Hotel. Room 410. I couldn't get any names. You know the clerks don't leave registration cards lying around these days. I didn't like to ask any questions. But I rode up in the elevator with them and spotted their room. I walked right on past them when the bellman put a key in their door, and walked down to the mezzanine and then downstairs with a bunch of women from the tea room. I didn't bother to take a room."

"What were they like?"

"They came up the ramp together but I didn't hear them speak. Both had briefcases, both wore quiet suits, nothing flashy. White shirts, starched, one blue tie, one black striped with gray. Black shoes. A couple of businessmen from the East Coast. They could be publishers, lawyers, doctors, account executives – no, cut the last; they weren't gaudy enough. You wouldn't look at them twice."

"Look at them twice. Faces."

"Both medium brown hair, one a bit darker than the other. Smooth faces, rather expressionless. One had gray eyes; the one with the lighter hair had blue eyes. Their eyes were interesting. Very quick to move, very observant, watching everything near them. That might have been wrong. They should have been a bit preoccupied with what they came out for or interested in California. They seemed more occupied with faces. It's a good thing I spotted them and not you. You don't look like a cop, but you don't look like a man who is not a cop. You have marks on you."

"Phooey. I'm a damn good-looking heart wrecker."

"Their features were strictly assembly line. Neither looked Italian. Each picked up a flight suitcase. One suitcase was gray with two red and white stripes up and down, about six or seven inches from the ends, the other a blue and white tartan. I didn't know there was such a tartan."

"There is, but I forget the name of it."

"I thought you knew everything."

"Just almost everything. Run along home now."

"Do I get a dinner and maybe a kiss?"

"Later, and if you're not careful you'll get more than you want."

"A rapist, eh? I'll carry a gun. You'll take over and follow them?"

"If they're the right men, they'll follow me. I already took an apartment across the street from Ikky. That block on Poynter and the two on each side of it have about six lowlife apartment houses to the block. I'll bet the incidence of chippies is very high."

"It's high everywhere these days."

"So long, Anne. See you."

"When you need help."

She hung up. I hung up. She puzzled me. Too wise to be so nice. I guess all nice women are wise too. I called Ikky. He was out. I had a drink from the office bottle, smoked for half an hour and called again. This time I got him.

I told him the score up to then, and said I hoped Anne had picked the right men. I told him about the apartment I had taken.

"Do I get expenses?" I asked.

"Five grand ought to cover the lot."

"If I earn it and get it. I heard you had a quarter of a million," I said at a wild venture.

"Could be, pal; but how do I get at it? The high boys know where it is. It'll have to cool a long time."

I said that was all right. I had cooled a long time myself. Of course I didn't expect to get the four thousand, even if I brought the job off. Men like Ikky Rosenstein would steal their mother's gold teeth. There seemed to be a little good in him somewhere – but little was the operative word.

I spent the next half hour trying to think of a plan. I couldn't think of one that looked promising. It was almost eight o'clock and I needed food. I didn't think the boys would move that night. Next morning they would drive past Ikky's place and scout the neighborhood.

I was ready to leave the office when the buzzer sounded from the door of my waiting room. I opened the communicating door. A small tight-looking man was standing in the middle of the floor rocking on his heels with his hands behind his back. He smiled at me, but he wasn't good at it. He walked towards me.

"You Marlowe?"

"Who else? What can I do for you?"

He was close now. He brought his right hand around fast with a gun in it. He stuck the gun in my stomach.

"You can lay off Ikky Rosenstein," he said in a voice that matched his face, "or you can get your belly full of lead."

4

HE WAS AN amateur. If he had stayed four feet away, he might have had something. I reached up and took the cigarette out of my mouth and held it carelessly.

"What makes you think I know any Ikky Rosenstein?"

He laughed a high-pitched laugh and pushed his gun into my stomach.

"Wouldn't you like to know?" The cheap sneer, the empty triumph of that feeling of power when you hold a fat gun in a small hand.

"It would be fair to tell me."

As his mouth opened for another crack, I dropped the cigarette and swept a hand. I can be fast when I have to. There are boys that are faster, but they don't stick guns in your stomach. I got my thumb behind the trigger and my hand over his. I kneed him in the groin. He bent over with a whimper. I twisted his arm to the right and I had his gun. I hooked a heel behind his heel and he was on the floor. He lay there blinking with surprise and pain, his knees drawn up against his stomach. He rolled from side to side groaning. I reached down and grabbed his left hand and yanked him to his feet. I had six inches and forty pounds on him. They ought to have sent a bigger, better-trained messenger.

"Let's go into my thinking parlor," I said. "We could have a chat and you could have a drink to pick you up. Next time don't get near enough to a prospect for him to get your gun hand. I'll just see if you have any more iron on you."

He hadn't. I pushed him through the door and into a chair. His breath wasn't quite so rasping. He grabbed out a handkerchief and mopped at his face.

"Next time," he said between his teeth. "Next time."

"Don't be an optimist. You don't look the part."

I poured him a drink of Scotch in a paper cup, set it down in front of him. I broke his .38 and dumped the cartridges into the desk drawer. I clicked the chamber back and laid the gun down.

"You can have it when you leave – if you leave."

"That's a dirty way to fight," he said, still gasping.

"Sure. Shooting a man is so much cleaner. Now, how did you get here?"

"Screw yourself."

"Don't be a crumb. I have friends. Not many, but some. I can get you for armed assault, and you know what would happen then. You'd be out on a writ or on bail and that's the last anyone would hear of you. The biggies don't go for failures. Now who sent you and how did you know where to come?"

"Ikky was covered," he said sullenly. "He's dumb. I trailed him here without no trouble at all. Why would he go see a private eye? People want to know."

"More."

"Go to hell."

"Come to think of it, I don't have to get you for armed assault. I can smash it out of you right here and now."

I got up from the chair and he put a flat hand out.

"If I get knocked about, a couple of real tough monkeys will drop around. If I don't report back, same thing. You ain't holding no real high cards. They just look high," he said.

"You haven't anything to tell. If this Ikky guy came to see me, you don't know why, nor whether I took him on. If he's a mobster, he's not my type of client."

"He come to get you to try to save his hide."

"Who from?"

"That'd be talking."

"Go right ahead. Your mouth seems to work fine. And tell the boys any time I front for a hood, that will be the day."

You have to lie a little once in a while in my business. I was lying a little. "What's Ikky done to get himself disliked? Or would that be talking?"

"You think you're a lot of man," he sneered, rubbing the place where I had kneed him. "In my league you wouldn't make pinch runner."

I laughed in his face. Then I grabbed his right wrist and twisted it behind his back. He began to squawk. I reached into his breast pocket with my left hand and hauled out a wallet. I let him go. He reached for his gun on the desk and I bisected his upper arm with a hard cut. He fell into the customer's chair and grunted.

"You can have your gun," I told him. "When I give it to you. Now be good or I'll have to bounce you just to amuse myself."

In the wallet I found a driver's license made out to Charles Hickon. It did me no good at all. Punks of his type always have slangy pseudonyms. They probably called him Tiny, or Slim, or Marbles, or even just "you." I tossed the wallet back to him. It fell to the floor. He couldn't even catch it.

"Hell," I said, "there must be an economy campaign on, if they sent you to do more than pick up cigarette butts."

"Screw yourself."

"All right, mug. Beat it back to the laundry. Here's your gun."

He took it, made a business of shoving it into his waistband, stood up, gave me as dirty a look as he had in stock, and strolled to the door, nonchalant as a hustler with a new mink stole. He turned at the door and gave me the beady eye.

"Stay clean, tinhorn. Tin bends easy."

With this blinding piece of repartee he opened the door and drifted out.

After a little while I locked my other door, cut the buzzer, made the office dark, and left. I saw no one who looked like a life-taker. I drove to my house, packed a suitcase, drove to a service station where they were almost fond of me, stored my car and picked up a Hertz Chevrolet. I drove this to Poynter Street, dumped my suitcase in the sleazy apartment I had rented early in the afternoon, and went to dinner at Victor's. It was nine o'clock, too late to drive to Bay City and take Anne to dinner. She'd have cooked her own long ago.

I ordered a double Gibson with fresh limes and drank it, and I was as hungry as a schoolboy.

5

ON THE WAY back to Poynter Street I did a good deal of weaving in and out and circling blocks and stopping, with a gun on the seat beside me. As far as I could tell, no one was trying to tail me.

I stopped on Sunset at a service station and made two calls from the box. I caught Bernie Ohls just as he was leaving to go home.

"This is Marlowe, Bernie. We haven't had a fight in years. I'm getting lonely."

"Well, get married. I'm chief investigator for the Sheriff's Office now. I rank acting-captain until I pass the exam. I don't hardly speak to private eyes."

"Speak to this one. I could need help. I'm on a ticklish job where I could get killed."

"And you expect me to interfere with the course of nature?"

"Come off it, Bernie. I haven't been a bad guy. I'm trying to save an ex-mobster from a couple of executioners."

"The more they mow each other down, the better I like it."

"Yeah. If I call you, come running or send a couple of good boys. You'll have had time to teach them."

We exchanged a couple of mild insults and hung up. I dialed Ikky Rosenstein's number. His rather unpleasant voice said: "Okay, talk."

"Marlowe. Be ready to move out about midnight. We've spotted your boy friends and they are holed up at the Beverly-Western. They won't move to your street tonight. Remember, they don't know you've been tipped."

"Sounds chancy."

"Good God, it wasn't meant to be a Sunday School picnic. You've been careless, Ikky. You were followed to my office. That cuts the time we have."

He was silent for a moment. I heard him breathing. "Who by?" he asked.

"Some little tweezer who stuck a gun in my belly and gave me the trouble of taking it away from him. I can only figure why they sent a punk on the theory that they don't want me to know too much, in case I don't know it already."

"You're in for trouble, friend."

"When not? I'll come over to your place about midnight. Be ready. Where's your car?"

"Out front."

"Get it on a side street and make a business of locking it up. Where's the back door of your flop?"

"In back. Where would it be? On the alley."

"Leave your suitcase there. We walk out together and go to your car. We drive the alley and pick up the suitcase or cases."

"Suppose some guy steals them?"

"Yeah. Suppose you get dead. Which do you like better?"

"Okay," he grunted. "I'm waiting. But we're taking big chances."

"So do race drivers. Does that stop them? There's no way to get out but fast. Douse your lights about ten and rumple the bed well. It would be good if you could leave some baggage behind. Wouldn't look so planned."

He grunted another okay and I hung up. The telephone box was well lighted outside. They usually are, at service stations. I took a good long gander around while I pawed over the collection of giveaway maps inside the station. I saw nothing to worry me. I took a map of San Diego just for the hell of it and got into my rent car.

On Poynter I parked around the corner and went up to my second-floor sleazy apartment and sat in the dark watching from my window. I saw nothing to worry about. A couple of medium-class chippies came out of Ikky's apartment house and were picked up in a late model car. A man about Ikky's height and build went into the apartment house. Various people came and went. The street was fairly quiet. Since they put in the Hollywood Freeway nobody much uses the off-the-boulevard streets unless they live in the neighborhood.

It was a nice fall night – or as nice as they get in Los Angeles' spoiled climate – clearish but not even crisp. I don't know what's happened to the weather in our overcrowded city, but it's not the weather I knew when I came to it.

It seemed like a long time to midnight. I couldn't spot anybody watching anything, and no couple of quiet-suited men paged any of the six apartment houses available. I was pretty sure they'd try mine first when they came, and if Anne had picked the right men, and if anybody had come at all, and if the tweezer's message back to his bosses had done me any good or otherwise. In spite of the hundred ways Anne could be wrong, I had a hunch she was right. The killers had no reason to be cagey if they didn't know Ikky had been warned. No reason but one. He had come to my office and been tailed there. But the Outfit, with all its arrogance of power, might laugh at the idea he had been tipped off or come to me for help. I was so small they would hardly be able to see me.

At midnight I left the apartment, walked two blocks watching for a tail, crossed the street and went into Ikky's dive. There was no locked door, and no elevator. I climbed steps to the third floor and looked for his apartment. I knocked lightly. He opened the door with a gun in his hand. He probably looked scared.

There were two suitcases by the door and another against the far wall. I went over and lifted it. It was heavy enough. I opened it. It was unlocked.

"You don't have to worry," he said. "It's got everything a guy could need for three-four nights, and nothing except some clothes that I couldn't glom off in any ready to wear place."

I picked up one of the other suitcases. "Let's stash this by the back door."

"We can leave by the alley too."

"We leave by the front door. Just in case we're covered – though I don't think so – we're just two guys going out together. Just one thing. Keep both hands in your coat pockets and the gun in your right. If anybody calls out your name behind you, turn fast and shoot. Nobody but a life-taker will do it. I'll do the same."

"I'm scared," he said in his rusty voice.

"Me too, if it helps any. But we have to do it. If you're braced, they'll have guns in their hands. Don't bother asking them questions. They wouldn't answer in words. If it's just my small friend, we'll cool him and dump him inside the door. Got it?"

He nodded, licking his lips. We carried the suitcases down and put them outside the back door. I looked along the alley. Nobody, and only a short distance to the side street. We went back in and along the hall to the front. We walked out on Poynter Street with all the casualness of a wife buying her husband a birthday tie.

Nobody made a move. The street was empty. We walked around the corner to Ikky's rent car. He unlocked it. I went back with him for the suitcases. Not a stir. We put the suitcases in the car and started up and drove to the next street.

A traffic light not working, a boulevard stop or two, the entrance to the Freeway. There was plenty of traffic on it even at midnight. California is loaded with people going places and making speed to get there. If you don't drive eighty miles an hour, everybody passes you. If you do, you have to watch the rear-view mirror for highway patrol cars. It's the rat race of rat races.

Ikky did a quiet seventy. We reached the junction to Route 66 and he took it. So far nothing. I stayed with him to Pomona.

"This is far enough for me," I said. "I'll grab a bus back if there is one, or park myself in a motor court. Drive to a service station and we'll ask for the bus stop. It should be close to the Freeway. Take us towards the business section."

He did that and stopped midway of a block. He reached out his pocketbook, and held out four thousand-dollar bills to me.

"I don't really feel I've earned all that. It was too easy."

He laughed with a kind of wry amusement on his pudgy face. "Don't be a sap. I have it made. You didn't know what you was walking into. What's more, your troubles are just beginning. The Outfit has eyes and ears everywhere. Perhaps I'm safe if I'm damn careful. Perhaps I ain't as safe as I think I am. Either way, you did what I asked. Take the dough. I got plenty."

I took it and put it away. He drove to an all-night service station and we were told where to find the bus stop. "There's a cross-country Greyhound at 2.25 A.M.," the attendant said, looking at a schedule. "They'll take you, if they got room."

Ikky drove to the bus stop. We shook hands and he went gunning down the road towards the Freeway. I looked at my watch and found a liquor store still open and bought a pint of Scotch. Then I found a bar and ordered a double with water.

My troubles were just beginning, Ikky had said. He was so right.

I got off at the Hollywood bus station, grabbed a taxi and drove to my office. I asked the driver to wait a few moments. At that time of night he was glad to. The colored night man let me into the building.

"You work late, Mr. Marlowe. But you always did, didn't you?"

"It's that sort of a business," I said. "Thanks, Jasper."

Up in my office I pawed the floor for mail and found nothing but a longish narrowish box, Special Delivery, with a Glendale postmark.

It contained nothing at all but a new freshly-sharpened pencil, the mobster's mark of death.

6

I DIDN'T TAKE it too hard. When they mean it, they don't send it to you. I took it as a sharp warning to lay off. There might be a beating arranged. From their point of view, that would be good discipline. "When we pencil a guy, any guy that tries to help him is in for a smashing." That could be the message.

I thought of going to my house on Yucca Avenue. Too lonely. I thought of going to Anne's place in Bay City. Worse. If they got wise to her, real hoods would think nothing of raping her and then beating her up.

It was the Poynter Street flop for me. Easily the safest place now. I went down to the waiting taxi and had him drive me to within three blocks of the so-called apartment house. I went upstairs, undressed and slept raw. Nothing bothered me but a broken spring. That bothered my back. I lay until 3.30 pondering the situation with my massive brain. I went to sleep with a gun under the pillow, which is a bad place to keep a gun when you have one pillow as thick and soft as a typewriter pad. It bothered me, so I transferred it to my right hand. Practice had taught me to keep it there even in sleep.

I woke up with the sun shining. I felt like a piece of spoiled meat. I struggled into the bathroom and doused myself with cold water and wiped off with a towel you couldn't have seen if you held it sideways. This was a really gorgeous apartment.

All it needed was a set of Chippendale furniture to graduate it into the slum class.

There was nothing to eat and if I went out, Miss-Nothing Marlowe might miss something. I had a pint of whiskey. I looked at it and smelled it, but I couldn't take it for breakfast, on an empty stomach, even if I could reach my stomach, which was floating around near the ceiling. I looked into the closets in case a previous tenant might have left a crust of bread in a hasty departure. Nope. I wouldn't have liked it anyhow, not even with whiskey on it. So I sat in the window. An hour of that and I was ready to bite a piece off a bellhop.

I dressed and went around the corner to the rent car and drove to an eatery. The waitress was sore too. She swept a cloth over the counter in front of me and let me have the last customer's crumbs in my lap.

"Look, sweetness," I said, "don't be so generous. Save the crumbs for a rainy day. All I want is two eggs three minutes – no more – a slice of your famous concrete toast, a tall glass tomato juice with a dash of Lea and Perrins, a big happy smile, and don't give anybody else any coffee. I might need it all."

"I got a cold," she said. "Don't push me around. I might crack you one on the kisser."

"Let's be pals. I had a rough night too."

She gave me a half-smile and went through the swing door sidewise. It showed more of her curves, which were ample, even excessive. But I got the eggs the way I liked them. The toast had been painted with melted butter past its bloom.

"No Lea and Perrins," she said, putting down the tomato juice. "How about a little Tabasco? We're fresh out of arsenic too."

I used two drops of Tabasco, swallowed the eggs, drank two cups of coffee and was about to leave the toast for a tip, but I went soft and left a quarter instead. That really brightened her. It was a joint where you left a dime or nothing. Mostly nothing.

Back on Poynter nothing had changed. I got to my window again and sat. At about 8.30 the man I had seen go into the apartment house across the way – the one with the same sort of height and build as Ikky – came out with a small briefcase and turned east. Two men got out of a dark blue sedan. They were of the same height and very quietly dressed and had soft hats pulled low over their foreheads. Each jerked out a revolver.

"Hey, Ikky!" one of them called out.

The man turned. "So long, Ikky," the other man said. Gunfire racketed between the houses. The man crumpled and lay motionless. The two men rushed for their car and were off, going west. Halfway down the block I saw a Caddy pull out and start ahead of them.

In no time at all they were completely gone.

It was a nice swift clean job. The only thing wrong with it was that they hadn't given it enough time for preparation.

They had shot the wrong man.

7

I GOT OUT of there fast, almost as fast as the two killers. There was a smallish crowd grouped around the dead man. I didn't have to look at him to know he was dead – the boys were pros. Where he lay on the sidewalk on the other side of the street I couldn't see him; people were in the way. But I knew just how he would look and I already heard sirens in the distance. It could have been just the routine shrieking from Sunset, but it wasn't. So somebody had telephoned. It was too early for the cops to be going to lunch.

I strolled around the corner with my suitcase and jammed into the rent car and went away from there. The neighborhood was not my piece of shortcake any more. I could imagine the questions.

"Just what took you over there, Marlowe? You got a flop of your own, ain't you?"

"I was hired by an ex-mobster in trouble with the Outfit. They'd sent killers after him."

"Don't tell us he was trying to go straight."

"I don't know. But I liked his money."

"Didn't do much to earn it, did you?"

"I got him away last night. I don't know where he is now. I don't want to know."

"You got him away?"

"That's what I said."

"Yeah – only he's in the morgue with multiple bullet wounds. Try something better. Or somebody's in the morgue."

And on and on. Policeman's dialogue. It comes out of an old shoe box. What they say doesn't mean anything, what they ask doesn't mean anything. They just keep boring in until you are so exhausted you flip on some detail. Then they smile happily and rub their hands, and say: "Kind of careless there, weren't you? Let's start all over again."

The less I had of that, the better. I parked in my usual parking slot and went up to the office. It was full of nothing but stale air. Every time I went into the dump it felt more and more tired. Why the hell hadn't I got myself a government job ten years ago? Make it fifteen years. I had brains enough to get a mail-order law degree. The country's full of lawyers that couldn't write a complaint without the book.

So I sat in my office chair and disadmired myself. After a while I remembered the pencil. I made certain arrangements with a forty-five gun, more gun than I ever carry – too much weight. I dialed the Sheriff's Office and asked for Bernie Ohls. I got him. His voice was sour.

"Marlowe. I'm in trouble – real trouble."

"Why tell me?" he growled. "You must be used to it by now."

"This kind of trouble you don't get used to. I'd like to come over and tell you."

"You in the same office?"

"The same."

"Have to go over that way. I'll drop in."

He hung up. I opened two windows. The gentle breeze wafted a smell of coffee and stale fat to me from Joe's Eats next door. I hated it, I hated myself, I hated everything.

Ohls didn't bother with my elegant waiting room. He rapped on my own door and I let him in. He scowled his way to the customer's chair.

"Okay. Give."

"Ever hear of a character named Ikky Rosenstein?"

"Why would I? Record?"

"An ex-mobster who got disliked by the mob. They put a pencil through his name and sent the usual two tough boys on a plane. He got tipped and hired me to help him get away."

"Nice clean work."

"Cut it out, Bernie." I lit a cigarette and blew smoke in his face. In retaliation he began to chew a cigarette. He never lit one, but he certainly mangled them.

"Look," I went on. "Suppose the man wants to go straight and suppose he doesn't. He's entitled to his life as long as he hasn't killed anyone. He told me he hadn't."

"And you believed the hood, huh? When do you start teaching Sunday School?"

"I neither believed him nor disbelieved him. I took him on. There was no reason not to. A girl I know and I watched the planes yesterday. She spotted the boys and tailed them to a hotel. She was sure of what they were. They looked it right down to their black shoes. They got off the plane separately and then pretended to know each other and not to have noticed on the plane. This girl – "

"Would she have a name?"

"Only for you."

"I'll buy, if she hasn't cracked any laws."

"Her name is Anne Riordan. She lives in Bay City. Her father was once Chief of Police there. And don't say that makes him a crook, because he wasn't."

"Uh-huh. Let's have the rest. Make a little time too."

"I took an apartment opposite Ikky. The killers were still at the hotel. At midnight I got Ikky out and drove with him as far as Pomona. He went on in his rent car and I came back by Greyhound. I moved into the apartment on Poynter Street, right across from his dump."

"Why — if he was already gone?"

I opened the middle desk drawer and took out the nice sharp pencil. I wrote my name on a piece of paper and ran the pencil through it.

"Because someone sent me this. I didn't think they'd kill me, but I thought they planned to give me enough of a beating to warn me off any more pranks."

"They knew you were in on it?"

"Ikky was tailed here by a little squirt who later came around and stuck a gun in my stomach. I knocked him around a bit, but I had to let him go. I thought Poynter Street was safer after that. I live lonely."

"I get around," Bernie Ohls said. "I hear reports. So they gunned the wrong guy."

"Same height, same build, same general appearance. I saw them gun him. I couldn't tell if it was the two guys from the Beverly-Western. I'd never seen them. It was just two guys in dark suits with hats pulled down. They jumped into a blue Pontiac sedan, about two years old, and lammed off, with a big Caddy running crash for them."

Bernie stood up and stared at me for a long moment. "I don't think they'll bother with you now," he said. "They've hit the wrong guy. The mob will be very quiet for a while. You know something? This town is getting to be almost as lousy as New York, Brooklyn and Chicago. We could end up real corrupt."

"We've made a hell of a good start."

"You haven't told me anything that makes me take action, Phil. I'll talk to the city homicide boys. I don't guess you're in any trouble. But you saw the shooting. They'll want that."

"I couldn't identify anybody, Bernie. I didn't know the man who was shot. How did *you* know it was the wrong man?"

"You told me, stupid."

"I thought perhaps the city boys had a make on him."

"They wouldn't tell me, if they had. Besides, they ain't hardly had time to go out for breakfast. He's just a stiff in the morgue to them until the ID comes up with something. But they'll want to talk to you, Phil. They just love their tape recorders."

He went out and the door whooshed shut behind him. I sat there wondering whether I had been a dope to talk to him. Or to take Ikky's troubles on. Five thousand green men said no. But they can be wrong too.

Somebody banged on my door. It was a uniform holding a telegram. I receipted for it and tore it loose.

It said: "On my way to Flagstaff. Mirador Motor Court. Think I've been spotted. Come fast."

I tore the wire into small pieces and burned them in my big ashtray.

8

I CALLED ANNE RIORDAN.

"Funny thing happened," I told her, and told her about the funny thing.

"I don't like the pencil," she said. "And I don't like the wrong man being killed, probably some poor bookkeeper in a cheap business or he wouldn't be living in that neighborhood. You should never have touched it, Phil."

"Ikky had a life. Where he's going he might make himself decent. He can change his name. He must be loaded or he wouldn't have paid me so much."

"I said I didn't like the pencil. You'd better come down here for a while. You can have your mail readdressed – if you get any mail. You don't have to work right away anyhow. And L.A. is oozing with private eyes."

"You don't get the point. I'm not through with the job. The city dicks have to know where I am, and if they do, all the crime beat reporters will know too. The cops might even decide to make me a suspect. Nobody who saw the shooting is going to put out a description that means anything. The American people know better than to be witnesses to gang killings."

"All right, loud brain. But my offer stands."

The buzzer sounded in the outside room. I told Anne I had to hang up. I opened the communicating door and a well-dressed – I might say elegantly dressed – middle-aged man stood six feet inside the outer door. He had a pleasantly dishonest smile on his face. He wore a white Stetson and one of those narrow ties that go through an ornamental buckle. His cream-colored flannel suit was beautifully tailored.

He lit a cigarette with a gold lighter and looked at me over the first puff of smoke.

"Mr. Marlowe?"

I nodded.

"I'm Foster Grimes from Las Vegas. I run the Rancho Esperanza on South Fifth. I hear you got a little involved with a man named Ikky Rosenstein."

"Won't you come in?"

He strolled past me into my office. His appearance told me nothing. A prosperous man who liked or felt it good business to look a bit western. You see them by the dozen in the Palm Springs winter season. His accent told me he was an easterner, but not New England. New York or

Baltimore, likely. Long Island, the Berkshires – no, too far from the city.

I showed him the customer's chair with a flick of the wrist and sat down in my antique swivel-squeaker. I waited.

"Where is Ikky now, if you know?"

"I don't know, Mr. Grimes."

"How come you messed with him?"

"Money."

"A damned good reason," he smiled. "How far did it go?"

"I helped him leave town. I'm telling you this, although I don't know who the hell you are, because I've already told an old friend-enemy of mine, a top man in the Sheriff's Office."

"What's a friend-enemy?"

"Law men don't go around kissing me, but I've known him for years, and we are as much friends as a private star can be with a law man."

"I told you who I was. We have a unique set-up in Vegas. We own the place except for one lousy newspaper editor who keeps climbing our backs and the backs of our friends. We let him live because letting him live makes us look better than knocking him off. Killings are not good business any more."

"Like Ikky Rosenstein."

"That's not a killing. It's an execution. Ikky got out of line."

"So your gun boys had to rub the wrong guy. They could have hung around a little to make sure."

"They would have, if you'd kept your nose where it belonged. They hurried. We don't appreciate that. We want cool efficiency."

"Who's this great big fat 'we' you keep talking about?"

"Don't go juvenile on me, Marlowe."

"Okay. Let's say I know."

"Here's what we want." He reached into his pocket and drew out a loose bill. He put it on the desk on his side. "Find Ikky and tell him to get back in line and everything is oke. With an innocent bystander gunned, we don't want any trouble or any extra publicity. It's that simple. You get this now." He nodded at the bill. It was a grand. Probably the smallest bill they had. "And another when you find Ikky and give him the message. If he holds out – curtains."

"Suppose I say take your goddam grand and blow your nose with it?"

"That would be unwise." He flipped out a Colt Woodsman with a short silencer on it. A Colt Woodsman will take one without jamming. He was fast too, fast and smooth. The genial expression on his face didn't change.

"I never left Vegas," he said calmly. "I can prove it. You're dead in your office chair and nobody knows anything. Just another private eye that tried the wrong pitch. Put your hands on the desk and think a little. Incidentally, I'm a crack shot even with this damned silencer."

"Just to sink a little lower in the social scale, Mr. Grimes, I ain't putting no hands on no desk. But tell me about this."

I flipped the nicely sharpened pencil across to him. He grabbed for it after a swift change of the gun to his left hand – very swift. He held the pencil up so that he could look at it without taking his eyes off me.

I said: "It came to me by Special Delivery mail. No message, no return address. Just the pencil. Think I've never heard about the pencil, Mr. Grimes?"

He frowned and tossed the pencil down. Before he could shift his long lithe gun back to his right hand I dropped mine under the desk and grabbed the butt of the .45 and put my finger hard on the trigger.

"Look under the desk, Mr. Grimes. You'll see a .45 in an open-end holster. It's fixed there and it's pointing at your belly. Even if you could shoot me through the heart the .45 would still go off from a convulsive movement of my hand. And your belly would be hanging by a shred and you would be knocked out of that chair. A .45 slug can throw you back six feet. Even the movies learned that at last."

"Looks like a Mexican stand-off," he said quietly. He holstered his gun. He grinned. "Nice smooth work, Marlowe. We could use you. But it's a long time for you and no time at all to us. Find Ikky and don't be a drip. He'll listen to reason. He doesn't really want to be on the run for the rest of his life. We'd trace him eventually."

"Tell me something, Mr. Grimes. Why pick on me? Apart from Ikky, what did I ever do to make you dislike me?"

Not moving, he thought a moment, or pretended to. "The Larsen case. You helped send one of our boys to the gas chamber. That we don't forget. We had you in mind as a fall guy for Ikky. You'll always be a fall guy, unless you play it our way. Something will hit you when you least expect it."

"A man in my business is always a fall guy, Mr. Grimes. Pick up your grand and drift out quietly. I might decide to do it your way, but I have to think. As for the Larsen case, the cops did all the work. I just happened to know where he was. I don't guess you miss him terribly."

"We don't like interference." He stood up. He put the grand note casually back in his pocket. While he was doing it I let go of the .45 and jerked out my Smith & Wesson five-inch .38.

He looked at it contemptuously. "I'll be in Vegas, Marlowe. In fact I never left Vegas. You can catch me at the Esperanza. No, we don't give a damn about Larsen personally. Just another gun handler. They come in gross lots. We *do* give a damn that some punk private eye fingered him."

He nodded and went out by my office door.

I did some pondering. I knew Ikky wouldn't go back to the Outfit. He wouldn't trust them enough if he got the chance. But there was another reason now. I called Anne Riordan again.

"I'm going to look for Ikky. I have to. If I don't call you in three days, get hold of Bernie Ohls. I'm going to Flagstaff, Arizona. Ikky says he will be there."

"You're a fool," she wailed. "It's some sort of trap."

"A Mr. Grimes of Vegas visited me with a silenced gun. I beat him to the punch, but I won't always be that lucky. If I find Ikky and report to Grimes, the mob will let me alone."

"You'd condemn a man to death?" Her voice was sharp and incredulous.

"No. He won't be there when I report. He'll have to hop a plane to Montreal, buy forged papers – Montreal is almost as crooked as we are – and plane to Europe. He may be fairly safe there. But the Outfit has long arms and Ikky will have a damned dull life staying alive. He hasn't any choice. For him it's either hide or get the pencil."

"So clever of you, darling. What about your own pencil?"

"If they meant it, they wouldn't have sent it. Just a bit of scare technique."

"And you don't scare, you wonderful handsome brute."

"I scare. But it doesn't paralyze me. So long. Don't take any lovers until I get back."

"Damn you, Marlowe!"

She hung up on me. I hung up on myself.

Saying the wrong thing is one of my specialties.

I beat it out of town before the homicide boys could hear about me. It would take them quite a while to get a lead. And Bernie Ohls wouldn't give a city dick a used paper bag. The Sheriff's men and the City Police co-operate about as much as two tomcats on a fence.

9

I MADE PHOENIX by evening and parked myself in a motor court on the outskirts. Phoenix was damned hot. The motor court had a dining room, so I had dinner. I collected some quarters and dimes from the cashier and shut myself in a phone booth and started to call the Mirador in Flagstaff. How silly could I get? Ikky might be registered under any name from Cohen to Cordileone, from Watson to Woichehovski. I called anyway and got nothing but as much of a smile as you can get on the phone. So I asked for a room the following night. Not a chance unless someone checked out, but they would put me down for a cancellation or something. Flagstaff is too near the Grand Canyon. Ikky must have arranged in advance. That was something to ponder too.

I bought a paperback and read it. I set my alarm watch for 6.30. The paperback scared me so badly that I put two guns under my pillow. It was about a guy who bucked the hoodlum boss of Milwaukee and got beaten up every fifteen minutes. I figured that his head and face would be nothing but a piece of bone with a strip of skin hanging from it. But in the next chapter he was as gay as a meadow lark. Then I asked myself why I was reading this drivel when I could have been memorizing *The Brothers Karamazov*. Not knowing any good answers, I turned the light out and went to sleep. At 6.30 I shaved and showered and had breakfast and took off for Flagstaff. I got there by lunchtime, and there was Ikky in the restaurant eating mountain trout. I sat down across from him. He looked surprised to see me.

I ordered mountain trout and ate it from the outside in, which is the proper way. Boning spoils it a little.

"What gives?" he asked me with his mouth full. A delicate eater.

"You read the papers?"

"Just the sporting section."

"Let's go to your room and talk about it. There's more than that."

We paid for our lunches and went along to a nice double. The motor courts are getting so good that they make a lot of hotels look cheap. We sat down and lit cigarettes.

"The two hoods got up too early and went over to Poynter Street. They parked outside your apartment house. They hadn't been briefed carefully enough. They shot a guy who looked a little like you."

"That's a hot one." He grinned. "But the cops will find out, and the Outfit will find out. So the tag for me stays on."

"You must think I'm dumb," I said. "I am."

"I thought you did a first-class job, Marlowe. What's dumb about that?"

"What job did I do?"

"You got me out of there pretty slick."

"Anything about it you couldn't have done yourself?"

"With luck – no. But it's nice to have a helper."

"You mean sucker."

His face tightened. And his rusty voice growled. "I don't catch. And give me back some of that five grand, will you? I'm shorter than I thought."

"I'll give it back to you when you find a hummingbird in a salt shaker."

"Don't be like that," he almost sighed, and flicked a gun into his hand. I didn't have to flick. I was holding one in my side pocket.

"I oughtn't to have boobed off," I said. "Put the heater away. It doesn't pay any more than a Vegas slot machine."

"Wrong. Them machines pay the jackpot every so often. Otherwise – no customers."

"Every so seldom, you mean. Listen, and listen good."

He grinned. His dentist was tired waiting for him.

"The set-up intrigued me," I went on, debonair as Milo Vance in a Van Dyne story and a lot brighter in the head. "First off, could it be done? Second, if it could be done, where would I be? But gradually I saw the little touches that flaw the picture. Why would you come to me at all? The Outfit isn't that naïve. Why would they send a little punk like this Charles Hickon or whatever name he uses on Thursdays? Why would an old hand like you let anybody trail you to a dangerous connection?"

"You slay me, Marlowe. You're so bright I could find you in the dark. You're so dumb you couldn't see a red white and blue giraffe. I bet you were back there in your unbrain emporium playing with that five grand like a cat with a bag of catnip. I bet you were kissing the notes."

"Not after you handled them. Then why the pencil that was sent to me? Big dangerous threat. It reinforced the rest. But like I told your choir boy from Vegas, they don't send them when they mean them. By the way, he had a gun too. A Woodsman .22 with a silencer. I had to make him put it away. He was nice about that. He started waving grands at me to find out where you were and tell him. A well-dressed, nice-looking front man for a pack of dirty rats. The Women's Christian Temperance Association and some bootlicking politicians gave them the money to be big, and they learned how to use it and make it grow. Now they're pretty well unstoppable. But they're still a pack of dirty rats. And they're always where they can't make a mistake. That's inhuman. Any man has a right to a few mistakes. Not the rats. They have to be perfect all the time. Or else they get stuck with *you*."

"I don't know what the hell you're talking about. I just know it's too long."

"Well, allow me to put it in English. Some poor jerk from the East Side gets involved with the lower echelons of a mob. You know what an echelon is, Ikky?"

"I been in the Army," he sneered.

"He grows up in the mob, but he's not all rotten. He's not rotten enough. So he tries to break loose. He comes out here and gets himself a cheap job of some sort and changes his name or names and lives quietly in a cheap apartment house. But the mob by now has agents in many places. Somebody spots him and recognizes him. It might be a pusher, a front man for a bookie joint, a night girl, even a cop that's on the take. So the mob, or call them the Outfit, say through their cigar smoke: 'Ikky can't do this to us. It's a small operation because he's small. But it annoys us. Bad for discipline. Call a couple of boys and have them pencil him.' But what boys do they call? A couple they're tired of. Been around too long. Might make a mistake or get chilly toes. Perhaps they like killing. That's bad too. That makes recklessness. The best boys are the ones that don't care either way. So although they don't know it, the boys they call are on their way out. But it would be kind of cute to frame a guy they already don't like, for fingering a hood named Larsen. One of these puny little jokes the Outfit takes big. 'Look guys, we even got time to play footies with a private eye. Jesus, we can do anything. We could even suck our thumbs.' So they send a ringer."

"The Torri brothers ain't ringers. They're real hard boys. They proved it – even if they did make a mistake."

"Mistake nothing. They got Ikky Rosenstein. You're just a singing commercial in this deal. And as of now you're under arrest for murder. You're worse off than that. The Outfit will habeas corpus you out of the clink and blow you down. You've served your purpose and you failed to finger me into a patsy."

His finger tightened on the trigger. I shot the gun out of his hand. My gun in my coat pocket was small, but at that distance accurate. And it was one of my days to be accurate myself.

He made a faint moaning sound and sucked at his hand. I went over and kicked him hard in the chest. Being nice to killers is not part of my repertoire. He went over backwards and sidewise and stumbled four or five steps. I picked up his gun and held it on him while I tapped all the places – not just pockets or holsters – where a man could stash a second gun. He was clean – that way anyhow.

"What are you trying to do to me?" he said whiningly. "I paid you. You're clear. I paid you damn well."

"We both have problems there. Yours is to stay alive." I took a pair of cuffs out of my pocket and wrestled his hands behind him and snapped them on. His hand was bleeding. I tied his show handkerchief around it. I went to the telephone.

Flagstaff was big enough to have a police force. The D.A. might even have his office there. This was Arizona, a poor state, relatively. The cops might even be honest.

10

I HAD TO stick around for a few days, but I didn't mind that as long as I could have trout caught eight or nine thousand feet up. I called Anne and Bernie Ohls. I called my answering service. The Arizona D.A. was a young keen-eyed man and the Chief of Police was one of the biggest men I ever saw.

I got back to L.A. in time and took Anne to Romanoff's for dinner and champagne.

"What I can't see," she said over a third glass of bubbly, "is why they dragged you into it, why they set up the fake Ikky Rosenstein. Why didn't they just let the two life-takers do their job?"

"I couldn't really say. Unless the big boys feel so safe they're developing a sense of humor. And unless this Larsen guy that went to the gas chamber was bigger than he seemed to be. Only three or four important mobsters have made the electric chair or the rope or the gas chamber. None that I know of in the life-imprisonment states like Michigan. If Larsen was bigger than anyone thought, they might have had my name on a waiting list."

"But why wait?" she asked me. "They'd go after you quickly."

"They can afford to wait. Who's going to bother them – Kefauver? He did his best, but do you notice any change in the set-up – except when they make one themselves?"

"Costello?"

"Income tax rap – like Capone. Capone may have had several hundred men killed, and killed a few of them himself, personally. But it took the Internal Revenue boys to get him. The Outfit won't make that mistake often."

"What I like about you, apart from your enormous personal charm, is that when you don't know an answer you make one up."

"The money worries me," I said. "Five grand of their dirty money. What do I do with it?"

"Don't be a jerk all your life. You earned the money and you risked your life for it. You can buy Series E Bonds. They'll make the money clean. And to me that would be part of the joke."

"*You* tell *me* one good reason why they pulled the switch."

"You have more of a reputation than you realize. And how would it be if the false Ikky pulled the switch? He sounds like one of these over-clever types that can't do anything simple."

"The Outfit will get him for making his own plans – if you're right."

"If the D.A. doesn't. And I couldn't care less about what happens to him. More champagne, please."

ENGLISH SUMMER
A Gothic Romance

Bury me where the soldiers of retreat
Are buried, underneath the faded star.

–Stephen Vincent Benét

1

IT WAS ONE of those old, old cottages in the country which
are supposed to be picturesque, which the English go to for
weekends or for a month in the summer in a year when they
can't afford the high Alps or Venice or Sicily or Greece or the
Riviera, a year when they don't want to see their infernal gray
ocean.

In the winter who lives in such places? Who would slog
through the long, dreadful wet silence to find out? But probably some peaceful old woman with apple cheeks and two
earthen hot-water bottles in her bed and not a care in the
world, not even for death.

It was summer now, however, and the Crandalls were there
for a month, I, as a guest for a vague few days. Edward
Crandall had invited me himself, and I had gone, a little to be
near her, a little because his asking me was a sort of insult, and
I like insults, from some people.

I don't think he hoped to catch me making love to her.
I don't think he would have cared. He was too busy on the
tiles of the roofs, on the walls of the barnyards, in the shadows
of the hayricks. He wouldn't have paid either of us that compliment anyhow.

But I never had made love to her, so he couldn't have
caught us – not in the three years, off and on, I had known
them. It was a curious, a very naïve, a very decrepit delicacy
on my part. In the circumstances, while she continued to
endure him in utter silence, I thought it would have been too
callous a gesture. Perhaps I was wrong. Probably I was wrong.
She was very lovely.

It was a small cottage, at the extreme edge of a village called Buddenham, but in spite of its natural seclusion it had those unnecessary walls that some English gardens have, as though the flowers might be caught in embarrassing postures. The part in the back, nearest the house, they liked to call the "close." It had that almost unbearable fragrance of English flowers in summer. On the sunny side nectarines grew in espaliers, and there was a table put there on the firm, ancient lawn, and rustic chairs for tea, if it was warm enough for tea outdoors. It never was while I was there.

In front there was more garden, another walled-in space smelling of roses and mignonettes, drowsy with striped bumblebees. There was a walk and a hedge and a fence and a gate. That was outside. I liked all of that. Inside I hated one thing, the stairs. They had a sort of deadly cold ingenuity of wrongness, as though designed for your six months' bride to fall down and break her neck, and make one of those sudden tragedies that people used to gloat over, licking their tear-wet lips.

I didn't even mind there being only one bathroom and no shower. After ten years of visiting in England, for long periods at a time, I knew there were few houses, even large ones, with more. And you get used to being wakened in the morning by a discreet tapping, then the door opening softly without your having answered, then the curtains being rasped back, and then by the dull thud of a copper utensil of quaint shape, full of hot water, being deposited in a wide shallow tray, in which you can just manage to sit — if you put your wet feet out on the floor. This is old-fashioned now, but it persists in some places.

That was all right, but not the stairs. In the first place there was a sort of very vague half-turn at the top, in complete darkness, and a totally unnecessary half-step there, at exactly the worst possible angle. I always stumbled over it.

Then at the straight upper reach of the main flight, before the half-turn, there was a newel post as hard and sharp as a steel girder and about the size of a well-grown oak. It was carved, the story went, from the rudder stem of some Spanish galleon which a very English storm had cast upon a very English lee shore. After the usual few centuries, part of the rudder-stem had got to Buddenham and got itself made into a newel post.

One more thing – the two steel engravings. They hung out at an absurd angle from the wall right on the straight part of the stairs – and the stairs were already cramped. They hung side by side, framed in that very monumental manner steel engravings used to love. One corner would lay your skull open like an axe. They were the Stag Drinking and the Stag at Bay. They seemed to be exactly the same, except for the position of the stag's head. But I never really saw them. I just crawled past them. The only place from which you could really see them was the passage to the kitchen and the scullery. From there, if you had any business there, and if you liked steel engravings after Landseer, you could look up through the banisters and gaze your fill. It may have been a lot of fun, but not to me.

This particular afternoon I came down these stairs stumbling and dodging about as usual, swinging my cherry-wood stick in a brisk and British manner, getting it caught in the banisters, and inhaling the faint sour aroma of the paste behind the wallpaper.

The house seemed unusually still. I missed the cracked monotone of old Bessie's humming in the kitchen. Old Bessie went with the cottage and looked very much as though she had come ashore with the Spanish galleon, through a lot of rocks.

I peeped into the drawing room, and that was empty, so I went on back through the French doors to the "close." Millicent was sitting there, in a garden chair. Just sitting. It seems that I must describe her, and I shall probably overdo it, like the rest.

She was, I suppose, very English, but more fragile than the English. She had that sort of ceramic delicacy and grace, like certain very lovely kinds of china. She was rather tall – quite tall, in fact, and from certain angles may have appeared a trifle sharp. But I had never thought so. And above all she had the flowing movement, the infinite, effortless grace of a fairy tale. She had the pale hair, so pale, so gold, so fine that you never saw a separate strand of it. It was the hair of a princess in a remote and bitter tower. It was the hair an old nurse would have brushed, hour after hour by candlelight, in a vast dim room, holding it softly in tired old hands, while the princess sat before a polished silver mirror, half asleep, and glanced into the burnished metal occasionally, but not to see herself. She had dreams for that mirror. That was the sort of hair Millicent Crandall had. I touched it only once and then it was too late.

She had lovely arms too, and they seemed to know it, without, as it were, her knowing it. So that they always seemed poised in just the right way, in the most languid and gracious curves, along a mantelpiece, with the wrist trailing, or the edge of a rather severe sleeve falling away so straightly that the curve it let you glimpse gained strength and lost no loveliness. And at tea, her hands would make gracious, unheeded, beautiful motions over the silver. That would be in London, particularly in the long, gray upstairs drawing room they had there. It would be half raining, and the light would be the color of rain, and the paintings on the wall, whatever color they had in them, would be gray. Even if they were van Goghs they would be gray. But her hair would not be gray.

Today, however, I just looked at her and waggled the cherrywood stick and said, "No use asking you to walk over to the lake and let me row you about, I suppose?"

She half smiled. Her half smile was negative.

"Where's Edward? Golfing?"

The same half smile, but derision in it now.

"Something about rabbits today, with a gamekeeper he met in the village pub. It *would* be a gamekeeper. It seems a lot of them get around a sort of clearing in a spinney, a warren, and the ferrets are sent down into the rabbits' holes, and so the rabbits have to come up."

"I know," I said. "Then they drink the blood."

"That should have been my line, if you ever left me one. Run along now, and don't be too late back for tea."

"It must be fun," I said, "just waiting for tea. In a warm spot, in a nice garden, with the bees droning around you not too close, and the nectarines perfuming the air. Waiting for tea — as if it were a revolution."

She just looked at me with her pale blue English eyes. Not tired eyes, but eyes that had looked at the same things too long.

"Revolution? What in the world does that mean?"

"I don't know," I said frankly. "It just sounded like a good gag line. So long."

To the English, Americans are always a trifle stupid.

I walked over to the lake too fast. It wasn't much of a lake, as American lakes go, but it had a lot of tiny islands on it, and these made vistas and gave a false impression of length, and the water birds swooped and clattered or just sat on reeds growing out of the water and looked supercilious. In places the old backwoods strolled down very close to the gray water. In these places there were no water birds. Somebody's cracked but not somehow leaky old tub was tied to a log by a short rope, stiff with age and paint. I used to row that among the little islands. Nothing lived on them, but there were things growing, and now and again some old gaffer would stop hoeing and shade his eyes and stare at me. I would call out a polite semi-English greeting. He would not answer. He was too old, too deaf and had other uses for his energy.

I got more tired than usual that day. The old boat seemed as cumbersome as a water-logged barn in a Mississippi flood. The always too short oars were shorter than ever. So I loafed going back, and there were shafts of yellow light through the beeches, distantly, in another world. It got cold on the water.

I dragged the boat up high enough to tie the painter to the log and straightened, sucking a finger the knot hadn't been kind to.

I hadn't heard a sound of her or of her big black horse or even of the clinking rings at the end of the bit. Last year's leaves must have been very soft around there, or she had a magic with horses.

But when I straightened and turned she was not more than nine feet away.

She wore a black riding habit, a white hunting stock at her throat, and the horse looked wicked as she sat astride of him. A stallion. She smiled, a black-eyed woman, young, but not a girl. I had never seen her before. She was terribly handsome.

"Like rowing?" she inquired in that offhand English way that is utterly beyond mere ease. Her voice was the voice of a thrush, an American thrush.

The black stallion looked at me red-eyed and quietly pawed a leaf or two, then stood like a rock, quietly swinging one ear.

"Hate it," I said. "All hard work and blisters. Then three miles home for tea."

"Then why do you do it? I never do anything I don't like." She touched the stallion's neck with a gauntleted glove as black as his coat.

I shrugged. "I must like it in a way. Exercise. Takes the nerves out of you. Beats up an appetite. I can't think of any clever reasons."

"You should," she said. "Being an American."

"Am I an American?"

"Of course. I watched you rowing. So fierce. I knew even then. And of course, your accent."

My eyes must have been a little avid on her face, but she didn't seem to mind.

"Staying with some people called Crandall, at Buddenham, aren't you, Mr. American? Gossip does get around so in these country places. I'm Lady Lakenham, from Lakeview."

Something must have stiffened in my face. As if I had said out loud: Oh, you're *that* woman!

She noticed it, I dare say. She would notice most things. Perhaps all things. But not even a very small new shadow was born in her deep black, depthless eyes.

"That lovely Tudor place – I've seen it already – from a distance."

"See it closer and get a shock," she said. "Try my tea. The name, if you please?"

"Paringdon. John Paringdon."

"John's a nice sturdy name," she said. "A trifle on the dull side. I'll have to put up with it, during the brief moments of our acquaintance. Take hold of Romeo's stirrup leather, John – above the iron and lightly."

The stallion fretted a little when I touched the leather, but she cooed at him and he began to walk homeward, up a rise, slowly, his ears very alert. Even when some bird suddenly whirred across the glade, low under the trees, only his ears jumped.

"Nice manners," I said.

She arched her black eyebrows.

"Romeo? That depends. We meet all sorts of people, don't we, Romeo? And our manners vary."

She swung her short whip lightly.

"But that wouldn't concern you, would it?"

"I don't know," I said. "It might."

She laughed. I found out later that she very seldom laughed.

My hand on the stirrup leather was inches above her foot. I wanted to touch her foot. I didn't know why; I thought she wanted me to touch her foot. I didn't know the why of that either.

"Oh, you have nice manners too," she said. "I can see that."

I said, "I'm still not sure. They are swift like the swallow, and slow like the ox, but always in the wrong place."

The whip flicked around idly, but not at me, nor at the black stallion who obviously didn't expect it to flick at him.

"I'm afraid you're flirting with me," she said.

"I'm afraid I am."

It was the stallion's fault. He stopped too suddenly. My hand slipped to her ankle. I kept it there.

I hadn't seen her move either, hadn't any idea how she had stopped the horse. He stood now like a casting in bronze.

She looked down very slowly at my hand on her ankle.

"Intentional?" she inquired.

"Very," I said.

"You have at least courage," she said. Her voice was distant, like a wood call. That kind of distance. I shook like a leaf.

She leaned down very very slowly until her head was almost as low as mine. The stallion didn't seem to move a muscle of his great body.

"I could do three things," she said. "Guess them."

"Easy. Ride on, use the whip on me, or just laugh."

"I was wrong," she said, in a suddenly taut voice. "Four things."

"Give me your lips," I said.

2

THE PLACE APPEARED suddenly, down the slope from a wide, grassy circle, which was supposed to be what remained of a

Roman camp. Down the slope was Lakeview, which, charac-
teristically, had no view of the lake.

It lay in an utterness of neglect you don't see in England,
in a jungle of tangled vines, a wilderness of long, weed-
grown lawns. Even the sunken garden had become a pit of
shame. Grass grew almost knee high on the Elizabethan
bowling lawn at the side. The house itself was a lovely time-
darkened red brick, in the traditional Elizabethan form,
with outward-jutting, heavily leaded windows. Fat spiders
slept behind them like bishops, and their webs mottled the
glass, and they gazed out somnolently where once the
hawk-faced dandies in slashed doublets had looked out at
England, unappeased, in their furious days, by its cloistered
charm.

Stables appeared, tottering in moss and neglect. A gnome,
all hands and nose and riding breeches, came out of a shadowy stall and held the stallion.

She dropped to the bricks of the stable yard, walked away
without a word.

"It's not neglect," she said, when we were out of the
gnome's hearing. "It's simple murder. He knew I loved the
place."

"Your husband?" I moved my lips softly, one inside the
other, hating him.

"Let's go in the front way. You get the loveliest view of
the main staircase. He excelled himself there. He gave that his
personal attention."

There was a wide space in front, ringed with a drive. Ancient
oaks closed it in. Its turf was worse than the rest because it had
been scythed roughly and looked yellow. The oaks sent long
shadows stealing insidiously across the ruined lawn, silent, dark,
probing fingers of hate. Shadows, yet more than shadows, as the
shadow on a sundial is more than a shadow.

A crone as aged and badly hung together as the stable
gnome answered the remote, fretful jangling of the bell. The

English of her sort seem never to go into a house. They must be admitted. The old woman muttered to herself in some obscure dialect, as though laying curses.

We stepped through the door, and the riding crop went up again.

"Now there," she said, in a voice than which nothing was ever harder, "you have his best work in the middle period, as painters say. Sir Henry Lakenham, Baronet, mind you, and please remember that a baronet is much more than a baron or viscount in our regard — Sir Henry Lakenham, one of our oldest baronets and one of our oldest staircases, meeting on somewhat unequal terms."

"You mean the axe was new," I said.

The main staircase, or what was left of it, was before us. It had been built for a royal descent, for a great lady with a retinue in velvet and stars, for an ingenuity of shadows on the vast paneled ceiling, for a victory or a triumph or a homecoming, and for, on occasion, just a staircase.

It was enormously broad and sweeping, it had the slow, indomitable curve of time. The balustrade alone must have been worth a fortune, but I merely guessed that. It had been hacked to jagged, dark splinters.

I turned away from it after quite a long time. There was a name now from which my stomach would always recoil.

"Wait a minute," I said. "You're still his — "

"Oh, that's part of the revenge."

The crone had gone mumbling away.

"What did you do to him?"

At first she said nothing. Then, very negligently: "I only wish I could do it again and again, forever, and that he might always hear of it down the dark places he will ultimately wander in."

"You don't mean that. Not all of it."

"No? Let's go this way. Our Romneys are famous — for their absence."

We went along what might have been a picture gallery. There were darker, plum-colored oblongs on the damask of the walls. Our footsteps echoed on a bare, dusty floor.

"Swine!" I said to the echoes and the emptiness. "Swine!"

"You don't really care," she said. "Do you?"

"No," I said. "Not as much as I pretend."

Beyond the gallery there was what might have been a gun room. From that a narrow, secret door led to a narrow, secret staircase, curved and intimate and gracious. We went up that. So we came at last to a room that was at least furnished.

She pulled her hard black hat off and fluffed her hair carelessly and threw her hat and gloves and whip on a bench. There was a huge canopied bed. Charles the Second had probably slept in it – not alone. There was a dressing table with wing mirrors and the usual chorus of glittering bottles. She went past all this, without a glance, to a table in the corner where she mixed Scotch and soda, tepid of course, and came back with two glasses in her hands.

Sinewy hands, the hands of a horsewoman. Not the lovely plastic things that were the hands of Millicent Crandall. These were hands that could be desperately tight, that could hurt. That could take a hunter over an impossible fence or a man over an aching abyss. Hands that almost shattered the fragile glasses she held. I saw their knuckles, as white as new ivory.

I was standing just inside the big old door and hadn't moved a muscle since I stepped into the room. She handed me a drink. It shook a little, and danced in the glass.

Her eyes – they were those far-off, unobtainable eyes. Those ancient eyes. They say nothing, they are utterly withdrawn. They are the last window that never opens in a house otherwise not secret.

Somewhere, I suppose, there was still the rather distant scent of sweet peas in an English garden, nectarines on a sunny wall, another fragrance and another head.

I reached back clumsily and turned the huge key, as big as a monkey wrench, in a lock the size of a cupboard door.

The lock creaked and we didn't laugh. We drank. Before I could put my glass down she was pressed against me so tightly that I stopped breathing.

Her skin was sweet and wild, like wildflowers on a sun-baked slope, in spring, in the hard white sun of my own country. Our lips burned together, almost fused. Then hers opened and her tongue drove hard against my teeth and her body shook convulsively.

"Please," she said in a strangled voice, her mouth buried in mine. "Please, oh please – "

There could be only one ending.

3

I DON'T REMEMBER what time it was when I got back to the Crandalls' cottage. I had to put a time on it afterward, for a reason, but I never really knew. The English summer afternoons last, like the English themselves, forever. I knew that Old Bessie was back because I could hear her humming monotone in the kitchen, like a fly caught in a pane of glass.

Perhaps even the almost infinite hour of tea had not been laid away.

I turned from the foot of the stairs and made myself go into the drawing room. That which I carried with me was neither all triumph nor all defeat, but it seemed to have no place there, where Millicent was.

She stood there, of course, as if waiting for me, her back to the futile lace curtains at the French doors. They were still, as she was. There was not, for the moment, enough life

in the air to move them. She stood as if she had been waiting for silent, immobile hours. I felt somehow that the light
had scarcely stirred along her arm or in the almost shadow
of her throat.

She didn't say anything at once. Her not saying anything
seemed very thunderous. Then her marble-smooth voice said,
surprisingly, "You've loved me for three years now, haven't
you, John?"

That was very swell, that was.

"Yes," I said. It was too late, far too late to be saying anything at all.

"I always knew it. You meant me to know it, didn't you,
John?"

"I suppose so. Yes." The croak I heard seemed to be my
voice.

Her pale blue eyes were placid as a pond under a full
moon.

"I've always liked knowing it," she said.

I didn't move nearer to her. I just stood there, not exactly
toeing holes in the carpet.

Quite suddenly, in that still, greenish late-afternoon light
her frail body began to ripple from head to foot.

There was another silence. I did nothing to end it. At last
she reached out to the frayed bell cord. The bell tinkled at the
back of the house like a child crying.

"Well, we can always have tea," she said.

I got out of the room, as one does, without seeming to use
the door.

I made the stairs without a fumble this time, the whole
straight flight and the turn. But I was another man now. I was
a smooth, quiet little man who had been put in his place and
didn't matter at all, but wouldn't have anything to worry
about either. All taken care of. Finished. A little man about
two feet high who rolled his eyes when you shook him hard
enough. Put him back in his box, dear, and let's go riding.

Then, just at the very top, where there was no step at all, I stumbled, and as if that made a draft, a door fell open, softly, like a leaf falling. Just half-open. Edward Crandall's bedroom door.

He was in there. The bed inside the door was very high and had at least two eiderdown mattresses on it, as they have in that part of the country. That was all I really looked at – the bed. He was sprawled all over it, on his face, as if eating it. Dead drunk. Passed out. A little early, even for him.

I stood there in the elf light that was neither afternoon nor dusk and looked in at him. The big black handsome brute, the conquering one. Filthy drunk, before it was even dark.

To hell with him. I reached over softly and shut the door again and almost tiptoed on to my own room, and washed up in the hand basin, with cold water. How cold it was, as cold as the morning after a battle.

I groped down the stairs again. In the meantime, tea had been served. She sat behind the low table, behind the large, polished urn, holding a sleeve away from it as she poured, so that her bare white arm seemed to shoot out of the sleeve.

"You must be tired," she said. "You must be terribly hungry," she said, in that flat, offhand, utterly dead voice that reminded me of the leave trains at Victoria during the war, the careless English women on the platform by the first-class carriages, saying those unimportant things, so easily, to the faces they would never see again. So careless, so smooth, so utterly dead inside.

It was like that. I took a cup of tea and a piece of scone.

"He's upstairs," I said. "Blotto. Of course you know that."

"Oh, yes." Her sleeve swirled a little, very delicately.

"Do I put him to bed?" I asked. "Or do I just let him decompose where he is?"

Her head jerked queerly. There was for the moment an expression she never meant me to see.

"John!" Quite smooth again now. "You've never talked like that about him before."

"Never talked much about him at all," I said. "Funny. He asked me down, too. And I came. Funny people – people are. It's been nice here too. I'm leaving."

"John!"

"The hell with it," I said. "I'm leaving. Thank him – when he's sober. Thank him a lot for asking me."

"John!" For the third time, just like that. "Aren't you being just a little strange?"

"It's the American gutturals creeping out," I said, "after a long hibernation."

"Have you hated him so much?"

"If you'll pardon an old friend," I said. "There are too many exclamation points in this conversation. Forget my bad manners. Of course I'll put him to bed – and then I'll take myself some English air."

But she was hardly listening to me now. She was leaning forward, and her eyes had an almost clairvoyant look, and she began to talk quickly, as if something had to be said and there wasn't much time and interruptions might come.

"There's a woman over at Lakeview," she said. "A Lady Lakenham. A terrible woman. A man-eater. He's been seeing her. This morning they had some sort of quarrel. He shouted all this at me, while we were alone in the house, contemptuously, over glasses of brandy he spilled all down his coat. She hit him in the face with a whip and rode him down on her horse."

Of course I wasn't hearing her either, not with my conscious ears. Instantly, as you'd snap your fingers, I had become a wooden man. It was as if all time were distilled into one instant and I had swallowed that, like a pill. It had made a wooden man of me. I could even feel a wooden grin pulling my face.

So even there he had to be first.

She stopped talking, it seemed, and she was looking at me across the tea urn. I saw her. I could see. One can, even in those moments. Her hair was ever so pale, her melancholy ever so distinct. She made the usual motions, slow, lovely curves of the arm and hand and wrist and cheek, which at the time had an almost unbearable seductiveness, but which in retrospect would have only the faded and uncertain grace of wisps of mist.

It seemed that I had handed her my cup and she was pouring me more tea.

"She lashed him with a hunting crop," she said. "Imagine! Edward! Then she rode him down, knocked him over with her big horse."

"On a big black stallion," I said. "She rode him down like a bundle of dirty rags."

Her breath caught in the stillness.

"Yes, she has her points," I said brutally. "And she loves the house. Lakeview. You ought to see what Lakenham did to the inside of it. He did his best lick on the main staircase – somebody else's heel of a husband."

Did her breath stay caught, or did someone laugh behind an arras, some court fool hiding from a wicked king?

"I knew her too," I said. "Intimately."

It seemed to dawn on her a little too slowly, as if a native had to be waked in a grass hut in Sumatra, and then run mile after mile through the jungle, and then a man had to ride a horse across a vast desert, and then a sailing ship had to battle storm after storm around the Horn, bringing the news home. It seemed to take all that time.

Her eyes got very large and very still and like gray glass. There was no color in them and no light.

"He must have thought he had the morning," I said. "I had an afternoon appointment. It just didn't – " I stopped. That wasn't funny, not in any company.

I stood up. "I'm sorry. So uselessly sorry. I'm just as easy to take as the next guy, for all my visions. I'm sorry. Sorry, and I know it's just a word."

She stood up too. She was coming around the table, very slowly. We were quite close together then, but no part of us touched.

Then she touched my sleeve, very lightly, as though a butterfly had lighted on it, and I was very still, not wanting to frighten the butterfly.

It floated away. It hovered in midair. It settled once more on my sleeve. Her voice said, as softly as the butterfly had moved, "We don't have to talk about it. We understand. We understand everything, you and I. We don't have to say a word."

"It could happen to anybody," I said. "The hell of it is when it does."

There was something else behind her eyes. They were not blank any more, but neither were they soft. Little doors were opening far back, at the ends of dark corridors. Doors that had been shut so long. So unutterably long. Steps came, along a stone corridor. They shuffled, without haste, without hope. A thread of smoke was caught in a draft and spiraled to nothing. All these things I seemed to see and know behind her eyes. Nonsense, of course.

"You're mine," she whispered, "all mine now."

She clutched my head and pulled it down. Her lips fumbling unskillfully on my mouth were as cold and remote as Arctic snow.

"Go upstairs and see if he is all right," she whispered secretly, "before you go."

"Sure." I spoke like a man who has been shot through the lungs.

So I went out of that room again, and up those stairs again.

Fumbling this time, fumbling with ancient caution. An old man whose bones were brittle. I got to my room and shut the door. I panted against it for a little while. Then I changed my clothes and put on the only lounge suit I had with me, tucked the rest of my stuff into a suitcase, closed the suitcase, and locked it very softly. Listening, moving very softly, a little boy who has been bad, bad, bad.

And in the silence I helped to make, steps came up the stairs and went into a room and came out of a room and went down the stairs again. Very slowly, all this, creeping like my thoughts.

Sounds came back. The cracked, incessant humming of the old woman in the kitchen, the buzzing of a late bee under my window, the creaking of an old countryman's cart far down the road. I picked up my suitcase and went out of my room. I shut its door softly, softly.

And at the top of the stairs *his* door had to be wide open again. Wide open, as if somebody had come up deliberately and opened it and left it open.

I put the suitcase down and leaned against the wall and stared in. He didn't seem to have moved much. Pretty complete case. He looked as if he had taken a running dive onto the high bed and grabbed two big handfuls of the counterpane and so passed into the large alcoholic beyond.

Then in the gray stillness I was aware of a lack of sound. The stertorous breathing, half snore, half mutter of the unconscious drunk. I listened – oh, very carefully. It was missing – his breathing. He didn't make any sound at all, sprawled on his face on that high bed.

Yet it wasn't even that that brought me into the room like a panther, crouching, noiseless, holding my own breath. It was something I had already looked at and not observed. His left ring finger. Funny, that was. It was half an inch longer than the middle finger next to it, as his hand hung limp against the spread. It should have been half an inch shorter.

It was half an inch longer. The extra length happened to be a congealed icicle of blood.

It had come all the way from his throat, soundless, implacable, and made that funny icicle there.

He had been dead, of course, for hours.

4

I SHUT THE door of the drawing room very politely, very carefully, like an old family priest departing into his funk hole, in the days of one of the anti-Catholic persecutions.

Then I stole over and shut the French doors. I suppose a little last fragrance of the roses and the nectarines crept in at me, mockingly, as I did this.

She was leaning back in a low chair, smoking a cigarette not skillfully, her pale gold head against a cushion. Her eyes — I didn't know what was in her eyes. I had had enough of what was in eyes, anyhow.

"Where's the gun? It should be in his hand."

I made it sharp but not loud, not a carrying voice. But there was no gentle English grayness in me now.

She smiled very faintly and pointed to one of those spindly articles of furniture on insecure logs which sometimes have drawers but are really to hold an array of little glazed cups and mugs emblazoned in gilt: "A Present from Bognor Regis," or wherever it was, and a coat of arms.

This particular sideboy, or whatever it was, had a stiff curved drawer, which I pulled out, rattling the glazed mugs a little.

It was in there, on a sheet of pink shelf paper, against a fringed doily. A Webley revolver. Innocent as a fish knife.

I put my nose down and sniffed at it. There seemed to be that harsh smell of cordite. I didn't touch the gun — yet.

"So you knew," I said. "You knew all the time I was making a prissy fool of myself. You knew while we had tea. You knew he was lying up there on that bed. Dripping blood slowly, slowly, slowly — the dead *do* bleed, but so slowly — from a wound in his throat, down under his shirt, down his arm, down his hand, down his finger. You knew all the time."

"That beast," she said in an utterly calm voice. "That offal. Have you any idea what he has subjected me to?"

"All right," I said. "I get that too. I'm not squeamish either, about his sort. But things have to be done. The gun shouldn't have been touched at all. Where it was it probably looked all right. Now you've handled it. Fingerprints, you know. You know about fingerprints?"

I wasn't talking to a child or being sarcastic either. I was just getting an idea over, in case it hadn't got over. She had somehow discarded the cigarette without my observing a movement. She could do those things. She sat now very still, her hands on the arms of her chair, slim, separate, as delicate as dawn.

"You were here alone," I said. "It was while Old Bessie had gone out. Nobody heard the shot, or would have thought of it as anything but a hunting gun."

She laughed then. It was a low, ecstatic laugh, the laugh of a woman nestling back among pillows, in a great canopied bed.

As she laughed, the lines of her throat sharpened a little. And they never softened again, that I saw.

"Why," she asked, "are you worrying about all that?"

"You should have told me before. What are you laughing at? Do you think this English law of yours is funny? . . . And you went up and opened that door – you. So I wouldn't leave without knowing. Why?"

"I loved you," she said. "After a fashion. I'm a cold woman, John. Did you know I was a cold woman?"

"I suspected it, but it didn't happen to be any of my business. You're not answering my question."

"Your business, as it were, lay elsewhere."

"That's a thousand years ago. Ten thousand. That lies with the Pharaohs. Crumbling in an ancient shroud. This is for now." I pointed upward, a hard stiff finger.

"It's beautiful," she sighed. "Let's not make a cheap sensation of it. It's a beautiful tragedy." She touched her slim, delicate neck caressingly.

"They'll hang me, John. They do – in England."

I stared at her with what eyes I had and what was in them.

"Deliberately," she said coolly. "With due formality. And some faint, summary regrets. And the governor of the prison will have a perfect crease in his trousers, put there as deliberately, as carefully, as coldly as – as I shot him."

I kept on breathing enough to stay alive. "On purpose?" It was a useless question. I already knew.

"Of course. I've been intending to for months. Today seemed somehow a little more brutal than usual. This woman over at Lakeview didn't improve his self-esteem. She made him cheap. He was always nasty. So I did what I did."

"But you could stand his being just nasty," I said.

She nodded that head. I heard a strange, clanking noise like nothing else on earth. Something swayed, hooded. Very gently it swayed, in a cold light, from a long, hidden exquisite neck.

"No," I said, without breath. "Never. This is easy. Will you play it my way?"

She stood up all in one smooth motion and came to me. I took her in my arms. I kissed her. I touched her hair.

"My knight," she whispered. "My plumed knight. My glistening one."

"How?" I asked, pointing into the drawer at the gun. "They'll test his hand for powder nitrates. That is, leakage of gas when the gun is fired. It's something that stays in the skin for a while and makes a chemical reaction. That has to be arranged."

She stroked my hair. "They will, my love. They will find what you mean. I put the gun in his own hand, and held it there, and soothed him. My finger was over his finger. He was so drunk he didn't even know what he was doing."

She went on stroking my hair.

"My plumed, glistening knight," she said.

I wasn't holding her now; she was holding me. I squeezed my brains slowly, slowly. Into a clot.

"It may not make a very good test," I said. "And they might test your hand as well. So we must do two things. Are you listening to me?"

"My plumed knight!" Her eyes shone.

"You must wash your right hand with good, harsh laundry soap and hot water, for a long time. It may hurt, but keep it up as long as you dare without taking the skin off. That would show. I mean that. It's important. The other thing is — I'm leaving with the gun. That should throw them off. I don't think that nitrate test is any good after about forty-eight hours. Understand?"

She said the same things, in the same way, and her eyes shone with the same light. Her hand on my head was the same soft, lingering hand.

I didn't hate her. I didn't love her. It was just something I had to do. I got the Webley and the pink paper under it, because that was slightly oil-stained. I looked closely at the wood of the drawer. That seemed clean. I put the gun and the paper away in my pockets.

"You don't sleep in the same room with him," I pounded on. "He's drunk — sleeping it off. Nothing new, nothing to get excited or worried about. You heard a shot, of course, at somewhere around the right time, but not too close and not too evasive either. You thought it was a gun in the woods."

She held my arm. I had to smooth hers. Her eyes demanded it.

"You're pretty disgusted with him," I said. "It's happened often enough, so that you got an overload today. So he's to be left alone till morning. Then Old Bessie — "

"Oh, not Old Bessie," she said beautifully. "Not poor Old Bessie."

It may have been a nice touch. It slid past me. I started to go.

"The main things — washing your hand, but not enough to inflame it — and me off with the gun. All set?"

She clutched me again, with that fierce, unskillful clutch.
"And afterwards – ?"
"And afterwards – " I breathed dreamily against her icy lips.
I pried myself loose from her and left that house.

5

FOR ALMOST THREE weeks I stayed clear of them, or they let
me. I was pretty good, for an amateur, in a small tight country
like England.

I ditched my runabout late at night, in the loneliest copse
I could drive to without lights. It seemed a thousand wind-
swept solitary miles from anywhere. It wasn't, of course.
I dragged my suitcase across infinite English landscapes,
through the dark, through fields of drowsy cattle, past the
fringes of silent villages where not a single lamp warmed the
night.

Not too early I reached a railway station and rode it to
London. I knew where to go, a small lodging house in
Bloomsbury, north of Russell Square, a place where no one
was what he should be or wanted to be, and no one cared,
least of all the slattern who called herself the landlady.

Breakfast, a cold, greasy mess on a tray outside your door.
Lunch, ale and bread and cheddar, if you wanted it. Dinner, if
you were in the dining class, you went out and foraged for. If
you came home late at night, the white-faced specters of
Russell Square haunted you, creeping along where the iron
railings had been, as though the mere memory of them
brought some shelter from the policeman's lantern. They
haunted you all night with the ache of their "Listen, dearies,"
with the remembrance of their pinched lips, gnawed thin
from within, their large hollow eyes in which a world was
already dead.

There was a man at the digs who played Bach, a little too
much and a little too loud; but he did it for his own soul.

There was a lonely old man with a poised, delicate face and a filthy mind. There were two young wooden butterflies who thought of themselves as actors.

I got sick of all that soon enough. I bought a knapsack and went on a walking tour down to Devonshire. I was in the papers, of course, but not prominently. No sensation, no blurred reproduction of my passport photograph, which made me look like an Armenian rug merchant with the toothache. Just a discreet paragraph about my being missing, age, height, weight, color of eyes, American, believed to have information which might aid the authorities. There was some brief biographical stuff about Edward Crandall, not more than three lines. He was not important to them. Merely a well-to-do man who happened to be dead. Calling me an American clinched it. My accent, when I tried it, was almost good enough for Bloomsbury. It would be more than good enough for the rural districts.

They caught up with me at Chagford, near the edge of Dartmoor. I was having tea, of course, the parlor boarder at a small farmhouse, a writer down from London for a bit of a rest. Nice manners, but no talker. Fond of cats.

They had two fat ones, a black and a white, who liked Devonshire cream as much as I did. The cats and I had our tea together. It was a dismal afternoon, as gray as a prison yard. A hangman's day. Mists would be hanging in low clumps on the hard yellow gorse of the moor.

There were two of them, a Constable Tressider, local man, though with a Cornish name, and the Scotland Yard man. This one was the enemy. The local man merely sat in the corner and smelled of his uniform.

The other was fiftyish, beautifully built, as they are over there when they are, red-faced, a warrant officer of the Guards without the ruthless, deadly detached voice. He was soft and quiet and friendly. He put his hat on the far end of the long dinner table and picked up the black cat.

"Glad to find you in, sir. Inspector Knight from the Yard. You've given us a very nice run for our money."

"Have tea," I said. I went over to pull the bell and leaned against the wall. "Have tea – with a murderer."

He laughed. Constable Tressider did not laugh. His face expressed nothing but the bitter wind on the moor.

"Gladly – but we won't talk of that other now, if you please. But just to ease your mind – nobody's in any real trouble over the affair."

I must have turned pretty white. He jumped for a bottle of Dewar's on the mantel and shook some of it into a glass faster than I would have thought such a big man could have moved. He had it against my mouth. I gulped.

A hand felt me over, a hand as neat and questing as a hummingbird's bill, as sharp, as thorough.

I grinned at him. "You'll have it," I said. "I just don't wear it to tea."

The constable had his tea in the corner, and the Scotland Yard man at the table, with the black cat in his lap. Rank, after all, is rank.

I went back to London with him that same evening.

And there was nothing to it – absolutely nothing.

They had been foxed and they knew it, and as the English always do, they lost as if they were winning. Outwardly, it was, why had I taken the gun? Because she had foolishly handled it, and that frightened me. Oh yes, I see. But it would really have been much better – you see, the Crown – and the inquest being adjourned at the request of the police makes a hint of something wrong, don't you think? I thought so, contritely.

That was outwardly. Inwardly, I saw it behind the cold gray stone walls of their eyes. The idea had come to them just too late and it was my fault. Just too late had arrived in their bleak, keen minds the possibility of his being just drunk enough and just silly enough to let somebody put a gun in his hand and point it (where he couldn't see it) and say "Bang!" and make him pull the trigger, with a finger over his lax finger, and then let him fall back – not laughing.

I saw Millicent Crandall at the adjourned inquest, a woman in black I had met somewhere, long ago. We did not speak to each other. I never saw her again. She must have looked ravishing in black chiffon nightgowns. She could wear one now, any day or any year.

I saw Lady Lakenham once, in Piccadilly, by the Green Park, strolling with a man and a dog. She sent them on and stopped. I think the dog was some sort of bob-tailed sheep-dog type, but much smaller. We shook hands. She looked marvelous.

We stood in the middle of the sidewalk, and the English moved around us meticulously, as the English do.

Her eyes were black marble, opaque, calm, at peace.

"You were swell to go to bat for me," I said.

"Why, darling, I had the grandest time with the Assistant Commissioner at Scotland Yard. The whole place simply swam with Scotch and soda."

"Without you," I said, "they might have tried to pin it on me."

"Tonight," she said, very quickly, very busily, "I'm terribly afraid I'm all booked up. But tomorrow – I'm staying at Claridge's. You'll call?"

"Tomorrow," I said. "Oh, definitely." (I was leaving England tomorrow.) "So you rode him down on Romeo. I'm being impertinent. Why?"

This on Piccadilly, by the Green Park, while the careful pedestrians eddied.

"Did I? Why, how utterly abominable of me. Don't you know why?" A thrush, as calm as the Green Park itself.

"Of course," I said. "Men of his type make that mistake. They think they own every woman who smiles at them." The wild perfume of her skin came to me a little, as if a desert wind brought it a thousand miles to me.

"Tomorrow," she said. "About four. You needn't even tele-phone, really."

"Tomorrow," I lied.

I stared at her until she was quite out of sight. Motionless, utterly motionless. They moved around me politely, those English, as though I were a monument, or a Chinese sage, or a life-sized doll in Dresden china.

Quite motionless. A chill wind blew leaves and bits of paper across the now lusterless grass of Green Park, across the trim walks, almost over the high curbing into Piccadilly itself.

I stood there for what seemed a long, long time, looking after nothing. There was nothing to look after.

CHINUA ACHEBE
Things Fall Apart

THE ARABIAN NIGHTS
(2 vols, tr. Husain Haddawy)

AUGUSTINE
The Confessions

JANE AUSTEN
Emma
Mansfield Park
Northanger Abbey
Persuasion
Pride and Prejudice
Sanditon and Other Stories
Sense and Sensibility

HONORÉ DE BALZAC
Cousin Bette
Eugénie Grandet
Old Goriot

SIMONE DE BEAUVOIR
The Second Sex

SAMUEL BECKETT
Molloy, Malone Dies,
The Unnamable

SAUL BELLOW
The Adventures of Augie March

HECTOR BERLIOZ
The Memoirs of Hector Berlioz

WILLIAM BLAKE
Poems and Prophecies

JORGE LUIS BORGES
Ficciones

JAMES BOSWELL
The Life of Samuel Johnson
The Journal of a Tour to
the Hebrides

CHARLOTTE BRONTË
Jane Eyre
Villette

EMILY BRONTË
Wuthering Heights

MIKHAIL BULGAKOV
The Master and Margarita

SAMUEL BUTLER
The Way of all Flesh

ITALO CALVINO
If on a winter's night a traveler

ALBERT CAMUS
The Stranger

WILLA CATHER
Death Comes for the Archbishop
My Ántonia

MIGUEL DE CERVANTES
Don Quixote

RAYMOND CHANDLER
The novels (2 vols)
Collected Stories

GEOFFREY CHAUCER
Canterbury Tales

ANTON CHEKHOV
My Life and Other Stories
The Steppe and Other Stories

KATE CHOPIN
The Awakening

CARL VON CLAUSEWITZ
On War

SAMUEL TAYLOR
COLERIDGE
Poems

WILKIE COLLINS
The Moonstone
The Woman in White

CONFUCIUS
The Analects

JOSEPH CONRAD
Heart of Darkness
Lord Jim
Nostromo
The Secret Agent
Typhoon and Other Stories
Under Western Eyes
Victory

DANTE ALIGHIERI
The Divine Comedy

DANIEL DEFOE
Moll Flanders
Robinson Crusoe

CHARLES DICKENS
Bleak House
David Copperfield